Sons and Lovers was first published in Great Britain, 1913; in the United States, 1913.
The Fox was first published in Great Britain, 1923; in the United States, 1923.
Love Among the Haystacks was first published in Great Britain, 1930;
in the United States, 1933.
Women in Love was first published in Great Britain, 1921; in the United States, 1920.
Aaron's Rod was first published in Great Britain, 1922; in the United States, 1922.
The Ladybird was first published in Great Britain, 1923; in the United States, 1923.

This edition first published in the United States of America
in 1979 jointly by

William Heinemann Inc
450 Park Avenue, New York, NY 10022

and

Octopus Books Inc
The Olympic Towers, 654 Fifth Avenue,
New York, NY 10022

Published by arrangement with The Viking Press

ISBN 0 905712 42 0

Printed in the United States of America
by R. R. Donnelley and Sons Company.

D.H. LAWRENCE

SONS AND LOVERS

THE FOX

LOVE AMONG
THE HAYSTACKS

AARON'S ROD

THE LADYBIRD

WOMEN IN LOVE

Octopus / Heinemann

D. H.
LAWRENCE

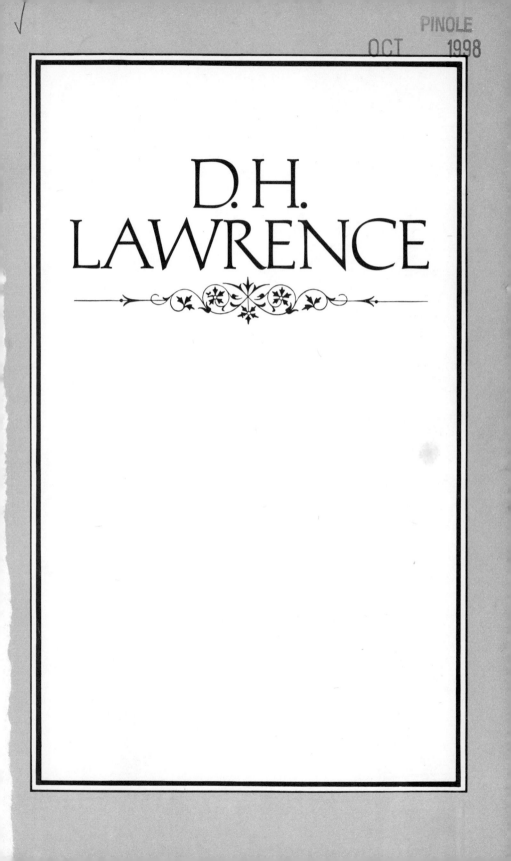

CONTENTS

D.H. LAWRENCE

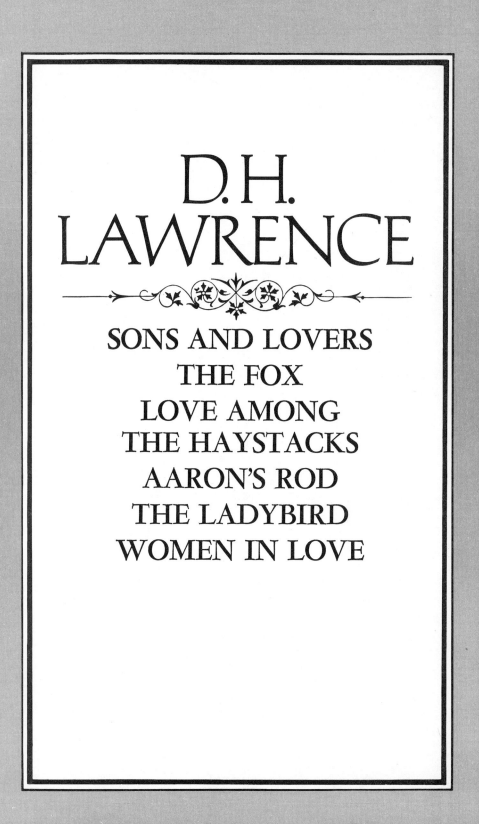

SONS AND LOVERS

THE FOX

LOVE AMONG
THE HAYSTACKS

AARON'S ROD

THE LADYBIRD

WOMEN IN LOVE

PART I

1

THE EARLY MARRIED LIFE OF THE MORELS

'The Bottoms' succeeded to 'Hell Row'. Hell Row was a block of thatched, bulging cottages that stood by the brookside on Greenhill Lane. There lived the colliers who worked in the little gin-pits two fields away. The brook ran under the alder-trees, scarcely soiled by these small mines, whose coal was drawn to the surface by donkeys that plodded wearily in a circle round a gin. And all over the countryside were these same pits, some of which had been worked in the time of Charles II, the few colliers and the donkeys burrowing down like ants into the earth, making queer mounds and little black places among the corn-fields and the meadows. And the cottages of these coalminers, in blocks and pairs here and there, together with odd farms and homes of the stockingers, straying over the parish, formed the village of Bestwood.

Then, some sixty years ago, a sudden change took place. The gin-pits were elbowed aside by the large mines of the financiers. The coal and iron field of Nottinghamshire and Derbyshire was discovered. Carston, Waite and Co appeared. Amid tremendous excitement, Lord Palmerston formally opened the company's first mine at Spinney Park, on the edge of Sherwood Forest.

About this time the notorious Hell Row, which through growing old had acquired an evil reputation, was burned down, and much dirt was cleansed away.

Carston, Waite and Co found they had struck on a good thing, so, down the valleys of the brooks from Selby and Nuttall, new mines were sunk, until soon there were six pits working. From Nuttall, high up on the sandstone among the woods, the railway ran, past the ruined priory of the Carthusians and past Robin Hood's Well, down to Spinney Park, then on to Minton, a large mine among corn-fields; from Minton across the farm-lands of the valleyside to Bunker's Hill, branching off there, and running north to Beggarlee and Selby, that looks over at Crich and the hills of Derbyshire; six mines like black studs on the countryside, linked by a loop of fine chain, the railway.

To accommodate the regiments of miners, Carston, Waite and Co built the Squares, great quadrangles of dwellings on the hillside of Bestwood, and then, in the brook valley, on the site of Hell Row, they erected the Bottoms.

The Bottoms consisted of six blocks of miners' dwellings, two rows of three, like the dots on a blank-six domino, and twelve houses in a block. This double row of dwellings sat at the foot of the rather sharp slope from Bestwood, and looked out, from the attic windows at least, on the slow climb of the valley towards Selby.

The houses themselves were substantial and very decent. One could walk all round, seeing little front gardens with auriculas and saxifrage in the shadow of the bottom block, sweet-williams and pinks in the sunny top block; seeing neat front windows, little porches, little privet hedges, and dormer windows for the attics. But that was outside; that was the view on to the uninhabited parlours of all the colliers' wives. The dwelling-room, the kitchen, was at the back of the house, facing inward between the blocks, looking at a scrubby back garden, and then at the ash-pits. And between the rows, between the long lines of ash-pits, went the alley, where the children played and the women gossiped and the men smoked. So, the actual conditions of living in the Bottoms, that was so well built and that looked so nice, were quite unsavoury because people must live in the kitchen, and the kitchens opened on to that nasty alley of ash-pits.

Mrs Morel was not anxious to move into the Bottoms, which was already twelve years old and on the downward path, when she descended to it from Bestwood. But it was the best she could do. Moreover, she had an end house in one of the top blocks, and thus had only one neighbour; on the other side an extra strip of garden. And, having an end house, she enjoyed a kind of aristocracy among the other women of the 'between' houses, because her rent was five shillings and sixpence instead of five shillings a week. But this superiority in station was not much consolation to Mrs Morel.

She was thirty-one years old, and had been married eight years. A rather small woman, of delicate mould but resolute bearing, she shrank a little from the first contact with the Bottoms women. She came down in the July, and in the September expected her third baby.

Her husband was a miner. They had only been in their new home three weeks when the wakes, or fair, began. Morel, she knew, was sure to make a holiday of it. He went off early on the Monday morning, the day of the fair. The two children were highly excited. William, a boy of seven, fled off immediately after breakfast, to prowl round the wakes ground, leaving Annie, who was only five, to whine all morning to go also. Mrs Morel did her work. She scarcely knew her neighbours yet, and knew no one with whom to trust the little girl. So she promised to take her to the wakes after dinner.

William appeared at half-past twelve. He was a very active lad, fair-haired, freckled, with a touch of the Dane or Norwegian about him.

'Can I have my dinner, mother?' he cried, rushing in with his cap on. ''Cause it begins at half-past one, the man says so.'

'You can have your dinner as soon as it's done,' replied the mother.

'Isn't it done?' he cried, his blue eyes staring at her in indignation. 'Then I'm goin' be-out it.'

'You'll do nothing of the sort. It will be done in five minutes. It is only half-past twelve.'

'They'll be beginnin',' the boy half cried, half shouted.

'You won't die if they do,' said the mother. 'Besides, it's only half-past twelve, so you've a full hour.'

The lad began hastily to lay the table, and directly the three sat down. They were eating batter-pudding and jam, when the boy jumped off his chair and stood perfectly still. Some distance away could be heard the first small braying of a merry-go-round, and the tooting of a horn. His face quivered as he looked at his mother.

'I told you!' he said, running to the dresser for his cap.

'Take your pudding in your hand – and it's only five past one, so you were wrong – you haven't got your twopence,' cried the mother in a breath.

The boy came back, bitterly disappointed, for his twopence; then went off without a word.

'I want to go, I want to go,' said Annie, beginning to cry.

'Well, and you shall go, whining, wizzening little stick!' said the mother. And later in the afternoon she trudged up the hill under the tall hedge with her child. The hay was gathered from the fields, and cattle were turned on to the eddish. It was warm, peaceful.

Mrs Morel did not like the wakes. There were two sets of horses, one going by steam, one pulled round by a pony; three organs were grinding, and there came odd cracks of pistol-shots, fearful screeching of the coconut man's rattle, shouts of the Aunt Sally man, screeches from the peep-show lady. The mother perceived her son gazing enraptured outside the Lion Wallace booth, at the pictures of this famous lion that had killed a negro and maimed for life two white men. She left him alone, and went to get Annie a spin of toffee. Presently the lad stood in front of her, wildly excited.

'You never said you was coming – isn't the' a lot of things? – that lion's killed three men – I've spent my tuppence – an' look here.'

He pulled from his pocket two egg cups, with pink moss-roses on them.

'I got these from that stall where y'ave ter get them marbles in them holes. An' I got these two in two goes – 'aepenny a go – they've got moss-roses on, look here. I wanted these.'

She knew he wanted them for her.

'H'm!' she said, pleased. 'They *are* pretty!'

'Shall you carry 'em, 'cause I'm frightened o' breakin' 'em?'

He was tipful of excitement now she had come, led her about the ground, showed her everything. Then, at the peepshow, she explained the pictures, in a sort of story, to which he listened as if spellbound. He would not leave her. All the time he stuck close to her, bristling with a small boy's pride of her. For no other woman looked such a lady as she did, in her little black bonnet and her cloak. She smiled when she saw women she knew. When she was tired she said to her son:

'Well, are you coming now, or later?'

'Are you goin' a'ready?' he cried, his face full of reproach.

'Already? It is past four, *I* know.'

'What are you goin' a'ready for?' he lamented.

'You needn't come if you don't want,' she said.

And she went slowly away with her little girl, whilst her son stood watching her, cut to the heart to let her go, and yet unable to leave the wakes. As she crossed the open ground in front of the Moon and Stars she heard men shouting, and smelled the beer, and hurried a little, thinking her husband was probably in the bar.

At about half-past six her son came home, tired now, rather pale, and somewhat wretched. He was miserable, though he did not know it, because he had let her go alone. Since she had gone, he had not enjoyed his wakes.

'Has my dad been?' he asked.

'No,' said the mother.

'He's helping to wait at the Moon and Stars. I see him through that black tin stuff wi' holes in, on the window, wi' his sleeves rolled up.'

'Ha!' exclaimed the mother shortly. 'He's got no money. An' he'll be satisfied if he gets his 'lowance, whether they give him more or not.'

When the light was fading, and Mrs Morel could see no more to sew, she rose and went to the door. Everywhere was the sound of excitement, the restlessness of the holiday, that at last infected her. She went out into the side garden. Women were coming home from the wakes, the children hugging a white lamb with green legs, or a wooden horse. Occasionally a man lurched past, almost as full as he could carry. Sometimes a good husband came along with his family, peacefully. But usually the women and children were alone. The stay-at-home mothers stood gossiping at the corners of the alley, as the twilight sank, folding their arms under their white aprons.

Mrs Morel was alone but she was used to it. Her son and her little girl slept upstairs; so, it seemed, her home was there behind her, fixed and stable. But she felt wretched with the coming child. The world seemed a dreary place, where nothing else would happen for her – at least until William grew up. But for herself, nothing but this dreary endurance – till the children grew up. And the children! She could not afford to have this third. She did not want it. The father serving beer in a public-house, swilling himself drunk. She despised him, and was tied to him. This coming child was too much for her. If it were not for William and Annie, she was sick of it, the struggle with poverty and ugliness and meanness.

She went into the front garden, feeling too heavy to take herself out, yet unable to stay indoors. The heat suffocated her. And looking ahead, the prospect of her life made her feel as if she were buried alive.

The front garden was a small square with a privet hedge. There she stood, trying to soothe herself with the scent of flowers and the fading, beautiful evening. Opposite her small gate was the stile that led uphill, under the tall hedge, between the burning glow of the cut pastures. The sky overhead throbbed and pulsed with light. The glow sank quickly off the field; the earth and the hedges smoked dusk. As it grew dark, a ruddy glare came out on the hill-top, and out of the glare the diminished commotion of the fair.

Sometimes, down the trough of darkness formed by the path under the hedges, men came lurching home. One young man lapsed into a run down the steep bit that ended the hill, and went with a crash into the stile. Mrs Morel shuddered. He picked himself up, swearing viciously, rather pathetically, as if he thought the stile had wanted to hurt him.

She went indoors, wondering if things were never going to alter. She was beginning by now to realize that they would not. She seemed so far away from her girlhood, she wondered if it were the same person walking heavily up the back garden at the Bottoms as had run so lightly on the breakwater at Sheerness ten years before.

'What have *I* to do with it?' she said to herself. 'What have I to do with all this? Even the child I am going to have! It doesn't seem as if *I* were taken into account.'

Sometimes life takes hold of one, carries the body along, accomplishes one's history, and yet is not real, but leaves oneself as it were slurred over.

'I wait,' Mrs Morel said to herself – 'I wait, and what I wait for can never come.'

Then she straightened the kitchen, lit the lamp, mended the fire, looked out the washing for the next day, and put it to soak. After which she sat down to her sewing. Through the long hours her needle flashed regularly through the stuff. Occasionally she sighed, moving to relieve herself. And all the time she was thinking how to make the most of what she had, for the children's sakes.

At half-past eleven her husband came. His cheeks were very red and very shiny above his black moustache. His head nodded slightly. He was pleased with himself.

'Oh! Oh! waitin' for me, lass? I've bin 'elpin' Anthony, an' what's think he's gen me? Nowt b'r a lousy hae'f-crown, an' that's ivry penny –'

'He thinks you've made the rest up in beer,' she said shortly.

'An' I 'aven't – that I 'aven't. You b'lieve me. I've 'ad very little this day, I have an' all.' His voice went tender. 'Here, an' I browt thee a bit o' brandysnap, an' a coconut for th' children.' He laid the gingerbread and the coconut, a hairy object, on the table. 'Nay, tha niver said thankyer for nowt i' thy life, did ter?'

As a compromise, she picked up the coconut and shook it, to see if it had any milk.

'It's a good 'un, you may back yer life o' that. I got it fra' Bill Hodgkisson. "Bill," I says, "tha non wants them three nuts, does ter? Arena ter for gi'ein' me one for my bit of a lad an' wench?" "I ham, Walter, my lad," 'e says; "ta'e which on 'em ter's a mind." An' so I took one, an' thanked 'im. I didn't like ter shake it afore 'is eyes, but 'e says, "Tha'd better ma'e sure it's a good un, Walt." An' so, yer see, I knowed it was. He's a nice chap, is Bill Hodgkisson, 'e's a nice chap!'

'A man will part with anything so long as he's drunk, and you're drunk along with him,' said Mrs Morel.

'Eh, tha mucky little 'ussy, who's drunk, I sh'd like ter know?' said Morel. He was extraordinarily pleased with himself, because of this day's helping to wait in the Moon and Stars. He chattered on.

Mrs Morel, very tired, and sick of his babble, went to bed as quickly as possible, while he raked the fire.

Mrs Morel came of a good old burgher family, famous independents who had fought with Colonel Hutchinson, and who remained stout Congregationalists. Her grandfather had gone bankrupt in the lace-market at a time when so many lace-manufacturers were ruined in Nottingham. Her father, George Coppart, was an engineer – a large, handsome, haughty man, proud of his fair skin and blue eyes, but more proud still of his integrity. Gertrude resembled her mother in her small build. But her temper, proud and unyielding, she had from the Coppards.

George Coppard was bitterly galled by his own poverty. He became foreman of the engineers in the dockyard at Sheerness. Mrs Morel – Gertrude – was the second daughter. She favoured her mother, loved her mother best of all; but she had the Coppards' clear, defiant blue eyes and their broad brow. She remembered to have hated her father's overbearing manner towards her gentle, humorous, kindly souled mother. She remembered running over the breakwater at Sheerness and finding the boat. She remembered to have been petted and flattered by all the men when she had gone to the dockyard, for she was a delicate, rather proud child. She remembered the funny old mistress, whose assistant she had become, whom she had loved to help in the private school. And she still had the Bible that John Field had given her. She used to walk home from chapel with John Field when she was nineteen. He was the son of a well-to-do tradesman, had been to college in London, and was to devote himself to business.

She could always recall in detail a September Sunday afternoon, when they had sat under the vine at the back of her father's house. The sun came through the chinks in the vineleaves and made beautiful patterns, like a lace scarf, falling on her and on him. Some of the leaves were clean yellow, like yellow flat flowers.

'Now sit still,' he had cried. 'Now your hair, I don't know what it *is* like! It's as bright as copper and gold, as red as burnt copper, and it has gold threads where the sun shines on it. Fancy their saying it's brown. Your mother calls it mouse-colour.'

She had met his brilliant eyes, but her clear face scarcely showed the elation which rose within her.

'But you say you don't like business,' she pursued.

'I don't. I hate it!' he cried hotly.

'And you would like to go into the ministry,' she half implored.

'I should. I should love it, if I thought I could make a first-rate preacher.'

'Then why don't you – why *don't* you?' Her voice rang with defiance. 'If *I* were a man, nothing would stop me.'

She held her head erect. He was rather timid before her.

'But my father's so stiff-necked. He means to put me into the business, and I know he'll do it.'

'But if you're a *man*?' she had cried.

'Being a man isn't everything,' he replied, frowning with puzzled helplessness.

Now, as she moved about her work at the Bottoms, with some experience of what being a man meant, she knew that it was *not* everything.

At twenty, owing to her health, she had left Sheerness. Her father had retired home to Nottingham. John Field's father had been ruined; the son had gone as a teacher in Norwood. She did not hear of him until, two years later, she made determined inquiry. He had married his landlady, a woman of forty, a widow with property.

And still Mrs Morel preserved John Field's Bible. She did not now believe him to be – Well, she understood pretty well what he might or might not have been. So she preserved his Bible and kept his memory intact in her heart, for her own sake. To her dying day, for thirty-five years, she did not speak of him.

When she was twenty-three years old, she met, at a Christmas party, a young man from the Erewash Valley. Morel was then twenty-seven years old. He was well set-up, erect, and very smart. He had wavy black hair that shone again, and a vigorous black beard that had never been shaved. His cheeks were ruddy, and his red, moist mouth was noticeable because he laughed so often and so heartily. He had that rare thing, a rich, ringing laugh. Gertrude Coppard had watched him, fascinated. He was so full of colour and animation, his voice ran so easily into comic grotesque, he was so ready and so pleasant with everybody. Her own father had a rich fund of humour, but it was satiric. This man's was different: soft, non-intellectual, warm, a kind of gambolling.

She herself was opposite. She had a curious, receptive mind, which found much pleasure and amusement in listening to other folk. She was clever in leading folk on to talk. She loved ideas, and was considered very intellectual. What she liked most of all was an argument on religion or philosophy or politics with some educated man. This she did not often enjoy. So she always had people tell her about themselves, finding her pleasure so.

In her person she was rather small and delicate, with a large brow, and dropping bunches of brown silk curls. Her blue eyes were very straight, honest, and searching. She had the beautiful hands of the Coppards. Her dress was always subdued. She wore dark blue silk, with a peculiar silver chain of silver scallops. This, and a heavy brooch of twisted gold, was her only ornament. She was still perfectly intact, deeply religious, and full of beautiful candour.

Walter Morel seemed melted away before her. She was to the miner that thing of mystery and fascination, a lady. When she spoke to him, it was with a southern pronunciation and a purity of English which thrilled him to hear. She watched him. He danced well, as if it were natural and joyous in him to dance. His grandfather was a French refugee who had married an English barmaid – if it had been a marriage. Gertrude Coppard watched the young miner as he danced, a certain subtle exultation like glamour in his movement, and his face the flower of his body, ruddy, with tumbled black hair, and laughing alike whatever partner he bowed above. She thought him rather wonderful, never having met anyone like him. Her father was to her the type of all men. And George Coppard, proud in his bearing, handsome, and rather bitter; who preferred theology in reading, and who drew near in sympathy only to one man, the Apostle Paul; who was harsh in government, and in familiarity ironic; who ignored all sensuous pleasure; – he was very different from the miner. Gertrude herself was rather contemptuous of dancing; she had not the slightest inclination towards that accomplishment, and had never learned even a Roger de Coverley. She was a puritan, like her father, high-minded, and really stern. Therefore the dusky, golden softness of this man's sensuous flame of life, that flowed off his flesh like the flame from a candle, not baffled and gripped into incandescence by thought and spirit as her life was, seemed to her something wonderful, beyond her.

He came and bowed above her. A warmth radiated through her as if she had drunk wine.

'Now do come and have this one wi' me,' he said caressively. 'It's easy, you know. I'm pining to see you dance.'

She had told him before she could not dance. She glanced at his humility and smiled. Her smile was very beautiful. It moved the man so that he forgot everything.

'No, I won't dance,' she said softly. Her words came clean and ringing.

Not knowing what he was doing – he often did the right thing by instinct – he sat beside her, inclining reverentially.

'But you mustn't miss your dance,' she reproved.

'Nay, I don't want to dance that – it's not one as I care about.'

'Yet you invited me to it.'

He laughed very heartily at this.

'I never thought o' that. Tha'rt not long in taking the curl out of me.'

It was her turn to laugh quickly.

'You don't look as if you'd come much uncurled,' she said.

'I'm like a pig's tail, I curl because I canna help it,' he laughed, rather boisterously.

'And you are a miner!' she exclaimed in surprise.

'Yes. I went down when I was ten.'

She looked at him in wondering dismay.

'When you were ten! And wasn't it very hard?' she asked.

'You soon get used to it. You live like th' mice, an' you pop out at night to see what's going on.'

'It makes me feel blind,' she frowned.

'Like a moudiwarp!' he laughed. 'Yi, an' there's some chaps as does go round like moudiwarps.' He thrust his face forward in the blind, snout-like way of a mole, seeming to sniff and peer for direction. 'They dun though!' he protested naïvely. 'Tha niver seen such a way they get in. But tha mun let me ta'e thee down some time, an' tha can see for thysen.'

She looked at him, startled. This was a new tract of life suddenly opened before her. She realized the life of the miners, hundreds of them toiling below earth and coming up at evening. He seemed to her noble. He risked his life daily, and with gaiety. She looked at him, with a touch of appeal in her pure humility.

'Shouldn't ter like it?' he asked tenderly. ''Appen not, it 'ud dirty thee.'

She had never been 'thee'd' and 'thou'd' before.

The next Christmas they were married, and for three months she was perfectly happy: for six months she was very happy.

He had signed the pledge, and wore the blue ribbon of a teetotaller: he was nothing if not showy. They lived, she thought, in his own house. It was small, but convenient enough, and quite nicely furnished, with solid, worthy stuff that suited her honest soul. The women, her neighbours, were rather foreign to her, and Morel's mother and sisters were apt to sneer at her lady-like ways. But she could perfectly well live by herself, so long as she had her husband close.

Sometimes, when she herself wearied of love-talk, she tried to open her heart seriously to him. She saw him listen deferentially, but without understanding. This killed her efforts at a finer intimacy, and she had flashes of fear. Sometimes he was restless of an evening: it was not enough for him just to be near her, she realized. She was glad when he set himself to little jobs.

He was a remarkably handy man – could make or mend anything. So she would say:

'I do like that coal-rake of your mother's – it is small and natty.'

'Does ter, my wench? Well, I made that, so I can make thee one.'

'What! why, it's a steel one!'

'An' what if it is! Tha s'lt ha'e one very similar, if not exactly same.'

She did not mind the mess, nor the hammering and noise. He was busy and happy.

But in the seventh month, when she was brushing his Sunday coat, she felt papers in the breast-pocket, and, seized with a sudden curiosity, took them out to read. He very rarely wore the frock-coat he was married in: and it had not occurred to her before to feel curious concerning the papers. They were the bills of the household furniture, still unpaid.

'Look here,' she said at night, after he was washed and had had his dinner. 'I found these in the pocket of your wedding-coat. Haven't you settled the bills yet?'

'No. I haven't had a chance.'

'But you told me all was paid. I had better go into Nottingham on Saturday and settle them. I don't like sitting on another man's chairs and eating from an unpaid table.'

He did not answer.

'I can have your bank-book, can't I?'

'Tha can ha'e it, for what good it'll be to thee.'

'I thought –' she began. He had told her he had a good bit of money left over. But she realized it was no use asking questions. She sat rigid with bitterness and indignation.

The next day she went down to see his mother.

'Didn't you buy the furniture for Walter?' she asked.

'Yes, I did,' tartly retorted the elder woman.

'And how much did he give you to pay for it?'

The elder woman was stung with fine indignation.

'Eighty pound, if you're so keen on knowin',' she replied.

'Eighty pounds! But there are forty-two pounds still owing!'

'I can't help that.'

'But where has it all gone?'

'You'll find all the papers, I think, if you look – beside ten pound as he owed me, an' six pound as the wedding cost down here.'

'Six pounds!' echoed Gertrude Morel. It seemed to her monstrous that, after her own father had paid so heavily for her wedding, six pounds more should have been squandered in eating and drinking at Walter's parents' house, at his expense.

'And how much has he sunk in his houses?' she asked.

'His houses – which houses?'

Gertrude Morel went white to the lips. He had told her the house he lived in, and the next one, was his own.

'I thought the house we live in –' she began.

'They're my houses, those two,' said the mother-in-law. 'And not clear either. It's as much as I can do to keep the mortgage interest paid.'

Gertrude sat white and silent. She was her father now.

'Then we ought to be paying you rent,' she said coldly.

'Walter is paying me rent,' replied the mother.

'And what rent?' asked Gertrude.

'Six-and-six a week,' retorted the mother.

It was more than the house was worth. Gertrude held her head erect, looked straight before her.

'It is lucky to be you,' said the elder woman, bitingly, 'to have a husband as takes all the worry of the money, and leaves you a free hand.'

The young wife was silent.

She said very little to her husband, but her manner had changed towards him. Something in her proud, honourable soul had crystallized out hard as rock.

When October came in, she thought only of Christmas. Two years ago, at Christmas, she had met him. Last Christmas she had married him. This Christmas she would bear him a child.

'You don't dance yourself, do you, missis?' asked her nearest neighbour, in October, when there was great talk of opening a dancing-class over the Brick and Tile Inn at Bestwood.

'No – I never had the least inclination to,' Mrs Morel replied.

'Fancy! An' how funny as you should ha' married your Mester. You know he's quite a famous one for dancing.'

'I didn't know he was famous,' laughed Mrs Morel.

'Yea, he is though! Why, he run that dancing-class in the Miners' Arms club-room for over five year.'

'Did he?'

'Yes, he did.' The other woman was defiant. 'An' it was thronged every Tuesday, and Thursday, an' Sat'day – an' there *was* carryin's-on, accordin' to all accounts.'

This kind of thing was gall and bitterness to Mrs Morel, and she had a fair share of it. The women did not spare her, at first; for she was superior, though she could not help it.

He began to be rather late in coming home.

'They're working very late now, aren't they?' she said to her washer-woman.

'No later than they allers do, I don't think. But they stop to have their pint at Ellen's, an' they get talkin', an' there you are! Dinner stone cold – an' it serves 'em right.'

'But Mr Morel does not take any drink.'

The woman dropped the clothes, looked at Mrs Morel, then went on with her work, saying nothing.

Gertrude Morel was very ill when the boy was born. Morel was good to her, as good as gold. But she felt very lonely, miles away from her own people. She felt lonely with him now, and his presence only made it more intense.

The boy was small and frail at first, but he came on quickly. He was a beautiful child, with dark gold ringlets, and dark-blue eyes which changed gradually to a clear blue. His mother loved him passionately. He came just when her own bitterness of disillusion was hardest to bear; when her faith in life was shaken, and her soul felt dreary and lonely. She made much of the child, and the father was jealous.

At last Mrs Morel despised her husband. She turned to the child; she turned from the father. He had begun to neglect her; the novelty of his own home was gone. He had no grit, she said bitterly to herself. What he felt just at the minute, that was all to him. He could not abide by anything. There was nothing at the back of all his show.

There began a battle between the husband and wife – a fearful, bloody battle that ended only with the death of one. She fought to make him undertake his own responsibilities, to make him fulful his obligations. But he was too different from her. His nature was purely sensuous, and she strove to make him moral, religious. She tried to force him to face things. He could not endure it – it drove him out of his mind.

While the baby was still tiny, the father's temper had become so irritable that it was not to be trusted. The child had only to give a little trouble when the man began to bully. A little more, and the hard hands of the collier hit the baby. Then Mrs Morel loathed her husband, loathed him for days; and he went out and drank; and she cared very little what he did. Only, on his return, she scathed him with her satire.

The estrangement between them caused him, knowingly or unknowingly, grossly to offend her where he would not have done.

William was only one year old, and his mother was proud of him, he was so pretty. She was not well off now, but her sisters kept the boy in clothes. Then, with his little white hat curled with an ostrich feather, and his white coat, he was a joy to her, the twining wisps of hair clustering round his head. Mrs Morel lay listening, one Sunday morning, to the chatter of the father and child downstairs. Then she dozed off. When she came downstairs, a great fire glowed in the grate, the room was hot, the breakfast was roughly laid, and seated in his armchair, against the chimney-piece, sat Morel, rather timid; and standing between his legs, the child – cropped like a sheep, with such an odd round poll – looking, wondering at her; and on a newspaper spread out upon the hearthrug, a myriad of crescent-shaped curls, like the petals of a marigold scattered in the reddening firelight.

Mrs Morel stood still. It was her first baby. She went very white, and was unable to speak.

'What dost think o' 'im?' Morel laughed uneasily.

She gripped her two fists, lifted them, and came forward. Morel shrank back.

'I could kill you, I could!' she said. She choked with rage, her two fists uplifted.

'Yer non want ter make a wench on 'im,' Morel said, in a frightened tone, bending his head to shield his eyes from hers. His attempt at laughter had vanished.

The mother looked down at the jagged, close-clipped head of her child. She put her hands on his hair, and stroked and fondled his head.

'Oh – my boy!' she faltered. Her lips trembled, her face broke, and, snatching up the child, she buried her face in his shoulder and cried painfully. She was one of those women who cannot cry; whom it hurts as it hurts a man. It was like ripping something out of her, her sobbing.

Morel sat with his elbows on his knees, his hands gripped together till the knuckles were white. He gazed in the fire, feeling almost stunned, as if he could not breathe.

Presently she came to an end, soothed the child and cleared away the breakfast-table. She left the newspaper, littered with curls, spread upon the hearthrug. At last her husband gathered it up and put it at the back of the fire. She went about her work with closed mouth and very quiet. Morel was subdued. He crept about wretchedly, and his meals were a misery that day. She spoke to him, civilly, and never alluded to what he had done. But he felt something final had happened.

Afterwards she said she had been silly, that the boy's hair would have had to be cut, sooner or later. In the end, she even brought herself to say to her husband it was just as well he had played barber when he did. But she knew, and Morel knew, that that act had caused something momentous to take place in her soul. She remembered the scene all her life, as one in which she had suffered the most intensely.

This act of masculine clumsiness was the spear through the side of her love for Morel. Before, while she had striven against him bitterly, she had fretted after him, as if he had gone astray from her. Now she ceased to fret for his love: he was an outsider to her. This made life much more bearable.

Nevertheless, she still continued to strive with him. She still had her high moral sense, inherited from generations of Puritans. It was now a religious instinct, and she was almost a fanatic with him, because she loved him, or had loved him. If he sinned, she tortured him. If he drank, and lied, was often a poltroon, sometimes a knave, she wielded the lash unmercifully.

The pity was, she was too much his opposite. She could not be content with the little he might be; she would have him the much that he ought to be. So, in seeking to make him nobler than he could be, she destroyed him. She injured and hurt and scarred herself, but she lost none of her worth. She also had the children.

He drank rather heavily, though not more than many miners, and always beer, so that whilst his health was affected, it was never injured. The week-end was his chief carouse. He sat in the Miners' Arms until turning-out time every Friday, every Saturday, and every Sunday evening. On Monday and Tuesday he had to get up and reluctantly leave towards ten o'clock. Sometimes he stayed at home on Wednesday and Thursday evenings, or was only out for an hour. He practically never had to miss work owing to his drinking.

But although he was very steady at work his wages fell off. He was blab-mouthed, a tongue-wagger. Authority was hateful to him, therefore he could only abuse the pit-managers. He would say, in the Palmerston:

'Th' gaffer come down to our stall this morning, an' 'e says, "You know, Walter, this 'ere'll not do. What about these props?" An' I says to him, "Why, what art talkin' about? What d'st mean about th' props?" "It'll never do, this 'ere," 'e says. "You'll be havin' th' roof in, one o' these days." An' I says, "Tha'd better stan' on a bit o' clunch, then, an' hold it up wi' thy 'ead." So 'e wor that mad, 'e cossed an' 'e swore, an' t'other chaps they did laugh.' Morel was a good mimic. He imitated the manager's fat, squeaky voice, with its attempt at good English.

'"I shan't have it, Walter. Who knows more about it, me or you?" So I says, "I've niver fun out how much tha' knows, Alfred. It'll 'appen carry thee ter bed an' back."'

So Morel would go on to the amusement of his boon companions. And some of this would be true. The pit-manager was not an educated man. He had been a boy along with Morel, so that, while the two disliked each other, they more or less took each other for granted. But Alfred Charlesworth did not forgive the butty these public-house sayings. Consequently, although Morel was a good miner, sometimes earning as much as five pounds a week when he married, he came gradually to have worse and worse stalls, where the coal was thin, and hard to get, and unprofitable.

Also, in summer, the pits were slack. Often, on bright sunny mornings, the men are seen trooping home again at ten, eleven or twelve o'clock. No empty trucks stand at the pit-mouth. The women on the hillside look across as they shake the hearthrug against the fence, and count the wagons the engine is taking along the line up the valley. And the children, as they come from school at dinner-time, looking down the fields and seeing the wheels on the headstocks standing, say:

'Minton's knocked off. My dad'll be at home.'

And there is a sort of shadow over all, women and children and men, because money will be short at the end of the week.

Morel was supposed to give his wife thirty shillings a week, to provide everything – rent, food, clothes, clubs, insurance, doctors. Occasionally, if he were flush, he gave her thirty-five. But these occasions by no means balanced those when he gave her twenty-five. In winter, with a decent stall, the miner might earn fifty or fifty-five shillings a week. Then he was happy. On Friday night, Saturday, and Sunday, he spent royally, getting rid of his sovereign or thereabouts. And out of so much, he scarcely spared the children an extra penny or brought them a pound of apples. It all went in drink. In the bad times, matters were more worrying, but he was not so often drunk, so that Mrs Morel used to say:

'I'm not sure I wouldn't rather be short, for when he's flush, there isn't a minute of peace.'

If he earned forty shillings he kept ten; from thirty-five he kept five; from thirty-two he kept four; from twenty-eight he kept three; from twenty-four he kept two; from twenty he kept one-and-six; from eighteen he kept a shilling; from sixteen he kept sixpence. He never saved a penny, and he gave his wife no opportunity of saving; instead, she had occasionally to pay his debts; not public-house debts, for those never were passed on to the women, but debts when he had bought a canary, or a fancy walking-stick.

At the wakes time, Morel was working badly, and Mrs Morel was trying to save against her confinement. So it galled her bitterly to think he should be out taking his pleasure and spending money, whilst she remained at home, harassed. There were two days' holiday. On the Tuesday morning Morel rose early. He was in good spirits. Quite early, before six o'clock, she heard him whistling away to himself downstairs. He had a pleasant way of whistling, lively and musical. He nearly always whistled hymns. He had been a choir-boy with a beautiful voice, and had taken solos in Southwell Cathedral. His morning whistling alone betrayed it.

His wife lay listening to him tinkering away in the garden, his whistling ringing out as he sawed and hammered away. It always gave her a sense of warmth and peace to hear him thus as she lay in bed, the children not yet awake, in the bright early morning, happy in his man's fashion.

At nine o'clock, while the children with bare legs and feet were sitting playing on the sofa, and the mother was washing up, he came in from his carpentry, his sleeves rolled up, his waistcoat hanging open. He was still a good-looking man, with black, wavy-hair, and a large black moustache. His face was perhaps too much inflamed, and there was about him a look almost of peevishness. But now he was jolly. He went straight to the sink where his wife was washing up.

'What, are thee there!' he said boisterously. 'Sluther off an' let me wesh mysen.'

'You may wait till I've finished,' said his wife.

'Oh, mun I? An' what if I shonna?'

This good-humoured threat amused Mrs Morel.

'Then you can go and wash yourself in the soft-water tub.'

'Ha! I can an' a', tha mucky little 'ussy.'

With which he stood watching her a moment, then went away to wait for her.

When he chose he could still make himself again a real gallant. Usually he preferred to go out with a scarf round his neck. Now, however, he made a toilet. There seemed so much gusto in the way he puffed and swilled as he washed himself, so much alacrity with which he hurried to the mirror in the kitchen, and, bending because it was too low for him, scrupulously parted his wet black hair, that it irritated Mrs Morel. He put on a turn-down collar, a black bow, and wore his Sunday tail-coat. As such, he looked spruce, and what his clothes would not do, his instinct for making the most of his good looks would.

At half-past nine Jerry Purdy came to call for his pal. Jerry was Morel's bosom friend, and Mrs Morel disliked him. He was a tall, thin man, with a rather foxy face, the kind of face that seems to lack eyelashes. He walked with a stiff, brittle dignity, as if his head were on a wooden spring. His nature was cold and shrewd. Generous where he intended to be generous, he seemed to be very fond of Morel, and more or less to take charge of him.

Mrs Morel hated him. She had known his wife, who had died of consumption, and who had, at the end, conceived such a violent dislike of her husband, that if he came into her room it caused her haemorrhage. None of which Jerry had seemed to mind. And now his eldest daughter, a girl of fifteen, kept a poor house for him, and looked after the two younger children.

'A mean, wizzen-hearted stick!' Mrs Morel said of him.

'I've never known Jerry mean in *my* life,' protested Morel. 'A opener-handed and more freer chap you couldn't find anywhere, accordin' to my knowledge.'

'Open-handed to you,' retorted Mrs Morel. 'But his fist is shut tight enough to his children, poor things.'

'Poor things! And what for are they poor things, I should like to know?'

But Mrs Morel would not be appeased on Jerry's score.

The subject of argument was seen, craning his thin neck over the scullery curtain. He caught Mrs Morel's eye.

'Mornin', missis! Mester in?'

'Yes – he is.'

Jerry entered unasked, and stood by the kitchen doorway. He was not invited to sit down, but stood there, coolly asserting the rights of men and husbands.

'A nice day,' he said to Mrs Morel.

'Yes.'

'Grand out this morning – grand for a walk.'

'Do you mean *you're* going for a walk?' she asked.

'Yes. We mean walkin' to Nottingham,' he replied.

'H'm!'

The two men greeted each other, both glad: Jerry, however, full of assurance, Morel rather subdued, afraid to seem too jubilant in presence of his wife. But he laced his boots quickly, with spirit. They were going for a ten-mile walk across the fields to Nottingham. Climbing the hillside from the Bottoms, they mounted gaily into the morning. At the Moon and Stars they had their first drink, then on to the Old Spot. Then a long five miles of drought to carry them into Bulwell to a glorious pint of bitter. But they stayed in a field with some haymakers whose gallon bottle was full, so that, when they came in sight of the city, Morel was sleepy. The town spread upwards before them, smoking vaguely in the midday glare, fringing the crest away to the south with spires and factory bulks and chimneys. In the last field Morel lay down under an oak-tree and slept soundly for over an hour. When he rose to go forward he felt queer.

The two had dinner in the Meadows, with Jerry's sister, then repaired to the Punch Bowl, where they mixed in the excitement of pigeon-racing. Morel never in his life played cards, considering them as having some occult, malevolent power – 'the devil's pictures', he called them! But he was a master of skittles and of dominoes. He took a challenge from a Newark man, on skittles. All the men in the old, long bar took sides, betting either one way or the other. Morel took off his coat. Jerry held the hat containing the money. The men at the tables watched. Some stood with their mugs in their hands. Morel felt his big wooden ball carefully, then launched it. He played havoc among the nine-pins, and won half-a-crown, which restored him to solvency.

By seven o'clock the two were in good condition. They caught the 7.30 train home.

In the afternoon the Bottoms was intolerable. Every inhabitant remaining was out of doors. The women, in twos and threes, bare-headed and in white aprons, gossiped in the alley between the blocks. Men, having a rest between drinks, sat on their heels and talked. The place smelled stale; the slate roofs glistered in the arid heat.

Mrs Morel took the little girl down to the brook in the meadows, which were not more than two hundred yards away. The water ran quickly over stones and broken pots. Mother and child leaned on the rail of the old sheep-bridge, watching. Up at the dipping-hole, at the other end of the meadows, Mrs Morel could see the naked forms of boys flashing round the deep yellow water, or an occasional bright figure dart glittering over the blackish stagnant meadow. She knew William was at the dipping-hole, and it was the dread of her life lest he should get drowned. Annie played under the tall old hedge, picking up alder cones, that she called currants. The child required much attention, and the flies were teasing.

The children were put to bed at seven o'clock. Then she worked awhile.

When Walter Morel and Jerry arrived at Bestwood they felt a load off their minds; a railway journey no longer impended, so they could put the finishing touches to a glorious day. They entered the Nelson with the satisfaction of returned travellers.

The next day was a work-day, and the thought of it put a damper on the men's spirits. Most of them, moreover, had spent their money. Some were already rolling dismally home, to sleep in preparation for the morrow. Mrs Morel, listening to their mournful singing, went indoors. Nine o'clock passed, and ten, and still 'the pair' had not returned. On a doorstep somewhere a man was singing loudly, in a drawl, 'Lead, kindly Light'. Mrs Morel was always indignant with the drunken men that they must sing that hymn when they got maudlin.

'As if "Genevieve" weren't good enough,' she said.

The kitchen was full of the scent of boiled herbs and hops. On the hob a large black saucepan steamed slowly. Mrs Morel took a panchion, a great bowl of thick red earth, streamed a heap of white sugar into the bottom, and then, straining herself to the weight, was pouring in the liquor.

Just then Morel came in. He had been very jolly in the Nelson, but coming home had grown irritable. He had not quite got over the feeling of irritability and pain, after having slept on the ground when he was so hot; and a bad conscience afflicted him as he neared the house. He did not know he was angry. But when the garden-gate resisted his attempts to open it, he kicked it and broke the latch. He entered just as Mrs Morel was pouring the infusion of herbs out of the saucepan. Swaying slightly, he lurched against the table. The boiling liquor pitched. Mrs Morel started back.

'Good gracious,' she cried, 'coming home in his drunkenness!'

'Comin' home in his what?' he snarled, his hat over his eye.

Suddenly her blood rose in a jet.

'Say you're *not* drunk!' she flashed.

She had put down her saucepan, and was stirring the sugar into the beer. He dropped his two hands heavily on the table, and thrust his face forward at her.

'"Say you're not drunk,"' he repeated. 'Why, nobody but a nasty little bitch like you 'ud 'ave such a thought.'

He thrust his fact forward at her.

'There's money to bezzle with, if there's money for nothing else.'

'I've not spent a two-shillin' bit this day,' he said.

'You don't get as drunk as a lord on nothing,' she replied. 'And,' she cried, flashing into sudden fury, 'if you've been sponging on your beloved Jerry, why, let him look after his children, for they need it.'

'It's a lie, it's a lie. Shut your face, woman.'

They were now at battle-pitch. Each forgot everything save the hatred of the other and the battle between them. She was fiery and furious as he. They went on till he called her a liar.

'No,' she cried, starting up, scarce able to breathe. 'Don't call me that – you, the most despicable liar that ever walked in shoe-leather.' She forced the last words out of suffocated lungs.

'You're a liar!' he yelled, banging the table with his fist. 'You're a liar, you're a liar.'

She stiffened herself with clenched fists.

'The house is filthy with you,' she cried.

'Then get out of it – it's mine. Get out of it!' he shouted. 'It's me as brings th' money whoam, not thee. It's my house, not thine. Then get out on't – get out on't!'

'And I would,' she cried, suddenly shaken into tears of impotence. 'Ah, wouldn't I, wouldn't I have gone long ago, but for those children. Ay, haven't I repented not going years ago, when I'd only the one' – suddenly drying into rage. 'Do you think it's for *you* I stop – do you think I'd stop one minute for *you?*'

'Go, then,' he shouted, beside himself. 'Go!'

'No!' she faced round. 'No,' she cried loudly, 'you shan't have it *all* your own way; you shan't do *all* you like. I've got those children to see to. My word,' she laughed, 'I should look well to leave them to you.'

'Go,' he cried thickly, lifting his fist. He was afraid of her. 'Go!'

'I should be only too glad. I should laugh, laugh, my lord, if I could get away from you,' she replied.

He came up to her, his red face, with its bloodshot eyes, thrust forward, and gripped her arms. She cried in fear of him, struggled to be free. Coming slightly to himself, panting, he pushed her roughly to the outer door, and thrust her forth, slotting the bolt behind her with a bang. Then he went back into the kitchen, dropped into his armchair, his head, bursting full of blood, sinking between his knees. Thus he dipped gradually into a stupor, from exhaustion and intoxication.

The moon was high and magnificent in the August night. Mrs Morel, seared with passion, shivered to find herself out there in a great white light, that fell cold on her, and gave a shock to her inflamed soul. She stood for a few moments helplessly staring at the glistening great rhubarb leaves near the door. Then she got the air into her breast. She walked down the garden path, trembling in every limb, while the child boiled within her. For a while she could not control her consciousness; mechanically she went over the last scene, then over it again, certain phrases, certain moments coming each time like a brand red-hot down on her soul; and each time she enacted again the past hour, each time the brand came down at the same points, till the mark was burnt in, and the pain burnt out, and at last she came to herself. She must have been half an hour in this delirious condition. Then the presence of the night came again to her. She glanced round in fear. She had wandered to the side garden, where she was walking up and down the path beside the currant bushes under the long wall. The garden was a narrow strip, bounded from the road, that cut transversely between the blocks, by a thick thorn hedge.

She hurried out of the side garden to the front, where she could stand as if in an immense gulf of white light, the moon streaming high in face of her, the moonlight standing up from the hills in front, and filling the valley where the Bottoms crouched, almost blindingly. There panting and half weeping in reaction from the stress, she murmured to herself over and over again: 'The nuisance! the nuisance!'

She became aware of something about her. With an effort she roused herself to see what it was that penetrated her consciousness. The tall while lilies were reeling in the moonlight, and the air was charged with their perfume, as with a presence. Mrs Morel gasped slightly in fear. She touched the big, pallid flowers on their petals, then shivered. They seemed to be stretching in the moonlight. She put her hand into one white bin: the gold scarcely showed on her fingers by moonlight. She bent down to look at the binful of yellow pollen; but it only appeared dusky. Then she drank a deep draught of the scent. It almost made her dizzy.

Mrs Morel leaned on the garden gate, looking out, and she lost herself awhile. She did not know what she thought. Except for a slight feeling of sickness, and her consciousness in the child, herself melted out like scent into the shiny, pale air. After a time the child, too, melted with her in the mixing-pot of moonlight, and she rested with the hills and lilies and houses, all swum together in a kind of swoon.

When she came to herself she was tired for sleep. Languidly she looked about her; the clumps of white phlox seemed like bushes spread with linen; a moth ricocheted over them, and right across the garden. Following it with her eye roused her. A few whiffs of the raw, strong scent of phlox invigorated her. She passed along the path, hesitating at the white rosebush. It smelled sweet and simple. She touched the white ruffles of the roses. Their fresh scent and cool, soft leaves reminded her of the morning-time and sunshine. She was very fond of them. But she was tired, and wanted to sleep. In the mysterious out-of-doors she felt forlorn.

There was no noise anywhere. Evidently the children had not been wakened, or had gone to sleep again. A train, three miles away, roared across the valley. The night was very large, and very strange, stretching its hoary distances infinitely. And out of the silver-grey fog of darkness came sounds vague and hoarse: a corncrake not far off, sound of a train like a sigh, and distant shouts of men.

Her quietened heart beginning to beat quickly again, she hurried down the side garden to the back of the house. Softly she lifted the latch; the door was still bolted, shut hard against her. She rapped gently, waited, then rapped again. She must not rouse the children, nor the neighbours. He must be asleep, and he would not wake easily. Her heart began to burn to be indoors. She clung to the door-handle. Now it was cold; she would take a chill, and in her present condition!

Putting her apron over her head and her arms, she hurried again to the side garden, to the window of the kitchen. Leaning on the sill, she could just see, under the blind, her husband's arms spread out on the table, and his black head on the board. He was sleeping with his face lying on the table. Something in his attitude made her feel tired of things. The lamp was burning smokily; she could tell by the colour of the light. She tapped at the window more and more noisily. Almost it seemed as if the glass would break. Still he did not wake up.

After vain efforts, she began to shiver, partly from contact with the stone, and from exhaustion. Fearful always for the unborn child, she wondered what she could do for warmth. She went down to the coal-house, where was an old hearthrug she had carried out for the rag-man the day before. This she wrapped over her shoulders. It was warm, if grimy. Then she walked up and down the garden path, peeping every now and then under the blind, knocking, and telling herself that in the end the very strain of his position must wake him.

At last, after about an hour, she rapped long and low at the window. Gradually the sound penetrated to him. When, in despair, she had ceased to tap, she saw him stir, then lift his face blindly. The labouring of his heart hurt him into consciousness. She rapped imperatively at the window. He started awake. Instantly she saw his fists set and his eyes glare. He had not a grain of physical fear. If it had been twenty burglars, he would have gone blindly for them. He glared round, bewildered, but prepared to fight.

'Open the door, Walter,' she said coldly.

His hands relaxed. It dawned on him what he had done. His head dropped, sullen and dogged. She saw him hurry to the door, heard the bolt chock. He tried the latch. It opened – and there stood the silver-grey night, fearful to him, after the tawny light of the lamp. He hurried back.

When Mrs Morel entered, she saw him almost running through the door to the stairs. He had ripped his collar off his neck in his haste to be gone ere she came in, and there it lay with bursten button-holes. It made her angry.

She warmed and soothed herself. In her weariness forgetting everything, she moved about at the little tasks that remained to be done, set his breakfast, rinsed his pit-bottle, put his pit-clothes on the hearth to warm, set his pit-boots beside them, put him out a clean scarf and snap-bag and two apples, raked the fire, and went to bed. He was already dead asleep. His narrow black eyebrows were drawn up in a sort of peevish misery into his forehead, while his cheeks' downstrokes, and his sulky mouth, seemed to be saying: 'I don't care who you are or what you are, I *shall* have my own way.'

Mrs Morel knew him too well to look at him. As she unfastened her brooch at the mirror, she smiled faintly to see her face all smeared with the yellow dust of lilies. She brushed it off, and at last lay down. For some time her mind continued snapping and jetting sparks, but she was asleep before her husband awoke from the first sleep of his drunkenness.

2

THE BIRTH OF PAUL, AND ANOTHER BATTLE

After such a scene as the last, Walter Morel was for some days abashed and ashamed, but he soon regained his old bullying indifference. Yet there was a slight shrinking, a diminishing in his assurance. Physically even, he shrank, and his fine full presence waned. He never grew in the least stout, so that, as he sank from his erect, assertive bearing, his physique seemed to contract along with his pride and moral strength.

But now he realized how hard it was for his wife to drag about at her work, and, his sympathy quickened by penitence, hastened forward with his help. He came straight home from the pit, and stayed in at evening till Friday, and then he could not remain at home. But he was back again by ten o'clock, almost quite sober.

He always made his own breakfast. Being a man who rose early and had plenty of time he did not, as some miners do, drag his wife out of bed at six o'clock. At five, sometimes earlier, he woke, got straight out of bed, and went downstairs. When she could not sleep, his wife lay waiting for this time, as for a period of peace. The only real rest seemed to be when he was out of the house.

He went downstairs in his shirt and then struggled into the pit-trousers, which were left on the hearth to warm all night. There was always a fire, because Mrs Morel raked. And the first sound in the house was the bang, bang of the poker against the raker, as Morel smashed the remainder of the coal to make the kettle, which was filled and left on the hob, finally boil. His cup and knife and fork, all he wanted except just the food, was laid ready on the table on a newspaper. Then he got his breakfast, made the tea, packed the bottom of the doors with rugs to shut out the draught, piled a big fire, and sat down to an hour of joy. He toasted his bacon on a fork and caught the drops of fat on his bread; then he put the rasher on his thick slice of bread, and cut off chunks with a clasp-knife, poured his tea into his saucer, and was happy. With his family about, meals were never so pleasant. He loathed a fork; it is a modern introduction which has still scarcely reached common people. What Morel preferred was a clasp-knife. Then, in solitude, he ate and drank, often sitting, in cold weather, on a little stool with his back to the warm chimney-piece, his food on the fender, his cup on the hearth. And then he read the last night's newspaper – what of it he could – spelling it over laboriously. He preferred to keep the blinds down and the candle lit even when it was daylight; it was the habit of the mine.

At a quarter to six he rose, cut two thick slices of bread-and-butter, and put them in the white calico snap-bag. He filled his tin bottle with tea. Cold tea without milk or sugar was the drink he preferred for the pit. Then he pulled off his shirt, and put on his pit-singlet, a vest of thick flannel cut low round the neck, and with short sleeves like a chemise.

Then he went upstairs to his wife with a cup of tea because she was ill, and because it occurred to him.

'I've brought thee a cup o' tea, lass,' he said.

'Well, you needn't, for you know I don't like it,' she replied.

'Drink it up; it'll pop thee off to sleep again.'

She accepted the tea. It pleased him to see her take it and sip it.

'I'll back my life there's no sugar in,' she said.

'Yi – there's one big un,' he replied, injured.

'It's a wonder,' she said, sipping again.

She had a winsome face when her hair was loose. He loved her to grumble at him in this manner. He looked at her again, and went, without any sort of leave-taking. He never took more than two slices of bread and butter to eat in the pit, so an apple or an orange was a treat to him. He always liked it when she put one out for him. He tied a scarf round his neck, put on his great, heavy boots, his coat, with the big pocket, that carried his snap-bag and his bottle of tea, and went forth into the fresh morning air, closing, without locking, the door behind him. He loved the early morning, and the walk across the fields. So he appeared at the pit-top, often with a stalk from the hedge between his teeth, which he chewed all day to keep his mouth moist, down the mine, feeling quite as happy as when he was in the field.

Later, when the time for the baby grew nearer, he would bustle round in his slovenly fashion, poking out the ashes, rubbing the fireplace, sweeping the house before he went to work. Then, feeling very self-righteous, he went upstairs.

'Now I'm cleaned up for thee; tha's no 'casions ter stir a peg all day, but sit and read thy books.'

Which made her laugh, in spite of her indignation.

'And the dinner cooks itself?' she answered.

'Eh, I know nowt about th' dinner.'

'You'd know if there weren't any.'

'Ay, 'appen so,' he answered, departing.

When she got downstairs, she would find the house tidy, but dirty. She could not rest until she had thoroughly cleaned; so she went down to the ash-pit with her dust-pan. Mrs Kirk, spying her, would contrive to have to go to her own coalplace at that minute. Then, across the wooden fence, she would call:

'So you keep wagging on, then?'

'Ay,' answered Mrs Morel deprecatingly. 'There's nothing else for it.'

'Have you seen Hose?' called a very small woman from across the road. It was Mrs Anthony, a black-haired, strange little body, who always wore a brown velvet dress, tight fitting.

'I haven't,' said Mrs Morel.

'Eh, I wish he'd come. I've got a copperful of clothes, an' I'm sure I heered his bell.'

'Hark! He's at the end.'

The two women looked down the alley. At the end of the Bottoms a man stood in a sort of old-fashioned trap, bending over bundles of cream-coloured stuff; while a cluster of women held up their arms to him, some with bundles. Mrs Anthony herself had a heap of creamy, undyed stockings hanging over her arm.

'I've done ten dozen this week,' she said proudly to Mrs Morel.

'T-t-t!' went the other. 'I don't know how you can find time.'

'Eh!' said Mrs Anthony. 'You can find time if you make time.'

'I don't know how you do it,' said Mrs Morel. 'And how much shall you get for those many?'

'Tuppence-ha'penny a dozen,' replied the other.

'Well,' said Mrs Morel, 'I'd starve before I'd sit down and seam twenty-four stockings for twopence ha'penny.'

'Oh, I don't know,' said Mrs Anthony. 'You can rip along with 'em.'

Hose was coming along, ringing his bell. Women were waiting at the yard-ends with their seamed stockings hanging over their arms. The man, a common fellow, made jokes with them, tried to swindle them, and bullied them. Mrs Morel went up her yard disdainfully.

It was an understood thing that if one woman wanted her neighbour, she should put the poker in the fire and bang at the back of the fireplace, which, as the fires were back to back, would make a great noise in the adjoining house. One morning Mrs Kirk, mixing a pudding, nearly started out of her skin as she heard the thud, thud in her grate. With her hands all floury, she rushed to the fence.

'Did you knock, Mrs Morel?'

'If you wouldn't mind, Mrs Kirk.'

Mrs Kirk climbed on to her copper, got over the wall on to Mrs Morel's copper, and ran in to her neighbour.

'Eh, dear, how are you feeling?' she cried in concern.

'You might fetch Mrs Bower,' said Mrs Morel.

Mrs Kirk went into the yard, lifted up her strong, shrill voice, and called:

'Ag-gie – Ag-gie!'

The sound was heard from one end of the Bottoms to the other. At last Aggie came running up, and was sent for Mrs Bower, whilst Mrs Kirk left her pudding and stayed with her neighbour.

Mrs Morel went to bed. Mrs Kirk had Annie and William for dinner. Mrs Bower, fat and waddling, bossed the house.

'Hash some cold meat up for the master's dinner, and make him an apple-charlotte pudding,' said Mrs Morel.

'He may go without pudding *this* day,' said Mrs Bower.

Morel was not as a rule one of the first to appear at the bottom of the pit, ready to come up. Some men were there before four o'clock, when the whistle blew loose-all; but Morel, whose stall, a poor one, was at this time about a mile and a half away from the bottom, worked usually till the first mate stopped, then he finished also. This day, however, the miner was sick of the work. At two o'clock he looked at his watch, by the light of the green candle – he was in a safe working – and again at half-past two. He was hewing at a piece of rock that was in the way for the next day's work. As he sat on his heels, or kneeled, giving hard blows with his pick, 'Uszza – uszza!' he went.

'Shall ter finish, Sorry?'* cried Barker, his fellow butty.

'Finish? Niver while the world stands!' growled Morel.

And he went on striking. He was tired.

'It's a heart-breaking job,' said Barker.

But Morel was too exasperated, at the end of his tether, to answer. Still he struck and hacked with all his might.

'Tha might as well leave it, Walter,' said Barker. 'It'll do tomorrow, without thee hackin' thy guts out.'

'I'll lay no b— finger on this tomorrow, Isr'el!' cried Morel.

'Oh, well, if tha wunna, someb'dy else 'll ha'e to,' said Israel.

Then Morel continued to strike.

'Hey-up there – *loose-a*'!' cried the men, leaving the next stall.

Morel continued to strike.

'Tha'll happen catch me up,' said Barker, departing.

When he had gone, Morel, left alone, felt savage. He had not finished his job. He had overworked himself into a frenzy. Rising, wet with sweat, he threw his tool down, pulled on his coat, blew out his candle, took his lamp, and went. Down the main road the lights of the other men went swinging. There was a hollow sound of many voices. It was a long, heavy tramp underground.

He sat at the bottom of the pit, where the great drops of water fell plash. Many colliers were waiting their turns to go up, talking noisily. Morel gave his answers short and disagreeable.

'It's rainin', Sorry,' said old Giles, who had had the news from the top.

Morel found one comfort. He had his old umbrella, which he loved, in the lamp cabin. At last he took his stand on the chair, and was at the top in a moment. Then he handed in his lamp and got his umbrella, which he had bought at an auction for one-and-six. He stood on the edge of the pit-bank for a moment, looking out over the fields; grey rain was falling. The trucks stood full of wet, bright coal. Water ran down the sides of the wagons, over the white 'C.W. and Co'. Colliers, walking indifferent to the rain, were streaming down the line and up the field, a grey, dismal host. Morel put up his umbrella, and took pleasure from the peppering of the drops thereon.

* 'Sorry' is a common form of address. It is, perhaps, a corruption of 'sirrah'.

All along the road to Bestwood the miners tramped, wet and grey and dirty, but their red mouths talking with animation. Morel also walked with a gang, but he said nothing. He frowned peevishly as he went. Many men passed into the Prince of Wales or into Ellen's. Morel, feeling sufficiently disagreeable to resist temptation, trudged along under the dripping trees that overhung the park wall, and down the mud of Greenhill Lane.

Mrs Morel lay in bed, listening to the rain, and the feet of the colliers from Minton, their voices, and the bang, bang of the gates as they went through the stile up the field.

'There's some herb beer behind the pantry-door,' she said. 'Th' master'll want a drink, if he doesn't stop.'

But he was late, so she concluded he had called for a drink, since it was raining. What did he care about the child or her?

She was very ill when her children were born.

'What is it?' she asked, feeling sick to death.

'A boy.'

And she took consolation in that. The thought of being the mother of men was warming to her heart. She looked at the child. It had blue eyes, and a lot of fair hair, and was bonny. Her love came up hot, in spite of everything. She had it in bed with her.

Morel, thinking nothing, dragged his way up the garden path, wearily and angrily. He closed his umbrella, and stood it in the sink; then he sluthered his heavy boots into the kitchen. Mrs Bowers appeared in the inner doorway.

'Well,' she said, 'she's about as bad as she can be. It's a boy child.'

The miner grunted, put his empty snap-bag and his tin bottle on the dresser, went back into the scullery and hung up his coat, then came and dropped into his chair.

'Han yer got a drink?' he asked.

The woman went into the pantry. There was heard the oop of a cork. She set the mug, with a little, disgusted rap, on the table before Morel. He drank, gasped, wiped his big moustache on the end of his scarf, drank, gasped, and lay back in his chair. The woman would not speak to him again. She set his dinner before him, and went upstairs.

'Was that the master?' asked Mrs Morel.

'I've gave him his dinner,' replied Mrs Bower.

After he had sat with his arms on the table – he resented the fact that Mrs Bower put no cloth on for him, and gave him a little plate instead of a full-sized dinner-plate – he began to eat. The fact that his wife was ill, that he had another boy, was nothing to him at that moment. He was too tired; he wanted his dinner; he wanted to sit with his arms lying on the board; he did not like having Mrs Bower about. The fire was too small to please him.

After he had finished his meal, he sat for twenty minutes; then he stoked up a big fire. Then, in his stockinged feet, he went reluctantly upstairs. It was a struggle to face his wife at this moment and he was tired. His face was black, and smeared with sweat. His singlet had dried again, soaking the dirt in. He had a dirty woollen scarf round his throat. So he stood at the foot of the bed.

'Well, how are ter, then?' he asked.

'I s'll be all right,' she answered.

'H'm!'

He stood at a loss what to say next. He was tired, and this bother was rather a nuisance to him, and he didn't quite know where he was.

'A lad, tha says,' he stammered.

She turned down the sheet and showed the child.

'Bless him!' he murmured. Which made her laugh, because he blessed by rote – pretending paternal emotion, which he did not feel just then.

'Go now,' she said.

'I will, my lass,' he answered, turning away.

Dismissed, he wanted to kiss her, but he dared not. She half wanted him to kiss her, but could not bring herself to give any sign. She only breathed freely when he was gone out of the room again, leaving behind him a faint smell of pit-dirt.

Mrs Morel had a visit every day from the Congregational clergyman. Mr Heaton was young, and very poor. His wife had died at the birth of his first baby, so he remained alone in the manse. He was a Bachelor of Arts of Cambridge, very shy and no preacher. Mrs Morel was fond of him, and he depended on her. For hours he talked to her, when she was well. He became the god-parent of the child.

Occasionally, the minister stayed to tea with Mrs Morel. Then she laid the cloth early, got out her best cups, with a little green rim, and hoped Morel would not come too soon; indeed, if he stayed for a pint, she would not mind this day. She had always two dinners to cook, because she believed children should have their chief meal at midday, whereas Morel needed his at five o'clock. So Mr Heaton would hold the baby, whilst Mrs Morel beat up a batter-pudding or peeled the potatoes, and he, watching her all the time, would discuss his next sermon. His ideas were quaint and fantastic. She brought him judiciously to earth. It was a discussion of the wedding at Cana.

'When He changed the water into wine at Cana,' he said, 'that is a symbol that the ordinary life, even the blood, of the married husband and wife, which had before been uninspired, like water, became filled with the Spirit, and was as wine, because, when love enters, the whole spiritual constitution of a man changes, is filled with the Holy Ghost, and almost his form is altered.'

Mrs Morel thought to herself:

'Yes, poor fellow, his young wife is dead; that is why he makes his love into the Holy Ghost.'

They were halfway down their first cup of tea when they heard the sluther of pit-boots.

'Good gracious!' exclaimed Mrs Morel, in spite of herself. The minister looked rather scared. Morel entered. He was feeling rather savage. He nodded a 'How d'yer do' to the clergyman, who rose to shake hands with him.

'Nay,' said Morel, showing his hand, 'look thee at it! Tha niver wants ter shake hands wi' a hand like that, does ter? There's too much pick-halft and shovel-dirt on it.'

The minister flushed with confusion, and sat down again. Mrs Morel rose, carried out the steaming saucepan. Morel took off his coat, dragged his armchair to the table and sat down, heavily.

'Are you tired?' asked the clergyman.

'Tired? I ham that,' replied Morel. '*You* don't know what it is to be tired, as *I'm* tired.'

'No,' replied the clergyman.

'Why, look yer 'ere,' said the miner, showing the shoulders of his singlet. 'It's a bit dry now, but it's wet as a clout with sweat even yet. Feel it.'

'Goodness!' cried Mrs Morel. 'Mr Heaton doesn't want to feel your nasty singlet.'

The clergyman put out his hand gingerly.

'No, perhaps he doesn't,' said Morel; 'But it's all come out of *me* whether or not. An' iv'ry day alike my singlet's wringin' wet. 'Aven't you got a drink, Missis, for a man when he comes home barkled up from the pit?'

'You know you drank all the beer,' said Mrs Morel, pouring out his tea.

'An' was there no more to be got?' Turning to the clergyman – 'A man gets that caked up wi' th' dust, you know – that clogged up down a coalmine, he *needs* a drink when he comes home.'

'I am sure he does,' said the clergyman.

'But it's ten to one if there's owt for him.'

'There's water – and there's tea,' said Mrs Morel.

'Water! It's not water as'll clear his throat.'

He poured out a saucerful of tea, blew it, and sucked it up through his great black moustache, sighing afterwards. Then he poured out another saucerful, and stood his cup on the table.

'My cloth!' said Mrs Morel, putting it on a plate.

'A man as comes home as I do's too tired to care about cloths,' said Morel.

'Pity!' exclaimed his wife, sarcastically.

The room was full of the smell of meat and vegetables and pit-clothes.

He leaned over to the minister, his great moustache thrust forward, his mouth very red in his black face.

'Mr Heaton,' he said, 'a man as has been down the black hole all day, dingin' away at a coal face, yi, a sight harder than that wall –'

'Needn't make a moan of it,' put in Mrs Morel.

She hated her husband because, whenever he had an audience, he whined and played for sympathy. William, sitting nursing the baby, hated him, with a boy's hatred for false sentiment, and for the stupid treatment of his mother. Annie had never liked him, she merely avoided him.

When the minister had gone, Mrs Morel looked at her cloth.

'A fine mess!' she said.

'Dos't think I'm goin' to sit wi' my arms danglin', cos tha's got a parson for tea wi' thee?' he bawled.

They were both angry, but she said nothing. The baby began to cry, and Mrs Morel, picking up a saucepan from the hearth, accidentally knocked Annie on the head, whereupon the girl began to whine, and Morel to shout at her. In the midst of this pandemonium, William looked up at the big glazed text over the mantelpiece and read distinctly:

'God Bless Our Home!'

Whereupon Mrs Morel, trying to soothe the baby, jumped up, rushed at him, boxed his ears, saying:

'What are *you* putting in for?'

And then she sat down and laughed, till tears ran over her cheeks, while William kicked the stool he had been sitting on, and Morel growled:

'I canna see what there is so much to laugh at.'

One evening, directly after the parson's visit, feeling unable to bear herself after another display from her husband, she took Annie and the baby and went out. Morel had kicked William, and the mother would never forgive him.

She went over the sheep-bridge and across a corner of the meadow to the cricket-ground. The meadows seemed one space of ripe, evening light, whispering with the distant mill-race. She sat on a seat under the alders in the cricket-ground, and fronted the evening. Before her, level and solid, spread the big green cricket-field, like the bed of a sea of light. Children played in the bluish shadow of the pavilion. Many rooks, high up, came cawing home across the softly-woven sky. They stooped in a long curve down into the golden glow, concentrating, cawing, wheeling, like black flakes on a slow vortex, over a tree-clump that made a dark boss among the pasture.

A few gentlemen were practising, and Mrs Morel could hear the chock of the ball, and the voices of men suddenly roused; could see the white forms of men shifting silently over the green, upon which already the under shadows were smouldering. Away at the grange, one side of the hay-stacks was lit up, the other sides blue-grey. A wagon of sheaves rocked small across the melting yellow light.

The sun was going down. Every open evening, the hills of Derbyshire were blazed over with red sunset. Mrs Morel watched the sun sink from the glistening sky, leaving a soft flower-blue overhead, while the western space went red, as if all the fire had swum down there, leaving the bell cast flawless blue. The mountain-ash berries across the field stood fierily out from the dark leaves, for a moment. A few shocks of corn in a corner of the fallow stood up as if alive; she imagined them bowing; perhaps her son would be a Joseph. In the east, a mirrored sunset floated pink opposite the west's scarlet. The big haystacks on the hillside, that butted into the glare, went cold.

With Mrs Morel it was one of those still moments when the small frets vanish, and the beauty of things stands out, and she had the peace and the strength to see herself. Now and again, a swallow cut close to her. Now and again, Annie came up with a handful of alder-currants. The baby was restless on his mother's knee, clambering with his hands at the light.

Mrs Morel looked down at him. She had dreaded this baby like a catastrophe, because of her feeling for her husband. And now she felt strangely towards the infant. Her heart was heavy because of the child, almost as if it were unhealthy, or malformed. Yet it seemed quite well. But she noticed the peculiar knitting of the baby's brows, and the peculiar heaviness of its eyes, as if it were trying to understand something that was pain. She felt, when she looked at her child's dark, brooding pupils, as if a burden were on her heart.

'He looks as if he was thinking about something – quite sorrowful,' said Mrs Kirk.

Suddenly, looking at him, the heavy feeling at the mother's heart melted into passionate grief. She bowed over him, and a few tears shook swiftly out of her very heart. The baby lifted his fingers.

'My lamb!' she cried softly.

And at that moment she felt, in some far inner place of her soul, that she and her husband were guilty.

The baby was looking up at her. It had blue eyes like her own, but its look was heavy, steady, as if it had realized something that had stunned some point of its soul.

In her arms lay the delicate baby. Its deep blue eyes, always looking up at her unblinking, seemed to draw her innermost thoughts out of her. She no longer loved her husband; she had not wanted this child to come, and there it lay in her arms and pulled at her heart. She felt as if the navel string that had connected its frail little body with hers had not been broken. A wave of hot love went over her to the infant. She held it close to her face and breast. With all her force, with all her soul she would make up to it for having brought it into the world unloved. She would love it all the more now it was here; carry it in her love. Its clear, knowing eyes gave her pain and fear. Did it know all about her? When it lay under her heart, had it been listening then? Was there a reproach in the look? She felt the marrow melt in her bones, with fear and pain.

Once more she was aware of the sun lying red on the rim of the hill opposite. She suddenly held up the child in her hands.

'Look!' she said. 'Look, my pretty!'

She thrust the infant forward to the crimson, throbbing sun, almost with relief. She saw him lift his little fist. Then she put him to her bosom again, ashamed of her impulse to give him back again whence he came.

'If he lives,' she thought to herself, 'what will become of him – what will he be?'

Her heart was anxious.

'I will call him "Paul",' she said suddenly; she knew not why.

After a while she went home. A fine shadow was flung over the deep green meadow, darkening all.

As she expected, she found the house empty. But Morel was home by ten o'clock, and that day, at least, ended peacefully.

Walter Morel was, at this time, exceedingly irritable. His work seemed to exhaust him. When he came home he did not speak civilly to anybody. If the fire were rather low he bullied about that; he grumbled about his dinner; if the children made a chatter he shouted at them in a way that made their mother's blood boil, and made them hate him.

On the Friday, he was not home by eleven o'clock. The baby was unwell, and was restless, crying if he were put down. Mrs Morel, tired to death, and still weak, was scarcely under control.

'I wish the nuisance would come,' she said wearily to herself.

The child at last sank down to sleep in her arms. She was too tired to carry him to the cradle.

'But I'll say nothing, whatever time he comes,' she said. 'It only works me up: I won't say anything. But I know if he does anything it'll make my blood boil,' she added to herself.

She sighed, hearing him coming, as if it were something she could not bear. He, taking his revenge, was nearly drunk. She kept her head bent over the child as he entered, not wishing to see him. But it went through her like a flash of hot fire when, in passing, he lurched against the dresser, setting the tins rattling, and clutched at the white pot knobs for support. He hung up his hat and coat, then returned, stood glowering from a distance at her, as she sat bowed over the child.

'Is there nothing to eat in the house?' he asked, insolently, as if to a servant. In certain stages of his intoxication he affected the clipped, mincing speech of the towns. Mrs Morel hated him most in this condition.

'You know what there is in the house,' she said, so coldly it sounded impersonal.

He stood and glared at her without moving a muscle.

'I asked a civil question, and I expect a civil answer,' he said affectedly.

'And you got it,' she said, still ignoring him.

He glowered again. Then he came unsteadily forward. He leaned on the table with one hand, and with the other jerked at the table drawer to get a knife to cut bread. The drawer stuck because he pulled sideways. In a temper he dragged it, so that it flew out bodily, and spoons, forks, knives, and a hundred metallic things, spashed with a clatter and a clang unon the brick floor. The baby gave a little convulsed start.

'What are you doing, clumsy, drunken fool?' the mother cried.

'Then tha should get the flamin' thing thysen. Tha should get up, like other women have to, an' wait on a man.'

'Wait on you – wait on you?' she cried. 'Yes, I see myself.'

'Yis, an' I'll learn thee tha's got to. Wait on *me*, yes, tha sh'lt wait on me –'

'Never, milord. I'd wait on a dog at the door first.'

'What – what?'

He was trying to fit in the drawer. At her last speech he turned round. His face was crimson, his eyes bloodshot. He stared at her one silent second in threat.

'P-h!' she went quickly, in contempt.

He jerked at the drawer in his excitement. It fell, cut sharply on his shin, and on the reflex he flung it at her.

One of the corners caught her brow as the shallow drawer crashed into the fireplace. She swayed, almost fell stunned from her chair. To her very soul she was sick; she clasped the child tightly to her bosom. A few moments elapsed; then, with an effort, she brought herself to. The baby was crying plaintively. Her left brow was bleeding rather profusely. As she glanced down at the child, her brain reeling, some drops of blood soaked into its white shawl; but the baby was at least not hurt. She balanced her head to keep equilibrium, so that the blood ran into her eye.

Walter Morel remained as he had stood, leaning on the table with one hand, looking blank. When he was sufficiently sure of his balance, he went across to her, swayed, caught hold of the back of her rocking-chair, almost tipping her out; then, leaning forward over her, and swaying as he spoke, he said, in a tone of wondering concern:

'Did it catch thee?'

He swayed again, as if he would pitch on to the child. With the catastrophe he had lost all balance.

'Go away,' she said, struggling to keep her presence of mind.

He hiccoughed. 'Let's – let's look at it,' he said, hiccoughing again.

'Go away!' she cried.

'Lemme – lemme look at it, lass.'

She smelled him of drink, felt the unequal pull of his swaying grasp on the back of her rocking-chair.

'Go away,' she said, and weakly she pushed him off.

He stood, uncertain in balance, gazing upon her. Summoning all her strength she rose, the baby on one arm. By a cruel effort of will, moving as if in sleep, she went across to the scullery, where she bathed her eye for a minute in cold water; but she was too dizzy. Afraid lest she should swoon, she returned to her rocking-chair, trembling in every fibre. By instinct, she kept the baby clasped.

Morel, bothered, had succeeded in pushing the drawer back into its cavity, and was on his knees, groping, with numb paws, for the scattered spoons.

Her brow was still bleeding. Presently Morel got up and came craning his neck towards her.

'What has it done to thee, lass?' he asked, in a very wretched, humble tone.

'You can see what it's done,' she answered.

He stood, bending forward, supported on his hands, which grasped his legs just above the knee. He peered to look at the wound. She drew away from the thrust of his face with its great moustache, averting her own face as much as possible. As he looked at her, who was cold and impassive as stone, with mouth shut tight, he sickened with feebleness and hopelessness of spirit. He was turning drearily away, when he saw a drop of blood fall from the averted wound into the baby's fragile, glistening hair. Fascinated he watched the heavy dark drop hang in the glistening cloud, and pull down the gossamer. Another drop fell. It would soak through to the baby's scalp. He watched, fascinated, feeling it soak in; then, finally, his manhood broke.

'What of this child?' was all his wife said to him. But her low, intense tones brought his head lower. She softened: 'Get me some wadding out of the middle drawer,' she said.

He stumbled away very obediently, presently returning with a pad, which she singed before the fire, then put on her forehead, as she sat with the baby on her lap.

'Now that clean pit-scarf.'

Again he rummaged and fumbled in the drawer, returning presently with a red, narrow scarf. She took it, and with trembling fingers proceeded to bind it round her head.

'Let me tie it for thee,' he said humbly.

'I can do it myself,' she replied. When it was done she went upstairs, telling him to rake the fire and lock the door.

In the morning Mrs Morel said:

'I knocked against the latch of the coal-place, when I was getting a raker in the dark, because the candle blew out.' Her two small children looked up at her with wide, dismayed eyes. They said nothing, but their parted lips seemed to express the unconscious tragedy they felt.

Walter Morel lay in bed next day until nearly dinner-time. He did not think of the previous evening's work. He scarcely thought of anything, but he would not think of that. He lay and suffered like a sulking dog. He had hurt himself most; and he was the more damaged because he would never say a word to her, or express his sorrow. He tried to wriggle out of it. 'It was her own fault,' he said to himself. Nothing, however, could prevent his inner consciousness inflicting on him the punishment which ate into his spirit like rust, and which he could only alleviate by drinking.

He felt as if he had not the initiative to get up, or to say a word, or to move, but could only lie like a log. Moreover, he had himself violent pains in the head. It was Saturday. Towards noon he rose, cut himself food in the pantry, ate it with his head dropped, then pulled on his boots, and went out, to return at three o'clock slightly tipsy and relieved; then once more straight to bed. He rose again at six in the evening, had tea and went straight out.

Sunday was the same: bed till noon, the Palmerston Arms till 2.30, dinner, and bed; scarcely a word spoken. When Mrs Morel went upstairs, towards four o'clock, to put on her Sunday dress, he was fast asleep. She would have felt sorry for him, if he had once said, 'Wife, I'm sorry.' But no; he insisted to himself it was her fault. And so he broke himself. So she merely left him alone. There was this deadlock of passion between them, and she was stronger.

The family began tea. Sunday was the only day when all sat down to meals together.

'Isn't my father going to get up?' asked William.

'Let him lie,' the mother replied.

There was a feeling of misery over all the house. The children breathed the air that was poisoned, and they felt dreary. They were rather disconsolate, did not know what to do, what to play at.

Immediately Morel woke he got straight out of bed. That was characteristic of him all his life. He was all for activity. The prostrated inactivity of two mornings was stifling him.

It was near six o'clock when he got down. This time he entered without hesitation, his wincing sensitiveness having hardened again. He did not care any longer what the family thought or felt.

The tea-things were on the table. William was reading aloud from 'The Child's Own', Annie listening and asking eternally 'Why?' Both children hushed into silence as they heard the approaching thud of their father's stockinged feet, and shrank as he entered. Yet he was usually indulgent to them.

Morel made the meal alone, brutally. He ate and drank more noisily than he had need. No one spoke to him. The family life withdrew, shrank away, and became hushed as he entered. But he cared no longer about his alienation.

Immediately he had finished tea he rose with alacrity to go out. It was this alacrity, this haste to be gone, which so sickened Mrs Morel. As she heard him sousing heartily in cold water, heard the eager scratch of the steel comb on the side of the bowl, as he wetted his hair, she closed her eyes in disgust. As he bent over, lacing his boots, there was a certain vulgar gusto in his movement that divided him from the reserved, watchful rest of the family. He always ran away from the battle with himself. Even in his own heart's privacy, he excused himself, saying, 'If she hadn't said so-and-so, it would never have happened. She asked for what she's got.' The children waited in restraint during his preparations. When he had gone, they sighed with relief.

He closed the door behind him, and was glad. It was a rainy evening. The Palmerston would be the cosier. He hastened forward in anticipation. All the slate roofs of the Bottoms shone black with wet. The roads, always dark with coal-dust, were full of blackish mud. He hastened along. The Palmerston windows were steamed over. The passage was paddled with wet feet. But the air was warm, if foul, and full of the sound of voices and the smell of beer and smoke.

'What shollt ha'e, Walter?' cried a voice, as soon as Morel appearerd in the doorway.

'Oh, Jim, my lad, wheriver has thee sprung frae?'

The men made a seat for him, and took him in warmly. He was glad. In a minute or two they had thawed all responsibility out of him, all shame, all trouble, and he was clear as a bell for a jolly night.

On the Wednesday following, Morel was penniless. He dreaded his wife. Having hurt her, he hated her. He did not know what to do with himself that evening, having not even twopence with which to go to the Palmerston, and being already rather deeply in debt. So, while his wife was down the garden with the child, he hunted in the top drawer of the dresser where she kept her purse, found it, and looked inside. It contained a half-crown, two half-pennies, and a sixpence. So he took the sixpence, put the purse carefully back, and went out.

The next day, when she wanted to pay the greengrocer, she looked in the purse for her sixpence, and her heart sank to her shoes. Then she sat down and thought: '*Was* there a sixpence? I hadn't spent it, had I? And I hadn't left it anywhere else?'

She was much put about. She hunted round everywhere for it. And, as she thought, the conviction came into her heart that her husband had taken it. What she had in her purse was all the money she possessed. But that he should sneak it from her thus was unbearable. He had done so twice before. The first time she had not accused him, and at the week-end he had put the shilling again into her purse. So that was how she had known he had taken it. The second time he had not paid back.

This time she felt it was too much. When he had had his dinner – he came home early that day – she said to him coldly:

'Did you take sixpence out of my purse last night?'

'Me!' he said, looking up in an offended way. 'No, I didna! I niver clapped eyes on your purse.'

But she could detect the lie.

'Why, you know you did,' she said quietly.

'I tell you I didna,' he shouted. 'Yer at me again, are yer? I've had about enough on't.'

'So you filch sixpence out of my purse while I'm taking the clothes in.'

'I'll make yer pay for this,' he said, pushing back his chair in desperation. He bustled and got washed, then went determinedly upstairs. Presently he came down dressed, and with a big bundle in a blue-checked, enormous handkerchief.

'And now,' he said, 'you'll see me again when you do.'

'It'll be before I want to,' she replied; and at that he marched out of the house with his bundle. She sat trembling slightly, but her heart brimming with contempt. What would she do if he went to some other pit, obtained work, and got in with another woman? But she knew him too well – he couldn't. She was dead sure of him. Nevertheless her heart was gnawed inside her.

'Where's my dad?' said William, coming in from school.

'He says he's run away,' replied the mother.

'Where to?'

'Eh, I don't know. He's taken a bundle in the blue handkerchief, and says he's not coming back.'

'What shall we do?' cried the boy.

'Eh, never trouble, he won't go far.'

'But if he doesn't come back,' wailed Annie.

And she and William retired to the sofa and wept. Mrs Morel sat and laughed.

'You pair of gabeys!' she exclaimed. 'You'll see him before the night's out.'

But the children were not to be consoled. Twilight came on. Mrs Morel grew anxious from very weariness. One part of her said, it would be a relief to see the last of him; another part fretted because of keeping the children; and inside

sewing – she did all her sewing by hand, made all shirts and children's clothing
– he would read to her from the newspaper, slowly pronouncing and delivering
the words like a man pitching quoits. Often she hurried him on, giving him a
phrase in anticipation. And then he took her words humbly.

The silences between them were peculiar. There would be the swift, slight
'cluck' of her needle, the sharp 'pop' of his lips as he let out the smoke, the
warmth, the sizzle on the bars as he spat in the fire. Then her thoughts turned
to William. Already he was getting a big boy. Already he was top of the class,
and the master said he was the smartest lad in the school. She saw him a man,
young, full of vigour, making the world glow again for her.

And Morel sitting there, quite alone, and having nothing to think about,
would be feeling vaguely uncomfortable. His soul would reach out in its blind
way to her and find her gone. He felt a sort of emptiness, almost like a vacuum
in his soul. He was unsettled and restless. Soon he could not live in that
atmosphere, and he affected his wife. Both felt an oppression on their
breathing when they were left together for some time. Then he went to bed and
she settled down to enjoy herself alone, working, thinking, living.

Meanwhile another infant was coming, fruit of this little peace and
tenderness between the separating parents. Paul was seventeen months old
when the new baby was born. He was then a plump, pale child, quiet, with
heavy blue eyes, and still the peculiar slight knitting of the brows. The last child
was also a boy, fair and bonny. Mrs Morel was sorry when she knew she was
with child for economic reasons and because she did not love her husband; but
not for the sake of the infant.

They called the baby Arthur. He was very pretty, with a mop of gold curls,
and he loved his father from the first. Mrs Morel was glad this child loved the
father. Hearing the miner's footsteps, the baby would put up his arms and
crow. And if Morel were in a good temper, he called back immediately, in his
hearty, mellow voice:

'What then, my beauty? I sh'll come to thee in a minute.'

And as soon as he had taken off his pit-coat, Mrs Morel would put an apron
round the child, and give him to his father.

'What a sight the lad looks!' she would exclaim sometimes, taking back the
baby, that was smutted on the face from his father's kisses and play. Then
Morel laughed joyfully.

'He's a little collier, bless his bit o' mutton!' he exclaimed.

And these were the happy moments of her life now, when the child included
the father in her heart.

Meanwhile William grew bigger and stronger and more active, while Paul,
always rather delicate and quiet, got slimmer, and trotted after his mother like
her shadow. He was usually active and interested, but sometimes he would
have fits of depression. Then the mother would find the boy of three or four
crying on the sofa.

'What's the matter?' she asked, and got no answer.

'What's the matter?' she insisted, getting cross.

'I don't know,' sobbed the child.

So she tried to reason him out of it, or to amuse him, but without effect. It
made her feel beside herself. Then the father, always impatient, would jump
from his chair and shout:

'If he doesn't stop, I'll smack him till he does.'

'You'll do nothing of the sort,' said the mother coldly. And then she carried the child into the yard, plumped him into his little chair, and said: 'Now cry there, Misery!'

And then a butterfly on the rhubarb-leaves perhaps caught his eye, or at last he cried himself to sleep. These fits were not often, but they caused a shadow in Mrs Morel's heart, and her treatment of Paul was different from that of the other children.

Suddenly one morning as she was looking down the valley of the Bottoms for the barm-man, she heard a voice calling her. It was the thin little Mrs Anthony in brown velvet.

'Here, Mrs Morel, I want to tell you about your Willie.'

'Oh, do you?' replied Mrs Morel. 'Why, what's the matter?'

'A lad as gets 'old of another an' rips his clothes off'n 'is back,' Mrs Anthony said, 'wants showing something.'

'Your Alfred's as old as my William,' said Mrs Morel.

''Appen 'e is, but that doesn't give him a right to get hold of the boy's collar, an' fair rip it clean off his back.'

'Well,' said Mrs Morel. 'I don't thrash my children, and even if I did, I should want to hear their side of the tale.'

'They'd happen be a bit better if they did get a good hiding,' retorted Mrs Anthony. 'When it comes ter rippin' a lad's clean collar off'n 'is back a-purpose –'

'I'm sure he didn't do it on purpose,' said Mrs Morel.

'Make me a liar!' shouted Mrs Anthony.

Mrs Morel moved away and closed her gate. Her hand trembled as she held her mug of barm.

'But I s'll let your mester know,' Mrs Anthony cried after her.

At dinner-time, when William had finished his meal and wanted to be off again – he was then eleven years old – his mother said to him:

'What did you tear Alfred Anthony's collar for?'

'When did I tear his collar?'

'I don't know when, but his mother says you did.'

'Why – it was yesterday – an' it was torn a'ready.'

'But you tore it more.'

'Well, I'd got a cobbler as 'ad licked seventeen – an' Alfy Ant'ny 'e says:

> '"Adam an' Eve an' pinch-me,
> Went down to a river to bade.
> Adam an' Eve got drownded,
> Who do yer think got saved?"

An' so I says, "Oh, Pinch-*you*," an' so I pinched 'im, an' 'e was mad, an' so he snatched my cobbler an' run off with it. An' so I run after 'im, an' when I was getting hold of him, 'e dodged, an' it ripped 'is collar. But I got my cobbler –'

He pulled from his pocket a black old horse-chestnut hanging on a string. This old cobbler had 'cobbled' – hit and smashed – seventeen other cobblers on similar strings. So the boy was proud of his veteran.

'Well,' said Mrs Morel, 'you know you've got no right to rip his collar.'

'Well, our mother!' he answered. 'I never meant tr'a done it – an' it was on'y an old indiarubber collar as was torn a'ready.'

'Next time,' said his mother, '*you* be more careful I shouldn't like it if you came home with *your* collar torn off.'

'I don't care, our mother; I never did it a-purpose.'

The boy was rather miserable at being reprimanded.

'No – well, you be more careful.'

William fled away, glad to be exonerated. And Mrs Morel, who hated any bother with the neighbours, thought she would explain to Mrs Anthony, and the business would be over.

But that evening Morel came in from the pit looking very sour. He stood in the kitchen and glared round, but did not speak for some minutes. Then:

'Wheer's that Willy?' he asked.

'What do you want *him* for?' asked Mrs Morel, who had guessed.

'I'll let 'im know when I get him,' said Morel, banging his pit-bottle on to the dresser.

'I suppose Mrs Anthony's got hold of you and been yarning to you about their Alfy's collar,' said Mrs Morel, rather sneering.

'Niver mind who's got hold of me,' said Morel. 'When I get hold of *'im* I'll make his bones rattle.'

'It's a poor tale,' said Mrs Morel, 'that you're so ready to side with any snipey vixen who likes to come telling tales against your own children.'

'I'll learn 'im!' said Morel. 'It none matters to me whose lad 'e is; 'e's none goin' rippin' an' tearin' about just as he's a mind.'

'"Ripping and tearing about!"' repeated Mrs Morel. 'He was running after that Alfy, who'd taken his cobbler, and he accidentally got hold of his collar, because the other dodged – as an Anthony would.'

'I know!' shouted Morel threateningly.

'You would, before you're told,' replied his wife bitingly.

'Niver you mind,' stormed Morel, 'I know my business.'

'That's more than doubtful,' said Mrs Morel, 'supposing some loud mouthed creature had been getting you to thrash your own children.'

'I know,' repeated Morel.

And he said no more, but sat and nursed his bad temper. Suddenly William ran in, saying:

'Can I have my tea, mother?'

'Tha can ha'e more than that!' shouted Morel.

'Hold your noise, man,' said Mrs Morel; 'and don't look so ridiculous.'

'He'll look ridiculous before I've done wi' him!' shouted Morel, rising from his chair and glaring at his son.

William, who was a tall lad for his years, but very sensitive, had gone pale, and was looking in a sort of horror at his father.

'Go out!' Mrs Morel commanded her son.

William had not the wit to move. Suddenly Morel clenched his fist, and crouched.

'I'll gi'e him "go out"!' he shouted like an insane thing.

'What!' cried Mrs Morel, panting with rage. 'You shall not touch him for *her* telling, you shall not!'

'Shonna I?' shouted Morel. 'Shonna I?'

And, glaring at the boy, he ran forward. Mrs Morel sprang in between them, with her fist lifted.

'Don't you *dare*!' she cried.

'What!' he shouted, baffled for the moment. 'What!'

She spun round to her son.

'*Go* out of the house!' she commanded him in fury.

The boy, as if hypnotized by her, turned suddenly and was gone. Morel rushed to the door, but was too late. He returned, pale under his pit-dirt with fury. But now his wife was fully roused.

'Only dare!' she said in a loud, ringing voice. 'Only dare, milord, to lay a finger on that child! You'll regret it for ever.'

He was afraid of her. In a towering rage, he sat down.

When the children were old enough to be left, Mrs Morel joined the Women's Guild. It was a little club of women attached to the Co-operative Wholesale Society, which met on Monday night in the long room over the grocery shop of the Bestwood 'Co-op'. The women were supposed to discuss the benefits to be derived from co-operation, and other social questions. Sometimes Mrs Morel read a paper. It seemed queer to the children to see their mother, who was always busy about the house, sitting writing in her rapid fashion, thinking, referring to books, and writing again. They felt for her on such occasions the deepest respect.

But they loved the Guild. It was the only thing to which they did not grudge their mother – and that partly because she enjoyed it, partly because of the treats they derived from it. The Guild was called by some hostile husbands, who found their wives getting too independent, the 'clat-fart' shop – that is, the gossip-shop. It is true, from off the basis of the Guild, the women could look at their homes, at the conditions of their own lives, and find fault. So the colliers found their women had a new standard of their own, rather disconcerting. And also, Mrs Morel always had a lot of news on Monday nights, so that the children liked William to be in when their mother came home, because she told him things.

Then, when the lad was thirteen, she got him a job in the 'Co-op' office. He was a very clever boy, frank, with rather rough features and real viking blue eyes.

'What dost want ter ma'e a stool-harsed Jack on 'im for?' said Morel. 'All he'll do is to wear his britches behind out, an' earn nowt. What's 'e startin' wi?'

'It doesn't matter what he's starting with,' said Mrs Morel.

'It wouldna! Put 'im i' th' pit wi' me, an' e'll earn a easy ten shillin' a wik from th' start. But six shillin' wearin' his truck-end out on a stool's better than ten shillin' i' th' pit wi' me, I know.'

'He is *not* going in the pit,' said Mrs Morel, 'and there's an end of it.'

'It wor good enough for me, but it's non good enough for 'im.'

'If your mother put you in the pit at twelve, it's no reason why I should do the same with my lad.'

'Twelve! It wor a sight afore that!'

'Whenever it was,' said Mrs Morel.

She was very proud of her son. He went to the night-school, and learned shorthand, so that by the time he was sixteen he was the best shorthand clerk and book-keeper on the place, except one. Then he taught in the night-schools. But he was so fiery that only his good-nature and his size protected him.

All the things that men do – the decent things – William did. He could run like the wind. When he was twelve he won a first prize in a race; an inkstand of glass, shaped like an anvil. It stood proudly on the dresser, and gave Mrs Morel a keen pleasure. The boy only ran for her. He flew home with his anvil, breathless, with a 'Look, mother!' That was the first real tribute to herself. She took it like a queen.

'How pretty!' she exclaimed.

Then he began to get ambitious. He gave all his money to his mother. When he earned fourteen shillings a week, she gave him back two for himself, and, as he never drank, he felt himself rich. He went about with the bourgeois of Bestwood. The townlet contained nothing higher than the clergyman. Then came the bank manager, then the doctors, then the tradespeople, and after that the hosts of colliers. William began to consort with the sons of the chemist, the schoolmaster, and the tradesmen. He played billiards in the Mechanics Hall. Also he danced – this in spite of his mother. All the life that Bestwood offered he enjoyed, from the sixpenny-hops down Church Street, to sports and billiards.

Paul was treated to dazzling descriptions of all kinds of flower-like ladies, most of whom lived like cut blooms in William's heart for a brief fortnight.

Occasionally some flame would come in pursuit of her errant swain. Mrs Morel would find a strange girl at the door, and immediately she sniffed the air.

'Is Mr Morel in?' the damsel would ask appealingly.

'My husband is at home,' Mrs Morel replied.

'I – I mean *young* Mr Morel,' repeated the maiden painfully.

'Which one? There are several.'

Whereupon much blushing and stammering from the fair one.

'I – I met Mr Morel – at Ripley,' she explained.

'Oh – at a dance?'

'Yes.'

'I don't approve of the girls my son meets at dances. And he is *not* at home.'

Then he came home angry with his mother for having turned the girl away so rudely. He was a careless, yet eager-looking fellow, who walked with long strides, sometimes frowning, often with his cap pushed jollily to the back of his head. Now he came in frowning. He threw his cap on to the sofa, and took his strong jaw in his hand, and glared down at his mother. She was small, with her hair taken straight back from her forehead. She had a quiet air of authority, and yet of rare warmth. Knowing her son was angry, she trembled inwardly.

'Did a lady call for me yesterday, mother?' he asked.

'I don't know about a lady. There was a girl came.'

'And why didn't you tell me?'

'Because I forgot, simply.'

He fumed a little.

'A good-looking girl – seemed a lady.'

'I didn't look at her.'

'Big brown eyes?'

'I did *not* look. And tell your girls, my son, that when they're running after you, they're not to come and ask your mother for you. Tell them that – brazen baggages you meet at dancing-classes.'

'I'm sure she was a nice girl.'

'And I'm sure she wasn't.'

There ended the altercation. Over the dancing there was a great strife between the mother and the son. The grievance reached its height when William said he was going to Hucknall Torkard – considered a low town – to a fancy-dress ball. He was to be a Highlander. There was a dress he could hire, which one of his friends had had, and which fitted him perfectly. The Highland suit came home. Mrs Morel received it coldly and would not unpack it.

'My suit come?' cried William.

'There's a parcel in the front-room.'

He rushed in and cut the string.

'How do you fancy your son in this!' he said, enraptured, showing her the suit.

'You know I don't want to fancy you in it.'

On the evening of the dance, when he had come home to dress, Mrs Morel put on her coat and bonnet.

'Aren't you going to stop and see me, mother?' he asked.

'No; I don't want to see you,' she replied.

She was rather pale, and her face was closed and hard. She was afraid of her son's going the same way as his father. He hesitated a moment, and his heart stood still with anxiety. Then he caught sight of the Highland bonnet with its ribbons. He picked it up gleefully, forgetting her. She went out.

When he was nineteen he suddenly left the Co-op office and got a situation in Nottingham. In his new place he had thirty shillings a week instead of eighteen. This was indeed a rise. His mother and his father were brimmed up with pride. Everybody praised William. It seemed he was going to get on rapidly. Mrs Morel hoped, with his aid, to help her younger sons. Annie was now studying to be a teacher. Paul, also very clever, was getting on well, having lessons in French and German from his godfather, the clergyman who was still a friend to Mrs Morel. Arthur, a spoilt and very good-looking boy, was at the Board-school, but there was talk of his trying to get a scholarship for the High School in Nottingham.

William remained a year at his new post in Nottingham. He was studying hard, and growing serious. Something seemed to be fretting him. Still he went out to the dances and the river parties. He did not drink. The children were all rabid teetotallers. He came home very late at night, and sat yet longer studying. His mother implored him to take more care, to do one thing or another.

'Dance, if you want to dance, my son; but don't think you can work in the office, and then amuse yourself, and *then* study on top of all. You can't; the human frame won't stand it. Do one thing or the other – amuse yourself or learn Latin; but don't try to do both.'

Then he got a place in London, at a hundred and twenty a year. This seemed a fabulous sum. His mother doubted almost whether to rejoice or to grieve.

'They want me in Lime Street on Monday week, mother,' he cried, his eyes blazing as he read the letter. Mrs Morel felt everything go silent inside her. He read the letter: '"And will you reply by Thursday whether you accept. Yours faithfully –" They want me, mother, at a hundred and twenty a year, and don't even ask to see me. Didn't I tell you I could do it! Think of me in London! And I can give you twenty pounds a year, mater. We s'll all be rolling in money.'

'We shall, my son,' she answered sadly.

It never occurred to him that she might be more hurt at his going away than glad of his success. Indeed, as the days drew near for his departure, her heart began to close and grow dreary with despair. She loved him so much! More than that, she hoped in him so much. Almost she lived by him. She liked to do things for him: she liked to put a cup for his tea and iron his collars, of which he was so proud. It was a joy to her to have him proud of his collars. There was no laundry. So she used to rub away at them with her little convex iron, to polish them, till they shone from the sheer pressure of her arm. Now she would not do it for him. Now he was going away. She felt almost as if he were going as well out of her heart. He did not seem to leave her inhabited with himself. That was the grief and the pain to her. He took nearly all himself away.

A few days before his departure – he was just twenty – he burned his love-letters. They had hung on a file at the top of the kitchen cupboard. From some of them he had read extracts to his mother. Some of them she had taken the trouble to read herself. But most were too trivial.

Now, on the Saturday morning he said:

'Come on, Postle, let's go through my letters, and you can have the birds and flowers.'

Mrs Morel had done her Saturday's work on the Friday, because he was having a last day's holiday. She was making him a rice cake, which he loved, to take with him. He was scarcely conscious that she was so miserable.

He took the first letter off the file. It was mauve-tinted, and had purple and green thistles. William sniffed the page.

'Nice scent! Smell.'

And he thrust the sheet under Paul's nose.

'Um!' said Paul, breathing in. 'What d'you call it? Smell, mother.'

His mother ducked her small, fine nose down to the paper.

'*I* don't want to smell their rubbish,' she said, sniffing.

'This girl's father,' said William, 'is as rich as Croesus. He owns property without end. She calls me Lafayette, because I know French. "You will see, I've forgiven you" – I like *her* forgiving me. "I told mother about you this morning, and she will have much pleasure if you come to tea on Sunday, but she will have to get father's consent also. I sincerely hope he will agree. I will let you know how it transpires. If, however, you –"'

'"Let you know how it" what?' interrupted Mrs Morel.

'"Transpires" – oh, yes!'

'"Transpires!"' repeated Mrs Morel mockingly. 'I thought she was so well educated!'

William felt slightly uncomfortable, and abandoned this maiden, giving Paul the corner with the thistles. He continued to read extracts from his letters, some of which amused his mother, some of which saddened her and made her anxious for him.

'My lad,' she said, 'they're very wise. They know they've only got to flatter your vanity, and you press up to them like a dog that has its head scratched.'

'Well, they can't go on scratching for ever,' he replied. 'And when they've done, I trot away.'

'But one day you'll find a string round your neck that you can't pull off,' she answered.

'Not me! I'm equal to any of 'em, mater, they needn't flatter themselves.'

'You flatter *yourself*,' she said quietly.

Soon there was a heap of twisted black pages, all that remained of the file of scented letters, except that Paul had thirty or forty pretty tickets from the corners of the notepaper – swallows and forget-me-nots and ivy sprays. And William went to London to start a new life.

THE YOUNG LIFE OF PAUL

Paul would be built like his mother, slightly and rather small. His fair hair went reddish, and then dark brown; his eyes were grey. He was a pale, quiet child, with eyes that seemed to listen, and with a full, dropping underlip.

As a rule he seemed old for his years. He was so conscious of what other people felt, particularly his mother. When she fretted he understood, and could have no peace. His soul seemed always attentive to her.

As he grew older he became stronger. William was too far removed from him to accept him as a companion. So the smaller boy belonged at first almost entirely to Annie. She was a tomboy and a 'flybie-skybie', as her mother called her. But she was intensely fond of her second brother. So Paul was towed round at the heels of Annie, sharing her game. She raced wildly at lerky with the other young wild-cats of the Bottoms. And always Paul flew beside her, living her share of the game, having as yet no part of his own. He was quiet and not noticeable. But his sister adored him. He always seemed to care for things if she wanted him to.

She had a big doll of which she was fearfully proud, though not so fond. So she laid the doll on the sofa, and covered it with an antimacassar, to sleep. Then she forgot it. Meantime Paul must practise jumping off the sofa arm. So he jumped crash into the face of the hidden doll. Annie rushed up, uttered a loud wail, and sat down to weep a dirge. Paul remained quite still. 'You couldn't tell it was there, mother; you couldn't tell it was there,' he repeated over and over. So long as Annie wept for the doll he sat helpless with misery. Her grief wore itself out. She forgave her brother – he was so much upset. But a day or two afterwards she was shocked.

'Let's make a sacrifice of Arabella,' he said. 'Let's burn her.'

She was horrified, yet rather fascinated. She wanted to see what the boy would do. He made an altar of bricks, pulled some of the shavings out of Arabella's body, poured on a little paraffin, and set the whole thing alight. He watched with wicked satisfaction the drops of wax melt off the broken forehead of Arabella, and drop like sweat into the flame. So long as the stupid big doll burned he rejoiced in silence. At the end he poked among the embers with a stick, fished out the arms and legs, all blackened, and smashed them under stones.

'That's the sacrifice of Missis Arabella,' he said. 'An' I'm glad there's nothing left of her.'

Which disturbed Annie inwardly, although she could say nothing. He seemed to hate the doll so intensely, because he had broken it.

All the children, but particularly Paul, were peculiarly *against* their father, along with their mother. Morel continued to bully and to drink. He had periods, months at a time, when he made the whole life of the family a misery. Paul never forgot coming home from the Band of Hope one Monday evening and finding his mother with her eye swollen and discoloured, his father standing on the hearthrug, feet astride, his head down, and William, just home from work, glaring at his father. There was a silence as the young children entered, but none of the elders looked round.

William was white to the lips, and his fists were clenched. He waited until the children were silent, watching with children's rage and hate; then he said:

'You coward, you daren't do it when I was in.'

But Morel's blood was up. He swung round on his son. William was bigger, but Morel was hard-muscled, and mad with fury.

'Dossn't I?' he shouted. 'Dossn't I? Ha'e much more o' thy chelp, my young jockey, an' I'll rattle my fist about thee. Ay, an' I sholl that, dost see.'

Morel crouched at the knees and showed his fist in an ugly, almost beast-like fashion. William was white with rage.

'Will yer?' he said, quiet and intense. 'It 'ud be the last time, though.'

Morel danced a little nearer, crouching, drawing back his fist to strike. William put his fists ready. A light came into his blue eyes, almost like a laugh. He watched his father. Another word, and the men would have begun to fight. Paul hoped they would. The three children sat pale on the sofa.

'Stop it, both of you,' cried Mrs Morel in a hard voice. 'We've had enough for *one* night. And *you*,' she said, turning on to her husband, 'look at your children!'

Morel glanced at the sofa.

'Look at the children, you nasty little bitch!' he sneered. 'Why, what have *I* done to the children, I should like to know? But they're like yourself; you've put 'em up to your own tricks and nasty ways – you've learned 'em in it, you 'ave.'

She refused to answer him. No one spoke. After a while he threw his boots under the table and went to bed.

'Why didn't you let me have a go at him?' said William, when his father was upstairs. 'I could easily have beaten him.'

'A nice thing – your own father,' she replied.

'"*Father!*"' repeated William. 'Call *him my* father!'

'Well, he is – and so –'

'But why don't you let me settle him? I could do, easily.'

'The idea!' she cried. 'It hasn't come to *that* yet.'

'No,' he said, 'it's come to worse. Look at yourself. *Why* didn't you let me give it him?'

'Because I couldn't bear it, so never think of it,' she cried quickly.

And the children went to bed, miserably.

When William was growing up, the family moved from the Bottoms to a house on the brow of the hill, commanding a view of the valley, which spread out like a convex cockleshell, or a clamp-shell, before it. In front of the house was a huge old ash-tree. The west wind, sweeping from Derbyshire, caught the houses with full force, and the tree shrieked again. Morel liked it.

'It's music,' he said. 'It sends me to sleep.'

But Paul and Arthur and Annie hated it. To Paul it became almost a demoniacal noise. The winter of their first year in the new house their father was very bad. The children played in the street, on the brim of the wide, dark valley, until eight o'clock. Then they went to bed. Their mother sat sewing below. Having such a great space in front of the house gave the children a feeling of night, of vastness, and of terror. This terror came in from the shrieking of the tree and the anguish of the home discord. Often Paul would wake up, after he had been asleep a long time, aware of thuds downstairs. Instantly he was wide awake. Then he heard the booming shouts of his father, come home nearly drunk, then the sharp replies of his mother, then the bang, bang of his father's fist on the table, and the nasty snarling shout as the man's voice got higher. And then the whole was drowned in a piercing medley of shrieks and cries from the great, windswept ash-tree. The children lay silent in suspense, waiting for a lull in the wind to hear what their father was doing. He might hit their mother again. There was a feeling of horror, a kind of bristling in the darkness, and a sense of blood. They lay with their hearts in the grip of an intense anguish. The wind came through the tree fiercer and fiercer. All the cords of the great harp hummed, whistled, and shrieked. And then came the horror of the sudden silence, silence everywhere, outside and downstairs. What was it? Was it a silence of blood? What had he done?

The children lay and breathed the darkness. And then, at last, they heard their father throw down his boots and tramp upstairs in his stockinged feet. Still they listened. Then at last, if the wind allowed, they heard the water of the tap drumming into the kettle, which their mother was filling for morning, and they could go to sleep in peace.

So they were happy in the morning – happy, very happy playing, dancing at night round the lonely lamp-post in the midst of the darkness. But they had one tight place of anxiety in their hearts, one darkness in their eyes, which showed all their lives.

Paul hated his father. As a boy he had a fervent private religion.

'Make him stop drinking,' he prayed every night. 'Lord let my father die,' he prayed very often. 'Let him not be killed at pit,' he prayed when, after tea, the father did not come home from work.

That was another time when the family suffered intensely. The children came from school and had their teas. On the hob the big black saucepan was simmering, the stew-jack was in the oven, ready for Morel's dinner. He was expected at five o'clock. But for months he would stop and drink every night on his way from work.

In the winter nights, when it was cold, and grew dark early, Mrs Morel would put a brass candlestick on the table, light a tallow candle to save the gas. The children finished their bread-and-butter, or dripping, and were ready to go out to play. But if Morel had not come they faltered. The sense of his sitting in all his pit-dirt, drinking, after a long day's work, not coming home and eating and washing, but sitting, getting drunk, on an empty stomach, made Mrs Morel unable to bear herself. From her the feeling was transmitted to the other children. She never suffered alone any more: the children suffered with her.

Paul went out to play with the rest. Down in the great trough of twilight, tiny clusters of lights burned where the pits were. A few last colliers struggled up the dim field-path. The lamplighter came along. No more colliers came. Darkness shut down over the valley; work was gone. It was night.

Then Paul ran anxiously into the kitchen. The one candle still burned on the table, the big fire glowed red. Mrs Morel sat alone. On the hob the saucepan steamed; the dinner-plate lay waiting on the table. All the room was full of the sense of waiting, waiting for the man who was sitting in his pit-dirt, dinnerless, some miles away from home, across the darkness, drinking himself drunk. Paul stood in the doorway.

'Has my dad come?' he asked.

'You can see he hasn't,' said Mrs Morel, cross with the futility of the question.

Then the boy dawdled about near this mother. They shared the same anxiety. Presently Mrs Morel went out and strained the potatoes.

'They're ruined and black,' she said; 'but what do I care?'

Not many words were spoken. Paul almost hated his mother for suffering because his father did not come home from work.

'What do you bother yourself for?' he said. 'If he wants to stop and get drunk, why don't you let him?'

'Let him!' flashed Mrs Morel. 'You may well say "let him".'

She knew that the man who stops on the way home from work is on a quick way to ruining himself and his home. The children were yet young, and depended on the breadwinner. William gave her the sense of relief, providing her at last with someone to turn to if Morel failed. But the tense atmosphere of the room on these waiting evenings was the same.

The minutes ticked away. At six o'clock still the cloth lay on the table, still the dinner stood waiting, still the same sense of anxiety and expectation in the room. The boy could not stand it any longer. He could not go out and play. So he ran in to Mrs Inger, next door but one, for her to talk to him. She had no children. Her husband was good to her, but was in a shop, and came home late. So, when she saw the lad at the door, she called:

'Come in, Paul.'

The two sat talking for some time, when suddenly the boy rose, saying:

'Well, I'll be going and seeing if my mother wants an errand doing.'

He pretended to be perfectly cheerful, and did not tell his friend what ailed him. Then he ran indoors.

Morel at these times came in churlish and hateful.

'This is a nice time to come home,' said Mrs Morel.

'What's it matter to yo' what time I come whoam?' he shouted.

And everybody in the house was still, because he was dangerous. He ate his food in the most brutal manner possible and, when he had done, pushed all the pots in a heap away from him, to lay his arms on the table. Then he went to sleep.

Paul hated his father so. The collier's small, mean head, with its black hair slightly soiled with grey, lay on the bare arms, and the face, dirty and inflamed, with a fleshy nose and thin, paltry brows, was turned sideways, asleep with beer and weariness and nasty temper. If anyone entered suddenly, or a noise were made, the man looked up and shouted:

'I'll lay my fist about thy y'ead, I'm tellin' thee, if tha doesna stop that clatter! Dost hear?'

And the two last words, shouted in a bullying fashion, usually at Annie, made the family writhe with hate of the man.

He was shut out from all family affairs. No one told him anything. The children, alone with their mother, told her all about the day's happenings, everything. Nothing had really taken place in them until it was told to their mother. But as soon as the father came in, everything stopped. He was like the scotch in the smooth, happy machinery of the home. And he was always aware of this fall of silence on his entry, the shutting off of life, the unwelcome. But now it was gone too far to alter.

He would dearly have liked the children to talk to him, but they could not. Sometimes Mrs Morel would say:

'You ought to tell your father.'

Paul won a prize in a competition in a child's paper. Everybody was highly jubilant.

'Now you'd better tell your father when he comes in,' said Mrs Morel. 'You know how he carries on and says he's never told anything.'

'All right,' said Paul. But he would almost rather have forfeited the prize than have to tell his father.

'I've won a prize in a competition, dad,' he said.

Morel turned round to him.

'Have you, my boy? What sort of a competition?'

'Oh, nothing – about famous women.'

'And how much is the prize, then, as you've got?'

'It's a book.'

'Oh, indeed!'

'About birds.'

'Hm – hm!'

And that was all. Conversation was impossible between the father and any other member of the family. He was an outsider. He had denied the God in him.

The only times when he entered again into the life of his own people was when he worked, and was happy at work. Sometimes, in the evening, he cobbled the boots or mended the kettle or his pit-bottle. Then he always wanted several attendants, and the children enjoyed it. They united with him in the work, in the actual doing of something, when he was his real self again.

He was a good workman, dexterous, and one who, when he was in a good humour, always sang. He had whole periods, months, almost years, of friction and nasty temper. Then sometimes he was jolly again. It was nice to see him run with a piece of red-hot iron into the scullery, crying:

'Out of my road – out of my road!'

Then he hammered the soft, red-glowing stuff on his iron goose, and made the shape he wanted. Or he sat absorbed for a moment, soldering. Then the children watched with joy as the metal sank suddenly molten, and was shoved about against the nose of the soldering-iron, while the room was full of a scent of burnt resin and hot tin, and Morel was silent and intent for a minute. He always sang when he mended boots because of the jolly sound of hammering. And he was rather happy when he sat putting great patches on his moleskin pit trousers, which he would often do, considering them too dirty, and the stuff too hard, for his wife to mend.

But the best time for the young children was when he made fuses. Morel fetched a sheaf of long sound wheat-straws from the attic. These he cleaned with his hand, till each one gleamed like a stalk of gold, after which he cut the straws into lengths of about six inches, leaving, if he could, a notch at the bottom of each piece. He always had a beautifully sharp knife that could cut a straw clean without hurting it. Then he set in the middle of the table a heap of gunpowder, a little pile of black grains upon the white-scrubbed board. He made and trimmed the straws while Paul and Annie filled and plugged them. Paul loved to see the black grains trickle down a crack in his palm into the mouth of the straw, peppering jollily downwards till the straw was full. Then he bunged up the mouth with a bit of soap – which he got in his thumb-nail from a pat in a saucer – and the straw was finished.

'Look, dad!' he said.

'That's right, my beauty,' replied Morel, who was peculiarly lavish of endearments to his second son. Paul popped the fuse into the powder-tin, ready for the morning, when Morel would take it to the pit, and use it to fire a shot what would blast the coal down.

Meantime Arthur, still fond of his father, would lean on the arm of Morel's chair, and say:

'Tell us about down pit, daddy.'

This Morel loved to do.

'Well, there's one little 'oss – we call 'im Taffy,' he would begin. 'An he's a fawce un!'

Morel had a warm way of telling a story. He made one feel Taffy's cunning.

'He's a brown un,' he would answer, 'an' not very high. Well, he comes i' th' stall wi' a rattle, an' then yo' 'ear 'im sneeze. "'Ello, Taff," you say, "what art sneezin' for? Bin ta' ein' some snuff?"'

'An' 'e sneezes again. Then he slives up an' shoves 'is 'ead-on yer, that cadin'. '"What's want, Taff?" yo' say.'

'And what does he?' Arthur always asked.

'He wants a bit o' bacca, my duckey.'

This story of Taffy would go on interminably, and everybody loved it.

Or sometimes it was a new tale.

'An' what dost think, my darlin'? When I went to put my coat on at snap-time, what should go runnin' up my arm but a mouse.

'"Hey up, theer!" I shouts.

'An' I wor just in time ter get 'im by th' tail.'

'And did you kill it?'

'I did, for they're a nuisance. The place is fair snied wi' 'em.'

'An' what do they live on?'

'The corn as the 'osses drops – and they'll get in your pocket an' eat your snap, if you'll let 'em – no matter where yo' hing your coat – the slivin', nibblin' little nuisances, for they are.'

These happy evenings could not take place unless Morel had some job to do. And then he always went to bed very early, often before the children. There was nothing remaining for him to stay up for, when he had finished tinkering, and had skimmed the headlines of the newspaper.

And the children felt secure when their father was in bed. They lay and talked softly awhile. Then they started as the lights went suddenly sprawling over the ceiling from the lamps that swung in the hands of the colliers tramping by outside, going to take the nine o'clock shift. They listened to the voices of the men, imagined them dipping down into the dark valley. Sometimes they went to the window and watched the three or four lamps growing tinier and tinier, swaying down the fields in the darkness. Then it was a joy to rush back to bed and cuddle closely in the warmth.

Paul was rather a delicate boy, subject to bronchitis. The others were all quite strong; so this was another reason for his mother's difference in feeling for him. One day he came home at dinner-time feeling ill. But it was not a family to make any fuss.

'What's the matter with *you*?' his mother asked sharply.

'Nothing,' he replied.

But he ate no dinner.

'If you eat no dinner, you're not going to school,' she said.

'Why?' he asked.

'That's why.'

So after dinner he lay down on the sofa, on the warm chintz cushions the children loved. Then he fell into a kind of doze. That afternoon Mrs Morel was ironing. She listened to the small, restless noise the boy made in his throat as she worked. Again rose in her heart the old, almost weary feeling towards him. She had never expected him to live. And yet he had a great vitality in his young body. Perhaps it would have been a little relief to her if he had died. She always felt a mixture of anguish in her love for him.

He, in his semi-conscious sleep, was vaguely aware of the clatter of the iron on the iron-stand, of the faint thud, thud of the ironing-board. Once roused, he opened his eyes to see his mother standing on the hearthrug with the hot iron near her cheek, listening, as it were, to the heat. Her still face, with the mouth closed tight from suffering and disillusion and self-denial, and her nose, the smallest bit on one side, and her blue eyes so young, quick, and warm, made his heart contract with love. When she was quiet, so, she looked brave and rich with life, but as if she had been done out of her rights. It hurt the boy keenly, this feeling about her that she had never had her life's fulfilment: and his own incapability to make up to her hurt him with a sense of impotence, yet made him patiently dogged inside. It was his childish aim.

She spat on the iron, and a little ball of spit bounded, raced off the dark, glossy surface. Then, kneeling, she rubbed the iron on the sack lining of the hearthrug vigorously. She was warm in the ruddy firelight. Paul loved the way she crouched and put her head on one side. Her movements were light and quick. It was always a pleasure to watch her. Nothing she ever did, no movement she ever made, could have been found fault with by her children. The room was warm and full of the scent of hot linen. Later on the clergyman came and talked softly with her.

Paul was laid up with an attack of bronchitis. He did not mind much. What happened happened, and it was no good kicking against the pricks. He loved the evenings, after eight o'clock, when the light was put out, and he could watch the fire-flames spring over the darkness of the walls and ceiling; could watch huge shadows waving and tossing, till the room seemed full of men who battled silently.

On retiring to bed, the father would come into the sickroom. He was always very gentle if anyone were ill. But he disturbed the atmosphere for the boy.

'Are ter asleep, my darlin'?' Morel asked softly.

'No; is my mother comin'?'

'She's just finishin' foldin' the clothes. Do you want anything?' Morel rarely 'thee'd' his son.

'I don't want nothing. But how long will she be?'

'Not long, my duckie.'

The father waited undecidedly on the hearthrug for a moment or two. He felt his son did not want him. Then he went to the top of the stairs and said to his wife:

'This childt's axin' for thee; how long art goin' to be?'

'Until I've finished, good gracious! Tell him to go to sleep.'

'She says you're to go to sleep,' the father repeated gently to Paul.

'Well, I want *her* to come,' insisted the boy.

'He says he can't go off till you come,' Morel called downstairs.

'Eh, dear! I shan't be long. And do stop shouting downstairs. There's the other children –'

Then Morel came again, and crouched before the bedroom fire. He loved a fire dearly.

'She says she won't be long,' he said.

He loitered about indefinitely. The boy began to get feverish with irritation. His father's presence seemed to aggravate all his sick impatience. At last Morel, after having stood looking at his son awhile, said softly:

'Good night, my darling.'

'Good night,' Paul replied, turning round in relief to be alone.

Paul loved to sleep with his mother. Sleep is still most perfect, in spite of hygienists, when it is shared with a beloved. The warmth, the security and peace of soul, the utter comfort from the touch of the other, knits the sleep, so that it takes the body and soul completely in its healing. Paul lay against her and slept, and got better; whilst she, always a bad sleeper, fell later on into a profound sleep that seemed to give her faith.

In convalescence he would sit up in bed, see the fluffy horses feeding at the troughs in the field, scattering their hay on the trodden yellow snow; watch the miners troop home – small, black figures trailing slowly in gangs across the white field. Then the night came up in dark blue vapour from the snow.

In convalescence everything was wonderful. The snowflakes suddenly arriving on the window-pane, clung there a moment like swallows, then were gone, and a drop of water was crawling down the glass. The snowflakes whirled round the corner of the house, like pigeons dashing by. Away across the valley the little black train crawled doubtfully over the great whiteness.

While they were so poor, the children were delighted if they could do anything to help economically. Annie and Paul and Arthur went out early in the morning, in summer, looking for mushrooms, hunting through the wet grass, from which the larks were rising, for the white-skinned, wonderful naked bodies crouched secretly in the green. And if they got half a pound they felt exceedingly happy: there was the joy of finding something, the joy of accepting something straight from the hand of Nature, and the joy of contributing to the family exchequer.

But the most important harvest, after gleaning for frumenty, was the blackberries. Mrs Morel must buy fruit for puddings on the Saturdays; also she liked blackberries. So Paul and Arthur scoured the coppices and woods and old quarries, so long as a blackberry was to be found, every weekend going on their search. In that region of mining villages blackberries became a comparative rarity. But Paul hunted far and wide. He loved being out in the country, among the bushes. But he also could not bear to go home to his mother empty. That, he felt, would disappoint her, and he would have died rather.

'Good gracious!' she would exclaim as the lads came in, late, and tired to death, and hungry, 'wherever have you been?'

'Well,' replied Paul, 'there wasn't any, so we went over Misk Hills. And look here, our mother!'

She peeped into the basket.

'Now, those are fine ones!' she exclaimed.

'And there's over two pounds – isn't there over two pounds?'

She tried the basket.

'Yes,' she answered doubtfully.

Then Paul fished out a little spray. He always brought her one spray, the best he could find.

'Pretty!' she said, in a curious tone, of a woman accepting a love-token.

The boy walked all day, went miles and miles, rather than own himself beaten and come home to her empty-handed. She never realized this, whilst he was young. She was a woman who waited for her children to grow up. And William occupied her chiefly.

But when William went to Nottingham, and was not so much at home, the mother made a companion of Paul. The latter was unconsciously jealous of his brother, and William was jealous of him. At the same time, they were good friends.

Mrs Morel's intimacy with her second son was more subtle and fine, perhaps not so passionate as with her eldest. It was the rule that Paul should fetch the money on Friday afternoons. The colliers of the five pits were paid on Fridays, but not individually. All the earnings of each stall were put down to the chief butty, as contractor, and he divided the wages again, either in the public-house or in his own home. So that the children could fetch the money, school closed early on Friday afternoons. Each of the Morel children – William, then Annie, then Paul – had fetched the money on Friday afternoons, until they went themselves to work. Paul used to set off at half-past three, with a little calico bag in his pocket. Down all the paths, women, girls, children, and men were seen trooping to the offices.

These offices were quite handsome: a new, red-brick building, almost like a mansion, standing in its own well-kept grounds at the end of Greenhill Lane. The waiting-room was the hall, a long, bare room paved with blue brick, and having a seat all round, against the wall. Here sat the colliers in their pit-dirt. They had come up early. The women and children usually loitered about on the red gravel paths. Paul always examined the grass border, and the big grass bank, because in it grew tiny pansies and tiny forget-me-nots. There was a sound of many voices. The women had on their Sunday hats. The girls chattered loudly. Little dogs ran here and there. The green shrubs were silent all around.

Then from inside came the cry 'Spinney Park – Spinney Park'. All the folk for Spinney Park trooped inside. When it was time for Bretty to be paid, Paul went in among the crowd. The pay-room was quite small. A counter went across, dividing it into half. Behind the counter stood two men – Mr Braithwaite and his clerk, Mr Winterbottom. Mr Braithwaite was large, somewhat of the stern patriarch in appearance, having a rather thin white beard. He was usually muffled in an enormous silk neckerchief, and right up to the hot summer a huge fire burned in the open grate. No window was open. Sometimes in winter the air scorched the throats of the people, coming in from the freshness. Mr Winterbottom was rather small and fat, and very bald. He made remarks that were not witty, whilst his chief launched forth patriarchal admonitions against the colliers.

The room was crowded with miners in their pit-dirt, men who had been home and changed, and women, and one or two children, and usually a dog. Paul was quite small, so it was often his fate to be jammed behind the legs of the men, near the fire which scorched him. He knew the order of the names – they went according to stall number.

'Holliday,' came the ringing voice of Mr Braithwaite. Then Mrs Holliday stepped silently forward, was paid, drew aside.

'Bower – John Bower.'

A boy stepped to the counter. Mr Braithwaite, large and irascible, glowered at him over his spectacles.

'John Bower!' he repeated.

'It's me,' said the boy.

'Why, you used to 'ave a different nose than that,' said glossy Mr Winterbottom, peering over the counter. The people tittered thinking of John Bower senior.

'How is it your father's not come?' said Mr Braithwaite, in a large and magisterial voice.

'He's badly,' piped the boy.

'You should tell him to keep off the drink,' pronounced the great cashier.

'An' niver mind if he puts his foot through yer,' said a mocking voice from behind.

All the men laughed. The large and important cashier looked down at his next sheet.

'Fred Pilkington!' he called, quite indifferent.

Mr Braithwaite was an important shareholder in the firm.

Paul knew his turn was next but one, and his heart began to beat. He was pushed against the chimney-piece. His calves were burning. But he did not hope to get through the wall of men.

'Walter Morel!' came the ringing voice.

'Here!' piped Paul, small and inadequate.

'Morel – Walter Morel!' the cashier repeated, his finger and thumb on the invoice, ready to pass on.

Paul was suffering convulsions of self-consciousness, and could not or would not shout. The backs of the men obliterated him. Then Mr Winterbottom came to the rescue.

'He's here. Where is he? Morel's lad?'

The fat, red, bald little man peered round with keen eyes. He pointed at the fireplace. The colliers looked round, moved aside, and disclosed the boy.

'Here he is!' said Mr Winterbottom.

Paul went to the counter.

'Seventeen pounds eleven and fivepence. Why don't you shout up when you're called?' said Mr Braithwaite. He banged on to the invoice a five-pound bag of silver, then in a delicate and pretty movement, picked up a little ten-pound column of gold, and plumped it beside the silver. The gold slid in a bright stream over the paper. The cashier finished counting off the money; the boy dragged the whole down the counter to Mr Winterbottom, to whom the stoppages for rent and tools must be paid. Here he suffered again.

'Sixteen an' six,' said Mr Winterbottom.

The lad was too much upset to count. He pushed forward some loose silver and half a sovereign.

'How much do you think you've given me?' asked Mr Winterbottom.

The boy looked at him, but said nothing. He had not the faintest notion.

'Haven't you got a tongue in your head?'

Paul bit his lip, and pushed forward some more silver.

'Don't they teach you to count at the Board-school?' he asked.

'Nowt but Algebra an' French,' said a collier.

'An' cheek an' impidence,' said another.

Paul was keeping someone waiting. With trembling fingers he got his money into the bag and slid out. He suffered the tortures of the damned on these occasions.

His relief, when he got outside, and was walking along the Mansfield Road, was infinite. On the park wall the mosses were green. There were some gold and some white fowls pecking under the apple-trees of an orchard. The colliers were walking home in a stream. The boy went near the wall, selfconsciously. He knew many of the men, but could not recognize them in their dirt. And this was a new torture to him.

When he got down to the New Inn, at Bretty, his father was not yet come. Mrs Wharmby, the landlady, knew him. His grandmother, Morel's mother, had been Mrs Wharmby's friend.

'Your father's not come yet,' said the landlady, in the peculiar half-scornful, half-patronizing voice of a woman who talks chiefly to grown men. 'Sit you down.'

Paul sat down on the edge of the bench in the bar. Some colliers were reckoning – sharing out their money – in a corner; others came in. They all glanced at the boy without speaking. At last Morel came; brisk, and with something of an air, even in his blackness.

'Hello!' he said rather tenderly to his son. 'Have you bested me? Shall you have a drink of something?'

Paul and all the children were bred up fierce anti-alcoholists, and he would have suffered more in drinking a lemonade before all the men than in having a tooth drawn.

The landlady looked at him *de haut en bas*, rather pitying, and at the same time, resenting his clear, fierce morality. Paul went home, glowering. He entered the house silently. Friday was baking day, and there was usually a hot bun. His mother put it before him.

Suddenly he turned on her in a fury, his eyes flashing:

'I'm *not* going to the office any more,' he said.

'Why, what's the matter?' his mother asked in surprise. His sudden rages rather amused her.

'I'm *not* going any more,' he declared.

'Oh, very well, tell your father so.'

He chewed his bun as if he hated it.

'I'm not – I'm not going to fetch the money.'

'Then one of Carlin's children can go; they'd be glad enough of the sixpence,' said Mrs Morel.

This sixpence was Paul's only income. It mostly went in buying birthday presents; but it *was* an income, and he treasured it. But –!

'They can have it, then!' he said. 'I don't want it.'

'Oh, very well,' said his mother. 'But you needn't bully *me* about it.'

'They're hateful, and common, and hateful, they are, and I'm not going any more. Mr Braithwaite drops his "h's", an' Mr Winterbottom says "You was".'

'And is that why you won't go any more?' smiled Mrs Morel.

The boy was silent for some time. His face was pale, his eyes dark and furious. His mother moved about at her work, taking no notice of him.

'They always stan' in front of me, so's I can't get out,' he said.

'Well, my lad, you've only to *ask* them,' she replied.

'An' then Alfred Winterbottom says, "What do they teach you at the Board-school"?'

'They never taught *him* much,' said Mrs Morel, 'that is a fact – neither manners nor wit – and his cunning he was born with.'

So, in her own way, she soothed him. His ridiculous hyper-sensitiveness made her heart ache. And sometimes the fury in his eyes roused her, made her sleeping soul lift up its head a moment, surprised.

'What was the cheque?' she asked.

'Seventeen pounds eleven and fivepence, and sixteen and six stoppages,' replied the boy. 'It's a good week; and only five shillings stoppages for my father.'

So she was able to calculate how much her husband had earned, and could call him to account if he gave her short money. Morel always kept to himself the secret of the week's amount.

Friday was the baking night and market night. It was the rule that Paul should stay at home and bake. He loved to stop in and draw or read; he was very fond of drawing. Annie always 'gallivanted' on Friday nights; Arthur was enjoying himself as usual. So the boy remained alone.

Mrs Morel loved her marketing. In the tiny market-place on the top of the hill, where four roads from Nottingham and Derby, Ilkeston and Mansfield, meet, many stalls were erected. Brakes ran in from surrounding villages. The market-place was full of women, the streets packed with men. It was amazing to see so many men everywhere in the streets. Mrs Morel usually quarrelled with her lace woman, sympathized with her fruit man – who was a gabey, but his wife was a bad un – laughed with the fish man – who was a scamp but so droll – put the linoleum man in his place, was cold with the odd-wares man, and only went to the crockery man when she was driven – or drawn by the cornflowers on a little dish; then she was coldly polite.

'I wondered how much that little dish was,' she said.

'Sevenpence to you.'

'Thank you.'

She put the dish down and walked away; but she could not leave the market-place without it. Again she went by where the pots lay coldly on the floor, and she glanced at the dish furtively, pretending not to.

She was a little woman, in a bonnet and a black costume. Her bonnet was in its third year; it was a great grievance to Annie.

'Mother!' the girl implored, 'don't wear that nubbly little bonnet.'

'Then what else shall I wear?' replied the mother tartly. 'And I'm sure it's right enough.'

It had started with a tip; then had had flowers; now was reduced to black lace and a bit of jet.

'It looks rather come down,' said Paul. 'Couldn't you give it a pick-me-up?'

'I'll jowl your head for impudence,' said Mrs Morel, and she tied the strings of the black bonnet valiantly under her chin.

She glanced at the dish again. Both she and her enemy, the pot man, had an uncomfortable feeling, as if there were something between them. Suddenly he shouted:

'Do you want it for fivepence?'

She started. Her heart hardened; but then she stopped and took up her dish.

'I'll have it,' she said.

'Yer'll do me the favour, like?' he said. 'Yer'd better spit in it, like yer do when y'ave something give yer.'

Mrs Morel paid him the fivepence in a cold manner.

'I don't see you give it me,' she said. 'You wouldn't let me have it for fivepence if you didn't want to.'

'In this flamin', scrattlin' place you may count yerself lucky if you can give your things away,' he growled.

'Yes; there are bad times, and good,' said Mrs Morel.

But she had forgiven the pot man. They were friends. She dare now finger his pots. So she was happy.

Paul was waiting for her. He loved her home-coming. She was always her best so – triumphant, tired, laden with parcels, feeling rich in spirit. He heard her quick, light step in the entry and looked up from his drawing.

'Oh!' she sighed, smiling at him from the doorway.

'My word, you *are* loaded!' he exclaimed, putting down his brush.

'I am!' she gasped. 'That brazen Annie said she'd meet me. *Such* a weight!' She dropped her string bag and her packages on the table.

'Is the bread done?' she asked, going to the oven.

'The last one is soaking,' he replied. 'You needn't look, I've not forgotten it.'

'Oh, that pot man!' she said, closing the oven door. 'You know what a wretch I've said he was? Well, I don't think he's quite so bad.'

'Don't you?'

The boy was attentive to her. She took off her little black bonnet.

'No. I think he can't make any money – well, it's everybody's cry alike nowadays – and it makes him disagreeable.'

'It would *me*,' said Paul.

'Well, one can't wonder at it. And he let me have – how much do you think he let me have *this* for?'

She took the dish out of its rag of newspaper, and stood looking on it with joy.

'Show me!' said Paul.

The two stood together gloating over the dish.

'I *love* cornflowers on things,' said Paul.

'Yes, and I thought of the teapot you bought me –'

'One and three,' said Paul.

'Fivepence!'

'It's not enough, mother.'

'No. Do you know, I fairly sneaked off with it. But I'd been extravagant, I couldn't afford any more. And he needn't have let me have it if he hadn't wanted to.'

'No, he needn't, need he,' said Paul, and the two comforted each other from the fear of having robbed the pot man.

'We c'n have stewed fruit in it,' said Paul.

'Or custard, or a jelly,' said his mother.

'Or radishes and lettuce,' said he.

'Don't forget that bread,' she said, her voice bright with glee.

Paul looked in the oven; tapped the loaf on the base.

'It's done,' he said, giving it to her.

She tapped it also.

'Yes,' she replied, going to unpack her bag. 'Oh, and I'm a wicked, extravagant woman. I know I s'll come to want.'

He hopped to her side eagerly, to see her latest extravagance. She unfolded another lump of newspaper and disclosed some roots of pansies and of crimson daisies.

'Four penn'orth!' she moaned.

'How *cheap!*' he cried.

'Yes, but I couldn't afford it *this* week of all weeks.'

'But lovely!' he cried.

'Aren't they!' she exclaimed, giving way to pure joy. 'Paul, look at this yellow one, isn't it – and a face just like an old man!'

'Just!' cried Paul, stooping to sniff. 'And smells that nice! But he's a bit splashed.'

He ran in the scullery, came back with the flannel, and carefully washed the pansy.

'*Now* look at him now he's wet!' he said.

'Yes!' she exclaimed, brimful of satisfaction.

The children of Scargill Street felt quite select. At the end where the Morels lived there were not many young things. So the few were more united. Boys and girls played together, the girls joining in the fights and the rough games, the boys taking part in the dancing games and rings and make-belief of the girls.

Annie and Paul and Arthur loved the winter evenings, when it was not wet. They stayed indoors till the colliers were all gone home, till it was thick dark, and the street would be deserted. Then they tied their scarves round their necks, for they scorned overcoats, as all the colliers' children did, and went out. The entry was very dark, and at the end the whole great night opened out, in a hollow, with a little tangle of lights below where Minton pit lay, and another far away opposite for Selby. The farthest tiny lights seemed to stretch out the darkness for ever. The children looked anxiously down the road at the one lamp-post, which stood at the end of the field path. If the little, luminous space were deserted, the two boys felt genuine desolation. They stood with their hands in their pockets under the lamp, turning their backs on the night, quite miserable, watching the dark houses. Suddenly a pinafore under a short coat was seen, and a long-legged girl came flying up.

'Where's Billy Pillins an' your Annie an' Eddie Dakin?'

'I don't know.'

But it did not matter so much – there were three now. They set up a game round the lamp-post, till the others rushed up, yelling. Then the play went fast and furious.

There was only this one lamp-post. Behind was the great scoop of darkness, as if all the night were there. In front, another wide, dark way opened over the hill brow. Occasionally somebody came out of his way and went into the field down the path. In a dozen yards the night had swallowed them. The children played on.

They were brought exceedingly close together owing to their isolation. If a quarrel took place, the whole play was spoilt. Arthur was very touchy, and Billy Pillins – really Philips – was worse. Then Paul had to side with Arthur, and on Paul's side went Alice, while Billy Pillins always had Emmie Limb and Eddie Dakin to back him up. Then the six would fight, hate with a fury of hatred, and flee home in terror. Paul never forgot, after one of these fierce internecine fights, seeing a big red moon lift itself up, slowly, between the waste road over the hill-top, steadily, like a great bird. And he thought of the Bible, that the moon should be turned to blood. And the next day he made haste to be friends with Billy Pillins, and then the wild, intense games went on again under the lamp-post, surrounded by so much darkness. Mrs Morel, going into her parlour, would hear the children singing away:

'My shoes are made of Spanish leather,
  My socks are made of silk;
I wear a ring on every finger,
  I wash myself in milk.'

They sounded so perfectly absorbed in the game as their voices came out of the night, that they had the feel of wild creatures singing. It stirred the mother; and she understood when they came in at eight o'clock, ruddy, with brilliant eyes, and quick, passionate speech.

They all loved the Scargill Street house for its openness, for the great scallop of the world it had in view. On summer evenings the women would stand against the field fence, gossiping, facing the west, watching the sunsets flare quickly out, till the Derbyshire hills ridged across the crimson far away, like the black crest of a newt.

In this summer season the pits never turned full time, particularly the soft coal. Mrs Dakin, who lived next door to Mrs Morel, going to the field fence to shake her hearthrug, would spy men coming slowly up the hill. She saw at once they were colliers. Then she waited, a tall, thin, shrew-faced woman, standing on the hill brow, almost like a menace to the poor colliers who were toiling up. It was only eleven o'clock. From the far-off wooded hills the haze that hangs like fine black crape at the back of a summer morning had not yet dissipated. The first man came to the stile. 'Chock-chock!' went the gate under his thrust.

'What, han' yer knocked off?' cried Mrs Dakin.

'We han, missis.'

'It's a pity as they letn yer goo,' she said sarcastically.

'It is that,' replied the man.

'Nay, you know you're flig to come up again,' she said.

And the man went on. Mrs Dakin, going up her yard, spied Mrs Morel taking the ashes to the ash-pit.

'I reckon Minton's knocked off, missis,' she cried.

'Isn't it sickenin'!' exclaimed Mrs Morel in wrath.

'Ha! But I'n just seed Jont Hutchby.'

'They might as well have saved their shoe-leather,' said Mrs Morel. And both women went indoors disgusted.

The colliers, their faces scarcely blackened, were trooping home again. Morel hated to go back. He loved the sunny morning. But he had gone to pit to work, and to be sent home again spoilt his temper.

'Good gracious, at this time!' exclaimed his wife, as he entered.

'Can I help it, woman?' he shouted.

'And I've not done half enough dinner.'

'Then I'll eat my bit o' snap as I took with me,' he bawled pathetically. He felt ignominious and sore.

And the children coming home from school, would wonder to see their father eating with his dinner the two thick slices of dry and dirty bread-and-butter that had been to pit and back.

'What's my dad eating his snap for now?' asked Arthur.

'I should ha'e it holled at me if I didna,' snorted Morel.

'What a story!' exclaimed his wife.

'An' is it goin' to be wasted?' said Morel. 'I'm not such a extravagant mortal as you lot, with your waste. If I drop a bit of bread at pit, in all the dust an' dirt, I pick it up an' eat it.'

'The mice would eat it,' said Paul. 'It wouldn't be wasted.'

'Good bread-an'-butter's not for mice, either,' said Morel. 'Dirty or not dirty, I'd eat it rather than it should be wasted.'

'You might leave it for the mice and pay for it out of your next pint,' said Mrs Morel.

'Oh, might I?' he exclaimed.

They were very poor that autumn. William had just gone away to London, and his mother missed his money. He sent ten shillings once or twice, but he had many things to pay for at first. His letters came regularly once a week. He wrote a good deal to his mother, telling her all his life, how he made friends, and was exchanging lessons with a Frenchman, how he enjoyed London. His mother felt again he was remaining to her just as when he was at home. She wrote to him every week her direct, rather witty letters. All day long, as she cleaned the house, she thought of him. He was in London: he would do well. Almost, he was like her knight who wore *her* favour in the battle.

He was coming at Christmas for five days. There had never been such preparations. Paul and Arthur scoured the land for holly and evergreens. Annie made the pretty paper hoops in the old-fashioned way. And there was unheard-of-extravagance in the larder. Mrs Morel made a big and magnificent cake. Then, feeling queenly, she showed Paul how to blanch almonds. He skinned the long nuts reverently, counting them all, to see not one was lost. It was said that eggs whisked better in a cold place. So the boy stood in the scullery, where the temperature was nearly at freezing-point, and whisked and whisked, and flew in excitement to his mother as the white of egg grew stiffer and more snowy.

'Just look, mother! Isn't it lovely?'

And he balanced a bit on his nose, then blew it in the air.

'Now, don't waste it,' said the mother.

Everybody was mad with excitement. William was coming on Christmas Eve. Mrs Morel surveyed the pantry. There was a big plum cake, and a rice cake, jam tarts, lemon tarts, and mince-pies – two enormous dishes. She was finishing cooking – Spanish tarts and cheese-cakes. Everywhere was decorated. The kissing bunch of berried holly hung with bright and glittering things spun slowly over Mrs Morel's head as she trimmed her little tarts in the kitchen. A great fire roared. There was a scent of cooked pastry. He was due at seven o'clock, but he would be late. The three children had gone to meet him. She was alone. But at a quarter to seven Morel came in again. Neither wife nor husband spoke. He sat in his armchair, quite awkward with excitement, and she quietly went on with her baking. Only by the careful way in which she did things could it be told how much moved she was. The clock ticked on.

'What time dost say he's coming?' Morel asked for the fifth time.

'The train gets in at half-past six,' she replied emphatically.

'Then he'll be here at ten past seven.'

'Eh, bless you, it'll be hours late on the Midland,' she said indifferently. But she hoped, by expecting him late, to bring him early. Morel went down the entry to look for him. Then he came back.

'Goodness, man!' she said. 'You're like an ill-sitting hen.'

'Hadna you better be gettin' him summat t'eat ready?' asked the father.

'There's plenty of time,' she answered.

'There's not much as I can see on,' he answered, turning crossly in his chair. She began to clear the table. The kettle was singing. They waited and waited.

Meantime the three children were on the platform at Sethley Bridge, on the

Midland main line, two miles from home. They waited one hour. A train came
– he was not there. Down the line the red and green lights shone. It was very
dark and very cold.

'Ask him if the London train's come,' said Paul to Annie, when they saw a
man in a tip cap.

'I'm not,' said Annie. 'You be quiet – he might send us off.'

But Paul was dying for the man to know they were expecting someone by
the London train: it sounded so grand. Yet he was much too much scared of
broaching any man, let alone one in a peaked cap, to dare to ask. The three
children could scarcely go into the waiting-room for fear of being sent away,
and for fear something should happen whilst they were off the platform. Still
they waited in the dark and cold.

'It's an hour an' a half late,' said Arthur pathetically.

'Well,' said Annie, 'it's Christmas Eve.'

They all grew silent. He wasn't coming. They looked down the darkness of
the railway. There was London! It seemed the uttermost of distance. They
thought anything might happen if one came from London. They were all too
troubled to talk. Cold and unhappy, and silent, they huddled together on the
platform.

At last, after more than two hours, they saw the lights of an engine peering
round, away down the darkness. A porter ran out. The children drew back
with beating hearts. A great train bound for Manchester drew up. Two doors
opened, and from one of them, William. They flew to him. He handed parcels
to them cheerily, and immediately began to explain that this great train had
stopped for *his* sake at such a small station as Sethley Bridge: it was not
booked to stop.

Meanwhile the parents were getting anxious. The table was set, the chop
was cooked, everything was ready. Mrs Morel put on her black apron. She was
wearing her best dress. Then she sat, pretending to read. The minutes were a
torture to her.

'H'm!' said Morel. 'It's an hour an' a ha'ef.'

'And those children waiting!' she said.

'Th' train canna ha' come in yet,' he said.

'I tell you, on Christmas Eve they're *hours* wrong.'

They were both a bit cross with each other, so gnawed with anxiety. The ash-
tree moaned outside in a cold, raw wind. And all that space of night from
London home! Mrs Morel suffered. The slight click of the works inside the
clock irritated her. It was getting so late; it was getting unbearable.

At last there was a sound of voices, and a footstep in the entry.

'Ha's here!' cried Morel, jumping up.

Then he stood back. The mother ran a few steps towards the door and
waited. There was a rush and a patter of feet, the door burst open. William was
there. He dropped his Gladstone bag and took his mother in his arms.

'Mater!' he said.

'My boy!' she cried.

And for two seconds, no longer, she clasped him and kissed him. Then she
withdrew and said, trying to be quite normal:

'But how late you are!'

'Aren't I!' he cried, turning to his father. 'Well, dad!'

The two men shook hands.

'Well, my lad!'

Morel's eyes were wet.

'We thought tha'd niver be commin',' he said.

'Oh, I'd come!' exclaimed William.

Then the son turned round to his mother.

'But you look well,' she said proudly, laughing.

'Well!' he exclaimed. 'I should think so – coming home!'

He was a fine fellow, big, straight, and fearless-looking. He looked round at the evergreens and the kissing bunch, and the little tarts that lay in their tins on the hearth.

'By jove! mother, it's not different!' he said, as if in relief.

Everybody was still for a second. Then he suddenly sprang forward, picked a tart from the hearth, and pushed it whole into his mouth.

'Well, did iver you see such a parish oven!' the father exclaimed.

He had brought them endless presents. Every penny he had he had spent on them. There was a sense of luxury overflowing in the house. For his mother there was an umbrella with gold on the pale handle. She kept it to her dying day, and would have lost anything rather than that. Everybody had something gorgeous, and besides, there were pounds of unknown sweets: Turkish delight, crystallized pineapple, and such-like things which, the children thought, only the splendour of London could provide. And Paul boasted of these sweets among his friends.

'Real pineapple, cut off in slices, and then turned into crystal – fair grand!'

Everybody was mad with happiness in the family. Home was home, and they loved it with a passion of love, whatever the suffering had been. There were parties, there were rejoicings. People came in to see William, to see what difference London had made to him. And they all found him 'such a gentleman, and *such* a fine fellow, my word!'

When he went away again the children retired to various places to weep alone. Morel went to bed in misery, and Mrs Morel felt as if she were numbed by some drug, as if her feelings were paralysed. She loved him passionately.

He was in the office of a lawyer connected with a large shipping firm, and at the midsummer his chief offered him a trip in the Mediterranean on one of the boats, for quite a small cost. Mrs Morel wrote: 'Go, go, my boy. You may never have a chance again, and I should love to think of you cruising there in the Mediterranean almost better than to have you at home.' But William came home for his fortnight's holiday. Not even the Mediterranean, which pulled at all his young man's desire to travel, and at his poor man's wonder at the glamorous south, could take him away when he might come home. That compensated his mother for much.

5

PAUL LAUNCHES INTO LIFE

Morel was rather a heedless man, careless of danger. So he had endless accidents. Now, when Mrs Morel heard the rattle of an empty coal-cart cease at her entry-end, she ran into the parlour to look, expecting almost to see her husband seated in the wagon, his face grey under his dirt, his body limp and sick with some hurt or other. If it were he, she would run out to help.

About a year after William went to London, and just after Paul had left school before he got work, Mrs Morel was upstairs and her son was painting in the kitchen – he was very clever with his brush – when there came a knock at the door. Crossly he put down his brush to go. At the same moment his mother opened a window upstairs and looked down.

A pit-lad in his dirt stood on the threshold.

'Is this Walter Morel's?' he asked.

'Yes,' said Mrs Morel. 'What is it?'

But she had guessed already.

'Your mester's got hurt,' he said.

'Eh, dear me!' she exclaimed. 'It's a wonder if he hadn't, lad. And what's he done this time?'

'I don't know for sure, but it's 'is leg somewhere. They ta'ein' 'im ter th' 'ospital.'

'Good gracious me!' she exclaimed. 'Eh, dear, what a one he is! There's not five minutes of peace. I'll be hanged if there is! His thumb's nearly better, and now – Did you see him?'

'I seed him at th' bottom. An' I seed 'em bring 'im up in a tub, an' 'e wor in a dead faint. But he shouted like anythink when Doctor Fraser examined him i' th' lamp cabin – an' cossed an' swore, an' said as 'e wor goin' to be ta'en whoam – 'e worn't goin' ter th' 'ospital.'

The boy faltered to an end.

'He *would* want to come home, so that I can have all the bother. Thank you, my lad. Eh, dear, if I'm not sick – sick and surfeited, I am!'

She came downstairs. Paul had mechanically resumed his painting.

'And it must be pretty bad if they've taken him to the hospital,' she went on. 'But what a *careless* creature he is! *Other* men, don't have all these accidents. Yes, he *would* want to put all the burden on me. Eh, dear, just as we *were* getting easy a bit at last. Put those things away, there's no time to be painting now. What time is there a train? I know I s'll have to go trailing to Keston. I s'll have to leave that bedroom.'

'I can finish it,' said Paul.

'You needn't. I shall catch the seven o'clock back, I should think. Oh, my blessed heart, the fuss and commotion he'll make! And those granite setts at Tinder Hill – he might well call them kidney pebbles – they'll jolt him almost to bits. I wonder why they can't mend them, the state they're in, an' all the men as go across in that ambulance. You'd think they'd have a hospital here. The men bought the ground, and, my sirs, there'd be accidents enough to keep it going. But no, they must trail them ten miles in a slow ambulance to Nottingham. It's a crying shame! Oh, and the fuss he'll make! I know he will! I wonder who's with him. Barker, I s'd think. Poor beggar, he'll wish himself anywhere rather. But he'll look after him, I know. Now, there's no telling how long he'll be stuck in that hospital – and *won't* he hate it! But if it's only his leg it's not so bad.'

All the time she was getting ready. Hurriedly taking off her bodice, she crouched at the boiler while the water ran slowly into her lading-can.

'I wish this boiler was at the bottom of the sea!' she exclaimed, wriggling the handle impatiently. She had very handsome, strong arms, rather surprising on a smallish woman.

Paul cleared away, put on the kettle, and set the table.

'There isn't a train till four-twenty,' he said. 'You've time enough.'

'Oh no I haven't!' she cried, blinking at him over the towel as she wiped her face.

'Yes you have. You must drink a cup of tea at any rate. Should I come with you to Keston?'

'Come with me? What for, I should like to know? Now, what have I to take him? Eh, dear! His clean shirt – and it's a blessing it *is* clean. But it had better be aired. And stockings – he won't want them – and a towel, I suppose; and handkerchiefs. Now what else?'

'A comb, a knife and fork and spoon,' said Paul. His father had been in the hospital before.

'Goodness knows what sort of state his feet were in,' continued Mrs Morel, as she combed her long brown hair, that was fine as silk, and was touched now with grey. 'He's very particular to wash himself to the waist, but below he thinks doesn't matter. But there, I suppose they see plenty like it.'

Paul had laid the table. He cut his mother one or two pieces of very thin bread-and-butter.

'Here you are,' he said, putting her cup of tea in her place.

'I can't be bothered!' she exclaimed crossly.

'Well, you've got to, so there, now it's put out ready,' he insisted.

So she sat down and sipped her tea, and ate a little, in silence. She was thinking.

In a few minutes she was gone, to walk the two and a half miles to Keston Station. All the things she was taking him she had in her bulging string bag. Paul watched her go up the road between the hedges – a little, quick-stepping figure, and his heart ached for her, that she was thrust forward again into pain and trouble. And she, tripping so quickly in her anxiety, felt at the back of her, her son's heart waiting on her, felt him bearing what part of the burden he could, even supporting her. And when she was at the hospital, she thought: 'It *will* upset that lad when I tell him how bad it is. I'd better be careful.' And when she was trudging home again, she felt he was coming to share her burden.

'Is it bad?' asked Paul, as soon as she entered the house.

'It's bad enough,' she replied.

'What?'

She sighed and sat down, undoing her bonnet-strings. Her son watched her face as it was lifted, and her small, work-hardened hands fingering at the bow under her chin.

'Well,' she answered, 'it's not really dangerous, but the nurse says it's a dreadful smash. You see, a great piece of rock fell on his leg – here – and it's a compound fracture. There are pieces of bone sticking through –'

'Ugh – how horrid!' exclaimed the children.

'And,' she continued, 'of course he says he's going to die – it wouldn't be him if he didn't. "I'm done for, my lass!" he said, looking at me. "Don't be so silly," I said to him. "You're not going to die of a broken leg, however badly it's smashed." "I s'll niver come out of 'ere but in a wooden box," he groaned. "Well," I said, "if you want them to carry you into the garden in a wooden box, when you're better, I've no doubt they will." "If we think it's good for him," said the Sister. She's an awfully nice Sister, but rather strict.'

Mrs Morel took off her bonnet. The children waited in silence.

'Of course, he *is* bad,' she continued, 'and he will be. It's a great shock, and he's lost a lot of blood; and, of course, it *is* a very dangerous smash. It's not at all sure that it will mend so easily. And then there's the fever and the mortification – if it took bad ways he'd quickly be gone. But there, he's a clean-blooded man, with a wonderful healing flesh, and so I see no reason why it *should* take bad ways. Of course there's a wound –'

She was pale now with emotion and anxiety. The three children realized that it was very bad for their father, and the house was silent, anxious.

'But he always gets better,' said Paul after a while.

'That's what I tell him,' said the mother.

Everybody moved about in silence.

'And he really looked nearly done for,' she said. 'But the Sister says that is the pain.'

Annie took away her mother's coat and bonnet.

'And he looked at me when I came away! I said: "I s'll have to go now, Walter, because of the train – and the children." And he looked at me. It seems hard.'

Paul took up his brush again and went on painting. Arthur went outside for some coal. Annie sat looking dismal. And Mrs Morel, in her little rocking-chair that her husband had made for her when the first baby was coming, remained motionless, brooding. She was grieved, and bitterly sorry for the man who was hurt so much. But still, in her heart of hearts, where the love should have burned, there was a blank. Now, when all her woman's pity was roused to its full extent, when she would have slaved herself to death to nurse him and to save him, when she would have taken the pain herself, if she could, somewhere far away inside her, she felt indifferent to him and his suffering. It hurt her most of all, this failure to love him, even when he roused her strong emotions. She brooded awhile.

'And there,' she said suddenly, 'when I'd got half-way to Keston, I found I'd come out in my working-boots – and *look* at them.' They were an old pair of Paul's, brown and rubbed through the toes. 'I didn't know what to do with myself, for shame,' she added.

In the morning, when Annie and Arthur were at school, Mrs Morel talked again to her son, who was helping her with her housework.

'I found Barker at the hospital. He did look bad, poor little fellow! "Well," I said to him, "what sort of journey did you have with him?" "Dunna ax me, missis!" he said. "Ay," I said, "I know what he'd be." "But it *wor* bad for him, Mrs Morel, it *wor* that!" he said. "I know," I said. "At ivry jolt I thought my 'eart would ha' flown clean out o' my mouth," he said. "An' the scream 'e gives sometimes! Missis, not for a fortune would I go through wi' it again." "I can quite understand it," I said. "It's a nasty job, though," he said, "an' one as'll be a long while afore it's right again." "I'm afraid it will," I said. I like Mr Barker – I *do* like him. There's something so manly about him.'

Paul resumed his task silently.

'And of course,' Mrs Morel continued, 'for a man like your father, the hospital *is* hard. He *can't* understand rules and regulations. And he won't let anybody else touch him, not if he can help it. When he smashed the muscles of his thigh, and it had to be dressed four times a day, *would* he let anybody but me or his mother do it? He wouldn't. So, of course, he'll suffer in there with the nurses. And I didn't like leaving him. I'm sure, when I kissed him an' came away, it seemed a shame.'

So she talked to her son, almost as if she were thinking aloud to him, and he took it in as best he could, by sharing her trouble to lighten it. And in the end she shared almost everything with him without knowing.

Morel had a very bad time. For a week he was in a critical condition. Then he began to mend. And then, knowing he was going to get better, the whole family sighed with relief, and proceeded to live happily.

They were not badly off whilst Morel was in the hospital. There were fourteen shillings a week from the pit, ten shillings from the sick club, and five shillings from the Disability Fund; and then every week the butties had something for Mrs Morel – five or seven shillings – so that she was quite well to do. And whilst Morel was progressing favourably in the hospital, the family was extraordinarily happy and peaceful. On Saturdays and Wednesdays Mrs Morel went to Nottingham to see her husband. Then she always brought back some little thing: a small tube of paint for Paul, or some thick paper; a couple of postcards for Annie, that the whole family rejoiced over for days before the girl was allowed to send them away; or a fret-saw for Arthur, or a bit of pretty wood. She described her adventures into the big shops with joy. Soon the folk in the picture-shop knew her, and knew about Paul. The girl in the book-shop took a keen interest in her. Mrs Morel was full of information when she got home from Nottingham. The three sat round till bed-time, listening, putting in, arguing. Then Paul often raked the fire.

'I'm the man in the house now,' he used to say to his mother with joy. They learned how perfectly peaceful the home could be. And they almost regretted – though none of them would have owned to such callousness – that their father was soon coming back.

Paul was now fourteen, and was looking for work. He was a rather small and rather finely-made boy, with dark brown hair and light blue eyes. His face had already lost its youthful chubbiness, and was becoming somewhat like William's – rough-featured, almost rugged – and it was extraordinarily mobile. Usually he looked as if he saw things, was full of life, and warm; then his smile, like his mother's, came suddenly and was very lovable; and then, when there was any clog in his soul's quick running, his face went stupid and ugly. He was the sort of boy that becomes a clown and a lout as soon as he is not understood, or feels himself held cheap; and, again, is adorable at the first touch of warmth.

He suffered very much from the first contact with anything. When he was seven, the starting school had been a nightmare and a torture to him. But afterwards he liked it. And now that he felt he had to go out into life, he went through agonies of shrinking self-consciousness. He was quite a clever painter for a boy of his years, and he knew some French and German and mathematics that Mr Heaton had taught him. But nothing he had was of any commercial value. He was not strong enough for heavy manual work, his mother said. He did not care for making things with his hands, preferred racing about or making excursions into the country, or reading, or painting.

'What do you want to be?' his mother asked.

'Anything.'

'That is no answer,' said Mrs Morel.

But it was quite truthfully the only answer he could give. His ambition, as far as this world's gear went, was quietly to earn his thirty or thirty-five shillings a week somewhere near home, and then, when his father died, have a cottage with his mother, paint and go out as he liked, and live happy ever after. That was his programme as far as doing things went. But he was proud within himself, measuring people against himself, and placing them, inexorably. And he thought that *perhaps* he might also make a painter, the real thing. But that he left alone.

'Then,' said his mother, 'you must look in the paper for the advertisements.'

He looked at her. It seemed to him a bitter humiliation and an anguish to go through. But he said nothing. When he got up in the morning, his whole being was knotted up over this one thought:

'I've got to go and look for advertisements for a job.'

It stood in front of the morning, that thought, killing all joy and even life, for him. His heart felt like a tight knot.

And then, at ten o'clock, he set off. He was supposed to be a queer, quiet child. Going up the sunny streets of the little town, he felt as if all the folk he met said to themselves: 'He's going to the Co-op reading-room to look in the papers for a place. He can't get a job. I suppose he's living on his mother.' Then he crept up the stone stairs behind the drapery shop at the Co-op, and peeped in the reading-room. Usually one or two men were there, either old, useless fellows, or colliers 'on the club'. So he entered, full of shrinking and suffering when they looked up, seated himself at the table, and pretended to scan the news. He knew they would think, 'What does a lad of thirteen want in a reading-room with a newspaper?' and he suffered.

Then he looked wistfully out of the window. Already he was a prisoner of industrialism. Large sunflowers stared over the old red wall of the garden opposite, looking in their jolly way down on the women who were hurrying with something for dinner. The valley was full of corn, brightening in the sun. Two collieries, among the fields, waved their small white plumes of stream. Far off on the hills were the woods of Annesley, dark and fascinating. Already his heart went down. He was being taken into bondage. His freedom in the beloved home valley was going now.

The brewers' wagons came rolling from Keston with enormous barrels, four a side, like beans in a burst bean-pod. The wagoner, throned aloft, rolling massively in his seat, was not much below Paul's eye. The man's hair, on his small, bullet head, was bleached almost white by the sun, and on his thick red arms, rocking idly on his sack apron, the white hairs glistened. His red face shone and was almost asleep with sunshine. The horses, handsome and brown, went on by themselves, looking by far the master of the show.

Paul wished he were stupid. 'I wish,' he thought to himself, 'I was fat like him, and like a dog in the sun. I wish I was a pig and a brewer's wagoner.'

Then, the room being at last empty, he would hastily copy an advertisement on a scrap of paper, then another, and slip out in immense relief. His mother would scan over his copies.

'Yes,' she said, 'you may try.'

William had written out a letter of application, couched in admirable business language, which Paul copied, with variations. The boy's handwriting was execrable, so that William, who did all things well, got into a fever of impatience.

The elder brother was becoming quite swanky. In London he found that he could associate with men far above his Bestwood friends in station. Some of the clerks in the office had studied for the law, and were more or less going through a kind of apprenticeship. William always made friends among men wherever he went, he was so jolly. Therefore he was soon visiting and staying in houses of men who, in Bestwood, would have looked down on the unapproachable bank manager, and would merely have called indifferently on the Rector. So he began to fancy himself as a great gun. He was, indeed, rather surprised at the ease with which he became a gentleman.

His mother was glad, he seemed so pleased. And his lodging in Walthamstow was so dreary. But now there seemed to come a kind of fever into the young man's letter. He was unsettled by all the change, he did not stand firm on his own feet, but seemed to spin rather giddily on the quick current of the new life. His mother was anxious for him. She could feel him losing himself. He had danced and gone to the theatre, boated on the river, been out with friends; and she knew he sat up afterwards in his cold bedroom grinding away at Latin, because he intended to get on in his office, and in the law as much as he could. He never sent his mother any money now. It was all taken, the little he had, for his own life. And she did not want any, except sometimes, when she was in a tight corner, and when ten shillings would have saved her much worry. She still dreamed of William, and of what he would do, with herself behind him. Never for a minute would she admit to herself how heavy and anxious her heart was because of him.

Also he talked a good deal now of a girl he had met at a dance, a handsome brunette, quite young, and a lady, after whom the men were running thick and fast.

'I wonder if you would run, my boy,' his mother wrote to him, 'unless you saw all the other men chasing her too. You feel safe enough and vain enough in a crowd. But take care, and see how you feel when you find yourself alone, and in triumph.'

William resented these things, and continued the chase. He had taken the girl on the river. 'If you saw her, mother, you would know how I feel. Tall and elegant, with the clearest of clear, transparent olive complexions, hair as black as jet, and such grey eyes – bright, mocking, like lights on water at night. It is all very well to be a bit satirical till you see her. And she dresses as well as any woman in London. I tell you, your son doesn't half put his head up when she goes walking down Piccadilly with him.'

Mrs Morel wondered, in her heart, if her son did not go walking down Piccadilly with an elegant figure and fine clothes, rather than with a woman who was near to him. But she congratulated him in her doubtful fashion. And, as she stood over the washing-tub, the mother brooded over her son. She saw him saddled with an elegant and expensive wife, earning little money, dragging along and getting draggled in some small, ugly house in a suburb. 'But there,' she told herself, 'I am very likely a silly – meeting trouble half-way.' Nevertheless, the load of anxiety scarcely ever left her heart, lest William should do the wrong thing by himself.

Presently, Paul was bidden call upon Thomas Jordan, Manufacturer of Surgical Appliances, at 21 Spaniel Row, Nottingham. Mrs Morel was all joy.

'There, you see!' she cried, her eyes shining. 'You've only written four letters, and the third is answered. You're lucky, my boy, as I always said you were.'

Paul looked at the picture of a wooden leg, adorned with elastic stockings and other appliances, that figured on Mr Jordan's notepaper, and he felt alarmed. He had not known that elastic stockings existed. And he seemed to feel the business world, with its regulated system of values, and its impersonality, and he dreaded it. It seemed monstrous also that a business could be run on wooden legs.

Mother and son set off together one Tuesday morning. It was August and blazing hot. Paul walked with something screwed up tight inside him. He would have suffered much physical pain rather than this unreasonable suffering at being exposed to strangers, to be accepted or rejected. Yet he chattered away with his mother. He would never have confessed to her how he suffered over these things, and she only partly guessed. She was gay, like a sweetheart. She stood in front of the ticket-office at Bestwood, and Paul watched her take from her purse the money for the tickets. As he saw her hands in their old black kid gloves getting the silver out of the worn purse, his heart contracted with pain of love of her.

She was quite excited, and quite gay. He suffered because she *would* talk aloud in presence of the other travellers.

'Now look at that silly cow!' she said, 'careering round as if it thought it was a circus.'

'It's most likely a bottfly,' he said very low.

'A what?' she asked brightly and unashamed.

They thought a while. He was sensible all the time of having her opposite him. Suddenly their eyes met, and she smiled to him – a rare, intimate smile, beautiful with brightness and love. Then each looked out of the window.

The sixteen slow miles of railway journey passed. The mother and son walked down Station Street, feeling the excitement of lovers having an adventure together. In Carrington Street they stopped to hang over the parapet and look at the barges on the canal below.

'It's just like Venice,' he said, seeing the sunshine on the water that lay between high factory walls.

'Perhaps,' she answered smiling.

They enjoyed the shops immensely.

'Now you see that blouse,' she would say, 'wouldn't that just suit our Annie? And for one-and-eleven-three. Isn't that cheap?'

'And made of needlework as well,' he said.

'Yes.'

They had plenty of time, so they did not hurry. The town was strange and delightful to them. But the boy was tied up inside a knot of apprehension. He dreaded the interview with Thomas Jordan.

It was nearly eleven o'clock by St Peter's Church. They turned up a narrow street that led to the Castle. It was gloomy and old-fashioned, having low dark shops and dark green house-doors with brass knockers, and yellow-ochred doorsteps projecting on to the pavement; then another old shop whose small window looked like a cunning, half-shut eye. Mother and son went cautiously, looking everywhere for 'Thomas Jordan and Son'. It was like hunting in some wild place. They were on tiptoe of excitement.

Suddenly they spied a big, dark archway, in which were names of various firms, Thomas Jordan among them.

'Here it is!' said Mrs Morel. 'But now *where* is it?'

They looked round. On one side was a queer, dark, cardboard factory, on the other a Commercial Hotel.

'It's up the entry,' said Paul.

And they ventured under the archway, as into the jaws of the dragon. They emerged into a wide yard, like a well, with buildings all round. It was littered with straw and boxes, and cardboard. The sunshine actually caught one crate whose straw was streaming on to the yard like gold. But elsewhere the place was like a pit. There were several doors, and two flights of steps. Straight in front, on a dirty glass door at the top of a staircase, loomed the ominous words 'Thomas Jordan and Son – Surgical Appliances'. Mrs Morel went first, her son followed her. Charles I mounted his scaffold with a lighter heart than had Paul

Morel as he followed his mother up the dirty steps to the dirty door.

She pushed open the door, and stood in pleased surprise. In front of her was a big warehouse, with creamy paper parcels everywhere, and clerks, with their shirt-sleeves rolled back, were going about in an at-home sort of way. The light was subdued, the glossy cream parcels seemed luminous, the counters were of dark brown wood. All was quiet and very homely. Mrs Morel took two steps forward, then waited. Paul stood behind her. She had on her Sunday bonnet and a black veil; he wore a boy's broad white collar and a Norfolk suit.

One of the clerks looked up. He was thin and tall, with a small face. His way of looking was alert. Then he glanced round to the other end of the room, where there was a glass office. And then he came forward. He did not say anything, but leaned in a gentle, inquiring fashion towards Mrs Morel.

'Can I see Mr Jordan?' she asked.

'I'll fetch him,' answered the young man.

He went down to the glass office. A red-faced, white-whiskered old man looked up. He reminded Paul of a pomeranian dog. Then the same little man came up the room. He had short legs, was rather stout, and wore an alpaca jacket. So, with one ear up, as it were, he came stoutly and inquiringly down the room.

'Good morning!' he said, hesitating before Mrs Morel, in doubt as to whether she were a customer or not.

'Good morning. I came with my son, Paul Morel. You asked him to call this morning.'

'Come this way,' said Mr Jordan, in a rather snappy little manner intended to be businesslike.

They followed the manufacturer into a grubby little room, upholstered in black American leather, glossy with the rubbing of many customers. On the table was a pile of trusses, yellow wash-leather hoops tangled together. They looked new and living. Paul sniffed the odour of new wash-leather. He wondered what the things were. By this time he was so much stunned that he only noticed the outside things.

'Sit down!' said Mr Jordan, irritably pointing Mrs Morel to a horse-hair chair. She sat on the edge in an uncertain fashion. Then the little old man fidgeted and found a paper.

'Did you write this letter?' he snapped, thrusting what Paul recognized as his own notepaper in front of him.

'Yes,' he answered.

At that moment he was occupied in two ways: first, on feeling guilty for telling a lie, since William had composed the letter; second, in wondering why his letter seemed so strange and different, in the fat, red hand of the man, from what it had been when it lay on the kitchen table. It was like part of himself, gone astray. He resented the way the man held it.

'Where did you learn to write?' said the old man crossly.

Paul merely looked at him shamedly, and did not answer.

'He *is* a bad writer,' put in Mrs Morel apologetically. Then she pushed up her veil. Paul hated her for not being prouder with this common little man, and he loved her face clear of the veil.

'And did you say you know French?' inquired the little man, still sharply.

'Yes,' said Paul.

'What school did you go to?'

'The Board-school.'

'And did you learn it there?'

'No – I –' The boy went crimson and got no further.

'His godfather gave him lessons,' said Mrs Morel, half-pleading and rather distant.

Mr Jordan hesitated. Then, in his irritable manner – he always seemed to keep his hands ready for action – he pulled another sheet of paper from his pocket, unfolded it. The paper made a crackling noise. He handed it to Paul.

'Read that,' he said.

It was a note in French, in thin, flimsy foreign handwriting that the boy could not decipher. He stared blankly at the paper.

'"Monsieur,"' he began; then he looked in great confusion at Mr Jordan. 'It's the – it's the –'

He wanted to say 'handwriting', but his wits would no longer work even sufficiently to supply him with the word. Feeling an utter fool, and hating Mr Jordan, he turned desperately to the paper again.

'"Sir – Please send me" – er – er – I can't tell the – er – "two pairs – *gris fil bas* – grey thread stockings" – er – er – "*sans* – without" – er – I can't tell the words – er – "*doigts* – fingers" – er – I can't tell the –'

He wanted to say 'handwriting', but the word still refused to come. Seeing him stuck, Mr Jordan snatched the paper from him.

'"Please send by return two pairs grey thread stockings without *toes*."'

'Well,' flashed Paul, ' "*doigts*" means "fingers" – as well – as a rul – e –'

The little man looked at him. He did not know whether '*doigts*' meant 'fingers'; he knew that for all *his* purposes it meant 'toes'.

'Fingers to stockings!' he snapped.

'Well, it *does* mean fingers,' the boy persisted.

He hated the little man, who made such a clod of him. Mr Jordan looked at the pale, stupid, defiant boy, then at the mother, who sat quiet and with that peculiar shut-off look of the poor who have to depend on the favour of others.

'And when could he come?' he asked.

'Well,' said Mrs Morel, 'as soon as you wish. He has finished school now.'

'He would live in Bestwood?'

'Yes; but he could be in – at the station – at quarter to eight.'

'H'm!'

It ended by Paul's being engaged as junior spiral clerk at eight shillings a week. The boy did not open his mouth to say another word, after having insisted that '*doigts*' meant 'fingers'. He followed his mother down the stairs. She looked at him with her bright blue eyes full of love and joy.

'I think you'll like it,' she said.

' "*Doigts*" does mean "fingers", mother, and it was the writing. I couldn't read the writing.'

'Never mind, my boy. I'm sure he'll be all right, and you won't see much of him. Wasn't that first young fellow nice? I'm sure you'll like them.'

'But wasn't Mr Jordan common, mother? Does he own it all?'

'I suppose he was a workman who has got on,' she said. 'You mustn't mind people so much. They're not being disagreeable to *you* – it's their way. You always think people are meaning things for you. But they don't.'

It was very sunny. Over the big desolate space of the market-place the blue sky shimmered, and the granite cobbles of the pavings glistened. Shops down the Long Row were deep in obscurity, and the shadow was full of colour. Just where the horse trams trundled across the market was a row of fruit stalls, with fruit blazing in the sun – apples and piles of reddish oranges, small greengage plums and bananas. There was a warm scent of fruit as mother and son passed. Gradually his feeling of ignominy and of rage sank.

'Where should we go for dinner?' asked the mother.

It was felt to be a reckless extravagance. Paul had only been in an eating-house once or twice in his life, and then only to have a cup of tea and a bun. Most of the people of Bestwood considered that tea and bread-and-butter, and perhaps potted beef, was all they could afford to eat in Nottingham. Real cooked dinner was considered great extravagance. Paul felt rather guilty.

They found a place that looked quite cheap. But when Mrs Morel scanned the bill of fare, her heart was heavy, things were so dear. So she ordered kidney pies and potatoes as the cheapest available dish.

'We oughtn't to have come here, mother,' said Paul.

'Never mind,' she said. 'We won't come again.'

She insisted on his having a small currant tart, because he liked sweets.

'I don't want it, mother,' he pleaded.

'Yes,' she insisted, 'you'll have it.'

And she looked round for the waitress. But the waitress was busy, and Mrs Morel did not like to bother her then. So the mother and son waited for the girl's pleasure, whilst she flirted among the men.

'Brazen hussy!' said Mrs Morel to Paul. 'Look now, she's taking that man *his* pudding, and he came long after us.'

'It doesn't matter, mother,' said Paul.

Mrs Morel was angry. But she was too poor, and her orders were too meagre, so that she had not the courage to insist on her rights just then. They waited and waited.

'Should we go, mother?' he said.

Then Mrs Morel stood up. The girl was passing near.

'Will you bring one currant tart?' said Mrs Morel clearly.

The girl looked round insolently.

'Directly,' she said.

'We have waited long enough,' said Mrs Morel.

In a moment the girl came back with the tart. Mrs Morel asked coldly for the bill. Paul wanted to sink through the floor. He marvelled at his mother's hardness. He knew that only years of battling had taught her to insist even so little on her rights. She shrank as much as he.

'It's the last time I go *there* for anything!' she declared, when they were outside the place, thankful to be clear.

'We'll go,' she said, 'and look at Keep's and Boot's, and one or two places, shall we?'

They had discussions over the pictures, and Mrs Morel wanted to buy him a little sable brush that he hankered for. But this indulgence he refused. He stood in front of milliners' shops and drapers' shops almost bored, but content for her to be interested. They wandered on.

'Now, just look at those black grapes!' she said. 'They make your mouth water. I've wanted some of those for years, but I s'll have to wait a bit before I get them.'

Then she rejoiced in the florists, standing in the doorway sniffing.

'Oh! oh! Isn't it simply lovely!'

Paul saw, in the darkness of the shop, an elegant young lady in black peering over the counter curiously.

'They're looking at you,' he said, trying to draw his mother away.

'But what *is* it!' she exclaimed, refusing to be moved.

'Stocks!' he answered, sniffing hastily. 'Look, there's a tubful.'

'So there is – red and white. But really, I never knew stocks to smell like it!' And, to his great relief, she moved out of the doorway, but only to stand in front of the window.

'Paul!' she cried to him, who was trying to get out of sight of the elegant young lady in black – the shop-girl. 'Paul! Just look here!'

He came reluctantly back.

'Now, just look at that fuchsia!' she exclaimed, pointing.

'H'm!' He made a curious, interested sound. 'You'd think every second as the flowers were going to fall off, they hang so big an' heavy.'

'And such an abundance!' she cried.

'And the way they drop downwards with their threads, and knots!'

'Yes!' she exclaimed. 'Lovely!'

'I wonder who'll buy it!' he said.

'I wonder!' she answered. 'Not us.'

'It would die in our parlour.'

'Yes, beastly cold, sunless hole; it kills every bit of plant you put in, and the kitchen chokes them to death.'

They bought a few things, and set off towards the station. Looking up the canal, through the dark pass of the buildings, they saw the Castle on its bluff of brown, green-bushed rock, in a positive miracle of delicate sunshine.

'Won't it be nice to come out at dinner-times?' said Paul. 'I can go all round here and see everything. I s'll love it.'

'You will,' assented his mother.

He had spent a perfect afternoon with his mother. They arrived home in the mellow evening, happy, and glowing, and tired.

In the morning he filled in the form for his season-ticket and took it to the station. When he got back, his mother was just beginning to wash the floor. He sat crouched up on the sofa.

'He says it'll be here by Saturday,' he said.

'And how much will it be?'

'About one pound eleven,' he said.

She went on washing her floor in silence.

'Is it a lot?' he asked.

'It's no more than I thought,' she answered.

'An I s'll earn eight shillings a week,' he said.

She did not answer, but went on with her work. At last she said:

'That William promised me, when he went to London, as he'd give me a pound a month. He has given me ten shillings – twice; and now I know he hasn't a farthing if I asked him. Not that I want it. Only just now you'd think he might be able to help with this ticket, which I'd never expected.'

'He earns a lot,' said Paul.

'He earns a hundred and thirty pounds. But they're all alike. They're large in promises, but it's precious little fulfilment you get.'

'He spends over fifty shillings a week on himself,' said Paul.

'And I keep this house on less than thirty,' she replied; 'and am supposed to find money for extras. But they don't care about helping you, once they've gone. He'd rather spend it on that dressed-up creature.'

'She should have her own money, if she's so grand,' said Paul.

'She should, but she hasn't. I asked him. And *I* know he doesn't buy her a gold bangle for nothing. I wonder whoever bought *me* a gold bangle.'

William was succeeding with his 'Gypsy', as he called her. He asked the girl – her name was Louisa Lily Denys Western – for a photograph to send to his mother. The photo came – a handsome brunette, taken in profile, smirking slightly – and, it might be, quite naked, for on the photograph not a scrap of clothing was to be seen, only a naked bust.

'Yes,' wrote Mrs Morel to her son, 'the photograph of Louie is very striking, and I can see she must be attractive. But do you think, my boy, it was very good taste of a girl to give her young man that photo to send to his mother – the first? Certainly the shoulders are beautiful, as you say. But I hardly expected to see so much of them at the first view.'

Morel found the photograph standing on the chiffonier in the parlour. He came out with it between his thick thumb and finger.

'Who dost reckon this is?' he asked of his wife.

'It's the girl our William is going with,' replied Mrs Morel.

'H'm! 'Er's a bright spark, from th' look on 'er, an' one as wunna do him owermuch good neither. Who is she?'

'Her name is Louisa Lily Denys Western.'

'An' come again tomorrer!' exclaimed the miner. 'An' is 'er an actress?'

'She is not. She's supposed to be a lady.'

'I'll bet!' he exclaimed, still staring at the photo. 'A lady, is she? An' how much does she reckon ter keep up this sort o' game on?'

'On nothing. She lives with an old aunt, whom she hates, and takes what bit of money's given her.'

'H'm!' said Morel, laying down the photograph. 'Then he's a fool to ha' ta'en up wi' such a one as that.'

'Dear Mater,' William replied. 'I'm sorry you didn't like the photograph. It never occurred to me when I sent it, that you mightn't think it decent. However, I told Gyp that it didn't quite suit your prim and proper notions, so she's going to send you another, that I hope will please you better. She's always being photographed; in fact the photographers *ask* her if they may take her for nothing.'

Presently the new photograph came, with a little silly note from the girl. This time the young lady was seen in a black satin evening bodice, cut square, with little puff sleeves, and black lace hanging down her beautiful arms.

'I wonder if she ever wears anything except evening clothes,' said Mrs Morel sarcastically. 'I'm sure I *ought* to be impressed.'

'You are disagreeable, mother,' said Paul. 'I think the first one with bare shoulders is lovely.'

'Do you?' answered his mother. 'Well, I don't.'

On the Monday morning the boy got up at six to start work. He had the season-ticket, which had cost such bitterness, in his waistcoat pocket. He loved it with its bars of yellow across. His mother packed his dinner in a small, shut-up basket, and he set off at a quarter to seven to catch the 7.15 train. Mrs Morel came to the entry-end to see him off.

It was a perfect morning. From the ash-tree the slender green fruits that the children call 'pigeons' were twinkling gaily down on a little breeze, into the front gardens of the houses. The valley was full of a lustrous dark haze, through which the ripe corn shimmered, and in which the steam from Minton pit melted swiftly. Puffs of wind came. Paul looked over the high woods of

Aldersley, where the country gleamed, and home had never pulled at him so powerfully.

'Good morning, mother,' he said, smiling, but feeling very unhappy.

'Good morning,' she replied cheerfully and tenderly.

She stood in her white apron on the open road, watching him as he crossed the field. He had a small, compact body that looked full of life. She felt, as she saw him trudging over the field, that where he determined to go he would get. She thought of William. He would have leaped the fence instead of going round to the stile. He was away in London, doing well. Paul would be working in Nottingham. Now she had two sons in the world. She could think of two places, great centres of industry, and feel that she had put a man into each of them, that these men would work out what *she* wanted; they were derived from her, they were of her, and their works also would be hers. All the morning long she thought of Paul.

At eight o'clock he climbed the dismal stairs of Jordan's Surgical Appliance Factory, and stood helplessly against the first great parcel-rack, waiting for somebody to pick him up. The place was still not awake. Over the counters were great dust sheets. Two men only had arrived, and were heard talking in a corner, as they took off their coats and rolled up their shirtsleeves. It was ten past eight. Evidently there was no rush of punctuality. Paul listened to the voices of the two clerks. Then he heard someone cough, and saw in the office at the end of the room an old, decaying clerk, in a round smoking-cap of black velvet embroidered with red and green, opening letters. He waited and waited. One of the junior clerks went to the old man, greeted him cheerily and loudly. Evidently the old 'chief' was deaf. Then the young fellow came striding importantly down to his counter. He spied Paul.

'Hello!' he said. 'You the new lad?'

'Yes,' said Paul.

'H'm! What's your name?'

'Paul Morel.'

'Paul Morel? All right, you come on round here.'

Paul followed him round the rectangle of counters. The room was second storey. It had a great hole in the middle of the floor, fenced as with a wall of counters, and down this wide shaft the lifts went, and the light for the bottom storey. Also there was a corresponding big, oblong hole in the ceiling, and one would see above, over the fence of the top floor, some machinery; and right away overhead was the glass roof, and all light for the three storeys came downwards, getting dimmer, so that it was always night on the ground floor and rather gloomy on the second floor. The factory was the top floor, the warehouse the second, the storehouse the ground floor. It was an insanitary, ancient place.

Paul was led round to a very dark corner.

'This is the "Spiral" corner,' said the clerk. 'You're Spiral, with Pappleworth. He's your boss, but he's not come yet. He doesn't get here till half-past eight. So you can fetch the letters, if your like, from Mr Melling down there.'

The young man pointed to the old clerk in the office.

'All right,' said Paul.

'Here's a peg to hang your cap on. Here are your entry ledgers. Mr Pappleworth won't be long.'

And the thin young man stalked away with long, busy strides over the hollow wooden floor.

After a minute or two Paul went down and stood in the door of the glass office. The old clerk in the smoking-cap looked down over the rim of his spectacles.

'Good morning,' he said, kindly and impressively. 'You want the letters for the Spiral department, Thomas?'

Paul resented being called 'Thomas'. But he took the letters and returned to his dark place, where the counter made an angle, where the great parcel-rack came to an end, and where there were three doors in the corner. He sat on a high stool and read the letters – those whose handwriting was not too difficult. They ran as follows:

'Will you please send me at once a pair of lady's silk spiral thigh-hose, without feet, such as I had from you last year; length, thigh to knee, etc.' Or 'Major Chamberlain wishes to repeat his previous order for a silk non-elastic suspensory bandage.'

Many of the letters, some of them in French or Norwegian, were a great puzzle to the boy. He sat on his stool nervously awaiting the arrival of his 'boss'. He suffered tortures of shyness when, at half-past eight, the factory girls for upstairs trooped past him.

Mr Pappleworth arrived, chewing a chlorodyne gum, at about twenty to nine, when all the other men were at work. He was a thin, sallow man with a red nose, quick, staccato, and smartly but stiffly dressed. He was about thirty-six years old. There was something rather 'doggy', rather smart, rather 'cute and shrewd, and something warm, and something slightly contemptible about him.

'You my new lad?' he said.

Paul stood up and said he was.

'Fetched the letters?'

Mr Pappleworth gave a chew to his gum.

'Yes.'

'Copied 'em?'

'No.'

'Well, come on then, let's look slippy. Changed your coat?'

'No.'

'You want to bring an old coat and leave it here.' He pronounced the last words with the chlorodyne gum between his side teeth. He vanished into darkness behind the great parcel-rack, reappeared coatless, turning up a smart striped shirt-cuff over a thin and hairy arm. Then he slipped into his coat. Paul noticed how thin he was, and that his trousers were in folds behind. He seized a stool, dragged it beside the boy's, and sat down.

'Sit down,' he said.

Paul took a seat.

Mr Pappleworth was very close to him. The man seized the letters, snatched a long entry-book out of a rack in front of him, flung it open, seized a pen, and said:

'Now look here. You want to copy these letters in here.' He sniffed twice, gave a quick chew at his gum, stared fixedly at a letter, then went very still and absorbed, and wrote the entry rapidly, in a beautiful flourishing hand. He glanced quickly at Paul.

'See that?'

'Yes.'

'Think you can do it all right?'

'Yes.'

'All right then, let's see you.'

He sprang off his stool; Paul took a pen. Mr Pappleworth disappeared. Paul rather liked copying the letters, but he wrote slowly, laboriously, and exceedingly badly. He was doing the fourth letter, and feeling quite busy and happy, when Mr Pappleworth reappeared.

'Now then, how'r yer getting on? Done 'em?'

He leaned over the boy's shoulder, chewing, and smelling of chlorodyne.

'Strike my bob, lad, you're a beautiful writer!' he exclaimed satirically. 'Ne'er mind, how many h'yer done? Only three! I'd a eaten 'em. Get on, my lad, an' put numbers on 'em. Here, look! Get on!'

Paul ground away at the letters, while Mr Pappleworth fussed over various jobs. Suddenly the boy started as a shrill whistle sounded near his ear. Mr Pappleworth came, took a plug out of a pipe, and said, in an amazingly cross and bossy voice:

'Yes?'

Paul heard a faint voice, like a woman's, out of the mouth of the tube. He gazed in wonder, never having seen a speaking-tube before.

'Well,' said Mr Pappleworth disagreeably into the tube, 'you'd better get some of your back work done, then.'

Again the woman's tiny voice was heard, sounding petty and cross.

'I've not time to stand here while you talk,' said Mr Pappleworth, and he pushed the plug into the tube.

'Come, my lad,' he said imploringly to Paul, 'there's Polly crying out for them orders. Can't you buck up a bit? Here, come out!'

He took the book, to Paul's immense chagrin, and began the copying himself. He worked quickly and well. This done, he seized some strips of long yellow paper, about three inches wide, and made out the day's orders for the work-girls.

'You'd better watch me,' he said to Paul, working all the while rapidly. Paul watched the weird little drawings of legs, and thighs, and ankles, with the strokes across and the numbers, and the few brief directions which his chief made upon the yellow paper. Then Mr Pappleworth finished and jumped up.

'Come on with me,' he said, and the yellow papers flying in his hands, he dashed through a door and down some stairs, into the basement where the gas was burning. They crossed the cold, damp storeroom, then a long, dreary room with a long table on trestles, into a smaller, cosy apartment, not very high, which had been built on to the main building. In this room a small woman with a red serge blouse, and her black hair done on top of her head, was waiting like a proud little bantam.

'Here y'are!' said Pappleworth.

'I think it is "here you are!"' exclaimed Polly. 'The girls have been here nearly half an hour waiting. Just think of the time wasted!'

'*You* think of getting your work done and not talking so much,' said Mr Pappleworth. 'You could ha' been finishing off.'

'You know quite well we finished everything off on Saturday!' cried Polly, flying at him, her dark eyes flashing.

'Tu-tu-tu-tu-terterter!' he mocked. 'Here's your new lad. Don't ruin him as you did the last.'

'"As we did the last!"' repeated Polly. 'Yes, *we* do a lot of ruining, we do. My word, a lad would *take* some ruining after he'd been with you.'

'It's time for work now, not for talk,' said Mr Pappleworth severely and coldly.

'It was time for work some time back,' said Polly, marching away with her head in the air. She was an erect little body of forty.

In that room were two round spiral machines on the bench under the window. Through the inner doorway was another longer room, with six more machines. A little group of girls, nicely dressed and in white aprons, stood talking together.

'Have you nothing else to do but talk?' said Mr Pappleworth.

'Only wait for you,' said one handsome girl, laughing.

'Well, get on, get on,' he said. 'Come on, my lad. You'll know your road down here again.'

And Paul ran upstairs after his chief. He was given some checking and invoicing to do. He stood at the desk, labouring in his execrable handwriting. Presently Mr Jordan came strutting down from the glass office and stood behind him, to the boy's great discomfort. Suddenly a red and fat finger was thrust on the form he was filling in.

'*Mr* J. A. Bates, Esquire!' exclaimed the cross voice just behind his ear.

Paul looked at 'Mr J. A. Bates, Esquire' in his own vile writing, and wondered what was the matter now.

'Didn't they teach you any better than *that* while they were at it? If you put "Mr" you don't put "Esquire" – a man can't be both at once.'

The boy regretted his too-much generosity in disposing of honours, hesitated, and with trembling fingers, scratched out the 'Mr'. Then all at once Mr Jordan snatched away the invoice.

'Make another! Are you going to send *that* to a gentleman?' And he tore up the blue form irritably.

Paul, his ears red with shame, began again. Still Mr Jordan watched.

'I don't know what they *do* teach in school. You'll have to write better than that. Lads learn nothing nowadays, but how to recite poetry and play the fiddle. Have you seen his writing?' he asked of Mr Pappleworth.

'Yes; prime, isn't it?' replied Mr Pappleworth, indifferently.

Mr Jordan gave a little grunt, not unamiable. Paul divined that his master's bark was worse than his bite. Indeed, the little manufacturer, although he spoke bad English, was quite gentleman enough to leave his men alone and to take no notice of trifles. But he knew he did not look like the boss and owner of the show, so he had to play his role of proprietor at first, to put things on a right footing.

'Let's see, *what's* your name?' asked Mr Pappleworth of the boy.

'Paul Morel.'

It is curious that children suffer so much at having to pronounce their own names.

'Paul Morel, is it? All right, you Paul-Morel through them things there, and then –'

Mr Pappleworth subsided on to a stool, and began writing. A girl came up from out of a door just behind, put some newly pressed elastic web appliances on the counter, and returned. Mr Pappleworth picked up the whitey-blue knee-band, examined it and its yellow order-paper quickly, and put it on one side. Next was a flesh-pink 'leg'. He went through the few things, wrote out a couple of orders, and called to Paul to accompany him. This time they went through the door whence the girl had emerged. There Paul found himself at the top of a little wooden flight of steps, and below him saw a room with windows round two sides, and at the farther end half a dozen girls sitting bending over the benches in the light from the window, sewing. They were singing together 'Two Little Girls in Blue'. Hearing the door opened, they all turned round, to see Mr Pappleworth and Paul looking down on them from the far end of the room. They stopped singing.

'Can't you make a bit less row?' said Mr Pappleworth. 'Folk'll think we keep cats.'

A hunchback woman on a high stool turned her long, rather heavy face towards Mr Pappleworth, and said, in a contralto voice:

'They're all tom-cats then.'

In vain Mr Pappleworth tried to be impressive for Paul's benefit. He descended the steps into the finishing-off room, and went to the hunchback Fanny. She had such a short body on her high stool that her head, with its great bands of bright brown hair, seemed over large, as did her pale, heavy face. She wore a dress of green-black cashmere, and her wrists, coming out of the narrow cuffs, were thin and flat, as she put down her work nervously. He showed her something that was wrong with a knee-cap.

'Well,' she said, 'you needn't come blaming it on to me. It's not my fault.' Her colour mounted to her cheek.

'I never said it *was* your fault. Will you do as I tell you?' replied Mr Pappleworth shortly.

'You don't say it's my fault, but you'd like to make out as it was,' the hunchback woman cried, almost in tears. Then she snatched the knee-cap from her 'boss', saying: 'Yes, I'll do it for you, but you needn't be snappy.'

'Here's your new lad,' said Mr Pappleworth.

Fanny turned, smiling very gently on Paul.

'Oh!' she said.

'Yes; don't make a softy of him between you.'

'It's not us 'ud make a softy of him,' she said indignantly.

'Come on then, Paul,' said Mr Pappleworth.

'*Au revoy*, Paul,' said one of the girls.

There was a titter of laughter. Paul went out, blushing deeply, not having spoken a word.

The day was very long. All morning the work-people were coming to speak to Mr Pappleworth. Paul was writing or learning to make up parcels, ready for the midday post. At one o'clock, or, rather, at a quarter to one, Mr Pappleworth disappeared to catch his train: he lived in the suburbs. At one o'clock, Paul, feeling very lost, took his dinner-basket down into the stockroom in the basement, that had the long table on trestles, and ate his meal hurriedly, alone in that cellar of gloom and desolation. Then he went out of doors. The brightness and the freedom of the streets made him feel adventurous and happy. But at two o'clock he was back in the corner of the big room. Soon the work-girls went trooping past, making remarks. It was the commoner girls who worked upstairs at the heavy tasks of truss-making and the finishing of artificial limbs. He waited for Mr Pappleworth, not knowing what to do, sitting scribbling on the yellow order-paper. Mr Pappleworth came at twenty minutes to three. Then he sat and gossiped with Paul, treating the boy entirely as an equal, even in age.

In the afternoon there was never very much to do, unless it were near the weekend, and the accounts had to be made up. At five o'clock all the men went down into the dungeon with the table on trestles, and there they had tea, eating bread-and-butter on the bare, dirty boards, talking with the same kind of ugly haste and slovenliness with which they ate their meal. And yet upstairs the atmosphere among them was always jolly and clear. The cellar and the trestles affected them.

After tea, when all the gases were lighted, *work* went more briskly. There was the big evening post to get off. The hose came up warm and newly pressed from the workrooms. Paul had made out the invoices. Now he had the packing up and addressing to do, then he had to weigh his stock of parcels on the scales. Everywhere voices were calling weights, there was the chink of metal, the rapid snapping of string, the hurrying to old Mr Melling for stamps. And at last the postman came with his sack, laughing and jolly. Then everything slacked off, and Paul took his dinner-basket and ran to the station to catch the eight-twenty train. The day in the factory was just twelve hours long.

His mother sat waiting for him rather anxiously. He had to walk from Keston, so he was not home until about twenty past nine. And he left the house before seven in the morning, Mrs Morel was rather anxious about his health. But she herself had had to put up with so much that she expected her children to take the same odds. They must go through with what came. And Paul stayed at Jordan's, although all the time he was there his health suffered from the darkness and lack of air and the long hours.

He came in pale and tired. His mother looked at him. She saw he was rather pleased, and her anxiety all went.

'Well, and how was it?' she asked.

'Ever so funny, mother,' he replied. 'You don't have to work a bit hard, and they're nice with you.'

'And did you get on all right?'

'Yes; they only say my writing's bad. But Mr Pappleworth – he's my man – said to Mr Jordan I should be all right. I'm Spiral, mother; you just come and see. It's ever so nice.'

Soon he liked Jordan's Mr Pappleworth, who had a certain 'saloon bar' flavour about him, he was always natural, and treated him as if he had been a comrade. Sometimes the 'Spiral boss' was irritable, and chewed more lozenges than ever. Even then, however, he was not offensive, but one of those people who hurt themselves by their own irritability more than they hurt other people.

'Haven't you done that *yet*?' he would cry. 'Go on, be a month of Sundays.'

Again, and Paul could understand him least then, he was jocular and in high spirits.

'I'm going to bring my little Yorkshire terrier bitch tomorrow,' he said jubilantly to Paul.

'What's a Yorkshire terrier?'

'*Don't* know what a Yorkshire terrier is? *Don't know a Yorkshire* –' Mr Pappleworth was aghast.

'Is it a little silky one – colours of iron and rusty silver?'

'*That's* it, my lad. She's a gem. She's had five pounds worth of pups already, and she's worth over seven pounds herself; and she doesn't weigh twenty ounces.'

The next day the bitch came. She was a shivering, miserable morsel. Paul did not care for her; she seemed so like a wet rag that would never dry. Then a man called for her, and began to make coarse jokes. But Mr Pappleworth nodded his head in the direction of the boy, and the talk went on *sotto voce*.

Mr Jordan only made one more excursion to watch Paul, and then the only fault he found was seeing the boy lay his pen on the counter.

'Put your pen in your ear, if you're going to be a clerk. Pen in your ear!' And one day he said to the lad, 'Why don't you hold your shoulders straighter? Come down here,' when he took him into the glass office and fitted him with special braces for keeping the shoulders square.

But Paul liked the girls best. The men seemed common and rather dull. He liked them all, but they were uninteresting. Polly, the little brisk overseer downstairs, finding Paul eating in the cellar, asked him if she could cook him anything on her little stove. Next day his mother gave him a dish that could be heated up. He took it into the pleasant, clean room to Polly. And very soon it grew to be an established custom that he should have dinner with her. When he came in at eight in the morning he took his basket to her, and when he came down at one o'clock she had his dinner ready.

He was not very tall, and pale, with thick chestnut hair, irregular features, and a wide, full mouth. She was like a small bird. He often called her a 'robinet'. Though naturally rather quiet, he would sit and chatter with her for hours telling her about his home. The girls all liked to hear him talk. They often gathered in a little circle while he sat on a bench, and held forth to them, laughing. Some of them regarded him as a curious little creature, so serious, yet so bright and jolly, and always so delicate in his way with them. They all liked him, and he adored them. Polly he felt he belonged to. Then Connie, with her mane of red hair, her face of apple-blossom, her murmuring voice, such a lady in her shabby black frock, appealed to his romantic side.

'When you sit winding,' he said, 'it looks as if you were spinning at a spinning-wheel – it looks ever so nice. You remind me of Elaine in the "Idylls of the King". I'd draw you if I could.'

And she glanced at him blushing shyly. And later on he had a sketch he prized very much: Connie sitting on the stool before the wheel, her flowing mane of red hair on her rusty black frock, her red mouth shut and serious, running the scarlet thread off the hank on to the reel.

With Louie, handsome and brazen, who always seemed to thrust her lip at him, he usually joked.

Emma was rather plain, rather old, and condescending. But to condescend to him made her happy, and he did not mind.

'How do you put needles in?' he asked.

'Go away and don't bother.'

'But I ought to know how to put needles in.'

She ground at her machine all the while steadily.

'There are many things you ought to know,' she replied.

'Tell me, then, how to stick needles in the machine.'

'Oh, the boy, what a nuisance he is! Why, *this* is how you do it.'

He watched her attentively. Suddenly a whistle piped. Then Polly appeared, and said in a clear voice:

'Mr Pappleworth wants to know how much longer you're going to be down here playing with the girls, Paul.'

Paul flew upstairs, calling 'Good-bye!' and Emma drew herself up.

'It wasn't *me* who wanted him to play with the machine,' she said.

As a rule, when all the girls came back at two o'clock, he ran upstairs to Fanny, the hunchback, in the finishing-off room. Mr Pappleworth did not appear till twenty to three, and he often found his boy sitting beside Fanny, talking, or drawing, or singing with the girls.

Often, after a minute's hesitation, Fanny would begin to sing. She had a fine contralto voice. Everybody joined in the chorus, and it went well. Paul was not at all embarrassed, after a while, sitting in the room with the half a dozen workgirls.

At the end of the song Fanny would say:

'I know you've been laughing at me.'

'Don't be so soft, Fanny!' cried one of the girls.

Once there was mention of Connie's red hair.

'Fanny's is better, to my fancy,' said Emma.

'You needn't try to make a fool of me,' said Fanny, flushing deeply.

'No, but she has, Paul; she's got beautiful hair.'

'It's a treat of a colour,' said he. 'That coldish colour like earth, and yet shiny. It's like bog-water.'

'Goodness me!' exclaimed one girl, laughing.

'How I do but get criticized,' said Fanny.

'But you should see it down, Paul,' said Emma earnestly. 'It's simply beautiful. Put it down for him, Fanny, if he wants something to paint.'

Fanny would not, and yet she wanted to.

'Then I'll take it down myself,' said the lad.

'Well, you can if you like,' said Fanny.

And he carefully took the pins out of the knot, and the rush of hair, of uniform dark brown, slid over the humped back.

'What a lovely lot!' he exclaimed.

The girls watched. There was silence. The youth shook the hair loose from the coil.

'It's splendid!' he said, smelling its perfume. 'I'll bet it's worth pounds.'

'I'll leave it to you when I die, Paul,' said Fanny, half joking.

'You look just like anybody else, sitting drying their hair,' said one of the girls to the long-legged hunchback.

Poor Fanny was morbidly sensitive, always imagining insults. Polly was curt and businesslike. The two departments were for ever at war, and Paul was always finding Fanny in tears. Then he was made the recipient of all her woes, and he had to plead her cause with Polly.

So the time went along happily enough. The factory had a homely feel. No one was rushed or driven. Paul always enjoyed it when the work got faster, towards post-time, and all the men united in labour. He liked to watch his fellow-clerks at work. The man was the work and the work was the man, one thing, for the time being. It was different with the girls. The real woman never seemed to be there at the task, but as if left out, waiting.

From the train going home at night he used to watch the lights of the town, sprinkled thick on the hills, fusing together in a blaze in the valleys. He felt rich in life and happy. Drawing farther off, there was a patch of lights at Bulwell like myriad petals shaken to the ground from the shed stars; and beyond was the red glare of the furnaces, playing like hot breath on the clouds.

He had to walk two and more miles from Keston home, up two long hills, down two short hills. He was often tired, and he counted the lamps climbing the hill above him, how many more to pass. And from the hilltop, on pitch-dark nights, he looked round on the villages five or six miles away, that shone like swarms of glittering living things, almost a heaven against his feet.

Marlpool and Heanor scattered the far-off darkness with brilliance. And occasionally the black valley space between was traced, violated by a great train rushing south to London or north to Scotland. The trains roared by like projectiles level on the darkness, fuming and burning, making the valley clang with their passage. They were gone, and the lights of the towns and villages glittered in silence.

And then he came to the corner at home, which faced the other side of the night. The ash-tree seemed a friend now. His mother rose with gladness as he entered. He put his eight shillings proudly on the table.

'It'll help, mother?' he asked wistfully.

'There's precious little left,' she answered, 'after your ticket and dinners and such are taken off.'

Then he told her the budget of the day. His life-story, like an Arabian Nights, was told night after night to his mother. It was almost as if it were her own life.

6

DEATH IN THE FAMILY

Arthur Morel was growing up. He was a quick, careless, impulsive boy, a good deal like his father. He hated study, made a great moan if he had to work and escaped as soon as possible to his sport again.

In appearance he remained the flower of the family, being well made, graceful, and full of life. His dark brown hair and fresh colouring, and his exquisite dark blue eyes shaded with long lashes, together with his generous manner and fiery temper, made him a favourite. But as he grew older his temper became uncertain. He flew into rages over nothing, seemed unbearably raw and irritable.

His mother, whom he loved, wearied of him sometimes. He thought only of himself. When he wanted amusement, all that stood in his way he hated, even if it were she. When he was in trouble he moaned to her ceaselessly.

'Goodness, boy!' she said, when he groaned about a master who, he said, hated him, 'if you don't like it, alter it, and if you can't alter it, put up with it.'

And his father, whom he had loved and who had worshipped him, he came to detest. As he grew older Morel fell into a slow ruin. His body, which had been beautiful in movement and in being, shrank, did not seem to ripen with the years, but to get mean and rather despicable. There came over him a look of meanness and of paltriness. And when the mean-looking elderly man bullied or ordered the boy about, Arthur was furious. Moreover, Morel's manners got worse and worse, his habits somewhat disgusting. When the children were growing up and in the crucial stage of adolescence, the father was like some ugly irritant to their souls. His manners in the house were the same as he used among the colliers down pit.

'Dirty nuisance!' Arthur would cry, jumping up and going straight out of the house when his father disgusted him. And Morel persisted the more because his children hated it. He seemed to take a kind of satisfaction in disgusting them, and driving them nearly mad, while they were so irritably sensitive at the age of fourteen or fifteen. So that Arthur, who was growing up when his father was degenerate and elderly, hated him worst of all.

Then, sometimes, the father would seem to feel the contemptuous hatred of his children.

'There's not a man tries harder for his family!' he would shout. 'He does his best for them, and then gets treated like a dog. But I'm not going to stand it, I tell you!'

But for the threat and the fact that he did not try so hard as he imagined, they would have felt sorry. As it was, the battle now went on nearly all between father and children, he persisting in his dirty and disgusting ways, just to assert his independence. They loathed him.

Arthur was so inflamed and irritable at last, that when he won a scholarship for the Grammar School in Nottingham, his mother decided to let him live in town, with one of her sisters, and only come home at week-ends.

Annie was still a junior teacher in the Board-school, earning about four shillings a week. But soon she would have fifteen shillings, since she had passed her examination, and there would be financial peace in the house.

Mrs Morel clung now to Paul. He was quiet and not brilliant. But still he stuck to his painting, and still he stuck to his mother. Everything he did was for her. She waited for his coming home in the evening, and then she unburdened herself of all she had pondered, or of all that had occurred to her during the day. He sat and listened with his earnestness. The two shared lives.

William was engaged now to his brunette, and had bought her an engagement ring that cost eight guineas. The children gasped at such a fabulous price.

'Eight guineas!' said Morel. 'More fool him! If he'd gen me some on't, it'ud ha' looked better on 'im.'

'Given *you* some of it!' cried Mrs Morel. 'Why give *you* some of it!'

She remembered *he* had bought no engagement ring at all, and she preferred William, who was not mean, if he were foolish. But now the young man talked only of the dances to which he went with his betrothed, and the different resplendent clothes she wore; or he told his mother with glee how they went to the theatre like great swells.

He wanted to bring the girl home. Mrs Morel said she should come at the Christmas. This time William arrived with a lady, but with no presents. Mrs Morel had prepared supper. Hearing footsteps, she rose and went to the door. William entered.

'Hello, mother!' He kissed her hastily, then stood aside to present a tall, handsome girl, who was wearing a costume of fine black-and-white check, and furs.

'Here's Gyp!'

Miss Western held out her hand and showed her teeth in a small smile.

'Oh, how do you do, Mrs Morel!' she exclaimed.

'I am afraid you will be hungry,' said Mrs Morel.

'Oh, no, we had dinner in the train. Have you got my gloves, Chubby?'

William Morel, big and raw-boned, looked at her quickly.

'How should I?' he said.

'Then I've lost them. Don't be cross with me.'

A frown went over his face, but he said nothing. She glanced round the kitchen. It was small and curious to her, with its glittering kissing-bunch, its evergreens behind the pictures, its wooden chairs and little deal table. At that moment Morel came in.

'Hello, dad!'

'Hello, my son! Tha's let on me!'

The two shook hands, and William presented the lady. She gave the same smile that showed her teeth.

'How do you do, Mr Morel?'

Morel bowed obsequiously.

'I'm very well, and I hope so are you. You must make yourself very welcome.'

'Oh, thank you,' she replied, rather amused.

'You will like to go upstairs,' said Mrs Morel.

'If you don't mind; but not if it is any trouble to you.'

'It is no trouble. Annie will take you. Walter, carry up this box.'

'And don't be an hour dressing yourself up,' said William to his betrothed.

Annie took a brass candlestick, and, too shy almost to speak, preceded the young lady to the front bedroom, which Mr and Mrs Morel had vacated for her. It, too, was small and cold by candlelight. The colliers' wives only lit fires in bedrooms in case of extreme illness.

'Shall I unstrap the box?' asked Annie.

'Oh, thank you very much!'

Annie played the part of maid, then went downstairs for hot water.

'I think she's rather tired, mother,' said William. 'It's a beastly journey, and we had such a rush.'

'Is there anything I can give her?' asked Mrs Morel.

'Oh no, she'll be all right.'

But there was a chill in the atmosphere. After half an hour Miss Western came down, having put on a purplish-coloured dress, very fine for the collier's kitchen.

'I told you you'd no need to change,' said William to her.

'Oh, Chubby!' Then she turned with that sweetish smile to Mrs Morel. 'Don't you think he's always grumbling, Mrs Morel?'

'Is he?' said Mrs Morel. 'That's not very nice of him.'

'It isn't, really!'

'You are cold,' said the mother. 'Won't you come near the fire?'

Morel jumped out of his arm-chair.

'Come and sit you here!' he said. 'Come and sit you here!'

'No, dad, keep your own chair. Sit on the sofa, Gyp,' said William.

'No, no!' cried Morel. 'This cheer's warmest. Come and sit here, Miss Wesson.'

'Thank you *so* much,' said the girl, seating herself in the collier's arm-chair, the place of honour. She shivered, feeling the warmth of the kitchen penetrate her.

'Fetch me a hanky, Chubby dear!' she said, putting up her mouth to him, and using the same intimate tones as if they were alone; which made the rest of the family feel as if they ought not to be present. The young lady evidently did not realize them as people; they were creatures to her for the present. William winced.

In such a household, in Streatham, Miss Western would have been a lady condescending to her inferiors. These people were, to her, certainly clownish – in short, the working classes. How was she to adjust herself?

'I'll go,' said Annie.

Miss Western took no notice, as if a servant had spoken. But when the girl came downstairs again with the handkerchief, she said, 'Oh, thank you!' in a gracious way.

She sat and talked about the dinner on the train, which had been so poor; about London, about dances. She was really very nervous and chattered from fear. Morel sat all the time smoking his thick twist tobacco, watching her, and listening to her glib London speech, as he puffed. Mrs Morel dressed up in her best black silk blouse, answered quietly and rather briefly. The three children sat round in silence and admiration. Miss Western was the princess. Everything of the best was got out for her; the best cups, the best spoons, the best tablecloth, the best coffee-jug. The children thought she must find it quite grand. She felt strange, not able to realize the people, not knowing how to treat them. William joked, and was slightly uncomfortable.

At about ten o'clock he said to her:

'Aren't you tired, Gyp?'

'Rather, Chubby,' she answered, at once in the intimate tones and putting her head slightly on one side.

'I'll light her candle, mother,' he said.

'Very well,' replied the mother.

Miss Western stood up, held out her hand to Mrs Morel.

'Good night, Mrs Morel,' she said.

Paul sat at the boiler, letting the water run from the tap into a stone beer-bottle. Annie swathed the bottle in an old flannel pit-singlet, and kissed her mother good night. She was to share the room with the lady, because the house was full.

'You wait a minute,' said Mrs Morel to Annie. And Annie sat nursing the hot-water bottle. Miss Western shook hands all round, to everybody's discomfort, and took her departure, preceded by William. In five minutes he was downstairs again. His heart was rather sore: he did not know why. He talked very little till everybody had gone to bed, but himself and his mother. Then he stood with his legs apart, in his old attitude on the hearthrug, and said hesitatingly:

'Well, mother?'

'Well, my son?'

She sat in the rocking-chair, feeling somehow hurt and humiliated, for his sake.

'Do you like her?'

'Yes,' came the slow answer.

'She's shy yet, mother. She's not used to it. It's different from her aunt's house, you know.'

'Of course it is, my boy; and she must find it difficult.'

'She does.' Then he frowned swiftly. 'If only she wouldn't put on her *blessed* airs!'

'It's only her first awkwardness, my boy. She'll be all right.'

'That's it, mother,' he replied gratefully. But his brow was gloomy. 'You know, she's not like you, mother. She's not serious, and she can't think.'

'She's young, my boy.'

'Yes; and she's had no sort of show. Her mother died when she was a child. Since then she's lived with her aunt, whom she can't bear. And her father was a rake. She's had no love.'

'No! Well, you must make up to her.'

'And so – you have to forgive her a lot of things.'

'*What* do you have to forgive her, my boy?'

'I dunno. When she seems shallow, you have to remember she's never had anybody to bring her deeper side out. And she's *fearfully* fond of me.'

'Anybody can see that.'

'But you know, mother – she's – she's different from us. Those sort of people, like those she lives amongst, they don't seem to have the same principles.'

'You mustn't judge too hastily,' said Mrs Morel.

But he seemed uneasy within himself.

In the morning, however, he was up singing and larking round the house.

'Hello!' he called, sitting on the stairs. 'Are you getting up?'

'Yes,' her voice called faintly.

'Merry Christmas!' he shouted to her.

Her laugh, pretty and tinkling, was heard in the bedroom. She did not come down in half an hour.

'Was she *really* getting up when she said she was?' he asked of Annie.

'Yes, she was,' replied Annie.

He waited awhile, then went to the stairs again.

'Happy New Year,' he called.

'Thank you, Chubby dear!' came the laughing voice, far away.

'Buck up!' he implored.

It was nearly an hour, and still he was waiting for her. Morel, who always rose before six, looked at the clock.

'Well, it's a winder!' he exclaimed.

The family had breakfast, all but William. He went to the foot of the stairs.

'Shall I have to send you an Easter egg up there?' he called, rather crossly. She only laughed. The family expected, after that time of preparation, something like magic. At last she came, looking very nice in a blouse and skirt.

'Have you *really* been all this time getting ready?' he asked.

'Chubby dear! That question is not permitted, is it, Mrs Morel?'

She played the grand lady at first. When she went with William to chapel, he in his frock coat and silk hat, she in her furs and London-made costume, Paul and Arthur and Annie expected everybody to bow to the ground in admiration. And Morel, standing in his Sunday suit at the end of the road, watching the gallant pair go, felt he was the father of princes and princesses.

And yet she was not so grand. For a year now she had been a sort of secretary or clerk in a London office. But while she was with the Morels she queened it. She sat and let Annie or Paul wait on her as if they were her servants. She treated Mrs Morel with a certain glibness and Morel with patronage. But after a day or so she began to change her tune.

William always wanted Paul or Annie to go along with them on their walks. It was so much more interesting. And Paul really *did* admire 'Gypsy' wholeheartedly; in fact, his mother scarcely forgave the boy for the adulation with which he treated the girl.

On the second day, when Lily said, 'Oh Annie, do you know where I left my muff?' William replied:

'You know it is in your bedroom. Why do you ask Annie?'

And Lily went upstairs with a cross, shut mouth. But it angered the young man that she made a servant of his sister.

On the third evening William and Lily were sitting together in the parlour by the fire in the dark. At a quarter to eleven Mrs Morel was heard raking the fire. William came out to the kitchen, followed by his beloved.

'Is it as late as that, mother?' he said. She had been sitting alone.

'It is not *late*, my boy, but it is as late as I usually sit up.'

'Won't you go to bed, then?' he asked.

'And leave you two? No, my boy, I don't believe in it.'

'Can't you trust us, mother?'

'Whether I can or not, I won't do it. You can stay till eleven if you like, and I can read.'

'Go to bed, Gyp,' he said to his girl. 'We won't keep mater waiting.'

'Annie has left the candle burning, Lily,' said Mrs Morel; 'I think you will see.'

'Yes, thank you. Good night, Mrs Morel.'

William kissed his sweetheart at the foot of the stairs, and she went. He returned to the kitchen.

'Can't you trust us, mother?' he repeated, rather offended.

'My boy, I tell you I don't *believe* in leaving two young things like you alone downstairs when everyone else is in bed.'

And he was forced to take this answer. He kissed his mother good night.

At Easter he came over alone. And then he discussed his sweetheart endlessly with his mother.

'You know, mother, when I'm away from her I don't care for her a bit. I shouldn't care if I never saw her again. But, then, when I'm with her in the evenings I am awfully fond of her.'

'It's a queer sort of love to marry on,' said Mrs Morel, 'if she holds you no more than that!'

'It *is* funny!' he exclaimed. It worried and perplexed him. 'But yet – there's so much between us now I couldn't give her up.'

'You know best,' said Mrs Morel. 'But if it is as you say, I wouldn't call it *love* – at any rate, it doesn't look much like it.'

'Oh, I don't know, mother. She's an orphan, and –'

They never came to any sort of conclusion. He seemed puzzled and rather fretted. She was rather reserved. All his strength and money went in keeping this girl. He could scarcely afford to take his mother to Nottingham when he came over.

Paul's wages had been raised at Christmas to ten shillings, to his great joy. He was quite happy at Jordan's, but his health suffered from the long hours and the confinement. His mother, to whom he became more and more significant, thought how to help.

His half-day holiday was on Monday afternoon. On a Monday morning in May, as the two sat alone at breakfast, she said:

'I think it will be a fine day.'

He looked up in surprise. This meant something.

'You know Mr Leivers has gone to live on a new farm. Well, he asked me last week if I wouldn't go and see Mrs Leivers, and I promised to bring you on Monday if it's fine. Shall we go?'

'I say, little woman, how lovely!' he cried. 'And we'll go this afternoon?'

Paul hurried off to the station jubilant. Down Derby Road was a cherry-tree that glistened. The old brick wall by the Statutes ground burned scarlet, spring was a very flame of green. And the steep sweep of highroad lay, in its cool morning dust, splendid with patterns of sunshine and shadow, perfectly still.

The trees sloped their great green shoulders proudly; and inside the warehouse all the morning, the boy had a vision of spring outside.

When he came home at dinner-time his mother was rather excited.

'Are we going?' he asked.

'When I'm ready,' she replied.

Presently he got up.

'Go and get dressed while I wash up,' he said.

She did so. He washed the pots, straightened, and then took her boots. They were quite clean. Mrs Morel was one of those naturally exquisite people who can walk in mud without dirtying their shoes. But Paul had to clean them for her. They were kid boots at eight shillings a pair. He, however, thought them the most dainty boots in the world, and he cleaned them with as much reverence as if they had been flowers.

Suddenly she appeared in the inner doorway rather shyly. She had got a new cotton blouse on. Paul jumped up and went forward.

'Oh, my stars!' he exclaimed. 'What a bobby-dazzler!'

She sniffed in a little haughty way, and put her head up.

'It's not a bobby-dazzler at all!' she replied. 'It's very quiet.'

She walked forward, whilst he hovered round her.

'Well,' she asked, quite shy, but pretending to be high and mighty, 'do you like it?'

'Awfully! You *are* a fine little woman to go jaunting out with!'

He went and surveyed her from the back.

'Well,' he said, 'if I was walking down the street behind you, I should say, "Doesn't *that* little person fancy herself!"'

'Well, she doesn't,' replied Mrs Morel. 'She's not sure it suits her.'

'Oh no! she wants to be in dirty black, looking as if she was wrapped in burnt paper. It *does* suit you, and *I* say you look nice.'

She sniffed in her little way, pleased, but pretending to know better.

'Well,' she said, 'it's cost me just three shillings. You couldn't have got it ready-made for that price, could you?'

'I should think you couldn't,' he replied.

'And, you know, it's good stuff.'

'Awfully pretty,' he said.

The blouse was white, with a little sprig of heliotrope and black.

'Too young for me, though, I'm afraid,' she said.

'Too young for you!' he exclaimed in disgust. 'Why don't you buy some false white hair and stick it on your head?'

'I s'll soon have no need,' she replied. 'I'm going white fast enough.'

'Well, you've no business to,' he said. 'What do I want with a white-haired mother?'

'I'm afraid you'll have to put up with one, my lad,' she said rather strangely.

They set off in great style, she carrying the umbrella William had given her, because of the sun. Paul was considerably taller than she, though he was not big. He fancied himself.

On the fallow land the young wheat shone silkily. Minton pit waved its plumes of white steam, coughed, and rattled hoarsely.

'Now look at that!' said Mrs Morel. Mother and son stood on the road to watch. Along the ridge of the great pit-hill crawled a little group in silhouette against the sky, a horse, a small truck, and a man. They climbed the incline against the heavens. At the end the man tipped the wagon. There was an undue rattle as the waste fell down the sheer slope of the enormous bank.

'You sit a minute, mother,' he said, and she took a seat on a bank, whilst he sketched rapidly. She was silent whilst he worked, looking round at the afternoon, the red cottages shining among their greenness.

'The world is a wonderful place,' she said, 'and wonderfully beautiful.'

'And so's the pit,' he said. 'Look how it heaps together, like something alive almost – a big creature that you don't know.'

'Yes,' she said. 'Perhaps.'

'And all the trucks standing waiting, like a string of beasts to be fed,' he said.

'And very thankful I am they *are* standing,' she said, 'for that means they'll turn middling time this week.'

'But I like the feel of *men* on things, while they're alive. There's a feel of men about trucks, because they've been handled with men's hands, all of them.'

'Yes,' said Mrs Morel.

They went along under the trees of the highroad. He was constantly informing her, but she was interested. They passed the end of Nethermere, that was tossing its sunshine like petals lightly in its lap. Then they turned on a private road, and in some trepidation approached a big farm. A dog barked furiously. A woman came out to see.

'Is this the way to Willey Farm?' Mrs Morel asked.

Paul hung behind in terror of being sent back. But the woman was amiable, and directed them. The mother and son went through the wheat and oats, over a little bridge into a wild meadow. Peewits, with their white breasts glistening, wheeled and screamed about them. The lake was still and blue. High overhead a heron floated. Opposite, the wood heaped on the hill, green and still.

'It's a wild road, mother,' said Paul. 'Just like Canada.'

'Isn't it beautiful!' said Mrs Morel, looking round.

'See that heron – see – see her legs?'

He directed his mother, what she must see and what not. And she was quite content.

'But now,' she said, 'which way? He told me through the wood.'

The wood, fenced and dark, lay on their left.

'I can feel a bit of a path on this road,' said Paul. 'You've got town feet, somehow or other, you have.'

They found a little gate, and soon were in a broad green alley of the wood, with a new thicket of fir and pine on one hand, an old oak glade dipping down on the other. And among the oaks, the bluebells stood in pools of azure, under the new green hazels, upon a pale fawn floor of oak-leaves. He found flowers for her.

'Here's a bit of new-mown hay,' he said; then, again, he brought her forget-me-nots. And, again, his heart hurt with love, seeing her hand, used with work, holding the little bunch of flowers he gave her. She was perfectly happy.

But at the end of the riding was a fence to climb. Paul was over in a second.

'Come,' he said, 'let me help you.'

'No, go away. I will do it in my own way.'

He stood below with his hands up ready to help her. She climbed cautiously.

'What a way to climb!' he exclaimed scornfully, when she was safely to earth again.

'Hateful stiles!' she cried.

'Duffer of a little woman,' he replied, 'who can't get over 'em.'

In front, along the edge of the wood, was a cluster of low red farm buildings.

The two hastened forward. Flush with the wood was the apple orchard, where blossom was falling on the grindstone. The pond was deep under a hedge and over-hanging oak-trees. Some cows stood in the shade. The farm and buildings, three sides of a quadrangle, embraced the sunshine towards the wood. It was very still.

Mother and son went into the small railed garden, where was a scent of red gillivers. By the open door were some floury loaves, put out to cool. A hen was just coming to peck them. Then, in the doorway, suddenly appeared a girl in a dirty apron. She was about fourteen years old, had a rosy dark face, a bunch of short black curls, very fine and free, and dark eyes; shy, questioning, a little resentful of the strangers, she disappeared. In a minute another figure appeared, a small, frail woman, rosy, with great dark brown eyes.

'Oh!' she exclaimed, smiling with a little glow, 'you've come, then. I *am* glad to see you.' Her voice was intimate and rather sad.

The two women shook hands.

'Now are you sure we're not a bother to you?' said Mrs Morel. 'I know what a farming life is.'

'Oh no! We're only too thankful to see a new face, it's so lost up here.'

'I suppose so,' said Mrs Morel.

They were taken through into the parlour – a long, low room, with a great bunch of guelder-roses in the fireplace. There the women talked, whilst Paul went out to survey the land. He was in the garden smelling the gillivers and looking at the plants, when the girl came out quickly to the heap of coal which stood by the fence.

'I suppose these are cabbage-roses?' he said to her, pointing to the bushes along the fence.

She looked at him with startled, big brown eyes.

'I suppose they are cabbage-roses when they come out?' he said.

'I don't know,' she faltered. 'They're white with pink middles.'

'Then they're maiden-blush.'

Miriam flushed. She had a beautiful warm colouring.

'I don't know,' she said.

'You don't have *much* in your garden,' he said.

'This is our first year here,' she answered, in a distant, rather superior way, drawing back and going indoors. He did not notice, but went his round of exploration. Presently his mother came out, and they went through the buildings. Paul was hugely delighted.

'And I suppose you have the fowls and calves and pigs to look after?' said Mrs Morel to Mrs Leivers.

'No,' replied the little woman. 'I can't find time to look after cattle, and I'm not used to it. It's as much as I can do to keep going in the house.'

'Well, I suppose it is,' said Mrs Morel.

Presently the girl came out.

'Tea is ready, mother,' she said in a musical, quiet voice.

'Oh, thank you, Miriam, then we'll come,' replied her mother, almost ingratiatingly. 'Would you *care* to have tea now, Mrs Morel?'

'Of course,' said Mrs Morel. 'Whenever it's ready.'

Paul and his mother and Mrs Leivers had tea together. Then they went out into the wood that was flooded with bluebells, while fumy forget-me-nots were in the paths. The mother and son were in ecstasy together.

When they got back to the house, Mr Leivers and Edgar, the eldest son, were in the kitchen. Edgar was about eighteen. Then Geoffrey and Maurice, big lads of twelve and thirteen, were in from school. Mr Leivers was a good-looking man in the prime of life, with a golden-brown moustache, and blue eyes screwed up against the weather.

The boys were condescending, but Paul scarcely observed it. They went round for eggs, scrambling into all sorts of places. As they were feeding the fowls Miriam came out. The boys took no notice of her. One hen, with her yellow chickens, was in a coop. Maurice took his hand full of corn and let the hen peck from it.

'Durst you do it?' he asked Paul.

'Let's see,' said Paul.

He had a small hand, warm, and rather capable-looking. Miriam watched. He held the corn to the hen. The bird eyed it with her hard, bright eye, and suddenly made a peck into his hand. He started, and laughed. 'Rap, rap, rap!' went the bird's beak in his palm. He laughed again, and the other boys joined.

'She knocks you, and nips you, but never hurts,' said Paul, when the last corn had gone.

'Now, Miriam,' said Maurice, 'you come an' 'ave a go.'

'No,' she cried, shrinking back.

'Ha! baby. The mardy-kid!' said her brothers.

'It doesn't hurt a bit,' said Paul. 'It only just nips rather nicely.'

'No,' she still cried, shaking her black curls and shrinking.

'She dursn't,' said Geoffrey. 'She niver durst do anything except recite poitry.'

'Dursn't jump off a gate, dursn't tweedle, dursn't go on a slide, dursn't stop a girl hittin' her. She can do nowt but go about thinkin' herself somebody. "The Lady of the Lake". Yah!' cried Maurice.

Miriam was crimson with shame and misery.

'I dare do more than you,' she cried. 'You're never anything but cowards and bullies.'

'Oh, cowards and bullies!' they repeated, mincingly, mocking her speech.

'Not such a clown shall anger me,
A boor is answered silently.'

he quoted against her, shouting with laughter.

She went indoors. Paul went with the boys into the orchard, where they had rigged up a parallel bar. They did feats of strength. He was more agile than strong, but it served. He fingered a piece of apple-blossom that hung low on a swinging bough.

'I wouldn't get the apple-blossom,' said Edgar, the eldest brother. 'There'll be no apples next year.'

'I wasn't going to get it,' replied Paul, going away.

The boys felt hostile to him; they were more interested in their own pursuits. He wandered back to the house to look for his mother. As he went round the back, he saw Miriam kneeling in front of the hen-coop, some maize in her hand, biting her lip, and crouching in an intense attitude. The hen was eyeing her wickedly. Very gingerly she put forward her hand. The hen bobbed for her. She drew back quickly with a cry, half of fear, half of chagrin.

'It won't hurt you,' said Paul.

She flushed crimson and started up.

'I only wanted to try,' she said in a low voice.

'See, it doesn't hurt,' he said, and, putting only two corns in his palm, he let the hen peck, peck, peck at his bare hand. 'It only makes you laugh,' he said.

She put her hand forward, and dragged it away, tried again, and started back with a cry. He frowned.

'Why, I'd let her take corn from my face,' said Paul, 'only she bumps a bit. She's ever so neat. If she wasn't, look how much ground she'd peck up every day.'

He waited grimly, and watched. At last Miriam let the bird peck from her hand. She gave a little cry – fear, and pain because of fear – rather pathetic. But she had done it, and she did it again.

'There, you see,' said the boy. 'It doesn't hurt, does it?'

She looked at him with dilated dark eyes.

'No,' she laughed, trembling.

Then she rose and went indoors. She seemed to be in some way resentful of the boy.

'He thinks I'm only a common girl,' she thought, and she wanted to prove she was a grand person like the 'Lady of the Lake'.

Paul found his mother ready to go home. She smiled on her son. He took the great bunch of flowers. Mr and Mrs Leivers walked down the fields with them. The hills were golden with evening; deep in the wood showed the darkening purple of bluebells. It was everywhere perfectly still, save for the rustling of leaves and birds.

'But it is a beautiful place,' said Mrs Morel.

'Yes,' answered Mr Leivers; 'it's a nice little place, if only it weren't for the rabbits. The pasture's bitten down to nothing. I dunno if ever I s'll get the rent off it.'

He clapped his hands, and the field broke into motion near the woods, brown rabbits hopping everywhere.

'Would you believe it!' exclaimed Mrs Morel.

She and Paul went on alone together.

'Wasn't it lovely, mother?' he said quietly.

A thin moon was coming out. His heart was full of happiness till it hurt. His mother had to chatter because she, too, wanted to cry, with happiness.

'Now *wouldn't* I help that man!' she said. '*Wouldn't* I see to the fowls and the young stock! And *I'd* learn to milk, and *I'd* talk with him, and *I'd* plan with him. My word, if I were his wife, the farm would be run, I know! But there, she hasn't the strength – she simply hasn't the strength. She ought never to have been burdened like it, you know. I'm sorry for her, and I'm sorry for him too. My word, if *I'd* had him, I shouldn't have thought him a bad husband! Not that she does either; and she's very lovable.'

William came home again with his sweetheart at the Whitsuntide. He had one week of his holidays then. It was beautiful weather. As a rule, William and Lily and Paul went out in the morning together for a walk. William did not talk to his beloved much, except to tell her things from his boyhood. Paul talked endlessly to both of them. They lay down, all three, in a meadow by Minton Church. On one side, by the Castle Farm, was a beautiful quivering screen of poplars. Hawthorn was dropping from the hedges; penny daisies and ragged robin were in the field, like laughter. William a big fellow of twenty-three, thinner now and even a bit gaunt, lay back in the sunshine and dreamed, while she fingered with his hair. Paul went gathering the big daisies. She had taken off her hat; her hair was black as a horse's mane. Paul came back and threaded daisies in her jet-black hair – big spangles of white and yellow, and just a pink touch of ragged robin.

'Now you look like a young witch-woman,' the boy said to her. 'Doesn't she, William?'

Lily laughed. William opened his eyes and looked at her. In his gaze was a certain baffled look of misery and fierce appreciation.

'Has he made a sight of me?' she asked, laughing down on her lover.

'That he has!' said William, smiling.

He looked at her. Her beauty seemed to hurt him. He glanced at her flower-decked head and frowned.

'You look nice enough, if that's what you want to know,' he said.

And she walked without her hat. In a little while William recovered and was rather tender to her. Coming to a bridge, he carved her initials and his in a heart.

L.L.W.
W.M.

She watched his strong, nervous hand, with its glistening hairs and freckles, as he carved, and she seemed fascinated by it.

All the time there was a feeling of sadness and warmth, and a certain tenderness in the house, whilst William and Lily were at home. But often he got irritable. She had brought, for an eight-days' stay, five dresses and six blouses.

'Oh, would you mind,' she said to Annie, 'washing me these two blouses, and these things?'

And Annie stood washing when William and Lily went out the next morning. Mrs Morel was furious. And sometimes the young man, catching a glimpse of his sweetheart's attitude towards his sister, hated her.

On Sunday morning she looked very beautiful in a dress of foulard, silky and sweeping, and blue as a jay-bird's feather, and in a large cream hat covered with many roses, mostly crimson. Nobody could admire her enough. But in the evening, when she was going out, she asked again:

'Chubby, have you got my gloves?'

'Which?' asked William.

'My new black *suede*.'

'No.'

There was a hunt. She had lost them.

'Look here, mother,' said William, 'that's the fourth pair she's lost since Christmas – at five shillings a pair!'

'You only gave me *two* of them,' she remonstrated.

And in the evening, after supper, he stood on the hearthrug whilst she sat on the sofa, and he seemed to hate her. In the afternoon he had left her whilst he went to see some old friend. She had sat looking at a book. After supper William wanted to write a letter.

'Here is your book, Lily,' said Mrs Morel. 'Would you care to go on with it for a few minutes?'

'No, thank you,' said the girl. 'I will sit still.'

'But it is so dull.'

William scribbled irritably at a great rate. As he sealed the envelope he said:

'Read a book! Why, she's never read a book in her life.'

'Oh, go along!' said Mrs Morel, cross with the exaggeration.

'It's true, mother – she hasn't,' he cried, jumping up and taking his old position on the hearthrug. 'She's never read a book in her life.'

' 'Er's like me,' chimed in Morel. ' 'Er canna see what there is i' books, ter sit borin' your nose in 'em for, nor more can I.'

'But you shouldn't say these things,' said Mrs Morel to her son.

'But it's true, mother – she *can't* read. What did you give her?'

'Well, I gave her a little thing of Annie Swan's. Nobody wants to read dry stuff on Sunday afternoon.'

'Well, I'll bet she didn't read ten lines of it.'

'You are mistaken,' said his mother.

All the time Lily sat miserably on the sofa. He turned to her swiftly.

'*Did* you read any?' he asked.

'Yes, I did,' she replied.

'How much?'

'I don't know how many pages.'

'Tell me *one* thing you read.'

She could not.

She never got beyond the second page. He read a great deal, and had a quick, active intelligence. She could understand nothing but love-making and chatter. He was accustomed to having all his thoughts sifted through his mother's mind; so, when he wanted companionship, and was asked to reply to be the billing and twittering lover, he hated his betrothed.

'You know, mother,' he said, when he was alone with her at night, 'she's no idea of money, she's so wessel-brained. When she's paid, she'll suddenly buy such rot as *marrons glacés*, and then *I* have to buy her season-ticket, and her extras, even her underclothing. And she wants to get married, and I think myself we might as well get married next year. But at this rate –'

'A fine mess of a marriage it would be,' replied his mother. 'I should consider it again, my boy.'

'Oh, well, I've gone too far to break off now,' he said, 'and so I shall get married as soon as I can.'

'Very well, my boy. If you will, you will, and there's no stopping you; and I tell you, *I* can't sleep when I think about it.'

'Oh, she'll be all right, mother. We shall manage.'

'And she lets you buy her underclothing?' asked the mother.

'Well,' he began apologetically, 'she didn't ask me; but one morning – and it *was* cold – I found her on the station shivering, not able to keep still; so I asked her if she was well wrapped up. She said: "I think so." So I said: "Have you got warm underthings on?" and she said No, they were cotton. I asked her why on earth she hadn't got something thicker on in weather like that, and she said because she *had* nothing. And there she is – a bronchial subject. I *had* to take her and get some warm things. Well, mother, I shouldn't mind the money if we had any. And, you know, she *ought* to keep enough to pay for her season-ticket; but no, she comes to me about that, and I have to find the money.'

'It's a poor lookout,' said Mrs Morel bitterly.

He was pale, and his rugged face, that used to be so perfectly careless and laughing, was stamped with conflict and despair.

'But I can't give her up now, it's gone too far,' he said. 'And, besides, for *some* things I couldn't do without her.'

'My boy, remember you're taking your life in your hands,' said Mrs Morel.

'*Nothing* is as bad as a marriage that's a hopeless failure. Mine was bad enough, God knows, and ought to teach you something; but it might have been worse by a long chalk.'

He leaned with his back against the side of the chimney-piece, his hands in his pockets. He was a big, raw-boned man, who looked as if he would go to the world's end if he wanted to. But she saw the despair on his face.

'I couldn't give her up now,' he said.

'Well,' she said, 'remember there are worse wrongs than breaking off an engagement.'

'I can't give her up *now*,' he said.

The clock ticked on; mother and son remained in silence, a conflict between them; but he would say no more. At last she said:

'Well, go to bed, my son. You'll feel better in the morning, and perhaps you'll know better.'

He kissed her, and went. She raked the fire. Her heart was heavy now as it had never been. Before, with her husband, things had seemed to be breaking down in her, but they did not destroy her power to live. Now her soul felt lamed in itself. It was her hope that was struck.

And so often William manifested the same hatred towards his betrothed. On the last evening at home he was railing against her.

'Well,' he said, 'if you don't believe me, what she's like, would you believe she has been confirmed three times?'

'Nonsense!' laughed Mrs Morel.

'Nonsense or not, she *has*! That's what confirmation means for her – a bit of a theatrical show where she can cut a figure.'

'I haven't, Mrs Morel!' cried the girl – 'I haven't! It is not true!'

'What!' he cried, flashing on her. 'Once in Bromley, once in Beckenham, and once somewhere else.'

'Nowhere else!' she said, in tears – 'nowhere else!'

'It *was*! And, if it wasn't, why were you confirmed *twice*?'

'Once I was only fourteen, Mrs Morel,' she pleaded, tears in her eyes.

'Yes,' said Mrs Morel; 'I can quite understand it, child. Take no notice of him. You ought to be ashamed, William, saying such things.'

'But it's true. She's religious – she had blue velvet Prayer-Books – and she's not so much religion, or anything else, in her than that table-leg. Gets confirmed three times for show to show herself off, and that's how she is in *everything – everything*!'

The girl sat on the sofa, crying. She was not strong.

'As for *love*!' he cried, 'you might as well ask a fly to love you! It'll love settling on you –'

'Now, say no more,' commanded Mrs Morel. 'If you want to say these things, you must find another place than this. I am ashamed of you, William! Why don't you be more manly. To do nothing but to find fault with a girl, and then pretend you're engaged to her!'

Mrs Morel subsided in wrath and indignation.

William was silent, and later he repented, kissed and comforted the girl. Yet it was true, what he had said. He hated her.

When they were going away, Mrs Morel accompanied them as far as Nottingham. It was a long way to Keston station.

'You know, mother,' he said to her, 'Gyp's shallow. Nothing goes deep with her.'

'William, I *wish* you wouldn't say these things,' said Mrs Morel, very uncomfortable for the girl who walked beside her.

'But it doesn't, mother. She's very much in love with me *now*, but if I died she'd have forgotten me in three months.'

Mrs Morel was afraid. Her heart beat furiously, hearing the quiet bitterness of her son's last speech.

'How do you know?' she replied. 'You *don't* know, and therefore you've no right to say such a thing.'

'He's always saying these things!' cried the girl.

'In three months after I was buried, you'd have somebody else, and I should be forgotten,' he said. 'And that's your love!'

Mrs Morel saw them into the train in Nottingham, then she returned home.

'There's one comfort,' she said to Paul – 'he'll never have any money to marry on, that I *am* sure of. And so she'll save him that way.'

So she took cheer. Matters were not yet very desperate. She firmly believed William would never marry his Gypsy. She waited, and she kept Paul near to her.

All summer long, William's letters had a feverish tone; he seemed unnatural and intense. Sometimes he was exaggeratedly jolly, usually he was flat and bitter in his letter.

'Ay,' his mother said, 'I'm afraid he's running himself against that creature, who isn't worthy of his love – no, no more than a rag doll.'

He wanted to come home. The midsummer holiday was gone; it was a long while to Christmas. He wrote in wild excitement, saying he could come for Saturday and Sunday at Goose Fair, the first week in October.

'You are not well, my boy,' said his mother, when she saw him.

She was almost in tears at having him to herself again.

'No, I've not been well,' he said. 'I've seemed to have a dragging cold all the last month, but it's going, I think.'

It was sunny October weather. He seemed wild with joy, like a schoolboy escaped; then again he was silent and reserved. He was more gaunt than ever, and there was a haggard look in his eyes.

'You are doing too much,' said his mother to him.

He was doing extra work, trying to make some money to marry on, he said. He only talked to his mother once on the Saturday night; then he was sad and tender about his beloved.

'And yet, you know, mother, for all that, if I died she'd be broken-hearted for two months, and then she'd start to forget me. You'd see, she'd never come home here to look at my grave, not even once.'

'Why, William,' said his mother, 'you're not going to die, so why talk about it?'

'But whether or not –' he replied.

'And she can't help it. She is like that, and if you choose her – well, you can't grumble,' said his mother.

On the Sunday morning, as he was putting his collar on:

'Look,' he said to his mother, holding up his chin, 'what a rash my collar's made under my chin!'

Just at the junction of chin and throat was a big red inflammation.

'It ought not to do that,' said his mother. 'Here, put a bit of this soothing ointment on. You should wear different collars.'

He went away on Sunday midnight, seeming better and more solid for his two days at home.

On Tuesday morning came a telegram from London that he was ill. Mrs Morel got off her knees from washing the floor, read the telegram, called a neighbour, went to her landlady and borrowed a sovereign, put on her things, and set off. She hurried to Keston, caught an express for London in Nottingham. She had to wait in Nottingham nearly an hour. A small figure in her black bonnet, she was anxiously asking the porters if they knew how to get to Elmers End. The journey was three hours. She sat in her corner in a kind of stupor, never moving. At King's Cross still no one could tell her how to get to Elmers End. Carrying her string bag, that contained her nightdress, comb and brush, she went from person to person. At last they sent her underground to Cannon Street.

It was six o'clock when she arrived at William's lodging. The blinds were not down.

'How is he?' she asked.

'No better,' said the landlady.

She followed the woman upstairs. William lay on the bed, with bloodshot eyes, his face rather discoloured. The clothes were tossed about, there was no fire in the room, a glass of milk stood on the stand at his bedside. No one had been with him.

'Why, my son!' said the mother bravely.

He did not answer. He looked at her, but did not see her. Then he began to say, in a dull voice, as if repeating a letter from dictation: 'Owing to a leakage in the hold of this vessel, the sugar had set, and become converted into rock. It needed hacking –'

He was quite unconscious. It had been his business to examine some such cargo of sugar in the Port of London.

'How long has he been like this?' the mother asked the landlady.

'He got home at six o'clock on Monday morning, and he seemed to sleep all day; then in the night we heard him talking, and this morning he asked for you. So I wired, and we fetched the doctor.'

'Will you have a fire made?'

Mrs Morel tried to soothe her son, to keep him still.

The doctor came. It was pneumonia, and, he said, a peculiar erysipelas, which had started under the chin where the collar chafed, and was spreading over the face. He hoped it would not get to the brain.

Mrs Morel settled down to nurse. She prayed for William, prayed that he would recognize her. But the young man's face grew more discoloured. In the night she struggled with him. He raved, and raved, and would not come to consciousness. At two o'clock, in a dreadful paroxysm, he died.

Mrs Morel sat perfectly still for an hour in the lodging bedroom; then she roused the household.

At six o'clock, with the aid of the charwoman, she laid him out; then she went round the dreary London village to the registrar and the doctor.

At nine o'clock to the cottage on Scargill Street came another wire:

'William died last night. Let father come, bring money.'

Annie, Paul, and Arthur were at home; Mr Morel was gone to work. The three children said not a word. Annie began to whimper with fear; Paul set off for his father.

It was a beautiful day. At Brinsley pit the white steam melted slowly in the sunshine of a soft blue sky; the wheels of the headstocks twinkled high up; the screen, shuffling its coal into the trucks, made a busy noise.

'I want my father, he's got to go to London,' said the boy to the first man he met on the bank.

'Tha wants Walter Morel? Go in theer an' tell Joe Ward.'

Paul went into the little top office.

'I want my father; he's got to go to London.'

'Thy feyther? Is he down? What's his name?'

'Mr Morel.'

'What, Walter? Is owt amiss?'

'He's got to go to London.'

The man went to the telephone and rang up the bottom office.

'Walter Morel's wanted. Number 42, Hard. Summat's amiss; there's his lad here.'

Then he turned round to Paul.

'He'll be up in a few minutes,' he said.

Paul wandered out to the pit-top. He watched the chair come up, with its wagon of coal. The great iron cage sank back on its rest, a full carfle was hauled off, an empty tram run on to the chair, a bell ting'ed somewhere, the chair heaved, then dropped like a stone.

Paul did not realize William was dead; it was impossible, with such a bustle going on. The puller-off swung the small truck on to the turn-table, another man ran with it along the bank down the curving lines.

'And William is dead, and my mother's in London, and what will she be doing?' the boy asked himself, as if it were a conundrum.

He watched chair after chair come up, and still no father. At last, standing beside a wagon, a man's form! The chair sank on its rests, Morel stepped off. He was slightly lame from an accident.

'Is it thee, Paul? Is 'e worse?'

'You've got to go to London.'

The two walked off the pit-bank, where men were watching curiously. As they came out and went along the railway, with the sunny autumn field on one side and a wall of trucks on the other, Morel said in a frightened voice:

''E's niver gone, child?'

'Yes.'

'When wor't?'

The miner's voice was terrified.

'Last night. We had a telegram from my mother.'

Morel walked on a few strides, then leaned up against a truck side, his hand over his eyes. He was not crying. Paul stood looking round, waiting. On the weighing-machine a truck trundled slowly. Paul saw everything, except his father leaning against the truck as if he were tired.

Morel had only once before been to London. He set off, scared and peaked, to help his wife. That was on Tuesday. The children were left alone in the house. Paul went to work, Arthur went to school, and Annie had in a friend to be with her.

On Saturday night, as Paul was turning the corner, coming home from Keston, he saw his mother and father, who had come to Sethley Bridge Station. They were walking in silence in the dark, tired, straggling apart. The boy waited.

'Mother,' he said, in the darkness.

Mrs Morel's small figure seemed not to observe. He spoke again.

'Paul!' she said, uninterestedly.

She let him kiss her, but she seemed unaware of him.

In the house she was the same – small, white, and mute. She noticed nothing, she said nothing, only:

'The coffin will be here tonight, Walter. You'd better see about some help.' Then turning to the children: 'We're bringing him home.'

Then she relapsed into the same mute looking into space, her hands folded on her lap. Paul, looking at her, felt he could not breathe. The house was dead silent.

'I went to work, mother,' he said, plaintively.

'Did you?' she answered dully.

After half an hour Morel, troubled and bewildered, came in again.

'Wheer s'll we ha'e him when he *does* come?' he asked his wife.

'In the front room.'

'Then I'd better shift th' table?'

'Yes.'

'An' ha'e him across th' chairs?'

'You know there – Yes, I suppose so.'

Morel and Paul went, with a candle, into the parlour. There was no gas there. The father unscrewed the top of the big mahogany oval table, and cleared the middle of the room; then he arranged six chairs opposite each other, so that the coffin could stand on their beds.

'You niver seed such a length as he is!' said the miner, and watching anxiously as he worked.

Paul went to the bay window and looked out. The ash-tree stood monstrous and black in front of the wide darkness. It was a faintly luminous night. Paul went back to his mother.

At ten o'clock Morel called:

'He's here!'

Everyone started. There was a noise of unbarring and unlocking the front door, which opened straight from the night into the room.

'Bring another candle,' called Morel.

Annie and Arthur went. Paul followed with his mother. He stood with his arm round her waist in the inner doorway. Down the middle of the cleared room waited six chairs, face to face. In the window, against the lace curtains, Arthur held up one candle, and by the open door, against the night, Annie stood leaning forward, her brass candlestick glittering.

There was the noise of wheels. Outside in the darkness of the street below Paul could see horses and a black vehicle, one lamp and a few pale faces; then some men, miners, all in their shirtsleeves, seemed to struggle in the obscurity. Presently two men appeared, bowed beneath a great weight. It was Morel and his neighbour.

'Steady!' called Morel, out of breath.

He and his fellow mounted the steep garden step, heaved into the candle-light with their gleaming coffin-end. Limbs of other men were seen struggling behind. Morel and Burns, in front, staggered; the great dark weight swayed.

'Steady, steady!' cried Morel, as if in pain.

All the six bearers were up in the small garden, holding the great coffin aloft. There were three more steps to the door. The yellow lamp of the carriage shone alone down in the black road.

'Now then!' said Morel.

The coffin swayed, the men began to mount the three steps, with their load. Annie's candle flickered, and she whimpered as the first men appeared, and the limbs and bowed heads of six men struggled to climb into the room, bearing the coffin that rode like sorrow on their living flesh.

'Oh, my son – my son!' Mrs Morel sang softly, and each time the coffin swung to the unequal climbing of the men: 'Oh, my son – my son – my son!'

'Mother!' Paul whimpered, his hand round her waist. 'Mother!'

She did not hear.

'Oh, my son – my son!' she repeated.

Paul saw drops of sweat fall from his father's brow. Six men were in the room – six coatless men, with yielding, struggling limbs, filling the room and knocking against the furniture. The coffin veered, and was gently lowered on to the chairs. The sweat fell from Morel's face on its boards.

'My word, he's a weight!' said a man, and the five miners sighed, bowed, and, trembling with the struggle, descended the steps again, closing the door behind them.

The family was alone in the parlour with the great polished box. William, when laid out, was six feet four inches long. Like a monument lay the bright brown, ponderous coffin. Paul thought it would never be got out of the room again. His mother was stroking the polished wood.

They buried him on the Monday in the little cemetery on the hillside that looks over the fields at the big church and the houses. It was sunny, and the white chrysanthemums frilled themselves in the warmth.

Mrs Morel could not be persuaded. after this. to talk and take her old bright interest in life. She remained shut off. All the way home in the train she had said to herself: 'If only it would have been me!'

When Paul came home at night he found his mother sitting, her day's work done, with hands folded in her lap upon her coarse apron. She always used to have changed her dress and put on a black apron, before. Now Annie set his supper, and his mother sat looking blankly in front of her, her mouth shut tight. Then he beat his brains for news to tell her.

'Mother, Miss Jordan was down today, and she said my sketch of a colliery at work was beautiful.'

But Mrs Morel took no notice. Night after night he forced himself to tell her things, although she did not listen. It drove him almost insane to have her thus. At last:

'What's a-matter, mother?' he asked.

She did not hear.

'What's a-matter?' he persisted. 'Mother, what's a-matter?'

'You know what's the matter,' she said irritably, turning away.

The lad – he was sixteen years old – went to bed drearily. He was cut off and wretched through October, November, and December. His mother tried, but she could not rouse herself. She could only brood on her dead son; he had been let to die so cruelly.

At last, on December 23, with his five shillings Christmas-box in his pocket, Paul wandered blindly home. His mother looked at him, and her heart stood still.

'What's the matter?' she asked.

'I'm badly, mother!' he replied. 'Mr Jordan gave me five shillings for a Christmas-box!'

He handed it to her with trembling hands. She put it on the table.

'You aren't glad!' he reproached her; but he trembled violently.

'Where hurts you?' she said, unbuttoning his overcoat.

It was the old question.

'I feel badly, mother.'

She undressed him and put him to bed. He had pneumonia dangerously, the doctor said.

'Might he never have had it if I'd kept him at home, not let him go to Nottingham?' was one of the first things she asked.

'He might not have been so bad,' said the doctor.

Mrs Morel stood condemned on her own ground.

'I should have watched the living, not the dead,' she told herself.

Paul was very ill. His mother lay in bed at nights with him; they could not afford a nurse. He grew worse, and the crisis approached. One night he tossed into consciousness in the ghastly, sickly feeling of dissolution, when all the cells in the body seem in intense irritability to be breaking down, and consciousness makes a last flare of struggle, like madness.

'I s'll die, mother!' he cried, heaving for breath on the pillow.

She lifted him up, crying in a small voice:

'Oh, my son – my son!'

That brought him to. He realized her. His whole will rose up and arrested him. He put his head on her breast, and took ease of her for love.

'For some things,' said his aunt, 'it was a good thing Paul was ill that Christmas. I believed it saved his mother.'

Paul was in bed for seven weeks. He got up white and fragile. His father had bought him a pot of scarlet and gold tulips. They used to flame in the window in the March sunshine as he sat on the sofa chattering to his mother. The two knitted together in perfect intimacy. Mrs Morel's life now rooted itself in Paul.

William had been a prophet. Mrs Morel had a little present and a letter from Lily at Christmas. Mrs Morel's sister had a letter at the New Year.

'I was at a ball last night. Some delightful people were there, and I enjoyed myself thoroughly,' said the letter. 'I had every dance – did not sit out one.'

Mrs Morel never heard any more of her.

Morel and his wife were gentle with each other for some time after the death of their son. He would go into a kind of daze, staring wide-eyed and blank across the room. Then he got up suddenly and hurried out to the Three Spots, returning in his normal state. But never in his life would he go for a walk up Shepstone, past the office where his son had worked, and he always avoided the cemetery.

PART II

7

LAD-AND-GIRL LOVE

Paul had been many times up to Willey Farm during the autumn. He was friends with the two youngest boys. Edgar, the eldest, would not condescend at first. And Miriam also refused to be approached. She was afraid of being set at nought, as by her own brothers. The girl was romantic in her soul. Everywhere was a Walter Scott heroine being loved by men with helmets or with plumes in their caps. She herself was something of a princess turned into a swine-girl in her own imagination. And she was afraid lest this boy, who, nevertheless, looked something like a Walter Scott hero, who could paint and speak French, and knew what algebra meant, and who went by train to Nottingham every day, might consider her simply as the swine-girl, unable to perceive the princess beneath; so she held aloof.

Her great companion was her mother. They were both brown-eyed, and inclined to be mystical, such women as treasure religion inside them, breathe it in their nostrils, and see the whole of life in a mist thereof. So to Miriam, Christ and God made one great figure, which she loved tremblingly and passionately when a tremendous sunset burned out the western sky, and Ediths, and Lucys, and Rowenas, Brian de Bois Guilberts, Rob Roys, and Guy Mannerings, rustled the sunny leaves in the morning, or sat in her bedroom aloft, alone, when it snowed. That was life to her. For the rest, she drudged in the house, which work she would not have minded had not her clean red floor been mucked up immediately by the trampling farm-boots of her brothers. She madly wanted her little brother of four to let her swathe him and stifle him in her love; she went to church reverently, with bowed head, and quivered in anguish from the vulgarity of the other choir-girls and from the common-sounding voice of the curate; she fought with her brothers, whom she considered brutal louts; and she held not her father in too high esteem because he did not carry any mystical ideals cherished in his heart but only wanted to have as easy a time as he could, and his meals when he was ready for them.

She hated her position as swine-girl. She wanted to be considered. She wanted to learn, thinking that if she could read, as Paul said he could read, 'Colomba', or the 'Voyage autour de ma Chambre' the world would have a different face for her and a deepened respect. She could not be princess by wealth or standing. So she was mad to have learning whereupon to pride herself. For she was different from other folk, and must not be scooped up among the common fry. Learning was the only distinction to which she thought to aspire.

Her beauty – that of a shy, wild, quiveringly sensitive thing – seemed nothing to her. Even her soul, so strong for rhapsody, was not enough. She must have something to reinforce her pride, because she felt different from other people. Paul she eyed rather wistfully. On the whole, she scorned the male sex. But here was a new specimen, quick, light, graceful, who could be gentle and who could be sad, and who was clever, and who knew a lot, and who had a death in the family. The boy's poor morsel of learning exalted him almost sky-high in her esteem. Yet she tried hard to scorn him, because he would not see in her the princess but only the swine-girl! And he scarcely observed her.

Then he was so ill, and she felt he would be weak. Then she would be stronger than he. Then she could love him. If she could be mistress of him in his weakness, take care of him, if he could depend on her, if she could, as it were, have him in her arms, how she could love him!

As soon as the skies brightened and plum-blossom was out, Paul drove off in the milkman's heavy float up to Willey Farm. Mr Leivers shouted in a kindly fashion at the boy, then clicked to the horses as they climbed the hill slowly, in the freshness of the morning. White clouds went on their way, crowding to the back of the hills that were rousing in the spring-time. The water of Nethermere lay below, very blue against the seared meadows and the thorn-trees.

It was four and a half miles' drive. Tiny buds on the hedges, vivid as copper-green, were opening into rosettes; and thrushes called, and blackbirds shrieked and scolded. It was a new, glamorous world.

Miriam, peeping through the kitchen window, saw the horse walk through the big white gate into the farmyard that was backed by the oak-wood, still bare. Then a youth in a heavy overcoat climbed down. He put up his hands for the whip and the rug that the good-looking, ruddy farmer handed down to him.

Miriam appeared in the doorway. She was nearly sixteen, very beautiful, with her warm colouring, her gravity, her eyes dilating suddenly like an ecstasy.

'I say,' said Paul, turning shyly aside, 'your daffodils are nearly out. Isn't it early? But don't they look cold?'

'Cold!' said Miriam, in her musical, caressing voice.

'The green on their buds –' and he faltered into silence timidly.

'Let me take the rug,' said Miriam over-gently.

'I can carry it,' he answered, rather injured. But he yielded it to her.

Then Mrs Leivers appeared.

'I'm sure you're tired and cold,' she said. 'Let me take your coat. It *is* heavy. You mustn't walk far in it.'

She helped him off with his coat. He was quite unused to such attention. She was almost smothered under its weight.

'Why, mother,' laughed the farmer as he passed through the kitchen, swinging the great-milk churns, 'you've got almost more than you can manage there.'

She beat up the sofa cushions for the youth.

The kitchen was very small and irregular. The farm had been originally a labourer's cottage. And the furniture was old and battered. But Paul loved it – loved the sack-bag that formed the hearthrug, and the funny little corner under the stairs, and the small window deep in the corner, through which, bending a little, he could see the plum-trees in the back-garden and the lovely round hills beyond.

'Won't you lie down?' said Mrs Leivers.

'Oh no; I'm not tired,' he said. 'Isn't it lovely coming out, don't you think? I saw a sloe-bush in blossom and a lot of celandines. I'm glad it's sunny.'

'Can I give you anything to eat or to drink?'

'No, thank you.'

'How's your mother?'

'I think she's tired now. I think she's had too much to do. Perhaps in a little while she'll go to Skegness with me. Then she'll be able to rest. I s'll be glad if she can.'

'Yes,' replied Mrs Leivers. 'It's a wonder she isn't ill herself.'

Miriam was moving about preparing dinner. Paul watched everything that happened. His face was pale and thin, but his eyes were quick and bright with life as ever. He watched the strange, almost rhapsodic way in which the girl moved about, carrying a great stew-jar to the oven, or looking in the saucepan. The atmosphere was different from that of his own home, where everything seemed so ordinary. When Mr Leivers called loudly outside to the horse, that was reaching over to feed on the rose-bushes in the garden, the girl started, looked round with dark eyes, as if something had come breaking in on her world. There was a sense of silence inside the house and out. Miriam seemed as in some dreamy tale, a maiden in bondage, her spirit dreaming in a land far away and magical. And her discoloured, old blue frock and her broken boots seemed only like the romantic rags of King Cophetua's beggar-maid.

She suddenly became aware of his keen blue eyes upon her, taking her all in. Instantly her broken boots and her frayed old frock hurt her. She resented his seeing everything. Even he knew that her stocking was not pulled up. She went into the scullery, blushing deeply. And afterwards her hands trembled slightly at her work. She nearly dropped all she handled. When her inside dream was shaken, her body quivered with trepidation. She resented that he saw so much.

Mrs Leivers sat for some time talking to the boy, although she was needed at her work. She was too polite to leave him. Presently she excused herself and rose. After a while she looked into the tin saucepan.

'Oh *dear*, Miriam,' she cried, 'these potatoes have boiled dry!'

Miriam started as if she had been stung.

'*Have* they, mother?' she cried.

'I shouldn't care, Miriam,' said the mother, 'if I hadn't trusted them to you.' She peered into the pan.

The girl stiffened as if from a blow. Her dark eyes dilated; she remained standing in the same spot.

'Well,' she answered, gripped tight in self-conscious shame, 'I'm sure I looked at them five minutes since.'

'Yes,' said the mother. 'I know it's easily done.'

'They're not much burned,' said Paul. 'It doesn't matter, does it?'

Mrs Leivers looked at the youth with her brown, hurt eyes.

'It wouldn't matter but for the boys,' she said to him. 'Only Miriam knows what a trouble they make if the potatoes are "caught".'

'Then,' thought Paul to himself, 'you shouldn't let them make a trouble.'

After a while Edgar came in. He wore leggings, and his boots were covered with earth. He was rather small, rather formal, for a farmer. He glanced at Paul, nodded to him distantly, and said:

'Dinner ready?'

'Nearly, Edgar,' replied the mother apologetically.

'I'm ready for mine,' said the young man, taking up the newspaper and reading. Presently the rest of the family trooped in. Dinner was served. The meal went rather brutally. The over-gentleness and apologetic tone of the mother brought out all the brutality of manner in the sons. Edgar tasted the potatoes, moved his mouth quickly like a rabbit, looked indignantly at his mother, and said:

'These potatoes are burnt, mother.'

'Yes, Edgar, I forgot them for a minute. Perhaps you'll have bread if you can't eat them.'

Edgar looked in anger across at Miriam.

'What was Miriam doing that she couldn't attend to them?' he said.

Miriam looked up. Her mouth opened, her dark eyes blazed and winced, but she said nothing. She swallowed her anger and her shame, bowing her dark head.

'I'm sure she was trying hard,' said the mother.

'She hasn't got sense even to boil the potatoes,' said Edgar. 'What is she kept at home for?'

'On'y for eating everything that's left in th' pantry,' said Maurice.

'They don't forget that potato-pie against our Miriam,' laughed the father.

She was utterly humiliated. The mother sat in silence, suffering, like some saint out of place at the brutal board.

It puzzled Paul. He wondered vaguely why all this intense feeling went running because of a few burnt potatoes. The mother exalted everything – even a bit of housework – to the plane of a religious trust. The sons resented this; they felt themselves cut away underneath, and they answered with brutality and also with a sneering superciliousness.

Paul was just opening out from childhood into manhood. This atmosphere, where everything took a religious value, came with a subtle fascination to him. There was something in the air. His own mother was logical. Here there was something different, something he loved, something that at times he hated.

Miriam quarrelled with her brother fiercely. Later in the afternoon, when they had gone away again, her mother said:

'You disappointed me at dinner-time, Miriam.'

The girl dropped her head.

'They are such *brutes*!' she suddenly cried, looking up with flashing eyes.

'But hadn't you promised not to answer them?' said the mother. 'And I believed in you. I *can't* stand it when you wrangle.'

'But they're so hateful!' cried Miriam, 'and – and *low*.'

'Yes, dear. But how often have I asked you not to answer Edgar back? Can't you let him say what he likes?'

'But why should he say what he likes?'

'Aren't you strong enough to bear it, Miriam, if even for my sake? Are you so weak that you must wrangle with them?'

Mrs Leivers stuck unflinchingly to this doctrine of 'the other cheek'. She could not instil it at all into the boys. With the girls she succeeded better, and Miriam was the child of her heart. The boys loathed the other cheek when it was presented to them. Miriam was often sufficiently lofty to turn it. Then they spat on her and hated her. But she walked in her proud humility, living within herself.

There was always this feeling of jangle and discord in the Leivers family. Although the boys resented so bitterly this eternal appeal to their deeper feelings of resignation and proud humility, yet it had its effect on them. They could not establish between themselves and an outsider just the ordinary human feeling and unexaggerated friendship; they were always restless for the something deeper. Ordinary folk seemed shallow to them, trivial and inconsiderable. And so they were unaccustomed, painfully uncouth in the simplest social intercourse, suffering, and yet insolent in their superiority. Then beneath was the yearning for the soul-intimacy to which they could not attain because they were too dumb, and every approach to close connexion was blocked by their clumsy contempt of other people. They wanted genuine intimacy, but they could not get even normally near to anyone, because they scorned to take the first steps, they scorned the triviality which forms common human intercourse.

Paul fell under Mrs Leivers' spell. Everything had a religious and intensified meaning when he was with her. His soul, hurt, highly developed, sought her as if for nourishment. Together they seemed to sift the vital fact from an experience.

Miriam was her mother's daughter. In the sunshine of the afternoon mother and daughter went down the fields with him. They looked for nests. There was a jenny wren's in the hedge by the orchard.

'I *do* want you to see this,' said Mrs Leivers.

He crouched down and carefully put his finger through the thorns into the round door of the nest.

'It's almost as if you were feeling inside the live body of the bird,' he said, 'it's so warm. They say a bird makes its nest round like a cup with pressing its breast on it. Then how did it make the ceiling round, I wonder?'

The nest seemed to start to life for the two women. After that, Miriam came to see it every day. It seemed so close to her. Again, going down the hedgeside with the girl, he noticed the celandines, scalloped splashes of gold, on the side of the ditch.

'I like them,' he said, 'when their petals go flat back with the sunshine. They seem to be pressing themselves at the sun.'

And then the celandines ever after drew her with a little spell. Anthropomorphic as she was, she stimulated him into appreciating things thus, and then they lived for her. She seemed to need things kindling in her imagination or in her soul before she felt she had them. And she was cut off from ordinary life by her religious intensity which made the world for her either a nunnery garden or a paradise, where sin and knowledge were not, or else an ugly, cruel thing.

So it was in this atmosphere of subtle intimacy, this meeting in their common feeling for something in Nature, that their love started.

Personally, he was a long time before he realized her. For ten months he had to stay at home after his illness. For a while he went to Skegness with his mother, and was perfectly happy. But even from the seaside he wrote long letters to Mrs Leivers about the shore and the sea. And he brought back his beloved sketches of the flat Lincoln coast, anxious for them to see. Almost they would interest the Leivers more than they interested his mother. It was not his art Mrs Morel cared about; it was himself and his achievement. But Mrs Leivers and her children were almost his disciples. They kindled him and made him glow to his work, whereas his mother's influence was to make him quietly determined, patient, dogged, unwearied.

He soon was friends with the boys, whose rudeness was only superficial.

They had all, when they could trust themselves, a strange gentleness and lovableness.

'Will you come with me on to the fallow?' asked Edgar, rather hesitatingly.

Paul went joyfully, and spent the afternoon helping to hoe or to single turnips with his friend, He used to lie with the three brothers in the hay piled up in the barn and tell them about Nottingham and about Jordan's. In return, they taught him to milk, and let him do little jobs – chopping hay or pulping turnips – just as much as he liked. At midsummer he worked all through hay-harvest with them, and then he loved them. The family was so cut off from the world actually. They seemed, somehow, like 'les derniers fils d'une race épuisée'. Though the lads were strong and healthy, yet they had all that oversensitiveness and hanging-back which made them so lonely, yet also such close, delicate friends once their intimacy was won. Paul loved them dearly, and they him.

Miriam came later. But he had come into her life before she made any mark on his. One dull afternoon, when the men were on the land and the rest at school, only Miriam and her mother at home, the girl said to him, after having hesitated for some time:

'Have you seen the swing?'

'No,' he answered. 'Where?'

'In the cowshed,' she replied.

She always hesitated to offer or to show him anything. Men have such different standards of worth from women, and her dear things – the valuable things to her – her brothers had so often mocked or flouted.

'Come on, then,' he replied, jumping up.

There were two cowsheds, one on either side of the barn. In the lower, darker shed there was standing for four cows. Hens flew scolding over the manger-wall as the youth and girl went forward for the great thick rope which hung from the beam in the darkness overhead, and was pushed back over a peg in the wall.

'It's something like a rope!' he exclaimed appreciatively; and he sat down on it, anxious to try it. Then immediately he rose.

'Come on, then, and have first go,' he said to the girl.

'See,' she answered, going into the farm, 'we put some bags on the seat'; and she made the swing comfortable for him. That gave her pleasure. He held the rope.

'Come on, then,' he said to her.

'No, I won't go first,' she answered.

She stood aside in her still, aloof fashion.

'Why?'

'You go,' she pleaded.

Almost for the first time in her life she had the pleasure of giving up to a man, of spoiling him. Paul looked at her.

'All right,' he said, sitting down. 'Mind out!'

He set off with a spring, and in a moment was flying through the air, almost out of the door of the shed, the upper half of which was open, showing outside the drizzling rain, the filthy yard, the cattle standing disconsolate against the black cart-shed, and at the back of all the grey-green wall of the wood. She stood below in her crimson tam-o'-shanter and watched. He looked down at her, and she saw his blue eyes sparkling.

'It's a treat of a swing,' he said.

'Yes.'

He was swinging through the air, every bit of him swinging, like a bird that swoops for joy of movement. And he looked down at her. Her crimson cap hung over her dark curls, her beautiful warm face, so still in a kind of brooding, was lifted towards him. It was dark and rather cold in the shed. Suddenly a swallow came down from the high roof and darted out of the door.

'I didn't know a bird was watching,' he called.

He swung negligently. She could feel him falling and lifting through the air, as if he were lying on some force.

'Now I'll die,' he said, in a detached, dreamy voice, as though he were the dying motion of the swing. She watched him, fascinated. Suddenly he put on the brake and jumped out.

'I've had a long turn,' he said. 'But it's a treat of a swing – it's a real treat of a swing!'

Miriam was amused that he took a swing so seriously and felt so warmly over it.

'No; you go on,' she said.

'Why, don't you want one?' he asked, astonished.

'Well, not much. I'll have just a little.'

She sat down, whilst he kept the bags in place for her.

'It's so ripping!' he said, setting her in motion. 'Keep your heels up, or they'll bang the manger-wall.'

She felt the accuracy with which he caught her, exactly at the right moment, and the exactly proportionate strength of his thrust, and she was afraid. Down to her bowels went the hot wave of fear. She was in his hands. Again, firm and inevitable came the thrust at the right moment. She gripped the rope, almost swooning.

'Ha!' she laughed in fear. 'No higher!'

'But you're not a *bit* high,' he remonstrated.

'But no higher.'

He heard the fear in her voice, and desisted. Her heart melted in hot pain when the moment came for him to thrust her forward again. But he left her alone. She began to breathe.

'Won't you really go any farther?' he asked. 'Should I keep you there?'

'No; let me go by myself,' she answered.

He moved aside and watched her.

'Why, you're scarcely moving,' he said.

She laughed slightly with shame, and in a moment got down.

'They say if you can swing you won't be sea-sick,' he said, as he mounted again. 'I don't believe I should ever be sea-sick.'

Away he went. There was something fascinating to her in him. For the moment he was nothing but a piece of swinging stuff; not a particle of him that did not swing. She could never lose herself, so, nor could her brothers. It roused a warmth in her. It were almost as if he were a flame that had lit a warmth in her whilst he swung in the middle air.

And gradually the intimacy with the family concentrated for Paul on three persons – the mother, Edgar, and Miriam. To the mother he went for that sympathy and that appeal which seemed to draw him out. Edgar was his very close friend. And to Miriam he more or less condescended, because she seemed so humble.

But the girl gradually sought him out. If he brought up his sketch-book, it was she who pondered longest over the last picture. Then she would look up at him. Suddenly, her dark eyes alight like water that shakes with a stream of gold in the dark, she would ask:

'Why do I like this so?'

Always something in her breast shrank from these close, intimate, dazzled looks of hers.

'Why *do* you?' he asked.

'I don't know. It seems so true.'

'It's because – it's because there is scarcely any shadow in it; it's more shimmery, as if I'd painted the shimmering protoplasm in the leaves and everywhere, and not the stiffness of the shape. That seems dead to me. Only this shimmeriness is the real living. The shape is a dead crust. The shimmer is inside really.'

And she, with her little finger in her mouth, would ponder these sayings. They gave her a feeling of life again, and vivified things which had meant nothing to her. She managed to find some meaning in his struggling, abstract speeches. And they were the medium through which she came distinctly at her beloved objects.

Another day she sat at sunset whilst he was painting some pine-trees which caught the red glare from the west. He had been quiet.

'There you are!' he said suddenly. 'I wanted that. Now, look at them and tell me, are they pine-trunks or are they red coals, standing-up pieces of fire in that darkness? There's God's burning bush for you, that burned not away.'

Miriam looked, and was frightened. But the pine-trunks were wonderful to her, and distinct. He packed his box and rose. Suddenly he looked at her.

'Why are you always sad?' he asked her.

'Sad!' she exclaimed, looking up at him with startled, wonderful brown eyes.

'Yes,' he replied. 'You are always, always sad.'

'I am not – oh, not a bit!' she cried.

'But even your joy is like a flame coming off of sadness,' he persisted. 'You're never jolly, or even just all right.'

'No,' she pondered. 'I wonder – why.'

'Because you're not; because you're different inside, like a pine-tree, and then you flare up; but you're not just like an ordinary tree, with fidgety leaves and jolly –'

He got tangled up in his own speech; but she brooded on it, and he had a strange, roused sensation, as if his feelings were new. She got so near him. It was a strange stimulant.

Then sometimes he hated her. Her youngest brother was only five. He was a frail lad, with immense brown eyes in his quaint fragile face – one of Reynolds's 'Choir of Angels', with a touch of elf. Often Miriam knelt to the child and drew him to her.

'Eh, my Hubert!' she sang, in a voice heavy and surcharged with love. 'Eh, my Hubert!'

And, folding him in her arms, she swayed slightly from side to side with love, her face half lifted, her eyes half closed, her voice drenched with love.

'Don't!' said the child, uneasy – 'don't, Miriam!'

'Yes; you love me, don't you?' she murmured deep in her throat, almost as if she were in a trance, and swaying also as if she were swooned in an ecstasy of love.

'Don't!' repeated the child, a frown on his clear brow.

'You love me, don't you!' she murmured.

'What do you make such a *fuss* for?' cried Paul, all in suffering because of her extreme emotion. 'Why can't you be ordinary with him?'

She let the child go, and rose, and said nothing. Her intensity, which would leave no emotion on a normal plane, irritated the youth into a frenzy. And this fearful, naked contact of her on small occasions shocked him. He was used to his mother's reserve. And on such occasions he was thankful in his heart and soul that he had his mother, so sane and wholesome.

All the life of Miriam's body was in her eyes, which were usually dark as a dark church, but could flame with light like a conflagration. Her face scarcely even altered from its look of brooding. She might have been one of the women who went with Mary when Jesus was dead. Her body was not flexible and living. She walked with a swing, rather heavily, her head bowed forward, pondering. She was not clumsy, and yet none of her movements seemed quite *the* movement. Often, when wiping the dishes, she would stand in bewilderment and chagrin because she had pulled in two halves a cup or a tumbler. It was as if, in her fear and self-mistrust, she put too much strength into the effort. There was no looseness or abandon about her. Everything was gripped stiff with intensity, and her effort, overcharged, closed in on itself.

She rarely varied from her swinging, forward, intense walk. Occasionally she ran with Paul down the fields. Then her eyes blazed naked in a kind of ecstasy that frightened him. But she was physically afraid. If she were getting over a stile, she gripped his hands in a little hard anguish, and began to lose her presence of mind. And he could not persuade her to jump from even a small height. Her eyes dilated, became exposed and palpitating.

'No!' she cried, half laughing in terror – 'no!'

'You shall!' he cried once, and jerking her forward, he brought her falling from the fence. But her wild 'Ah!' of pain, as if she were losing consciousness, cut him. She landed on her feet safely, and afterwards had courage in this respect.

She was very much dissatisfied with her lot.

'Don't you like being at home?' Paul asked her, surprised.

'Who would?' she answered, low and intense. 'What is it? I'm all day cleaning what the boys make just as bad in five minutes. I don't *want* to be at home.'

'What do you want, then?'

'I want to do something. I want a chance like anybody else. Why should I, because I'm a girl, be kept at home and not allowed to be anything? What chance *have* I?'

'Chance of what?'

'Of knowing anything – of learning, of doing anything. It's not fair, because I'm a woman.'

She seemed very bitter. Paul wondered. In his own home Annie was almost glad to be a girl. She had not so much responsibility; things were lighter for her. She never wanted to be other than a girl. But Miriam almost fiercely wished she were a man. And yet she hated men at the same time.

'But it's as well to be a woman as a man,' he said, frowning.

'Ha! Is it! Men have everything.'

'I should think women ought to be as glad to be women as men are to be men,' he answered.

'No!' she shook her head – 'no! Everything the men have.'

'But what do you want?' he asked.

'I want to learn. Why *should* it be that I know nothing?'

'What! such as mathematics and French?'

'Why *shouldn't* I know mathematics? Yes!' she cried, her eye expanding in a kind of defiance.

'Well, you can learn as much as I know,' he said. 'I'll teach you, if you like.' Her eyes dilated. She mistrusted him as a teacher.

'Would you?' he asked.

Her head had dropped, and she was sucking her finger broodingly.

'Yes,' she said hesitatingly.

He used to tell his mother all these things.

'I'm going to teach Miriam algebra,' he said.

'Well,' replied Mrs Morel, 'I hope she'll get fat on it.'

When he went up to the farm on the Monday evening, it was drawing twilight. Miriam was just sweeping up the kitchen, and was kneeling at the hearth when he entered. Everyone was out but her. She looked round at him, flushed, her dark eyes shining, her fine hair falling about her face.

'Hello!' she said, soft and musical. 'I knew it was you.'

'How?'

'I knew your step. Nobody treads so quick and firm.'

He sat down, sighing.

'Ready to do some algebra?' he asked, drawing a little book from his pocket.

'But —'

He could feel her backing away.

'You said you wanted,' he insisted.

'Tonight, though?' she faltered.

'But I came on purpose. And if you want to learn it, you must begin.'

She took up her ashes in the dustpan and looked at him, half tremulously, laughing.

'Yes, but tonight! You see, I haven't thought of it.'

'Well, my goodness! Take the ashes and come.'

He went and sat on the stone bench in the back-yard, where the big milk-cans were standing, tipped up, to air. The men were in the cowsheds. He could hear the little sing-song of the milk spurting into the pails. Presently she came, bringing some big greenish apples.

'You know you like them,' she said.

He took a bite.

'Sit down,' he said, with his mouth full.

She was short-sighted, and peering over his shoulder. It irritated him. He gave her the book quickly.

'Here,' he said. 'It's only letters for figures. You put down "a" instead of "2" or "6".'

They worked, he talking, she with her head down on the book. He was quick and hasty. She never answered. Occasionally, when he demanded of her, 'Do you see?' she looked up at him, her eyes wide with the half-laugh that comes of fear. 'Don't you?' he cried.

He had been too fast. But she said nothing. He questioned her more, then got hot. It made his blood rouse to see her there, as it were, at his mercy, her mouth open, her eyes dilated with laughter that was afraid, apologetic, ashamed. Then Edgar came along with two buckets of milk.

'Hello!' he said. 'What are you doing?'

'Algebra,' replied Paul.

'Algebra!' repeated Edgar curiously. Then he passed on with a laugh. Paul took a bite at his forgotten apple, looked at the miserable cabbages in the garden, pecked into lace by the fowls, and he wanted to pull them up. Then he glanced at Miriam. She was poring over the book, seemed absorbed in it, yet trembling lest she could not get at it. It made him cross. She was ruddy and beautiful. Yet her soul seemed to be intensely supplicating. The algebra-book she closed, shrinking, knowing he was angered; and at the same instant he grew gentle, seeing her hurt because she did not understand.

But things came slowly to her. And when she held herself in a grip, seemed so utterly humble before the lesson, it made his blood rouse. He stormed at her, got ashamed, continued the lesson, and grew furious again, abusing her. She listened in silence. Occasionally, very rarely, she defended herself. Her liquid dark eyes blazed at him.

'You don't give me time to learn it,' she said.

'All right,' he answered, throwing the book on the table and lighting a cigarette. Then, after a while, he went back to her repentant. So the lessons went. He was always either in a rage or very gentle.

'What do you tremble your *soul* before it for?' he cried. 'You don't learn algebra with your blessed soul. Can't you look at it with your clear simple wits?'

Often, when he went again into the kitchen, Mrs Leivers would look at him reproachfully, saying:

'Paul, don't be so hard on Miriam. She may not be quick, but I'm sure she tries.'

'I can't help it,' he said rather pitiably. 'I go off like it.'

'You don't mind me, Miriam, do you?' he asked of the girl later.

'No,' she reassured him in her beautiful deep tones – 'no, I don't mind.'

'Don't mind me; it's my fault.'

But, in spite of himself, his blood began to boil with her. It was strange that no one else made him in such fury. He flared against her. Once he threw the pencil in her face. There was a silence. She turned her face slightly aside.

'I didn't –' he began, but got no further, feeling weak in all his bones. She never reproached him or was angry with him. He was often cruelly ashamed. But still again his anger burst like a bubble surcharged and still, when he saw her eager, silent, as it were, blind face, he felt he wanted to throw the pencil in it; and still, when he saw her hand trembling and her mouth parted with suffering, his heart was scalded with pain for her. And because of the intensity to which she roused him, he sought her.

Then he often avoided her and went with Edgar. Miriam and her brother were naturally antagonistic. Edgar was a rationalist, who was curious, and had a sort of scientific interest in life. It was a great bitterness to Miriam to see herself deserted by Paul for Edgar, who seemed so much lower. But the youth was very happy with her elder brother. The two men spent afternoons together on the land or in the loft doing carpentry, when it rained. And they talked together, or Paul taught Edgar the songs he himself had learned from Annie at the piano. And often all the men, Mr Leivers as well, had bitter debates on the nationalizing of the land and similar problems. Paul had already heard his mother's views, and as these were as yet his own, he argued for her. Miriam attended and took part, but was all the time waiting until it should be over and a personal communication might begin.

'After all,' she said within herself, 'if the land were nationalized, Edgar and Paul and I would be just the same.' So she waited for the youth to come back to her.

He was studying for his painting. He loved to sit at home, alone with his mother, at night, working and working. She sewed or read. Then, looking up from his task, he would rest his eyes for a moment on her face, that was bright with living warmth, and he returned gladly to his work.

'I can do my best things when you sit there in your rocking-chair, mother,' he said.

'I'm sure!' she exclaimed, sniffing with mock scepticism. But she felt it was so, and her heart quivered with brightness. For many hours she sat still, slightly conscious of him labouring away, whilst she worked or read her book. And he, with all his soul's intensity directing his pencil, could feel her warmth inside him like strength. They were both very happy so, and both unconscious of it. These times, that meant so much, and which were real living, they almost ignored.

He was conscious only when stimulated. A sketch finished, he always wanted to take it to Miriam. Then he was stimulated into knowledge of the work he had produced unconsciously. In contact with Miriam he gained insight; his vision went deeper. From his mother he drew the life-warmth, the strength to produce; Miriam urged this warmth into intensity like a white light.

When he returned to the factory the conditions of work were better. He had Wednesday afternoon off to go to the Art school – Miss Jordan's provision – returning in the evening. Then the factory closed at six instead of at eight on Thursday and Friday evenings.

One evening in the summer Miriam and he went over the fields by Herod's Farm on their way from the library home. So it was only three miles to Willey Farm. There was a yellow glow over the mowing-grass, and the sorrel-heads burned crimson. Gradually, as they walked along the high land, the gold in the west sank down to red, the red to crimson, and then the chill blue crept up against the glow.

They came out upon the high road to Alfreton, which ran white between the darkening fields. There Paul hesitated. It was two miles home for him, one mile forward for Miriam. They both looked up the road that ran in shadow right under the glow of the north-west sky. On the crest of the hill, Selby, with its stark houses and the up-pricked headstocks of the pit, stood in black silhouette small against the sky.

He looked at his watch.

'Nine o'clock!' he said.

The pair stood, loth to part, hugging their books.

'The wood is so lovely now,' she said. 'I wanted you to see it.'

He followed her slowly across the road to the white gate.

'They grumble so if I'm late,' he said.

'But you're not doing anything wrong,' she answered impatiently.

He followed her across the nibbled pasture in the dusk. There was a coolness in the wood, a scent of leaves, of honeysuckle, and a twilight. The two walked in silence. Night came wonderfully there, among the throngs of dark-trunks. He looked round, expectant.

She wanted to show him a certain wild-rose bush she had discovered. She knew it was wonderful. And yet, till he had seen it, she felt it had not come into her soul. Only he could make it her own, immortal. She was dissatisfied.

Dew was already on the paths. In the old oak-wood a mist was rising, and he hesitated, wondering whether one whiteness were a strand of fog or only campion-flowers pallid in a cloud.

By the time they came to the pine-trees Miriam was getting very eager and very intense. Her bush might be gone. She might not be able to find it; and she wanted it so much. Almost passionately she wanted to be with him when he stood before the flowers. They were going to have a communion together – something that thrilled her, something holy. He was walking beside her in silence. They were very near to each other. She trembled, and he listened, vaguely anxious.

Coming to the edge of the wood, they saw the sky in front, like mother-of-pearl, and the earth growing dark. Somewhere on the outermost branches of the pine-wood the honeysuckle was streaming scent.

'Where?' he asked.

'Down the middle path,' she murmured, quivering.

When they turned the corner of the path she stood still. In the wide walk between the pines, gazing rather frightened, she could distinguish nothing for some moments; the greying light robbed things of their colour. Then she saw her bush.

'Ah!' she cried, hastening forward.

It was very still. The tree was tall and straggling. It had thrown its briers over a hawthorn-bush, and its long streamers trailed thick right down to the grass, splashing the darkness everywhere with great split stars, pure white. In bosses of ivory and in large splashed stars the roses gleamed on the darkness of foliage and stems of grass. Paul and Miriam stood close together, silent, and watched. Point after point the steady roses shone out of them, seeming to kindle something in their souls. The dusk came like smoke around, and still did not put out the roses.

Paul looked into Miriam's eyes. She was pale and expectant with wonder, her lips were parted, and her dark eyes lay open to him. His look seemed to travel down into her. Her soul quivered. It was the communion she wanted. He turned aside, as if pained. He turned to the bush.

'They seems as if they walk like butterflies, and shake themselves.' he said.

She looked at her roses. They were white. some incurved and holy. others expanded in an ecstasy. The tree was dark as a shadow. She lifted her hand impulsively to the flowers; she went forward and touched them in worship.

'Let us go,' he said.

There was a cool scent of ivory roses – a white, virgin scent. Something made him feel anxious and imprisoned. The two walked in silence.

''Till Sunday,' he said quietly, and left her; and she walked home slowly, feeling her soul satisfied with the holiness of the night. He stumbled down the path. And as soon as he was out of the wood, in the free open meadow, where he could breathe, he started to run as fast as he could. It was like a delicious delirium in his veins.

Always when he went with Miriam, and it grew rather late, he knew his mother was fretting and getting angry about him – why, he could not understand. As he went into the house, flinging down his cap, his mother looked up at the clock. She had been sitting thinking, because a chill to her eyes prevented her reading. She could feel Paul being drawn away by this girl. And she did not care for Miriam. 'She is one of those who will want to suck a man's soul out till he had none of his own left,' she said to herself; 'and he is just such a gaby as to let himself be absorbed. She will never let him become a man; she never will.' So, while he was away with Miriam, Mrs Morel grew more and more worked up.

She glanced at the clock, and said, coldly and rather tired: 'You have been far enough tonight.'

His soul, warm and exposed from contact with the girl, shrank.

'You must have been right home with her,' his mother continued.

He would not answer. Mrs Morel, looking at him quickly, saw his hair was damp on his forehead with haste, saw him frowning in his heavy fashion, resentfully.

'She must be wonderfully fascinating, that you can't get away from her, but must go trailing eight miles at this time of night.'

He was hurt between the past glamour with Miriam and the knowledge that his mother fretted. He had meant not to say anything, to refuse to answer. But he could not harden his heart or ignore his mother.

'I *do* like to talk to her,' he answered irritably.

'Is there nobody else to talk to?'

'You wouldn't say anything if I went with Edgar.'

'You know I should. You know, whoever you went with, I should say it was too far for you to go trailing, late at night, when you've been to Nottingham. Besides' – her voice suddenly flashed into anger and contempt – 'it is disgusting – bits of lads and girls courting.'

'It is *not* courting,' he cried.

'I don't know what else you call it.'

'It's not! Do you think we *spoon* and do? We only talk.'

' 'Till goodness knows what time and distance,' was the sarcastic rejoinder.

Paul snapped at the laces of his boots angrily.

'What are you so mad about?' he asked. 'Because you don't like her.'

'I don't say I don't like her. But I don't hold with children keeping company, and never did.'

'But you don't mind our Annie going out with Jim Inger.'

'They've more sense than you two.'

'Why?'

'Our Annie's not one of the deep sort.'

He failed to see the meaning of this remark. But his mother looked tired. She was never so strong after William's death; and her eyes hurt her.

'Well,' he said, 'it's so pretty in the country. Mr Sleath asked about you. He said he'd missed you. Are you a bit better?'

'I ought to have been in bed a long time ago,' she replied.

'Why, mother, you know you wouldn't have gone before quarter-past ten.'

'Oh yes, I should!'

'Oh, little woman, you'd say anything now you're disagreeable with me, wouldn't you?'

He kissed her forehead that he knew so well: the deep marks between the brows, the rising of the fine hair, greying now, and the proud setting of the temples. His hand lingered on her shoulder after his kiss. Then he went slowly to bed. He had forgotten Miriam; he only saw how his mother's hair was lifted back from her warm, broad brow. And somehow, she was hurt.

Then the next time he saw Miriam he said to her:

'Don't let me be late tonight – not later than ten o'clock. My mother gets so upset.'

Miriam dropped her head, brooding.

'Why does she get upset?' she asked.

'Because she says I oughtn't to be out late when I have to get up early.'

'Very well!' said Miriam, rather quietly, with just a touch of a sneer.

He resented that. And he was usually late again.

That there was any love growing between him and Miriam neither of them would have acknowledged. He thought he was too sane for such sentimentality, and she thought herself too lofty. They both were late in coming to maturity, and psychical ripeness was much behind even the physical. Miriam was exceedingly sensitive, as her mother had always been. The slightest grossness made her recoil almost in anguish. Her brothers were brutal, but never coarse in speech. The men did all the discussing of farm matters outside. But, perhaps, because of the continual business of birth and of begetting which goes on upon every farm, Miriam was the more hypersensitive to the matter, and her blood was chastened almost to disgust of the faintest suggestion of such intercourse. Paul took his pitch from her, and their intimacy went on in an utterly blanched and chaste fashion. It could never be mentioned that the mare was in foal.

When he was nineteen, he was earning only twenty shillings a week, but he was happy. His painting went well, and life went well enough. On the Good Friday he organized a walk to the Hemlock Stone. There were three lads of his own age, then Annie and Arthur, Miriam and Geoffrey. Arthur, apprenticed as an electrician in Nottingham, was home for the holiday. Morel, as usual, was up early, whistling and sawing in the yard. At seven o'clock the family heard him buy threepennyworth of hot-cross buns, he talked with gusto to the little girl who brought them, calling her 'my darling'. He turned away several boys who came with more buns, telling them they had been 'kested' by a little lass. Then Mrs Morel got up, and the family straggled down. It was an immense luxury to everybody, this lying in bed just beyond the ordinary time on a weekday. And Paul and Arthur read before breakfast, and had the meal unwashed, sitting in their shirtsleeves. This was another holiday luxury. The room was warm. Everything felt free of care and anxiety. There was a sense of plenty in the house.

While the boys were reading, Mrs Morel went into the garden. They were now in another house, an old one, near the Scargill Street home, which had been left soon after William had died. Directly came an excited cry from the garden:

'Paul, Paul! come and look!'

It was his mother's voice. He threw down his book and went out. There was a long garden that ran to a field. It was a grey, cold day, with a sharp wind blowing out of Derbyshire. Two fields away Bestwood began, with a jumble of roofs and red house-ends, out of which rose the church tower and the spire of the Congregational Chapel. And beyond went woods and hills, right away to the pale grey heights of the Pennine Chain. Paul looked down the garden for his mother. Her head appeared among the young currant-bushes.

'Come here!' she cried.

'What for?' he answered.

'Come and see.'

She had been looking at the buds on the currant-trees. Paul went up.

'To think,' she said, 'that here I might never have seen them!'

Her son went to her side. Under the fence, in a little bed, was a ravel of poor grassy leaves, such as come from very immature bulbs, and three scyllas in bloom. Mrs Morel pointed to the deep blue flowers.

'Now, just see those!' she exclaimed. 'I was looking at the currant-bushes, when, thinks I to myself, "There's something very blue; is it a bit of sugar-bag?" and there, behold you! Sugar-bag! Three glories of the snow, and *such* beauties! But where on earth did they come from?'

'I don't know,' said Paul.

'Well, that's a marvel, now! I *thought* I knew every weed and blade in this garden. But *haven't* they done well? You see, that gooseberry-bush just shelters them. Not nipped, not touched!'

He crouched down and turned up the bells of the little blue flowers.

'They're a glorious colour!' he said.

'Aren't they!' she cried. 'I guess they come from Switzerland, where they say they have such lovely things. Fancy them against the snow! But where have they come from? They can't have *blown* here, can they?'

Then he remembered having set here a lot of little trash of bulbs to mature.

'And you never told me,' she said.

'No; I thought I'd leave it till they might flower.'

'And now, you see! I might have missed them. And I've never had a glory of the snow in my garden in my life.'

She was full of excitement and elation. The garden was an endless joy to her. Paul was thankful for her sake at last to be in a house with a long garden that went down to a field. Every morning after breakfast she went out and was happy pottering about in it. And it was true, she knew every weed and blade.

Everybody turned up for the walk. Food was packed, and they set off, a merry, delighted party. They hung over the wall of the mill-race, dropped paper in the water on one side of the tunnel and watched it shoot out on the other. They stood on the footbridge over Boathouse Station and looked at the metals gleaming coldly.

'You should see the Flying Scotchman come through at half-past six!' said Leonard, whose father was a signalman. 'Lad, but she doesn't half buzz!' and the little party looked up the lines one way, to London, and the other way, to Scotland, and they felt the touch of these two magical places.

In Ilkeston the colliers were waiting in gangs for the public-houses to open. It was a town of idleness and lounging. At Stanton Gate the iron foundry blazed. Over everything there was great discussions. At Trowell they crossed again from Derbyshire into Nottinghamshire. They came to the Hemlock Stone at dinner-time. Its field was crowded with folk from Nottingham and Ilkeston.

They had expected a venerable and dignified monument. They found a little, gnarled, twisted stump of rock, something like a decayed mushroom, standing out pathetically on the side of a field. Leonard and Dick immediately proceeded to carve their initials, 'L. W.' and 'R. P.', in the old red sandstone; but Paul desisted, because he had read in the newspaper satirical remarks about initial-carvers, who could find no other road to immortality. Then all the lads climbed to the top of the rock to look round.

Everywhere in the field below, factory girls and lads were eating lunch or sporting about. Beyond was the garden of an old manor. It had yew-hedges and thick clumps and borders of yellow crocuses round the lawn.

'See,' said Paul to Miriam, 'what a quiet garden!'

She saw the dark yews and the golden crocuses, then she looked at him gratefully. He had not seemed to belong to her among all these others; he was different then – not her Paul, who understood the slightest quiver of her innermost soul, but something else speaking another language than hers. How it hurt her, and deadened her very perceptions. Only when he came right back to her, leaving his other, his lesser self, as she thought, would she feel alive again. And now he asked her to look at this garden, wanting the contact with her again. Impatient of the set in the field, she turned to the quiet lawn, surrounded by sheaves of shut-up crocuses. A feeling of stillness, almost of ecstasy, came over her. It felt almost as if she were alone with him in this garden.

Then he left her again and joined the others. Soon they started home. Miriam loitered behind, alone. She did not fit in with the others; she could very rarely get into human relations with anyone: so her friend, her companion, her lover, was Nature. She saw the sun declining wanly. In the dusky, cold hedgerows were some red leaves. She lingered to gather them, tenderly, passionately. The love in her finger-tips caressed the leaves; the passion in her heart came to a glow upon the leaves.

Suddenly she realized she was alone in a strange road, and she hurried forward. Turning a corner in the lane, she came upon Paul, who stood bent over something, his mind fixed on it, working away steadily, patiently, a little hopelessly. She hesitated in her approach, to watch.

He remained concentrated in the middle of the road. Beyond, one rift of rich gold in that colourless grey evening seemed to make him stand out in dark relief. She saw him, slender and firm, as if the setting sun had given him to her. A deep pain took hold of her, and she knew she must love him. And she had discovered him, discovered in him a rare potentiality, discovered his loneliness. Quivering as at some 'annunciation', she went slowly forward.

At last he looked up.

'Why,' he exclaimed gratefully, 'have you waited for me!'

She saw a deep shadow in his eyes.

'What is it?' she asked.

'The spring's broken here'; and he showed her where his umbrella was injured.

Instantly, with some shame, she knew he had not done the damage himself, but that Geoffrey was responsible.

'It is only an old umbrella isn't it?' she asked.

She wondered why he, who did not usually trouble over trifles, made such a mountain of this molehill.

'But it was William's, an' my mother can't help but know,' he said quietly, still patiently working the umbrella.

The words went through Miriam like a blade. This, then, was the confirmation of her vision of him! She looked at him. But there was about him a certain reserve, and she dared not comfort him, not even speak softly to him.

'Come on,' he said. 'I can't do it'; and they went in silence along the road.

That same evening they were walking along under the trees by Nether Green. He was talking to her fretfully, seemed to be struggling to convince himself.

'You know,' he said, with an effort, 'if one person loves, the other does.'

'Ah!' she answered. 'Like mother said to me when I was little, "Love begets love."'

'Yes, something like that, I think it *must* be.'

'I hope so, because if it were not, love might be a very terrible thing,' she said.

'Yes, but it *is* – at least with most people,' he answered.

And Miriam, thinking he had assured himself, felt strong in herself. She always regarded that sudden coming upon him in the lane as a revelation. And this conversation remained graven in her mind as one of the letters of the law.

Now she stood with him and for him. When, about this time, he outraged the family feeling at Willey Farm by some overbearing insult, she stuck to him, and believed he was right. And at this time she dreamed dreams of him, vivid, unforgettable. These dreams came again later on, developed to a more subtle psychological stage.

On the Easter Monday the same party took an excursion to Wingfield Manor. It was great excitement to Miriam to catch a train at Sethley Bridge, amid all the bustle of the Bank Holiday crowd. They left the train at Alfreton. Paul was interested in the street and in the colliers with their dogs. Here was a new race of miners. Miriam did not live till they came to the church. They were all rather timid of entering, with their bags of food, for fear of being turned out. Leonard, a comic, thin fellow, went first; Paul, who would have died rather than be sent back, went last. The place was decorated for Easter. In the font hundreds of white narcissi seemed to be growing. The air was dim and coloured from the windows, and thrilled with a subtle scent of lilies and narcissi. In that atmosphere Miriam's soul came into a glow. Paul was afraid of the things he mustn't do; and he was sensitive to the feel of the place. Miriam turned to him. He answered. They were together. He would not go beyond the Communion-rail. She loved him for that. Her soul expanded into prayer beside him. He felt the strange fascination of shadowy religious places. All his latent mysticism quivered into life. She was drawn to him. He was a prayer along with her.

Miriam very rarely talked to the other lads. They at once became awkward in conversation with her. So usually she was silent.

It was past midday when they climbed the steep path to the manor. All things shone softly in the sun, which was wonderfully warm and enlivening. Celandines and violets were out. Everybody was tip-top full with happiness. The glitter of the ivy, the soft, atmospheric grey of the castle walls, the gentleness of everything near the ruin, was perfect.

The manor is of hard, pale grey stone, and the outer walls are blank and calm. The younger folk were in raptures. They went in trepidation, almost afraid that the delight of exploring this ruin might be denied them. In the first courtyard, within the high broken walls, were farm-carts, with their shafts lying idle on the ground, the tyres of the wheels brilliant with gold-red rust. It was very still.

All eagerly paid their sixpences, and went timidly through the fine clean arch of the inner courtyard. They were shy. Here on the pavement, where the hall had been, an old thorn-tree was budding. All kinds of strange openings and broken rooms were in the shadow around them.

After lunch they set off once more to explore the ruin. This time the girls went with the boys, who could act as guides and expositors. There was one tall tower in a corner, rather tottering, where they say Mary Queen of Scots was imprisoned.

'Think of the Queen going up here!' said Miriam in a low voice, as she climbed the hollow stairs.

'If she could get up,' said Paul, 'for she had rheumatism like anything. I reckon they treated her rottenly.'

'You don't think she deserved it?' asked Miriam.

'No, I don't. She was only lively.'

They continued to mount the winding staircase. A high wind, blowing through the loopholes, went rushing up the shaft, and filled the girl's skirts like a balloon, so that she was ashamed, until he took the hem of her dress and held it down for her. He did it perfectly simply, as he would have picked up her glove. She remembered this always.

Round the broken top of the tower the ivy bushed out, old and handsome. Also, there were a few chill gillivers, in pale cold bud. Miriam wanted to lean over for some ivy, but he would not let her. Instead, she had to wait behind him, and take from him each spray as he gathered it and held it to her, each one separately, in the purest manner of chivalry. The tower seemed to rock in the wind. They looked over miles and miles of wooded country, and country with gleams of pasture.

The crypt underneath the manor was beautiful, and in perfect preservation. Paul made a drawing: Miriam stayed with him. She was thinking of Mary Queen of Scots looking with her strained, hopeless eyes, that could not understand misery, over the hills whence no help came, or sitting in this crypt, being told of a God as cold as the place she sat in.

They set off again gaily, looking round on their beloved manor that stood so clean and big on its hill.

'Supposing you could have *that* farm,' said Paul to Miriam.

'Yes!'

'Wouldn't it be lovely to come and see you!'

They were now in the bare country of stone walls, which he loved, and which, though only ten miles from home, seemed so foreign to Miriam. The party was straggling. As they were crossing a large meadow that sloped away from the sun, along a path embedded with innumerable tiny glittering points, Paul, walking alongside, laced his fingers in the strings of the bag Miriam was carrying, and instantly she felt Annie behind, watchful and jealous. But the meadow was bathed in a glory of sunshine, and the path was jewelled, and it was seldom that he gave her any sign. She held her fingers very still among the strings of the bag, his fingers touching; and the place was golden as a vision.

At last they came into the straggling grey village of Crich, that lies high. Beyond the village was the famous Crich Stand that Paul could see from the garden at home. The party pushed on. Great expanse of country spread around and below. The lads were eager to get to the top of the hill. It was capped by a round knoll, half of which was by now cut away, and on the top of which stood an ancient monument, sturdy and squat, for signalling in old days far down into the level lands of Nottinghamshire and Leicestershire.

It was blowing so hard, high up there in the exposed place, that the only way to be safe was to stand nailed by the wind to the wall of the tower. At their feet fell the precipice where the limestone was quarried away. Below was a jumble of hills and tiny villages – Matlock, Ambergate, Stoney Middleton. The lads were eager to spy out the church of Bestwood, far away among the rather crowded country on the left. They were disgusted that it seemed to stand on a plane. They saw the hills of Derbyshire fall into the monotony of the Midlands that swept away South.

Miriam was somewhat scared by the wind, but the lads enjoyed it. They went on, miles and miles, to Whatstandwell. All the food was eaten, everybody was hungry, and there was very little money to get home with. But they managed to procure a loaf and a currant-loaf, which they hacked into pieces with shut-knives, and ate sitting on the wall near the bridge, watching the bright Derwent rushing by, and the brakes from Matlock pulling up at the inn.

Paul was now pale with weariness. He had been responsible for the party all day, and now he was done. Miriam understood, and kept close to him, and he left himself in her hands.

They had an hour to wait at Ambergate Station. Trains came, crowded with excursionists returning to Manchester, Birmingham and London.

'We might be going there – folk easily might think we're going that far,' said Paul.

They got back rather late. Miriam, walking home with Geoffrey, watched the moon rise big and red and misty. She felt something was fulfilled in her.

She had an elder sister, Agatha, who was a school-teacher. Between the two girls was a feud. Miriam considered Agatha worldly. And she wanted herself to be a school-teacher.

One Saturday afternoon Agatha and Miriam were upstairs dressing. Their bedroom was over the stable. It was a low room, not very large, and bare. Miriam had nailed on the wall a reproduction of Veronese's 'St Catherine'. She loved the woman who sat in the window, dreaming. Her own windows were too small to sit in. But the front one was dripped over with honeysuckle and virginia creeper, and looked upon the tree-tops of the oak-wood across the yard, while the little back window, no bigger than a handkerchief, was a loophole to the east, to the dawn beating up against the beloved round hills.

The two sisters did not talk much to each other. Agatha, who was fair and small and determined, had rebelled against the home atmosphere, against the doctrine of 'the other cheek'. She was out in the world now, in a fair way to be independent. And she insisted on worldly values, on appearance, on manners, on position, which Miriam would fain have ignored.

Both girls liked to be upstairs, out of the way, when Paul came. They preferred to come running down, open the stair-foot door, and see him watching, expectant of them. Miriam stood painfully pulling over her head a rosary he had given her. It caught in the fine mesh of her hair. But at last she had it on, and the red-brown wooden beads looked well against her cool brown neck. She was a well-developed girl, and very handsome. But in the little looking-glass nailed against the whitewashed wall she could only see a fragment of herself at a time. Agatha had bought a little mirror of her own which she propped up to suit herself. Miriam was near the window. Suddenly she heard the well-known click of the chain, and she saw Paul fling open the gate, push his bicycle into the yard. She saw him look at the house, and she shrank away. He walked in a nonchalant fashion, and his bicycle went with him as if it were a live thing.

'Paul's come!' she exclaimed.

'Aren't you glad?' said Agatha cuttingly.

Miriam stood still in amazement and bewilderment.

'Well, aren't you?' she asked.

'Yes, but I'm not going to let him see it, and think I wanted him.'

Miriam was startled. She heard him putting his bicycle in the stable underneath, and talking to Jimmy, who had been a pit-horse and who was seedy.

'Well, Jimmy my lad, how are ter? Nobbut sick an' sadly, like? Why, then, it's a shame, my owd lad.'

She heard the rope run through the hole as the horse lifted its head from the lad's caress. How she loved to listen when he thought only the horse could hear. But there was a serpent in her Eden. She searched earnestly in herself to see if she wanted Paul Morel. She felt there would be some disgrace in it. Full of twisted feeling, she was afraid she did want him. She stood self-convicted. Then came an agony of new shame. She shrank within herself in a coil of torture. Did she want Paul Morel, and did he know she wanted him? What a subtle infamy upon her! She felt as if her whole soul coiled into knots of shame.

Agatha was dressed first, and ran downstairs. Miriam heard her greet the lad gaily, knew exactly how brilliant her grey eyes became with that tone. She herself would have felt it bold to have greeted him in such wise. Yet there she stood under the self-accusation of wanting him, tied to that stake of torture. In bitter perplexity she knelt down and prayed:

'O Lord, let me not love Paul Morel. Keep me from loving him, if I ought not to love him.'

Something anomalous in the prayer arrested her. She lifted her head and pondered. How could it be wrong to love him? Love was God's gift. And yet it caused her shame. That was because of him, Paul Morel. But then, it was not his affair, it was her own, between herself and God. She was to be a sacrifice. But it was God's sacrifice, not Paul Morel's or her own. After a few minutes she hid her face in the pillow again, and said:

'But, Lord, if it is Thy will that I should love him, make me love him – as Christ would, who died for the souls of men. Make me love him splendidly, because he is Thy son.'

She remained kneeling for some time, quite still, and deeply moved, her black hair against the red squares and the lavender-sprigged squares of the patchwork-quilt. Prayer was almost essential to her. Then she fell into that rapture of self-sacrifice, identifying herself with a God who was sacrificed, which gives to so many human souls their deepest bliss.

When she went downstairs Paul was lying back in an armchair, holding forth with much vehemence to Agatha, who was scorning a little painting he had brought to show her. Miriam glanced at the two, and avoided their levity. She went into the parlour to be alone.

It was tea-time before she was able to speak to Paul, and then her manner was so distant he thought he had offended her.

Miriam discontinued her practice of going each Thursday evening to the library in Bestwood. After calling for Paul regularly during the whole spring, a number of trifling incidents and tiny insults from his family awakened her to their attitude towards her, and she decided to go no more. So she announced to Paul one evening she would not call at his house again for him on Thursday nights.

'Why?' he asked, very short.

'Nothing. Only I'd rather not.'

'Very well.'

'But,' she faltered, 'if you'd care to meet me, we could still go together.'

'Meet you where?'

'Somewhere – where you like.'

'I shan't meet you anywhere. I don't see why you shouldn't keep calling for me. But if you won't, I don't want to meet you.'

So the Thursday evenings which had been so precious to her, and to him, were dropped. He worked instead. Mrs Morel sniffed with satisfaction at this arrangement.

He would not have it that they were lovers. The intimacy between them had been kept so abstract, such a matter of the soul, all thought and weary struggle into consciousness, that he saw it only as a platonic friendship. He stoutly denied there was anything else between them. Miriam was silent, or else she very quietly agreed. He was a fool who did not know what was happening to himself; by tacit agreement they ignored the remarks and insinuations of their acquaintances.

'We aren't lovers, we are friends,' he said to her. '*We* know it. Let them talk. What does it matter what they say?'

Sometimes, as they were walking together, she slipped her arm timidly into his. But he always resented it, and she knew it. It caused a violent conflict in him. With Miriam he was always on the high plane of abstraction, when his natural fire of love was transmitted into the fine stream of thought. She would have it so. If he were jolly and, as she put it, flippant, she waited till he came back to her, till the change had taken place in him again, and he was wrestling with his own soul, frowning, passionate in his desire for understanding. And in this passion for understanding her soul lay close to his; she had him all to herself. But he must be made abstract first.

Then, if she put her arm in his, it caused him almost torture. His consciousness seemed to split. The place where she was touching him ran hot with friction. He was one internecine battle, and he became cruel to her because of it.

One evening in midsummer Miriam called at the house, warm from climbing. Paul was alone in the kitchen; his mother could be heard moving about upstairs.

'Come and look at the sweet-peas,' he said to the girl.

They went into the garden. The sky behind the townlet and the church was orange-red; the flower-garden was flooded with a strange warm light that lifted every leaf into significance. Paul passed along a fine row of sweet-peas, gathering a blossom here and there, all cream and pale blue. Miriam followed, breathing the fragrance. To her, flowers appeared with such strength she felt she must make them part of herself. When she bent and breathed a flower, it was as if she and the flower were loving each other. Paul hated her for it. There seemed a sort of exposure about the action, something too intimate.

When he had got a fair bunch, they returned to the house. He listened for a moment to his mother's quiet movements upstairs, then he said:

'Come here, and let me pin them in for you.' He arranged them two or three at a time in the bosom of her dress, stepping back now and then to see the effect. 'You know,' he said, taking the pin out of his mouth, 'a woman ought always to arrange her flowers before her glass.'

Miriam laughed. She thought flowers ought to be pinned in one's dress without any care. That Paul should take pains to fix her flowers for her was his whim.

He was rather offended at her laughter.

'Some women do – those who look decent,' he said.

Miriam laughed again, but mirthlessly, to hear him thus mix her up with women in a general way. From most men she would have ignored it. But from him it hurt her.

He had nearly finished arranging the flowers when he heard his mother's footsteps on the stairs. Hurriedly he pushed in the last pin and turned away.

'Don't let mater know,' he said.

Miriam picked up her books and stood in the doorway looking with chagrin at the beautiful sunset. She would call for Paul no more, she said.

'Good evening, Mrs Morel,' she said, in a deferential way. She sounded as if she had no right to be there.

'Oh, is it you, Miriam?' replied Mrs Morel coolly.

But Paul insisted on everybody's accepting his friendship with the girl, and Mrs Morel was too wise to have any open rupture.

It was not till he was twenty years old that the family could ever afford to go away for a holiday. Mrs Morel had never been away for a holiday, except to see her sister, since she had been married. Now at last Paul had saved enough money, and they were all going. There was to be a party: some of Annie's friends, one friend of Paul's, a young man in the same office where William had previously been, and Miriam.

It was great excitement writing for rooms. Paul and his mother debated it endlessly between them. They wanted a furnished cottage for two weeks. She thought one week would be enough, but he insisted on two.

At last they got an answer from Mablethorpe, a cottage such as they wished for thirty shillings a week. There was immense jubilation. Paul was wild with joy for his mother's sake. She would have a real holiday now. He and she sat at evening picturing what it would be like. Annie came in, and Leonard, and Alice, and Kitty. There was wild rejoicing and anticipation. Paul told Miriam. She seemed to brood with joy over it. But the Morels' house rang with excitement.

They were to go on Saturday morning by the seven train. Paul suggested that Miriam should sleep at his house, because it was so far for her to walk. She came down for supper. Everybody was so excited that even Miriam was accepted with warmth. But almost as soon as she entered the feeling in the family became close and tight. He had discovered a poem by Jean Ingelow which mentioned Mablethorpe, and so he must read it to Miriam. He would never have got so far in the direction of sentimentality as to read poetry to his own family. But now they condescended to listen. Miriam sat on the sofa absorbed in him. She always seemed absorbed in him, and by him, when he was present. Mrs Morel sat jealously on her own chair. She was going to hear also. And even Annie, and the father attended, Morel with his head cocked on one side like somebody listening to a sermon and feeling conscious of the fact. Paul ducked his head over the book. He had got now all the audience he cared for. And Mrs Morel and Annie almost contested with Miriam who should listen best and win his favour. He was in very high feather.

'But,' interrupted Mrs Morel, 'what *is* the "Bride of Enderby" that the bells are supposed to ring?'

'It's an old tune they used to play on the fells for a warning against water. I suppose the Bride of Enderby was drowned in a flood,' he replied. He had not the faintest knowledge what it really was, but would never have sunk so low as to confess that to his womenfolk. They listened and believed him. He believed himself.

'And the people knew what that tune meant?' said his mother.

'Yes, just like the Scotch when they heard "The Flowers o' the Forest" – and when they used to ring the bells backward for alarm.'

'How?' said Annie. 'A bell sounds the same whether it's rung backwards or forwards.'

'But,' he said, 'if you start with the deep bell and ring up to the high one – der – der – der – der – der – der – der – der!'

He ran up the scale. Everybody thought it clever. He thought so too. Then, waiting a minute, he continued the poem.

'H'm!' said Mrs Morel curiously, when he finished. 'But I wish everything that's written weren't so sad.'

'*I* canna see what they want drownin' theirselves for,' said Morel.

There was a pause. Annie got up to clear the table.

Miriam rose to help with the pots.

'Let *me* help to wash up,' she said.

'Certainly not,' cried Annie. 'You sit down again. There aren't many.'

And Miriam, who could not be familiar and insist, sat down again to look at the book with Paul.

He was master of the party; his father was no good. And great tortures he suffered lest the tin box should be put out at Firsby instead of at Mablethorpe. And he wasn't equal to getting a carriage. His bold little mother did that.

'Here!' she cried to a man. 'Here!'

Paul and Annie got behind the rest, convulsed with shamed laughter.

'How much will it be to drive to Brook Cottage?' said Mrs Morel.

'Two shillings.'

'Why, how far is it?'

'A good way.'

'I don't believe it,' she said.

But she scrambled in. There were eight crowded in one old seaside carriage.

'You see,' said Mrs Morel, 'it's only threepence each, and if it were a tram car –'

They drove along. Each cottage they came to, Mrs Morel cried:

'Is it this? Now, this is it!'

Everybody sat breathless. They drove past. There was a universal sigh.

'I'm thankful it wasn't that brute,' said Mrs Morel. 'I *was* frightened.' They drove on and on.

At last they descended at a house that stood alone over the dyke by the highroad. There was wild excitement because they had to cross a little bridge to get into the front garden. But they loved the house that lay so solitary, with a sea-meadow on one side, and immense expanse of land patched in white barley, yellow oats, red wheat, and green root-crops, flat and stretching level to the sky.

Paul kept accounts. He and his mother ran the show. The total expenses – lodging, food, everything – was sixteen shillings a week per person. He and Leonard went bathing in the morning. Morel was wandering abroad quite early.

'You, Paul,' his mother called from the bedroom, 'eat a piece of bread-and-butter.'

'All right,' he answered.

And when he got back he saw his mother presiding in state at the breakfast-table. The woman of the house was young. Her husband was blind, and she did laundry work. So Mrs Morel always washed the pots in the kitchen and made the beds.

'But you said you'd have a real holiday,' said Paul, 'and now you work.'

'Work!' she exclaimed. 'What are you talking about!'

He loved to go with her across the fields to the village and the sea. She was afraid of the plank bridges, and he abused her for being a baby. On the whole he stuck to her if he were *her* man.

Miriam did not get much of him, except, perhaps, when all the others went to the 'Coons'. Coons were insufferably stupid to Miriam, so he thought they were to himself also, and he preached priggishly to Annie about the fatuity of listening to them. Yet he, too, knew all their songs, and sang them along the roads roisterously. And if he found himself listening, the stupidity pleased him very much. Yet to Annie he said:

'Such rot! there isn't a grain of intelligence in it. Nobody with more gumption than a grasshopper could go and sit and listen.' And to Miriam he said, with much scorn of Annie and the others: 'I suppose they're at the "Coons".'

It was queer to see Miriam singing coon songs. She had a straight chin that went in a perpendicular line from the lower lip to the turn. She always reminded Paul of some sad Botticelli angel when she sang, even when it was:

> 'Come down lover's lane
> For a walk with me, talk with me.'

Only when he sketched, or at evening when the others were at the 'Coons', she had him to herself. He talked to her endlessly about his love of horizontals: how they, the great levels of sky and land in Lincolnshire, meant to him the eternality of the will, just as the bowed Norman arches of the church, repeating themselves, meant the dogged leaping forward of the persistent human soul, on and on, nobody knows where; in contradiction to the perpendicular lines and to the Gothic arch, which, he said, leapt up at heaven and touched the ecstasy and lost itself in the divine. Himself, he said, was Norman, Miriam was Gothic. She bowed in consent even to that.

One evening he and she went up the great sweeping shore of sand towards Theddlethorpe. The long breakers plunged and ran in a hiss of foam along the coast. It was a warm evening. There was not a figure but themselves on the far reaches of sand, no noise but the sound of the sea. Paul loved to see it clanging at the land. He loved to feel himself between the noise of it and the silence of the sandy shore. Miriam was with him. Everything grew very intense. It was quite dark when they turned again. The way home was through a gap in the sandhills, and then along a raised grass road between two dykes. The country was black and still. From behind the sandhills came the whisper of the sea. Paul and Miriam walked in silence. Suddenly he started. The whole of his blood seemed to burst into flame, and he could scarcely breathe. An enormous orange moon was staring at them from the rim of the sandhills. He stood still, looking at it.

'Ah!' cried Miriam, when she saw it.

He remained perfectly still, staring at the immense and ruddy moon, the only thing in the far-reaching darkness of the level. His heart beat heavily, the muscles of his arms contracted.

'What is it?' murmured Miriam, waiting for him.

He turned and looked at her. She stood beside him, for ever in shadow. Her face, covered with the darkness of her hat, was watching him unseen. But she was brooding. She was slightly afraid – deeply moved and religious. That was her best state. He was impotent against it. His blood was concentrated like a flame in his chest. But he could not get across to her. There were flashes in his blood. But somehow she ignored them. She was expecting some religious state in him. Still yearning she was half aware of his passion, and gazed at him, troubled.

'What is it?' she murmured again.

'It's the moon,' he answered, frowning.

'Yes,' she assented. 'Isn't it wonderful?' She was curious about him. The crisis was past.

He did not know himself what was the matter. He was naturally so young, and their intimacy was so abstract, he did not know he wanted to crush her to on his breast to ease the ache there. He was afraid of her. The fact that he might want her as a man wants a woman had in him been suppressed into a shame. When she shrank in her convulsed, coiled torture from the thought of such a thing, he had winced to the depths of his soul. And now this 'purity' prevented even their first love-kiss. It was as if she could scarcely stand the shock of physical love, even a passionate kiss, and then he was too shrinking and sensitive to give it.

As they walked along the dark fen-meadow he watched the moon and did not speak. She plodded beside him. He hated her, for she seemed in some way to make him despise himself. Looking ahead – he saw the one light in the darkness, the window of their lamp-lit cottage.

He loved to think of his mother, and the other jolly people.

'Well, everybody else has been in long ago!' said his mother as they entered.

'What does that matter!' he cried irritably. 'I can go a walk if I like, can't I?'

'And I should have thought you could get in to supper with the rest,' said Mrs Morel.

'I shall please myself,' he retorted. 'It's not *late*. I shall do as I like.'

'Very well,' said his mother cuttingly, 'then *do* as you like.'

And she took no further notice of him that evening. Which he pretended neither to notice nor to care about, but sat reading. Miriam read also, obliterating herself. Mrs Morel hated her for making her son like this. She watched Paul growing irritable, priggish, and melancholic. For this she put the blame on Miriam. Annie and all her friends joined against the girl. Miriam had no friend of her own, only Paul. But she did not suffer so much, because she despised the triviality of these other people.

And Paul hated her because, somehow, she spoilt his ease and naturalness. And he writhed himself with a feeling of humiliation.

8

STRIFE IN LOVE

Arthur finished his apprenticeship, and got a job on the electrical plant at Minton Pit. He earned very little, but had a good chance of getting on. But he was wild and restless. He did not drink nor gamble. Yet he somehow contrived to get into endless scrapes, always through some hot-headed thoughtlessness. Either he went rabbiting in the woods, like a poacher, or he stayed in Nottingham all night instead of coming home, or he miscalculated his dive into the canal at Bestwood, and scored his chest into one mass of wounds on the raw stones and tins at the bottom.

He had not been at his work many months when again he did not come home one night.

'Do you know where Arthur is?' asked Paul at breakfast.

'I do not,' replied his mother.

'He is a fool,' said Paul. 'And if he *did* anything I shouldn't mind. But no, he simply can't come away from a game of whist, or else he must see a girl home from the skating-rink – quite proprietously – and so can't get home. He's a fool.'

'I don't know that it would make it any better if he did something to make us all ashamed,' said Mrs Morel.

'Well, *I* should respect him more,' said Paul.

'I very much doubt it,' said his mother coldly.

They went on with breakfast.

'Are you fearfully fond of him?' Paul asked his mother.

'What do you ask that for?'

'Because they say a woman always likes the youngest best.'

'She may do – but I don't. No, he wearies me.'

'And you'd actually rather he was good?'

'I'd rather he showed some of a man's common sense.'

Paul was raw and irritable. He also wearied his mother very often. She saw the sunshine going out of him, and she resented it.

As they were finishing breakfast came the postman with a letter from Derby. Mrs Morel screwed up her eyes to look at the address.

'Give it here, blind eye!' exclaimed her son, snatching it away from her.

She started, and almost boxed his ears.

'It's from your son, Arthur,' he said.

'What now –!' cried Mrs Morel.

'"My dearest Mother,"' Paul read, '"I don't know what made me such a fool. I want you to come and fetch me back from here. I came with Jack Bredon yesterday, instead of going to work, and enlisted. He said he was sick of wearing the seat of a stool out, and, like the idiot you know I am, I came away with him.

'"I have taken the King's shilling, but perhaps if you came for me they would let me go back with you, I was a fool when I did it. I don't want to be in the army. My dear mother, I am nothing but a trouble to you. But if you get me out of this, I promise I will have more sense and consideration..."'

Mrs Morel sat down in her rocking-chair.

'Well, *now*,' she cried, 'let him stop!'

'Yes,' said Paul, 'let him stop.'

There was silence. The mother sat with her hands folded in her apron, her face set, thinking.

'If I'm not *sick*!' she cried suddenly. 'Sick!'

'Now,' said Paul, beginning to frown, 'you're not going to worry your soul out about this, do you hear.'

'I suppose I'm to take it as a blessing,' she flashed, turning on her son.

'You're not going to mount it up to a tragedy, so there,' he retorted.

'The *fool*! – the young fool!' she cried.

'He'll look well in uniform,' said Paul irritatingly.

His mother turned on him like a fury.

'Oh, will he!' she cried. 'Not in my eyes!'

'He should get in a cavalry regiment; he'll have the time of his life, and will look an awful swell.'

'Swell – *swell*! – a mighty swell indeed! – a common soldier!'

'Well,' said Paul, 'what am I but a common clerk?'

'A good deal, my boy!' cried his mother, stung.

'What?'

'At any rate, a *man*, and not a thing in a red coat.'

'I shouldn't mind being in a red coat – or dark blue, that would suit me better – if they didn't boss me about too much.'

But his mother had ceased to listen.

'Just as he was getting on, or might have been getting on, at his job – a young nuisance – here he goes and ruins himself for life. What good will he be, do you think, after *this*?'

'It may lick him into shape beautifully,' said Paul.

'Lick him into shape! – lick what marrow there *was* out of his bones. A *soldier*! – a common *soldier*! – nothing but a body that makes movements when it hears a shout! It's a fine thing!'

'I can't understand why it upsets you,' said Paul.

'No, perhaps you can't. But *I* understand'; and she sat back in her chair, her chin in one hand, holding her elbow with the other, brimmed up with wrath and chagrin.

'And shall you go to Derby?' asked Paul.

'Yes.'

'It's no good.'

'I'll see for myself.'

'And why on earth don't you let him stop? It's just what he wants.'

'Of course,' cried the mother, '*you* know what he wants!'

She got ready and went by the first train to Derby, where she saw her son and the sergeant. It was, however, no good.

When Morel was having his dinner in the evening, she said suddenly:

'I've had to go to Derby today.'

The miner turned up his eyes, showing the whites in his black face.

'Has ter, lass. What took thee there?'

'That Arthur!'

'Oh – an' what's agate now?'

'He's only enlisted.'

Morel put down his knife and leaned back in his chair.

'Nay,' he said, 'that he niver 'as!'

'And is going down to Aldershot tomorrow.'

'Well!' exclaimed the miner. 'That's a winder.' He considered it a moment, said 'H'm!' and proceeded with his dinner. Suddenly his face contracted with wrath. 'I hope he may never set foot i' my house again,' he said.

'The idea!' cried Mrs Morel. 'Saying such a thing!'

'I do,' repeated Morel. 'A fool as runs away for a soldier let 'im look after 'issen; I s'll do no more for 'im.'

'A fat sight you have done as it is,' she said.

And Morel was almost ashamed to go to his public-house that evening.

'Well, did you go?' said Paul to his mother when he came home.

'I did.'

'And could you see him?'

'Yes.'

'And what did he say?'

'He blubbered when I came away.'

'H'm!'

'And so did I, so you needn't "h'm!"'

Mrs Morel fretted after her son. She knew he would not like the army. He did not. The discipline was intolerable to him.

'But the doctor,' she said with some pride to Paul, 'said he was perfectly proportioned – almost exactly: all his measurements were correct. He *is* good-looking, you know.'

'He's awfully nice-looking. But he doesn't fetch the girls like William, does he?'

'No; it's a different character. He's a good deal like his father, irresponsible.'

To console his mother, Paul did not go much to Willey Farm at this time. And in the autumn exhibition of students' work in the Castle he had two studies, a landscape in water-colour and a still life in oil, both of which had first-prize awards. He was highly excited.

'What do you think I've got for my pictures, mother?' he asked, coming home one evening. She saw by his eyes he was glad. Her face flushed.

'Now, how should I know, my boy!'

'A first prize for those glass jars –'

'H'm!'

'And a first prize for that sketch up at Willey Farm.'

'Both first?'

'Yes.'

'H'm!'

There was a rosy, bright look about her, though she said nothing.

'It's nice,' he said, 'isn't it?'

'It is.'

'Why don't you praise me up to the skies?'

She laughed.

'I should have the trouble of dragging you down again,' she said.

But she was full of joy, nevertheless. William had brought her his sporting trophies. She kept them still, and she did not forgive his death. Arthur was handsome – at least, a good specimen – and warm and generous, and probably would do well in the end. But Paul was going to distinguish himself. She had a great belief in him, the more because he was unaware of his own powers. There was so much to come out of him. Life for her was rich with promise. She was to see herself fulfilled. Not for nothing had been her struggle.

Several times during the exhibition Mrs Morel went to the Castle unknown to Paul. She wandered down the long room looking at the other exhibits. Yes, they were good. But they had not in them a certain something which she demanded for her satisfaction. Some made her jealous, they were so good. She looked at them a long time trying to find fault with them. Then suddenly she had a shock that made her heart beat. There hung Paul's picture! She knew it as if it were printed on her heart.

'Name – Paul Morel – First Prize.'

It looked so strange, there in public, on the walls of the Castle gallery, where in her lifetime she had seen so many pictures. And she glanced round to see if anyone had noticed her again in front of the same sketch.

But she felt a proud woman. When she met well-dressed ladies going home to the Park, she thought to herself:

'Yes, you look very well – but I wonder if *your* son has two first prizes in the Castle.'

And she walked on, as proud a little woman as any in Nottingham. And Paul felt he had done something for her, if only a trifle. All his work was hers.

One day, as he was going up Castle Gate, he met Miriam. He had seen her on the Sunday, and had not expected to meet her in town. She was walking with a rather striking woman, blonde, with a sullen expression, and a defiant carriage. It was strange how Miriam in her bowed, meditative bearing, looked dwarfed beside this woman with the handsome shoulders. Miriam watched Paul searchingly. His gaze was on the stranger, who ignored him. The girl saw his masculine spirit rear its head.

'Hello!' he said, 'you didn't tell me you were coming to town.'

'No,' replied Miriam, half apologetically. 'I drove in to Cattle Market with father.'

He looked at her companion.

'I've told you about Mrs Dawes,' said Miriam huskily; she was nervous. 'Clara, do you know Paul?'

'I think I've seen him before,' replied Mrs Dawes indifferently, as she shook hands with him. She had scornful grey eyes, a skin like white honey, and a full mouth, with a slightly lifted upper lip that did not know whether it was raised in scorn of all men or out of eagerness to be kissed, but which believed the former. She carried her head back, as if she had drawn away in contempt, perhaps from men also. She wore a large, dowdy hat of black beaver, and a sort of slightly affected simple dress that made her look rather sack-like. She was evidently poor, and had not much taste. Miriam usually looked nice.

'Where have you seen me?' Paul asked of the woman.

She looked at him as if she would not trouble to answer. Then:

'Walking with Louie Travers,' she said.

Louie was one of the 'spiral' girls.

'Why, do you know her?' he asked.

She did not answer. He turned to Miriam.

'Where are you going?' he asked.

'To the Castle.'

'What train are you going home by?'

'I am driving with father. I wish you could come too. What time are you free?'

'You know not till eight tonight, damn it!'

And directly the two women moved on.

Paul remembered that Clara Dawes was the daughter of an old friend of Mrs Leivers. Miriam had sought her out because she had once been spiral overseer at Jordan's, and because her husband, Baxter Dawes, was smith for the factory, making the irons for cripple instruments, and so on. Through her Miriam felt she got into direct contact with Jordan's, and could estimate better Paul's position. But Mrs Dawes was separated from her husband, and had taken up Women's Rights. She was supposed to be clever. It interested Paul.

Baxter Dawes he knew and disliked. The smith was a man of thirty-one or thirty-two. He came occasionally through Paul's corner – a big, well-set man, also striking to look at, and handsome. There was a peculiar similarity between himself and his wife. He had the same white skin, with a clear, golden tinge. His hair was of soft brown, his moustache was golden. And he had a similar defiance in his bearing and manner. But then came the difference. His eyes, dark brown and quick-shifting, were dissolute. They protruded very slightly, and his eyelids hung over them in a way that was half hate. His mouth, too, was sensual. His whole manner was of cowed defiance, as if he were ready to knock anybody down who disapproved of him – perhaps because he really disapproved of himself.

From the first day he had hated Paul. Finding the lad's impersonal, deliberate gaze of an artist on his face, he got into a fury.

'What are yer lookin' at?' he sneered, bullying.

The boy glanced away. But the smith used to stand behind the counter and talk to Mr Pappleworth. His speech was dirty, with a kind of rottenness. Again he found the youth with his cool, critical gaze fixed on his face. The smith started round as if he had been stung.

'What'r yer lookin' at, three hap'orth o' pap?' he snarled.

The boy shrugged his shoulders slightly.

'Why yer –!' shouted Dawes.

'Leave him alone,' said Mr Pappleworth, in that insinuating voice which means, 'he's only one of your good little sops who can't help it.'

Since that time the boy used to look at the man every time he came through with the same curious criticism, glancing away before he met the smith's eye. It made Dawes furious. They hated each other in silence.

Clara Dawes had no children. When she had left her husband the home had been broken up, and she had gone to live with her mother. Dawes lodged with his sister. In the same house was a sister-in-law, and somehow Paul knew that this girl, Louie Travers, was now Dawes's woman. She was a handsome, insolent hussy who mocked at the youth, and yet flushed if he walked along to the station with her as she went home.

The next time he went to see Miriam it was Saturday evening. She had a fire in the parlour, and was waiting for him. The others, except her father and mother and the young children, had gone out, so the two had the parlour together. It was a long, low, warm room. There were three of Paul's small sketches on the wall, and his photo was on the mantelpiece. On the table and on the high old rose-wood piano were bowls of coloured leaves. He sat in the armchair, she crouched on the hearthrug near his feet. The glow was warm on her handsome, pensive face as she kneeled there like a devotee.

'What did you think of Mrs Dawes?' she asked quietly.

'She doesn't look very amiable,' he replied.

'No, but don't you think she's a fine woman?' she said, in a deep tone.

'Yes – in stature. But without a grain of taste. I like her for some things. *Is* she disagreeable?'

'I don't think so. I think she's dissatisfied.'

'What with?'

'Well – how would *you* like to be tied for life to a man like that?'

'Why did she marry him, then, if she was to have revulsions so soon?'

'Ay, why did she!' repeated Miriam bitterly.

'And I should have thought she had enough fight in her to match him,' he said.

Miriam bowed her head.

'Ay?' she queried satirically. 'What makes you think so?'

'Look at her mouth – made for passion – and the very set-back of her throat –' He threw his head back in Clara's defiant manner.

Miriam bowed a little lower.

'Yes,' she said.

There was a silence for some moments, while he thought of Clara.

'And what were the things you liked about her?' she asked.

'I don't know – her skin and the texture of her – and her – I don't know – there's a sort of fierceness somewhere in her. I appreciate her as an artist, that's all.'

'Yes.'

He wondered why Miriam crouched there brooding in that strange way. It irritated him.

'You don't really like her, do you?' he asked the girl.

She looked at him with her great, dazzled dark eyes.

'I do,' she said.

'You don't – you can't – not really.'

'Then what?' she asked slowly.

'Eh, I don't know – perhaps you like her because she's got a grudge against men.'

That was more probably one of his own reasons for liking Mrs Dawes, but this did not occur to him. They were silent. There had come into his forehead a knitting of the brows which was becoming habitual with him, particularly when he was with Miriam. She longed to smooth it away, and she was afraid of it. It seemed the stamp of a man who was not her man in Paul Morel.

There were some crimson berries among the leaves in the bowl. He reached over and pulled out a bunch.

'If you put red berries in your hair,' he said, 'why would you look like some witch or priestess, and never like a reveller?'

She laughed with a naked, painful sound.

'I don't know,' she said.

His vigorous warm hands were playing excitedly with the berries.

'Why can't you laugh?' he said. 'You never laugh laughter. You only laugh when something is odd or incongruous and then it almost seems to hurt you.'

She bowed her head as if he were scolding her.

'I wish you could laugh at me for just one minute – just for one minute. I feel as if it would set something free.'

'But' – and she looked up at him with eyes frightened and struggling – 'I do laugh at you – I *do*.'

'Never! There's always a kind of intensity. When you laugh I could always cry; it seems as if it shows up your suffering. Oh, you make me knit the brows of my very soul and cogitate.'

Slowly she shook her head despairingly.

'I'm sure I don't want to,' she said.

'I'm so damned spiritual with *you* always!' he cried.

She remained silent, thinking. 'Then why don't you be otherwise?' But he saw her crouching, brooding figure, and it seemed to tear him in two.

'But, there, it's autumn,' he said, 'and everybody feels like a disembodied spirit then.'

There was still another silence. This peculiar sadness between them thrilled her soul. He seemed so beautiful with his eyes gone dark, and looking as if they were deep as the deepest well.

'You make me so spiritual!' he lamented. 'And I don't want to be spiritual.'

She took her finger from her mouth with a little pop, and looked up at him almost challenging. But still her soul was naked in her great dark eyes, and there was the same yearning appeal upon her. If he could have kissed her in abstract purity he would have done so. But he could not kiss her thus – and she seemed to leave no other way. And she yearned to him.

He gave a brief laugh.

'Well,' he said, 'get that French and we'll do some – some Verlaine.'

'Yes,' she said in a deep tone, almost of resignation. And she rose and got the books. And her rather red, nervous hands looked so pitiful, he was mad to comfort her and kiss her. But then he dared not – or could not. There was something prevented him. His kisses were wrong for her. They continued the reading till ten o'clock, when they went into the kitchen, and Paul was natural and jolly again with the father and mother. His eyes were dark and shining; there was a kind of fascination about him.

When he went into the barn for his bicycle he found the front wheel punctured.

'Fetch me a drop of water in a bowl,' he said to her. 'I shall be late, and then I s'll catch it.'

He lighted the hurricane lamp, took off his coat, turned up the bicycle, and set speedily to work. Miriam came with the bowl of water and stood close to him, watching. She loved to see his hands doing things. He was slim and vigorous, with a kind of easiness even in his most hasty movements. And busy at his work he seemed to forget her. She loved him absorbedly. She wanted to run her hands down his sides. She always wanted to embrace him, so long as he did not want her.

'There!' he said, rising suddenly. 'Now, could you have done it quicker?'

'No!' she laughed.

He straightened himself. His back was towards her. She put her two hands on his sides, and ran them quickly down.

'You are so *fine*!' she said.

He laughed, hating her voice, but his blood roused to a wave of flame by her hands. She did not seem to realize *him* in all this. He might have been an object. She never realized the male he was.

He lighted his bicycle-lamp, bounced the machine on the barn floor to see that the tyres were sound, and buttoned his coat.

'That's all right!' he said.

She was trying the brakes, that she knew were broken.

'Did you have them mended?' she asked.

'No!'

'But why didn't you?'

'The back one goes on a bit.'

'But it's not safe.'

'I can use my toe.'

'I wish you'd had them mended,' she murmured.

'Don't worry – come to tea tomorrow, with Edgar.'

'Shall we?'

'Do – about four. I'll come to meet you.'

'Very well.'

She was pleased. They went across the dark yard to the gate. Looking across, he saw through the uncurtained window of the kitchen the heads of Mr and Mrs Leivers in the warm glow. It looked very cosy. The road, with pine-trees, was quite black in front.

''Till tomorrow,' he said, jumping on his bicycle.

'You'll take care, won't you?' she pleaded.

'Yes.'

His voice already came out of the darkness. She stood a moment watching the light from his lamp race into obscurity along the ground. She turned very slowly indoors. Orion was wheeling up over the wood, his dog twinkling after him, half smothered. For the rest of the world was full of darkness, and silent, save for the breathing of cattle in their stalls. She prayed earnestly for his safety that night. When he left her, she often lay in anxiety, wondering if he had got home safely.

He dropped down the hills on his bicycle. The roads were greasy, so he had to let it go. He felt a pleasure as the machine plunged over the second, steeper drop in the hill. 'Here goes!' he said. It was risky, because of the curve in the darkness at the bottom, and because of the brewers' wagons with drunken wagoners asleep. His bicycle seemed to fall beneath him, and he loved it. Recklessness is almost a man's revenge on his woman. He feels he is not valued, so he will risk destroying himself to deprive her altogether.

The stars on the lake seemed to leap like grasshoppers, silver upon the blackness, as he spun past. Then there was the long climb home.

'See, mother!' he said, as he threw her the berries and leaves on the table.

'H'm!' she said, glancing at them, then away again. She sat reading, alone, as she always did.

'Aren't they pretty?'

'Yes.'

He knew she was cross with him. After a few minutes he said:

'Edgar and Miriam are coming to tea tomorrow.'

She did not answer.

'You don't mind?'

Still she did not answer.

'Do you?' he asked.

'You know whether I mind or not.'

'I don't see why you should. I have plenty of meals there.'

'You do?'

'Then why do you grudge them tea?'

'I begrudge whom tea?'

'What are you so horrid for?'

'Oh, say no more! You've asked her to tea, it's quite sufficient. She'll come.'

He was very angry with his mother. He knew it was merely Miriam she objected to. He flung off his boots and went to bed.

Paul went to meet his friends the next afternoon. He was glad to see them coming. They arrived home at about four o'clock. Everywhere was clean and still for Sunday afternoon. Mrs Morel sat in her black dress and black apron. She rose to meet the visitors. With Edgar she was cordial, but with Miriam cold and rather grudging. Yet Paul thought the girl looked so nice in her brown cashmere frock.

He helped his mother to get the tea ready. Miriam would have gladly proffered, but was afraid. He was rather proud of his home. There was about it now, he thought, a certain distinction. The chairs were only wooden, and the sofa was old. But the hearthrug and cushions were cosy; the pictures were prints in good taste; there was a simplicity in everything, and plenty of books. He was never ashamed in the least of his home, nor was Miriam of hers, because both were what they should be, and warm. And then he was proud of the table; the china was pretty, the cloth was fine. It did not matter that the spoons were not silver nor the knives ivory-handled; everything looked nice. Mrs Morel had managed wonderfully while her children were growing up, so that nothing was out of place.

Miriam talked books a little. That was her unfailing topic. But Mrs Morel was not cordial, and turned soon to Edgar.

At first Edgar and Miriam used to go into Mrs Morel's pew. Morel never went to chapel, preferring the public-house. Mrs Morel, like a little champion, sat at the head of her pew, Paul at the other end; and at first Miriam sat next to him. Then the chapel was like home. It was a pretty place, with dark pews and slim, elegant pillars, and flowers. And the same people had sat in the same places ever since he was a boy. It was wonderfully sweet and soothing to sit there for an hour and a half, next to Miriam, and near to his mother, uniting his two loves under the spell of the place of worship. Then he felt warm and happy and religious at once. And after chapel he walked home with Miriam, whilst Mrs Morel spent the rest of the evening with her old friend, Mrs Burns. He was keenly alive on his walks on Sunday nights with Edgar and Miriam. He never went past the pits at night, by the lighted lamp-house, the tall black headstocks and lines of trucks, past the fans spinning slowly like shadows, without the feeling of Miriam returning to him, keen and almost unbearable.

She did not very long occupy the Morels' pew. Her father took one for themselves once more. It was under the little gallery, opposite the Morels'. When Paul and his mother came in the chapel the Leivers' pew was always empty. He was anxious for fear she would not come: it was so far, and there were so many rainy Sundays. Then, often very late indeed, she came in, with her long stride, her head bowed, her face hidden under her hat of dark green velvet. Her face, as she sat opposite, was always in shadow. But it gave him a very keen feeling, as if all his soul stirred within him, to see her there. It was not the same glow, happiness, and pride, that he felt in having his mother in charge: something more wonderful, less human, and tinged to intensity by a pain, as if there were something he could not get to.

At this time he was beginning to question the orthodox creed. He was twenty-one, and she was twenty. She was beginning to dread the spring: he became so wild, and hurt her so much. All the way he went cruelly smashing her beliefs. Edgar enjoyed it. He was by nature critical and rather dispassionate. But Miriam suffered exquisite pain, as, with an intellect like a knife, the man she loved examined her religion in which she lived and moved and had her being. But he did not spare her. He was cruel. And when they went alone he was even more fierce, as if he would kill her soul. He bled her beliefs till she almost lost consciousness.

'She exults – she exults as she carries him off from me,' Mrs Morel cried in her heart when Paul had gone. 'She's not like an ordinary woman, who can leave me my share in him. She wants to absorb him. She wants to draw him out and absorb him till there is nothing left of him, even for himself. He will never be a man on his own feet – she will suck him up.' So the mother sat, and battled and brooded bitterly.

And he, coming home from his walks with Miriam, was wild with torture. He walked biting his lips and with clenched fists, going at a great rate. Then, brought up against a stile, he stood for some minutes, and did not move. There was a great hollow of darkness fronting him, and on the black up-slopes patches of tiny lights, and in the lowest trough of the night, a flare of the pit. It was all weird and dreadful. Why was he torn so, almost bewildered, and unable to move? Why did his mother sit at home and suffer? He knew she suffered badly. But why should she? And why did he hate Miriam, and feel so cruel towards her, at the thought of his mother? If Miriam caused his mother suffering, then he hated her – and he easily hated her. Why did she make him feel as if he were uncertain of himself, insecure, an indefinite thing, as if he had not sufficient sheathing to prevent the night and the space breaking into him? How he hated her! And then, what a rush of tenderness and humility!

Suddenly he plunged on again, running home. His mother saw on him the marks of some agony, and she said nothing. But he had to make her talk to him. Then she was angry with him for going so far with Miriam.

'Why don't you like her, mother?' he cried in despair.

'I don't know, my boy,' she replied piteously. 'I'm sure I've tried to like her. I've tried and tried, but I can't – I can't!'

And he felt dreary and hopeless between the two.

Spring was the worst time. He was changeable, and intense and cruel. So he decided to stay away from her. Then came the hours when he knew Miriam was expecting him. His mother watched him growing restless. He could not go on with his work. He could do nothing. It was as if something were drawing his soul out towards Willey Farm. Then he put on his hat and went, saying nothing. And his mother knew he was gone. And as soon as he was on the way he sighed with relief. And when he was with her he was cruel again.

One day in March he lay on the banks of Nethermere, with Miriam sitting beside him. It was a glistening, white-and-blue day. Big clouds, so brilliant, went by overhead, while shadows stole along on the water. The clear spaces in the sky were of clean, cold blue. Paul lay on his back in the old grass, looking up. He could not bear to look at Miriam. She wanted to want him, and he resisted. He resisted all the time. He wanted now to give her passion and tenderness, and he could not. He felt that she wanted the soul out of his body, and not him. All his strength and energy she drew into herself through some channel which united them. She did not want to meet him, so that there were two of them, man and woman together. She wanted to draw all of him into her.

It urged him to an intensity like madness, which fascinated him, as drug-taking might.

He was discussing Michelangelo. It felt to her as if she were fingering the very quivering tissue, the very protoplasm of life, as she heard him. It gave her her deepest satisfaction. And in the end it frightened her. There he lay in the white intensity of his search, and his voice gradually filled her with fear, so level it was, almost inhuman, as if in a trance.

'Don't talk any more,' she pleaded softly, laying her hand on his forehead.

He lay quite still, almost unable to move. His body was somewhere discarded.

'Why not? Are you tired?'

'Yes, and it wears you out.'

He laughed shortly, realizing.

'Yet you always make me like it,' he said.

'I don't wish to,' she said, very low.

'Now when you've gone too far, and you feel you can't bear it. But your unconscious self always asks it of me. And I suppose I want it.'

He went on, in his dead fashion:

'If only you could want *me*, and not want what I can reel off for you!'

'I!' she cried bitterly – 'I! Why, when would you let me take you?'

'Then it's my fault,' he said, and, gathering himself together, he got up and began to talk trivialities. He felt insubstantial. In a vague way he hated her for it. And he knew he was as much to blame himself. This, however, did not prevent his hating her.

One evening about this time he had walked along the home road with her. They stood by the pasture leading down to the wood, unable to part. As the stars came out the clouds closed. They had glimpses of their own constellation, Orion, towards the west. His jewels glimmered for a moment, his dog ran low, struggling with difficulty through the spume of cloud.

Orion was for them chief in significance among the constellations. They gazed at him in their strange, surcharged hours of feeling, until they seemed themselves to live in every one of his stars. This evening Paul had been moody and perverse. Orion had seemed just an ordinary constellation to him. He had fought against his glamour and fascination. Miriam was watching her lover's mood carefully. But he said nothing that gave him away, till the moment came to part, when he stood frowning gloomily at the gathered clouds, behind which the great constellation must be striding still.

There was to be a little party at his house the next day, at which she was to attend.

'I shan't come and meet you,' he said.

'Oh, very well; it's not very nice,' she replied slowly.

'It's not that – only they don't like me to. They say I care more for you than for them. And you understand, don't you? You know it's only friendship.'

Miriam was astonished and hurt for him. It had cost him an effort. She left him, wanting to spare him any further humiliation. A fine rain blew in her face as she walked along the road. She was hurt deep down; and she despised him for being blown about by any wind of authority. And in her heart of hearts, unconsciously, she felt that he was trying to get away from her. This she would never have acknowledged. She pitied him.

At this time Paul became an important factor in Jordan's warehouse. Mr Pappleworth left to set up a business of his own, and Paul remained with Mr

Jordan as spiral overseer. His wages were to be raised to thirty shillings at the year-end, if things went well.

Still on Friday night Miriam often came down for her French lesson. Paul did not go so frequently to Willey Farm, and she grieved at the thought of her education's coming to an end; moreover, they both loved to be together, in spite of discords. So they read Balzac, and did compositions, and felt highly cultured.

Friday night was reckoning night for the miners. Morel 'reckoned' – shared up the money of the stall – either in the New Inn at Bretty or in his own house, according as his fellow-butties wished. Barker had turned a non-drinker, so now the men reckoned at Morel's house.

Annie, who had been teaching away, was at home again. She was still a tomboy; and she was engaged to be married. Paul was studying design.

Morel was always in good spirits on Friday evening, unless the week's earnings were small. He bustled immediately after his dinner, prepared to get washed. It was decorum for the women to absent themselves while the men reckoned. Women were not supposed to spy into such a masculine privacy as the butties' reckoning, nor were they to know the exact amount of the week's earnings. So, whilst her father was spluttering in the scullery, Annie went out to spend an hour with a neighbour. Mrs Morel attended to her baking.

'Shut that doo-er!' bawled Morel furiously.

Annie banged it behind her, and was gone.

'If tha oppens it again while I'm weshin' me, I'll ma'e thy jaw rattle,' he threatened from the midst of his soapsuds. Paul and the mother frowned to hear him.

Presently he came running out of the scullery, with the soapy water dripping from him, dithering with cold.

'Oh, my sirs!' he said. 'Wheer's my towel?'

It was hung on a chair to warm before the fire, otherwise he would have bullied and blustered. He squatted on his heels before the hot baking-fire to dry himself.

'F-ff-f!' he went, pretending to shudder with cold.

'Goodness, man, don't be such a kid!' said Mrs Morel! 'It's not cold.'

'Thee strip thysen stark nak'd to wesh thy flesh i' that scullery,' said the miner, as he rubbed his hair; 'nowt b'r a ice-'ouse!'

'And I shouldn't make that fuss,' replied his wife.

'No, tha'd drop down stiff, as dead as a door-knob, wi' thy nesh sides.'

'Why is a door-knob deader than anything else?' asked Paul, curious.

'Eh, I dunno; that's what they say,' replied his father. 'But there's that much draught i' yon scullery, as it blows through your ribs like through a five-barred gate.'

'It would have some difficulty in blowing through yours,' said Mrs Morel.

Morel looked down ruefully at his sides.

'Me!' he exclaimed. 'I'm nowt b'r a skinned rabbit. My bones fair juts out on me.'

'I should like to know where,' retorted his wife.

'Iv'ry-wheer! I'm nobbut a sack o' faggots.'

Mrs Morel laughed. He had still a wonderfully young body, muscular, without any fat. His skin was smooth and clear. It might have been the body of a man of twenty-eight, except that there were, perhaps, too many blue scars, like tattoo marks, where the coal-dust remained under the skin, and that his chest was too hairy. But he put his hand on his sides ruefully. It was his fixed belief that, because he did not get fat, he was as thin as a starved rat.

Paul looked at his father's thick, brownish hands all scarred, with broken nails rubbing the fine smoothness of his sides, and the incongruity struck him. It seemed strange they were the same flesh.

'I suppose,' he said to his father, 'you had a good figure once.'

'Eh!' exclaimed the miner, glancing round, startled and timid, like a child.

'He had,' exclaimed Mrs Morel, 'if he didn't hurtle himself up as if he was trying to get in the smallest space he could.'

'Me!' exclaimed Morel – 'me a good figure! I wor niver much more n'r a skeleton.'

'Man!' cried his wife, 'don't be such a pulamiter!'

''Strewth!' he said. 'Tha's niver knowed me but what I looked as if I wor goin' off in a rapid decline.'

She sat and laughed.

'You've had a constitution like iron,' she said, 'and never a man had a better start, if it was body that counted. You should have seen him as a young man,' she cried suddenly to Paul, drawing herself up to imitate her husband's once handsome bearing.

Morel watched her shyly. He saw again the passion she had had for him. It blazed upon her for a moment. He was shy, rather scared, and humble. Yet again he felt his old glow. And then immediately he felt the ruin he had made during these years. He wanted to bustle about, to run away from it.

'Gi'e my back a bit of a wesh,' he asked her.

His wife brought a well-soaped flannel and clapped it on his shoulders. He gave a jump.

'Eh, tha mucky little 'ussy!' he cried. 'Cowd as death!'

'You ought to have been a salamander,' she laughed, washing his back. It was very rarely she would do anything so personal for him. The children did those things.

'The next world won't be half hot enough for you,' she added.

'No,' he said; 'tha'lt see as it's draughty for me.'

But she had finished. She wiped him in a desultory fashion, and went upstairs, returning immediately with his shifting-trousers. When he was dried he struggled into his shirt. Then, ruddy and shiny, with hair on end, and his flannelette shirt hanging over his pit-trousers, he stood warming the garments he was going to put on. He turned them, he pulled them inside out, he scorched them.

'Goodness, man!' cried Mrs Morel; 'get dressed!'

'Should thee like to clap thysen into britches as cowd as a tub o' water?' he said.

At last he took off his pit-trousers and donned decent black. He did all this on the hearthrug, as he would have done if Annie and her familiar friends had been present.

Mrs Morel turned the bread in the oven. Then from the red earthenware panchion of dough that stood in a corner she took another handful of paste, worked it to the proper shape, and dropped it into a tin. As she was doing so Barker knocked and entered. He was a quiet, compact little man, who looked as if he would go through a stone wall. His black hair was cropped short, his head was bony. Like most miners, he was pale, but healthy and taut.

'Evenin', missis,' he nodded to Mrs Morel, and he seated himself with a sigh.

'Good evening,' she replied cordially.

'Tha's made thy heels crack,' said Morel. 'I dunno as I have,' said Barker. He sat, as the men always did in Mrs Morel's kitchen, effacing himself rather.

'How's missis?' she asked of him.

He had told her some time back:

'We're expectin' us third just now, you see.'

'Well,' he answered, rubbing his head, 'she keeps pretty middlin', I think.'

'Let's see – when?' asked Mrs Morel.

'Well, I shouldn't be surprised any time now.'

'Ah! And she's kept fairly?'

'Yes, tidy.'

'That's a blessing, for she's none too strong.'

'No. An' I've done another silly trick.'

'What's that?'

Mrs Morel knew Barker wouldn't do anything very silly.

'I'm come be-out th' market-bag.'

'You can have mine.'

'Nay, you'll be wantin' that yourself.'

'I shan't. I take a string bag always.'

She saw the determined little collier buying in the week's groceries and meat on the Friday nights, and she admired him. 'Barker's little, but he's ten times the man you are,' she said to her husband.

Just then Wesson entered. He was thin, rather frail-looking, with a boyish ingenuousness and a slightly foolish smile, despite his seven children. But his wife was a passionate woman.

'I see you've kested me,' he said, smiling rather vapidly.

'Yes,' replied Barker.

The newcomer took off his cap and his big woollen muffler. His nose was pointed and red.

'I'm afraid you're cold, Mr Wesson,' said Mrs Morel.

'It's a bit nippy,' he replied.

'Then come to the fire.'

'Nay, I s'll do where I am.'

Both colliers sat away back. They could not be induced to come on the hearth. The hearth is sacred to the family.

'Go thy ways i' th' arm-chair,' cried Morel cheerily.

'Nay, thank yer; I'm very nicely here.'

'Yes, come, of course,' insisted Mrs Morel.

He rose and went awkwardly. He sat in Morel's arm-chair awkwardly. It was too great a familiarity. But the fire made him blissfully happy.

'And how's that chest of yours?' demanded Mrs Morel.

He smiled again, with his blue eyes rather sunny.

'Oh, it's very middlin',' he said.

'Wi' a rattle in it like a kettle drum,' said Barker shortly.

'T-t-t-t!' went Mrs Morel rapidly with her tongue. 'Did you have that flannel singlet made?'

'Not yet,' he smiled.

'Then, why didn't you?' she cried.

'It'll come,' he smiled.

'Ah, an' Doomsday!' exclaimed Barker.

Barker and Morel were both impatient of Wesson. But, then, they were both as hard as nails, physically.

When Morel was nearly ready he pushed the bag of money to Paul.

'Count it, boy,' he asked humbly.

Paul impatiently turned from his books and pencil, tipped the bag upside down on the table. There was a five-pound bag of silver, sovereigns and loose money. He counted quickly, referred to the checks – the written papers giving amount of coal – put the money in order. Then Barker glanced at the checks.

Mrs Morel went upstairs, and the three men came to table, Morel, as master of the house, sat in his arm-chair, with his back to the hot fire. The two butties had cooler seats. None of them counted the money.

'What did we say Simpson's was?' asked Morel; and the butties cavilled for a minute over the dayman's earnings. Then the amount was put aside.

'An' Bill Naylor's?'

This money also was taken from the pack.

Then, because Wesson lived in one of the company's houses, and his rent had been deducted, Morel and Barker took four-and-six each. And because Morel's coals had come, and the leading was stopped, Barker and Wesson took four shillings each. Then it was plain sailing. Morel gave each of them a sovereign till there were no more sovereigns; each half a crown till there were no more half-crowns; each a shilling till there were no more shillings. If there was anything at the end that wouldn't split, Morel took it and stood drinks.

Then the three men rose and went. Morel scuttled out of the house before his wife came down. She heard the door close, and descended. She looked hastily at the bread in the oven. Then, glancing on the table, she saw her money lying. Paul had been working all the time. But now he felt his mother counting the week's money and her wrath rising.

'T-t-t-t!' went her tongue.

He frowned. He could not work when she was cross. She counted again.

'A measly twenty-five shillings!' she exclaimed. 'How much was the cheque?'

'Ten pounds eleven,' said Paul irritably. He dreaded what was coming.

'And he gives me a scrattlin' twenty-five, an' his club this week! But I know him. He thinks because *you're* earning he needn't keep the house any longer. No, all he has to do with his money is to guttle it. But I'll show him!'

'Oh, mother, don't!' cried Paul.

'Don't what, I should like to know?' she exclaimed.

'Don't carry on again, I can't work.'

She went very quiet.

'Yes, it's all very well,' she said; 'but how do you think I'm going to manage?'

'Well, it won't make it any better to whittle about it.'

'I should like to know what you'd do if you had it to put up with.'

'It won't be long. You can have my money. Let him go to hell.'

He went back to his work and she tied her bonnet-strings grimly. When she was fretted he could not bear it. But now he began to insist on her recognizing him.

'The two loaves at the top,' she said, 'will be done in twenty minutes. Don't forget them.'

'All right,' he answered; and she went to the market.

He remained alone working. But his usual intense concentration became unsettled. He listened for the yard-gate. At a quarter-past seven came a low knock, and Miriam entered.

'All alone?' she said.

'Yes.'

As if at home, she took off her tam-o'-shanter and her long coat, hanging them up. It gave him a thrill. This might be their own house, his and hers. Then she came back and peered over his work.

'What is it?' she asked.

'Still design, for decorating stuffs, and for embroidery.'

She bent short-sightedly over the drawings.

It irritated him that she peered so into everything that was his, searching him out. He went into the parlour and returned with a bundle of brownish linen. Carefully unfolding it, he spread it on the floor. It proved to be a curtain or *portière*, beautifully stencilled with a design on roses.

'Ah, how beautiful!' she cried.

The spread cloth, with its wonderful reddish roses and dark green stems, all so simple, and somehow so wicked-looking, lay at her feet. She went on her knees before it, her dark curls dropping. He saw her crouched voluptuously before his work, and his heart beat quickly. Suddenly she looked up at him.

'Why does it seem cruel?' she cried.

'What?'

'There seems a feeling of cruelty about it,' she said.

'It's jolly good, whether or not,' he replied, folding up his work with a lover's hands.

She rose slowly, pondering.

'And what will you do with it?' she asked.

'Send it to Liberty's. I did it for my mother, but I think she'd rather have the money.'

'Yes,' said Miriam. He had spoken with a touch of bitterness, and Miriam sympathized. Money would have been nothing to *her*.

He took the cloth back into the parlour. When he returned, he threw to Miriam a smaller piece. It was a cushion-cover with the same design.

'I did that for you,' he said.

She fingered the work with trembling hands, and did not speak. He became embarrassed.

'By Jove, the bread!' he cried.

He took the top loaves out, tapped them vigorously. They were done. He put them on the hearth to cool. Then he went to the scullery, wetted his hands, scooped the last white dough out of the punchion, and dropped it into a baking-tin. Miriam was still bent over her painted cloth. He stood rubbing the bits of dough from his hands.

'You do like it?' he asked.

She looked up at him, with her dark eyes one flame of love. He laughed uncomfortably. Then he began to talk about the design. There was for him the most intense pleasure in talking about his work to Miriam. All his passion, all his wild blood, went into this intercourse with her, when he talked and conceived his work. She brought forth to him his imaginations. She did not understand, any more than a woman understands when she conceives a child in her womb. But this was life for her and for him.

While they were talking, a young woman of about twenty-two, small and pale, hollow-eyed, yet with a relentless look about her, entered the room. She was a friend at the Morels'.

'Take your things off,' said Paul.

'No, I'm not stopping.'

She sat down in the arm-chair opposite Paul and Miriam, who were on the sofa. Miriam moved a little farther from him. The room was hot, with a scent of new bread. Brown, crisp loaves stood on the hearth.

'I shouldn't have expected to see you here tonight, Miriam Leivers,' said Beatrice wickedly.

'Why not?' murmured Miriam huskily.

'Why, let's look at your shoes.'

Miriam remained uncomfortably still.

'If tha doesna tha durs'na,' laughed Beatrice.

Miriam put her feet from under her dress. Her boots had that queer, irresolute, rather pathetic look about them, which showed how self-conscious and self-mistrustful she was. And they were covered with mud.

'Glory! You're a positive muck-heap,' exclaimed Beatrice. 'Who cleans your boots?'

'I clean them myself.'

'Then you wanted a job,' said Beatrice. 'It would ha' taken a lot of men to ha' brought me down here tonight. But love laughs at sludge, doesn't it, 'Postle, my duck?'

'*Inter alia*,' he said.

'Oh, Lord! are you going to spout foreign languages? What does it mean, Miriam?'

There was a fine sarcasm in the last question, but Miriam did not see it.

'"Among other things," I believe,' she said humbly.

Beatrice put her tongue between her teeth and laughed wickedly.

'"Among other things," 'Postle?' she repeated. 'Do you mean love laughs at mothers, and fathers, and sisters, and brothers, and men friends, and lady friends, and even at the b'loved himself?'

She affected a great innocence.

'In fact, it's one big smile,' he replied.

'Up its sleeve, 'Postle Morel – you believe me,' she said; and she went off into another burst of wicked, silent laughter.

Miriam sat silent, withdrawn into herself. Every one of Paul's friends delighted in taking sides against her, and he left her in the lurch – seemed almost to take a sort of revenge upon her then.

'Are you still at school?' asked Miriam of Beatrice.

'Yes.'

'You've not had your notice then?'

'I expect it at Easter.'

'Isn't it an awful shame, to turn you off merely because you didn't pass the exam?'

'I don't know,' said Beatrice coldly.

'Agatha says you're as good as any teacher anywhere. It seems to me ridiculous. I wonder why you didn't pass.'

'Short of brains, eh, 'Postle?' said Beatrice briefly.

'Only brains to bite with,' replied Paul, laughing.

'Nuisance!' she cried; and, springing from her seat, she rushed and boxed his ears. She had beautiful small hands. He held her wrists while she wrestled with him. At last she broke free, and seized two handfuls of his thick, dark brown hair, which she shook.

'Beat!' he said, as he pulled his hair straight with his fingers. 'I hate you!'

She laughed with glee.

'Mind!' she said. 'I want to sit next to you.'

'I'd as lief be neighbours with a vixen,' he said, nevertheless making place for her between him and Miriam.

'Did it ruffle his pretty hair, then!' she cried; and, with her haircomb, she combed him straight. 'And his nice little moustache!' she exclaimed. She tilted his head back and combed his young moustache. 'It's a wicked moustache, 'Postle,' she said. 'It's a red for danger. Have you got any of those cigarettes?'

He pulled his cigarette-case from his pocket. Beatrice looked inside it.

'And fancy me having Connie's last cig,' said Beatrice, putting the thing between her teeth. He held a lit match to her, and she puffed daintily.

'Thanks so much, darling,' she said mockingly.

It gave her a wicked delight.

'Don't you think he does it nicely, Miriam?' she asked.

'Oh very!' said Miriam.

He took a cigarette for himself.

'Light, old boy?' said Beatrice, tilting her cigarette at him.

He bent forward to her to light his cigarette at hers. She was winking at him as he did so. Miriam saw his eyes trembling with mischief, and his full, almost sensual, mouth quivering. He was not himself and she could not bear it. As he was now, she had no connexion with him; she might as well not have existed. She saw the cigarette dancing on his full lips. She hated his thick hair for being tumbled loose on his forehead.

'Sweet boy!' said Beatrice, tipping up his chin and giving him a little kiss on the cheek.

'I s'll kiss thee back, Beat,' he said.

'Tha wunna!' she giggled, jumping up and going away. 'Isn't he shameless, Miriam?'

'Quite,' said Miriam. 'By the way, aren't you forgetting the bread?'

'By Jove!' he cried, flinging open the oven-door.

Out puffed the bluish smoke and a smell of burned bread.

'Oh, golly!' cried Beatrice, coming to his side. He crouched before the oven, she peered over his shoulder. 'This is what comes of the oblivion of love, my boy.'

Paul was ruefully removing the loaves. One was burnt black on the hot side; another was hard as a brick.

'Poor Mater!' said Paul.

'You want to grate it,' said Beatrice. 'Fetch me the nutmeg-grater.'

She arranged the bread in the oven. He brought the grater, and she grated the bread on to a newspaper on the table. He set the doors open to blow away the smell of burned bread. Beatrice grated away, puffing her cigarette, knocking the charcoal off the poor loaf.

'My word, Miriam! You're in for it this time,' said Beatrice.

'I!' exclaimed Miriam in amazement.

'You'd better be gone when his mother comes in. *I* know why King Alfred burned the cakes. Now I see it! 'Postle would fix up a tale about his work making him forget, if he thought it would wash. If that old woman had come in a bit sooner, she'd have boxed the brazen thing's ears who made the oblivion, instead of poor Alfred's.'

She giggled as she scraped the loaf. Even Miriam laughed in spite of herself. Paul mended the fire ruefully.

The garden-gate was heard to bang.

'Quick!' cried Beatrice, giving Paul the scraped loaf. 'Wrap it up in a damp towel.'

Paul disappeared into the scullery. Beatrice hastily blew her scrapings into the fire, and sat down innocently. Annie came bursting in. She was an abrupt, quite smart young woman. She blinked in the strong light.

'Smell of burning!' she exclaimed.

'It's the cigarettes,' replied Beatrice demurely.

'Where's Paul?'

Leonard had followed Annie. He had a long comic face and blue eyes, very sad.

'I suppose he's left you to settle it between you,' he said. He nodded sympathetically to Miriam, and became gently sarcastic to Beatrice.

'No,' said Beatrice, 'he's gone off with number nine.'

'I just met number five inquiring for him,' said Leonard.

'Yes – we're going to share him up like Solomon's baby,' said Beatrice. Annie laughed.

'Oh, ay,' said Leonard. 'And which bit should you have?'

'I don't know,' said Beatrice. 'I'll let all the others pick first.'

'An' you'd have the leavings, like?' said Leonard, twisting up a comic face. Annie was looking in the oven. Miriam sat ignored. Paul entered.

'This bread's a fine sight, our Paul,' said Annie.

'Then you should stop an' look after it,' said Paul.

'You mean *you* should do what you're reckoning to do,' replied Annie.

'He should, shouldn't he!' cried Beatrice.

'I s'd think he'd got plenty on hand,' said Leonard.

'You had a nasty walk, didn't you, Miriam?' said Annie.

'Yes – but I'd been in all week –'

'And you wanted a bit of a change, like,' insinuated Leonard kindly.

'Well, you can't be stuck in the house for ever,' Annie agreed. She was quite amiable. Beatrice pulled on her coat, and went out with Leonard and Annie. She would meet her own boy.

'Don't forget that bread, our Paul,' cried Annie. 'Good night, Miriam. I don't think it will rain.'

When they had all gone, Paul fetched the swathed loaf, unwrapped it, and surveyed it sadly.

'It's a mess!' he said.

'But,' answered Miriam impatiently, 'what is it, after all – twopence ha'penny.'

'Yes, but – it's the mater's precious baking, and she'll take it to heart. However, it's no good bothering.'

He took the loaf back into the scullery. There was a little distance between him and Miriam. He stood balanced opposite her for some moments considering, thinking of his behaviour with Beatrice. He felt guilty inside himself, and yet glad. For some inscrutable reason it served Miriam right. He was not going to repent. She wondered what he was thinking of as he stood suspended. His thick black hair was tumbled over his forehead. Why might she not push it back for him, and remove the marks of Beatrice's comb? Why might she not press his body with her two hands? It looked so firm and every whit living. And he would let other girls, why not her?

Suddenly he started into life. It made her quiver almost with terror as he quickly pushed the hair off his forehead and came towards her.

'Half-past eight!' he said. 'We'd better buck up. Where's your French?'

Miriam shyly and rather bitterly produced her exercise-book. Every week she wrote for him a sort of diary of her inner life, in her own French. He had found this was the only way to get her to do compositions. And her diary was mostly a love-letter. He would read it now; she felt as if her soul's history were going to be desecrated by him in his present mood. He sat beside her. She watched his hand, firm and warm, rigorously scoring her work. He was reading only the French, ignoring her soul that was there. But gradually his hand forgot its work. He read in silence, motionless. She quivered.

'"*Ce matin les oiseaux m'ont éveillé,*"' he read. '"*Il faisait encore un crépuscule. Mais la petite fenêtre de ma chambre était blême, et puis jaune, et tous les oiseaux de bois éclatèrent dans un chanson vif et résonnant. Tout l'aube tressaillit. J'avais rêvé de vous. Est-ce que vous voyez aussi l'aube? Les oiseaux m'éveillent presque tous les matins et toujours il y a quelque chose de terreur dans le cri des grives. Il est si clair –*"'

Miriam sat tremulous, half ashamed. He remained quite still, trying to understand. He only knew she loved him. He was afraid of her love for him. It was too good for him, and he was inadequate. His own love was at fault, not hers. Ashamed, he corrected her work humbly writing above her words.

'Look,' he said, 'the past participle conjugated with *avoir* agrees with the direct object when it precedes.'

She bent forward, trying to see and to understand. Her free, fine curls tickled his face. He started as if they had been red hot, shuddering. He saw her peering forward at the page, her red lips parted piteously, the black hair springing in fine strands across her tawny, ruddy cheek. She was coloured like a pomegranate for richness. His breath came short as he watched her. Suddenly she looked up at him. Her dark eyes were naked with their love, afraid, and yearning. His eyes, too, were dark, and they hurt her. They seemed to master her. She lost all her self-control, was exposed in fear. And he knew, before he could kiss her, he must drive something out of himself. And a touch of hate for her crept back again into his heart. He returned to her exercise.

Suddenly he flung down the pencil, and was at the oven in a leap, turning the bread. For Miriam he was too quick. She started violently, and it hurt her with real pain. Even the way he crouched before the oven hurt her. There seemed to be something cruel in it, something cruel in the swift way he pitched the bread out of the tins, caught it up again. If only he had been gentle in his movements she would have felt so rich and warm. As it was, she was hurt.

He returned and finished the exercise.

'You've done well this week,' he said.

She saw he was flattered by her diary. It did not repay her entirely.

'You really do blossom out sometimes,' he said. 'You ought to write poetry.'

She lifted her head with joy, then she shook it mistrustfully. 'I don't trust myself,' she said.

'You should try!'

Again she shook her head.

'Shall we read or is it too late?' he asked.

'It is late – but we can read just a little,' she pleaded.

She was really getting now the food for her life during the next week. He made her copy Baudelaire's 'Le Balcon'. Then he read it for her. His voice was soft and caressing, but growing almost brutal. He had a way of lifting his lips and showing his teeth, passionately and bitterly, when he was much moved. This he did now. It made Miriam feel as if he were trampling on her. She dared not look at him, but sat with her head bowed. She could not understand why he got into such a tumult and fury. It made her wretched. She did not like Baudelaire, on the whole – nor Verlaine.

> 'Behold her singing in the field
> Yon solitary highland lass.'

That nourished her heart. So did 'Fair Ines'. And –

> 'It is a beauteous evening, calm and free,
> The holy time is quiet as a nun.'

These were like herself. And there was he, saying in his throat bitterly:

> *'Tu te rappelleras la beauté des caresses.'*

The poem was finished; he took the bread out of the oven, arranging the burnt loaves at the bottom of the panchion, the good ones at the top. The desiccated loaf remained swathed up in the scullery.

'Mater needn't know till morning,' he said. 'It won't upset her so much then as at night.'

Miriam looked in the bookcase, saw what postcards and letters he had received, saw what books were there. She took one that interested him. Then he turned down the gas and they set off. He did not trouble to lock the door.

He was not home again until a quarter to eleven. His mother was seated in the rocking-chair. Annie, with a rope of hair hanging down her back, remained sitting on a low stool before the fire, her elbows on her knees, gloomily. On the table stood the offending loaf unswathed. Paul entered rather breathless. No one spoke. His mother was reading the little local newspaper. He took off his coat, and went to sit down on the sofa. His mother moved curtly aside to let him pass. No one spoke. He was uncomfortable. For some minutes he sat pretending to read a piece of paper he found on the table. Then –

'I forgot that bread mother,' he said.

There was no answer from either woman.

'Well,' he said, 'it's only twopence ha'penny. I can pay you for that.'

Being angry he put three pennies on the table, and slid them towards his mother. She turned away her head. Her mouth was shut tightly.

'Yes,' said Annie, 'you don't know how badly my mother is!'

The girl sat staring into the fire.

'Why is she badly?' asked Paul, in his overbearing way.

'Well!' said Annie. 'She could scarcely get home.'

He looked closely at his mother. She looked ill.

'*Why* could she scarcely get home?' he asked her, still sharply. She would not answer.

'I found her as white as a sheet sitting here,' said Annie, with a suggestion of tears in her voice.

'Well, why?' insisted Paul. His brows were knitting, his eyes dilating passionately.

'It was enough to upset anybody,' said Mrs Morel, 'hugging those parcels – meat, and greengroceries, and a pair of curtains –'

'Well, why *did* you hug them; you needn't have done.'

'Then who would?'

'Let Annie fetch the meat.'

'Yes, and I *would* fetch the meat, but how was I to know? You were off with Miriam, instead of being in when my mother came.'

'And what was the matter with you?' asked Paul of his mother.

'I suppose it's my heart,' she replied. Certainly she looked bluish round the mouth.

'And have you felt it before?'

'Yes – often enough.'

'Then why haven't you told me? – and why haven't you seen a doctor?'

Mrs Morel shifted in her chair, angry with him for his hectoring.

'You'd never notice anything,' said Annie. 'You're too eager to be off with Miriam.'

'Oh, am I – and any worse than you with Leonard?'

'*I* was in at a quarter to ten.'

There was silence in the room for a time.

'I should have thought,' said Mrs Morel bitterly, 'that she wouldn't have occupied you so entirely as to burn a whole ovenful of bread.'

'Beatrice was here as well as she.'

'Very likely. But we know why the bread is spoilt.'

'Why?' he flashed.

'Because you were engrossed with Miriam,' replied Mrs Morel hotly.

'Oh, very well – then it was *not*!' he replied angrily.

He was distressed and wretched. Seizing a paper, he began to read. Annie, her blouse unfastened, her long ropes of hair twisted into a plait, went up to bed, bidding him a very curt good night.

Paul sat pretending to read. He knew his mother wanted to upbraid him. He also wanted to know what had made her ill, for he was troubled. So, instead of running away to bed, as he would have liked to do, he sat and waited. There was a tense silence. The clock ticked loudly.

'You'd better go to bed before your father comes in,' said the mother harshly. 'And if you're going to have anything to eat, you'd better get it.'

'I don't want anything.'

It was his mother's custom to bring in some trifle for supper on Friday night, the night of luxury for the colliers. He was too angry to go and find it in the pantry this night. This insulted her.

'If I *wanted* you to go to Selby on Friday night, I can imagine the scene,' said Mrs Morel. 'But you're never too tired to go if *she* will come for you. Nay, but you neither want to eat nor drink then.'

'I can't let her go alone.'

'Can't you? And why does she come?'

'Not because I ask her.'

'She doesn't come without you want her –'

'Well, what if I *do* want her –' he replied.

'Why, nothing, if it was sensible or reasonable. But to go trapesing up there miles and miles in the mud, coming home at midnight, and got to go to Nottingham in the morning –'

'If I hadn't, you'd be just the same.'

'Yes, I should, because there's no sense in it. Is she *so* fascinating that you must follow her all that way?' Mrs Morel was bitterly sarcastic. She sat still, with averted face, stroking, with a rhythmic, jerked movement, the black sateen of her apron. It was a movement that hurt Paul to see.

'I do like her,' he said, 'but –'

'*Like* her!' said Mrs Morel, in the same biting tones. 'It seems to me you like nothing and nobody else. There's neither Annie, nor me, nor anyone now for you.'

'What nonsense, Mother – you know I don't love her – I – I tell you I *don't* love her – she doesn't even walk with my arm, because I don't want her to.'

'Then why do you fly to her so often!'

'I *do* like to talk to her – I never said I didn't. But I *don't* love her.'

'Is there nobody else to talk to?'

'Not about the things we talk of. There's lots of things that you're not interested in, that –'

'What things?'

Mrs Morel was so intense that Paul began to pant.

'Why – painting – and books. *You* don't care about Herbert Spencer.'

'No,' was the sad reply. 'And *you* won't at my age.'

'Well, but I do know – and Miriam does –'

'And how do you know,' Mrs Morel flashed defiantly, 'that *I* shouldn't? Do you ever try me?'

'But you don't, Mother, you know you don't care whether a picture's decorative or not, you don't care what *manner* it is in.'

'How do you know I don't care? Do you ever try me? Do you ever talk to me about these things, to try?'

'But it's not that that matters to you, Mother, you know it's not.'

'What is it, then – what is it, then, that matters to me?' she flashed. He knitted his brows with pain.

'You're old, Mother, and we're young.'

He only meant that the interests of *her* age were not the interests of his. But he realized the moment he had spoken that he had said the wrong thing.

'Yes, I know it well – I am old. And therefore I may stand aside; I have nothing more to do with you. You only want me to wait on you – the rest is for Miriam.'

He could not bear it. Instinctively he realized that he was life to her. And, after all, she was the chief thing to him, the only supreme thing.

'You know it isn't, Mother, you know it isn't!'

She was moved to pity by his cry.

'It looks a great deal like it,' she said, half putting aside her despair.

'No, mother – I really *don't* love her. I talk to her, but I want to come home to you.'

He had taken off his collar and tie, and rose, bare-throated to go to bed. As he stooped to kiss his mother, she threw her arms round his neck, hid her face on his shoulder, and cried, in a whimpering voice, so unlike her own that he writhed in agony:

'I can't bear it. I could let another woman – but not her. She'd leave me no room, not a bit of room –'

And immediately he hated Miriam bitterly.

'And I've never – you know, Paul – I've never had a husband – not really –' He stroked his mother's hair, and his mouth was on her throat.

'And she exults so in taking you from me – she's not like ordinary girls.'

'Well, I don't love her, Mother,' he murmured, bowing his head and hiding his eyes on her shoulder in misery. His mother kissed him a long, fervent kiss.

'My boy!' she said, in a voice trembling with passionate love.

Without knowing, he gently stroked her face.

'There,' said his mother, 'now go to bed. You'll be *so* tired in the morning.' As she was speaking she heard her husband coming. 'There's your father – now go.' Suddenly she looked at him almost as if in fear. 'Perhaps I'm selfish. If you want her, take her, my boy.'

His mother looked so strange. Paul kissed her, trembling, 'Ha – Mother!' he said softly.

Morel came in, walking unevenly. His hat was over one corner of his eye. He balanced in the doorway.

'At your mischief again?' he said venomously.

Mrs Morel's emotion turned into sudden hate of the drunkard who had come in thus upon her.

'At any rate, it is sober,' she said.

'H'm – h'm! H'm – h'm!' he sneered. He went into the passage, hung up his hat and coat. Then they heard him go down three steps to the pantry. He returned with a piece of pork-pie in his fist. It was what Mrs Morel had bought for her son.

'Nor was that bought for you. If you can give me no more than twenty-five shillings, I'm sure I'm not going to buy you pork-pie to stuff, after you've swilled a bellyful of beer.'

'Wha-at – wha-at!' snarled Morel, toppling in his balance.

'Wha-at – not for me?' He looked at the piece of meat and crust, and suddenly, in a vicious spurt of temper, flung it into the fire.

Paul started to his feet.

'Waste your own stuff!' he cried.

'What – what!' suddenly shouted Morel, jumping up and clenching his fist. 'I'll show yer, yer young jockey!'

'All right!' said Paul viciously, putting his head on one side. 'Show me!'

He would at that moment dearly have loved to have a smack at something. Morel was half crouching, fists up, ready to spring. The young man stood, smiling with his lips.

'Ussha!' hissed the father, swiping round with a great stroke just past his son's face. He dared not, even though so close, really touch the young man, but swerved an inch away.

'Right!' said Paul, his eyes upon the side of his father's mouth, where in another instant his fist would have hit. He ached for that stroke. But he heard a faint moan from behind. His mother was deadly pale, and dark at the mouth. Morel was dancing up to deliver another blow.

'Father!' said Paul, so that the word rang.

Morel started, and stood at attention.

'Mother!' moaned the boy, 'Mother!'

She began to struggle with herself. Her open eyes watched him, although she could not move. Gradually she was coming to herself. He laid her down on the sofa, and ran upstairs for a little whisky, which at last she could sip. The tears were hopping down his face. As he kneeled in front of her he did not cry, but the tears ran down his face quietly. Morel, on the opposite side of the room, sat with his elbows on his knees glaring across.

'What's a-matter with 'er?' he asked.

'Faint!' replied Paul.

'H'm!'

The elderly man began to unlace his boots. He stumbled off to bed. His last fight was fought in that home.

Paul kneeled there, stroking his mother's hand.

'Don't be poorly, Mother – don't be poorly!' he said time after time.

'It's nothing, my boy,' she murmured.

At last he rose, fetched in a large piece of coal, and raked the fire. Then he cleared the room, put everything straight, laid the things for breakfast, and brought his mother's candle.

'Can you go to bed, Mother?'

'Yes, I'll come.'

'Sleep with Annie, Mother, not with him.'

'No, I'll sleep in my own bed.'

'Don't sleep with him, Mother.'

'I'll sleep in my own bed.'

She rose, and he turned out the gas, then followed her closely upstairs, carrying her candle. On the landing he kissed her close.

'Good night, Mother.'

'Good night!' she said.

He pressed his face upon the pillow in a fury of misery. And yet, somewhere in his soul, he was at peace because he still loved his mother best. It was the bitter peace of resignation.

The efforts of his father to conciliate him next day were a great humiliation to him.

Everybody tried to forget the scene.

9

DEFEAT OF MIRIAM

Paul was dissatisfied with himself and with everything. The deepest of his love belonged to his mother. When he felt he had hurt her, or wounded his love for her, he could not bear it. Now it was spring, and there was battle between him and Miriam. This year he had a good deal against her. She was vaguely aware of it. The old feeling that she was to be a sacrifice to this love, which she had had when she prayed, was mingled in all her emotions. She did not at the bottom believe she ever would have him. She did not believe in herself primarily; doubted whether she could ever be what he would demand of her. Certainly she never saw herself living happily through a lifetime with him. She saw tragedy, sorrow, and sacrifice ahead. And in sacrifice she was proud, in renunciation she was strong, for she did not trust herself to support everyday life. She was prepared for the big things and the deep things, like tragedy. It was the sufficiency of the small day-life she could not trust.

The Easter holidays began happily. Paul was his own frank self. Yet she felt it would go wrong. On the Sunday afternoon she stood at her bedroom window, looking across at the oak-trees of the wood, in whose branches a twilight was tangled, below the bright sky of the afternoon. Grey-green rosettes of honeysuckle leaves hung before the window, some already, she fancied, showing bud. It was spring, which she loved and dreaded.

Hearing the clack of the gate she stood in suspense. It was a bright grey day, Paul came into the yard with his bicycle, which glittered as he walked. Usually he rang his bell and laughed towards the house. Today he walked with shut lips and cold, cruel bearing, that had something of a slouch and a sneer in it. She knew him well by now, and could tell from that keen-looking, aloof young body of his what was happening inside him. There was a cold correctness in the way he put his bicycle in its place, that made her heart sink.

She came downstairs nervously. She was wearing a new net blouse that she thought became her. It had a high collar with a tiny ruff, reminding her of Mary Queen of Scots, and making her, she thought, look wonderfully a woman, and dignified. At twenty she was full-breasted and luxuriously formed. Her face was still a soft rich mask, unchangeable. But her eyes, once fitted, were wonderful. She was afraid of him. He would notice her new blouse.

He, being in a hard, ironical mood, was entertaining the family to a description of a service given in the Primitive Methodist Chapel, conducted by one of the well-known preachers of the sect. He sat at the head of the table, his mobile face, with eyes that could be so beautiful, shining with tenderness or dancing with laughter, now taking on one expression and then another, in imitation of various people he was mocking. His mockery always hurt her; it was too near the reality. He was too clever and cruel. She felt that when his eyes were like this, hard with mocking hate, he would spare neither himself nor anybody else. But Mrs Leivers was wiping her eyes with laughter, and Mr Leivers, just awake from his Sunday nap, was rubbing his head in amusement. The three brothers sat with ruffled, sleepy appearance in their shirtsleeves, giving a guffaw from time to time. The whole family loved a 'take-off' more than anything.

He took no notice of Miriam. Later, she saw him remark her new blouse, saw that the artist approved, but it won from him not a spark of warmth. She was nervous, could hardly reach the teacups from the shelves.

When the men went out to milk, she ventured to address him personally.

'You were late,' she said.

'Was I?' he answered.

There was silence for a while.

'Was it rough riding?' she asked.

'I didn't notice it.'

She continued quickly to lay the table. When she had finished –

'Tea won't be for a few minutes. Will you come and look at the daffodils?' she said.

He rose without answering. They went out into the back garden under the budding damson-trees. The hills and the sky were clean and cold. Everything looked washed, rather hard. Miriam glanced at Paul. He was pale and impassive. It seemed cruel to her that his eyes and brows, which she loved, could look so hurting.

'Has the wind made you tired?' she asked. She detected an underneath feeling of weariness about him.

'No, I think not,' he answered.

'It must be rough on the road – the wood moans so.'

'You can see by the clouds it's a south-west wind; that helps me here.'

'You see, I don't cycle, so I don't understand,' she murmured.

'Is there need to cycle to know that? he said.

She thought his sarcasms were unnecessary. They went forward in silence. Round the wild, tussocky lawn at the back of the house was a thorn hedge, under which daffodils were craning forward from among their sheaves of grey-green blades. The cheeks of the flowers were greenish with cold. But still some had burst, and their gold ruffled and glowed. Miriam went on her knees before one cluster, took a wild-looking daffodil between her hands, turned up its face of gold to her, and bowed down, caressing it with her mouth and cheeks and brows. He stood aside, with his hands in his pockets watching her. One after another she turned up to him the faces of the yellow, bursten flowers appealingly, fondling them lavishly all the while.

'Aren't they magnificent?' she murmured.

'Magnificent! it's a bit thick – they're pretty!'

She bowed again to her flowers at his censure of her praise. He watched her crouching, sipping the flowers with fervid kisses.

'Why must you always be fondling things!' he said irritably.

'But I love to touch them,' she replied, hurt.

'Can you never like things without clutching them as if you wanted to pull the heart out of them? Why don't you have a bit more restraint, or reserve, or something?'

She looked up at him full of pain, then continued slowly to stroke her lips against a ruffled flower. Their scent, as she smelled it, was much kinder than he; it almost made her cry.

'You wheedle the soul out of things,' he said. 'I would never wheedle – at any rate, I'd go straight.'

He scarcely knew what he was saying. These things came from him mechanically. She looked at him. His body seemed one weapon, firm and hard against her.

'You're always begging for things to love you,' he said, 'as if you were a beggar for love. Even the flowers, you have to fawn on them –'

Rhythmically, Miriam was swaying and stroking the flower with her mouth, inhaling the scent which ever after made her shudder as it came to her nostrils.

'You don't want to love – your eternal and abnormal craving is to be loved. You aren't positive, you're negative. You absorb, absorb, as if you must fill yourself up with love, because you've got a shortage somewhere.'

She was stunned by his cruelty, and did not hear. He had not the faintest notion of what he was saying. It was as if his fretted, tortured soul, run hot by thwarted passion, jetted off these sayings like sparks from electricity. She did not grasp anything he said. She only sat crouched beneath his cruelty and his hatred of her. She never realized in a flash. Over everything she brooded and brooded.

After tea he stayed with Edgar and the brother, taking no notice of Miriam. She, extremely unhappy on this looked-for holiday, waited for him. And at last he yielded and came to her. She was determined to track this mood of his to its origin. She counted it not much more than a mood.

'Shall we go through the wood a little way?' she asked him, knowing he never refused a direct request.

They went down to the warren. On the middle path they passed a trap, a narrow horseshoe hedge of small fir-boughs, baited with the guts of a rabbit. Paul glanced at it frowning. She caught his eye.

'Isn't it dreadful?' she asked.

'I don't know? Is it worse than a weasel with its teeth in a rabbit's throat? One weasel or many rabbits? One or the other must go!'

He was taking the bitterness of life badly. She was rather sorry for him.

'We will go back to the house,' he said. 'I don't want to walk out.'

They went past the lilac-tree, whose bronze leaf-buds were coming unfastened. Just a fragment remained of the haystack, a monument squared and brown, like a pillar of stone. There was a little bed of hay from the last cutting.

'Let us sit here a minute,' said Miriam.

He sat down against his will, resting his back against the hard wall of hay. They faced the amphitheatre of round hills that glowed with sunset, tiny white farms standing out, the meadows golden, the woods dark and yet luminous, tree-tops folded over tree-tops, distinct in the distance. The evening had cleared, and the east was tender with a magenta flush under which the land lay still and rich.

'Isn't it beautiful?' she pleaded.

But he only scowled. He would rather have had it ugly just then.

At that moment a big bull-terrier came rushing up, open-mouthed, pranced his two paws on the youth's shoulders, licking his face. Paul drew back, laughing. Bill was a great relief to him. He pushed the dog aside, but it came leaping back.

'Get out,' said the lad, 'or I'll dot thee one.'

But the dog would not be pushed away. So Paul had a little battle with the creature, pitching poor Bill away from him, who, however, only floundered tumultuously back again, wild with joy. The two fought together, the man laughing grudgingly, the dog grinning all over. Miriam watched them. There was something pathetic about the man. He wanted so badly to love, to be tender. The tough way he bowled the dog over was really loving. Bill got up, panting with happiness, his brown eyes rolling in his white face, and lumbered back again. He adored Paul. The lad frowned.

'Bill, I've had enough o' thee,' he said.

But the dog only stood with two heavy paws, that quivered with love, upon his thigh, and flicked a red tongue at him. He drew back.

'No,' he said – 'no – I've had enough.'

And in a minute the dog trotted off happily, to vary the fun.

He remained staring miserably across at the hills, whose still beauty he begrudged. He wanted to go and cycle with Edgar. Yet he had not the courage to leave Miriam.

'Why are you sad?' she asked humbly.

'I'm not sad; why should I be?' he answered. 'I'm only normal.'

She wondered why he always claimed to be normal when he was disagreeable.

'But what is the matter?' she pleaded, coaxing him soothingly.

'Nothing!'

'Nay!' she murmured.

He picked up a stick and began to stab the earth with it.

'You'd far better not talk,' he said.

'But I wish to know –' she replied.

He laughed resentfully.

'You always do,' he said.

'It's not fair to me,' she murmured.

He thrust, thrust, thrust at the ground with the pointed stick, digging up little clods of earth as if he were in a fever of irritation. She gently and firmly laid her hand on his wrist.

'Don't!' she said. 'Put it away.'

He flung the stick into the currant-bushes, and leaned back. Now he was bottled up.

'What is it?' she pleaded softly.

He lay perfectly still, only his eyes alive, and they full of torment.

'You know,' he said at length, rather wearily – 'you know – we'd better break it off.'

It was what she dreaded. Swiftly everything seemed to darken before her eyes.

'Why?' she murmured. 'What has happened?'

'Nothing has happened. We only realize where we are. It's no good –'

She waited in silence, sadly, patiently. It was no good being impatient with him. At any rate, he would tell her now what ailed him.

'We agreed on friendship,' he went on in a dull, monotonous voice. 'How often *have* we agreed for friendship! and yet – it neither stops there, nor gets anywhere else.'

He was silent again. She brooded. What did he mean? He was so wearing. There was something he would not yield. Yet she must be patient with him.

'I can only give friendship – it's all I'm capable of – it's a flaw in my make-up. The thing overbalances to one side – I hate a toppling balance. Let us have done.'

There was warmth of fury in his last phrases. He meant she loved him more than he her. Perhaps he could not love her. Perhaps she had not in herself that which he wanted. It was the deepest motive of her soul, this self-mistrust. It was so deep she dared neither realize nor acknowledge it. Perhaps she was deficient. Like an infinitely subtle shame, it kept her always back. It if were so, she would do without him. She would never let herself want him. She would merely see.

'But what has happened?' she said.

'Nothing – it's all myself – it only comes out just now. We're always like this towards Easter-time.'

He grovelled so helplessly, she pitied him. At least she never floundered in such a pitiable way. After all, it was he who was chiefly humiliated.

'What do you want?' she asked.

'Why – I mustn't come often – that's all. Why should I monopolize you when I'm not – You see, I'm deficient in something with regard to you –'

He was telling her he did not love her, and so sought to leave her a chance with another man. How foolish and blind and shamefully clumsy he was! What were other men to her! What were men to her at all! But he, ah! she loved his soul. Was *he* deficient in something? Perhaps he was.

'But I don't understand,' she said huskily. 'Yesterday –'

The night was turning jangled and hateful to him as the twilight faded. And she bowed under her suffering.

'I know,' he cried, 'you never will! You'll never believe that I can't – can't physically, any more than I can fly up like a skylark –'

'What?' she murmured. Now she dreaded.

'Love you.'

He hated her bitterly at that moment because he made her suffer. Love her! She knew he loved her. He really belonged to her. This about not loving her, physically, bodily, was a mere perversity on his part, because he knew she loved him. He was stupid like a child. He belonged to her. His soul wanted her. She guessed somebody had been influencing him. She felt upon him the hardness the foreignness of another influence.

'What have they been saying at home?' she asked.

'It's not that,' he answered.

And then she knew it was. She despised them for their commonness, his people. They did not know what things were really worth.

He and she talked very little more that night. After all he left her to cycle with Edgar.

He had come back to his mother. Hers was the strongest tie in his life. When he thought round, Miriam shrank away. There was a vague, unreal feel about her. And nobody else mattered. There was one place in the world that stood solid and did not melt into unreality: the place where his mother was. Everybody else could grow shadowy, almost non-existent to him, but she could not. It was as if the pivot of his life, from which he could not escape, was his mother.

And in the same way she waited for him. In him was established her life now. After all, the life beyond offered very little to Mrs Morel. She saw that our chance for *doing* is here, and doing counted with her. Paul was going to prove that she had been right; he was going to make a man whom nothing should shift off his feet; he was going to alter the face of the earth in some way which mattered. Wherever he went she felt her soul went with him. Whatever he did she felt her soul stood by him, ready, as it were, to hand him his tools. She could not bear it when he was with Miriam. William was dead. She would fight to keep Paul.

And he came back to her. And in his soul was a feeling of the satisfaction of self-sacrifice because he was faithful to her. She loved him first; he loved her first. And yet it was not enough. His new young life, so strong and imperious, was urged towards something else. It made him mad with restlessness. She saw this, and wished bitterly that Miriam had been a woman who could take this new life of his, and leave her the roots. He fought against his mother almost as he fought against Miriam.

It was a week before he went again to Willey Farm. Miriam had suffered a great deal, and was afraid to see him again. Was she now to endure the ignominy of his abandoning her? That would only be superficial and temporary. He would come back. She held the keys to his soul. But meanwhile, how he would torture her with his battle against her. She shrank from it.

However, the Sunday after Easter he came to tea. Mrs Leivers was glad to see him. She gathered something was fretting him, that he found things hard. He seemed to drift to her for comfort. And she was good to him. She did him that great kindness of treating him almost with reverence.

He met her with the young children in the front garden.

'I'm glad you've come,' said the mother, looking at him with her great appealing brown eyes. 'It is such a sunny day. I was just going down to the fields for the first time this year.'

He felt she would like him to come. That soothed him. They went, talked simply, he gentle and humble. He could have wept with gratitude that she was deferential to him. He was feeling humiliated.

At the bottom of the Mow Close they found a thrush's nest.

'Shall I show you the eggs?' he said.

'Do!' replied Mrs Leivers. 'They seem *such* a sign of spring, and so hopeful.'

He put aside the thorns, and took out the eggs, holding them in the palm of his hand.

'They are quite hot – I think we frightened her off them,' he said.

'Ay, poor thing!' said Mrs Leivers.

Miriam could not help touching the eggs, and his hand which, it seemed to her, cradled them so well.

'Isn't it a strange warmth!' she murmured, to get near him.

'Blood heat,' he answered.

She watched him putting them back, his body pressed against the hedge, his arm reaching slowly through the thorns, his hand folded carefully over the eggs. He was concentrated on the act. Seeing him so, she loved him; he seemed so simple and sufficient to himself. And she could not get to him.

After tea she stood hesitating at the bookshelf. He too 'Tartarin de Tarascon'. Again they sat on the bank of hay at the foot of the stack. He read a couple of pages, but without any heart for it. Again the dog came racing up to repeat the fun of the other day. He shoved his muzzle in the man's chest. Paul fingered his ear for a moment. Then he pushed him away.

'Go away, Bill,' he said. 'I don't want you!'

Bill slunk off, and Miriam wondered and dreaded what was coming. There was a silence about the youth that made her still with apprehension. It was not his furies, but his quiet resolutions that she feared.

Turning his face a little to one side, so that she could not see him, he began, speaking slowly and painfully:

'Do you think – if I didn't come up so much – you might get to like somebody else – another man?'

So this was what he was still harping on.

'But I don't know any other men. Why do you ask?' she replied, in a low tone that should have been a reproach to him.

'Why,' he blurted, 'because they say I've no right to come up like this – without we mean to marry –'

Miriam was indignant at anybody forcing the issues between them. She had been furious with her own father for suggesting to Paul, laughingly, that he knew why he came so much.

'Who says?' she asked, wondering if her people had anything to do with it. They had not.

'Mother – and the others. They say at this rate everybody will consider me engaged, and I ought to consider myself so, because it's not fair to you. And I've tried to find out – and I don't think I love you as a man ought to love his wife. What do *you* think about it?'

Miriam bowed her head moodily. She was angry at having this struggle. People should leave him and her alone.

'I don't know,' she murmured.

'Do you think we love each other enough to marry?' he asked definitely. It made her tremble.

'No,' she answered truthfully. 'I don't think so – we're too young.'

'I thought perhaps,' he went on miserably, 'that you, with your intensity in things, might have given me more – than I could ever make up to you. And even now – if you think it better – we'll get engaged.'

Now Miriam wanted to cry. And she was angry, too. He was always such a child for people to do as they liked with.

'No, I don't think so,' she said firmly.

He pondered a minute.

'You see,' he said, 'with me – I don't think one person would ever monopolize me – be everything to me – I think never.'

This she did not consider.

'No,' she murmured. Then, after a pause, she looked at him, and her dark eyes flashed.

'This is your mother,' she said. 'I know she never liked me.'

'No, no, it isn't,' he said hastily. 'It was for your sake she spoke this time. She only said, if I was going on, I ought to consider myself engaged.' There was a silence. 'And if I ask you to come down any time, you won't stop away, will you?'

She did not answer. By this time she was very angry.

'Well, what shall we do?' she said shortly. 'I suppose I'd better drop French. I was just beginning to get on with it. But I suppose I can go on alone.'

'I don't see that we need,' he said. 'I can give you a French lesson, surely.'

'Well – and there are Sunday nights. I shan't stop coming to chapel, because I enjoy it, and it's all the social life I get. But you've no need to come home with me. I can go alone.'

'All right,' he answered, rather taken aback. 'But if I ask Edgar, he'll always come with us, and then they can say nothing.'

There was silence. After all, then, she would not lose much. For all their talk down at his home there would not be much difference. She wished they would mind their own business.

'And you won't think about it, and let it trouble you, will you?' he asked.

'Oh no,' replied Miriam, without looking at him.

He was silent. She thought him unstable. He had no fixity of purpose, no anchor of righteousness that held him.

'Because,' he continued, 'a man gets across his bicycle – and goes to work – and does all sorts of things. But a woman broods.'

'No, I shan't bother,' said Miriam. And she meant it.

It had gone rather chilly. They went indoors.

'How white Paul looks!' Mrs Leivers exclaimed. 'Miriam, you shouldn't have let him sit out of doors. Do you think you've taken cold, Paul?'

'Oh, no!' he laughed.

But he felt done up. It wore him out, the conflict in himself. Miriam pitied him now. But quite early, before nine o'clock, he rose to go.

'You're not going home, are you?' asked Mrs Leivers anxiously.

'Yes,' he replied, 'I said I'd be early.' He was very awkward.

'But this *is* early,' said Mr Leivers.

Miriam sat in the rocking-chair, and did not speak. He hesitated, expecting her to rise and go with him to the barn as usual for his bicycle. She remained as she was. He was at a loss.

'Well – good night all!' he faltered.

She spoke her good night along with all the others. But as he went past the window he looked in. She saw him pale, his brows knit slightly in a way that had become constant with him, his eyes dark with pain.

She rose and went to the doorway to wave good-bye to him as he passed through the gate. He rode slowly under the pine-trees, feeling a cur and a miserable wretch. His bicycle went tilting down the hills at random. He thought it would be a relief to break one's neck.

Two days later he sent up a book and a little note, urging her to read and to be busy.

At that time he gave all his friendship to Edgar. He loved the family so much, he loved the farm so much; it was the dearest place on earth to him. His home was not so lovable. It was his mother. But then he would have been just as happy with his mother anywhere. Whereas Willey Farm he loved passionately. He loved the little pokey kitchen, where men's boots tramped, and the dog slept with one eye open for fear of being trodden on; where the lamp hung over the table at night, and everything was so silent. He loved Miriam's long, low parlour, with its atmosphere of romance, its flowers, its books, its high rosewood piano. He loved the gardens and the buildings that stood with their scarlet roofs on the naked edges of the fields, crept towards the wood as if for cosiness, the wild country scooping down a valley and up the uncultured hills of the other side. Only to be there was an exhilaration and a joy to him. He loved Mrs Leivers, with her unworldliness and her quaint cynicism; he loved Mr Leivers, so warm and young and lovable; he loved Edgar, who lit up when he came, and the boys and the children and Bill – even the sow Circe and the Indian game-cock called Tippoo. All this besides Miriam. He could not give it up.

So he went as often, but he was usually with Edgar. Only all the family, including the father, joined in charades and games at evening. And later, Miriam drew them together, and they read 'Macbeth' out of penny books, taking parts. It was great excitement. Miriam was glad, and Mrs Leivers was glad, and Mr Leivers enjoyed it. Then they all learned songs together from tonic solfa, singing in a circle round the fire. But now Paul was very rarely alone with Miriam. She waited. When she and Edgar and he walked home together from chapel or from the literary society in Bestwood, she knew this talk, so passionate and so unorthodox nowadays, was for her. She did envy Edgar, however, his cycling with Paul, his Friday nights, his days working in the fields. For her Friday nights and her French lessons were gone. She was nearly always alone, walking, pondering in the wood, reading, studying, dreaming, waiting. And he wrote to her frequently.

One Sunday evening they attained to their old rare harmony. Edgar had stayed to Communion – he wondered what it was like – with Mrs Morel. So Paul came on alone with Miriam to his home. He was more or less under her spell again. As usual, they were discussing the sermon. He was setting now full sail towards Agnosticism, but such a religious Agnosticism that Miriam did not suffer so badly. They were at the Renan 'Vie de Jésus' stage. Miriam was the threshing-floor on which he threshed out all his beliefs. While he trampled his ideas upon her soul, the truth came out for him. She alone was his threshing floor. She alone helped him towards realization. Almost impassive, she submitted to his argument and expounding. And somehow, because of her, he gradually realized where he was wrong. And what he realized, she realized. She felt he could not do without her.

They came to the silent house. He took the key out of the scullery window, and they entered. All the time he went on with his discussion. He lit the gas, mended the fire, and brought her some cakes from the pantry. She sat on the sofa, quietly, with a plate on her knee. She wore a large white hat with some pinkish flowers. It was a cheap hat, but he liked it. Her face beneath was still and pensive, golden-brown and ruddy. Always her ears were hid in her short curls. She watched him.

She liked him on Sundays. Then he wore a dark suit that showed the lithe movement of his body. There was a clean, clear-cut look about him. He went on with his thinking to her. Suddenly he reached for a Bible. Miriam liked the way he reached up – so sharp, straight to the mark. He turned the pages quickly, and read her a chapter of St John. As he sat in the arm-chair reading, intent, his voice only thinking, she felt as if he were using her unconsciously as a man uses his tools at some work he is bent on. She loved it. And the wistfulness of his voice was like a reaching to something, and it was as if she were what he reached with. She sat back on the sofa away from him, and yet feeling herself the very instrument his hand grasped. It gave her great pleasure.

Then he began to falter and to get self-conscious. And when he came to the verse, 'A woman, when she is in travail, hath sorrow because her hour is come', he missed it out. Miriam had felt him growing uncomfortable. She shrank when the well-known words did not follow. He went on reading, but she did not hear. A grief and shame made her bend her head. Six months ago he would have read it simply. Now there was a scotch in his running with her. Now she felt there was really something hostile between them, something of which they were ashamed.

She ate her cake mechanically. He tried to go on with his argument, but could not get back the right note. Soon Edgar came in. Mrs Morel had gone to the friends'. The three set off to Willey Farm.

Miriam brooded over his split with her. There was something else he wanted. He could not be satisfied; he could give her no peace. There was between them now always a ground for strife. She wanted to prove him. She believed that his chief need in life was herself. If she could prove it, both to herself and to him, the rest might go; she could simply trust to the future.

So in May she asked him to come to Willey Farm and meet Mrs Dawes. There was something he hankered after. She saw him, whenever they spoke of Clara Dawes, rouse and get slightly angry. He said he did not like her. Yet he was keen to know about her. Well, he should put himself to the test. She believed that there were in him desires for higher things, and desires for lower, and that the desire for the higher would conquer. At any rate, he should try. She forgot that her 'higher' and 'lower' were arbitrary.

He was rather excited at the idea of meeting Clara at Willey Farm. Mrs Dawes came for the day. Her heavy, dun-coloured hair was coiled on top of her head. She wore a white blouse and navy skirt, and somehow, wherever she was, seemed to make things look paltry and insignificant. When she was in the room, the kitchen seemed too small and mean altogether. Miriam's beautiful twilightly parlour looked stiff and stupid. All the Leivers were eclipsed like candles. They found her rather hard to put up with. Yet she was perfectly amiable, but indifferent, and rather hard.

Paul did not come till afternoon. He was early. As he swung off his bicycle, Miriam saw him look round at the house eagerly. He would be disappointed if the visitor had not come. Miriam went out to meet him, bowing her head because of the sunshine. Nasturtiums were coming out crimson under the cool green shadow of their leaves. The girl stood, dark-haired, glad to see him.

'Hasn't Clara come?' he asked.

'Yes,' replied Miriam in her musical tone. 'She's reading.'

He wheeled his bicycle into the barn. He had put on a handsome tie, of which he was rather proud, and socks to match.

'She came this morning?' he asked.

'Yes,' replied Miriam, as she walked at his side. 'You said you'd bring me that letter from the man at Liberty's. Have you remembered?'

'Oh dash, no!' he said. 'But nag at me till you get it.'

'I don't like to nag at you.'

'Do it whether or not. And is she any more agreeable?' he continued.

'You know I always think she is quite agreeable.'

He was silent. Evidently his eagerness to be early today had been the newcomer. Miriam already began to suffer. They went together towards the house. He took the clips off his trousers, but was too lazy to brush the dust from his shoes, in spite of the socks and tie.

Clara sat in the cool parlour reading. He saw the nape of her white neck, and the fine hair lifted from it. She rose, looking at him indifferently. To shake hands she lifted her arm straight, in a manner that seemed at once to keep him at a distance, and yet to fling something to him. He noticed how her breasts swelled inside her blouse, and how her shoulder curved handsomely under the thin muslin at the top of her arm.

'You have chosen a fine day,' he said.

'It happens so,' she said.

'Yes,' he said; 'I am glad.'

She sat down, not thanking him for his politeness.

'What have you been doing all morning?' asked Paul of Miriam.

'Well, you see,' said Miriam, coughing huskily, 'Clara only came with father – and so – she's not been here very long.'

Clara sat leaning on the table, holding aloof. He noticed her hands were large, but well kept. And the skin on them seemed almost coarse, opaque, and white, with fine golden hairs. She did not mind if he observed her hands. She intended to scorn him. Her heavy arm lay negligently on the table. Her mouth was closed as if she were offended, and she kept her face slightly averted.

'You were at Margaret Bonford's meeting the other evening,' he said to her.

Miriam did not know this courteous Paul. Clara glanced at him.

'Yes,' she said.

'Why,' asked Miriam, 'how do you know?'

'I went in for a few minutes before the train came,' he answered.

Clara turned away again rather disdainfully.

'I think she's a lovable little woman,' said Paul.

'Margaret Bonford!' exclaimed Clara. 'She's a great deal cleverer than most men.'

'Well, I didn't say she wasn't,' he said, deprecating. 'She's lovable for all that.'

'And of course, that is all that matters,' said Clara witheringly.

He rubbed his head, rather perplexed, rather annoyed.

'I suppose it matters more than her cleverness,' he said: 'which after all, would never get her to heaven.'

'It's not heaven she wants to get – it's her fair share on earth,' retorted Clara. She spoke as if he were responsible for some deprivation which Miss Bonford suffered.

'Well,' he said, 'I thought she was warm, and awfully nice – only too frail. I wished she was sitting comfortably in peace –'

'"Darning her husband's stockings,"' said Clara scathingly.

'I'm sure she wouldn't mind darning even my stockings,' he said. 'And I'm sure she'd do them well. Just as I wouldn't mind blacking her boots if she wanted me to.'

But Clara refused to answer this sally of his. He talked to Miriam for a little while. The other woman held aloof.

'Well,' he said, 'I think I'll go and see Edgar. Is he on the land?'

'I believe,' said Miriam, 'he's gone for a load of coal. He should be back directly.'

'Then,' he said, 'I'll go and meet him.'

Miriam dared not propose anything for the three of them. He rose and left.

On the top road, where the gorse was out, he saw Edgar walking lazily beside the mare, who nodded her white-starred forehead as she dragged the clanking load of coal. The young farmer's face lighted up as he saw his friend. Edgar was good-looking, with dark, warm eyes. His clothes were old and rather disreputable, and he walked with considerable pride.

'Hello!' he said, seeing Paul bareheaded. 'Where are you going?'

'Came to meet you. Can't stand "Nevermore".'

Edgar's teeth flashed in a laugh of amusement.

'Who is "Nevermore"?' he asked.

'The lady – Mrs Dawes – it ought to be Mrs The Raven that quoted "Nevermore".'

Edgar laughed with glee.

'Don't you like her?' he asked.

'Not a fat lot,' said Paul. 'Why, do you?'

'No!' The answer came with a deep ring of conviction. 'No!' Edgar pursed up his lips. 'I can't say she's much in my line.' He mused a little. Then: 'But why do you call her "Nevermore"?' he asked.

'Well,' said Paul, 'if she looks at a man she says haughtily "Nevermore", and if she looks at herself in the looking-glass she says disdainfully "Nevermore", and if she thinks back she says it in disgust, and if she looks forward she says it cynically.'

Edgar considered this speech, failed to make much out of it, and said, laughingly,

'You think she's a man-hater?'

'*She* thinks she is,' replied Paul.

'But you don't think so?'

'No,' replied Paul.

'Wasn't she nice with you, then?'

'Could you imagine her *nice* with anybody?' asked the young man.

Edgar laughed. Together they unloaded the coal in the yard. Paul was rather self-conscious, because he knew Clara could see if she looked out of the window. She didn't look.

On Saturday afternoons the horses were brushed down and groomed. Paul and Edgar worked together, sneezing with the dust that came from the pelts of Jimmy and Flower.

'Do you know a new song to teach me?' said Edgar.

He continued to work all the time. The back of his neck was sun-red when he bent down, and his fingers that held the brush were thick. Paul watched him sometimes.

'"Mary Morrison"?' suggested the younger.

Edgar agreed. He had a good tenor voice, and he loved to learn all the songs his friend could teach him, so that he could sing whilst he was carting. Paul had a very indifferent baritone voice, but a good ear. However, he sang softly, for fear of Clara. Edgar repeated the line in a clear tenor. At times they both broke off to sneeze, and first one, then the other, abused his horse.

Miriam was impatient of men. It took so little to amuse them – even Paul. She thought it anomalous in him that he could be so thoroughly absorbed in a triviality.

It was tea-time when they had finished.

'What song was that?' asked Miriam.

Edgar told her. The conversation turned to singing.

'We have such jolly times,' Miriam said to Clara.

Mrs Dawes ate her meal in a slow dignified way. Whenever the men were present she grew distant.

'Do you like singing?' Miriam asked her.

'If it is good,' she said.

Paul, of course, coloured.

'You mean if it is high class and trained?' he said.

'I think a voice needs training before the singing is anything,' she said.

'You might as well insist on having people's voices trained before you allow them to talk,' he replied. 'Really, people sing for their own pleasure, as a rule.'

'And it may be for other people's discomfort.'

'Then the other people should have flaps on their ears,' he replied.

The boys laughed. There was a silence. He flushed deeply, and ate in silence.

After tea, when all the men had gone but Paul, Mrs Leivers said to Clara:

'And you find life happier now?'

'Infinitely.'

'And you are satisfied?'

'So long as I can be free and independent.'

'And you don't *miss* anything in your life?' asked Mrs Leivers gently.

'I've put all that behind me.'

Paul had been feeling uncomfortable during this discourse. He got up.

'You'll find you're always tumbling over things you've put behind you,' he said. Then he took his departure to the cowsheds. He felt he had been witty, and his manly pride was high. He whistled as he went down the brick track.

Miriam came for him a little later to know if he would go with Clara and her for a walk. They set off down to Strelley Mill Farm. As they were going beside the brook, on the Willey Water side, looking through the break at the edge of the wood, where pink campions glowed under a few sunbeams, they saw, beyond the tree-trunks and the thin hazel bushes, a man leading a great bay horse through the gullies. The big red beast seemed to dance romantically through that dimness of green hazel drift, away there where the air was shadowy, as if it were in the past, among the fading bluebells that might have bloomed for Deirdre or Iseult.

The three stood charmed.

'What a treat to be a knight,' he said, 'and to have a pavilion here.'

'And to have us shut up safely?' replied Clara.

'Yes,' he answered, 'singing with your maids at your broidery. I would carry your banner of white and green and heliotrope. I would have "W.S.P.U." emblazoned on my shield, beneath a woman rampant.'

'I have no doubt,' said Clara, 'that you would much rather fight for a woman than let her fight for herself.'

'I would. When she fights for herself she seems like a dog before a looking-glass, gone into a mad fury with its own shadow.'

'And *you* are the looking-glass?' she asked, with a curl of the lip.

'Or the shadow,' he replied.

'I am afraid,' she said, 'that you are too clever.'

'Well, I leave it to you to be *good*,' he retorted, laughing. 'Be good, sweet maid, and just let *me* be clever.'

But Clara wearied of his flippancy. Suddenly, looking at her, he saw that the upward lifting of her face was misery and not scorn. His heart grew tender for everybody. He turned and was gentle with Miriam, whom he had neglected till then.

At the wood's edge they met Limb, a thin, swarthy man of forty, tenant of Strelley Mill, which he ran as a cattle-raising farm. He held the halter of the powerful stallion indifferently, as if he were tired. The three stood to let him pass over the stepping-stones of the first brook. Paul admired that so large an animal should walk on such springy toes, with an endless excess of vigour. Limb pulled up before them.

'Tell your father, Miss Leivers,' he said, in a peculiar piping voice, 'that his young beas'es' as broke that bottom fence three days an' runnin'.'

'Which?' asked Miriam, tremulous.

The great horse breathed heavily, shifting round its red flanks, and looking suspiciously with its wonderful big eyes upwards from under its lowered head and falling mane.

'Come along a bit,' replied Limb, 'an' I'll show you.'

The man and the stallion went forward. It danced sideways, shaking its white fetlocks and looking frightened, as it felt itself in the brook.

'No hanky-pankyin',' said the man affectionately to the beast.

It went up the bank in little leaps, then splashed finely through the second brook. Clara, walking with a kind of sulky abandon, watched it half-fascinated, half-contemptuous. Limb stopped and pointed to the fence under some willows.

'There, you see where they got through,' he said. 'My man's druv'em back three times.'

'Yes,' answered Miriam, colouring as if she were at fault.

'Are you comin' in?' asked the man.

'No, thanks, but we should like to go by the pond.'

'Well, just as you've a mind,' he said.

The horse gave little whinneys of pleasure at being so near home.

'He is glad to be back,' said Clara, who was interested in the creature.

'Yes – 'e's been a tidy step today.'

They went through the gate, and saw approaching them from the big farmhouse a smallish, dark, excitable-looking woman of about thirty-five. Her hair was touched with grey, her dark eyes looked wild. She walked with her hands behind her back. Her brother went forward. As it saw her, the big bay stallion whinneyed again. She came up excitedly.

'Are you home again, my boy!' she said tenderly to the horse, not to the man. The great beast shifted round to her, ducking his head. She smuggled into his mouth the wrinkled yellow apple she had been hiding behind her back, then she kissed him near the eyes. He gave a big sigh of pleasure. She held his head in her arms against her breast.

'Isn't he splendid!' said Miriam to her.

Miss Limb looked up. Her dark eyes glanced straight at Paul.

'Oh, good evening, Miss Leivers,' she said. 'It's ages since you've been down.' Miriam introduced her friends.

'Your horse *is* a fine fellow!' said Clara.

'Isn't he!' Again she kissed him. 'As loving as any man!'

'More loving than most men, I should think,' replied Clara.

'He's a nice boy!' cried the woman, again embracing the horse.

Clara, fascinated by the big beast, went up to stroke his neck.

'He's quite gentle,' said Miss Limb. 'Don't you think big fellows are?'

'He's a beauty!' replied Clara.

She wanted to look in his eyes. She wanted him to look at her.

'It's a pity he can't talk,' she said.

'Oh, but he can – all but,' replied the other woman.

Then her brother moved on with the horse.

'Are you coming in? *Do* come in, Mr – I didn't catch it.'

'Morel,' said Miriam. 'No, we won't come in, but we should like to go by the mill-pond.'

'Yes – yes, do. Do you fish, Mr Morel?'

'No,' said Paul.

'Because if you do you might come and fish any time,' said Miss Limb. 'We scarcely see a soul from week's end to week's end. I should be thankful.'

'What fish are there in the pond?' he asked.

They went through the front garden, over the sluice, and up the steep bank to the pond, which lay in shadow, with its two wooded islets. Paul walked with Miss Limb.

'I shouldn't mind swimming here,' he said.

'Do,' she replied. 'Come when you like. My brother will be awfully pleased to talk with you. He is so quiet, because there is no one to talk to. Do come and swim.'

Clara came up.

'It's a fine depth,' she said, 'and so clear.'

'Yes,' said Miss Limb.

'Do you swim?' said Paul. 'Miss Limb was just saying we could come when we liked.'

'Of course there's the farm hands,' said Miss Limb.

They talked a few moments, then went on up the wild hill, leaving the lonely, haggard-eyed woman on the bank.

The hillside was all ripe with sunshine. It was wild and tussocky, given over to rabbits. The three walked in silence. Then:

'She makes me feel uncomfortable,' said Paul.

'You mean Miss Limb?' asked Miriam. 'Yes.'

'What's a matter with her? Is she going dotty with being too lonely?'

'Yes,' said Miriam. 'It's not the right sort of life for her. I think it's cruel to bury her there. *I* really ought to go and see her more. But – she upsets me.'

'She makes me feel sorry for her – yes, and she bothers me,' she said.

'I suppose,' blurted Clara suddenly, 'she wants a man.'

The other two were silent for a few moments.

'But it's the loneliness sends her cracked,' said Paul.

Clara did not answer, but strode on uphill. She was walking with her head hanging, her legs swinging as she kicked through the dead thistles and the tussocky grass, her arms hanging loose. Rather than walking, her handsome body seemed to be blundering up the hill. A hot wave went over Paul. He was curious about her. Perhaps life had been cruel to her. He forgot Miriam, who was walking beside him talking to him. She glanced at him, finding he did not answer her. His eyes were fixed ahead on Clara.

'Do you still think she is disagreeable?' she asked.

He did not notice that the question was sudden. It ran with his thoughts.

'Something's the matter with her,' he said.

'Yes,' answered Miriam.

They found at the top of the hill a hidden wild field, two sides of which were backed by the wood, the other sides by high loose hedges of hawthorn and elder-bushes. Between these overgrown bushes were gaps that the cattle might have walked through had there been any cattle now. There the turf was smooth as velveteen, padded and holed by the rabbits. The field itself was coarse, and crowded with tall, big cowslips that had never been cut. Clusters of strong flowers rose everywhere above the coarse tussocks of bent. It was like a roadstead crowded with tall, fairy shipping.

'Ah!' cried Miriam, and she looked at Paul, her dark eyes dilating. He smiled. Together they enjoyed the field of flowers. Clara, a little way off, was looking at the cowslips disconsolately. Paul and Miriam stayed close together, talking in subdued tones. He kneeled on one knee, quickly gathering the best blossoms, moving from tuft to tuft restlessly, talking softly all the time. Miriam plucked the flowers lovingly, lingering over them. He always seemed to her too quick, and almost scientific. Yet his bunches had a natural beauty more than hers. He loved them, but as if they were his and he had a right to them. She had more reverence for them: they held something she had not.

The flowers were very fresh and sweet. He wanted to drink them. As he gathered them, he ate the little yellow trumpets. Clara was still wandering about disconsolately. Going towards her, he said:

'Why don't you get some?'

'I don't believe in it. They look better growing.'

'But you'd like some?'

'They want to be left.'

'I don't believe they do.'

'I don't want the corpses of flowers about me,' she said.

'That's a stiff, artificial notion,' he said. 'They don't die any quicker in water than on their roots. And besides, they *look* nice in a bowl – they look jolly. And you only call a thing a corpse because it looks corpse-like.'

'Whether it is one or not?' she argued.

'It isn't one to me. A dead flower isn't a corpse of a flower.' Clara now ignored him.

'And even so – what right have you to pull them?' she asked.

'Because I like them, and want them – and there's plenty of them.'

'And that is sufficient?'

'Yes. Why not? I'm sure they'd smell nice in your room in Nottingham.'

'And I should have the pleasure of watching them die.'

'But then – it does not matter if they do die.'

Whereupon he left her, and went stooping over the clumps of tangled flowers which thickly sprinkled the field like pale, luminous foam-clots. Miriam had come close. Clara was kneeling, breathing some scent from the cowslips.

'I think,' said Miriam, 'if you treat them with reverence you don't do them any harm. It is the spirit you pluck them in that matters.'

'Yes,' he said. 'But no, you get 'em because you want 'em and that's all.' He held out his bunch.

Miriam was silent. He picked some more.

'Look at these!' he continued; 'sturdy and lusty like little trees and like boys with fat legs.'

Clara's hat lay on the grass not far off. She was kneeling, bending forward still to smell the flowers. Her neck gave him a sharp pang, such a beautiful thing, yet not proud of itself just now. Her breasts swung slightly in her blouse. The arching curve of her back was beautiful and strong; she wore no stays. Suddenly, without knowing, he was scattering a handful of cowslips over her hair and neck saying:

> 'Ashes to ashes, and dust to dust,
> If the Lord won't have you the devil must.'

The chill flowers fell on her neck. She looked up at him, with almost pitiful, scared grey eyes, wondering what he was doing. Flowers fell on her face, and she shut her eyes.

Suddenly, standing there above her, he felt awkward.

'I thought you wanted a funeral,' he said, ill at ease.

Clara laughed strangely, and rose, picking the cowslips from her hair. She took up her hat and pinned it on. One flower had remained tangled in her hair. He saw, but would not tell her. He gathered up the flowers he had sprinkled over her.

At the edge of the wood the bluebells had flowed over into the field and stood there like flood-water. But they were fading now. Clara strayed up to them. He wandered after her. The bluebells pleased him.

'Look how they've come out of the wood!' he said.

Then she turned with a flash of warmth and of gratitude.

'Yes,' she smiled.

His blood beat up.

'It makes me think of the wild men of the woods, how terrified they would be when they got breast to breast with the open space.'

'Do you think they were?' she asked.

'I wonder which was more frightened among old tribes – those bursting out of their darkness of woods upon all the space of light, or those from the open tiptoeing into the forests.'

'I should think the second,' she answered.

'Yes, you *do* feel like one of the open space sort, trying to force yourself into the dark, don't you?'

'How should I know?' she answered queerly.

The conversation ended there.

The evening was deepening over the earth. Already the valley was full of shadow. One tiny space of light stood opposite at Crossleigh Bank Farm. Brightness was swimming on the top of the hills. Miriam came up slowly, her face in her big, loose bunch of flowers, walking ankle-deep through the scattered froth of the cowslips. Beyond her the trees were coming into shape, all shadow.

'Shall we go?' she asked.

And the three turned away. They were all silent. Going down the path they could see the light of home right across, and on the ridge of the hill a thin dark outline with little lights, where the colliery village touched the sky.

'It has been nice, hasn't it?' he asked.

Miriam murmured assent, Clara was silent.

'Don't you think so?' he persisted.

But she walked with her head up, and still did not answer. He could tell by the way she moved, as if she didn't care, that she suffered.

At this time Paul took his mother to Lincoln. She was bright and enthusiastic as ever, but as he sat opposite her in the railway carriage, she seemed to look frail. He had a momentary sensation as if she were slipping away from him. Then he wanted to get hold of her, to fasten her, almost to chain her. He felt he must keep hold of her with his hand.

They drew near to the city. Both were at the window looking at the cathedral.

'There she is, mother!' he cried.

They saw the great cathedral lying couchant above the plain.

'Ah!' she exclaimed. 'So she is!'

He looked at his mother. Her blue eyes were watching the cathedral quietly. She seemed again to be beyond him. Something in the eternal repose of the uplifted cathedral, blue and noble against the sky, was reflected in her, something of the fatality. What was, *was*. With all his young will he could not alter it. He saw her face, the skin still fresh and pink and downy, but crow's-feet near her eyes, her eyelids steady, sinking a little, her mouth always closed with disillusion; and there was on her the same eternal look, as if she knew fate at last. He beat against it with all the strength of his soul.

'Look mother, how big she is above the town! Think, there are streets and streets below her! She looks bigger than the city altogether.'

'So she does!' exclaimed his mother, breaking bright into life again. But he had seen her sitting. looking steady out of the window at the cathedral, her face and eyes fixed, reflecting the relentlessness of life. And the crow's-feet near her eyes, and her mouth shut so hard, made him feel he would go mad.

They ate a meal that she considered wildly extravagant.

'Don't imagine I like it,' she said, as she ate her cutlet. 'I *don't* like it, I really don't! Just *think* of your money wasted!'

'You never mind my money,' he said. 'You forget I'm a fellow taking his girl for an outing.'

And he bought her some blue violets.

'Stop it at once, sir!' she commanded. 'How can I do it?'

'You've got nothing to do. Stand still!'

And in the middle of High Street he stuck the flowers in her coat.

'An old thing like me!' she said, sniffing.

'You see,' he said, 'I want people to think we're awful swells. So look ikey.'

'I'll jowl your head,' she laughed.

'Strut!' he commanded. 'Be a fantail pigeon.'

It took him an hour to get her through the street. She stood above Glory Hole, she stood before Stone Bow, she stood everywhere, and exclaimed.

A man came up, took off his hat, and bowed to her.

'Can I show you the town, madam?'

'No, thank you,' she answered. 'I've got my son.'

Then Paul was cross with her for not answering with more dignity.

'You go away with you!' she exclaimed. 'Ha! that's the Jew's House. Now, do you remember that lecture, Paul –?'

But she could scarcely climb the cathedral hill. He did not notice. Then suddenly he found her unable to speak. He took her into a little public-house, where she rested.

'It's nothing,' she said. 'My heart is only a bit old; one must expect it.'

He did not answer, but looked at her. Again his heart was crushed in a hot grip. He wanted to cry, he wanted to smash things in fury.

They set off again, pace by pace, so slowly. And every step seemed like a weight on his chest. He felt as if his heart would burst. At last they came to the top. She stood enchanted, looking at the castle gate, looking at the cathedral front. She had quite forgotten herself.

'Now *this* is better than I thought it could be!' she cried.

But he hated it. Everywhere he followed her, brooding. They sat together in the cathedral. They attended a little service in the choir. She was timid.

'I suppose it is open to anybody?' she asked him.

'Yes,' he replied. 'Do you think they'd have the damn cheek to send us away?'

'Well, I'm sure,' she exclaimed, 'they would if they heard your language.'

Her face seemed to shine again with joy and peace during the service. And all the time he was wanting to rage and smash things and cry.

Afterwards, when they were leaning over the wall, looking at the town below, he blurted suddenly:

'Why can't a man have a *young* mother? What is the old for?'

'Well,' his mother laughed, 'she can scarcely help it.'

'And why wasn't I the oldest son? Look – they say the young ones have the advantage – but look, *they* had the young mother. You should have had me for your eldest son.'

'*I* didn't arrange it,' she remonstrated. 'Come to consider, you're as much to blame as me.'

He turned on her, white, his eyes furious.

'What are you old for?' he said, mad with his impotence. '*Why* can't you walk? *Why* can't you come with me to places?'

'At one time,' she replied, 'I could have run up that hill a good deal better than you.'

'What's the good of that to *me*?' he cried, hitting his fist on the wall. Then he became plaintive. 'It's too bad of you to be ill. Little, it is –'

'Ill!' she cried. 'I'm a bit old, and you'll have to put up with it, that's all.'

They were quiet. But it was as much as they could bear. They got jolly again over tea. As they sat by Brayford, watching the boats, he told her about Clara. His mother asked him innumerable questions.

'Then who does she live with?'

'With her mother, on Bluebell Hill.'

'And they have enough to keep them?'

'I don't think so. I think they do lace work.'

'And wherein lies her charm, my boy?'

'I don't know that she's charming, mother. But she's nice. And she seems straight, you know – not a bit deep, not a bit.'

'But she's a good deal older than you.'

'She's thirty, I'm going on twenty-three.'

'You haven't told me what you like her for.'

'Because I don't know – a sort of defiant way she's got – a sort of angry way.'

Mrs Morel considered. She would have been glad now for her son to fall in love with some woman who would – she did not know what. But he fretted so, got so furious suddenly, and again was melancholic. She wished he knew some nice woman – She did not know what she wished, but left it vague. At any rate she was not hostile to the idea of Clara.

Annie, too, was getting married. Leonard had gone away to work in Birmingham. One week-end when he was home she had said to him:

'You don't look very well, my lad.'

'I dunno,' he said. 'I feel anyhow or nohow, ma.' He called her 'ma' already in his boyish fashion.

'Are you sure they're good lodgings?' she asked.

'Yes – yes. Only – it's a winder when you have to pour your own tea out – an' nobody to grouse if you teem it in your saucer and sup it up. It somehow takes a' the taste out of it.'

Mrs Morel laughed.

'And so it knocks you up?' she said.

'I dunno. I want to get married,' he blurted, twisting his fingers and looking down at his boots. There was silence.

'But,' she exclaimed, 'I thought you said you'd wait another year.'

'Yes, I did say so,' he replied stubbornly.

Again she considered.

'And you know,' she said, 'Annie's a bit of a spendthrift. She's saved no more than eleven pounds. And I know, lad, you haven't had much chance.'

He coloured up to his ears.

'I've got thirty-four quid,' he said.

'It doesn't go far,' she answered.

He said nothing but twisted his fingers.

'And you know,' she said, 'I've nothing –'

'I didn't want, ma!' he cried, very red, suffering and remonstrating.

'No my lad, I know. I was only wishing I had. And take away five pounds for the wedding and things – it leaves twenty-nine pounds. You won't do much on that.'

He twisted still, impotent, stubborn, not looking up.

'But do you really want to get married?' she asked. 'Do you feel as if you ought?'

He gave her one straight look from his blue eyes.

'Yes,' he said.

'Then,' she replied, 'we must all do the best we can for it, lad.'

The next time he looked up there were tears in his eyes.

'I don't want Annie to feel handicapped,' he said, struggling.

'My lad,' she said, 'you're steady – you've got a decent place. If a man had *needed* me I'd have married him on his last week's wages. She may find it a bit hard to start humbly. Young girls *are* like that. They look forward to the fine home they think they'll have. But *I* had expensive furniture. It's not everything.'

So the wedding took place almost immediately. Arthur came home, and was splendid in uniform. Annie looked nice in a dove-grey dress that she could take for Sundays. Morel called her a fool for getting married, and was cool with his son-in-law. Mrs Morel had white tips in her bonnet, and some white on her blouse, and was teased by both her sons for fancying herself so grand. Leonard was jolly and cordial, and felt a fearful fool. Paul could not quite see what Annie wanted to get married for. He was fond of her, and she of him. Still, he hoped rather lugubriously that it would turn out all right. Arthur was astonishingly handsome in his scarlet and yellow, and he knew it well, but was secretly ashamed of the uniform. Annie cried her eyes out in the kitchen, on leaving her mother. Mrs Morel cried a little, then patted her on the back and said:

'But don't cry, child, he'll be good to you.'

Morel stamped and said she was a fool to go and tie herself up. Leonard looked white and overwrought. Mrs Morel said to him:

'I s'll trust her to you, my lad, and hold you responsible for her.'

'You can,' he said, nearly dead with the ordeal. And it was all over.

When Morel and Arthur were in bed, Paul sat talking, as he often did, with his mother.

'You're not sorry she's married, mother, are you?' he asked.

'I'm not sorry she's married – but – it seems strange that she should go from me. It even seems to me hard that she can prefer to go with Leonard. That's how mothers are – I know it's silly.'

'And shall you be miserable about her?'

'When I think of my own wedding day,' his mother answered, 'I can only hope her life will be different.'

'But you can trust him to be good to her?'

'Yes, yes. They say he's not good enough for her. But I say if a man is *genuine*, as he is, and a girl is fond of him – then – it should be all right. He's as good as she.'

'So you don't mind?'

'I would *never* have let a daughter of mine marry a man I didn't *feel* to be genuine through and through. And yet, there's a gap now she's gone.'

They were both miserable, and wanted her back again. It seemed to Paul his mother looked lonely, in her new black silk blouse with its bit of white trimming.

'At any rate, mother, I s'll never marry,' he said.

'Ay, they all say that, my lad. You've not met the one yet. Only wait a year or two.'

'But I shan't marry, mother. I shall live with you, and we'll have a servant.'

'Ah, my lad, it's easy to talk. We'll see when the time comes.'

'What time? I'm nearly twenty-three.'

'Yes, you're not one that would marry young. But in three years' time –'

'I shall be with you just the same.'

'We'll see, my boy, we'll see.'

'But you don't want me to marry?'

'I shouldn't like to think of you going through your life without anybody to care for you and do – no.'

'And you think I ought to marry?'

'Sooner or later every man ought.'

'But you'd rather it were later.'

'It would be hard – and very hard. It's as they say:

> "A son's my son till he takes him a wife,
> But my daughter's my daughter the whole of her life".'

'And you think I'd let a wife take me from you?'

'Well, you wouldn't ask her to marry your mother as well as you.' Mrs Morel smiled.

'She could do what she liked; she wouldn't have to interfere.'

'She wouldn't – till she'd got you – and then you'd see.'

'I never will see. I'll never marry while I've got you – I won't.'

'But I shouldn't like to leave you with nobody, my boy,' she cried.

'You're not going to leave me. What are you? Fifty-three! I'll give you till seventy-five. There you are, I'm fat and forty-four. Then I'll marry a staid body. See!'

His mother sat and laughed.

'Go to bed,' she said – 'go to bed.'

'And we'll have a pretty house, you and me, and a servant, and it'll be just all right. I s'll perhaps be rich with my painting.'

'Will you go to bed!'

'And then you s'll have a pony-carriage. See yourself – a little Queen Victoria trotting round.'

'I tell you to go to bed,' she laughed.

He kissed her and went. His plans for the future were always the same.

Mrs Morel sat brooding – about her daughter, about Paul, about Arthur. She fretted at losing Annie. The family was very closely bound. And she felt she *must* live now, to be with her children. Life was so rich for her. Paul wanted her, and so did Arthur. Arthur never knew how deeply he loved her. He was a creature of the moment. Never yet had he been forced to realize himself. The army had disciplined his body, but not his soul. He was in perfect health and very handsome. His dark, vigorous hair sat close to his smallish head. There was something childish about his nose, something almost girlish about his dark blue eyes. But he had the full red mouth of a man under his brown moustache, and his jaw was strong. It was his father's mouth; it was the nose and eyes of her own mother's people – good-looking, weak-principled folk. Mrs Morel was anxious about him. Once he had really run the rig he was safe. But how far would he go?

The army had not really done him any good. He resented bitterly the authority of the petty officers. He hated having to obey as if he were an animal. But he had too much sense to kick. So he turned his attention to getting the best out of it. He could sing, he was a boon-companion. Often he got into scrapes, but they were the manly scrapes that are easily condoned. So he made a good time out of it, whilst his self-respect was in suppression. He trusted to his good looks and handsome figure, his refinement, his decent education to get him most of what he wanted, and he was not disappointed. Yet he was restless. Something seemed to gnaw him inside. He was never still, he was never alone. With his mother he was rather humble. Paul he admired and loved and despised slightly. And Paul admired and loved and despised him, slightly.

Mrs Morel had had a few pounds left to her by her father, and she decided to buy her son out of the army. He was wild with joy. Now he was like a lad taking a holiday.

He had always been fond of Beatrice Wyld, and during his furlough he picked up with her again. She was stronger and better in health. The two often went long walks together, Arthur taking her arm in soldier's fashion, rather stiffly. And she came to play the piano whilst he sang. Then Arthur would unhook his tunic collar. He grew flushed, his eyes were bright, he sang in a manly tenor. Afterwards they sat together on the sofa. He seemed to flaunt his body: she was aware of him so – the strong chest, the sides, the thighs in their close-fitting trousers.

He liked to lapse into the dialect when he talked to her. She would sometimes smoke with him. Occasionally she would only take a few whiffs at his cigarette.

'Nay,' he said to her one evening, when she reached for his cigarette. 'Nay, tha doesna. I'll gi'e thee a smoke kiss if ter's a mind.'

'I want a whiff, no kiss at all,' she answered.

'Well, an' tha s'lt ha'e a whiff,' he said, 'along wi' t' kiss.'

'I want a draw at thy fag,' she cried, snatching for the cigarette between his lips.

He was sitting with his shoulder touching her. She was small and quick as lightning. He just escaped.

'I'll gi'e thee a smoke kiss,' he said.

'Tha'rt a knivey nuisance, Arty Morel,' she said, sitting back.

'Ha'e a smoke kiss?'

The soldier leaned forward to her, smiling. His face was near hers.

'Shonna!' she replied, turning away her head.

He took a draw at his cigarette, and pursed up his mouth, and put his lips close to her. His dark-brown cropped moustache stood out like a brush. She looked at the puckered crimson lips, then suddenly snatched the cigarette from his fingers and darted away. He, leaping after her, seized the comb from her back hair. She turned, threw the cigarette at him. He picked it up, put it in his mouth, and sat down.

'Nuisance!' she cried. 'Give me my comb!'

She was afraid that her hair, specially done for him, would come down. She stood with her hands to her head. He hid the comb between his knees.

'I've non got it,' he said.

The cigarette trembled between his lips with laughter as he spoke.

'Liar!' she said.

''S true as I'm here!' he laughed, showing his hands.

'You brazen imp!' she exclaimed, rushing and scuffling for the comb, which he had under his knees. As she wrestled with him, pulling at his smooth, tight-covered knees, he laughed till he lay back on the sofa shaking with laughter. The cigarette fell from his mouth, almost singeing his throat. Under his delicate tan the blood flushed up, and he laughed till his blue eyes were blinded, his throat swollen almost to choking. Then he sat up. Beatrice was putting in her comb.

'Tha tickled me, Beat,' he said thickly.

Like a flash her small white hand went out and smacked his face. He started up, glaring at her. They stared at each other. Slowly the flush mounted her cheek, she dropped her eyes, then her head. He sat down sulkily. She went into the scullery to adjust her hair. In private there she shed a few tears, she did not know what for.

When she returned she was pursed up close. But it was only a film over her fire. He, with ruffled hair, was sulking upon the sofa. She sat down opposite, in the arm-chair, and neither spoke. The clock ticked in the silence like blows.

'You are a little cat,' he said at length, half apologetically.

'Well, you shouldn't be brazen,' she replied.

There was again a long silence. He whistled to himself, like a man much agitated but defiant. Suddenly she went across to him and kissed him.

'Did it, pore fing!' she mocked.

He lifted his face, smiling curiously.

'Kiss?' he invited her.

'Daren't I?' she asked.

'Go on!' he challenged, his mouth lifted to her.

Deliberately, and with a peculiar quivering smile that seemed to overspread her whole body, she put her mouth on his. Immediately his arms folded round her. As soon as the long kiss was finished she drew back her head from him, put her delicate fingers on his neck, through the open collar. Then she closed her eyes, giving herself up again in a kiss.

She acted of her own free will. What she would do she did, and made nobody responsible.

Paul felt life changing around him. The conditions of youth were gone. Now it was a home of grown-up people. Annie was a married woman, Arthur was following his own pleasure in a way unknown to his folk. For so long they had all lived at home, and gone out to pass their time. But now, for Annie and Arthur, life lay outside their mother's house. They came home for holiday and for rest. So there was that strange, half-empty feeling about the house, as if the birds had flown. Paul became more and more unsettled. Annie and Arthur had gone. He was restless to follow. Yet home was for him beside his mother. And still there was something else, something outside, something he wanted.

He grew more and more restless. Miriam did not satisfy him. His old mad desire to be with her grew weaker. Sometimes he met Clara in Nottingham, sometimes he went to meetings with her, sometimes he saw her at Willey Farm. But on these last occasions the situation became strained. There was a triangle of antagonism between Paul and Clara and Miriam. With Clara he took on a smart, worldly, mocking tone very antagonistic to Miriam. It did not matter what went before. She might be intimate and sit with him. Then as soon as Clara appeared, it all vanished, and he played to the newcomer.

Miriam had one beautiful evening with him in the hay. He had been on the horse-rake, and, having finished, came to help her to put the hay in cocks. Then he talked to her of his hopes and despairs, and his whole soul seemed to lie bare before her. She felt as if she watched the very quivering stuff of life in him. The moon came out: they walked home together: he seemed to have come to her because he needed her so badly, and she listened to him, gave him all her love and her faith. It seemed to her he brought her the best of himself to keep, and that she would guard it all her life. Nay, the sky did not cherish the stars more surely and eternally than she would guard the good in the soul of Paul Morel. She went on home alone, feeling exalted, glad in her faith.

And then, the next day, Clara came. They were to have tea in the hayfield. Miriam watched the evening drawing to gold and shadow. And all the time

Paul was sporting with Clara. He made higher and higher heaps of hay that they were jumping over. Miriam did not care for the game, and stood aside. Edgar and Geoffrey and Maurice and Clara and Paul jumped. Paul won, because he was light. Clara's blood was roused. She could run like an Amazon. Paul loved the determined way she rushed at the haycock and leaped, landed on the other side, her breasts shaken, her thick hair coming undone.

'You touched!' he cried. 'You touched!'

'No!' she flashed, turning to Edgar. 'I didn't touch, did I? Wasn't I clear?'

'I couldn't say,' laughed Edgar.

None of them could say.

'But you touched,' said Paul. 'You're beaten.'

'I did *not* touch!' she cried.

'As plain as anything,' said Paul.

'Box his ears for me!' she cried to Edgar.

'Nay,' Edgar laughed. 'I daren't. You must do it yourself.'

'And nothing can alter the fact that you touched,' laughed Paul.

She was furious with him. Her little triumph before these lads and men was gone. She had forgotten herself in the game. Now he was to humble her.

'I think you are despicable!' she said.

And again he laughed, in a way that tortured Miriam.

'And I *knew* you couldn't jump that heap,' he teased.

She turned her back on him. Yet everybody could see that the only person she listened to, or was conscious of, was he, and he of her. It pleased the men to see this battle between them. But Miriam was tortured.

Paul could choose the lesser in place of the higher, she saw. He could be unfaithful to himself, unfaithful to the real, deep Paul Morel. There was a danger of his becoming frivolous, of his running after his satisfactions like any Arthur, or like his father. It made Miriam bitter to think that he should throw away his soul for this flippant traffic of triviality with Clara. She walked in bitterness and silence, while the other two rallied each other, and Paul sported.

And afterwards, he would not own it, but he was rather ashamed of himself, and prostrated himself before Miriam. Then again he rebelled.

'It's not religious to be religious,' he said. 'I reckon a crow is religious when it sails across the sky. But it only does it because it feels itself carried to where it's going, not because it thinks it is being eternal.'

But Miriam knew that one should be religious in everything, have God, whatever God might be, present in everything.

'I don't believe God knows such a lot about Himself,' he cried. 'God doesn't *know* things, He *is* things. And I'm sure He's not soulful.'

And then it seemed to her that Paul was arguing God on to his own side, because he wanted his own way and his own pleasure. There was a long battle between him and her. He was utterly unfaithful to her even in her own presence; then he was ashamed, then repentant; then he hated her, and went off again. Those were the ever-recurring conditions.

She fretted him to the bottom of his soul. There she remained – sad, pensive, a worshipper. And he caused her sorrow. Half the time he grieved for her, half the time he hated her. She was his conscience; and he felt, somehow, he had got a conscience that was too much for him. He could not leave her, because in one way she did hold the best of him. He could not stay with her because she did not take the rest of him, which was three-quarters. So he chafed himself into rawness over her.

When she was twenty-one he wrote her a letter which could only have been written to her.

'May I speak of our old, worn love, this last time. It, too, is changing, it it not? Say, has not the body of that love died, and left you its invulnerable soul? You see, I can give you a spirit love, I have given it you this long, long time; but not embodied passion. See, you are a nun. I have given you what I would give a holy nun – as a mystic monk to a mystic nun. Surely you esteem it best. Yet you regret – no, have regretted – the other. In all our relations no body enters. I do not talk to you through the senses – rather through the spirit. That is why we cannot love in the common sense. Ours is not an everyday affection. As yet we are mortal, and to live side by side with one another would be dreadful, for somehow with you I cannot long be trivial, and, you know, to be always beyond this mortal state would be to lose it. If people marry, they must live together as affectionate humans, who may be commonplace with each other without feeling awkward – not as two souls. So I feel it.

'Ought I to send this letter – I doubt it. But there – it is best to understand. Au revoir.'

Miriam read this letter twice, after which she sealed it up. A year later she broke the seal to show her mother the letter.

'You are a nun – you are a nun.' The words went into her heart again and again. Nothing he ever had said had gone into her so deeply, fixedly, like a mortal wound.

She answered him two days after the party.

'"Our intimacy would have been all-beautiful but for one little mistake,"' she quoted. 'Was the mistake mine?'

Almost immediately he replied to her from Nottingham, sending her at the same time a little 'Omar Khayyam'.

'I am glad you answered; you are so calm and natural you put me to shame. What a ranter I am! We are often out of sympathy. But in fundamentals we may always be together I think.

'I must thank you for your sympathy with my painting and drawing. Many a sketch is dedicated to you. I do look forward to your criticisms, which, to my shame and glory, are always grand appreciations. It is a lovely joke, that. Au revoir.'

This was the end of the first phase of Paul's love-affair. He was now about twenty-three years old, and, though still virgin, the sex instinct that Miriam had over-refined for so long now grew particularly strong. Often, as he talked to Clara Dawes, came that thickening and quickening of his blood, that peculiar concentration in the breast, as if something were alive there, a new self or a new centre of consciousness, warning him that sooner or later, he would have to ask one woman or another. But he belonged to Miriam. Of that she was so fixedly sure that he allowed her right.

10

CLARA

When he was twenty-three years old Paul sent in a landscape to the winter exhibition at Nottingham Castle. Miss Jordan had taken a good deal of interest in him, had invited him to her house, where he met other artists. He was beginning to grow ambitious.

One morning the postman came just as he was washing in the scullery. Suddenly he heard a wild noise from his mother. Rushing into the kitchen, he found her standing on the hearthrug wildly waving a letter and crying 'Hurrah!' as if she had gone mad. He was shocked and frightened.

'Why, mother!' he exclaimed.

She flew to him, flung her arms round him for a moment, then waved the letter crying:

'Hurrah, my boy! I knew we should do it!'

He was afraid of her – the small, severe woman with greying hair suddenly bursting out in such frenzy. The postman came running back, afraid something had happened. They saw his tipped cap over the short curtain. Mrs Morel rushed to the door.

'His picture's got first prize, Fred,' she cried, 'and is sold for twenty guineas.'

'My word, that's something like!' said the young postman, whom they had known all his life.

'And Major Moreton has bought it!' she cried.

'It looks like meanin' something, that does, Mrs Morel,' said the postman, his blue eyes bright. He was glad to have brought such a lucky letter. Mrs Morel went indoors and sat down, trembling. Paul was afraid lest she might have misread the letter, and might be disappointed after all. He scrutinized it once, twice. Yes, he became convinced it was true. Then he sat down, his heart beating with joy.

'Mother!' he exclaimed.

'Didn't I *say* we should do it!' she said, pretending she was not crying.

He took the kettle off the fire and mashed the tea.

'You didn't think, mother –' he began tentatively.

'No, my son – not so much – but I expected a good deal.'

'But not so much,' he said.

'No – no – but I knew we should do it.'

And then she recovered her composure, apparently at least. He sat with his shirt turned back, showing his young throat almost like a girl's, and the towel in his hand, his hair sticking up wet.

'Twenty guineas, mother! That's just what you wanted to buy Arthur out. Now you needn't borrow any. It'll just do.'

'Indeed, I shan't take it all,' she said.

'But why?'

'Because I shan't.'

'Well – you have twelve pounds, I'll have nine.'

They cavilled about sharing the twenty guineas. She wanted to take only the five pounds she needed. He would not hear of it. So they got over the stress of emotion by quarrelling.

Morel came home at night from the pit, saying:

'They tell me Paul's got first prize for his picture, and sold it to Lord Henry Bentley for fifty pound.'

'Oh, what stories people do tell!' she cried.

'Ha!' he answered. 'I said I wor sure it wor a lie. But they said tha'd told Fred Hodgkisson.'

'As if I would tell him such stuff!'

'Ha!' assented the miner.

But he was disappointed nevertheless.

'It's true he has got the first prize,' said Mrs Morel.

The miner sat heavily in his chair.

'Has he, beguy!' he exclaimed.

He stared across the room fixedly.

'But as for fifty pounds – such nonsense!' She was silent awhile. 'Major Moreton bought it for twenty guineas, that's true.'

'Twenty guineas! Tha niver says!' exclaimed Morel.

'Yes, and it was worth it.'

'Ay!' he said. 'I don't misdoubt it. But twenty guineas for a bit of a paintin' as he knocked off in an hour or two!'

He was silent with conceit of his son. Mrs Morel sniffed, as if it were nothing.

'And when does he handle th' money?' asked the collier.

'That I couldn't tell you. When the picture is sent home, I suppose.'

There was silence. Morel stared at the sugar-basin instead of eating his dinner. His black arm, with the hand all gnarled with work, lay on the table. His wife pretended not to see him rub the back of his hand across his eyes, nor the smear in the coal-dust on his black face.

'Yes, an' that other lad 'ud 'a done as much if they hadna ha' killed 'im,' he said quietly.

The thought of William went through Mrs Morel like a cold blade. It left her feeling she was tired, and wanted rest.

Paul was invited to dinner at Mr Jordan's. Afterwards he said:

'Mother, I want an evening suit.'

'Yes, I was afraid you would,' she said. She was glad. There was a moment or two of silence. 'There's that one of William's,' she continued, 'that I know cost four pounds ten and which he'd only worn three times.'

'Should you like me to wear it, mother?' he asked.

'Yes, I think it would fit you – at least the coat. The trousers would want shortening.'

He went upstairs and put on the coat and vest. Coming down, he looked strange in a flannel collar and a flannel shirt-front, with an evening coat and vest. It was rather large.

'The tailor can make it right,' she said, smoothing her hand over his shoulder. 'It's beautiful stuff. I never could find in my heart to let your father wear the trousers, and very glad I am now.'

And as she smoothed her hand over the silk collar she thought of her eldest son. But this son was living enough inside the clothes. She passed her hand down his back to feel him. He was alive and hers. The other was dead.

He went out to dinner several times in his evening suit that had been William's. Each time his mother's heart was firm with pride and joy. He was started now. The studs she and the children had bought for William were in his shirt-front; he wore one of William's dress shirts. But he had an elegant figure. His face was rough, but warm-looking and rather pleasing. He did not look particularly a gentleman, but she thought he looked quite a man.

He told her everything that took place, everything that was said. It was as if she had been there. And he was dying to introduce her to these friends who had dinner at seven-thirty in the evening.

'Go along with you!' she said. 'What do they want to know me for?'

'They do!' he cried indignantly. 'If they want to know me – and they say they do – then they want to know you, because you are quite as clever as I am.'

'Go along with you, child!' she laughed.

But she began to spare her hands. They, too, were work-gnarled now. The skin was shiny with so much hot water, the knuckles rather swollen. But she began to be careful to keep them out of soda. She regretted what they had been – so small and exquisite. And when Annie insisted on her having more stylish blouses to suit her age, she submitted. She even went so far as to allow a black velvet bow to be placed on her hair. Then she sniffed in her sarcastic manner, and was sure she looked a sight. But she looked a lady, Paul declared, as much as Mrs Major Moreton, and far, far nicer. The family was coming on. Only Morel remained unchanged, or rather, lapsed slowly.

Paul and his mother now had long discussions about life. Religion was fading into the background. He had shovelled away all the beliefs that would hamper him, had cleared the ground, and come more or less to the bedrock of belief that one should feel inside oneself for right and wrong, and should have the patience to gradually realize one's God. Now life interested him more.

'You know,' he said to his mother, 'I don't want to belong to the well-to-do middle class. I like my common people best. I belong to the common people.'

'But if anyone else said so, my son, wouldn't you be in a tear. *You* know you consider yourself equal to any gentleman.'

'In myself,' he answered, 'not in my class or my education or my manners. But in myself I am.'

'Very well, then. Then why talk about the common people?'

'Because – the difference between people isn't in their class, but in themselves. Only from the middle classes one gets ideas, and from the common people – life itself, warmth. You feel their hates and loves.'

'It's all very well, my boy. But, then, why don't you go and talk to your father's pals?'

'But they're rather different.'

'Not at all. They're the common people. After all, whom do you mix with now – among the common people? Those that exchange ideas, like the middle class. The rest don't interest you.'

'But – there's the life –'

'I don't believe there's a lot more life from Miriam than you could get from any educated girl – say Miss Moreton. It is *you* who are snobbish about class.'

She frankly *wanted* him to climb into the middle class, a thing not very difficult, she knew. And she wanted him in the end to marry a lady.

Now she began to combat him in his restless fretting. He still kept up his connexion with Miriam, could neither break free nor go the whole length of engagement. And this indecision seemed to bleed him of his energy. Moreover, his mother suspected him of an unrecognized leaning towards Clara, and, since the latter was a married woman, she wished he would fall in love with one of the girls in a better station of life. But he was stupid, and would refuse to love or even to admire a girl much, just because she was his social superior.

'My boy,' said his mother to him, 'all your cleverness, your breaking away from old things, and taking life in your own hands, doesn't seem to bring you much happiness.'

'What is happiness!' he cried. 'It's nothing to me! How *am* I to be happy?' The plump question disturbed her.

'That's for you to judge, my lad. But if you could meet some *good* woman who would *make* you happy – and you began to think of settling your life – when you have the means – so that you could work without all this fretting – it would be much better for you.'

He frowned. His mother caught him on the raw of his wound of Miriam. He pushed the tumbled hair off his forehead, his eyes full of pain and fire.

'You mean easy, mother,' he cried. 'That's a woman's whole doctrine for life – ease of soul and physical comfort. And I do despise it.'

'Oh, do you!' replied his mother. 'And do you call yours a divine discontent?'

'Yes, I don't care about its divinity. But damn your happiness! So long as life's full, it doesn't matter whether it's happy or not. I'm afraid your happiness would bore me.'

'You never give it a chance,' she said. Then suddenly all her passion of grief over him broke out. 'But it does matter!' she cried. 'And you *ought* to be happy, you ought to try to be happy, to live to be happy. How could I bear to think your life wouldn't be a happy one!'

'Your own's been bad enough, mater, but it hasn't left you so much worse off than the folk who've been happier. I reckon you've done well. And I am the same. Aren't I well enough off?'

'You're not, my son. Battle – battle – and suffer. It's about all you do, as far as I can see.'

'But why not, my dear? I tell you it's the best –'

'It isn't. And one *ought* to be happy, one *ought*.'

By this time Mrs Morel was trembling violently. Struggles of this kind often took place between her and her son, when she seemed to fight for his very life against his own will to die. He took her in his arms. She was ill and pitiful.

'Never mind, Little,' he murmured. 'So long as you don't feel life's paltry and a miserable business, the rest doesn't matter, happiness or unhappiness.'

She pressed him to her.

'But I want you to be happy,' she said pathetically.

'Eh, my dear – say rather you want me to live.'

Mrs Morel felt as if her heart would break for him. At this rate she knew he would not live. He had that poignant carelessness about himself, his own suffering, his own life, which is a form of slow suicide. It almost broke her heart. With all the passion of her strong nature she hated Miriam for having in this subtle way undermined his joy. It did not matter to her that Miriam could not help it. Miriam did it, and she hated her.

She wished so much he would fall in love with a girl equal to be his mate – educated and strong. But he would not look at anybody above him in station. He seemed to like Mrs Dawes. At any rate that feeling was wholesome. His mother prayed and prayed for him, that he might not be wasted. That was all her prayer – not for his soul or his righteousness, but that he might not be wasted. And while he slept, for hours and hours she thought and prayed for him.

He drifted away from Miriam imperceptibly, without knowing he was going. Arthur only left the army to be married. The baby was born six months after his wedding. Mrs Morel got him a job under the firm again, at twenty-one shillings a week. She furnished for him, with the help of Beatrice's mother, a little cottage of two rooms. He was caught now. It did not matter how he kicked and struggled, he was fast. For a time he chafed, was irritable with his young wife, who loved him; he went almost distracted when the baby, which was delicate, cried or gave trouble. He grumbled for hours to his mother. She only said, 'Well, my lad, you did it yourself, now you must make the best of it.' And then the grit came out in him. He buckled to work, undertook his responsibilities, acknowledged that he belonged to his wife and child, and did make a good best of it. He had never been very closely inbound into the family. Now he was gone altogether.

The months went slowly along. Paul had more or less got into connexion with the Socialist, Suffragette, Unitarian people in Nottingham, owing to his acquaintance with Clara. One day a friend of his and of Clara's, in Bestwood, asked him to take a message to Mrs Dawes. He went in the evening across Sneinton Market to Bluebell Hill. He found the house in a mean little street paved with granite cobbles and having causeways of dark blue, grooved bricks. The front door went up a step from off this rough pavement, where the feet of the passers-by rasped and clattered. The brown paint on the door was so old that the naked wood showed between the rents. He stood on the street below and knocked. There came a heavy footstep; a large, stout woman of about sixty towered above him. He looked up at her from the pavement. She had a rather severe face.

She admitted him into the parlour, which opened on to the street. It was a small, stuffy, defunct room, of mahogany, and deathly enlargements of photographs of departed people done in carbon. Mrs Radford left him. She was stately, almost martial, In a moment Clara appeared. She flushed deeply, and he was covered with confusion. It seemed as if she did not like being discovered in her home circumstances.

'I thought it couldn't be your voice,' she said.

But she might as well be hung for a sheep as for a lamb. She invited him out of the mausoleum of a parlour into the kitchen.

That was a little, darkish room too, but it was smothered in white lace. The mother had seated herself again by the cupboard, and was drawing thread from a vast web of lace. A clump of fluff and ravelled cotton was at her right hand, a heap of three-quarter-inch lace lay on her left, whilst in front of her was the mountain of the lace web, piling the hearthrug. Threads of curly cotton, pulled out from between the lengths of lace, strewed over the fender and the fireplace. Paul dared not go forward, for fear of treading on piles of white stuff.

On the table was a jenny for carding the lace. There was a pack of brown cardboard squares, a pack of cards of lace, a little box of pins, and on the sofa lay a heap of drawn lace.

The room was all lace, and it was so dark and warm that the white, snowy stuff seemed the more distinct.

'If you're coming in you won't have to mind the work,' said Mrs Radford. 'I know we're about blocked up. But sit you down.'

Clara, much embarrassed, gave him a chair against the wall opposite the white heaps. Then she herself took her place on the sofa, shamedly.

'Will you drink a bottle of stout?' Mrs Radford asked. 'Clara, get him a bottle of stout.'

He protested, but Mrs Radford insisted.

'You look as if you could do with it,' she said. 'Haven't you never any more colour than that?'

'It's only a thick skin I've got that doesn't show the blood through,' he answered.

Clara, ashamed and chagrined, brought him a bottle of stout and a glass. He poured out some of the black stuff.

'Well,' he said, lifting the glass, 'here's health!'

'And thank you,' said Mrs Radford.

He took a drink of stout.

'And light yourself a cigarette, so long as you don't set the house on fire,' said Mrs Radford.

'Thank you,' he replied.

'Nay, you needn't thank me,' she answered. 'I s'll be glad to smell a bit of smoke in th' 'ouse again. A house o' women is as dead as a house wi' no fire, to my thinkin'. I'm not a spider as likes a corner to myself. I like a man about, if he's only something to snap at.'

Clara began to work. Her jenny spun with a subdued buzz; the white lace hopped from between her fingers on to the card. It was filled; she snipped off the length and pinned the end down to the banded lace. Then she put a new card in her jenny. Paul watched her. She sat square and magnificent. Her throat and arms were bare. The blood still mantled below her ears; she bent her head in shame of her humility. Her face was set on her work. Her arms were creamy and full of life beside the white lace; her large, well-kept hands worked with a balanced movement, as if nothing would hurry them. He, not knowing, watched her all the time. He saw the arch of her neck from the shoulder, as she bent her head; he saw the coil of dun hair; he watched her moving, gleaming arms.

'I've heard a bit about you from Clara,' continued the mother. 'You're in Jordan's, aren't you?' She drew her lace unceasingly.

'Yes.'

'Ay, well, and I can remember when Thomas Jordan used to ask *me* for one of my toffies.'

'Did he?' laughed Paul. 'And did he get it?'

'Sometimes he did, sometimes he didn't – which was latterly. For he's the sort that takes all and gives naught, he is – or used to be.'

'I think he's very decent,' said Paul.

'Yes; well, I'm glad to hear it.'

Mrs Radford looked across at him steadily. There was something determined about her that he liked. Her face was falling loose, but her eyes were calm, and there was something strong in her that made it seem she was not old; merely her wrinkles and loose cheeks were an anachronism. She had the strength and sang-froid of a woman in the prime of life. She continued drawing the lace with slow, dignified movements. The big web came up inevitably over her apron; the length of lace fell away at her side. Her arms were finely shapen, but glossy and yellow as old ivory. They had not the peculiar dull gleam that made Clara's so fascinating to him.

'And you've been going with Miriam Leivers!' the mother asked him.

'Well –' he answered.

'Yes, she's a nice girl,' she continued. 'She's very nice, but she's a bit too much above this world to suit my fancy.'

'She is a bit like that,' he agreed.

'She'll never be satisfied till she's got wings and can fly over everybody's head, she won't,' she said.

Clara broke in, and he told her his message. She spoke humbly to him. He had surprised her in her drudgery. To have her humble made him feel as if he were lifting his head in expectation.

'Do you like jennying?' he asked.

'What can a woman do!' she replied bitterly.

'Is it sweated?'

'More or less. Isn't *all* woman's work? That's another trick the men have played, since we force ourselves into the labour market.'

'Now then, you shut up about the men,' said her mother. 'If the women wasn't fools, the men wouldn't be bad uns, that's what I say. No man was ever that bad wi' me but what he got it back again. Not but what they're a lousy lot, there's no denying it.'

'But they're all right really, aren't they?' he asked.

'Well, they're a bit different from women,' she answered.

'Would you care to be back at Jordan's?' he asked Clara.

'I don't think so,' she replied.

'Yes, she would!' cried her mother; 'thank her stars if she could get back. Don't you listen to her. She's for ever on that 'igh horse of hers, an' its back's that thin an' starved it'll cut her i' two one of these days.'

Clara suffered badly from her mother. Paul felt as if his eyes were coming very wide open. Wasn't he to take Clara's fulminations so seriously, after all? She spun steadily at her work. He experienced a thrill of joy, thinking she might need his help. She seemed denied and deprived of so much. And her arm moved mechanically, that should never have been subdued to a mechanism, and her head was bowed to the lace, that never should have been bowed. She seemed to be stranded there among the refuse that life has thrown away, doing her jennying. It was a bitter thing to her to be put aside by life, as if it had no use for her. No wonder she protested.

She came with him to the door. He stood below in the mean street, looking up at her. So fine she was in her stature and her bearing, she reminded him of Juno dethroned. As she stood in the doorway, she winced from the street, from her surroundings.

'And you will go with Mrs Hodgkisson to Hucknall?'

He was talking quite meaninglessly, only watching her. Her grey eyes at last met his. They looked dumb with humiliation, pleading with a kind of captive misery. He was shaken and at a loss. He had thought her high and mighty.

When he left her, he wanted to run. He went to the station in a sort of dream, and was at home without realizing he had moved out of her street.

He had an idea that Susan, the overseer of the spiral girls, was about to be married. He asked her the next day.

'I say, Susan, I heard a whisper of your getting married. What about it?'

Susan flushed red.

'Who's been talking to you?' she replied.

'Nobody. I merely heard a whisper that you *were* thinking –'

'Well, I am, though you needn't tell anybody. What's more, I wish I wasn't!'

'Nay, Susan, you won't make me believe that.'

'Shan't I? You *can* believe it, though. I'd rather stop here a thousand times.'

Paul was perturbed.

'Why, Susan?'

The girl's colour was high, and her eyes flashed.

'That's why!'

'And must you?'

For answer, she looked at him. There was about him a candour and gentleness which made the women trust him. He understood.

'Ah, I'm sorry,' he said.

Tears came to her eyes.

'But you'll see it'll turn out all right. You'll make the best of it,' he continued rather wistfully.

'There's nothing else for it.'

'Yes, there's making the worst of it. Try and make it all right.'

He soon made occasion to call again on Clara.

'Would you,' he said, 'care to come back to Jordan's?'

She put down her work, laid her beautiful arms on the table, and looked at him for some moments without answering. Gradually the flush mounted her cheek.

'Why?' she asked.

Paul felt rather awkward.

'Well, because Susan is thinking of leaving,' he said.

Clara went on with her jennying. The white lace leaped in little jumps and bounds on to the card. He waited for her. Without raising her head, she said at last, in a peculiar low voice:

'Have you said anything about it?'

'Except to you, not a word.'

There was again a long silence.

'I will apply when the advertisement is out,' she said.

'You will apply before that. I will let you know exactly when.'

She went on spinning her little machine, and did not contradict him.

Clara came to Jordan's. Some of the older hands, Fanny among them, remembered her earlier rule, and cordially disliked the memory. Clara had always been 'ikey', reserved, and superior. She had never mixed with the girls as one of themselves. If she had occasion to find fault, she did it coolly and with perfect politeness, which the defaulter felt to be a bigger insult than crossness. Towards Fanny, the poor, over-strung hunchback, Clara was unfailingly compassionate and gentle, as a result of which Fanny shed more bitter tears than ever the rough tongues of the other overseers had caused her.

There was something in Clara that Paul disliked, and much that piqued him. If she were about, he always watched her strong throat or her neck, upon which the blonde hair grew low and fluffy. There was a fine down, almost invisible, upon the skin of her face and arms, and when once he had perceived it, he saw it always.

When he was at his work, painting in the afternoon, she would come and stand near to him, perfectly motionless. Then he felt her, though she neither spoke nor touched him. Although she stood a yard away he felt as if he were in contact with her. Then he could paint no more. He flung down the brushes, and turned to talk to her.

Sometimes she praised his work; sometimes she was critical and cold.

'You are affected in that piece,' she would say; and, as there was an element of truth in her condemnation, his blood boiled with anger.

Again: 'What of this?' he would ask enthusiastically.

'H'm!' She made a small doubtful sound. 'It doesn't interest me much.'

'Because you don't understand it,' he retorted.

'Then why ask me about it?'

'Because I thought you would understand.'

She would shrug her shoulders in scorn of his work. She maddened him. He was furious. Then he abused her, and went into passionate exposition of his stuff. This amused and stimulated her. But she never owned that she had been wrong.

During the ten years that she had belonged to the women's movement she had acquired a fair amount of education, and, having had some of Miriam's passion to be instructed, had taught herself French, and could read in that language with a struggle. She considered herself as a woman apart, and particularly apart, from her class. The girls in the spiral department were all of good homes. It was a small, special industry, and had a certain distinction. There was an air of refinement in both rooms. But Clara was aloof also from her fellow-workers.

None of these things, however, did she reveal to Paul. She was not the one to give herself away. There was a sense of mystery about her. She was so reserved, he felt she had much to reserve. Her history was open on the surface, but its inner meaning was hidden from everybody. It was exciting. And then sometimes he caught her looking at him from under her brows with an almost furtive, sullen scrutiny, which made him move quickly. Often she met his eyes. But then her own were, as it were, covered over, revealing nothing. She gave him a little, lenient smile. She was to him extraordinarily provocative, because of the knowledge she seemed to possess, and gathered fruit of experience he could not attain.

One day he picked up a copy of 'Lettres de mon Moulin' from her work-bench.

'You read French, do you?' he cried.

Clara glanced round negligently. She was making an elastic stocking of heliotrope silk, turning the spiral machine with slow, balanced regularity, occasionally bending down to see her work or to adjust the needles; then her magnificent neck, with its down and fine pencils of hair, shone white against the lavender, lustrous silk. She turned a few more rounds, and stopped.

'What did you say?' she asked, smiling sweetly.

Paul's eyes glittered at her insolent indifference to him.

'I did not know you read French,' he said, very polite.

'Did you not?' she replied, with a faint, sarcastic smile.

'Rotten swank!' he said, but scarcely loud enough to be heard.

He shut his mouth angrily as he watched her. She seemed to scorn the work she mechanically produced; yet the hose she made were as nearly perfect as possible.

'You don't like spiral work,' he said.

'Oh, well, all work is work,' she answered, as if she knew all about it.

He marvelled at her coldness. He had to do everything hotly. She must be something special.

'What would you prefer to do?' he asked.

She laughed at him indulgently, as she said:

'There is so little likelihood of my ever being given a choice, that I haven't wasted time considering.'

'Pah!' he said, contemptuous on his side now. 'You only say that because you're too proud to own up what you want and can't get.'

'You know me very well,' she replied coldly.

'I know you think you're terrific great shakes, and that you live under the eternal insult of working in a factory.'

He was very angry and very rude. She merely turned away from him in disdain. He walked whistling down the room, flirted and laughed with Hilda.

Later on he said to himself:

'What was I so impudent to Clara for?' He was rather annoyed with himself, at the same time glad. 'Serve her right; she stinks with silent pride,' he said to himself angrily.

In the afternoon he came down. There was a certain weight on his heart which he wanted to remove. He thought to do it by offering her chocolates.

'Have one?' he said. 'I bought a handful to sweeten me up.'

To his great relief, she accepted. He sat on the work-bench beside her machine, twisting a piece of silk round his finger. She loved him for his quick, unexpected movements, like a young animal. His feet swung as he pondered. The sweets lay strewn on the bench. She bent over her machine, grinding rhythmically, then stooping to see the stocking that hung beneath, pulled down by the weight. He watched the handsome crouching of her back, and the apron-strings curling on the floor.

'There is always about you,' he said, 'a sort of waiting. Whatever I see you doing, you're not really there: you are waiting – like Penelope when she did her weaving.' He could not help a spurt of wickedness. 'I'll call you Penelope,' he said.

'Would it make any difference?' she said, carefully removing one of her needles.

'That doesn't matter, so long as it pleases me. Here, I say, you seem to forget I'm your boss. It just occurs to me.'

'And what does that mean?' she asked coolly.

'It means I've got a right to boss you.'

'Is there anything you want to complain about?'

'Oh, I say, you needn't be nasty,' he said angrily.

'I don't know what you want,' she said, continuing her task.

'I want you to treat me nicely and respectfully.'

'Call you "sir", perhaps?' she asked quietly.

'Yes, call me "sir". I should love it.'

'Then I wish you would go upstairs, sir.'

His mouth closed, and a frown came on his face. He jumped suddenly down.

'You're too blessed superior for anything,' he said.

And he went away to the other girls. He felt he was being angrier than he had any need to be. In fact, he doubted slightly that he was showing off. But if he were, then he would. Clara heard him laughing, in a way she hated, with the girls down the next room.

When at evening he went through the department after the girls had gone, he saw his chocolates lying untouched in front of Clara's machine. He left them. In the morning they were still there, and Clara was at her work. Later on Minnie, a little brunette they called Pussy, called to him:

'Hey, haven't you got a chocolate for anybody?'

'Sorry, Pussy,' he replied. 'I meant to have offered them; then I went and forgot 'em.'

'I think you did,' she answered.

'I'll bring you some this afternoon. You don't want them after they've been lying about, do you?'

'Oh, I'm not particular,' smiled Pussy.

'Oh no,' he said. 'They'll be dusty.'

He went up to Clara's bench.

'Sorry I left these things littering about,' he said.

She flushed scarlet. He gathered them together in his fist.

'They'll be dirty now,' he said. 'You should have taken them. I wonder why you didn't. I meant to have told you I wanted you to.'

He flung them out of the window into the yard below. He just glanced at her. She winced from his eyes.

In the afternoon he brought another packet.

'Will you take some?' he said, offering them first to Clara. 'These are fresh.'

She accepted one, and put it on to the bench.

'Oh, take several – for luck,' he said.

She took a couple more, and put them on the bench also. Then she turned in confusion to her work. He went on up the room.

'Here you are, Pussy,' he said. 'Don't be greedy!'

'Are they all for her?' cried the others, rushing up.

'Of course they're not,' he said.

The girls clamoured round. Pussy drew back from her mates.

'Come out!' she cried. 'I can have first pick, can't I, Paul?'

'Be nice with 'em,' he said, and went away.

'You *are* a dear,' the girls cried.

'Tenpence,' he answered.

He went past Clara without speaking. She felt the three chocolate creams would burn her if she touched them. It needed all her courage to slip them into the pocket of her apron.

The girls loved him and were afraid of him. He was so nice while he was nice, but if he was offended, so distant, treating them as if they scarcely existed, or not more than the bobbins of thread. And then, if they were impudent, he said quietly: 'Do you mind going on with your work,' and stood and watched.

When he celebrated his twenty-third birthday, the house was in trouble. Arthur was just going to be married. His mother was not well. His father, getting an old man, and lame from his accidents, was given a paltry, poor job. Miriam was an eternal reproach. He felt he owed himself to her, yet could not give himself. The house, moreover, needed his support. He was pulled in all directions. He was not glad it was his birthday. It made him bitter.

He got to work at eight o'clock. Most of the clerks had not turned up. The girls were not due till 8.30. As he was changing his coat he heard a voice behind him say:

'Paul, Paul, I want you.'

It was Fanny, the hunchback, standing at the top of her stairs, her face radiant with a secret. Paul looked at her in astonishment.

'I want you,' she said.

He stood, at a loss.

'Come on,' she coaxed. 'Come before you begin on the letters.'

He went down the half-dozen steps into her dry, narrow, 'finishing-off' room. Fanny walked before him: her black bodice was short – the waist was under her armpits – and her green-black cashmere skirt seemed very long, as she strode with big strides before the young man, himself so graceful. She went to her seat at the narrow end of the room, where the window opened on to chimney-pots. Paul watched her thin hands and her flat red wrists as she excitedly twitched her white apron, which was spread on the bench in front of her.

She hesitated.

'You didn't think we'd forget you?' she asked reproachful.

'Why?' he asked. He had forgotten his birthday himself.

'"Why", he says! "Why!" Why, look here!' She pointed to the calendar, and he saw, surrounding the big black number '21', hundreds of little crosses in blacklead.

'Oh, kisses for my birthday,' he laughed. 'How did you know?'

'Yes, you want to know, don't you?' Fanny mocked, hugely delighted. 'There's one from everybody – except Lady Clara – and two from some. But I shan't tell you how many I put.'

'Oh, I know, you're spooney,' he said.

'There you *are* mistaken!' she cried indignant. 'I could never be so soft.' Her voice was strong and contralto.

'You always pretend to be such a hard-hearted hussy,' he laughed. 'And you know you're as sentimental –'

'I'd rather be called sentimental than frozen meat,' Fanny blurted. Paul knew she referred to Clara, and he smiled.

'Do you say such nasty things about me?' he laughed.

'No, my duck,' the hunchback woman answered, lavishly tender. She was thirty-nine. 'No, my duck, because you don't think yourself a fine figure in marble and us nothing but dirt. I'm as good as you, aren't I, Paul?' and the question delighted her.

'Why, we're not better than one another, are we?' he replied.

'But I'm as good as you, aren't I, Paul?' she persisted daringly.

'Of course you are. If it comes to goodness, you're better.'

She was rather afraid of the situation. She might get hysterical.

'I thought I'd get here before the others – won't they say I'm deep! Now shut your eyes –' she said.

'And open your mouth, and see what God sends you,' he continued, suiting action to words, and expecting a piece of chocolate. He heard the rustle of the apron, and a faint clink of metal. 'I'm going to look,' he said.

He opened his eyes. Fanny, her long cheeks flushed, her blue eyes shining, was gazing at him. There was a little bundle of paint-tubes on the bench before him. He turned pale.

'No, Fanny,' he said quickly.

'From us all,' she answered hastily.

'No, but –'

'Are they the right sort?' she asked, rocking herself with delight.

'Jove! they're the best in the catalogue.'

'But they're the right sorts?' she cried.

'They're off the little list I'd made to get when my ship came in.' He bit his lip.

Fanny was overcome with emotion. She must turn the conversation.

'They was all on thorns to do it; they all paid their shares, all except the Queen of Sheba.'

The Queen of Sheba was Clara.

'And wouldn't she join?' Paul asked.

'She didn't get the chance; we never told her; we wasn't going to have *her* bossing *this* show. We didn't *want* her to join.'

Paul laughed at the woman. He was much moved. At last he must go. She was very close to him. Suddenly she flung her arms round his neck and kissed him vehemently.

'I can give you a kiss today,' she said apologetically. 'You've looked so white, it's made my heart ache.'

Paul kissed her, and left her. Her arms were so pitifully thin that his heart ached also.

That day he met Clara as he ran downstairs to wash his hands at dinner-time.

'You have stayed to dinner!' he exclaimed. It was unusual for her.

'Yes; and I seem to have dined an old surgical-appliance stock. I *must* go out now, or I shall feel stale india-rubber right through.'

She lingered. He instantly caught at her wish.

'You are going anywhere?' he asked.

They went together up to the Castle. Outdoors she dressed very plainly, down to ugliness; indoors she always looked nice. She walked with hesitating steps alongside Paul, bowing and turning away from him. Dowdy in dress, and drooping, she showed to great disadvantage. He could scarcely recognize her strong form, that seemed to slumber with power. She appeared almost insignificant, drowning her stature in her stoop, as she shrank from the public gaze.

The Castle grounds were very green and fresh. Climbing the precipitous ascent, he laughed and chattered, but she was silent, seeming to brood over something. There was scarcely time to go inside the squat, square building that crowns the bluff rock. They leaned upon the wall where the cliff runs sheer down to the Park. Below them, in their holes in the sandstone, pigeons preened themselves and cooed softly. Away down upon the boulevard at the foot of the rock, tiny trees stood in their own pools of shadow, and tiny people went scurrying about in almost ludicrous importance.

'You feel as if you could scoop up the folk like tadpoles, and have a handful of them,' he said.

She laughed, answering:

'Yes; it is necessary to get far off in order to see us proportionately. The trees are much more significant.'

'Bulk only,' he said.

She laughed cynically.

Away beyond the boulevard the thin stripes of the metals showed upon the railway track, whose margin was crowded with little stacks of timber, beside which smoking toy engines fussed. Then the silver string of the canal lay at random among the black heaps. Beyond, the dwellings, very dense on the river flat, looked like black, poisonous herbage, in thick rows and crowded beds, stretching right away, broken now and then by taller plants, right to where the river glistened in a hieroglyph across the country. The steep scarp cliffs across the river looked puny. Great stretches of country darkened with trees and faintly brightened with corn-land, spread towards the haze, where the hills rose blue beyond grey.

'It is comforting,' said Mrs Dawes, 'to think the town goes no farther. It is only a *little* sore upon the country yet.'

'A little scab,' Paul said.

She shivered. She loathed the town. Looking drearily across at the country which was forbidden her, her impassive face, pale and hostile, she reminded Paul of one of the bitter, remorseful angels.

'But the town's all right,' he said; 'it's only temporary. This is the crude, clumsy make-shift we've practised on, till we find out what the idea is. The town will come all right.'

The pigeons in the pockets of rock, among the perched bushes, cooed comfortably. To the left the large church of St Mary rose into space, to keep close company with the Castle, above the heaped rubble of the town. Mrs Dawes smiled brightly as she looked across the country.

'I feel better,' she said.

'Thank you,' he replied. 'Great compliment!'

'Oh, my brother!' she laughed.

'H'm! that's snatching back with the left hand what you gave with the right, and no mistake,' he said.

She laughed in amusement at him.

'But what was the matter with you?' he asked. 'I know you were brooding something special. I can see the stamp of it on your face yet.'

'I think I will not tell you,' she said.

'All right, hug it,' he answered.

She flushed and bit her lip.

'No,' she said, 'it was the girls.'

'What about 'em?' Paul asked.

'They have been plotting something for a week now, and today they seem particularly full of it. All alike; they insult me with their secrecy.'

'Do they?' he asked in concern.

'I do not mind,' she went on, in the metallic, angry tone, 'if they did not thrust it into my face – the fact that they have a secret.'

'Just like women,' said he.

'It is hateful, their mean gloating,' she said tensely.

Paul was silent. He knew what the girls gloated over. He was sorry to be the cause of this new dissension.

'They can have all the secrets in the world,' she went on, brooding bitterly; 'but they might refrain from glorying in them, and making me feel more out of it than ever. It is – it is almost unbearable.'

Paul thought for a few moments. He was much perturbed.

'I will tell you what it's all about,' he said, pale and nervous. 'It's my birthday, and they've bought me a fine lot of paints, all the girls. They're jealous of you' – he felt her stiffen coldly at the word 'jealous' – 'merely because I sometimes bring you a book,' he added slowly. 'But, you see, it's only a trifle. Don't bother about it, will you – because' – he laughed quickly – 'well, what would they say if they saw us here now, in spite of their victory?'

She was angry with him for his clumsy reference to their present intimacy. It was almost insolent of him. Yet he was so quiet, she forgave him, although it cost her an effort.

Their two hands lay on the rough stone parapet of the Castle wall. He had inherited from his mother a fineness of mould, so that his hands were small and vigorous. Hers were large, to march her large limbs, but white and powerful looking. As Paul looked at them he knew her. 'She is wanting somebody to take her hands – for all she is so contemptuous of us,' he said to himself. And she saw nothing but his two hands, so warm and alive, which seemed to live for her. He was brooding now, staring out over the country from under sullen brows. The little, interesting diversity of shapes had vanished from the scene; all that remained was a vast, dark matrix of sorrow and tragedy, the same in all the houses and the river-flats and the people and the birds; they were only shapen differently. And now that the forms seemed to have melted away, there remained the mass from which all the landscape was composed, a dark mass of struggle and pain. The factory, the girls, his mother, the large, uplifted church, the thicket of the town, merged into one atmosphere – dark, brooding, and sorrowful, every bit.

'Is that two o'clock striking?' Mrs Dawes said in surprise.

Paul started, and everything sprang into form, regained its individuality, its forgetfulness, and its cheerfulness.

They hurried back to work.

When he was in a rush of preparing for the night's post, examining the work up from Fanny's room, which smelt of ironing, the evening postman came in.

'"Mr Paul Morel",' he said, smiling, handing Paul a package. 'A lady's handwriting! Don't let the girls see it.'

The postman, himself a favourite, was pleased to make fun of the girls' affection for Paul.

It was a volume of verse with a brief note: 'You will allow me to send you this, and so spare me my isolation. I also sympathize and wish you well. – C.D.'

Paul flushed hot.

'Good Lord! Mrs Dawes. She can't afford it. Good Lord, who ever'd have thought it!'

He was suddenly intensely moved. He was filled with the warmth of her. In the glow he could almost feel her as if she were present – her arms, her shoulders, her bosom, see them, feel them, almost contain them.

This move on the part of Clara brought them into closer intimacy. The other girls noticed that when Paul met Mrs Dawes his eyes lifted and gave that peculiar bright greeting which they could interpret. Knowing he was unaware, Clara made no sign, save that occasionally she turned aside her face from him when he came upon her.

They walked out together very often at dinner-time; it was quite open, quite frank. Everybody seemed to feel that he was quite unaware of the state of his own feeling, and that nothing was wrong. He talked to her now with some of the old fervour with which he had talked to Miriam, but he cared less about the talk; he did not bother about his conclusions.

One day in October they went out to Lambley for tea. Suddenly they came to a halt on the top of the hill. He climbed and sat on a gate, she sat on the stile. The afternoon was perfectly still, with a dim haze, and yellow sheaves glowing through. They were quiet.

'How old were you when you married?' he asked quietly.

'Twenty-two.'

Her voice was subdued, almost submissive. She would tell him now.

'It is eight years ago?'

'Yes.'

'And when did you leave him?'

'Three years ago.'

'Five years! Did you love him when you married him?'

She was silent for some time; then she said slowly:

'I thought I did – more or less. I didn't think much about it. And he wanted me. I was very prudish then.'

'And you sort of walked into it without thinking?'

'Yes. I seemed to have been asleep nearly all my life.'

'Somnambule? But – when did you wake up?'

'I don't know that I ever did, or ever have – since I was a child.'

'You went to sleep as you grew to be a woman? How queer! And he didn't wake you?'

'No, he never got there,' she replied, in a monotone.

The brown birds dashed over the hedges where the rose-hips stood naked and scarlet.

'Got where?' he asked.

'At me. He never really mattered to me.'

The afternoon was so gently warm and dim. Red roofs of the cottages burned among the blue haze. He loved the day. He could feel, but he could not understand, what Clara was saying.

'But why did you leave him? Was he horrid to you?'

She shuddered lightly.

'He – he sort of degraded me. He wanted to bully me because he hadn't got me. And then I felt as if I wanted to run, as if I was fastened and bound up. And he seemed dirty.'

'I see.'

He did not at all see.

'And was he always dirty?' he asked.

'A bit,' she replied slowly. 'And then he seemed as if he couldn't get *at* me, really. And then he got brutal – he *was* brutal!'

'And why did you leave him, finally?'

'Because – because he was unfaithful to me –'

They were both silent for some time. Her hand lay on the gate-post as she balanced. He put his own over it. His heart beat quickly.

'But did you – were you ever – did you ever give him a chance?'

'Chance? How?'

'To come near to you.'

'I married him – and I was willing –'

They both strove to keep their voices steady.

'I believes he loves you,' he said.

'It looks like it,' she replied.

He wanted to take his hand away, and could not. She saved him by removing her own. After a silence, he began again:

'Did you leave him out of count all along?'

'He left me,' she said.

'And I suppose he couldn't *make* himself mean everything to you?'

'He tried to bully me into it.'

But the conversation had got them both out of their depth. Suddenly Paul jumped down.

'Come on,' he said. 'Let's go and get some tea.'

They found a cottage, where they sat in the cold parlour. She poured out his tea. She was very quiet. He felt she had withdrawn again from him. After tea, she stared broodingly into her teacup, twisting her wedding ring all the time. In her abstraction she took the ring off her finger, stood it up, and spun it upon the table. The gold became a diaphanous glittering globe. It fell, and the ring was quivering upon the table. She spun it again and again. Paul watched, fascinated.

But she was a married woman, and he believed in simple friendship. And he considered that he was perfectly honourable with regard to her. It was only friendship between man and woman, such as any civilized persons might have.

He was like so many young men of his own age. Sex had become so complicated in him that he would have denied that he ever could want Clara or Miriam or any woman whom he *knew*. Sex desire was a sort of detached thing, that did not belong to a woman. He loved Miriam with his soul. He grew warm at the thought of Clara, he battled with her, he knew the curves of her breast and shoulders as if they had been moulded inside him; and yet he did not positively desire her. He would have denied it for ever. He believed himself really bound to Miriam. If ever he should marry, some time in the far future, it would be his duty to marry Miriam. That he gave Clara to understand, and she said nothing, but left him to his courses. He came to her, Mrs Dawes, whenever he could. Then he wrote frequently to Miriam, and visited the girl occasionally. So he went on through the winter; but he seemed not so fretted. His mother was easier about him. She thought he was getting away from Miriam.

Miriam knew now how strong was the attraction of Clara for him; but still she was certain that the best in him would triumph. His feeling for Mrs Dawes – who, moreover, was a married woman – was shallow and temporal, compared with his love for herself. He would come back to her, she was sure; with some of his young freshness gone, perhaps, but cured of his desire for the lesser things which other women than herself could give him. She could bear all if he were inwardly true to her and must come back.

He saw none of the anomaly of his position. Miriam was his old friend, lover, and she belonged to Bestwood and home and his youth. Clara was a newer friend, and she belonged to Nottingham, to life, to the world. It seemed to him quite plain.

Mrs Dawes and he had many periods of coolness, when they saw little of each other; but they always came together again.

'Were you horrid with Baxter Dawes?' he asked her. It was a thing that seemed to trouble him.

'In what way?'

'Oh, I don't know. But weren't you horrid with him? Didn't you do something that knocked him to pieces?'

'What, pray?'

'Making him feel as if he were nothing – *I* know,' Paul declared.

'You are so clever, my friend,' she said coolly.

The conversation broke off there. But it made her cool with him for some time.

She very rarely saw Miriam now. The friendship between the two women was not broken off, but considerably weakened.

'Will you come in to the concert on Sunday afternoon?' Clara asked him just after Christmas.

'I promised to go up to Willey Farm,' he replied.

'Oh, very well.'

'You don't mind, do you?' he asked.

'Why should I?' she answered.

Which almost annoyed him.

'You know,' he said, 'Miriam and I have been a lot to each other ever since I was sixteen – that's seven years now.'

'It's a long time,' Clara replied.

'Yes; but somehow she – it doesn't go right –'

'How?' asked Clara.

'She seems to draw me and draw me, and she wouldn't leave a single hair of me free to fall out and blow away – she'd keep it.'

'But you like to be kept.'

'No,' he said, 'I don't. I wish it could be normal, give and take – like me and you. I want a woman to keep me, but not in her pocket.'

'But if you love her, it couldn't be normal, like me and you.'

'Yes; I should love her better then. She sort of wants me so much that I can't give myself.'

'Wants you how?'

'Wants the soul out of my body. I can't help shrinking back from her.'

'And yet you love her!'

'No, I don't love her. I never even kiss her.'

'Why not?' Clara asked.

'I don't know.'

'I suppose you're afraid,' she said.

'I'm not. Something in me shrinks from her like hell – she's so good, when I'm not good.'

'How do you know what she is?'

'I do! I know she wants a sort of soul union.'

'But how do you know what she wants?'

'I've been with her for seven years.'

'And you haven't found out the very first thing about her.'

'What's that?'

'That she doesn't want any of your soul communion. That's your own imagination. She wants you.'

He pondered over this. Perhaps he was wrong.

'But she seems –' he began.

'You've never tried,' she answered.

11

THE TEST OF MIRIAM

With the spring came again the old madness and battle. Now he knew he would have to go to Miriam. But what was his reluctance? He told himself it was only a sort of overstrong virginity in her and him which neither could break through. He might have married her; but his circumstances at home made it difficult, and, moreover, he did not want to marry. Marriage was for life, and because they had become close companions, he and she, he did not see that it should inevitably follow they should be man and wife. He did not feel that he wanted marriage with Miriam. He wished he did. He would have given his head to have felt a joyous desire to marry her and to have her. Then why couldn't he bring it off? There was some obstacle; and what was the obstacle?

It lay in the physical bondage. He shrank from the physical contact. But why? With her he felt bound up inside himself. He could not go out to her. Something struggled in him, but he could not get to her. Why? She loved him. Clara said she even wanted him; then why couldn't he go to her, make love to her, kiss her? Why, when she put her arm in his, timidly, as they walked did he feel he would burst forth in brutality and recoil? He owed himself to her; he wanted to belong to her. Perhaps the recoil and the shrinking from her was love in its first fierce modesty. He had no aversion for her. No, it was the opposite; it was a strong desire battling with a still stronger shyness and virginity. It seemed as if virginity were a positive force, which fought and won in both of them. And with her he felt it so hard to overcome; yet he was nearest to her, and with her alone could he deliberately break through. And he owed himself to her. Then, if they could get things right, they would marry; but he would not marry unless he could feel strong in the joy of it – never. He could not have faced his mother. It seemed to him that to sacrifice himself in a marriage he did not want would be degrading, and would undo all his life, make it a nullity. He would try what he *could* do.

And he had a great tenderness for Miriam. Always, she was sad, dreaming her religion; and he was nearly a religion to her. He could not bear to fail her. It would all come right if they tried.

He looked round. A good many of the nicest men he knew were like himself, bound in by their own virginity, which they could not break out of. They were so sensitive to their women that they would go without them for ever rather than do them a hurt, an injustice. Being the sons of mothers whose husbands had blundered rather brutally through their feminine sanctities, they were themselves too diffident and shy. They could easier deny themselves than incur any reproach from a woman; for a woman was like their mother, and they were full of the sense of their mother. They preferred themselves to suffer the misery of celibacy, rather than risk the other person.

He went back to her. Something in her, when he looked at her, brought the tears almost to his eyes. One day he stood behind her as she sang. Annie was playing a song on the piano. As Miriam sang her mouth seemed hopeless. She sang like a nun singing to heaven. It reminded him so much of the mouth and eyes of one who sings beside a Botticelli Madonna, so spiritual. Again, hot as steel, came up the pain in him. Why must he ask her for the other thing? Why was there his blood battling with her? If only he could have been always gentle, tender with her, breathing with her the atmosphere of reverie and religious dreams, he would give his right hand. It was not fair to hurt her. There seemed an eternal maidenhood about her; and when he thought of her mother, he saw the great brown eyes of a maiden who was nearly scared and shocked out of her virgin maidenhood, but not quite, in spite of her seven children. They had been born almost leaving her out of count, not of her, but upon her. So she could never let them go, because she never had possessed them.

Mrs Morel saw him going again frequently to Miriam, and was astonished. He said nothing to his mother. He did not explain nor excuse himself. If he came home late, and she reproached him, he frowned and turned on her in an overbearing way.

'I shall come home when I like,' he said: 'I am old enough.'

'Must she keep you till this time?'

'It is I who stay,' he answered.

'And she lets you? But very well,' she said.

And she went to bed, leaving the door unlocked for him; but she lay listening until he came, often long after. It was a great bitterness to her that he had gone back to Miriam. She recognized, however, the uselessness of any further interference. He went to Willey Farm as a man now, not as a youth. She had no right over him. There was a coldness between him and her. He hardly told her anything. Discarded, she waited on him, cooked for him still, and loved to slave for him; but her face closed again like a mask. There was nothing for her to do now but the housework; for all the rest he had gone to Miriam. She could not forgive him. Miriam killed the joy and the warmth in him. He had been such a jolly lad, and full of the warmest affection; now he grew colder, more and more irritable and gloomy. It reminded her of William; but Paul was worse. He did things with more intensity, and more realization of what he was about. His mother knew how he was suffering for want of a woman, and she saw him going to Miriam. If he had made up his mind, nothing on earth would alter him. Mrs Morel was tired. She began to give up at last; she had finished. She was in the way.

He went on determinedly. He realized more or less what his mother felt. It only hardened his soul. He made himself callous towards her; but it was like being callous to his own health. It undermined him quickly; yet he persisted.

He lay back in the rocking-chair at Willey Farm one evening. He had been talking to Miriam for some weeks, but had not come to the point. Now he said suddenly:

'I am twenty-four, almost.'

She had been brooding. She looked up at him suddenly in surprise.

'Yes. What makes you say it?'

There was something in the charged atmosphere that she dreaded.

'Sir Thomas More says one can marry at twenty-four.'

She laughed quaintly, saying:

'Does it need Sir Thomas More's sanction?'

'No; but one ought to marry about then.'

'Ay,' she answered broodingly; and she waited.

'I can't marry you,' he continued slowly, 'not now, because we've no money, and they depend on me at home.'

She sat half-guessing what was coming.

'But I want to marry now –'

'You want to marry?' she repeated.

'A woman – you know what I mean.'

She was silent.

'Now, at last, I must,' he said.

'Ay,' she answered.

'And you love me?'

She laughed bitterly.

'Why are you ashamed of it?' he answered. 'You wouldn't be ashamed before your God, why are you before people?'

'Nay,' she answered deeply, 'I am not ashamed.'

'You are,' he replied bitterly; 'and it's my fault. But you know I can't help being – as I am – don't you?'

'I know you can't help it,' she replied.

'I love you an awful lot – then there is something short.'

'Where?' she answered, looking at him.

'Oh, in me! It is I who ought to be ashamed – like a spiritual cripple. And I am ashamed. It is misery. Why is it?'

'I don't know,' replied Miriam.

'And I don't know,' he repeated. 'Don't you think we have been too fierce in our what they call purity? Don't you think that to be so much afraid and averse is a sort of dirtiness?'

She looked at him with startled dark eyes.

'You recoiled away from anything of the sort, and I took the motion from you, and recoiled also, perhaps worse.'

There was silence in the room for some time.

'Yes,' she said, 'it is so.'

'There is between us,' he said 'all these years of intimacy. I feel naked enough before you. Do you understand?'

'I think so,' she answered.

'And you love me?'

She laughed.

'Don't be bitter,' he pleaded.

She looked at him and was sorry for him; his eyes were dark with torture. She was sorry for him; it was worse for him to have this deflected love than for herself, who could never be properly mated. He was restless, for ever urging forward and trying to find a way out. He might do as he liked, and have what he liked of her.

'Nay,' she said softly, 'I am not bitter.'

She felt she could bear anything for him; she would suffer for him. She put her hand on his knee as he leaned forward in his chair. He took it and kissed it; but it hurt to do so. He felt he was putting himself aside. He sat there sacrificed to her purity, which felt more like nullity. How could he kiss her hand passionately, when it would drive her away, and leave nothing but pain? Yet slowly he drew her to him and kissed her.

They knew each other too well to pretend anything. As she kissed him, she watched his eyes; they were staring across the room, with a peculiar dark blaze in them that fascinated her. He was perfectly still. She could feel his heart throbbing heavily in his breast.

'What are you thinking about?' she asked.

The blaze in his eyes shuddered, became uncertain.

'I was thinking, all the while, I love you. I have been obstinate.'

She sank her head on his breast.

'Yes,' she answered.

'That's all,' he said, and his voice seemed sure, and his mouth was kissing her throat.

Then she raised her head and looked into his eyes with her full gaze of love. The blaze struggled, seemed to try to get away from her, and then was quenched. He turned his head quickly aside. It was a moment of anguish.

'Kiss me,' she whispered.

He shut his eyes, and kissed her, and his arms folded her closer and closer.

When she walked home with him over the fields, he said:

'I am glad I came back to you. I feel so simple with you – as if there was nothing to hide. We will be happy?'

'Yes,' she murmured, and the tears came to her eyes.

'Some sort of perversity in our souls,' he said, 'makes us not want, get away from, the very thing we want. We have to fight against that.'

'Yes,' she said, and she felt stunned.

As she stood under the drooping thorn-tree, in the darkness by the roadside, he kissed her, and his fingers wandered over her face. In the darkness, where he could not see her but only feel her, his passion flooded him. He clasped her very close.

'Sometime you will have me?' he murmured, hiding his face on her shoulder. It was so difficult.

'Not now,' she said.

His hopes and his heart sank. A dreariness came over him.

'No,' he said.

His clasp of her slackened.

'I love to feel your arm *there*!' she said, pressing his arm against her back, where it went round her waist. 'It rests me so.'

He tightened the pressure of his arm upon the small of her back to rest her.

'We belong to each other,' he said.

'Yes.'

'Then why shouldn't we belong to each other altogether?'

'But –' she faltered.

'I know it's a lot to ask,' he said; 'but there's not much risk for you really – not in the Gretchen way. You can trust me there?'

'Oh, I can trust you,' the answer came quick and strong. 'It's not that – it's not that at all – but –'

'What?'

She hid her face in his neck with a little cry of misery.

'I don't know!' she cried.

She seemed slightly hysterical, but with a sort of horror. His heart died in him.

'You don't think it ugly?' he asked.

'No, not now. You have *taught* me it isn't.'

'You are afraid?'

She calmed herself hastily.

'Yes, I am only afraid,' she said.

He kissed her tenderly.

'Never mind,' he said. 'You shall please yourself.'

Suddenly she gripped his arms round her, and clenched her body stiff.

'You *shall* have me,' she said, through her shut teeth.

His heart beat up again like fire. He folded her close, and his mouth was on her throat. She could not bear it. She drew away. He disengaged her.

'Won't you be late?' she asked gently.

He sighed, scarcely hearing what she said. She waited, wishing he would go. At last he kissed her quickly and climbed the fence. Looking round he saw the pale blotch of her face down in the darkness under the hanging tree. There was no more of her but this pale blotch.

'Good-bye!' he called softly. She had no body, only a voice and a dim face. He turned away and ran down the road, his fists clenched; and when he came to the wall over the lake he leaned there, almost stunned, looking up the black water.

Miriam plunged home over the meadows. She was not afraid of people, what they might say; but she dreaded the issue with him. Yes, she would let him have her if he insisted; and then, when she thought of it afterwards, her heart went down. He would be disappointed, he would find no satisfaction, and then he would go away. Yet he was so insistent; and over this, which did not seem so all-important to her, was their love to break down. After all, he was only like other men, seeking his satisfaction. Oh, but there was something more in him, something deeper! She could trust to it, in spite of all desires. He said that possession was a great moment in life. All strong emotions concentrated there. Perhaps it was so. There was something divine in it; then she would submit, religiously, to the sacrifice. He should have her. And at the thought her whole body clenched itself involuntarily, hard, as if against something; but Life forced her through this gate of suffering, too, and she would submit. At any rate, it would give him what he wanted, which was her deepest wish. She brooded and brooded and brooded herself towards accepting him.

He courted her now like a lover. Often, when he grew hot, she put his face from her, held it between her hands, and looked in his eyes. He could not meet her gaze. Her dark eyes, full of love, earnest and searching, made him turn away. Not for an instant would she let him forget. Back again he had to torture himself into a sense of his responsibility and hers. Never any relaxing, never any leaving himself to the great hunger and inpersonality of passion; he must be brought back to a deliberate, reflective creature. As if from a swoon of passion she called him back to the littleness, the personal relationship. He could not bear it. 'Leave me alone – leave me alone!' he wanted to cry; but she wanted him to look at her with eyes full of love. His eyes, full of the dark, impersonal fire of desire, did not belong to her.

There was a great crop of cherries at the farm. The trees at the back of the house, very large and tall, hung thick with scarlet and crimson drops, under the dark leaves. Paul and Edgar were gathering the fruit one evening. It had been a hot day, and now the clouds were rolling in the sky, dark and warm. Paul climbed high in the tree, above the scarlet roofs of the buildings. The wind, moaning steadily, made the whole tree rock with a subtle, thrilling motion that stirred the blood. The young man, perched insecurely in the slender branches, rocked till he felt slightly drunk, reached down the boughs where the scarlet beady cherries hung thick underneath, and tore off handful after handful of the sleek, cool-fleshed fruit. Cherries touched his ears and his neck as he stretched forward, their chill finger-tips sending a flash down his blood. All shades of red, from a golden vermilion to a rich crimson, glowed and met his eyes under a darkness of leaves.

The sun, going down, suddenly caught the broken clouds. Immense piles of gold flared out of the south-east, heaped in soft, glowing yellow right up the sky. The world, till now dusk and grey, reflected the gold glow, astonished. Everywhere the trees, and the grass, and the far-off water, seemed roused from the twilight and shining.

Miriam came out wondering.

'Oh!' Paul heard her mellow voice call, 'isn't it wonderful?'

He looked down. There was a faint glimmer on her face, that looked very soft, turned up at him.

'How high you are!' she said.

Beside her, on the rhubarb leaves, were four dead birds, thieves that had been shot. Paul saw some cherry-stones hanging quite bleached, like skeletons, picked clear of flesh. He looked down again to Miriam.

'Clouds are on fire,' he said.

'Beautiful!' she cried.

She seemed so small, so soft, so tender, down there. He threw a handful of cherries at her. She was startled and frightened. He laughed with a low, chuckling sound, and pelted her. She ran for shelter, picking up some cherries. Two fine pairs she hung over her ears; then she looked up again.

'Haven't you got enough?' she asked.

'Nearly. It is like being on a ship up here.'

'And how long will you stay?'

'While the sunset lasts.'

She went to the fence and sat there, watching the gold clouds fall to pieces, and go in immense, rose-coloured ruin towards the darkness. Gold flamed to scarlet, like pain in its intense brightness. Then the scarlet sank to rose, and rose to crimson, and quickly the passion went out of the sky. All the world was dark grey. Paul scrambled quickly down with his basket, tearing his shirt-sleeve as he did so.

'They are lovely,' said Miriam, fingering the cherries.

'I've torn my sleeve,' he answered.

She took the three-cornered rip, saying:

'I shall have to mend it.' It was near the shoulder. She put her fingers through the tear. 'How warm!' she said.

He laughed. There was a new strange note in his voice, one that made her pant.

'Shall we stay out?' he said.

'Won't it rain?' she asked.

'No, let us walk a little way.'

They went down the fields and into the thick plantation of fir-trees and pines.

'Shall we go in among the trees?' he asked.

'Do you want to?'

'Yes.'

It was very dark among the firs, and the sharp spines pricked her face. She was afraid. Paul was silent and strange.

'I like the darkness,' he said. 'I wish it were thicker – good, thick darkness.'

He seemed to be almost unaware of her as a person: she was only to him then a woman. She was afraid.

He stood against a pine-tree trunk and took her in his arms. She relinquished herself to him, but it was a sacrifice in which she felt something of horror. This thick-voiced, oblivious man was a stranger to her.

Later it began to rain. The pine-trees smelled very strong. Paul lay with his head on the ground, on the dead pine-needles, listening to the sharp hiss of the rain – a steady, keen noise. His heart was down, very heavy. Now he realized that she had not been with him all the time, that her soul had stood apart, in a sort of horror. He was physically at rest, but not more. Very dreary at heart, very sad, and very tender, his fingers wandered over her face pitifully. Now again she loved him deeply. He was tender and beautiful.

'The rain!' he said.

'Yes – it is coming on you?'

She put her hands over him, on his hair, on his shoulders, to feel if the raindrops fell on him. She loved him dearly. He, as he lay with his face on the dead pine-leaves, felt extraordinarily quiet. He did not mind if the raindrops came on him; he would have lain and got wet through; he felt as if nothing mattered, as if his living were smeared away into the beyond, near and quite lovable. This strange, gentle reaching-out to death was new to him.

'We must go,' said Miriam.

'Yes,' he answered, but did not move.

To him now, life seemed a shadow, day a white shadow; night, and death, and stillness, and inaction, this seemed like *being*. To be alive, to be urgent and insistent – that was *not-to-be*. The highest of all was to melt out into the darkness and sway there, identified with the great Being.

'The rain is coming in on us,' said Miriam.

He rose, and assisted her.

'It is a pity,' he said.

'What?'

'To have to go. I feel so still.'

'Still!' she repeated.

'Stiller than I have ever been in my life.'

He was walking with his hand in hers. She pressed his fingers, feeling a slight fear. Now he seemed beyond her; she had a fear lest she should lose him.

'The fir-trees are like presences on the darkness: each one only a presence.'

She was afraid, and said nothing.

'A sort of hush: the whole night wondering and asleep: I suppose that's what we do in death – sleep in wonder.'

She had been afraid before of the brute in him: now of the mystic. She trod beside him in silence. The rain fell with a heavy 'Hush!' on the trees. At last they gained the cart-shed.

'Let us stay here awhile,' he said.

There was a sound of rain everywhere, smothering everything.

'I feel so strange and still,' he said; 'along with everything.'

'Ay,' she answered patiently.

He seemed again unaware of her, though he held her hand close.

'To be rid of our individuality, which is our will, which is our effort – to live effortless, a kind of conscious sleep – that is very beautiful, I think that is our after-life – our immortality.'

'Yes?'

'Yes – and very beautiful to have.'

'You don't usually say that.'

'No.'

In a while they went indoors. Everybody looked at them curiously. He still kept the quiet, heavy look in his eyes, the stillness of his voice. Instinctively, they all left him alone.

About this time Miriam's grandmother, who lived in a tiny cottage in Woodlinton, fell ill, and the girl was sent to keep house. It was a beautiful little place. The cottage had a big garden in front, with red brick walls, against which the plum-trees were nailed. At the back another garden was separated from the fields by a tall old hedge. It was very pretty. Miriam had not much to do, so she found time for her beloved reading, and for writing introspective pieces which interested her.

At the holiday-time her grandmother, being better, was driven to Derby to stay with her daughter for a day or two. She was a crotchety old lady, and might return the second day or the third; so Miriam stayed alone in the cottage, which also pleased her.

Paul used often to cycle over, and they had as a rule peaceful and happy times. He did not embarrass her much; but then on the Monday of the holiday he was to spend a whole day with her.

It was perfect weather. He left his mother, telling her where he was going. She would be alone all the day. It cast a shadow over him; but he had three days that were all his own, when he was going to do as he liked. It was sweet to rush through the morning lanes on his bicycle.

He got to the cottage at about eleven o'clock. Miriam was busy preparing dinner. She looked so perfectly in keeping with the little kitchen, ruddy and busy. He kissed her and sat down to watch. The room was small and cosy. The sofa was covered all over with a sort of linen in squares of red and pale blue, old, much washed, but pretty. There was a stuffed owl in a case over a corner cupboard. The sunlight came through the leaves of the scented geraniums in the window. She was cooking a chicken in his honour. It was their cottage for the day, and they were man and wife. He beat the eggs for her and peeled the potatoes. He thought she gave a feeling of home almost like his mother; and no one could look more beautiful, with her tumbled curls, when she was flushed from the fire.

The dinner was a great success. Like a young husband, he carved. They talked all the time with unflagging zest. Then he wiped the dishes she had washed, and they went out down the fields. There was a bright little brook that ran into a bog at the foot of a very steep bank. Here they wandered, picking still a few marsh-marigolds and many big blue forget-me-nots. Then she sat on the bank with her hands full of flowers, mostly golden water-blobs. As she put her face down into the marigolds, it was all overcast with a yellow shine.

'Your face is bright,' he said, 'like a transfiguration.'

She looked at him, questioning. He laughed pleadingly to her, laying his hand on hers. Then he kissed her fingers, then her face.

The world was all steeped in sunshine, and quite still, yet not asleep, but quivering with a kind of expectancy.

'I have never seen anything more beautiful than this,' he said. He held her hand fast all the time.

'And the water singing to itself as it runs – do you love it?' She looked at him full of love. His eyes were very dark, very bright.

'Don't you think it's a great day?' he asked.

She murmured her assent. She *was* happy, and he saw it.

'And our day – just between us,' he said.

They lingered a little while. Then they stood up upon the sweet thyme, and he looked down at her simply.

'Will you come?' he asked.

They went back to the house, hand-in-hand, in silence. The chickens came scampering down the path to her. He locked the door, and they had the little house to themselves.

He never forgot seeing her as she lay on the bed, when he was unfastening his collar. First he saw only her beauty, and was blind with it. She had the most beautiful body he had ever imagined. He stood unable to move or speak, looking at her, his face half smiling with wonder. And then he wanted her, but as he went forward to her, her hands lifted in a little pleading movement, and he looked at her face, and stopped. Her big brown eyes were watching him, still and resigned and loving; she lay as if she had given herself up to sacrifice: there was her body for him; but the look at the back of her eyes, like a creature awaiting immolation, arrested him, and all his blood fell back.

'You are sure you want me?' he asked, as if a cold shadow had come over him.

'Yes, quite sure.'

She was very quiet, very calm. She only realized that she was doing something for him. He could hardly bear it. She lay to be sacrificed for him because she loved him so much. And he had to sacrifice her. For a second, he wished he were sexless or dead. Then he shut his eyes again to her, and his blood beat back again.

And afterwards he loved her – loved her to the last fibre of his being. He loved her. But he wanted, somehow, to cry. There was something he could not bear for her sake. He stayed with her till quite late at night. As he rode home he felt that he was finally initiated. He was a youth no longer. But why had he the dull pain in his soul? Why did the thought of death, the after-life, seem so sweet and consoling?

He spent the week with Miriam, and wore her out with his passion before it was gone. He had always, almost wilfully, to put her out of count, and act from the brute strength of his own feelings. And he could not do it often, and there remained afterwards always the sense of failure and of death. If he were really with her, he had to put aside himself and his desire. If he would have her, he had to put her aside.

'When I come to you,' he asked her, his eyes dark with pain and shame, 'you don't really want me, do you?'

'Ah, yes!' she replied quickly.

He looked at her.

'Nay,' he said.

She began to tremble.

'You see,' she said, taking his face and shutting it out against her shoulder – 'you see – as we are – how can I get used to you? It would come all right if we were married.'

He lifted her head and looked at her.

'You mean, now, it is always too much shock?'

'Yes – and –'

'You are always clenched against me.'

She was trembling with agitation.

'You see,' she said, 'I'm not used to the thought –'

'You are lately,' he said.

'But all my life. Mother said to me, "There is one thing in marriage that is always dreadful, but you have to bear it." And I believed it.'

'And still believe,' he said.

'No!' she cried hastily. 'I believe, as you do, that loving, even in *that* way, is the high-water mark of living.'

'That doesn't alter the fact that you never *want* it.'

'No,' she said, taking his head in her arms and rocking in despair. 'Don't say so! You don't understand.' She rocked with pain. 'Don't I want your children?'

'But not me.'

'How can you say so? But we must be married to have children –'

'Shall we be married, then? *I* want you to have my children.' He kissed her hand reverently. She pondered sadly, watching him.

'We are too young,' she said at length.

'Twenty-four and twenty-three –'

'Not yet,' she pleaded, as she rocked herself in distress.

'When you will,' he said.

She bowed her head gravely. The tone of hopelessness in which he said these things grieved her deeply. It had always been a failure between them. Tacitly, she acquiesced in what he felt.

And after a week of love he said to his mother suddenly one Sunday night, just as they were going to bed:

'I shan't go so much to Miriam's mother.'

She was surprised, but she would not ask him anything.

'You please yourself,' she said.

So he went to bed. But there was a new quietness about him which she had wondered at. She almost guessed. She would leave him alone, however. Precipitation might spoil things. She watched him in his loneliness, wondering where he would end. He was sick, and much too quiet for him. There was a perpetual little knitting of his brows, such as she had seen when he was a small baby, and which had been gone for many years. Now it was the same again. And she could do nothing for him. He had to go on alone, make his own way.

He continued faithful to Miriam. For one day he had loved her utterly. But it never came again. The sense of failure grew stronger. At first it was only a sadness. Then he began to feel he could not go on. He wanted to run, to go abroad, anything. Gradually he ceased to ask her to have him. Instead of drawing them together, it put them apart. And then he realized, consciously, that it was no good. It was useless trying: it would never be a success between them.

For some months he had seen very little of Clara. They had occasionally walked out for half an hour at dinner-time. But he always reserved himself for Miriam. With Clara, however, his brow cleared, and he was gay again. She treated him indulgently, as if he were a child. He thought he did not mind. But deep below the surface it piqued him.

Sometimes Miriam said:

'What about Clara? I hear nothing of her lately.'

'I walked with her about twenty minutes yesterday,' he replied.

'And what did she talk about?'

'I don't know. I suppose I did all the jawing – I usually do. I think I was telling her about the strike, and how the women took it.'

'Yes.'

So he gave the account of himself.

But insidiously, without his knowing it, the warmth he felt for Clara drew him away from Miriam, for whom he felt responsible, and to whom he felt he belonged. He thought he was being quite faithful to her. It is not easy to estimate exactly the strength and warmth of one's feelings for a woman till they have run away with one.

He began to give more time to his friends. There was Jessop, at the Art School; Swain, who was chemistry demonstrator at the University; Newton, who was a teacher; besides Edgar and Miriam's younger brothers. Pleading work, he sketched and studied with Jessop. He called in the University for Swain, and the two went 'down town' together. Having come home in the train with Newton, he called and had a game of billiards with him in the Moon and Stars. If he gave to Miriam the excuse of his men friends, he felt quite justified. His mother began to be relieved. He always told her where he had been.

During the summer, Clara wore sometimes a dress of soft cotton stuff with loose sleeves. When she lifted her hands, her sleeves fell back, and her beautiful strong arms shone out.

'Half a minute,' he cried. 'Hold your arm still.'

He made sketches of her hand and arm, and the drawings contained some of the fascination the real thing had for him. Miriam, who always went scrupulously through his books and papers, saw the drawings.

'I think Clara has such beautiful arms,' he said.

'Yes! When did you draw them?'

'On Tuesday, in the work-room. You know, I've got a corner where I can work. Often I can do every single thing they need in the department, before dinner. Then I work for myself in the afternoon, and just see to things at night.'

'Yes,' she said, turning the leaves of his sketch-book.

Frequently he hated Miriam. He hated her as she bent forward and pored over his things. He hated her way of patiently casting him up, as if he were an endless psychological account. When he was with her, he hated her for having got him, and yet not got him, and he tortured her. She took all and gave nothing, he said. At least, she gave no living warmth. She was never alive, and giving off life. Looking for her was like looking for something which did not exist. She was only his conscience, not his mate. He hated her violently, and was more cruel to her. They dragged on till the next summer. He saw more and more of Clara.

At last he spoke. He had been sitting working at home one evening. There was between him and his mother a peculiar condition of people frankly finding fault with each other. Mrs Morel was strong on her feet again. He was not going to stick to Miriam. Very well; then she would stand aloof till he said something. It had been coming a long time, this bursting of the storm in him, when he would come back to her. This evening there was between them a peculiar condition of suspense. He worked feverishly and mechanically, so that he could escape from himself. It grew late. Through the open door, stealthily, came the scent of madonna lilies, almost as if it were prowling abroad. Suddenly he got up and went out of doors.

The beauty of the night made him want to shout. A half-moon, dusky gold, was sinking behind the black sycamore at the end of the garden, making the sky dull purple with its glow. Nearer, a dim white fence of lilies went across the garden, and the air all round seemed to stir with scent, as if it were alive. He went across the bed of pinks, whose keen perfume came sharply across the rocking, heavy scent of the lilies, and stood alongside the white barrier of flowers. They flagged all loose, as if they were panting. The scent made him drunk. He went down to the field to watch the moon sink under.

A corncrake in the hay-close called insistently. The moon slide quickly downwards, growing more flushed. Behind him the great flowers leaned as if they were calling. And then, like a shock, he caught another perfume, something raw and coarse. Hunting round, he found the purple iris, touched their fleshy throats and their dark, grasping hands. At any rate, he had found something. They stood stiff in the darkness. Their scent was brutal. The moon was melting down upon the crest of the hill. It was gone; all was dark. The corncrake called still.

Breaking off a pink, he suddenly went indoors.

'Come, my boy,' said his mother. 'I'm sure it's time you went to bed.'

He stood with the pink against his lips.

'I shall break off with Miriam, mother,' he answered calmly.

She looked up at him over her spectacles. He was staring back at her, unswerving. She met his eyes for a moment, then took off her glasses. He was white. The male was up in him, dominant. She did not want to see him too clearly.

'But I thought –' she began.

'Well,' he answered, 'I don't love her. I don't want to marry her – so I shall have done.'

'But,' exclaimed his mother, amazed, 'I thought lately you had made up your mind to have her, and so I said nothing.'

'I had – I wanted to – but now I don't want. It's no good. I shall break off on Sunday. I ought to, oughtn't I?'

'You know best. You know I said so long ago.'

'I can't help that now. I shall break off on Sunday.'

'Well,' said his mother. 'I think it will be best. But lately I decided you had made up your mind to have her, so I said nothing, and should have said nothing. But I say as I have always said, I *don't* think she is suited to you.'

'On Sunday I break off,' he said, smelling the pink. He put the flower in his mouth. Unthinking, he bared his teeth, closed them on the blossom slowly, and had a mouthful of petals. These he spat into the fire, kissed his mother, and went to bed.

On Sunday he went up to the farm in the early afternoon. He had written Miriam that they would walk over the fields to Hucknall. His mother was very tender with him. He said nothing. But she saw the effort it was costing. The peculiar set look on his face stilled her.

'Never mind, my son,' she said. 'You will be so much better, when it is all over.'

Paul glanced swiftly at his mother in surprise and resentment. He did not want sympathy.

Miriam met him at the lane-end. She was wearing a new dress of figured muslin that had short sleeves. Those short sleeves, and Miriam's brown-skinned arms beneath them – such pitiful, resigned arms – gave him so much pain that they helped to make him cruel. She had made herself look so beautiful and fresh for him. She seemed to blossom for him alone. Every time he looked at her – a mature young woman now, and beautiful in her new dress – it hurt so much that his heart seemed almost to be bursting with the restraint he put on it. But he had decided, and it was irrevocable.

On the hills they sat down, and he lay with his head in her lap, whilst she fingered his hair. She knew that 'he was not there', as she put it. Often, when she had him with her, she looked for him, and could not find him. But this afternoon she was not prepared.

It was nearly five o'clock when he told her. They were sitting on the bank of a stream, where the lip of turf hung over a hollow bank of yellow earth, and he was hacking away with a stick, as he did when he was perturbed and cruel.

'I have been thinking,' he said, 'we ought to break off.'

'Why?' she cried in surprise.

'Because it's no good going on.'

'Why is it no good?'

'It isn't. I don't want to marry. I don't want ever to marry. And if we're not going to marry, it's no good going on.'

'But why do you say this now?'

'Because I've made up my mind.'

'And what about these last months, and the things you told me then?'

'I can't help it; I don't want to go on.'

'You don't want any more of me?'

'I want us to break off – you be free of me, I free of you.'

'And what about these last months?'

'I don't know. I've not told you anything but what I thought was true.'

'Then why are you different now?'

'I'm not – I'm the same – only I know it's no good going on.'

'You haven't told me why it's no good.'

'Because I don't want to go on – and I don't want to marry.'

'How many times have you offered to marry me, and I wouldn't?'

'I know; but I want us to break off.'

There was silence for a moment or two, while he dug viciously at the earth. She bent her head, pondering. He was an unreasonable child. He was like an infant which, when it has drunk its fill, throws away and smashes the cup. She looked at him, feeling she could get hold of him and *wring* some consistency out of him. But she was helpless. Then she cried.

'I have said you were only fourteen – you are only *four*!'

He still dug at the earth viciously. He heard.

'You are a child of four,' she repeated in her anger.

He did not answer, but said in his heart: 'All right; if I'm a child of four, what do you want me for? *I* don't want another mother.' But he said nothing to her, and there was silence.

'And have you told your people?' she asked.

'I have told my mother.'

There was another long interval of silence.

'Then what do you *want*?' she asked.

'Why, I want us to separate. We have lived on each other all these years; now let us stop. I will go my own way without you, and you will go your way without me. You will have an independent life of your own then.'

There was in it some truth that, in spite of her bitterness, she could not help registering. She knew she felt in a sort of bondage to him, which she hated because she could not control it. She had hated her love for him from the moment it grew too strong for her. And, deep down, she had hated him because she loved him and he dominated her. She had resisted his domination. She had fought to keep herself free of him in the last issue. And she *was* free of him, even more than he of her.

'And,' he continued, 'we shall always be more or less each other's work. You have done a lot for me, I for you. Now let us start and live by ourselves.'

'Very well,' he said; 'I will say no more.'

'What do you want to do?' she asked.

'Nothing – only be free,' he answered.

She, however, knew in her heart that Clara's influence was over him to liberate him. But she said nothing.

'And what have I to tell my mother?' she asked.

'I told my mother,' he answered, 'that I was breaking off – clean and altogether.'

'I shall not tell them at home,' she said.

Frowning, 'You please yourself,' he said.

He knew he had landed her in a nasty hole, and was leaving her in the lurch. It angered him.

'Tell them you wouldn't and won't marry me, and have broken off,' he said. 'It's true enough.'

She bit her finger moodily. She thought over their whole affair. She had known it would come to this; she had seen it all along. It chimed with her bitter expectation.

'Always – it has always been so!' she cried. 'It has been one long battle between us – you fighting away from me.'

It came from her unawares, like a flash of lightning. The man's heart stood still. Was this how she saw it?

'But we've had *some* perfect hours, *some* perfect times, when we were together!' he pleaded.

'Never!' she cried, 'never! It has always been you fighting me off.'

'Not always – not at first!' he pleaded.

'Always, from the very beginning – always the same!'

She had finished, but she had done enough. He sat aghast. He had wanted to say, 'It has been good, but it is at an end.' And she – she whose love he had believed in when he had despised himself – denied that their love had ever been love. 'He had always fought away from her?' Then it had been monstrous. There had never been anything really between them; all the time he had been imagining something where there was nothing. And she had known. She had known so much, and had told him so little. She had known all the time. All the time this was at the bottom of her!

He sat silent in bitterness. At last the whole affair appeared in a cynical aspect to him. She had really played with him, not he with her. She had hidden all her condemnation from him, had flattered him, and despised him. She despised him now. He grew intellectual and cruel.

'You ought to marry a man who worships you,' he said; 'then you could do as you liked with him. Plenty of men will worship you, if you get on the private side of their natures. You ought to marry one such. They would never fight you off.'

'Thank you!' she said. 'But don't advise me to marry someone else any more. You've done it before.'

'Very well,' he said; 'I will say no more.'

He sat still, feeling as if he had had a blow, instead of giving one. Their eight years of friendship and love, *the* eight years of his life, were nullified.

'When did you think of this?' she asked.

'I thought definitely on Thursday night.'

'I knew it was coming,' she said.

That pleased him bitterly. 'Oh, very well! If she knew then it doesn't come as a surprise to her,' he thought.

'And have you said anything to Clara?' she asked.

'No; but I shall tell her now.'

There was a silence.

'Do you remember the things you said this time last year, in my grandmother's house – nay last month even?'

'Yes,' he said; 'I do! And I meant them! I can't help that it's failed.'

'It has failed because you want something else.'

'It would have failed whether or not. *You* never believed in me.'

She laughed strangely.

He sat in silence. He was full of a feeling that she had deceived him. She had despised him when he thought she worshipped him. She had let him say wrong things, and had not contradicted him. She had let him fight alone. But it stuck in his throat that she had despised him whilst he thought she worshipped him. She should have told him when she found fault with him. She had not played fair. He hated her. All these years she had treated him as if he were a hero, and thought of him secretly as an infant, a foolish child. Then why had she left the foolish child to his folly? His heart was hard against her.

She sat full of bitterness. She had known – oh, well she had known! All the time he was away from her she had summed him up, seen his littleness, his meanness, and his folly. Even she had guarded her soul against him. She was not overthrown, nor prostrated, not even much hurt. She had known. Only why, as he sat there, had he still this strange dominance over her? His very movements fascinated her as if she were hypnotized by him. Yet he was despicable, false, inconsistent, and mean. Why this bondage for her? Why was it the movement of his arm stirred her as nothing else the world could? Why was she fastened to him? Why, even now, if he looked at her and commanded her, would she have to obey? She would obey him in his trifling commands. But once he was obeyed, then she had him in her power, she knew, to lead him where she would. She was sure of herself. Only, this new influence! Ah, he was not a man! He was a baby that cries for the newest toy. And all the attachment of his soul would not keep him. Very well, he would have to go. But he would come back when he had tired of his new sensation.

He hacked at the earth till she was fretted to death. She rose. He sat flinging lumps of earth in the stream.

'We will go and have tea here?' he asked.

'Yes,' she answered.

They chattered over irrelevant subjects during tea. He held forth on the love of ornament – the cottage parlour moved him thereto – and its connexion with aesthetics. She was cold and quiet. As they walked home, she asked:

'And we shall not see each other?'

'No – or rarely,' he answered.

'Nor write?' she asked, almost sarcastically.

'As you will,' he answered. 'We're not strangers – never should be, whatever happened. I will write to you now and again. You please yourself.'

'I see!' she answered cuttingly.

But he was at that stage at which nothing else hurts. He had made a great cleavage in his life. He had had a great shock when she had told him their love had been always a conflict. Nothing more mattered. If it had never been much, there was no need to make a fuss that it was ended.

He left her at the lane-end. As she went home, solitary, in her new frock, having her people to face at the other end, he stood still with shame and pain in the highroad, thinking of the suffering he caused her.

In the reaction towards restoring his self-esteem, he went into the Willow Tree for a drink. There were four girls who had been out for the day, drinking a modest glass of port. They had some chocolates on the table. Paul sat near with his whisky. He noticed the girls whispering and nudging. Presently one, a bonny dark hussy, leaned to him and said:

'Have a chocolate?'

The others laughed loudly at her impudence.

'All right,' said Paul. 'Give me a hard one – nut, I don't like creams.'

'Here you are, then,' said the girl; 'here's an almond for you.'

She held the sweet between her fingers. He opened his mouth. She popped it in, and blushed.

'You *are* nice!' he said.

'Well,' she answered, 'we thought you looked overcast, and they dared me offer you a chocolate.'

'I don't mind if I have another – another sort,' he said.

And presently they were all laughing together.

It was nine o'clock when he got home, falling dark. He entered the house in silence. His mother, who had been waiting, rose anxiously.

'I told her,' he said.

'I'm glad,' replied the mother, with great relief.

He hung up his cap wearily.

'I said we'd have done altogether,' he said.

'That's right, my son,' said the mother. 'It's hard for her now, but best in the long run. I know. You weren't suited for her.'

He laughed shakily as he sat down.

'I've had such a lark with some girls in a pub,' he said.

His mother looked at him. He had forgotten Miriam now. He told her about the girls in the Willow Tree. Mrs Morel looked at him. It seemed unreal, his gaiety. At the back of it was too much horror and misery.

'Now have some supper,' she said very gently.

Afterwards he said wistfully:

'She never thought she'd have me, Mother, not from the first, and so she's not disappointed.'

'I'm afraid,' said his mother, 'she doesn't give up hopes of you yet.'

'No,' he said, 'perhaps not.'

'You'll find it's better to have done,' she said.

'*I* don't know,' he said desperately.

'Well, leave her alone,' replied his mother.

So he left her, and she was alone. Very few people cared for her, and she for very few people. She remained alone with herself, waiting.

12

PASSION

He was gradually making it possible to earn a livelihood by his art. Liberty's had taken several of his painted designs on various stuffs, and he could sell designs for embroideries, for altar-cloths, and similar things, in one or two places. It was not very much he made at present, but he might extend it. He had also made friends with the designer for a pottery firm, and was gaining some knowledge of his new acquaintance's art. The applied arts interested him very much. At the same time he laboured slowly at his pictures. He loved to paint large figures, full of light, but not merely made up of lights and cast shadows, like the Impressionists; rather definite figures that had a certain luminous quality, like some of Michelangelo's people. And these he fitted into a landscape, in what he thought true proportion. He worked a great deal from memory, using everybody he knew. He believed firmly in his work, that it was good and valuable. In spite of fits of depression, shrinking, everything, he believed in his work.

He was twenty-four when he said his first confident thing to his mother.

'Mother,' he said, I s'll make a painter that they'll attend to.'

She sniffed in her quaint fashion. It was like a half-pleased shrug of the shoulders.

'Very well, my boy, we'll see,' she said.

'You shall see, my pigeon! You see if you're not swanky one of these days!'

'I'm quite content, my boy,' she smiled.

'But you'll have to alter. Look at you with Minnie!'

Minnie was the small servant, a girl of fourteen.

'And what about Minnie?' asked Mrs Morel, with dignity.

'I heard her this morning: "Eh, Mrs Morel! I was going to do that," when you went out in the rain for some coal,' he said. 'That looks a lot like your being able to manage servants!'

'Well, it was only the child's niceness,' said Mrs Morel.

'And you apologizing to her: "You can't do two things at once, can you?"'

'She *was* busy washing up,' replied Mrs Morel.

'And what did she say? "It could easy have waited a bit. Now look how your feet paddle!"'

'Yes – brazen young baggage!' said Mrs Morel, smiling.

He looked at his mother, laughing. She was quite warm and rosy again with love of him. It seemed as if all the sunshine were on her for a moment. He continued his work gladly. She seemed so well when she was happy that he forgot her grey hair.

And that year she went with him to the Isle of Wight for a holiday. It was too exciting for them both, and too beautiful. Mrs Morel was full of joy and wonder. But he would have her walk with him more than she was able. She had a bad fainting bout. So grey her face was, so blue her mouth! It was agony to him. He felt as if someone were pushing a knife in his chest. Then she was better again, and he forgot. But the anxiety remained inside him, like a wound that did not close.

After leaving Miriam he went almost straight to Clara. On the Monday following the day of the rupture he went down to the workroom. She looked up at him and smiled. They had grown very intimate unawares. She saw a new brightness about him.

'Well, Queen of Sheba!' he said, laughing.

'But why?' she asked.

'I think it suits you. You've got a new frock on.'

She flushed, asking:

'And what of it?'

'Suits you – awfully! *I* could design you a dress.'

'How would it be?'

He stood in front of her, his eyes glittering as he expounded. He kept her eyes fixed with his. Then suddenly he took hold of her. She half started back. He drew the stuff of her blouse tighter, smoothed it over her breast.

'More *so*!' he explained.

But they were both of them flaming with blushes, and immediately he ran away. He had touched her. His whole body was quivering with the sensation.

There was already a sort of secret understanding between them. The next evening he went into the cinematograph with her for a few minutes before train-time. As they sat, he saw her hand lying near him. For some moments he dared not touch it. The pictures danced and dithered. Then he took her hand in his. It was large and firm; it filled his grasp. He held it fast. She neither moved nor made any sign. When they came out his train was due. He hesitated.

'Good night,' she said. He darted away across the road.

The next day he came again, talking to her. She was rather superior with him.

'Shall we go a walk on Monday?' he asked.

She turned her face aside.

'Shall you tell Miriam?' she replied sarcastically.

'I have broken with her,' he said.

'When?'

'Last Sunday.'

'You quarrelled?'

'No! I had made up my mind. I told her quite definitely I should consider myself free.'

Clara did not answer, and he returned to his work. She was so quiet and so superb!

On the Saturday evening he asked her to come and drink coffee with him in a restaurant, meeting him after work was over. She came, looking very reserved and very distant. He had three-quarters of an hour to train-time.

'We will walk a little while,' he said.

She agreed, and they went past the Castle into the Park. He was afraid of her. She walked moodily at his side, with a kind of resentful, reluctant, angry walk. He was afraid to take her hand.

'Which way shall we go?' he asked as they walked in darkness.

'I don't mind.'

'Then we'll go up the steps.'

He suddenly turned round. They had passed the Park steps. She stood still in resentment at his suddenly abandoning her. He looked at her. She stood aloof. He caught her suddenly in his arms, held her strained for a moment, kissed her. Then he let her go.

'Come along,' he said, penitent.

She followed him. He took her hand and kissed her fingertips. They went in silence. When they came to the light, he let go her hand. Neither spoke till they reached the station. Then they looked each other in the eyes.

'Good night,' she said.

And he went for his train. His body acted mechanically. People talked to him. He heard faint echoes answering them. He was in a delirium. He felt that he would go mad if Monday did not come at once. On Monday he would see her again. All himself was pitched there, ahead. Sunday intervened. He could not bear it. He could not see her till Monday. And Sunday intervened – hour after hour of tension. He wanted to beat his head against the door of the carriage. But he sat still. He drank some whisky on the way home, but it only made it worse. His mother must not be upset, that was all. He dissembled, and got quickly to bed. There he sat, dressed, with his chin on his knees, staring out of the window at the far hill, with its few lights. He neither thought nor slept, but sat perfectly still, staring. And when at last he was so cold that he came to himself, he found his watch had stopped at half-past two. It was after three o'clock. He was exhausted, but still there was the torment of knowing it was only Sunday morning. He went to bed and slept. Then he cycled all day long, till he was fagged out. And he scarcely knew where he had been. But the day after was Monday. He slept till four o'clock. Then he lay and thought. He was coming nearer to himself – he could see himself, real, somewhere in front. She would go a walk with him in the afternoon. Afternoon! It seemed years ahead.

Slowly the hours crawled. His father got up; he heard him pottering about. Then the miner set off to the pit, his heavy boots scraping the yard. Cocks were still crowing. A cart went down the road. His mother got up. She knocked the fire. Presently she called him softly. He answered as if he were asleep. This shell of himself did well.

He was walking to the station – another mile! The train was near Nottingham. Would it stop before the tunnels? But it did not matter; it would get there before dinner-time. He was at Jordan's. She would come in half an hour. At any rate, she would be near. He had done the letters. She would be there. Perhaps she had not come. He ran downstairs. Ah! he saw her through the glass door. Her shoulders stopping a little to her work made him feel he could not go forward; he could not stand. He went in. He was pale, nervous, awkward, and quite cold. Would she misunderstand him? He could not write his real self with this shell.

'And this afternoon,' he struggled to say. 'You will come?'

'I think so,' she replied, murmuring.

He stood before her, unable to say a word. She hid her face from him. Again came over him the feeling that he would lose consciousness. He set his teeth and went upstairs. He had done everything correctly yet, and he would do so. All the morning things seemed a long way off, as they do to a man under chloroform. He himself seemed under a tight band of constraint. Then there was his other self, in the distance, doing things, entering stuff in a ledger, and he watched that far-off him carefully to see he made no mistake.

But the ache and strain of it could not go on much longer. He worked incessantly. Still it was only twelve o'clock. As if he had nailed his clothing against the desk, he stood there and worked, forcing every stroke out of himself. It was a quarter to one; he could clear away. Then he ran downstairs.

'You will meet me at the Fountain at two o'clock,' he said.

'I can't be there till half past.'

'Yes!' he said.

She saw his dark, mad eyes.

'I will try at a quarter past.'

And he had to be content. He went and got some dinner. All the time he was still under chloroform, and every minute was stretched out indefinitely. He walked miles of street. Then he thought he would be late at the meeting-place. He was at the Fountain at five past two. The torture of the next quarter of an hour was refined beyond expression. It was the anguish of combining the living self with the shell. Then he saw her. She came! And he was there.

'You are late,' he said.

'Only five minutes,' she answered.

'I'd never have done it to you,' he laughed.

She was in a dark blue costume. He looked at her beautiful figure.

'You want some flowers,' he said, going to the nearest florists.

She followed him in silence. He bought her a bunch of scarlet, brick-red carnations. She put them in her coat, flushing.

'That's a fine colour!' he said.

'I'd rather have had something softer,' she said.

He laughed.

'Do you feel like a blot of vermilion walking down the street?' he said.

She hung her head, afraid of the people they met. He looked sideways at her as they walked. There was a wonderful close down on her face near the ear that he wanted to touch. And a certain heaviness, the heaviness of a very full ear of corn that dips slightly in the wind, that there was about her, made his brain spin. He seemed to be spinning down the street, everything going round.

As they sat in the tramcar, she leaned her heavy shoulder against him, and he took her hand. He felt himself coming round from the anaesthetic, beginning to breathe. Her ear, half hidden among her blonde hair, was near to him. The temptation to kiss it was almost to great. But there were other people on top of the car. It still remained to him to kiss it. After all, he was not himself, he was some attribute of her, like the sunshine that fell on her.

He looked quickly away. It had been raining. The big bluff of the Castle rock was streaked with rain, as it reared above the flat of the town. They crossed the wide, black space of the Midland Railway, and passed the cattle enclosure that stood out white. Then they ran down sordid Wilford Road.

She rocked slightly to the tram's motion, and as she leaned against him, rocked upon him. He was a vigorous, slender man, with exhaustless energy. His face was rough, with rough-hewn features, like the common people's; but his eyes under the deep brows were so full of life that they fascinated her. They seemed to dance, and yet they were still, trembling on the finest balance of laughter. His mouth, the same, was just going to spring into a laugh of triumph, yet did not. There was a sharp suspense about him. She bit her lip moodily. His hand was hard clenched over hers.

They paid their two halfpennies at the turnstile and crossed the bridge. The Trent was very full. It swept silent and insidious under the bridge, travelling in a soft body. There had been a great deal of rain. On the river levels were flat gleams of flood water. The sky was grey, with glisten of silver here and there. In Wilford Churchyard the dahlias were sodden with rain – wet black-crimson balls. No one was on the path that went along the green river meadow, along the elm-tree colonnade.

There was the faintest haze over the silvery-dark water and the green meadow-banks, and the elm-trees that were spangled with gold. The river slid by in a body, utterly silent and swift, intertwining among itself like some subtle, complex creature. Clara walked moodily beside him.

'Why,' she asked at length, in rather a jarring tone, 'did you leave Miriam?' He frowned.

'Because I *wanted* to leave her,' he said.

'Why?'

'Because I didn't want to go on with her. And I didn't want to marry.'

She was silent for a moment. They picked their way down the muddy path. Drops of water fell from the elm-trees.

'You didn't want to marry Miriam, or you didn't want to marry at all?' she asked.

'Both,' he answered – 'both!'

They had to manoeuvre to get to the stile, because of the pools of water.

'And what did she say?' Clara asked.

'Miriam? She said I was a baby of four, and that I always *had* battled her off.'

Clara pondered over this for a time.

'But you have really been going with her for some time?' she asked.

'Yes.'

'And now you don't want any more of her?'

'No. I know it's no good.'

She pondered again.

'Don't you think you've treated her rather badly?' she asked.

'Yes; I ought to have dropped it years back. But it would have been no good going on. Two wrongs don't make a right.'

'How old *are* you?' Clara asked.

'Twenty-five.'

'And I am thirty,' she said.

'I know you are.'

'I shall be thirty-one – or *am* I thirty-one?'

'I neither know nor care. What does it matter!'

They were at the entrance to the Grove. The wet, red track, already sticky with fallen leaves, went up the steep bank between the grass. On either side stood the elm-trees like pillars along a great aisle, arching over and making high up a roof from which the dead leaves fell. All was empty and silent and wet. She stood on top of the stile, and he held both her hands. Laughing, she looked down into his eyes. Then she leaped. Her breast came against his; he held her, and covered her face with kisses.

They went on up the slippery, steep red path. Presently she released his hand and put it round her waist.

'You press the vein in my arm, holding it so tightly,' she said.

They walked along. His finger-tips felt the rocking of her breast. All was silent and deserted. On the left the red wet plough-land showed through the doorways between the elm-boles and their branches. On the right, looking down, they could see the tree-tops of elms growing far beneath them, hear occasionally the gurgle of the river. Sometimes there below they caught glimpses of the full, soft-sliding Trent, and of water-meadows dotted with small cattle.

'It has scarcely altered since little Kirke White used to come,' he said.

But he was watching her throat below the ear, where the flush was fusing into the honey-white, and her mouth that pouted disconsolate. She stirred against him as she walked, and his body was like a taut string.

Half-way up the big colonnade of elms, where the Grove rose highest above the river, their forward movement faltered to an end. He led her across to the grass, under the trees at the edge of the path. The cliff of red earth sloped swiftly down, through trees and bushes, to the river that glimmered and was dark between the foliage. The far-below water-meadows were very green. He and she stood leaning against one another, silent, afraid, their bodies touching all along. There came a quick gurgle from the river below.

'Why', he asked at length, 'did you hate Baxter Dawes?'

She turned to him with a splendid movement. Her mouth was offered him, and her throat; her eyes were half shut; her breast was tilted as if it asked for him. He flashed with a small laugh, shut his eyes, and met her in a long, whole kiss. Her mouth fused with his; their bodies were sealed and annealed. It was some minutes before they withdrew. They were standing beside the public path.

'Will you go down to the river?' he asked.

She looked down at him, leaving herself in his hands. He went over the brim of the declivity and began to climb down.

'It is slippery,' he said.

'Never mind,' she replied.

The red clay went down almost sheer. He slid, went from one tuft of grass to the next, hanging on to the bushes, making for a little platform at the foot of a tree. There he waited for her, laughing with excitement. Her shoes were clogged with red earth. It was hard for her. He frowned. At last he caught her hand, and she stood beside him. The cliff rose above them and fell away below. Her colour was up, her eyes flashed. He looked at the big drop below them.

'It's risky,' he said; 'or messy, at any rate. Shall we go back?'

'Not for my sake,' she said quickly.

'All right. You see, I can't help you; I should only hinder. Give me that little parcel and your gloves. Your poor shoes!'

They stood perched on the face of the declivity, under the trees.

'Well, I'll go again,' he said.

Away he went, slipping, staggering, sliding to the next tree, into which he fell with a slam that nearly shook the breath out of him. She came after cautiously, hanging on to the twigs and grasses. So they descended, stage by stage, to the river's brink. There, to his disgust, the flood had eaten away the path, and the red decline ran straight into the water. He dug in his heels and brought himself up violently. The string of the parcel broke with a snap; the brown parcel bounded down, leaped into the water, and sailed smoothly away. He hung on to his tree.

'Well, I'll be damned!' he cried crossly. Then he laughed. She was coming perilously down.

'Mind!' he warned her. He stood with his back to the tree, waiting. 'Come now,' he called, opening his arms.

She let herself run. He caught her, and together they stood watching the dark water scoop at the raw edge of the bank. The parcel had sailed out of sight.

'It doesn't matter,' she said.

He held her close and kissed her. There was only room for their four feet.

'It's a swindle!' he said. 'But there's a rut where a man has been, so if we go on I guess we shall find the path again.'

The river slid and twined its great volume. On the other bank cattle were feeding on the desolate flats. The cliff rose high above Paul and Clara on their right hand. They stood against the tree in the watery silence.

'Let us try going forward,' he said; and they struggled in the red clay along the groove a man's nailed boots had made. They were hot and flushed. Their barkled shoes hung heavy on their steps. At last they found the broken path. It was littered with rubble from the water, but at any rate it was easier. They cleaned their boots with twigs. His heart was beating thick and fast.

Suddenly, coming on to the little level, he saw two figures of men standing silent at the water's edge. His heart leaped. They were fishing. He turned and put his hand up warningly to Clara. She hesitated, buttoned her coat. The two went on together.

The fishermen turned curiously to watch the two intruders on their privacy and solitude. They had had a fire, but it was nearly out. All kept perfectly still. The men turned again to their fishing, stood over the grey glinting river like statues. Clara went with bowed head, flushing; he was laughing to himself. Directly they passed out of sight behind the willows.

'Now, they ought to be drowned,' said Paul softly.

Clara did not answer. They toiled forward along a tiny path on the river's lip. Suddenly it vanished. The bank was sheer red solid clay in front of them, sloping straight into the river. He stood and cursed beneath his breath, setting his teeth.

'It is impossible!' said Clara.

He stood erect, looking round. Just ahead were two islets in the stream, covered with osiers. But they were unattainable. The cliff came down like a sloping wall from far above their heads. Behind, not far back, were the fishermen. Across the river the distant cattle fed silently in the desolate afternoon. He cursed again deeply under his breath. He gazed up the great steep bank. Was there no hope but to scale back to the public path?

'Stop a minute,' he said, and, digging his heels sideways into the steep bank of red clay, he began nimbly to mount. He looked across at every tree-foot. At last he found what he wanted. Two beech-trees side by side on the hill held a little level on the upper face between their roots. It was littered with damp leaves, but it would do. The fishermen were perhaps sufficiently out of sight. He threw down his rainproof and waved to her to come.

She toiled to his side. Arriving there, she looked at him heavily, dumbly, and laid her head on his shoulder. He held her fast as he looked round. They were safe enough from all but the small, lonely cows over the river. He sunk his mouth on her throat, where he felt her heavy pulse beat under his lips. Everything was perfectly still. There was nothing in the afternoon but themselves.

When she arose, he, looking on the ground all the time, saw suddenly sprinkled on the black wet beech-roots many scarlet carnation petals, like splashed drops of blood; and red, small splashes fell from her bosom, streaming down her dress to her feet.

'Your flowers are smashed,' he said.

She looked at him heavily as she put back her hair. Suddenly he put his finger-tips on her cheek.

'Why dost look so heavy?' he reproached her.

She smiled sadly, as if she felt alone in herself. He caressed her cheek with his fingers, and kissed her.

'Nay!' he said. 'Never thee bother!'

She gripped his fingers tight, and laughed shakily. Then she dropped her hand. He put the hair back from her brows, stroking her temples, kissing them lightly.

'But tha shouldna worrit!' he said softly, pleading.

'No, I don't worry!' she laughed tenderly and resigned.

'Yea, tha does! Dunna thee worrit,' he implored, caressing.

'No!' she consoled him, kissing him.

They had a stiff climb to get to the top again. It took them a quarter of an hour. When he got on to the level grass, he threw off his cap, wiped the sweat from his forehead, and sighed.

'Now we're back at the ordinary level,' he said.

She sat down, panting, on the tussocky grass. Her cheeks were flushed pink. He kissed her, and she gave way to joy.

'And now I'll clean thy boots and make thee fit for respectable folk,' he said.

He kneeled at her feet, worked away with a stick and tufts of grass. She put her fingers in his hair, drew his head to her, and kissed it.

'What am I supposed to be doing,' he said, looking at her laughing; 'cleaning shoes or dibbling with love? Answer me that!'

'Just whichever I please,' she replied.

'I'm your boot-boy for the time being, and nothing else!' But they remained looking into each other's eyes and laughing. Then they kissed with little nibbling kisses.

'T-t-t!' he went with his tongue, like his mother. 'I tell you, nothing gets done when there's a woman about.'

And he returned to his boot-cleaning, singing softly. She touched his thick hair, and he kissed her fingers. He worked away at her shoes. At last they were quite presentable.

'There you are, you see!' he said. 'Aren't I a great hand at restoring you to respectability? Stand up! There, you look as irreproachable as Britannia herself!'

He cleaned his own boots a little, washed his hands in a puddle, and sang. They went on into Clifton village. He was madly in love with her; every movement she made, ever crease in her garments, sent a hot flush through him and seemed adorable.

The old lady at whose house they had tea was roused into gaiety by them.

'I could wish you'd had something of a better day,' she said, hovering round.

'Nay!' he laughed. 'We've been saying how nice it is.'

The old lady looked at him curiously. There was a peculiar glow and charm about him. His eyes were dark and laughing. He rubbed his moustache with a glad movement.

'Have you been saying *so*!' she exclaimed, a light rousing in her old eyes.

'Truly!' he laughed.

'Then I'm sure the day's good enough,' said the old lady.

She fussed about, and did not want to leave them.

'I don't know whether you'd like some radishes as well,' she said to Clara; 'but I've got some in the garden – *and* a cucumber.'

Clara flushed. She looked very handsome.

'I should like some radishes,' she answered.

And the old lady pottered off gleefully.

'If she knew!' said Clara quietly to him.

'Well, she doesn't know; and it shows we're nice in ourselves, at any rate. You look quite enough to satisfy an archangel, and I'm sure I feel harmless – so – if it makes you look nice, and makes folk happy when they have us, and makes us happy – why, we're not cheating them out of much!'

They went on with the meal. When they were going away, the old lady came timidly with three tiny dahlias in full blow, neat as bees, and speckled scarlet and white. She stood before Clara, pleased with herself, saying:

'I don't know whether –' and holding the flowers forward in her old hand.

'Oh, how pretty!' cried Clara, accepting the flowers.

'Shall she have them all?' asked Paul reproachfully of the old woman.

'Yes, she shall have them all,' she replied, beaming with joy. 'You have got enough for your share.'

'Ah, but I shall ask her to give me one!' he teased.

'Then she does as she pleases,' said the old lady, smiling. And she bobbed a little curtsey of delight.

Clara was rather quiet and uncomfortable. As they walked along, he said.

'You don't feel criminal, do you?'

She looked at him with startled grey eyes.

'Criminal!' she said. 'No.'

'But you seem to feel you have done a wrong?'

'No,' she said. 'I only think, "If they knew!"'

'If they knew, they'd cease to understand. As it is, they do understand, and they like it. What do they matter? Here, with only the trees and me, you don't feel not the least bit wrong, do you?'

He took her by the arm, held her facing him, holding her eyes with his. Something fretted him.

'Not sinners, are we?' he said, with an uneasy little frown.

'No,' she replied.

He kissed her, laughing.

'You like your little bit of guiltiness, I believe,' he said. 'I believe Eve enjoyed it, when she went cowering out of Paradise.'

But there was a certain glow and quietness about her that made him glad. When he was alone in the railway-carriage, he found himself tumultuously happy, and the people exceedingly nice, and the night lovely, and everything good.

Mrs Morel was sitting reading when he got home. Her health was not good now, and there had come that ivory pallor into her face when he never noticed, and which afterwards he never forgot. She did not mention her own ill-health to him. After all, she thought, it was not much.

'You are late!' she said, looking at him.

His eyes were shining; his face seemed to glow. He smiled to her.

'Yes; I've been down Clifton Grove with Clara.'

His mother looked at him again.

'But won't people talk?' she said.

'Why? They know she's a suffragette, and so on. And what if they do talk.'

'Of course, there may be nothing wrong in it,' said his mother. 'But you know what folk are, and if once she gets talked about –'

'Well, I can't help it. Their jaw isn't so almighty important, after all.'

'I think you ought to consider *her*.'

'So I *do*! What can people say? – that we take a walk together. I believe you're jealous.'

'You know, I should be *glad* if she weren't a married woman.'

'Well, my dear, she lives separate from her husband, and talks on platforms; so she's already singled out from the sheep, and, as far as I can see, hasn't much to lose. No; her life's nothing to her, so what's the worth of nothing? She goes with me – it becomes something. Then she must pay – we both must pay! Folk are so frightened of paying; they'd rather starve and die.'

'Very well, my son. We'll see how it will end.'

'Very well, my mother. I'll abide by the end.'

'We'll see!'

'And she's – she's *awfully* nice, mother; she is really! You don't know!'

'That's not the same as marrying her.'

'It's perhaps better.'

There was a silence for a while. He wanted to ask his mother something, but was afraid.

'Should you like to know her?' he hesitated.

'Yes,' said Mrs Morel, coolly. 'I should like to know what she's like.'

'But she's nice, mother, she is! And not a bit common!'

'I never suggested she was.'

'But you seem to think she's – not as good as – She's better than ninety-nine folk out of a hundred, I tell you! She's *better*, she is! She's fair, she's honest, she's straight! There isn't anything underhand or superior about her. Don't be mean about her!'

Mrs Morel flushed.

'I am sure I am not mean about her. She may be quite as you say, but –'

'You don't approve,' he finished.

'And do you expect me to?' she answered coldly.

'Yes! – yes! – if you'd anything about you, you'd be glad! Do you *want* to see her?'

'I said I did.'

'Then I'll bring her – shall I bring her here?'

'You please yourself.'

'Then I *will* bring her here – on Sunday – to tea. If you think a horrid thing about her, I shan't forgive you.'

His mother laughed.

'As if it would make any difference!' she said. He knew he had won.

'Oh, but it feels so fine, mother, when she's there! She's such a queen in her way.'

Occasionally he still walked a little way from chapel with Miriam and Edgar. He did not go up to the farm. She, however, was very much the same with him, and he did not feel embarrassed in her presence. One evening she was alone when he accompanied her. They began by talking books: it was their unfailing topic. Mrs Morel had said that his and Miriam's affair was like a fire fed on books – if there were no more volumes it would die out. Miriam, for her part, boasted that she could read him like a book, could place her finger any minute on the chapter and the line. He, easily taken in, believed that Miriam knew more about him than anyone else. So it pleased him to talk to her about himself, like the simplest egoist. Very soon the conversation drifted to his own doings. It flattered him immensely that he was of such supreme interest.

'And what have you been doing lately?'

'I – oh, not much! I made a sketch of Bestwood from the garden, that is nearly right at last. It's the hundredth try.'

So they went on. Then she said:

'You've not been out, then, lately?'

'Yes; I went up Clifton Grove on Monday afternoon with Clara.'

'It was not very nice weather,' said Mirian, 'was it?'

'But I wanted to go out, and it was all right. The Trent *is* full.'

'And did you go to Barton?' she asked.

'No, we had tea in Clifton.'

'*Did* you! That would be nice.'

'It was! The jolliest old woman! She gave us several pom-pom dahlias, as pretty as you like.'

Miriam bowed her head and brooded. He was quite unconscious of concealing anything from her.

'What made her give them you?' she asked.

He laughed.

'Because she liked us – because we were jolly, I should think.'

Miriam put her finger in her mouth.

'Were you late home?' she asked.

At last he resented her tone.

'I caught the seven-thirty.'

'Ha!'

They walked on in silence, and he was angry.

'And how *is* Clara?' asked Miriam.

'Quite all right, I think.'

'That's good!' she said, with a tinge of irony. 'By the way, what of her husband? One never hears anything of him.'

'He's got some other woman, and is also quite all right,' he replied. 'At least, so I think.'

'I see – you don't know for certain. Don't you think a position like that is hard on a woman?'

'Rottenly hard!'

'It's so unjust!' said Miriam. 'The man does as he likes –'

'Then let the woman also,' he said.

'How can she? And if she does, look at her position!'

'What of it?'

'Why, it's impossible! You don't understand what a woman forfeits –'

'No, I don't. But if a woman's got nothing but her fair fame to feed on, why, it's thin tack, and a donkey would die of it!'

So she understood his moral attitude, at least, and she knew he would act accordingly.

She never asked him anything direct, but she got to know enough.

Another day, when he saw Miriam, the conversation turned to marriage, then to Clara's marriage with Dawes.

'You see,' he said, 'she never knew the fearful importance of marriage. She thought it was all in the day's march – it would have to come – and Dawes – well, a good many women would have given their souls to get him; so why not him? Then she developed into the *femme incomprise*, and treated him badly, I'll bet my boots.'

'And she left him because he didn't understand her?'

'I suppose so. I suppose she had to. It isn't altogether a question of understanding; it's a question of living. With him, she was only half alive; the rest was dormant, deadened. And the dormant woman was the *femme incomprise*, and she *had* to be awakened.'

'And what about him?'

'I don't know. I rather think he loves her as much as he can, but he's a fool.'

'It was something like your mother and father,' said Miriam.

'Yes; but my mother, I believe, got *real* joy and satisfaction out of my father at first. I believe she had a passion for him; that's why she stayed with him. After all, they were bound to each other.'

'Yes,' said Miriam.

'That's what one *must have*, I think,' he continued – 'the real, real flame of feeling through another person – once, only once, if it only last three months. See, my mother looks as if she'd *had* everything that was necessary for her living and developing. There's not a tiny bit of feeling of sterility about her.'

'No,' said Miriam.

'And with my father, at first, I'm sure she had the real thing. She knows; she has been there. You can feel it about her, and about him, and about hundreds of people you meet every day; and, once it has happened to you, you can go on with anything and ripen.'

'What has happened, exactly?' asked Miriam.

'It's so hard to say, but the something big and intense that changes you when you really come together with somebody else. It almost seems to fertilize your soul and make it that you can go on and mature.'

'And you think your mother had it with your father?'

'Yes; and at the bottom she feels grateful to him for giving it her, even now, though they are miles apart.'

'And you think Clara never had it?'

'I'm sure.'

Miriam pondered this. She saw what he was seeking – a sort of baptism of fire in passion, it seemed to her. She realized that he would never be satisfied till he had it. Perhaps it was essential to him, as to some men, to sow wild oats; and afterwards, when he was satisfied, he would not rage with restlessness any more, but could settle down and give her his life into her hands. Well, then, if he must go, let him go and have his fill – something big and intense, he called it. At any rate, when he had got it, he would not want it – that he said himself; he would want the other thing that she could give him. He would want to be owned, so that he could work. It seemed to her a bitter thing that he must go, but she could let him go into an inn for a glass of whisky, so she could let him go to Clara, so long as it was something that would satisfy a need in him, and leave him free for herself to possess.

'Have you told your mother about Clara?' she asked.

She knew this would be a test of the seriousness of his feeling for the other woman; she knew he was going to Clara for something vital, not as a man goes for pleasure to a prostitute, if he told his mother.

'Yes,' he said, 'and she is coming to tea on Sunday.'

'To your house?'

'Yes; I want mater to see her.'

'Ah!'

There was a silence. Things had gone quicker than she thought. She felt a sudden bitterness that he could leave her so soon and so entirely. And was Clara to be accepted by his people, who had been so hostile to herself?

'I may call in as I go to chapel,' she said. 'It is a long time since I saw Clara.'

'Very well,' he said, astonished, and unconsciously angry.

On the Sunday afternoon he went to Keston to meet Clara at the station. As he stood on the platform he was trying to examine in himself if he had a premonition.

'Do I *feel* as if she'd come?' he said to himself, and he tried to find out. His heart felt queer and contracted. That seemed like foreboding. Then he *had* a foreboding she would not come! Then she would not come, and instead of taking her over the fields home, as he had imagined, he would have to go alone. The train was late; the afternoon would be wasted, and the evening. He hated her for not coming. Why had she promised, then, if she could not keep her promise? Perhaps she had missed her train – he himself was always missing trains – but that was no reason why she should miss this particular one. He was angry with her; he was furious.

Suddenly he saw the train crawling, sneaking round the corner. Here, then, was the train, but of course she had not come. The green engine hissed along the platform, the row of brown carriages drew up, several doors opened. No;

she had not come! No! Yes; ah, there she was! She had a big black hat on! He was at her side in a moment.

'I thought you weren't coming,' he said.

She was laughing rather breathlessly as she put out her hand to him; their eyes met. He took her quickly along the platform, talking at a great rate to hide his feelings. She looked beautiful. In her hat were large silk roses, coloured like tarnished gold. Her costume of dark cloth fitted so beautifully over her breast and shoulders. His pride went up as he walked with her. He felt the station people, who knew him, eyed her with awe and admiration.

'I was sure you weren't coming,' he laughed shakily.

She laughed in answer, almost with a little cry.

'And I wondered, when I was in the train, what*ever* I should do if you weren't there!' she said.

He caught her hand impulsively, and they went along the narrow twitchel. They took the road into Nuttall and over the Reckoning House Farm. It was a blue, mild day. Everywhere the brown leaves lay scattered; many scarlet hips stood upon the hedge beside the wood. He gathered a few for her to wear.

'Though, really,' he said, as he fitted them into the breast of her coat, 'you ought to object to my getting them, because of the birds. But they don't care much for rose-hips in this part, where they can get plenty of stuff. You often find the berries going rotten in the springtime.'

So he chattered, scarcely aware of what he said, only knowing he was putting berries in the bosom of her coat, while she stood patiently for him. And she watched his quick hands, so full of life, and it seemed to her she had never *seen* anything before. Till now, everything had been indistinct.

They came near to the colliery. It stood quite still and black among the cornfields, its immense heap of slag seen rising almost from the oats.

'What a pity there is a coal-pit here where it is so pretty!' said Clara.

'Do you think so?' he answered. 'You see, I am so used to it I should miss it. No; and I like the pits here and there. I like the rows of trucks, and the headstocks, and the steam in the daytime, and the lights at night. When I was a boy, I always thought a pillar of cloud by day and a pillar of fire by night was a pit, with its steam, and its lights, and the burning bank – and I thought the Lord was always at the pit-top.'

As they drew near home she walked in silence, and seemed to hang back. He pressed her fingers in his own. She flushed, but gave no response.

'Don't you want to come home?' he asked.

'Yes, I want to come,' she replied.

It did not occur to him that her position in his home would be rather a peculiar and difficult one. To him it seemed just as if one of his men friends were going to be introduced to his mother, only nicer.

The Morels lived in a house in an ugly street that ran down a steep hill. The street itself was hideous. The house was rather superior to most. It was old, grimy, with a big bay window, and it was semi-detached, but it looked gloomy. Then Paul opened the door to the garden, and all was different. The sunny afternoon was there, like another land. By the path grew tansy and little trees. In front of the window was a plot of sunny grass, with old lilacs round it. And away went the garden, with heaps of dishevelled chrysanthemums in the sunshine, down to the sycamore-tree, and the field, and beyond one looked over a few red-roofed cottages to the hills with all the glow of the autumn afternoon.

Mrs Morel sat in her rocking-chair, wearing her black silk blouse. Her grey-brown hair was taken smooth back from her brow and high temples; her face was rather pale. Clara, suffering, followed Paul into the kitchen. Mrs Morel rose. Clara thought her a lady, even rather stiff. The young woman was very nervous. She had almost a wistful look, almost resigned.

'Mother – Clara,' said Paul.

Mrs Morel held out her hand and smiled.

'He has told me a good deal about you,' she said.

The blood flamed in Clara's cheek.

'I hope you don't mind my coming,' she faltered.

'I was pleased when he said he would bring you,' replied Mrs Morel.

Paul, watching, felt his heart contract with pain. His mother looked so small, and sallow, and done-for beside the luxuriant Clara.

'It's such a pretty day, mother!' he said. 'And we saw a jay.'

His mother looked at him; he had turned to her. She thought what a man he seemed, in his dark, well-made clothes. He was pale and detached-looking; it would be hard for any woman to keep him. Her heart glowed; then she was sorry for Clara.

'Perhaps you'll leave your things in the parlour,' said Mrs Morel nicely to the young woman.

'Oh, thank you,' she replied.

'Come on,' said Paul, and he led the way into the little front-room, with its old piano, its mahogany furniture, its yellowing marble mantelpiece. A fire was burning; the place was littered with books and drawing-boards. 'I leave my things lying about,' he said. 'It's so much easier.'

She loved his artist's paraphernalia, and the books, and the photos of people. Soon he was telling her: this was William, this was William's young lady in the evening dress, this was Annie and her husband, this was Arthur and his wife and the baby. She felt as if she were being taken into a family. He showed her photos, books, sketches, and they talked a little while. Then they returned to the kitchen. Mrs Morel put aside her book. Clara wore a blouse of fine silk chiffon, with narrow black-and-white stripes; her hair was done simply, coiled on top of her head. She looked rather stately and reserved.

'You have gone to live down Sneinton Boulevard!' said Mrs Morel. 'When I was a girl – girl, I say! – when I was a young woman *we* lived in Minerva Terrace.'

'Oh, did you!' said Clara. 'I have a friend in Number 6.'

And the conversation had started. They talked Nottingham and Nottingham people; it interested them both. Clara was still rather nervous; Mrs Morel was still somewhat on her dignity. She clipped her language very clear and precise. But they were going to get on well together, Paul saw.

Mrs Morel measured herself against the younger woman, and found herself easily stronger. Clara was deferential. She knew Paul's surprising regard for his mother, and she had dreaded the meeting, expecting someone rather hard and cold. She was surprised to find this little interested woman chatting with such readiness; and then she felt, as she felt with Paul, that she would not care to stand in Mrs Morel's way. There was something so hard and certain in his mother, as if she never had a misgiving in her life.

Presently Morel came down, ruffled and yawning, from his afternoon sleep. He scratched his grizzled head, he plodded in his stockinged feet, his waistcoat hung open over his shirt. He seemed incongruous.

'This is Mrs Dawes, father,' said Paul.

Then Morel pulled himself together. Clara saw Paul's manner of bowing and shaking hands.

'Oh, indeed!' exclaimed Morel. 'I am very glad to see you – I am, I assure you. But don't disturb yourself. No, no, make yourself quite comfortable, and be very welcome.'

Clara was astonished at this flood of hospitality from the old collier. He was so courteous, so gallant! She thought him most delightful.

'And may you have come far?' he asked.

'Only from Nottingham,' she said.

'From Nottingham! Then you have had a beautiful day for your journey.'

Then he strayed into the scullery to wash his hands and face, and from force of habit came on to the hearth with the towel to dry himself.

At tea Clara felt the refinement and sang-froid of the household. Mrs Morel was perfectly at her ease. The pouring out of tea and attending to the people went on unconsciously, without interrupting her in her talk. There was a lot of room at the oval table; the china of dark blue willow-pattern looked pretty on the glossy cloth. There was a little bowl of small, yellow chrysanthemums. Clara felt she completed the circle, and it was a pleasure to her. But she was rather afraid of the self-possession of the Morels, father and all. She took their tone; there was a feeling of balance. It was a cool, clear atmosphere, where everyone was himself, and in harmony. Clara enjoyed it, but there was a fear deep at the bottom of her.

Paul cleared the table whilst his mother and Clara talked. Clara was conscious of his quick, vigorous body as it came and went, seeming blown by a wind at its work. It was almost like the hither and thither of a leaf that comes unexpected. Most of herself went with him. By the way she leaned forward, as if listening, Mrs Morel could see she was possessed elsewhere as she talked, and again the elder woman was sorry for her.

Having finished, he strolled down the garden, leaving the two women to talk. It was a hazy, sunny afternoon, mild and soft. Clara glanced through the window after him as he loitered among the chrysanthemums. She felt as if something almost tangible fastened her to him; yet he seemed so easy in his graceful, indolent movement, so detached as he tied up the too-heavy flower-branches to their stakes, that she wanted to shriek in her helplessness.

Mrs Morel rose.

'You will let me help you wash up,' said Clara.

'Eh, there are so few, it will only take me a minute,' said the other.

Clara, however, dried the tea-things, and was glad to be on such good terms with his mother; but it was torture not to be able to follow him down the garden. At last she allowed herself to go; she felt as if a rope were taken off her ankle.

The afternoon was golden over the hills of Derbyshire. He stood across in the other garden, beside a bush of pale Michaelmas daisies, watching the last bees crawl into the hive. Hearing her coming, he turned to her with an easy motion, saying:

'It's the end of the run with these chaps.'

Clara stood near him. Over the low red wall in front was the country and the far-off hills, all golden dim.

At that moment Miriam was entering through the garden-door. She saw Clara go up to him, saw him turn, and saw them come to rest together.

Something in their perfect isolation together made her know that it was accomplished between them, that they were, as she put it, married. She walked very slowly down the cinder-track of the long garden.

Clara had pulled a button from a hollyhock spire, and was breaking it to get the seeds. Above her bowed head the pink flowers stared, as if defending her. The last bees were falling down to the hive.

'Count your money,' laughed Paul, as she broke the flat seeds one by one from the roll of coin. She looked at him.

'I'm well off,' she said, smiling.

'How much? Pf!' He snapped his fingers. 'Can I turn them into gold?'

'I'm afraid not,' she laughed.

They looked into each other's eyes, laughing. At that moment they became aware of Miriam. There was a click, and everything had altered.

'Hello, Miriam!' he exclaimed. 'You said you'd come!'

'Yes. Had you forgotten?'

She shook hands with Clara, saying:

'It seems strange to see you here.'

'Yes,' replied the other; 'it seems strange to be here.'

There was a hesitation.

'It is pretty, isn't it?' said Miriam.

'I like it very much,' replied Clara.

Then Miriam realized that Clara was accepted as she had never been.

'Have you come down alone?' asked Paul.

'Yes; I went to Agatha's to tea. We are going to chapel. I only called in for a moment to see Clara.'

'You should have come in here to tea,' he said.

Miriam laughed shortly, and Clara turned impatiently aside.

'Do you like the chrysanthemums?' he asked.

'Yes; they are very fine,' replied Miriam.

'Which sort do you like best?' he asked.

'I don't know. The bronze, I think.'

'I don't think you've seen all the sorts. Come and look. Come and see which are *your* favourites, Clara.'

He led the two women back to his own garden, where the towzled bushes of flowers of all colours stood raggedly along the path down to the field. The situation did not embarrass him, to his knowledge.

'Look, Miriam; these are the white ones that came from your garden. They aren't so fine here, are they?'

'No,' said Miriam.

'But they're hardier. You're so sheltered; things grow big and tender, and then die. These little yellow ones I like. Will you have some?'

While they were out there the bells began to ring in the church, sounding loud across the town and the field. Miriam looked at the tower, proud among the clustering roofs, and remembered the sketches he had brought her. It had been different then, but he had not left her even yet. She asked him for a book to read. He ran indoors.

'What! Is that Miriam?' asked his mother coldly.

'Yes; she said she'd call and see Clara.'

'You told her, then?' came the sarcastic answer.

'Yes; why shouldn't I?'

'There's certainly no reason why you shouldn't,' said Mrs Morel, and she returned to her book. He winced from his mother's irony, frowned irritably, thinking: 'Why can't I do as I like?'

'You've not seen Mrs Morel before?' Miriam was saying to Clara.

'No; but she's *so* nice!'

'Yes,' said Miriam, dropping her head; 'in some ways she's very fine.'

'I should think so.'

'Had Paul told you much about her?'

'He had talked a good deal.'

'Ha!'

There was a silence until he returned with the book.

'When will you want it back?' Miriam asked.

'When you like,' he answered.

Clara turned to go indoors, whilst he accompanied Miriam to the gate.

'When will you come up to Willey Farm?' the latter asked.

'I couldn't say,' replied Clara.

'Mother asked me to say she'd be pleased to see you any time, if you cared to come.'

'Thank you; I should like to, but I can't say when.'

'Oh, very well!' exclaimed Miriam rather bitterly, turning away.

She went down the path with her mouth to the flowers he had given her.

'You're sure you won't come in?' he said.

'No, thanks.'

'We are going to chapel.'

'Ha, I shall see you, then!' Miriam was very bitter.

'Yes.'

They parted. He felt guilty towards her. She was bitter, and she scorned him. He still belonged to herself, she believed; yet he could have Clara, take her home, sit with her next his mother in chapel, give her the same hymn-book he had given herself years before. She heard him running quickly indoors.

But he did not go straight in. Halting on the plot of grass he heard his mother's voice, then Clara's answer:

'What I hate is the bloodhound quality in Miriam.'

'Yes,' said his mother quickly, 'yes; *doesn't* it make you hate her, now!'

His heart went hot, and he was angry with them for talking about the girl. What right had they to say that? Something in the speech itself stung him into a flame of hate against Miriam. Then his own heart rebelled furiously at Clara's taking the liberty of speaking so about Miriam. After all, the girl was the better woman of the two, he thought, if it came to goodness. He went indoors. His mother looked excited. She was beating with her hand rhythmically on the sofa-arm, as women do who are wearing out. He could never bear to see the movement. There was a silence; then he began to talk.

In chapel Miriam saw him find the place in the hymn-book for Clara, in exactly the same way as he used for herself. And during the sermon he could see the girl across the chapel, her hat throwing a dark shadow over her face. What did she think, seeing Clara with him? He did not stop to consider. He felt himself cruel towards Miriam.

After chapel he went over Pentrich with Clara. It was a dark autumn night. They had said good-bye to Miriam, and his heart had smitten him as he left the girl alone. 'But it serves her right,' he said inside himself, and it almost gave him pleasure to go off under her eyes with this other handsome woman.

There was a scent of damp leaves in the darkness. Clara's hand lay warm and inert in his own as they walked. He was full of conflict. The battle that raged inside him made him feel desperate.

Up Pentrich Hill Clara leaned against him as he went. He slid his arm round her waist. Feeling the strong motion of her body under his arm as she walked, the tightness in his chest because of Miriam relaxed, and the hot blood bathed him. He held her closer and closer.

Then: 'You still keep on with Miriam,' she said quietly.

'Only talk. There never *was* a great deal more than talk between us,' he said bitterly.

'Your mother doesn't care for her,' said Clara.

'No, or I might have married her. But it's all up, really!'

Suddenly his voice went passionate with hate.

'If I was with her now, we should be jawing about the "Christian Mystery", or some such tack. Thank God, I'm not!'

They walked on in silence for some time.

'But you can't really give her up,' said Clara.

'I don't give her up, because there's nothing to give,' he said.

'There is for her.'

'I don't know why she and I shouldn't be friends as long as we live,' he said. 'But it'll only be friends.'

Clara drew away from him, leaning away from contact with him.

'What are you drawing away for?' he asked.

She did not answer, but drew farther from him.

'Why do you want to walk alone?' he asked.

Still there was no answer. She walked resentfully, hanging her head.

'Because I said I would be friends with Miriam!' he exclaimed.

She would not answer him anything.

'I tell you it's only words that go between us,' he persisted, trying to take her again.

She resisted. Suddenly he strode across in front of her, barring her way.

'Damn it!' he said. 'What do you want now?'

'You'd better run after Miriam,' mocked Clara.

The blood flamed up in him. He stood showing his teeth. She dropped sulkily. The lane was dark, quite lonely. He suddenly caught her in his arms, stretched forward, and put his mouth on her face in a kiss of rage. She turned frantically to avoid him. He held her fast. Hard and relentless his mouth came for her. Her breasts hurt against the wall of his chest. Helpless, she went loose in his arms, and he kissed her, and kissed her.

He heard people cóming down the hill.

'Stand up! Stand up!' he said thickly, gripping her arm till it hurt. If he had let go, she would have sunk to the ground.

She sighed and walked dizzily beside him. They went on in silence.

'We will go over the fields,' he said; and then she woke up.

But she let herself be helped over the stile, and she walked in silence with him over the first dark field. It was the way to Nottingham and to the station, she knew. He seemed to be looking about. They came out on a bare hilltop where stood the dark figure of the ruined windmill. There he halted. They stood together high up on the darkness, looking at the lights scattered on the night before them, handfuls of glittering points, villages lying high and low on the dark, here and there.

'Like treading among the stars,' he said with a quaky laugh.

Then he took her in his arms, and held her fast. She moved aside her mouth to ask, dogged and low:

'What time is it?'

'It doesn't matter,' he pleaded thickly.

'Yes it does – yes! I must go!'

'It's early yet,' he said.

'What time is it?' she insisted.

All round lay the black night, speckled and spangled with lights.

'I don't know.'

She put her hand on his chest, feeling for his watch. He felt the joints fuse into fire. She groped in his waistcoat pocket, while he stood panting. In the darkness she could see the round pale face of the watch, but not the figures. She stopped over it. He was panting till he could take her in his arms again.

'I can't see,' she said.

'Then don't bother.'

'Yes; I'm going!' she said, turning away.

'Wait! I'll look!' But he could not see. 'I'll strike a match.'

He secretly hoped it was too late to catch the train. She saw the glowing lantern of his hands as he cradled the light; then his face lit up, his eyes fixed on the watch. Instantly all was dark again. All was black before her eyes; only a glowing match was red near her feet. Where was he?

'What is it?' she asked, afraid.

'You can't do it,' his voice answered out of the darkness.

There was a pause. She felt in his power. She had heard the ring in his voice. It frightened her.

'What time is it?' she asked, quiet, definite, hopeless.

'Two minutes to nine,' he replied, telling the truth with a struggle.

'And can I get from here to the station in fourteen minutes?'

'No. At any rate –'

She could distinguish his dark form again a yard or so away. She wanted to escape.

'But can't I do it?' she pleaded.

'If you hurry,' he said brusquely. 'But you could easily walk it, Clara; it's only seven miles to the tram. I'll come with you.'

'No; I want to catch the train.'

'But why?'

'I do – I want to catch the train.'

Suddenly his voice altered.

'Very well,' he said, dry and hard. 'Come along then.'

And he plunged ahead into the darkness. She ran after him, wanting to cry. Now he was hard and cruel to her. She ran over the rough, dark fields behind him, out of breath, ready to drop. But the double row of lights at the station drew nearer. Suddenly:

'There she is!' he cried, breaking into a run.

There was a faint rattling noise. Away to the right the train, like a luminous caterpillar, was threading across the night. The rattling ceased.

'She's over the viaduct. You'll just do it.'

Clara ran, quite out of breath, and fell at last into the train. The whistle blew. He was gone. Gone! – and she was in a carriage full of people. She felt the cruelty of it.

He turned round and plunged home. Before he knew where he was he was in the kitchen at home. He was very pale. His eyes were dark and dangerous-looking, as if her were drunk. His mother looked at him.

'Well, I must say your boots are in a nice state!' she said.

He looked at his feet. Then he tore off his overcoat. His mother wondered if he were drunk.

'She caught the train then?' she said.

'Yes.'

'I hope *her* feet weren't so filthy. Where on earth you dragged her I don't know!'

He was silent and motionless for some time.

'Did you like her?' he asked grudgingly at last.

'Yes, I liked her. But you'll tire of her, my son; you know you will.'

He did not answer. She noticed how he laboured in his breathing.

'Have you been running?' she asked.

'We had to run for the train.'

'You'll go and knock yourself up. You'd better drink hot milk.'

It was as good a stimulant as he could have, but he refused and went to bed. There he lay face down on the counterpane, and shed tears of rage and pain. There was a physical pain that made him bite his lips till they bled, and the chaos inside him left him unable to think, almost to feel.

'This is how she serves me, is it?' he said in his heart, over and over, pressing his face in the quilt. And he hated her. Again he went over the scene, and again he hated her.

The next day there was a new aloofness about him. Clara was very gentle, almost loving. But he treated her distantly, with a touch of contempt. She sighed, continuing to be gentle. He came round.

One evening of that week Sarah Bernhardt was the the Theatre Royal in Nottingham, giving 'La Dame aux Camélias'. Paul wanted to see this old and famous actress, and he asked Clara to accompany him. He told his mother to leave the key in the window for him.

'Shall I book seats?' he asked Clara.

'Yes. And put on an evening suit, will you! I've never seen you in it.'

'But, good Lord, Clara! Think of *me* in evening suit at the theatre!' he remonstrated.

'Would you rather not?' she asked.

'I will if you *want* me to: but I s'll feel a fool.'

She laughed at him.

'Then feel a fool for my sake, won't you?'

The request made his blood flush up.

'I suppose I s'll have to.'

'What are you taking a suit-case for?' his mother asked.

He blushed furiously.

'Clara asked me,' he began.

'And what seats are you going in?'

'Circle – three-and-six each!'

'Well, I'm sure!' exclaimed his mother sarcastically.

'It's only once in the bluest of blue moons,' he said.

He dressed at Jordan's, put on an overcoat and a cap, and met Clara in a café. She was with one of her suffragette friends. She wore an old long coat, which did not suit her, and had a little wrap over her head, which he hated. The three went to the theatre together.

Clara took off her coat on the stairs, and he discovered she was in a sort of semi-evening dress, that left her arms and neck and part of her breast bare. Her hair was done fashionably. The dress, a simple thing of green crape, suited her. She looked quite grand, he thought. He could see her figure inside the frock, as if that were wrapped closely round her. The firmness and softness of her upright body could almost be felt as he looked at her. He clenched his fists.

And he was to sit all the evening beside her beautiful naked arm, watching the strong throat rise from the strong chest, watching the breasts under the green stuff, the curve of her limbs in the tight dress. Something in him hated her again for submitting him to this torture of nearness. And he loved her as she balanced her head and stared straight in front of her, pouting, wistful, immobile, as if she yielded herself to her fate because it was too strong for her. She could not help herself; she was in the grip of something bigger than herself. A kind of eternal look about her, as if she were a wistful sphinx, made it necessary for him to kiss her. He dropped his programme, and crouched down on the floor to get it, so that he could kiss her hand and wrist. Her beauty was a torture to him. She sat immobile. Only, when the lights went down, she sank a little against him, and he caressed her hand and arm with his fingers. He could smell her faint perfume. All the time his blood kept sweeping up in great white-hot waves that killed his consciousness momentarily.

The drama continued. He saw it all in the distance, going on somewhere; he did not know where, but it seemed far away inside him. He was Clara's white heavy arms, her throat, her moving bosom. That seemed to be himself. Then away somewhere the play went on, and he was identified with that also. There was no himself. The grey and black eyes of Clara, her bosom coming down on his, her arm that he held gripped between his hands, were all that existed. Then he felt himself small and helpless, her towering in her force above him.

Only the intervals, when the lights came up, hurt him expressibly. He wanted to run anywhere, so long as it would be dark again. In a maze, he wandered out for a drink. Then the lights were out, and the strange, insane reality of Clara and the drama took hold of him again.

The play went on. But he was obsessed by the desire to kiss the tiny blue vein that nestled in the bend of her arm. He could feel it. His whole life seemed suspended till he had put his lips there. It must be done. And the other people! At last he bent quickly forward and touched it with his lips. His moustache brushed the sensitive flesh. Clara shivered, drew away her arm.

When all was over, the lights up, the people clapping, he came to himself and looked at his watch. His train was gone.

'I s'll have to walk home!' he said.

Clara looked at him.

'Is it too late?' she asked.

He nodded. Then he helped her on with her coat.

'I love you! You look beautiful in that dress,' he murmured over her shoulder, among the throng of bustling people.

She remained quiet. Together they went out of the theatre. He saw cabs waiting, the people passing. It seemed he met a pair of brown eyes which hated him. But he did not know. He and Clara turned away, mechanically taking the direction to the station.

The train had gone. He would have to walk the ten miles home.

'It doesn't matter,' he said. 'I shall enjoy it.'

'Won't you,' she said, flushing, 'come home for the night? I can sleep with mother.'

He looked at her. Their eyes met.

'What will your mother say?' he asked.

'She won't mind.'

'You're sure?'

'Quite!'

'*Shall* I come?'

'If you will.'

'Very well.'

And they turned away. At the first stopping-place they took the car. The wind blew fresh in their faces. The town was dark; the tram tipped in its haste. He sat with her hand fast in his.

'Will your mother be gone to bed?' he asked.

'She may be. I hope not.'

They hurried along the silent, dark little street, the only people out of doors. Clara quickly entered the house. He hesitated.

'Come in,' she said.

He leaped up the step and was in the room. Her mother appeared in the inner doorway, large and hostile.

'Who have you got here?' she asked.

'It's Mr Morel; he missed his train. I thought we might put him up for the night, and save him a ten-mile walk.'

'H'm!' exclaimed Mrs Radford. 'That's *your* look-out! If you've invited him, he's very welcome as far as I'm concerned. *You* keep the house!'

'If you don't like me, I'll go away again,' he said.

'Nay, nay, you needn't! Come along in! I dunno what you'll think of the supper I'd got her.'

It was a little dish of chip potatoes and a piece of bacon. The table was roughly laid for one.

'You can have some more bacon,' continued Mrs Radford. 'More chips you can't have.'

'It's a shame to bother you,' he said.

'Oh, don't you be apologetic! It doesn't *do* wi' me! You treated her to the theatre, didn't you?' There was a sarcasm in the last question.

'Well?' laughed Paul uncomfortably.

'Well, and what's an inch of bacon! Take your coat off.'

The big, straight-standing woman was trying to estimate the situation. She moved about the cupboard. Clara took his coat. The room was very warm and cosy in the lamplight.

'My sirs!' exclaimed Mrs Radford, 'but you two's a pair of bright beauties, I must say! What's all that get-up for?'

'I believe we don't know,' he said, feeling a victim.

'There isn't room in *this* house for two such bobby-dazzlers, if you fly your kites *that* high!' she rallied them. It was a nasty thrust.

He in his dinner jacket, and Clara in her green dress and bare arms, were confused. They felt they must shelter each other in that little kitchen.

'And look at *that* blossom!' continued Mrs Radford, pointing to Clara. 'What does she reckon she did it for?'

Paul looked at Clara. She was rosy; her neck was warm with blushes. There was a moment of silence.

'You like to see it, don't you?' he asked.

The mother had them in her power. All the time his heart was beating hard, and he was tight with anxiety. But he would fight her.

'Me like to see it!' exclaimed the old woman. 'What should I like to see her make a fool of herself for?'

'I've seen people look bigger fools,' he said. Clara was under his protection now.

'Oh, ay! And when was that?' came the sarcastic rejoinder.

'When they made frights of themselves,' he answered.

Mrs Radford, large and threatening, stood suspended on the hearthrug, holding her fork.

'They're fools either road,' she answered at length, turning to the Dutch oven.

'No,' he said, fighting stoutly. 'Folk ought to look as well as they can.'

'And do you call *that* looking nice!' cried the mother, pointing a scornful fork at Clara. 'That – that looks as if it wasn't properly dressed!'

'I believe you're jealous that you can't swank as well,' he said laughing.

'Me! I could have worn evening dress with anybody, if I'd wanted to!' came the scornful answer.

'And why didn't you want to?' he asked pertinently. 'Or *did* you wear it?'

There was a long pause. Mrs Radford readjusted the bacon in the Dutch oven. His heart beat fast, for fear he had offended her.

'Me!' she exclaimed at last. 'No, I didn't! And when I was in service, I knew as soon as one of the maids came out in bare shoulders what sort *she* was, going to her sixpenny hop!'

'Were you too good to go to a sixpenny hop?' he said.

Clara sat with bowed head. His eyes were dark and glittering. Mrs Radford took the Dutch oven from the fire, and stood near him, putting bits of bacon on his plate.

'*There's* a nice crozzly bit!' she said.

'Don't give me the best!' he said.

'*She's* got what *she* wants,' was the answer.

There was a sort of scornful forbearance in the woman's tone that made Paul know she was mollified.

'But *do* have some!' he said to Clara.

She looked up at him with her grey eyes, humiliated and lonely.

'No thanks!' she said.

'Why won't you?' he answered caressively.

The blood was beating up like fire in his veins. Mrs Radford sat down again, large and impressive and aloof. He left Clara altogether to attend to the mother.

'They say Sarah Bernhardt's fifty,' he said.

'Fifty! She's turned sixty!' came the answer.

'Well,' he said, 'you'd never think it! She made me want to howl even now.'

'I should like to see myself howling at *that* bad old baggage!' said Mrs Radford. 'It's time she began to think herself a grandmother, not a shrieking catamaran –'

He laughed.

'A catamaran is a boat the Malays use,' he said.

'And it's a word as *I* use,' she retorted.

'My mother does sometimes, and it's no good my telling her,' he said.

'I s'd think she boxes your ears,' said Mrs Radford, good-humouredly.

'She'd like to, and she says she will, so I give her a little stool to stand on.'

'That's the worst of my mother,' said Clara. 'She never wants a stool for anything.'

'But she often can't touch *that* lady with a long prop,' retorted Mrs Radford to Paul.

'I s'd think she doesn't want touching with a prop,' he laughed. '*I* shouldn't.'

'It might do the pair of you good to give you a crack on the head with one,' said the mother, laughing suddenly.

'Why are you so vindictive towards me?' he said. 'I've not stolen anything from you.'

'No; I'll watch that,' laughed the older woman.

Soon the supper was finished. Mrs Radford sat in her chair. Paul lit a cigarette, Clara went upstairs, returning with a sleeping-suit, which she spread on the fender to air.

'Why, I'd forgot all about *them*,' said Mrs Radford. 'Where have they sprung from?'

'Out of my drawer.'

'H'm! You bought 'em for Baxter, an' he wouldn't wear 'em, would he?' – laughing. 'Said he reckoned to do wi'out trousers i' bed.' She turned confidentially to Paul saying:

'He couldn't *bear* 'em, them pyjama things.'

The young man sat making rings of smoke.

'Well, it's everybody to his taste,' he laughed.

Then followed a little discussion of the merits of pyjamas.

'My mother loves me in them,' he said. 'She says I'm a pierrot.'

'I can imagine they'd suit you,' said Mrs Radford.

After a while he glanced at the little clock that was ticking on the mantelpiece. It was half-past twelve.

'It is funny,' he said, 'but it takes hours to settle down to sleep after the theatre.'

'It's about time you did,' said Mrs Radford, clearing the table.

'Are *you* tired?' he asked Clara.

'Not the least bit,' she answered, avoiding his eyes.

'Shall we have a game of cribbage?' he said.

'I've forgotten it.'

'Well, I'll teach you again. May we play crib, Mrs Radford?' he asked.

'You'll please yourselves,' she said, 'but it's pretty late.'

'A game or so will make us sleepy,' he answered.

Clara brought the cards, and sat spinning her wedding-ring whilst he shuffled them. Mrs Radford was washing up in the scullery. As it grew later Paul felt the situation getting more and more tense.

'Fifteen two, fifteen four, fifteen six, and two's eight –!'

The clock struck one. Still the game continued. Mrs Radford had done all the little jobs preparatory to going to bed, had locked the door and filled the kettle. Still Paul went on dealing and counting. He was obsessed by Clara's arms and throat. He believed he could see where the division was just beginning for her breasts. He could not leave her. She watched his hands, and felt her joints melt as they moved quickly. She was so near; it was almost as if he touched her, and yet not quite. His mettle was aroused. He hated Mrs Radford. She sat on, nearly dropping asleep, but determined and obstinate on her chair. Paul glanced at her, then at Clara. She met his eyes, that were angry, mocking, and hard as steel. Her own answered him in shame. He knew *she*, at any rate, was of his mind. He played on.

At last Mrs Radford roused herself stiffly, and said:

'Isn't it nigh on time you two was thinking o' bed?'

Paul played on without answering. He hated her sufficiently to murder her.

'Half a minute,' he said.

The elder woman rose and sailed stubbornly into the scullery, returning with his candle, which she put on the mantelpiece. Then she sat down again. The hatred of her went so hot down his veins, he dropped his cards.

'We'll stop, then,' he said, but his voice was still a challenge.

Clara saw his mouth shut hard. Again he glanced at her. It seemed like an agreement. She bent over the cards, coughing, to clear her throat.

'Well, I'm glad you've finished,' said Mrs Radford. 'Here, take your things' – she thrust the warm suit in his hand – 'and this is your candle. Your room's over this; there's only two, so you can't go wrong. Well, good night. I hope you'll rest well.'

'I'm sure I shall: I always do,' he said.

'Yes; and so you ought at your age,' she replied.

He bade good night to Clara, and went. The twisting stairs of white, scrubbed wood creaked and clanged at every step. He went doggedly. The two doors faced each other. He went in his room, pushed the door to, without fastening the latch.

It was a small room with a large bed. Some of Clara's hairpins were on the dressing-table – her hair brush. Her clothes and some skirts hung under a cloth in a corner. There was actually a pair of stockings over a chair. He explored the room. Two books of his own were there on the shelf. He undressed, folded his suit, and sat on the bed, listening. Then he blew out the candle, lay down, and in two minutes was almost asleep. Then click! – he was wide awake and writhing in torment. It was as if, when he had nearly got to sleep, something had bitten him suddenly and sent him mad. He sat up and looked at the room in the darkness, his feet doubled under him, perfectly motionless, listening. He heard a cat somewhere away outside; then the heavy, poised tread of the mother; then Clara's distinct voice:

'Will you unfasten my dress?'

There was silence for some time. At last the mother said:

'Now then! Aren't you coming up?'

'No, not yet,' replied the daughter calmly.

'Oh, very well then! If it's not late enough, stop a bit longer. Only you needn't come waking me up when I've got to sleep.'

'I shan't be long,' said Clara.

Immediately afterwards Paul heard the mother slowly mounting the stairs. The candle-light flashed through the cracks in his door. Her dress brushed the door, and his heart jumped. Then it was dark, and he heard the clatter of her latch. She was very leisurely indeed in her preparations for sleep. After a long time it was quite still. He sat strung up on the bed, shivering slightly. His door was an inch open. As Clara came upstairs, he would intercept her. He waited. All was dead silence. The clock struck two. Then he heard a slight scrape of the fender downstairs. Now he could not help himself. His shivering was uncontrollable. He felt he must go or die.

He stepped off the bed, and stood a moment, shuddering. Then he went straight to the door. He tried to step lightly. The first stair cracked like a shot. He listened. The old woman stirred in her bed. The staircase was dark. There was a slit of light under the stair-foot door, which opened into the kitchen. He stood a moment. Then he went on, mechanically. Every step creaked, and his back was creeping, lest the old woman's door should open behind him up above. He fumbled with the door at the bottom. The latch opened with a loud click. He went through into the kitchen, and shut the door noisily behind him. The old woman daren't come now.

Then he stood, arrested. Clara was kneeling on a pile of white underclothing, on the hearthrug, her back towards him, warming herself. She did not look around, but sat crouching on her heels, and her rounded, beautiful back was towards him, and her face was hidden. She was warming her body at the fire for consolation. The glow was rosy on one side, the shadow was dark and warm on the other. Her arms hung slack.

He shuddered violently, clenching his teeth and fists hard to keep control. Then he went forward to her. He put one hand on her shoulder, the fingers of the other hand under the chin to raise her face. A convulsed shiver ran through her, once, twice, at his touch. She kept her head bent.

'Sorry!' he murmured, realizing that his hands were very cold.

Then she looked up at him, frightened, like a thing that is afraid of death.

'My hands are so cold,' he murmured.

'I like it,' she whispered, closing her eyes.

The breath of her words was on his mouth. Her arms clasped his knees. The cord of his sleeping-suit dangled against her and made her shiver. As the warmth went into him, his shuddering became less.

At length, unable to stand any more, he raised her, and she buried her head on his shoulder. His hands went over her slowly with an infinite tenderness of caress. She clung close to him, trying to hide herself against him. He clasped her very fast. Then at last she looked at him, mute, imploring, looking to see if she must be ashamed.

His eyes were dark, very deep, and very quiet. It was as if her beauty and his taking it hurt him, made him sorrowful. He looked at her with a little pain, and was afraid. He was so humble before her. She kissed him fervently on the eyes, first one, then the other, and she folded herself to him. She gave herself. He held her fast. It was a moment intense almost to agony.

She stood letting him adore her and tremble with joy of her. It healed her hurt pride. It healed her; it made her glad. It made her feel erect and proud again. Her pride had been wounded inside her. She had been cheapened. Now she radiated with joy and pride again. It was her restoration and her recognition.

Then he looked at her, his face radiant. They laughed to each other, and he strained her to his chest. The seconds ticked off, the minutes passed, and still the two stood clasped rigid together, mouth to mouth, like a statue in one block.

But again his fingers went seeking over her, restless, wandering, dissatisfied. The hot blood came up wave upon wave. She laid her head on his shoulder.

'Come you to my room,' he murmured.

She looked at him and shook her head, her mouth pouting disconsolately, her eyes heavy with passion. He watched her fixedly.

'Yes!' he said.

Again she shook her head.

'Why not?' he asked.

She looked at him still heavily, sorrowfully, and again she shook her head. His eyes hardened, and he gave way.

When, later on, he was back in bed, he wondered why she had refused to come to him openly, so that her mother would know. At any rate, then things would have been definite. And she could have stayed with him the night, without having to go, as she was, to her mother's bed. It was strange, and he could not understand it. And almost immediately he fell asleep.

He awoke in the morning with someone speaking to him. Opening his eyes, he saw Mrs Radford, big and stately, looking down on him. She held a cup of tea in her hand.

'Do you think you're going to sleep till Doomsday?' she said.

He laughed at once.

'It ought only to be about five o'clock,' he said.

'Well,' she answered, 'it's half-past seven, whether or not. Here, I've brought you a cup of tea.'

He rubbed his face, pushed the tumbled hair off his forehead, and roused himself.

'What's it so late for!' he grumbled.

He resented being awakened. It amused her. She saw his neck in the flannel sleeping-jacket, as white and round as a girl's. He rubbed his hair crossly.

'It's not good your scratching your head,' she said. 'It won't make it no earlier. Here, an' how long d'you think I'm going to stand waiting wi' this here cup?'

'Oh, dash the cup!' he said.

'You should go to bed earlier,' said the woman.

He looked up at her, laughing with impudence.

'I went to bed before *you* did,' he said.

'Yes, my Guyney, you did!' she exclaimed.

'Fancy,' he said, stirring his tea, 'having tea brought to bed to me! My mother'd think I'm ruined for life.'

'Don't she never do it?' asked Mrs Radford.

'She'd as leave think of flying.'

'Ah, I always spoilt my lot! That's why they've turned out such bad uns,' said the elderly woman.

'You'd only Clara,' he said. 'And Mr Radford's in heaven. So I suppose there's only you left to be the bad un.'

'I'm not bad; I'm only soft,' she said, as she went out of the bedroom. 'I'm only a fool, I am!'

Clara was very quiet at breakfast, but she had a sort of air of proprietorship over him that pleased him infinitely. Mrs Radford was evidently fond of him. He began to talk of his painting.

'What's the good,' exclaimed the mother, 'of your whittling and worrying and twistin' and too-in' at that painting of yours? What *good* does it do you, I should like to know? You'd better be enjoyin' yourself.'

'Oh, but,' exclaimed Paul, 'I made over thirty guineas last year.'

'Did you! Well, that's a consideration, but it's nothing to the time you put in.'

'And I've got four pounds owing. A man said he'd give me five pounds if I'd paint him and his missis and the dog and the cottage. And I went and put the fowls in instead of the dog, and he was waxy, so I had to knock a quid off. I was sick of it, and I didn't like the dog. I made a picture of it. What shall I do when he pays me the four pounds?'

'Nay! You know your own uses for your money,' said Mrs Radford.

'But I'm going to bust this four pounds. Should we go to the seaside for a day or two?'

'Who?'

'You and Clara and me.'

'What, on your money!' she exclaimed, half wrathful.

'Why not?'

'*You* wouldn't be long in breaking your neck at a hurdle race,' she said.

'So long as I get a good run for my money! Will you?'

'Nay; you may settle that between you.'

'And you're willing?' he asked, amazed and rejoicing.

'You'll do as you like,' said Mrs Radford, 'whether I'm willing or not.'

13

BAXTER DAWES

Soon after Paul had been to the theatre with Clara, he was drinking in the Punch Bowl with some friends of his when Dawes came in. Clara's husband was growing stout; his eye-lids were getting slack over his brown eyes; he was losing his healthy firmness of flesh. He was very evidently on the downward track. Having quarrelled with his sister, he had gone into cheap lodgings. His mistress had left him for a man who would marry her. He had been in prison one night for fighting when he was drunk, and there was a shady betting episode in which he was concerned.

Paul and he were confirmed enemies, and yet there was between them that peculiar feeling of intimacy, as if they were secretly near to each other, which sometimes exists between two people, although they never speak to one another. Paul often thought of Baxter Dawes, often wanted to get at him and be friends with him. He knew Dawes often thought about him, and that the man was drawn to him by some bond or other. And yet the two never looked at each other save in hostility.

Since he was a superior employee at Jordan's, it was the thing for Paul to offer Dawes a drink.

'What'll you have?' he asked of him.

'Nowt wi' a bleeder like you!' replied the man.

Paul turned away with a slight disdainful movement of the shoulders, very irritating.

'The aristocracy,' he continued, 'is a really military institution. Take Germany, now. She's got thousands of aristocrats whose only means of existence is the army. They're deadly poor, and life's deadly slow. So they hope for war. They look for war as a chance of getting on. Till there's a war they're idle good-for-nothings. When there's a war, they are leaders and commanders. There you are then – they *want* war!'

He was not a favourite debater in the public-house, being too quick and overbearing. He irritated the older men by his assertive manner, and his cocksureness. They listened in silence, and were not sorry when he finished.

Dawes interrupted the young man's flow of eloquence by asking, in a loud sneer:

'Did you learn all that at th' theatre th' other night?'

Paul looked at him; their eyes met. Then he knew Dawes had seen him coming out of the theatre with Clara.

'Why, what about th' theatre?' asked one of Paul's associates, glad to get a dig at the young fellow, and sniffing something tasty.

'Oh, him in a bob-tailed evening suit, on the lardy-da!' sneered Dawes, jerking his head contemptuously at Paul.

'That's comin' it strong,' said the mutual friend. 'Tart an' all?'

'Tart, begod!' said Dawes.

'Go on; let's have it!' cried the mutual friend.

'You've got it,' said Dawes, 'an' I reckon Morelly had it an' all.'

'Well, I'll be jiggered!' said the mutual friend. 'An' was it a proper tart?'

'Tart, God blimey – yes!'

'How do you know?'

'Oh,' said Dawes, 'I reckon he spent th' night –'

There was a good deal of laughter at Paul's expense.

'But who *was* she? D'you know her?' asked the mutual friend.

'I should *shay sho*,' said Dawes.

This brought another burst of laughter.

'Then spit it out,' said the mutual friend.

Dawes shook his head, and took a gulp of beer.

'It's a wonder he hasn't let on himself,' he said. 'He'll be braggin' of it in a bit.'

'Come on, Paul,' said his friend: 'it's no good. You might just as well own up.'

'Own up what? That I happened to take a friend to the theatre?'

'Oh well, if it was all right, tell us who she was, lad,' said the friend.

'She *was* all right,' said Dawes.

Paul was furious. Dawes wiped his golden moustache with his fingers, sneering.

'Strike me –! One o' that sort?' said the mutual friend. 'Paul, boy, I'm surprised at you. And do you know her, Baxter?'

'Just a bit, like!'

He winked at the other men.

'Oh, well,' said Paul, 'I'll be going!'

The mutual friend laid a detaining hand on his shoulder.

'Nay,' he said, 'you don't get off as easy as that, my lad. We've got to have a full account of this business.'

'Then get it from Dawes,' he said.

'You shouldn't funk your own deeds, man,' remonstrated the friend.

Then Dawes made a remark which caused Paul to throw half a glass of beer in his face.

'Oh, Mr Morel!' cried the barmaid, and she rang the bell for the 'chucker-out'.

Dawes spat and rushed for the young man. At that minute a brawny fellow with his shirtsleeves rolled up and his trousers tight over his haunches intervened.

'Now, then!' he said, pushing his chest in front of Dawes.

'Come out!' cried Dawes.

Paul was leaning, white and quivering, against the brass rail of the bar. He hated Dawes, wished something could exterminate him at that moment; and at the same time, seeing the wet hair on the man's forehead, he thought he looked pathetic. He did not move.

'Come out, you –' said Dawes.

'That's enough, Dawes,' cried the barmaid.

'Come on,' said the 'chucker-out', with kindly insistence, 'you'd better be getting on.'

And, by making Dawes edge away from his own close proximity, he worked him to the door.

'*That's* the little sod as started it!' cried Dawes, half cowed, pointing to Paul Morel.

'Why, what a story, Mr Dawes!' said the barmaid. 'You know it was you all the time.'

Still the 'chucker-out' kept thrusting his chest forward at him, still he kept edging back, until he was in the doorway and on the steps outside; then he turned round.

'All right,' he said, nodding straight at his rival.

Paul had a curious sensation of pity, almost of affection, mingled with a violent hate, for the man. The coloured door swung to; there was silence in the bar.

'Serve him jolly well right!' said the barmaid.

'But it's a nasty thing to get a glass of beer in your eyes,' said the mutual friend.

'I tell you *I* was glad he did,' said the barmaid. 'Will you have another, Mr Morel?'

She held up Paul's glass questioningly. He nodded.

'He's a man as doesn't care for anything, is Baxter Dawes,' said one.

'Pooh! Is he?' said the barmaid. 'He's a loud-mouthed one, he is, and they're never much good. Give me a pleasant-spoken chap, if you want a devil!'

'Well, Paul my lad,' said the friend, 'you'll have to take care of yourself now for a while.'

'You won't have to give him a chance over you, that's all,' said the barmaid.

'Can you box?' asked a friend.

'Not a bit,' he answered, still very white.

'I might give you a turn or two,' said the friend.

'Thanks, I haven't time.'

And presently he took his departure.

'Go along with him, Mr Jenkinson,' whispered the barmaid, tipping Mr Jenkinson the wink.

The man nodded, took his hat, said 'Good night· all!' very heartily, and followed Paul calling:

'Half a minute, old man. You an' me's going the same road, I believe.'

'Mr Morel doesn't like it,' said the barmaid. 'You'll see, we shan't have him in much more. I'm sorry; he'd good company. And Baxter Dawes wants locking up, that's what he wants.'

Paul would have died rather than his mother should get to know of this affair. He suffered tortures of humiliation and self-consciousness. There was now a good deal of his life of which necessarily he could not speak to his mother. He had a life apart from her – his sexual life. The rest she still kept. But he felt he had to conceal something from her, and it irked him. There was a certain silence between them, and he felt he had, in that silence, to defend himself against her; he felt condemned by her. Then sometimes he hated her, and pulled at her bondage. His life wanted to free itself of her. It was like a circle where life turned back on itself, and got no farther. She bore him, loved him, kept him, and his love turned back into her, so that he could not be free to go forward with his own life, really love another woman. At this period, unknowingly, he resisted his mother's influence. He did not tell her things; there was a distance between them.

Clara was happy, almost sure of him. She felt she had at had at last got him for herself; and then again came the uncertainty. He told her jestingly of the affair with her husband. Her colour came up, her grey eyes flashed.

'That's him to a "T",' she cried – 'like a navvy! He's not fit for mixing with decent folk.'

'Yet you married him,' he said.

It made her furious that he reminded her.

'I did!' she cried. 'But how was I to know!'

'I think he might have been rather nice,' he said.

'You think *I* made him what he is!' she exclaimed.

'Oh no! He made himself. But there's something about him –'

Clara looked at her lover closely. There was something in him she hated, a sort of detached criticism of herself, a coldness which made her woman's soul harden against him.

'And what are you going to do?' she asked.

'How?'

'About Baxter.'

'There's nothing to do, is there?' he replied.

'You can fight him if you have to, I suppose?' she said.

'No; I haven't the least sense of the "fist". It's funny. With most men there's the instinct to clench the fist and hit. It's not so with me. I should want a knife or a pistol or something to fight with.'

'Then you'd better carry something,' she said.

'Nay,' he laughed; 'I'm not daggeroso.'

'But he'll do something to you. You don't know him.'

'All right,' he said, 'we'll see.'

'And you'll let him?'

'Perhaps, if I can't help it.'

'And if he kills you?' she said.

'I should be sorry, for his sake and mine.'

Clara was silent for a moment.

'You *do* make me angry!' she exclaimed.

'That's nothing afresh,' he laughed.

'But why are you so silly? You don't know him.'

'And don't want.'

'Yes, but you're not going to let a man do as he likes with you?'

'What must I do?' he replied, laughing.

'*I* should carry a revolver,' she said. 'I'm sure he's dangerous.'

'I might blow my fingers off,' he said.

'No; but won't you?' she pleaded.

'No.'

'Not anything?'

'No.'

'And you leave him to –?'

'Yes.'

'You are a fool!'

'Fact!'

She set her teeth with anger.

'I could *shake* you!' she cried, trembling with passion.

'Why?'

'Let a man like *him* do as he likes with you.'

'You can go back to him if he triumphs,' he said.

'Do you want me to hate you?' she asked.

'Well, I only tell you,' he said.

'And *you* say you *love* me!' she exclaimed, low and indignant.

'Ought I to slay him to please you?' he said. 'But if I did, see what a hold he'd have over me.'

'Do you think I'm a fool!' she exclaimed.

'Not at all. But you don't understand me, my dear.'

There was a pause between them.

'But you ought *not* to expose yourself,' she pleaded.

He shrugged his shoulders.

> 'The man in righteousness arrayed,
>   The pure and blameless liver,
> Needs nor the keen Toledo blade,
>   Nor venom-freighted quiver,'

he quoted.

She looked at him searchingly.

'I wish I could understand you,' she said.

'There's simply nothing to understand,' he laughed.

She bowed her head, brooding.

He did not see Dawes for several days; then one morning as he ran upstairs from the spiral room he almost collided with the burly metal-worker.

'What the –!' cried the smith.

'Sorry!' said Paul, and passed on.

'*Sorry!*' sneered Dawes.

Paul whistled lightly, 'Put Me among the Girls.'

'I'll stop your whistle, my jockey!' he said.

The other took no notice.

'You're goin' to answer for that job of the other night.'

Paul went to his desk in his corner, and turned over the leaves of the ledger.

'Go and tell Fanny I want order 907, quick!' he said to the boy.

Dawes stood in the doorway, tall and threatening, looking at the top of the young man's head.

'Six and five's eleven and seven's one-and-six,' Paul added aloud.

'An' you hear, do you!' said Dawes.

'*Five and ninepence!*' He wrote a figure. 'What's that?' he said.

'I'm going to show you what it is,' said the smith.

The other went on adding the figures aloud.

'Yer crawlin' little – yer daresn't face me proper!'

Paul quickly snatched the heavy ruler. Dawes started. The young man ruled some lines in his ledger. The elder man was infuriated.

'But wait till I light on you, no matter where it is, I'll settle your hash for a bit, yer little swine!'

'All right,' said Paul.

At that the smith started heavily from the doorway. Just then a whistle piped shrilly. Paul went to the speaking-tube.

'Yes!' he said, and he listened. 'Er – yes!' He listened, then he laughed. 'I'll come down directly. I've got a visitor just now.'

Dawes knew from his tone he had been speaking to Clara. He stepped forward.

'Yer little devil!' he said. 'I'll visitor you, inside of two minutes! Think I'm goin' ter have *you* whipperty-snappin' round?'

The other clerks in the warehouse looked up. Paul's office-boy appeared, holding some white article.

'Fanny says you could have had it last night if you'd let her know,' he said.

'All right,' answered Paul, looking at the stocking. 'Get if off.'

Dawes stood frustrated, helpless with rage. Morel turned round.

'Excuse me a minute,' he said to Dawes, and he would have run downstairs.

'By God, I'll stop your gallop!' shouted the smith, seizing him by the arm. He turned quickly.

'Hey! Hey!' cried the office-boy, alarmed.

Thomas Jordan started out of his little glass office, and came running down the room.

'What's a-matter, what's a-matter?' he said, in his old man's sharp voice.

'I'm just goin' ter settle this little –, that' all,' said Dawes desperately.

'What do you mean?' snapped Thomas Jordan.

'What I say,' said Dawes, but he hung fire.

Morel was leaning against the counter, ashamed, half grinning.

'What's it all about?' snapped Thomas Jordan.

'Couldn't say,' said Paul, shaking his head and shrugging his shoulders.

'Couldn't yer, couldn't yer!' cried Dawes, thrusting forward his handsome furious face, and squaring his fist.

'Have you finished?' cried the old man, strutting. 'Get off about your business, and don't come here tipsy in the morning.'

Dawes turned his big frame slowly upon him.

'Tipsy!' he said. 'Who's tipsy? I'm no more tipsy than *you* are!'

'We've heard that song before,' snapped the old man. 'Now you get off, and don't be long about it. Comin' *here* with your rowdying.'

The smith looked down contemptuously on his employer. His hands, large and grimy, and yet well shaped for his labour, worked restlessly. Paul remembered they were the hands of Clara's husband, and a flash of hate went through him.

'Get out before you're turned out!' snapped Thomas Jordan.

'Why, who'll turn me out?' said Dawes, beginning to sneer.

Mr Jordan started, marched up to the smith, waving him off, thrusting his stout little figure at the man, saying:

'Get off my premises – get off!'

He seized and twitched Dawes' arm.

'Come off!' said the smith, and with a jerk of the elbow he sent the little manufacturer staggering backwards.

Before anyone could help him, Thomas Jordan had collided with the flimsy spring-door. It had given way, and let him crash down the half-dozen steps into Fanny's room. There was a second of amazement; then men and girls were running. Dawes stood a moment looking bitterly on the scene, then he took his departure.

Thomas Jordan was shaken and bruised, not otherwise hurt. He was, however, beside himself with rage. He dismissed Dawes from his employment, and summoned him for assault.

At the trial Paul Morel had to give evidence. Asked how the trouble began, he said:

'Dawes took occasion to insult Mrs Dawes and me because I accompanied her to the theatre one evening; then I threw some beer at him, and he wanted his revenge.'

'Cherchez la femme!' smiled the magistrate.

The case was dismissed after the magistrate had told Dawes he thought him a skunk.

'You gave the case away,' snapped Mr Jordan to Paul.

'I don't think I did,' replied the latter. 'Besides, you didn't really want a conviction, did you?'

'What do you think I took the case up for?'

'Well,' said Paul, 'I'm sorry if I said the wrong thing.' Clara was also very angry.

'Why need *my* name have been dragged in?' she said.

'Better speak it openly than leave it to be whispered.'

'There was no need for anything at all,' she declared.

'We are none the poorer,' he said indifferently.

'*You* may not be,' she said.

'And you?' he asked.

'I need never have been mentioned.'

'I'm sorry,' he said; but he did not sound sorry.

He told himself easily: 'She will come round.' And she did.

He told his mother about the fall of Mr Jordan and the trial of Mr Dawes. Mrs Morel watched him closely.

'And what do you think of it all?' she asked him.

'I think he's a fool,' he said.

But he was very uncomfortable, nevertheless.

'Have you ever considered where it will end?' his mother said.

'No,' he answered; 'things work out of themselves.'

'They do, in a way one doesn't like, as a rule,' said his mother.

'And then one has to put up with them,' he said.

'You'll find you're not as good at "putting up" as you imagine,' she said.

He went on working rapidly at his design.

'Do you ever ask *her* opinion?' she said at length.

'What of?'

'Of you, and the whole thing.'

'I don't care what her opinion of me is. She's fearfully in love with me, but it's not very deep.'

'But quite as deep as your feeling for her.'

He looked up at his mother curiously.

'Yes,' he said. 'You know, mother. I think there must be something the matter with me, that I *can't* love. When she's there, as a rule, I *do* love her. Sometimes, when I see her just as *the woman*, I love her, mother; but then, when she talks and criticizes, I often don't listen to her.'

'Yet she's as much sense as Miriam.'

'Perhaps; and I love her better than Miriam. But *why* don't they hold me?'

The last question was almost a lamentation. His mother turned away her face, sat looking across the room, very quiet, grave, with something of renunciation.

'But you wouldn't want to marry Clara?' she said.

'No; at first perhaps I would. But why – why don't I want to marry her or anybody? I feel sometimes as if I wronged my women, mother.'

'How wronged them, my son?'

'I don't know.'

He went on painting rather despairingly; he had touched the quick of the trouble.

'And as for wanting to marry,' said his mother, 'there's plenty of time yet.'

'But no, mother. I even love Clara, and I did Miriam; but to *give* myself to them in marriage I couldn't. I couldn't belong to them. They seem to want *me*, and I can't ever give it them.'

'You haven't met the right woman.'

'And I never shall meet the right woman while you live,' he said.

She was very quiet. Now she began to feel again tired, as if she were done.

'We'll see, my son,' she answered.

The feeling that things were going in a circle made him mad.

Clara was, indeed, passionately in love with him, and he with her, as far as passion went. In the daytime he forgot her a good deal. She was working in the same building, but he was not aware of it. He was busy, and her existence was of no matter to him. But all the time she was in the spiral room she had a sense that he was upstairs, a physical sense of his person in the same building. Every second she expected him to come through the door, and when he came it was a shock to her. But he was often short and offhand with her. He gave her his directions in an official manner, keeping her at bay. With what wits she had left she listened to him. She dared not misunderstand or fail to remember, but it was a cruelty to her. She wanted to touch his chest. She knew exactly how this breast was shapen under the waistcoat, and she wanted to touch it. It maddened her to hear his mechanical voice giving orders about the work. She wanted to break through the sham of it, smash the trivial coating of business which covered him with hardness, get at the man again; but she was afraid, and before she could feel one touch of his warmth he was gone, and she ached again.

He knew that she was dreary every evening she did not see him, so he gave her a good deal of his time. The days were often a misery to her, but the evenings and the nights were usually a bliss to them both. Then they were silent. For hours they sat together, or walked together in the dark, and talked only a few, almost meaningless words. But he had her hand in his, and her bosom left its warmth in his chest, making him feel whole.

One evening they were walking down by the canal, and something was troubling him. She knew she had not got him. All the time he whistled softly and persistently to himself. She listened, feeling she could learn more from his whistling than from his speech. It was a sad dissatisfied tune – a tune that made her feel he would not stay with her. She walked on in silence. When they came to the swing bridge he sat down on the great pole, looking at the stars in the water. He was a long way from her. She had been thinking.

'Will you always stay at Jordan's?' she asked.

'No,' he answered without reflecting. 'No; I s'll leave Nottingham and go abroad – soon.'

'Go abroad! What for?'

'I dunno! I feel restless.'

'But what shall you do?'

'I shall have to get some steady designing work, and some sort of sale for my pictures first,' he said. 'I am gradually making my way. I know I am.'

'And when do you think you'll go?'

'I don't know. I shall hardly go for long, while there's my mother.'

'You couldn't leave her?'

'Not for long.'

She looked at the stars in the black water. They lay very white and staring. It was an agony to know he would leave her, but it was almost an agony to have him near her.

'And if you made a nice lot of money, what would you do?' she asked.

'Go somewhere in a pretty house near London with my mother.'

'I see.'

There was a long pause.

'I could still come and see you,' he said, 'I don't know. Don't ask me what I should do; I don't know.'

There was a silence. The stars shuddered and broke upon the water. There came a breath of wind. He went suddenly to her, and put his hand on her shoulder.

'Don't ask me anything about the future,' he said miserably. 'I don't know anything. Be with me now, will you, no matter what it is?'

And she took him in her arms. After all, she was a married woman, and she had no right even to what he gave her. He needed her badly. She had him in her arms, and he was miserable. With her warmth she folded him over, consoled him, loved him. She would let the moment stand for itself.

After a moment he lifted his head as if he wanted to speak.

'Clara,' he said, struggling.

She caught him passionately to her, pressed his head down on her breast with her hand. She could not bear the suffering in his voice. She was afraid in her soul. He might have anything of her – anything; but she did not want to *know*. She felt she could not bear it. She wanted him to be soothed upon her – soothed. She stood clasping him and caressing him, and he was something unknown to her – something almost uncanny. She wanted to soothe him into forgetfulness.

And soon the struggle went down in his soul, and he forgot. But then Clara was not there for him, only a woman, warm, something he loved and almost worshipped, there in the dark. But it was not Clara, and she submitted to him. The naked hunger and inevitability of his loving her, something strong and blind and ruthless in his primitiveness, made the hour almost terrible to her. She knew how stark and alone he was, and she felt it was great that he came to her; and she took him simply because his need was bigger either than her or him, and her soul was still within her. She did this for him in his need, even if he left her, for she loved him.

All the while the peewits were screaming in the field. When he came to, he wondered what was near his eyes, curving and strong with life in the dark, and what voice it was speaking. Then he realized it was the grass, and the peewit was calling. The warmth was Clara's breathing heaving. He lifted his head, and looked into her eyes. They were dark and shining and strange, life wild at the source staring into his life, stranger to him, yet meeting him; and he put his face down on her throat, afraid. What was she? A strong, strange, wild life, that breathed with his in the darkness through this hour. It was all so much bigger than themselves that he was hushed. They had met, and included in their meeting the thrust of the manifold grass-stems, the cry of the peewit, the wheel of the stars.

When they stood up they saw other lovers stealing down the opposite hedge. It seemed natural they were there; the night contained them.

And after such an evening they both were very still, having known the immensity of passion. They felt small, half afraid, childish, and wondering, like Adam and Eve when they lost their innocence and realized the magnificence of the power which drove them out of Paradise and across the great night and the great day of humanity. It was for each of them an initiation and a satisfaction. To know their own nothingness, to know the tremendous living flood which carried them always, gave them rest within themselves. If so great a magnificent power could overwhelm them, identify them altogether with itself, so that they knew they were only grains in the tremendous heave that lifted every grass-blade its little height, and every tree, and living thing, then why fret about themselves? They could let themselves be carried by life, and they felt a sort of peace each in the other. There was a verification which they had had together. Nothing could nullify it, nothing could take it away; it was almost their belief in life.

But Clara was not satisfied. Something great was there, she knew; something great enveloped her. But it did not keep her. In the morning it was not the same. They had *known*, but she could not keep the moment. She wanted it again; she wanted something permanent. She had not realized fully. She thought it was he whom she wanted. He was not safe to her. This that had been between them might never be again; he might leave her. She had not got him; she was not satisfied. She had been there, but she had not gripped the – the something – she knew not what – which she was mad to have.

In the morning he had considerable peace, and was happy in himself. It seemed almost as if he had known the baptism of fire in passion, and it left him at rest. But it was not Clara. It was something that happened because of her, but it was not her. They were scarcely any nearer each other. If was as if they had been blind agents of a great force.

When she saw him that day at the factory her heart melted like a drop of fire. It was his body, his brows. The drop of fire grew more intense in her breast; she must hold him. But he, very quiet, very subdued this morning, went on giving his instructions. She followed him into the dark, ugly basement, and lifted her arms to him. He kissed her, and the intensity of passion began to burn him again. Somebody was at the door. He ran upstairs; she returned to her room, moving as if in a trance.

After that the fire slowly went down. He felt more and more that his experience had been impersonal, and not Clara. He loved her. There was a big tenderness, as after a strong emotion they had known together; but it was not she who could keep his soul steady. He had wanted her to be something she could not be.

And she was mad with desire of him. She could not see him without touching him. In the factory, as he talked to her about spiral hose, she ran her hand secretly along his side. She followed him out into the basement for a quick kiss;

her eyes, always mute and yearning, full of unrestrained passion, she kept fixed on his. He was afraid of her, lest she should too flagrantly give herself away before the other girls. She invariably waited for him at dinner-time for him to embrace her before she went. He felt as if she were helpless, almost a burden to him, and it irritated him.

'But what do you always want to be kissing and embracing for?' he said. 'Surely there's a time for everything.'

She looked up at him, and the hate came into her eyes.

'*Do* I always want to be kissing you?' she said.

'Always, even if I come to ask you about the work. I don't want anything to do with love when I'm at work. Work's work —'

'And what is love?' she asked. 'Has it to have special hours?'

'Yes; out of work hours.'

'And you'll regulate it according to Mr Jordan's closing time?'

'Yes; and according to the freedom from business of any sort.'

'It is only to exist in spare time?'

'That's all, and not always then — not the kissing sort of love.'

'And that's all you think of it?'

'It's quite enough.'

'I'm glad you think so.'

And she was cold to him for some time – she hated him; and while she was cold and contemptuous, he was uneasy till she had forgiven him again. But when they started afresh they were not any nearer. He kept her because he never satisfied her.

In the spring they went together to the seaside. They had rooms at a little cottage near Theddlethorpe, and lived as man and wife. Mrs Radford sometimes went with them.

It was known in Nottingham that Paul Morel and Mrs Dawes were going together, but as nothing was very obvious, and Clara was always a solitary person, and he seemed so simple and innocent, it did not make much difference.

He loved the Lincolnshire coast, and she loved the sea. In the early morning they often went out together to bathe. The grey of the dawn, the far, desolate reaches of the fenland smitten with winter, the sea-meadows rank with herbage, were stark enough to rejoice his soul. As they stepped on to the highroad from their plank bridge. and looked round at the endless monotony of levels, the land a little darker than the sky, the sea sounding small beyond the sandhills, his heart filled strong with the sweeping restlessness of life. She loved him then. He was solitary and strong, and his eyes had a beautiful light.

They shuddered with cold; then he raced her down the road to the green turf bridge. She could run well. Her colour soon came, her throat was bare, her eyes shone. He loved her for being so luxuriously heavy, and yet so quick. Himself was light; she went with a beautiful rush. They grew warm, and walked hand in hand.

A flush came into the sky, the wan moon, half-way down the west, sank into insignificance. On the shadowy land things began to take life, plants with great leaves became distinct. They came through a pass in the big, cold sandhills on to the beach. The long waste of foreshore lay moaning under the dawn and the sea; the ocean was a flat dark strip with a white edge. Over the gloomy sea the sky was red. Quickly the fire spread among the clouds and scattered them. Crimson burned to orange, orange to dull gold, and in a golden glitter the sun came up, dribbling fierily over the waves in little splashes, as if someone had gone along and the light had spilled from her pail as she walked.

The breakers ran down the shore in long, hoarse strokes. Tiny seagulls, like specks of spray, wheeled above the line of surf. Their crying seemed larger than they. Far away the coast reached out, and melted into the morning, the tussocky sandhills seeming to sink to a level with the beach. Mablethorpe was tiny on their right. They had alone the space of all this level shore, the sea, and the upcoming sun, the faint noise of the waters, the sharp crying of the gulls.

They had a warm hollow in the sandhills where the wind did not come. He stood looking out to sea.

'It's very fine,' he said.

'Now don't get sentimental,' she said.

It irritated her to see him standing gazing at the sea, like a solitary and poetic person. He laughed. She quickly undressed.

'There are some fine waves this morning,' she said triumphantly.

She was a better swimmer than he; he stood idly watching her.

'Aren't you coming?' she said.

'In a minute,' he answered.

She was white and velvet skinned, with heavy shoulders. A little wind, coming from the sea, swept across her body and ruffled her hair.

The morning was of a lovely limpid gold colour. Veils of shadow seemed to be drifting away on the north and the south. Clara stood shrinking slightly from the touch of the wind, twisting her hair. The sea-grass rose behind the white stripped woman. She glanced at the sea, then looked at him. He was watching her with dark eyes which she loved and could not understand. She hugged her breasts between her arms, cringing, laughing:

'Oo, it will be so cold!' she said.

He bent forward and kissed her, held her suddenly close, and kissed her again. She stood waiting. He looked into her eyes, then away at the pale sands.

'Go, then!' he said quietly.

She flung her arms round his neck, drew him against her, kissed him passionately, and went, saying:

'But you'll come in?'

'In a minute.'

She went plodding heavily over the sand that was soft as velvet. He, on the sandhills, watched the great pale coast envelop her. She grew smaller, lost proportion, seemed only like a large white bird toiling forward.

'Not much more than a big white pebble on the beach, not much more than a slot of foam being blown and rolled over the sand,' he said to himself.

She seemed to move very slowly across the vast sounding shore. As he watched, he lost her. She was dazzled out of sight by the sunshine. Again he saw her, the merest white speck moving against the white, muttering sea-edge.

'Look how little she is!' he said to himself. 'She's lost like a grain of sand in the beach – just a concentrated speck blown along, a tiny white foam-bubble, almost nothing among the morning. Why does she absorb me?'

The morning was altogether interrupted: she was gone in the water. Far and wide the beach, the sandhills with their blue marrain, the shining water, glowed together in immense, unbroken solitude.

'What is she, after all?' he said to himself. 'Here's the seacoast morning, big and permanent and beautiful; there is she, fretting, always unsatisfied, and temporary as a bubble of foam. What does she mean to me, after all? She represents something, like a bubble of foam represents the sea. But what is *she*? It's not her I care for.'

Then, startled by his own unconscious thoughts, that seemed to speak so distinctly that all the morning could hear, he undressed and ran quickly down the sands. She was watching for him. Her arm flashed up to him, she heaved on a wave, subsided, her shoulders in a pool of liquid silver. He jumped through the breakers, and in a moment her hand was on his shoulder.

He was a poor swimmer, and could not stay long in the water. She played round him in triumph, sporting with her superiority, which he begrudged her. The sunshine stood deep and fine on the water. They laughed in the sea for a minute or two, then raced each other back to the sandhills.

When they were drying themselves, panting heavily, he watched her laughing, breathless face, her bright shoulders, her breasts that swayed and made him frightened as she rubbed them, and he thought again:

'But she is magnificent, and even bigger than the morning and the sea. Is she – ? Is she – ?'

She, seeing his dark eyes fixed on her, broke off from her drying with a laugh.

'What are you looking at?' she said.

'You,' he answered, laughing.

Her eyes met his, and in a moment he was kissing her white 'goose-fleshed' shoulder, and thinking:

What is she? What is she?

She loved him in the morning. There was something detached, hard, and elemental about his kisses then, as if he were only conscious of his own will, not in the least of her and her wanting him.

Later in the day he went out sketching.

'You,' he said to her, 'go with your mother to Sutton. I am so dull.'

She stood and looked at him. He knew she wanted to come with him, but he preferred to be alone. She made him feel imprisoned when she was there, as if he could not get a free deep breath, as if there were something on top of him. She felt his desire to be free of her.

In the evening he came back to her. They walked down the shore in the darkness, then sat for awhile in the shelter of the sandhills.

'It seems,' she said, as they stared over the darkness of the sea, where no light was to be seen – 'it seems as if you only loved me at night – as if you didn't love me in the daytime.'

He ran the cold sand through his fingers, feeling guilt under the accusation.

'The night is free to you,' he replied. 'In the daytime I want to be by myself.'

'But why?' she said. 'Why, even now, when we are on this short holiday?'

'I don't know. Love-making stifles me in the daytime.'

'But it needn't be always love-making,' she said.

'It always is,' he answered, 'when you and I are together.'

She sat feeling very bitter.

'Do you ever want to marry me?' he asked curiously.

'Do you me?' she replied.

'Yes, yes; I should like us to have children,' he answered slowly.

She sat with her head bent, fingering the sand.

'But you don't really want a divorce from Baxter, do you?' he said.

It was some minutes before she replied.

'No,' she said, very deliberately; 'I don't think I do.'

'Why?'

'I don't know.'

'Do you feel as if you belonged to him?'

'No; I don't think so.'

'What, then?'

'I think he belongs to me,' she replied.

He was silent for some minutes, listening to the wind blowing over the hoarse, dark sea.

'And you never really intended to belong to *me*?' he said.

'Yes, I do belong to you,' she answered.

'No,' he said; 'because you don't want to be divorced.'

It was a knot they could not untie, so they left it, took what they could get, and what they could not attain they ignored.

'I consider you treated Baxter rottenly,' he said another time.

He half expected Clara to answer him, as his mother would: 'You consider your own affairs, and don't know so much about other people's.' But she took him seriously, almost to his own surprise.

'Why?' she said.

'I suppose you thought he was a lily of the valley, and so you put him in an appropriate pot, and tended him according. You made up your mind he was a lily of the valley, and it was no good his being a cow-parsnip. You wouldn't have it.'

'I certainly never imagined him a lily of the valley.'

'You imagined him something he wasn't. That's just what a woman is. She thinks she knows what's good for a man, and she's going to see he gets it; and no matter if he's starving, he may sit and whistle for what he needs, while she's got him, and is giving him what's good for him.'

'And what are you doing?' she asked.

'I'm thinking of what tune I shall whistle,' he laughed.

And instead of boxing his ears, she considered him in earnest.

'You think I want to give you what's good for you?' she asked.

'I hope so; but love should give a sense of freedom, not of prison. Miriam made me feel tied up like a donkey to a stake. I must feed on her patch, and nowhere else. It's sickening!'

'And would *you* let a *woman* do as she likes?'

'Yes; I'll see that she *likes* to love me. If she doesn't – well, I don't hold her.'

'If you were as wonderful as you say –' replied Clara.

'I should be the marvel I am,' he laughed.

There was a silence in which they hated each other, though they laughed.

'Love's a dog in the manger,' he said.

'And which of us is the dog?' she asked.

'Oh well, you, of course.'

So there went on a battle between them. She knew she never fully had him. Some part, big and vital in him, she had no hold over; nor did she ever try to get it, or even to realize what it was. And he knew in some way that she held herself still as Mrs Dawes. She did not love Dawes, never had loved him; but she believed he loved her, at least depended on her. She felt a certain surety about him that she never felt with Paul Morel. Her passion for the young man has filled her soul, given her a certain satisfaction, eased her of her self-mistrust, her doubt. Whatever else she was, she was inwardly assured. It was almost as if she had gained *herself*, and stood now distinct and complete. She had received her confirmation; but she never believed that her life belonged to Paul Morel, nor his to her. They would separate in the end, and the rest of her life would be an ache after him. But at any rate, she *knew* now, she was sure of herself. And the same could almost be said of him. Together they had received the baptism of life, each through the other; but now their missions were separate. Where he wanted to go she could not come with him. They would have to part sooner or later. Even if they married, and were faithful to each other, still he would have to leave her, go on alone, and she would only have to attend to him when he came home. But it was not possible. Each wanted a mate to go side by side with.

Clara had gone to live with her mother upon Mapperley Plains. One evening, as Paul and she were walking along Woodborough Road, they met Dawes. Morel knew something about the bearing of the man approaching, but he was absorbed in his thinking at the moment, so that only his artist's eye watched the form of the stranger. Then he suddenly turned to Clara with a laugh, and put his hand on her shoulder, saying, laughing:

'But we walk side by side, and yet I'm in London arguing with an imaginary Orpen; and where are you?'

At that instant Dawes passed, almost touching Morel. The young man glanced, saw the dark brown eyes burning, full of hate and yet tired.

'Who was that?' he asked of Clara.

'It was Baxter,' she replied.

Paul took his hand from her shoulder and glanced round; then he saw again distinctly the man's form as it approached him. Dawes still walked erect, with his fine shoulders flung back, and his face lifted; but there was a furtive look in his eyes that gave one the impression he was trying to get unnoticed past every person he met, glancing suspiciously to see what they thought of him. And his hands seemed to be wanting to hide. He wore old clothes, the trousers were torn at the knee, and the handkerchief tied round his throat was dirty; but his cap was still defiantly over one eye. As she saw him, Clara felt guilty. There was a tiredness and despair on his face that made her hate him, because it hurt her.

'He looks shady,' said Paul.

But the note of pity in his voice reproached her, and made her feel hard.

'His true commonness comes out,' she answered.

'Do you hate him?' he asked.

'You talk,' she said, 'about the cruelty of women; I wish you knew the cruelty of men in their brute force. They simply don't know that the woman exists.'

'Don't *I*?' he said.

'No,' she answered.

'Don't I know you exist?'

'About *me* you know nothing,' she said bitterly – 'about *me*!'

'Not more than Baxter knew?' he asked.

'Perhaps not as much.'

He felt puzzled, and helpless, and angry. There she walked unknown to him, though they had been through such experience together.

'But you know *me* pretty well,' he said.

She did not answer.

'Did you know Baxter as well as you know me?' he asked. 'He wouldn't let me,' she said.

'And I have let you know me?'

'It's what men *won't* let you do. They won't let you get really near to them,' she said.

'And haven't I let you?'

'Yes,' she answered slowly; 'but you've never come near to me. You can't come out of yourself, you can't. Baxter could do that better than you.'

He walked on pondering. He was angry with her for preferring Baxter to him.

'You begin to value Baxter now you've not got him,' he said.

'No; I can only see where he was different from you.'

But he felt she had a grudge against him.

One evening, as they were coming home over the fields, she startled him by asking:

'Do you think it's worth it – the – the sex part?'

'The act of loving, itself?'

'Yes; is it worth anything to you?'

'But how can you separate it?' he said. 'It's the culmination of everything. All our intimacy culminates then.'

'Not for me,' she said.

He was silent. A flash of hate for her came up. After all, she was dissatisfied with him, even there, where he thought they fulfilled each other. But he believed her too implicitly.

'I feel,' she continued slowly, 'as if I hadn't got you, as if all you weren't there, and as if it weren't *me* you were taking –'

'Who, then?'

'Something just for yourself. It has been fine, so that I daren't think of it. But is it *me* you want, or is it *It*?'

He again felt guilty. Did he leave Clara out of count, and take simply woman? But he thought that was splitting a hair.

'When I had Baxter, actually had him, then I *did* feel as if I had all of him,' she said.

'And it was better?' he asked.

'Yes, yes; it was more whole. I don't say you haven't given me more than he ever gave me.'

'Or could give you.'

'Yes, perhaps; but you've never given me yourself.'

He knitted his brows angrily.

'If I start to make love to you,' he said, 'I just go like a leaf down the wind.'

'And leave me out of count,' she said.

'And then it is nothing to you?' he asked, almost rigid with chagrin.

'It's something; and sometimes you have carried me away – right away – I know – and – I reverence you for it – but –'

'Don't "but" me,' he said, kissing her quickly, as a fire ran through him. She submitted, and was silent.

It was true as he said. As a rule, when he started love-making, the emotion was strong enough to carry with it everything –reason, soul, blood – in a great sweep, like the Trent carries bodily its black-swirls and intertwinings, noiselessly. Gradually the little criticism, the little sensations, were lost, thought also went, everything borne along in one flood. He became, not a man with a mind, but a great instinct. His hands were like creatures, living; his limbs, his body, were all life and consciousness, subject to no will of his, but living in themselves. Just as he was, so it seemed the vigorous, wintry stars were strong also with life. He and they struck with the same pulse of fire, and the same body of strength which held the bracken-frond stiff near his eyes held his own body firm. If was as if he, and the stars, and the dark herbage, and Clara were licked up in an immense tongue of flame, which tore onwards and upwards. Everything rushed along in living beside him; everything was still, perfect in itself, along with him. This wonderful stillness in each thing in itself, while it was being borne along in a very ecstasy of living, seemed the highest point of bliss.

And Clara knew this held him to her, so she trusted altogether to the passion. It, however, failed her very often. They did not often reach again the height of that once when the peewits had called. Gradually, some mechanical effort spoilt their loving, or, when they had splendid moments, they had them separately, and not so satisfactorily. So often he seemed merely to be running on alone; often they realized it had been a failure, not what they had wanted. He left her, knowing *that* evening had only made a little split between them. Their loving grew more mechanical, without the marvellous glamour. Gradually they began to introduce novelties, to get back some of the feeling of satisfaction. They would be very near, almost dangerously near to the river, so that the black water ran not far from his face, and it gave a little thrill; or they loved sometimes in a little hollow below the fence of the path where people were passing occasionally, on the edge of the town, and they heard footsteps coming, almost felt the vibration of the tread, and they heard what the passers-by said – strange little things that were never intended to be heard. And afterwards each of them was rather ashamed, and these things caused a distance between the two of them. He began to despise her a little, as if she had merited it!

One night he left her to go to Daybrook Station over the fields. It was very dark, with an attempt at snow, although the spring was so far advanced. Morel had not much time; he plunged forward. The town ceases almost abruptly on the edge of a steep hollow; there the houses with their yellow lights stand up against the darkness. He went over the stile, and dropped quickly into the hollow of the fields. Under the orchard one warm window shone in Swineshead Farm. Paul glanced round. Behind, the houses stood on the brim of the dip, black against the sky, like wild beasts glaring curiously with yellow eyes down into the darkness. It was the town that seemed savage and uncouth, glaring on the clouds at the back of him. Some creature stirred under the willows of the farm pond. It was too dark to distinguish anything.

He was close up to the next stile before he saw a dark shape leaning against it. The man moved aside.

'Good evening!' he said.

'Good evening!' Morel answered, not noticing.

'Paul Morel?' said the man.

Then he knew it was Dawes. The man stopped his way.

'I've got yer, have I?' he said awkwardly.

'I shall miss my train,' said Paul.

He could see nothing of Dawes's face. The man's teeth seemed to chatter as he talked.

'You're going to get it from me now,' said Dawes.

Morel attempted to move forward; the other man stepped in front of him.

'Are yer goin' to take that top-coat off,' he said, 'or are you goin' to lie down to it?'

Paul was afraid the man was mad.

'But,' he said, 'I don't know how to fight.'

'All right, then,' answered Dawes, and before the younger man knew where he was he was staggering backwards from a blow across the face.

The whole night went black. He tore off his overcoat and coat, dodging a blow, and flung the garments over Dawes. The latter swore savagely. Morel in his shirtsleeves, was now alert and furious. He felt his whole body unsheath itself like a claw. He could not fight, so he would use his wits. The other man became more distinct to him; he could see particularly the shirt-breast. Dawes stumbled over Paul's coats, then came rushing forward. The young man's mouth was bleeding. It was the other man's mouth he was dying to get at, and the desire was anguish in its strength. He stepped quickly through the stile, and as Dawes was coming through after him, like a flash he got a blow in over the other's mouth. He shivered with pleasure. Dawes advanced slowly, spitting. Paul was afraid; he moved round to get to the stile again. Suddenly, from out of nowhere, came a great blow against his ear, that sent him falling helpless backwards. He heard Dawes's heavy panting, like a wild beast's; then came a kick on the knee, giving him such agony that he got up and, quite blind, leapt clean under his enemy's guard. He felt blows and kicks, but they did not hurt. He hung on to the bigger man like a wild cat, till at last Dawes fell with a crash, losing his presence of mind. Paul went down with him. Pure instinct brought his hands to the man's neck, and before Dawes, in frenzy and agony, could wrench him free, he had got his fists twisted in the scarf and his knuckles dug in the throat of the other man. He was a pure instinct, without reason or feeling. His body, hard and wonderful in itself, cleaved against the struggling body of the other man; not a muscle in him relaxed. He was quite unconscious, only his body had taken upon itself to kill this other man. For himself, he had neither feeling nor reason. He lay pressed hard against his adversary, his body adjusting itself to its one pure purpose of choking the other man, resisting exactly at the right moment, with exactly the right amount of strength, the struggles of the other, silent, intent, unchanging, gradually pressing its knuckles deeper, feeling the struggles of the other body become wilder and more frenzied. Tighter and tighter grew his body, like a screw that is gradually increasing in pressure, till something breaks.

Then suddenly he relaxed, full of wonder and misgiving. Dawes had been yielding. Morel felt his body flame with pain, as he realized what he was doing; he was all bewildered. Dawes's struggles suddenly renewed themselves in a furious spasm. Paul's hands were wrenched, torn out of the scarf in which they were knotted, and he was flung away, helpless. He heard the horrid sound of the other's gasping, but he lay stunned; then, still dazed, he felt the blows of the other's feet, and lost consciousness.

Dawes, grunting with pain like a beast, was kicking the prostrate body of his rival. Suddenly the whistle of the train shrieked two fields away. He turned round and glared suspiciously. What was coming? He saw the lights of the train draw across his vision. It seemed to him people were approaching. He made off across the field into Nottingham, and dimly in his consciousness as he went, he felt on his foot the place where his boot had knocked against one of the lad's bones. The knock seemed to re-echo inside him; he hurried to get away from it.

Morel gradually came to himself. He knew where he was and what had happened, but he did not want to move. He lay still, with tiny bits of snow tickling his face. It was pleasant to lie quite, quite still. The time passed. It was the bits of snow that kept rousing him when he did not want to be roused. At last his will clicked into action.

'I mustn't lie here,' he said; 'it's silly.'

But still he did not move.

'I said I was going to get up,' he repeated. 'Why don't I?'

And still it was some time before he had sufficiently pulled himself together to stir; then gradually he got up. Pain made him sick and dazed, but his brain was clear. Reeling, he groped for his coats and got them on, buttoning his overcoat up to his ears. It was some time before he found his cap. He did not know whether his face was still bleeding. Walking blindly, every step making him sick with pain, he went back to the pond and washed his face and hands. The icy water hurt, but helped to bring him back to himself. He crawled back up the hill to the tram. He wanted to get to his mother – he must get to his mother – that was his blind intention. He covered his face as much as he could, and struggled sickly along. Continually the ground seemed to fall away from him as he walked, and he felt himself dropping with a sickening feeling into space; so, like a nightmare, he got through with the journey home.

Everybody was in bed. He looked at himself. His face was discoloured and smeared with blood, almost like a dead man's face. He washed it, and went to bed. The night went by in delirium. In the morning he found his mother looking at him. Her blue eyes – they were all he wanted to see. She was there; he was in her hands.

'It's not much, mother,' he said. 'It was Baxter Dawes.'

'Tell me where it hurts you,' she said quietly.

'I don't know – my shoulder. Say it was a bicycle accident, mother.'

He could not move his arm. Presently Minnie, the little servant, came upstairs with some tea.

'Your mother's nearly frightened me out of my wits – fainted away,' she said.

He felt he could not bear it. His mother nursed him; he told her about it.

'And now I should have done with them all,' she said quietly.

'I will, mother.'

She covered him up.

'And don't think about it,' she said – 'only try to go to sleep. The doctor won't be here till eleven.'

He had a dislocated shoulder, and the second day acute bronchitis set in. His mother was pale as death now, and very thin. She would sit and look at him, then away into space. There was something between them that neither dared mention. Clara came to see him. Afterwards he said to his mother:

'She makes me tired, mother.'

'Yes; I wish she wouldn't come,' Mrs Morel replied.

Another day Miriam came, but she seemed almost like a stranger to him.

'You know, I don't care about them, mother,' he said.

'I'm afraid you don't, my son,' she replied sadly.

It was given out everywhere that it was a bicycle accident. Soon he was able to go to work again, but now there was a constant sickness and gnawing at his heart. He went to Clara, but there seemed, as it were, nobody there. He could not work. He and his mother seemed almost to avoid each other. There was some secret between them which they could not bear. He was not aware of it. He only knew that his life seemed unbalanced, as if it were going to smash into pieces.

Clara did not know what was the matter with him. She realized that he seemed unaware of her. Even when he came to her he seemed unaware of her; always he was somewhere else. She felt she was clutching for him, and he was somewhere else. It tortured her, and so she tortured him. For a month at a time she kept him at arm's length. He almost hated her, and was driven to her in spite of himself. He went mostly into the company of men, was always at the George or the White Horse. His mother was ill, distant, quiet, shadowy. He was terrified of something; he dared not look at her. Her eyes seemed to grow darker, her face more waxen; still she dragged about at her work.

At Whitsuntide he said he would go to Blackpool for four days with his friend Newton. The latter was a big, jolly fellow, with a touch of the bounder about him. Paul said his mother must go to Sheffield to stay a week with Annie, who lived there. Perhaps the change would do her good. Mrs Morel was attending a woman's doctor in Nottingham. He said her heart and her digestion were wrong. She consented to go to Sheffield, though she did not want to; but now she would do everything her son wished of her. Paul said he would come for her on the fifth day, and stay also in Sheffield till the holiday was up. It was agreed.

The two young men set off gaily for Blackpool. Mrs Morel was quite lively as Paul kissed her and left her. Once at the station, he forgot everything. Four days were clear – not an anxiety, not a thought. The two young men simply enjoyed themselves. Paul was like another man. None of himself remained – no Clara, no Miriam, no mother that fretted him. He wrote to them all, and long letters to his mother; but they were jolly letters that made her laugh. He was having a good time, as young fellows will in a place like Blackpool. And underneath it all was a shadow for her.

Paul was very gay, excited at the thought of staying with his mother in Sheffield. Newton was to spend the day with them. Their train was late. Joking, laughing, with their pipes between their teeth, the young men swung their bags on to the tram-car. Paul had bought his mother a little collar of real lace that he wanted to see her wear, so that he could tease her about it.

Annie lived in a nice house, and had a little maid. Paul ran gaily up the steps. He expected his mother laughing in the hall, but it was Annie who opened to him. She seemed distant to him. He stood a second in dismay. Annie let him kiss her cheek.

'Is my mother ill?' he said.

'Yes, she's not very well. Don't upset her.'

'Is she in bed?'

'Yes.'

And then the queer feeling went over him, as if all the sunshine had gone out of him, and it was all shadow. He dropped the bag and ran upstairs. Hesitating, he opened the door. His mother sat up in bed, wearing a dressing-gown of old rose colour. She looked at him almost as if she were ashamed of herself, pleading to him, humble. He saw the ashy look about her.

'Mother!' he said.

'I thought you were never coming,' she answered gaily.

But he only fell on his knees at the bedside, and buried his face in the bedclothes, crying in agony, and saying:

'Mother – mother – mother!'

She stroked his hair slowly with her thin hand.

'Don't cry,' she said. 'Don't cry – it's nothing.'

But he felt as if his blood was melting into tears, and he cried in terror and pain.

'Don't – don't cry,' his mother faltered.

Slowly she stroked his hair. Shocked out of himself, he cried, and the tears hurt in every fibre of his body. Suddenly he stopped, but he dared not lift his face out of the bedclothes.

'You *are* late. Where have you been?' his mother asked.

'The train was late,' he replied, muffled in the sheet.

'Yes; that miserable Central! Is Newton come?'

'Yes.'

'I'm sure you must be hungry, and they've kept dinner waiting.'

With a wrench he looked up at her.

'What is it, mother?' he asked brutally.

She averted her eyes as she answered:

'Only a bit of a tumour, my boy. You needn't trouble. It's been there – the lump has – a long time.'

Up came the tears again. His mind was clear and hard, but his body was crying.

'Where?' he said.

She put her hand on her side.

'Here. But you know they can sweal a tumour away.'

He stood feeling dazed and helpless, like a child. He thought perhaps it was as she said. Yes; he reassured himself it was so. But all the while his blood and his body knew definitely what it was. He sat down on the bed, and took her hand. She had never had but the one ring – her wedding ring.

'When were you poorly?' he asked.

'It was yesterday it began,' she answered submissively.

'Pains!'

'Yes; but not more than I've often had at home. I believe Dr Ansell is an alarmist.'

'You ought not to have travelled alone,' he said, to himself more than to her.

'As if that had anything to do with it!' she answered quickly.

They were silent for a while.

'Now go and have your dinner,' she said. 'You *must* be hungry.'

'Have you had yours?'

'Yes; a beautiful sole I had. Annie *is* good to me.'

They talked a little while, then he went downstairs. He was very white and strained. Newton sat in miserable sympathy.

After dinner he went into the scullery to help Annie to wash up. The little maid had gone on an errand.

'Is it really a tumour?' he asked.

Annie began to cry again.

'The pain she had yesterday – I never saw anybody suffer like it!' she cried. 'Leonard ran like a madman for Dr Ansell, and when she'd got to bed she said to me: "Annie, look at this lump on my side. I wonder what it is?" And there I looked, and I thought I should have dropped. Paul, as true as I'm here, it's a lump as big as my double fist. I said: "Good gracious, mother, whenever did that come?" "Why, child," she said, "it's been there a long time." I thought I should have died, our Paul, I did. She's been having these pains for months at home, and nobody looking after her.'

The tears came to his eyes, then dried suddenly.

'But she's been attending the doctor in Nottingham – and she never told me,' he said.

'If I'd have been at home,' said Annie, 'I should have seen for myself.'

He felt like a man walking in unrealities. In the afternoon he went to see the doctor. The latter was a shrewd, lovable man.

'But what is it?' he said.

The doctor looked at the young man, then knitted his fingers.

'It may be a large tumour which has formed in the membrane,' he said slowly, 'and which we *may* be able to make go away.'

'Can't you operate?' asked Paul.

'Not there,' replied the doctor.

'Are you sure?'

'Quite!'

Paul meditated a while.

'Are you sure it's a tumour?' he asked. 'Why did Dr Jameson in Nottingham never find out anything about it? She's been going to him for weeks, and he's treated her for heart and indigestion.'

'Mrs Morel never told Dr Jameson about the lump,' said the doctor.

'And do you *know* it's a tumour?'

'No, I am not sure.'

'What else *might* it be? You asked my sister if there was cancer in the family. Might it be cancer?'

'I don't know.'

'And what shall you do?'

'I should like an examination, with Dr Jameson.'

'Then have one.'

'You must arrange about that. His fees wouldn't be less than ten guineas to come here from Nottingham.'

'When would you like him to come?'

'I will call in this evening, and we will talk it over.'

Paul went away, biting his lip.

His mother could come downstairs for tea, the doctor said. Her son went upstairs to help her. She wore the old-rose dressing-gown that Leonard had given Annie, and, with a little colour in her face, was quite young again.

'But you look quite pretty in that,' he said.

'Yes; they make me so fine, I hardly know myself,' she answered.

But when she stood up to walk, the colour went. Paul helped her, half carrying her. At the top of the stairs she was gone. He lifted her up and carried her quickly downstairs; laid her on the couch. She was light and frail. Her face looked as if she were dead, with the blue lips shut tight. Her eyes opened – her blue, unfailing eyes – and she looked at him pleadingly, almost wanting him to forgive her. He held brandy to her lips, but her mouth would not open. All the time she watched him lovingly. She was only sorry for him. The tears ran down his face without ceasing, but not a muscle moved. He was intent on getting a little brandy between her lips. Soon she was able to swallow a teaspoonful. She lay back so tired. The tears continued to run down his face.

'But,' she panted, 'it'll go off. Don't cry!'

'I'm not doing,' he said.

After a while she was better again. He was kneeling beside the couch. They looked into each other's eyes.

'I don't want you to make a trouble of it,' she said.

'No, mother. You'll have to be quite still, and then you'll get better soon.'

But he was white to the lips, and their eyes as they looked at each other understood. Her eyes were so blue – such a wonderful forget-me-not blue! He felt if only they had been of a different colour he could have borne it better. His heart seemed to be ripping slowly in his breast. He kneeled there, holding her hand, and neither said anything. Then Annie came in.

'Are you all right?' she murmured timidly to her mother.

'Of course,' said Mrs Morel.

Paul sat down and told her about Blackpool. She was curious.

A day or two after, he went so see Dr Jameson in Nottingham, to arrange for a consultation. Paul had practically no money in the world. But he could borrow.

His mother had been used to go to the public consultation on Saturday morning, when she could see the doctor for only a nominal sum. Her son went on the same day. The waiting-room was full of poor women, who sat patiently on a bench around the wall. Paul thought of his mother, in her little black costume, sitting waiting likewise. The doctor was late. The women all looked rather frightened. Paul asked the nurse in attendance if he could see the doctor immediately he came. It was arranged so. The women sitting patiently round the walls of the room eyed the young man curiously.

At last the doctor came. He was about forty, good-looking, brown-skinned. His wife had died, and he, who had loved her, had specialized on women's ailments. Paul told his name and his mother's. The doctor did not remember.

'Number forty-six M,' said the nurse; and the doctor looked up the case in his book.

'There is a big lump that may be a tumour,' said Paul. 'But Dr Ansell was going to write you a letter.'

'Ah, yes!' replied the doctor, drawing the letter from his pocket. He was very friendly, affable, busy, kind. He would come to Sheffield the next day.

'What is your father?' he asked.

'He is a coal-miner,' replied Paul.

'Not very well off, I suppose?'

'This – I see after this,' said Paul.

'And you?' smiled the doctor.

'I am a clerk in Jordan's Appliance Factory.'

The doctor smiled at him.

'Er – to go to Sheffield!' he said, putting the tips of his fingers together, and smiling with his eyes. 'Eight guineas?'

'Thank you!' said Paul, flushing and rising. 'And you'll come tomorrow?'

'Tomorrow – Sunday? Yes! Can you tell me about what time there is a train in the afternoon?'

'There is a Central gets in at four-fifteen.'

'And will there be any way of getting up to the house? Shall I have to walk?' The doctor smiled.

'There is the tram,' said Paul; 'the Western Park tram.'

The doctor made a note of it.

'Thank you!' he said, and shook hands.

Then Paul went on home to see his father, who was left in the charge of Minnie. Walter Morel was getting very grey now. Paul found him digging in the garden. He had written him a letter. He shook hands with his father.

'Hello, son! Tha has landed, then?' said the father.

'Yes,' replied the son. 'But I'm going back tonight.'

'Are ter, beguy!' exclaimed the collier. 'An' has ter eaten owt?'

'No.'

'That's just like thee,' said Morel. 'Come thy ways in.'

The father was afraid of the mention of his wife. The two went indoors. Paul ate in silence; his father, with earthy hands, and sleeves rolled up, sat in the arm-chair opposite and looked at him.

'Well, an' how is she?' asked the miner at length, in a little voice.

'She can sit up; she can be carried down for tea,' said Paul.

'That's a blessin'!' exclaimed Morel. 'I hope we s'll soon be havin' her whoam, then. An' what's that Nottingham doctor say?'

'He's going tomorrow to have an examination of her.'

'Is he beguy! That's a tidy penny, I'm thinkin'!'

'Eight guineas.'

'Eight guineas!' The miner spoke breathlessly. 'Well, we mun find it from somewhere.'

'I can pay that,' said Paul.

There was a silence between them for some time.

'She says she hopes you're getting on all right with Minnie,' Paul said.

'Yes, I'm all right, an' I wish as she was,' answered Morel. 'But Minnie's a good little wench, bless 'er heart!' He sat looking dismal.

'I s'll have to be going at half-past three,' said Paul.

'It's a trapse for thee, lad! Eight guineas! An' when dost think she'll be able to get as far as this?'

'We must see what the doctors say tomorrow,' Paul said.

Morel sighed deeply. The house seemed strangely empty, and Paul thought his father looked lost, forlorn, and old.

'You have to go and see her next week, father,' he said.

'I hope she'll be a-whoam by that time,' said Morel.

'If she's not,' said Paul, 'then you must come.'

'I dunno wheer I s'll find th' money,' said Morel.

'And I'll write to you what the doctor says,' said Paul.

'But tha writes i' such a fashion, I canna ma'e it out,' said Morel.

'Well, I'll write plain.'

It was no good asking Morel to answer, for he could scarcely do more than write his own name.

The doctor came. Leonard felt it his duty to meet him with a cab. The examination did not take long. Annie, Arthur, Paul, and Leonard were waiting in the parlour anxiously. The doctors came down. Paul glanced at them. He had never had any hope, except when he had deceived himself.

'It *may* be a tumour; we must wait and see,' said Dr Jameson.

'And if it is,' said Annie, 'can you sweal it away?'

'Probably,' said the doctor.

Paul put eight sovereigns and half a sovereign on the table. The doctor counted them, took a florin out of his purse, and put that down.

'Thank you!' he said. 'I'm sorry Mrs Morel is so ill. But we must see what we can do.'

'There can't be an operation?' said Paul.

The doctor shook his head.

'No,' he said; 'and even if there could, her heart wouldn't stand it.'

'Is her heart risky?' asked Paul.

'Yes; you must be careful with her.'

'Very risky?'

'No – er – no, no! Just take care.'

And the doctor was gone.

Then Paul carried his mother downstairs. She lay simply, like a child. But when he was on the stairs, she put her arms round his neck, clinging.

'I'm so frightened of these beastly stairs,' she said.

And he was frightened, too. He would let Leonard do it another time. He felt he could not carry her.

'He think's it's only a tumour!' cried Annie to her mother. 'And he can sweal it away.'

'I *knew* he could,' protested Mrs Morel scornfully.

She pretended not to notice that Paul had gone out of the room. He sat in the kitchen, smoking. Then he tried to brush some grey ash off his coat. He looked again. It was one of his mother's grey hairs. It was so long! He held it up, and it drifted into the chimney. He let go. The long grey hair floated and was gone in the blackness of the chimney.

The next day he kissed her before going back to work. It was very early in the morning, and they were alone.

'You won't fret, my boy!' she said.

'No, mother.'

'No; it would be silly. And take care of yourself.'

'Yes,' he answered. Then, after a while: 'And I shall come next Saturday, and shall bring my father?'

'I suppose he wants to come,' she replied. 'At any rate, if he does you'll have to let him.'

He kissed her again, and stroked the hair from her temples, gently, tenderly, as if she were a lover.

'Shan't you be late?' she murmured.

'I'm going,' he said, very low.

Still he sat a few minutes, stroking the brown and grey hair from her temples.

'And you won't be any worse, mother?'

'No, my son.'

'You promise me?'

'Yes; I won't be any worse.'

He kissed her, held her in his arms for a moment, and was gone. In the early sunny morning he ran to the station, crying all the way; he did not know what for. And her blue eyes were wide and staring as she thought of him.

In the afternoon he went a walk with Clara. They sat in the little wood where bluebells were standing. He took her hand.

'You'll see,' he said to Clara, 'she'll never be better.'

'Oh, you don't know!' replied the other.

'I do,' he said.

She caught him impulsively to her breast.

'Try and forget it, dear,' she said; 'try and forget it.'

'I will,' he answered.

Her breast was there, warm for him; her hands were in his hair. It was comforting and he held his arms round her. But he did not forget. He only talked to Clara of something else. And it was always so. When she felt it coming, the agony, she cried to him:

'Don't think of it, Paul! Don't think of it, Paul! Don't think of it, my darling!'

And she pressed him to her breast, rocked him, soothed him like a child. So he put the trouble aside for her sake, to take it up again immediately he was alone. All the time, as he went about, he cried mechanically. His mind and hands were busy. He cried, he did not know why. It was his blood weeping. He was just as much alone whether he was with Clara or with the men in the White Horse. Just himself and this pressure inside him, that was all that existed. He read sometimes. He had to keep his mind occupied. And Clara was a way of occupying his mind.

On the Saturday Walter Morel went to Sheffield. He was a forlorn figure, looking rather as if nobody owned him. Paul ran upstairs.

'My father's come,' he said, kissing his mother.

'Has he?' she answered weariedly.

The old collier came rather frightened into the bedroom.

'How dun I find thee, lass?' he said, going forward and kissing her in a hasty, timid fashion.

'Well, I'm middlin',' she replied.

'I see tha art,' he said. He stood looking down on her. Then he wiped his eyes with his handkerchief. Helpless, and as if nobody owned him, he looked.

'Have you gone on all right?' asked the wife, rather wearily, as if it were an effort to talk to him.

'Yis,' he answered. ''Er's a bit behint-hand now and again, as yer might expect.'

'Does she have your dinner ready?' asked Mrs Morel.

'Well, I've 'ad to shout at 'er once' or twice,' he said.

'And you *must* shout at her if she's not ready. She *will* leave things to the last minute.

She gave him a few instructions. He sat looking at her as if she were almost a stranger to him, before whom he was awkward and humble, and also as if he had lost his presence of mind, and wanted to run. This feeling that he wanted to run away, that he was on thorns to be gone from so trying a situation, and yet must linger because it looked better, made his presence so trying. He put up his eyebrows for misery, and clenched his fists on his knees, feeling so awkward in presence of a big trouble.

Mrs Morel did not change much. She stayed in Sheffield for two months. If anything, at the end she was rather worse. But she wanted to go home. Annie had her children. Mrs Morel wanted to go home. So they got a motor-car from Nottingham – for she was too ill to go by train – and she was driven through the sunshine. It was just August; everything was bright and warm. Under the blue sky they could all see she was dying. Yet she was jollier than she had been for weeks. They all laughed and talked.

'Annie,' she exclaimed, 'I saw a lizard dart on that rock!'

Her eyes were so quick; she was still so full of life.

Morel knew she was coming. He had the front-door open. Everybody was on tiptoe. Half the street turned out. They heard the sound of the great motor-car. Mrs Morel, smiling, drove home down the street.

'And just look at them all come out to see me!' she said. 'But there, I suppose I should have done the same. How do you do, Mrs Matthews? How are you, Mrs Harrison?'

They none of them could hear, but they saw her smile and nod. And they all saw death on her face, they said. It was a great event in the street.

Morel wanted to carry her indoors, but he was too old. Arthur took her as if she were a child. They had set her a big, deep chair by the hearth where her rocking-chair used to stand. When she was unwrapped and seated, and had drunk a little brandy, she looked round the room.

'Don't think I didn't like your house, Annie,' she said; 'but it's nice to be in my own home again.'

And Morel answered huskily:

'It is, lass, it is.'

And Minnie, the little quaint maid, said:

'An' we glad t' 'ave yer.'

There was a lovely yellow ravel of sunflowers in the garden. He looked out of the window.

'There are my sunflowers!' she said.

14

THE RELEASE

'By the way,' said Dr Ansell one evening when Morel was in Sheffield, 'we've got a man in the fever hospital here who comes from Nottingham – Dawes. He doesn't seem to have many belongings in this world.'

'Baxter Dawes!' Paul exclaimed.

'That's the man – has been a fine fellow, physically, I should think. Been in a bit of a mess lately. You know him?'

'He used to work at the place where I am.'

'Did he? Do you know anything about him? He's just sulking, or he'd be a lot better than he is by now.'

'I don't know anything of his home circumstances, except that he's separated from his wife and has been a bit down, I believe. But tell him about me, will you? Tell him I'll come and see him.'

The next time Morel saw the doctor he said:

'And what about Dawes?'

'I said to him,' answered the other, '"Do you know a man from Nottingham named Morel?" and he looked at me as if he'd jump at my throat. So I said, "I see you know the name; it's Paul Morel." Then I told him about your saying you would go and see him. "What does he want?" he said, as if you were a policeman.'

'And did he say he would see me?' asked Paul.

'He wouldn't say anything – good, bad, or indifferent,' replied the doctor.

'Why not?'

'That's what I want to know. There he lies and sulks, day in, day out. Can't get a word of information out of him.'

'Do you think I might go?' asked Paul.

'You might.'

There was a feeling of connexion between the rival men, more than ever since they had fought. In a way Morel felt guilty towards the other, and more or less responsible. And being in such a state of soul himself, he felt an almost painful nearness to Dawes, who was suffering and despairing, too. Besides, they had met in a naked extremity of hate, and it was a bond. At any rate, the elemental man in each had met.

He went down to the isolation hospital, with Dr Ansell's card. The sister, a healthy young Irishwoman, led him down the ward.

'A visitor to see you, Jim Crow,' she said.

Dawes turned suddenly over with a startled grunt.

'Eh?'

'Caw!' she mocked. 'He can only say "Caw!" I have brought you a gentleman to see you. Now say "Thank you," and show some manners.'

Dawes looked swiftly with his dark, startled eyes beyond the sister at Paul. His look was full of fear, mistrust, hate, and misery. Morel met the swift, dark eyes, and hesitated. The two men were afraid of the naked selves they had been.

'Dr Ansell told me you were here,' said Morel, holding out his hand.

Dawes mechanically shook hands.

'So I thought I'd come in,' continued Paul.

There was no answer. Dawes lay staring at the opposite wall.

'Say "Caw!"' mocked the nurse. 'Say "Caw!" Jim Crow.'

'He is getting on all right?' said Paul to her.

'Oh yes! He lies and imagines he's going to die,' said the nurse, 'and it frightens every word out of his mouth.'

'And you *must* have somebody to talk to,' laughed Morel.

'That's it!' laughed the nurse. 'Only two old men and a boy who always cries. It *is* hard lines! Here am I dying to hear Jim Crow's voice, and nothing but an odd "Caw!" will he give!'

'So rough on you!' said Morel.

'Isn't it?' said the nurse.

'I suppose I am a godsend,' he laughed.

'Oh, dropped straight from heaven!' laughed the nurse.

Presently she left the two men alone. Dawes was thinner, and handsome again, but life seemed low in him. As the doctor said, he was lying sulking, and would not move forward towards convalescence. He seemed to grudge every beat of his heart.

'Have you had a bad time?' asked Paul.

Suddenly again Dawes looked at him.

'What are you doing in Sheffield?' he asked.

'My mother was taken ill at my sister's in Thurston Street. What are you doing here?'

There was no answer.

'How long have you been in?' Morel asked.

'I couldn't say for sure,' Dawes answered grudgingly.

He lay staring across at the wall opposite, as if trying to believe Morel was not there. Paul felt his heart go hard and angry.

'Dr Ansell told me you were here,' he said coldly.

The other man did not answer.

'Typhoid's pretty bad, I know,' Morel persisted.

Suddenly Dawes said:

'What did you come for?'

'Because Dr Ansell said you didn't know anybody here. Do you?'

'I know nobody nowhere,' said Dawes.

'Well,' said Paul, 'it's because you don't choose to, then.'

There was another silence.

'We s'll be taking my mother home as soon as we can,' said Paul.

'What's a-matter with her?' asked Dawes, with a sick man's interest in illness.

'She's got a cancer.'

There was another silence.

'But we want to get her home,' said Paul. We s'll have to get a motor-car.'

Dawes lay thinking.

'Why don't you ask Thomas Jordan to lend you his?' said Dawes.

'It's not big enough,' Morel answered.

Dawes blinked his dark eyes as he lay thinking.

'Then ask Jack Pilkington; he'd lend it you. You know him.'

'I think I s'll hire one,' said Paul.

'You're a fool if you do,' said Dawes.

The sick man was gaunt and handsome again. Paul was sorry for him because his eyes looked so tired.

'Did you get a job here?' he asked.

'I was only here a day or two before I was taken bad,' Dawes replied.

'You want to get in a convalescent home,' said Paul.

The other's face clouded again.

'I'm goin' in no convalescent home,' he said.

'My father's been in the one at Seathorpe, an' he liked it. Dr Ansell would get you a recommend.'

Dawes lay thinking. It was evident he dared not face the world again.

'The seaside would be all right just now,' Morel said. 'Sun on those sandhills, and the waves not far out.'

The other did not answer.

'By Gad!' Paul concluded, too miserable to bother much; 'it's all right when you know you're going to walk again, and swim!'

Dawes glanced at him quickly. The man's dark eyes were afraid to meet any other eyes in the world. But the real misery and helplessness in Paul's tone gave him a feeling of relief.

'Is she far gone?' he asked.

'She's going like wax,' Paul answered; 'but cheerful – lively!'

He bit his lip. After a minute he rose.

'Well, I'll be going,' he said. 'I'll leave you this half-crown.'

'I don't want it,' Dawes muttered.

Morel did not answer, but left the coin on the table.

'Well,' he said, 'I'll try and run in when I'm back in Sheffield. Happen you might like to see my brother-in-law? He works in Pyecrofts.'

'I don't know him,' said Dawes.

'He's all right. Should I tell him to come? He might bring you some papers to look at.'

The other man did not answer. Paul went. The strong emotion that Dawes aroused in him, repressed, made him shiver.

He did not tell his mother, but next day he spoke to Clara about this interview. It was in the dinner-hour. The two did not often go out together now, but this day he asked her to go with him to the Castle grounds. There they sat while the scarlet geraniums and the yellow calceolarias blazed in the sunlight. She was now always rather protective, and rather resentful towards him.

'Did you know Baxter was in Sheffield hospital with typhoid?' he asked.

She looked at him with startled grey eyes, and her face went pale.

'No,' she said, frightened.

'He's getting better. I went to see him yesterday – the doctor told me.'

Clara seemed stricken by the news.

'Is he very bad?' she asked guiltily.

'He has been. He's mending now.'

'What did he say to you?'

'Oh, nothing! He seems to be sulking.'

There was a distance between the two of them. He gave her more information.

She went about shut up and silent. The next time they took a walk together, she disengaged herself from his arm, and walked at a distance from him. He was wanting her comfort badly.

'Won't you be nice with me?' he asked.

She did not answer.

'What's the matter?' he said, putting his arm across her shoulder.

'Don't!' she said, disengaging herself.

He left her alone, and returned to his own brooding.

'Is it Baxter that upsets you?' he asked at length.

'I *have* been *vile* to him!' she said.

'I've said many a time you haven't treated him well,' he replied.

And there was a hostility between them. Each pursued his own train of thought.

'I've treated him – no, I've treated him badly,' she said. 'And now you treat *me* badly. It serves me right.'

'How do I treat you badly?' he said.

'It serves me right,' she repeated. 'I never considered him worth having, and now you don't consider *me*. But it serves me right. He loved me a thousand times better than you ever did.'

'He didn't!' protested Paul.

'He did! At any rate, he did respect me, and that's what you don't do.'

'It looked as if he respected you!' he said.

'He did! And I *made* him horrid – I know I did! You've taught me that. And he loved me a thousand times better than ever you do.'

'All right,' said Paul.

He only wanted to be left alone now. He had his own trouble, which was almost too much to bear. Clara only tormented him and made him tired. He was not sorry when he left her.

She went on the first opportunity to Sheffield to see her husband. The meeting was not a success. But she left him roses and fruit and money. She wanted to make restitution. It was not that she loved him. As she looked at him lying there her heart did not warm with love. Only she wanted to humble herself to him, to kneel before him. She wanted now to be self-sacrificial. After all, she had failed to make Morel really love her. She was morally frightened. She wanted to do penance. So she kneeled to Dawes, and it gave him a subtle pleasure. But the distance between them was still very great – too great. It frightened the man. It almost pleased the woman. She liked to feel she was serving him across an insuperable distance. She was proud now.

Morel went to see Dawes once or twice. There was a sort of friendship between the two men, who were all the while deadly rivals. But they never mentioned the woman who was between them.

Mrs Morel got gradually worse. At first they used to carry her downstairs, sometimes even into the garden. She sat propped in her chair, smiling, and so pretty. The gold wedding-ring shone on her white hand; her hair was carefully brushed. And she watched the tangled sunflowers dying, the chrysanthemums coming out, and the dahlias.

Paul and she were afraid of each other. He knew, and she knew, that she was dying. But they kept up a pretence of cheerfulness. Every morning, when he got up, he went into her room in his pyjamas.

'Did you sleep, my dear?' he asked.

'Yes,' she answered.

'Not very well?'

'Well, yes!'

Then he knew she had lain awake. He saw her hand under the bedclothes, pressing the place on her side where the pain was.

'Has it been bad?' he asked.

'No. It hurt a bit, but nothing to mention.'

And she sniffed in her old scornful way. As she lay she looked like a girl. And all the while her blue eyes watched him. But there were the dark pain-circles beneath that made him ache again.

'It's a sunny day,' he said.

'It's a beautiful day.'

'Do you think you'll be carried down?'

'I shall see.'

Then he went away to get her breakfast. All day long he was conscious of nothing but her. It was a long ache that made him feverish. Then, when he got home in the early evening, he glanced through the kitchen window. She was not there; she had not got up.

He ran straight upstairs and kissed her. He was almost afraid to ask:

'Didn't you get up, pigeon?'

'No,' she said. 'It was that morphia; it made me tired.'

'I think he gives you too much,' he said.

'I think he does,' she answered.

He sat down by the bed, miserably. She had a way of curling and lying on her side, like a child. The grey and brown hair was loose over her ear.

'Doesn't it tickle you?' he said, gently putting it back.

'It does,' she replied.

His face was near hers. Her blue eyes smiled straight into his, like a girl's – warm, laughing with tender love. It made him pant with terror, agony and love.

'You want your hair doing in a plait,' he said. 'Lie still.'

And going behind her, he carefully loosened her hair, brushed it out. It was like fine long silk of brown and grey. Her head was snuggled between her shoulders. As he lightly brushed and plaited her hair, he bit his lip and felt dazed. It all seemed unreal, he could not understand it.

At night he often worked in her room, looking up from time to time. And so often he found her blue eyes fixed on him. And when their eyes met, she smiled. He worked away again mechanically, producing good stuff without knowing what he was doing.

Sometimes he came in, very pale and still, with watchful, sudden eyes, like a man who is drunk almost to death. They were both afraid of the veils that were ripping between them.

Then she pretended to be better, chattered to him gaily, made a great fuss over some scraps of news. For they had both come to the condition when they had to make much of the trifles, lest they should give in to the big thing, and their human independence would go smash. They were afraid, so they made light of things and were gay.

Sometimes as she lay he knew she was thinking of the past. Her mouth gradually shut hard in a line. She was holding herself rigid, so that she might die without ever uttering the great cry that was tearing from her. He never forgot that hard, utterly lonely and stubborn clenching of her mouth, which persisted for weeks. Sometimes, when it was lighter, she talked about her husband. Now she hated him. She did not forgive him. She could not bear him to be in the room. And a few things, the things that had been most bitter to her, came up again so strongly that they broke from her, and she told her son.

He felt as if his life were being destroyed, piece by piece, within him. Often the tears came suddenly. He ran to the station, the tear-drops falling on the pavement. Often he could not go on with his work. The pen stopped writing. He sat staring, quite unconscious. And when he came round again he felt sick, and trembled in his limbs. He never questioned what it was. His mind did not try to analyse or understand. He merely submitted, and kept his eyes shut; let the thing go over him.

His mother did the same. She thought of the pain, of the morphia, of the next day; hardly ever of the death. That was coming, she knew. She had to submit to it. But she would never entreat it or make friends with it. Blind, with her face shut hard and blind, she was pushed towards the door. The days passed, the weeks, the months.

Sometimes, in the sunny afternoons, she seemed almost happy.

'I try to think of the nice times – when we went to Mablethorpe, and Robin Hood's Bay, and Shanklin,' she said. 'After all, not everybody has seen those beautiful places. And wasn't it beautiful! I try to think of that, not of the other things.'

Then, again, for a whole evening she spoke not a word; neither did he. They were together, rigid, stubborn, silent. He went into his room at last to go to bed, and leaned against the doorway as if paralysed, unable to go any farther. His consciousness went. A furious storm, he knew not what, seemed to ravage inside him. He stood leaning there, submitting, never questioning.

In the morning they were both normal again, though her face was grey with the morphia, and her body felt like ash. But they were bright again, nevertheless. Often, especially if Annie or Arthur were at home, he neglected her. He did not see much of Clara. Usually he was with men. He was quick and active and lively; but when his friends saw him go white to the gills, his eyes dark and glittering, they had a certain mistrust of him. Sometimes he went to Clara, but she was almost cold to him.

'Take me!' he said simply.

Occasionally she would. But she was afraid. When he had her then, there was something in it that made her shrink away from him – something unnatural. She grew to dread him. He was so quiet, yet so strange. She was afraid of the man who was not there with her, whom she could feel behind this make-belief lover; somebody sinister, that filled her with horror. She began to have a kind of horror of him. It was almost as if he were a criminal. He wanted her – he had her – and it made her feel as if death itself had her in its grip. She lay in horror. There was no man there loving her. She almost hated him. Then came little bouts of tenderness. But she dared not pity him.

Dawes had come to Colonel Seely's Home near Nottingham. There Paul visited him sometimes, Clara very occasionally. Between the two men the friendship had developed peculiarly. Dawes, who mended very slowly and seemed very feeble, seemed to leave himself in the hands of Morel.

In the beginning of November Clara reminded Paul that it was her birthday.

'I'd nearly forgotten,' he said.

'I thought quite,' she replied.

'No. Shall we go to the seaside for the week-end?'

They went. It was cold and rather dismal. She waited for him to be warm and tender with her, instead of which he seemed hardly aware of her. He sat in the railway-carriage, looking out, and was startled when she spoke to him. He was not definitely thinking. Things seemed as if they did not exist. She went across to him.

'What is it, dear?' she asked.

'Nothing!' he said. 'Don't those windmill sails look monotonous?'

He sat holding her hand. He could not talk nor think. It was a comfort, however, to sit holding her hand. She was dissatisfied and miserable. He was not with her; she was nothing.

And in the evening they sat among the sandhills, looking at the black, heavy sea.

'She will never give in,' he said quietly.

Clara's heart sank.

'No,' she replied.

'There are different ways of dying. My father's people are frightened, and have to be hauled out of life into death like cattle into a slaughter-house, pulled by the neck; but my mother's people are pushed from behind, inch by inch. They are stubborn people, and won't die.'

'Yes,' said Clara.

'And she won't die. She can't. Mr Renshaw, the parson, was in the other day. "Think!" he said to her; "you will have your mother and father, and your sisters, and your son, in the Other Land." And she said: "I have done without them for a long time, and *can* do without them now. It is the living I want, not the dead." She wants to live even now.'

'Oh, how horrible!' said Clara, too frightened to speak.

'And she looks at me, and she wants to say with me,' he went on monotonously. 'She's got such a will, it seems as if she would never go – never!'

'Don't think of it!' cried Clara.

'And she looks at me, and she wants to stay with me,' he went on won't give in. And do you know, I said to her on Thursday, "Mother, if I had to die, I'd die. I'd *will* to die." And she said to me, sharp: "Do you think I haven't? Do you think you can die when you like?"'

His voice ceased. He did not cry, only went on speaking monotonously. Clara wanted to run. She looked round. There was the black, re-echoing shore, the dark sky down on her. She got up terrified. She wanted to be where there was light, where there were other people. She wanted to be away from him. He sat with his head dropped, not moving a muscle.

'And I don't want her to eat,' he said, 'and she knows it. When I ask her, "Shall you have anything?" she's almost afraid to say "Yes." "I'll have a cup of

Benger's," she says. "It'll only keep your strength up," I said to her. "Yes" – and she almost cried –"but there's such a gnawing when I eat nothing. I can't bear it." So I went and made her the food. It's the cancer that gnaws like that at her. I wish she'd die.'

'Come!' said Clara roughly. 'I'm going.'

He followed her down the darkness of the sands. He did not come to her. He seemed scarcely aware of her existence. And she was afraid of him, and disliked him.

In the same acute daze they went back to Nottingham. He was always busy, always doing something, always going from one to the other of his friends.

On the Monday he went to see Baxter Dawes. Listless and pale, the man rose to greet the other, clinging to his chair as he held out his hand.

'You shouldn't get up,' said Paul.

Dawes sat down heavily, eyeing Morel with a sort of suspicion.

'Don't you waste your time on me,' he said, 'if you've owt better to do.'

'I wanted to come,' said Paul. 'Here! I brought you some sweets.'

The invalid put them aside.

'It's not been much of a week-end,' said Morel.

'How's your mother?' asked the other.

'Hardly any different.'

'I thought she was perhaps worse, being as you didn't come on Sunday.'

'I was at Skegness,' said Paul. 'I wanted a change.'

The other looked at him with dark eyes. He seemed to be waiting, not quite daring to ask, trusting to be told.

'I went with Clara,' said Paul.

'I knew as much,' said Dawes quietly.

'It was an old promise,' said Paul.

'You have it your own way,' said Dawes.

This was the first time Clara had been definitely mentioned between them.

'Nay,' said Morel slowly; 'she's tired of me.'

Again Dawes looked at him.

'Since August she's been getting tired of me,' Morel repeated.

The two men were very quiet together. Paul suggested a game of draughts. They played in silence.

'I s'll go abroad when my mother's dead,' said Paul.

'Abroad!' repeated Dawes.

'Yes; I don't care what I do.'

They continued the game. Dawes was winning.

'I s'll have to begin a new start of some sort,' said Paul; 'and you as well, I suppose.'

He took one of Dawes's pieces.

'I dunno where,' said the other.

'Things have to happen,' Morel said. 'It's no good doing anything – at least – no, I don't know. Give me some toffee.'

The two men ate sweets, and began another game of draughts.

'What made that scar on your mouth?' asked Dawes.

Paul put his hand hastily to his lips, and looked over the garden.

'I had a bicycle accident,' he said.

Dawes's hand trembled as he moved the piece.

'You shouldn't ha' laughed at me,' he said very low.

'When?'

'That night on Woodborough Road, when you and her passed me – you with your hand on her shoulder.'

'I never laughed at you,' said Paul.

Dawes kept his fingers on the draught-piece.

'I never knew you were there till the very second when you passed,' said Morel.

'It was that as did me,' he said, very low.

Paul took another sweet.

'I never laughed,' he said, 'except as I'm always laughing.'

They finished the game.

That night Morel walked home from Nottingham, in order to have something to do. The furnaces flared in a red blotch over Bulwell; the black clouds were like a low ceiling. As he went along the ten miles of highroad, he felt as if he were walking out of life, between the black levels of the sky and the earth. But at the end was only the sick-room. If he walked and walked for ever, there was not only that place to come to.

He was not tired when he got near home, or he did not know it. Across the field he could see the red firelight leaping in her bedroom window.

'When she's dead,' he said to himself, 'that fire will go out.'

He took off his boots quietly and crept upstairs. His mother's door was wide open, because she slept alone still. The red firelight dashed its glow on the landing. Soft as a shadow, he peeped in her doorway.

'Paul!' she murmured.

His heart seemed to break again. He went in and sat by the bed.

'How late you are!' she murmured.

'Not very,' he said.

'Why, what time is it?' The murmur came plaintive and helpless.

'It's only just gone eleven.'

That was not true; it was nearly one o'clock.

'Oh!' she said; 'I thought it was later.'

And he knew the unutterable misery of her nights that would not go.

'Can't you sleep, my pigeon?' he said.

'No, I can't,' she wailed.

'Never mind, Little!' he said, crooning. 'Never mind, my love. I'll stop with you half an hour, my pigeon; then perhaps it will be better.'

And he sat by the bedside, slowly, rhythmically stroking her brows with his finger-tips, stroking her eyes shut, soothing her, holding her fingers in his free hand. They could hear the sleepers' breathing in the other rooms.

'Now go to bed,' she murmured, lying quite still under his fingers and his love.

'Will you sleep?' he asked.

'Yes, I think so.'

'You feel better, my Little, don't you?'

'Yes,' she said, like a fretful, half-soothed child.

Still the days and the weeks went by. He hardly ever went to see Clara now. But he wandered restlessly from one person to another for some help, and there was none anywhere. Miriam had written to him tenderly. He went to see her. Her heart was very sore when she saw him, white, gaunt, with his eyes dark and bewildered. Her pity came up, hurting her till she could not bear it.

'How is she?' she asked.

'The same – the same!' he said. 'The doctors says she can't last, but I know she will. She'll be here at Christmas.'

Miriam shuddered. She drew him to her; she pressed him to her bosom; she kissed him and kissed him. He submitted, but it was torture. She could not kiss his agony. That remained alone and apart. She kissed his face, and roused his blood, while his soul was apart, writhing with the agony of death. And she kissed him and fingered his body, till at last, feeling he would go mad, he got away from her. It was not that he wanted just then – not that. And she thought she had soothed him and done him good.

December came, and some snow. He stayed at home all the while now. They could not afford a nurse. Annie came to look after her mother; the parish nurse, whom they loved, came in morning and evening. Paul shared the nursing with Annie. Often, in the evenings, when friends were in the kitchen with them, they all laughed together and shook with laughter. It was reaction. Paul was so comical. Annie was so quaint. The whole party laughed till they cried, trying to subdue the sound. And Mrs Morel, lying alone in the darkness heard them, and among her bitterness was a feeling of relief.

Then Paul would go upstairs gingerly, guiltily, to see if she had heard.

'Shall I give you some milk?' he asked.

'A little,' she replied plaintively.

And he would put some water with it, so that it should not nourish her. Yet he loved her more than his own life.

She had morphia every night, and her heart got fitful. Annie slept beside her. Paul would go in in the early morning, when his sister got up. His mother was wasted and almost ashen in the morning with the morphia. Darker and darker grew her eyes, all pupil, with the torture. In the mornings the weariness and ache was too much to bear. Yet she could not – would not – weep, or even complain much.

'You slept a bit later this morning, little one,' he would say to her.

'Did I?' she answered, with fretful weariness.

'Yes; it's nearly eight o'clock.'

He stood looking out of the window. The whole country was bleak and pallid under the snow. Then he felt her pulse. There was a strong stroke and a weak one, like a sound and its echo. That was supposed to betoken the end. She let him feel her wrist, knowing what he wanted.

Sometimes they looked in each other's eyes. Then they almost seemed to make an agreement. It was almost as if he were agreeing to die also. But she did not consent to die; she would not. Her body was wasted to a fragment of ash. Her eyes were dark and full of torture.

'Can't you give her something to put an end to it?' he asked the doctor at last.

But the doctor shook his head.

'She can't last many days now, Mr Morel,' he said.

Paul went indoors.

'I can't bear it much longer; we shall all go mad,' said Annie.

The two sat down to breakfast.

'Go and sit with her while we have breakfast, Minnie,' said Annie. But the girl was frightened.

Paul went through the country, through the woods, over the snow. He saw the marks of rabbits and birds in the white snow. He wandered miles and miles. A smoky red sunset came on slowly, painfully, lingering. He thought she would die that day. There was a donkey that came up to him over the snow by the wood's edge, and put its head against him, and walked with him alongside. He put his arms round the donkey's neck, and stroked his cheeks against his ears.

His mother, silent, was still alive, with her hard mouth gripped grimly, her eyes of dark torture only living.

It was nearing Christmas; there was more snow. Annie and he felt as if they could go on no more. Still her dark eyes were alive. Morel, silent and frightened, obliterated himself. Sometimes he would go into the sick-room and look at her. Then he backed out, bewildered.

She kept her hold on life still. The miners had been out on strike, and returned a fortnight or so before Christmas. Minnie went upstairs with the feeding-cup. It was two days after the men had been in.

'Have the men been saying their hands are sore, Minnie?' she asked, in the faint, querulous voice that would not give in. Minnie stood surprised.

'Not as I know of, Mrs Morel,' she answered.

'But I'll bet they are sore,' said the dying woman, as she moved her head with a sigh of weariness. 'But, at any rate, there'll be something to buy in with this week.'

Not a thing did she let slip.

'Your father's pit things will want well airing, Annie,' she said, when the men were going back to work.

'Don't you bother about that, my dear,' said Annie.

One night Annie and Paul were alone. Nurse was upstairs.

'She'll live over Christmas,' said Annie. They were both full of horror.

'She won't,' he replied grimly. 'I s'll give her morphia.'

'Which?' said Annie.

'All that came from Sheffield,' said Paul.

'Ay – do!' said Annie.

The next day he was painting in the bedroom. She seemed to be asleep. He stepped softly backwards and forwards at his painting. Suddenly her small voice wailed:

'Don't walk about, Paul.'

He looked round. Her eyes, like dark bubbles in her face, were looking at him.

'No, my dear,' he said gently. Another fibre seemed to snap in his heart.

That evening he got all the morphia pills there were, and took them downstairs. Carefully he crushed them to powder.

'What are you doing?' said Annie.

'I s'll put 'em in her night milk.'

Then they both laughed together like two conspiring children. On top of all their horror flickered this little sanity.

Nurse did not come that night to settle Mrs Morel down. Paul went up with the hot milk in a feeding-cup. It was nine o'clock.

She was reared up in bed, and he put the feeding-cup between her lips that he would have died to save from any hurt. She took a sip, then put the spout of the cup away and looked at him with her dark, wondering eyes. He looked at her.

'Oh, it *is* bitter, Paul!' she said, making a little grimace.

'It's a new sleeping draught the doctor gave me for you,' he said. 'He thought it wouldn't leave you in such a state in the morning.'

'And I hope it won't,' she said, like a child.

She drank some more of the milk.

'But it *is* horrid!' she said.

He saw her frail fingers over the cup, her lips making a little move.

'I know – I tasted it,' he said. 'But I'll give you some clean milk afterwards.'

'I think so,' she said, and she went on with the draught. She was obedient to him like a child. He wondered if she knew. He saw her poor wasted throat moving as she drank with difficulty. Then he ran downstairs for more milk. There were no grains in the bottom of the cup.

'Has she had it?' whispered Annie.

'Yes – and she said it was bitter.'

'Oh!' laughed Annie, putting her under lip between her teeth.

'And I told her it was a new draught. Where's that milk?'

They both went upstairs.

'I wonder why nurse didn't come to settle me down?' complained the mother, like a child, wistfully.

'She said she was going to a concert, my love,' replied Annie.

'Did she?'

They were silent a minute. Mrs Morel gulped the little clean milk.

'Annie, that draught *was* horrid!' she said plaintively.

'Was it, my love? Well, never mind.'

The mother sighed again with weariness. Her pulse was very irregular.

'Let *us* settle you down,' said Annie. 'Perhaps nurse will be so late.'

'Ay,' said the mother – 'try.'

They turned the clothes back. Paul saw his mother like a girl curled up in her flannel nightdress. Quickly they made one half of the bed, moved her, made the other, straightened her nightgown over her small feet, and covered her up.

'There,' said Paul, stroking her softly. 'There! – now you'll sleep.'

'Yes,' she said. 'I didn't think you could do the bed so nicely,' she added, almost gaily. Then she curled up, with her cheek on her hand, her head snugged between her shoulders. Paul put the long thin plait of grey hair over her shoulder and kissed her.

'You'll sleep, my love,' he said.

'Yes,' she answered trustfully. 'Good night.'

They put out the light, and it was still.

Morel was in bed. Nurse did not come. Annie and Paul came to look at her about eleven. She seemed to be sleeping as usual after her draught. Her mouth had come a bit open.

'Shall we sit up?' said Paul.

'I s'll lie with her as I always do,' said Annie. 'She might wake up.'

'All right. And call me if you see any difference.'

'Yes.'

They lingered before the bedroom fire, feeling the night big and black and snowy outside, their two selves alone in the world. At last he went into the next room and went to bed.

He slept almost immediately, but kept waking every now and again. Then he went sound asleep. He started awake at Annie's whispered, 'Paul, Paul!' He saw his sister in her white nightdress, with her long plait of hair down her back, standing in the darkness.

'Yes?' he whispered, sitting up.

'Come and look at her.'

He slipped out of bed. A bud of gas was burning in the sick chamber. His mother lay with her cheek on her hand, curled up as she had gone to sleep. But her mouth had fallen open, and she breathed with great hoarse breaths, like snoring, and there were long intervals between.

'She's going!' he whispered.

'Yes,' said Annie.

'How long has she been like it?'

'I only just woke up.'

Annie huddled into the dressing-gown, Paul wrapped himself in a brown blanket. It was three o'clock. He mended the fire. Then the two sat waiting. The great, snoring breath was taken – held awhile – then given back. There was a space – a long space. Then they started. The great, snoring breath was taken again. He bent close down and looked at her.

'Isn't it awful!' whispered Annie.

He nodded. They sat down again helplessly. Again came the great, snoring breath. Again they hung suspended. Again it was given back, long and harsh. The sound, so irregular, at such wide intervals, sounded through the house. Morel, in his room, slept on. Paul and Annie sat crouched, huddled, motionless. The great, snoring sound began again – there was a painful pause while the breath was held – back came the rasping breath. Minute after minute passed. Paul looked at her again, bending low over her.

'She may last like this,' he said.

They were both silent. He looked out of the window, and could faintly discern the snow on the garden.

'You go to my bed,' he said to Annie. 'I'll sit up.'

'No,' she said, 'I'll stop with you.'

'I'd rather you didn't,' he said.

At last Annie crept out of the room, and he was alone. He hugged himself in his brown blanket, crouched in front of his mother, watching. She looked dreadful, with the bottom jaw fallen back. He watched. Sometimes he thought the great breath would never begin again. He could not bear it – the waiting. Then suddenly, startling him, came the great harsh sound. He mended the fire again, noiselessly. She must not be disturbed. The minutes went by. The night was going, breath by breath. Each time the sound came he felt it wring him, till at last he could not feel so much.

His father got up. Paul heard the miner drawing his stocking on, yawning. Then Morel, in shirt and stockings, entered.

'Hush!' said Paul.

Morel stood watching. Then he looked at his son, helplessly, and in horror.

'Had I better stop a-whoam?' he whispered.

'No. Go to work. She'll last through tomorrow.'

'I don't think so.'

'Yes. Go to work.'

The miner looked at her again, in fear, and went obediently out of the room. Paul saw the tape of his garters swinging against his legs.

After another half-hour Paul went downstairs and drank a cup of tea, then returned. Morel, dressed for the pit, came upstairs again.

'Am I to go?' he said.

'Yes.'

And in a few minutes Paul heard his father's heavy steps go thudding over the deadening snow. Miners called in the street as they tramped in gangs to work. The terrible, long-drawn breaths continued – heave – heave – heave; then a long pause – then ah – ah-h-h-h-h! as it came back. Far away over the snow sounded the hooters of the ironworks. One after another they crowed and boomed, some small and far away, some near, the blowers of the collieries and the other works. Then there was silence. He mended the fire. The great breaths broke the silence – she looked just the same. He put back the blind and peered out. Still it was dark. Perhaps there was a lighter tinge. Perhaps the snow was bluer. He drew up the blind and got dressed. Then, shuddering, he drank brandy from the bottle on the washstand: The snow *was* growing blue. He heard a cart clanking down the street. Yes, it was seven o'clock and it was coming a little bit light. He heard some people calling. The world was waking. A grey, deathly dawn crept over the snow. Yes, he could see the houses. He put out the gas. It seemed very dark. The breathing came still, but he was almost used to it. He could see her. She was just the same. He wondered if he piled heavy clothes on top of her it would make it heavier and the horrible breathing would stop. He looked at her. That was not her – not her a bit. If he piled the blanket and heavy coats on her –

Suddenly the door opened, and Annie entered. She looked at him questioningly.

'Just the same,' he said calmly.

They whispered together a minute, then he went downstairs to get breakfast. It was twenty to eight. Soon Annie came down.

'Isn't it awful! Doesn't she look awful!' she whispered, dazed with horror.

He nodded.

'If she looks like that!' said Annie.

'Drink some tea,' he said.

They went upstairs again. Soon the neighbours came with their frightened question:

'How is she?'

It went on just the same. She lay with her cheek in her hand, her mouth fallen open, and the great, ghastly snores came and went.

At ten o'clock nurse came. She looked strange and woebegone.

'Nurse,' cried Paul, 'she'll last like this for days?'

'She can't, Mr Morel,' said nurse. 'She can't.'

There was a silence.

'Isn't it dreadful!' wailed the nurse. 'Who would have thought she could stand it? Go down now, Mr Morel, go down.'

At last, at about eleven o'clock, he went downstairs and sat in the neighbour's house. Annie was downstairs also. Nurse and Arthur were upstairs. Paul sat with his head in his hands. Suddenly Annie came flying across the yard crying, half mad:

'Paul – Paul – she's gone!'

In a second he was back in his own house and upstairs. She lay curled up and still, with her face on her hand, and nurse was wiping her mouth. They all stood back. He kneeled down, and put his face to hers and his arms round her:

'My love – my love – oh, my love!' he whispered again and again. 'My love – oh, my love!'

Then he heard the nurse behind him, crying, saying:

'She's better, Mr Morel, she's better.'

When he took his face up from his warm, dead mother he went straight downstairs and began blacking his boots.

There was a good deal to do, letters to write, and so on. The doctor came and glanced at her, and sighed.

'Ay – poor thing!' he said, then turned away. 'Well, call at the surgery about six for the certificate.'

The father came home from work at about four o'clock. He dragged silently into the house and sat down. Minnie bustled to give him his dinner. Tired, he laid his black arms on the table. There were swede turnips for his dinner, which he liked. Paul wondered if he knew. It was some time, and nobody had spoken. At last the son said:

'You noticed the blinds were down?'

Morel looked up.

'No,' he said. 'Why – has she gone?'

'Yes.'

'When wor that?'

'About twelve this morning.'

'H'm!'

The miner sat still for a moment, then began his dinner. It was as if nothing had happened. He ate his turnips in silence. Afterwards he washed and went upstairs to dress. The door of her room was shut.

'Have you seen her?' Annie asked of him when he came down.

'No,' he said.

In a little while he went out. Annie went away, and Paul called on the undertaker, the clergyman, the doctor, the registrar. It was a long business. He got back at nearly eight o'clock. The undertaker was coming soon to measure for the coffin. The house was empty except for her. He took a candle and went upstairs.

The room was cold, that had been warm for so long. Flowers, bottles, plates, all sick-room litter was taken away; everything was harsh and austere. She lay raised on the bed, the sweep of the sheet from the raised feet was like a clean curve of snow, so silent. She lay like a maiden asleep. With his candle in his hand, he bent over her. She lay like a girl asleep and dreaming of her love. The mouth was a little open, as if wondering from the suffering, but her face was young, her brow clear and white as if life had never touched it. He looked again at the eyebrows, at the small, winsome nose a bit on one side. She was young again. Only the hair as it arched so beautifully from her temples was mixed with silver, and the two simple plaits that lay on her shoulders were filigree of silver and brown. She would wake up. She would lift her eyelids. She was with him still. He bent and kissed her passionately. But there was coldness against his mouth. He bit his lip with horror. Looking at her, he felt he could never, never let her go. No! He stroked the hair from her temples. That, too, was cold. He saw the mouth so dumb and wondering at the hurt. Then he crouched on the floor, whispering to her:

'Mother, mother!'

He was still with her when the undertakers came, young men who had been to school with him. They touched her reverently, and in a quiet, businesslike fashion. They did not look at her. He watched jealously. He and Annie guarded her fiercely. They would not let anybody come to see her, and the neighbours were offended.

After a while Paul went out of the house, and played cards at a friend's. It was midnight when he got back. His father rose from the couch as he entered, saying in a plaintive way:

'I though tha wor niver comin', lad.'

'I didn't think you'd sit up,' said Paul.

His father looked so forlorn. Morel had been a man without fear – simply nothing frightened him. Paul realized with a start that he had been afraid to go to bed, alone in the house with his dead. He was sorry.

'I forgot you'd be alone, father,' he said.

'Dost want owt to eat?' asked Morel.

'No.'

'Sithee – I made thee a drop o' hot milk. Get it down thee; it's cold enough for owt.'

Paul drank it.

'I must go to Nottingham tomorrow,' he said.

After a while Morel went to bed. He hurried past the closed door, and left his own door open. Soon the son came upstairs also. He went in to kiss her good night, as usual. It was cold and dark. He wished they had kept her fire burning. Still she dreamed her young dream. But she would be cold.

'My dear!' he whispered. 'My dear!'

And he did not kiss her, for fear she should be cold and strange to him. It eased him she slept so beautifully. He shut the door softly, not to wake her, and went to bed.

In the morning Morel summoned his courage, hearing Annie downstairs and Paul coughing in his room across the landing. He opened her door, and went into the darkened room. He saw the white uplifted form in the twilight, but her he dared not see. Bewildered, too frightened to possess any of his faculties, he got out of the room again and left her. He never looked at her again. He had not seen her for months, because he had not dared to look. And she looked like his young wife again.

'Have you seen her?' Annie asked of him sharply after breakfast.

'Yes,' he said.

'And don't you think she looks nice?'

'Yes.'

He went out of the house soon after. And all the time he seemed to be creeping aside to avoid it.

Paul went about from place to place, doing the business of the death. He met Clara in Nottingham, and they had tea together in a café, when they were quite jolly again. She was infinitely relieved to find he did not take it tragically.

Later, when the relatives began to come for the funeral, the affair became public, and the children became social beings. They put themselves aside. They buried her in a furious storm of rain and wind. The wet clay glistened, all the white flowers were soaked. Annie gripped his arms and leaned forward. Down below she saw a dark corner of William's coffin. The oak box sank steadily. She was gone. The rain poured in the grave. The procession of black, with its umbrellas glistening, turned away. The cemetery was deserted under the drenching cold rain.

Paul went home and busied himself supplying the guests with drinks. His father sat in the kitchen with Mrs Morel's relatives, 'superior' people, and wept, and said what a good lass she'd been, and how he'd tried to do everything he could for her – everything. He had striven all his life to do what he could for her, and he'd nothing to reproach himself with. She was gone, but he'd done his best for her. He wiped his eyes with his white handkerchief. He'd nothing to reproach himself for, he repeated. All his life he'd done his best for her.

And that was how he tried to dismiss her. He never thought of her personally. Everything deep in him he denied. Paul hated his father for sitting sentimentalizing over her. He knew he would do it in the public-houses. For the real tragedy went on in Morel in spite of himself. Sometimes, later, he came down from his afternoon sleep, white and cowering.

'I *have* been dreaming of thy mother,' he said in a small voice.

'Have you, father? When I dream of her it's always just as she was when she was well. I dream of her often, but it seems quite nice and natural, as if nothing had altered.'

But Morel crouched in front of the fire in terror.

The weeks passed half real, not much pain, not much of anything, perhaps a little relief, mostly a *nuit blanche*. Paul went restlessly from place to place. For some months, since his mother had been worse, he had not made love to Clara. She was, as it were, dumb to him, rather distant. Dawes saw her very occasionally, but the two could not get an inch across the great distance between them. The three of them were drifting forward.

Dawes mended very slowly. He was in the convalescent home at Skegness at Christmas, nearly well again. Paul went to the seaside for a few days. His father was with Annie in Sheffield. Dawes came to Paul's lodgings. His time in the home was up. The two men, between whom was such a big reserve, seemed faithful to each other. Dawes depended on Morel now. He knew Paul and Clara had practically separated.

Two days after Christmas Paul was to go back to Nottingham. The evening before he sat with Dawes smoking before the fire.

'You know Clara's coming down for the day tomorrow?' he said.

The other man glanced at him.

'Yes, you told me,' he replied.

Paul drank the remainder of his glass of whisky.

'I told the landlady your wife was coming,' he said.

'Did you?' said Dawes, shrinking, but almost leaving himself in the other's hands. He got up rather stiffly, and reached for Morel's glass.

'Let me fill you up,' he said.

Paul jumped up.

'You sit still,' he said.

But Dawes, with rather shaky hand, continued to mix the drink. 'Say when,' he said.

'Thanks!' replied the other. 'But you've no business to get up.'

'It does me good, lad,' replied Dawes. 'I began to think I'm right again, then.'

'You are about right, you know.'

'I am, certainly I am,' said Dawes, nodding to him.

'And Len says he can get you on in Sheffield.'

Dawes glanced at him again, with dark eyes that agreed with everything the other would say, perhaps a trifle dominated by him.

'It's funny,' said Paul, 'starting again. I feel in a lot bigger mess than you.'

'In what way, lad?'

'I don't know. I don't know. It's as if I was in a tangled sort of hole, rather dark and dreary, and no road anywhere.'

'I know – I understand it,' Dawes said, nodding. But you'll find it'll come all right.'

He spoke caressingly.

'I suppose so,' said Paul.

Dawes knocked his pipe in a hopeless fashion.

'You've not done for yourself like I have,' he said.

Morel saw the wrist and the white hand of the other man gripping the stem of the pipe and knocking out the ash, as if he had given up.

'How old are you?' Paul asked.

'Thirty-nine,' replied Dawes, glancing at him.

Those brown eyes, full of the consciousness of failure, almost pleading for reassurance, for someone to re-establish the man in himself, to warm him, to set him up firm again, troubled Paul.

'You'll just be in your prime,' said Morel. 'You don't look as if much life had gone out of you.'

The brown eyes of the other flashed suddenly.

'It hasn't,' he said. 'The go is there.'

Paul looked up and laughed.

'We've both got plenty of life in us yet to make things fly,' he said.

The eyes of the two men met. They exchanged one look. Having recognized the stress of passion each in the other, they both drank their whisky.

'Yes, begod!' said Dawes, breathless.

There was a pause.

'And I don't see,' said Paul, 'why you shouldn't go on where you left off.'

'What –' said Dawes, suggestively.

'Yes – fit your old home together again.'

Dawes hid his face, and shook his head.

'Couldn't be done,' he said, and he looked up with an ironic smile.

'Why? Because you don't want?'

'Perhaps.'

They smoked in silence. Dawes showed his teeth as he bit his pipe stem.

'You mean you don't want her?' asked Paul.

Dawes stared up at the picture with a caustic expression on his face.

'I hardly know,' he said.

The smoke floated softly up.

'I believe she wants you,' said Paul.

'Do you?' replied the other, soft, satirical, abstract.

'Yes. She never really hitched on to me – you were always there in the background. That's why she wouldn't get a divorce.'

Dawes continued to stare in a satirical fashion at the picture over the mantelpiece.

'That's how women are with me,' said Paul. 'They want me like mad, but they don't want to belong to me. And she *belonged* to you all the time. I knew.'

The triumphant male came up in Dawes. He showed his teeth more distinctly.

'Perhaps I was a fool,' he said.

'You were a big fool,' said Morel.

'But perhaps even *then* you were a bigger fool,' said Dawes. There was a touch of triumph and malice in it.

'Do you think so?' said Paul.

They were silent for some time.

'At any rate, I'm clearing out tomorrow,' said Morel.

'I see,' answered Dawes.

Then they did not talk any more. The instinct to murder each other had returned. They almost avoided each other.

They shared the same bedroom. When they retired Dawes seemed abstract, thinking of something. He sat on the side of the bed in his shirt, looking at his legs.

'Aren't you getting cold?' asked Morel.

'I was lookin' at these legs,' replied the other.

'What's up with 'em? They look all right,' replied Paul, from his bed.

'They look all right. But there's some water in 'em yet.'

'And what about it?'

'Come and look.'

Paul reluctantly got out of bed and went to look at the rather handsome legs of the other man that were covered with glistening, dark gold hair.

'Look here,' said Dawes, pointing to his shin. 'Look at the water under here.'

'Where?' said Paul.

The man pressed his finger-tips. They left little dents that filled up slowly.

'It's nothing,' said Paul.

'You feel,' said Dawes.

Paul tried with his fingers. It made little dents.

'H'm!' he said.

'Rotten, isn't it?' said Dawes.

'Why? It's nothing much.'

'You're not much of a man with water in your legs.'

'I can't see as it makes any difference,' said Morel. 'I've got a weak chest.' He returned to his own bed.

'I suppose the rest of me's all right,' said Dawes, and he put out the light.

In the morning it was raining. Morel packed his bag. The sea was grey and shaggy and dismal. He seemed to be cutting himself off from life more and more. It gave him a wicked pleasure to do it.

The two men were at the station. Clara stepped out of the train, and came along the platform, very erect and coldly composed. She wore a long coat and a tweed hat. Both men hated her for her composure. Paul shook hands with her at the barrier. Dawes was leaning against the bookstall, watching. His black overcoat was buttoned up to the chin because of the rain. He was pale, with almost a touch of nobility in his quietness. He came forward, limping slightly.

'You ought to look better than this,' she said.

'Oh, I'm all right now.'

The three stood at a loss. She kept the two men hesitating near her.

'Shall we go to the lodging straight off,' said Paul, 'or somewhere else?'

'We may as well go home,' said Dawes.

Paul walked on the outside of the pavement, then Dawes, then Clara. They made polite conversation. The sitting-room faced the sea, whose tide, grey and shaggy, hissed not far off.

Morel swung up the big arm-chair.

'Sit down, Jack,' he said.

'I don't want the chair,' said Dawes.

'Sit down!' Morel repeated.

Clara took off her things and laid them on the couch. She had a slight air of resentment. Lifting her hair with her fingers, she sat down, rather aloof and composed. Paul ran downstairs to speak to the landlady.

'I should think you're cold,' said Dawes to his wife. 'Come nearer to the fire.'

'Thank you, I'm quite warm,' she answered.

She looked out of the window at the rain and at the sea.

'When are you going back?' she asked.

'Well, the rooms are taken until tomorrow, so he wants me to stop. He's going back tonight.'

'And then you're thinking of going to Sheffield?'

'Yes.'

'Are you fit to start work?'

'I'm going to start.'

'You've really got a place?'

'Yes – begin on Monday.'

'You don't look fit.'

'Why don't I?'

She looked again out of the window instead of answering.

'And have you got lodgings in Sheffield?'

'Yes.'

Again she looked away out of the window. The panes were blurred with streaming rain.

'And can you manage all right?' she asked.

'I s'd think so. I s'll have to!'

They were silent when Morel returned.

'I shall go by the four-twenty,' he said as he entered.

Nobody answered.

'I wish you'd take your boots off,' he said to Clara. 'There's a pair of slippers of mine.'

'Thank you,' she said. 'They aren't wet.'

He put the slippers near her feet. She left them there.

Morel sat down. Both the men seemed helpless, and each of them had a rather hunted look. But Dawes now carried himself quietly, seemed to yield himself, while Paul seemed to screw himself up. Clara thought she had never seen him look so small and mean. He was as if trying to get himself into the smallest possible compass. And as he went about arranging, and as he sat talking, there seemed something false about him and out of tune. Watching him unknown, she said to herself there was no stability about him. He was fine in his way, passionate, and able to give her drinks of pure life when he was in one mood. And now he looked paltry and insignificant. There was nothing stable about him. Her husband had more manly dignity. At any rate *he* did not waft about with any wind. There was something evanescent about Morel, she thought, something shifting and false. He would never make sure ground for any woman to stand on. She despised him rather for his shrinking together, getting smaller. Her husband at least was manly, and when he was beaten gave in. But this other would never own to being beaten. He would shift round and round, prowl, get smaller. She despised him. And yet she watched him rather than Dawes, and it seemed as if their three fates lay in his hands. She hated him for it.

She seemed to understand better now about men, and what they could or would do. She was less afraid of them, more sure of herself. That they were not the small egoists she had imagined them made her more comfortable. She had learned a good deal – almost as much as she wanted to learn. Her cup had been full. It was still as full as she could carry. On the whole, she would not be sorry when he was gone.

They had dinner, and sat eating nuts and drinking by the fire. Not a serious word had been spoken. Yet Clara realized that Morel was withdrawing from the circle, leaving her the option to stay with her husband. It angered her. He was a mean fellow, after all, to take what he wanted and then give her back. She did not remember that she herself had had what she wanted, and really, at the bottom of her heart, wished to be given back.

Paul felt crumpled up and lonely. His mother had really supported his life. He had loved her; they two had, in fact, faced the world together. Now she was gone, and for ever behind him was the gap in life, the tear in the veil, through which his life seemed to drift slowly, as if he were drawn towards death. He wanted someone of their own free initiative to help him. The lesser things he began to let go from him, for fear of this big thing, the lapse towards death, following in the wake of his beloved. Clara could not stand for him to hold on to. She wanted him, but not to understand him. He felt she wanted the man on top, not the real him that was in trouble. That would be too much trouble to her; he dared not give it her. She could not cope with him. It made him ashamed. So, secretly ashamed because he was in such a mess, because his own hold on life was so unsure, because nobody held him, feeling unsubstantial, shadowy, as if he did not count for much in this concrete world, he drew himself together smaller and smaller. He did not want to die; he would not give in. But he was not afraid of death. If nobody would help, he would go on alone.

Dawes had been driven to the extremity of life, until he was afraid. He could go to the brink of death, he could lie on the edge and look in. Then, cowed, afraid, he had to crawl back, and like a beggar take what offered. There was a certain nobility in it. As Clara saw, he owned himself beaten, and he wanted to be taken back whether or not. That she could do for him.

It was three o'clock.

'I am going by the four-twenty,' said Paul again to Clara. 'Are you coming then or later?'

'I don't know,' she said.

'I'm meeting my father in Nottingham at seven-fifteen,' he said.

'Then,' she answered. 'I'll come later.'

Dawes jerked suddenly, as if he had been held on a strain. He looked out over the sea, but he saw nothing.

'There are one or two books in the corner,' said Morel. 'I've done with 'em.'

At about four o'clock he went.

'I shall see you both later,' he said, as he shook hands.

'I suppose so,' said Dawes. 'An' perhaps – one day – I s'll be able to pay you back the money as –'

'I shall come for it, you'll see,' laughed Paul. 'I s'll be on the rocks before I'm very much older.'

'Ay – well –' said Dawes.

'Good-bye,' he said to Clara.

'Good-bye,' she said, giving him her hand. Then she glanced at him for the last time, dumb and humble.

He was gone. Dawes and his wife sat down again.

'It's a nasty day for travelling,' said the man.

'Yes,' she answered.

They talked in a desultory fashion until it grew dark. The landlady brought in the tea. Dawes drew up his chair to the table without being invited, like a husband. Then he sat humbly waiting for his cup. She served him as she would, like a wife, not consulting his wish.

After tea, as it drew near to six o'clock, he went to the window. All was dark outside. The sea was roaring.

'It's raining yet,' he said.

'Is it?' she answered.

'You won't go tonight, shall you?' he said, hesitating.

She did not answer. He waited.

'I shouldn't go in this rain,' he said.

'Do you *want* me to stay?' she asked.

His hand as he held the dark curtain trembled.

'Yes,' he said.

He remained with his back to her. She rose and went slowly to him. He let go the curtain, turned, hesitating, towards her. She stood with her hands behind her back, looking up at him in a heavy, inscrutable fashion.

'Do you want me, Baxter?' she asked.

His voice was hoarse as he answered:

'Do you want to come back to me?'

She made a moaning noise, lifted her arms, and put them round his neck, drawing him to her. He hid his face on her shoulder, holding her clasped.

'Take me back!' she whispered, ecstatic. 'Take me back, take me back!' And she put her fingers through his fine, thin dark hair, as if she were only semiconscious. He tightened his grasp on her.

'Do you want me again?' he murmured, broken.

15

DERELICT

Clara went with her husband to Sheffield, and Paul scarcely saw her again. Walter Morel seemed to have let all the trouble go over him, and there he was, crawling about on the mud of it, just the same. There was scarcely any bond between father and son, save that each felt he must not let the other go in any actual want. As there was no one to keep on the home, and as they could neither of them bear the emptiness of the house, Paul took lodgings in Nottingham, and Morel went to live with a friendly family in Bestwood.

Everything seemed to have gone smash for the young man. He could not paint. The picture he finished on the day of his mother's death – one that satisfied him – was the last thing he did. At work there was no Clara. When he came home he could not take up his brushes again. There was nothing left.

So he was always in the town at one place or another, drinking, knocking about with the men he knew. It really wearied him. He talked to barmaids, to almost any woman, but there was that dark, strained look in his eyes, as if he were hunting something.

Everything seemed so different, so unreal. There seemed no reason why people would go along the street, and houses pile up in the daylight. There seemed no reason why these things should occupy the space, instead of leaving it empty. His friends talked to him; he heard the sounds, and he answered. But why there should be the noise of speech he could not understand.

He was most himself when he was alone, or working hard and mechanically at the factory. In the latter case there was pure forgetfulness, when he lapsed from consciousness. But it had to come to an end. It hurt him so, that things had lost their reality. The first snowdrops came. He saw the tiny drop-pearls among the grey. They would have given him the liveliest emotion at one time. Now they were there, but they did not seem to mean anything. In a few moments they would cease to occupy that place, and just the space would be, where they had been. Tall, brilliant tram-cars ran along the street at night. It seemed almost a wonder they should trouble to rustle backwards and forwards. 'Why trouble to go tilting down to Trent Bridges?' he asked of the big trams. It seemed they just as well might *not* be as be.

The realest thing was the thick darkness at night. That seemed to him whole and comprehensible and restful. He could leave himself to it. Suddenly a piece of paper started near his feet and blew along down the pavement. He stood still, rigid, with clenched fists, a flame of agony going over him. And he saw again the sick-room, his mother, her eyes. Unconsciously he had been with her, in her company. The swift hop of the paper reminded him she was gone. But he had been with her. He wanted everything to stand still, so that he could be with her again.

The days passed, the weeks. But everything seemed to have fused, gone into a conglomerated mass. He could not tell one day from another, one week from another, hardly one place from another. Nothing was distinct or distinguishable. Often he lost himself for an hour at a time, could not remember what he had done.

One evening he came home late to his lodging. The fire was burning low; everybody was in bed. He threw on some more coal, glanced at the table, and decided he wanted no supper. Then he sat down in the arm-chair. It was perfectly still. He did not know anything, yet he saw the dim smoke wavering up the chimney. Presently two mice came out, cautiously, nibbling the fallen crumbs. He watched them as it were from a long way off. The church clock struck two. Far away he could hear the sharp clinking of the trucks on the railway. No, it was not they that were far away. They were there in their places. But where was he himself?

The time passed. The two mice, careering wildly, scampered cheekily over his slippers. He had not moved a muscle. He did not want to move. He was not thinking of anything. It was easier so. There was no wrench of knowing anything. Then, from time to time, some other consciousness, working mechanically, flashed into sharp phrases.

'What am I doing?'

And out of the semi-intoxicated trance came the answer:

'Destroying myself.'

Then a dull, live feeling, gone in an instant, told him that it was wrong. After a while, suddenly came the question:

'Why wrong?'

Again there was no answer, but a stroke of hot stubbornness inside his chest resisted his own annihilation.

There was a sound of a heavy cart clanking down the road. Suddenly the electric light went out; there was a bruising thud in the penny-in-the-slot meter. He did not stir, but sat gazing in front of him. Only the mice had scuttled, and the fire glowed red in the dark room.

Then, quite mechanically and more distinctly, the conversation began again inside him.

'She's dead. What was it all for – her struggle?'

That was his despair wanting to go after her.

'You're alive.'

'She's not.'

'She is – in you.'

Suddenly he felt tired with the burden of it.

'You've got to keep alive for her sake,' said his will in him.

Something felt sulky, as if it would not rouse.

'You've got to carry forward her living, and what she had done, go on with it.'

But he did not want to. He wanted to give up.

'But you can go on with your painting,' said the will in him. 'Or else you can beget children. They both carry on her effort.'

'Painting is not living.'

'Then live.'

'Marry whom?' came the sulky question.

'As best you can.'

'Miriam?'

But he did not trust that.

He rose suddenly, went straight to bed. When he got inside his bedroom and closed the door, he stood with clenched fists.

'Mater, my dear –' he began, with the whole force of his soul. Then he stopped. He would not say it. He would not admit that he wanted to die, to have done. He would not own that life had beaten him, or that death had beaten him.

Going straight to sleep, he slept at once, abandoning himself to the sleep.

So the weeks went on. Always alone, his soul oscillated, first on the side of death, then on the side of life, doggedly. The real agony was that he had nowhere to go, nothing to do, nothing to say, and *was* nothing himself. Sometimes he ran down the streets as if he were mad: sometimes he was mad; things weren't there, things were there. It made him pant. Sometimes he stood before the bar of the public-house where he had called for a drink. Everything suddenly stood back away from him. He saw the face of the barmaid, the gabbling drinkers, his own glass on the slopped, mahogany board, in the distance. There was something between him and them. He could not get into touch. He did not want them; he did not want his drink. Turning abruptly, he went out. On the threshold he stood and looked at the lighted street. But he was not of it or in it. Something separated him. Everything went on there below those lamps, shut away from him. He could not get at them. He felt he couldn't touch the lamp-posts, not if he reached. Where could he go? There was nowhere to go, neither back into the inn, or forward anywhere. He felt stifled. There was nowhere for him. The stress grew inside him; he felt he should smash.

'I mustn't,' he said; and, turning blindly, he went in and drank. Sometimes the drink did him good; sometimes it made him worse. He ran down the road. For ever restless, he went here, there, everywhere. He determined to work. But when he had made six strokes, he loathed the pencil violently, got up, and went away, hurried off to a club where he could play cards or billiards, to a place where he could flirt with a barmaid who was no more to him than the brass pump-handle she drew.

He was very thin and lantern-jawed. He dared not meet his own eyes in the mirror; he never looked at himslef. He wanted to get away from himself, but there was nothing to get hold of. In despair he thought of Miriam. Perhaps – perhaps –?

Then, happening to go into the Unitarian Church one Sunday evening, when they stood up to sing the second hymn he saw her before him. The light glistened on her lower lip as she sang. She looked as if she had got something, at any rate; some hope in heaven, if not in earth. Her comfort and her life seemed in the after-world. A warm, strong feeling for her came up. She seemed to yearn, as she sang, for the mystery and comfort. He put his hope in her. He longed for the sermon to be over, to speak to her.

The throng carried her out just before him. He could nearly touch her. She did not know he was there. He saw the brown humble nape of her neck under its black curls. He would leave himself to her. She was better and bigger than he. He would depend on her.

She went wandering, in her blind way, through the little throng of people outside the church. She always looked so lost and out of place among people. He went forward and put his hand on her arm. She started violently. Her great brown eyes dilated with fear, then went questioning at the sight of him. He shrank slightly from her.

'I didn't know –' she faltered.

'Nor I,' he said.

He looked away. His sudden, flaring hope shrank again.

'What are you doing in town?' he asked.

'I'm staying at Cousin Annie's.'

'Ha! For long?'

'No; only till tomorrow.'

'Must you go straight home?'

She looked at him, then hid her face under her hat-brim.

'No,' she said – 'no: it's not necessary.'

He turned away, and she went with him. They threaded through the throng of church-people. The organ was still sounding in St Mary's. Dark figures came through the lighted doors; people were coming down the steps. The large coloured windows glowed up in the night. The church was like a great lantern suspended. They went down Hollow Stone, and he took the car for the Bridges.

'You will just have supper with me,' he said; 'then I'll bring you back.'

'Very well,' she replied, low and husky.

They scarcely spoke while they were on the car. The Trent ran dark and full under the bridge. Away towards Colwick all was black night. He lived down Holme Road, on the naked edge of the town, facing across the river meadows towards Sneinton Hermitage and the steep scarp of Colwick Wood. The floods were out. The silent water and the darkness spread away on their left. Almost afraid, they hurried along by the houses.

Supper was laid. He swung the curtain over the window. There was a bowl of freesias and scarlet anemones on the table. She bent to them. Still touching them with her finger-tips, she looked at him, saying:

'Aren't they beautiful?'

'Yes,' he said. 'What will you drink – coffee?'

'I should like it,' she said.

'Then excuse me a moment.'

He went out to the kitchen.

Miriam took off her things and looked round. It was a bare, severe room. Her photo, Clara's, Annie's, were on the wall. She looked on the drawing-board to see what he was doing. There were only a few meaningless lines. She looked to see what book he was reading. Evidently just an ordinary novel. The letters in the rack she saw were from Annie, Arthur, and from some men or other she did not know. Everything he had touched, everything that was in the least personal to him, she examined with lingering absorption. He had been gone from her for so long, she wanted to rediscover him, his position, what he was now. But there was not much in the room to help her. It only made her feel rather said, it was so hard and comfortless.

She was curiously examining a sketch-book when he returned with the coffee.

'There's nothing new in it,' he said, 'and nothing very interesting.'

He put down the tray, and went to look over her shoulder. She turned the pages slowly, intent on examining everything.

'H'm!' he said, as she paused at a sketch. 'I'd forgotten that. It's not bad, is it?'

'No,' she said. 'I don't quite understand it.'

He took the book from her and went through it. Again he made a curious sound of surprise and pleasure.

'There's some not bad stuff in there,' he said.

'Not at all bad,' she answered gravely.

He felt again her interest in his work. Or was it for himself? Why was she always most interested in him as he appeared in his work?

They sat down to supper.

'By the way,' he said, 'didn't I hear something about your earning your own living?'

'Yes,' she replied, bowing her dark head over her cup.

'And what of it?'

'I'm merely going to the farming college at Broughton for three months, and I shall probably be kept on as a teacher there.'

'I say – that sounds all right for you! You always wanted to be independent.'

'Yes.'

'Why didn't you tell me?'

'I only knew last week.'

'But I heard a month ago,' he said.

'Yes, but nothing was settled then.'

'I should have thought,' he said, 'you'd have told me you were trying.'

She ate her food in the deliberate, constrained way, almost as if she recoiled a little from doing anything so publicly, that he knew so well.

'I suppose you're glad,' he said.

'Very glad.'

'Yes – it will be something.'

He was rather disappointed.

'I think it will be a great deal,' she said, almost haughtily, resentfully.

He laughed shortly.

'Why do you think it won't?' she asked.

'Oh, I don't think it won't be a great deal. Only you'll find earning your own living isn't everything.'

'No,' she said, swallowing with difficulty; 'I don't suppose it is.'

'I suppose work *can* be nearly everything to a man,' he said, 'though it isn't to me. But a woman only works with a part of herself. The real and vital part is covered up.'

'But a man can give *all* himself to a work?' she asked.

'Yes, practically.'

'And a woman only the unimportant part of herself?'

'That's it.'

She looked up at him, and her eyes dilated with anger.

'Then,' she said, 'if it's true, it's a great shame.'

'It is. But I don't know everything,' he answered.

After supper they drew up to the fire. He swung her a chair facing him, and they sat down. She was wearing a dress of dark claret colour, that suited her dark complexion and her large features. Still, the curls were fine and free, but her face was much older, the grown throat much thinner. She seemed old to him, older than Clara. Her bloom of youth had quickly gone. A sort of stiffness, of woodenness, had come upon her. She meditated a little while, then looked at him.

'And how are things with you?' she asked.

'About all right,' he answered.

She looked at him, waiting.

'Nay,' she said, very low.

Her brown, nervous hands were clasped over her knee. They had still the lack of confidence or repose, the almost hysterical look. He winced as he saw them. Then he laughed mirthlessly. She put her fingers between her lips. His slim, black, tortured body lay quite still in the chair. She suddenly took her finger out of her mouth and looked at him.

'And you have broken off with Clara?'

'Yes.'

His body lay like an abandoned thing, strewn in the chair.

'You know,' she said, 'I think we ought to get married.'

He opened his eyes for the first time since many months, and attended to her with respect.

'Why?' he said.

'See,' she said, 'how you waste yourself! You might be ill, you might die, and I never know – be no more then than if I had never known you.'

'And if we married?' he asked.

'At any rate, I could prevent you wasting yourself and being a prey to other women – like – like Clara.'

'A prey?' he repeated smiling.

She bowed her head in silence. He lay feeling his despair come up again.

'I'm not sure,' he said slowly, 'that marriage would be much good.'

'I only think of you,' she replied.

'I know you do. But – you love me so much, you want to put me in your pocket. And I should die there smothered.'

She bent her head, put her finger between her lips, while the bitterness surged up in her heart.

'And what will you do otherwise?' she asked.

'I don't know – go on, I suppose. Perhaps I shall soon go abroad.'

The despairing doggedness in his tone made her go on her knees on the rug before the fire, very near to him. There she crouched as if she were crushed by something, and could not raise her head. His hands lay quite inert on the arms of his chair. She was aware of them. She felt that now he lay at her mercy. If she could rise, take him, put her arms round him, and say, 'You are mine,' then he would leave himself to her. But dare she? She could easily sacrifice herself. But dare she assert herself? She was aware of his dark-clothed, slender body, that seemed one stroke of life, sprawled in the chair close to her. But no she dared not put her arms round it, take it up, and say, 'It is mine, this body. Leave it to me.' And she wanted to. It called to all her woman's instinct. But she crouched, and dared not. She was afraid he would not let her. She was afraid it was too much. It lay there, his body, abandoned. She knew she ought to take it up and claim it, and claim every right to it. But – could she do it? Her impotence before him, before the strong demand of some unknown thing in him, was her extremity. Her hands fluttered; she half lifted her head. Her eyes, shuddering, appealing, gone almost distracted, pleaded to him suddenly. His heart caught with pity. He took her hands, drew her to him, and comforted her.

'Will you have me, to marry me?' he said, very low.

Oh, why did not he take her? Her very soul belonged to him. Why should he not take what was his? She had borne so long the cruelty of belonging to him and not being claimed by him. Now he was straining her again. It was too much for her. She drew back her head, held his face between her hands, and looked him in the eyes. No, he was hard. He wanted something else. She pleaded to him with all her love not to make it *her* choice. She could not cope with it, with him, she knew not with what. But it strained her till she felt she would break.

'Do you want it?' she asked, very gravely.

'Not much,' he replied, with pain.

She turned her face aside; then, raising herself with dignity, she took his head to her bosom, and rocked him softly. She was not to have him, then! So she could comfort him. She put her fingers through his hair. For her, the anguished sweetness of self-sacrifice. For him, the hate and misery of another failure. He could not bear it – that breast which was warm and which cradled him without taking the burden of him. So much he wanted to rest on her that the feint of rest only tortured him. He drew away.

'And without marriage we can do nothing?' he asked.

His mouth was lifted from his teeth with pain. She put her little finger between her lips.

'No,' she said, low and like the toll of a bell. 'No, I think not.'

It was the end then between them. She could not take him and relieve him of the responsibility of himself. She could only sacrifice herself to him – sacrifice herself every day, gladly. And that he did not want. He wanted her to hold him and say, with joy and authority: 'Stop all this restlessness and beating against death. You are mine for a mate.' She had not the strength. Or was it a mate she wanted? or did she want a Christ in him?

He felt, in leaving her, he was defrauding her of life. But he knew that, in staying, stifling the inner, desperate man, he was denying his own life. And he did not hope to give life to her by denying his own.

She sat very quiet. He lit a cigarette. The smoke went up from it, wavering. He was thinking of his mother, and had forgotten Miriam. She suddenly looked at him. Her bitterness came surging up. Her sacrifice, then, was useless. He lay there aloof, careless about her. Suddenly she saw again his lack of religion, his restless instability. He would destroy himself like a perverse child. Well, then, he would!

'I think I must go,' she said, softly.

By her tone he knew she was despising him. He rose quietly.

'I'll come with you,' he answered.

She stood before the mirror pinning on her hat. How bitter, how unutterably bitter, it made her that he rejected her sacrifice! Life ahead looked dead, as if the glow were gone out. She bowed her face over the flowers – the freesias so sweet and spring-like, the scarlet anemones flaunting over the table. It was like him to have those flowers.

He moved about the room with a certain sureness of touch, swift and relentless and quiet. She knew she could not cope with him. He would escape like a weasel out of her hands. Yet without him in her life would trail on lifeless. Brooding, she touched the flowers.

'Have them!' he said; and he took them out of the jar, dripping as they were, and went quickly into the kitchen. She waited for him, took the flowers, and they went out together, he talking, she feeling dead.

She was going from him now. In her misery she leaned against him as they sat on the car. He was unresponsive. Where would he go? What would be the end of him? She could not bear it, the vacant feeling where he should be. He was so foolish, so wasteful, never at peace with himself. And now where would he go? And what did he care that he wasted her? He had no religion; it was all for the moment's attraction that he cared, nothing else, nothing deeper. Well, she would wait and see how it turned out with him. When he had had enough he would give in and come to her.

He shook hands and left her at the door of her cousin's house. When he turned away he felt the last hold for him had gone. The town, as he sat upon the car, stretched away over the bay of railway, a level fume of lights. Beyond the town the country, little smouldering spots for more towns – the sea – the night – on and on! And he had no place in it! Whatever spot he stood in, there he stood alone. From his breast, from his mouth, sprang the endless space, and it was there behind him, everywhere. The people hurrying along the streets offered no obstruction to the void in which he found himself. They were small shadows whose footsteps and voices could be heard, but in each of them the same night, the same silence. He got off the car. In the country all was dead still. Little stars shone high up; little stars spread far away in the flood-waters, a firmament below. Everywhere the vastness and terror of the immense night which is roused and stirred for a brief while by the day, but which returns, and will remain at last eternal, holding everything in its silence and its living gloom. There was no Time, only Space. Who could say his mother had lived and did not live? She had been in one place, and was in another; that was all. And his soul could not leave her, wherever she was. Now she was gone abroad into the night, and he was with her still. They were together. But yet there was his body, his chest, that leaned against the stile, his hands on the wooden bar. They seemed something. Where was he? – one tiny upright speck of flesh, less than an ear of wheat lost in the field. He could not bear it. On every side the immense dark silence seemed pressing him, so tiny a spark, into extinction, and yet, almost nothing, he could not be extinct. Night, in which everything was lost, went reaching out, beyond stars and sun. Stars and sun, a few bright grains, went spinning round for terror, and holding each other in embrace, there in a darkness that outpassed them all, and left them tiny and daunted. So much, and himself, infinitesimal, at the core a nothingness, and yet not nothing.

'Mother!' he whispered – 'mother!'

She was the only thing that held him up, himself, amid all this. And she was gone, intermingled herself. He wanted her to touch him, have him alongside with her.

But no, he would not give in. Turning sharply, he walked towards the city's gold phosphorescence. His fists were shut, his mouth set fast. He would not take that direction, to the darkness, to follow her. He walked towards the faintly humming, glowing town, quickly.

D.H. LAWRENCE

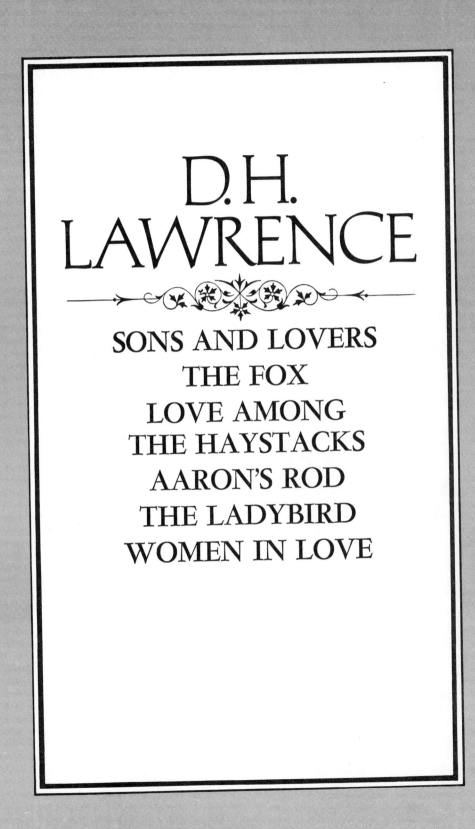

SONS AND LOVERS

THE FOX

LOVE AMONG
THE HAYSTACKS

AARON'S ROD

THE LADYBIRD

WOMEN IN LOVE

The two girls were usually known by their surnames, Banford and March. They had taken the farm together, intending to work it all by themselves: that is, they were going to rear chickens, make a living by poultry, and add to this by keeping a cow, and raising one or two young beasts. Unfortunately, things did not turn out well.

Banford was a small, thin, delicate thing with spectacles. She, however, was the principal investor, for March had little or no money. Banford's father, who was a tradesman in Islington, gave his daughter the start, for her health's sake, and because he loved her, and because it did not look as if she would marry. March was more robust. She had learned carpentry and joinery at the evening classes in Islington. She would be the man about the place. They had, moreover, Banford's old grandfather living with them at the start. He had been a farmer. But unfortunately the old man died after he had been at Bailey Farm for a year. Then the two girls were left alone.

They were neither of them young: that is, they were near thirty. But they certainly were not old. They set out quite gallantly with their enterprise. They had numbers of chickens, black Leghorns and white Leghorns, Plymouths and Wyandottes; also some ducks; also two heifers in the fields. One heifer, unfortunately, refused absolutely to stay in the Bailey Farm closes. No matter how March made up the fences, the heifer was out, wild in the woods, or trespassing on the neighbouring pasture, and March and Banford were away, flying after her, with more haste than success. So this heifer they sold in despair. Then, just before the other beast was expecting her first calf, the old man died, and the girls, afraid of the coming event, sold her in a panic, and limited their attentions to fowls and ducks.

In spite of a little chagrin, it was a relief to have no more cattle on hand. Life was not made merely to be slaved away. Both girls agreed in this. The fowls were quite enough trouble. March had set up her carpenter's bench at the end of the open shed. Here she worked, making coops and doors and other appurtenances. The fowls were housed in the bigger building, which had served as barn and cow-shed in old days. They had a beautiful home, and should have been perfectly content. Indeed, they looked well enough. But the girls were disgusted at their tendency to strange illnesses, at their exacting way of life, and at their refusal, obstinate refusal to lay eggs.

March did most of the outdoor work. When she was out and about, in her puttees and breeches, her belted coat and her loose cap, she looked almost like some graceful, loose-balanced young man, for her shoulders were straight, and her movements easy and confident, even tinged with a little indifference or irony. But her face was not a man's face, ever. The wisps of her crisp dark hair blew about her as she stooped, her eyes were big and wide and dark, when she looked up again, strange, startled, shy and sardonic at once. Her mouth, too, was almost pinched as if in pain and irony. There was something odd and unexplained about her. She would stand balanced on one hip, looking at the fowls pattering about in the obnoxious fine mud of the sloping yard, and calling to her favourite white hen, which came in answer to her name. But there was an almost satirical flicker in March's big, dark eyes as she looked at her three-toed flock pottering about under her gaze, and the same slight dangerous satire in her voice as she spoke to the favoured Patty, who pecked at March's boot by way of friendly demonstration.

Fowls did not flourish at Bailey Farm, in spite of all that March did for them. When she provided hot food for them in the morning, according to rule, she noticed that it made them heavy and dozy for hours. She expected to see them lean against the pillars of the shed in their languid processes of digestion. And she knew quite well that they ought to be busily scratching and foraging about, if they were to come to any good. So she decided to give them their hot food at night, and let them sleep on it. Which she did. But it made no difference.

War conditions, again, were very unfavourable to poultry-keeping. Food was scarce and bad. And when the Daylight Saving Bill was passed, the fowls obstinately refused to go to bed as usual, about nine o'clock in the summertime. That was late enough, indeed, for there was no peace till they were shut up and asleep. Now they cheerfully walked around, without so much as glancing at the barn, until ten o'clock or later. Both Banford and March disbelieved in living for work alone. They wanted to read or take a cycle-ride in the evening, or perhaps March wished to paint curvilinear swans on porcelain, with green background, or else make a marvellous fire-screen by processes of elaborate cabinet work. For she was a creature of odd whims and unsatisfied tendencies. But from all these things she was prevented by the stupid fowls.

One evil there was greater than any other. Bailey Farm was a little homestead, with ancient wooden barn and low-gabled farm-house, lying just one field removed from the edge of the wood. Since the war the fox was a demon. He carried off the hens under the very noses of March and Banford. Banford would start and stare through her big spectacles with all her eyes, as another squawk and flutter took place at her heels. Too late! Another white Leghorn gone. It was disheartening.

They did what they could to remedy it. When it became permitted to shoot foxes, they stood sentinel with their guns, the two of them, at the favoured hours. But it was no good. The fox was too quick for them. So another year passed, and another, and they were living on their losses, as Banford said. They let their farm-house one summer, and retired to live in a railway-carriage that was deposited as a sort of out-house in a corner of the field. This amused them, and helped their finances. None the less, things looked dark.

Although they were usually the best of friends, because Banford, though nervous and delicate, was a warm, generous soul, and March, though so odd and absent in herself, had a strange magnanimity, yet, in the long solitude, they were apt to become a little irritable with one another, tired of one another. March had four-fifths of the work to do, and though she did not mind, there seemed no relief, and it made her eyes flash curiously sometimes. Then

Banford, feeling more nerve-worn than ever, would become despondent, and March would speak sharply to her. They seemed to be losing ground, somehow, losing hope as the months went by. There alone in the fields by the wood, with the wide country stretching hollow and dim to the round hills of the White Horse, in the far distance, they seemed to have to live too much off themselves. There was nothing to keep them up – and no hope.

The fox really exasperated them both. As soon as they had let the fowls out, in the early summer mornings, they had to take their guns and keep guard: and then again as soon as evening began to mellow, they must go once more. And he was so sly. He slid along in the deep grass; he was difficult as a serpent to see. And he seemed to circumvent the girls deliberately. Once or twice March had caught sight of the white tip of his brush, or the ruddy shadow of him in the deep grass, and she had let fire at him. But he made no account of this.

One evening March was standing with her back to the sunset, her gun under her arm, her hair pushed under her cap. She was half watching, half musing. It was her constant state. Her eyes were keen and observant, but her inner mind took no notice of what she saw. She was always lapsing into this odd, rapt state, her mouth rather screwed up. It was a question whether she was there, actually conscious present, or not.

The trees on the wood-edge were a darkish, brownish green in the full light – for it was the end of August. Beyond, the naked, copper-like shafts and limbs of the pine trees shone in the air. Nearer the rough grass, with its long, brownish stalks all agleam, was full of light. The fowls were round about – the ducks were still swimming on the pond under the pine trees. March looked at it all, saw it all, and did not see it. She heard Banford speaking to the fowls in the distance – and she did not hear. What was she thinking about? Heaven knows. Her consciousness was, as it were, held back.

She lowered her eyes, and suddenly saw the fox. He was looking up at her. His chin was pressed down, and his eyes were looking up. They met her eyes. And he knew her. She was spellbound – she knew he knew her. So he looked into her eyes, and her soul failed her. He knew her, he was not daunted.

She struggled, confusedly she came to herself, and saw him making off, with slow leaps over some fallen boughs, slow, impudent jumps. Then he glanced over his shoulder, and ran smoothly away. She saw his brush held smooth like a feather, she saw his white buttocks twinkle. And he was gone, softly, soft as the wind.

She put her gun to her shoulder, but even then pursed her mouth, knowing it was nonsense to pretend to fire. So she began to walk slowly after him, in the direction he had gone, slowly, pertinaciously. She expected to find him. In her heart she was determined to find him. What she would do when she saw him again she did not consider. But she was determined to find him. So she walked abstractedly about on the edge of the wood, with wide, vivid dark eyes, and a faint flush in her cheeks. She did not think. In strange mindlessness she walked hither and thither.

At last she became aware that Banford was calling her. She made an effort of attention, turned, and gave some sort of screaming call in answer. Then again she was striding off towards the homestead. The red sun was setting, the fowls were retiring towards their roost. She watched them, white creatures, black creatures, gathering to the barn. She watched them spellbound, without seeing them. But her automatic intelligence told her when it was time to shut the door.

She went indoors to supper, which Banford had set on the table. Banford chatted easily. March seemed to listen, in her distant, manly way. She answered a brief word now and then. But all the time she was as if spellbound. And as soon as supper was over, she rose again to go out, without saying why.

She took her gun again and went to look for the fox. For he had lifted his eyes upon her, and his knowing look seemed to have entered her brain. She did not so much think of him: she was possessed by him. She saw his dark, shrewd, unabashed eye looking into her, knowing her. She felt him invisibly master her spirit. She knew the way he lowered his chin as he looked up, she knew his muzzle, the golden brown, and the greyish white. And again she saw him glance over his shoulder at her, half inviting, half contemptuous and cunning. So she went, with her great startled eyes glowing, her gun under her arm, along the wood edge. Meanwhile the night fell, and a great moon rose above the pine trees. And again Banford was calling.

So she went indoors. She was silent and busy. She examined her gun, and cleaned it, musing abstractedly by the lamp-light. Then she went out again, under the great moon, to see if everything was right. When she saw the dark crests of the pine trees against the blood-red sky, again her heart beat to the fox, the fox. She wanted to follow him, with her gun.

It was some days before she mentioned the affair to Banford. Then suddenly one evening she said:

'The fox was right at my feet on Saturday night.'

'Where?' said Banford, her eyes opening behind her spectacles.

'When I stood just above the pond.'

'Did you fire?' cried Banford.

'No, I didn't.'

'Why not?'

'Why, I was too much surprised, I suppose.'

It was the same old, slow, laconic way of speech March always had. Banford stared at her friend for a few moments.

'You saw him?' she cried.

'Oh yes! He was looking up at me, cool as anything.'

'I tell you,' cried Banford – 'the cheek! They're not afraid of us, Nellie.'

'Oh no,' said March.

'Pity you didn't get a shot at him,' said Banford.

'Isn't it a pity! I've been looking for him ever since. But I don't suppose he'll come so near again.'

'I don't suppose he will,' said Banford.

And she proceeded to forget about it, except that she was more indignant than ever at the impudence of the beggar. March also was not conscious that she thought of the fox. But whenever she fell into her half-musing, when she was half rapt and half intelligently aware of what passed under her vision, then it was the fox which somehow dominated her unconsciousness, possessed the blank half of her musing. And so it was for weeks, and months. No matter whether she had been climbing the trees for the apples, or beating down the last of the damsons, or whether she had been digging out the ditch from the duck-pond, or clearing out the barn, when she had finished, or when she straightened herself, and pushed the wisps of hair away again from her forehead, and pursed up her mouth again in an odd, screwed fashion, much too old for her years, there was sure to come over her mind the old spell of the fox, as it came when he was looking at her. It was as if she could smell him at these times. And it always recurred, at unexpected moments, just as she was going to sleep at night, or just as she was pouring the water into the tea-pot to make tea – it was the fox, it came over her like a spell.

So the months passed. She still looked for him unconsciously when she went towards the wood. He had become a settled effect in her spirit, a state permanently established, not continuous, but always recurring. She did not know what she felt or thought: only the state came over her, as when he looked at her.

The months passed, the dark evenings came, heavy, dark November, when March went about in high boots, ankle deep in mud, when the night began to fall at four o'clock, and the day never properly dawned. Both girls dreaded these times. They dreaded the almost continuous darkness that enveloped them on their desolate little farm near the wood. Banford was physically afraid. She was afraid of tramps, afraid lest someone should come prowling around. March was not so much afraid as uncomfortable, and disturbed. She felt discomfort and gloom in all her physique.

Usually the two girls had tea in the sitting-room. March lighted a fire at dusk, and put on the wood she had chopped and sawed during the day. Then the long evening was in front, dark, sodden, black outside, lonely and rather oppressive inside, a little dismal. March was content not to talk, but Banford could not keep still. Merely listening to the wind in the pines outside, or the drip of water, was too much for her.

One evening the girls had washed up the tea-cups in the kitchen, and March had put on her house-shoes, and taken up a roll of crochet-work, which she worked at slowly from time to time. So she lapsed into silence. Banford stared at the red fire, which, being of wood, needed constant attention. She was afraid to begin to read too early, because her eyes would not bear any strain. So she sat staring at the fire, listening to the distant sounds, sound of cattle lowing, of a dull, heavy moist wind, of the rattle of the evening rain on the little railway not far off. She was almost fascinated by the red glow of the fire.

Suddenly both girls started, and lifted their heads. They heard a footstep – distinctly a footstep. Banford recoiled in fear. March stood listening. Then rapidly she approached the door that led into the kitchen. At the same time they heard the footsteps approach the back door. They waited a second. The back door opened softly. Banford gave a loud cry. A man's voice said softly:

'Hello!'

March recoiled, and took a gun from a corner.

'What do you want?' she cried, in a sharp voice.

Again the soft, softly-vibrating man's voice said:

'Hello! What's wrong?'

'I shall shoot!' cried March. 'What do you want?'

'Why, what's wrong? What's wrong?' came the soft, wondering, rather scared voice: and a young soldier, with his heavy kit on his back, advanced into the dim light.

'Why,' he said, 'who lives here then?'

'We live here,' said March. 'What do you want?'

'Oh!' came the long, melodious, wonder-note from the young soldier. 'Doesn't William Grenfel live here then?'

'No – you know he doesn't.'

'Do I? Do I? I don't, you see. He *did* live here, because he was my grandfather, and I lived here myself five years ago. What's become of him then?'

The young man – or youth, for he would not be more than twenty – now advanced and stood in the inner doorway. March, already under the influence of his strange, soft, modulated voice, stared at him spellbound. He had a ruddy, roundish face, with fairish hair, rather long, flattened to his forehead with sweat. His eyes were blue, and very bright and sharp. On his cheeks, on the fresh ruddy skin were fine, fair hairs, like a down, but sharper. It gave him a slightly glistening look. Having his heavy sack on his shoulders, he stooped, thrusting his head forward. His hat was loose in one hand. He stared brightly, very keenly from girl to girl, particularly at March, who stood pale, with great dilated eyes, in her belted coat and puttees, her hair knotted in a big crisp knot behind. She still had the gun in her hand. Behind her, Banford, clinging to the sofa-arm, was shrinking away, with half-averted head.

'I thought my grandfather still lived here? I wonder if he's dead.'

'We've been here for three years,' said Banford, who was beginning to recover her wits, seeing something boyish in the round head with its rather long, sweaty hair.

'Three years! You don't say so! And you don't know who was here before you?'

'I know it was an old man, who lived by himself.'

'Ay! Yes, that's him! And what became of him then?'

'He died. I know he died.'

'Ay! He's dead then!'

The youth stared at them without changing colour or expression. If he had any expression, besides a slight baffled look of wonder, it was one of sharp curiosity concerning the two girls; sharp, impersonal curiosity, the curiosity of that round young head.

But to March he was the fox. Whether it was the thrusting forward of his head, or the glisten of fine whitish hairs on the ruddy cheek-bones, or the bright, keen eyes, that can never be said: but the boy was to her the fox, and she could not see him otherwise.

'How is it you didn't know if your grandfather was alive or dead?' asked Banford, recovering her natural sharpness.

'Ay, that's it,' replied the softly-breathing youth. 'You see, I joined up in Canada, and I hadn't heard for three or four years. I ran away to Canada.'

'And now have you just come from France?'

'Well – from Salonika really.'

There was a pause, nobody knowing quite what to say.

'So you've nowhere to go now?' said Banford rather lamely.

'Oh, I know some people in the village. Anyhow, I can go to the "Swan".'

'You came on the train, I suppose. Would you like to sit down a bit?'

'Well – I don't mind.'

He gave an odd little groan as he swung off his kit. Banford looked at March.

'Put the gun down,' she said. 'We'll make a cup of tea.'

'Ay,' said the youth. 'We've seen enough of rifles.'

He sat down rather tired on the sofa, leaning forward.

March recovered her presence of mind, and went into the kitchen. There she heard the soft young voice musing:

'Well, to think I should come back and find it like this!' He did not seem sad, not at all – only rather interestedly surprised.

'And what a difference in the place, eh?' he continued, looking round the room.

'You see a difference, do you?' said Banford.

'Yes – don't I!'

His eyes were unnaturally clear and bright, though it was the brightness of abundant health.

March was busy in the kitchen preparing another meal. It was about seven o'clock. All the time, while she was active, she was attending to the youth in the sitting-room, not so much listening to what he said as feeling the soft run of his voice. She primmed up her mouth tighter and tighter, puckering it as if it were sewed, in her effort to keep her will uppermost. Yet her large eyes dilated and glowed in spite of her; she lost herself. Rapidly and carelessly she prepared the meal, cutting large chunks of bread and margarine – for there was no butter. She racked her brain to think of something else to put on the tray – she had only bread, margarine, and jam, and the larder was bare. Unable to conjure anything up, she went into the sitting-room with her tray.

She did not want to be noticed. Above all, she did not want him to look at her. But when she came in, and was busy setting the table just behind him, he pulled himself up from his sprawling, and turned and looked over his shoulder. She became pale and wan.

The youth watched her as she bent over the table, looked at her slim, well-shapen legs, at the belted coat cropping around her thighs, at the knot of dark hair, and his curiosity, vivid and widely alert, was again arrested by her.

The lamp was shaded with a dark-green shade, so that the light was thrown downwards and the upper half of the room was dim. His face moved bright under the light, but March loomed shadowy in the distance.

She turned round, but kept her eyes sideways, dropping and lifting her dark lashes. Her mouth unpuckered as she said to Banford:

'Will you pour out?'

Then she went into the kitchen again.

'Have your tea where you are, will you?' said Banford to the youth – 'unless you'd rather come to the table.'

'Well,' said he, 'I'm nice and comfortable here, aren't I? I will have it here, if you don't mind.'

'There's nothing but bread and jam,' she said. And she put his plate on a stool by him. She was very happy now, waiting on him. For she loved company. And now she was no more afraid of him than if he were her own younger brother. He was such a boy.

'Nellie,' she cried. 'I've poured you a cup out.'

March appeared in the doorway, took her cup, and sat down in a corner, as far from the light as possible. She was very sensitive in her knees. Having no skirts to cover them, and being forced to sit with them boldly exposed, she suffered. She drank and shrank, trying not to be seen. And the youth, sprawling low on the couch, glanced up at her, with long, steady, penetrating looks, till she was almost ready to disappear. Yet she held her cup balanced, she drank her tea, screwed up her mouth and held her head averted. Her desire to be invisible was so strong that it quite baffled the youth. He felt he could not see her distinctly. She seemed like a shadow within the shadow. And ever his eyes came back to her, searching, unremitting, with unconscious fixed attention.

Meanwhile he was talking softly and smoothly to Banford, who loved nothing so much as gossip, and who was full of perky interest, like a bird. Also he ate largely and quickly and voraciously, so that March had to cut more chunks of bread and margarine, for the roughness of which Banford apologized.

'Oh, well,' said March, suddenly speaking, 'if there's no butter to put on it, it's no good trying to make dainty pieces.'

Again the youth watched her, and he laughed, with a sudden, quick laugh, showing his teeth and wrinkling his nose.

'It isn't, is it,' he answered in his soft, near voice.

It appeared he was Cornish by birth and upbringing. When he was twelve years old he had come to Bailey Farm with his grandfather, with whom he had never agreed very well. So he had run away to Canada, and worked far away in the West. Now he was here – and that was the end of it.

He was very curious about the girls, to find out exactly what they were doing. His questions were those of a farm youth; acute, practical, a little mocking. He was very much amused by their attitude to their losses; for they were amusing on the score of heifers and fowls.

'Oh, well,' broke in March, 'we don't believe in living for nothing but work.'

'Don't you?' he answered. And again the quick young laugh came over his face. He kept his eyes steadily on the obscure woman in the corner.

'But what will you do when you've used up all your capital?' he said.

'Oh, I don't know,' answered March laconically. 'Hire ourselves out for land-workers, I suppose.'

'Yes, but there won't be any demand for women landworkers now the war's over,' said the youth.

'Oh, we'll see. We shall hold on a bit longer yet,' said March, with a plangent, half-sad, half-ironical indifference.

'There wants a man about the place,' said the youth softly.

Banford burst out laughing.

'Take care what you say,' she interrupted. 'We consider ourselves quite efficient.'

'Oh,' came March's slow plangent voice, 'it isn't a case of efficiency, I'm afraid. If you're going to do farming you must be at it from morning till night, and you might as well be a beast yourself.'

'Yes, that's it,' said the youth. 'You aren't willing to put yourselves into it.'

'We aren't,' said March, 'and we know it.'

'We want some of our time for ourselves,' said Banford.

The youth threw himself back on the sofa, his face tight with laughter, and laughed silently but thoroughly. The calm scorn of the girls tickled him tremendously.

'Yes,' he said, 'but why did you begin then?'

'Oh,' said March, 'we had a better opinion of the nature of fowls then than we have now.'

'Of nature altogether, I'm afraid,' said Banford. 'Don't talk to me about Nature.'

Again the face of the youth tightened with delighted laughter.

'You haven't a very high opinion of fowls and cattle, haven't you?' he said.

'Oh no – quite a low one,' said March.

He laughed out.

'Neither fowls nor heifers,' said Banford, 'nor goats nor the weather.'

The youth broke into a sharp yap of laughter, delighted. The girls began to laugh too, March turning aside her face and wrinkling her mouth in amusement.

'Oh, well,' said Banford, 'we don't mind, do we, Nellie?'

'No,' said March, 'we don't mind.'

The youth was very pleased. He had eaten and drunk his fill. Banford began to question him. His name was Henry Grenfel – no, he was not called Harry, always Henry. He continued to answer with courteous simplicity, grave and charming. March, who was not included, cast long, slow glances at him from her recess, as he sat there on the sofa, his hands clasping his knees, his face under the lamp bright and alert, turned to Banford. She became almost peaceful at last. He was identified with the fox – and he was here in full presence. She need not go after him any more. There in the shadow of her corner she gave herself up to a warm, relaxed peace, almost like sleep, accepting the spell that was on her. But she wished to remain hidden. She was only fully at peace whilst he forgot her, talking to Banford. Hidden in the shadow of the corner, she need not any more be divided in herself, trying to keep up two planes of consciousness. She could at last lapse into the odour of the fox.

For the youth, sitting before the fire in his uniform, sent a faint but distinct odour into the room, indefinable, but something like a wild creature. March no longer tried to reserve herself from it. She was still and soft in her corner like a passive creature in its cave.

At last the talk dwindled. The youth relaxed his clasp of his knees, pulled himself together a little, and looked around. Again he became aware of the silent, half-invisible woman in the corner.

'Well,' he said unwillingly, 'I suppose I'd better be going, or they'll be in bed at the "Swan".'

'I'm afraid they're in bed, anyhow,' said Banford. 'They've all got this influenza.'

'Have they!' he exclaimed. And he pondered. 'Well,' he continued, 'I shall find a place somewhere.'

'I'd say you could stay here, only –' Banford began.

He turned and watched her, holding his head forward.

'What?' he asked.

'Oh, well,' she said, 'propriety, I suppose.' She was rather confused.

'It wouldn't be improper, would it?' he said, gently surprised.

'Not as far as we're concerned,' said Banford.

'And not as far as *I'm* concerned,' he said, with grave naiveté. 'After all, it's my own home, in a way.'

Banford smiled at this.

'It's what the village will have to say,' she said.

There was a moment's blank pause.

'What do you say, Nellie?' asked Banford.

'I don't mind,' said March, in her distinct tone. 'The village doesn't matter to me, anyhow.'

'No,' said the youth, quick and soft. 'Why should it? I mean, what should they say?'

'Oh, well,' came March's plangent, laconic voice, 'they'll easily find something to say. But it makes no difference what they say. We can look after ourselves.'

'Of course you can,' said the youth.

'Well then, stop if you like,' said Banford. 'The spare room is quite ready.'

His face shone with pleasure.

'If you're quite sure it isn't troubling you too much,' he said, with that soft courtesy which distinguished him.

'Oh, it's no trouble,' they both said.

He looked, smiling with delight, from one to another.

'It's awfully nice not to have to turn out again, isn't it?' he said gratefully.

'I suppose it is,' said Banford.

March disappeared to attend the room. Banford was as pleased and thoughtful as if she had her own young brother home from France. It gave her just the same kind of gratification to attend on him, to get out the bath for him, and everything. Her natural warmth and kindliness had now an outlet. And the youth luxuriated in her sisterly attention. But it puzzled him slightly to know that March was silently working for him too. She was so curiously silent and obliterated. It seemed to him he had not really seen her. He felt he should not know her if he met her in the road.

That night March dreamed vividly. She dreamed she heard a singing outside which she could not understand, a singing that roamed round the house, in the fields, and in the darkness. It moved her so that she felt she must weep. She went out, and suddenly she knew it was the fox singing. He was very yellow and bright, like corn. She went nearer to him, but he ran away and ceased singing. He seemed near, and she wanted to touch him. She stretched out her hand, but suddenly he bit her wrist, and at the same instant, as she drew back, the fox, turning round to bound away, whisked his brush across her face, and it seemed his brush was on fire, for it seared and burned her mouth with a great pain. She awoke with the pain of it, and lay trembling as if she were really seared.

In the morning, however, she only remembered it as a distant memory. She arose and was busy preparing the house and attending to the fowls. Banford flew into the village on her bicycle to try and buy food. She was a hospitable soul. But alas, in the year 1918 there was not much food to buy. The youth came downstairs in his shirt-sleeves. He was young and fresh, but he walked with his head thrust forward, so that his shoulders seemed raised and rounded, as if he had a slight curvature of the spine. It must have been only a manner of bearing himself, for he was young and vigorous. He washed himself and went outside, whilst the women were preparing breakfast.

He saw everything, and examined everything. His curiosity was quick and insatiable. He compared the state of things with that which he remembered before, and cast over in his mind the effect of the changes. He watched the fowls and the ducks, to see their condition; he noticed the flight of wood-pigeons overhead: they were very numerous; he saw the few apples high up, which March had not been able to reach; he remarked that they had borrowed a draw-pump, presumably to empty the big soft-water cistern which was on the north side of the house.

'It's a funny, dilapidated old place,' he said to the girls, as he sat at breakfast.

His eyes were wise and childish, with thinking about things. He did not say much, but ate largely. March kept her face averted. She, too, in the early morning could not be aware of him, though something about the glint of his khaki reminded her of the brilliance of her dream-fox.

During the day the girls went about their business. In the morning he attended to the guns, shot a rabbit and a wild duck that was flying high towards the wood. That was a great addition to the empty larder. The girls felt that already he had earned his keep. He said nothing about leaving, however. In the afternoon he went to the village. He came back at tea-time. He had the same alert, forward-reaching look on his roundish face. He hung his hat on a peg with a little swinging gesture. He was thinking about something.

'Well,' he said to the girls, as he sat at table. 'What am I going to do?'

'How do you mean – what are you going to do?' said Banford.

'Where am I going to find a place in the village to stay?' he said.

'I don't know,' said Banford. 'Where do you think of staying?'

'Well' – he hesitated – 'at the "Swan" they've got this 'flu, and at the "Plough and Harrow" they got the soldiers who are collecting the hay for the army: besides, in the private houses, there's ten men and a corporal altogether billeted in the village, they tell me. I'm not sure where I could get a bed.'

He left the matter to them. He was rather calm about it. March sat with her elbows on the table, her two hands supporting her chin, looking at him unconsciously. Suddenly he lifted his clouded blue eyes, and unthinking looked straight into March's eyes. He was startled as well as she. He, too, recoiled a little. March felt the same sly, taunting, knowing spark leap out of his eyes, as he turned his head aside, and fall into her soul, as it had fallen from the dark eyes of the fox. She pursed her mouth as if in pain, as if asleep too.

'Well, I don't know,' Banford was saying. She seemed reluctant, as if she were afraid of being imposed upon. She looked at March. But, with her weak, troubled sight, she only saw the usual semi-abstraction on her friend's face. 'Why don't you speak, Nellie?' she said.

But March was wide-eyed and silent, and the youth, as if fascinated, was watching her without moving his eyes.

'Go on – answer something,' said Banford. And March turned her head slightly aside, as if coming to consciousness, or trying to. come to consciousness.

'What do you expect me to say?' she asked automatically.

'Say what you think,' said Banford.

'It's all the same to me,' said March.

And again there was silence. A pointed light seemed to be on the boy's eyes, penetrating like a needle.

'So it is to me,' said Banford. 'You can stop on here if you like.'

A smile like a cunning little flame came over his face, suddenly and involuntarily. He dropped his head quickly to hide it, and remained with his head dropped, his face hidden.

'You can stop on here if you like. You can please yourself, Henry,' Banford concluded.

Still he did not reply, but remained with his head dropped. Then he lifted his face. It was bright with a curious light, as if exultant, and his eyes were strangely clear as he watched March. She turned her face aside, her mouth suffering as if wounded, and her consciousness dim.

Banford became a little puzzled. She watched the steady, pellucid gaze of the youth's eyes as he looked at March, with the invisible smile gleaming on his face. She did not know how he was smiling, for no feature moved. It seemed only in the gleam, almost the glitter of the fine hairs on his cheeks. Then he looked with quite a changed look at Banford.

'I'm sure,' he said in his soft, courteous voice, 'you're awfully good. You're too good. You don't want to be bothered with me, I'm sure.'

'Cut a bit of bread, Nellie,' said Banford uneasily, adding: 'It's no bother, if you like to stay. It's like having my own brother here for a few days. He's a boy like you are.'

'That's awfully kind of you,' the lad repeated. 'I should like to stay ever so much, if you're sure I'm not a trouble to you.'

'No, of course you're no trouble. I tell you, it's a pleasure to have somebody in the house besides ourselves,' said warm-hearted Banford.

'But Miss March?' he said in his soft voice, looking at her.

'Oh, it's quite all right as far as I'm concerned,' said March vaguely.

His face beamed, and he almost rubbed his hands with pleasure.

'Well then,' he said, 'I should love it, if you'd let me pay my board and help with the work.'

'You've no need to talk about board,' said Banford.

One or two days went by, and the youth stayed on at the farm. Banford was quite charmed by him. He was so soft and courteous in speech, not wanting to say much himself, preferring to hear what she had to say, and to laugh in his quick, half-mocking way. He helped readily with the work – but not too much. He loved to be out alone with the gun in his hands, to watch, to see. For his sharp-eyed, impersonal curiosity was insatiable, and he was most free when he was quite alone, half-hidden, watching.

Particularly he watched March. She was a strange character to him. Her figure, like a graceful young man's, piqued him. Her dark eyes made something rise in his soul, with a curious elate excitement, when he looked into them, an excitement he was afraid to let be seen, it was so keen and secret. And then her odd, shrewd speech made him laugh outright. He felt he must go further, he was inevitably impelled. But he put away the thought of her and went off towards the wood's edge with the gun.

The dusk was falling as he came home, and with the dusk, a fine, late November rain. He saw the fire-light leaping in the window of the sitting-room, a leaping light in the little cluster of the dark buildings. And he thought to himself it would be a good thing to have this place for his own. And then the thought entered him shrewdly: Why not marry March? He stood still in the middle of the field for some moments, the dead rabbit hanging still in his hand, arrested by this thought. His mind waited in amazement – it seemed to calculate – and then he smiled curiously to himself in acquiescence. Why not? Why not indeed? It was a good idea. What if it was rather ridiculous? What did it matter? What if she was older than he? It didn't matter. When he thought of her dark, startled, vulnerable eyes he smiled subtly to himself. He was older than she, really. He was master of her.

He scarcely admitted his intention even to himself. He kept it as a secret even from himself. It was all too uncertain as yet. He would have to see how things went. Yes, he would have to see how things went. If he wasn't careful, she would just simply mock at the idea. He knew, sly and subtle as he was, that if he went to her plainly and said: 'Miss March, I love you and want you to marry me,' her inevitable answer would be: 'Get out. I don't want any of that tomfoolery.' This was her attitude to men and their 'tomfoolery'. If he was not careful, she would turn round on him with her savage, sardonic ridicule, and dismiss him from the farm and from her own mind for ever. He would have to go gently. He would have to catch her as you catch a deer or a woodcock when you go out shooting. It's no good walking out into the forest and saying to the deer: 'Please fall to my gun.' No, it is a slow, subtle battle. When you really go out to get a deer, you gather yourself together, you coil yourself inside yourself, and you advance secretly, before dawn, into the mountains. It is not so much what you do, when you go out hunting, as how you feel. You have to be subtle and cunning and absolutely fatally ready. It becomes like a fate. Your own fate overtakes and determines the fate of the deer you are hunting. First of all, even before you come in sight of your quarry, there is a strange battle, like mesmerism. Your own soul, as a hunter, has gone out to fasten on the soul of the deer, even before you see any deer. And the soul of the deer fights to escape. Even before the deer has any wind of you, it is so. It is a subtle, profound battle of wills which takes place in the invisible. And it is a battle never finished till your bullet goes home. When you are *really* worked up to the true pitch, and you come at last into range, you don't then aim as you do when you are firing at a bottle. It is your own *will* which carries the bullet into the heart of your quarry. The bullet's flight home is a sheer projection of your own fate into the fate of the deer. It happens like a supreme wish, a supreme act of volition, not as a dodge of cleverness.

He was a huntsman in spirit, not a farmer, and not a soldier stuck in a regiment. And it was as a young hunter that he wanted to bring down March as his quarry, to make her his wife. So he gathered himself subtly together, seemed to withdraw into a kind of invisibility. He was not quite sure how he would go on. And March was suspicious as a hare. So he remained in appearance just the nice, odd, stranger-youth, staying for a fortnight on the place.

He had been sawing logs for the fire in the afternoon. Darkness came very early. It was still a cold, raw mist. It was getting almost too dark to see. A pile of short sawed logs lay beside the trestle. March came to carry them indoors, or into the shed, as he was busy sawing the last log. He was working in his shirt-sleeves, and did not notice her approach; she came unwillingly, as if shy. He saw her stooping to the brightened logs, and he stopped sawing. A fire like lightning flew down his legs in the nerves.

'March?' he said in his quiet, young voice.

She looked up from the logs she was piling.

'Yes!' she said.

He looked down on her in the dusk. He could see her not too distinctly.

'I wanted to ask you something,' he said.

'Did you? What was it?' she said. Already the fright was in her voice. But she was too much mistress of herself.

'Why' – his voice seemed to draw out soft and subtle, it penetrated her nerves – 'why, what do you think it is?'

She stood up, placed her hands on her hips, and stood looking at him transfixed, without answering. Again he burned with a sudden power.

'Well,' he said, and his voice was so soft it seemed rather like a subtle touch, like the merest touch of a cat's paw, a feeling rather than a sound. 'Well – I wanted to ask you to marry me.'

March felt rather than heard him. She was trying in vain to turn aside her face. A great relaxation seemed to have come over her. She stood silent, her head slightly on one side. He seemed to be bending towards her, invisibly smiling. It seemed to her fine sparks came out of him.

Then very suddenly she said:

'Don't try any of your tomfoolery on me.'

A quiver went over his nerves. He had missed. He waited a moment to collect himself again. Then he said, putting all the strange softness into his voice, as if he were imperceptibly stroking her.

'Why, it's not tomfoolery. It's not tomfoolery. I mean it. I mean it. What makes you disbelieve me?'

He sounded hurt. And his voice had such a curious power over her; making her feel loose and relaxed. She struggled somewhere for her own power. She felt for a moment that she was lost – lost – lost. The word seemed to rock in her as if she were dying. Suddenly again she spoke.

'You don't know what you are talking about,' she said, in a brief and transient stroke of scorn. 'What nonsense! I'm old enough to be your mother.'

'Yes, I do know what I'm talking about. Yes, I do,' he persisted softly, as if he were producing his voice in her blood. 'I know quite well what I'm talking about. You're not old enough to be my mother. That isn't true. And what does it matter even if it was. You can marry me whatever age we are. What is age to me? And what is age to you! Age is nothing.'

A swoon went over her as he concluded. He spoke rapidly – in the rapid Cornish fashion – and his voice seemed to sound in her somewhere where she was helpless against it. 'Age is nothing!' The soft, heavy insistence of it made her sway dimly out there in the darkness. She could not answer.

A great exultance leaped like fire over his limbs. He felt he had won.

'I want to marry you, you see. Why shouldn't I?' he proceeded, soft and rapid. He waited for her to answer. In the dusk he saw her almost phosphorescent. Her eyelids were dropped, her face half-averted and unconscious. She seemed to be in his power. But he waited, watchful. He dared not yet touch her.

'Say then,' he said, 'say then you'll marry me. Say – say!' He was softly insistent.

'What?' she asked, faint, from a distance, like one in pain. His voice was now unthinkably near and soft. He drew very near to her.

'Say yes.'

'Oh, I can't,' she wailed helplessly, half-articulate, as if semi-conscious, and as if in pain, like one who dies. 'How can I?'

'You can,' he said softly, laying his hand gently on her shoulder as she stood with her head averted and dropped, dazed. 'You can. Yes, you can. What makes you say you can't? You can. You can.' And with awful softness he bent forward and just touched her neck with his mouth and his chin.

'Don't!' she cried, with a faint mad cry like hysteria, starting away and facing round on him. 'What do you mean?' But she had no breath to speak with. It was as if she was killed.

'I mean what I say,' he persisted softly and cruelly. 'I want you to marry me. I want you to marry me. You know that, now, don't you? You know that, now? Don't you? Don't you?'

'What?' she said.

'Know,' he replied.

'Yes,' she said. 'I know you say so.'

'And you know I mean it, don't you?'

'I know you say so.'

'You believe me?' he said.

She was silent for some time. Then she pursed her lips.

'I don't know what I believe,' she said.

'Are you out there?' came Banford's voice, calling from the house.

'Yes, we're bringing in the logs,' he answered.

'I thought you'd gone lost,' said Banford disconsolately. 'Hurry up, do, and come and let's have tea. The kettle's boiling.'

He stooped at once to take an armful of little logs and carry them into the kitchen, where they were piled in a corner. March also helped, filling her arms and carrying the logs on her breast as if they were some heavy child. The night had fallen cold.

When the logs were all in, the two cleaned their boots noisily on the scraper outside, then rubbed them on the mat. March shut the door and took off her old felt hat – her farm-girl hat. Her thick, crisp, black hair was loose, her face was pale and strained. She pushed back her hair vaguely and washed her hands. Banford came hurrying into the dimly-lighted kitchen, to take from the oven the scones she was keeping hot.

'Whatever have you been doing all this time?' she asked fretfully. 'I thought you were never coming in. And it's ages since you stopped sawing. What were you doing out there?'

'Well,' said Henry, 'we had to stop that hole in the barn to keep the rats out.'

'Why, I could see you standing there in the shed I could see your shirt-sleeves,' challenged Banford.

'Yes, I was just putting the saw away.'

They went in to tea. March was quite mute. Her face was pale and strained and vague. The youth, who always had the same ruddy, self-contained look on his face, as though he were keeping himself to himself, had come to tea in his shirt-sleeves as if he were at home. He bent over his plate as he ate his food.

'Aren't you cold?' said Banford spitefully. 'In your shirt-sleeves.'

He looked up at her, with his chin near his plate, and his eyes very clear, pellucid, and unwavering as he watched her.

'No, I'm not cold,' he said with his usual soft courtesy. 'It's much warmer in here than it is outside, you see.'

'I hope it is,' said Banford, feeling nettled by him. He had a strange, suave assurance and a wide-eyed bright look that got on her nerves this evening.

'But perhaps,' he said softly and courteously, 'you don't like me coming to tea without my coat. I forgot that.'

'Oh, I don't mind,' said Banford: although she *did*.

'I'll go and get it, shall I?' he said.

March's dark eyes turned slowly down to him.

'No, don't you bother,' she said in her queer, twanging tone. 'If you feel all right as you are, stop as you are.' She spoke with a crude authority.

'Yes,' said he, 'I *feel* all right, if I'm not rude.'

'It's usually considered rude,' said Banford. 'But we don't mind.'

'Go along, "considered rude",' ejaculated March. 'Who considers it rude?'

'Why, you do, Nellie, in anybody else,' said Banford, bridling a little behind her spectacles, and feeling her food stick in her throat.

But March had again gone vague and unheeding, chewing her food as if she did not know she was eating at all. And the youth looked from one to another, with bright, watching eyes.

Banford was offended. For all his suave courtesy and soft voice, the youth seemed to her impudent. She did not like to look at him. She did not like to meet his clear, watchful eyes, she did not like to see the strange glow in his face, his cheeks with their delicate fine hair, and his ruddy skin that was quite dull and yet which seemed to burn with a curious heat of life. It made her feel a little ill to look at him: the quality of his physical presence was too penetrating, too hot.

After tea the evening was very quiet. The youth rarely went into the village. As a rule, he read: he was a great reader, in his own hours. That is, when he did begin, he read absorbedly. But he was not very eager to begin. Often he walked about the fields and along the hedges alone in the dark at night, prowling with a queer instinct for the night, and listening to the wild sounds.

Tonight, however, he took a Captain Mayne Reid book from Banford's shelf and sat down with knees wide apart and immersed himself in his story. His brownish fair hair was long, and lay on his head like a thick cap, combed sideways. He was still in his shirt-sleeves, and bending forward under the lamp-light, with his knees stuck wide apart and the book in his hand and his whole figure absorbed in the rather strenuous business of reading, he gave Banford's sitting-room the look of a lumber-camp. She resented this. For on her sitting-room floor she had a red Turkey rug and dark stain round, the fire-place had fashionable green tiles, the piano stood open with the latest dance music: she played quite well: and on the walls were March's hand-painted swans and water-lilies. Moreover, with the logs nicely, tremulously burning in the grate, the thick curtains drawn, the doors all shut, and the pine trees hissing and shuddering in the wind outside, it was cosy, it was refined and nice. She resented the big, raw, long-legged youth sticking his khaki knees out and sitting there with his soldier's shirt-cuffs buttoned on his thick red wrists. From time to time he turned a page, and from time to time he gave a sharp look at the fire, settling the logs. Then he immersed himself again in the intense and isolated business of reading.

March, on the far side of the table, was spasmodically crochetting. Her mouth was pursed in an odd way, as when she had dreamed the fox's brush burned it, her beautiful, crisp black hair strayed in wisps. But her whole figure was absorbed in its bearing, as if she herself was miles away. In a sort of semi-dream she seemed to be hearing the fox singing round the house in the wind, singing wildly and sweetly and like a madness. With red but well-shaped hands she slowly crochetted the white cotton, very slowly, awkwardly.

Banford was also trying to read, sitting in her low chair. But between those two she felt fidgetty. She kept moving and looking round and listening to the wind, and glancing secretly from one to the other of her companions. March, seated on a straight chair, with her knees in their close breeches crossed, and slowly, laboriously crochetting, was also a trial.

'Oh dear!' said Banford. 'My eyes are bad tonight.' And she pressed her fingers on her eyes.

The youth looked up at her with his clear, bright look, but did not speak.

'Are they, Jill?' said March absently.

Then the youth began to read again, and Banford perforce returned to her book. But she could not keep still. After a while she looked up at March, and a queer, almost malignant little smile was on her thin face.

'A penny for them, Nell,' she said suddenly.

March looked round with big, startled black eyes, and went pale as if with terror. She had been listening to the fox singing so tenderly, so tenderly, as he wandered round the house.

'What?' she said vaguely.

'A penny for them,' said Banford sarcastically. 'Or twopence, if they're as deep as all that.'

The youth was watching with bright, clear eyes from beneath the lamp.

'Why,' came March's vague voice, 'what do you want to waste your money for?'

'I thought it would be well spent,' said Banford.

'I wasn't thinking of anything except the way the wind was blowing,' said March.

'Oh dear,' replied Banford, 'I could have had as original thought as that myself. I'm afraid I *have* wasted my money this time.'

'Well, you needn't pay,' said March.

The youth suddenly laughed. Both women looked at him: March rather surprised-looking, as if she had hardly known he was there.

'Why, do you ever pay up on these occasions?' he asked.

'Oh yes,' said Banford. 'We always do. I've sometimes had to pass a shilling a week to Nellie, in the winter-time. It costs much less in summer.'

'What, paying for each other's thoughts?' he laughed.

'Yes, when we've absolutely come to the end of everything else.'

He laughed quickly, wrinkling his nose sharply like a puppy and laughing with quick pleasure, his eyes shining.

'It's the first time I ever heard of that,' he said.

'I guess you'd hear of it often enough if you stayed a winter on Bailey Farm,' said Banford lamentably.

'Do you get so tired, then?' he asked.

'So bored,' said Banford.

'Oh!' he said gravely. 'But why should you be bored?'

'Who wouldn't be bored?' said Banford.

'I'm sorry to hear that,' he said gravely.

'You must be, if you were hoping to have a lively time here,' said Banford.

He looked at her long and gravely.

'Well,' he said, with his odd, young seriousness, 'it's quite lively enough for me.'

'I'm glad to hear it,' said Banford.

And she returned to her book. In her thin, frail hair were already many threads of grey, though she was not yet thirty. The boy did not look down, but turned his eyes to March, who was sitting with pursed mouth laboriously crochetting, her eyes wide and absent. She had a warm, pale, fine skin and a delicate nose. Her pursed mouth looked shrewish. But the shrewish look was contradicted by the curious lifted arch of her dark brows, and the wideness of her eyes; a look of startled wonder and vagueness. She was listening again for the fox, who seemed to have wandered farther off into the night.

From under the edge of the lamp-light the boy sat with his face looking up, watching her silently, his eyes round and very clear and intent. Banford, biting her fingers irritably, was glancing at him under her hair. He sat there perfectly still, his ruddy face tilted up from the low level under the light, on the edge of the dimness, and watching with perfect abstract intentness. March suddenly lifted her great, dark eyes from her crochetting and saw him. She started, giving a little exclamation.

'There he is!' she cried involuntarily, as if terribly startled.

Banford looked around in amazement, sitting up straight.

'Whatever has got you, Nellie?' she cried.

But March, her face flushed a delicate rose colour, was looking away to the door.

'Nothing! Nothing!' she said crossly. 'Can't one speak?'

'Yes, if you speak sensibly,' said Banford. 'Whatever did you mean?'

'I don't know what I meant,' cried March testily.

'Oh, Nellie, I hope you aren't going jumpy and nervy. I feel I can't stand another *thing*! Whoever did you mean? Did you mean Henry?' cried poor, frightened Banford.

'Yes. I suppose so,' said March laconically. She would never confess to the fox.

'Oh dear, my nerves are all gone for tonight,' wailed Banford.

At nine o'clock March brought in a tray with bread and cheese and tea – Henry had confessed that he liked a cup of tea. Banford drank a glass of milk and ate a little bread. And soon she said:

'I'm going to bed, Nellie. I'm all nerves tonight. Are you coming?'

'Yes, I'm coming the minute I've taken the tray away,' said March.

'Don't be long then,' said Banford fretfully. 'Good night, Henry. You'll see the fire is safe, if you come up last, won't you?'

'Yes, Miss Banford, I'll see it's safe,' he replied in his reassuring way.

March was lighting the candle to go to the kitchen. Banford took her candle and went upstairs. When March came back to the fire, she said to him:

'I suppose we can trust you to put out the fire and everything?' She stood there with her hand on her hip, and one knee loose, her head averted shyly, as if she could not look at him. He had his face lifted, watching her.

'Come and sit down a minute,' he said softly.

'No, I'll be going. Jill will be waiting, and she'll get upset, if I don't come.'

'What made you jump like that this evening?' he asked.

'When did I jump?' she retorted, looking at him.

'Why, just now you did,' he said. 'When you cried out.'

'Oh!' she said. 'Then! – Why, I thought you were the fox!' And her face screwed into a queer smile, half-ironic.

'The fox! Why the fox?' he asked softly.

'Why, one evening last summer when I was out with the gun I saw the fox in the grass nearly at my feet, looking straight up at me. I don't know – I suppose he made an impression on me.' She turned aside her head again and let one foot stray loose, self-consciously.

'And did you shoot him?' asked the boy.

'No, he gave me such a start, staring straight at me as he did, and then stopping to look back at me over his shoulder with a laugh on his face.'

'A laugh on his face!' repeated Henry, also laughing. 'He frightened you, did he?'

'No, he didn't frighten me. He made an impression on me, that's all.'

'And you thought I was the fox, did you?' he laughed, with the same queer, quick little laugh, like a puppy wrinkling his nose.

'Yes, I did, for the moment,' she said. 'Perhaps he'd been in my mind without my knowing.'

'Perhaps you think I've come to steal your chickens or something,' he said, with the same young laugh.

But she only looked at him with a wide, dark, vacant eye.

'It's the first time,' he said, 'that I've ever been taken for a fox. Won't you sit down for a minute?' His voice was very soft and cajoling.

'No,' she said. 'Jill will be waiting.' But still she did not go, but stood with one foot loose and her face turned aside, just outside the circle of light.

'But won't you answer my question?' he said, lowering his voice still more.

'I don't know what question you mean.'

'Yes, you do. Of course you do. I mean the question of you marrying me.'

'No, I shan't answer that question,' she said flatly.

'Won't you?' The queer, young laugh came on his nose again. 'Is it because I'm like the fox? Is that why?' And still he laughed.

She turned and looked at him with a long, slow look.

'I wouldn't let that put you against me,' he said. 'Let me turn the lamp low, and come and sit down a minute.'

He put his red hand under the glow of the lamp and suddenly made the light very dim. March stood there in the dimness quite shadowy, but unmoving. He rose silently to his feet, on his long legs. And now his voice was extraordinarily soft and suggestive, hardly audible.

'You'll stay a moment,' he said. 'Just a moment.' And he put his hand on her shoulder. She turned her face from him. 'I'm sure you don't really think I'm like the fox,' he said, with the same softness and with a suggestion of laughter in his tone, a subtle mockery. 'Do you now?' And he drew her gently towards him and kissed her neck, softly. She winced and trembled and hung away. But his strong, young arm held her, and he kissed her softly again, still on the neck, for her face was averted.

'Won't you answer my question? Won't you now?' came his soft, lingering voice. He was trying to draw her near to kiss her face. And he kissed her cheek softly, near the ear.

At that moment Banford's voice was heard calling fretfully, crossly from upstairs.

'There's Jill!' cried March, starting and drawing erect.

And as she did so, quick as lightning he kissed her on the mouth, with a quick, brushing kiss. It seemed to burn through her every fibre. She gave a queer little cry.

'You will, won't you? You will?' he insisted softly.

'Nellie! *Nellie!* Whatever are you so long for?' came Banford's faint cry from the outer darkness.

But he held her fast, and was murmuring with that intolerable softness and insistency:

'You will, won't you? Say yes! Say yes!'

March, who felt as if the fire had gone through her and scathed her, and as if she could do no more, murmured:

'Yes! Yes! Anything you like! Anything you like! Only let me go! Only let me go! Jill's calling.'

'You know you've promised,' he said insidiously.

'Yes! Yes! I do!' Her voice suddenly rose into a shrill cry. 'All right, Jill, I'm coming.'

Startled, he let her go, and she went straight upstairs.

In the morning at breakfast, after he had looked round the place and attended to the stock and thought to himself that one could live easily enough here, he said to Banford:

'Do you know what, Miss Banford?'

'Well, what?' said the good-natured, nervy Banford.

He looked at March, who was spreading jam on her bread.

'Shall I tell?' he said to her.

She looked up at him, and a deep pink colour flushed over her face.

'Yes, if you mean Jill,' she said. 'I hope you won't go talking all over the village, that's all.' And she swallowed her dry bread with difficulty.

'Whatever's coming?' said Banford, looking up with wide, tired, slightly reddened eyes. She was a thin, frail little thing, and her hair, which was delicate and thin, was bobbed, so it hung softly by her worn face in its faded brown and grey.

'Why, what do you think?' he said, smiling like one who has a secret.

'How do I know!' said Banford.

'Can't you guess?' he said, making bright eyes and smiling, pleased with himself.

'I'm sure I can't. What's more, I'm not going to try.'

'Nellie and I are going to be married.'

Banford put down her knife out of her thin, delicate fingers, as if she would never take it up to eat any more. She stared with blank, reddened eyes.

'You what?' she exclaimed.

'We're going to get married. Aren't we, Nellie?' and he turned to March.

'You say so, anyway,' said March, laconically. But again she flushed with an agonised flush. She, too, could swallow no more.

Banford looked at her like a bird that has been shot: a poor, little sick bird. She gazed at her with all her wounded soul in her face, at the deep-flushed March.

'Never!' she exclaimed, helpless.

'It's quite right,' said the bright and gloating youth.

Banford turned aside her face, as if the sight of the food on the table made her sick. She sat like this for some moments, as if she were sick. Then, with one hand on the edge of the table, she rose to her feet.

'I'll *never* believe it, Nellie,' she cried. 'It's absolutely impossible!'

Her plaintive, fretful voice had a thread of hot anger and despair.

'Why? Why shouldn't you believe it?' asked the youth, with all his soft, velvety impertinence in his voice.

Banford looked at him from her wide, vague eyes, as if he were some creature in a museum.

'Oh,' she said languidly, 'because she can never be such a fool. She can't lose her self-respect to such an extent.' Her voice was cold and plaintive, drifting.

'In what way will she lose her self-respect?' asked the boy.

Banford looked at him with vague fixity from behind her spectacles.

'If she hasn't lost it already,' she said.

He became very red, vermilion, under the slow, vague stare from behind the spectacles.

'I don't see it at all,' he said.

'Probably you don't. I shouldn't expect you would,' said Banford, with that straying mild tone of remoteness which made her words even more insulting.

He sat stiff in his chair, staring with hot, blue eyes from his scarlet face. An ugly look had come on his brow.

'My word, she doesn't know what she's letting herself in for,' said Banford, in her plaintive, drifting, insulting voice.

'What has it got to do with you, anyway?' said the youth, in a temper.

'More than it has to do with you, probably,' she replied, plaintive and venomous.

'Oh, has it! I don't see that at all,' he jerked out.

'No, you wouldn't,' she answered, drifting.

'Anyhow,' said March, pushing back her hair and rising uncouthly. 'It's no good arguing about it.' And she seized the bread and the tea-pot and strode away to the kitchen.

Banford let her fingers stray across her brow and along her hair, like one bemused. Then she turned and went away upstairs.

Henry sat stiff and sulky in his chair, with his face and his eyes on fire. March came and went, clearing the table. But Henry sat on, stiff with temper. He took no notice of her. She had regained her composure and her soft, even, creamy complexion. But her mouth was pursed up. She glanced at him each time as she came to take things from the table, glanced from her large, curious eyes, more in curiosity than anything. Such a long, red-faced, sulky boy! That was all he was. He seemed as remote from her as if his red face were a red chimney-pot on a cottage across the fields, and she looked at him just as objectively, as remotely.

At length he got up and stalked out into the fields with the gun. He came in only at dinner-time, with the devil still in his face, but his manners quite polite. Nobody said anything particular; they sat each one at the sharp corner of a triangle, in obstinate remoteness. In the afternoon he went out again at once with the gun. He came in at nightfall with a rabbit and a pigeon. He stayed in all the evening, but hardly opened his mouth. He was in the devil of a temper, feeling he had been insulted.

Banford's eyes were red, she had evidently been crying. But her manner was more remote and supercilious than ever; the way she turned her head if he spoke at all, as if he were some tramp or inferior intruder of that sort, made his blue eyes go almost black with rage. His face looked sulkier. But he never forgot his polite intonation, if he opened his mouth to speak.

March seemed to flourish in this atmosphere. She seemed to sit between the two antagonists with a little wicked smile on her face, enjoying herself. There was even a sort of complacency in the way she laboriously crochetted this evening.

When he was in bed, the youth could hear the two women talking and arguing in their room. He sat up in bed and strained his ears to hear what they said. But he could hear nothing, it was too far off. Yet he could hear the soft, plaintive drip of Banford's voice, and March's deeper note.

The night was quiet, frosty. Big stars were snapping outside, beyond the ridge-tops of the pine trees. He listened and listened. In the distance he heard a fox yelping: and the dogs from the farms barking in answer. But it was not that he wanted to hear. It was what the two women were saying.

He got stealthily out of bed and stood by his door. He could hear no more than before. Very, very carefully he began to lift the door latch. After quite a time he had his door open. Then he stepped stealthily out into the passage. The old oak planks were cold under his feet, and they creaked preposterously. He crept very, very gently up the one step, and along by the wall, till he stood outside their door. And there he held his breath and listened. Banford's voice:

'No, I simply couldn't stand it. I should be dead in a month. Which is just what he would be aiming at, of course. That would just be his game, to see me in the churchyard. No, Nellie, if you were to do such a thing as to marry him, you could never stop here. I couldn't, I couldn't live in the same house with him. Oh! – h! I feel quite sick with the smell of his clothes. And his red face simply turns me over. I can't eat my food when he's at the table. What a fool I was ever to let him stop. One ought *never* to try to do a kind action. It always flies back in your face like a boomerang.'

'Well, he's only got two more days,' said March.

'Yes, thank heaven. And when he's gone he'll never come in this house again. I feel so bad while he's here. And I know, I know he's only counting what he can get out of you. I *know* that's all it is. He's just a good-for-nothing, who doesn't want to work, and who thinks he'll live on us. But he won't live on me. If you're such a fool, then it's your own look-out. Mrs Burgess knew him all the time he was here. And the old man could never get him to do any steady work. He was off with the gun on every occasion, just as he is now. Nothing but the gun! Oh, I do hate it. You don't know what you're doing, Nellie, you don't. If you marry him he'll just make a fool of you. He'll go off and leave you stranded. I know he will, if he can't get Bailey Farm out of us – and he's not going to, while I live. While I live he's never going to set foot here. I know what it would be. He'd soon think he was master of both of us, as he thinks he's master of you already.'

'But he isn't,' said Nellie.

'He thinks he is, anyway. And that's what he wants: to come and be master here. Yes, imagine it! That's what we've got the place together for, is it, to be bossed and bullied by a hateful, red-faced boy, a beastly labourer. Oh, we *did* make a mistake when we let him stop. We ought never to have lowered ourselves. And I've had such a fight with all the people here, not to be pulled down to their level. No, he's not coming here. And then you see – if he can't have the place, he'll run off to Canada or somewhere again, as if he'd never known you. And here you'll be, absolutely ruined and made a fool of. I know I shall never have any peace of mind again.'

'We'll tell him he can't come here. We'll tell him that,' said March.

'Oh, don't you bother; I'm going to tell him that, and other things as well, before he goes. He's not going to have all his own way while I've got the strength left to speak. Oh, Nellie, he'll despise you, he'll despise you, like the awful little beast he is, if you give way to him. I'd no more trust him than I'd trust a cat not to steal. He's deep, he's deep, and he's bossy, and he's selfish through and through, as cold as ice. All he wants is to make use of you. And when you're no more use to him, then I pity you.'

'I don't think he's as bad as all that,' said March.

'No, because he's been playing up to you. But you'll find out, if you see much of him. Oh, Nellie, I can't bear to think of it.'

'Well, it won't hurt you, Jill, darling.'

'Won't it! Won't it! I shall never know a moment's peace again while I live, nor a moment's happiness. No, Nellie –' and Banford began to weep bitterly.

The boy outside could hear the stifled sound of the woman's sobbing, and could hear March's soft, deep, tender voice comforting, with wonderful gentleness and tenderness, the weeping woman.

His eyes were so round and wide that he seemed to see the whole night, and his ears were almost jumping off his head. He was frozen stiff. He crept back to bed, but felt as if the top of his head were coming off. He could not sleep. He could not keep still. He rose, quietly dressed himself, and crept out on to the landing once more. The women were silent. He went softly downstairs and out to the kitchen.

Then he put on his boots and his overcoat and took the gun. He did not think to go away from the farm. No, he only took the gun. As softly as possible he unfastened the door and went out into the frosty December night. The air was still, the stars bright, the pine trees seemed to bristle audibly in the sky. He went stealthily away down a fenceside, looking for something to shoot. At the same time he remembered that he ought not to shoot and frighten the women.

So he prowled round the edge of the gorse cover, and through the grove of tall old hollies, to the woodside. There he skirted the fence, peering through the darkness with dilated eyes that seemed to be able to grow black and full of sight in the dark, like a cat's. An owl was slowly and mournfully whooing round a great oak tree. He stepped stealthily with his gun, listening, listening, watching.

As he stood under the oaks of the wood-edge he heard the dogs from the neighbouring cottage up the hill yelling suddenly and startlingly, and the wakened dogs from the farms around barking answer. And suddenly it seemed to him England was little and tight, he felt the landscape was constricted even in the dark, and that there were too many dogs in the night, making a noise like a fence of sound, like the network of English hedges netting the view. He felt the fox didn't have a chance. For it must be the fox that had started all this hullabaloo.

Why not watch for him, anyhow! He would, no doubt, be coming sniffing round. The lad walked downhill to where the farmstead with its few pine trees crouched blackly. In the angle of the long shed, in the black dark, he crouched down. He knew the fox would be coming. It seemed to him it would be the last of the foxes in this loudly-barking, thick-voiced England, tight with innumerable little houses.

He sat a long time with his eyes fixed unchanging upon the open gateway, where a little light seemed to fall from the stars or from the horizon, who knows. He was sitting on a log in a dark corner with the gun across his knees. The pine trees snapped. Once a chicken fell off its perch in the barn with a loud crawk and cackle and commotion that startled him, and he stood up, watching with all his eyes, thinking it might be a rat. But he *felt* it was nothing. So he sat down again with the gun on his knees and his hands tucked in to keep them warm, and his eyes fixed unblinking on the pale reach of the open gateway. He felt he could smell the hot, sickly, rich smell of live chickens on the cold air.

And then – a shadow. A sliding shadow in the gateway. He gathered all his vision into a concentrated spark, and saw the shadow of the fox, the fox creeping on his belly through the gate. There he went, on his belly like a snake. The boy smiled to himself and brought the gun to his shoulder. He knew quite well what would happen. He knew the fox would go to where the fowl door was boarded up and sniff there. He knew he would lie there for a minute, sniffing the fowls within. And then he would start again prowling under the edge of the old barn, waiting to get in.

The fowl door was at the top of a slight incline. Soft, soft as a shadow the fox slid up this incline, and crouched with his nose to the boards. And at the same moment there was the awful crash of a gun reverberating between the old buildings, as if all the night had gone smash. But the boy watched keenly. He saw even the white belly of the fox as the beast beat his paws in death. So he went forward.

There was a commotion everywhere. The fowls were scuffling and crawking, the ducks were quark-quarking, the pony had stamped wildly to his feet. But the fox was on his side, struggling in his last tremors. The boy bent over him and smelt his foxy smell.

There was a sound of a window opening upstairs, then March's voice calling:

'Who is it?'

'It's me,' said Henry; 'I've shot the fox.'

'Oh, goodness! You nearly frightened us to death.'

'Did I? I'm awfully sorry.'

'Whatever made you get up?'

'I heard him about.'

'And have you shot him?'

'Yes, he's here,' and the boy stood in the yard holding up the warm, dead brute. 'You can't see, can you? Wait a minute.' And he took his flash-light from his pocket and flashed it on to the dead animal. He was holding it by the brush. March saw, in the middle of the darkness, just the reddish fleece and the white belly and the white underneath of the pointed chin, and the queer, dangling paws. She did not know what to say.

'He's a beauty,' he said. 'He will make you a lovely fur.'

'You don't catch me wearing a fox fur,' she replied.

'Oh!' he said. And he switched off the light.

'Well, I should think you'll come in and go to bed again now,' she said.

'Probably I shall. What time is it?'

'What time is it, Jill?' called March's voice. It was a quarter to one.

That night March had another dream. She dreamed that Banford was dead, and that she, March, was sobbing her heart out. Then she had to put Banford into her coffin. And the coffin was the rough wood-box in which the bits of chopped wood were kept in the kitchen, by the fire. This was the coffin, and there was no other, and March was in agony and dazed bewilderment, looking for something to line the box with, something to make it soft with, something to cover up the poor, dead darling. Because she couldn't lay her in there just in her white, thin night-dress, in the horrible wood-box. So she hunted and hunted, and picked up thing after thing, and threw it aside in the agony of dream-frustration. And in her dream-despair all she could find that would do was a fox-skin. She knew that it wasn't right, that this was not what she should have. But it was all she could find. And so she folded the brush of the fox, and laid her darling Jill's head on this, and she brought round the skin of the fox and laid it on the top of the body, so that it seemed to make a whole ruddy, fiery coverlet, and she cried and cried, and woke to find the tears streaming down her face.

The first thing that both she and Banford did in the morning was to go out to see the fox. Henry had hung it up by the heels in the shed, with its poor brush falling backwards. It was a lovely dog-fox in its prime, with a handsome, thick, winter coat: a lovely golden-red colour, with grey as it passed to the belly, and belly all white, and a great full brush with a delicate black and grey and pure white tip.

'Poor brute!' said Banford. 'If it wasn't such a thieving wretch, you'd feel sorry for it.'

March said nothing, but stood with her foot trailing aside, one hip out; her face was pale and her eyes big and black, watching the dead animal that was suspended upside down. White and soft as snow his belly: white and soft as snow. She passed her hand softly down it. And his wonderful black-glinted brush was full and frictional, wonderful. She passed her hand down this also, and quivered. Time after time she took the full fur of that thick tail between her fingers, and passed her hand slowly downwards. Wonderful, sharp, thick, splendour of a tail. And he was dead! She pursed her lips, and her eyes went black and vacant. Then she took the head in her hand.

Henry was sauntering up, so Banford walked rather pointedly away. March stood there bemused, with the head of the fox in her hand. She was wondering, wondering, wondering over his long, fine muzzle. For some reason it reminded her of a spoon or a spatula. She felt she could not understand it. The beast was a strange beast to her, incomprehensible, out of her range. Wonderful silver whiskers he had, like ice-threads. And pricked ears with hair inside. But that long, long, slender spoon of a nose! – and the marvellous white teeth beneath! It was to thrust forward and bite with, deep, deep, deep into the living prey, to bite and bite the blood.

'He's a beauty, isn't he?' said Henry, standing by.

'Oh yes, he's a fine big fox. I wonder how many chickens he's responsible for,' she replied.

'A good many. Do you think he's the same one you saw in the summer?'

'I should think very likely he is,' she replied.

He watched her, but he could make nothing of her. Partly she was so shy and virgin, and partly she was so grim, matter-of-fact, shrewish. What she said seemed to him so different from the look of her big, queer, dark eyes.

'Are you going to skin him?' she asked.

'Yes, when I've had breakfast, and got a board to peg him on.'

'My word, what a strong smell he's got! Pooo! It'll take some washing off one's hands. I don't know why I was so silly as to handle him.' And she looked at her right hand, that had passed down his belly and along his tail, and had even got a tiny streak of blood from one dark place in his fur.

'Have you seen the chickens when they smell him, how frightened they are?' he said.

'Yes, aren't they!'

'You must mind you don't get some of his fleas.'

'Oh, fleas!' she replied, nonchalant.

Later in the day she saw the fox's skin nailed flat on a board, as if crucified. It gave her an uneasy feeling.

The boy was angry. He went about with his mouth shut, as if he had swallowed part of his chin. But in behaviour he was polite and affable. He did not say anything about his intention. And he left March alone.

That evening they sat in the dining-room. Banford wouldn't have him in her sitting-room any more. There was a very big log on the fire. And everybody was busy. Banford had letters to write, March was sewing a dress, and he was mending some little contrivance.

Banford stopped her letter-writing from time to time to look round and rest her eyes. The boy had his head down, his face hidden over his job.

'Let's see,' said Banford. 'What train do you go by, Henry?'

He looked up straight at her.

'The morning train. In the morning,' he said.

'What, the eight-ten or the eleven-twenty?'

'The eleven-twenty, I suppose,' he said.

'That is the day after tomorrow?' said Banford.

'Yes, the day after tomorrow.'

'Mm!' murmured Banford, and she returned to her writing. But as she was licking her envelope, she asked:

'And what plans have you made for the future, if I may ask?'

'Plans?' he said, his face very bright and angry.

'I mean about you and Nellie, if you are going on with this business. When do you expect the wedding to come off?' She spoke in a jeering tone.

'Oh, the wedding!' he replied. 'I don't know.'

'Don't you know anything?' said Banford. 'Are you going to clear out on Friday and leave things no more settled than they are?'

'Well, why shouldn't I? We can always write letters.'

'Yes, of course you can. But I wanted to know because of this place. If Nellie is going to get married all of a sudden, I shall have to be looking round for a new partner.'

'Couldn't she stay on here if she were married?' he said. He knew quite well what was coming.

'Oh,' said Banford, 'this is no place for a married couple. There's not enough work to keep a man going, for one thing. And there's no money to be made. It's quite useless your thinking of staying on here if you marry. Absolutely!'

'Yes, but I wasn't thinking of staying on here,' he said.

'Well, that's what I want to know. And what about Nellie, then? How long is *she* going to be here with me, in that case?'

The two antagonists looked at one another.

'That I can't say,' he answered.

'Oh, go along,' she cried petulantly. 'You must have some idea what you are going to do, if you ask a woman to marry you. Unless it's all a hoax.'

'Why should it be a hoax? I am going back to Canada.'

'And taking her with you?'

'Yes, certainly.'

'You hear that, Nellie?' said Banford.

March, who had had her head bent over her sewing, now looked up with a sharp, pink blush on her face, and a queer, sardonic laugh in her eyes and on her twisted mouth.

'That's the first time I've heard that I was going to Canada,' she said.

'Well, you have to hear it for the first time, haven't you?' said the boy.

'Yes, I suppose I have,' she said nonchalantly. And she went back to her sewing.

'You're quite ready, are you, to go to Canada? Are you, Nellie?' asked Banford.

March looked up again. She let her shoulders go slack, and let her hand that held the needle lie loose in her lap.

'It depends on *how* I'm going,' she said. 'I don't think I want to go jammed up in the steerage, as a soldier's wife. I'm afraid I'm not used to that way.'

The boy watched her with bright eyes.

'Would you rather stay over here while I go first?' he asked.

'I would, if that's the only alternative,' she replied.

'That's much the wisest. Don't make it any fixed engagement,' said Banford. 'Leave yourself free to go or not after he's got back and found you a place, Nellie. Anything else is madness, madness.'

'Don't you think,' said the youth, 'we ought to get married before I go – and then go together, or separate, according to how it happens?'

'I think it's a terrible idea,' cried Banford.

But the boy was watching March.

'What do you think?' he asked her.

She let her eyes stray vaguely into space.

'Well, I don't know,' she said. 'I shall have to think about it.'

'Why?' he asked pertinently.

'Why?' She repeated his question in a mocking way and looked at him laughing, though her face was pink again. 'I should think there's plenty of reasons why.'

He watched her in silence. She seemed to have escaped him. She had got into league with Banford against him. There was again the queer, sardonic look about her; she would mock stoically at everything he said or which life offered.

'Of course,' he said, 'I don't want to press you to do anything you don't wish to do.'

'I should think not, indeed,' cried Banford indignantly.

At bed-time Banford said plaintively to March:

'You take my hot bottle up for me, Nellie, will you?'

'Yes, I'll do it,' said March, with the kind of willing unwillingness she so often showed towards her beloved but uncertain Jill.

The two women went upstairs. After a time March called from the top of the stairs: 'Good night, Henry. I shan't be coming down. You'll see to the lamp and the fire, won't you?'

The next day Henry went about with the cloud on his brow and his young cub's face shut up tight. He was cogitating all the time. He had wanted March to marry him and go back to Canada with him. And he had been sure she would do it. Why he wanted her he didn't know. But he did want her. He had set his mind on her. And he was convulsed with a youth's fury at being thwarted. To be thwarted, to be thwarted! It made him so furious inside that he did not know what to do with himself. But he kept himself in hand. Because even now things might turn out differently. She might come over to him. Of course she might. It was her business to do so.

Things drew to a tension again towards evening. He and Banford had avoided each other all day. In fact, Banford went in to the little town by the 11.20 train. It was market day. She arrived back on the 4.25. Just as the night was falling Henry saw her little figure in a dark-blue coat and a dark-blue tam-o'-shanter hat crossing the first meadow from the station. He stood under one of the wild pear trees, with the old dead leaves round his feet. And he watched the little blue figure advancing persistently over the rough winter-ragged meadow. She had her arms full of parcels, and advanced slowly, frail thing she was, but with that devilish little certainty which he so detested in her. He stood invisible under the pear tree, watching her every step. And if looks could have affected her, she would have felt a log of iron on each of her ankles as she made her way forward. 'You're a nasty little thing, you are,' he was saying softly, across the distance. 'You're a nasty little thing. I hope you'll be paid back for all the harm you've done me for nothing. I hope you will – you nasty little thing. I hope you'll have to pay for it. You will, if wishes are anything. You nasty little creature that you are.'

She was toiling slowly up the slope. But if she had been slipping back at every step towards the Bottomless Pit, he would not have gone to help her with her parcels. Aha, there went March, striding with her long, land stride in her breeches and her short tunic! Striding downhill at a great pace, and even running a few steps now and then, in her great solicitude and desire to come to the rescue of the little Banford. The boy watched her with rage in his heart. See her leap a ditch, and run, run as if a house was on fire, just to get to that creeping, dark little object down there! So, the Banford just stood still and waited. And March strode up and took *all* the parcels except a bunch of yellow chrysanthemums. These the Banford still carried – yellow chrysanthemums!

'Yes, you look well, don't you?' he said softly into the dusk air. 'You look well, pottering up there with a bunch of flowers, you do. I'd make you eat them for your tea if you hug them so tight. And I'd give them you for breakfast again, I would. I'd give you flowers. Nothing but flowers.'

He watched the progress of the two women. He could hear their voices: March always outspoken and rather scolding in her tenderness, Banford murmuring rather vaguely. They were evidently good friends. He could not hear what they said till they came to the fence of the home meadow, which they must climb. Then he saw March manfully climbing over the bars with all her packages in her arms, and on the still air he heard Banford's fretful:

'Why don't you let me help you with the parcels?' She had a queer, plaintive hitch in her voice. Then came March's robust and reckless:

'Oh, I can manage. Don't you bother about me. You've all you can do to get yourself over.'

'Yes, that's all very well,' said Banford fretfully, 'You say, *Don't you bother about me*, and then all the while you feel injured because nobody thinks of you.'

'When do I feel injured?' said March.

'Always. You always feel injured. Now you're feeling injured because I won't have that boy to come and live on the farm.'

'I'm not feeling injured at all,' said March.

'I know you are. When he's gone you'll sulk over it. I know you will.'

'Shall I?' said March. 'We'll see.'

'Yes, we *shall* see, unfortunately. I can't think how you can make yourself so cheap. I can't *imagine* how you can lower yourself like it.'

'I haven't lowered myself,' said March.

'I don't know what you call it, then. Letting a boy like that come so cheeky and impudent and make a mug of you. I don't know what you think of yourself. How much respect do you think he's going to have for you afterwards? My word, I wouldn't be in your shoes, if you married him.'

'Of course you wouldn't. My boots are a good bit too big for you, and not half dainty enough,' said March, with rather a misfire sarcasm.

'I thought you had too much pride, really I did. A woman's got to hold herself high, especially with a youth like that. Why, he's impudent. Even the way he forced himself on us at the start.'

'We asked him to stay,' said March.

'Not till he'd almost forced us to. And then he's so cocky and self-assured. My word, he puts my back up. I simply can't imagine how you can let him treat you so cheaply.'

'I don't let him treat me cheaply,' said March. 'Don't you worry yourself, nobody's going to treat me cheaply. And even you aren't, either.' She had a tender defiance and a certain fire in her voice.

'Yes, it's sure to come back to me,' said Banford bitterly. 'That's always the end of it. I believe you only do it to spite me.'

They went now in silence up the steep, grassy slope and over the brow, through the gorse bushes. On the other side of the hedge the boy followed in the dusk, at some little distance. Now and then, through the huge ancient hedge of hawthorn, risen into trees, he saw the two dark figures creeping up the hill. As he came to the top of the slope he saw the homestead dark in the twilight, with a huge old pear tree leaning from the near gable, and a little yellow light twinkling in the small side windows of the kitchen. He heard the clink of the latch and saw the kitchen door open into light as the two women went indoors. So they were at home.

And so! – this was what they thought of him. It was rather in his nature to be a listener, so he was not at all surprised whatever he heard. The things people said about him always missed him personally. He was only rather surprised at the women's way with one another. And he disliked the Banford with an acid dislike. And he felt drawn to the March again. He felt again irresistibly drawn to her. He felt there was a secret bond, a secret thread between him and her, something very exclusive, which shut out everybody else and made him and her possess each other in secret.

He hoped again that she would have him. He hoped with his blood suddenly firing up that she would agree to marry him quite quickly: at Christmas, very likely. Christmas was not far off. He wanted, whatever else happened, to snatch her into a hasty marriage and a consummation with him. Then for the future, they could arrange later. But he hoped it would happen as he wanted it. He hoped that tonight she would stay a little while with him, after Banford had gone upstairs. He hoped he could touch her soft, creamy cheek, her strange, frightened face. He hoped he could look into her dilated, frightened dark eyes, quite near. He hoped he might even put his hand on her bosom and feel her soft breasts under her tunic. His heart beat deep and powerful as he thought of that. He wanted very much to do so. He wanted to make sure of her soft woman's breasts under her tunic. She always kept the brown linen coat buttoned so close up to her throat. It seemed to him like some perilous secret, that her soft woman's breasts must be buttoned up in that uniform. It seemed to him, moreover, that they were so much softer, tenderer, more lovely and lovable, shut up in that tunic, than were the Banford's breasts, under her soft blouses and chiffon dresses. The Banford would have little iron breasts, he said to himself. For all her frailty and fretfulness and delicacy, she would have tiny iron breasts. But March, under her crude, fast, workman's tunic, would have soft, white breasts, white and unseen. So he told himself, and his blood burned.

When he went into tea, he had a surprise. He appeared at the inner door, his face very ruddy and vivid and his blue eyes shining, dropping his head forward as he came in, in his usual way, and hesitating in the doorway to watch the inside of the room, keenly and cautiously, before he entered. He was wearing a long-sleeved waistcoat. His face seemed extraordinarily like a piece of the out-of-doors come indoors: as holly-berries do. In his second of pause in the doorway he took in the two women sitting at table, at opposite ends, saw them sharply. And to his amazement March was dressed in a dress of dull, green silk crape. His mouth came open in surprise. If she had suddenly grown a moustache he could not have been more surprised.

'Why,' he said, 'do you a wear a dress, then?'

She looked up, flushing a deep rose colour, and twisting her mouth with a smile, said:

'Of course I do. What else do you expect me to wear but a dress?'

'A land girl's uniform, of course,' said he.

'Oh,' she cried, nonchalant, 'that's only for this dirty, mucky work about here.'

'Isn't it your proper dress, then?' he said.

'No, not indoors it isn't,' she said. But she was blushing all the time as she poured out his tea. He sat down in his chair at table, unable to take his eyes off her. Her dress was a perfectly simple slip of bluey-green crape, with a line of gold stitching round the top and round the sleeves, which came to the elbow. It was cut just plain and round at the top, and showed her white, soft throat. Her arms he knew, strong and firm muscled, for he had often seen her with her sleeves rolled up. But he looked her up and down, up and down.

Banford, at the other end of the table, said not a word, but piggled with the sardine on her plate. He had forgotten her existence. He just simply stared at March while he ate his bread and margarine in huge mouthfuls, forgetting even his tea.

'Well, I never knew anything make such a difference!' he murmured, across his mouthfuls.

'Oh, goodness!' cried March, blushing still more. 'I might be a pink monkey!'

And she rose quickly to her feet and took the tea-pot to the fire, to the kettle. And as she crouched on the hearth with her green slip about her, the boy stared more wide-eyed than ever. Through the crape her woman's form seemed soft and womanly. And when she stood up and walked he saw her legs move soft within her modernly short skirt. She had on black silk stockings, and small patent shoes with little gold buckles.

No, she was another being. She was something quite different. Seeing her always in the hard-cloth breeches, wide on the hips, buttoned on the knee, strong as armour, and in the brown puttees and thick boots, it had never occurred to him that she had a woman's legs and feet. Now it came upon him. She had a woman's soft, skirted legs, and she was accessible. He blushed to the roots of his hair, shoved his nose in his tea-cup and drank his tea with a little noise that made Banford simply squirm: and strangely, suddenly he felt a man, no longer a youth. He felt a man, with all a man's grave weight of responsibility. A curious quietness and gravity came over his soul. He felt a man, quiet, with a little of the heaviness of male destiny upon him.

She was soft and accessible in her dress. The thought went home in him like an everlasting responsibility.

'Oh, for goodness' sake, say something, somebody,' cried Banford fretfully. 'It might be a funeral.' The boy looked at her, and she could not bear his face.

'A funeral!' said March, with a twisted smile. 'Why, that breaks my dream.'

Suddenly she had thought of Banford in the wood-box for a coffin.

'What, have you been dreaming of a wedding?' said Banford sarcastically.

'Must have been,' said March.

'Whose wedding?' asked the boy.

'I can't remember,' said March.

She was shy and rather awkward that evening, in spite of the fact that, wearing a dress, her bearing was much more subdued than in her uniform. She felt unpeeled and rather exposed. She felt almost improper.

They talked desultorily about Henry's departure next morning, and made the trivial arrangement. But of the matter on their minds, none of them spoke.

They were rather quiet and friendly this evening; Banford had practically nothing to say. But inside herself she seemed still, perhaps kindly.

At nine o'clock March brought in the tray with the everlasting tea and a little cold meat which Banford had managed to procure. It was the last supper, so Banford did not want to be disagreeable. She felt a bit sorry for the boy, and felt she must be as nice as she could.

He wanted her to go to bed. She was usually the first. But she sat on in her chair under the lamp, glancing at her book now and then, and staring into the fire. A deep silence had come into the room. It was broken by March asking, in a rather small tone:

'What time is it, Jill?'

'Five past ten,' said Banford, looking at her wrist.

And then not a sound. The boy had looked up from the book he was holding between his knees. His rather wide, cat-shaped face had its obstinate look, his eyes were watchful.

'What about bed?' said March at last.

'I'm ready when you are,' said Banford.

'Oh, very well,' said March. 'I'll fill your bottle.'

She was as good as her word. When the hot-water bottle was ready, she lit a candle and went upstairs with it. Banford remained in her chair, listening acutely. March came downstairs again.

'There you are, then,' she said. 'Are you going up?'

'Yes, in a minute,' said Banford. But the minute passed, and she sat on in her chair under the lamp.

Henry, whose eyes were shining like a cat's as he watched from under his brows, and whose face seemed wider, more chubbed and cat-like with unalterable obstinacy, now rose to his feet to try his throw.

'I think I'll go and look if I can see the she-fox,' he said. 'She may be creeping round. Won't you come as well for a minute, Nellie, and see if we see anything?'

'Me!' cried March, looking up with her startled, wondering face.

'Yes. Come on,' he said. It was wonderful how soft and warm and coaxing his voice could be, how near. The very sound of it made Banford's blood boil. 'Come on for a minute,' he said, looking down into her uplifted, unsure face.

And she rose to her feet as if drawn up by his young, ruddy face that was looking down on her.

'I should think you're never going out at this time of night, Nellie!' cried Banford.

'Yes, just for a minute,' said the boy, looking round on her, and speaking with an odd, sharp yelp in his voice.

March looked from one to the other, as if confused, vague. Banford rose to her feet for battle.

'Why, it's ridiculous. It's bitter cold. You'll catch your death in that thin frock. And in those slippers. You're not going to do any such thing.'

There was a moment's pause. Banford turtled up like a little fighting cock, facing March and the boy.

'Oh, I don't think you need worry yourself,' he replied. 'A moment under the stars won't do anybody any damage. I'll get the rug off the sofa in the dining-room. You're coming, Nellie.'

His voice had so much anger and contempt and fury in it as he spoke to Banford: and so much tenderness and proud authority as he spoke to March, that the latter answered.

'Yes, I'm coming.'

And she turned with him to the door.

Banford, standing there in the middle of the room, suddenly burst into a long wail and a spasm of sobs. She covered her face with her poor, thin hands, and her thin shoulders shook in an agony of weeping. March looked back from the door.

'Jill!' she cried in a frantic tone, like someone just coming awake. And she seemed to start towards her darling.

But the boy had March's arm in his grip, and she could not move. She did not know why she could not move. It was as in a dream when the heart strains and the body cannot stir.

'Never mind,' said the boy softly. 'Let her cry. Let her cry. She will have to cry sooner or later. And the tears will relieve her feelings. They will do her good.'

So he drew March slowly through the doorway. But her last look was back to the poor little figure which stood in the middle of the room with covered face and thin shoulders shaken with bitter weeping.

In the dining-room he picked up the rug and said:

'Wrap yourself up in this.'

She obeyed – and they reached the kitchen door, he holding her soft and firm by the arm, though she did not know it. When she saw the night outside she started back.

'I must go back to Jill,' she said. 'I *must*! Oh yes, I must.'

Her tone sounded final. The boy let go of her and she turned indoors. But he seized her again and arrested her.

'Wait a minute,' he said. 'Wait a minute. Even if you go, you're not going yet.'

'Leave go! Leave go!' she cried. 'My place is at Jill's side. Poor little thing, she's sobbing her heart out.'

'Yes,' said the boy bitterly. 'And your heart too, and mine as well.'

'Your heart?' said March. He still gripped her and detained her.

'Isn't it as good as her heart?' he said. 'Or do you think it's not?'

'Your heart?' she said again, incredulous.

'Yes, mine! Mine! Do you think I haven't *got* a heart?' And with his hot grasp he took her hand and pressed it under his left breast. 'There's my heart,' he said, 'if you don't believe in it.'

It was wonder which made her attend. And then she felt the deep, heavy, powerful stroke of his heart, terrible, like something from beyond. It was like something from beyond, something awful from outside, signalling to her. And the signal paralysed her. It beat upon her very soul, and made her helpless. She forgot Jill. She could not think of Jill any more. She could not think of her. That terrible signalling from outside!

The boy put his arm round her waist.

'Come with me,' he said gently. 'Come and let us say what we've got to say.'

And he drew her outside, closed the door. And she went with him darkly down the garden path. That he should have a beating heart! And that he should have his arm round her, outside the blanket! She was too confused to think who he was or what he was.

He took her to a dark corner of the shed, where there was a tool-box with a lid, long and low.

'We'll sit here a minute,' he said.

And obediently she sat down by his side.

'Give me your hand,' he said.

She gave him both her hands, and he held them between his own. He was young, and it made him tremble.

'You'll marry me. You'll marry me before I go back, won't you?' he pleaded.

'Why, aren't we both a pair of fools?' she said.

He had put her in the corner, so that she should not look out and see the lighted window of the house across the dark garden. He tried to keep her all there inside the shed with him.

'In what way a pair of fools?' he said. 'If you go back to Canada with me, I've got a job and a good wage waiting for me, and it's a nice place, near the mountains. Why shouldn't you marry me? Why shouldn't we marry? I should like to have you there with me. I should like to feel I'd got somebody there, at the back of me, all my life.'

'You'd easily find somebody else who'd suit you better,' she said.

'Yes, I might easily find another girl. I know I could. But not one I really wanted. I've never met one I really wanted for good. You see, I'm thinking of all my life. If I marry, I want to feel it's for all my life. Other girls: well, they're just girls, nice enough to go a walk with now and then. Nice enough for a bit of play. But when I think of my life, then I should be very sorry to have to marry one of them, I should indeed.'

'You mean they wouldn't make you a good wife.'

'Yes, I mean that. But I don't mean they wouldn't do their duty by me. I mean – I don't know what I mean. Only when I think of my life, and of you, then the two things go together.'

'And what if they didn't?' she said, with her odd, sardonic touch.

'Well, I think they would.'

They sat for some time silent. He held her hands in his, but he did not make love to her. Since he had realized that she was a woman, and vulnerable, accessible, a certain heaviness had possessed his soul. He did not want to make love to her. He shrank from any such performance, almost with fear. She was a woman, and vulnerable, accessible to him finally, and he held back from that which was ahead, almost with dread. It was a kind of darkness he knew he would enter finally, but of which he did not want as yet even to think. She was the woman, and he was responsible for the strange vulnerability he had suddenly realized in her.

'No,' she said at last, 'I'm a fool. I know I'm a fool.'

'What for?' he asked.

'To go on with this business.'

'Do you mean me?' he asked.

'No, I mean myself. I'm making a fool of myself, and a big one.'

'Why, because you don't want to marry me, really?'

'Oh, I don't know whether I'm against it, as a matter of fact. That's just it. I don't know.'

He looked at her in the darkness, puzzled. He did not in the least know what she meant.

'And don't you know whether you like to sit here with me this minute or not?' he asked.

'No, I don't really. I don't know whether I wish I was somewhere else, or whether I like being here. I don't know, really.'

'Do you wish you were with Miss Banford? Do you wish you'd gone to bed with her?' he asked, as a challenge.

She waited a long time before she answered.

'No,' she said at last. 'I don't wish that.'

'And do you think you would spend all your life with her – when your hair goes white, and you are old?' he said.

'No,' she said, without much hesitation. 'I don't see Jill and me two old women together.'

'And don't you think, when I'm an old man and you're an old woman, we might be together still, as we are now?' he said.

'Well, not as we are now,' she replied. 'But I could imagine – no, I can't. I can't imagine you an old man. Besides, it's dreadful!'

'What, to be an old man?'

'Yes, of course.'

'Not when the time comes,' he said. 'But it hasn't come. Only it will. And when it does, I should like to think you'd be there as well.'

'Sort of old age pensions,' she said dryly.

Her kind of witless humour always startled him. He never knew what she meant. Probably she didn't quite know herself.

'No,' he said, hurt.

'I don't know why you harp on old age,' she said. 'I'm not ninety.'

'Did anybody ever say you were?' he asked, offended.

They were silent for some time, pulling different ways in the silence.

'I don't want you to make fun of me,' he said.

'Don't you?' she replied, enigmatic.

'No, because just this minute I'm serious. And when I'm serious, I believe in not making fun of it.'

'You mean nobody else must make fun of you,' she replied.

'Yes, I mean that. And I mean I don't believe in making fun of it myself. When it comes over me so that I'm serious, then – there it is, I don't want it to be laughed at.'

She was silent for some time. Then she said, in a vague, almost pained voice:

'No, I'm not laughing at you.'

A hot wave rose in his heart.

'You believe me, do you?' he asked.

'Yes, I believe you,' she replied, with a twang of her old, tired nonchalance, as if she gave in because she was tired. But he didn't care. His heart was hot and clamorous.

'So you agree to marry me before I go? – perhaps at Christmas?'

'Yes, I agree.'

'There!' he exclaimed. 'That's settled it.'

And he sat silent, unconscious, with all the blood burning in all his veins, like fire in all the branches and twigs of him. He only pressed her two hands to his chest, without knowing. When the curious passion began to die down, he seemed to come awake to the world.

'We'll go in, shall we?' he said: as if he realized it was cold.

She rose without answering.

'Kiss me before we go, now you've said it,' he said.

And he kissed her gently on the mouth, with a young, frightened kiss. It made her feel so young, too, and frightened, and wondering: and tired, tired, as if she were going to sleep.

They went indoors. And in the sitting-room, there, crouched by the fire like a queer little witch, was Banford. She looked round with reddened eyes as they entered, but did not rise. He thought she looked frightening, unnatural, crouching there and looking round at them. Evil he thought her look was, and he crossed his fingers.

Banford saw the ruddy, elate face on the youth: he seemed strangely tall and bright and looming. And March had a delicate look on her face; she wanted to hide her face, to screen it, to let it not be seen.

'You've come at last,' said Banford uglily.

'Yes, we've come,' said he.

'You've been long enough for anything,' she said.

'Yes, we have. We've settled it. We shall marry as soon as possible,' he replied.

'Oh, you've settled it, have you! Well, I hope you won't live to repent it,' said Banford.

'I hope so too,' he replied.

'Are you going to bed *now*, Nellie?' said Banford.

'Yes, I'm going now.'

'Then for goodness' sake come along.'

March looked at the boy. He was glancing with his very bright eyes at her and at Banford. March looked at him wistfully. She wished she could stay with him. She wished she had married him already, and it was all over. For oh, she felt suddenly so safe with him. She felt so strangely safe and peaceful in his presence. If only she could sleep in his shelter, and not with Jill. She felt afraid of Jill. In her dim, tender state, it was agony to have to go with Jill and sleep with her. She wanted the boy to save her. She looked again at him.

And he, watching with bright eyes, divined something of what she felt. It puzzled and distressed him that she must go with Jill.

'I shan't forget what you've promised,' he said, looking clear into her eyes, right into her eyes, so that he seemed to occupy all herself with his queer, bright look.

She smiled to him faintly, gently. She felt safe again – safe with him.

But in spite of all the boy's precautions, he had a setback. The morning he was leaving the farm he got March to accompany him to the market-town, about six miles away, where they went to the registrar and had their names stuck up as two people who were going to marry. He was to come at Christmas, and the wedding was to take place then. He hoped in the spring to be able to take March back to Canada with him, now the war was really over. Though he was so young, he had saved some money.

'You never have to be without *some* money at the back of you, if you can help it,' he said.

So she saw him off in the train that was going West: his camp was on Salisbury Plain. And with big, dark eyes she watched him go, and it seemed as if everything real in life was retreating as the train retreated with his queer, chubby, ruddy face, that seemed so broad across the cheeks, and which never seemed to change its expression, save when a cloud of sulky anger hung on the brow, or the bright eyes fixed themselves in their stare. This was what happened now. He leaned there out of the carriage window as the train drew off, saying goodbye and staring back at her, but his face quite unchanged. There was no emotion on his face. Only his eyes tightened and became fixed and intent in their watching like a cat's when suddenly she sees something and stares. So the boy's eyes stared fixedly as the train drew away, and she was left feeling intensely forlorn. Failing his physical presence, she seemed to have nothing of him. And she had nothing of anything. Only his face was fixed in her mind: the full, ruddy, unchanging cheeks, and the straight snout of a nose and the two eyes staring above. All she could remember was how he suddenly wrinkled his nose when he laughed, as a puppy does when he is playfully growling. But him, himself, and what he was – she knew nothing, she had nothing of him when he left her.

On the ninth day after he had left her he received this letter.

Dear Henry,

I have been over it all again in my mind, this business of me and you, and it seems to me impossible. When you aren't there I see what a fool I am. When you are there you seem to blind me to things as they actually are. You make me see things all unreal, and I don't know what. Then when I am alone again with Jill I seem to come to my own senses and realize what a fool I am making of myself, and how I am treating you unfairly. Because it must be unfair to you for me to go on with this affair when I can't feel in my heart that I really love you. I know people talk a lot of stuff and nonsense about love, and I don't want to do that. I want to keep to plain facts and act in a sensible way. And that seems to me what I'm not doing. I don't see on what grounds I am going to marry you. I know I am not head over heels in love with you, as I have fancied myself to be with fellows when I was a young fool of a girl. You are an absolute stranger to me, and it seems to me you will always be one. So on what grounds am I going to marry you? When I think of Jill, she is ten times more real to me. I know her and I'm awfully fond of her, and I hate myself for a beast if I ever hurt her little finger. We have a life together. And even if it can't last for ever, it is a life while it does last. And it might last as long as either of us lives. Who knows how long we've got to live? She is a delicate little thing, perhaps nobody but me knows how delicate. And as for me, I feel I might fall down the well any day. What I don't seem to see at all is you. When I think of what I've been and what I've done with you, I'm afraid I am a few screws loose. I should be sorry to think that softening of the brain is setting in so soon, but that is what it seems like. You are such an absolute stranger, and so different from what I'm used to, and we don't seem to have a thing in common. As for love, the very word seems impossible. I know what love means even in Jill's case, and I know that in this affair with you it's an absolute impossibility. And then going to Canada. I'm sure I must have been clean off my chump when I promised such a thing. It makes me feel fairly frightened of myself. I feel I might do something really silly that I wasn't responsible for – and end my days in a lunatic asylum. You may think that's all I'm fit for after the way I've gone on, but it isn't a very nice thought for me. Thank goodness Jill is here, and her being here makes me feel sane again, else I don't know what I might do; I might have an accident with the gun one evening. I love Jill, and she makes me feel safe and sane, with her loving anger against me for being such a fool. Well, what I want to say is, won't you let us cry the whole thing off? I can't marry you, and really, I won't do such a thing if it seems to me wrong. It is all a great mistake. I've made a complete fool of myself, and all I can do is to apologize to you and ask you please to forget it, and please to take no further notice of me. Your fox-skin is nearly ready, and seems all right. I will post it to you if you will let me know if this address is still right, and if you will accept my apology for the awful and lunatic way I have behaved with you, and then let the matter rest.

Jill sends her kindest regards. Her mother and father are staying with us over Christmas.

Yours very sincerely,

ELLEN MARCH.

The boy read this letter in camp as he was cleaning his kit. He set his teeth, and for a moment went almost pale, yellow round the eyes with fury. He said nothing and saw nothing and felt nothing but a livid rage that was quite unreasoning. Baulked! Baulked again! Baulked! He wanted the woman, he had fixed like doom upon having her. He felt that was his doom, his destiny, and his reward, to have this woman. She was his heaven and hell on earth, and he would have none elsewhere. Sightless with rage and thwarted madness he got through the morning. Save that in his mind he was lurking and scheming towards an issue, he would have committed some insane act. Deep in himself he felt like roaring and howling and gnashing his teeth and breaking things.

But he was too intelligent. He knew society was on top of him, and he must scheme. So with his teeth bitten together, and his nose curiously slightly lifted, like some creature that is vicious, and his eyes fixed and staring, he went through the morning's affairs drunk with anger and suppression. In his mind was one thing – Banford. He took no heed of all March's outpouring: none. One thorn rankled, stuck in his mind. Banford. In his mind, in his soul, in his whole being, one thorn rankling to insanity. And he would have to get it out. He would have to get the thorn of Banford out of his life, if he died for it.

With this one fixed idea in his mind, he went to ask for twenty-four hours' leave of absence. He knew it was not due to him. His consciousness was supernaturally keen. He knew where he must go – he must go to the captain. But how could he get at the captain? In that great camp of wooden huts and tents he had no idea where his captain was.

But he went to the officers' canteen. There was his captain standing talking with three other officers. Henry stood in the doorway at attention.

'May I speak to Captain Berryman?' The captain was Cornish like himself.

'What do you want?' called the captain.

'May I speak to you, Captain?'

'What do you want?' replied the captain, not stirring from among his group of fellow officers.

Henry watched his superior for a minute without speaking.

'You won't refuse me, sir, will. you?' he asked gravely.

'It depends what it is.'

'Can I have twenty-four hours' leave?'

'No, you've no business to ask.'

'I know I haven't. But I must ask you.'

'You've had your answer.'

'Don't send me away, Captain.'

There was something strange about the boy as he stood there so everlasting in the doorway. The Cornish captain felt the strangeness at once, and eyed him shrewdly.

'Why, what's afoot?' he said, curious.

'I'm in trouble about something. I must go to Blewbury,' said the boy.

'Blewbury, eh? After the girls?'

'Yes, it is a woman, Captain.' And the boy, as he stood there with his head reaching forward a little, went suddenly terribly pale, or yellow, and his lips seemed to give off pain. The captain saw and paled a little also. He turned aside.

'Go on, then,' he said. 'But for God's sake don't cause any trouble of any sort.'

'I won't, Captain, thank you.'

He was gone. The captain, upset, took a gin and bitters. Henry managed to hire a bicycle. It was twelve o'clock when he left the camp. He had sixty miles of wet and muddy crossroads to ride. But he was in the saddle and down the road without a thought of food.

At the farm, March was busy with a work she had had some time in hand. A bunch of Scotch fir trees stood at the end of the open shed, on a little bank where ran the fence between two of the gorse-shaggy meadows. The farthest of these trees was dead – it had died in the summer, and stood with all its needles brown and sere in the air. It was not a very big tree. And it was absolutely dead. So March determined to have it, although they were not allowed to cut any of the timber. But it would make such splendid firing, in these days of scarce fuel.

She had been giving a few stealthy chops at the trunk for a week or more, every now and then hacking away for five minutes, low down, near the ground, so no one should notice. She had not tried the saw, it was such hard work, alone. Now the tree stood with a great yawning gap in his base, perched, as it were, on one sinew, and ready to fall. But he did not fall.

It was late in the damp December afternoon, with cold mists creeping out of the woods and up the hollows, and darkness waiting to sink in from above. There was a bit of yellowness where the sun was fading away beyond the low woods of the distance. March took her axe and went to the tree. The small thud-thud of her blows resounded rather ineffectual about the wintry homestead. Banford came out wearing her thick coat, but with no hat on her head, so that her thin, bobbed hair blew on the uneasy wind that sounded in the pines and in the wood.

'What I'm afraid of,' said Banford, 'is that it will fall on the shed and we sh'll have another job repairing that.'

'Oh, I don't think so,' said March, straightening herself and wiping her arm over her hot brow. She was flushed red, her eyes were very wide open and queer, her upper lip lifted away from her two white, front teeth with a curious, almost rabbit look.

A little stout man in a black overcoat and a bowler hat came pottering across the yard. He had a pink face and a white beard and smallish, pale-blue eyes. He was not very old, but nervy, and he walked with little short steps.

'What do you think, father?' said Banford. 'Don't you think it might hit the shed in falling?'

'Shed, no!' said the old man. 'Can't hit the shed. Might as well say the fence.'

'The fence doesn't matter,' said March, in her high voice.

'Wrong as usual, am I!' said Banford, wiping her straying hair from her eyes.

The tree stood as it were on one spelch of itself, leaning, and creaking in the wind. It grew on the bank of a little dry ditch between the two meadows. On the top of the bank straggled one fence, running to the bushes up-hill. Several trees clustered there in the corner of the field near the shed and near the gate which led into the yard. Towards this gate, horizontal across the weary meadows, came the grassy, rutted approach from the high road. There trailed another rickety fence, long split poles joining the short, thick, wide-apart uprights. The three people stood at the back of the tree, in the corner of the shed meadow, just above the yard gate. The house, with its two gables and its porch, stood tidy in a little grassed garden across the yard. A little, stout, rosy-faced woman in a little red woollen shoulder shawl had come and taken her stand in the porch.

'Isn't it down yet,' she cried, in a high little voice.

'Just thinking about it,' called her husband. His tone towards the two girls was always rather mocking and satirical. March did not want to go on with her hitting while he was there. As for him, he wouldn't lift a stick from the ground if he could help it, complaining, like his daughter, of rheumatics in his shoulder. So the three stood there a moment silent in the cold afternoon, in the bottom corner near the yard.

They heard the far-off taps of a gate, and craned to look. Away across, on the green horizontal approach, a figure was just swinging on to a bicycle again, and lurching up and down over the grass, approaching.

'Why, it's one of our boys – it's Jack,' said the old man.

'Can't be,' said Banford.

March craned her head to look. She alone recognized the khaki figure. She flushed, but said nothing.

'No, it isn't Jack, I don't think,' said the old man, staring with little round blue eyes under his white lashes.

In another moment the bicycle lurched into sight, and the rider dropped off at the gate. It was Henry, his face wet and red and spotted with mud. He was altogether a muddy sight.

'Oh!' cried Banford, as if afraid. 'Why, it's Henry!'

'What!' muttered the old man. He had a thick, rapid, muttering way of speaking, and was slightly deaf. 'What? What? Who is it? Who is it, do you say? That young fellow? That young fellow of Nellie's? Oh! Oh!' And the satiric smile came on his pink face and white eyelashes.

Henry, pushing the wet hair off his steaming brow, had caught sight of them and heard what the old man said. His hot, young face seemed to flame in the cold light.

'Oh, are you all there!' he said, giving his sudden, puppy's little laugh. He was so hot and dazed with cycling he hardly knew where he was. He leaned the bicycle against the fence and climbed over into the corner on to the bank, without going into the yard.

'Well, I must say, we weren't expecting *you*,' said Banford laconically.

'No, I suppose not,' said he, looking at March.

She stood aside, slack, with one knee drooped and the axe resting its head loosely on the ground. Her eyes were wide and vacant, and her upper lip lifted from her teeth in that helpless, fascinated rabbit look. The moment she saw his glowing, red face it was all over with her. She was as helpless as if she had been bound. The moment she saw the way his head seemed to reach forward.

'Well, who is it? Who is it, anyway?' asked the smiling, satiric old man in his muttering voice.

'Why, Mr Grenfel, whom you've heard us tell about, father,' said Banford coldly.

'Heard you tell about, I should think so. Heard of nothing else practically,' muttered the elderly man, with his queer little jeering smile on his face. 'How do you do,' he added, suddenly reaching out his hand to Henry.

The boy shook hands just as startled. Then the two men fell apart.

'Cycled over from Salisbury Plain, have you?' asked the old man.

'Yes.'

'Hm! Longish ride. How long d'it take you, eh? Some time, eh? Several hours, I suppose.'

'About four.'

'Eh? Four! Yes, I should have thought so. When are you going back, then?'

'I've got till tomorrow evening.'

'Till tomorrow evening, eh? Yes. Hm! Girls weren't expecting you, were they?'

And the old man turned his pale-blue, round little eyes under their white lashes mockingly towards the girls. Henry also looked round. He had become a little awkward. He looked at March, who was still staring away into the distance as if to see where the cattle were. Her hand was on the pommel of the axe, whose head rested loosely on the ground.

'What were you doing there?' he asked in his soft, courteous voice. 'Cutting a tree down?'

March seemed not to hear, as if in a trance.

'Yes,' said Banford. 'We've been at it for over a week.'

'Oh! And have you done it all by yourselves then?'

'Nellie's done it all, I've done nothing,' said Banford.

'Really! You must have worked quite hard,' he said, addressing himself in a curious gentle tone direct to March. She did not answer, but remained half averted staring away towards the woods above as if in a trance.

'*Nellie!*' cried Banford sharply. 'Can't you answer?'

'What – me?' cried March, starting round and looking from one to the other. 'Did anyone speak to me?'

'Dreaming!' muttered the old man, turning aside to smile. 'Must be in love, eh, dreaming in the day-time!'

'Did you say anything to me?' said March, looking at the boy as from a strange distance, her eyes wide and doubtful, her face delicately flushed.

'I said you must have worked hard at the tree,' he replied courteously.

'Oh, that! Bit by bit. I thought it would have come down by now.'

'I'm thankful it hasn't come down in the night, to frighten us to death,' said Banford.

'Let me just finish it for you, shall I?' said the boy.

March slanted the axe-shaft in his direction.

'Would you like to?' she said.

'Yes, if you wish it,' he said.

'Oh, I'm thankful when the thing's down, that's all,' she replied, nonchalant.

'Which way is it going to fall?' said Banford. 'Will it hit the shed?'

'No, it won't hit the shed,' he said. 'I should think it will fall there – quite clear. Though it might give a twist and catch the fence.'

'Catch the fence!' cried the old man. 'What, catch the fence! When it's leaning at that angle? Why, it's farther off than the shed. It won't catch the fence.'

'No,' said Henry, 'I don't suppose it will. It has plenty of room to fall quite clear, and I suppose it will fall clear.'

'Won't tumble backwards on top of *us*, will it?' asked the old man, sarcastic.

'No, it won't do that,' said Henry, taking off his short overcoat and his tunic. 'Ducks! Ducks! Go back!'

A line of four brown-speckled ducks led by a brown-and-green drake were stemming away downhill from the upper meadow, coming like boats running on a ruffled sea, cockling their way top speed downwards towards the fence and towards the little group of people, and cackling as excitedly as if they brought news of the Spanish Armada.

'Silly things! Silly things!' cried Banford, going forward to turn them off. But they came eagerly towards her, opening their yellow-green beaks and quacking as if they were so excited to say something.

'There's no food. There's nothing here. You must wait a bit,' said Banford to them. 'Go away. Go away. Go round to the yard.'

They didn't go, so she climbed the fence to swerve them round under the gate and into the yard. So off they waggled in an excited string once more, wagging their rumps like the stems of little gondolas, ducking under the bar of the gate. Banford stood on the top of the bank, just over the fence, looking down on the other three.

Henry looked up at her, and met her queer, round-pupilled, weak eyes staring behind her spectacles. He was perfectly still. He looked away, up at the weak, leaning tree. And as he looked into the sky, like a huntsman who is watching a flying bird, he thought to himself: 'If the tree falls in just such a way, and spins just so much as it falls, then the branch there will strike her exactly as she stands on top of that bank.'

He looked at her again. She was wiping the hair from her brow again, with that perpetual gesture. In his heart he had decided her death. A terrible still force seemed in him, and a power that was just his. If he turned even a hair's breadth in the wrong direction, he would lose the power.

'Mind yourself, Miss Banford,' he said. And his heart held perfectly still, in the terrible pure will that she should not move.

'Who, me, mind myself?' she cried, her father's jeering tone in her voice. 'Why, do you think you might hit me with the axe?'

'No, it's just possible the tree might, though,' he answered soberly. But the tone of his voice seemed to her to imply that he was only being falsely solicitous, and trying to make her move because it was his will to move her.

'Absolutely impossible,' she said.

He heard her. But he held himself icy still, lest he should lose his power.

'No, it's just possible. You'd better come down this way.'

'Oh, all right. Let us see some crack Canadian tree-felling,' she retorted.

'Ready, then,' he said, taking the axe, looking round to see he was clear.

There was a moment of pure motionless suspense, when the world seemed to stand still. Then suddenly his form seemed to flash up enormously tall and fearful, he gave two swift, flashing blows, in immediate succession, the tree was severed, turning slowly, spinning strangely in the air and coming down like a sudden darkness on the earth. No one saw what was happening except himself. No one heard the strange little cry which the Banford gave as the dark end of the bough swooped down, down on her. No one saw her crouch a little and receive the blow on the back of the neck. No one saw her flung outwards and laid, a little twitching heap, at the foot of the fence. No one except the boy. And he watched with intense bright eyes, as he would watch a wild goose he had shot. Was it winged or dead? Dead!

Immediately he gave a loud cry. Immediately March gave a wild shriek that went far, far down the afternoon. And the father started a strange bellowing sound.

The boy leapt the fence and ran to the fringe. The back of the neck and head was a mass of blood, of horror. He turned it over. The body was quivering with little convulsions. But she was dead really. He knew it, that it was so. He knew it in his soul and his blood. The inner necessity of his life was fulfilling itself, it was he who was to live. The thorn was drawn out of his bowels. So he put her down gently. She was dead.

He stood up. March was standing there petrified and absolutely motionless. Her face was dead white, her eyes big black pools. The old man was scrambling horribly over the fence.

'I'm afraid it's killed her,' said the boy.

The old man was making curious, blubbering noises as he huddled over the fence. 'What!' cried March, starting electric.

'Yes, I'm afraid,' repeated the boy.

March was coming forward. The boy was over the fence before she reached it.

'What do you say, killed her?' she asked in a sharp voice.

'I'm afraid so,' he answered softly.

She went still whiter, fearful. The two stood facing one another. Her black eyes gazed on him with the last look of resistance. And then in a last agonized failure she began to grizzle, to cry in a shivery little fashion of a child that doesn't want to cry, but which is beaten from within, and gives that little first shudder of sobbing which is not yet weeping, dry and fearful.

He had won. She stood there absolutely helpless, shuddering her dry sobs and her mouth trembling rapidly. And then, as in a child, with a little crash came the tears and the blind agony of sightless weeping. She sank down on the grass, and sat there with her hands on her breast and her face lifted in sightless, convulsed weeping. He stood above her, looking down on her, mute, pale, and everlasting seeming. He never moved, but looked down on her. And among all the torture of the scene, the torture of his own heart and bowels, he was glad, he had won.

After a long time he stooped to her and took her hands.

'Don't cry,' he said softly. 'Don't cry.'

She looked up at him with tears running from her eyes, a senseless look of helplessness and submission. So she gazed on him as if sightless, yet looking up to him. She would never leave him again. He had won her. And he knew it and was glad, because he wanted her for his life. His life must have her. And now he had won her. It was what his life must have.

But if he had won her, he had not yet got her. They were married at Christmas as he had planned, and he got again ten days' leave. They went to Cornwall, to his own village, on the sea. He realized that it was awful for her to be at the farm any more.

But though she belonged to him, though she lived in his shadow, as if she could not be away from him, she was not happy. She did not want to leave him: and yet she did not feel free with him. Everything round her seemed to watch her, seemed to press on her. He had won her, he had her with him, she was his wife. And she – she belonged to him, she knew it. But she was not glad. And he was still foiled. He realized that though he was married to her and possessed her in every possible way, apparently, and though she *wanted* him to possess her, she wanted it, she wanted nothing else, now, still he did not quite succeed.

Something was missing. Instead of her soul swaying with new life, it seemed to droop, to bleed, as if it were wounded. She would sit for a long time with her hand in his, looking away at the sea. And in her dark, vacant eyes was a sort of wound, and her face looked a little peaked. If he spoke to her, she would turn to him with a faint new smile, the strange, quivering little smile of a woman who has died in the old way of love, and can't quite rise to the new way. She still felt she ought to *do* something, to strain herself in some direction. And there was nothing to do, and no direction in which to strain herself. And she could not quite accept the submergence which his new love put upon her. If she was in love, she ought to *exert* herself, in some way, loving. She felt the weary need of our day to *exert* herself in love. But she knew that in fact she must no more exert herself in love. He would not have the love which exerted itself towards him. It made his brow go black. No, he wouldn't let her exert her love towards him. No, she had to be passive, to acquiesce, and to be submerged under the surface of love. She had to be like the seaweeds she saw as she peered down from the boat, swaying forever delicately under water, with all their delicate fibrils put tenderly out upon the flood, sensitive, utterly sensitive and receptive within the shadowy sea, and never, never rising and looking forth above water while they lived. Never. Never looking forth from the water until they died, only then washing, corpses, upon the surface. But while they lived, always submerged, always beneath the wave. Beneath the wave they might have powerful roots, stronger than iron; they might be tenacious and dangerous in their soft waving within the flood. Beneath the water they might be stronger, more indestructible than resistant oak trees are on land. But it was always under-water, always under-water. And she, being a woman, must be like that.

And she had been so used to the very opposite. She had to take all the thought for love and for life, and all the responsibility. Day after day she had been responsible for the coming day, for the coming year: for her dear Jill's health and happiness and well-being. Verily, in her own small way, she had felt herself responsible for the well-being of the world. And this had been her great stimulant, this grand feeling that, in her own small sphere, she was responsible for the well-being of the world.

And she had failed. She knew that, even in her small way, she had failed. She had failed to satisfy her own feeling of responsibility. It was so difficult. It seemed so grand and easy at first. And the more you tried, the more difficult it became. It had seemed so easy to make one beloved creature happy. And the more you tried, the worse the failure. It was terrible. She had been all her life reaching, reaching, and what she reached for seemed so near, until she had stretched to her utmost limit. And then it was always beyond her.

Always beyond her, vaguely, unrealizably beyond her, and she was left with nothingness at last. The life she reached for, the happiness she reached for, the well-being she reached for all slipped back, became unreal, the farther she stretched her hand. She wanted some goal, some finality – and there was none. Always this ghastly reaching, reaching, striving for something that might be just beyond. Even to make Jill happy. She was glad Jill was dead. For she had realized that she could never make her happy. Jill would always be fretting herself thinner and thinner, weaker and weaker. Her pains grew worse instead of less. It would be so for ever. She was glad she was dead.

And if Jill had married a man it would have been just the same. The woman striving, striving to make the man happy, striving within her own limits for the well-being of her world. And always achieving failure. Little, foolish successes in money or in ambition. But at the very point where she most wanted success, in the anguished effort to make some one beloved human being happy and perfect, there the failure was almost catastrophic. You wanted to make your beloved happy, and his happiness seemed always achievable. If only you did just this, that and the other. And you did this, that, and the other, in all good faith, and every time the failure became a little more ghastly. You could love yourself to ribbons and strive and strain yourself to the bone, and things would go from bad to worse, bad to worse, as far as happiness went. The awful mistake of happiness.

Poor March, in her good-will and her responsibility, she had strained herself till it seemed to her that the whole of life and everything was only a horrible abyss of nothingness. The more you reached after the fatal flower of happiness, which trembles so blue and lovely in a crevice just beyond your grasp, the more fearfully you become aware of the ghastly and awful gulf of the precipice below you, into which you will inevitably plunge, as into the bottomless pit, if you reach any farther. You pluck flower after flower – it is never *the* flower. The flower itself – its calyx is a horrible gulf, it is the bottomless pit.

That is the whole history of the search for happiness, whether it be your own or somebody else's that you want to win. It ends, and it always ends, in the ghastly sense of the bottomless nothingness into which you will inevitably fall if you strain any farther.

And women? – what goal can any woman conceive, except happiness? Just happiness for herself and the whole world. That, and nothing else. And so, she assumes the responsibility and set off towards her goal. She can see it there, at the foot of the rainbow. Or she can see it a little way beyond, in the blue distance. Not far, not far.

But the end of the rainbow is a bottomless gulf down which you can fall forever without arriving, and the blue distance is a void pit which can swallow you and all your efforts into its emptiness, and still be no emptier. You and all your efforts. So, the illusion of attainable happiness!

Poor March, she had set off so wonderfully towards the blue goal. And the farther and farther she had gone, the more fearful had become the realization of emptiness. An agony, an insanity at last.

She was glad it was over. She was glad to sit on the shore and look westwards over the sea, and know the great strain had ended. She would never strain for love and happiness any more. And Jill was safely dead. Poor Jill, poor Jill. It must be sweet to be dead.

For her own part, death was not her destiny. She would have to leave her destiny to the boy. But then, the boy. He wanted more than that. He wanted her to give herself without defences, to sink and become submerged in him. And she – she wanted to sit still, like a woman on the last milestone, and watch. She wanted to see, to know, to understand. She wanted to be alone: with him at her side.

And he! He did not want her to watch any more, to see any more, to understand any more. He wanted to veil her woman's spirit, as Orientals veil the woman's face. He wanted her to commit herself to him, and to put her independent spirit to sleep. He wanted to take away from her all her effort, all that seemed her very *raison d'être*. He wanted to make her submit, yield, blindly pass away out of all her strenuous consciousness. He wanted to take away her consciousness, and make her just his woman. Just his woman.

And she was so tired, so tired, like a child that wants to go to sleep, but which fights against sleep as if sleep were death. She seemed to stretch her eyes wider in the obstinate effort and tension of keeping awake. She *would* keep awake. She *would* know. She *would* consider and judge and decide. She *would* have the reins of her own life between her own hands. She *would* be an independent woman to the last. But she was so tired, so tired of everything. And sleep seemed near. And there was such rest in the boy.

Yet there, sitting in a niche of the high, wild cliffs of West Cornwall, looking over the westward sea, she stretched her eyes wider and wider. Away to the West, Canada, America. She *would* know and she *would* see what was ahead. And the boy, sitting beside her, staring down at the gulls, had a cloud between his brows and the strain of discontent in his eyes. He wanted her asleep, at peace in him. He wanted her at peace, asleep in him. And *there* she was, dying with the strain of her own wakefulness. Yet she would not sleep: no, never. Sometimes he thought bitterly that he ought to have left her. He ought never to have killed Banford. He should have left Banford and March to kill one another.

But that was only impatience: and he knew it. He was waiting, waiting to go West. He was aching almost in torment to leave England, to go West, to take March away. To leave this shore! He believed that as they crossed the seas, as they left this England which he so hated, because in some way it seemed to have stung him with poison, she would go to sleep. She would close her eyes at last and give in to him.

And then he would have her, and he would have his own life at last. He chafed, feeling he hadn't got his own life. He would never have it till she yielded and slept in him. Then he would have all his own life as a young man and a male, and she would have all her own life as a woman and a female. There would be no more of this awful straining. She would not be a man any more, an independent woman with a man's responsibility. Nay, even the responsibility for her own soul she would have to commit to him. He knew it was so, and obstinately held out against her, waiting for the surrender.

'You'll feel better when once we get over the seas to Canada over there,' he said to her as they sat among the rocks on the cliff.

She looked away to the sea's horizon, as if it were not real. Then she looked round at him, with the strained, strange look of a child that is struggling against sleep.

'Shall I?' she said.

'Yes,' he answered quietly.

And her eyelids dropped with the slow motion, sleep weighing them unconscious. But she pulled them open again to say:

'Yes, I may. I can't tell. I can't tell what it will be like over there.'

'If only we could go soon!' he said, with pain in his voice.

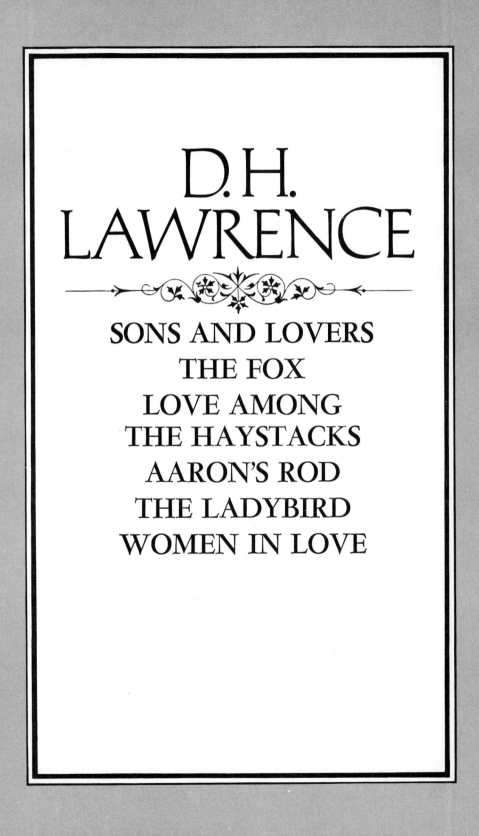

D.H. LAWRENCE

SONS AND LOVERS

THE FOX

LOVE AMONG
THE HAYSTACKS

AARON'S ROD

THE LADYBIRD

WOMEN IN LOVE

1

The two large fields lay on a hillside facing south. Being newly cleared of hay, they were golden green, and they shone almost blindingly in the sunlight. Across the hill, halfway up, ran a high hedge, that flung its black shadow finely across the molten glow of the sward. The stack was being built just above the hedge. It was of great size, massive, but so silvery and delicately bright in tone that it seemed not to have weight. It rose dishevelled and radiant among the steady, golden-green glare of the field. A little farther back was another, finished stack.

The empty wagon was just passing through the gap in the hedge. From the far-off corner of the bottom field, where the sward was still striped grey with winrows, the loaded wagon launched forward to climb the hill to the stack. The white dots of the hay-makers showed distinctly among the hay.

The two brothers were having a moment's rest, waiting for the load to come up. They stood wiping their brows with their arms, sighing from the heat and the labour of placing the last load. The stack they rode was high, lifting them up above the hedge-tops, and very broad, a great slightly-hollowed vessel into which the sunlight poured, in which the hot, sweet scent of hay was suffocating. Small and inefficacious the brothers looked, half-submerged in the loose, great trough, lifted high up as if on an altar reared to the sun.

Maurice, the younger brother, was a handsome young fellow of twenty-one, careless and debonair, and full of vigour. His grey eyes, as he taunted his brother, were bright and baffled with a strong emotion. His swarthy face had the same peculiar smile, expectant and glad and nervous, of a young man roused for the first time in passion.

'Tha sees,' he said, as he leaned on the pommel of his fork, 'tha thowt as tha'd done me one, didna ter?' He smiled as he spoke, then fell again into his pleasant torment of musing.

'I thought nowt – tha knows so much,' retorted Geoffrey, with the touch of a sneer. His brother had the better of him. Geoffrey was a very heavy, hulking fellow, a year older than Maurice. His blue eyes were unsteady, they glanced away quickly; his mouth was morbidly sensitive. One felt him wince away, through the whole of his great body. His inflamed self-consciousness was a disease in him.

'Ah, but though, I know tha did,' mocked Maurice. 'Tha went slinkin' off' – Geoffrey winced convulsively – 'thinking as that wor the last night as any of us'ud ha'e ter stop here, an' so tha'd leave me to sleep out, though it wor thy turn –'

He smiled to himself, thinking of the result of Geoffrey's ruse.

'I didna go slinkin' off neither,' retorted Geoffrey, in his heavy, clumsy manner, wincing at the phrase. 'Didna my feyther send me to fetch some coal –'

'Oh yes, oh yes – we know all about it. But tha sees what tha missed, my lad.'

Maurice, chuckling, threw himself on his back in the bed of hay. There was absolutely nothing in his world, then, except the shallow ramparts of the stack, and the blazing sky. He clenched his fists tight, threw his arms across his face, and braced his muscles again. He was evidently very much moved, so acutely that it was hardly pleasant, though he still smiled. Geoffrey, standing behind him, could just see his red mouth, with the young moustache like black fur, curling back and showing the teeth in a smile. The elder brother leaned his chin on the pommel of his fork, looking out across the country.

Far away was the faint blue heap of Nottingham. Between, the country lay under a haze of heat, with here and there a flag of colliery smoke waving. But near at hand, at the foot of the hill, across the deep-hedged high road, was only the silence of the old church and the castle farm, among their trees. The large view only made Geoffrey more sick. He looked away, to the wagons crossing the field below him, the empty cart like a big insect moving down-hill, the load coming up, rocking like a ship, the brown head of the horse ducking, the brown knees lifted and planted strenuously. Geoffrey wished it would be quick.

'Tha didna think –'

Geoffrey started, coiled within himself, and looked down at the handsome lips moving in speech below the brown arms of his brother.

'Tha didna think 'er'd be thur wi' me – or tha wouldna ha' left me to it,' Maurice said, ending with a little laugh of excited memory. Geoffrey flushed with hate, and had an impulse to set his foot on that moving, taunting mouth, which was there below him. There was silence for a time, then, in a peculiar tone of delight, Maurice's voice came again, spelling out the words, as it were:

'Ich bin klein, mein Herz ist rein,
Ist niemand d'rin als Christ allein.'

Maurice chuckled, then, convulsed at a twinge of recollection, keen as pain, he twisted over, pressed himself into the hay.

'Can thee say thy prayers in German?' came his muffled voice.

'I non want,' growled Geoffrey.

Maurice chuckled. His face was quite hidden, and in the dark he was going over again his last night's experiences.

'What about kissing 'er under th' ear, Sonny,' he said, in a curious, uneasy tone. He writhed, still startled and inflamed by his first contact with love.

Geoffrey's heart swelled within him, and things went dark. He could not see the landscape.

'An' there's just a nice two-handful of her bosom,' came the low, provocative tones of Maurice, who seemed to be talking to himself.

The two brothers were both fiercely shy of women, and until this hay harvest, the whole feminine sex had been represented by their mother and in presence of any other women they were dumb louts. Moreover, brought up by a proud mother, a stranger in the country, they held the common girls as beneath them, because beneath their mother, who spoke pure English, and was very quiet. Loud-mouthed and broad-tongued the common girls were. So these two young men had grown up virgin but tormented.

Now again Maurice had the start of Geoffrey, and the elder brother was deeply mortified. There was a danger of his sinking into a morbid state, from sheer lack of living, lack of interest. The foreign governess at the Vicarage, whose garden lay beside the top field, had talked to the lads through the hedge, and had fascinated them. There was a great elder bush, with its broad creamy flowers crumbling on to the garden path, and into the field. Geoffrey never smelled elder-flower without starting and wincing, thinking of the strange foreign voice that had so startled him as he mowed out with the scythe in the hedge bottom. A baby had run through the gap, and the Fräulein, calling in German, had come brushing down the flowers in pursuit. She had started so on seeing a man standing there in the shade, that for a moment she could not move: and then she had blundered into the rake which was lying by his side. Geoffrey, forgetting she was a woman when he saw her pitch forward, had picked her up carefully, asking: 'Have you hurt you?'

Then she had broken into a laugh, and answered in German, showing him her arms, and knitting her brows. She was nettled rather badly.

'You want a dock leaf,' he said. She frowned in a puzzled fashion.

'A dock leaf?' she repeated. He had rubbed her arms with the green leaf.

And now, she had taken to Maurice. She had seemed to prefer himself at first. Now she had sat with Maurice in the moonlight, and had let him kiss her. Geoffrey sullenly suffered, making no fight.

Unconsciously, he was looking at the Vicarage garden. There she was, in a golden-brown dress. He took off his hat, and held up his right hand in greeting to her. She, a small, golden figure, waved her hand negligently from among the potato rows. He remained, arrested, in the same posture, his hat in his left hand, his right arm upraised, thinking. He could tell by the negligence of her greeting that she was waiting for Maurice. What did she think of himself? Why wouldn't she have him?

Hearing the voice of the wagoner leading the load, Maurice rose. Geoffrey still stood in the same way, but his face was sullen, and his upraised hand was slack with brooding. Maurice faced up-hill. His eyes lit up and he laughed. Geoffrey dropped his own arm, watching.

'Lad!' chuckled Maurice. 'I non knowed 'er wor there.' He waved his hand clumsily. In these matters Geoffrey did better. The elder brother watched the girl. She ran to the end of the path, behind the bushes, so that she was screened from the house. Then she waved her handkerchief wildly. Maurice did not notice the manoeuvre. There was the cry of a child. The girl's figure vanished, reappeared holding up a white childish bundle, and came down the path. There she put down her charge, sped up-hill to a great ash tree, climbed quickly to a large horizontal bar that formed the fence there, and, standing poised, blew kisses with both her hands, in a foreign fashion that excited the brothers. Maurice laughed aloud, as he waved his red handkerchief.

'Well, what's the danger?' shouted a mocking voice from below. Maurice collapsed, blushing furiously.

'Nowt!' he called.

There was a hearty laugh from below.

The load rode up, sheered with a hiss against the stack, then sank back again upon the scotches. The brothers ploughed across the mass of hay, taking the forks. Presently a big burly man, red and glistening, climbed to the top of the load. Then he turned round, scrutinized the hillside from under his shaggy brows. He caught sight of the girl under the ash tree.

'Oh, that's who it is,' he laughed. 'I thought it was some such bird, but I couldn't see her.'

The father laughed in a hearty, chaffing way, then began to teem the load. Geoffrey, on the stack above, received his great forkfuls, and swung them over to Maurice, who took them, placed them, building the stack. In the intense sunlight, the three worked in silence, knit together in a brief passion of work. The father stirred slowly for a moment, getting the hay from under his feet. Geoffrey waited, the blue tines of his fork glittering in expectation: the mass rose, his fork swung beneath it, there was a light clash of blades, then the hay was swept on to the stack, caught by Maurice, who placed it judiciously. One after another, the shoulders of the three men bowed and braced themselves. All wore light blue, bleached shirts, that stuck close to their backs. The father moved mechanically, his thick, rounded shoulders bending and lifting dully: he worked monotonously. Geoffrey flung away his strength. His massive shoulders swept and flung the hay extravagantly.

'Dost want to knock me ower?' asked Maurice angrily. He had to brace himself against the impact. The three men worked intensely, as if some will urged them. Maurice was light and swift at the work, but he had to use his judgment. Also, when he had to place the hay along the far ends, he had some distance to carry it. So he was too slow for Geoffrey. Ordinarily, the elder would have placed the hay as far as possible where his brother wanted it. Now, however, he pitched his forkfuls into the middle of the stack. Maurice strode swiftly and handsomely across the bed, but the work was too much for him. The other two men, clenched in their receive and deliver, kept up a high pitch of labour. Geoffrey still flung the hay at random. Maurice was perspiring heavily with heat and exertion, and was getting worried. Now and again, Geoffrey wiped his arm across his brow, mechanically, like an animal. Then he glanced with satisfaction at Maurice's moiled condition, and caught the next forkful.

'Wheer dost think thou'rt hollin' it, fool!' panted Maurice, as his brother flung a forkful out of reach.

'Wheer I've a mind,' answered Geoffrey.

Maurice toiled on, now very angry. He felt the sweat trickling down his body: drops fell into his long black lashes, blinding him, so that he had to stop and angrily dash his eyes clear. The veins stood out in his swarthy neck. He felt he would burst, or drop, if the work did not soon slacken off. He heard his father's fork dully scrape the cart bottom.

'There, the last,' the father panted. Geoffrey tossed the last light lot at random, took off his hat, and, steaming in the sunshine as he wiped himself, stood complacently watching Maurice struggle with clearing the bed.

'Don't you think you've got your bottom corner a bit far out?' came the father's voice from below. 'You'd better be drawing in now, hadn't you?'

'I thought you said next load,' Maurice called sulkily.

'Aye! All right. But isn't this bottom corner –?'

Maurice, impatient, took no notice.

Geoffrey strode over the stack, and stuck his fork in the offending corner. 'What – here?' he bawled in his great voice.

'Aye – isn't it a bit loose?' came the irritating voice.

Geoffrey pushed his fork in the jutting corner, and, leaning his weight on the handle, shoved. He thought it shook. He thrust again with all his power. The mass swayed.

'What art up to, tha fool!' cried Maurice, in a high voice.

'Mind who tha'rt callin' a fool,' said Geoffrey, and he prepared to push again. Maurice sprang across, and elbowed his brother aside. On the yielding, swaying bed of hay, Geoffrey lost his foothold and fell grovelling. Maurice tried the corner.

'It's solid enough,' he shouted angrily.

'Aye – all right,' came the conciliatory voice of the father; 'you do get a bit of rest now there's such a long way to cart it,' he added reflectively.

Geoffrey had got to his feet.

'Tha'll mind who tha'rt nudging, I can tell thee,' he threatened heavily; adding, as Maurice continued to work, 'an' tha non ca's him a fool again, dost hear?'

'Not till next time,' sneered Maurice.

As he worked silently round the stack, he neared where his brother stood like a sullen statue, leaning on his fork-handle, looking out over the countryside. Maurice's heart quickened in its beat. He worked forward, until a point of his fork caught in the leather of Geoffrey's boot, and the metal rang sharply.

'Are ter going ta shift thysen?' asked Maurice threateningly. There was no reply from the great block. Maurice lifted his upper lips like a dog. Then he put out his elbow and tried to push his brother into the stack, clear of his way.

'Who are ter shovin'?' came the deep, dangerous voice.

'Thaïgh,' replied Maurice, with a sneer, and straightway the two brothers set themselves against each other, like opposing bulls, Maurice trying his hardest to shift Geoffrey from his footing, Geoffrey leaning all his weight in resistance. Maurice, insecure in his footing, staggered a little, and Geoffrey's weight followed him. He went slithering over the edge of the stack.

Geoffrey turned white to the lips, and remained standing, listening. He heard the fall. Then a flush of darkness came over him, and he remained standing only because he was planted. He had not strength to move. He could hear no sound from below, was only faintly aware of a sharp shriek from a long way off. He listened again. Then he filled with sudden panic.

'Feyther!' he roared, in his tremendous voice: 'Feyther! Feyther!'

The valley re-echoed with the sound. Small cattle on the hillside looked up. Men's figures came running from the bottom field, and much nearer a woman's figure was racing across the upper field. Geoffrey waited in terrible suspense.

'Ah-h!' he heard the strange, wild voice of the girl cry out. 'Ah-h!' – and then some foreign wailing speech. Then: 'Ah-h! Are you dea-ed!'

He stood sullenly erect on the stack, not daring to go down, longing to hide in the hay, but too sullen to stoop out of sight. He heard his eldest brother come up, panting:

'Whatever's amiss!' and then the labourer, and then his father.

'Whatever have you been doing?' he heard his father ask, while yet he had not come round the corner of the stack. And then, in a low, bitter tone:

'Eh, he's done for! I'd no business to ha' put it all on that stack.'

There was a moment or two of silence, then the voice of Henry, the eldest brother, said crisply:

'He's not dead – he's coming round.'

Geoffrey heard, but was not glad. He had as lief Maurice were dead. At least that would be final: better than meeting his brother's charges, and of seeing his mother pass to the sick-room. If Maurice was killed, he himself would not explain, no, not a word, and they could hang him if they liked. If Maurice were only hurt, then everybody would know, and Geoffrey could never lift his face again. What added torture, to pass along, everybody knowing. He wanted something that he could stand back to, something definite, if it were only the knowledge that he had killed his brother. He *must* have something firm to back up to, or he would go mad. He was so lonely, he who above all needed the support of sympathy.

'No, he's commin' to; I tell you he is,' said the labourer.

'He's not dea-ed, he's not dea-ed,' came the passionate, strange sing-song of the foreign girl. 'He's not dead – no-o.'

'He wants some brandy – look at the colour of his lips,' said the crisp, cold voice of Henry. 'Can you fetch some?'

'Wha-at? Fetch?' Fräulein did not understand.

'Brandy,' said Henry, very distinct.

'Brrandy!' she re-echoed.

'You go, Bill,' groaned the father.

'Aye, I'll go,' replied Bill, and he ran across the field.

Maurice was not dead, nor going to die. This Geoffrey now realized. He was glad after all that the extreme penalty was revoked. But he hated to think of himself going on. He would always shrink now. He had hoped and hoped for the time when he would be careless, bold as Maurice, when he would not wince and shrink. Now he would always be the same, coiling up in himself like a tortoise with no shell.

'Ah-h! He's getting better!' came the wild voice of the Fräulein, and she began to cry, a strange sound, that startled the men, made the animal bristle within them. Geoffrey shuddered as he heard, between her sobbing, the impatient moaning of his brother as the breath came back.

The labourer returned at a run, followed by the Vicar. After the brandy, Maurice made more moaning, hiccuping noise. Geoffrey listened in torture. He heard the Vicar asking for explanations. All the united, anxious voices replied in brief phrases.

'It was that other,' cried the Fräulein. 'He knocked him over – Ha!'

She was shrill and vindictive.

'I don't think so,' said the father to the Vicar, in a quite audible but private tone, speaking as if the Fräulein did not understand his English.

The Vicar addressed his children's governess in bad German. She replied in a torrent which he would not confess was too much for him. Maurice was making little moaning, sighing noises.

'Where's your pain, boy, eh?' the father asked pathetically.

'Leave him alone a bit,' came the cool voice of Henry. 'He's winded, if no more.'

'You'd better see that no bones are broken,' said the anxious Vicar.

'It wor a blessing as he should a dropped on that heap of hay just there,' said the labourer. 'If he'd happened to ha' catched hisself on this nog o' wood 'e wouldna ha' stood much chance.'

Geoffrey wondered when he would have courage to venture down. He had wild notions of pitching himself head foremost from the stack: if he could only extinguish himself, he would be safe. Quite frantically, he longed not to be. The idea of going through life thus coiled up within himself in morbid self-consciousness, always lonely, surly, and a misery, was enough to make him cry out. What would they all think when they knew he had knocked Maurice off that high stack?

They were talking to Maurice down below. The lad had recovered in great measure, and was able to answer faintly.

'Whatever was you doin'?' the father asked gently. 'Was you playing about with our Geoffrey? – Aye, and where is he?'

Geoffrey's heart stood still.

'I dunno,' said Henry, in a curious, ironic tone.

'Go an' have a look,' pleaded the father, infinitely relieved over one son, anxious now concerning the other. Geoffrey could not bear that his eldest brother should climb up and question him in his high-pitched drawl of curiosity. The culprit doggedly set his feet on the ladder. His nailed boots slipped a rung.

'Mind yourself,' shouted the over-wrought father.

Geoffrey stood like a criminal at the foot of the ladder, glancing furtively at the group. Maurice was lying, pale and slightly convulsed, upon a heap of hay. The Fräulein was kneeling beside his head. The Vicar had the lad's shirt full open down the breast, and was feeling for broken ribs. The father kneeled on the other side, the labourer and Henry stood aside.

'I can't find anything broken,' said the Vicar, and he sounded slightly disappointed.

'There's nowt broken to find,' murmured Maurice, smiling.

The father started. 'Eh?' he said. 'Eh?' and he bent over the invalid.

'I say it's not hurt me,' repeated Maurice.

'What were you doing?' asked the cold, ironic voice of Henry. Geoffrey turned his head away: he had not yet raised his face.

'Nowt as I know on,' he muttered in a surly tone.

'Why!' cried Fräulein in a reproachful tone. 'I see him – knock him over!' She made a fierce gesture with her elbow. Henry curled his long moustache sardonically.

'Nay lass, niver,' smiled the wan Maurice. 'He was fur enough away from me when I slipped.'

'Oh, ah!' cried the Fräulein, not understanding.

'Yi,' smiled Maurice indulgently.

'I think you're mistaken,' said the father, rather pathetically, smiling at the girl as if she were 'wanting'.

'Oh no,' she cried. 'I *see* him.'

'Nay, lass,' smiled Maurice quietly.

She was a Pole, named Paula Jablonowsky: young, only twenty years old, swift and light as a wild cat, with a strange wild-cat way of grinning. Her hair was blonde and full of life, all crisped into many tendrils with vitality, shaking round her face. Her fine blue eyes were peculiarly lidded, and she seemed to look piercingly, then languorously, like a wild cat. She had somewhat Slavonic cheek-bones, and was very much freckled. It was evident that the Vicar, a pale, rather cold man, hated her.

Maurice lay pale and smiling in her lap, whilst she cleaved to him like a mate. One felt instinctively that they were mated. She was ready at any minute to fight with ferocity in his defence, now he was hurt. Her looks at Geoffrey were full of fierceness. She bowed over Maurice and caressed him with her foreign-sounding English.

'You say what you lai-ike,' she laughed, giving him lordship over her.

'Hadn't you better be going and looking what has become of Margery?' asked the Vicar in tones of reprimand.

'She is with her mother – I heard her. I will go in a whai-ile,' smiled the girl coolly.

'Do you feel as if you could stand?' asked the father, still anxiously.

'Aye, in a bit,' smiled Maurice.

'You want to get up?' caressed the girl, bowing over him, till her face was not far from his.

'I'm in no hurry,' he replied, smiling brilliantly.

This accident had given him quite a strange new ease, an authority. He felt extraordinarily glad. New power had come to him all at once.

'You in no hurry,' she repeated, gathering his meaning. She smiled tenderly: she was in his service.

'She leaves us in another month – Mrs Inwood could stand no more of her,' apologized the Vicar quietly to the father.

'Why, is she –'

'Like a wild thing – disobedient and insolent.'

'Ha!'

The father sounded abstract.

'No more foreign governesses for me.'

Maurice stirred, and looked up at the girl.

'You stand up?' she asked brightly. 'You well?'

He laughed again, showing his teeth winsomely. She lifted his head, sprang to her feet, her hands still holding his head, then she took him under the armpits and had him on his feet before anyone could help. He was much taller than she. He grasped her strong shoulders heavily, leaned against her, and, feeling her round, firm breast doubled up against his side, he smiled, catching his breath.

'You see, I'm all right,' he gasped. 'I was only winded.'

'You all raïght?' she cried, in great glee.

'Yes, I am.'

He walked a few steps after a moment.

'There's nowt ails me, father,' he laughed.

'Quite well, you?' she cried in a pleading tone. He laughed outright, looked down at her, touching her cheek with his fingers.

'That's it – if tha likes.'

'If I lai-ike!' she repeated, radiant.

'She's going at the end of three weeks,' said the Vicar consolingly to the farmer.

2

While they were talking, they heard the far-off hooting of a pit.

'There goes th' loose 'a,' said Henry coldly. 'We're *not* going to get that corner up today.'

The father looked round anxiously.

'Now, Maurice, are you sure you're all right?' he asked.

'Yes, I'm all right. Haven't I told you?'

'Then you sit down there, and in a bit you can be getting dinner out. Henry, you go on the stack. Wheer's Jim? Oh, he's minding the hosses. Bill, and you, Geoffrey, you can pick while Jim loads.'

Maurice sat down under the wych elm to recover. The Fräulein had fled back. He made up his mind to ask her to marry him. He had got fifty pounds of his own, and his mother would help him. For a long time he sat musing, thinking what he would do. Then, from the float he fetched a big basket covered with a cloth, and spread the dinner. There was an immense rabbit-pie, a dish of cold potatoes, much bread, a great piece of cheese, and a solid rice pudding.

These two fields were four miles from the home farm. But they had been in the hands of the Wookeys for several generations, therefore the father kept them on, and everyone looked forward to the hay harvest at Greasley: it was a kind of picnic. They brought dinner and tea in the milk-float, which the father drove over in the morning. The lads and the labourers cycled. Off and on, the harvest lasted a fortnight. As the high road from Alfreton to Nottingham ran at the foot of the fields, someone usually slept in the hay under the shed to guard the tools. The sons took it in turns. They did not care for it much, and were for that reason anxious to finish the harvest on this day. But work went slack and disjointed after Maurice's accident.

When the load was teemed, they gathered round the white cloth, which was spread under a tree between the hedge and the stack, and, sitting on the ground, ate their meal. Mrs Wookey sent always a clean cloth, and knives and forks and plates for everybody. Mr Wookey was always rather proud of this spread: everything was so proper.

'There now,' he said, sitting down jovially. 'Doesn't this look nice now – eh?'

They all sat round the white spread, in the shadow of the tree and the stack, and looked out up the fields as they ate. From their shady coolness, the gold sward seemed liquid, molten with heat. The horse with the empty wagon wandered a few yards, then stood feeding. Everything was still as a trance. Now and again, the horse between the shafts of the load that stood propped beside the stack, jingled his loose bit as he ate. The men ate and drank in silence, the father reading the newspaper, Maurice leaning back on a saddle, Henry reading the *Nation*, the others eating busily.

Presently 'Helloa!' 'Er's 'ere again!' exclaimed Bill. All looked up. Paula was coming across the field carrying a plate.

'She's bringing something to tempt your appetite, Maurice,' said the eldest brother ironically. Maurice was midway through a large wedge of rabbit-pie and some cold potatoes.

'Aye, bless me if she's not,' laughed the father. 'Put that away, Maurice, it's a shame to disappoint her.'

Maurice looked round very shamefaced, not knowing what to do with his plate.

'Give it over here,' said Bill. 'I'll polish him off.'

'Bringing something for the invalid?' laughed the father to the Fräulein. 'He's looking up nicely.'

'I bring him some chicken, him!' She nodded her head at Maurice childishly. He flushed and smiled.

'Tha doesna mean ter bust 'im,' said Bill.

Everybody laughed aloud. The girl did not understand, so she laughed also. Maurice ate his portion very sheepishly.

The father pitied his son's shyness.

'Come here and sit by me,' he said. 'Eh, Fräulein! Is that what they call you?'

'I sit by you, father,' she said innocently.

Henry threw his head back and laughed long and noiselessly.

She settled near to the big, handsome man.

'My name,' she said, 'is Paula Jablonowsky.'

'Is what?' said the father, and the other men went into roars of laughter.

'Tell me again,' said the father. 'Your name –'

'Paula.'

'Paula? Oh – well, it's a rum sort of name, eh? His name –' he nodded at his son.

'Maurice – I know.' She pronounced it sweetly, then laughed into the father's eyes. Maurice blushed to the roots of his hair.

They questioned her concerning her history, and made out that she came from Hanover, that her father was a shopkeeper, and that she had run away from home because she did not like her father. She had gone to Paris.

'Oh,' said the father, now dubious. 'And what did you do there?'

'In school – in a young ladies' school.'

'Did you like it?'

'Oh no – no laïfe – no life!'

'What?'

'When we go out – two and two – all together – no more. Ah, no life, no life.'

'Well, that's a winder!' exclaimed the father. 'No life in Paris! And have you found much life in England?'

'No – ah no. I don't like it.' She made a grimace at the Vicarage.

'How long have you been in England?'

'Chreestmas – so.'

'And what will you do?'

'I will go to London, or to Paris. Ah, Paris! – Or get married!' She laughed into the father's eyes.

The father laughed heartily.

'Get married, eh? And who to?'

'I don't know. I am going away.'

'The country's too quiet for you?' asked the father.

'Too quiet – hm!' she nodded in assent.

'You wouldn't care for making butter and cheese?'

'Making butter – hm!' She turned to him with a glad, bright gesture. 'I like it.'

'Oh,' laughed the father. 'You would, would you?'

She nodded vehemently, with glowing eyes.

'She'd like anything in the shape of a change,' said Henry judicially.

'I think she would,' agreed the father. It did not occur to them that she fully understood what they said. She looked at them closely, then thought with bowed head.

'Hullo!' exclaimed Henry, the alert. A tramp was slouching towards them through the gap. He was a very seedy, slinking fellow, with a tang of horsey braggadocio about him. Small, thin, and ferrety, with a week's red beard bristling on his pointed chin, he came slouching forward.

'Have yer got a bit of a job goin'?' he asked.

'A bit of a job,' repeated the father. 'Why, can't you see as we've a'most done?'

'Aye – but I noted you was a hand short, an' I thowt as 'appen you'd gie me half a day.'

'What, are *you* any good in a hay close?' asked Henry, with a sneer.

The man stood slouching against the haystack. All the others were seated on the floor. He had an advantage.

'I could work aside any on yer,' he bragged.

'Tha looks it,' laughed Bill.

'And what's your regular trade?' asked the father.

'I'm a jockey by rights. But I did a bit o' dirty work for a boss o' mine, an' I was landed. '*E* got the benefit, *I* got kicked out. '*E* axed me – an' then 'e looked as if 'e'd never seed me.'

'Did he, though!' exclaimed the father sympathetically.

''E did that!' asserted the man.

'But we've got nothing for you,' said Henry coldly.

'What does the boss say?' asked the man, impudent.

'No, we've no work you can do,' said the father. 'You can have a bit o' something to eat, if you like.'

'I should be glad of it,' said the man.

He was given the chunk of rabbit-pie that remained. This he ate greedily. There was something debased, parasitic, about him, which disgusted Henry. The others regarded him as a curiosity.

'That was nice and tasty,' said the tramp, with gusto.

'Do you want a piece of bread 'n' cheese?' asked the father.

'It'll help to fill up,' was the reply.

The man ate this more slowly. The company was embarrassed by his presence, and could not talk. All the men lit their pipes, the meal over.

'So you dunna want any help?' said the tramp at last.

'No – we can manage what bit there is to do.'

'You don't happen to have a fill of bacca to spare, do you?'

The father gave him a good pinch.

'You're all right here,' he said, looking round. They resented this familiarity. However, he filled his clay pipe and smoked with the rest.

As they were sitting silent, another figure came through the gap in the hedge, and noiselessly approached. It was a woman. She was rather small and finely made. Her face was small, very ruddy, and comely, save for the look of bitterness and aloofness that it wore. Her hair was drawn tightly back under a sailor hat. She gave an impression of cleanness, of precision and directness.

'Have you got some work?' she asked of her man. She ignored the rest. He tucked his tail between his legs.

'No, they haven't got no work for me. They've just gave me a draw of bacca.'

He was a mean crawl of a man.

'An' am I goin' to wait for you out there on the lane all day?'

'You needn't if you don't like. You could go on.'

'Well, are you coming?' she asked contemptuously. He rose to his feet in a rickety fashion.

'You needn't be in such a mighty hurry,' he said. 'If you'd wait a bit you might get summat.'

She glanced for the first time over the men. She was quite young, and would have been pretty, were she not so hard and callous-looking.

'Have you had your dinner?' asked the father.

She looked at him with a kind of anger and turned away. Her face was so childish in its contours, contrasting strangely with her expression.

'Are you coming?' she said to the man.

'He's had his tuck-in. Have a bit, if you want it,' coaxed the father.

'What have you had?' she flashed to the man.

'He's had all what was left o' th' rabbit-pie,' said Geoffrey, in an indignant, mocking tone, 'and a great hunk o' bread an' cheese.'

'Well, it was gave me,' said the man.

The young woman looked at Geoffrey, and he at her. There was a sort of kinship between them. Both were at odds with the world. Geoffrey smiled satirically. She was too grave, too deeply incensed even to smile.

'There's a cake here, though – you can have a bit o' that,' said Maurice blithely.

She eyed him with scorn.

Again she looked at Geoffrey. He seemed to understand her. She turned, and in silence departed. The man remained obstinately sucking at his pipe. Everybody looked at him with hostility.

'We'll be getting to work,' said Henry, rising, pulling off his coat. Paula got to her feet. She was a little bit confused by the presence of the tramp.

'I go,' she said, smiling brilliantly. Maurice rose and followed her sheepishly.

'A good grind, eh?' said the tramp, nodding after the Fräulein. The men only half understood him, but they hated him.

'Hadn't you better be getting off?' said Henry.

The man rose obediently. He was all slouching, parasitic insolence. Geoffrey loathed him, longed to exterminate him. He was exactly the worst foe of the hypersensitive: insolence without sensibility, preying on sensibility.

'Aren't you goin' to give me summat for her? It's nowt she's had all day, to my knowin'. She'll 'appen eat it if I take it 'er – though she gets more than I've any knowledge of' – this with a lewd wink of jealous spite. 'And then tries to keep a tight hand on me,' he sneered, taking the bread and cheese, and stuffing it in his pocket.

3

Geoffrey worked sullenly all the afternoon, and Maurice did the horse-raking. It was exceedingly hot. So the day wore on, the atmosphere thickened, and the sunlight grew blurred. Geoffrey was picking with Bill – helping to load the wagons from the winrows. He was sulky, though extraordinarily relieved: Maurice would not tell. Since the quarrel neither brother had spoken to the other. But their silence was entirely amicable, almost affectionate. They had both been deeply moved, so much so that their ordinary intercourse was interrupted: but underneath, each felt a strong regard for the other. Maurice was peculiarly happy, his feeling of affection swimming over everything. But Geoffrey was still sullenly hostile to the most part of the world. He felt isolated. The free and easy inter-communication between the other workers left him distinctly alone. And he was a man who could not bear to stand alone, he was too much afraid of the vast confusion of life surrounding him, in which he was helpless. Geoffrey mistrusted himself with everybody.

The work went on slowly. It was unbearably hot, and everyone was disheartened.

'We s'll have getting-on-for another day of it,' said the father at tea-time, as they sat under the tree.

'Quite a day,' said Henry.

'Somebody'll have to stop, then,' said Geoffrey. 'It 'ud better be me.'

'Nay, lad, I'll stop,' said Maurice, and he hid his head in confusion.

'Stop again tonight!' exclaimed the father. 'I'd rather you went home.'

'Nay, I'm stoppin',' protested Maurice.

'He wants to do his courting,' Henry enlightened them.

The father thought seriously about it.

'I don't know ...' he mused, rather perturbed.

But Maurice stayed. Towards eight o'clock, after sundown, the men mounted their bicycles, the father put the horse in the float, and all departed. Maurice stood in the gap of the hedge and watched them go, the cart rolling and swinging down-hill, over the grass stubble, the cyclists dipping swiftly like shadows in front. All passed through the gate, there was a quick clatter of hoofs on the roadway under the lime trees, and they were gone. The young man was very much excited, almost afraid, at finding himself alone.

Darkness was rising from the valley. Already, up the steep hill the cart-lamps crept indecisively, and the cottage windows were lit. Everything looked strange to Maurice, as if he had not seen it before. Down the hedge a large lime tree teemed with scent that seemed almost like a voice speaking. It startled him. He caught a breath of the over-sweet fragrance, then stood still, listening expectantly.

Up-hill, a horse whinneyed. It was the young mare. The heavy horses went thundering across to the far hedge.

Maurice wondered what to do. He wandered round the deserted stacks restlessly. Heat came in wafts, in thick strands. The evening was a long time cooling. He thought he would go and wash himself. There was a trough of pure water in the hedge bottom. It was filled by a tiny spring that filtered over the brim of the trough down the lush hedge bottom of the lower field. All round the trough, in the upper field, the land was marshy, and there the meadow-sweet stood like clots of mist, very sickly-smelling in the twilight. The night did not darken, for the moon was in the sky, so that as the tawny colour drew off the heavens they remained pallid with a dimmed moon. The purple bell-flowers in the hedge went black, the ragged robin turned its pink to a faded white, the meadow-sweet gathered light as if it were phosphorescent, and it made the air ache with scent.

Maurice kneeled on the slab of stone bathing his hands and arms, then his face. The water was deliciously cool. He had still an hour before Paula would come: she was not due till nine. So he decided to take his bath at night instead of waiting till morning. Was he not sticky, and was not Paula coming to talk to him? He was delighted the thought had occurred to him. As he soused his head in the trough, he wondered what the little creatures that lived in the velvety silt at the bottom would think of the taste of soap. Laughing to himself, he squeezed his cloth into the water. He washed himself from head to foot, standing in the fresh, forsaken corner of the field, where no one could see him by daylight, so that now, in the veiled grey tinge of moonlight, he was no more noticeable than the crowded flowers. The night had on a new look: he never remembered to have seen the lustrous grey sheen of it before, nor to have noticed how vital the lights looked, like live folk inhabiting the silvery spaces. And the tall trees, wrapped obscurely in their mantles, would not have surprised him had they begun to move in converse. As he dried himself, he discovered little wanderings in the air, felt on his sides soft touches and caresses that were peculiarly delicious: sometimes they startled him, and he laughed as if he were not alone. The flowers, the meadow-sweet particularly, haunted him. He reached to put his hand over their fleeciness. They touched his thighs. Laughing, he gathered them and dusted himself all over with their cream dust and fragrance. For a moment he hesitated in wonder at himself: but the subtle glow in the hoary black night reassured him. Things never had looked so personal and full of beauty, he had never known the wonder in himself before.

At nine o'clock he was waiting under the elder bush, in a state of high trepidation, but feeling that he was worthy, having a sense of his own wonder. She was late. At a quarter-past nine she came, flitting swiftly, in her own eager way.

'No, she would *not* go to sleep,' said Paula, with a world of wrath in her tone. He laughed bashfully. They wandered out into the dim, hill-side field.

'I have sat – in that bedroom – for an hour, for hours,' she cried indignantly. She took a deep breath: 'Ah, breathe!' she smiled.

She was very intense, and full of energy.

'I want' – she was clumsy with the language – 'I want – I should laike – to run – there!' She pointed across the field.

'Let's run, then,' he said curiously.

'Yes!'

And in an instant she was gone. He raced after her. For all he was so young and limber, he had difficulty in catching her. At first he could scarcely see her, though he could hear the rustle of her dress. She sped with astonishing fleetness. He overtook her, caught her by the arm, and they stood panting, facing one another with laughter.

'I could win,' she asserted blithely.

'Tha couldna,' he replied, with a peculiar, excited laugh. They walked on, rather breathless. In front of them suddenly appeared the dark shapes of the three feeding horses.

'We ride a horse?' she said.

'What, bareback?' he asked.

'You say?' She did not understand.

'With no saddle?'

'No saddle – yes – no saddle.'

'Coop, lass!' he said to the mare, and in a minute he had her by the forelock, and was leading her down to the stacks, where he put a halter on her. She was a big, strong mare. Maurice seated the Fräulein, clambered himself in front of the girl, using the wheel of the wagon as a mount, and together they trotted uphill, she holding lightly round his waist. From the crest of the hill they looked round.

The sky was darkening with an awning of cloud. On the left the hill rose black and wooded, made cosy by a few lights from cottages along the highway. The hill spread to the right, and tufts of trees shut round. But in front was a great vista of night, a sprinkle of cottage candles, a twinkling cluster of lights, like an elfish fair in full swing, at the colliery an encampment of light at a village, a red flare on the sky far off, above an iron-foundry, and in the farthest distance the dim breathing of town lights. As they watched the night stretch far out, her arms tightened round his waist, and he pressed his elbows to his side, pressing her arms closer still. The horse moved restlessly. They clung to each other.

'Tha daesna want to go right away?' he asked the girl behind him.

'I stay with you,' she answered softly, and he felt her crouching close against him. He laughed curiously. He was afraid to kiss her, though he was urged to do so. They remained still, on the restless horse, watching the small lights lead deep into the night, an infinite distance.

'I don't want to go,' he said, in a tone half pleading.

She did not answer. The horse stirred restlessly.

'Let him run,' cried Paula, 'fast!'

She broke the spell, startled him into a little fury. He kicked the mare, hit her, and away she plunged down-hill. The girl clung tightly to the young man. They were riding bareback down a rough, steep hill. Maurice clung hard with hands and knees. Paula held him fast round the waist, leaning her head on his shoulders, and thrilling with excitement.

'We shall be off, we shall be off,' he cried, laughing with excitement; but she only crouched behind and pressed tight to him. The mare tore across the field. Maurice expected every moment to be flung on to the grass. He gripped with all the strength of his knees. Paula tucked herself behind him, and often wrenched him almost from his hold. Man and girl were taut with effort.

At last the mare came to a standstill, blowing. Paula slid off, and in an instant Maurice was beside her. They were both highly excited. Before he knew what he was doing, he had her in his arms, fast, and was kissing her, and laughing. They did not move for some time. Then, in silence, they walked towards the stacks.

It had grown quite dark, the night was thick with cloud. He walked with his arm round Paula's waist, she with her arm round him. They were near the stacks when Maurice felt a spot of rain.

'It's going to rain,' he said.

'Rain!' she echoed, as if it were trivial.

'I s'll have to put the stack-cloth on,' he said gravely. She did not understand.

When they got to the stacks, he went round to the shed, to return staggering in the darkness under the burden of the immense and heavy cloth. It had not been used once during the hay harvest.

'What are you going to do?' asked Paula, coming close to him in the darkness.

'Cover the top of the stack with it,' he replied. 'Put it over the stack, to keep the rain out.'

'Ah!' she cried, 'up there!' He dropped his burden. 'Yes,' he answered.

Fumblingly he reared the long ladder up the side of the stack. He could not see the top.

'I hope it's solid,' he said softly.

A few smart drops of rain sounded drumming on the cloth. They seemed like another presence. It was very dark indeed between the great buildings of hay. She looked up the black wall and shrank to him.

'You carry it up there?' she asked.

'Yes,' he answered.

'I help you?' she said.

And she did. They opened the cloth. He clambered first up the steep ladder, bearing the upper part, she followed closely, carrying her full share. They mounted the shaky ladder in silence, stealthily.

4

As they climbed the stacks a light stopped at the gate on the high road. It was Geoffrey, come to help his brother with the cloth. Afraid of his own intrusion, he wheeled his bicycle silently towards the shed. This was a corrugated iron erection, on the opposite side of the hedge from the stacks. Geoffrey let his light go in front of him, but there was no sign from the lovers. He thought he saw a shadow slinking away. The light of the bicycle lamp sheered yellowly across the dark, catching a glint of raindrops, a mist of darkness, shadow of leaves and strokes of long grass. Geoffrey entered the shed – no one was there. He walked slowly and doggedly round to the stacks. He had passed the wagon, when he heard something sheering down upon him. Starting back under the wall of hay, he saw the long ladder slither across the side of the stack, and fall with a bruising ring.

'What wor that?' he heard Maurice, aloft, ask cautiously.

'Something fall,' came the curious, almost pleased voice of the Fräulein.

'It wor niver th' ladder,' said Maurice. He peered over the side of the stack. He lay down, looking.

'It is an' a'!' he exclaimed. 'We knocked it down with the cloth, dragging it over.'

'We fast up here?' she exclaimed with a thrill.

'We are that – without I shout and make 'em hear at the Vicarage.'

'Oh no,' she said quickly.

'I don't want to,' he replied, with a short laugh. There came a swift clatter of raindrops on the cloth. Geoffrey crouched under the wall of the other stack.

'Mind where you tread – here, let me straighten this end,' said Maurice, with a peculiar intimate tone – a command and an embrace. 'We s'll have to sit under it. At any rate, we shan't get wet.'

'Not get wet!' echoed the girl, pleased, but agitated.

Geoffrey heard the slide and rustle of the cloth over the top of the stack, heard Maurice telling her to 'Mind!'

'Mind!' she repeated. 'Mind! you say "Mind!"'

'Well, what if I do?' he laughed. 'I don't want you to fall over th' side, do I?' His tone was masterful, but he was not quite sure of himself.

There was silence a moment or two.

'Maurice!' she said plaintively.

'I'm here,' he answered tenderly, his voice shaky with excitement that was near to distress. 'There, I've done. Now should we – we'll sit under this corner.'

'Maurice!' she was rather pitiful.

'What? You'll be all right,' he remonstrated, tenderly indignant.

'I be all raïght,' she repeated, 'I be all raïght, Maurice?'

'Tha knows tha will – I canna ca' thee Powla. Should I ca' thee Minnie?'

It was the name of a dead sister.

'Minnie?' she exclaimed in surprise.

'Aye, should I?'

She answered in full-throated German. He laughed shakily.

'Come on – come on under. But do yer wish you was safe in th' Vicarage? Should I shout for somebody?' he asked.

'I don't wish, no!' She was vehement.

'Art sure?' he insisted, almost indignantly.

'Sure – I quite sure.' She laughed.

Geoffrey turned away at the last words. Then the rain beat heavily. The lonely brother slouched miserably to the hut, where the rain played a mad tattoo. He felt very miserable, and jealous of Maurice.

His bicycle lamp, downcast, shone a yellow light on the stark floor of the shed or hut with one wall open. It lit up the trodden earth, the shafts of tools lying piled under the beam, beside the dreary grey metal of the building. He took off the lamp, shone it round the hut. There were piles of harness, tools, a big sugar-box, a deep bed of hay – then the beams across the corrugated iron, all very dreary and stark. He shone the lamp into the night: nothing but the furtive glitter of raindrops through the mist of darkness, and black shapes hovering round.

Geoffrey blew out the light and flung himself on to the hay. He would put the ladder up for them in a while, when they would be wanting it. Meanwhile he sat and gloated over Maurice's felicity. He was imaginative, and now he had something concrete to work upon. Nothing in the whole of life stirred him so profoundly, and so utterly, as the thought of this woman. For Paula was strange, foreign, different from the ordinary girls: the rousing, feminine quality seemed in her concentrated, brighter, more fascinating than in anyone he had known, so that he felt most like a moth near a candle. He would have loved her wildly – but Maurice had got her. His thoughts beat the same course, round and round. What was it like when you kissed her, when she held you tight round the waist, how did she feel towards Maurice, did she love to touch him, was he fine and attractive to her; what did she think of himself – she merely disregarded him, as she would disregard a horse in a field; why would she do so, why couldn't he make her regard himself, instead of Maurice: he would never command a woman's regard like that, he always gave in to her too soon; if only some woman would come and take him for what he was worth, though he was such a stumbler and showed to such disadvantage, ah, what a grand thing it would be; how he would kiss her. Then round he went again in the same course, brooding almost like a madman. Meanwhile the rain drummed deep on the shed, then grew lighter and softer. There came the drip, drip of the drops falling outside.

Geoffrey's heart leaped up his chest, and he clenched himself, as a black shape crept round the post of the shed and, bowing, entered silently. The young man's heart beat so heavily in plunges, he could not get his breath to speak. It was shock, rather than fear. The form felt towards him. He sprang up, gripped it with his great hand's panting 'Now, then!'

There was no resistance, only a little whimper of despair.

'Let me go,' said a woman's voice.

'What are you after?' he asked, in deep, gruff tones.

'I thought 'e was 'ere,' she wept despairingly, with little, stubborn sobs.

'An' you've found what you didn't expect, have you?'

At the sound of his bullying she tried to get away from him.

'Let me go,' she said.

'Who did you expect to find here?' he asked, but more his natural self.

'I expected my husband – him as you saw at dinner. Let me go.'

'Why, is it you?' exclaimed Geoffrey. 'Has he left you?'

'Let me go,' said the woman sullenly, trying to draw away. He realized that her sleeve was very wet, her arm slender under his grasp. Suddenly he grew ashamed of himself: he had no doubt hurt her, gripping her so hard. He relaxed, but did not let her go.

'An' are you searching round after that snipe as was here at dinner?' he asked. She did not answer.

'Where did he leave you?'

'I left him – here. I've seen nothing of him since.'

'I s'd think it's good riddance,' he said. She did not answer. He gave a short laugh, saying:

'I should ha' thought you wouldn't ha' wanted to clap eyes on him again.'

'He's my husband – an' he's not go n' to run off if I can stop him.'

Geoffrey was silent, not knowing what to say.

'Have you got a jacket on?' he asked at last.

'What do you think? You've got hold of it.'

'You're wet through, aren't you?'

'I shouldn't be dry, comin' through that teemin' rain. But 'e's not here, so I'll go.'

'I mean,' he said humbly, 'are you wet through?'

She did not answer. He felt her shiver.

'Are you cold?' he asked, in surprise and concern.

She did not answer. He did not know what to say.

'Stop a minute,' he said, and he fumbled in his pocket for his matches. He struck a light, holding it in the hollow of his large, hard palm. He was a big man, and he looked anxious. Shedding the light on her, he saw she was rather pale, and very weary looking. Her old sailor hat was sodden and drooping with rain. She wore a fawn-coloured jacket of smooth cloth. This jacket was black-wet where the rain had beaten, her skirt hung sodden, and dripped on to her boots. The match went out.

'Why, you're wet through!' he said.

She did not answer.

'Shall you stop in here while it gives over?' he asked. She did not answer.

''Cause if you will, you'd better take your things off, an' have th' rug. There's a horse-rug in the box.'

He waited, but she would not answer. So he lit his bicycle lamp, and rummaged in the box, pulling out a large brown blanket, striped with scarlet and yellow. She stood stock still. He shone the light on her. She was very pale, and trembling fitfully.

'Are you that cold?' he asked in concern. 'Take your jacket off, and your hat, and put this right over you.'

Mechanically, she undid the enormous fawn-coloured buttons, and unpinned her hat. With her black hair drawn back from her low, honest brow, she looked little more than a girl, like a girl driven hard with womanhood by stress of life. She was small, and natty, with neat little features. But she shivered convulsively.

'Is something a-matter with you?' he asked.

'I've walked to Bulwell and back,' she quivered, 'looking for him – an' I've not touched a thing since this morning.' She did not weep – she was too dreary-hardened to cry. He looked at her in dismay, his mouth half open: 'Gormin' as Maurice would have said.

"Aven't you had nothing to eat?' he said.

Then he turned aside to the box. There, the bread remaining was kept, and the great piece of cheese, and such things as sugar and salt, with all table utensils: there was some butter.

She sat down drearily on the bed of hay. He cut her a piece of bread and butter, and a piece of cheese. This she took, but ate listlessly.

'I want a drink,' she said.

'We 'aven't got no beer,' he answered. 'My father doesn't have it.'

'I want water,' she said.

He took a can and plunged through the wet darkness, under the great black hedge, down to the trough. As he came back he saw her in the half-lit little cave sitting bunched together. The soaked grass wet his feet – he thought of her. When he gave her a cup of water, her hand touched his and he felt her fingers hot and glossy. She trembled so she spilled the water.

'Do you feel badly?' he asked.

'I can't keep myself still – but it's only with being tired and having nothing to eat.'

He scratched his head contemplatively, waited while she ate her piece of bread and butter. Then he offered her another piece.

'I don't want it just now,' she said.

'You'll have to eat summat,' he said.

'I couldn't eat any more just now.'

He put the piece down undecidedly on the box. Then there was another long pause. He stood up with bent head. The bicycle, like a restful animal, glittered behind him, turning towards the wall. The woman sat hunched on the hay, shivering.

'Can't you get warm?' he asked.

'I shall by an' by – don't you bother. I'm taking your seat – are you stopping here all night?'

'Yes.'

'I'll be goin' in a bit,' she said.

'Nay, I non want you to go. I'm thinkin' how you could get warm.'

'Don't you bother about me,' she remonstrated, almost irritably.

'I just want to see as the stacks is all right. You take your shoes an' stockin's an' all your wet things off: you can easy wrap yourself all over in that rug, there's not so much of you.'

'It's raining – I s'll be all right – I s'll be going in a minute.'

'I've got to see as the stacks is safe. Take your wet things off.'

'Are you coming back?' she asked.

'I mighn't, not till morning.'

'Well, I s'll be gone in ten minutes, then. I've no rights to be here, an' I s'll not let anybody be turned out for me.'

'You won't be turning me out.'

'Whether or no, I shan't stop.'

'Well, shall you if I come back?' he asked. She did not answer.

He went. In a few moments, she blew the light out. The rain was falling steadily, and the night was a black gulf. All was intensely still. Geoffrey listened everywhere: no sound save the rain. He stood between the stacks but only heard the trickle of water, and the light swish of rain. Everything was lost in blackness. He imagined death was like that, many things dissolved in silence and darkness, blotted out, but existing. In the dense blackness he felt himself almost extinguished. He was afraid he might not find things the same. Almost frantically, he stumbled, feeling his way, till his hand touched the wet metal. He had been looking for a gleam of light.

'Did you blow the lamp out?' he asked, fearful lest the silence should answer him.

'Yes,' she answered humbly. He was glad to hear her voice. Groping into the pitch-dark shed, he knocked against the box, part of whose cover served as table. There was a clatter and fall.

'That's the lamp, an' the knife, an' the cup,' he said. He struck a match.

'Th' cup's not broke.' He put it into the box.

'But th' oil's spilled out o' th' lamp. It always was a rotten old thing.' He hastily blew out his match, which was burning his fingers. Then he struck another light.

'You don't want a lamp, you know you don't, and I s'll be going directly, so you come an' lie down an' get your night's rest. I'm not taking any of your place.'

He looked at her by the light of another match. She was a queer little bundle, all brown, with gaudy border folding in and out, and her little face peering at him. As the match went out she saw him beginning to smile.

'I can sit right at his end,' she said. 'You lie down.'

He came and sat on the hay, at some distance from her. After a spell of silence:

'Is he really your husband?' he asked.

'He is!' she answered grimly.

'Hm!' Then there was silence again.

After a while: 'Are you warm now?'

'Why do you bother yourself?'

'I don't bother myself – do you follow him because you like him?' He put it very timidly. He wanted to know.

'I don't – I wish he was dead,' this with bitter contempt. Then doggedly: 'But he's my husband.'

He gave a short laugh.

'By Gad!' he said.

Again, after a while: 'Have you been married long?'

'Four years.'

'Four years – why, how old are you?'

'Twenty-three.'

'Are you turned twenty-three?'

'Last May.'

'Then you're four month older than me.' He mused over it. They were only two voices in the pitch-black night. It was eerie silence again.

'And do you just tramp about?' he asked.

'He reckons he's looking for a job. But he doesn't like work in any shape or form. He was a stableman when I married him, at Greenhalgh's, the horse-dealers, at Chesterfield, where I was housemaid. He left that job when the baby was only two months, and I've been badgered about from pillar to post ever sin'. They say a rolling stone gathers no moss...'

'An' where's the baby?'

'It died when it was ten months old.'

Now the silence was clinched between them. It was quite a long time before Geoffrey ventured to say sympathetically: 'You haven't much to look forward to.'

'I've wished many a score time when I've started shiverin' an' shakin' at nights, as I was taken bad for death. But we're not that handy at dying.'

He was silent. 'But whatever shall you do?' he faltered.

'I s'll find him, if I drop by th' road.'

'Why?' he asked, wondering, looking her way, though he saw nothing but solid darkness.

'Because I shall. He's not going to have it all his own road.'

'But why don't you leave him?'

'Because he's *not goin' to have it all his own road.*'

She sounded very determined, even vindictive. He sat in wonder, feeling uneasy, and vaguely miserable on her behalf. She sat extraordinarily still. She seemed like a voice only, a presence.

'Are you warm now?' he asked, half afraid.

'A bit warmer – but my feet!' She sounded pitiful.

'Let me warm them with my hands,' he asked her. 'I'm hot enough.'

'No, thank you,' she said coldly.

Then, in the darkness, she felt she had wounded him. He was writhing under her rebuff, for his offer had been pure kindness.

'They're 'appen dirty,' she said, half mocking.

'Well – mine is – an' I have a bath a'most every day,' he answered.

'I don't know when they'll get warm,' she moaned to herself.

'Well, then, put them in my hands.'

She heard him faintly rattling the match-box, and then a phosphorescent glare began to fume in his direction. Presently he was holding two smoking, blue-green blotches of light towards her feet. She was afraid. But her feet ached so, and the impulse drove her on, so she placed her soles lightly on the two blotches of smoke. His large hands clasped over her instep, warm and hard.

'They're like ice!' he said, in deep concern.

He warmed her feet as best he could, putting them close against him. Now and again convulsive tremors ran over her. She felt his warm breath on the balls of her toes, that were bunched up in his hands. Leaning forward, she touched his hair delicately with her fingers. He thrilled. She fell to gently stroking his hair, with timid, pleading finger-tips.

'Do they feel any better?' he asked, in a low voice, suddenly lifting his face to her. This sent her hand sliding softly over his face, and her finger-tips caught on his mouth. She drew quickly away. He put his hand out to find hers, in his other palm holding both her feet. His wandering hand met her face. He touched it curiously. It was wet. He put his big fingers cautiously on her eyes, into two little pools of tears.

'What's a matter?' he asked in a low, choked voice.

She leaned down to him and gripped him tightly round the neck, pressing him to her bosom in a little frenzy of pain. Her bitter disillusionment with life, her unalleviated shame and degradation during the last four years, had driven her into loneliness, and hardened her till a large part of her nature was caked and sterile. Now she softened again, and her spring might be beautiful. She had been in a fair way to make an ugly old woman.

She clasped the head of Geoffrey to her breast, which heaved and fell, and heaved again. He was bewildered, full of wonder. He allowed the woman to do as she would with him. Her tears fell on his hair, as she wept noiselessly; and he breathed deep as she did. At last she let go her clasp. He put his arms round her.

'Come and let me warm you,' he said, folding up on his knee and lapping her with his heavy arms against himself. She was small and *câline*. He held her very warm and close. Presently she stole her arms round him.

'You *are* big,' she whispered.

He gripped her hard, started, put his mouth down wanderingly, seeking her out. His lips met her temple. She slowly, deliberately turned her mouth to his, and with opened lips, met him in a kiss, his first love kiss.

5

It was breaking cold dawn when Geoffrey woke. The woman was still sleeping in his arms. Her face in sleep moved all his tenderness: the tight shutting of her mouth, as if in resolution to bear what was very hard to bear, contrasted so pitifully with the small mould of her features. Geoffrey pressed her to his bosom: having her, he felt he could bruise the lips of the scornful, and pass on erect, unabateable. With her to complete him, to form the core of him, he was firm and whole. Needing her so much, he loved her fervently.

Meanwhile the dawn came like death, one of those slow, livid mornings that seem to come in a cold sweat. Slowly, and painfully, the air began to whiten. Geoffrey saw it was not raining. As he was watching the ghastly transformation outside, he felt aware of something. He glanced down: she was open-eyed, watching him; she had golden-brown, calm eyes, that immediately smiled into his. He also smiled, bowed softly down and kissed her. They did not speak for some time. Then:

'What's thy name?' he asked curiously.

'Lydia,' she said.

'Lydia!' he repeated wonderingly. He felt rather shy.

'Mine's Geoffrey Wookey,' he said.

She merely smiled at him.

They were silent for a considerate time. By morning light, things look small. The huge trees of the evening were dwindled to hoary, small, uncertain things, trespassing in the sick pallor of the atmosphere. There was a dense mist, so that the light could scarcely breathe. Everything seemed to quiver with cold and sickliness.

'Have you often slept out?' he asked her.

'Not so very,' she answered.

'You won't go after *him*?' he asked.

'I s'll have to,' she replied, but she nestled in to Geoffrey. He felt a sudden panic.

'You mustn't,' he exclaimed, and she saw he was afraid for himself. She let it be, was silent.

'We couldn't get married?' he asked thoughtfully.

'No.'

He brooded deeply over this. At length:

'Would you go to Canada with me?'

'We'll see what you think in two months' time,' she replied quietly, without bitterness.

'I s'll think the same,' he protested, hurt.

She did not answer, only watched him steadily. She was there for him to do as he liked with; but she would not injure his fortunes; no, not to save his soul.

'Haven't you got no relations?' he asked.

'A married sister at Crick.'

'On a farm?'

'No – married a farm labourer – but she's very comfortable. I'll go there, if you want me to, just till I can get another place in service.'

He considered this.

'Could you get on a farm?' he asked wistfully.

'Greenhalgh's was a farm.'

He saw the future brighten: she would be a help to him. She agreed to go to her sister, and to get a place of service – until spring, he said, when they would sail for Canada. He waited for her assent.

'You will come with me, then?' he asked.

'When the time comes,' she said.

Her want of faith made him bow his head: she had reason for it.

'Shall you walk to Crick, or go from Langley Mill to Ambergate? But it's only ten mile to walk. So we can go together up Hunt's Hill – you'd have to go past our lane-end, then I could easy nip down an' fetch you some money,' he said humbly.

'I've got half a sovereign by me – it's more than I s'll want.'

'Let's see it,' he said.

After a while, fumbling under the blanket, she brought out the piece of money. He felt she was independent of him. Brooding rather bitterly, he told himself she'd forsake him. His anger gave him courage to ask:

'Shall you go in service in your maiden name?'

'No.'

He was bitterly wrathful with her – full of resentment.

'I bet I s'll niver see you again,' he said, with a short, hard laugh. She put her arms round him, pressed him to her bosom, while the tears rose to her eyes. He was reassured, but not satisfied.

'Shall you write to me tonight?'

'Yes, I will.'

'And can I write to you – who shall I write to?'

'Mrs Bredon.'

'"Bredon"!' he repeated bitterly.

He was exceedingly uneasy.

The dawn had grown quite wan. He saw the hedges drooping wet down the grey mist. Then he told her about Maurice.

'Oh, you *shouldn't*!' she said. 'You should ha' put the ladder up for them, you *should*.'

'Well – I don't care.'

'Go and do it now – and I'll go.'

'No, don't you. Stop an' see our Maurice; go on, stop an' see him – then I'll be able to tell him.'

She consented in silence. He had her promise she would not go before he returned. She adjusted her dress, found her way to the trough, where she performed her toilet.

Geoffrey wandered round to the upper field. The stacks looked wet in the mist, the hedge was drenched. Mist rose like steam from the grass, and the near hills were veiled almost to a shadow. In the valley, some peaks of black poplar showed fairly definite, jutting up. He shivered with chill.

There was no sound from the stacks, and he could see nothing. After all, he wondered, were they up there? But he reared the ladder to the place whence it had been swept, then went down the hedge to gather dry sticks. He was breaking off thin dead twigs under a holly tree when he heard, on the perfectly still air: 'Well, I'm dashed!'

He listened intently. Maurice was awake.

'Sithee here!' the lad's voice exclaimed. Then, after a while, the foreign sound of the girl:

'What – oh, thair!'

'Aye, th' ladder's there, right enough.'

'You said it had fall down.'

'Well, I heard it drop – an' I couldna feel it nor see it.'

'You said it had fall down – you lie, you liar.'

'Nay, as true as I'm here –'

'You tell me lies – make me stay here – you tell me lies –' She was passionately indignant.

'As true as I'm standing here –' he began.

'Lies! – lies! – lies!' she cried. 'I don't believe you, never. You *mean*, you *mean, mean, mean*!'

'A' raïght, then!' He was now incensed, in his turn.

'You are bad, mean, mean, mean.'

'Are ter commin' down?' asked Maurice coldly.

'No – I will not come with you – mean, to tell me lies.'

'Are ter commin' down?'

'No, I don't want you.'

'A' raïght, then!'

Geoffrey, peering through the holly tree, saw Maurice negotiating the ladder. The top rung was below the brim of the stack, and rested on the cloth, so it was dangerous to approach. The Fräulein watched him from the end of the stack, where the cloth thrown back showed the light, dry hay. He slipped slightly, she screamed. When he had got on to the ladder, he pulled the cloth away, throwing it back, making it easy for her to descend.

'Now are ter commin'?' he asked.

'No!' She shook her head violently, in a pet.

Geoffrey felt slightly contemptuous of her. But Maurice waited.

'Are ter commin'?' he called again.

'No,' she flashed, like a wild cat.

'All right, then I'm going.'

He descended. At the bottom, he stood holding the ladder.

'Come on, while I hold it steady,' he said.

There was no reply. For some minutes he stood patiently with his foot on the bottom rung of the ladder. He was pale, rather washed-out in his appearance, and he drew himself together with cold.

'Are ter commin', or aren't ter?' he asked at length. Still there was no reply.

'Then stop up till tha'rt ready,' he muttered, and he went away. Round the other side of the stacks he met Geoffrey.

'What, are thaïgh here?' he exclaimed.

'Bin here a' naïght,' replied Geoffrey. 'I come to help thee wi' th' cloth, but I found it on, an' th' ladder down, so I thowt tha'd gone.'

'Did ter put th' ladder up?'

'I did a bit sin'.'

Maurice brooded over this, Geoffrey struggled with himself to get out his own news. At last he blurted:

'Tha knows that woman as wor here yis'day dinner – 'er come back, an' stopped i' th' shed a' night, out o' th' rain.'

'Oh – ah!' said Maurice, his eye kindling, and a smile crossing his pallor.

'An' I s'll gi'e her some breakfast.'

'Oh – ah!' repeated Maurice.

'It's th' man as is good-for-nowt, not her,' protested Geoffrey. Maurice did not feel in a position to cast stones.

'Tha pleases thysen,' he said, 'what ter does.' He was very quiet, unlike himself. He seemed bothered and anxious, as Geoffrey had not seen him before.

'What's up wi thee?' asked the elder brother, who in his own heart was glad, and relieved.

'Nowt,' was the reply.

They went together to the hut. The woman was folding the blanket. She was fresh from washing, and looked very pretty. Her hair, instead of being screwed tightly back, was coiled in a knot low down, partly covering her ears. Before she had deliberately made herself plain-looking: now she was neat and pretty, with a sweet, womanly gravity.

'Hello. I didn't think to find you here,' said Maurice, very awkwardly, smiling. She watched him gravely without reply. 'But it was better in shelter than outside last night,' he added.

'Yes,' she replied.

'Shall you get a few more sticks?' Geoffrey asked him. It was a new thing for Geoffrey to be leader. Maurice obeyed. He wandered forth into the damp, raw morning. He did not go to the stack, as he shrank from meeting Paula.

At the mouth of the hut, Geoffrey was making the fire. The woman got out coffee from the box: Geoffrey set the tin to boil. They were arranging breakfast when Paula appeared. She was hatless. Bits of hay stuck in her hair, and she was white-faced – altogether, she did not show to advantage.

'Ah – you!' she exclaimed, seeing Geoffrey.

'Hello!' he answered. 'You're out early.'

'Where's Maurice?'

'I dunno, he should be back directly.'

Paula was silent.

'When have you come?' she asked.

'I come last night, but I could see nobody about. I got up half an hour sin', an' put th' ladder up ready to take the stack-cloth up.

Paula understood, and was silent. When Maurice returned with the faggots, she was crouched warming her hands. She looked up at him, but he kept his eyes averted from her. Geoffrey met the eyes of Lydia, and smiled. Maurice put his hands to the fire.

'You cold?' asked Paula tenderly.

'A bit,' he answered, quite friendly, but reserved. And all the while the four sat round the fire, drinking their smoked coffee, eating each a small piece of toasted bacon, Paula watched eagerly for the eyes of Maurice, and he avoided her. He was gentle, but would not give his eyes to her looks. And Geoffrey smiled constantly to Lydia, who watched gravely.

The German girl succeeded in getting safely into the Vicarage, her escapade unknown to anyone save the housemaid. Before a week was out, she was openly engaged to Maurice, and when her month's notice expired, she went to live at the farm.

Geoffrey and Lydia kept faith one with the other.

D.H. LAWRENCE

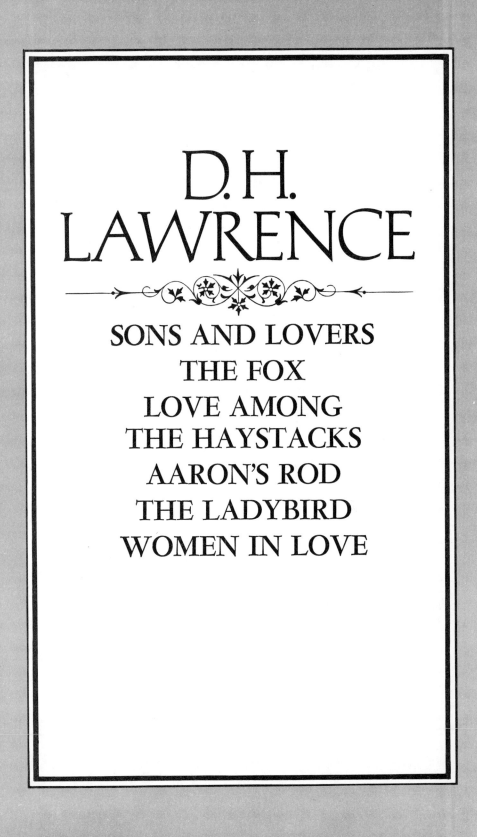

SONS AND LOVERS

THE FOX

LOVE AMONG
THE HAYSTACKS

AARON'S ROD

THE LADYBIRD

WOMEN IN LOVE

1

THE BLUE BALL

There was a large, brilliant evening star in the early twilight, and underfoot the earth was half frozen. It was Christmas Eve. Also the war was over, and there was a sense of relief that was almost a new menace. A man felt the violence of the nightmare released now into the general air. Also there had been another wrangle among the men on the pit-bank that evening.

Aaron Sisson was the last man on the little black railway-line climbing the hill home from work. He was late because he had attended a meeting of the men on the bank. He was secretary to the Miners' Union for his colliery, and had heard a good deal of silly wrangling that left him nettled.

He strode over a stile, crossed two fields, strode another stile, and was in the long road of colliers' dwellings. Just across was his own house: he had built it himself. He went through the little gate, up past the side of the house to the back. There he hung a moment, glancing down the dark, wintry garden.

'My father – my father's come!' cried a child's excited voice, and two little girls in white pinafores ran out in front of his legs.

'Father, shall you set the Christmas Tree?' they cried. 'We've got one!'

'Afore I have my dinner?' he answered amiably.

'Set it now. Set it now. We got it through Fred Alton.'

'Where is it?'

The little girls were dragging a rough, dark object out of a corner of the passage into the light of the kitchen door.

'It's a beauty!' exclaimed Millicent.

'Yes, it is,' said Marjory.

'I should think so,' he replied, striding over the dark bough. He went to the back kitchen to take off his coat.

'Set it now, father. Set it now,' clamoured the girls.

'You might as well. You've left your dinner so long, you might as well do it now before you have it,' came a woman's plangent voice, out of the brilliant light of the middle room.

Aarom Sisson had taken off his coat and waistcoat and his cap. He stood bare-headed in his shirt and braces, contemplating the tree.

'What am I to put in?' he queried. He picked up the tree, and held it erect by the top-most twig. He felt the cold as he stood in the yard coat-less, and he twitched his shoulders.

'Isn't it a beauty!' repeated Millicent.

'Ay! – lop-sided though.'

'Put something on, you two!' came the woman's high imperative voice from the kitchen.

'We aren't cold,' protested the girls from the yard.

'Come and put something on,' insisted the voice.

The man started off down the path; the little girls ran grumbling indoors. The sky was clear; there was still a crystalline, non-luminous light in the under air.

Aaron rummaged in his shed at the bottom of the garden, and found a spade and a box that was suitable. Then he came out to his neat, bare, wintry garden. The girls flew towards him, putting the elastic of their hats under their chins as they ran. The tree and the box lay on the frozen earth. The air breathed dark, frosty, electric.

'Hold it up straight,' he said to Millicent, as he arranged the tree in the box. She stood silent and held the top bough; he filled in round the roots.

When it was done, and pressed in, he went for the wheelbarrow. The girls were hovering excited round the tree. He dropped the barrow and stooped to the box. The girls watched him hold back his face – the boughs pricked him.

'Is it very heavy?' asked Millicent.

'Ay!' he replied, with a little grunt.

Then the procession set off – the trundling wheelbarrow, the swinging, hissing tree, the two excited little girls. They arrived at the door. Down went the legs of the wheelbarrow on the yard. The man looked at the box.

'Where are you going to have it?' he called.

'Put it in the back kitchen,' cried his wife.

'You'd better have it where it's going to stop. I don't want to hawk it about.'

'Put it on the floor against the dresser, father. Put it there,' urged Millicent.

'You come and put some paper down, then,' called the mother hastily.

The two children ran indoors; the man stood contemplative in the cold, shrugging his uncovered shoulders slightly. The open inner door showed a bright linoleum on the floor, and the end of a brown side-board on which stood an aspidistra.

Again with a wrench Aaron Sisson lifted the box. The tree pricked and stung. His wife watched him as he entered staggering, with his face averted.

'Mind where you make a lot of dirt,' she said.

He lowered the box with a little jerk on to the spread-out newspaper on the floor. Soil scattered.

'Sweep it up,' he said to Millicent.

His ear was lingering over the sudden, clutching hiss of the tree-boughs.

A stark white incandescent light filled the room and made everything sharp and hard. In the open fire-place a hot fire burned red. All was scrupulously clean and perfect. A baby was cooing in a rocker-less wicker cradle by the hearth. The mother, a slim, neat woman with dark hair, was sewing a child's frock. She put this aside, rose, and began to take her husband's dinner from the oven.

'You stopped confabbing long enough tonight,' she said.

'Yes,' he answered, going to the back kitchen to wash his hands.

In a few minutes he came and sat down to the table. The doors were shut close, but there was a draught, because the settling of the mines under the house made the doors not fit. Aaron moved his chair, to get out of the draught. But he still sat in his shirt and trousers.

He was a good-looking man, fair, and pleasant, about thirty-two years old.

He did not talk much, but seemed to think about something. His wife resumed her sewing: She was acutely aware of her husband, but he seemed not very much aware of her.

'What were they on about today, then?' she said.

'About the throw-in.'

'And did they settle anything?'

'They're going to try it – and they'll come out if it isn't satisfactory.'

'The butties won't have it, I know,' she said.

He gave a short laugh, and went on with his meal.

The two children were squatted on the floor by the tree. They had a wooden box, from which they had taken many little newspaper packets which they were spreading out like wares.

'Don't open any. We won't open any of them till we've taken them all out – and then we'll undo one in our turns. Then we s'll both undo equal,' Millicent was saying.

'Yes, we'll take them *all* out first,' re-echoed Marjory.

'And what are they going to do about Job Arthur Freer? – Do they want him?'

A faint smile came on her husband's face.

'Nay, I don't know what they want. Some of 'em want him – whether they're a majority, I don't know.'

She watched him closely.

'Majority! I'd give 'em majority. They want to get rid of you, and make a fool of you, and you want to break your heart over it. Strikes me you need something to break your heart over.'

He laughed silently.

'Nay,' he said. 'I s'll never break my heart.'

'You'll go nearer to it over that, than over anything else: just because a lot of ignorant monkeys want a monkey of their own sort to do the Union work, and jabber to them, they want to get rid of you, and you eat your heart out about it. More fool you, that's all I say – more fool you. If you cared for your wife and children half what you care about your Union, you'd be a lot better pleased in the end. But you care about nothing but a lot of ignorant colliers, who don't know what they want except it's more money just for themselves. Self, self, self – that's all it is with them – and ignorance.'

'You'd rather have self without ignorance?' he said, smiling finely.

'I would, if I've got to have it. But what I should like to see is a man that has thought for others, and isn't all self and politics.'

Her colour had risen, her hand trembled with anger as she sewed. A blank look had come over the man's face, as if he did not hear or heed any more. He drank his tea in a long draught, wiped his moustache with two fingers, and sat looking abstractedly at the children.

They had laid all the little packets on the floor, and Millicent was saying: 'Now I'll undo the first, and you can have the second. I'll take this –'

She unwrapped the bit of newspaper and disclosed a silvery ornament for a Christmas tree: a frail thing like a silver plum, with deep rosy indentations on each side.

'Oh!' she exclaimed. 'Isn't it *lovely*!'

Her fingers cautiously held the long bubble of silver and glowing rose, cleaving to it with a curious, irritating possession. The man's eyes moved away from her. The lesser child was fumbling with one of the little packets.

'Oh!' – a wail went up from Millicent – 'You've taken one! – You didn't wait.' Then her voice changed to a motherly admonition, and she began to interfere. 'This is the way to do it, look! Let me help you.'

But Marjory drew back with resentment.

'Don't, Millicent! – Don't!' came the childish cry. But Millicent's finger itched.

At length Marjory had got her treasure – a little silvery bell, with a glass drop hanging inside. The bell was made of frail glassy substance, light as air.

'Oh, the bell!' rang out Millicent's clanging voice. 'The bell! It's my bell. My bell! It's mine! Don't break it, Marjory. Don't break it, will you?'

Marjory was shaking the bell against her ear. But it was dumb, it made no sound.

'You'll break it, I know you will. You'll break it. Give it *me* –' cried Millicent, and she began to take away the bell. Marjory set up an expostulation.

'*Let her alone,*' said the father.

Millicent let go as if she had been stung, but still her brassy, impudent voice persisted:

'She'll break it. She'll break it. It's *mine* –'

'You undo another,' said the mother, politic.

Millicent began with hasty, itching fingers to unclose another package.

'Aw – aw, mother, my peacock – aw, my peacock, my green peacock!' Lavishly she hovered over a sinuous greenish bird, with wings and tail of spun glass, pearly, and body of deep electric green.

'It's *mine* – my green peacock! It's mine, because Marjory's had one wing off, and mine hadn't. My green peacock that I love! I love it!' She swung it softly from the little ring on its back. Then she went to her mother.

'Look, mother, isn't it a beauty?'

'Mind the ring doesn't come out,' said her mother. 'Lovely!'

The girl passed on to her father.

'Look, father, don't you love it!'

'Love it?' he re-echoed, ironical over the word love.

She stood for some moments, trying to force his attention. Then she went back to her place.

Marjory had brought forth a golden apple, red on one cheek, rather garish.

'Oh!' exclaimed Millicent feverishly, instantly seized with desire for what she had not got, indifferent to what she had. Her eye ran quickly over the packages. She took one.

'Now!' she exclaimed loudly, to attract attention. 'Now! What's this? – What's this? What will this beauty be?'

With finicky fingers she removed the newspaper. Marjory watched her wide-eyed. Millicent was self-important.

'The blue ball!' she cried in a climax of rapture. 'I've got *the blue ball.*'

She held it gloating in the cup of her hands. It was a little globe of hardened glass, of a magnificent full dark blue colour. She rose and went to her father.

'It was *your* blue ball, wasn't it, father?'

'Yes.'

'And you had it when you were a little boy, and now I have it when I'm a little girl.'

'Ay,' he replied dryly.

'And it's never been broken all those years.'

'No, not yet.'

'And perhaps it never will be broken?'

To this she received no answer.

'Won't it break?' she persisted. 'Can't you break it?'

'Yes, if you hit it with a hammer,' he said.

'Aw!' she cried. 'I don't mean that. I mean if you just drop it. It won't break if you drop it, will it?'

'I dare say it won't.'

'But *will* it?'

'I sh'd think not.'

'Should I try?'

She proceeded gingerly to let the blue ball drop. It bounced dully on the floor-covering.

'Oh-h-h!' she cried, catching it up. 'I love it.'

'Let *me* drop it,' cried Marjory, and there was a performance of admonition and demonstration from the elder sister.

But Millicent must go further. She became excited.

'It won't break,' she said, 'even if you toss it up in the air.'

She flung it up, it fell safely. But her father's brow knitted slightly. She tossed it wildly: it fell with a little splashing explosion: it had smashed. It had fallen on the sharp edge of the tiles that protruded under the fender.

'*Now* what have you done!' cried the mother.

The child stood with her lip between her teeth, a look, half of pure misery and dismay, half of satisfaction, on her pretty, sharp face.

'She wanted to break it,' said the father.

'No, she didn't! What do you say that for!' said the mother. And Millicent burst into a flood of tears.

He rose to look at the fragments that lay splashed on the floor.

'You must mind the bits,' he said, 'and pick 'em all up.' He took one of the pieces to examine it. It was fine and thin and hard, lined with pure silver, brilliant. He looked at it closely. So – this was what it was. And this was the end of it. He felt the curious soft explosion of its breaking still in his ears. He threw his piece in the fire.

'Pick all the bits up,' he said. 'Give-over! give over! Don't cry any more.'

The good-natured tone of his voice quieted the child, as he intended it should.

He went away to the back kitchen to wash himself. As he was bending his head over the sink before the little mirror, lathering to shave, there came from outside the dissonant voices of boys, pouring out the dregs of carol-singing.

'While Shep-ep-ep-ep-herds watched –'

He held his soapy brush suspended for a minute. They called this singing! His mind flitted back to early carol music. Then again he heard the vocal violence outside.

'Aren't you off there!' he called out, in masculine menace. The noise stopped, there was a scuffle. But the feet returned and the voices resumed. Almost immediately the door opened, boys were heard muttering among themselves. Millicent had given them a penny. Feet scraped on the yard, then went thudding along the side of the house to the street.

To Aaron Sisson this was home, this was Christmas: the unspeakably familiar. The war over, nothing was changed. Yet everything changed. The scullery in which he stood was painted green, quite fresh, very clean, the floor was red tiles. The wash-copper of red bricks was very red, the mangle with its put-up board was white-scrubbed, the American oil-cloth on the table had a gay pattern, there was a warm fire, the water in the boiler hissed faintly. And in front of him, beneath him as he leaned forward shaving, a drop of water fell with strange, incalculable rhythm from the bright brass tap into the white enamelled bowl, which was now half full of pure, quivering water. The war was over, and everything just the same. The acute familiarity of this house, which had been built for his marriage twelve years ago, the changeless pleasantness of it all seemed unthinkable. It prevented his thinking.

When he went into the middle room to comb his hair he found the Christmas tree sparkling, his wife was making pastry at the table, the baby was sitting up propped in cushions.

'Father,' said Millicent, approaching him with a flat blue-and-white angel of cotton-wool, and two ends of cotton – 'tie the angel at the top.'

'Tie it at the top?' he said, looking down.

'Yes. At the very top – because it's just come down from the sky.'

'Ay, my word!' he laughed. And he tied the angel.

Coming downstairs after changing he went into the icy cold parlour, and took his music and a small handbag. With this he retreated again to the back kitchen. He was still in trousers and shirt and slippers: but now it was a clean white shirt, and his best black trousers, and new pink and white braces. He sat under the gas-jet of the back kitchen, looking through his music. Then he opened the bag, in which were sections of a flute and a piccolo. He took out the flute and adjusted it. As he sat he was physically aware of the sounds of the night: the bubbling of water in the boiler, the faint sound of the gas, the sudden crying of the baby in the next room, then noises outside, distant boys shouting, distant rags of carols, fragments of voices of men. The whole country was roused and excited.

The little room was hot. Aaron rose and opened a square ventilator over the copper, letting in a stream of cold air which was grateful to him. Then he cocked his eye over the sheet of music spread out on the table before him. He tried his flute. And then at last, with the odd gesture of a diver taking a plunge, he swung his head and began to play. A stream of music, soft and rich and fluid, came out of the flute. He played beautifully. He moved his head and his raised bare arms with slight, intense movements, as the delicate music poured out. It was sixteenth-century Christmas melody, very limpid and delicate.

The pure, mindless, exquisite motion and fluidity of the music delighted him with a strange exasperation. There was something tense, exasperated to the point of intolerable anger, in his good-humoured breast, as he played the finely-spun peace-music. The more exquisite the music, the more perfectly he produced it, in sheer bliss; and at the same time, the more intense was the maddened exasperation within him.

Millicent appeared in the room. She fidgeted at the sink. The music was a bugbear to her, because it prevented her from saying what was on her own mind. At length it ended, her father was turning over the various books and sheets. She looked at him quickly, seizing her opportunity.

'Are you going out, father?' she said.

'Eh?'

'Are you going out?' She twisted nervously.

'What do you want to know for?'

He made no other answer, and turned again to the music. His eye went down a sheet – then over it again – then more closely over it again.

'Are you?' persisted the child, balancing on one foot. He looked at her, and his eyes were angry under knitted brows.

'What are you bothering about?' he said.

'I'm not bothering – I only wanted to know if you were going out,' she pouted, quivering to cry.

'I expect I am,' he said quietly.

She recovered at once, but still with timidity asked:

'We haven't got any candles for the Christmas tree – shall *you* buy some, because mother isn't going out?'

'Candles!' he repeated, settling his music and taking up the piccolo.

'Yes – shall you buy us some, father? Shall you?'

'Candles!' he repeated, putting the piccolo to his mouth and blowing a few piercing, preparatory notes.

'Yes, little Christmas-tree candles – blue ones and red ones, in boxes – shall you, father?'

'We'll see – if I see any –'

'But *shall* you?' she insisted desperately. She wisely mistrusted his vagueness.

But he was looking unheeding at the music. Then suddenly the piccolo broke forth, wild, shrill, brilliant. He was playing Mozart. The child's face went pale with anger at the sound. She turned and went out, closing both doors behind her to shut out the noise.

The shrill, rapid movements of the piccolo music seemed to possess the air, it was useless to try to shut it out. The man went on playing to himself, measured and insistent. In the frosty evening the sound carried. People passing down the street hesitated, listening. The neighbours knew it was Aaron practising his piccolo. He was esteemed a good player: was in request at concerts and dances, also at swell balls. So the vivid piping sound tickled the darkness.

He played on till about seven o'clock: he did not want to go out too soon, in spite of the early closing of the public-houses. He never went with the stream, but made a side current of his own. His wife said he was contrary. When he went into the middle room to put on his collar and tie, the two little girls were having their hair brushed, the baby was in bed, there was a hot smell of mince-pies baking in the oven.

'You won't forget our candles, will you, father?' asked Millicent, with assurance now.

'I'll see,' he answered.

His wife watched him as he put on his overcoat and hat. He was well-dressed, handsome-looking. She felt there was a curious glamour about him. It made her feel bitter. He had an unfair advantage – he was free to go off, while she must stay at home with the children.

'There's no knowing what time you'll be home,' she said.

'I shan't be late,' he answered.

'It's easy to say so,' she retorted, with some contempt. He took his stick and turned towards the door.

'Bring the children some candles for their tree, and don't be so selfish,' she said.

'All right,' he said, going out.

'Don't say *All right* if you never mean to do it,' she cried, with sudden anger, following him to the door.

His figure stood large and shadowy in the darkness.

'How many do you want?' he said.

'A dozen,' she said. 'And holders, too, if you get them,' she added, with barren bitterness.

'Yes – all right.' He turned and melted into the darkness. She went indoors, worn with a strange and bitter flame.

He crossed the fields towards the little town, which once more fumed its lights under the night. The country ran away, rising on its right hand. It was no longer a great bank of darkness. Lights twinkled freely here and there, though forlornly, now that the war-time restrictions were removed. It was no glitter of pre-war nights, pit-heads glittering far off with electricity. Neither was it the black gulf of the war darkness: instead, this forlorn sporadic twinkling.

Everybody seemed to be out of doors. The hollow dark country-side re-echoed like a shell with shouts and calls and excited voices. Restlessness and nervous excitement, nervous hilarity were in the air. There was a sense of electric surcharge everywhere, frictional, a neurasthenic haste for excitement.

Every moment Aaron Sisson was greeted with Good night – Good night, Aaron – Good night, Mr Sisson. People carrying parcels, children, women, thronged home on the dark paths. They were all talking loudly, declaiming loudly about what they could and could not get, and what this or the other had cost.

When he got into the main street, the only street of shops, it was crowded. There seemed to have been some violent but quiet contest, a subdued fight, going on all the afternoon and evening: people struggling to buy things, to get things. Money was spent like water, there was a frenzy of money-spending. Though the necessities of life were in abundance, still the people struggled in frenzy for cheese, sweets, raisins, pork-stuff, even for flowers and holly, all of which were scarce, and for toys and knick-knacks, which were sold out. There was a wild grumbling, but a deep satisfaction in the fight, the struggle. The same fight and the same satisfaction in the fight was witnessed whenever a tram-car stopped, or when it heaved its way into sight. Then the struggle to mount on board became desperate and savage, but stimulating. Souls surcharged with hostility found now some outlet for their feelings.

As he came near the little market-place he bethought himself of the Christmas-tree candles. He did not intend to trouble himself. And yet, when he glanced in passing into the sweet-shop window, and saw it bare as a board, the very fact that he probably *could not* buy the things made him hesitate, and try.

'Have you got any Christmas-tree candles?' he asked as he entered the shop.

'How many do you want?'

'A dozen.'

'Can't let you have a dozen. You can have two boxes – four in a box – eight. Sixpence a box.'

'Got any holders?'

'Holders? Don't ask. Haven't seen one this year.'

'Got any toffee –?'

'Cough-drops – twopence an ounce – nothing else left.'

'Give me four ounces.'

He watched her weighing them in the little brass scales.

'You've not got much of a Christmas show,' he said.

'Don't talk about Christmas, as far as sweets is concerned. They ought to have allowed us six times the quantity – there's plenty of sugar, why didn't they? We s'll have to enjoy ourselves with what we've got. We mean to, anyhow.'

'Ay,' he said.

'Time we had a bit of enjoyment, *this* Christmas. They ought to have made things more plentiful.'

'Yes,' he said, stuffing his package in his pocket.

2

ROYAL OAK

The war had killed the little market of the town. As he passed the market-place on the brow, Aaron noticed that there were only two miserable stalls. But people crowded just the same. There was a loud sound of voices, men's voices. Men pressed round the doorways of the public-houses.

But he was going to a pub out of town. He descended the dark hill. A street-lamp here and there shed parsimonious light. In the bottoms, under the trees, it was very dark. But a lamp glimmered in front of the 'Royal Oak'. This was a low, white house sunk three steps below the highway. It was darkened, but sounded crowded.

Opening the door, Sisson found himself in the stone passage. Old Bob, carrying three cans, stopped to see who had entered – then went on into the public bar on the left. The bar itself was a sort of little window-sill on the right: the pub was a small one. In this window-opening stood the landlady, drawing and serving to her husband. Behind the bar was a tiny parlour or den, the landlady's preserve.

'Oh, it's you!' she said, bobbing down to look at the newcomer. None entered her bar-parlour unless invited.

'Come in,' said the landlady.

There was a peculiar intonation in her complacent voice, which showed she had been expecting him, a little irritably.

He went across into her bar-parlour. It would not hold more than eight or ten people, all told – just the benches along the walls, the fire between – and two little round tables.

'I began to think you weren't coming,' said the landlady, bringing him a whisky.

She was a large, stout, high-coloured woman, with a fine profile, probably Jewish. She had chestnut-coloured eyes, quick, intelligent. Her movements were large and slow, her voice laconic.

'I'm not so late, am I?' asked Aaron.

'Yes, you *are* late, I should think.' She looked up at the little clock. 'Close on nine.'

'I did some shopping,' said Aaron, with a quick smile.

'Did you indeed! That's new, I'm sure. May we ask what you bought?'

This he did not like. But he had to answer.

'Christmas-tree candles, and toffee.'

'For the little children? Well, you've done well for once! I must say I recommend you. I didn't think you had so much in you.'

She sat herself down in her seat at the end of the bench and took up her knitting. Aaron sat next to her. He poured water into his glass and drank.

'It's warm in here,' he said, when he had swallowed the liquor.

'Yes, it is. You won't want to keep that thick, good overcoat on,' replied the landlady.

'No,' he said, 'I think I'll take it off.'

She watched him as he hung up his overcoat. He wore black clothes, as usual. As he reached up to the pegs, she could see the muscles of his shoulders, and the form of his legs. Her reddish-brown eyes seemed to burn, and her nose, that had a subtle, beautiful Hebraic curve, seemed to arch itself. She made a little place for him by herself, as he returned. She carried her head thrown back, with dauntless self-sufficiency.

There were several colliers in the room, talking quietly. They were the superior type all, favoured by the landlady, who loved intellectual discussion. Opposite, by the fire, sat a little, greenish man – evidently an Oriental.

'You're very quiet all at once, Doctor,' said the landlady in her slow, laconic voice.

'Yes. May I have another whisky, please?'

She rose at once, powerfully energetic.

'Oh, I'm sorry,' she said. And she went to the bar.

'Well,' said the little Hindu doctor, 'and how are things going now, with the men?'

'The same as ever,' said Aaron.

'Yes,' said the stately voice of the landlady. 'And I'm afraid they will always be the same as ever. When will they learn wisdom?'

'But what do you call wisdom?' asked Sherardy, the Hindu. He spoke with a little, childish lisp.

'What do I call wisdom?' repeated the landlady. 'Why, all acting together for the common good. That is wisdom in my idea.'

'Yes, very well, that is so. But what do you call the common good?' replied the little doctor, with childish pertinence.

'Ay,' said Aaron, with a laugh, 'that's it.'

The miners were all stirring now, to take part in the discussion.

'What do I call the common good?' repeated the landlady. 'That all people should study the welfare of other people, and not only their own.'

'They are not to study their own welfare?' said the doctor.

'Ah, that I did not say,' replied the landlady. 'Let them study their own welfare, and that of others also.'

'Well then,' said the doctor, 'what is the welfare of a collier?'

'The welfare of a collier,' said the landlady, 'is that he shall earn sufficient wages to keep himself and his family comfortable, to educate his children, and to educate himself; for that is what he wants, education.'

'Ay, happen so,' put in Brewitt, a big, fine, good-humoured collier. 'Happen so, Mrs Houseley. But what if you haven't got much education, to speak of?'

'You can *always* get it,' she said, patronizing.

'Nay – I'm blest if you can. It's no use tryin' to educate a man over forty – not by book-learning. That isn't saying he's a fool, neither.'

'And what better is them that's got education?' put in another man. 'What better is the manager, or th' under-manager, than we are? – Pender's yaller enough i' th' face.'

'He is that,' assented the men in chorus.

'But because he's yellow in the face, as you say, Mr Kirk,' said the landlady largely, 'that doesn't mean he has no advantages higher than what you have got.'

'Ay,' said Kirk. 'He can ma'e more money than I can – that's about a' as it comes to.'

'He can make more money,' said the landlady. 'And when he's made it, he knows better how to use it.'

''Appen so, an' a'! – What does he do, more than eat and drink and work? – an' take it out of hissel a sight harder than I do, by th' looks of him. – What's it matter, if he eats a bit more or drinks a bit more –'

'No,' reiterated the landlady. 'He not only eats and drinks. He can read, and he can converse.'

'Me an' a' –,' said Tom Kirk, and the men burst into a laugh. 'I can read – an' I've had many a talk an' conversation with you in this house, Mrs Houseley – am havin' one at this minute, seemingly.'

'*Seemingly*, you are,' said the landlady ironically. 'But do you think there would be no difference between your conversation and Mr Pender's, if he were here, so that I could *enjoy* his conversation?'

'An' what difference would there be?' asked Tom Kirk. 'He'd go home to his bed just the same.'

'*There*, you are mistaken. He would be the better, and so should I, a great deal better, for a little genuine conversation.'

'If it's conversation as ma'es his behind drop –' said Tom Kirk.

'An' puts th' bile in his face –' said Brewitt:

There was a general laugh.

'I can see it's no use talking about it any further,' said the landlady, lifting her head dangerously.

'But look here, Mrs Houseley, do you really think it makes much difference to a man, whether he can hold a serious conversation or not?' asked the doctor.

'I do indeed, all the difference in the world. To me, there is no greater difference than between an educated man and an uneducated man.'

'And where does it come in?' asked Kirk.

'But wait a bit, now,' said Aaron Sisson. 'You take an educated man – take Pender. What's his education for? What does he scheme for? What does he contrive for? What does he talk for?'

'For all the purposes of his life,' replied the landlady.

'Ay, an' what's the purpose of his life?' insisted Aaron Sisson.

'The purpose of his life,' repeated the landlady, at a loss. 'I should think he knows that best himself.'

'No better than I know it – and you know it,' said Aaron.

'Well,' said the landlady, 'if you know, then speak out. What is it?'

'To make more money for the firm – and so make his own chance of a rise better.'

The landlady was baffled for some moments. Then she said:

'Yes, and suppose that he does. Is there any harm in it? Isn't it his duty to do what he can for himself? Don't you try to earn all you can?'

'Ay,' said Aaron. 'But there's soon a limit to what I can earn. It's like this. When you work it out, everything comes to money. Reckon it as you like, it's money on both sides. It's money we live for, and money is what our lives is worth – nothing else. Money we live for, and money we are when we're dead:

that or nothing. An' it's money as is between the masters and us. There's a few educated ones got hold of one end of the rope, and all the lot of us hanging on to th' other end, an' we s'll go on pulling our guts out, time in, time out –'

'But they've got th' long end o' th' rope, th' masters has,' said Brewitt.

'For as long as one holds, the other will pull,' concluded Aaron Sisson philosophically.

'An' I'm almighty sure o' that,' said Kirk.

There was a little pause.

'Yes, that's all there is in the minds of *you men*,' said the landlady. 'But what can be done with the money: that you never think of – the education of the children, the improvement of conditions –'

'Educate the children, so that they can lay hold of the long end of the rope, instead of the short end,' said the doctor, with a little giggle.

'Ay, that's it,' said Brewitt. 'I've pulled at th' short end, an' my lads may do th' same.'

'A selfish policy,' put in the landlady.

'Selfish or not, they may do it.'

'Till the crack o' doom,' said Aaron, with a glistening smile.

'Or the crack o' th' rope,' said Brewitt.

'Yes, and *then what*?' cried the landlady.

'Then we s'll all drop on our backsides,' said Kirk.

There was a general laugh, and an uneasy silence.

'All I can say of you men,' said the landlady, 'is that you have a narrow, selfish policy. Instead of thinking of the children, instead of thinking of improving the world you live in –'

'We hang on, British bulldog breed,' said Brewitt.

There was a general laugh.

'Yes, and little wiser than dogs, wrangling for a bone,' said the landlady.

'Are we to let t'other side run off wi' th' bone, then, while we sit on our stunts an' yowl for it?' asked Brewitt.

'No indeed. There can be wisdom in everything. It's what you *do* with the money, when you've got it,' said the landlady, 'that's where the importance lies.'

'It's Missis as gets it,' said Kirk. 'It doesn't stop wi' us.'

'Ay, it's the wife as gets it, ninety per cent,' they all concurred.

'And who *should* have the money, indeed, if not your wives? They have everything to *do* with the money. What idea have *you*, but to waste it!'

'Women waste nothing – they couldn't if they tried,' said Aaron Sisson.

There was a lull for some minutes. The men were all stimulated by drink. The landlady kept them going. She herself sipped a glass of brandy – but slowly. She sat near to Sisson – and the great fierce warmth of her presence enveloped him particularly. He loved so to luxuriate, like a cat, in the presence of a violent woman. He knew that tonight she was feeling very nice to him – a female glow that came out of her to him. Sometimes when she put down her knitting, or took it up again from the bench beside him, her fingers just touched his thigh, and the fine electricity ran over his body, as if he were a cat tingling at a caress.

And yet he was not happy – nor comfortable. There was a hard, opposing core in him, that neither the whisky nor the woman could dissolve or soothe, tonight. It remained hard, nay became harder and more deeply antagonistic to his surroundings, every moment. He recognized it as a secret malady he suffered from: this strained, unacknowledged opposition to his surroundings, a hard core of irrational, exhausting withholding of himself. Irritating, because he still *wanted* to give himself. A woman and whisky, these were usually a remedy – and music. But lately these had begun to fail him. No, there was something in him that would not give in – neither to the whisky, nor the woman, nor even the music. Even in the midst of his best music, it sat deep established in him, this obstinate black dog, and growled and was never cajoled. He knew of its presence – and was a little uneasy. For, of course, he *wanted* to let himself go; to feel rosy and loving and all that. But at the very thought, the black dog showed its teeth.

He sipped his whisky with gratification, he luxuriated in the presence of the landlady, very confident of the strength of her liking for him. He glanced at her profile – that fine throwback of her hostile head, wicked in the midst of her philanthropy; that subtle, really very beautiful delicate curve of her nose, that moved him exactly like a piece of pure sound. But tonight it did not overcome him. There was a devilish little cold eye in his brain that was not taken in by what he saw.

A terrible obstinacy located itself in him. He saw the fine, rich-coloured, secretive face of the Hebrew woman, so loudly self-righteous, and so dangerous, so destructive, so lustful – and he waited for his blood to melt with passion for her. But not tonight. Tonight his heart was hard and cold as ice. The very danger and lustfulness of her, which had so pricked his senses, now left him colder. He disliked her at her tricks. He had come to her once too often. To her and to every woman. Bah, the love game! And the whisky that was to help the game. He had drowned himself once too often in the whisky and in love. Now he floated like a corpse in both, with a cold, hostile eye.

And at least half of his inward fume was anger because he could no longer drown. Nothing would have pleased him better than to have felt his senses swimming and flowing into darkness. But impossible! Cold, with a cold white fury inside him, he floated wide-eyed and apart as a corpse. He thought of the gentle love of his first married years, and became only whiter and colder, set in a more intense obstinacy. A wave of revulsion lifted him.

He became aware that he was deadly antagonistic to the landlady, that he disliked the whole circumstances. A cold, diabolical consciousness detached itself from his state of semi-intoxication.

'Is it pretty much the same out there in India?' he asked of the doctor, suddenly.

The doctor started, and attended to him on his own level.

'Probably,' he answered, 'it is worse.'

'Worse!' exclaimed Aaron Sisson. 'How's that?'

'Why, because, in a way the people of India have an easier time even than the people of England. Because they have no responsibility. The British Government takes the responsibility. And the people have nothing to do, except their bit of work – and talk perhaps about national rule, just for a pastime.'

'They have to earn their living?' said Sisson.

'Yes,' said the little doctor, who had lived for some years among the colliers, and become quite familiar with them. 'Yes, they have to earn their living – and then no more. That's why the British Government is the worst thing possible for them. It is the worst thing possible. And not because it is a bad government. Really, it is not a bad government. It is a good one – and they know it – much better than they would make for themselves, probably. But for that reason it is so very bad.'

The little oriental laughed a queer, sniggering laugh. His eyes were very bright, dilated, completely black. He was looking into the ice-blue, pointed eyes of Aaron Sisson. They were both intoxicated – but grimly so. They looked at each other in elemental difference.

The whole room was now attending to this new conversation: which they all accepted as serious. For Aaron was considered a special man, a man of peculiar understanding, even though as a rule he said little.

'If it is a good government, doctor, how can it be so bad for the people?' said the landlady.

The doctor's eyes quivered for the fraction of a second, as he watched the other man. He did not look at the landlady.

'It would not matter what kind of mess they made – and they would make a mess, if they governed themselves, the people of India. They would probably make the greatest muddle possible – and start killing one another. But it wouldn't matter if they exterminated half the population, so long as they did it themselves, and were responsible for it.'

Again his eyes dilated, utterly black, to the eyes of the other man, and an arch little smile flickered on his face.

'I think it would matter very much indeed,' said the landlady. 'They had far better *not* govern themselves.'

She was, for some reason, becoming angry. The little greenish doctor emptied his glass, and smiled again.

'But what difference does it make,' said Aaron Sisson, 'whether they govern themselves or not? They only live till they die, either way.' And he smiled faintly. He had not really listened to the doctor. The terms 'British Government', and 'bad for the people – good for the people', made him malevolently angry.

The doctor was nonplussed for a moment. Then he gathered himself together.

'It matters,' he said, 'it matters. People should always be responsible for themselves. How can any people be responsible for another race, for a race which is even older than they are, and not at all little children?'

Aaron Sisson watched the other dark face, with its utterly exposed eyes. He was in a state of semi-intoxicated anger and clairvoyance. He saw in the black void, glistening eyes of the oriental only the same danger, the same menace which he saw in the landlady. Fair, wise, even benevolent words: always the human good speaking, and always underneath, something hateful, something detestable and murderous. Wise speech, and good intentions – they were invariably maggoty with these secret lustful inclinations to destroy the man in a man. Whenever he heard anyone holding forth: the landlady, this doctor, the spokesman at the miners' meeting – or the all-benevolent newspaper – his soul curdled with revulsion as from something foul. Even the infernal good-will and love of his wife. To hell with good-will. It was more hateful than ill-will. All righteous bullying, like poison gas!

The landlady looked at the clock.

'Ten minutes to, gentlemen,' she said, coldly. For she too knew that Aaron was spoiled for her that night.

The men began to take their leave, shakily. The little doctor seemed to evaporate. The landlady helped Aaron on with his coat. She saw the curious whiteness round his nostrils and his eyes, the fixed hellish look on his face.

'You'll eat a mince-pie in the kitchen with us, for luck?' she said to him, detaining him till last.

But he turned laughing to her.

'Nay,' he said. 'I must be getting home.'

He turned and went straight out of the house. Watching him, the landlady's face became yellow with passion and rage.

'That little poisonous Indian viper,' she said aloud, attributing Aaron's mood to the doctor. Her husband was noisily bolting the door.

Outside it was dark and frosty. A gang of men lingered in the road near the closed door. Aaron found himself among them, his heart bitterer than steel.

The men were dispersing. He should take the road home. But the devil was in it, if he could take a stride in the homeward direction. There seemed a wall in front of him. He veered. But neither could he take a stride in the opposite direction. So he was destined to veer round, like some sort of weather-cock, there in the middle of the dark road outside the Royal Oak.

But as he turned, he caught sight of a third exit. Almost opposite was the mouth of Shottle Lane, which led off under trees, at right angles to the high-road, up to New Brunswick Colliery. He veered towards the off-chance of this opening, in a delirium of icy fury, and plunged away into the dark lane, walking slowly, on firm legs.

3

THE LIGHTED TREE

It is remarkable how many odd or extraordinary people there are in England. We hear continual complaints of the stodgy dullness of the English. It would be quite as just to complain of their freakish, unusual characters. Only *en masse* the metal is all Britannia.

In an ugly little mining town we find the odd ones just as distinct as anywhere else. Only it happens that dull people invariably meet dull people, and odd individuals always come across odd individuals, no matter where they may be. So that to each kind society seems all of a piece.

At one end of the dark, tree-covered Shottle Lane stood the Royal Oak public house; and Mrs Houseley was certainly an odd woman. At the other end of the lane was Shottle House, where the Bricknells lived; the Bricknells were odd, also. Alfred Bricknell, the old man, was one of the partners in the colliery firm. His English was incorrect, his accent broad Derbyshire, and he was not a gentleman in the snobbish sense of the word. Yet he was well-to-do, and very stuck-up. His wife was dead.

Shottle House stood two hundred yards beyond New Brunswick Colliery. The colliery was embedded in a plantation, whence its burning pit-hill glowed, fumed, and stank sulphur in the nostrils of the Bricknells. Even war-time efforts had not put out this refuse-fire. Apart from this, Shottle House was a pleasant, square house, rather old, with shrubberies and lawns. It ended the lane in a dead-end. Only a field-path trekked away to the left.

On this particular Christmas Eve Alfred Bricknell had only two of his children at home. Of the others, one daughter was unhappily married, and away in India weeping herself thinner; another was nursing her babies in Streatham. Jim, the hope of the house, and Julia, now married to Robert Cunningham, had come home for Christmas.

The party was seated in the drawing-room, that the grown-up daughters had made very fine during their periods of courtship. Its walls were hung with fine grey canvas, it had a large, silvery-grey, silky carpet, and the furniture was covered with dark green silky material. Into this reticence pieces of futurism, Omega cushions and Van-Gogh-like pictures exploded their colours. Such *chic* would certainly not have been looked for up Shottle Lane.

The old man sat in his high grey arm-chair very near an enormous coal fire. In this house there was no coal-rationing. The finest coal was arranged to obtain a gigantic glow such as a coal-owner may well enjoy, a great, intense mass of pure red fire. At this fire Alfred Bricknell toasted his tan, lambswool-lined slippers.

He was a large man, wearing a loose grey suit, and sprawling in the large grey arm-chair. The soft lamp-light fell on his clean, bald, Michelangelo head, across which a few pure hairs glittered. His chin was sunk on his breast, so that his sparse but strong-haired white beard, in which every strand stood distinct, like spun glass, lithe and elastic, curved now upwards and inwards, in a curious curve returning upon him. He seemed to be sunk in stern, prophet-like meditation. As a matter of fact, he was asleep after a heavy meal.

Across, seated on a pouffe on the other side of the fire, was a cameo-like girl with neat black hair done tight and bright in the French mode. She had strangely-drawn eyebrows, and her colour was brilliant. She was hot, leaning back behind the shaft of old marble of the mantelpiece, to escape the fire. She wore a simple dress of apple-green satin, with full sleeves and ample skirt and a tiny bodice of green cloth. This was Josephine Ford, the girl Jim was engaged to.

Jim Bricknell himself was a tall big fellow of thirty-eight. He sat in a chair in front of the fire, some distance back, and stretched his long legs far in front of him. His chin, too, was sunk on his breast, his young forehead was bald, and raised in odd wrinkles, he had a silent half-grin on his face, a little tipsy, a little satyr-like. His small moustache was reddish.

Behind him a round table was covered with cigarettes, sweets, and bottles. It was evident Jim Bricknell drank beer for choice. He wanted to get fat – that was his idea. But he couldn't bring it off: he was thin, though not too thin, except to his own thinking.

His sister Julia was bunched up in a low chair between him and his father. She, too, was a tall stag of a thing, but she sat hunched up like a witch. She wore a wine-purple dress, her arms seemed to poke out of the sleeves, and she had dragged her brown hair into straight, untidy strands. Yet she had real beauty. She was talking to the young man, who was not her husband: a fair, pale, fattish young fellow in pincenez and dark clothes. This was Cyril Scott, a friend.

The only other person stood at the round table pouring out red wine. He was a fresh, stoutish young Englishman in khaki, Julia's husband. Robert Cunningham was a lieutenant about to be demobilized, when he would become a sculptor once more. He drank red wine in large throatfuls, and his eyes grew a little moist. The room was hot and subdued, everyone was silent.

'I say,' said Robert suddenly, from the rear, 'anybody have a drink? Don't you find it rather hot?'

'Is there another bottle of beer there?' said Jim, without moving, too settled even to stir an eye-lid.

'Yes – I think there is,' said Robert.

'Thanks – don't open it yet,' murmured Jim.

'Have a drink, Josephine?' said Robert.

'No thank you,' said Josephine, bowing slightly.

Finding the drinks did not go, Robert went round with the cigarettes. Josephine Ford looked at the white rolls.

'Thank you,' she said, and taking one, suddenly licked her rather full, dry red lips with the rapid tip of her tongue. It was an odd movement, suggesting a snake's flicker. She put her cigarette between her lips, and waited. Her movements were very quiet and well bred; but perhaps too quiet, they had the dangerous impassivity of the Bohemian, Parisian or American, rather than English.

'Cigarette, Julia?' said Robert to his wife.

She seemed to start or twitch, as if dazed. Then she looked up at her husband with a queer smile, puckering the corners of her eyes. He looked at the cigarettes, not at her. His face had the blunt, voluptuous gravity of a young lion, a great cat. She kept him standing for some moments impassively. Then suddenly she hung her long, delicate fingers over the box, in doubt, and spasmodically jabbed at the cigarettes, clumsily raking one out at last.

'Thank you, dear – thank you,' she cried, rather high, looking up and smiling once more. He turned calmly aside, offering the cigarettes to Scott, who refused.

'Oh!' said Julia, sucking the end of her cigarette. 'Robert is so happy with all the good things – aren't you, dear?' She sang, breaking into a hurried laugh. 'We aren't used to such luxurious living, we aren't – *are we, dear*? No, we're not such swells as this, we're not. Oh *Robbie*, isn't it all right, isn't it just all right?' She tailed off into her hurried, wild, repeated laugh. 'We're so happy in a land of plenty, *aren't we, dear*?'

'Do you mean I'm greedy, Julia?' said Robert.

'Greedy! Oh, greedy! – he asks if he's greedy? No, you're not greedy, Robbie, you're not greedy. I want you to be happy.'

'I'm quite happy,' he returned.

'Oh, he's happy! Really! – he's happy! Oh, what an accomplishment! Oh, my word!' Julia puckered her eyes and laughed herself into a nervous twitching silence.

Robert went round with the matches. Julia sucked her cigarette.

'Give us a light, Robbie, if you *are* happy!' she cried.

'It's coming,' he answered.

Josephine smoked with short, sharp puffs. Julia sucked wildly at her light. Robert returned to his red wine. Jim Bricknell suddenly roused up, looked round on the company, smiling a little vacuously and showing his odd, pointed teeth.

'Where's the beer?' he asked, in deep tones, smiling full into Josephine's face, as if she were going to produce it by some sleight of hand. Then he wheeled round to the table, and was soon pouring beer down his throat as down a pipe. Then he dropped supine again. Cyril Scott was silently absorbing gin and water.

'I say,' said Jim, from the remote depth of his sprawling. 'Isn't there something we could do to while the time away?'

Everybody suddenly laughed – it sounded so remote and absurd.

'What, play bridge or poker or something conventional of that sort?' said Josephine in her distinct voice, speaking to him as if he were a child.

'Oh, damn bridge,' said Jim in his sleep-voice. Then he began pulling his powerful length together. He sat on the edge of his chair-seat, leaning forward, peering into all the faces and grinning.

'Don't look at me like that – so long –' said Josephine, in her self-contained voice. 'You make me uncomfortable.' She gave an odd little grunt of a laugh, and the tip of her tongue went over her lips as she glanced sharply, half furtively, round the room.

'I like looking at you,' said Jim, his smile becoming more malicious.

'But you shouldn't, when I tell you not,' she returned.

Jim twisted round to look at the state of the bottles. The father also came awake. He sat up.

'Isn't it time,' he said, 'that you all put away your glasses and cigarettes, and thought of bed?'

Jim rolled slowly round towards his father, sprawling in the long chair.

'Ah, Dad,' he said, 'tonight's the night! Tonight's some night, Dad. You can sleep any time –' his grin widened – 'but there aren't many nights to sit here – like this – eh?'

He was looking up all the time into the face of his father, full and nakedly lifting his face to the face of his father, and smiling fixedly. The father, who was perfectly sober, except for the contagion from the young people, felt a wild tremor go through his heart as he gazed on the face of his boy. He rose stiffly.

'You want to stay?' he said. 'You want to stay! Well then – well then, I'll leave you. But don't be long.' The old man rose to his full height, rather majestic. The four younger people also rose respectfully – only Jim lay still prostrate in his chair, twisting up his face towards his father.

'You won't stay long,' said the old man, looking round a little bewildered. He was seeking a responsible eye. Josephine was the only one who had any feeling for him.

'No, we won't stay long, Mr Bricknell,' she said gravely.

'Good night, Dad,' said Jim, as his father left the room.

Josephine went to the window. She had rather a stiff *poupée* walk.

'How is the night?' she said, as if to change the whole feeling in the room. She pushed back the thick grey silk curtains. 'Why?' she exclaimed. 'What is that light burning? A red light?'

'Oh, that's only the pit-bank on fire,' said Robert, who had followed her.

'How strange! Why is it burning now?'

'It always burns, unfortunately – it is most consistent at it. It is the refuse from the mines. It has been burning for years, in spite of all efforts to the contrary.'

'How very curious! May we look at it?' Josephine now turned the handle of the french windows, and stepped out.

'Beautiful!' they heard her voice exclaim from outside. In the room, Julia laid her hand gently, protectively over the hand of Cyril Scott.

'Josephine and Robert are admiring the night together!' she said, smiling with subtle tenderness to him.

'Naturally! Young people always do these romantic things,' replied Cyril

Scott. He was twenty-two years old, so he could afford to be cynical.

'Do they? Don't you think it's nice of them?' she said, gently removing her hand from his. His eyes were moist with pleasure.

'I do. I envy them enormously. One only needs to be sufficiently naïve,' he said.

'One does, doesn't one!' cooed Julia.

'I say, do you hear the bells?' said Robert, poking his head into the room.

'No, dear! Do you?' replied Julia.

'Bells! Hear the bells! Bells!' exclaimed the half-tipsy and self-conscious Jim. He rolled in his chair in an explosion of sudden, silent laughter, showing his mouthful of pointed teeth, like a dog. Then he gradually gathered himself together, found his feet, smiling fixedly.

'Pretty cool night!' he said aloud, when he felt the air on his almost bald head. The darkness smelt of sulphur.

Josephine and Robert moved out of sight. Julia was abstracted, following them with her eyes. With almost supernatural keenness she seemed to catch their voices from the distance.

'Yes, Josephine, *wouldn't* that be *awfully* romantic!' she suddenly called shrilly.

The pair in the distance started.

'What – !' they heard Josephine's sharp exclamation.

'What's that? What would be romantic?' said Jim, as he lurched up and caught hold of Cyril Scott's arm.

'Josephine wants to make a great illumination of the grounds of the estate,' said Julia, magniloquent.

'No – no – I didn't say it,' remonstrated Josephine.

'What Josephine said,' explained Robert, 'was simply that it would be pretty to put candles on one of the growing trees, instead of having a Christmas tree indoors.'

'Oh Josephine, how sweet of you!' cried Julia.

Cyril Scott giggled.

'Good egg! Champion idea, Josey, my lass. Eh? What!' cried Jim. 'Why not carry it out – eh? Why not? Most attractive.' He leaned forward over Josephine, and grinned.

'Oh no!' expostulated Josephine. 'It all sounds so silly now. No. Let us go indoors and go to bed.'

'*No*, Josephine dear – *no*! It's a *lovely* idea!' cried Julia. 'Let's get candles and lanterns and things –'

'Let's!' grinned Jim. 'Let's everybody – let's!'

'Shall we really?' asked Robert. 'Shall we illuminate one of the fir trees by the lawn?'

'Yes! How lovely!' cried Julia. 'I'll fetch the candles.'

'The women must put on warm cloaks,' said Robert.

They trooped indoors for coats and wraps and candles and lanterns. Then, lighted by a bicycle lamp, they tropped off to the shed to twist wire round the candles for holders. They clustered round the bench.

'I say,' said Julia, 'doesn't Cyril look like a pilot on a stormy night! Oh I say!' and she went into one of her hurried laughs.

They all looked at Cyril Scott, who was standing sheepishly in the background, in a very large overcoat, smoking a large pipe. The young man was uncomfortable, but assumed a stoic air of philosophic indifference.

Soon they were busy round a prickly fir tree at the end of the lawn. Jim stood in the background vaguely staring. The bicycle lamp sent a beam of strong white light deep into the uncanny foliage, heads clustered and hands worked. The night above was silent, dim. There was no wind. In the near distance they could hear the panting of some engine at the colliery.

'Shall we light them as we fix them,' asked Robert, 'or save them for one grand rocket at the end?'

'Oh, as we do them,' said Cyril Scott, who had lacerated his fingers and wanted to see some reward.

A match spluttered. One naked little flame sprang alight among the dark foliage. The candle burned tremulously, naked. They all were silent.

'We ought to do a ritual dance! We ought to worship the tree,' sang Julia, in her high voice.

'Hold on a minute. We'll have a little more illumination,' said Robert.

'Why, yes. We want more than one candle,' said Josephine.

But Julia had dropped the cloak in which she was huddled, and with arms slung asunder was sliding, waving, crouching in a *pas seul* before the tree, looking like an animated bough herself.

Jim, who was hugging his pipe in the background, broke into a short, harsh, cackling laugh.

'Aren't we fools!' he cried. 'What? Oh God's love, aren't we fools!'

'No – why?' cried Josephine, amused but resentful.

But Jim vouchsafed nothing further, only stood like a Red Indian, gripping his pipe.

The beam of the bicycle lamp moved and fell about the hands and faces of the young people, and penetrated the recesses of the secret trees. Several little tongues of flame clipped sensitive and ruddy on the naked air, sending a faint glow over the needle foliage. They gave a strange, perpendicular aspiration in the night. Julia waved slowly in her tree dance. Jim stood apart, with his legs straddled, a motionless figure.

The party round the tree became absorbed and excited as more ruddy tongues of flame pricked upward from the dark tree. Pale candles became evident, the air was luminous. The illumination was becoming complete, harmonious.

Josephine suddenly looked round.

'Why-y-y!' came her long note of alarm.

A man in a bowler hat and a black overcoat stood on the edge of the twilight.

'What is it?' cried Julia.

'*Homo sapiens!*' said Robert, the lieutenant. 'Hand the light, Cyril.'

He played the beam of light full on the intruder: a man in a bowler hat, with a black overcoat buttoned to his throat, a pale, dazed, blinking face. The hat was tilted at a slightly jaunty angle over the left eye, the man was well-featured. He did not speak.

'Did you want anything?' asked Robert, from behind the light.

Aaron Sisson blinked, trying to see who addressed him. To him they were all illusory. He did not answer.

'Anything you wanted?' repeated Robert, military, rather peremptory.

Jim suddenly doubled himself up and burst into a loud, harsh cackle of laughter. Whoop! he went, and doubled himself up with laughter. Whoop! whoop! he went, and fell on the ground, and writhed with laughter. He was in that state of intoxication when he could find no release from maddening self-consciousness. He knew what he was doing, he did it deliberately. And yet he was also beside himself, in a sort of hysterics. He could not help himself, in exasperated self-consciousness.

The others all began to laugh, unavoidably. It was a contagion. They laughed helplessly and foolishly. Only Robert was anxious.

'I'm afraid he'll wake the house,' he said, looking at the doubled-up figure of Jim writhing on the grass and whooping loudly.

'No – no!' cried Josephine, weak with laughing in spite of herself. 'No – it's too long – I'm like to die laughing –'

Jim embraced the earth in his convulsions. Even Robert shook quite weakly with laughter. His face was red, his eyes full of dancing water. Yet he managed to articulate:

'I say, you know, you'll bring the old man down.' Then he went off again into spasms.

'Hu! Hu!' whooped Jim, subsiding. 'Hu!' He rolled over on to his back and lay silent. The others also became weakly silent.

'What's amiss?' said Aaron Sisson, breaking this spell. They all began to laugh again, except Jim, who lay on his back looking up at the strange sky.

'What're you laughing at?' repeated Aaron.

'We're laughing at the man on the grass,' replied Josephine. 'I think he's drunk a little too much.'

'Or not enough,' put in Cyril Scott. He twigged Jim's condition.

'Ay,' said Aaron, standing mute and obstinate.

'Did you want anything?' Robert inquired once more.

'Eh?' Aaron looked up. 'Me? No, not me.' A sort of inertia kept him rooted. The young people looked at one another and began to laugh, rather embarrassed.

'Another!' said Cyril Scott cynically.

They wished the stranger would go away. There was a pause.

'What do you reckon stars are?' asked the sepulchral voice of Jim. He still lay flat on his back on the grass.

Josephine went to him and pulled at his coat.

'Get up,' she said. 'You'll take cold. Get up now, we're going indoors.'

'What do you reckon stars are?' he persisted.

Aaron Sisson stood on the edge of the light, smilingly staring at the scene, like a boy out of his place, but stubbornly keeping his ground.

'Get up now,' said Josephine. 'We've had enough.' But Jim would not move.

Robert went with the bicycle lamp and stood at Aaron's side.

'Shall I show you a light to the road – you're off your track,' he said. 'You're in the grounds of Shottle House.'

'I can find my road,' said Aaron. 'Thank you.'

Jim suddenly got up and went to peer at the stranger, poking his face close to Aaron's face.

'Right-o,' he remarked. 'You're not half a bad sort of chap. Cheeri-o! What's your drink?'

'Mine – whisky,' said Aaron.

'Come and have one. We're the only sober couple in the bunch – what?' cried Jim.

Aaron stood unchanged, static in everything. Jim took him by the arm affectionately. The stranger looked at the flickering tree, with its tiers of lights.

'A Christmas tree,' he said jerking his head and smiling.

'That's right, old man,' said Jim, seeming thoroughly sober now. 'Come indoors and have a drink.'

Aaron Sisson negatively allowed himself to be led off. The others followed in silence, leaving the tree to flicker the night through. The stranger stumbled at the open window-door.

'Mind the step,' said Jim affectionately.

They crowded to the fire, which was still hot. The newcomer looked round vaguely. Jim took Aaron's bowler hat and gave him a chair. He sat without looking round, a remote, abstract look on his face. He was very pale, and seemed inwardly absorbed.

The party threw off their wraps and sat around. Josephine turned to Aaron Sisson, who sat with a glass of whisky in his hand, rather slack in his chair, in his thickish overcoat. He did not want to drink. His hair was blond, quite tidy, his mouth and chin handsome, but a little obstinate, his eyes inscrutable. His pallor was not natural to him. Though he kept the appearance of a smile, underneath he was hard and opposed. He did not wish to be with these people, and yet, mechanically, he stayed.

'Do you feel quite well?' Josephine asked him.

He looked at her quickly.

'Me?' he said. He smiled faintly. 'Yes, I'm all right.' Then he dropped his head again and seemed oblivious.

'Tell us your name,' said Jim affectionately.

The stranger looked up.

'My name's Aaron Sisson, if it's anything to you,' he said.

Jim began to grin.

'It's a name I don't know,' he said. Then he named all the party present. But the stranger hardly heeded, though his eyes looked curiously from one to the other, slow, shrewd, clairvoyant.

'Were you on your way home?' asked Robert, huffy.

The stranger lifted his head and looked at him.

'Home!' he repeated. 'No. The other road.' He indicated the direction with his head, and smiled faintly.

'Beldover!' inquired Robert.

'Yes.'

He had dropped his head again, as if he did not want to look at them.

To Josephine, the pale, impassive, blank-seeming face, the blue eyes with the smile which wasn't a smile, and the continual dropping of the well-shaped head was curiously affecting. She wanted to cry.

'Are you a miner?' Robert asked, *de haute en bas*.

'No,' cried Josephine. She had looked at his hands.

'Men's check weighman,' replied Aaron. He had emptied his glass. He put it on the table.

'Have another?' said Jim, who was attending fixedly, with curious absorption, to the stranger.

'No,' cried Josephine, 'no more.'

Aaron looked at Jim, then at her, and smiled slowly, with remote bitterness. Then he lowered his head again. His hands were loosely clasped between his knees.

'What about the wife?' said Robert – the young lieutenant. 'What about the wife and kiddies! You're a married man, aren't you?'

The sardonic look of the stranger rested on the subaltern.

'Yes,' he said.

'Won't they be expecting you?' said Robert, trying to keep his temper and his tone of authority.

'I expect they will.'

'Then you'd better be getting along, hadn't you?'

The eyes of the intruder rested all the time on the flushed subaltern. The look on Aaron's face became slowly satirical.

'Oh, dry up the army touch,' said Jim contemptuously to Robert. 'We're all civvies here. We're all right, aren't we?' he said loudly, turning to the stranger with a grin that showed his pointed teeth.

Aaron gave a brief laugh of acknowledgment.

'How many children have you?' sang Julia from her distance.

'Three.'

'Girls or boys?'

'Girls.'

'All girls? Dear little things! How old?'

'Oldest's eight – youngest nine months –'

'So small!' sang Julia, with real tenderness now.

Aaron dropped his head.

'But you're going home to them, aren't you?' said Josephine, in whose eyes the tears had already risen. He looked up at her, at her tears. His face had the same pale, perverse smile.

'Not tonight,' he said.

'But why? You're wrong!' cried Josephine.

He dropped his head and became oblivious.

'Well!' said Cyril Scott, rising at last with a bored exclamation, 'I think I'll retire.'

'Will you?' said Julia, also rising. 'You'll find your candle outside.'

She went out. Scott bade good night, and followed her. The four people remained in the room, quite silent. Then Robert rose and began to walk about, agitated.

'Don't you go back to 'em. Have a night out. You stop here tonight,' Jim said suddenly, in a quiet, intimate tone.

The stranger turned his head and looked at him, considering.

'Yes?' he said. He seemed to be smiling coldly.

'Oh, but!' cried Josephine. 'Your wife and your children! Won't they be awfully bothered? Isn't it awfully unkind to them?'

She rose in her eagerness. He sat turning up his face to her. She could not understand his expression.

'Won't you go home to them?' she said, hysterical.

'Not tonight,' he replied quietly, again smiling.

'You're wrong!' she cried. 'You're wrong!'

And so she hurried out of the room in tears.

'Er – what bed do you propose to put him in?' asked Robert, rather officer-life.

'Don't propose at all, my lad,' replied Jim ironically – he did not like Robert. Then to the stranger he said: 'You'll be all right on the couch in my room? – It's a good couch, big enough, plenty of rugs –' His voice was easy and intimate.

Aaron looked at him and nodded.

They had another drink each, and at last the two set off, rather stumbling, upstairs. Aaron carried his bowler hat with him.

Robert remained pacing in the drawing-room for some time. Then he went out, to return in a little while. He extinguished the lamps and saw that the fire was safe. Then he went to fasten the window-doors securely. Outside he saw the uncanny glimmer of candles across the lawn. He had half a mind to go out and extinguish them – but he did not. So he went upstairs and the house was quiet. Faint crumbs of snow were falling outside.

When Jim woke in the morning Aaron had gone. Only on the floor were two packets of Christmas-tree candles, fallen from the stranger's pockets. He had gone through the drawing-room door, as he had come. The housemaid said that while she was cleaning the grate in the dining-room she heard someone go into the drawing-room: a parlourmaid had even seen someone come out of Jim's bedroom. But they had both thought it was Jim himself, for he was an unsettled housemate.

There was a thin film of snow, a lovely Christmas morning.

4

THE PILLAR OF SALT

Our story will not yet see daylight. A few days after Christmas, Aaron sat in the open shed at the bottom of his own garden, looking out on the rainy darkness. No one knew he was there. It was some time after six in the evening.

From where he sat, he looked straight up the garden to the house. The blind was not drawn in the middle kitchen, he could see the figures of his wife and one child. There was a light also in the upstairs window. His wife was gone upstairs again. He wondered if she had the baby ill. He could see her figure vaguely behind the lace curtains of the bedroom. It was like looking at his home through the wrong end of a telescope. Now the little girls had gone from the middle room: only to return in a moment.

His attention strayed. He watched the light falling from the window of the next-door house. Uneasily, he looked along the whole range of houses. The street sloped down-hill, and the backs were open to the fields. So he saw a curious succession of lighted windows, between which jutted the intermediary back premises, scullery and out-house, in dark little blocks. It was something like the keyboard of a piano: more still, like a succession of musical notes. For the rectangular planes of light were of different intensities, some bright and keen, some soft, warm, like candle-light, and there was one surface of pure red light, one or two were almost invisible, dark green. So the long scale of lights seemed to trill across the darkness, now bright, now dim, swelling and sinking. The effect was strange.

And thus the whole private life of the street was threaded in lights. There was a sense of indecent exposure, from so many backs. He felt himself almost in physical contact with this contiguous stretch of back premises. He heard the familiar sound of water gushing from the sink into the grating, the dropping of a pail outside the door, the clink of a coal-shovel, the banging of a door, the sound of voices. So many houses cheek by jowl, so many squirming lives, so many back yards, back doors giving on to the night. It was revolting.

Away in the street itself, a boy was calling the newspaper: *–'ning Post! – 'ning Po-o-ost!* It was a long, melancholy howl, and seemed to epitomize the whole of the dark, wet, secretive, thickly-inhabited night. A figure passed the window of Aaron's own house, entered and stood inside the room talking to Mrs Sisson. It was a young woman in a brown mackintosh and a black hat. She stood under the incandescent light, and her hat nearly knocked the globe. Next door a man had run out in his shirt-sleeves: a young, dark-headed collier running to the gate for a newspaper running bareheaded, coatless, slippered, in the rain. He had got his news-sheet, and was returning. And just at that moment the young man's wife came out, shading her candle with a lading tin. She was going to the coal-house for some coal. Her husband passed her on the threshold. She could be heard breaking the bits of coal and placing them on the dustpan. The light from her candle fell faintly behind her. Then she went back, blown by a swirl of wind. But again she was at the door, hastily standing her iron shovel against the wall. Then she shut the back door with a bang. These noises seemed to scrape and strike the night.

In Aaron's own house, the young person was still talking to his wife. Millicent came out, sheltering a candle with her hand. The candle blew out. She ran indoors, and emerged again, her white pinafore fluttering. This time she performed her little journey safely. He could see the faint glimmer of her candle emerging secretly from the closet.

The young person was taking her leave. He could hear her sympathetic – 'Well – good night! I hope she'll be no worse. Good night, Mrs Sisson!' She was gone – he heard the windy bang of the street gate. Presently Millicent emerged again, flitting indoors.

So he rose to his feet, balancing, swaying a little before he started into motion, as so many colliers do. Then he moved along the path towards the house, in the rain and darkness, very slowly edging forwards.

Suddenly the door opened. His wife emerged with a pail. He stepped quietly aside, on to his side garden, among the sweet herbs. He could smell rosemary and sage and hyssop. A low wall divided his garden from his neighbour's. He put his hand on it, on its wetness, ready to drop over should his wife come forward. But she only threw the contents of her pail on the garden and retired again. She might have seen him had she looked. He remained standing where he was, listening to the trickle of rain in the water-butt. The hollow countryside lay beyond him. Sometimes in the windy darkness he could see the red burn of New Brunswick bank, or the brilliant jewels of light clustered at Bestwood Colliery. Away in the dark hollow, nearer, the glare of the electric power station disturbed the night. So again the wind swirled the rain across all these hieroglyphs of the countryside, familiar to him as his own breast.

A motor-car was labouring up the hill. His trained ear attended to it unconsciously. It stopped with a jar. There was a bang of the yard gate. A shortish, dark figure in a bowler hat passed the window. Millicent was drawing down the blind. It was the doctor. The blind was drawn, he could see no more.

Stealthily he began to approach the house. He stood by the climbing rose of the porch, listening. He heard voices upstairs. Perhaps the children would be downstairs. He listened intently. Voices were upstairs only. He quietly opened the door. The room was empty, save for the baby, who was cooing in her cradle. He crossed to the hall. At the foot of the stairs he could hear the voice of the Indian doctor: 'Now, little girl, you must keep still and warm in bed, and not cry for the moon.' He said '*de* moon,' just as ever. Marjory must be ill.

So Aaron quietly entered the parlour. It was a cold, clammy room, dark. He could hear footsteps passing outside on the asphalt pavement below the window, and the wind howling with familiar cadence. He began feeling for something in the darkness of the music-rack beside the piano. He touched and felt – he could not find what he wanted. Perplexed, he turned and looked out of the window. Through the iron railing of the front wall he could see the little motor-car sending its straight beams of light in front of it, up the street.

He sat down on the sofa by the window. The energy had suddenly left all his limbs. He sat with his head sunk, listening. The familiar room, the familiar voice of his wife and his children – he felt weak as if he were dying. He felt weak, like a drowning man who acquiesces in the waters. His strength was gone, he was sinking back. He would sink back to it all, float henceforth like a drowned man.

So he heard voices coming nearer from upstairs, feet moving. They were coming down.

'No, Mrs Sisson, you needn't worry,' he heard the voice of the doctor on the stairs. 'If she goes on as she is, she'll be all right. Only she must be kept warm and quiet – warm and quiet – that's the chief thing.'

'Oh, when she has these little bouts I can't bear it.' Aaron heard his wife's voice.

They were downstairs. Their feet click-clicked on the tiled passage. They had gone into the middle room. Aaron sat and listened.

'She won't have any more bouts. If she does, give her a few drops from the little bottle, and raise her up. But she won't have any more,' the doctor said.

'If she does, I s'll go off my head, I know I shall.'

'No you won't. No you won't do anything of the sort. You won't go off your head. You'll keep your head on your shoulders, where it ought to be,' protested the doctor.

'But it nearly drives me mad.'

'Then don't let it. The child won't die, I tell you. She will be all right, with care. Who have you got sitting up with her? You're not to sit up with her tonight, I tell you. Do you hear me?'

'Miss Smitham's coming in. But it's no good – I shall have to sit up. I shall *have* to.'

'I tell you you won't. You obey *me*. I know what's good for you as well as for her. I am thinking of you as much as of her.'

'But I can't bear it – all alone.' This was with the beginning of tears. There was a dead silence – then a sound of Millicent weeping with her mother. As a matter of fact, the doctor was weeping too, for he was an emotional, sympathetic soul, over forty.

'Never mind – never mind – you aren't alone,' came the doctor's matter-of-fact voice, after a loud nose-blowing. 'I am here to help you. I will do whatever I can – whatever I can.'

'I can't bear it. I can't bear it,' wept the woman. Another silence, another nose-blowing, and again the doctor:

'You'll *have* to bear it – I tell you there's nothing else for it. You'll have to bear it – but we'll do our best for you. I will do my best for you – always – *always* – in sickness or out of sickness – There!'

He pronounced *there* oddly, not quite *dhere.*

'You haven't heard from your husband?' he added.

'I had a letter' – sobs – 'from the bank this morning.'

'*From de bank?*'

'Telling me they were sending me so much per month, from him, as an allowance, and that he was quite well, but he was travelling.'

'Well then, why not let him travel? You can live.'

'But to leave me *alone*,' there was burning indignation in her voice. 'To go off and leave me with every responsibility, to leave me with all the burden.'

'Well, I wouldn't trouble about him. Aren't you better off without him?'

'I am. I am,' she cried fiercely. 'When I got that letter this morning, I said, *May evil befall you, you selfish demon.* And I hope it may.'

'Well – well, well – well, don't fret. Don't be angry, it won't make it any better, I tell you.'

'Angry! I *am* angry. I'm worse than angry. A week ago I hadn't a grey hair in my head. Now look here –' There was a pause.

'Well – well, well – well, never mind. You will be all right, don't you bother. Your hair is beautiful, anyhow.'

'What makes me so mad is that he should go off like that – never a word – coolly takes his hook. I could kill him for it.'

'Were you ever happy together?'

'We were all right at first. I know I was fond of *him.* But he'd kill anything. He kept himself back, always kept himself back, couldn't give himself –'

There was a pause.

'Ah well,' sighed the doctor. 'Marriage is a mystery. I'm glad I'm not entangled in it.'

'Yes, to make some woman's life a misery. I'm sure it was death to live with him, he seemed to kill everything off inside you. He was a man you couldn't quarrel with, and get it over. Quiet – quiet in his tempers, and selfish through and through. I've lived with him twelve years – I know what it is. Killing! You don't know what he was –'

'I think I knew him. A fair man? Yes?' said the doctor.

'Fair to look at. There's a photograph of him in the parlour – taken when he was married – and one of me. Yes, he's fair-haired.'

Aaron guessed that she was getting a candle to come into the parlour. He was tempted to wait and meet them – and accept it all again. Devilishly tempted, he was. Then he thought of her voice, and his heart went cold. Quick as thought he obeyed his first impulse. He felt behind the couch, on the floor where the curtains fell. Yes – the bag was there. He took it at once. In the next breath he stepped out of the room and tiptoed into the passage. He retreated to the far end, near the street door, and stood behind the coats that hung on the hall-stand.

At that moment his wife came into the passage, holding a candle. She was red-eyed with weeping, and looked frail.

'Did you leave the parlour door open?' she asked of Millicent, suspiciously.

'No,' said Millicent from the kitchen.

The doctor, with his soft, Oriental tread, followed Mrs Sisson into the parlour. Aaron saw his wife hold up the candle before his portrait, and begin to weep. But he knew her. The doctor laid his hand softly on her arm, and left it there, sympathetically. Nor did he remove it when Millicent stole into the room, looking very woebegone and important. The wife wept silently, and the child joined in.

'Yes, I know him,' said the doctor. 'If he thinks he will be happier when he's gone away, you must be happier too, Mrs Sisson. That's all. Don't let him triumph over you by making you miserable. You enjoy yourself as well. You're only a girl.'

But a tear came from his eye, and he blew his nose vigorously on a large white silk handkerchief, and began to polish his pince-nez. Then he turned, and they all bundled out of the room.

The doctor took his departure. Mrs Sisson went almost immediately upstairs, and Millicent shortly crept after her. Then Aaron, who had stood motionless as if turned to a pillar of salt, went quietly down the passage and into the living-room. His face was very pale, ghastly-looking. He caught a glimpse of himself in the mirror over the mantel, as he passed, and felt weak, as if he were really a criminal. But his heart did not relax, nevertheless. So he hurried into the night, down the garden, climbed the fence into the field, and went away across the field in the rain, towards the high-road.

He felt sick in every fibre. He almost hated the little handbag he carried, which held his flute and piccolo. It seemed a burden just then – a millstone round his neck. He hated the scene he had left – and he hated the hard, inviolable heart that stuck unchanging in his own breast.

Coming to the high-road, he saw a tall, luminous tram-car roving along through the town. The trams ran across country from town to town. He dared not board, because people knew him. So he took a side road, and walked in a detour for two miles. Then he came out on the high-road again, and waited for a tram-car. The rain blew on his face. He waited a long time for the last car.

5

AT THE OPERA

A friend had given Josephine Ford a box at the opera for one evening: our story continues by night. The box was large and important, near the stage. Josephine and Julia were there, with Robert and Jim – also two more men. The women sat in front of the box, conspicuously. They were both poor, they were rather excited. But they belonged to a set which looked on social triumphs as a downfall that one allows oneself. The two men, Lilly and Struthers, were artists, the former literary, the latter a painter. Lilly sat by Josephine in front of the box: he was her little lion of the evening.

Few women can sit in front of a big box, on a crowded and noisy opera night, without thrilling and dilating. There is an intoxication in being thus thrust forward, conspicuous and enhanced, right in the eye of the vast crowd that lines the hollow shell of the auditorium. Thus even Josephine and Julia leaned their elbows and poised their heads regally, looking condescendingly down upon the watchful world. They were two poor women, having nothing to do with society. Half Bohemians.

Josephine was an artist. In Paris she was a friend of a very fashionable dressmaker and decorator, master of modern elegance. Sometimes she designed dresses for him, and sometimes she accepted from him a commission to decorate a room. Usually at her last sou, it gave her pleasure to dispose of costly and exquisite things for other people, and then be rid of them.

This evening her dress was a simple, but a marvellously poised thing of black and silver: in the words of the correct journal. With her tight, black, bright hair, her arched brows, her dusky-ruddy face and her bare shoulders; her strange equanimity, her long, slow, slanting looks; she looked foreign and frightening, clear as a cameo, but dark, far off. Julia was the English beauty, in a lovely blue dress. Her hair was becomingly untidy on her low brow, her dark blue eyes wandered and got excited, her nervous mouth twitched. Her high-pitched, sing-song voice and her hurried laugh could be heard in the theatre. She twisted a beautiful little fan that a dead artist had given her.

Not being fashionable, they were in the box when the overture began. The opera was Verdi – *Aïda*. If it is impossible to be in an important box at the opera without experiencing the strange intoxication of fashionable pre-eminence, it is just as impossible to be there without some feeling of horror at the sight the stage presents.

Josephine leaned her elbow and looked down: she knew how arresting that proud, rather stiff bend of her head was. She had some aboriginal American in her blood. But as she looked, she pursed her mouth. The artist in her forgot everything, she was filled with disgust. The sham Egypt of *Aïda* hid from her nothing of its shame. The singers were all colour-washed, deliberately colour-washed to a bright orange tint. The men had oblong dabs of black wool under their lower lip; the beard of the mighty Pharaohs. This oblong dab shook and wagged to the singing.

The vulgar bodies of the fleshy women were unendurable. They all looked such good meat. Why were their haunches so prominent? It was a question Josephine could not solve. She scanned their really expensive, brilliant clothing. It was *nearly* right – nearly splendid. It only lacked that last subtlety which the world always lacks, the last final clinching which puts calm into a sea of fabric, and yet is the opposite pole to machine fixity.

But the leading tenor was the chief pain. He was large stout, swathed in a cummerbund, and looked like a eunuch. This fattish, emasculated look seems common in stage heroes – even the extremely popular. The tenor sang bravely, his mouth made a large coffin-shaped, yawning gap in his orange face, his little beard fluttered oddly, like a tail. He turned up his eyes to Josephine's box as he sang – that being the regulation direction. Meanwhile his abdomen shook as he caught his breath, the flesh of his fat naked arms swayed.

Josephine looked down with the fixed gravity of a Red Indian, immovable, inscrutable. It was not till the scene was ended that she lifted her head as if breaking a spell, sent the point of her tongue rapidly over her dried lips, and looked round into the box. Her brown eyes expressed shame, fear, and disgust. A curious grimace went over her face – a grimace only to be expressed by the exclamation *Merde!* But she was mortally afraid of society and its fixed institutions. Rapidly she scanned the eyes of her friends in the box. She rested on the eyes of Lilly, a dark, ugly man.

'Isn't it nasty?' she said.

'You shouldn't look so closely,' he said. But he took it calmly, easily, whilst she felt floods of burning disgust, a longing to destroy it all.

'Oh – ho – ho!' laughed Julia. 'It's so fu-nny – so funny!'

'Of course, we are too near,' said Robert.

'Say you admire that pink fondant over there,' said Struthers, indicating with his eyebrows a blonde large woman in white satin with pink edging, who sat in a box opposite, on the upper tier.

'Oh, the fondant – exactly – the fondant! Yes, I admire her immensely! Isn't she exactly *it*!' sang Julia.

Josephine was scanning the auditorium. So many myriads of faces – like beads on a bead-work pattern – all bead-work, in different layers. She bowed to various acquaintances – mostly Americans in uniform, whom she had known in Paris. She smiled to Lady Cochrane, two boxes off – Lady Cochrane had given her the box. But she felt rather coldly towards her.

The curtain rose, the opera wound its slow length along. The audience loved it. They cheered with mad enthusiasm. Josephine looked down on the choppy sea of applause, white gloves clapping, heads shaking. The noise was strange and rattling. What a curious multiple object a theatre audience was! It seemed to have a million heads, a million hands, and one monstrous, unnatural consciousness. The singers appeared before the curtain – the applause rose up like clouds of dust.

'Oh, isn't it too *wonderful*!' cried Julia. 'I am wild with excitement. Are you all of you?'

'Absolutely wild,' said Lilly laconically.

'Where is Scott tonight?' asked Struthers.

Julia turned to him and gave him a long, queer look from her dark blue eyes. 'He's in the country,' she said, rather enigmatic.

'Don't you know, he's got a house down in Dorset,' said Robert, verbally rushing in. 'He wants Julia to go down and stay.'

'Is she going?' said Lilly.

'She hasn't decided,' replied Robert.

'Oh! What's the objection?' asked Struthers.

'Well, none whatsoever, as far as can be seen, except that she can't make up her mind,' replied Robert.

'Julia's got no mind,' said Jim rudely.

'Oh! Hear the brotherly verdict!' laughed Julia hurriedly.

'You mean go down to Dorset alone?' said Struthers.

'Why not?' replied Robert, answering for her.

'And stay how long?'

'Oh – as long as it lasts,' said Robert again.

'Starting with eternity,' said Lilly, 'and working back to a fortnight.'

'And what's the matter? – Looks bad in the eyes of the world?'

'Yes – about that. Afraid of compromising herself –'

Lilly looked at them.

'Depends what you take the world to mean. Do you mean us in this box, or the crew outside there?' He jerked his head towards the auditorium.

'Do you think, Lilly, that we're the world?' said Robert ironically.

'Oh yes. I guess we're shipwrecked in this box, like Robinson Crusoes. And what we do on our own little island matters to us alone. As for the infinite crowds of howling savages outside there in the unspeakable, all you've got to do is to mind they don't scalp you.'

'But *won't* they?' said Struthers.

'Not unless you put your head in their hands,' said Lilly.

'I don't know –' said Jim.

But the curtain had risen, they hushed him into silence.

All through the next scene Julia puzzled herself, as to whether she should go down to the country and live with Scott. She had carried on a nervous kind of *amour* with him, based on soul sympathy and emotional excitement. But whether to go and live with him? She didn't know if she wanted to or not: and she couldn't for her life find out. She was in that nervous state when desire seems to evaporate the moment fulfilment is offered. When the curtain dropped she turned.

'You see,' she said, screwing up her eyes, 'I have to think of Robert.' She cut the word in two, with an odd little hitch in her voice – '*Rob*-ert.'

'My dear Julia, can't you believe that I'm *tired* of being thought of,' cried Robert, flushing.

Julia screwed up her eyes in a slow smile, oddly cogitating.

'Well, who *am* I to think of?' she asked.

'Yourself,' said Lilly.

'Oh yes! Why, yes! I never thought of that!' She gave a hurried little laugh. 'But then it's no *fun* to think about oneself,' she cried flatly. 'I think about *Rob*-ert, and *Scott*!' She screwed up her eyes and peered oddly at the company.

'Which of them will find you the greatest treat,' said Lilly sarcastically.

'Anyhow,' interjected Robert nervously, 'it will be something new for Scott.'

'Stale buns for you, old boy,' said Jim dryly.

'I don't say so. But –' exclaimed the flushed, full-blooded Robert, who was nothing if not courteous to women.

'How long ha' you been married? Eh?' asked Jim.

'Six years!' sang Julia sweetly.

'Good God!'

'You see,' said Robert, 'Julia can't decide anything for herself. She waits for someone else to decide, then she puts her spoke in.'

'Put it plainly –' began Struthers.

'But don't you know, it's no *use* putting it plainly,' cried Julia.

'But *do* you want to be with Scott, out and out, or *don't* you?' said Lilly.

'Exactly!' chimed Robert. 'That's the question for you to answer, Julia.'

'I *won't* answer it,' she cried. 'Why should I?'

And she looked away into the restless hive of the theatre. She spoke so wildly that she attracted attention. But it half pleased her. She stared abstractedly down at the pit.

The men looked at one another in some comic consternation.

'Oh, damn it all!' said the long Jim, rising and stretching himself. 'She's dead nuts on Scott. She's all over him. She'd have eloped with him weeks ago if it hadn't been so easy. She can't stand it that Robert offers to hand her into the taxi.'

He gave his malevolent grin round the company, then went out. He did not reappear for the next scene.

'Of course, if she loves Scott –' began Struthers.

Julia suddenly turned with wild desperation and cried:

'I like him tremendously – tre-men-dous-ly! He *does* understand.'

'Which we don't,' said Robert.

Julia smiled her long, odd smile in their faces: one might almost say she smiled in their teeth.

'What do *you* think, Josephine?' asked Lilly.

Josephine was leaning forward. She started. Her tongue went rapidly over her lips. 'Who? I?' she exclaimed.

'Yes.'

'I think Julia should go with Scott,' said Josephine. 'She'll bother with the idea till she's done it. She loves him, really.'

'Of course she does,' cried Robert.

Julia, with her chin resting on her arms, in a position which irritated the neighbouring Lady Cochrane sincerely, was gazing with unseeing eyes down upon the stalls.

'Well then –' began Struthers. But the music struck up softly. They were all rather bored. Struthers kept on making small, half-audible remarks – which was bad form, and displeased Josephine, the hostess of the evening.

When the curtain came down for the end of the act, the men got up. Lilly's wife, Tanny, suddenly appeared. She had come on after a dinner engagement.

'Would you like tea or anything?' Lilly asked.

The women refused. The men filtered out on to the crimson and white, curving corridor. Julia, Josephine and Tanny remained in the box. Tanny was soon hitched on to the conversation in hand.

'Of course,' she replied, 'one can't decide such a thing like drinking a cup of tea.'

'Of course one can't, dear Tanny,' said Julia.

'After all, one doesn't leave one's husband every day, to go and live with another man. Even if one looks on it as an experiment –'

'It's difficult!' cried Julia. 'It's difficult! I feel they all want to *force* me to decide. It's cruel.'

'Oh, men with their beastly logic, their either-this-or-that stunt, they are an awful bore. But, of course, Robert can't love you *really*, or he'd want to keep you. I can see Lilly discussing such a thing for *me*. But then you don't love Robert either,' said Tanny.

'I do! Oh, I do, Tanny! I *do* love him, I love him dearly. I think he's beautiful. Robert's beautiful. And he *needs* me. And I need him, too. I need his support. Yes, I do love him.'

'But you like Scott better,' said Tanny.

'Only because he – he's different,' sang Julia, in long tones. 'You see, Scott has his art. His art matters. And *Rob*-ert – Robert is a dilettante, don't you think – he's dilettante –' She screwed up her eyes at Tanny. Tanny cogitated.

'Of course, I don't think that matters,' she replied.

'But it does, it matters tremendously, dear Tanny, tremendously.'

'Of course,' Tanny sheered off, 'I can see Scott has great attractions – a great warmth somewhere –'

'Exactly!' cried Julia. 'He *understands* –'

'And I believe he's a real artist. You might even work together. You might write his librettos.'

'Yes! – Yes! –' Julia spoke with a long, pondering hiss.

'It might be *awfully* nice,' said Tanny rapturously.

'Yes! – It might! – It might! –' pondered Julia. Suddenly she gave herself a shake. Then she laughed hurriedly, as if breaking from her line of thought.

'And wouldn't Robert be an *awfully* nice lover for Josephine! Oh, wouldn't that be splendid!' she cried, with her high laugh.

Josephine, who had been gazing down into the orchestra, turned now, flushing darkly.

'But I don't want a lover, Julia,' she said, hurt.

'Josephine, dear! Dear old Josephine! Don't you really! Oh, yes you do. I want one so *badly*,' cried Julia, with her shaking laugh. 'Robert's awfully *good* to me. But we've been married six years. And it does make a difference, doesn't it, Tanny dear?'

'A great difference,' said Tanny.

'Yes, it makes a difference, it makes a difference,' mused Julia, 'dear old *Rob*-ert – I wouldn't hurt him for worlds. I wouldn't. Do you think it would hurt Robert?'

She screwed up her eyes, looking at Tanny.

'Perhaps it would do Robert good to be hurt a little,' said Tanny. 'He's so well nourished.'

'Yes! Yes! I see what you mean, Tanny? Poor old *Rob*-ert! Oh, poor old *Rob*-ert, he's so young.'

'He *does* seem young,' said Tanny. 'One doesn't forgive it.'

'He is young,' said Julia. 'I'm five years older than he. He's only twenty-seven. Poor old Robert.'

'Robert is young, and inexperienced,' said Josephine, suddenly turning with anger. 'But I don't know why you talk about him.'

'Is he inexperienced, Josephine dear? *Is* he?' sang Julia.

Josephine flushed darkly, and turned away.

'Ah, he's not so innocent as all that,' said Tanny roughly. 'Those young young men, who seem so fresh, they're deep enough, really. They're far less innocent really than men who *are* experienced.'

'They are, aren't they, Tanny,' repeated Julia softly. 'They're old – older than the Old Man of the Seas, sometimes, aren't they? Incredibly old, like little boys who know too much – aren't they? Yes!' She spoke quietly, seriously, as if it had struck her.

Below, the orchestra was coming in. Josephine was watching closely. Julia became aware of this.

'Do you see anybody we know, Josephine?' she asked.

Josephine started.

'No,' she said, looking at her friends quickly and furtively.

'Dear old Josephine, she knows all sorts of people,' sang Julia.

At that moment the men returned.

'Have you actually come back!' exclaimed Tanny to them. They sat down without answering. Jim spread himself as far as he could, in the narrow space. He stared upwards, wrinkling his ugly, queer face. It was evident he was in one of his moods.

'If somebody loved me!' he complained. 'If only somebody loved me I should be all right. I'm going to pieces.' He sat up and peered into the faces of the women.

'But we *all* love you,' said Josephine, laughing uneasily. 'Why aren't you satisfied!'

'I'm not satisfied. I'm not satisfied,' murmured Jim.

'Would you like to be wrapped in swaddling bands and laid at the breast?' asked Lilly, disagreeably.

Jim opened his mouth in a grin, and gazed long and malevolently at his questioner.

'Yes,' he said. Then he sprawled his long six foot of limb and body across the box again.

'You should try loving somebody, for a change,' said Tanny. 'You've been loved too often. Why not try and love somebody?'

Jim eyed her narrowly.

'I couldn't love *you*,' he said, in vicious tones.

'*A la bonne heure!*' said Tanny.

But Jim sank his chin on his chest, and repeated obstinately:

'I want to be loved.'

'How many times *have* you been loved?' Robert asked him. 'It would be rather interesting to know.'

Jim looked at Robert long and slow, but did not answer.

'Did you ever keep count?' Tanny persisted.

Jim looked up at her, malevolent.

'I believe I did,' he replied.

'Forty is the age when a man should begin to reckon up,' said Lilly.

Jim suddenly sprang to his feet, and brandished his fists.

'I'll pitch the lot of you over the bloody rail,' he said. He glared at them, from under his bald, wrinkled forehead. Josephine glanced round. She had become a dusky white colour. She was afraid of him, and disliked him intensely nowadays.

'Do you recognize anyone in the orchestra?' she asked.

The party in the box had become dead silent. They looked down. The conductor was at his stand. The music began. They all remained silent and motionless during the next scene, each thinking his own thoughts. Jim was uncomfortable. He wanted to make good. He sat with his elbows on his knees, grinning slightly, looking down. At the next interval he stood up suddenly.

'It *is* the chap – what?' he exclaimed excitedly, looking round at his friends.

'Who?' said Tanny.

'It *is* he!' said Josephine quietly, meeting Jim's eye.

'Sure!' he barked.

He was leaning forward over the ledge, rattling a programme in his hands, as if trying to attract attention. Then he made signals.

'There you are!' he exclaimed triumphantly. 'That's the chap.'

'Who? Who?' they cried.

But neither Jim nor Josephine would vouchsafe an answer.

The next was the long interval. Jim and Josephine gazed down at the orchestra. The musicians were laying aside their instruments and rising. The ugly fire-curtain began slowly to descend. Jim suddenly bolted out.

'Is it that man, Aaron Sisson?' asked Robert.

'Where? Where?' cried Julia. 'It can't be.'

But Josephine's face was closed and silent. She did not answer.

The whole party moved out on to the crimson-carpeted gangway. Groups of people stood about chatting, men and women were passing along, to pay visits or to find drinks. Josephine's party stared around, talking desultorily. And at length they perceived Jim stalking alone, leading Aaron Sisson by the arm. Jim was grinning, the flautist looked unwilling. He had a comely appearance, in his white shirt – a certain comely blondness and repose. And as much a gentleman as anybody.

'Well!' cried Josephine to him. 'How do you come here?'

'I play the flute,' he answered, as he shook hands.

The little crowd stood in the gangway and talked.

'How wonderful of you to be here!' cried Julia.

He laughed.

'Do you think so?' he answered.

'Yes, I do. It seems so *far* from Shottle House and Christmas Eve. Oh, wasn't it exciting!' cried Julia.

Aaron looked at her, but did not answer.

'We've heard all about you,' said Tanny playfully.

'Oh yes,' he replied.

'Come!' said Josephine, rather irritated. 'We crowd up the gangway.' And she led the way inside the box.

Aaron stood and looked down at the dishevelled theatre.

'You get all the view,' he said.

'We do, don't we!' cried Julia.

'More than we bargain for,' said Lilly.

'Tell us what you are doing. You've got a permanent job?' asked Josephine.

'Yes – at present.'

'Ah! It's more interesting for you than at Beldover.' She had taken her seat. He looked down at her dusky young face. Her voice was always clear and measured.

'It's a change,' he said, smiling.

'Oh, it must be more than that,' she said. 'Why, you must feel a whole difference. It's a whole new life.'

He smiled, as if he were laughing at her silently. She flushed.

'But isn't it?' she persisted.

'Yes. It can be,' he replied.

He looked as if he were quietly amused, but dissociated. None of the people in the box were quite real to him. He was not really amused. Julia found him dull, stupid. Tanny also was offended that he could not *perceive* her. The men remained practically silent.

'You're a chap I always hoped would turn up again,' said Jim.

'Oh yes!' replied Aaron, smiling as if amused.

'But perhaps he doesn't like us! Perhaps he's not glad that *we've* turned up,' said Julia, leaving her sting.

The flautist turned and looked at her.

'You can't *remember* us, can you?' she asked.

'Yes,' he said. 'I can remember you.'

'Oh,' she laughed. 'You *are* unflattering.'

He was annoyed. He did not know what she was getting at.

'How are your wife and children?' she asked spitefully.

'All right, I think.'

'But you've been back to them?' cried Josephine in dismay.

He looked at her, a slow, half-smiling look, but did not speak.

'Come an' have a drink. Damn the women,' said Jim uncouthly, seizing Aaron by the arm and dragging him off.

6

TALK

The party stayed to the end of the interminable opera. They had agreed to wait for Aaron. He was to come round to the vestibule for them, after the show. They trooped slowly downstairs into the crush of the entrance hall. Chattering, swirling people, red carpet, palms green against cream-and-gilt walls, small whirlpools of life at the open, dark doorways, men in opera hats steering decisively about – it was the old scene. But there were no taxis – absolutely no taxis. And it was raining. Fortunately the women had brought shoes. They slipped these on. Jim rocked through the crowd, in his tall hat, looking for the flautist.

At last Aaron was found – wearing a bowler hat. Julia groaned in spirit. Josephine's brows knitted. Not that anybody cared, really. But as one must frown at something, why not at the bowler hat. Acquaintances and elegant young men in uniforms insisted on rushing up and bowing and exchanging a few words, either with Josephine, or Jim, or Julia, or Lilly. They were coldly received. The party veered out into the night.

The women hugged their wraps about them, and set off sharply, feeling some repugnance for the wet pavements and the crowd. They had not far to go – only to Jim's rooms in the Adelphi. Jim was leading Aaron, holding him by the arm and slightly pinching his muscles. It gave him great satisfaction to have between his fingers the arm-muscles of a working man, one of the common people, the *fons et origo* of modern life. Jim was talking rather vaguely about Labour and Robert Smillie, and Bolshevism. He was all for revolution and the triumph of Labour.

So they arrived, mounted a dark stair, and entered a large, handsome room, one of the Adams rooms. Jim had furnished it from Heal's with striped hangings, green and white and yellow and dark purple, and with a green-and-black checked carpet, and great stripe-covered chairs and chesterfield. A big gas-fire was soon glowing in the handsome old fireplace, the panelled room seemed cosy.

While Jim was handing round drinks and sandwiches, and Josephine was making tea, Robert played Bach on the piano – the pianola, rather. The chairs and lounge were in a half-circle round the fire. The party threw off their wraps and sank deep into this expensive comfort of modern Bohemia. They needed the Bach to take away the bad taste that *Aïda* left in their mouths. They needed the whisky and curaçao to rouse their spirits. They needed the profound comfort in which to sink away from the world. All the men, except Aaron, had been through the war in some way or other. But here they were, in the old setting exactly, the old Bohemian routine.

The bell rang, Jim went downstairs. He returned shortly with a frail, elegant woman – fashionable rather than Bohemian. She was cream and auburn, Irish, with a slightly-lifted upper lip that gave her a pathetic look. She dropped her wrap and sat down by Julia, taking her hand delicately.

'How are you, darling?' she asked.

'Yes – I'm happy,' said Julia, giving her odd, screwed-up smile.

The pianola stopped, they all chatted indiscriminately. Jim was watching the newcomer – Mrs Browning – with a concentrated, wolfish grin.

'I like her,' he said at last. 'I've seen her before, haven't I? – I like her awfully.'

'Yes,' said Josephine, with a slight grunt of a laugh. 'He wants to be loved.'

'Oh,' cried Clariss. 'So do I!'

'Then there you are!' cried Tanny.

'Also no, there we aren't,' cried Clariss. She was beautiful too, with her lifted upper lip. 'We both want to be loved, and so we miss each other entirely. We run on in two parallel lines, that can never meet,' she laughed low and half sad.

'Doesn't *she* love you?' said Aaron to Jim, amused, indicating Josephine. 'I thought you were engaged.'

'*Her!*' leered Jim vindictively, glancing at Josephine. '*She* doesn't love me.'

'Is that true?' asked Robert hastily, of Josephine.

'Why,' she said, 'yes. Why should he make me say out here that I don't love him?'

'Got you, my girl,' said Jim.

'Then it's no engagement?' said Robert.

'Listen to the row fools make, rushing in,' said Jim maliciously.

'No, the engagement is broken,' said Josephine.

'World coming to pieces bit by bit,' said Lilly. Jim was twisting in his chair, and looking like a Chinese dragon, diabolical. The room was uneasy.

'What gives you such a belly-ache for love, Jim?' said Lilly, 'or for being loved? Why do you want so badly to be loved?'

'Because I like it, damn you,' barked Jim. 'Because I'm in need of it.'

None of them quite knew whether they ought to take it as a joke. It was just a bit too real to be quite pleasant.

'Why are you such a baby?' said Lilly. 'There you are, six foot in length, have been a cavalry officer and fought in two wars, and you spend your time crying for somebody to love you. You're a comic.'

'Am I though,' said Jim. 'I'm losing life. I'm getting thin.'

'You don't look as if you were losing life,' said Lilly.

'Don't I! I am though. I'm dying.'

'What of? Lack of life?'

'That's about it, my young cock. Life's leaving me.'

'Better sing. Tosti's "Farewell" to it.'

Jim, who had been sprawling full length in his arm-chair, the centre of interest of all the company, suddenly sprang forward and pushed his face, grinning, in the face of Lilly.

'You're a funny customer, you are,' he said.

Then he turned round in his chair, saw Clariss sitting at the feet of Julia, with one white arm over her friend's knee. Jim immediately stuck forward his muzzle and gazed at her. Clariss had loosened her masses of thick, auburn hair, so that it hung half down. Her face was creamy pale, her upper lip lifted with odd pathos. She had rose-rubies in her ears.

'I like *her*,' said Jim. 'What's her name?'

'Mrs Browning. Don't be so rude,' said Josephine.

'Browning for gravies. Any relation of Robert?'

'Oh yes! You ask my husband,' came the slow, plangent voice of Clariss.

'You've got a husband, have you?'

'Rather! Haven't I, Juley?'

'Yes,' said Julia, vaguely and wispily. 'Yes, dear, you have.'

'And two fine children,' put in Robert.

'No! You don't mean it!' said Jim. 'Who's your husband? Anybody?'

'Rather!' came the deep voice of Clariss. 'He sees to that.'

Jim stared, grinning, showing his pointed teeth, reaching nearer and nearer to Clariss who, in her frail scrap of an evening dress, amethyst and silver, was sitting still in the deep black hearth-rug, her arm over Julia's knee, taking very little notice of Jim, although he amused her.

'I like you awfully, I say,' he repeated.

'Thanks, I'm sure,' she said.

The others were laughing, sprawling in their chairs, and sipping curaçao and taking a sandwich or a cigarette. Aaron Sisson alone sat upright, smiling flickeringly. Josephine watched him, and her pointed tongue went from time to time over her lips.

'But I'm sure,' she broke in, 'this isn't very interesting for the others. Awfully boring! Don't be silly all the time, Jim, or we must go home.'

Jim looked at her with narrowed eyes. He hated her voice. She let her eye rest on his for a moment. Then she put her cigarette to her lips. Robert was watching them both.

Josephine took her cigarette from her lips again.

'Tell us about yourself, Mr Sisson,' she said. 'How do you like being in London?'

'I like London,' said Aaron.

Where did he live! Bloomsbury. Did he know many people? No – nobody except a man in the orchestra. How had he got his job? Through an agent. Etc. Etc.

'What do you make of the miners?' said Jim, suddenly taking a new line.

'Me?' said Sisson. 'I don't make anything of them.'

'Do you think they'll make a stand against the government?'

'What for?'

'Nationalisation.'

'They might, one day.'

'Think they'd fight?'

'Fight?'

'Yes.'

Aaron sat laughing.

'What have they to fight for?'

'Why, everything! What haven't they to fight for?' cried Josephine fiercely. 'Freedom. liberty, an escape from this rotten system. Won't they fight for that?'

Aaron sat smiling, slowly shaking his head.

'Nay,' he said, 'you mustn't ask me what they'll do – I've only just left them, for good. They'll do a lot of cavilling.'

'But won't they *act*?' cried Josephine.

'Act?' said Aaron. 'How, act?'

'Why, defy the government, and take things in their own hands,' said Josephine.

'They might, some time,' said Aaron, rather indifferent.

'I wish they would!' cried Josephine. 'My, wouldn't I love it if they'd make a bloody revolution.'

They were all looking now at her. Her black brows were twitching: in her black and silver dress she looked a symbol of young disaster.

'Must it be bloody, Josephine?' said Robert.

'Why, yes. I don't believe in revolutions that aren't bloody,' said Josephine. 'Wouldn't I love it! I'd go in front with a red flag.'

'It would be rather fun,' said Tanny.

'Wouldn't it?' cried Josephine.

'Oh Josey, dear!' cried Julia hysterically. 'Isn't she a red-hot Bolsher! *I* should be frightened.'

'No!' cried Josephine. 'I should love it.'

'So should I,' said Jim, in a luscious sort of voice. 'What price machine-guns at the end of the Strand! That's a day to live for, what?'

'Ha! Ha!' laughed Clariss, with her deep laugh. 'We'd all Bolsh together. I'd give the cheers.'

'I wouldn't mind getting killed. I'd love it, in a real fight,' said Josephine.

'But Josephine,' said Robert; 'don't you think we've had enough of that sort of thing in the war? Don't you think it all works out rather stupid and unsatisfying?'

'Ah, but a civil war would be different. I've no interest in fighting Germans. But a civil war would be different.'

'That's a fact, it would,' said Jim.

'Only rather worse,' said Robert.

'No, I don't agree,' cried Josephine. 'You'd feel you were doing something, in a civil war.'

'Pulling the house down,' said Lilly.

'Yes,' she cried. 'Don't you hate it, the house we live in – London – England – America! Don't you hate them?'

'I don't like them. But I can't get much fire in my hatred. They pall on me rather,' said Lilly.

'Ay!' said Aaron, suddenly stirring in his chair.

Lilly and he glanced at one another with a look of recognition.

'Still,' said Tanny, 'there's got to be a clearance some day or other.'

'Oh,' drawled Clariss. 'I'm all for a clearance. I'm all for pulling the house down. Only while it stands I do want central heating and a good cook.'

'May I come to dinner?' said Jim.

'Oh yes. You'd find it rather domestic.'

'Where do you live?'

'Rather far out now – Amersham.'

'Amersham? Where's that – ?'

'Oh, it's on the map.'

There was a little lull. Jim gulped down a drink, standing at the sideboard. He was a tall, fine, soldierly figure, and his face, with its little sandy moustache and bald forehead, was odd. Aaron Sisson sat watching him, unconsciously.

'Hello you!' said Jim. 'Have one?'

Aaron shook his head, and Jim did not press him. It saved the drinks.

'You believe in love, don't you?' said Jim, sitting down near Aaron, and grinning at him.

'Love!' said Aaron.

'*Love*! he says,' mocked Jim, grinning at the company.

'What about it, then?' asked Aaron.

'It's life! Love is life,' said Jim fiercely.

'It's a vice, like drink,' said Lilly.

'Eh? A vice!' said Jim. 'May be for you, old bird.'

'More so still for you,' said Lilly.

'It's life. It's life!' reiterated Jim. 'Don't you agree?' He turned wolfishly to Clariss.

'Oh yes – every time –' she drawled, nonchalant.

'Here, let's write it down,' said Lilly. He found a blue pencil and printed in large letters on the old creamy marble of the mantelpiece panel: – LOVE IS LIFE.

Julia suddenly rose and flung her arms asunder wildly.

'Oh, I hate love. I hate it,' she protested.

Jim watched her sardonically.

'Look at her!' he said. 'Look at Lesbia who hates love.'

'No, but perhaps it is a disease. Perhaps we are all wrong, and we can't love properly,' put in Josephine.

'Have another try,' said Jim. 'I know what love is. I've thought about it. Love is the soul's respiration.'

'Let's have that down,' said Lilly.

LOVE IS THE SOUL'S RESPIRATION. He printed it on the old mantelpiece.

Jim eyed the letters.

'It's right,' he said. 'Quite right. When you love, your soul breathes in. If you don't breathe in, you suffocate.'

'What about breathing out?' said Robert. 'If you don't breathe out, you asphyxiate.'

'Right you are, Mock Turtle –' said Jim maliciously.

'Breathing out is a bloody revolution,' said Lilly.

'You've hit the nail on the head,' said Jim solemnly.

'Let's record it then,' said Lilly. And with the blue pencil he printed:–
WHEN YOU LOVE, YOUR SOUL BREATHES IN.
And then on the next line:–
WHEN YOUR SOUL BREATHES OUT, IT'S A BLOODY REVOLUTION.

'I say, Jim,' he said. 'You must be busting yourself trying to breathe in.'

'Don't you be too clever. I've thought about it,' said Jim. 'When I'm in love, I get a great inrush of energy. I actually feel it rush in – here!' He poked his finger on the pit of his stomach. 'It's the soul's expansion. And if I can't get these rushes of energy, I'm dying, and I know I am.'

He spoke the last words with sudden ferocity and desperation.

'All *I* know is,' said Tanny, 'you don't look it.'

'I *am*. I *am*,' Jim protested. I'm dying. Life's leaving me.'

'Maybe you're choking with love,' said Robert. 'Perhaps you've breathed in so much, you don't know how to let it go again. Perhaps your soul's got a crick in it, with expanding so much.'

'You're a bloody young sucking-pig, you are,' said Jim.

'Even at that age, I've learned my manners,' replied Robert.

Jim looked round the party. Then he turned to Aaron Sisson.

'What do you make of 'em, eh?' he said.

Aaron shook his head, and laughed.

'Me?' he said.

But Jim did not wait for an answer.

'I've had enough,' said Tanny, suddenly rising. 'I think you're all silly. Besides, it's getting late.'

'She!' said Jim, rising and pointing luridly to Clarris, 'she's Love. And *he's* the working people. The hope is in those two –' He jerked a thumb at Aaron Sisson, after having indicated Mrs Browning.

'Oh, how awfully interesting. It's quite a long time since I've been a personification. I suppose you've never been one before?' said Clariss, turning to Aaron in conclusion.

'No, I don't think I have,' he answered.

'I hope personification is right. Ought it to be *allegory* or something else?' This from Clariss to Robert.

'Or a parable, Clariss,' laughed the young lieutenant.

'Good-bye,' said Tanny. 'I've been awfully bored.'

'Have you?' grinned Jim. 'Good-bye! Better luck next time.'

'We'd better look sharp,' said Robert, 'if we want to get the tube.'

The party hurried through the rainy narrow streets down to the Embankment station. Robert and Julia and Clariss were going west, Lilly and his wife, Tanny, were going to Hampstead, Josephine and Aaron Sisson were going both to Bloomsbury.

'I suppose,' said Robert, on the stairs, 'Mr Sisson will see you to your door, Josephine. He lives your way.'

'There's no need at all,' said Josephine.

The four who were going north went down to the low tube level. It was nearly the last train. The station was half deserted, half rowdy, several fellows were drunk, shouting and crowing. Down there in the bowels of London, after midnight, everything seemed horrible and unnatural.

'How I hate this London,' said Tanny. She was half Norwegian, and had spent a large part of her life in Norway, before she married Lilly.

'Yes, so do I,' said Josephine. 'But if one must earn one's living one must stay here. I wish I could get back to Paris. But there's nothing doing for me in France. When do you go back into the country, both of you?'

'Friday,' said Lilly.

'How lovely for you! And when will you go to Norway, Tanny?'

'In about a month,' said Tanny.

'You must be awfully pleased.'

'Oh – thankful – *thankful* to get out of England –'

'I know. That's how I feel. Everything is so awful – so dismal and dreary, I find it –'

They crowded into the train. Men were still yelling like wild beasts – others were asleep – soldiers were singing.

'Have you really broken your engagement with Jim?' shrilled Tanny in a high voice, as the train roared.

'Yes, he's impossible,' said Josephine. 'Perfectly hysterical and impossible.'

'And *selfish* –' cried Tanny.

'Oh terribly –' cried Josephine.

'Come up to Hampstead to lunch with us,' said Lilly to Aaron.

'Ay – thank you,' said Aaron.

Lilly scribbled directions on a card. The hot, jaded, midnight underground rattled on. Aaron and Josephine got down to change trains.

7

THE DARK SQUARE GARDEN

Josephine had invited Aaron Sisson to dinner at a restaurant in Soho, one Sunday evening. They had a corner to themselves, and with a bottle of burgundy she was getting his history from him.

His father had been a shaft-sinker, earning good money, but had been killed by a fall down the shaft when Aaron was only four years old. The widow had opened a shop: Aaron was her only child. She had done well in her shop. She had wanted Aaron to be a school-teacher. He had served three years' apprenticeship, then suddenly thrown it up and gone to the pit.

'But why?' said Josephine.

He had a curious quality of an intelligent, almost sophisticated mind, which had repudiated education. On purpose he kept the Midland accent in his speech. He understood perfectly what a personification was – and an allegory. But he preferred to be illiterate.

Josephine found out what a miner's checkweighman was. She tried to find out what sort of wife Aaron had – but, except that she was the daughter of a publican and was delicate in health, she could learn nothing.

'And do you send her money?' she asked.

'Ay,' said Aaron. 'The house is mine. And I allow her so much a week out of the money in the bank. My mother left me a bit over a thousand when she died.'

'You don't mind what I say, do you?' said Josephine.

'No, I don't mind,' he laughed.

He had this pleasant-seeming, courteous manner. But he really kept her at a distance. In some things he reminded her of Robert: blond, erect, nicely built, fresh and English-seeming. But there was a curious cold distance to him, which she could not get across. An inward indifference to her – perhaps to everything. Yet his laugh was so handsome.

'Will you tell me why you left your wife and children? Didn't you love them?'

Aaron looked at the odd, round, dark muzzle of the girl. She had had her hair bobbed, and it hung in odd dark folds, very black, over her ears.

'Why I left her?' he said. 'For no particular reason. They're all right without me.'

Josephine watched his face. She saw a pallor of suffering under his freshness, and a strange tension in his eyes.

'But you couldn't leave your little girls for no reason at all –'

'Yes, I did. For no reason – except I wanted to have a bit of free room round me – to loose myself.'

'You mean you wanted love?' flashed Josephine, thinking he said *lose*.

'No, I wanted fresh air. I don't know what I wanted. Why should I know?'

'But we must know: especially when other people are going to suffer so,' said she.

'Ah well! A breath of fresh air, by myself. I felt forced to love. I feel if I go back home now, I shall be *forced* – forced to love – or care – or something.'

'Perhaps you wanted more than your wife could give you,' she said.

'Perhaps less. She's made up her mind she loves me, and she's not going to let me off.'

'Did you never love her?' said Josephine.

'Oh yes. I shall never love anybody else. But I'm damned if I want to go on being a lover, to her or anybody. That's the top and bottom of it. I don't want to *care*, when care isn't in me. And I'm not going to be forced to it.'

The fat, aproned French waiter was hovering near. Josephine let him remove the plates and the empty bottle.

'Have more wine,' she said to Aaron. 'Do?'

But he refused. She liked him because of his dead-level indifference to his surroundings. French waiters and foreign food – he noticed them in his quick, amiable-looking fashion – but he was indifferent. Josephine was piqued. She wanted to pierce this amiable aloofness of his.

She ordered coffee and brandies.

'But you don't want to get away from *everything*, do you? I myself feel so *lost* sometimes – so dreadfully alone: not in a silly sentimental fashion, because men keep telling me they love me, don't you know. But my *life* seems alone, for some reason –'

'Haven't you got relations?' he said.

'No one, now mother is dead. Nothing nearer than aunts and cousins in America. I suppose I shall see them all again one day. But they hardly count over here.'

'Why don't you get married?' he said. 'How old are you?'

'I'm twenty-five. How old are you?'

'Thirty-three.'

'You might almost be any age. I don't know why I don't get married. In a way, I hate earning my own living – yet I go on – And I like my work –'

'What are you doing now?'

'I'm painting scenery for a new play – rather fun – I enjoy it. But I often wonder what will become of me.'

'In what way?'

She was almost affronted.

'What becomes of me? Oh, I don't know! And it doesn't matter, not to anybody but myself.'

'What becomes of anybody, anyhow? We live till we die. What do you want?'

'Why, I keep saying I want to get married and feel sure of something. But I don't know – I feel dreadful sometimes – as if every minute would be the last. I keep going on and on – I don't know what for – and *it* keeps going on and on – goodness knows what it's all for.'

'You shouldn't bother yourself,' he said. 'You should just let it go on and on –'

'But I *must* bother,' she said. 'I must think and feel –'

'You've no occasion,' he said.

'How – ?' she said, with a sudden grunting, unhappy laugh. Then she lit a cigarette.

'No,' she said. 'What I should really like more than anything would be an end of the world. I wish the world would come to an end.'

He laughed, and poured his drops of brandy down his throat.

'It won't, for wishing,' he said.

'No, that's the awful part of it. It'll just go on and on. Doesn't it make you feel you'd go mad?'

He looked at her, and shook his head.

'You see, it doesn't concern me,' he said. 'So long as I can float by myself.'

'But *are* you *satisfied*!' she cried.

'I like being by myself – I hate feeling and caring, and being forced into it. I want to be left alone –'

'You aren't very polite to your hostess of the evening,' she said, laughing a bit piqued.

'Oh, we're all right,' he said. 'You know what I mean –'

'You like your own company? Do you! Sometimes I think I'm nothing when I'm alone. Sometimes I think I surely must be nothing – nothingness.'

He shook his head.

'No,' he said. 'No. I only want to be left alone.'

'Not to have anything to do with anybody?' she queried ironically.

'Not to any extent.'

She watched him – and then she bubbled with a laugh.

'I think you're funny,' she said. 'You don't mind?'

'No – why – It's just as you see it. Jim Bricknell's a rare comic, to my eye.'

'Oh, him! – no, not actually. He's self-conscious and selfish and hysterical. It isn't a bit funny after a while.'

'I only know what I've seen,' said Aaron. 'You'd both of you like a bloody revolution, though.'

'Yes. Only when it came he wouldn't be there.'

'Would you?'

'Yes, indeed I would. I would give everything to be in it. I'd give heaven and earth for a great big upheaval – and then darkness.'

'Perhaps you'll get it, when you die,' said Aaron.

'Oh, but I don't want to die and leave all this standing. I hate it so.'

'Why do you?'

'But don't you?'

'No, it doesn't really bother me.'

'It makes me feel I can't live.'

'I can't see that.'

'But you always disagree with one!' said Josephine. 'How do you like Lilly? What do you think of him?'

'He seems sharp,' said Aaron.

'Yes! But he's more than sharp.'

'Oh yes. He's got his finger in most pies.'

'And doesn't like the plums in any of them,' said Josephine tartly.

'What does he do?'

'Write – stories and plays.'

'And makes it pay?'

'Hardly at all. They want us to go. Shall we?'

She rose from the table. The waiter handed her her cloak, and they went out into the blowy dark night. She folded her wrap round her, and hurried forward, with short, sharp steps. There was a certain Parisian *chic* and mincingness about her, even in her walk: but underneath, a striding, savage suggestion, as if she could leg it in great strides, like some savage squaw.

Aaron pressed his bowler hat down on his brow.

'Would you rather take a bus?' she said in a high voice, because of the wind.

'I'd rather walk.'

'So would I.'

They hurried across the Charing Cross Road, where great buses rolled and rocked, crammed with people. Her heels clicked sharply on the pavement as they walked east. They crossed Holborn, and passed the Museum. And neither of them said anything.

When they came to the corner, she held out her hand.

'Look!' she said. 'Don't come any farther: don't trouble.'

'I'll walk round with you: unless you'd rather not.'

'No – But do you want to bother?'

'It's no bother.'

So they pursued their way through the high wind, and turned at last into the old, beautiful square. It seemed dark and deserted, dark like a savage wilderness in the heart of London. The wind was roaring in the great bare trees of the centre, as if it were some wild, dark grove deep in a forgotten land.

Josephine opened the gate of the Square garden with her key, and let it slam to behind him.

'How wonderful the wind is!' she shrilled. 'Shall we listen to it for a minute?'

She led him across the grass past the shrubs to the big tree in the centre. There she climbed up to a seat. He sat beside her. They sat in silence, looking at the darkness. Rain was blowing in the wind. They huddled against the big tree-trunk, for shelter, and watched the scene.

Beyond the tall shrubs and the high, heavy railings the wet street gleamed silently. The houses of the Square rose like a cliff on this inner dark sea, dimly lighted at occasional windows. Boughs swayed and sang. A taxi-cab swirled round a corner like a cat, and purred to a standstill. There was a light of an open hall door. But all far away, it seemed, unthinkably far away. Aaron sat still and watched. He was frightened, it all seemed so sinister, this dark, bristling heart of London. Wind boomed and tore like waves ripping a shingle beach. The two white lights of the taxi stared round and departed, leaving the coast at the foot of the cliffs deserted, faintly spilled with light from the high lamp. Beyond there, on the outer rim, a policeman passed solidly.

Josephine was weeping steadily all the time, but inaudibly. Occasionally she blew her nose and wiped her face. But he had not realized. She hardly realized herself. She sat near the strange man. He seemed so still and remote – so fascinating.

'Give me your hand,' she said to him, subduedly.

He took her cold hand in his warm, living grasp. She wept more bitterly. He noticed at last.

'Why are you crying?' he said.

'I don't know,' she replied, rather matter-of-fact, through her tears.

So he let her cry, and said no more, but sat with her cold hand in his warm, easy clasp.

'You'll think me a fool,' she said. 'I don't know why I cry.'

'You can cry for nothing if you like, can't you?' he said.

'Why, yes, but it's not very sensible.'

He laughed shortly.

'Sensible!' he said.

'You are a strange man,' she said. But he took no notice.

'Did you ever intend to marry Jim Bricknell?' he asked.

'Yes, of course.'

'I can't imagine it,' he said.

'Why not?'

Both were watching blankly the roaring night of mid-London, the phantasmagoric old Bloomsbury square. They were still hand in hand.

'Such as you shouldn't marry,' he said.

'But why not? I want to.'

'You think you do.'

'Yes, indeed I do.'

He did not say any more.

'Why shouldn't I?' she persisted.

'I don't know –'

And again he was silent.

'You've known some life, haven't you?' he asked.

'Me? Why?'

'You seem to.'

'Do I? I'm sorry. Do I seem vicious? No, I'm not vicious. I've seen some life, perhaps – in Paris mostly. But not much. Why do you ask?'

'I wasn't thinking.'

'But what do you mean? What *are* you thinking?'

'Nothing. Nothing.'

'Don't be so irritating,' she said.

But he did not answer, and she became silent also. They sat hand in hand.

'Won't you kiss me?' came her voice out of the darkness.

He waited some moments, then his voice sounded gently, half mocking, half reproachful.

'Nay,' he said.

'Why not?'

'I don't want to.'

'Why not?' she asked.

He laughed, but did not reply.

She sat perfectly still for some time. She had ceased to cry. In the darkness her face was set and sullen. Sometimes a spray of rain blew across it. She drew her hand from his and rose to her feet.

'I'll go in now,' she said.

'You're not offended, are you?' he asked.

'No. Why?'

They stepped down in the darkness from their perch.

'I wondered.'

She strode off for some little way. Then she turned and said:

'Yes, I think it is rather insulting.'

'Nay,' he said. 'Not it! Not it!'

And he followed her to the gate.

She opened with her key, and they crossed the road to her door.

'Good night,' she said, turning and giving him her hand.

'You'll come and have dinner with me – or lunch – will you? When shall we make it?' he asked.

'Well, I can't say for certain. I'm very busy just now. I'll let you know.'

A policeman shed his light on the pair of them as they stood on the step.

'All right,' said Aaron, dropping back, and she hastily opened the big door and entered.

8

A PUNCH IN THE WIND

The Lillys had a labourer's cottage in Hampshire – pleasant enough. They were poor. Lilly was a little, dark, thin, quick fellow, his wife a fine blonde. They had known Robert and Julia for some years, but Josephine and Jim were new acquaintances – fairly new.

One day in early spring Lilly had a telegram, 'Coming to see you arrive 4.30

– Bricknell.' He was surprised, but he and his wife got the spare room ready. And at four o'clock Lilly went off to the station. He was a few minutes late, and saw Jim's tall, rather elegant figure stalking down the station path. Jim had been an officer in the regular army, and still spent hours with his tailor. But instead of being a soldier he was a sort of socialist, and a red-hot revolutionary of a very ineffectual sort.

'Good lad!' he exclaimed, as Lilly came up. 'Thought you wouldn't mind.'

'Not at all. Let me carry your bag.'

Jim had a bag and a knapsack.

'I had an inspiration this morning,' said Jim. 'I suddenly saw that if there was a man in England who could save me, it was you.'

'Save you from what?' asked Lilly, rather abashed.

'Eh –?' and Jim stopped grinning at the smaller man. Lilly was somewhat puzzled, but he had a certain belief in himself as a saviour. The two men tramped rather incongruously through the lanes to the cottage.

Tanny was in the doorway as they came up the garden path.

'So nice to see you! Are you all right?' she said.

'A1,' said Jim, grinning. 'Nice of you to have me.'

'Oh, we're awfully pleased.'

Jim dropped his knapsack on the broad sofa.

'I've brought some food,' he said.

'Have you! That's sensible of you. We can't get a great deal here, except just at week-ends,' said Tanny.

Jim fished out a pound of sausages and a pot of fish paste.

'How lovely the sausages,' said Tanny. 'We'll have them for dinner tonight – and we'll have the other for tea now. You'd like a wash?'

But Jim had already opened his bag, taken off his coat, and put on an old one: there before them all in the pretty cottage living-room.

'Thanks,' he said.

Lilly made the tea, and at length all sat down.

'Well, how unexpected this is – and how nice!' said Tanny.

'Jolly – eh?' said Jim. He ate rapidly, stuffing his mouth too full.

'How is everybody?' asked Tanny.

'All right. Julia's gone with Cyril Scott. Can't stand that fellow, can you? What?'

'Yes, I think he's rather nice,' said Tanny. 'What will Robert do?'

'Have a shot at Josephine, apparently.'

'Really? Is he in love with her? I thought so. And she likes him too, doesn't she?' said Tanny.

'Very likely,' said Jim.

'I suppose you're jealous,' laughed Tanny.

'Me!' Jim shook his head. 'Not a bit. Like to see the ball kept rolling.'

'What have you been doing lately?'

'Been staying a few days with my wife.'

'No, really! I can't believe it.'

Jim had a French wife, who had divorced him, and two children. Now he was paying visits to this wife again: purely friendly. Tanny did most of the talking. Jim excited her, with his way of looking in her face and grinning wolfishly, and at the same time asking to be saved.

After tea he wanted to send telegrams, so Lilly took him round to the village post office. Telegrams were a necessary part of his life. He had to be suddenly starting off to keep sudden appointments, or he felt he was a void in the atmosphere. He talked to Lilly about social reform, and so on, Jim's work in town was merely nominal. He spent his time wavering about and going to various meetings, philandering and weeping.

Lilly kept in the back of his mind the saving which James had come to look for. He intended to do his best. After dinner the three sat cosily round the kitchen fire.

'But what do you really think will happen to the world?' Lilly asked Jim, amid much talk.

'What? There's something big coming,' said Jim.

'Where from?'

'Watch Ireland, and watch Japan – they're the two poles of the world,' said Jim.

'I thought Russia and America,' said Lilly.

'Eh? What? Russia and America! They'll depend on Ireland and Japan. I know it. I've had a vision of it. Ireland on this side and Japan on the other – they'll settle it.'

'I don't see how,' said Lilly.

'*I* don't see *how* – but I had a vision of it.'

'What sort of vision?'

'Couldn't describe it.'

'But you don't think much of the Japanese, do you?' asked Lilly.

'Don't I! Don't I!' said Jim. 'What, don't you think they're wonderful?'

'No. I think they're rather unpleasant.'

'I think the salvation of the world lies with them.'

'Funny salvation,' said Lilly. 'I think they're anything but angels.'

'Do you though? Now that's funny. Why?'

'Looking at them even, I knew a Russian doctor who'd been through the Russo–Japanese War, and who had gone a bit cracked. He said he saw the Japs rush a trench. They threw everything away and flung themselves through the Russian fire, and simply dropped in masses. But those that reached the trenches jumped in with bare hands on the Russians and tore their faces apart and bit their throats out – fairly ripped the faces off the bone. It had sent the doctor a bit mad. He said the wounded were awful – their faces torn off and their throats mangled – and dead Japs with flesh between the teeth – God knows if it's true. But that's the impression the Japanese had made on this man – it had affected his mind really.'

Jim watched Lilly, and smiled as if he were pleased.

'No – really –!' he said.

'Anyhow, they're more demon than angel, I believe,' said Lilly.

'Oh no, Rawdon, but you always exaggerate,' said Tanny.

'Maybe,' said Lilly.

'I think Japanese are fascinating – fascinating – so quick, and such *force* in them –'

'Rather! – eh?' said Jim, looking with a quick smile at Tanny.

'I think a Japanese lover would be marvellous,' she laughed riskily.

'I s'd think he would,' said Jim, screwing up his eyes.

'Do you hate the normal British as much as I do?' she asked him.

'Hate them! Hate them!' he said, with an intimate grin.

'Their beastly virtue,' said she. 'And I believe there's nobody more vicious underneath.'

'Nobody!' said Jim.

'But you're British yourself,' said Lilly to Jim.

'No, I'm Irish. Family's Irish – my mother was a Fitzpatrick.'

'Anyhow, you live in England.'

'Because they won't let me go to Ireland.'

The talk drifted. Jim finished up all the beer, and they prepared to go to bed. Jim was a bit tipsy, grinning. He asked for bread and cheese to take upstairs.

'Will you have supper?' said Lilly. He was surprised, because Jim had eaten strangely much at dinner.

'No – where's the loaf?' And he cut himself about half of it. There was no cheese.

'Bread'll do,' said Jim.

'Sit down and eat it. Have cocoa with it,' said Tanny.

'No, I like to have it in my bedroom.'

'You don't eat bread in the night?' said Lilly.

'I do.'

'What a funny thing to do.'

The cottage was in darkness. The Lillys slept soundly. Jim woke up and chewed bread and slept again. In the morning at dawn he rose and went downstairs. Lilly heard him roaming about – heard the woman come in to clean – heard them talking. So he got up to look after his visitor, though it was not seven o'clock, and the woman was busy. But before he went down, he heard Jim come upstairs again.

Mrs Short was busy in the kitchen when Lilly went down.

'The other gentleman have been down, sir,' said Mrs Short. 'He asked me where the bread and butter were, so I said should I cut him a piece. But he wouldn't let me do it. I gave him a knife and he took it for himself, in the pantry.'

'I say, Bricknell,' said Lilly at breakfast-time, 'why do you eat so much bread?'

'I've got to feed up. I've been starved during this damned war.'

'But hunks of bread won't feed you up.'

'Gives the stomach something to work at, and prevents it grinding on the nerves,' said Jim.

'But surely you don't want to keep your stomach always full and heavy.'

'I do, my boy. I do. It needs keeping solid. I'm losing life, if I don't. I tell you I'm losing life. Let me put something inside me.'

'I don't believe bread's any use.'

During breakfast Jim talked about the future of the world.

'I reckon Christ's the finest thing time has ever produced,' said he; 'and will remain it.'

'But you don't want crucifixions *ad infinitum*,' said Lilly.

'What? Why not?'

'Once is enough – and have done.'

'Don't you think love and sacrifice are the finest things in life?' said Jim over his bacon.

'Depends *what* love, and what sacrifice,' said Lilly. 'If I really believe in an Almighty God, I am willing to sacrifice for Him. That is, I'm willing to yield my own personal interest to the bigger creative interest. But it's obvious Almighty God isn't mere Love.'

'I think it is. Love and only love,' said Jim. 'I think the greatest joy is sacrificing one's self to love.'

'To *someone* you love, you mean,' said Tanny.

'No, I don't. I don't mean someone at all. I mean love – love – love. I sacrifice myself to love. I reckon that's the highest man is capable of.'

'But you can't sacrifice yourself to an abstract principle,' said Tanny.

'That's just what you can do. And that's the beauty of it. Who represents the principle doesn't matter. Christ is the principle of love,' said Jim.

'But no!' said Tanny. 'It *must* be more individual. It must be *somebody* you love, not abstract love in itself. How can you sacrifice yourself to an abstraction?'

'Ha, I think Love and your Christ detestable,' said Lilly. 'A sheer ignominy.'

'Finest thing the world has produced,' said Jim.

'No. A thing which sets itself up to be betrayed! No, it's foul. Don't you see it's the Judas principle you really worship. Judas is the real hero. But for Judas the whole show would have been *manqué*.'

'Oh yes,' said Jim. 'Judas was inevitable. I'm not sure that Judas wasn't the greatest of the disciples – and Jesus knew it. I'm not sure Judas wasn't the disciple Jesus loved.'

'Jesus certainly encouraged him in his Judas tricks,' said Tanny.

Jim grinned knowingly at Lilly.

'Then it was a nasty combination. And anything which turns on a Judas climax is a dirty show, to my thinking. I think your Judas is a rotten, dirty worm, just a dirty little self-conscious sentimental twister. And out of all Christianity he is the hero today. When people say Christ they mean Judas. They find him luscious on the palate. And Jesus fostered him –' said Lilly.

'He's a profound figure, is Judas. It's taken two thousand years to begin to understand him,' said Jim, pushing the bread and marmalade into his mouth.

'A traitor is a traitor – no need to understand any further. And a system which rests all its weight on a piece of treachery makes that treachery not only inevitable but sacred. That's why I'm sick of Christianity – at any rate, this modern Christmongery.'

'The finest thing the world has produced, or ever will produce – Christ and Judas –' said Jim.

'Not to me,' said Lilly. 'Foul combination.'

It was a lovely morning in early March. Violets were out, and the first wild anemones. The sun was quite warm. The three were about to take out a picnic lunch. Lilly, however, was suffering from Jim's presence.

'Jolly nice here,' said Jim. 'Mind if I stay till Saturday?'

There was a pause. Lilly felt he was being bullied, almost obscenely bullied. Was he going to agree? Suddenly he looked up at Jim.

'I'd rather you went tomorrow,' he said.

Tanny, who was sitting opposite Jim, dropped her head in confusion.

'What's tomorrow?' said Jim.

'Thursday,' said Lilly.

'Thursday,' repeated Jim. And he looked up and got Lilly's eye. He wanted to say: 'Friday then?'

'Yes, I'd rather you went Thursday,' repeated Lilly.

'But Rawdon –!' broke in Tanny, who was suffering. She stopped, however.

'We can walk across country with you some way if you like,' said Lilly to Jim. It was a sort of compromise.

'Fine!' said Jim. 'We'll do that, then.'

It was lovely sunshine, and they wandered through the woods. Between Jim and Tanny was a sort of growing *rapprochement*, which got on Lilly's nerves.

'What the hell do you take that beastly tone for?' cried Lilly at Tanny, as the three sat under a leafless great beech tree.

'But I'm not personal at all, am I, Mr Bricknell?' said Tanny.

Jim watched Lilly, and grinned pleasedly.

'Why shouldn't you be, anyhow?' he said.

'Yes!' she retorted. 'Why not!'

'Not while I'm here. I loathe the slimy, creepy, personal intimacy:– *"Don't you think, Mr Bricknell, that it's lovely to be able to talk quite simply to somebody? Oh, it's such a relief, after most people –"'* Lilly mimicked his wife's last speech savagely.

'But I *mean* it,' cried Tanny. 'It *is* lovely.'

'Dirty messing,' said Lilly angrily.

Jim watched the dark, irascible little man with amusement.

They rose and went to look for an inn, and beer. Tanny still clung rather stickily to Jim's side.

But it was a lovely day, the first of all the days of spring, with crocuses and wallflowers in the cottage gardens, and white cocks crowing in the quiet hamlet.

When they got back in the afternoon to the cottage, they found a telegram for Jim. He let the Lillys see it – 'Meet you for a walk on your return journey – Lois.' At once Tanny wanted to know all about Lois. Lois was a nice girl, well-to-do middle-class, but also an actress, and she would do anything Jim wanted.

'I must get a wire to her to meet me tomorrow,' he said. 'Where shall I say?'

Lilly produced the map, and they decided on time and station at which Lois, coming out of London, should meet Jim. Then the happy pair could walk along the Thames valley, spending a night perhaps at Marlow, or some such place.

Off went Jim and Lilly once more to the post office. They were quite good friends. Having so inhospitably fixed the hour of departure, Lilly wanted to be nice. Arrived at the post office, they found it shut: half-day closing for the little shop.

'Well,' said Lilly. 'We'll go to the station.'

They proceeded to the station – found the station-master – were conducted down to the signal-box. Lilly naturally hung back from people, but Jim was hob-nob with the stationmaster and the signal-man, quite officer-and-my-men kind of thing. Lilly sat out on the steps of the signal-box, rather ashamed, while the long telegram was shouted over the telephone to the junction town – first the young lady and her address, then the message – 'Meet me X. station 3.40 tomorrow walk back great pleasure Jim.'

Anyhow, that was done. They went home to tea. After tea, as the evening fell, Lilly suggested a little stroll in the woods, while Tanny prepared the dinner. Jim agreed, and they set out. The two men wandered through the trees in the dusk, till they came to a bank on the farther edge of the wood. There they sat down.

And there Lilly said what he had to say. 'As a matter of fact,' he said, 'it's nothing but love and self-sacrifice which makes you feel yourself losing life.'

'You're wrong. Only love brings it back – and wine. If I drink a bottle of burgundy I feel myself restored at the middle – right here! I feel the energy back again. And if I can fall in love – But it's becoming so damned hard –'

'What, to fall in love?' asked Lilly.

'Yes.'

'Then why not leave off trying! What do you want to poke yourself and prod yourself into love for?'

'Because I'm *dead* without it. I'm dead. I'm dying.'

'Only because you force yourself. If you drop working yourself up –'

'I shall die. I only live when I can fall in love. Otherwise I'm dying by inches. Why, man you don't know what it was like. I used to get the most grand feelings – like a great rush of force, or light – a great rush – right here, as I've said, at the solar plexus. And it would come any time – anywhere – no matter where I was. And then I was all right.'

'All right for what? – for making love?'

'Yes, man, I was.'

'And now you aren't? Oh, well, leave love alone, as any twopenny doctor would tell you.'

'No, you're off it there. It's nothing technical. Technically I can make love as much as you like. It's nothing a doctor has any say in. It's what I feel inside me. I feel the life going. I know it's going. I never get those inrushes now, unless I drink a jolly lot, or if I possibly could fall in love.'

'You should leave yourself and your inrushes alone.'

'But you can't. It's a sort of ache.'

'Then you should stiffen your backbone. It's your backbone that matters. You shouldn't want to abandon yourself. You shouldn't want to fling yourself all loose into a woman's lap. You should stand by yourself and learn to be by yourself. Why don't you be more like the Japanese you talk about? Quiet, aloof little devils. They don't bother about being loved. They keep themselves taut in their own selves – there, at the bottom of the spine – the devil's own power they've got there.'

Jim mused a bit.

'Think they have?' he laughed. It seemed comic to him.

'Sure! Look at them. Why can't you gather yourself there?'

'At the tail?'

'Yes. Hold yourself firm there.'

Jim broke into a cackle of a laugh and rose. The two went through the dark woods back to the cottage. Jim staggered and stumbled like a drunken man: or worse, like a man with locomotor ataxy: as if he had no power in his lower limbs.

'Walk there –!' said Lilly, finding him the smoothest bit of the dark path. But Jim stumbled and shambled, in a state of nauseous weak relaxation. However, they reached the cottage: and food and beer – and Tanny, piqued with curiosity to know what the men had been saying privately to each other.

After dinner they sat once more talking round the fire. Lilly sat in a small chair facing the fire, the other two in the armchairs on either side of the hearth.

'How nice it will be for you, walking with Lois towards London tomorrow,' gushed Tanny sentimentally.

'Good God!' said Lilly. 'Why the dickens doesn't he walk by himself, without wanting a woman always there to hold his hand.'

'Don't be so spiteful,' said Tanny. '*You* see that you have a woman always there to hold *your* hand.'

'My hand doesn't need holding,' snapped Lilly.

'Doesn't it! More than most men's! But you're so beastly ungrateful and mannish. Because I hold you safe enough all the time, you like to pretend you're doing it all yourself.'

'All right. Don't drag yourself in,' said Lilly, detesting his wife at that moment. 'Anyhow,' and he turned to Jim, 'it's time you'd done slobbering yourself over a lot of little women, one after the other.'

'Why shouldn't I, if I like it,' said Jim.

'Yes, why not?' said Tanny.

'Because it makes a fool of you. Look at you, stumbling and staggering with no use in your legs. I'd be ashamed if I were you.'

'Would you?' said Jim.

'I would. And it's nothing but your wanting to be loved which does it. A maudlin crying to be loved, which makes your knees all go ricky.'

'Think that's it?' said Jim.

'What else is it. You haven't been here a day, but you must telegraph for some female to be ready to hold your hand the moment you go away. And before she lets go, you'll be wiring for another. *You want to be loved*, you want to be loved – a man of your years. It's disgusting.'

'I don't see it. I believe in love –' said Jim, watching and grinning oddly.

'Bah, love? Messing, that's what it is. It wouldn't matter if it did you no harm. But when you stagger and stumble down a road, out of sheer sloppy relaxation of your will –'

At this point Jim suddenly sprang from his chair at Lilly, and gave him two or three hard blows with his fists upon the front of the body. Then he sat down in his own chair again, saying sheepishly:

'I knew I should have to do it, if he said any more.'

Lilly sat motionless as a statue, his face like paper. One of the blows had caught him rather low, so that he was almost winded, and could not breathe. He sat rigid, paralysed as a winded man is. But he wouldn't let it be seen. With all his will he prevented himself from gasping. Only through his parted lips he drew tiny gasps, controlled, nothing revealed to the other two. He hated them both far too much.

For some minutes there was dead silence, whilst Lilly silently and viciously fought for his breath. Tanny opened her eyes wide in a sort of pleased bewilderment, and Jim turned his face aside and hung his clasped hands between his knees.

'There's a great silence, suddenly!' said Tanny.

'What is there to say?' ejaculated Lilly rapidly, with a spoonful of breath which he managed to compress and control into speech. Then he sat motionless again, concerned with the business of getting back his wind, and not letting the other two see.

Jim jerked in his chair and looked round.

'It isn't that I don't like the man,' he said, in a rather small voice. 'But I knew if he went on I should have to do it.'

To Lilly, rigid and physically preoccupied, there sounded a sort of self-consciousness in Jim's voice, as if the whole thing had been semi-deliberate. He detected the sort of maudlin deliberateness which goes with hysterics, and he was colder, more icy than ever.

Tanny looked at Lilly, puzzled, bewildered, but still rather pleased, as if she demanded an answer. None being forthcoming, she said:

'Of course, you mustn't expect to say all those things without rousing a man.'

Still Lilly did not answer. Jim glanced at him, then looked at Tanny.

'It isn't that I don't like him,' he said slowly. 'I like him better than any man I've never known, I believe.' He clasped his hands and turned aside his face.

'Judas!' flashed through Lilly's mind.

Again Tanny looked for her husband's answer.

'Yes, Rawdon,' she said. 'You can't say the things you do without their having an effect. You really ask for it, you know.'

'It's no matter.' Lilly squeezed the words out coldly. 'He wanted to do it, and he did it.'

A dead silence ensued now. Tanny looked from man to man.

'I could feel it coming to me,' said Jim.

'Of course!' said Tanny. 'Rawdon doesn't know the things he says.' She seemed pleased that he had had to pay for them for once.

It takes a man a long time to get his breath back, after a sharp blow in the wind. Lilly was managing by degrees. The others no doubt attributed his silence to deep or fierce thoughts. It was nothing of the kind: merely a cold struggle to get his wind back, without letting them know he was struggling: and a sheer, stock-stiff hatred of the pair of them.

'I like the man,' said Jim, 'never liked a man more than I like him.' He spoke as if with difficulty.

'The man' stuck safely in Lilly's ears.

'Oh well,' he managed to say. 'It's nothing. I've done my talking and had an answer, for once.'

'Yes, Rawdy, you've had an answer, for once. Usually you don't get an answer, you know – and that's why you go so far – in the things you say. Now you'll know how you make people feel.'

'Quite!' said Lilly.

'*I* don't feel anything. I don't mind what he says,' said Jim.

'Yes, but he ought to know the things he *does* say,' said Tanny. 'He goes on, without considering the person he's talking to. This time it's come back on him. He mustn't say such personal things, if he's not going to risk an answer.'

'I don't mind what he says. I don't mind a bit,' said Jim.

'Nor do I mind,' said Lilly indifferently. 'I say what I feel. You do as you feel. There's an end of it.'

A sheepish sort of silence followed this speech. It was broken by a sudden laugh from Tanny.

'The things that happen to us!' she said, laughing rather shrilly. 'Suddenly, like a thunderbolt, we're all struck into silence!'

'Rum game, eh!' said Jim, grinning.

'Isn't it funny! Isn't life too funny!' She looked again at her husband. 'But Rawdy, you must admit it was your own fault.'

Lilly's stiff face did not change.

'Why *fault*!' he said, looking at her coldly. 'What is there to talk about?'

'Usually there's so much,' she said sarcastically.

A few phrases dribbled out of the silence. In vain Jim tried to get Lilly to thaw, and in vain Tanny gave her digs at her husband. Lilly's stiff, inscrutable face did not change, he was polite and aloof. So they all went to bed.

In the morning, the walk was to take place, as arranged, Lilly and Tanny accompanying Jim to the third station, across country. The morning was lovely, the country beautiful. Lilly like the countryside and enjoyed the walk. But a hardness inside himself never relaxed. Jim talked a little again about the future of the world, and a higher state of Christlikeness in man. But Lilly only laughed. Then Tanny managed to get ahead with Jim, sticking to his side and talking sympathetic personalities. But Lilly, feeling it from afar, ran after them and caught them up. They were silent.

'What was the interesting topic?' he said cuttingly.

'Nothing at all!' said Tanny, nettled. 'Why must you interfere?'

'Because I intend to,' said Lilly.

And the two fell apart, as if severed with a knife. Jim walked rather sheepishly, as if cut out.

So they came at last past the canals to the wayside station: and at last Jim's train came. They all said good-bye. Jim and Tanny were both waiting for Lilly to show some sign of reconciliation. But none came. He was cheerful and aloof.

'Good-bye,' he said to Jim. 'Hope Lois will be there all right. Third station on. Good-bye! Good-bye!'

'You'll come to Rackham?' said Jim, leaning out of the train.

'We should love to,' called Tanny, after the receding train.

'All right,' said Lilly non-committal.

But he and his wife never saw Jim again. Lilly never intended to see him: a devil sat in the little man's breast.

'You shouldn't try to make a little Jesus of yourself, coming so near to people, wanting to help them,' was Tanny's last word.

9

LOW-WATER MARK

Tanny went away to Norway to visit her people, for the first time for three years. Lilly did not go: he did not want to. He came to London and settled in a room over Covent Garden market. The room was high up, a fair size, and stood at the corner of one of the streets and the market itself, looking down on the stalls and the carts and the arcade. Lilly would climb out of the window and sit for hours watching the behaviour of the great draught-horses which brought the mountains of boxes and vegetables. Funny half-human creatures they seemed, so massive and fleshy, yet so Cockney. There was one which could not bear donkeys, and which used to stretch out its great teeth like some massive serpent after every poor diminutive ass that came with a coster's barrow. Another great horse could not endure standing. It would shake itself and give little starts, and back into the heaps of carrots and broccoli, whilst the driver went into a frenzy of rage.

There was always something to watch. One minute it was two great loads of empty crates, which in passing had got entangled, and reeled, leaning to fall disastrously. Then the drivers cursed and swore and dismounted and stared at their jeopardized loads: till a thin fellow was persuaded to scramble up the airy mountains of cages, like a monkey. And he actually managed to put them to rights. Great sigh of relief when the vans rocked out of the market.

Again there was a particular page-boy in buttons, with a round and perky behind, who nimbly carried a tea-tray from somewhere to somewhere, under the arches beside the market. The great brawny porters would tease him, and he would stop to give them cheek. One afternoon a giant lunged after him: the boy darted gracefully among the heaps of vegetables, still bearing aloft his tea-tray, like some young blue-buttoned acolyte fleeing before a false god. The giant rolled after him – when alas, the acolyte of the tea-tray slipped among the vegetables, and down came the tray. Then tears, and a roar of unfeeling mirth from the giants. Lilly felt they were going to make it up to him.

Another afternoon a young swell sauntered persistently among the vegetables, and Lilly, seated in his high little balcony, wondered why. But at last, a taxi, and a very expensive female, in a sort of silver brocade gown and a great fur shawl and ospreys in her bonnet! Evidently an assignation. Yet what could be more conspicuous than this elegant pair, picking their way through the cabbage-leaves?

And then, one cold grey afternoon in early April, a man in a black overcoat and a bowler hat, walking uncertainly. Lilly had risen and was just retiring out of the chill, damp air. For some reason he lingered to watch the figure. The man was walking east. He stepped rather insecurely off the pavement, and wavered across the setts between the wheels of the standing vans. And suddenly he went down. Lilly could not see him on the floor, but he saw some vanmen go forward, and he saw one of them pick up the man's hat.

'I'd better go down,' said Lilly to himself.

So he began running down the four long flights of stone stairs, past the many doors of the multifarious business premises, and out into the market. A little crowd had gathered, and a large policeman was just rowing into the centre of the interest. Lilly, always a hoverer on the edge of public commotions, hung now hesitating on the outskirts of the crowd.

'What is it?' he said, to a rather sniffy messenger-boy.

'Drunk,' said the messenger boy: except that, in unblushing Cockney, he pronounced it: 'Drank!'

Lilly hung further back on the edge of the little crowd.

'Come on here. Where d'you want to go?' he heard the hearty tones of the policeman.

'I'm all right. I'm all right,' came the testy drunken answer.

'All right, are yer! All right, and *then* some. Come on, get on your pins.'

'I'm all right! I'm all right.'

The voice made Lilly peer between the people. And sitting on the granite setts, being hauled up by a burly policeman, he saw our acquaintance Aaron, very pale in the face and a little dishevelled.

'Like me to tuck the sheets round you, shouldn't you! Fancy yourself snug in bed, don't you. You won't believe you're right in the way of traffic, will you now, in Covent Garden Market. Come on, we'll see to you.' And the policeman hoisted the bitter and unwilling Aaron.

Lilly was quickly at the centre of the affair, unobtrusive like a shadow, different from the other people.

'Help him up to my room, will you?' he said to the constable. 'Friend of mine.'

The large constable looked down on the bare-headed, wispy, unobtrusive Lilly with good-humoured suspicion and incredulity. Lilly could not have borne it if the policeman had uttered any of this Cockney suspicion, so he watched him. There was a great gulf between the public official and the odd, quiet little individual – yet Lilly had his way.

'Which room?' said the policeman, dubious.

Lilly pointed quickly round. Then he said to Aaron:

'Were you coming to see me, Sisson? You'll come in, won't you?'

Aaron nodded rather stupidly and testily. His eyes looked angry. Somebody stuck his hat on his head for him, and made him look a fool. Lilly took it off again, and carried it for him. He turned, and the crowd eased. He watched Aaron sharply, and saw that it was with difficulty he could walk. So he caught him by the arm on the other side from the policeman, and they crossed the road to the pavement.

'Not so much of this sort of thing these days,' said the policeman.

'Not so much opportunity,' said Lilly.

'More than there was, though. Coming back to the old days, like. Working round, bit by bit.'

They had arrived at the stairs. Aaron stumbled up.

'Steady now! Steady does it!' said the policeman, steering his charge. There was a curious breach of distance between Lilly and the constable.

At last Lilly opened his own door. The room was pleasant. The fire burned warm, the piano stood open, the sofa was untidy with cushions and papers, books and papers covered the big writing-desk. Beyond the screen made by the book-shelves and the piano were two beds, with washstand by one of the large windows, the one through which Lilly had climbed.

The policeman looked round curiously.

'More cosy here than in the lock-up, sir!' he said.

Lilly laughed. He was hastily clearing the sofa.

'Sit on the sofa, Sisson,' he said.

The policeman lowered his charge, with a:

'Right we are, then!'

Lilly felt in his pocket, and gave the policeman half a crown. But he was watching Aaron, who sat stupidly on the sofa, very pale and semi-conscious.

'Do you feel ill, Sisson?' he said sharply.

Aaron looked back at him with heavy eyes, and shook his head slightly.

'I believe you are,' said Lilly, taking his hand.

'Might be a bit o' this flu, you know,' said the policeman.

'Yes,' said Lilly. 'Where is there a doctor?' he added, on reflection.

'The nearest?' said the policeman. And he told him. 'Leave a message for you, sir?'

Lilly wrote his address on a card, then changed his mind.

'No, I'll run round myself if necessary,' he said.

And the policeman departed.

'You'll go to bed, won't you?' said Lilly to Aaron, when the door was shut. Aaron shook his head sulkily.

'I would if I were you. You can stay here till you're all right. I'm alone, so it doesn't matter.'

But Aaron had relapsed into semi-consciousness. Lilly put the big kettle on the gas stove, and the little kettle on the fire. Then he hovered in front of the stupefied man. He felt uneasy. Again he took Aaron's hand and felt the pulse.

'I'm sure you aren't well. You must go to bed,' he said. And he kneeled and unfastened his visitor's boots. Meanwhile the kettle began to boil: he put a hot-water-bottle into the bed.

'Let us get your overcoat off,' he said to the stupefied man. 'Come along.' And with coaxing and pulling and pushing he got off the overcoat and coat and waistcoat.

At last Aaron was undressed and in bed. Lilly brought him tea. With a dim kind of obedience he took the cup and would drink. He looked at Lilly with heavy eyes.

'I gave in, I gave in to her, else I should ha' been all right,' he said.

'To whom?' said Lilly.

'I gave in to her – and afterwards I cried, thinking of Lottie and the children. I felt my heart break, you know. And that's what did it. I should have been all right if I hadn't given in to her –'

'To whom?' said Lilly.

'Josephine. I felt, the minute I was loving her, I'd done myself. And I had. Everything came back on me. If I hadn't given in to her, I should ha' kept all right.'

'Don't bother now. Get warm and still –'

'I felt it – I felt it go, inside me, the minute I gave in to her. It's perhaps killed me.'

'No, not it. Never mind, be still. Be still, and you'll be all right in the morning.'

'It's my own fault, for giving in to her. If I'd kept myself back, my liver wouldn't have broken inside me, and I shouldn't have been sick. And I knew –'

'Never mind now. Have you drunk your tea? Lie down. Lie down, and go to sleep.'

Lilly pushed Aaron down in the bed, and covered him over. Then he thrust his hands under the bedclothes and felt his feet – still cold. He arranged the water-bottle. Then he put another cover on the bed.

Aaron lay still, rather grey and peaked-looking, in a stillness that was not healthy. For some time Lilly went about stealthily, glancing at his patient from time to time. Then he sat down to read.

He was roused after a time by a moaning of troubled breathing and a fretful stirring in the bed. He went across. Aaron's eyes were open, and dark-looking.

'Have a little hot milk,' said Lilly.

Aaron shook his head faintly, not noticing.

'A little Bovril?'

The same faint shake.

Then Lilly wrote a note for the doctor, went into the office on the same landing, and got a clerk, who would be leaving in a few minutes, to call with the note. When he came back he found Aaron still watching.

'Are you here by yourself?' asked the sick man.

'Yes. My wife's gone to Norway.'

'For good?'

'No,' laughed Lilly. 'For a couple of months or so. She'll come back here: unless she joins me in Switzerland or somewhere.'

Aaron was still for a while.

'You've not gone with her,' he said at length.

'To see her people? No, I don't think they want me very badly – and I don't want very badly to go. Why should I? It's better for married people to be separated sometimes.'

'Ay –! said Aaron, watching the older man with fever-darkened eyes.

'I hate married people who are two in one – stuck together like two jujube lozenges,' said Lilly.

'Me an' all. I hate 'em myself,' said Aaron.

'Everybody ought to stand by themselves, in the first place – men and women as well. They can come together, in the second place, if they like. But nothing is any good unless each one stands alone, intrinsically.'

'I'm with you there,' said Aaron. 'If I'd kep' myself to myself I shouldn't be bad now. Though I'm not very bad. I s'll be all right in the morning. But I did myself in when I went with another woman. I felt myself go – as if the bile broke inside me, and I was sick.'

'Josephine seduced you?' laughed Lilly.

'Ay, right enough,' replied Aaron grimly. 'She won't be coming here, will she?'

'Not unless I ask her.'

'You won't ask her, though –?'

'No, not if you don't want her.'

'I don't.'

The fever made Aaron naïve and communicative, unlike himself. And he knew he was being unlike himself, he knew that he was not in proper control of himself, so he was unhappy, uneasy.

'I'll stop here the night then, if you don't mind,' he said.

'You'll have to,' said Lilly. 'I've sent for the doctor. I believe you've got the flu.'

'Think I have?' said Aaron frightened.

'Don't be scared,' laughed Lilly.

There was a long pause. Lilly stood at the window looking at the darkening market, beneath the street-lamps.

'I s'll have to go to the hospital, if I have,' came Aaron's voice.

'No, if it's only going to be a week or a fortnight's business, you can stop here. I've nothing to do,' said Lilly.

'There's no occasion for you to saddle yourself with me,' said Aaron dejectedly.

'You can go to your hospital if you like – or back to your lodgings – if you wish to,' said Lilly. 'You can make up your mind when you see how you are in the morning.'

'No use going back to my lodgings,' said Aaron.

'I'll send a telegram to your wife if you like,' said Lilly.

Aaron was silent, dead silent, for some time.

'Nay,' he said at length, in a decided voice. 'Not if I die for it.'

Lilly remained still, and the other man lapsed into a sort of semi-sleep, motionless and abandoned. The darkness had fallen over London, and away below the lamps were white. Lilly lit the green-shaded reading-lamp over the desk. Then he stood and looked at Aaron, who lay still, looking sick. Rather beautiful the bones of the countenance: but the skull too small for such a heavy jaw, and rather coarse mouth. Aaron half opened his eyes, and writhed feverishly, as if his limbs could not be in the right place. Lilly mended the fire, and sat down to write. Then he got up and went downstairs to unfasten the street door, so that the doctor could walk up. The business people had gone from their various holes, all the lower part of the tall house was in darkness.

Lilly waited and waited. He boiled an egg and made himself toast. Aaron said he might eat the same. Lilly cooked another egg and took it to the sick man. Aaron looked at it and pushed it away with nausea. He would have some tea. So Lilly gave him tea.

'Not much fun for you, doing this for somebody who is nothing to you,' said Aaron.

'I shouldn't if you were unsympathetic to me,' said Lilly. 'As it is, it's happened so, and so we'll let be.'

'What time is it?'

'Nearly eight o'clock.'

'Oh my Lord, the opera.'

And Aaron got half out of bed. But as he sat on the bedside he knew he could not safely get to his feet. He remained a picture of dejection.

'Perhaps we ought to let them know,' said Lilly.

But Aaron, blank with stupid misery, sat huddled there on the bedside without answering.

'I'll run round with a note,' said Lilly. 'I suppose others have had flu, besides you. Lie down!'

But Aaron stupidly and dejectedly sat huddled on the side of the bed, wearing old flannel pyjamas of Lilly's, rather small for him. He felt too sick to move.

'Lie down! Lie down!' said Lilly. 'And keep still while I'm gone. I shan't be more than ten minutes.'

'I don't care if I die,' said Aaron.

Lilly laughed.

'You're a long way from dying,' said he, 'or you wouldn't say it.'

But Aaron only looked up at him with queer, far-off, haggard eyes, something like a criminal who is just being executed.

'Lie down!' said Lilly, pushing him gently into the bed. 'You won't improve yourself sitting there, anyhow.'

Aaron lay down, turned away, and was quite still. Lilly quietly left the room on his errand.

The doctor did not come until ten o'clock: and worn out with work when he did come.

'Isn't there a lift on this establishment?' he said, as he groped his way up the stone stairs. Lilly had heard him, and run down to meet him.

The doctor poked the thermometer under Aaron's tongue and felt the pulse. Then he asked a few questions: listened to the heart and breathing.

'Yes, it's the flu,' he said curtly. 'Nothing to do but to keep warm in bed and not move, and take plenty of milk and liquid nourishment. I'll come round in the morning and give you an injection. Lungs are all right so far.'

'How long shall I have to be in bed?' said Aaron.

'Oh – depends. A week at least.'

Aaron watched him sullenly – and hated him. Lilly laughed to himself. The sick man was like a dog that is ill but which growls from a deep corner, and will bite if you put your hand in. He was in a state of black depression.

Lilly settled him down for the night, and himself went to bed. Aaron squirmed with heavy, pained limbs, the night through, and slept and had bad dreams. Lilly got up to give him drinks. The din in the market was terrific before dawn, and Aaron suffered bitterly.

In the morning he was worse. The doctor gave him injections against pneumonia.

'You wouldn't like me to wire to your wife?' said Lilly.

'No,' said Aaron abruptly. 'You can send me to the hospital. I'm nothing but a piece of carrion.'

'Carrion!' said Lilly. 'Why?'

'I know it. I feel it.'

'Oh, that's only the sort of nauseated feeling you get with flu.'

'I'm only fit to be thrown underground, and made an end of. I can't stand myself –'

He had a ghastly, grey look of self-repulsion.

'It's the germ that makes you feel like that,' said Lilly. 'It poisons the system for a time. But you'll work it off.'

At evening he was no better, the fever was still high. Yet there were no complications – except that the heart was irregular.

'The one thing I wonder,' said Lilly, 'is whether you hadn't better be moved out of the noise of the market. It's fearful for you in the early morning.'

'It makes no difference to me,' said Aaron.

The next day he was a little worse, if anything. The doctor knew there was nothing to be done. At evening he gave the patient a calomel pill. It was rather strong, and Aaron had a bad time. His burning, parched, poisoned inside was twisted and torn. Meanwhile carts banged, porters shouted, all the hell of the market went on outside, away down on the cobble setts. But this time the two men did not hear.

'You'll feel better now,' said Lilly, after the operation.

'It's done me harm,' cried Aaron fretfully. 'Send me to the hospital, or you'll repent it. Get rid of me in time.'

'Nay,' said Lilly. 'You get better. Damn it, you're only one among a million.'

Again over Aaron's face went the ghastly grimace of self-repulsion.

'My soul's gone rotten,' he said.

'No,' said Lilly. 'Only toxin in the blood.'

Next day the patient seemed worse, and the heart more irregular. He rested badly. So far, Lilly had got a fair night's rest. Now Aaron was not sleeping, and he seemed to struggle in the bed.

'Keep your courage up, man,' said the doctor sharply. 'You give way.'

Aaron looked at him blackly, and did not answer.

In the night Lilly was up time after time. Aaron would slip down on his back, and go semi-conscious. And then he would awake, as if drowning, struggling to move, mentally shouting aloud, yet making no sound for some moments, mentally shouting in frenzy, but unable to stir or make a sound. When at last he got some sort of physical control he cried: 'Lift me up! Lift me up!'

Lilly hurried and lifted him up, and he sat panting with a sobbing motion, his eyes gloomy and terrified, more than ever like a criminal who is just being executed. He drank brandy, and was laid down on his side.

'Don't let me lie on my back,' he said, terrified.

'No, I won't,' said Lilly.

Aaron frowned curiously on his nurse.

'Mind you don't let me,' he said, exacting and really terrified.

'No, I won't let you.'

And now Lilly was continually crossing over and pulling Aaron on to his side, whenever he found him slipped down on his back.

In the morning the doctor was puzzled. Probably it was the toxin in the blood which poisoned the heart. There was no pneumonia. And yet Aaron was clearly growing worse. The doctor agreed to send in a nurse for the coming night.

'What's the matter with you, man!' he said sharply to his patient. 'You give way! You give way! Can't you pull yourself together?'

But Aaron only became more gloomily withheld, retracting from life. And

Lilly began to be really troubled. He got a friend to sit with the pateint in the afternoon, whilst he himself went out and arranged to sleep in Aaron's room at his lodging.

The next morning, when he came in, he found the patient lying as ever, in a sort of heap in the bed. Nurse had had to lift him up and hold him up again. And now Aaron lay in a sort of semi-stupor of fear, frustrated anger, misery and self-repulsion: a sort of interlocked depression.

The doctor frowned when he came. He talked with the nurse, and wrote another prescription. Then he drew Lilly away to the door.

'What's the matter with the fellow?' he said. 'Can't you rouse his spirit? He seems to be sulking himself out of life. He'll drop out quite suddenly, you know, if he goes on like this. Can't you rouse him up?'

'I think it depresses him partly that his bowels won't work. It frightens him. He's never been ill in his life before,' said Lilly.

'His bowels won't work if he lets all his spirit go, like an animal dying of the sulks,' said the doctor impatiently. 'He might go off quite suddenly – dead before you can turn round –'

Lilly was properly troubled. Yet he did not quite know what to do. It was early afternoon, and the sun was shining into the room. There were daffodils and anemones in a jar, and freezias and violets. Down below in the market were two stalls of golden and blue flowers, gay.

'The flowers are lovely in the spring sunshine,' said Lilly. 'I wish I were in the country, don't you? As soon as you are better we'll go. It's been a terrible cold, wet spring. But now it's going to be nice. Do you like being in the country?'

'Yes,' said Aaron.

He was thinking of his garden. He loved it. Never in his life had he been away from a garden before.

'Make haste and get better, and we'll go.'

'Where?' said Aaron.

'Hampshire. Or Berkshire. Or perhaps you'd like to go home? Would you?'

Aaron lay still, and did not answer.

'Perhaps you want to, and you don't want to,' said Lilly. 'You can please yourself, anyhow.'

There was no getting anything definite out of the sick man – his soul seemed stuck, as if it would not move.

Suddenly Lilly rose and went to the dressing-table.

'I'm going to rub you with oil,' he said. 'I'm going to rub you as mothers do their babies whose bowels don't work.'

Aaron frowned slightly as he glanced at the dark, self-possessed face of the little man.

'What's the good of that?' he said irritably. 'I'd rather be left alone.'

'Then you won't be.'

Quickly he uncovered the blond lower body of his patient, and began to rub the abdomen with oil, using a slow, rhythmic, circulating motion, a sort of massage. For a long time he rubbed finely and steadily, then went over the whole of the lower body, mindless, as if in a sort of incantation. He rubbed every speck of the man's lower body – the abdomen, the buttocks, the thighs and knees, down to his feet, rubbed it all warm and glowing with camphorated oil, every bit of it, chafing the toes swiftly, till he was almost exhausted. Then Aaron was covered up again, and Lilly sat down in fatigue to look at his patient.

He saw a change. The spark had come back into the sick eyes, and the faint trace of a smile, faintly luminous, into the face. Aaron was regaining himself. But Lilly said nothing. He watched his patient fall into a proper sleep.

And he sat and watched him sleep. And he thought to himself, 'I wonder why I do it. I wonder why I bother with him. Jim ought to have taught me my lesson. As soon as this man's really better he'll punch me in the wind, metaphorically if not actually, for having interfered with him. And Tanny would say he was quite right to do it. She says I want power over them. What if I do? They don't care how much power the mob has over them, the nation, Lloyd George and Northcliffe and the police and money. They'll yield themselves up to that sort of power quickly enough, and immolate themselves *pro bono publico* by the million. And what's the *bonum publicum* but a mob power. Why can't they submit to a bit of healthy individual authority. The fool would die, without me; just as that fool Jim will die in hysterics one day. Why does he last so long?

'Tanny's the same. She does nothing really but resist me: my authority, or my influence, or just *me*. At the bottom of her heart she just blindly and persistently opposes me. God knows what it is she opposes: just me myself. She thinks I want her to submit to me. So I do, in a measure natural to our two selves. Somewhere, she ought to submit to me. But they all prefer to kick against the pricks. Not that *they* get many pricks. I get them. Damn them all, why don't I leave them alone. They only grin and feel triumphant when they've insulted one and punched one in the wind.

'This Aaron will do just the same. I like him, and he ought to like me. And he'll be another Jim: he *will* like me, if he can knock the wind out of me. A lot of little Stavrogins coming up to whisper affectionately, and biting one's ear.

'But anyhow I can soon see the last of this chap: and him the last of all the rest. I'll be damned for ever if I see their Jims and Roberts and Julias and Scotts any more. Let them dance round their insipid hell-broth. Thin tack it is.

'There's a whole world besides this little gang of wastrels. Except, dear God, that they've exterminated all the people worth knowing. I can't do with folk who teem by the billion, like the Chinese and Japs and Orientals altogether. Only vermin teem by the billion. Higher types breed slower. I would have loved the Aztecs and the Red Indians. I *know* they hold the element in life which I am looking for – they had living pride. Not like the flea-bitten Asiatics. Even niggers are better than Asiatics, though they are wallowers. The American races – and the South Sea Islanders – the Marquesans, the Maori blood. That was the true blood. It wasn't frightened. All the rest are craven – Europeans, Asiatics, Africans – everyone at his own individual quick craven and cringing: only conceited in the mass, the mob. How I hate them: the mass-bullies, the individual Judases.

'Well, if one will be a Jesus he must expect his Judas. That's why Abraham Lincoln gets shot. A Jesus makes a Judas inevitable. A man should remain himself, not try to spread himself over humanity. He should pivot himself on his own pride.

'I suppose really I ought to have packed this Aaron off to the hospital. Instead of which here I am rubbing him with oil to rub the life into him. And I *know* he'll bite me, like a warmed snake, the moment he recovers. And Tanny will say "Quite right too," I shouldn't have been so intimate. No, I should have left it to mechanical doctors and nurses.

'So I should. Everything to its own. And Aaron belongs to this little system, and Jim is waiting to be psycho-analysed, and Tanny is waiting for her own glorification.

'All right, Aaron. Last time I break my bread for anybody, this is. So get better, my flautist, so that I can go away.

'It was easy for the Red Indians and the others to take their hook into death. They might have stayed a bit longer to help one to defy the white masses.

'I'll make some tea –'

Lilly rose softly and went across to the fire. He had to cross a landing to a sort of little lavatory, with a sink and a tap, for water. The clerks peeped out at him from an adjoining office and nodded. He nodded and disappeared from their sight as quickly as possible with his kettle. His dark eyes were quick, his dark hair was untidy, there was something silent and withheld about him. People could never approach him quite ordinarily.

He put on the kettle and quietly set cups and plates on a tray. The room was clean and cosy and pleasant. He did the cleaning himself, and was as efficient and unobtrusive a housewife as any woman. While the kettle boiled, he sat darning the socks which he had taken off Aaron's feet when the flautist arrived, and which he had washed. He preferred that no outsider should see him doing these things. Yet he preferred to do them himself, so that he should be independent of outside aid.

His face was dark and hollow, he seemed frail, sitting there in the London afternoon darning the black woollen socks. His full brow was knitted slightly, there was a tension. At the same time there was an indomitable stillness about him, as it were in the atmosphere about him. His hands, though small, were not very thin. He bit off the wool as he finished his darn.

As he was making the tea he saw Aaron rouse up in bed.

'I've been to sleep. I feel better,' said the patient, turning round to look what the other man was doing. And the sight of water steaming in a jet into the teapot seemed attractive.'

'Yes,' said Lilly. 'You've slept for a good two hours.'

'I believe I have,' said Aaron.

'Would you like a little tea?'

'Ay – and a bit of toast.'

'You're not supposed to have solid food. Let me take your temperature.'

The temperature was down to a hundred, and Lilly, in spite of the doctor, gave Aaron a piece of toast with his tea, enjoining him not to mention it to the nurse.

In the evening the two men talked.

'You do everything for yourself, then?' said Aaron.

'Yes, I prefer it.'

'You like living all alone?'

'I don't know about that. I never have lived alone. Tanny and I have been very much alone in various countries: but that's two, not one.'

'You miss her then?'

'Yes, of course. I missed her horribly in the cottage, when she'd first gone. I felt my heart was broken. But here, where we've never been together, I don't notice it so much.'

'She'll come back,' said Aaron.

'Yes, she'll come back. But I'd rather meet her abroad than here – and get on a different footing.'

'Why?'

'Oh, I don't know. There's something wrong with marriage altogether, I think. *Égoïsme à deux –*'

'What's that mean?'

'*Égoïsme à deux?* Two people, one egoism. Marriage is a self-conscious egoistic state, it seems to me.'

'You've got no children?' said Aaron.

'No. Tanny wants children badly. I don't. I'm thankful we have none.'

'Why?'

'I can't quite say. I think of them as a burden. Besides, there *are* such millions and billions of children in the world. And we know well enough what sort of millions and billions of people they'll grow up into. I don't want to add my quota to the mass – It's against my instinct –'

'Ay –!' laughed Aaron, with a curt acquiescence.

'Tanny's furious. But then, when a woman has got children, she thinks the world wags only for them and her. Nothing else. The whole world wags for the sake of the children – and their sacred mother.'

'Ay, that's *damned* true,' said Aaron.

'And myself I'm sick of the children stunt. Children are all right, so long as you just take them for what they are; young immature things like kittens and half-grown dogs, nuisances, sometimes very charming. But I'll be hanged if I can see anything high and holy about children. I should be sorry to, it would be so bad for the children. Young brats, tiresome and amusing in turns.'

'When they don't give themselves airs,' said Aaron.

'Yes, indeed. Which they do half their time. Sacred children, and sacred motherhood, I'm absolutely fed stiff by it. That's why I'm thankful I have no children. Tanny can't come it over me there.'

'It's a fact. When a woman's got her children, by God, she's a bitch in the manger. You can starve while she sits on the hay. It's useful to keep her pups warm.'

'Yes.'

'Why, you know –' Aaron turned excitedly in the bed, 'they look on a man as if he was nothing but an instrument to get and rear children. If you have anything to do with a woman, she thinks it's because you want to get children by her. And I'm damned if it is. I want my own pleasure, or nothing: and children be damned.'

'Ah, women! – *they* must be loved at any price!' said Lilly. 'And if you just don't want to love them – and tell them so – what a crime!'

'A crime!' said Aaron. 'They make a criminal of you. Them and their children be cursed. Is my life given me for nothing but to get children, and work for a woman? See them all in hell first – they'd better die while they're children, if childhood's all that's important.'

'I quite agree,' said Lilly. 'If childhood is more important than manhood, then why live to be a man at all? Why not remain an infant?'

'Be damned and blasted to women and all their importances,' cried Aaron. 'They want to get you under, and children is their chief weapon.'

'Men have got to stand up to the fact that manhood is more than childhood – and then force women to admit it,' said Lilly. 'But the rotten whiners, they're all grovelling before a baby's napkin and a woman's petticoat.'

'It's a fact,' said Aaron. But he glanced at Lilly oddly, as if suspiciously. And Lilly caught the look. But he continued:

'And if they think you try to stand on your legs and walk with the feet of manhood, why, there isn't a blooming father and lover among them but will do his best to get you down and suffocate you – either with a baby's napkin or a woman's petticoat.'

Lilly's lips were curling, he was dark and bitter.

'Ay, it is like that,' said Aaron, rather subduedly.

'The man's spirit has gone out of the world. Men can't move an inch unless they can grovel humbly at the end of the journey.'

'No,' said Aaron, watching with keen, half-amused eyes.

'That's why marriage wants readjusting – or extending – to get men on to their own legs once more, and to give them the adventure again. But men won't stick together and fight for it. Because once a woman has climbed up with her children, she'll find plenty of grovellers ready to support her and suffocate any defiant spirit. And women will sacrifice eleven men, fathers, husbands, brothers and lovers, for one baby – or for her own female self-conceit.'

'She will that,' said Aaron.

'And can you find two men to stick together without feeling criminal, and without cringing, and without betraying one another? You can't. One is sure to go fawning round some female, then they both enjoy giving each other away, and doing a new grovel before a woman again.'

'Ay,' said Aaron.

After which Lilly was silent.

10

THE WAR AGAIN

'One is a fool,' said Lilly, 'to be lachrymose. The thing to do is to get a move on.'

Aaron looked up with a glimpse of a smile. The two men were sitting before the fire at the end of a cold, wet April day: Aaron convalescent, somewhat chastened in appearance.

'Ay,' he said rather sourly. 'A move back to Guilford Street.'

'Oh, I meant to tell you,' said Lilly. 'I was reading an old Baden history. They made a law in 1528 – not a law, but a regulation – that if a man forsakes his wife and children, as now so often happens, the said wife and children are at once to be despatched after him. I thought that would please you. Does it?'

'Yes,' said Aaron briefly.

'They would have arrived the next day, like a forwarded letter.'

'I should have had to get a considerable move on at that rate,' grinned Aaron.

'Oh no. You might quite like them here.' But Lilly saw the white frown of determined revulsion on the convalescent's face.

'Wouldn't you?' he asked.

Aaron shook his head.

'No,' he said. And it was obvious he objected to the topic. 'What are you going to do about your move on?'

'Me!' said Lilly. 'I'm going to sail away next week – or steam dirtily away on a tramp called the *Maud Allen Wing*.'

'Where to?'

'Malta.'

'Where from?'

'London Dock. I fixed up my passage this morning for ten pounds. I am cook's assistant, signed on.'

Aaron looked at him with a little admiration.

'You can take a sudden jump, can you?' he said.

'The difficulty is to refrain from jumping: overboard or anywhere.'

Aaron smoked his pipe slowly.

'And what good will Malta do you?' he asked, envious.

'Heaven knows. I shall cross to Syracuse and move up Italy.'

'Sounds as if you were a millionaire.'

'I've got thirty-five pounds in all the world. But something will come along.'

'I've got more than that,' said Aaron.

'Good for you,' replied Lilly.

He rose and went to the cupboard, taking out a bowl and a basket of potatoes. He sat down again, paring the potatoes. His busy activity annoyed Aaron.

'But what's the good of going to Malta? Shall *you* be any different in yourself, in another place? You'll be the same there as you are here.'

'How am I here?'

'Why, you're all the time grinding yourself against something inside you. You're never free. You're never content. You never stop chafing.'

Lilly dipped his potato into the water and cut out the eyes carefully. Then he cut it in two and dropped it in the clean water of the second bowl. He had not expected this criticism.

'Perhaps I don't,' said he.

'Then what's the use of going somewhere else. You won't change yourself.'

'I may in the end,' said Lilly.

'You'll be yourself, whether it's Malta or London,' said Aaron.

'There's a doom for me,' laughed Lilly. The water on the fire was boiling. He rose and threw in salt, then dropped in the potatoes with little plops. 'But there are lots of me's. I'm not only just one proposition. A new place brings out a new thing in a man. Otherwise you'd have stayed in your old place with your family.'

'The man in the middle of you doesn't change,' said Aaron.

'Do you find it so?' said Lilly.

'Ay. Every time.'

'Then, what's to be done?'

'Nothing, as far as I can see. You get as much amusement out of life as possible, and there's the end of it.'

'All right then, I'll get the amusement.'

'Ay, all right then,' said Aaron. 'But there isn't anything wonderful about it. You talk as if you were doing something special. You aren't. You're no more than a man who drops into a pub for a drink to liven himself up a bit. Only you give it a lot of names, and make out as if you were looking for the philosopher's stone, or something like that. When you're only killing time like the rest of folks, before time kills you.'

Lilly did not answer. It was not yet seven o'clock, but the sky was dark. Aaron sat in the firelight. Even the saucepan on the fire was silent. Darkness, silence, the firelight in the upper room, and the two men together.

'It isn't quite true,' said Lilly, leaning on the mantelpiece and staring down into the fire.

'Where isn't it? You talk, and you make a man believe you've got something he hasn't got. But where is it, when it comes to? What have you got, more than me or Jim Bricknell? Only a bigger choice of words, it seems to me.'

Lilly was motionless and inscrutable like a shadow.

'Does it, Aaron!' he said in a colourless voice.

'Yes. What else is there to it?' Aaron sounded testy.

'Why,' said Lilly at last, 'there's something. I agree, it's true what you say about me. But there's a bit of something else. There's just a bit of something in me, I think, which *isn't* a man running into a pub for a drink –'

'And what –?'

The question fell into the twilight like a drop of water falling down a deep shaft into a well.

'I think a man may come into possession of his own soul at last – as the Buddhists teach – but without ceasing to love, or even to hate. One loves, one hates – but somewhere beyond it all, one understands, and possesses one's soul in patience and in peace –'

'Yes,' said Aaron slowly, 'while you only stand and talk about it. But when you've got no chance to talk about it – and when you've got to live – you don't possess your soul neither in patience nor in peace, but any devil that likes possesses you and does what it likes with you, while you fridge yourself and fray yourself out like a worn rag.'

'I don't care,' said Lilly. 'I'm learning to possess my soul in patience and in peace, and I know it. And it isn't a negative Nirvana either. And if Tanny possesses her own soul in patience and peace as well – and if in this we understand each other at last – then there we are, together and apart at the same time, and free of each other, and eternally inseparable. I have my Nirvana – and I have it all to myself. But more than that. It coincides with her Nirvana.'

'Ah yes,' said Aaron. 'But I don't understand all that word-splitting.'

'I do, though. You learn to be quite alone and possess your own soul in isolation – and at the same time to be perfectly *with* someone else – that's all I ask.'

'Sort of sit on a mountain-top, back to back with somebody else, like a couple of idols.'

'No – because it isn't a case of sitting – or a case of back to back. It's what you get to after a lot of fighting and a lot of sensual fulfilment. And it never does away with the fighting and with the sensual passion. It flowers on top of them, and it would never flower save on top of them.'

'What wouldn't?'

'The possessing one's own soul – and the being together with someone else in silence, beyond speech.'

'And you've got them?'

'I've got a *bit* of the real quietness inside me.'

'So has a dog on a mat.'

'So I believe too.'

'Or a man in a pub.'

'Which I don't believe.'

'You prefer the dog?'

'Maybe.'

There was silence for a few moments.

'And I'm the man in the pub,' said Aaron.

'You aren't the dog on the mat, anyhow.'

'And you're the idol on the mountain-top, worshipping yourself.'

'You talk to me like a woman, Aaron.'

'How do you talk to *me*, do you think?'

'How do I?'

'Are the potatoes done?'

Lilly turned quickly aside and switched on the electric light. Everything changed. Aaron sat still before the fire, irritated. Lilly went about preparing the supper.

The room was pleasant at night. Two tall dark screens hid the two beds. In front, the piano was littered with music, the desk littered with papers. Lilly went out on to the landing and set the chops to grill on the gas-stove. Hastily he put a small table on the hearth-rug, spread it with a blue-and-white cloth, set plates and glasses. Aaron did not move. It was not his nature to concern himself with domestic matters – and Lilly did it best alone.

The two men had an almost uncanny understanding of one another – like brothers. They came from the same district, from the same class. Each might have been born into the other's circumstance. Like brothers, there was a profound hostility between them. But hostility is not antipathy.

Lilly's skilful housewifery always irritated Aaron: it was so self-sufficient. But most irritating of all was the little man's unconscious assumption of priority. Poor Lilly was actually unaware that he assumed this quiet predominance over others. He mashed the potatoes, he heated the plates, he warmed the red wine, he whisked eggs into the milk pudding, and served his visitor like a housemaid. But none of this detracted from the silent assurance with which he bore himself, and with which he seemed to domineer over his acquaintance.

At last the meal was ready. Lilly drew the curtains, switched off the central light, put the green-shaded electric lamp on the table, and the two men drew up to the meal. It was good food, well cooked and hot. Certainly Lilly's hands were no longer clean: but it was clean dirt, as he said.

Aaron sat in the low arm-chair at table. So his face was below, in the full light. Lilly sat high on a small chair, so that his face was in the green shadow. Aaron was handsome, and always had that peculiar well-dressed look of his type. Lilly was indifferent to his own appearance, and his collar was a rag.

So the two men ate in silence. They had been together alone for a fortnight only: but it was like a small eternity. Aaron was well now – only he suffered from the depression and the sort of fear that follows influenza.

'When are you going?' he asked irritably, looking up at Lilly, whose face hovered in that green shadow above, and worried him.

'One day next week. 'They'll send me a telegram. Not later than Thursday.'

'You're looking forward to going?' The question was half bitter.

'Yes. I want to get a new tune out of myself.'

'Had enough of this?'

'Yes.'

A flush of anger came on Aaron's face.

'You're easily on, and easily off,' he said, rather insulting.

'Am I?' said Lilly. 'What makes you think so?'

'Circumstances,' replied Aaron sourly.

To which there was no answer. The host cleared away the plates and put the pudding on the table. He pushed the bowl to Aaron.

'I suppose I shall never see you again, once you've gone,' said Aaron.

'It's your choice. I will leave you an address.'

After this, the pudding was eaten in silence.

'Besides, Aaron,' said Lilly, drinking his last sip of wine, 'what do you care whether you see me again or not? What do you care whether you see anybody again or not? You want to be amused. And now you're irritated because you think I am not going to amuse you any more: and you don't know who *is* going to amuse you. I admit it's a dilemma. But it's a hedonistic dilemma of the commonest sort.'

'I don't know hedonistic. And supposing I am as you say – are you any different?'

'No, I'm not very different. But I always persuade myself there's a bit of difference. Do you know what Josephine Ford confessed to me? She's had her lovers enough. "There isn't any such thing as love, Lilly," she said. "Men are simply afraid to be alone. That is absolutely all there is in it: fear of being alone."'

'What by that?' said Aaron.

'You agree?'

'Yes, on the whole.'

'So do I – on the whole. And then I asked her what about woman. And then she said with a woman it wasn't fear, it was just boredom. A woman is like a violinist: any fiddle, any instrument rather than empty hands and no tune going.'

'Yes – what I said before: getting as much amusement out of life as possible,' said Aaron.

'You amuse me – and I'll amuse you.'

'Yes – just about that.'

'All right, Aaron,' said Lilly. 'I'm not going to amuse you, or try to amuse you any more.'

'Going to try somebody else: and Malta.'

'Malta, anyhow.'

'Oh, and somebody else – in the next five minutes.'

'Yes – that also.'

'Good-bye and good luck to you.'

'Good-bye and good luck to you, Aaron.'

With which Lilly went aside to wash the dishes. Aaron sat alone under the zone of light, turning over a score of *Pelléas*. Though the noise of London was around them, it was far below, and in the room was a deep silence. Each of the men seemed invested in his own silence.

Aaron suddenly took his flute and began trying little passages from the opera on his knee. He had not played since his illness. The noise came out a little tremulous, but low and sweet. Lilly came forward with a plate and a cloth in his hand.

'Aaron's rod is putting forth again,' he said, smiling.

'What?' said Aaron, looking up.

'I said Aaron's rod is putting forth again.'

'What rod?'

'Your flute, for the moment.'

'It's got to put forth my bread and butter.'

'Is that all the buds it's going to have?'

'What else!'

'Nay – that's for you to show. What flowers do you imagine came out of the rod of Moses's brother?'

'Scarlet runners, I should think, if he'd got to live on them.'

'Scarlet enough, I'll bet.'

Aaron turned unnoticing back to his music. Lilly finished the wiping of the dishes, then took a book and sat on the other side of the table.

'It's all one to you then,' said Aaron suddenly, 'whether we ever see one another again?'

'Not a bit,' said Lilly, looking up over his spectacles. 'I very much wish there might be something that held us together.'

'Then if you wish it, why isn't there?'

'You might wish your flute to put out scarlet-runner flowers at the joints.'

'Ay – I might. And it would be all the same.'

The moment of silence that followed was extraordinary in its hostility.

'Oh, we shall run across one another again some time,' said Aaron.

'Sure,' said Lilly. 'More than that: I'll write you an address that will always find me. And when you write I will answer you.'

He took a bit of paper and scribbled an address. Aaron folded it and put it into his waistcoat pocket. It was an Italian address.

'But how can I live in Italy?' he said. 'You can shift about. I'm tied to a job.'

'You – with your budding rod, your flute – and your charm – you can always do as you like.'

'My what?'

'Your flute and your charm.'

'What charm?'

'Just your own. Don't pretend you don't know you've got it. I don't really like charm myself: too much of a trick about it. But whether or not, you've got it.'

'It's news to me.'

'Not it.'

'Fact, it is.'

'Ha! Somebody will always take a fancy to you. And you can live on that, as well as on anything else.'

'Why do you always speak so despisingly?'

'Why shouldn't I?'

'Have you any right to despise another man?'

'When did it go by rights?'

'No, not with you.'

'You answer me like a woman, Aaron.'

Again there was a space of silence. And again it was Aaron who at last broke it.

'We're in different positions, you and me,' he said.

'How?'

'You can live by your writing – but I've got to have a job.'

'Is that all?' said Lilly.

'Ay. And plenty. You've got the advantage of me.'

'Quite,' said Lilly. 'But why? I was a dirty-nosed little boy when you were a clean-nosed little boy. And I always had more patches on my breeches than you: neat patches too, my poor mother! So what's the good of talking about advantages. You had the start. And at this very moment you could buy me up, lock, stock, and barrel. So don't feel hard done by. It's a lie.'

'You've got your freedom.'

'I make it and I take it.'

'Circumstances make it for you.'

'As you like.'

'You don't do a man justice,' said Aaron.

'Does a man care?'

'He might.'

'Then he's no man.'

'Thanks again, old fellow.'

'Welcome,' said Lilly, grimacing.

Again Aaron looked at him, baffled, almost with hatred. Lilly grimaced at the blank wall opposite and seemed to ruminate. Then he went back to his book. And no sooner had he forgotten Aaron, reading the fantasies of a certain Leo Frobenius, than Aaron must stride in again.

'You can't say there isn't a difference between your position and mine,' he said pertinently.

Lilly looked darkly over his spectacles.

'No, by God,' he said. 'I should be in a poor way otherwise.'

'You can't say you haven't the advantage – your *job* gives you the advantage.'

'All right. Then leave it out with my job, and leave me alone.'

'That's your way of dodging it.'

'My dear Aaron, I agree with you perfectly. There is no difference between us, save the fictitious advantage given to me by my job. Save for my job – which is to write lies – Aaron and I are two identical little men in one and the same little boat. Shall we leave it at that, now?'

'Yes,' said Aaron. 'That's about it.'

'Let us shake hands on it – and go to bed, my dear chap. You are just recovering from influenza, and look paler than I like.'

'You mean you want to be rid of me,' said Aaron.

'Yes, I do mean that,' said Lilly.

'Ay,' said Aaron.

And after a few minutes more staring at the score of *Pelléas*, he rose, put the score away on the piano, laid his flute beside it, and retired behind the screen. In silence, the strange dim noise of London sounding from below, Lilly read on about the Kabyles. His soul had the faculty of divesting itself of the moment, and seeking further, deeper interests. These old Africans! And Atlantis! Strange, strange wisdom of the Kabyles! Old, old dark Africa, and the world before the flood! How jealous Aaron seemed! The child of a jealous God. A jealous God! Could any race be anything but despicable, with such an antecedent?

But no, persistent as a jealous God himself, Aaron reappeared in his pyjamas, and seated himself in his chair.

'What is the difference then between you and me, Lilly?' he said.

'Haven't we shaken hands on it – a difference of jobs.'

'You don't believe that though, do you?'

'Nay, now I reckon you're trespassing.'

'Why am I? I know you don't believe it.'

'What do I believe then?' said Lilly.

'You believe you know something better than me – and that you are something better than me. Don't you?'

'Do *you* believe it?'

'What?'

'That I *am* something better than you, and that I *know* something better?'

'No, because I don't see it,' said Aaron.

'Then if you don't see it, it isn't there. So go to bed and sleep the sleep of the just and the convalescent. I am not to be badgered any more.'

'Am I badgering you?' said Aaron.

'Indeed you are.'

'So I'm in the wrong again?'

'Once more, my dear.'

'You're a God Almighty in your way, you know.'

'So long as I'm not in anybody else's way. Anyhow, you'd be much better sleeping the sleep of the just. And I'm going out for a minute or two. Don't catch cold there with nothing on –'

'I want to catch the post,' he added, rising.

Aaron looked up at him quickly. But almost before there was time to speak, Lilly had slipped into his hat and coat, seized his letters, and gone.

It was a rainy night. Lilly turned down King Street to walk to Charing Cross. He liked being out of doors. He liked to post his letters at Charing Cross post office. He did not want to talk to Aaron any more. He was glad to be alone.

He walked quickly down Villiers Street to the river, to see it flowing blackly towards the sea. It had an endless fascination for him: never failed to soothe him and give him a sense of liberty. He liked the night, the dark rain, the river, and even the traffic. He enjoyed the sense of friction he got from the streaming of people who meant nothing to him. It was like a fox slipping alert among unsuspecting cattle.

When he got back, he saw in the distance the lights of a taxi standing outside the building where he lived, and heard a thumping and hallooing. He hurried forward.

It was a man called Herbertson.

'Oh, why, there you are!' exclaimed Herbertson, as Lilly drew near. 'Can I come up and have a chat?'

'I've got that man who's had flu. I should think he is gone to bed.'

'Oh!' The disappointment was plain. 'Well, look here! I'll just come up for a couple of minutes.' He laid his hand on Lilly's arm. 'I heard you were going away. Where are you going?'

'Malta.'

'Malta! Oh, I know Malta very well. Well now, it'll be all right if I come up for a minute? I'm not going to see much more of you, apparently.' He turned quickly to the taxi. 'What is it on the clock?'

The taxi was paid, the two men went upstairs. Aaron was in bed, but called as Lilly entered the room.

'Hullo!' said Lilly. 'Not asleep? Captain Herbertson has come in for a minute.'

'Hope I shan't disturb you,' said Captain Herbertson, laying down his stick and gloves, and his cap. He was in uniform. He was one of the few surviving officers of the Guards, a man of about forty-five, good-looking, getting rather stout. He settled himself in the chair where Aaron had sat, hitching up his trousers. The gold identity plate, with its gold chain, fell conspicuously over his wrist.

'Been to *Rosemary*,' he said. 'Rotten play, you know – but passes the time awfully well. Oh, I quite enjoyed it.'

Lilly offered him Sauterne – the only thing in the house.

'Oh yes! How awfully nice! Yes, thanks, I shall love it. Can I have it with soda? Thanks! Do you know, I think that's the very best drink in the tropics: sweet white wine, with soda. Yes – well! Well now, why are you going away?'

'For a change,' said Lilly.

'You're quite right, one needs a change now the damned thing is all over. As soon as I get out of khaki I shall be off. Malta! Yes! I've been in Malta several times. I think Valetta is quite enjoyable, particularly in winter, with the opera. Oh – er – how's your wife? All right? Yes! – glad to see her people again. Bound to be. Oh, by the way, I met Jim Bricknell. Sends you a message hoping you'll go down and stay – down at Captain Bingham's place in Surrey, you know. Awfully queer lot down there. Not my sort, no. You won't go down? No, I shouldn't. Not the right sort of people.'

Herbertson rattled away, rather spasmodic. He had been through the very front hill of the war – and like every man who had, he had the war at the back of his mind, like an obsession. But in the meantime, he skirmished.

'Yes. I was on guard the other day when the Queen gave one of her tea-parties to the blind. Awful affair. But the children are awfully nice children. Prince of Wales awfully nice, almost too nice. Prince Henry smart boy, too – oh, a smart boy. Queen Mary poured out the tea, and I handed round bread and butter. She told me I made a very good waiter. I said, "Thank you, Madam."'

The talk flowed on, about royalty and the Guards, Buckingham Palace and St James's.

'Rather a nice story about Queen Victoria. Man named Joyce, something or other, often used to dine at the Palace. And he was an awfully good imitator – really clever, you know. Used to imitate the Queen. "Mr Joyce," she said, "I hear your imitation is very amusing. Will you do it for us now, and let us see what it is like?" "Oh no, Madam! I'm afraid I couldn't do it now. I'm afraid I'm not in the humour." But she would have him do it. And it was really awfully funny. He had to do it. You know what he did? He used to take a table-napkin, and put it on with one corner over his forehead, and the rest hanging down behind, like her veil thing. And then he sent for the kettle lid. He always had the kettle lid, for that little crown of hers. And then he impersonated her. But he was awfully good – so clever. "Mr Joyce," she said. "We are not amused. Please leave the room." Yes, that is exactly what she said: "*We* are not amused – please leave the room." I like the *We*, don't you? And he a man of sixty or so. However, he left the room and for a fortnight or so he wasn't invited. Wasn't she wonderful – Queen Victoria?'

And so, by light transitions, to the Prince of Wales at the front, and thus into the trenches. And then Herbertson was on the subject he was obsessed by. He had come, unconsciously, for this and this only; to talk war to Lilly: or at Lilly. For the latter listened and watched, and said nothing. As a man at night helplessly takes a taxi to find some woman, some prostitute, Herbertson had almost unthinkingly got into a taxi and come battering at the door in Covent Garden, only to talk war to Lilly, whom he knew very little. But it was a driving instinct – to come and get it off his chest.

And on and on he talked, over his white wine and soda. He was not conceited – he was not showing off – far from it. It was the same thing here in this officer as it was with the privates, and the same with this Englishman as with a Frenchman or a German or an Italian. Lilly had sat in a cow-shed listening to a youth in the North Country: he had sat on the corn-straw that the oxen had been treading out, in Calabria, under the moon: he had sat in a farm-kitchen with a German prisoner: and every time it was the same thing, the same hot, blind, anguished voice of a man who has seen too much, experienced too much, and doesn't know where to turn. None of the glamour of returned heroes, none of the romance of war: only a hot, blind, mesmerized voice, going on and on, mesmerized by a vision that the soul cannot bear.

In this officer, of course, there was a lightness and an appearance of bright diffidence and humour. But underneath it all was the same as in the common men of all the combatant nations: the hot, seared burn of unbearable experience, which did not heal nor cool, and whose irration was not to be relieved. The experience gradually cooled on top: but only with a surface crust. The soul did not heal, did not recover.

'I used to be awfully frightened,' laughed Herbertson. 'Now you say, Lilly, you'd never have stood it. But you would. You're nervous – and it was just the nervous ones that did stand it. When nearly all our officers were gone, we had a man come out – a man called Margeritson, from India – big merchant people out there. They all said he was no good – not a bit of good – nervous chap. No good at all. But when you had to get out of the trench and go for the Germans he was perfect – perfect. It all came to him then, at the crisis, and he was perfect.

'Some things frighten one man, and some another. Now, shells would never frighten me. But I couldn't stand bombs. You could tell the difference between our machines and the Germans. Ours was a steady noise – drrrrrrrr! – but their's was heavy, drrrr*ruru*drrrrr*ruru* –! My word, that got on my nerves....

'No, I was never hit. The nearest thing was when I was knocked down by an exploding shell – several times that – you know. When you shout like mad for the men to come and dig you out, under all the earth. And my word, you do feel frightened then.' Herbertson laughed with a twinkling motion to Lilly. But between his brows there was a tension like madness.

'And a funny thing, you know – how you don't notice things. In – let me see – 1916 – the German guns were a lot better than ours. Ours were old, and when they're old you can't tell where they'll hit: whether they'll go beyond the mark, or whether they'll fall short. Well, this day our guns were firing short, and killing our own men. We'd had the order to charge, and were running forward, and I suddenly felt hot water spurting on my neck –' He put his hand to the back of his neck and glanced round apprehensively. 'It was a chap called Innes. Oh, an awfully decent sort – people were in the Argentine. He'd been calling out to me as we were running, and I was just answering. When I felt this hot water on my neck and saw him running past me with no head – he'd got no head, and he went running past me. I don't know how far, but a long way ... Blood, you know. Yes, well ...

'Oh, I hated Chelsea – I loathed Chelsea – Chelsea was purgatory to me. I had a corporal called Wallace – he was a fine chap – oh, he was a fine chap – six foot two – and about twenty-four years old. He was my stand-back. Oh, I hated Chelsea, and parades, and drills. You know, when it's drill, and you're giving orders, you forget what order you've just given – in front of the Palace there the crowd don't notice – but it's awful for *you*. And you know you daren't look round to see what the men are doing. But Wallace was splendid. He was just behind me, and I'd hear him, quite quiet, you know, "It's right wheel, sir." Always perfect, always perfect – yes – well ...

'You know you don't get killed if you don't think you will. Now I never thought I should get killed. And I never knew a man get killed if he hadn't been thinking he would. I said to Wallace I'd rather be out here, at the front, than at Chelsea. I hated Chelsea – I can't tell you how much. "Oh, no, sir!" he said. "I'd rather be at Chelsea than here. I'd rather be at Chelsea. There isn't hell like this at Chelsea." We'd had orders that we were to go back to the rear camp the next day. "Never mind, Wallace," I said. "We shall be out of this hell-on-earth tomorrow." And he took my hand. We weren't much for showing feeling or anything in the Guards. But he took my hand. We climbed out to charge. Poor fellow, he was killed –' Herbertson dropped his head, and for some moments seemed to go unconscious, as if struck. Then he lifted his face, and went on in the same animated, chatty fashion: 'You see, he had a presentiment. I'm sure he had a presentiment. None of the men got killed unless they had a presentiment – like that, you know ...'

Herbertson nodded keenly at Lilly, with his sharp, twinkling, yet obsessed eyes. Lilly wondered why he made the presentiment responsible for the death – which he obviously did – and not *vice versa*. Herbertson implied every time that you'd never get killed if you could keep yourself from having a presentiment. Perhaps there was something in it. Perhaps the soul issues its own ticket of death, when it can stand no more. Surely life controls life: and not accident.

'It's a funny thing what shock will do. We had a sergeant and he shouted to me. Both his feet were off – both his feet, clean at the ankle. I gave him morphia. You know officers aren't allowed to use the needle – might give the man blood poisoning. You give those tabloids. They say they act in a few minutes, but they *don't*. It's a quarter of an hour. And nothing is more demoralising than when you have a man, wounded, you know, and crying out. Well, this man I gave him the morphia before he got over the stunning, you know. So he didn't feel the pain. Well, they carried him in. I always used to like to look after my men. So I went next morning and I found he hadn't been removed to the Clearing Station. I got hold of the doctor and I said, "Look here! Why hasn't this man been taken to the Clearing Station?" I used to get excited. But after some years they'd got used to me. "Don't get excited, Herbertson, the man's dying." "But," I said, "he's just been talking to me as strong as you are." And he had – he'd talk as strong and well as you or me, then go quiet for a bit. I said I gave him the morphia before he came round from the stunning. So he'd felt nothing. But in two hours he was dead. The doctor says that the shock does it like that sometimes. You can do nothing for them. Nothing vital is injured – and yet the life is broken in them. Nothing can be done – funny thing. Must be something in the brain –'

'It's obviously not the brain,' said Lilly. 'It's deeper than the brain.'

'Deeper,' said Herbertson, nodding. 'Funny thing where life is. We had a lieutenant. You know we all buried our own dead. Well, he looked as if he was asleep. Most of the chaps looked like that.' Herbertson closed his eyes and laid his face aside, like a man asleep and dead peacefully. 'You very rarely see a man dead with any other look on his face – you know the other look –' And he clenched his teeth with a sudden, momentaneous, ghastly distortion. 'Well, you'd never have known this chap was dead. He had a wound here – in the back of his head – and a bit of blood on his hand – and nothing else, nothing.

Well, I said we'd give him a decent burial. He lay there waiting – and they'd wrapped him in a filthy blanket – you know. Well, I said he should have a proper blanket. He'd been dead lying there a day and a half you know. So I went and got a blanket, a beautiful blanket, out of his private kit – his people were Scotch, well-known family – and I got the pins, you know, ready to pin him up properly, for the Scots Guards to bury him. And I thought he'd be stiff, you see. But when I took him by the arms, to lift him on, he sat up. It gave me an awful shock. "Why he's alive!" I said. But they said he was dead. I couldn't believe it. It gave me an awful shock. He was as flexible as you or me, and looked as if he was asleep. You couldn't believe he was dead. But we pinned him up in his blanket. It was an awful shock to me. I couldn't believe a man could be like that after he'd been dead two days....

'The Germans were wonderful with the machine-guns – it's a wicked thing, a machine-gun. But they couldn't touch us with the bayonet. Every time the men came back they had bayonet practice, and they got awfully good. You know when you thrust at the Germans – so – if you miss him, you bring your rifle back sharp, with a round swing, so that the butt comes up and hits up under the jaw. It's one movement, following on with the stab, you see, if you miss him. It was too quick for them. But bayonet charge was worst, you know. Because your man cries out when you catch him, when you get him, you know. That's what does you....

'No, oh no, this was no war like other wars. All the machinery of it. No, you couldn't stand it, but for the men. The men are wonderful, you know. They'll be wiped out.... No, it's your men who keep you going, if you're an officer.... But there'll never be another war like this. Because the Germans are the only people who could make a war like this – and I don't think they'll ever do it again, do you?

'Oh, they were wonderful, the Germans. They were amazing. It was incredible, what they invented and did. We had to learn from them, in the first two years. But they were too methodical. That's why they lost the war. They were too methodical. They'd fire their guns every ten minutes – regular. Think of it! Of course, we knew when to run, and when to lie down. You got so that you knew almost exactly what they'd do – if you'd been out long enough. And then you could time what you wanted to do yourselves.

'They were a lot more nervous than we were, at the last. They sent up enough light at night from their trenches – you know, those things that burst in the air like electric light – we had none of that to do – they did it all for us – lit up everything. They were more nervous than we were....'

It was nearly two o'clock when Herbertson left. Lilly depressed, remained before the fire. Aaron got out of bed and came uneasily to the fire.

'It gives me the bellyache, that damned war,' he said.

'So it does me,' said Lilly. 'All unreal.'

'Real enough for those that had to go through it.'

'No, least of all for them,' said Lilly sullenly. 'Not as real as a bad dream. Why the hell don't they wake up and realize it!'

'That's a fact,' said Aaron. 'They're hypnotized by it.'

'And they want to hypnotize me. And I won't be hypnotized. The war was a lie and is a lie and will go on being a lie till somebody busts it.'

'It was a fact – you can't bust that. You can't bust the fact that it happened.'

'Yes, you can. It never happened. It never happened to me. No more than my dreams happen. My dreams don't happen: they only seem.'

'But the war did happen, right enough,' smiled Aaron palely.

'No, it didn't. Not to me or to any man, in his own self. It took place in the automatic sphere, like dreams do. But the *actual man* in every man was just absent – asleep – or drugged – inert – dream-logged. That's it.'

'You tell 'em so,' said Aaron.

'I do. But it's no good. Because they won't wake up now even – perhaps never. They'll all kill themselves in their sleep.'

'They wouldn't be any better if they did wake up and be themselves – that is, supposing they are asleep, which I can't see. They are what they are – and they're all alike – and never very different from what they are now.'

Lilly stared at Aaron with black eyes.

'Do you believe in them less than I do, Aaron?' he asked slowly.

'I don't even want to believe in them.'

'But in yourself?' Lilly was almost wistful – and Aaron uneasy.

'I don't know that I've any more right to believe in myself than in them,' he replied. Lilly watched and pondered.

'No,' he said. 'That's not true – I *knew* the war was false: humanly quite false. I always knew it was false. The Germans were false, we were false, everybody was false.'

'And not you?' asked Aaron shrewishly.

'There was a wakeful, self-possessed bit of me which knew that the war and all that horrible movement was false for me. And so I wasn't going to be dragged in. The Germans could have shot my mother or me or what they liked: I wouldn't have joined the *war*. I would like to kill my enemy. But become a bit of that huge obscene machine they called the war, that I never would, no, not if I died ten deaths and had eleven mothers violated. But I would like to kill my enemy: oh yes, more than one enemy. But not as a unit in a vast obscene mechanism. That, never: no, never.'

Poor Lilly was too earnest and vehement. Aaron made a fine nose. It seemed to him like a lot of words and a bit of wriggling out of a hole.

'Well,' he said, 'you've got men and nations, and you've got the machines of war – so how are you going to get out of it? League of Nations?'

'Damn all leagues. Damn all masses and groups, anyhow. All I want is to get *myself* out of their horrible heap: to get out of the swarm. The swarm to me is nightmare and nullity – horrible helpless writhing in a dream. I want to get myself awake, out of it all – all that mass-consciousness, all that mass-activity – it's the most horrible nightmare to me. No man is awake and himself. No man who was awake and in possession of himself would use poison gases: no man. His own awake self would scorn such a thing. It's only when the ghastly mob-sleep, the dream helplessness of the mass-psyche overcomes him, that he becomes completely base and obscene.'

'Ha! – well,' said Aaron. 'It's the wide-awake ones that invent the poison gas, and use it. Where should we be without it?'

Lilly started, went stiff and hostile.

'Do you mean that, Aaron?' he said, looking into Aaron's face with a hard, inflexible look.

Aaron turned aside half sheepishly.

'That's how it looks on the face of it, isn't it?' he said.

'Look here, my friend, it's too late for you to be talking to me about the face of things. If that's how you feel, put your things on and follow Herbertson. Yes – go out of my room. I don't put up with the face of things here.'

Aaron looked at him in cold amazement.

'It'll do tomorrow morning, won't it?' he asked, rather mocking.

'Yes,' said Lilly coldly. 'But please go tomorrow morning.'

'Oh, I'll go all right,' said Aaron. 'Everybody's got to agree with you – that's your price.'

But Lilly did not answer. Aaron turned into bed, his satirical smile under his nose. Somewhat surprised, however, at this sudden turn of affairs.

As he was just going to sleep, dismissing the matter, Lilly came once more to his bedside, and said, in a hard voice:

'I'm *not* going to pretend to have friends on the face of things. No, and I *don't* have friends who don't fundamentally agree with me. A friend means one who is at one with me in matters of life and death. And if you're at one with all the rest, then you're their friend, not mine. So be *their* friend. And please leave me in the morning. You owe me nothing, you have nothing more to do with me. I have had enough of these friendships where I pay the piper and the mob calls the tune.

'Let me tell you, moreover, your heroic Herbertsons lost us more than ever they won. A brave ant is damned cowardly individual. Your heroic officers are a sad sight, *afterwards*, when they come home. Bah, your Herbertson! The only justification for war is what you learn from it. And what have they learnt? Why did so many of them have presentiments, as he called it? Because they could feel inside them, there was nothing to come after. No life-courage: always death-courage. Nothing beyond this hell – only death or love-languishing –'

'What could they have seen, anyhow?' said Aaron.

'It's not what you see, actually. It's the kind of spirit you keep inside you: the life spirit. When Wallace had presentiments, Herbertson, being officer, should have said: "None of that, Wallace. You and I, we've got to live and make life smoke." Instead of which he let Wallace be killed, and his own heart be broken. Always the death choice. And we won't, we simply *will not* face the world as we've made it, and our own souls as we find them, and take the responsibility. We'll *never* get anywhere till we stand up man to man and face *everything* out, and break the old forms, but never let our own pride and courage of life be broken.'

Lilly broke off, and went silently to bed. Aaron turned over to sleep, rather resenting the sound of so many words. What difference did it make anyhow? In the morning, however, when he saw the other man's pale, closed, rather haughty face, he realized that something *had* happened. Lilly was courteous and even affable: but with a curious cold space between him and Aaron. Breakfast passed, and Aaron knew that he must leave. There was something in Lilly's bearing which just showed him the door. In some surprise and confusion, and in some anger, not unmingled with humorous irony, he put his things in his bag. He put on his hat and coat. Lilly was seated rather stiffly, writing.

'Well,' said Aaron. 'I suppose we shall meet again.'

'Oh, sure to,' said Lilly, rising from his chair. 'We are sure to run across one another.'

'When are you going?' asked Aaron.

'In a few days' time.'

'Oh well, I'll run in and see you before you go, shall I?'

'Yes, do.'

Lilly escorted his guest to the top of the stairs, shook hands, and then returned into his own room, closing the door on himself.

Aaron did not find his friend at home when he called. He felt it was a slap in the face. But then he knew perfectly well that Lilly had made a certain call upon his, Aaron's, soul: a call which he, Aaron, did not intend to obey. Rather he curled his fine nose, worldly-wise. People who make calls on other people's souls are bound to find the door shut. If in return the soul-caller chooses to shut his worldly house-door in the face of the world-caller, well, it is nearly quits. Aaron accepted the *quid pro quo*. He was not sure whether he felt superior to his unworldly enemy or not. He rather felt he did.

11

MORE PILLAR OF SALT

The opera season ended, Aaron was invited by Cyril Scott to join a group of musical people in a village by the sea. He accepted, and spent a pleasant month. It pleased the young men musically-inclined and Bohemian by profession to patronize the flautist, whom they declared marvellous. Bohemians with well-to-do parents, they could always afford to squander a little spasmodic and self-gratifying patronage. And Aaron did not mind being patronized. He had nothing else to do.

But the party broke up early in September. The flautist was detained a few days at a country house, for the amusement of the guests. Then he left for London.

In London he found himself at a loose end. A certain fretful dislike of the patronage of indifferent young men, younger than himself, and a certain distaste for regular work in the orchestra made him look round. He wanted something else. He wanted to disappear again. Qualms and emotions concerning his abandoned family overcame him. The early, delicate autumn affected him. He took a train to the Midlands.

And again, just after dark, he strolled with his little bag across the field which lay at the end of his garden. It had been mown, and the grass was already growing long. He stood and looked at the line of black windows, lighted once more. He smelled the scents of autumn, phlox and moist old vegetation and corn in sheaf. A nostalgia which was half at least revulsion affected him. The place, the home, at once fascinated him and revolted him.

Sitting in his shed, he scrutinized his garden carefully, in the starlight. There were two rows of beans, rather dishevelled. Near at hand the marrow plants sprawled from their old bed. He could detect the perfume of a few carnations. He wondered who it was had planted the garden, during his long absence. Anyhow, there it was, planted and fruited and waning into autumn.

The blind was not drawn. It was eight o'clock. The children were going to bed. Aaron waited in his shed, his bowels stirred with violent but only half-admitted emotions. There was his wife, slim and graceful, holding a little mug to the baby's mouth. And the baby was drinking. She looked lonely. Wild emotions attacked his heart. There was going to be a wild and emotional reconciliation.

Was there? It seemed like something fearful and imminent. A passion arose in him, a craving for the violent emotional reconciliation. He waited impatiently for the children to be gone to bed, gnawed with restless desire.

He heard the clock strike nine, then half-past, from the village behind. The children would be asleep. His wife was sitting sewing some little frock. He went lingering down the garden path, stooping to lift the fallen carnations, to see how they were. There were many flowers, but small. He broke one off, then threw it away. The golden rod was out. Even in the little lawn there were asters, as of old.

His wife started to listen, hearing his step. He was filled with a violent conflict of tenderness, like a sickness. He hesitated, tapping at the door, and entered. His wife started to her feet, at bay.

'What have you come for!' was her involuntary ejaculation.

But he, with the familiar odd jerk of his head towards the garden, asked with a faint smile:

'Who planted the garden?'

And he felt himself dropping into the twang of the vernacular, which he had discarded.

Lottie only stood and stared at him, objectively. She did not think to answer. He took his hat off, and put it on the dresser. Again the familiar act maddened her.

'What have you come for?' she cried again, with a voice full of hate. Or perhaps it was fear and doubt and even hope as well. He heard only hate.

This time he turned to look at her. The old dagger was drawn in her.

'I wonder,' he said, 'myself.'

Then she recovered herself, and with trembling hand picked up her sewing again. But she still stood at bay, beyond the table. She said nothing. He, feeling tired, sat down on the chair nearest the door. But he reached for his hat, and kept it on his knee. She, as she stood there unnaturally, went on with her sewing. There was silence for some time. Curious sensations and emotions went through the man's frame, seeming to destroy him. They were like electric shocks, which he felt she emitted against him. And an old sickness came in him again. He had forgotten it. It was the sickness of the unrecognized and incomprehensible strain between him and her.

After a time she put down her sewing, and sat again in her chair.

'Do you know how vilely you've treated me?' she said, staring across the space at him. He averted his face. Yet he answered, not without irony:

'I suppose so.'

'And why?' she cried. 'I should like to know why.'

He did not answer. The way she rushed in made him go vague.

'Justify yourself. Say why you've been so vile to me. Say what you had against me,' she demanded.

'What I *had* against her,' he mused to himself: and he wondered that she used the past tense. He made no answer.

'Accuse me,' she insisted. 'Say what I've done to make you treat me like this. Say it. You must *think* it hard enough.'

'Nay,' he said. 'I don't think it.'

This speech, by which he merely meant that he did not trouble to formulate any injuries he had against her, puzzled her.

'Don't come pretending you love me, *now*. It's too late,' she said with contempt. Yet perhaps also hope.

'You might wait till I start pretending,' he said.

This enraged her.

'You vile creature!' she exclaimed. 'Go! What have you come for?'

'To look at you,' he said sarcastically.

After a few minutes she began to cry, sobbing violently into her apron.

'What have I done! What have I done! I don't know what I've done that he should be like this to me,' she sobbed, into her apron. It was childish, and perhaps true. At least it was true from the childish part of her nature. He sat gloomy and uneasy.

She took the apron from her tear-stained face, and looked at him. It was true, in her moments of roused exposure she was a beautiful woman – a beautiful woman. At this moment, with her flushed, tear-stained, wilful distress, she was beautiful.

'Tell me,' she challenged. 'Tell me! Tell me what I've done. Tell me what you have against me. Tell me.'

Watching like a lynx, she saw the puzzled, hurt look in his face. Telling isn't so easy – especially when the trouble goes too deep for conscious comprehension. He couldn't *tell* what he had against her. And he had not the slightest intention of doing what she would have liked him to do, starting to pile up detailed grievances. He knew the detailed grievances were nothing in themselves.

'You *can't*,' she cried vindictively. 'You *can't*. You *can't* find anything real to bring against me, though you'd like to. You'd like to be able to accuse me of something, but you *can't*, because you know there isn't anything.'

She watched him, watched. And he sat in the chair near the door, without moving.

'You're unnatural, that's what you are,' she cried. 'You're unnatural. You're not a man. You haven't got a man's feelings. You're nasty, and cold, and unnatural. And you're a coward. You're a coward. You run away from me, without telling me what you've got against me.'

'When you've had enough, you go away and you don't care what you do,' he said, epigrammatic.

She paused a moment.

'Enough of what?' she said. 'What have you had enough of? Of me and your children? It's a nice manly thing to say. Haven't I loved you? Haven't I loved you for twelve years, and worked and slaved for you and tried to keep you right? Heavens knows where you'd have been but for me, evil as you are at the bottom. You're evil, that's what it is – and weak. You're too weak to love a woman and give her what she wants: too weak. Unmanly and cowardly, he runs away.'

'No wonder,' he said.

'No,' she cried. 'It *is* no wonder, with a nature like yours: weak and unnatural and evil. It *is* no wonder.'

She became quiet – and then started to cry again, into her apron. Aaron waited. He felt physically weak.

'And who knows what you've been doing all these months,' she wept. 'Who knows all the vile things you've been doing. And you're the father of my children – the father of my little girls – and who knows what vile things he's guilty of, all these months.'

'I shouldn't let my imagination run away with me,' he answered. 'I've been playing the flute in the orchestra of one of the theatres in London.'

'Ha!' she cried. 'It's more than that. Don't think I'm going to believe you. I know you, with your smooth-sounding lies. You're a liar, as you know. And I know you've been doing other things besides play a flute in an orchestra. You! – as if I don't know you. And then coming crawling back to me with your lies and your pretence. Don't think I'm taken in.'

'I should be sorry,' he said.

'Coming crawling back to me, and expecting to be forgiven,' she went on. 'But no – I don't forgive – and I can't forgive – never – not as long as I live shall I forgive what you've done to me.'

'You can wait till you're asked, anyhow,' he said.

'And you can wait,' she said. 'And you *shall* wait.'

She took up her sewing, and stitched steadily, as if calmly. Anyone glancing in would have imagined a quiet domestic hearth at that moment. He, too, feeling physically weak, remained silent, feeling his soul absent from the scene.

Again she suddenly burst into tears, weeping bitterly.

'And the children,' she sobbed, rocking herself with grief and chagrin. 'What have I been able to say to the children – what have I been able to tell them.'

'What *have* you told them?' he asked coldly.

'I told them you'd gone away to work,' she sobbed, laying her head on her arms on the table. 'What else could I tell them? I couldn't tell them the vile truth about their father. I couldn't tell *them* how evil you are.' She sobbed and moaned.

He wondered what exactly the vile truth would have been, had she *started* to tell it. And he began to feel, coldly and cynically, that among all her distress there was a luxuriating in the violent emotions of the scene in hand, and the situation altogether.

Then again she became quiet, and picked up her sewing. She stitched quietly, wistfully, for some time. Then she looked up at him – a long look of reproach, and sombre accusation, and wifely tenderness. He turned his face aside.

'You know you've been wrong to me, don't you?' she said, half wistfully, half menacing.

He felt her wistfulness and menace tearing him in his bowels and loins.

'You do know, don't you?' she insisted, still with the wistful appeal, and the veiled threat.

'You do, or you would answer,' she said. 'You've still got enough that's right in you, for you to know.'

She waited. He sat still, as if drawn by hot wires.

Then she slipped across to him, put her arms round him, sank on her knees at his side, and sank her face against his thigh.

'Say you know how wrong you are. Say you know how cruel you've been to me,' she pleaded. But under her female pleading and appeal he felt the iron of her threat.

'You *do* know it,' she murmured, looking up into his face as she crouched by his knee. 'You *do* know it. I can see in your eyes that you know it. And why have you come back to me, if you don't know it! Why have you come back to me? Tell me!' Her arms gave him a sharp, compulsory little clutch round the waist. 'Tell me! Tell me!' she murmured, with all her appeal liquid in her throat.

But him, it half overcame, and at the same time, horrified. He had a certain horror of her. The strange, liquid sound of her appeal seemed to him like the swaying of a serpent which mesmerizes the fated, fluttering, helpless bird. She clasped her arms round him, she drew him to her, she half roused his passion. At the same time she coldly horrified and repelled him. He had not the faintest feeling, at the moment, of his own wrong. But she wanted to win his own self-betrayal out of him. He could see himself as the fascinated victim, falling to this cajoling, artful woman, the wife of his bosom. But as well, he had a soul outside himself, which looked on the whole scene with cold revulsion, and which was as unchallengeable as time.

'No,' he said. 'I don't feel wrong.'

'You *do*!' she said, giving him a sharp, admonitory clutch. 'You *do*. Only you're silly, and obstinate, babyish and silly and obstinate. An obstinate little boy – you *do* feel wrong. And you *are* wrong. And you've got to say it.'

But quietly he disengaged himself and got to his feet, his face pale and set, obstinate as she said. He put his hat on, and took his little bag. She watched him curiously, still crouching by his chair.

'I'll go,' he said, putting his hand on the latch.

Suddenly she sprang to her feet and clutched him by the shirt-neck, her hand inside his soft collar, half strangling him.

'You villain,' she said, and her face was transfigured with passion as he had never seen it before, horrible. 'You villain!' she said thickly. 'What have you come here for?'

His soul went black as he looked at her. He broke her hand away from his shirt collar, bursting the stud-holes. She recoiled in silence. And in one black, unconscious movement he was gone, down the garden and over the fence and across the country, swallowed in a black unconsciousness.

She realizing, sank upon the hearth-rug and lay there curled upon herself. She was defeated. But she too would never yield. She lay quite motionless for some time. Then she got up, feeling the draught on the floor. She closed the door, and drew down the blind. Then she looked at her wrist which he had gripped, and which pained her. Then she went to the mirror and looked for a long time at her white, strained, determined face. Come life, come death, she too would never yield. And she realized now that he would never yield.

She was faint with weariness, and would be glad to get to bed and sleep.

Aaron meanwhile had walked across the country and was looking for a place to rest. He found a corn-field with a half-built stack, and sheaves in stook. Ten to one some tramp would have found the stack. He threw a dozen sheaves together and lay down, looking at the stars in the September sky. He too would never yield. The illusion of love was gone for ever. Love was a battle in which each party strove for the mastery of the other's soul. So far, man had yielded the mastery to women. Now he was fighting for it back again. And too late, for the woman would never yield.

But whether woman yielded or not, he would keep the mastery of his own soul and conscience and actions. He would never yield himself up to her judgment again. He would hold himself for ever beyond her jurisdiction.

Henceforth, life single, not life double.

He looked at the sky, and thanked the universe for the blessedness of being alone in the universe. To be alone, to be oneself, not to be driven or violated into something which is not oneself, surely it is better than anything. He thought of Lottie, and knew how much more truly herself she was when she was alone, with no man to distort her. And he was thankful for the division between them. Such scenes as the last were too horrible and unreal.

As for future unions, too soon to think about it. Let there be clean and pure division first, perfected singleness. That is the only way to final, living unison: through sheer, finished singleness.

12

NOVARA

Having no job for the autumn, Aaron fidgeted in London. He played at some concerts and some private shows. He was one of an odd quartette, for example, which went to play to Lady Artemis Hooper, when she lay in bed after her famous escapade of falling through the window of her taxi-cab. Aaron had that curious knack, which belongs to some people, of getting into the swim without knowing he was doing it. Lady Artemis thought his flute lovely, and had him again to play for her. Aaron looked at her, and she at him. She, as she reclined there in bed in a sort of half-light, well made-up, smoking her cigarettes and talking in a rather raucous voice, making her slightly rasping witty comments to the other men in the room – of course there were other men, the audience – was a shock to the flautist. This was the bride of the moment! Curious how raucous her voice sounded out of the cigarette smoke. Yet he liked her – the reckless note of the modern, social freebooter. In himself was a touch of the same quality.

'Do you love playing?' she asked him.

'Yes,' he said, with that shadow of irony which seemed like a smile on his face.

'Live for it, so to speak,' she said.

'I make my living by it,' he said.

'But that's not really how you take it?' she said. He eyed her. She watched him over her cigarette. It was a personal moment.

'I don't think about it,' he said.

'I'm sure you don't. You wouldn't be so good if you did. You're awfully lucky, you know, to be able to pour yourself down your flute.'

'You think I go down easy?' he laughed.

'Ah!' she replied, flicking her cigarette broadcast. 'That's the point. What should you say, Jimmy?' she turned to one of the men. He screwed his eyeglass nervously and stiffened himself to look at her.

'I – I shouldn't like to say, off-hand,' came the small-voiced, self-conscious answer. And Jimmy bridled himself and glanced at Aaron.

'Do you find it a tight squeeze, then?' she said, turning to Aaron once more.

'No, I can't say that,' he answered. 'What of me goes down goes down easy enough. It's what doesn't go down.'

'And how much is that?' she asked, eyeing him.

'A good bit, maybe,' he said.

'Slops over, so to speak,' she retorted sarcastically. 'And which do you enjoy more, trickling down your flute, or slopping over on to the lap of Mother Earth – or Miss, more probably?'

'Depends,' he said.

Having got him a few steps too far upon the personal ground, she left him to get off by himself.

So he found London got on his nerves. He felt it rubbed him the wrong way. He was flattered, of course, by his own success – and felt at the same time irritated by it. This state of mind was by no means acceptable. Wherever he was he liked to be given, tacitly, the first place – or a place among the first. Among the musical people he frequented, he found himself on a callow kind of equality with everybody, even the stars and aristocrats, at one moment, and a backstairs outsider the next. It was all just as the moment demanded. There was a certain excitement in slithering up and down the social scale, one minute chatting in a personal *tête-à-tête* with the most famous, or notorious, of the society beauties; and the next walking in the rain, with his flute in a bag, to his grubby lodging in Bloomsbury. Only the excitement roused all the savage sarcasm that lay at the bottom of his soul, and which burned there like an unhealthy bile.

Therefore he determined to clear out – to disappear. He had a letter from Lilly, from Novara. Lilly was drifting about. Aaron wrote to Novara, and asked if he should come to Italy, having no money to speak of. 'Come if you want to. Bring your flute. And if you've no money, put on a good suit of clothes and a big black hat, and play outside the best café in any Italian town, and you'll collect enough to get on with.'

It was a sporting chance. Aaron packed his bag and got a passport, and wrote to Lilly to say he would join him, as invited, at Sir William Franks's. He hoped Lilly's answer would arrive before he left London. But it didn't.

Therefore behold our hero alighting at Novara, two hours late, on a wet dark evening. He hoped Lilly would be there: but nobody. With some slight dismay he faced the big, crowded station. The stream of people carried him automatically through the barrier, a porter having seized his bag, and volleyed various unintelligible questions at him. Aaron understood not one word. So he just wandered after the blue blouse of the porter.

The porter deposited the bag on the steps of the station front, fired off more questions and gesticulated into the half-illuminated space of darkness outside the station. Aaron decided it meant a cab, so he nodded and said 'Yes.' But there were no cabs, so once more the blue-bloused porter slung the big bag and the little bag on the strap over his shoulder, and they plunged into the night, towards some lights and a sort of theatre place.

One carriage stood there in the rain – yes, and it was free.

'Keb? yes – orright – sir. Whe'to? Where you go? Sir William Franks – Yes, I know. Long way go – go long way. Sir William Franks.'

The cabman spattered his few words of English. Aaron gave the porter an English shilling. The porter let the coin lie in the middle of his palm, as if it were a live beetle, and darted to the light of the carriage to examine the beast, exclaiming volubly. The cabman, wild with interest, peered down from the box into the palm of the porter, and carried on an impassioned dialogue. Aaron stood with one foot on the step.

'What you give – he? One franc?' asked the driver.

'A shilling,' said Aaron.

'One sheeling. Yes, I know that. One sheeling English' – and the driver went off into impassioned exclamations in Torinese. The porter, still muttering and holding his hand as if the coin might sting him, filtered away.

'Orright. He know – sheeling – orright. English moneys, eh? Yes, he know. You get up, sir.'

And away went Aaron, under the hood of the carriage, clattering down the wide darkness of Novara, over a bridge apparently, past huge rain-wet statues, and through more rainy half-lit streets.

They stopped at last outside a sort of park wall with trees above. The big gates were just beyond.

'Sir William Franks – there –' in a mixture of Italian and English the driver told Aaron to get down and to ring the bell on the right. Aaron got down and in the darkness was able to read the name on the plate.

'How much?' said Aaron to the driver.

'Ten franc,' said the fat driver.

But it was his turn now to screw down and scrutinize the pink ten-shilling note. He waved it in his hand.

'Not good, eh? Not good moneys?'

'Yes,' said Aaron, rather indignantly. 'Good English money. Ten shillings. Better than ten francs, a good deal. Better – better –'

'Good – you say? Ten sheeling –' The driver muttered and muttered, as if dissatisfied. But as a matter of fact he stowed the note in his waistcoat pocket with considerable satisfaction, looked at Aaron curiously, and drove away.

Aaron stood there in the dark outside the big gates, and wished himself somewhere else. However, he rang the bell. There was a huge barking of dogs on the other side. Presently a light switched on, and a woman, followed by a man, appeared cautiously, in the half-opened doorway.

'Sir William Franks?' said Aaron.

'Si, signore.'

And Aaron stepped with his two bags inside the gate. Huge dogs jumped round. He stood in the darkness under the trees at the foot of the park. The woman fastened the gate – Aaron saw a door – and through an uncurtained window a man writing at a desk – rather like the clerk in an hotel office. He was going with his two bags to the open door, when the woman stopped him, and began talking to him in Italian. It was evident he must not go in. So he put down the bags. The man stood a few yards away, watchfully.

Aaron looked down at the woman and tried to make out something of what she was saying, but could not. The dogs still barked spasmodically, drops fell from the tall dark trees that rose overhead.

'Is Mr Lilly here? Mr Lilly?' he asked.

'Signor Lillee. No signore –'

And off the woman went in Italian. But it was evident Lilly was not at the house. Aaron wished more than ever he had not come, but had gone to an hotel.

He made out that the woman was asking him for his name – 'Meester –? Meester –?' she kept saying, with a note of interrogation.

'Sisson. Mr Sisson,' said Aaron, who was becoming impatient. And he found a visiting-card to give her. She seemed appeased – said something about telephone – and left him standing.

The rain had ceased, but big drops were shaken from the dark high trees. Through the uncurtained window he saw the man at the desk reach for the telephone. There was a long pause. At length the woman came back and motioned to him to go up – up the drive which curved and disappeared under the dark trees.

'Go up there?' said Aaron, pointing.

That was evidently the intention. So he picked up his bags and strode forward, from out of the circle of electric light, up the curved drive in the darkness. It was a steep incline. He saw trees and the grass slopes. There was a tang of snow in the air.

Suddenly, up ahead, a brilliant light switched on. He continued uphill through the trees along the path, towards it, and at length emerged at the foot of a great flight of steps, above which was a wide glass entrance, and an Italian manservant in white gloves hovering as if on the brink.

Aaron emerged from the drive and climbed the steps. The manservant came down two steps and took the little bag. Then he ushered Aaron and the big bag into a large, pillared hall, with thick Turkish carpet on the floor, and handsome appointments. It was spacious, comfortable and warm; but somewhat pretentious; rather like the imposing hall into which the heroine suddenly enters on the film.

Aaron dropped his heavy bag, with relief, and stood there, hat in hand, in his damp overcoat in the circle of light, looking vaguely at the yellow marble pillars, the gilded arches above, the shadowy distance and the great stairs. The butler disappeared – reappeared in another moment – and through an open doorway came the host. Sir William was a small, clean old man with a thin white beard and a courtly deportment, wearing a black velvet dinner-jacket faced with purple silk.

'How do you do, Mr Sisson. You come straight from England?'

Sir William held out his hand courteously and benevolently, smiling an old man's smile of hospitality.

'Mr Lilly has gone away?' said Aaron.

'Yes. He left us several days ago.'

Aaron hesitated.

'You didn't expect me, then?'

'Yes, oh yes. Yes, oh yes. Very glad to see you – Well now, come in and have some dinner –'

At this moment Lady Franks appeared – short, rather plump, but erect and definite, in a black silk dress and pearls round her throat.

'How do you do? We are just at dinner,' she said. 'You haven't eaten? No – well then – would you like a bath now, or –?'

It was evident the Franks had dispensed much hospitality: much of it charitable. Aaron felt it.

'No,' he said. 'I'll wash my hands and come straight in, shall I?'

'Yes, perhaps that would be better –'

'I'm afraid I am a nuisance –'

'Not at all – Beppe –' and she gave instructions in Italian.

Another footman appeared, and took the big bag. Aaron took the little one this time. They climbed the broad, turning stairs, crossed another handsome lounge, gilt and ormolu and yellow silk chairs and scattered copies of the *Graphic* or of *Country Life*, then they disappeared through a doorway into a much narrower flight of stairs. Man can so rarely keep it up all the way, the grandeur.

Two black-and-white chambermaids appeared. Aaron found himself in a blue silk bedroom, and a footman unstrapping his bag, which he did not want unstrapped. Next minute he was beckoned and allured by the Italian servants down the corridor, and presented to the handsome, spacious bathroom, which was warm and creamy-coloured and glittering with massive silver and mysterious with up-to-date conveniences. There he was left to his own devices, and felt like a small boy finding out how it works. For even the mere turning of the taps was a problem in silver mechanics.

In spite of all the splendours and the elaborated convenience, he washed himself in good hot water, and wished he were having a bath, chiefly because of the wardrobe of marvellous Turkish towels. Then he clicked his way back to his bedroom, changed his shirt and combed his hair in the blue silk bedroom with the Greuze picture, and felt a little dim and superficial surprise. He had fallen into country house parties before, but never into quite such a plushy sense of riches. He felt he ought to have his breath taken away. But alas, the cinema has taken our breath away so often, investing us in all the splendours of the splendidest American millionaire, or all the heroics and marvels of the Somme or the North Pole, that life has now no magnate richer than we, no hero nobler than we have been, on the film. *Connu! Connu!* Everything life has to offer is known to us, couldn't be known better, from the film.

So Aaron tied his tie in front of a big Venice mirror, and nothing was a surprise to him. He found a footman hovering to escort him to the dining-room – a real Italian footman, uneasy because milady's dinner was unsettled. He entered the rather small dining-room, and saw the people at table.

He was told various names: bowed to a young slim woman with big blue eyes and dark hair like a photograph, then to a smaller rather colourless young woman with a large nose: then to a stout rubicund, bald Colonel, and to a tall, thin, Oxford-looking Major with a black patch over his eye – both these men in khaki – finally to a good-looking, well-nourished young man in a dinner-jacket, and he sat down to his soup, on his hostess's left hand. The colonel sat on her right, and was confidential. Little Sir William, with his hair and his beard white like spun glass, his manner very courteous and animated, the purple facings of his velvet jacket very impressive, sat at the far end of the table jesting with the ladies and showing his teeth in an old man's smile, a little bit affected, but pleasant, wishing everybody to be happy.

Aaron ate his soup, trying to catch up. Milady's own confidential Italian butler, fidelity itself, hovered quivering near, spiritually helping the newcomer to catch up. Two nice little entrée dishes, specially prepared for Aaron to take the place of the bygone fish and vol-au-vents of the proper dinner, testified to the courtesy and charity of his hostess.

Well, eating rapidly, he had more or less caught up by the time the sweets came. So he swallowed a glass of wine and looked round. His hostess with her pearls, and her diamond star in her grey hair, was speaking of Lilly and then of music to him.

'I hear you are a musician. That's what I should have been if I had had my way.'

'What instrument?' asked Aaron.

'Oh, the piano. Yours is the flute, Mr Lilly says. I think the flute can be so attractive. But I feel, of course, you have more range with the piano. I love the piano – and orchestra.'

At that moment the Colonel and hostess-duties distracted her. But she came back in snatches. She was a woman who reminded him a little of Queen Victoria; so assured in her own room, a large part of her attention always given to the successful issue of her duties, the remainder at the disposal of her guests. It was an old-fashioned, not unpleasant feeling: like retrospect. But she had beautiful big, smooth emeralds and sapphires on her fingers. Money! What a curious thing it is! Aaron noticed the deference of all the guests at table: a touch of obsequiousness: before the money! And the host and hostess accepted the deference, nay, expected it, as their dues. Yet both Sir William and Lady Franks *knew* that it was only money and success. They had both a certain afterthought, knowing dimly that the game was but a game, and that they were the helpless leaders in the game. They had a certain basic ordinariness which prevented their making any great hits, and which kept them disillusioned all the while. They remembered their poor and insignificant days.

'And I hear you were playing in the orchestra at Covent Garden. We came back from London last week. I enjoyed Beecham's operas so much.'

'Which do you like best?' said Aaron.

'Oh, the Russians. I think *Ivan*. It is such fine music.'

'I find *Ivan* artificial.'

'Do you? Oh, I don't think so. No, I don't think you can say that.'

Aaron wondered at her assurance. She seemed to put him just a tiny bit in his place, even in an opinion on music. Money gave her that right too. Curious – the only authority left. And he deferred to her opinion: that is, to her money. He did it almost deliberately. Yes – what did he believe in, besides money? What does any man? He looked at the black patch over the Major's eye. What had he given his eye for? – the nation's money. Well, and very necessary too; otherwise we might be where the wretched Austrians are. Instead of which – how smooth his hostess's sapphires!

'Of course I myself prefer Moussorgsky,' said Aaron. 'I think he is a greater artist. But perhaps it is just personal preference.'

'Yes. *Boris* is wonderful. Oh, some of the scenes in *Boris*!'

'And even more *Kovantchina*,' said Aaron. 'I wish we could go back to melody pure and simple. Yet I find *Kovantchina*, which is all mass music practically, gives me more satisfaction than any other opera.'

'Do you really. I shouldn't say so: oh no. But you can't mean that you would like all music to go back to melody pure and simple! Just a flute – just a pipe! Oh, Mr Sisson, you are bigoted for your instrument. I just *live* in harmony – chords, chords!' She struck imaginary chords on the white damask, and her sapphires swam blue. But at the same time she was watching to see if Sir William had still got beside his plate the white medicine *cachet* which he must swallow at every meal. Because if so, she must remind him to swallow it. However, at that very moment, he put it on his tongue. So that she could turn her attention again to Aaron and the imaginary chord on the white damask; the thing she just lived in. But the rubicund bald Colonel, more rubicund after wine, most rubicund now the marsala was going, snatched her attention with a burly homage to her femininity, and shared his fear with her with a boyish gallantry.

When the women had gone up, Sir William came near and put his hand on Aaron's shoulder. It was evident the charm was beginning to work. Sir William was a self-made man, and not in the least a snob. He liked the fundamental ordinariness in Aaron, the commonness of the common man.

'Well now, Mr Sisson, we are very glad to see you: very glad indeed. I count Mr Lilly one of the most interesting men it has ever been my good fortune to know. And so for your own sake, and for Mr Lilly's sake, we are very glad to see you. Arthur, my boy, give Mr Sisson some marsala – and take some yourself.'

'Thank you sir,' said the well-nourished young man in nice evening clothes. 'You'll take another glass yourself, sir?'

'Yes, I will, I will. I will drink a glass with Mr Sisson. Major, where are you wandering off to? Come and take a glass with us, my boy.'

'Thanks, Sir William,' drawled the young Major with the black patch.

'Now, Colonel – I hope you are in good health and spirits.'

'Never better, Sir William, never better.'

'I'm very glad to hear it: very glad indeed. Try my marsala – I think it is quite good. Port is beyond us for the moment – for the moment –'

And the old man sipped his brown wine, and smiled again. He made quite a handsome picture: but he was frail.

'And where are you bound, Mr Sisson? Towards Rome?'

'I came to meet Lilly,' said Aaron.

'Ah! but Lilly has fled over the borders by this time. Never was such a man for crossing frontiers. Wonderful person, to be able to do it.'

'Where has he gone?' said Aaron.

'I think to Geneva for the moment. But he certainly talked of Venice. You yourself have no definite goal?'

'No.'

'Ah! You have not come to Italy to practise your art?'

'I shall *have* to practise it: or else – No, I haven't come for that.'

'Ah, you will *have* to practise it. Ah yes! We are all under the necessity to eat. And you have a family in England? Am I not right?'

'Quite. I've got a family depending on me.'

'Yes, then you must practise your art: you must practise your art. Well – shall we join the ladies? Coffee will no doubt be served.'

'Will you take my arm, sir?' said the well-nourished Arthur.

'Thank you, thank you,' the old man motioned him away.

So they went upstairs to where the three women were sitting in the library round the fire: chattering not very interested. The entry of Sir William at once made a stir.

The girl in white, with the biggish nose, fluttered round him. She was Arthur's wife. The girl in soft blue spread herself on the couch; she was the young Major's wife: and she had a blue band round her hair. The Colonel hovered stout and fidgety round Lady Franks and the liqueur stand. He and the Major were both in khaki – belonging to the service on duty in Italy still.

Coffee appeared – and Sir William doled out *crème de menthe*. There was no conversation – only tedious words. The little party was just commonplace and dull – boring. Yet Sir William, the self-made man, was a study. And the young Oxford-like Major, with his English diffidence and his one dark, pensive, baffled eye, was only waiting to be earnest, poor devil.

The girl in white had been a sort of companion to Lady Franks, so that Arthur was more or less a son-in-law. In this capacity he acted. Aaron strayed round uneasily, looking at the books, but not to read, and at the big pictures above. It was Arthur who fetched out the little boxes containing the orders conferred on Sir William for his war-work: and perhaps more, for the many thousands of pounds he had spent on his war-work.

There were three orders: one British, and quite important, a large silver star for the breast; one Italian, smaller, and silver and gold; and one from the state of Ruritania, in silver and red-and-green enamel, smaller than the others.

'Come now, William,' said Lady Franks, 'you must try them all on. You must try them all on together, and let us see how you look.'

The little, frail old man, with his strange old man's blue eyes and his old man's perpetual laugh, swelled out his chest and said:

'What, am I to appear in all my vanities?' And he laughed shortly.

'Of course you are. We want to see you,' said the white girl.

'Indeed we do! We shouldn't mind all appearing in such vanities – what, Lady Franks!' boomed the Colonel.

'I should think not,' replied his hostess. 'When a man has honours conferred on him, it shows a poor spirit if he isn't proud of them.'

'Of course I am proud of them!' said Sir William.

'Well then, come and have them pinned on. I think it's wonderful to have got so much in one lifetime – wonderful –' said Lady Franks.

'Oh, Sir William is a wonderful man,' said the Colonel.

'Well – we won't say so before him. But let us look at him in his orders.'

Arthur, always ready on these occasions, had taken the large and shining British star from its box, and drew near to Sir William, who stood swelling his chest, pleased, proud, and a little wistful.

'This one first, sir,' said Arthur.

Sir William stood very still, half tremulous, like a man undergoing an operation.

'And it goes just here – the level of the heart. This is where it goes' – and carefully he pinned the large, radiating ornament on the black velvet dinner-jacket of the old man.

'That is the first – and very becoming,' said Lady Franks.

'Oh, very becoming! Very becoming!' said the tall wife of the Major – she was a handsome young woman of the tall frail type.

'Do you think so, my dear?' said the old man, with his eternal smile: the curious smile of old people when they are dead.

'Not only becoming, sir,' said the Major, bending his tall slim figure forwards, 'but a reassuring sign that a nation knows how to distinguish her valuable men.'

'Quite!' said Lady Franks. 'I think it is a very great honour to have got it. The King was most gracious, too – Now the other. That goes beside it – the Italian.'

Sir William stood there undergoing the operation of the pinning-on. The Italian star being somewhat smaller than the British, there was a slight question as to where exactly it should be placed. However, Arthur decided it: and the old man stood before the company with his two stars on his breast.

'And now the Ruritanian,' said Lady Franks eagerly.

'That doesn't go on the same level with the others, Lady Franks,' said Arthur. 'That goes much lower down – about here.'

'Are you sure?' said Lady Franks. 'Doesn't it go more here.'

'No no, no, no, not at all. Here! Isn't it so, Sybil?'

'Yes, I think so,' said Sybil.

Old Sir William stood quite silent, his breast prepared, peering over the facings of his coat to see where the star was going. The Colonel was called in, and though he knew nothing about it, he agreed with Arthur, who apparently did know something. So the star was pinned quite low down. Sir William, peeping down, exclaimed:

'Well, that is most curious now! I wear an order over the pit of my stomach! I think that is very curious: a curious place to wear an order.'

'Stand up! Stand up and let us look!' said Lady Franks. 'There now, isn't it handsome? And isn't it a great deal of honour for one man? Could he have expected so much, in one lifetime? I call it wonderful. Come and look at yourself, dear' – and she led him to a mirror.

'What's more, all thoroughly deserved,' said Arthur.

'I should think so,' said the Colonel, fidgeting.

'Ah yes, nobody has deserved them better,' cooed Sybil.

'Nor on more humane and generous grounds,' said the Major, *sotto voce.*

'The effort to save life, indeed,' returned the Major's young wife: 'Splendid!'

Sir William stood naïvely before the mirror and looked at his three stars on his black velvet dinner-jacket.

'Almost directly over the pit of my stomach,' he said, 'I hope that it is not a decoration for my greedy *appetite.*' And he laughed at the young women.

'I assure you it is in position, sir,' said Arthur. 'Absolutely correct. I will read it out to you later.'

'Aren't you satisfied? Aren't you a proud man? Isn't it wonderful?' said Lady Franks. 'Why what more could a man want from life? He could never *expect* so much.'

'Yes, my dear. I *am* a proud man. Three countries have honoured me –' There was a little breathless pause.

'And not more than they ought to have done,' said Sybil.

'Well! Well! I shall have my head turned. Let me return to my own humble self. I am too much in the stars at the moment.'

Sir William turned to Arthur to have his decorations removed. Aaron, standing in the background, felt the whole scene strange, childish, a little touching. And Lady Franks was so obviously trying to *console* her husband: to console the frail excitable old man with his honours. But why console him? Did he need consolation? And did she? It was evident that only the hard-money-woman in her put any price on the decorations.

Aaron came forward and examined the orders, one after the other. Just metal playthings of curious shiny silver and gilt and enamel. Heavy the British one – but only like some heavy buckle, a piece of metal merely when one turned it over. Somebody dropped the Italian cross, and there was a moment of horror. But the lump of metal took no hurt. Queer to see the things stowed in their boxes again. Aaron had always imagined these mysterious decorations as shining by nature on the breasts of heroes. Pinned-on pieces of metal were a considerable come-down.

The orders were put away, the party sat round the fire in the comfortable library, the men sipping more *crème de menthe*, since nothing else offered, and the couple of hours in front promising the tedium of small-talk of tedious people who had really nothing to say and no particular originality in saying it.

Aaron, however, had reckoned without his host. Sir William sat upright in his chair, with all the determination of a frail old man who insists on being level with the young. The new guest sat in a lower chair, smoking, that curious glimmer on his face which made him so attractive, and which only meant that he was looking on the whole scene from the outside, as it were, from beyond a fence. Sir William came almost directly to the attack.

'And so, Mr Sisson, you have no definite purpose in coming to Italy!'

'No, none,' said Aaron. 'I wanted to join Lilly.'

'But when you had joined him –?'

'Oh, nothing – stay here a time, in this country, if I could earn my keep.'

'Ah! – earn your keep? So you hope to earn your keep here? May I ask how?'

'By my flute.'

'Italy is a poor country.'

'I don't want much.'

'You have a family to provide for.'

'They are provided for – for a couple of years.'

'Oh, indeed! Is that so?'

The old man got out of Aaron the detailed account of his circumstances – how he had left so much money to be paid over to his wife, and had reserved only a small amount for himself.

'I see you are like Lilly – you trust to Providence,' said Sir William.

'Providence or fate,' said Aaron.

'Lilly calls it Providence,' said Sir William. 'For my own part, I always advise Providence plus a banking account. I have every belief in Providence, plus a banking account. Providence, and no banking account I have observed to be almost invariably fatal. Lilly and I have argued it. He believes in casting his bread upon the waters. I sincerely hope he won't have to cast himself after his bread, one of these days. Providence with a banking account. Believe in Providence once you have secured enough to live on. I should consider it disastrous to believe in Providence *before*. One can never be *sure* of Providence.'

'What can you be sure of, then?' said Aaron.

'Well, in moderation, I can believe in a little hard cash, and in my own ability to earn a little hard cash.'

'Perhaps Lilly believes in his own ability too.'

'No. Not so. Because he will never directly work to earn money. He works – and works quite well, I am told: but only as the spirit moves him, and never with any eye to the market. Now I call that *tempting* Providence, myself. The spirit may move him in quite an opposite direction to the market – then where is Lilly? I have put it to him more than once.'

'The spirit generally does move him dead against the market,' said Aaron. 'But he manages to scrape along.'

'In a state of jeopardy: all the time in a state of jeopardy,' said the old man. 'His whole existence, and that of his wife, is completely precarious. I found, in my youth, the spirit moved me to various things which would have left me and my wife starving. So I realized in time, that was no good. I took my spirit in hand, therefore, and made him pull the cart which mankind is riding in. I harnessed him to the work of productive labour. And so he brought me my reward.'

'Yes,' said Aaron. 'But every man according to his belief.'

'I don't see,' said Sir William, 'how a man can *believe* in a Providence unless he sets himself definitely to the work of earning his daily bread, and making provision for future needs. That's what Providence means to me – making provision for oneself and one's family. Now Mr Lilly – and you yourself – you say you believe in a Providence that does *not* compel you to earn your daily bread, and make provision. I confess myself I cannot see it: and Lilly has never been able to convince me.'

'I don't believe in a kind-hearted Providence,' said Aaron, 'and I don't believe Lilly does. But I believe in chance. I believe, if I go my own way, without tying my nose to a job, chance will always throw something in my way: enough to get along with.'

'But on what do you base such a very unwarrantable belief?'

'I just feel like that.'

'And if you are ever quite without success – and nothing to fall back on?'

'I can work at something.'

'In case of illness, for example?'

'I can go to a hospital – or die.'

'Dear me! However, you are more logical than Lilly. He seems to believe that he has the Invisible – call it Providence if you will – on his side, and that this Invisible will never leave him in the lurch, or let him down, so long as he sticks to his own side of the bargain, and *never* works for his own ends. I don't quite see how he works. Certainly he seems to me a man who squanders a great deal of talent unworthily. Yet for some reason or other he calls this true, genuine activity, and has a contempt for actual work by which a man makes provision for his years and for his family. In the end, he will have to fall back on charity. But when I say so, he denies it, and says that in the end we, the men who work and make provision, will have to fall back on him. Well, all I can say is, that *so far* he is in far greater danger of having to fall back on me, than I on him.'

'The old man sat back in his chair, with a little laugh of triumph. But it smote almost devilishly on Aaron's ears, and for the first time in his life he felt that there existed a necessity for taking sides.

'I don't suppose he will do much falling back,' he said.

'Well, he is young yet. You are both young. You are squandering your youth. I am an old man and I see the end.'

'What end, Sir William?'

'Charity – and poverty – and some not very congenial "job", as you call it, to put bread in your mouth. No, no, I would not like to trust myself to your Providence, or to your Chance. Though I admit your Chance is a sounder proposition than Lilly's Providence. You speculate with your life and your talent. I admit the nature which is a born speculator. After all, with your flute you will speculate in other people's taste for luxury, as a man may speculate in theatres or *trains de luxe*. You are the speculator. That may be your way of wisdom. But Lilly does not even speculate. I cannot see his point. I cannot see his point. Yet I have the greatest admiration for his mentality.'

The old man had fired up during this conversation – and all the others in the room had gone silent. Lady Franks was palpably uneasy. She alone knew how frail the old man was – frailer by far than his years. She alone knew what fear of his own age, what fear of death haunted him now: fear of his own non-existence. His own old age was an agony to him: worse than an agony, a horror. He wanted to be young – to live, to live. And he was old, he was breaking up. The glistening youth of Aaron, the impetuousness of Lilly, fascinated him. And both these men seemed calmly to contradict his own wealth and honours.

Lady Franks tried to turn off the conversation to the trickles of normal chit-chat. The Colonel was horribly bored – so were all the women – Arthur was indifferent. Only the young Major was implicated, troubled in his earnest and philosophic spirit.

'What I can't see,' he said, 'is the place that others have in your scheme.'

'It isn't a scheme,' said Aaron.

'Well then, your way of life. Isn't it pretty selfish, to marry a woman and then expect her to live on very little indeed, and that always precarious, just because you happen to believe in Providence or in Chance: which I think worse? What I don't see is where others come in. What would the world be like if everybody lived that way?'

'Other people can please themselves,' said Aaron.

'No they can't – because you take first choice, it seems to me. Supposing your wife – or Lilly's wife – asks for security and for provision, as Sir William says. Surely she has a right to it?'

'If I've no right to it myself – and I *have* no right to it, if I don't want it – then what right has she?'

'Every right, I should say. All the more since you are improvident.'

'Then she must manage her rights for herself. It's no good her foisting her rights on to me.'

'Isn't that pure selfishness?'

'It may be. I shall send my wife money as long as I've money to send.'

'And supposing you have none?'

'Then I can't send it – and she must look out for herself.'

'I call that almost criminal selfishness.'

'I can't help it.'

The conversation with the young Major broke off.

'It is certainly a good thing for society that men like you and Mr Lilly are not common,' said Sir William, laughing.

'Becoming commoner every day, you'll find,' interjaculated the Colonel.

'Indeed! Indeed! Well. May we ask you another question, Mr Sisson. I hope you don't object to our catechism?'

'No. Nor your judgment afterwards,' said Aaron, grinning.

'Then upon what grounds did you abandon your family? I know it is a tender subject. But Lilly spoke of it to us, and as far as I could see ...'

'There were no grounds,' said Aaron. 'No, there weren't. I just left them.'

'Mere caprice?'

'If it's a caprice to be begotten – and a caprice to be born – and a caprice to die – then that was a caprice, for it was the same.'

'Like birth or death? – I don't follow.'

'It happened to me: a birth happened to me once – and death will happen. It was a sort of death too: or a sort of birth. But as undeniable as either. And without any more grounds.'

The old, tremulous man, and the young man, were watching one another.

'A natural event,' said Sir William.

'A natural event,' said Aaron.

'Not that you loved any other woman?'

'God save me from it.'

'You just left off loving?'

'Not even that. I went away.'

'What from?'

'From it all.'

'From the woman in particular?'

'Oh yes. Yes. Yes, that.'

'And you couldn't go back?'

Aaron shook his head.

'Yet you can give no reasons?'

'Not any reasons that would be any good. It wasn't a question of reasons. It was a question of her and me and what must be. What makes a child be born out of its mother, to the pain and trouble of both of them? I don't know.'

'But that is a natural process.'

'So is this – or nothing.'

'No,' interposed the Major. 'Because birth is a universal process – and yours is a specific, almost unique event.'

'Well, unique or not, it so came about. I didn't even leave off loving her – not as far as I know. I left her as I shall leave the earth when I die – because it has to be.'

'Do you know what I think it is, Mr Sisson?' put in Lady Franks. 'I think you are just in a wicked state of mind: just that. Mr Lilly too. And you must be very careful, or some great misfortune will happen to you.'

'It may,' said Aaron.

'And it will, mark my word, it will.'

'You almost wish it might, as a judgment on me,' smiled Aaron.

'Oh no, indeed. I should only be too sorry. But I feel it will, unless you are careful.'

'I'll be careful then.'

'Yes, and you can't be too careful.'

'You make me frightened.'

'I would like to make you very frightened indeed, so that you went back humbly to your wife and family.'

'It would *have* to be a big fright then, I assure you.'

'Ah, you are really heartless. It makes me angry.'

She turned angrily aside.

'Well, well! Well, well! Life! Life! Young men are a new thing to me!' said Sir William, shaking his head. 'Well, well! What do you say to whisky and soda, Colonel?'

'Why, delighted, Sir William,' said the Colonel, bouncing up.

'A night-cap, and then we retire,' said Lady Franks.

Aaron sat thinking. He knew Sir William liked him: and that Lady Franks didn't. One day he might have to seek help from Sir William. So he had better placate milady. Wrinkling the fine, half-mischievous smile on his face, and trading on his charm, he turned to his hostess.

'You wouldn't mind, Lady Franks, if I said nasty things about my wife and found a lot of fault with her. What makes you angry is that I know it is not a bit more her fault than mine, that we come apart. It can't be helped.

'Oh yes, indeed. I disapprove of your way of looking at things altogether. It seems to be altogether cold and unmanly and inhuman. Thank goodness my experience of a man has been different.'

'We can't all be alike, can we? And if I don't choose to let you see me crying, that doesn't prove I've never had a bad half hour, does it? I've had many – ay, and a many.'

'Then why are you so *wrong*, so wrong in your behaviour?'

'I suppose I've got to have my bout out: and when it's out, I can alter.'

'Then I hope you've almost had your bout out,' she said.

'So do I,' said he, with a half-repentant, half-depressed look on his attractive face. The corners of his mouth grimaced slightly under his moustache.

'The best thing you can do is to go straight back to England, and to her.'

'Perhaps I'd better ask her if she wants me, first,' he said dryly.

'Yes, you might do that too.' And Lady Franks felt she was quite getting on with her work of reform, and the restoring of woman to her natural throne. Best not go too fast, either.

'Say when,' shouted the Colonel, who was manipulating the syphon.

'When,' said Aaron.

The men stood up to their drinks.

'Will you be leaving in the morning, Mr Sisson?' asked Lady Franks.

'May I stay till Monday morning?' said Aaron. They were at Saturday evening.

'Certainly. And you will take breakfast in your room: we all do. At what time? Half-past eight?'

'Thank you very much.'

'Then at half-past eight the man will bring it in. Good night.'

Once more in his blue silk bedroom, Aaron grimaced to himself and stood in the middle of the room grimacing. His hostess's admonitions were like vitriol in his ears. He looked out of the window. Through the darkness of trees, the lights of a city below. Italy! The air was cold with snow. He came back into his soft warm room. Luxurious it was. And luxurious the deep warm bed.

He was still asleep when the man came noiselessly in with the tray: and it was morning. Aaron woke and sat up. He felt that the deep warm bed and the soft warm room had made him sleep too well: robbed him of his night, like a narcotic. He preferred to be more uncomfortable and more aware of the flight of the dark hours. It seemed numbing.

The footman in his grey house-jacket was neat and Italian and sympathizing. He gave good-morning in Italian – then softly arranged the little table by the bedside, and put out the toast and coffee and butter and boiled egg and honey, with silver and delicate china. Aaron watched the soft, catlike motions of the man. The dark eyes glanced once at the blond man, leaning on his elbow on the pillow. Aaron's face had that watchful, half-amused expression. The man said something in Italian. Aaron shook his head, laughed, and said:

'Tell me in English.'

The man went softly to the window curtains, and motioned them with his hand.

'Yes, do,' said Aaron.

So the man drew the buff-coloured silk curtains: and Aaron, sitting in bed, could see away beyond red roofs of a town, and in the farther heaven great snowy mountains.

'The Alps,' he said in surprise.

'Gli Alpi, si signore.' The man bowed, gathered up Aaron's clothes, and silently retired.

Aaron watched through the window. It was a frosty morning at the end of September, with a clear blue morning sky, Alpine, and the watchful, snow-streaked mountain-tops bunched in the distance, as if waiting. There they were, lowering round, circling, waiting. They reminded him of marvellous striped sky-panthers circling round a great camp: the red-roofed city. Aaron looked, and looked again. In the near distance, under the house, elm tree-tops were yellowing. He felt himself changing inside his skin.

So he hurried away to his coffee and eggs. A little silver egg-cup with a curious little frill round it: honey in a frail, iridescent glass bowl, gold-iridescent: the charm of delicate and fine things. He smiled half mockingly to himself. Two instincts played in him: the one, an instinct for fine delicate things: he had attractive hands; the other, an inclination to throw the dainty little table with all its niceties out of the window. It evoked a sort of devil in him.

He took his bath: the man had brought back his things: he dressed and went downstairs. No one in the lounge: he went down to the ground floor: no one in the big hall with its pillars of yellow marble and its gold arches, its enormous, dark, bluey-red carpet. He stood before the great glass doors. Some red flowers still were blooming in the tubs on the steps, handsome: and beautiful chrysanthemums in the wide portico. Beyond, yellow leaves were already falling on the green grass and the neat drive. Everywhere was silent and empty. He climbed the wide stairs, sat in the long upper lounge where the papers were. He wanted his hat and coat, and did not know where to find them. The windows looked on to a terraced garden, the hill rising steeply behind the house. He wanted to go out.

So he opened more doors, and in a long drawing-room came upon five or six men-servants, all in the grey house-jackets, all clean-shaven, neat, with neat black hair, all with dusters or brushes or feather brooms, and all frolicking, chattering, playing like so many monkeys. They were all of the same neat, smallish size. They were all laughing. They rolled back a great rug as if it were some football game, one flew at the curtains. And they merely looked at Aaron and went on chattering, and laughing and dusting.

Surprised, and feeling that he trespassed, he stood at the window a moment looking out. The noise went on behind him. So he turned, smiling, and asked for his hat, pointing to his head. They knew at once what he wanted. One of the fellows beckoned him away, down to the hall and to the long cupboard place where hats and coats and sticks were hung. There was his hat; he put it on, while the man chattered to him pleasantly and unintelligibly, and opened for him the back door, into the garden.

13

WIE ES IHNEN GEFÄLLT

The fresh morning air comes startling after a central-heated house. So Aaron found it. He felt himself dashing up the steps into the garden like a bird dashing out of a trap where it has been caught: that warm and luxurious house. Heaven bless us, we who want to save civilization. We had better make up our minds what of it we want to save. The kernel may be all well and good. But there is precious little kernel, to a lot of woolly stuffing and poisonous rind.

The gardens to Sir William's place were not imposing, and still rather war-neglected. But the pools of water lay smooth in the bright air, the flowers showed their colours beside the walks. Many birds dashed about, rather bewildered, having crossed the Alps in their migration southwards. Aaron noted with gratification a certain big magnificence, a certain reckless powerfulness in the still-blossoming, harsh-coloured, autumn flowers. Distinct satisfaction he derived from it.

He wandered upwards, up the succeeding flights of steps, till he came to the upper rough hedge, and saw the wild copse on the hill-crest just above. Passing through a space in the hedge, he climbed the steep last bit of Sir William's land. It was a little vineyard, with small vines and yellowing leaves. Everywhere the place looked neglected – but as if man had just begun to tackle it once more.

At the very top, by the wild hedge where spindle-berries hung pink, seats were placed, and from here the view was very beautiful. The hill dropped steep beneath him. A river wound on the near side of the city, crossed by a white bridge. The city lay close clustered, ruddy on the plains, glittering in the clear air with its flat roofs and domes and square towers, strangely naked-seeming in the clear, clean air. And massive in the farther nearness, snow-streaked mountains, the tiger-like Alps. Tigers prowling between the north and the south. And this beautiful city lying nearest exposed. The snow-wind brushed her this morning like the icy whiskers of a tiger. And clear in the light lay Novara, wide, fearless, violent Novara. Beautiful the perfect air, the perfect and unblemished Alp sky. And like the first southern flower, Novara.

Aaron sat watching in silence. Only the uneasy birds rustled. He watched the city and the winding river, the bridges, and the imminent Alps. He was on the south side. On the other side of the time barrier. His old sleepy English nature was startled in its sleep. He felt like a man who knows it is time to wake up, and who doesn't want to wake up, to face the responsibility of another sort of day.

To open his darkest eyes and wake up to a new responsibility. Wake up and enter on the responsibility of a new self in himself. Ach, the horror of responsibility! He had all his life slept and shelved the burden. And he wanted to go on sleeping. It was so hateful to have to get a new grip on his own bowels, a new hard recklessness into his heart, a new and responsible consciousness into his mind and soul. He felt some finger prodding, prodding, prodding him awake out of the sleep of pathos and tragedy and spasmodic passion, and he wriggled, unwilling, oh most unwilling to undertake the new business.

In fact he ran away again. He gave a last look at the town and its white-fanged mountains, and descended through the garden, round the way of the kitchen garden and garage and stables and pecking chickens, back to the house again. In the hall still no one. He went upstairs to the long lounge. There sat the rubicund, bald, boy-like Colonel reading the *Graphic*. Aaron sat down opposite him, and made a feeble attempt at conversation. But the Colonel wasn't having any. It was evident he didn't care for the fellow – Mr Aaron that is. Aaron therefore dried up, and began to sit him out, with the aid of the *Queen*. Came a servant, however, and said that the Signor Colonello was called up from the hospital, on the telephone. The Colonel once departed, Aaron fled again, this time out of the front doors and down the steep little park to the gates.

Huge dogs and little dogs came bounding forward. Out of the lodge came the woman with the keys, smiling very pleasantly this morning. So, he was in the street. The wide road let him inevitably to the big bridge, with the violent, physical stone statue-groups. Men and women were moving about, and he noticed for the first time the littleness and the momentaneousness of the Italians in the street. Perhaps it was the wideness of the bridge and the subsequent big open boulevard. But there it was: the people seemed little upright brisk figures moving in a certain isolation, like tiny figures on a big stage. And he felt himself moving in the space between. All the northern cosiness gone. He was set down with a space round him.

Little trams flitted down the boulevard in the bright sweet light. The barbers' shops were all busy, half the Novarese at that moment ambushed in lather, full in the public gaze. A shave is nothing if not a public act, in the south. At the little outdoor tables of the cafés a very few drinkers sat before empty coffee-cups. Most of the shops were shut. It was too soon after the war for life to be flowing very fast. The feeling of emptiness of neglect, of lack of supplies was evident everywhere.

Aaron strolled on, surprised himself at his gallant feeling of liberty: a feeling of bravado and almost swaggering carelessness which is Italy's best gift to an Englishman. He had crossed the dividing line, and the values of life, though ostensibly and verbally the same, were dynamically different. Alas, however, the verbal and the ostensible, the accursed mechanical ideal, gains day by day over the spontaneous life-dynamic, so that Italy becomes as idea-bound and as automatic as England: just a business proposition.

Coming to the station, he went inside. There he saw a money-changing window which was open, so he planked down a five-pound note and got two hundred and ten lire. Here was a start. At a bookstall he saw a man buy a big timetable with a large railway map in it. He immediately bought the same. Then he retired to a corner to get his whereabouts.

In the morning he must move: where? He looked on the map. The map seemed to offer two alternatives, Milan and Genoa. He chose Milan, because of its musical associations and its cathedral. Milano then. Strolling and still strolling, he found the boards announcing Arrivals and Departures. As far as he could make out, the train for Milan left at 9.0 in the morning.

So much achieved, he left the big desolating caravanserai of the station. Soldiers were camped in every corner, lying in heaps asleep. In their grey-green uniform, he was surprised at their sturdy limbs and uniformly small stature. For the first time he saw the cock-feathers of the Bersaglieri. There seemed a new life-quality everywhere. Many worlds, not one world. But alas, the one world triumphing more and more over the many worlds, the big oneness swallowing up the many small diversities in its insatiable gnawing appetite, leaving a dreary sameness throughout the world, that means at last complete sterility.

Aaron, however, was too new to the strangeness, he had no eye for the horrible sameness that was spreading like a disease over Italy from England and the north. He plunged into the space in front of the station, and took a new wide boulevard. To his surprise he ran towards a big and over-animated statue that stood resolutely with its back to the magnificent snow-domes of the wild Alps. Wolves in the street could not have startled him more than those magnificent fierce-gleaming mountains of snow at the street end, beyond the statue. He stood and wondered, and never thought to look who the gentleman was. Then he turned right round, and began to walk home.

Luncheon was at one o'clock. It was half-past twelve when he rang at the lodge gates. He climbed through the leaves of the little park, on a side-path, rather reluctantly towards the house. In the hall Lady Franks was discussing with Arthur a fat Pekingese who did not seem very well. She was sure the servants did not obey her orders concerning the Pekingese bitch. Arthur, who was more than indifferent, assured her they did. But she seemed to think that the whole of the male human race was in league against the miserable specimen of a she-dog. She almost cried, thinking her Queenie *might* by some chance meet with, perhaps, a harsh word or look. Queenie apparently fattened on the secret detestation of the male human species.

'I can't bear to think that a dumb creature might be ill-treated,' she said to Aaron. 'Thank goodness the Italians are better than they used to be.'

'Are they better than they used to be?'

'Oh, much. They have learnt it from us.'

She then inquired if her guest had slept, and if he were rested from his journey. Aaron, into whose face the faint snow-wind and the sun had brought a glow, replied that he had slept well and enjoyed the morning, thank you. Whereupon Lady Franks knitted her brows and said Sir William had had such a bad night. He had not been able to sleep, and had got up and walked about the room. The least excitement, and she dreaded a break-down. He must have absolute calm and restfulness.

'There's one for you and your jawing last night, Aaron, my boy!' said our hero to himself.

'I thought Sir William seemed so full of life and energy,' he said aloud.

'Ah, did you! No, he *wants* to be. But he can't do it. He's very much upset this morning. I have been very anxious about him.'

'I am sorry to hear that.'

Lady Franks departed to some duty. Aaron sat alone before the fire. It was a huge fireplace, like a dark chamber shut in by tall, finely-wrought iron gates. Behind these iron gates of curly iron the logs burned and flickered like leopards slumbering and lifting their heads within their cage. Aaron wondered who was the keeper of the savage element, who it was that would open the iron grille and throw on another log, like meat to the lions. To be sure the fire was only to be looked at: like wild beasts in the Zoo. For the house was warm from roof to floor. It was strange to see the blue air of sunlight outside, the yellow-edged leaves falling in the wind, the red flowers shaking.

The gong sounded softly through the house. The Colonel came in heartily from the garden, but did not speak to Aaron. The Major and his wife came pallid down the stairs. Lady Franks appeared, talking domestic-secretarial business with the wife of Arthur. Arthur, well-nourished and half at home, called down the stairs. And then Sir William descended, old and frail now in the morning, shaken: still he approached Aaron heartily, and asked him how he did, and how he had spent his morning. The old man who had made a fortune: how he expected homage: and how he got it! Homage, like most things, is just a convention and a social trick. Aaron found himself paying homage too to the old man who had made a fortune. But also, exacting a certain deference in return, from the old man who had made a fortune. Getting it too. On what grounds? Youth, maybe. But mostly scorn for fortunes and fortune-making. Did he scorn fortunes and fortune-making? Not he, otherwise whence this homage for the old man with much money. Aaron, like everybody else, was rather paralysed by a million sterling, personified in one old man. Paralysed, fascinated, overcome. All those three. Only having no final control over his own make-up, he could not drive himself into the money-making or even into the money-having habit. And he had just wit enough to threaten Sir William's golden king with his own ivory queen and knights of wilful life. And Sir William quaked.

'Well, and how have you spent your morning?' asked the host.

'I went first to look at the garden.'

'Ah, not much to see now. They have been beautiful with flowers, once. But for two and a half years the house has been a hospital for officers – and even tents in the park and garden – as many as two hundred wounded and sick at a time. We are only just returning to civil life. And flowers need time. Yes – yes – British officers – for two and a half years. But did you go up, now, to the belvedere?'

'To the top – where the vines are? I never expected the mountains.'

'You never expected the mountains? Pray, why not? They are always there.'

'But I was never there before. I never knew they were there, round the town. I didn't expect it like that.'

'Ah! So you found our city impressive?'

'Very! Ah, very! A new world to me. I feel I've come out of myself.'

'Yes, it is a wonderful sight – a wonderful sight – But you have not been *into* the town?'

'Yes. I saw the men being shaved, and all the soldiers at the station: and a statue, and mountains behind it. Oh, I've had a full morning.'

'A full morning! That is good, that is good!' The old man looked again at the younger man, and seemed to get life from him, to live in him vicariously.

'Come,' said the hostess. 'Luncheon.'

Aaron sat again on his hostess's left hand. The Colonel was more affable now it was meal-time. Sir William was again in a good humour, chaffing the young ladies with an old man's gallantry. But now he insisted on drawing Aaron into the play. And Aaron did not want to be drawn. He did not one bit want to chaffer gallantries with the young women. Between him and Sir William there was a curious rivalry – unconscious on both sides. The old knight had devoted an energetic, adventurous, almost an artistic nature to the making of his fortune and the developing of later philanthropics. He had no children. Aaron was devoting a similar nature to anything but fortune-making and philanthropy. The one held life to be a storing-up of produce and a conservation of energy: the other held life to be a sheer spending of energy and a storing-up of nothing but experience. There they were, in opposition, the old man and the young. Sir William kept calling Aaron into the chaffer at the other end of the table: and Aaron kept on refusing to join. He hated long-distance answers, anyhow. And in his mood of the moment he hated the young women. He had a conversation with Arthur about statues: concerning which Aaron knew nothing, and Arthur less than nothing. Then Lady Franks turned the conversation to the soldiers at the station, and said how Sir William had equipped rest-huts for the Italian privates near the station: but that such was the jealousy and spite of the Italian Red Cross – or some such body locally – that Sir William's huts had been left empty – standing unused – while the men had slept on the stone floor of the station, night after night, in icy winter. There was evidently much bitter feeling as a result of Sir William's philanthropy. Apparently even the honey of lavish charity had turned to gall in the Italian mouth: at least the official mouth. Which gall had been spat back at the charitable, much to his pain. It is in truth a difficult world, particularly when you have another race to deal with. After which came the beef-olives.

'Oh,' said Lady Franks, 'I had such a dreadful dream last night, such a dreadful dream. It upset me so much, I have not been able to get over it all day.'

'What was it?' said Aaron. 'Tell it, and break it.'

'Why,' said his hostess, 'I dreamed I was asleep in my room – just as I actually was – and that it was night, yet with a terrible sort of light, like the dead light before dawn, so that one could see. And my maid Giuseppina came running into my room saying: "Signora! Signora! Si alza! Subito! Signora! Vengono su!" – and I said: "Chi? Chi sono chi vengono? Chi?" – "I Novaresi! I Novaresi vengono su. Vengono qui!" – I got out of bed and went to the window. And there they were, in the dead light, rushing up to the house, through the trees. It was so awful, I haven't been able to forget it all day.'

'Tell me what the words are in English,' said Aaron.

'Why, she said: "Get up, get up – the Novaresi, the people of Novara are coming up – vengono su – they are coming up – the Novara people – work-people. I can't forget it. It was so real, I can't believe it didn't actually happen.'

'Ah,' said Aaron. 'It will never happen. I know, that whatever one foresees, and *feels* has happened, never happens in real life. It sort of works itself off through the imagining of it.'

'Well, it was almost more real to me than real life,' said his hostess.

'Then it will never happen in real life,' he said.

Luncheon passed, and coffee. The party began to disperse – Lady Franks to answer more letters, with the aid of Arthur's wife – some to sleep, some to walk. Aaron escaped once more through the big gates. This time he turned his back on the town and the mountains and climbed up the hill into the country. So he went between the banks and the bushes, watching for unknown plants and shrubs, hearing the birds, feeling the influence of a new soil. At the top of the hill he saw over into vineyards, and a new strange valley with a winding river, and jumbled, entangled hills. Strange wild country so near the town. It seemed to keep an almost virgin wildness – yet he saw the white houses dotted here and there.

Just below him was a peasant house: and on a little loggia in the sun two peasants in white shirt-sleeves and black Sunday suits were sitting drinking wine and talking, talking. Peasant youths in black hats, their sweethearts in dark stuff dresses, wearing no hat, but a black silk or a white silk scarf, passed slowly along the little road just below the ridge. None looked up to see Aaron sitting there alone. From some hidden place somebody was playing an accordion, a jerky sound in the still afternoon. And away beyond lay the unchanging, mysterious valley and the infolding, mysterious hills of Italy.

Returning back again another way, he lost himself at the foot of the hill in new and deserted suburb streets – unfinished streets of seemingly unfinished houses. Then a sort of boulevard where bourgeois families were taking the Sunday afternoon walk: stout papas, stout, pallid mamas in rather cheap black fur, little girls very much dressed, and long lads in short socks and round sailor caps, ribbons fluttering. Alien they felt, alien, alien, as a bourgeois crowd always does, but particularly a foreign, Sunday-best bourgeois crowd. Aaron wandered and wandered, finding the tram terminus and trying blank, unfinished street after street. He had a great disinclination to ask his way.

At last he recognized the bank and the little stream of water that ran along the street side. So he was back in time for tea. A hospital nurse was there, and two other strange women. Arthur played the part of host. Sir William came in from a walk with the dogs, but retired to his room without taking tea.

And so the evening fell. Aaron sat in the hall at some distance from the fire, which burned behind its wrought-iron gates. He was tired now with all his impressions, and dispirited. He thought of his wife and children at home: of the church-bells ringing so loudly across the field beyond his garden-end: of the dark-clad people trailing unevenly across the two paths, one to the left, one to the right, forking their way towards the houses of the town, to church or to chapel: mostly to chapel. At this hour he himself would be dressed in his best clothes, tying his bow, ready to go out to the public-house. And his wife would be resenting his holiday departure, whilst she was left fastened to the children.

Rather tired and dispirited in this alien place, he wondered if he wished himself back. But the moment he actually *realized* himself at home, and felt the tension of barrenness which it meant, felt the curious and deadly opposition of his wife's will against his own nature, the almost nauseating ache which it amounted to, he pulled himself together and rejoiced again in his new surroundings. Her will, her will, her terrible, implacable, cunning will! What was there in the female will so diabolical, he asked himself, that it could press like a flat sheet of iron against a man all the time? The female will! He realized now that he had a horror of it. It was flat and inflexible as a sheet of iron. But also it was cunning as a snake that could sing treacherous songs.

Of two people at a deadlock, he always reminded himself, there is not one only wholly at fault. Both must be at fault. Having a detached and logical soul, he never let himself forget this truth. Take Lottie! He had loved her. He had never loved any other woman. If he had had his other affairs – it was out of spite or defiance or curiosity. They meant nothing. He and Lottie had loved one another. And the love had developed almost at once into a kind of combat. Lottie had been the only child of head-strong, well-to-do parents. He also had been the only child of his widowed mother. Well then, both he and Lottie had been brought up to consider themselves the first in whatsoever company they found themselves. During the early months of the marriage he had, of course, continued the spoiling of the young wife. But this never altered the fact that, by his very nature, he considered himself as first and almost as single in any relationship. First and single he felt, and as such he bore himself. It had taken him years to realize that Lottie also felt herself first and single: under all her whimsicalness and fretfulness was a conviction as firm as steel: that she, as woman, was the centre of creation, the man was but an adjunct. She, as woman, and particularly as mother, was the first great source of life and being, and also of culture. The man was but the instrument and the finisher. She was the source and the substance.

Sure enough, Lottie had never formulated this belief inside herself. But it was formulated for her in the whole world. It is the substantial and professed belief of the whole white world. She did but inevitably represent what the whole world around her asserted: the life-centrality of woman. Woman, the life-bearer, the life-source.

Nearly all men agree to the assertion. Practically all men, even while demanding their selfish rights as superior males, tacitly agree to the fact of the sacred life-bearing priority of woman. Tacitly, they yield the worship to that which is female. Tacitly, they conspire to agree that all that is productive, all that is fine and sensitive and most essentially noble, is woman. This, in their productive and religious souls, they believe. And however much they may react against the belief, loathing their women, running to prostitutes, or beer or *anything*, out of reaction against this great and ignominious dogma of the sacred priority of women, still they do but profane the god they worship. Profaning woman, they still inversely worship her.

But in Aaron was planted another seed. He did not know it. He started off on the good old tack of worshipping his woman while his heart was honest, and profaning her in his fits of temper and revolt. But he made a bad show.

Born in him was a spirit which could not worship woman: no, and would not. Could not and would not. It was not in him. In early days, he tried to pretend it was in him. But through his plaintive and homage-rendering love of a young husband was always, for the woman, discernible the arrogance of self-unyielding male. He never yielded himself: never. All his mad loving was only an effort. Afterwards, he was as devilishly unyielded as ever. And it was an instinct in her that her man must yield to her, so that she should envelop him, yielding, in her all-beneficent love. She was quite sure that her love was all-beneficent. Of this no shadow of doubt. She was quite sure that the highest her man could ever know or ever reach, was to be perfectly enveloped in her all-beneficent love. This was her idea of marriage. She held it not as an idea, but as a profound impulse and instinct: an instinct developed in her by the age in which she lived. All that was deepest and most sacred in her feeling centred in this belief.

And he outraged her! Oh, from the first day and the first night, she felt he outraged her. True, for some time she had been taken in by his manifest love. But though you can deceive the conscious mind, you can never deceive the deep unconscious instinct. She could never understand whence arose in her, almost from the first days of marriage with him, her terrible paroxysms of hatred for him. She was in love with him: ah, heaven, how maddeningly she was in love with him: a certain unseizable beauty that was his, and which fascinated her as a snake a bird. But in revulsion, how she hated him! How she abhorred him! How she despised and shuddered at him! He seemed a horrible thing to her.

And then again, oh God, the agony of her desire for him. The agony of her long, long desire for him. He was a passionate lover. He gave her, ostensibly, all she asked for. He withheld from her nothing, no experience, no degree of intimacy. She was his intimate, or he hers.

And yet, oh horror for a woman, he withheld everything from her. He withheld the very centre of himself. For a long time she never realized. She was dazed and maddened only. But as months of married experience passed into years of married torment, she began to understand. It was that, after their most tremendous and, it seemed to her, heaven-rending passion – yea, when for her every veil seemed rent and a terrible and sacred creative darkness covered the earth – then – after all this wonder and miracle -- in crept a poisonous grey snake of disillusionment, a poisonous grey snake of disillusionment that bit her to madness, so that she really was a mad woman, demented.

Why? Why? He never gave himself. He never came to her, *really*. He withheld himself. Yes, in those supreme and sacred times which for her were the whole culmination of life and being, the ecstasy of unspeakable passional conjunction, he was not really hers. He was withheld. He withheld the central core of himself, like the devil and hell-fiend he was. He cheated and made play with her tremendous passional soul, her sacred sex passion, most sacred of all things for a woman. All the time, some central part of him stood apart from her, aside, looking on.

Oh, agony and horror for a passionate, fierce-hearted woman! She who loved him. She who loved him to madness. She who would have died for him. She who did die with him, many terrible and magnificent connubial deaths, in his arms, her husband.

Her husband! How bitter the word grew to her! Her husband! and him never once given, given wholly to her! Her husband – and in all the frenzied finality of desire, she never *fully* possessed him, not once. No, not once. As time went on, she learned it for inevitable. Not once!

And then, how she hated him! Cheated, foiled, betrayed, forced to love him or to hate him: never able to be at peace near him nor away from him: poor Lottie, no wonder she was as a mad woman. She was strictly as a woman demented, after the birth of her second child. For all her instinct, all her impulse, all her desire, and above all, all her *will*, was to possess her man in very fullness once: just once: and once and for all. Once, just once: and it would be once and for all.

But never! Never! Not once! Never! Not for one single solitary second! Was it not enough to send a woman mad. Was it not enough to make her demented! Yes, and mad she was. She made his life a hell for him. She bit him to the bone with her frenzy of rage, chagrin, and agony. She drove him mad too: mad, so that he beat her: mad so that he longed to kill her. But even in his greatest rages it was the same: he never finally lost himself: he remained, somewhere in the centre, in possession of himself. She sometimes wished he would kill her: or that she would kill him. Neither event happened.

And neither of them understood what was happening. How should they? They were both dazed, horrified, and mortified. He took to leaving her alone as much as was possible. But when he *had* to come home, there was her terrible will, like a flat cold snake coiled round his soul and squeezing him to death. Yes, she did not relent. She was a good wife and mother. All her duties she fulfilled. But she was not one to yield. *He* must yield. That was written in eternal letters, on the iron tablet of her will. *He* must yield. She the woman, the mother of his children, how should she ever even think to yield? It was unthinkable. He, the man, the weak, the false, the treacherous, the half-hearted, it was he who must yield. Was not hers the divine will and the divine right? Ha, she would be less than woman if she ever capitulated, abandoned her divine responsibility as woman! No, *he* must yield.

So, he was unfaithful to her. Piling reproach after reproach upon himself, he added adultery to his brutality. And this was the beginning of the end. She was more than maddened: but he began to grow silent, unresponsive, as if he did not hear her. He was unfaithful to her: and oh, in such a low way. Such shame, such shame! But he only smiled carelessly now, and asked her what she wanted. She had asked for all she got. That he reiterated. And that was all he would do.

Terrible was, that she found even his smile of insolent indifference half-beautiful. Oh, bitter chain to bear! But she summoned up all her strange woman's will. She fought against his fascination, the fascination he exerted over her. With fearful efforts of will she fought against it, and mastered it. And then, suddenly, horror and agony of it, up it would rush in her again, her unbearable desire for him, the longing for his contact, his quality of beauty.

That was a cross hard to bear. Yet even that she bore. And schooled herself into a fretful, petulant manner of indifference. Her odd, whimsical petulance hid a will which he, and he alone, knew to be stronger than steel, strong as a diabolical, cold grey snake that presses and presses and cannot relax; nay, cannot relax. She became the same as he. Even in her moments of most passionate desire for him, the cold and snake-like tension of her will never relaxed, and the cold, snake-like eye of her intention never closed.

So, till it reached a deadlock. Each will was wound tense, and so fixed. Fixed! There was neither any relaxing nor any increase of pressure. Fixed.

Hard like a numbness, a grip that was solidifying and turning to stone.

He realized, somehow, that at this terrible passive game of fixed tension she would beat him. Her fixed female soul, her wound-up female will would solidify into stone – whereas his must break. In him something must break. It was a cold and fatal deadlock, profitless. A life-automatism of fixed tension that suddenly, in him, did break. His will flew loose in a recoil: a recoil away from her. He left her, as inevitably as a broken spring flies out from its hold.

Not that he was broken. He would not do her even that credit. He had only flown loose from the old centre-fixture. His will was still entire and unabated. Only he did not know: he did not understand. He swung wildly about from place to place, as if he were broken.

Then suddenly, on this Sunday evening in the strange country, he realized something about himself. He realized that he had never intended to yield himself fully to her or to anything: that he did not intend ever to yield himself up entirely to her or to anything: that his very being pivoted on the fact of his isolate self-responsibility, aloneness. His intrinsic and central aloneness was the very centre of his being. Break it, and he broke his being. Break this central aloneness, and he broke everything. It was the great temptation, to yield himself: and it was the final sacrilege. Anyhow, it was something which, from his profoundest soul, he did not intend to do. By the innermost isolation and singleness of his own soul he would abide though the skies fell on top of one another, and seven heavens collapsed.

Vaguely he realized this. And vaguely he realized that this had been the root cause of his strife with Lottie: Lottie, the only person who had mattered at all to him in all the world: save perhaps his mother. And his mother had not mattered, no, not one-half nor one-fifth what Lottie had mattered. So it was: there was, for him, only her significant in the universe. And between him and her matters were as they were.

He coldly and terribly hated her for a moment. Then no more. There was no solution. It was a situation without a solution. But at any rate, it was now a defined situation. He could rest in peace.

Thoughts something in this manner ran through Aaron's subconscious mind as he sat in the strange house. He could not have fired it all off at any listener, as these pages are fired off at any chance reader. Nevertheless, there it was, risen to half-consciousness in him. All his life he had *hated* knowing what he felt. He had wilfully, if not consciously, kept a gulf between his passional soul and his open mind. In his mind was pinned up a nice description of himself, and a description of Lottie, sort of authentic passports to be used in the conscious world. These authentic passports, self-describing: nose short, mouth normal, etc.; he had insisted that they should do all the duty of the man himself. This ready-made and very banal idea of himself as a really quite nice individual: eyes blue, nose short, mouth normal, chin normal: this he had insisted was really himself. It was his conscious mask.

Now at last, after years of struggle, he seemed suddenly to have dropped his mask on the floor, and broken it. His authentic self-describing passport, his complete and satisfactory idea of himself suddenly became a rag of paper, ridiculous. What on earth did it matter if he was nice or not, his chin was normal or abnormal?

His mask, his idea of himself dropped and was broken to bits. There he sat now maskless and invisible. That was how he strictly felt: invisible and undefined, rather like Wells's *Invisible Man*. He had no longer a mask to present to people: he was present and invisible: they *could* not really think anything about him, because they could not really see him. What did they see when they looked at him? Lady Franks, for example. He neither knew nor cared. He only knew he was invisible to himself and everybody, and that all thinking about what he was like was only a silly game of Mrs Mackenzie's Dead.

So there. The old Aaron Sisson was as if painfully transmuted, as the Invisible Man when he underwent his transmutations. Now he was gone, and no longer to be seen. His visibility lost for ever.

And then what? Sitting there as an invisible presence, the preconceived world melted also and was gone. Lady Franks, Sir William, all the guests, they talked and manoeuvred with their visible personalities, manipulating the masks of themselves. And underneath there was something invisible and dying – something fading, wilting: the essential plasm of themselves: their invisible being.

Well now, and what next? Having in some curious manner tumbled from the tree of modern knowledge, and cracked and rolled out from the shell of the preconceived idea of himself like some dark, night-lustrous chestnut from the green ostensibility of the burr, he lay as it were exposed but invisible on the floor, knowing, but making no conceptions: knowing, but having no idea. Now that he was finally unmasked and exposed, the accepted idea of himself cracked and rolled aside like a broken chestnut-burr, the mask split and shattered, he was at last quiet and free. He had dreaded exposure: and behold, we cannot be exposed, for we are invisible. We cannot be exposed to the looks of others, for our very being is night-lustrous and unseeable. Like the Invisible Man, we are only revealed through our clothes and our masks.

In his own powerful but subconscious fashion Aaron realized this. He was a musician. And hence even his deepest *ideas* were not word-ideas, his very thoughts were not composed of words and ideal concepts. They too, his thoughts and his ideas, were dark and invisible, as electric vibrations are invisible no matter how many words they may purport. If I, as a word-user, must translate his deep conscious vibrations into finite words, that is my own business. I do but make a translation of the man. He would speak in music. I speak with words.

The inaudible music of his conscious soul conveyed his meaning in him quite as clearly as I convey it in words: probably much more clearly. But in his own mode only: and it was in his own mode only he realized what I must put into words. These words are my own affair. His mind was music.

Don't grumble at me then, gentle reader, and swear at me that this damned fellow wasn't half clever enough to think all these smart things, and realize all these fine-drawn-out subtleties. You are quite right, he wasn't, yet it all resolved itself in him as I say, and it is for you to prove that it didn't.

In his now silent, maskless state of wordless comprehension, he knew that he had never wanted to surrender himself utterly to Lottie: nor to his mother: nor to anybody. The last extreme of self-abandon in love was for him an act of false behaviour. His own nature inside him fated him not to take this last false step, over the edge of the abyss of selflessness. Even if he wanted to, he could not. He might struggle on the edge of the precipice like an assassin struggling with his own soul, but he could not conquer. For, according to all the current prejudice and impulse in one direction, he too had believed that the final achievement, the consummation of human life, was this flinging oneself over the precipice, down the bottomless pit of love. Now he realized that love, even in its intensest, was only an attribute of the human soul: one of its incomprehensible gestures. And to fling down the whole soul in one gesture of finality in love was as much a criminal suicide as to jump off a church-tower or a mountain-peak. Let a man give himself as much as he liked in love, to seven thousand extremities, he must never give himself *away*. The more generous and the more passionate a soul, the more it *gives* itself. But the more absolute remains the law, that it shall never give itself away. Give thyself, but give thyself not away. That is the lesson written at the end of the long strange lane of love.

The *idée fixe* of today is that every individual shall not only give himself, but shall achieve the last glory of giving himself away. And since this takes two – you can't even make a present of yourself unless you've got somebody to receive the present; since this last extra-divine act takes two people to perform it, you've got to take into count not only your giver but your receiver. Who is going to be the giver and who the receiver?

Why, of course, in our long-drawn-out Christian day, man is given and woman is recipient. Man is the gift, woman the receiver. This is the sacrament we live by; the holy communion we live for. That man give himself to woman in an utter and sacred abandon, all, all, all himself given, and taken. Woman, eternal woman, she is the communicant. She receives the sacramental body and spirit of the man.

And when she's got it, according to her passionate and all-too-sacred desire, completely, when she possesses her man at last finally and ultimately, without blemish or reservation in the perfection of the sacrament: then, also, poor woman, the blood and the body of which she has partaken become insipid or nauseous to her, she is driven mad by the endless meal of the marriage sacrament, poisoned by the sacred communion which was her goal and her soul's ambition.

We have pushed a process into a goal. The aim of any process is not the perpetuation of that process, but the completion thereof. Love is a process of the incomprehensible human soul: love also incomprehensible, but still only a process. The process should work to a completion, not to some horror of intensification and extremity wherein the soul and body ultimately perish. The completion of the process of love is the arrival at a state of simple, pure self-possession, for man and woman. Only that. Which isn't exciting enough for us sensationalists. We prefer abysses and maudlin self-abandon and self-sacrifice, the degeneration into a sort of slime and merge.

Perhaps, truly, the process of love is never accomplished. But it moves in great stages, and at the end of each stage a true goal, where the soul possesses itself in simple and generous singleness. Without this, love is a disease.

So Aaron, crossing a certain border-line and finding himself alone completely, accepted his loneliness or singleness as a fulfilment, a state of fulfilment. The long fight with Lottie had driven him at last to himself, so that he was quiet as a thing which has its root deep in life, and has lost its anxiety. As for considering the lily, it is not a matter of consideration. The lily toils and spins hard enough, in her own way. But without that strain and that anxiety with which we try to weave ourselves a life. The lily is life-rooted, life-central. She *cannot* worry. She is life itself, a little, delicate fountain playing creatively, for as long or as short a time as may be, and unable to be anxious. She may be sad or sorry, if the north wind blows. But even then, anxious she cannot be. Whether her fountain play or cease to play, from out the cold, damp earth, she cannot be anxious. She may only be glad or sorry, and continue her way. She is perfectly herself, whatever befall! even if frosts cut her off. Happy lily, never to be saddled with an *idée fixe*, never to be in the grip of a monomania for happiness or love or fulfilment. It is not *laisser aller*. It is life-rootedness. It is being by oneself, life-giving, like the much-mooted lily. One toils, one spins, one strives: just as the lily does. But like her, taking one's own life-way amidst everything, and taking one's own life-way alone. Love too. But there also, taking one's way alone, happily alone in all the wonders of communion, swept up on the winds, but never swept away from one's very self. Two eagles in mid-air, maybe like Whitman's Dalliance of Eagles. Two eagles in mid-air, grappling, whirling, coming to their intensification of love-oneness there in mid-air. In mid-air the love consummation. But all the time each lifted on its own wings: each bearing itself up on its own wings at every moment of the mid-air love consummation. That is the splendid love-way.

The party was festive at dinner-time, the women in their finest dresses, new flowers on the table, the best wine going. It was Sunday evening. Aaron too was dressed – and Lady Franks, in black lace and pearls, was almost gay.

There were quails for dinner. The Colonel was quite happy. An air of conviviality gathered round the table during the course of the meal.

'I hope,' said Aaron, 'that we shall have some music tonight.'

'I want so much to hear your flute,' said his hostess.

'And I your piano,' he said.

'I am very weak – very out of practice. I tremble at the thought of playing before a musician. But you must not be too critical.'

'Oh,' said Aaron. 'I am not a man to be afraid of.'

'Well, we will see,' said Lady Franks. 'But I am afraid of music itself.'

'Yes,' said Aaron. 'I think it is risky.'

'Immoral! I don't see that! Music risky? Bach? Beethoven! No, I don't agree. On the contrary, I think it is most elevating – most morally inspiring. No, I tremble before it because it *is* so wonderful and elevating.'

'I often find it makes me feel diabolical,' said he.

'That is your misfortune, I am sure,' said Lady Franks. 'Please do take another – but perhaps you don't like mushrooms?'

Aaron quite liked mushrooms, and helped himself to the entrée.

'But perhaps,' said she, 'you are too modern. You don't care for Bach or Beethoven or Chopin – dear Chopin.'

'I find them all quite as modern as I am.'

'Is that so? Yes. For myself I am quite old-fashioned – though I can appreciate Strauss and Stravinsky as well, some things. But my old things – ah, I don't think the moderns are so fine. They are not so deep. They haven't fathomed life so deeply.' Lady Franks sighed faintly.

'They don't care for depths,' said Aaron.

'No, they haven't the capacity. But I like big, deep music. Oh, I love orchestra. But my instrument is the piano. I like the great masters, Bach, Beethoven. They have such faith. You were talking of faith – believing that things would work out well for you in the end. Beethoven inspires that in me too.'

'He makes you feel that all will be well with you at last?'

'Yes, he does. He makes me feel faith in my *personal* destiny. And I do feel that there is something in one's special fate. I feel that I myself have a special kind of fate, that will always look after me.'

'And you can trust to it?'

'Yes, I can. It *always* turns out right. I think something has gone wrong – and then, it always turns out right. Why, when we were in London – when we were at lunch one morning it suddenly struck me, haven't I left my fur cloak somewhere? It was rather cold, so I had taken it with me, and then never put it on. And I hadn't brought it home. I had left it somewhere. But whether in a taxi, or in a shop, or in a little show of pictures I had been to, I couldn't remember. I *could not* remember. And I thought to myself: have I lost my cloak? I went round to everywhere I could think of: no trace of it. But I didn't give it up. Something prompted me not to give it up: quite distinctly, I felt something telling me that I should get it back. So I called at Scotland Yard and gave the information. Well, two days later I had a notice from Scotland Yard, so I went. And there was my cloak. I had it back. And that has happened to me almost every time. I almost *always* get my things back. And I always feel that something looks after me, do you know: almost takes care of me.'

'But do you mean when you lose things – or in your life?'

'I mean when I lose things – or when I want to get something I want – I am very nearly always successful. And I always feel there is some sort of higher power which does it for me.'

'Finds your cloak for you.'

'Yes. Wasn't it extraordinary? I felt when I saw my cloak in Scotland Yard: There, I *knew* I should recover you. And I always feel, as I say, that there is some higher power which helps me. Do you feel the same?'

'No, not that way, worse luck. I lost a batch of music a month ago which didn't belong to me – and which I couldn't replace. But I never could recover it: though I'm sure nobody wanted it.'

'How very unfortunate. Whereas my fur cloak was just the thing that gets stolen most.'

'I wished some power would trace my music: but apparently we aren't all gifted alike with guardian angels.'

'Apparently not. And that is how I regard it: almost as a gift, you know, that my fairy godmother gave me in my cradle.'

'For always recovering your property?'

'Yes – and succeeding in my undertakings.'

'I'm afraid I had no fairy godmother.'

'Well – I think I had. And very glad I am of it.'

'Why, yes,' said Aaron, looking at his hostess.

So the dinner sailed merrily on.

'But does Beethoven make you feel,' said Aaron as an afterthought, 'in the same way – that you will always find the things you have lost?'

'Yes – he makes me feel the same faith: that what I lose will be returned to me. Just as I found my cloak. And that if I enter into an understanding, it will be successful.'

'And your life has been always successful?'

'Yes – almost always. We have succeeded with almost everything.'

'Why, yes,' said Aaron, looking at her again.

But even so, he could see a good deal of hard wornness under her satisfaction. She had had her suffering, sure enough. But none the less, she was in the main satisfied. She sat there, a good hostess, and expected the homage due to her success. And, of course, she got it. Aaron himself did his little share of shoe-licking, and swallowed the taste of boot-polish with a grimace, knowing what he was about.

The dinner wound gaily to an end. The ladies retired. Sir William left his seat of honour at the end of the table and came and sat next to Aaron, summoning the other three men to cluster near.

'Now, Colonel,' said the host, 'send round the bottle.'

With a flourish of the elbow and shoulder, the Colonel sent on the port: actually port, in those bleak, post-war days.

'Well, Mr Sisson,' said Sir William, 'we will drink to your kind Providence: providing, of course, that we shall give no offence by so doing.'

'No sir – no sir! The Providence belonged to Mr Lilly. Mr Sisson put his money on kindly Fortune, I believe,' said Arthur, who, rosy and fresh with wine, looked as if he would make a marvellous *bonne bouche* for a finely-discriminating cannibal.

'Ah, yes, indeed! A much more ingratiating lady to lift our glasses to. Mr Sisson's kindly Fortune. Fortuna gentilissima! Well, Mr Sisson, and may your Lady Fortune ever smile on you.'

Sir William lifted his glass with an odd little smirk, some touch of a strange, prim old satyr lurking in his oddly inclined head. Nay, more than satyr: that curious, rather terrible iron demon that has fought with the world and wrung wealth from it, and which knows all about it. The devilish spirit of iron itself, and iron machines. So, with his strange, old smile showing his teeth rather terribly, the old knight glowered sightlessly over his glass at Aaron. Then he drank: the strange, careful, old-man's gesture in drinking.

'But,' said Aaron, 'if Fortune is a female –'

'Fortune! Fortune! Why, Fortune is a lady. What do you say, Major?'

'She has all the airs of one, Sir William,' said the Major, with the wistful grimness of his age and culture. And the young fellow stared like a crucified cyclop from his one eye: the black shutter being over the other.

'And all the graces,' capped Sir William, delighted with himself.

'Oh, quite!' said the Major. 'For some, all the airs, and for others, all the graces.'

'Faint heart ne'er won fair lady, my boy,' said Sir William. 'Not that your heart is faint. On the contrary – as we know, and your country knows. But with Lady Fortune you need another kind of stout heart – oh, quite another kind.'

'I believe it, sir: and the kind of stout heart which I am afraid I haven't got,' said the Major.

'What!' said the old man. 'Show the white feather before you've tackled the lady! Fill the Major's glass, Colonel. I am quite sure we will none of us ever say die.'

'Not likely. Not if we know it,' said the Colonel, stretching himself heartily inside his tunic. He was becoming ruddier than the cherry. All he cared about at the moment was his gay little port glass. But the Major's young cheek was hollow and sallow, his one eye terribly pathetic.

'And you, Mr Sisson,' said Sir William, 'mean to carry all before you by taking no thought for the morrow. Well now, we can only wish you success.'

'I don't want to carry all before me,' said Aaron. 'I should be sorry. I want to walk past most of it.'

'Can you tell us where to? I am intrigued, as Sybil says, to know where you will walk to. Come now. Enlighten us.'

'Nowhere, I suppose.'

'But is that satisfactory? Can you find it satisfactory?'

'Is it even true?' said the Major. 'Isn't it quite as positive an act to walk away from a situation as to walk towards it?'

'My dear boy, you can't merely walk away from a situation. Believe that. If you walk away from Rome, you walk into the Maremma, or into the Alban Hills or into the sea – but you walk into something. Now, if I am going to walk away from Rome, I prefer to choose my direction, and therefore my destination.'

'But you can't,' said the Major.

'What can't you?'

'Choose. Either your direction or your destination –' The Major was obstinate.

'Really!' said Sir William. 'I have not found it so. I have not found it so. I have had to keep myself hard at work, all my life, choosing between this or that.'

'And we,' said the Major, 'have no choice, except between this or nothing.'

'Really! I am afraid,' said Sir William, 'I am afraid I am too old – or too young – which shall I say? – to understand.'

'Too young, sir,' said Arthur sweetly. 'The child was always father to the man, I believe.'

'I confess the Major makes me feel childish,' said the old man. 'The choice between this or nothing is a puzzler to me. Can you help me out, Mr Sisson? What do you make of this this-or-nothing business? I can understand neck-or-nothing –'

'I prefer the *nothing* part of it to the *this* part of it,' said Aaron, grinning.

'Colonel,' said the old man, 'throw a little light on this nothingness.'

'No, Sir William,' said the Colonel. 'I am all right as I am.'

'As a matter of fact, so are we all, perfectly A1,' said Arthur.

Aaron broke into a laugh.

'That's the top and bottom of it,' he laughed, flushed with wine, and handsome. 'We're all as right as ninepence. Only it's rather nice to talk.'

'There!' said Sir William. 'We're all as right as ninepence! We're all as right as ninepence. So there we'll leave it, before the Major has time to say he is twopence short.' Laughing his strange old soundless laugh, Sir William rose and made a little bow. 'Come up and join the ladies in a minute or two,' he said. Arthur opened the door for him and he left the room.

The four men were silent for a moment – then the Colonel whipped up the decanter and filled his glass. Then he stood up and clinked glasses with Aaron, like a real old sport.

'Luck to you,' he said.

'Thanks,' said Aaron.

'You're going in the morning?' said Arthur.

'Yes,' said Aaron.

'What train?' said Arthur.

'Eight-forty.'

'Oh – then we shan't see you again. Well – best of luck.'

'Best of luck –' echoed the Colonel.

'Same to you,' said Aaron, and they all peered over their glasses and quite loved one another for a rosy minute.

'I should like to know, though,' said the hollow-cheeked young Major with the black flap over his eye, 'whether you do really mean you are all right – that it is all right with you – or whether you only say so to get away from the responsibility.'

'I mean I don't really care – I don't damn – let the devil take it all.'

'The devil doesn't want it, either,' said the Major.

'Then let him leave it. I don't care one single little curse about it all.'

'Be damned! What is there to care about?' said the Colonel.

'Ay, what?' said Aaron.

'It's all the same, whether you care or don't care. So I say it's much easier not to care,' said Arthur.

'Of course it is,' said the Colonel gaily.

'And I think so too,' said Aaron.

'Right, you are! We're all as right as ninepence – what? Good old sport! Here's your's!' cried the Colonel.

'We shall have to be going up,' said Arthur, wise in his generation.

As they went into the hall, Arthur suddenly put one arm round Aaron's waist, and one arm round the Colonel's, and the three did a sudden little barn-dance towards the stairs. Arthur was feeling himself quite let loose again, back in his old regimental mess.

Approaching the foot of the stairs, he let go again. He was in that rosy condition when united-we-stand. But unfortunately it is a complicated job to climb the stairs in unison. The whole lot tends to fall backwards. Arthur, therefore, rosy, plump, looking so good to eat, stood still a moment in order to find his own neatly-slippered feet. Having found them, he proceeded to put them carefully one before the other, and to his enchantment found that this procedure was carrying him magically up the stairs. The Colonel, like a drowning man, clutched feebly for the straw of the great stair-rail – and missed it. He would have gone under, but that Aaron's hand gripped his arm. So, orientating once more like a fragile tendril, he reached again for the banister rail, and got it. After which, lifting his feet as if they were little packets of sand tied to his trouser buttons, he manipulated his way upwards. Aaron was in that pleasant state when he saw what everybody else was doing and was unconscious of what he did himself. Whilst tall, gaunt, erect, like a murdered Hamlet resurrected in khaki, with the terrible black shutter over his eye, the young Major came last.

Arthur was making a stern fight for his composure. His whole future depended on it. But do what he would, he could not get the flushed, pleased, mess-happy look off his face. The Colonel, oh awful man, did a sort of plump roly-poly cakewalk, like a far boy, right to the very door of that sanctum-sanctorum, the library. Aaron was inwardly convulsed. Even the Major laughed.

But Arthur stiffened himself militarily and cleared his throat. All four started to compose themselves, like actors going on the stage, outside that library door. And then Arthur softly, almost wistfully, opened and held the door for the others to pass. The Colonel slunk meekly in, and sat in a chair in the background. The Major stalked in expressionless, and hovered towards the sofa where his wife sat.

There was rather a cold-water-down-your-back feeling in the library. The ladies had been waiting for coffee: Sir William was waiting too. Therefore in a little tension, half-silent, the coffee was handed round. Lady Franks was discussing something with Arthur's wife. Arthur's wife was in a cream lace dress, and looking what is called lovely. The Major's wife was in amethyst chiffon with dark-red roses, and was looking blindingly beautiful. The Colonel was looking into his coffee-cup as wistfully as if it contained the illusion of tawny port. The Major was looking into space, as if there and there alone, etc. Arthur was looking for something which Lady Franks had asked for, and which he was much too flushed to find. Sir William was looking at Aaron, and preparing for another *coeur à coeur.*

'Well,' he said, 'I doubt if you will care for Milan. It is one of the least Italian of all the towns, in my opinion. Venice, of course, is a thing apart. I cannot stand, myself, that miserable specimen the modern Roman. He has most of the vices of the old Romans and none of the virtues. The most congenial town, perhaps, for a stranger, is Florence. But it has a very bad climate.'

Lady Franks rose significantly and left the room, accompanied by Arthur's wife. Aaron knew, silently, that he was summoned to follow. His hostess had her eye on him this evening. But always postponing his obedience to the cool commands of women, he remained talking with his host in the library, and sipping *crème de menthe.* Came the ripple of the pianoforte from the open doorway down at the farther end of the room. Lady Franks was playing, in the large drawing-room. And the ripple of the music contained in it the hard insistence of the little woman's will. Coldly, and decidedly, she intended there should be no more unsettling conversations for the old Sir William. Aaron was to come forthwith into the drawing-room. Which Aaron plainly understood – and so he didn't go. No, he didn't go, though the pianoforte rippled and swelled in volume. No, and he didn't go even when Lady Franks left off playing and came into the library again. There he sat, talking with Sir William. Let us do credit to Lady Franks's will-power, and admit that the talk was quite empty and distracted – none of the depths and skirmishes of the previous occasions. None the less, the talk continued. Lady Franks retired. discomfited, to her piano again. She would never break in upon her lord.

So now Aaron relented. He became more and more distracted. Sir William wandered away like some restless, hunted soul. The Colonel still sat in his chair, nursing his last drop of *crème de menthe* resentfully. He did not care for the green toffee-stuff. Arthur was busy. The Major lay sprawled in the last stages of everything on the sofa, holding his wife's hand. And the music came pathetically through the open folding-doors. Of course, she played with feeling – it went without saying. Aaron's soul felt rather tired. But she had a touch of discrimination also.

He rose and went to the drawing-room. It was a large, vacant-seeming, Empire sort of drawing-room, with yellow silk chairs along the walls and yellow silk panels upon the walls, and a huge, vasty crystal chandelier hanging from a far-away-above ceiling. Lady Franks sat at a large black Bechstein piano at one end of this vacant yellow state-room. She sat, a little plump elderly lady in black lace, for all the world like Queen Victoria in Max Beerbohm's drawing of Alfred Tennyson reading to her Victorian Majesty, with space before her. Arthur's wife was bending over some music in a remote corner of the big room.

Aaron seated himself on one of the chairs by the wall, to listen. Certainly it was a beautiful instrument. And certainly, in her way, she loved it. But Aaron remembered an anthem in which he had taken part as a boy.

> His eye is on the sparrow
> So I know He watches me.

For a long time he had failed to catch the word *sparrow*, and had heard:

> His eye is on the spy-hole
> So I know He watches me.

Which was just how it had all seemed to him, as a boy.

Now, as ever, he felt the eye was on the spy-hole. There sat the woman playing music. But her inward eye was on the spy-hole of her vital affairs – her domestic arrangements, her control of her household, guests and husband included. The other eye was left for the music, don't you know.

Sir William appeared hovering in the doorway, not at all liking the defection of Mr Aaron. Then he retreated. He seemed not to care for music. The Major's wife hovered – felt it her duty to aude, or play audience – and entered, seating herself in a breath of lilac and amethyst again at the near distance. The Major, after a certain beating about the bush, followed and sat rapt in dim contemplation near his wife. Arthur luckily was still busy with something.

Aaron, of course, made proper musical remarks in the intervals – Arthur's wife sorted out more pieces. Arthur appeared – and then the Colonel. The Colonel tiptoed beautifully across the wide blank space of the Empire room, and seated himself on a chair, rather in the distance, with his back to the wall, facing Aaron. When Lady Franks finished her piece, to everybody's amazement the Colonel clapped gaily to himself and said Bravo! as if at a Café Chantant – looking around for his glass. But there was no glass. So he crossed his neatly-khakied legs, and looked rapt again.

Lady Franks started with a *vivace* Schumann piece. Everybody listened in sanctified silence, trying to seem to like it. When suddenly our Colonel began to spring and bounce in his chair, slinging his loose leg with a kind of rapture up and down in the air, and capering upon his posterior, doing a sitting-down jig to the Schumann *vivace*. Arthur, who had seated himself at the farthest extremity of the room, winked with wild bliss at Aaron. The Major tried to look as if he noticed nothing, and only succeeded in looking agonized. His wife studied the point of her silver shoe minutely, and peeped through her hair at the performance. Aaron grimly chuckled, and loved the Colonel with real tenderness.

And the game went on while the *vivace* lasted. Up and down bounced the plump Colonel on his chair, kicking with his bright, black-patent toe higher and higher, getting quite enthusiastic over his jig. Rosy and unabashed, he was worthy of the great nation he belonged to. The broad-seated Empire chair showed no signs of giving way. Let him enjoy himself, away there across the yellow Sahara of this silk-panelled salon. Aaron felt quite cheered up.

'Well, now,' he thought to himself, 'this man is in entire command of a very important branch of the British Service in Italy. We are a great race still.'

But Lady Franks must have twigged. Her playing went rather stiff. She came to the end of the *vivace* movement, and abandoned her piece.

'I always prefer Schumann in his *vivace* moods,' said Aaron.

'Do you?' said Lady Franks. 'Oh, I don't know.'

It was now the turn of Arthur's wife to sing. Arthur seemed to get farther away, if it was possible, for he was at the remotest remote end of the room, near the gallery doors. The Colonel became quiet, pensive. The Major's wife eyed the young woman in white lace, and seemed not to care for lace. Arthur seemed to be trying to push himself backwards through the wall. Lady Franks switched on more lights into the vast and voluminous crystal chandelier which hung like some glory-cloud above the room's centre. And Arthur's wife sang – sweet little French songs, and Ye Banks and Braes, and *Caro mio ben*, which goes without saying: and so on. She had quite a nice voice and was quite adequately trained. Which is enough said. Aaron had all his nerves on edge.

Then he had to play the flute. Arthur strolled upstairs with him, arm-in-arm, where he went to fetch his instrument.

'I find music in the home rather a strain, you know,' said Arthur.

'Cruel strain. I quite agree,' said Aaron.

'I don't mind it so much in the theatre – or even a concert – where there are a lot of people to take the edge off – But after a good dinner –'

'It's medicine,' said Aaron.

'Well, you know, it really is, to me. It affects my inside.'

Aaron laughed. And then, in the yellow drawing-room, blew into his pipe and played. He knew so well that Arthur, the Major, the Major's wife, the Colonel, and Sir William thought it merely an intolerable bore. However, he played. His hostess even accompanied him in a Mozart bit.

14

XX SETTEMBRE

Aaron was wakened in the morning by the soft entrance of the butler with the tray: it was just seven o'clock. Lady Franks's household was punctual as the sun itself.

But our hero roused himself with a wrench. The very act of lifting himself from the pillow was like a fight this morning. Why? He recognized his own wrench, the pain with which he struggled under the necessity to move. Why shouldn't he want to move? Why not? Because he didn't want the day in front – the plunge into a strange country, towards nowhere, with no aim in view. True, he said that ultimately he wanted to join Lilly. But this was hardly more than a sop, an excuse for his own irrational behaviour. He was breaking loose from one connection after another: and what for? Why break every tie? Snap, snap, snap went the bonds and ligatures which bound him to the life that had formed him, the people he had loved or liked. He found all his affections snapping off, all the ties which united him with his own people coming asunder. And why? In God's name, why? What was there instead?

There was nothingness. There was just himself, and blank nothingness. He had perhaps a faint sense of Lilly ahead of him: an impulse in that direction: or else merely an illusion. He could not persuade himself that he was seeking for love, for any kind of unison or communion. He knew well enough that the thought of any loving, any sort of real coming together between himself and anybody or anything, was just objectionable to him. No – he was not moving *towards* anything: he was moving almost violently away from everything. And that was what he wanted. Only that. Only let him *not* run into any sort of embrace with anything or anybody – this was what he asked. Let no new connections be made between himself and anything on earth. Let all old connections break. This was his craving.

Yet he struggled under it this morning as under the lid of a tomb. The terrible sudden weight of inertia! He knew the tray stood ready by the bed: he knew the automobile would be at the door at eight o'clock, for Lady Franks had said so, and he half divined that the servant had also said so: yet there he lay, in a kind of paralysis in this bed. He seemed for the moment to have lost his will. Why go forward into more nothingness, away from all that he knew, all he was accustomed to and all he belonged to?

However, with a click he sat up. And the very instant he had poured his coffee from the little silver coffee-pot into his delicate cup, he was ready for anything and everything. The sense of silent adventure took him, the exhilarated feeling that he was fulfilling his own inward destiny. Pleasant to taste was the coffee, the bread, the honey – delicious.

The man brought his clothes, and again informed him that the automobile would be at the door at eight o'clock: or at least so he made out.

'I can walk,' said Aaron.

'Milady ha comandato l'automobile,' said the man softly.

It was evident that if Milady had ordered it, so it must be.

So Aaron left the still-sleeping house, and got into the soft and luxurious car. As he dropped through the park he wondered that Sir William and Lady Franks should be so kind to him: a complete stranger. But so it was. There he sat in their car. He wondered, also, as he ran over the bridge and into the city, whether this soft-running automobile would ever rouse the socialistic bile of the work-people. For the first time in his life, as he sat among the snug cushions, he realized what it might be to be rich and uneasy: uneasy, even if not afraid, lurking there inside an expensive car. Well, it wasn't much of a sensation anyhow: and riches were stuffy, like wadded upholstery on everything. He was glad to get out into the fresh air of the common crowd. He was glad to be in the bleak, not-very-busy station. He was glad to be part of common life. For the very atmosphere of riches seems to be stuffed and wadded, never any real reaction. It was terrible, as if one's very body, shoulders and arms, were upholstered and made cushiony. Ugh, but he was glad to shake off himself the atmosphere of wealth and motor-cars, to get out of it all. It was like getting out of quilted clothes.

'Well,' thought Aaron, 'if this is all it amounts to, to be rich, you can have riches. They talk about money being power. But the only sort of power it has over me is to bring on a kind of numbness, which I fairly hate. No wonder rich people don't seem to be really alive.'

The relief of escaping quite took away his self-conscious embarrassment at the station. He carried his own bags, bought a third-class ticket, and got into the train for Milan without caring one straw for the comments or the looks of the porters.

It began to rain. The train ran across the great plain of north Italy. Aaron sat in his wood-seated carriage and smoked his pipe in silence, looking at the thick, short Lombards opposite him without heeding them. He paid hardly any outward attention to his surroundings, but sat involved in himself.

In Milan he had been advised to go to the Hotel Britannia, because it was not expensive, and English people went there. So he took a carriage, drove round the green space in front of Milan station, and away into the town. The streets were busy, but only half-heartedly so.

It must be confessed that every new move he made was rather an effort. Even he himself wondered why he was struggling with foreign porters and foreign cabmen, being talked at and not understanding a word. But there he was. So he went on with it.

The hotel was small and congenial. The hotel porter answered in English. Aaron was given a little room with a tiny balcony, looking on to a quiet street. So, he had a home of his own once more. He washed, and then counted his money. Thirty-seven pounds he had: and no more. He stood on the balcony and looked at the people going by below. Life seems to be moving so quick, when one looks down on it from above.

Across the road was a large stone house with its green shutters all closed. But from the flagpole under the eaves, over the central window of the uppermost floor – the house was four storeys high – waved the Italian flag in the melancholy damp air. Aaron looked at it – the red, white and green tricolor, with the white cross of Savoy in the centre. It hung damp and still. And there seemed a curious vacancy in the city – something empty and depressing in the great human centre. Not that there was really a lack of people. But the spirit of the town seemed depressed and empty. It was a national holiday. The Italian flag was hanging from almost every house front.

It was about three o'clock in the afternoon. Aaron sat in the restaurant of the hotel drinking tea, for he was rather tired, and looking through the thin curtains at the little square outside, where people passed, little groups of dark, aimless-seeming men, a little bit poorer-looking – perhaps rather shorter in stature – but very much like the people in any other town. Yet the feeling of the city was so different from that of London. There seemed a curious emptiness. The rain had ceased, but the pavements were still wet. There was a tension.

Suddenly there was a noise of two shots, fired in rapid succession. Aaron turned startled to look into the quiet piazza. And to his amazement, the pavements were empty, not a soul was in sight. Two minutes before the place was busy with passers-by, and a newspaper-man selling the *Corriere*, and little carriages rattling through. Now, as if by magic, nobody, nothing. It was as if they had all melted into thin air.

The waiter, too, was peeping behind the curtain. A carriage came trotting into the square – an odd man took his way alone – the traffic began to stir once more, and people reappeared as suddenly as they had disappeared. Then the waiter ran hastily and furtively out and craned his neck, peering round the square. He spoke with two youths – rather loutish youths. Then he returned to his duty in the hotel restaurant.

'What was it? What were the shots?' Aaron asked him.

'Oh – somebody shooting at a dog,' said the man negligently.

'At a dog!' said Aaron, with round eyes.

He finished his tea, and went out into the town. His hotel was not far from the cathedral square. Passing through the arcade, he came in sight of the famous cathedral with its numerous spines pricking into the afternoon air. He was not as impressed as he should have been. And yet there was something in the northern city – this big square with all the trams threading through, the little yellow Continental trams: and the spiny bulk of the great cathedral, like a grey-purple sea-urchin with many spines, on the one side, the ornamental grass-plots and flower-beds on the other: the big shops going all along the farther strands, all round: and the endless, restless, nervous drift of a north Italian crowd, so nervous, so twitchy; nervous and twitchy as the slipping past of the little yellow tram-cars; it all affected him with a sense of strangeness, nervousness, and approaching winter. It struck him the people were afraid of themselves: afraid of their own souls, and that which was in their own souls.

Turning up the broad steps of the cathedral, he entered the famous building. The sky had cleared, and the freshened light shone coloured in living tablets round the wonderful, towering, rose-hearted dusk of the great church. At some altars lights flickered uneasily. At some unseen side-altar mass was going on, and a strange ragged music fluttered out on the incense-dusk of the great and lofty interior, which was all shadow, all shadow, hung round with jewel tablets of light. Particularly beautiful the great east bay, above the great altar. And all the time, over the big-patterned marble floor, the faint click and rustle of feet coming and going, coming and going, like shallow uneasy water rustled back and forth in a trough. A white dog trotted pale through the under-dusk, over the pale, big-patterned floor. Aaron came to the side altar where mass was going on, candles ruddily wavering. There was a small cluster of kneeling women – a ragged handful of on-looking men – and people wandering up and wandering away, young women with neatly dressed black hair, and shawls, but without hats; fine young women in very high heels; young men with nothing to do; ragged men with nothing to do. All strayed faintly clicking over the slabbed floor, and glanced at the flickering altar where the white-surpliced boys were curtseying and the white-and-gold priest was bowing, his hands over his breast, in the candle-light. All strayed, glanced, lingered, and strayed away again, as if the spectacle were not sufficiently holding. The bell chimed for the elevation of the Host. But the thin trickle of people trickled the same, uneasily, over the slabbed floor of the vastly-upreaching, shadow-foliaged cathedral.

The smell of incense in his nostrils, Aaron went out again by a side door, and began to walk along the pavements of the cathedral square, looking at the shops. Some were closed, and had little notices pinned on them. Some were open, and seemed half-stocked with half-elegant things. Men were crying newspapers. In the cafés a few men were seated drinking Vermouth. In the doorway of the restaurants waiters stood inert, looking out on the streets. The curious heart-eating *ennui* of the big town on a holiday came over our hero. He felt he must get out, whatever happened. He could not bear it.

So he went back to his hotel and up to his room. It was still only five o'clock. And he did not know what to do with himself. He lay down on the bed, and looked at the painting on his bedroom ceiling. It was a terrible business in Reckitt's blue and browny gold, with awful heraldic beasts, rather worm-wriggly, displayed in a blue field.

As he lay thinking of nothing and feeling nothing except a certain weariness, or dreariness, or tension, or God-knows-what, he heard a loud hoarse noise of humanity in the distance, something frightening. Rising, he went on to his little balcony. It was a sort of procession or march of men, here and there a red flag fluttering from a man's hand. There had been a big meeting, and this was the issue. The procession was irregular, but powerful: men four abreast. They emerged irregularly from the small piazza into the street, calling and vociferating. They stopped before a shop and clotted into a crowd, shouting, becoming vicious. Over the shop-door hung a tricolor – a national flag. The shop was closed: men began to knock at the door. They were all workmen, some in railway-men's caps, mostly in black hats. Some wore red cotton neck-ties. They lifted their faces to the national flag, and as they shouted and gesticulated Aaron could see their strong teeth in their jaws. There was something frightening in their lean, strong Italian jaws, something inhuman and possessed-looking in their foreign, southern-shaped faces, so much more formed and demon-looking than northern faces. They had a demon-like fixed purpose and sharp will, and the noise of their voices was like a scraping of steel and copper weapons. Aaron wondered what they wanted. There were no women – all men; a strange male slashing sound. Vicious it was – the head of the procession clustering thick before the shop, the thick wedge of the procession beyond, flecked with red flags.

A window opened above the shop, and a frowsty-looking man, yellow-pale, was quickly and nervously hauling in the national flag. There were shouts of derision and mockery: a great overtone of derision, acrid. The flag and its owner ignominiously disappeared. And the procession moved on.

Almost every shop had a flag flying. And every one of these flags now began to disappear, quickly or slowly, sooner or later, in obedience to the command of the vicious, derisive crowd that marched and clotted slowly down the street, having its own way.

Only one flag remained flying: the big tricolor that floated from the top storey of the house opposite Aaron's hotel. The ground floor of this house consisted of shop premises – now closed. There was no sign of any occupant. The flag floated inert aloft.

The whole crowd had come to a stop immediately below the hotel, and all were now looking up at the green and white and red tricolor which stirred damply in the early evening light, from under the broad eaves of the house opposite. Aaron looked at the long flag, which drooped almost unmoved from the eaves-shadows, and he half-expected it to furl itself up of its own accord, in obedience to the will of the masses. Then he looked down at the packed black shoulders of the mob below, and at the curious clustering pattern of a sea of black hats. He could hardly see anything but hats and shoulders, uneasily moving like boiling pitch away beneath him. But the shouts began to come up hotter and hotter. There had been a great banging of the shop door and a ringing of the bell of the guilty house-door. The crowd – the swollen head of the procession – talked and shouted, occupying the centre of the street but leaving the pavement clear. A woman in a white blouse appeared in the shop-door. She came out and looked up at the flag and shook her head and gesti-culated with her hands. It was evidently not her flag: she had nothing to do with it. The leaders now turned again to the large house-door, and began to ring all the bells and to beat with their fists. But no good – there was no answer. Voices arose ragged and ironical. The woman explained again, with rapid gestures. Apparently there was nobody at home in the upper apartments – all entrances were locked – there was no caretaker to be found. Nobody owned the flag. There it hung under the broad eaves of the strong stone house, and didn't even know it was guilty. The woman went back into her shop and drew down the iron shutter from inside.

The crowd, nonplussed, now began to argue and shout and whistle. The voices rose in pitch and derision. Steam was getting up. There hung the gaudy flag. The mob crowded forward and filled the street in a mass below. All the rest of the street was empty and shut up. And still hung the showy rag, red and white and green, up aloft.

Suddenly there was a lull – then shouts, half-encouraging, half-derisive. And Aaron saw a smallish black figure of a youth, fair-haired, not more than seventeen years old, clinging like a monkey to the front of the house, and by the help of the heavy drain-pipe and the stonework ornamentation climbing up to the stone ledge that ran beneath the ground-floor windows, up like a sudden cat on to the projecting footing. There he did not stop, but continued his race like some frantic lizard running up the great wall-front, working his way from the noise below as if in a frenzy of fright. It was one unending wriggling movement, sheer up the front of the impassive, heavy stone house.

The flag hung from a pole under one of the windows of the top storey – the third floor. Up went the wriggling figure of the possessed youth. The cries of the crowd below were now wild, ragged ejaculations of excitement and encouragement. The youth seemed to be lifted up, almost magically, on the intense up-reaching excitement of the massed men below. He had passed the ledge of the first floor, like a lizard he wriggled up and passed the ledge or coping of the second floor, and there he was, like an upward-climbing shadow, scrambling on to the coping of the third floor. The crowd was for a second electrically still as the boy rose there erect, cleaving to the wall with the tips of his fingers.

But he did not hesitate for one breath. He was on his feet and running along the narrow coping that went across the house-front under the third-floor windows, running there on that narrow footing away above the street, straight to the flag. He had got it: he had clutched it in one hand, a handful of it. Exactly like a great flame rose the simultaneous yell of the crowd as the boy jerked and got the flag loose. He had torn it down, it was in his hand. A tremendous long yell, touched with a snarl of triumph and searing like a puff of flame, sounded as the boy remained for one moment with the flag in his fist looking down at the crowd below. His face was odd and elated and still. Then with the slightest gesture he threw the flag from him, and Aaron watched the gaudy remnant falling towards the many faces, whilst the noise of yelling rose up unheeded.

There was a great clutch and hiss in the crowd. The boy still stood unmoved, holding by one hand behind him, looking down from above, from his dangerous elevation, in a sort of abstraction.

And the next thing Aaron was conscious of was the sound of trumpets. A sudden startling challenge of trumpets, and out of nowhere a sudden rush of grey-green carabinieri battering the crowd wildly with truncheons. It was so sudden that Aaron *heard* nothing any more. He only saw.

In utmost amazement he saw the sturdy, greeny-grey carabinieri, like a posse of foot-soldiers, rushing thick and wild and indiscriminate on the crowd, with a frenzied excitement which must have been based on fear: a sudden, new, excited crowd in uniform attacking the civilian crowd and laying about blindly, furiously, with truncheons. There was a seething moment in the street below. And almost instantaneously the original crowd burst into it in a frenzy of panic. The mob broke as if something had exploded inside it. A few black-hatted men fought furiously to get themselves free of the hated soldiers; in the confusion bunches of men staggered, reeled, fell, and were struggling among the legs of their comrades and of the carabinieri. But the bulk of the crowd just burst and fled, in every direction. Like drops of water they seemed to fly up at the very walls themselves. They darted into any entry, any doorway. They sprang up the walls and clambered into the ground-floor windows. They sprang up the walls on to window-ledges, and then jumped down again and ran: clambering, wriggling, darting, running in every direction: some cut, blood on their faces, terror or frenzy of flight in their hearts. Not so much terror as the frenzy of running away. In a breath the street was empty.

And all the time there above on the stone coping stood the long-faced, fair-haired boy, while four stout carabinieri in the street below stood with uplifted revolvers and covered him, shouting that if he moved they would shoot. So there he stood, still looking down, still holding with his left hand behind him, covered by four revolvers. He was not so much afraid as twitchily self-conscious because of his false position.

Meanwhile down below the crowd had disappeared – melted momentaneously. The carabinieri were busy arresting the men who had fallen and been trodden underfoot, or who had let themselves foolishly be taken. Perhaps half a dozen men: half a dozen prisoners: less rather than more.

The sergeant ordered these to be secured between soldiers. And last of all the youth up above, still covered by the revolvers, was ordered to come down. He turned quite quietly, and quite humbly, cautiously picked his way along the coping to the drain-pipe. He reached this pipe and began in cautious dejection to climb down. It was a real climb down.

Once in the street he was seized by the grey uniforms. The soldiers formed up. The sergeant gave the order. And away marched authority, triumphant and thankful to have got off so lightly. The dejected youth was marched away between them.

Then were heard a few scattered yells of derision and protest against the carabinieri. There were once again more gangs of men and groups of youths along the street. They sent up an occasional shout or threat. But always over their shoulders, and ready to pretend it was not they who shouted. They were all cowed and hang-dog once more, and made not the slightest effort to save the youth. Nevertheless they prowled and watched ready for next time.

So, away went the prisoner and the grey-green soldiers, and the street was left to the little gangs and groups of hang-dog, discontented men, all thoroughly out of countenance. The scene was ended.

Aaron looked round, dazed. And then for the first time he noticed, on the next balcony to his own, two young men: young gentlemen, he would have said. The one was tall and handsome and well-coloured, might be Italian. But the other, with his pale thin face and his rimless monocle in his eye, he was surely an Englishman. He was surely one of the young officers shattered by the war. A look of strange, arch, bird-like pleasure was on his face at this moment: if one could imagine the gleaming smile of a white owl over the events that had just passed, this was the impression produced on Aaron by the face of the young man with the monocle. The other youth, the ruddy handsome one, had knitted his brows in mock distress, and was glancing with a look of shrewd curiosity at Aaron, and with a look of almost self-satisfied excitement first to one end of the street, then to the other.

'But imagine, Angus, it's all over!' he said, laying his hand on the arm of the monocled young man, and making great eyes – not without a shrewd glance in Aaron's direction.

'Did you see him fall!' replied Angus, with another strange gleam.

'Yes! But was he *hurt* –?'

'*I* don't know. I should think so. He fell right back out of that window on to those stones!'

'But how perfectly *awful*! Did you ever see anything like it?'

'No. It's quite one of the funniest things I ever did see. I saw nothing quite like it, even in the war –'

Here Aaron withdrew into his room. His mind and soul were in a whirl. He sat down in his chair, and did not move again for a great while. When he did move, he took his flute and played he knew not what. But strange, strange his soul passed into his instrument. Or passed half into his instrument. There was a big residue left, to go bitter, or to ferment into good old wine of wisdom.

He did not notice the dinner-gong, and only the arrival of the chamber-maid, to put the wash-table in order, sent him down to the restaurant. The first thing he saw, as he entered, was the two young Englishmen seated at a table in a corner just behind him. Their hair was brushed straight back from their foreheads, making the sweep of the head bright and impeccable, and leaving both the young faces clear as if in cameo. Angus had laid his monocle on the table, and was looking round the room with wide, light-blue eyes, looking hard, like some bird-creature, and seeming to see nothing. He had evidently been very ill: was still very ill. His cheeks and even his jaw seemed shrunken, almost withered. He forgot his dinner: or he did not care for it. Probably the latter.

'What do you think, Francis,' he said, 'of making a plan to see Florence and Siena and Orvieto on the way down, instead of going straight to Rome?' He spoke in precise, particularly-enunciated words, in a public-school manner, but with a strong twang of South Wales.

'Why, Angus,' came the grateful voice of Francis, 'I thought we had settled to go straight through via Pisa.' Francis was graceful in everything – in his tall, elegant figure, in the poses of his handsome head, in the modulation of his voice.

'Yes, but I see we can go either way – either Pisa or Florence. And I thought it might be nice to look at Florence and Siena and Orvieto. I believe they're very lovely,' came the soft, precise voice of Angus, ending in a touch of odd emotion on the words "very lovely", as if it were a new experience to him to be using them.

'I'm *sure* they're marvellous. I'm quite sure they're marvellously beautiful,' said Francis, in his assured, elegant way. 'Well then, Angus – suppose we do that, then? When shall we start?'

Angus was the nervous insister. Francis was quite occupied with his own thoughts and calculations and curiosity. For he was very curious, not to say inquisitive. And at the present moment he had a new subject to ponder.

This new subject was Aaron, who sat with his back to our new couple, and who, with his fine sharp eyes, caught every word that they said. Aaron's back was broad enough, and his shoulders square, and his head rather small and fairish and well-shaped – and Francis was intrigued. He wanted to know was the man English. He *looked* so English – yet he might be – he might perhaps be Danish, Scandinavian, or Dutch. Therefore the elegant young man watched and listened with all his ears.

The waiter who had brought Aaron his soup now came very free and easy, to ask for further orders.

'What would you like to drink? Wine? Chianti? Or white wine? Or beer?' The old-fashioned 'Sir' was dropped. It is too old-fashioned now, since the war.

'What *should* I drink?' said Aaron, whose acquaintance with wines was not very large.

'Half-litre of Chianti: that is very good,' said the waiter, with the air of a man who knew only too well how to bring up his betters, and train them in the way they should go.

'All right,' said Aaron.

The welcome sound of these two magic words, All Right! was what the waiter most desired. 'All Right! Yes! All Right!' This is the pith, the marrow, the sum and essence of the English language to a southerner. Of course it is not *all right*. It is *Or-rye* – and one word at that. The blow that would be given to most foreign waiters, if they were forced to realize that the famous *orye* was really composed of two words, and spelt *all right*, would be too cruel, perhaps.

'Half-litre Chianti. Orye,' said the waiter. And we'll let him say it.

'*English!*' whispered Francis melodramatically in the ear of Angus. 'I *thought* so. The flautist.'

Angus put in his monocle, and stared at the oblivious shoulders of Aaron, without apparently seeing anything.

'Yes. Obviously English,' said Angus, pursing like a bird.

'Oh, but I *heard* him,' whispered Francis emphatically.

'Quite,' said Angus. 'But quite inoffensive.'

'Oh, but Angus, my dear – he's the *flautist*. Don't you remember? The divine bit of Scriabin. At least I believe it was Scriabin. But *perfectly divine* ! ! ! I adore the flute above all things –' And Francis placed his hand on Angus's arm, and rolled his eyes – Lay this to the credit of a bottle of Lacrimae Christi, if you like.

'Yes. So do I,' said Angus, again looking archly through the monocle, and seeing nothing. 'I wonder what he's doing here.'

'Don't you think we might *ask* him?' said Francis, in a vehement whisper. 'After all, we are the only three English people in the place.'

'For the moment, apparently we are,' said Angus. 'But the English are all over the place wherever you go, like bits of orange-peel in the street. Don't forget that, Francesco.'

'No, Angus, I don't. The point is, his flute is *perfectly divine* – and he seems quite attractive in himself. Don't you think so?'

'Oh, quite,' said Angus, whose observations had got no further than the black cloth of the back of Aaron's jacket. That there was a man inside he had not yet paused to consider.

'Quite a musician,' said Francis.

'The hired sort,' said Angus, 'most probably.'

'But he *plays* – he *plays* most marvellously. *That* you can't get away from, Angus.'

'I quite agree,' said Angus.

'Well then? Don't you think we might hear him again? Don't you think we might get him to play for us? But I should love it more than anything.'

'Yes, I should too,' said Angus. 'You might ask him to coffee and a liqueur.'

'I should like to – most awfully. But do you think I might?'

'Oh, yes. He won't mind being offered a coffee and liqueur. We can give him something decent. Where's the waiter?' Angus lifted his pinched, ugly bare face and looked around with weird command for the waiter. The waiter, having not much to do, and feeling ready to draw these two weird young birds, allowed himself to be summoned.

'Where's the wine list? What liqueurs have you got?' demanded Angus abruptly.

The waiter rattled off a list, beginning with Strega and ending with cherry brandy.

'Grand Marnier,' said Angus. 'And leave the bottle.'

Then he looked with arch triumph at Francis, like a wicked bird. Francis bit his finger moodily, and glowered with handsome, dark-blue, uncertain eyes at Mr Aaron, who was just surveying the *frutta*: which consisted of two rather old pomegranates and various pale yellow apples, with a sprinkling of withered dried figs. At the moment, they all looked like a *natura morta* arrangement.

'But do you think I might –?' said Francis moodily. Angus pursed his lips with a reckless brightness.

'Why not? I see no reason why you shouldn't,' he said. Whereupon Francis cleared his throat, disposed of his serviette, and rose to his feet, slowly but gracefully. Then he composed himself, and took on the air he wished to assume at the moment. It was a nice dégagé air, half naïve and half enthusiastic. Then he crossed to Aaron's table, and stood on one lounging hip, gracefully, and bent forward in a confidential manner, and said:

'*Do* excuse me. But I *must* ask you if it was you we heard playing the flute so perfectly wonderfully, just before dinner.'

The voice was confidential and ingratiating. Aaron, relieved from the world's stress of seeing life anew in the rosy glow of half a litre of good old Chianti – the war was so near, but gone by – looked up at the dark-blue, ingenuous, well-adapted eyes of our friend Francis, and smiling said:

'Yes. I saw you on the balcony as well.'

'Oh, did you notice us?' plunged Francis. 'But wasn't it an extraordinary affair?'

'Very,' said Aaron. 'I couldn't make it out, could you?'

'Oh,' cried Francis. 'I never try. It's all much too new and complicated for me. But perhaps you know Italy?'

'No, I don't,' said Aaron.

'Neither do we. And we feel rather stunned. We had only just arrived – and then – Oh!' Francis put up his hand to his comely brow and rolled his eyes. 'I feel perfectly overwhelmed with it still.'

He here allowed himself to sink friendlily into the vacant chair opposite Aaron's.

'Yes, I thought it was a bit exciting,' said Aaron. 'I wonder what will become of him –'

'– Of the one who climbed for the flag, you mean? No! But wasn't it perfectly marvellous! Oh incredible, quite incredible? And then your flute to finish it all! Oh! I felt it only wanted that. I haven't got over it yet. But your playing was *marvellous*, really marvellous. Do you know, I can't forget it. You are a professional musician, of course?'

'If you mean I play for a living,' said Aaron. 'I have played in orchestras in London.'

'Of course! Of course! I knew you must be a professional. But don't you give private recitals too?'

'No, I never have.'

'Oh!' cried Francis, catching his breath. 'I can't believe it. But you play *marvellously*! Oh, but I just loved it, it simply swept me away, after that scene in the street. It seemed to sum it all up, you know.'

'Did it,' said Aaron, rather grimly.

'But won't you come and have coffee with us at our table?' said Francis. 'We should like it most awfully if you would.'

'Yes, thank you,' said Aaron, half rising.

'But you haven't had your dessert,' said Francis, laying a fatherly detaining hand on the arm of the other man. Aaron looked at the detaining hand.

'The dessert isn't much to stop for,' he said. 'I can take with me what I want.' And he picked out a handful of dried figs.

The two went across to Angus's table.

'We're going to take coffee together,' said Francis complacently, playing the host with a suave assurance that was rather amusing and charming in him.

'Yes. I'm very glad,' said Angus. Let us give the show away: he was being wilfully nice. But he was quite glad to be able to be so nice. Anything to have a bit of life going: especially a bit of pleased life. He looked at Aaron's comely, wine-warmed face with gratification.

'Have a Grand Marnier,' he said. 'I don't know how bad it is. Everything is bad now. They lay it down to the war as well. It used to be quite a decent drink. What the war has got to do with bad liqueurs, I don't know.'

Aaron sat down in a chair at their table.

'But let us introduce ourselves,' said Francis. 'I am Francis – or really Franz Dekker. And this is Angus Guest, my friend.'

'And my name is Aaron Sisson.'

'What! What did you say?' said Francis, leaning forward. He too had sharp ears.

'Aaron Sisson.'

'Aaron Sisson! Oh, but how amusing! What a nice name!'

'No better than yours, is it?'

'Mine! Franz Dekker! Oh, much more amusing, *I* think,' said Francis archly.

'Oh well, it's a matter of opinion. You're the double decker, not me.'

'The double decker!' said Francis archly. 'Why, what do you mean! –' He rolled his eyes significantly. 'But may I introduce my friend, Angus Guest.'

'You've introduced me already, Francesco,' said Angus.

'So sorry,' said Francis.

'Guest!' said Aaron

Francis suddenly began to laugh.

'May he not be Guest?' he said fatherly.

'Very likely,' said Aaron. 'Not that I was ever good at guessing.'

Francis tilted his eyebrows. Fortunately the waiter arrived with the coffee.

'Tell me,' said Francis, 'will you have your coffee black, or with milk?' He was determined to restore a tone of sobriety.

The coffee was sipped in sober solemnity.

'Is music your line as well, then?' asked Aaron.

'No we're painters. We're going to work in Rome.'

'To earn your living?'

'Not yet.'

The amount of discretion, modesty, and reserve which Francis put into these two syllables gave Aaron to think that he had two real young swells to deal with.

'No,' continued Francis. 'I was only *just* down from Oxford when the war came – and Angus had been about ten months at the Slade. But I have always painted. So now we are going to work, really hard, in Rome, to make up for lost time. Oh, one has lost so much time, in the war. And such *precious* time! I don't know if ever one will even be able to make it up again.' Francis tilted his handsome eyebrows and put his head on one side with a wise-distressed look.

'No,' said Angus. 'One will never be able to make it up. What is more, one will never be able to start again where one left off. We're shattered old men, now, in one sense. And in another sense, we're just pre-war babies.'

The speech was uttered with an odd abruptness and didacticism which made Aaron open his eyes. Angus had that peculiar manner: he seemed to be haranguing himself in the circle of his own thoughts, not addressing himself to his listener. So his listener listened on the outside edge of the young fellow's crowded thoughts. Francis put on a distressed air, and let his attention wander. Angus pursed his lips and his eyes were stretched wide with a kind of pleasure, like a wicked owl which has just joyfully hooted an ill omen.

'Tell me,' said Francis to Aaron. 'Where were *you* all the time during the war?'

'I was doing my job,' said Aaron. Which led to his explaining his origins.

'Really! So your music is quite new! But how interesting!' cried Francis.

Aaron explained further.

'And so the war hardly affected you? But what did you *feel* about it, privately?'

'I didn't feel much. I didn't know what to feel. Other folks did such a lot of feeling, I thought I'd better keep my mouth shut.'

'Yes, quite!' said Angus. 'Everybody has such a lot of feelings on somebody else's behalf, that nobody ever had time to realize what they felt themselves. I know I was like that. The feelings all came on to me from the outside: like flies settling on meat. Before I knew where I was I was eaten up with a swarm of feelings, and I found myself in the trenches. God knows what for. And ever since then I've been trying to get out of my swarm of feelings, which buzz in and out of me and have nothing to do with me. I realized it in hospital. It's exactly like trying to get out of a swarm of nasty, dirty flies. And every one you kill makes you sick, but doesn't make the swarm any less.'

Again Angus pursed and bridled and looked like a pleased, wicked white owl. Then he polished his monocle on a very choice silk handkerchief, and fixed it unseeing in his left eye.

But Francis was not interested in his friend's experiences. For Francis had had a job in the War Office – whereas Angus was a war-hero with shattered nerves. And let him depreciate his own experiences as much as he liked, the young man with the monocle kept tight hold on his prestige as a war hero. Only for himself, though. He by no means insisted that anyone else should be war-bitten.

Francis was one of those men who, like women, can set up the sympathetic flow and make a fellow give himself away without realizing what he is doing. So there sat our friend Aaron, amusingly unbosoming himself of all his history and experiences, drawn out by the arch, subtle attentiveness of the handsome Francis. Angus listened too with pleased amusedness on his pale, emaciated face, pursing his shrunken jaw. And Aaron sipped various glasses of the liqueur, and told all his tale as if it was a comedy. A comedy it seemed, too, at that hour. And a comedy no doubt it was. But mixed, like most things in this life. Mixed.

It was quite late before this séance broke up: and the waiter itching to get rid of the fellows.

'Well now,' said Francis as he rose from the table and settled his elegant waist, resting on one hip, as usual. 'We shall see you in the morning, I hope.

You say you are going to Venice. Why? Have you some engagement in Venice?'

'No,' said Aaron. 'I only was going to look for a friend – Rawdon Lilly.'

'Rawdon Lilly! Why, is he in Venice? Oh, I've heard *such* a lot about him. I should like *so* much to meet him. But I heard he was in Germany –'

'I don't know where he is.'

'Angus! Didn't we hear that Lilly was in Germany?'

'Yes, in Munich, being psycho-analysed, I believe it was.'

Aaron looked rather blank.

'But have you anything to take you to Venice? It's such a bad climate in the winter. Why not come with us to Florence?' said Francis.

Aaron wavered. He really did not know what to do.

'Think about it,' said Francis, laying his hand on Aaron's arm. 'Think about it tonight. And we'll meet in the morning. At what time?'

'Any time,' said Aaron.

'Well, say eleven. We'll meet in the lounge here at eleven. Will that suit you? All right then. It's so awfully nice meeting you. That marvellous flute. And think about Florence. But do come. Don't disappoint us.'

The two young men went elegantly upstairs.

15

A RAILWAY JOURNEY

The next day but one, the three set off for Florence. Aaron had made an excursion from Milan with the two young heroes, and dined with them subsequently at the most expensive restaurant in the town. Then they had all gone home – and had sat in the young men's bedroom drinking tea, whilst Aaron played the flute. Francis was really musical, and enchanted. Angus enjoyed the novelty, and the moderate patronage he was able to confer. And Aaron felt amused and pleased, and hoped he was paying for his treat.

So behold them setting off for Florence in the early morning. Angus and Francis had first-class tickets: Aaron took a third-class.

'Come and have lunch with us on the train,' said Angus. 'I'll order three places, and we can lunch together.'

'Oh, I can buy a bit of food at the station,' said Aaron.

'No, come and lunch with us. It will be much nicer. And we shall enjoy it as well,' said Angus.

'Of course! Ever so much nicer! Of course!' cried Francis. 'Yes, why not, indeed! Why should you hesitate?'

'All right then,' said Aaron, not without some feeling of constraint.

So they separated. The young men settled themselves amidst the red plush and crochet-work, looking, with their hair plastered smoothly back, quite as first-class as you could wish, creating quite the right impression on the porters and the travelling Italians. Aaron went to his third-class, farther up the train.

'Well then, *au revoir*, till luncheon,' cried Francis.

The train was fairly full in the third- and second-classes. However, Aaron got his seat, and the porter brought on his bags, after disposing of the young men's luggage. Aaron gave the tip uneasily. He always hated tipping – it seemed humiliating both ways. And the airy aplomb of the two young cavaliers, as they settled down among the red plush and the obsequiousness, and said, 'Well then, *au revoir* till luncheon,' was peculiarly unsettling: though they did not intend it so.

'The porter thinks I'm their servant – their valet,' said Aaron to himself, and a curious half-amused, half-contemptuous look flickered on his face. It annoyed him. The falsity occasioned by the difference in the price of the tickets was really humiliating. Aaron had lived long enough to know that as far as manhood and intellect went – nay, even education – he was not the inferior to the two young 'gentlemen'. He knew quite well that, as far as intrinsic nature went, they did not imagine him an inferior: rather the contrary. They had rather an exaggerated respect for him and his life-power, and even his origin. And yet – they had the inestimable cash advantage – and they were going to keep it. They knew it was nothing more than an artificial cash superiority. But they gripped it all the more intensely. They were the upper middle classes. They were Eton and Oxford. And they were going to hang on to their privileges. In these days, it was a fool who abdicates before he's forced to. And therefore:

'Well then – *au revoir* till luncheon.'

They were being so awfully nice. And inwardly they were *not* condescending. But socially, they just had to be. The world is made like that. It wasn't their own private fault. It was no fault at all. If was just the mode in which they were educated, the style of their living. And as we know, *le style, c'est l'homme.*

Angus came of very wealthy iron people near Merthyr. Already he had a very fair income of his own. As soon as the law-business concerning his father's and his grandfather's will was settled, he would be well off. And he knew it, and valued himself accordingly. Francis was the son of a highly-esteemed barrister and politician of Sydney, and in his day would inherit his father's lately-won baronetcy. But Francis had not very much money: and was much more class-flexible than Angus. Angus had been born in a house with a park, and of awful hard-willed, money-bound people. Francis came of a much more adventurous, loose, excitable family, and had the colonial newness and adaptability. He knew, for his own part, that class superiority was just a trick, nowadays. Still, it was a trick that paid. And a trick he was going to play as long as it did pay.

While Aaron sat, a little pale at the gills, immobile, ruminating these matters, a not very pleasant look about his nose-end, he heard a voice:

'Oh, there you *are*! I thought I'd better come and see, so that we can fetch you at lunch-time. You've got a seat? Are you quite comfortable? Is there anything I could get you? Why, you're in a non-smoker! But that doesn't matter, everybody will smoke. Are you sure you have everything? Oh, but wait just one moment –'

It was Francis, long and elegant, with his straight shoulders and his coat buttoned to show his waist, and his face so well-formed and so modern. So modern, altogether. His voice was pleasantly modulated, and never hurried. He looked as if a thought had struck him. He put a finger to his brow, and hastened back to his own carriage. In a minute he returned with a new London literary magazine.

'Something to read – I shall have to *fly* – see you at lunch,' and he had turned and elegantly hastened, but not too fast, back to his carriage. The porter was holding the door for him. So Francis looked pleasantly hurried, but by no means rushed. Oh dear no. He took his time. It was not for him to bolt and scramble like a mere Italian.

The people in Aaron's carriage had watched the apparition of the elegant youth intently. For them, he was a being from another sphere – no doubt a young milordo with power, wealth, and glamorous life behind him. Which was just what Francis intended to convey. So handsome – so very, very impressive in all his elegant calm showiness. He made such a *bella figura*. It was just what the Italians loved. Those in the first-class regions thought he might even be an Italian, he was so attractive.

The train in motion, the many Italian eyes in the carriage studied Aaron. He too was good-looking. But by no means so fascinating as the young milordo. Not half as sympathetic. No good at all at playing a rôle. Probably a servant of the young signori.

Aaron stared out of the window, and played the one single British rôle left to him, that of ignoring his neighbours, isolating himself in their midst, and minding his own business. Upon this insular trick our greatness and our predominance depends – such as it is. Yes, they might look at him. They might think him a servant or what they liked. But he was inaccessible to them. He isolated himself upon himself, and there remained.

It was a lovely day, a lovely, lovely day of early autumn. Over the great plain of Lombardy a magnificent blue sky glowed like mid-summer, the sun shone strong. The great plain, with its great stripes of cultivation – without hedges or boundaries – how beautiful it was! Sometimes he saw oxen ploughing. Sometimes, oh so beautiful, teams of eight, of ten, even of twelve pale, great soft oxen in procession, ploughing the dark velvety earth, a driver with a great whip at their head, a man far behind holding the plough-shafts. Beautiful the soft, soft plunging motion of oxen moving forwards. Beautiful the strange, snaky lifting of the muzzles, the swaying of the sharp horns. And the soft, soft crawling motion of a team of oxen, so invisible, almost, yet so inevitable. Now and again straight canals of water flashed blue. Now and again the great lines of grey-silvery poplars rose and made avenues or lovely grey airy quadrangles across the plain. Their top boughs were spangled with gold and green leaf. Sometimes the vine-leaves were gold and red, a patterning. And the great square farm-homesteads, white, red-roofed, with their out-buildings, stood naked amid the lands, without screen or softening. There was something big and exposed about it all. No more the cosy English ambushed life: no longer the cosy littleness of the landscape. A bigness – and nothing to shelter the unshrinking spirit. It was all exposed, exposed to the sweep of plain, to the high strong sky, and to human gaze. A kind of boldness, an indifference. Aaron was impressed and fascinated. He looked with a new interest at the Italians in the carriage with him – for this same boldness and indifference and exposed gesture. And he found it in them too. And again it fascinated him. It seemed so much bigger, as if the walls of life had fallen. Nay, the walls of English life will have to fall.

Sitting there in the third-class carriage, he became happy again. The *presence* of his fellow-passengers was not so hampering as in England. In England, everybody seems held tight and gripped, nothing is left free. Every passenger seems like a parcel who is holding his string as fast as he can about him, lest one corner of the wrapper should come undone and reveal what is inside. And every other passenger is forced, by the public will, to hold himself as tight-bound also. Which in the end becomes a sort of self-conscious madness.

But here, in the third-class carriage, there was no tight string round every man. They were not all trussed with self-conscious string as tight as capons. They had a sufficient amount of callousness and indifference and natural equanimity. True, one of them spat continually on the floor, in large spits. And another sat with boots all unlaced and his collar off, and various important buttons undone. They did not seem to care it bits of themselves did show, through the gaps in the wrapping. Aaron winced – but he preferred it to English tightness. He was pleased, he was happy with the Italians. He thought how generous and natural they were.

So the towns passed by, and the hours, and he seemed at last to have got outside himself and his old conditions. It seemed like a great escape. There was magic again in life – real magic. Was it illusion, or was it genuine? He thought it genuine, and opened his soul as if there was no danger.

Lunch-time came. Francis summoned Aaron down the rocking train. The three men had a table to themselves, and all felt they were enjoying themselves very much indeed. Of course Francis and Angus made a great impression again. But in the dining-car were mostly middle-class well-to-do Italians. And these did not look upon our two young heroes as two young wonders. No, rather with some criticism, and some class-envy. But they were impressed: oh, they were impressed! How should they not be, when our young gentlemen had such an air! Aaron was conscious all the time that the fellow-diners were being properly impressed by the flower of civilization and the salt of the earth, namely, young, well-to-do Englishmen. And he had a faint premonition, based on experience perhaps, that fellow-passengers in the end never forgive the man who has 'impressed' them. Mankind loves being impressed. It asks to be impressed. It almost forces those whom it can force to play a rôle and to make an impression. And afterwards, never forgives.

When the train ran into Bologna Station, they were still in the restaurant car. Nor did they go at once to their seats. Angus had paid the bill. There was three-quarters-of-an-hour's wait in Bologna.

'You may as well come down and sit with us,' said Francis. 'We've got nobody in our carriage, so why shouldn't we all stay together during the wait? You kept your own seat, I suppose?'

No, he had forgotten. So when he went to look for it, it was occupied by a stout man who was just taking off his collar and wrapping a white kerchief round his neck. The third-class carriages were packed. For those were early days after the war, while men still had pre-war notions and were poor. Ten months would steal imperceptibly by, and the mysterious revolution would be effected. Then, the second-class and the first-class would be packed, indescribably packed, crowded, on all great trains: and the third-class carriages, lo and behold, would be comparatively empty. Oh marvellous days of bankruptcy, when nobody will condescend to travel third!

However, these were still modest, sombre months immediately after the peace. So a large man with a fat neck and a white kerchief, and a collar over his knee, sat in Aaron's seat. Aaron looked at the man, and at his own luggage overhead. The fat man saw him looking and stared back: then stared also at the luggage overhead: and with his almost invisible north-Italian gesture said much plainer than words could have said it: 'Go to hell. I'm here and I'm going to stop here.'

There was something insolent and unbearable about the look – and about the rocky fixity of the large man. He sat as if he had insolently taken root in his seat. Aaron flushed slightly. Francis and Angus strolled along the train, outside, for the corridor was already blocked with the mad Bologna rush, and the baggage belonging. They joined Aaron as he stood on the platform.

'But where is your seat?' cried Francis, peering into the packed and jammed compartments of the third-class.

'That man's sitting in it.'

'Which?' cried Francis, indignant.

'The fat one there – with the collar on his knee.'

'But it was *your seat* –!'

Francis's gore rose in indignation. He mounted into the corridor. And in the doorway of the compartment he bridled like an angry horse rearing, bridling his head. Poising himself on one hip, he stared fixedly at the man with the collar on his knee, then at the baggage aloft. He looked down at the fat man as a bird looks down from the eaves of a house. But the man looked back with a solid, rock-like impudence, before which an Englishman quails: a jeering, immovable insolence, with a sneer round the nose and a solid-seated posterior.

'But,' said Francis in English – none of them had any Italian yet. 'But,' said Francis, turning round to Aaron, 'that was *your seat*?' and he flung his long forefinger in the direction of the fat man's thighs.

'Yes!' said Aaron.

'And he's *taken* it –!' cried Francis in indignation.

'And know it too,' said Aaron.

'But –!' – and Francis looked round imperiously, as if to summon his bodyguard. But bodyguards are no longer forthcoming, and train-guards are far from satisfactory. The fat man sat on, with a sneer-grin, very faint but very effective, round his nose, and a solidly-planted posterior. He quite enjoyed the pantomime of the young foreigners. The other passengers said something to him, and he answered laconic. Then they all had the faint sneer-grin round their noses. A woman in the corner grinned jeeringly straight in Francis's face. His charm failed entirely this time: and as for his commandingness, that was ineffectual indeed. Rage came up in him.

'Oh, well – something must be done,' said he decisively. 'But didn't you put something in the seat to *reserve* it?'

'Only that *New Statesman* – but he's moved it.'

The man still sat with the invisible sneer-grin on his face, and that peculiar and immovable plant of his Italian posterior.

'Mais – cette place était *réservée* –' said Francis, moving to the direct attack.

The man turned aside and ignored him utterly – then said something to the men opposite, and they all began to show their teeth in a grin.

Francis was not so easily foiled. He touched the man on the arm. The man looked round threateningly, as if he had been struck.

'Cette place est réservée – par ce Monsieur –' said Francis with hauteur, though still in an explanatory tone, and pointing to Aaron.

The Italian looked him, not in the eyes, but between the eyes, and sneered full in his face. Then he looked with contempt at Aaron. And then he said, in Italian, that there was room for such snobs in the first-class, and that they had not any right to come occupying the place of honest men in the third.

'Già! Già!' barked the other passengers in the carriage.

'Loro possono andare prima classa – *prima classa!*' said the woman in the corner, in a very high voice, as if talking to deaf people, and pointing at Aaron's luggage, then along the train to the first-class carriages.

'C'è posto là,' said one of the men, shrugging his shoulders.

There was a jeering quality in the hard insolence which made Francis go very red and Angus very white. Angus stared like a death's-head behind his monocle, with death-blue eyes.

'Oh, never mind. Come along to the first-class. I'll pay the difference. We shall be much better all together. Get the luggage down, Francis. It wouldn't be possible to travel with this lot, even if he gave up the seat. There's plenty of room in our carriage – and I'll pay the extra,' said Angus.

He knew there was one solution – and only one – Money.

But Francis bit his finger. He felt almost beside himself – and quite powerless. For he knew the guard of the train would jeer too. It is not so easy to interfere with honest third-class Bolognesi in Bologna Station, even if they *have* taken another man's seat. Powerless, his brow knitted, and looking just like Mephistopheles with his high forehead and slightly arched nose, Mephistopheles in a rage, he hauled down Aaron's bag and handed it to Angus. So they transferred themselves to the first-class carriage, while the fat man and his party in the third-class watched in jeering, triumphant silence. Solid, planted, immovable, in static triumph.

So Aaron sat with the others amid the red plush, whilst the train began its long slow climb of the Appenines, stinking sulphureous through tunnels innumerable. Wonderful the steep slopes, the great chestnut woods, and then the great distances glimpsed between the heights, Firenzuola away and beneath, Turneresque hills far off, built of heaven-bloom, not of earth. It was cold at the summit-station, ice and snow in the air, fierce. Our travellers shrank into the carriage again, and wrapped themselves round.

Then the train began its long slither downhill, still through a whole necklace of tunnels, which fortunately no longer stank. So down and down, till the plain appears in sight once more, the Arno valley. But then began the inevitable hitch that always happens in Italian travel. The train began to hesitate – to falter to a halt, whistling shrilly as if in protest: whistling pip-pip-pip in espostulation as it stood forlorn among the fields: then stealing forward again and stealthily making pace, gathering speed, till it had got up a regular spurt: then suddenly the brakes came on with a jerk, more falteringly to a halt, more whistling and pip-pip-pipping, as the engine stood jingling with impatience: after which another creep and splash, and another choking off. So on till they landed in Prato station: and there they sat. A fellow-passenger told them there was an hour to wait here: an hour. Something had happened up the line.

'Then I propose we make tea,' said Angus, beaming.

'Why not! Of course. Let us make tea. And I will look for water.'

So Aaron and Francis went to the restaurant bar and filled the little pan at the tap. Angus got down the red picnic-case, of which he was so fond, and spread out the various arrangements on the floor of the coupé. He soon had the spirit-lamp burning, the water heating. Francis proposed that he and Aaron should dash into Prato and see what could be bought, whilst the tea was in preparation. So off they went, leaving Angus like a busy old wizard manipulating his arrangements on the floor of the carriage, his monocle beaming with bliss. The one fat fellow-passenger with a lurid striped rug over his knees watched with acute interest. Everybody who passed the doorway stood to contemplate the scene with pleasure. Officials came and studied the situation with appreciation. Then Francis and Aaron returned with a large supply of roast chestnuts, piping hot, and hard dried plums, and good dried figs, and rather stale rusks. They found the water just boiling, Angus just throwing in the tea-egg, and the fellow-passenger just poking his nose right in, he was so thrilled.

Nothing pleased Angus so much as thus pitching camp in the midst of civilization. The scrubby newspaper packets of chestnuts, plums, figs and rusks were spread out: Francis flew for salt to the man at the bar, and came back with a little paper of rock-salt: the brown tea was dispensed in the silver-fitted glasses from the immortal luncheon-case: and the picnic was in full swing. Angus, being in the height of his happiness, now sat on the seat cross-legged, with his feet under him, in the authentic Buddha fashion, and on his face the queer rapt alert look, half a smile, also somewhat Buddhistic, holding his glass of brown tea in his hand. He was as rapt and immobile as if he really were in a mystic state. Yet it was only his delight in the tea-party. The fellow-passenger peered at the tea, and said in broken French, was it good? In equally fragmentary French Francis said very good, and offered the fat passenger some. He, however, held up his hand in protest, as if to say not for any money would he swallow the hot-watery stuff. And he pulled out a flask of wine. But a handful of chestnuts he accepted.

The train-conductor, ticket-collector, and the heavy green soldier who protected them, swung open the door and stared attentively. The fellow-passenger addressed himself to these newcomers, and they all began to smile good-naturedly. Then the fellow-passenger – he was stout and fifty and had a brilliant striped rug always over his knees – pointed out the Buddha-like position of Angus, and the three in-starers smiled again. And so the fellow-passenger thought he must try too. So he put aside his rug, and lifted his feet from the floor, and took his toes in his hands, and tried to bring his legs up and his feet under him. But his knees were fat, his trousers in the direst extreme of peril, and he could no more manage it than if he had tried to swallow himself. So he desisted suddenly, rather scared, whilst the three bunched and official heads in the doorway laughed and jested at him, showing their teeth and teasing him. But on our gipsy party they turned their eyes with admiration. They loved the novelty and the fun. And on the thin, elegant Angus in his new London clothes they looked really puzzled, as he sat there immobile, gleaming through his monocle like some Buddha going wicked, perched cross-legged and ecstatic on the red velvet seat. They marvelled that the lower half of him could so double up, like a foot-rule. So they stared till they had seen enough. When they suddenly said, 'Buon' appetito,' withdrew their heads and shoulders, slammed the door, and departed.

Then the train set off also – and shortly after six arrived in Florence. It was debated what should Aaron do in Florence. The young men had engaged a room at Bertolini's hotel, on the Lugarno. Bertolini's was not expensive – but Aaron knew that his friends would not long endure hotel life. However, he went along with the other two, trusting to find a cheaper place on the morrow.

It was growing quite dark as they drove to the hotel, but still was light enough to show the river rustling, the Ponte Vecchio spanning its little storeys across the flood, on its low, heavy piers: and some sort of magic of the darkening, varied houses facing, on the other side of the stream. Of course they were all enchanted.

'I knew,' said Francis, 'we should love it.'

Aaron was told he could have a little back room and pension terms for fifteen liras a day, if he stayed at least fifteen days. The exchange was then at forty-five. So fifteen liras meant just six-shillings-and-sixpence a day, without extras. Extras meant wine, tea, butter, and light. It was decided he should look for something cheaper next day.

By the tone of the young men, he now gathered that they would prefer it if he took himself off to a cheaper place. They wished to be on their own.

'Well then,' said Francis, 'you will be in to lunch here, won't you? Then we'll see you at lunch.'

It was as if both the young men had drawn in their feelers now. They were afraid of finding the new man an incubus. They wanted to wash their hands of him. Aaron's brow darkened.

> 'Perhaps it was right to dissemble your love
> But why did you kick me downstairs ...'

The morning then found him out early, before his friends had arisen. It was sunny again. The magic of Florence at once overcame him, and he forgot the bore of limited means and hotel costs. He went straight out of the hotel door, across the road, and leaned on the river parapet. There ran the Arno: not such a flood after all, but a green stream with shoals of pebbles in its course. Across, and in the delicate shadow of the early sun, stood the opposite Lugarno, the old flat houses, pink, or white, or grey stone, with their green shutters, some closed, some opened. It had a flowery effect, the skyline irregular against the morning light. To the right the delicate Trinità bridge, to the left the old bridge with its little shops over the river. Beyond, towards the sun, glimpses of green, sky-bloomed country: Tuscany.

There was a noise and clatter of traffic: boys pushing hand-barrows over the cobble-stones, slow bullocks, stepping side by side, and shouldering one another affectionately, drawing a load of country produce, then horses in great brilliant scarlet cloths, like vivid palls, slowly pulling the long narrow carts of the district and men hu-huing! – and people calling: all the sharp, clattering morning noise of Florence.

'Oh Angus! Do come and look! *Oh* so lovely!'

Glancing up, he saw the elegant figure of Francis, in fine coloured-silk pyjamas, perched on a small upper balcony, turning away from the river towards the bedroom again, his hand lifted to his lips, as if to catch there his cry of delight. The whole pose was classic and effective: and very amusing. How the Italians would love it!

Aaron slipped back across the road, and walked away under the houses towards the Ponte Vecchio. He passed the bridge – and passed the Uffizi – watching the green hills opposite, and San Miniato. Then he noticed the over-dramatic group of statuary in the Piazza Mentana – male and physical and melodramatic – and then the corner house. It was a big old Florentine house, with many green shutters, and wide eaves. There was a notice plate by the door – 'Pension Nardini'.

He came to a full stop. He stared at the notice-plate, stared at the glass door, and turning round, stared at the over-pathetic dead soldier on the arm of his over-heroic pistol-firing comrade; *Mentana* – and the date! Aaron wondered what and where Mentana was. Then at last he summoned his energy, opened the glass door, and mounted the first stairs.

He waited some time before anybody appeared. Then a maid-servant.

'Can I have a room?' said Aaron.

The bewildered, wild-eyed servant maid opened a door and showed him into a heavily-gilt, heavily-plush drawing-room with a great deal of frantic grandeur about it. There he sat and cooled his heels for half an hour. Arrived at length a stout young lady – handsome, with big dark-blue Italian eyes, but anaemic and too stout.

'Oh!' she said as she entered, not knowing what else to say.

'Good morning,' said Aaron awkwardly.

'Oh, good morning! English! Yes! Oh, I am so sorry to keep you, you know, to make you wait so long. I was upstairs, you know, with a lady. Will you sit?'

'Can I have a room?' said Aaron.

'A room! Yes, you can.'

'What terms?'

'Terms! Oh! Why, ten francs a day, you know, pension – if you stay – how long will you stay?'

'At least a month, I expect.'

'A month! Oh yes. Yes, ten francs a day.'

'For everything?'

'Everything. Yes, everything. Coffee, bread, honey or jam in the morning: lunch at half-past twelve; tea in the drawing-room, half-past four: dinner at half-past seven: all very nice. And a warm room with the sun – Would you like to see?'

So Aaron was led up the big, rambling old house to the top floor – then along a long old corridor – and at last into a big bedroom with two beds and a red-tiled floor – a little dreary, as ever – but the sun just beginning to come in, and a lovely view on to the river, towards the Ponte Vecchio, and at the hills with their pines and villas and verdure opposite.

Here he would settle. The signorina would send a man for his bags at half-past two in the afternoon.

At luncheon Aaron found the two friends, and told them of his move.

'How very nice for you! Ten francs a day – but that is nothing. I am so pleased you've found something. And when will you be moving in?' said Francis.

'At half-past two.'

'Oh, so soon. Yes, just as well. But we shall see you from time to time, of course. What did you say the address was? Oh yes – just near the awful statue. Very well. We can look you up any time – and you will find us here. Leave a message if we should happen not to be in – we've got lots of engagements –'

16

FLORENCE

The very afternoon after Aaron's arrival in Florence the sky became dark, the wind cold, and rain began steadily to fall. He sat in his big, bleak room above the river, and watched the pale green water fused with yellow, the many-threaded streams fuse into one, as swiftly the surface flood came down from the hills. Across, the dark green hills looked darker in the wet, the umbrella pines held up in vain above the villas. But away below on the Lugarno, traffic rattled as ever.

Aaron went down at five o'clock to tea, and found himself alone next a group of women, mostly Swedes or Danish or Dutch, drinking a peculiar brown herb-brew which tasted like nothing else on earth, and eating two thick bits of darkish bread smeared with a brown smear which hoped it was jam, but hoped in vain. Unhappily he sat in the gilt and red, massively ornate room, while the foreign women eyed him. Oh, bitter to be a male under such circumstances.

He escaped as soon as possible back to his far-off regions, lonely and cheerless, away above. But he rather liked the far-off remoteness in the big old Florentine house: he did not mind the peculiar dark, uncosy dreariness. It was not really dreary: only indifferent. Indifferent to comfort, indifferent to all homeliness and cosiness. The over-big furniture trying to be impressive, but never to be pretty or bright or cheerful. There it stood, ugly and apart. And there let it stand. Neither did he mind the lack of fire, the cold sombreness of his big bedroom. At home, in England, the bright grate and the ruddy fire, the thick hearth-rug and the man's arm-chair, these had been inevitable. And now he was glad to get away from it all. He was glad not to have a cosy hearth, and his own arm-chair. He was glad to feel the cold, and to breathe the unwarmed air. He preferred the Italian way of no fires, no heating. If the day was cold, he was willing to be cold too. If it was dark, he was willing to be dark. The cosy brightness of a real home – it had stifled him till he felt his lungs would burst. The horrors of real domesticity. No, the Italian brutal way was better.

So he put his overcoat over his knee, and studied some music he had bought in Milan: some Pergolesi and the Scarlatti he liked, and some Corelli. He preferred frail, sensitive, abstract music, with not much feeling in it, but a certain limpidity and purity. Night fell as he sat reading the scores. He would have liked to try certain pieces on his flute. But his flute was too sensitive, it winced from the new strange surroundings, and would not blossom.

Dinner sounded at last – at eight o'clock, or something after. He had to learn to expect the meals always forty minutes late. Down he went, down the long, dark, lonely corridors and staircases. The dining-room was right downstairs. But he had a little table to himself near the door, the elderly women were at some little distance. The only other men were Agostino, the unshapely waiter, and an Italian duke, with wife and child and nurse, the family sitting all together at a table half-way down the room, and utterly preoccupied with a little yellow dog.

However, the food was good enough, and sufficient, and the waiter and the maid-servant cheerful and bustling. Everything felt happy-go-lucky and informal, there was no particular atmosphere. Nobody put on any airs, because nobody in the Nardini took any notice if they did. The little ducal dog yapped, the ducal son shouted, the waiter dropped half a dozen spoons, the old women knitted during the waits, and all went off so badly that it was quite pleasant. Yes, Aaron preferred it to Bertolini's, which was trying to be efficient and correct: though not making any strenuous effort. Still, Bertolini's was much more up to the scratch, there was the tension of proper standards. Whereas here at Nardini's, nothing mattered very much.

It was November. When he got up to his far-off room again, Aaron felt almost as if he were in a castle with the drawbridge drawn up. Through the open window came the sound of the swelling Arno, as it rushed and rustled along over its gravel-shoals. Lights spangled the opposite side. Traffic sounded deep below. The room was not really cold, for the summer sun so soaks into these thick old buildings that it takes a month or two of winter to soak it out. The rain still fell.

In the morning it was still November, and the dawn came slowly. And through the open window was the sound of the river's rushing. But the traffic started before dawn, with a bang and a rattle of carts, and a bang and jingle of tram-cars over the not-distant bridge. Oh, noisy Florence! At half-past seven Aaron rang for his coffee: and got it at a few minutes past eight. The signorina had told him to take his coffee in bed.

Rain was still falling. But towards nine o'clock it lifted, and he decided to go out. A wet, wet world. Carriages going by, with huge wet shiny umbrellas, black and with many points, erected to cover the driver and the tail of the horse and the box-seat. The hood of the carriage covered the fare. Clatter-clatter through the rain. Peasants with long wagons and slow oxen, and pale-green huge umbrellas erected for the driver to walk beneath. Men tripping along in cloaks, shawls, umbrellas, anything, quite unconcerned. A man loading gravel in the river-bed, in spite of the wet. And innumerable bells ringing: but innumerable bells. The great soft trembling of the cathedral bell felt in all the air.

Anyhow it was a new world. Aaron went along close to the tall thick houses, following his nose. And suddenly he caught sight of the long slim neck of the Palazzo Vecchio up above, in the air. And in another minute he was passing between massive buildings, out into the Piazza della Signoria. There he stood still and looked round him in real surprise, and real joy. The flat, empty square with its stone paving was all wet. The great buildings rose dark. The dark, sheer front of the Palazzo Vecchio went up like a cliff, to the battlements, and the slim tower soared dark and hawk-like, crested, high above. And at the foot of the cliff stood the great naked David, white and stripped in the wet, white against the dark, warm-dark cliff of the building – and near, the heavy naked men of Bandinelli.

The first thing he had seen, as he turned into the square, was the back of one of these Bandinelli statues: a great naked man of marble, with a heavy back and strong naked flanks over which the water was trickling. And then to come immediately upon the David, so much whiter, glistening skin-white in the wet, standing a little forward, and shrinking.

He may be ugly, too naturalistic, too big, and anything else you like. But the David in the Piazza della Signoria, there under the dark great Palace, in the position Michelangelo chose for him, there, standing forward stripped and exposed and eternally half-shrinking, half-wishing to expose himself, he is the genius of Florence. The adolescent, the white, self-conscious, physical adolescent: enormous, in keeping with the stark, grim, enormous palace, which is dark and bare as he is white and bare. And behind, the big, lumpy Bandinelli men are in keeping too. They may be ugly – but they are there in their place, and they have their own lumpy reality. And this morning in the rain, standing unbroken, with the water trickling down their flanks and along the inner side of their great thighs, they were real enough, representing the undaunted physical nature of the heavier Florentines.

Aaron looked and looked at the three great naked men. David so much white, and standing forward, self-conscious: then at the great splendid front of the Palazzo Vecchio: and at the fountain splashing water upon its wet, wet figures; and the distant equestrian statue; and the stone-flagged space of the grim square. And he felt that here he was in one of the world's living centres, here, in the Piazza della Signoria. The sense of having arrived – of having reached a perfect centre of the human world: this he had.

And so, satisfied, he turned round to look at the bronze Perseus which rose just above him. Benvenuto Cellini's dark hero looked female, with his plump hips and his waist, female and rather insignificant: graceful, and rather vulgar. The clownish Bandinellis were somehow more to the point. Then all the statuary in the Loggia! But that is a mistake. It looks too much like the yard of a monumental mason.

The great, naked men in the rain, under the dark-grey November sky, in the dark, strong, inviolable square! The wonderful hawk-head of the old palace! The physical, self-conscious adolescent, Michelangelo's David, shrinking and exposing himself, with his white, slack limbs! Florence, passionate, fearless Florence had spoken herself out. Aaron was fascinated by the Piazza della Signoria. He never went into the town, nor returned from it to his lodging, without contriving to pass through the square. And he never passed through it without satisfaction. Here men had been at their intensest, most naked pitch, here, at the end of the old world and the beginning of the new. Since then, always rather pulling and apologetic.

Aaron felt a new self, a new life-urge rising inside himself. Florence seemed to start a new man in him. It was a town of men. On Friday morning, so early, he heard the traffic. Early, he watched the rather low, two-wheeled traps of the peasants spanking recklessly over the bridge, coming in to town. And then, when he went out, he found the Piazza della Signoria packed with men: but all, all men. And all farmers, land-owners and land-workers. The curious, fine-nosed Tuscan farmers, with their half-sardonic, amber-coloured eyes. Their curious individuality, their clothes worn so easy and reckless, their hats with the personal twist. Their curious full oval cheeks, their tendency to be too fat, to have a belly and heavy limbs. Their close-sitting dark hair. And above all, their sharp, almost acrid, mocking expression, the silent curl of the nose, the eternal challenge, the rock-bottom unbelief, and the subtle fearlessness. The dangerous, subtle, never-dying fearlessness, and the acrid unbelief. But men! Men! A town of men, in spite of everything. The one manly quality, undying, acrid fearlessness. The eternal challenge of the unquenched human soul. Perhaps too acrid and challenging today, when there is nothing left to challenge. But men – who existed without apology and without justification. Men who would neither justify themselves nor apologize for themselves. Just men. The rarest thing left in our sweet Christendom.

Altogether Aaron was pleased with himself, for being in Florence. Those were early days after the war, when as yet very few foreigners had returned, and the place had the native sombreness and intensity. So that our friend did not mind being alone.

The third day, however, Francis called on him. There was a tap at the bedroom door, and the young man entered, all eyes of curiosity.

'Oh, there you *are*!' he cried, flinging his hand and twisting his waist and then laying his hand on his breast. 'Such a *long* way up to you! But *miles* –! Well, how are you? Are you quite all right here? You are? I'm so glad – we've been so *rushed*, seeing people, that we haven't had a *minute*. But not a *minute*! People! People! People! Isn't it amazing how many there are, and how many one knows, and gets to know! But amazing! Endless acquaintances! – oh, and such quaint people here! so *odd*!! so *more* than odd! Oh, extraordinary –!' Francis chuckled to himself over the extraordinariness. Then he seated himself gracefully at Aaron's table. 'Oh, *music*! What? Corelli! So interesting! So very clever, these people, weren't they! Corelli and the younger Scarlatti and all that crowd.' Here he closed the score again. 'But now – *look*! Do you want to know anybody here, or don't you? I've told them about you, and of course they're dying to meet you and hear you play. But I thought it best not to mention anything about – about your being hard-up, and all that. I said you were just here on a visit. You see with this kind of people I'm sure it's much the best not to let them start off by thinking you will need them at all – or that you *might* need them. Why give yourself away, anyhow? Just meet them and take them for what they're worth – and then you can see. If they like to give you an engagement to play at some show or other – well, you can decide when the time comes whether you will accept. Much better that these kind of people shouldn't get it into their heads at once that they can hire your services. It doesn't do. They haven't enough discrimination for that. Much best make rather a favour of it, than sort of *ask* them to hire you. Don't you agree? Perhaps I'm wrong.'

Aaron sat and listened and wondered at the wisdom and the genuine kindness of the young *beau*. And more still, he wondered at the profound social disillusionment. This handsome collie dog was something of a social wolf, half showing his fangs at the moment. But with genuine kind-heartedness for another wolf. Aaron was touched.

'Yes, I think that's the best way,' he said.

'You do! Yes, so do I. Oh, they are such queer people! Why is it, do you think, that English people abroad go so very *queer* – so ultra-English – *incredible*! – and at the same time so perfectly impossible? But impossible! Pathological, I assure you. And as for their sexual behaviour – oh, dear, don't mention it. I assure you it doesn't bear mention. And all quite, flagrant, quite unabashed – under the cover of this fanatical Englishness. But I couldn't begin to *tell* you all the things. It's just incredible.'

Aaron wondered how on earth Francis had been able to discover and bear witness to so much that was incredible, in a bare two days. But a little gossip, and an addition of lurid imagination, will carry you anywhere.

'Well, now,' said Francis. 'What are you doing today?'

Aaron was not doing anything in particular.

'Then will you come and have dinner with us –?'

Francis fixed up the time and the place – a small restaurant at the other end of the town. Then he leaned out of the window.

'Fascinating place! Oh, fascinating place!' he said, in soliloquy. 'And you've got a superb view. Almost better than ours, I think. Well then, half-past seven. We're meeting a few other people, mostly residents or people staying some time. We're not inviting them. Just dropping in, you know – a little restaurant. We shall see you then! Well then, *a rivederci* till this evening. So glad you like Florence! I'm simply loving it – revelling. And the pictures! Oh –'

The party that evening consisted all of men: Francis and Angus, and a writer, James Argyle, and little Algy Constable, and tiny Louis Mee, and deaf Walter Rosen. They all snapped and rattled at one another, and were rather spiteful but rather amusing. Francis and Angus had to leave early. They had another appointment. And James Argyle got quite tipsy, and said to Aaron:

'But my body, don't let yourself be led astray by the talk of such people as Algy. Beware of them, my boy, if you've a soul to save. If you've a soul to save!' And he swallowed the remains of his litre.

Algy's nose trembled a little, and his eyes blinked.

'And if you've a soul to *lose*,' he said, 'I would warn you very earnestly against Argyle.' Whereupon Algy shut one eye and opened the other so wide, that Aaron was almost scared.

'Quite right, my boy. Ha! Ha! Never a truer thing said! Ha-Ha-Ha.' Argyle laughed his Mephistophelian tipsy laugh. 'They'll teach you to save. Never was such a lot of ripe old savers! Save their old trouser-buttons! Go to them if you want to learn to save. Oh yes, I advise it seriously. You'll lose nothing – not even a reputation. You may lose your *soul*, of course. But that's a detail, among such a hoard of banknotes and trouser-buttons. Ha-ha! What's a soul to them –?'

'What is it to you, is perhaps the more pertinent question,' said Algy, flapping his eyelids like some crazy owl. 'It is you who specialize in the matter of soul, and we who are in need of enlightenment –'

'Yes, very true, you *are*! You *are* in need of enlightenment. A set of benighted wise virgins. Ha-ha-ha! That's good, that – benighted wise virgins! What –' Argyle put his red face near to Aaron's, and made a *moue*, narrowing his eyes quizzically as he peered up from under his level grey eyebrows. 'Sit in the dark to save the lamp-oil! And all no good to them. When the bridegroom cometh –! Ha-ha! Good that! Good, my boy! The bridegroom –' he giggled to himself. 'What about the bridegroom, Algy, my boy? Eh? What about him? Better trim your wick, old man, if it's not too late –'

'We were talking of souls, not wicks, Argyle,' said Algy.

'Same thing. Upon my soul it all amounts to the same thing. Where's the soul in a man that hasn't got a bed-fellow – eh? – answer me that! Can't be done, you know. Might as well ask a virgin chicken to lay you an egg. But believe me, there's far more damned chastity in the world, than anything else. Even in this town. Call it chastity, if you like. I see nothing in it but sterility. It takes a rat to praise long tails. Impotence set up the praise of chastity – believe me or not – but that's the bottom of it. The virtue is made out of the necessity. Ha-ha-ha! They can't do it, and so they make a virtue of not doing it. Like them! Like them!'

There was a pause. Argyle was in his cups, which left no more to be said. Algy, quivering and angry, looked disconcertingly round the room as if he were quite calm and collected. The deaf Jewish Rosen was smiling down his nose and saying: 'What was that last? I didn't catch that last,' cupping his ear with his hand in the frantic hope that someone would answer. No one paid any heed.

'I shall be going,' said Algy, looking round. Then to Aaron he said, 'You play the flute, I hear. May we hear you some time?'

'Yes,' said Aaron, non-committal.

'Well, look here – come to tea tomorrow. I shall have some friends, and Del Torre will play the piano. Come to tea tomorrow, will you?'

'Thank you, I will.'

'And perhaps you'll bring your flute along.'

'Don't you do any such thing, my boy. Make them entertain *you*, for once. They're always squeezing an entertainment out of somebody' – and Argyle desperately emptied the remains of Algy's wine into his own glass: whilst Algy stood as if listening to something far off, and blinking terribly.

'Anyhow,' he said at length, 'you'll come, won't you? And bring the flute if you feel like it.'

'Don't you take that flute, my boy,' persisted Argyle. 'Don't think of such a thing. If they want a concert, let them buy their tickets and go to the Teatro Diana. Or to Marchesa del Torre's Saturday morning. She can afford to treat them.'

Algy looked at Argyle, and blinked.

'Well,' he said. 'I hope you'll get home all right, Argyle.'

'Thank you for your courtesy, Algy. Won't you lend me your arm?'

As Algy was small and frail, somewhat shaky: and as Argyle was a finely built, heavy man of fifty or more, the slap was unkind.

'Afraid I can't tonight. Good night –'

Algy departed, so did little Mee, who had sat with a little delighted disapproval on his tiny, bird-like face, without saying anything. And even the Jew Rosen put away his deaf-machine and began awkwardly to take his leave. His long nose was smiling to itself complacently at all the things Argyle had been saying.

When he too had gone, Argyle arched his brows at Aaron, saying:

'Oh, my dear fellow, what a lot they are! Little Mee – looking like an innocent little boy. He's over seventy if he's a day. Well over seventy. Well, you don't believe me. Ask his mother – ask his mother. She's ninety-five. Old lady of ninety-five –' Argyle even laughed himself at his own preposterousness.

'And then Algy – Algy's not a fool, you know. Oh, he can be most entertaining, most witty, and amusing. But he's out of place here. He should be in Kensington, dandling round the ladies' drawing-rooms and making his *mots*. They're rich, you know, the pair of them. Little Mee used to boast that he lived on eleven-and-threepence a week. Had to, poor chap. But then what does a white mouse like that need? Makes a heavy meal on a cheese-paring. Luck, you know – but, of course, he's come into money as well. Rich as Croesus, and still lives on nineteen and twopence a week. Though it's nearly double, of course, what it used to be. No wonder he looks anxious. They disapprove of me – oh, quite right, quite right from their own point of view. Where would their money be otherwise? It wouldn't last long if I laid my hands on it –' He made a devilish quizzing face. 'But you know, they get on my nerves. Little old maids, you know, little old maids. I'm sure I'm surprised at their patience with me. But when people are patient with you, you want to spit gall at them. Don't you? Ha-ha-ha! Poor old Algy. Did I lay it on him tonight, or did I miss him?'

'I think you got him,' said Aaron.

'He'll never forgive me. Depend on it, he'll never forgive me. Ha-ha! I like to be unforgiven. It adds *zest* to one's intercourse with people, to know that they'll never forgive me. Ha-ha-ha! Little old maids, who do their knitting with their tongues. Poor old Algy – he drops his stitches now. Ha-ha-ha! Must be eighty, I should say.'

Aaron laughed. He had never met a man like Argyle before – and he could not help being charmed. The other man had a certain wicked whimsicality that was very attractive, when levelled against someone else, and not against oneself. He must have been very handsome in his day, with his natural dignity, and his clean-shaven strong square face. But now his face was all red and softened and inflamed, his eyes had gone small and wicked under his bushy grey brows. Still he had a presence. And his grey hair, almost gone white, was still handsome.

'And what are you going to do in Florence?' asked Argyle.

Aaron explained.

'Well,' said Argyle, 'make what you can out of them, and then go. Go before they have time to do the dirty on you. If they think you want anything from them, they'll treat you like a dog, like a dog. Oh, they're very frightened of anybody who wants anything of them: frightened to death. I see nothing of them. Live by myself – see nobody. Can't stand it, you know: their silly little tea-parties – simply can't stand it. No, I live alone – and shall die alone. At least, I sincerely hope so. I should be sorry to have any of them hanging round.'

The restaurant was empty, the pale, malarial waiter – he had, of course, contracted malaria during the war – was looking purple round the eyes. But Argyle callously sat on. Aaron therefore rose to his feet.

'Oh, I'm coming, I'm coming,' said Argyle.

He got unsteadily to his feet. The waiter helped him on with his coat: and he put a disreputable-looking little curly hat on his head. Then he took his stick.

'Don't look at my appearance, my dear fellow,' said Argyle. 'I am frayed at the wrists – Look here!' He showed the cuffs of his overcoat, just frayed through. 'I've got a trunkful of clothes in London, if only somebody would bring it out to me. Ready then! Avanti!'

And so they passed out into the still rainy street. Argyle lived in the very centre of the town: in the cathedral square. Aaron left him at his hotel door.

'But come and see me,' said Argyle. 'Call for me at twelve o'clock – or just before twelve – and let us have luncheon together. What! Is that all right? Yes, come just before twelve. When? – tomorrow? Tomorrow morning? Will you come tomorrow?'

Aaron said he would come on Monday.

'Monday, eh! You say Monday! Very well then. Don't you forget now. Don't you forget. For I've a memory like a vice. *I* shan't forget – just before twelve then. And come right up. I'm right under the roof. In Paradise, as the porter always says. Siamo nel paradiso. But he's a *crétin*. As near Paradise as I care for, for it's devilish hot in summer, and damned cold in winter. Don't you forget now – Monday, twelve o'clock.'

And Argyle pinched Aaron's arm fast, then went unsteadily up the steps to his hotel door.

The next day at Algy's there was a crowd. Algy had a very pleasant flat indeed, kept more scrupulously neat and finicking than ever any woman's flat was kept. So today, with its bowls of flowers and its pictures and books and old furniture, and Algy, very nicely dressed, fluttering and blinking and making really a charming host, it was all very delightful to the little mob of visitors. They were a curious lot, it is true: everybody rather exceptional. Which, though it may be startling, is so very much better fun than everybody all alike. Aaron talked to an old, old Italian elegant in side-curls, who peeled off his grey gloves and studied his formalities with a delightful Mid-Victorian dash, and told stories about a *plaint* which Lady Surry had against Lord Marsh, and was quite incomprehensible. Out rolled the English words, like plums out of a burst bag, and all completely unintelligible. But the old *beau* was supremely satisfied. He loved talking English, and holding his listeners spellbound.

Next to Aaron on the sofa sat the Marchesa del Torre, an American woman from the Southern States, who had lived most of her life in Europe. She was about forty years of age, handsome, well-dressed, and quiet in the buzz of the tea-party. It was evident she was one of Algy's lionesses. Now she sat by Aaron, eating nothing, but taking a cup of tea and keeping still. She seemed sad – or not well perhaps. Her eyes were heavy. But she was very carefully made up, and very well dressed, though simply: and sitting there, full-bosomed, rather sad, remote-seeming, she suggested to Aaron a modern Cleopatra brooding, Antony-less.

Her husband, the Marchese, was a little intense Italian in a Colonel's grey uniform, cavalry, leather gaiters. He had blue eyes, his hair was cut very short, his head looked hard and rather military: he would have been taken for an Austrian officer, or even a German, had it not been for the peculiar Italian sprightliness and touch of grimace in his mobile countenance. He was rather like a gnome – not ugly, but odd.

Now he came and stood opposite to Signor di Lanti, and quizzed him in Italian. But it was evident, in quizzing the old buck, the little Marchese was hovering near his wife, in earshot. Algy came up with cigarettes, and she at once began to smoke, with that peculiar heavy intensity of a nervous woman.

Aaron did not say anything – did not know what to say. He was peculiarly conscious of the woman sitting next to him, her arm near his. She smoked heavily, in silence, as if abstracted, a sort of cloud on her level, dark brows. Her hair was dark, but a softish brown, not black, and her skin was fair. Her bosom would be white. Why Aaron should have had this thought, he could not for the life of him say.

Manfredi, her husband, rolled his blue eyes and grimaced as he laughed at old Lanti. But it was obvious that his attention was diverted sideways, towards his wife. Aaron, who was tired of nursing a tea-cup, placed it on a table and resumed his seat in silence. But suddenly the little Marchese whipped out his cigarette-case, and making a little bow, presented it to Aaron, saying:

'Won't you smoke?'

'Thank you,' said Aaron.

'Turkish that side – Virginia there – you see.'

'Thank you, Turkish,' said Aaron.

The little officer in his dove-grey and yellow uniform snapped his box shut again, and presented a light.

'You are new in Florence?' he said, as he presented the match.

'Four days,' said Aaron.

'And I hear you are musical.'

'I play the flute – no more.'

'Ah yes – but then you play it as an artist, not as an accomplishment.'

'But how do you know?' laughed Aaron.

'I was told so – and I believe it.'

'That's nice of you, anyhow. But you are a musician too.'

'Yes – we are both musicians – my wife and I.'

Manfredi looked at his wife. She flicked the ash off her cigarette.

'What sort?' said Aaron.

'Why, how do you mean, what sort? We are dilettanti, I suppose.'

'No – what is your instrument? The piano?'

'Yes – the pianoforte. And my wife sings. But we are very much out of practice. I have been at the war four years, and we have had our home in Rome. My wife was in Paris often, she did not wish to stay in Italy alone. And so – you see – everything goes –'

'But you will begin again?'

'Yes. We have begun already. We have music on Saturday mornings. Next Saturday a string quartette, and violin solos by a young Florentine woman – a friend – very good indeed, daughter of our Professor Tortoli, who composes – as you may know –'

'Yes,' said Aaron.

'Would you care to come and hear –?'

'Awfully nice if you would –' suddenly said the wife, quite simply, as if she had merely been tired, and not talking before.

'I should like to very much –'

'Do come then.'

While they were making the arrangements, Algy came up in his blandest manner.

'Now, Marchesa – might we hope for a song?'

'No – I don't sing any more,' came the slow, contralto reply.

'Oh, but you can't mean you say that deliberately –'

'Yes, quite deliberately –' She threw away her cigarette and opened her little gold case to take another.

'But what can have brought you to such a disastrous decision?'

'I can't say,' she replied, with a little laugh. 'The war, probably.'

'Oh, but don't let the war deprive us of this, as of everything else.'

'Can't be helped,' she said. 'I have no choice in the matter. The bird has flown –' She spoke with a certain heavy languor.

'You mean the bird of your voice? Oh, but that is quite impossible. One can hear it calling out the leaves every time you speak.'

'I'm afraid you can't get him to do any more than call out of the leaves.'

'But – but – pardon me – is it because you don't intend there should be any more song? Is that your intention?'

'That I couldn't say,' said the Marchesa, smoking, smoking.

'Yes,' said Manfredi. 'At the present time it is because she *will* not – not because she cannot. It is her will, as you say.'

'Dear me! Dear me! said Algy. 'But this is really another disaster added to the war list. But – but – will none of us ever be able to persuade you?' He smiled half cajoling, half pathetic, with a prodigious flapping of his eyes.

'I don't know,' said she. 'That will be as it must be.'

'Then can't we say it must be *song* once more?'

To this sally she merely laughed, and pressed out her half-smoked cigarette.

'How very disappointing! How very cruel of – of fate and the war – and – and all the sum total of evils,' said Algy.

'Perhaps –' here the little and piquant host turned to Aaron.

'Perhaps Mr Sisson, your flute might call out the bird of song. As thrushes call each other into challenge, you know. Don't you think that is very probable?'

'I have no idea,' said Aaron.

'But you, Marchesa. Won't you give us hope that it might be so?'

'I've no idea, either,' said she. 'But I should very much like to hear Mr Sisson's flute. It's an instrument I like extremely.'

'There now. You see you may work the miracle, Mr Sisson. Won't you play for us?'

'I'm afraid I didn't bring my flute along,' said Aaron. 'I didn't want to arrive with a little bag.'

'Quite!' said Algy. 'What a pity it wouldn't go in your pocket.'

'Not music and all,' said Aaron.

'Dear me! What a *comble* of disappointment. I never felt so strongly, Marchesa, that the old life and the old world had collapsed. Really – I shall soon have to try to give up being cheerful at all.'

'Don't do that,' said the Marchesa. 'It isn't worth the effort.'

'Ah! I'm glad you find it so. Then I have hope.'

She merely smiled, indifferent.

The tea-party began to break up – Aaron found himself going down the stairs with the Marchesa and her husband. They descended all three in silence, husband and wife in front. Once outside the door, the husband asked:

'How shall we go home, dear? Tram or carriage –?' It was evident he was economical.

'Walk,' she said, glancing over her shoulder at Aaron. 'We are all going the same way, I believe.'

Aaron said where he lived. They were just across the river. And so all three proceeded to walk through the town.

'You are sure it won't be too much for you – too far?' said the little officer, taking his wife's arm solicitously. She was taller than he. But he was a spirited fellow.

'No, I feel like walking.'

'So long as you don't have to pay for it afterwards.'

Aaron gathered that she was not well. Yet she did not look ill – unless it were nerves. She had that peculiar heavy remote quality of pre-occupation and neurosis.

The streets of Florence were very full this Sunday evening, almost impassable, crowded particularly with gangs of grey-green soldiers. The three made their way brokenly, and with difficulty. The Italian was in a constant state of returning salutes. The grey-green, sturdy, unsoldierly soldiers looked at the woman as she passed.

'I am sure you had better take a carriage,' said Manfredi.

'No – I don't mind it.'

'Do you feel at home in Florence?' Aaron asked her.

'Yes – as much as anywhere. Oh yes – quite at home.'

'Do you like it as well as anywhere?' he asked.

'Yes – for a time. Paris for the most part.'

'Never America?'

'No, never America. I came when I was quite a little girl to Europe – Madrid – Constantinople – Paris: I hardly knew America at all.'

Aaron remembered that Francis had told him, the Marchesa's father had been a famous figure in Europe.

'So you feel you have no country of your own?'

'I have Italy. I am Italian now, you know?'

Aaron wondered why she spoke so muted, so numbed. Manfredi seemed really attached to her – and she to him. They were so simple with one another.

They came towards the bridge where they should part.

'Won't you come and have a cocktail?' she said.

'Now?' said Aaron.

'Yes. This is the right time for a cocktail. What time is it, Manfredi?'

'Half-past six. Do come and have one with us,' said the Italian. 'We always take one about this time.'

Aaron continued with them over the bridge. They had the first floor of an old palazzo opposite, a little way up the hill. A man-servant opened the door.

'If only it will be warm,' she said. 'The apartment is almost impossible to keep warm. We will sit in the little room.'

Aaron found himself in a quite warm room with shaded lights and a mixture of old Italian stiffness and deep soft modern comfort. The Marchesa went away to take off her wraps, and the Marchese chatted with Aaron. The little officer was amiable and kind, and it was evident he liked his guest.

'Would you like to see the room where we have music?' he said. 'It is a fine room for the purpose – we used before the war to have music every Saturday morning, from ten to twelve: and all friends might come. Usually we had fifteen or twenty people. Now we are starting again. I enjoy it so much. I am afraid my wife isn't so enthusiastic as she used to be. I wish something would rouse her up, you know. The war seemed to take her life away. Here in Florence are so many amateurs. Very good indeed. We can have very good chamber-music indeed. I hope it will cheer her up and make her quite herself again. I was away for such long periods, at the front. And it was not good for her to be alone. I am hoping now all will be better.'

So saying, the little, odd officer switched on the lights of the long salon. It was a handsome room in the Italian mode of the Empire period – beautiful old faded tapestry panels – reddish – and some ormolu furniture – and other things mixed in – rather conglomerate, but pleasing, all the more pleasing. It was big, not too empty, and seemed to belong to human life, not to show and shutupedness. The host was happy showing it.

'Of course the flat in Rome is more luxurious than this,' he said, 'But I prefer this. I prefer it here.' There was a certain wistfulness as he looked round, then began to switch off the lights.

They returned to the little salotto. The Marchesa was seated in a low chair. She wore a very thin white blouse, that showed her arms and her throat. She was a full-breasted, soft-skinned woman, though not stout.

'Make the cocktails then, Manfredi,' she said. 'Do you find this room very cold?' she asked of Aaron.

'Not a bit cold,' he said.

'The stove goes all the time,' she said, 'but without much effect.'

'You wear such thin clothes,' he said.

'Ah no, the stove should give heat enough. Do sit down. Will you smoke? There are cigarettes – and cigars, if you prefer them.'

'No, I've got my own, thanks.'

She took her own cigarette from her gold case.

'It is a fine room, for music, the big room,' said he.

'Yes, quite. Would you like to play for us some time, do you think?'

'Do you want me to? I mean does it interest you?'

'What – the flute?'

'No – music altogether –'

'Music altogether –! Well! I used to love it. Now – I'm not sure. Manfredi lives for it, almost.'

'For that and nothing else?' asked Aaron.

'No, no! No, no! Other things as well.'

'But you don't like it much any more?'

'I don't know. Perhaps I don't. I'm not sure.'

'You don't look forward to the Saturday mornings?' he asked.

'Perhaps I don't – but for Manfredi's sake, of course, I do. But for his sake more than my own, I admit. And I think he knows it.'

'A crowd of people in one's house –' said Aaron.

'Yes, the people. But it's not only that. It's the music itself – I think I can't stand it any more. I don't know.'

'Too emotional? Too much feeling for you?'

'Yes, perhaps. But no. What I can't stand is chords, you know: harmonies. A number of sounds all sounding together. It just makes me ill. It makes me feel so sick.'

'What – do you want discords? – dissonances?'

'No – they are nearly as bad. No, it's just when any number of musical notes, different notes, come together, harmonies or discords. Even a single chord struck on the piano. It makes me feel sick. I just feel as if I should retch. Isn't it strange? Of course, I don't tell Manfredi. It would be too cruel to him. It would cut his life in two.'

'But then why do you have the music – the Sundays – then?'

'Oh, I just keep out of the way as much as possible. I'm sure you feel there is something wrong with me, that I take it as I do,' she added, as if anxious: but half ironical.

'No – I was just wondering – I believe I feel something the same myself. I know orchestra makes me blind with hate or I don't know what. But I want to throw bombs.'

'There now. It does that to me, too. Only now it has fairly got me down, and I feel nothing but helpless nausea. You know, like when you are seasick.'

Her dark-blue, heavy, haunted-looking eyes were resting on him as if she hoped for something. He watched her face steadily, a curious intelligence flickered on his own.

'Yes,' he said. 'I understand it. And I know, *at the bottom*, I'm like that. But I keep myself from realizing, don't you know. Else perhaps, where should I be? Because I make my life and my living at it, as well.'

'At music! Do you! But how bad for you. But perhaps the flute is different. I have a feeling that it is. I can think of one single pipe-note – yes, I can think of it quite, quite calmly. And I can't even think of the piano, or of the violin with its tremolo, or of orchestra, or of a string quartette – or even a military band – I can't think of it without a shudder. I can only bear drum-and-fife. Isn't it crazy of me. But from the other, from what we call music proper, I've endured too much. But bring your flute one day. Bring it, will you? And let me hear it quite alone. Quite, quite alone. I think it might do me an awful lot of good. I do really. I can imagine it.' She closed her eyes, and her strange, sing-song lapsing voice came to an end. She spoke almost like one in a trance – or a sleep-walker.

'I've got it now in my overcoat pocket,' he said, 'if you like.'

'Have you? Yes!' She never hurried: always slow and resonant, so that the echoes of her voice seemed to linger. 'Yes – do get it. Do get it. And play in the other room – quite – quite without accompaniment. Do – and try me.'

'And you will tell what you feel?'

'Yes.'

Aaron went out to his overcoat. When he returned with his flute, which he was screwing together, Manfredi had come with the tray and three cocktails. The Marchesa took her glass.

'Listen, Manfredi,' she said. 'Mr Sisson is going to play, quite alone in the sala. And I am going to sit here and listen.'

'Very well,' said Manfredi. 'Drink your cocktail first. Are you going to play without music?'

'Yes,' said Aaron.

'I'll just put on the lights for you.'

'No – leave it dark. There will be enough light come in from here.'

'Sure?' said Manfredi.

'Yes.'

The little soldier was an intruder at the moment. Both the others felt it so. But they bore him no grudge. They knew it was they who were exceptional, not he. Aaron swallowed his drink, and looked towards the door.

'Sit down, Manfredi. Sit still,' said the Marchesa.

'Won't you let me try some accompaniment?' said the soldier.

'No. I shall just play a little thing from memory,' said Aaron.

'Sit down, dear. Sit down,' said the Marchesa to her husband.

He seated himself obediently. The flash of bright yellow on the grey of his uniform seemed to make him like a chaffinch or a gnome.

Aaron retired to the other room, and waited awhile, to get back the spell which connected him with the woman, and gave the two of them this strange isolation, beyond the bounds of life, as it seemed.

He caught it again. And there, in the darkness of the big room, he put his flute to his lips, and began to play. It was a clear, sharp, lilted run-and-fall of notes, not a tune in any sense of the word, and yet a melody: a bright, quick sound of pure animation: a bright, quick, animate noise, running and pausing. It was like a bird's singing, in that it had no human emotion or passion or intention or meaning – a ripple and poise of animate sound. But it was unlike a bird's singing, in that the notes followed clear and single one after the other, in their subtle gallop. A nightingale is rather like that – a wild sound. To read all the human pathos into nightingales' singing is nonsense. A wild, savage, non-human lurch and squander of sound, beautiful, but entirely unaesthetic.

What Aaron was playing was not of his own invention. It was a bit of medieval phrasing written for the pipe and the viol. It made the piano seem a ponderous, nerve-wracking steam-roller of noise, and the violin, as we knew it, a hateful wire-drawn nerve-torturer.

After a little while, when he entered the smaller room again, the Marchesa looked full into his face.

'Good!' she said. 'Good!'

And a gleam almost of happiness seemed to light her up. She seemed like one who had been kept in a horrible enchanted castle – for years and years. Oh, a horrible enchanted castle, with wet walls of emotions and ponderous chains of feelings and a ghastly atmosphere of must-be. She felt she had seen through the opening door a crack of sunshine, and thin, pure, light outside air, outside, beyond this dank and beastly dungeon of feelings and moral necessity. Ugh! – she shuddered convulsively at what had been. She looked at her little husband. Chains of necessity all round him: a little jailer. Yet she was fond of him. If only he would throw away the castle keys. He was a little gnome. What did he clutch the castle keys so tight for?

Aaron looked at her. He knew that they understood one another, he and she. Without any moral necessity or any other necessity. Outside – they had got outside the castle of so-called human life. Outside the horrible, stinking human castle of life. A bit of true, limpid freedom. Just a glimpse.

'Charming!' said the Marchese. 'Truly charming! But what was it you played?'

Aaron told him.

'But truly delightful. I say, won't you play for us one of these Sundays? And won't you let me take the accompaniment? – I should be charmed, charmed if you would.'

'All right,' said Aaron.

'Do drink another cocktail,' said his hostess.

He did so. And then he rose to leave.

'Will you stay to dinner?' said the Marchesa. 'We have two people coming – two Italian relatives of my husband. But –'

No, Aaron declined to stay to dinner.

'Then won't you come on – let me see – on Wednesday? Do come on Wednesday. We are alone. And do bring the flute. Come at half-past six, as to-day, will you? Yes.'

Aaron promised – and then he found himself in the street. It was half-past seven. Instead of returning straight home, he crossed the Ponte Vecchio and walked straight into the crowd. The night was fine now. He had his overcoat over his arm, and in a sort of trance or frenzy, whirled away by his evening's experience, and by the woman, he strode swiftly forward, hardly heeding anything, but rushing blindly on through all the crowd, carried away by his own feelings, as much as if he had been alone, and all this many people merely trees.

Leaving the Piazza Vittorio Emmanuele a gang of soldiers suddenly rushed around him, buffeting him in one direction, whilst another gang, swinging round the corner, threw him back helpless again into the midst of the first gang. For some moments he struggled among the rude, brutal little mob of grey-green coarse uniforms that smelt so strong of soldiers. Then, irritated, he found himself free again, shaking himself and passing on towards the cathedral. Irritated, he now put on his overcoat and buttoned it to the throat, closing himself in, as it were, from the brutal insolence of the Sunday night mob of men. Before, he had been walking through them in a rush of naked feeling, all exposed to their tender mercies. He now gathered himself together.

As he was going home, suddenly, just as he was passing the Bargello, he stopped. He stopped, and put his hand to his breast pocket. His letter-case was gone. He had been robbed. It was as if lightning ran through him at that moment, as if a fluid electricity rushed down his limbs, through the sluice of his knees, and out at his feet, leaving him standing there almost unconscious. For a moment unconscious and super-conscious he stood there. He had been robbed. They had put their hand in his breast and robbed him. If they had stabbed him it could hardly have had a greater effect on him.

And he had known it. He had known it. When the soldiers jostled him so evilly they robbed him. And he knew it. He had known it as if it were fate. Even as if it were fated beforehand.

Feeling quite weak and faint, as if he had really been struck by some evil electric fluid, he walked on. And as soon as he began to walk, he began to reason. Perhaps his letter-case was in his other coat. Perhaps he had not had it with him at all. Perhaps he was feeling all this, just for nothing. Perhaps it was all folly.

He hurried forward. He wanted to make sure. He wanted relief. It was as if the power of evil had suddenly seized him and thrown him, and he wanted to say it was not so, that he had imagined it all, conjured it up. He did not want to admit the power of evil – particularly at that moment. For surely a very ugly evil spirit had struck him, in the midst of that gang of Italian soldiers. He knew it – it had pierced him. It had *got* him.

But he wanted to say it was not so. Reaching the house, he hastened upwards to his far-off, lonely room, through the dark corridors. Once in his own apartment, he shut the door and switched on the light, a sensation like fear at his heart. Then he searched his other pockets. He looked everywhere. In vain.

In vain, truly enough. For he *knew* the thing was stolen. He had known it all along. The soldiers had deliberately plotted, had deliberately rushed him and taken his purse. They must have watched him previously. They must have grinned, and jeered at him.

He sat down in a chair, to recover from the shock. The pocket-book contained four hundred francs, three one-pound notes, and various letters and private effects – Well, these were lost. But it was not so much the loss as the assault on his person that caused him to feel so stricken. He felt the jeering, gibing blows they had given as they jostled him.

And now he sat, weak in every limb, and said to himself: 'Yes – and if I hadn't rushed along so full of feeling: if I hadn't exposed myself: if I hadn't got worked up with the Marchesa, and then rushed all kindled through the streets without reserve: it would never have happened. I gave myself away: and there was someone ready to snatch what I gave. I gave myself away. It is my own fault. I should have been on my guard. I should be always on my guard: always, always, with God and the devil both, I should be on my guard. Godly or devilish, I should hold fast to my reserve and keep on the watch. And if I don't, I deserve what I get.'

But still he sat in his chair in his bedroom, dazed. One part of his soul was saying emphatically: It serves you right. It is nothing but right. It serves everybody right who rushes enkindled through the street, and trust implicitly in mankind and in the life-spirit, as if mankind and the life-spirit were a playground for enkindled individuals. It serves you right. You have paid about twelve pounds sterling for your lesson. Fool, you might have known beforehand, and then you needn't have paid at all. You can ill afford twelve pounds sterling, you fool. But since paid you have, then mind, mind the lesson is learned. Never again. Never expose yourself again. Never again absolute trust. It is blasphemy against life, is absolute trust. Has a wild creature ever absolute trust? It minds itself. Sleeping or waking it is on its guard. And so must you be, or you'll go under. Sleeping or waking, man or woman, God or the devil, keep your guard over yourself. Keep your guard over yourself, lest worse befall you. No man is robbed unless he incites a robber. No man is murdered unless he attracts a murderer. Then be not robbed: it lies within your own power. And be not murdered. Or if you are, you deserve it. Keep your guard over yourself, now, always and for ever. Yes, against God quite as hard as against the devil. He's fully as dangerous to you....

Thus thinking, not in his mind but in his soul, his active living soul, he gathered his equanimity once more, and accepted the fact. So he rose and tidied himself for dinner. His face was now set, and still. His heart also was still – and fearless. Because its sentinel was stationed. Stationed, stationed for ever.

And Aaron never forgot. After this, it became essential to him to feel that the sentinel stood guard in his own heart. He felt a strange unease the moment he was off his guard. Asleep or awake, in the midst of the deepest passion or the suddenest love, or in the throes of greatest excitement or bewilderment, somewhere, some corner of himself was awake to the fact that the sentinel of the soul must not sleep: no, never, not for one instant.

17

NEL PARADISO

Aaron and Lilly sat on Argyle's little loggia, high up under the eaves of the house, a sort of long attic-terrace just under the roof, where no one would have suspected it. It was level with the grey conical roof of the Baptistery. Here sat Aaron and Lilly in the afternoon, in the last of the lovely autumn sunshine. Below, the square was already cold in shadow, the pink and white and green Baptistery rose lantern-shaped as from some sea-shore, cool, cold and wan now the sun was gone. Black figures, innumerable black figures, curious because they were all on end, up on end – Aaron could not say why he expected them to be horizontal – little black figures up on end, like fishes that swim on their tails, wiggled endlessly across the piazza, little carriages on natural all-fours rattled tinily across, the yellow little tram-cars like dogs slipped round the corner. The balcony was so high up, that the sound was ineffectual. The upper space, above the houses, was nearer than the under-currents of the noisy town. Sunlight, lovely full sunlight, lingered warm and still on the balcony. It caught the façade of the cathedral sideways, like the tips of a flower, and sideways lit up the stem of Giotto's tower, like a lily stem, or a long, lovely pale pink and white and green pistil of the lily of the cathedral. Florence, the flowery town. Firenze – Fiorenze – the flowery town: the red lilies. The Fiorentini, the flower-souled. Flowers with good roots in the mud and muck, as should be: and fearless blossoms in air, like the cathedral and the tower and the David.

'I love it,' said Lilly. 'I love this place. I love the cathedral and the tower. I love its pinkness and its paleness. The gothic souls find fault with it, and say it is gimcrack and tawdry and cheap. But I love it; it is delicate and rosy, and the dark stripes are as they should be, like the tiger marks on a pink lily. It's a lily, not a rose: a pinky white lily with dark tigery marks. And heavy too, in its own substance: earth-substance, risen from earth into the air: and never forgetting the dark, black-fierce earth – I reckon here men for a moment were themselves, as a plant in flower is for the moment completely itself. Then it goes off. As Florence has gone off. No flowers now. But it *has* flowered. And I don't see why a race should be like an aloe tree, flower once and die. Why should it? Why Why not flower again? Why not?'

'If it's going to, it will,' said Aaron. 'Our deciding about it won't alter it.'

'The decision is part of the business.'

Here they were interrupted by Argyle, who put his head through one of the windows. He had flecks of lather on his reddened face.

'Do you think you're wise now,' he said, 'to sit in that sun?'

'So late in the year?' laughed Lilly.

'Always fear the sun when there's an "r" in the month,' said Argyle. 'Always fear it "r" or no "r", I say. I'm frightened of it. I've been in the south, I know what it is. I tell you I'm frightened of it. But if you think you can stand it – well –'

'It won't last much longer, anyhow,' said Lilly.

'Too long for me, my boy. I'm a shady bird, in all senses of the word, in all senses of the word. Now are you comfortable? What? Have another cushion? A rug for your knees? You're quite sure now? Well, wait just one moment till the waiter brings up a syphon, and you shall have a whisky and soda. Precious – oh yes, very precious these days – like drinking gold. Thirty-five liras a bottle, my boy!' Argyle pulled a long face, and made a noise with his lips. 'But I had this bottle given me, and luckily you've come while there's a drop left. Very glad you have! Very glad you have.'

Here he poked a little table through the window, and put a bottle and two glasses, one a tooth-glass, upon it. Then he withdrew again to finish shaving. The waiter presently hobbled up with the syphon and third glass. Argyle pushed his head through the window, that was only a little higher than the balcony. He was soon neatly shaved, and was brushing his hair.

'Go ahead, my boys, go ahead with that whisky!' he said.

'We'll wait for you,' said Lilly.

'No, no, don't think of it. However, if you will, I shall be one minute only – one minute only. I'll put on the water for the tea now. Oh, damned bad methylated spirit they sell now! And six francs a litre! Six francs a litre! I don't know what I'm going to do, the air I breathe costs money nowadays. Just one moment and I'll be with you! Just one moment –'

In a very little while he came from the tiny attic bedroom, through the tiniest cupboard of a sitting-room under the eaves, where his books were, and where he had hung his old red Indian tapestries – or silk embroideries – and he emerged there up above the world on the loggia.

'Now then – siamo nel Paradiso, eh? Paradisal enough for you, is it?'

'The devil looking over Lincoln,' said Lilly, laughing, glancing up into Argyle's face.

'The devil looking over *Florence* would feel sad,' said Argyle. 'The place is fast growing respectable. Oh, piety makes the devil chuckle. No doubt about it, no doubt whatever. There –!' He had just finished settling his tie and buttoning his waistcoat. 'How do I look, eh? Presentable? I've just had this suit turned. Clever little tailor across the way there. But he charged me a hundred and twenty francs.' Argyle pulled a face, and made the little trumping noise with his lips. 'However – not bad, is it? He had to let in a bit at the back of the waistcoat, and a gusset, my boy, a gusset in the trousers back. Well, well, might do worse. Is it all right?'

Lilly eyed the suit.

'Very nice. Very nice indeed. Such a good cloth! That makes all the difference.'

'Oh, my dear fellow, all the difference! This suit is eleven years old – eleven years old. But beautiful English cloth – before the war, before the war!'

'It looks quite wonderfully expensive and smart now,' said Lilly.

'Expensive and smart, eh! Ha-ha-ha! Well, it cost me a hundred and twenty francs to have it turned, and I found that expensive enough. Well now, come –' Here Argyle's voice took a new gay cheer. 'A whisky and soda, Lilly? Say when! Oh, nonsense, nonsense! You're going to have double that. You're no lily of the valley here, remember. Not with me. Not likely. *Siamo nel paradiso*, remember.'

'But why should we drink your whisky? Tea would do for us just as well.'

'Not likely! Not likely! When I have the pleasure of your company, my boy, we drink a glass of something, unless I am utterly stripped. Say when, Aaron.'

'When,' said Aaron.

Argyle at last seated himself heavily in a small chair. The sun had left the loggia, but was glowing still on Giotto's tower and the top of the cathedral façade, and on the remoter great red-tiled dome.

'Look at my little red monthly rose,' said Argyle. 'Wonderful little fellow! I wouldn't have anything happen to him for the world. Oh, a bacchic little chap. I made Pasquale wear a wreath of them on his hair. Very becoming they were, very. Oh, I've had a charming show of flowers. Wonderful creatures sunflowers are. They got up and put their heads over the balcony, looking down on the square below. Oh, great fun, great fun! The Blessed Damosel looked down – what? Lucky thing for her she wasn't on my balcony. Ha-ha-ha! Oh, you never know, she might have enjoyed it. Never believe a woman when she says she's chaste, nor a man when he says he's a – Yes, I had a charming show of flowers, charming – zinnias, petunias, ranunculus, sunflowers, white stocks – oh, charming. Look at that bit of honeysuckle. You see the berries where his flowers were! Delicious scent, I assure you.'

Under the little balcony wall Argyle had put square red-tiled pots, all round, and in these still blossomed a few pansies and asters, whilst in a corner a monthly rose hung flowers like round blood-drops. Argyle was as tidy and scrupulous in his tiny rooms and his balcony as if he were a first-rate seaman on a yacht. Lilly remarked on this.

'Do you see signs of the old maid coming out in me? Oh, I don't doubt it. I don't doubt it. We all end that way. Age makes old maids of us all. And Tanny is all right, you say? Bring her to see me.'

'All right, Argyle. Höflichkeiten.'

'What? gar keine Höflichkeiten. Wahrhaftiger Kerl, bin ich. When am I going to see Tanny? When are you coming to dine with me?'

'After you've dined with us – say the day after tomorrow –'

'Right you are. Delighted – Let me look if that water's boiling.' He got up and poked half himself inside the bedroom.

'Look,' said Lilly. 'There's Del Torre!'

'Like some sort of midge, in that damned grey-and-yellow uniform. I can't stand it, I tell you. I can't stand the sight of any more of these uniforms. Like a blight on the human landscape. Like a blight. Like green-flies on rose trees, smother-flies. Europe's got the smother-fly in these infernal shoddy militarists.'

'Del Torre's coming out of it as soon as he can,' said Lilly.

'I should think so too.'

'I like him myself – very much. Look, he's seen us! He wants to come up, Argyle.'

'What, in that uniform! I'll see him in his grandmother's crinoline first.'

'Don't be fanatical, it's bad taste. Let him come up a minute.'

'Not for my sake. But for yours, he shall.' Argyle stood at the parapet of the balcony and waved his arm. 'Yes, come up,' he said, 'come up, you little mistkäfer – what the Americans call a bug. Come up and be damned.'

Of course Del Torre was too far off to hear this exhortation. Lilly also waved to him – and watched him pass into the doorway far below.

'I'll rinse one of these glasses for him,' said Argyle.

The Marchese's step was heard on the stone stairs: then his knock.

'Come in! Come in!' cried Argyle from the bedroom, where he was rinsing the glass. The Marchese entered, grinning with his curious, half-courteous greeting. 'Go through – go through,' cried Argyle. 'Go on to the loggia – and mind your head. Good heavens, mind your head in that doorway.'

The Marchese just missed the top of the doorway as he climbed the abrupt steps on to the loggia. There he greeted Lilly and Aaron with hearty handshakes.

'Very glad to see you – very glad indeed!' he cried, grinning with excited courtesy and pleasure, and covering Lilly's hand with both his own gloved hands. 'When did you come to Florence?'

There was a little explanation. Argyle shoved the last chair – it was a luggage stool – through the window.

'All I can do for you in the way of a chair,' he said.

'Ah, that is all right,' said the Marchese. 'Well, it is very nice up here – and very nice company. Of the very best, the very best in Florence.'

'The highest, anyhow,' said Argyle grimly, as he entered with the glass. 'Have a whisky and soda, Del Torre. It's the bottom of the bottle, as you see.'

'The bottom of the bottle! Then I start with the tail-end, yes!' He stretched his blue eyes so that the whites showed all round, and grinned a wide, gnome-like grin.

'You made that start long ago, my dear fellow. Don't play the *ingénu* with me, you know it won't work. Say when, my man, say when!'

'Yes, when,' said Del Torre. 'When did I make that start, then?'

'At some unmentionably young age. Chicken such as you soon learn to cheep.'

'Chickens such as I soon learn to cheep,' repeated Del Torre, pleased with the verbal play. 'What is cheap, please? What is to *cheap*?'

'Cheep! Cheep!' squeaked Argyle, making a face at the little Italian, who was perched on one strap of the luggage-stool. 'It's what chickens say when they're poking their little noses into new adventures – naughty ones.'

'Are chickens naughty? Oh! I thought they could only be good!'

'Featherless chickens like yourself, my boy.'

'Oh, as for featherless. Then there is no saying what they will do –' And here the Marchese turned away from Argyle with the inevitable question to Lilly:

'Well, and how long will you stay in Florence?'

Lilly did not know: but he was not leaving immediately.

'Good! Then you will come and see us at once ...'

Argyle rose once more, and went to make the tea. He shoved a lump of cake

– or rather panetone, a good currant loaf – through the window, with a knife to cut it.

'Help yourselves to the panetone,' he said. 'Eat it up. The tea is coming at once. You'll have to drink it in your glasses, there's only one old cup.'

The Marchese cut the cake, and offered pieces. The two men took and ate.

'So you have already found Mr Sisson!' said Del Torre to Lilly.

'Ran straight into him in the Via Nazionale,' said Lilly.

'Oh, one always runs into everybody in Florence. We are all already acquainted: also with the flute. That is a great pleasure.'

'So I think. Does your wife like it too?'

'Very much indeed! She is quite *éprise*. I too shall have to learn to play it.'

'And run the risk of spoiling the shape of your mouth – like Alcibiades.'

'Is there a risk? Yes! Then I shan't play it. My mouth is too beautiful. But Mr Sisson has not spoilt his mouth.'

'Not yet,' said Lilly. 'Give him time.'

'Is he also afraid – like Alcibiades?'

'Are you, Aaron?' said Lilly.

'What?'

'Afraid of spoiling your beauty by screwing your mouth to the flute?'

'I look a fool, do I, when I'm playing?' said Aaron.

'Only the least little bit in the world,' said Lilly. 'The way you prance your head, you know, like a horse.'

'Ah well,' said Aaron. 'I've nothing to lose.'

'And were you surprised, Lilly, to find your friend here?' asked Del Torre.

'I ought to have been. But I wasn't really.'

'Then you expected him?'

'No. It came naturally though. But why did you come, Aaron? What exactly brought you?'

'Accident,' said Aaron.

'Ah no! No! There is no such thing as accident,' said the Italian. 'A man is drawn by his fate, where he goes.'

'You are right,' said Argyle, who came now with the teapot. 'A man is drawn – or driven. Driven, I've found it. Ah, my dear fellow, what is life but a search for a friend? A search for a friend – that sums it up.'

'Or a lover,' said the Marchese, grinning.

'Same thing. Same thing. My hair is white – but that is the sum of my whole experience. The search for a friend.' There was something at once real and sentimental in Argyle's tone.

'Are you not seeking any more, Lilly?' asked the Marchese. 'Do you seek nothing?'

'We married men who haven't left our wives, are we supposed to seek anything?' said Lilly. 'Aren't we perfectly satisfied and in bliss with the wonderful women who honour us as wives?'

'Ah yes, yes!' said the Marchese. 'But now we are not speaking to the world. Now we try to speak of that which we have in the centre of our hearts.'

'And what have we there?' said Lilly.

'Well – shall I say? We have unrest. We have another need. We have something that hurts and eats us, yes, eats us inside. Do I speak the truth?'

'Yes. But what is the something?'

'I don't know. I don't know. But it is something in love, I think. It is love itself which gnaws us inside, like a cancer,' said the Italian.

'But why should it? Is that the nature of love?' said Lilly.

'I don't know. Truly, I don't know. But perhaps it *is* in the nature of love – I don't know. But I tell you. I love my wife – she is very dear to me. I admire her, I trust her, I believe her. She is to me much more than any woman, more even than my mother. And so, I am very happy. I am very happy, she is very happy, in our love and our marriage. But wait. Nothing has changed – the love has not changed: it is the same. And yet we are *not* happy. No, we are not happy. I know she is not happy, I know I am not –'

'Why should you be?' said Lilly.

'Yes – and it is not even happiness,' said the Marchese, screwing up his face in a painful effort of confession. 'It is not even happiness. No, I do not ask to be happy. Why should I? It is childish. But there is for both of us, I know it, something which bites us, which eats us within, and drives us, drives us, somewhere, we don't know where. But it drives us, and eats away the life – and yet we love each other, and we must not be separate. Do you know what I mean? Do you understand me at all in what I say? I speak what is true –'

'Yes, I understand. I'm in the same dilemma myself. But what I want to hear is *why* you think it is so. Why is it?'

'Shall I say what I think? Yes? And you can tell me if it is foolish to you. Shall I tell you? Well. Because a woman, she now first wants the man, and he must go to her because he is wanted. Do you understand? You know – supposing I go to a woman – supposing she is my wife – and I go to her, yes, with my blood all ready, because it is I who want. Then she puts me off. Then she says, not now, not now, I am tired, I am not well. I do not feel like it. She puts me off – till I am angry or sorry or whatever I am – but till my blood has gone down again, you understand, and I don't want her any more. And then she puts her arms round me, and caresses me, and makes love to me – till she rouses me once more. So, and so she rouses me – and so I come to her. And I love her, it is very good, very good. But it was she who began, it was her initiative, you know. I do not think, in all my life, my wife has loved me from *my* initiative, you know. She will yield to me – because I insist, or because she wants to be a good submissive wife who loves me. So she will yield to me. But ah, what is it, you know? What is it, a woman who allows me, and who has no answer? It is something worse than nothing – worse than nothing. And so it makes me very discontented and unbelieving. If I say to her, she says it is not true. Then she says, all she wants is that I should desire her, that I should love her and desire her. But even that is putting *her* will first. And if I come to her so, if I come to her of my own desire, then she puts me off. She puts me off, or she only allows me to come to her. Even now it is the same, after ten years, as it was at first. But now I know, and for many years I did not know –'

The little man was intense. His face was strained, his blue eyes so stretched that they showed the whites all round. He gazed into Lilly's face.

'But does it matter?' said Lilly slowly, 'in which of you the desire initiates? Isn't the result the same?'

'It matters. It matters –' cried the Marchese.

'Oh, my dear fellow, how *much* it matters –' interrupted Argyle sagely.

'Ay!' said Aaron.

The Marchese looked from one to the other of them.

'It matters!' he cried. 'It matters life or death. It used to be that desire started in the man, and the woman answered. It used to be so for a long time in Italy. For this reason the women were kept away from the men. For this reason our

Catholic religion tried to keep the young girls in convents, and innocent, before marriage. So that with their minds they should not know, and should not start this terrible thing, this woman's desire over a man, beforehand. This desire which starts in a woman's head, when she knows, and which takes a man for her use, for her service. This is Eve. Ah, I hate Eve. I hate her, when she knows, and when she *wills*. I hate her when she will make of me that which serves her desire. She may love me, she may be soft and kind to me, she may give her life for me. But why? Only because I am *hers*. I am that thing which does her most intimate service. She can see no other in me. And I may be no other to her –'

'Then why not let it be so, and be satisfied?' said Lilly.

'Because I cannot. I cannot. I would. But I cannot. The Borghesia – the citizens – the bourgeoisie, they are the ones who can. Oh yes. The bourgeoisie, the shopkeepers, these serve their wives so, and their wives love them. They are the marital maquereaux – the husband-maquereaux, you know. Their wives are so stout and happy, and they dote on their husbands and always betray them. So it is with the bourgeoisie. She loves her husband so much, and is always seeking to betray him. Or she is a Madame Bovary, seeking for a scandal. But the bourgeois husband, he goes on being the same. He is the horse, and she the driver. And when she says gee-up, you know – then the comes ready, like a hired maquereau. Only he feels so good, like a good little boy at her breast. And then there are the nice little children. And so they keep the world going – But for me –' he spat suddenly and with frenzy on the floor.

'You are quite right my boy,' said Argyle. 'You are quite right. They've got the start of us, the women: and we've got to canter when they say gee-up. I – oh, I went through it all. But I broke the shafts and smashed the matrimonial cart, I can tell you, and I didn't care whether I smashed her up along with it or not. I didn't care one single bit, I assure you. And here I am. And she is dead and buried these dozen years. Well – well! Life, you know, life. And Women. Oh, they are the very hottest hell once they get the start of you. There's *nothing* they won't do to you, once they've got you. Nothing they won't do to you. Especially if they love you. Then you may as well give up the ghost: or smash the cart behind you, and her in it. Otherwise she will just harry you into submission, and make a dog of you, and cuckold you under your nose. And you'll submit. Oh, you'll submit, and go on calling her my darling. Or else, if you won't submit, she'll do for you. Your only chance is to smash the shafts, and the whole matrimonial cart. Or she'll do for you. For a woman has an uncanny, hellish strength – she's a she-bear and a wolf, is a woman when she's got the start of you. Oh, it's a terrible experience, if you're not a bourgeois, and not one of the knuckling-under, money-making sort.'

'Knuckling-under sort. Yes. That is it,' said the Marchese.

'But can't there be a balancing of wills?' said Lilly.

'My dear boy, the balance lies in that, that when one goes up, the other goes down. One acts, the other takes. It is the only way in love. And the women are nowadays the active party. Oh yes, not a shadow of doubt about it. They take the initiative, and the man plays up. That's how it is. The man just plays up. Nice manly proceeding, what!' cried Argyle.

'But why can't man accept it as the natural order of things?' said Lilly. 'Science makes it the natural order.'

'All my – to science,' said Argyle. 'No man with one drop of real spunk in him can stand it long.'

'Yes! Yes! Yes!' cried the Italian. 'Most men want it so. Most men want only that a woman shall want them, and they shall then play up to her when she has roused them. Most men want only this: that a woman shall choose one man out, to be her man, and he shall worship her and come up when she shall provoke him. Otherwise he is to keep still. And the woman, she is quite sure of her part. She must be loved and adored, and above all, obeyed: particularly in her sex desire. There she must not be thwarted, or she becomes a devil. And if she is obeyed, she becomes a misunderstood woman with nerves, looking round for the next man whom she can bring under. So it is.'

'Well,' said Lilly. 'And then what?'

'Nay,' interrupted Aaron. 'But do you think it's true what he says? Have you found it like that? You're married. Has your experience been different, or the same?'

'What was yours?' asked Lilly.

'Mine was the same. Mine was the same, if ever it was,' said Aaron.

'And mine was *extremely* similar,' said Argyle with a grimace.

'And yours, Lilly?' asked the Marchese anxiously.

'Not very different,' said Lilly.

'Ah!' cried Del Torre, jerking up erect as if he had found something.

'And what's your way out?' Aaron asked him.

'I'm not out – so I won't holloa,' said Lilly. 'But Del Torre puts it best. What do you say is the way out, Del Torre?'

'The way out is that it should change: that the man should be the asker and the woman the answerer. It *must* change.'

'But it *doesn't*. Prrr!' Argyle made his trumping noise.

'Does it?' asked Lilly of the Marchese.

'No. I think it does not.'

'And will it ever again?'

'Perhaps never.'

'And then what?'

'Then? Why then man seeks a *pis-aller*. Then he seeks something which will give him answer, and which will not only draw him, draw him, with a terrible sexual will. So he seeks young girls, who know nothing, and so cannot force him. He thinks he will possess them while they are young, and they will be soft and responding to his wishes. But in this too he is mistaken. Because now a baby of one year, if it be a female, is like a woman of forty, so is its will made up, so it will force a man.'

'And so young girls are no good, even as a *pis-aller*.'

'No good – because they are all modern women. Every one, a modern woman. Not one who isn't.'

'Terrible thing, the modern woman,' put in Argyle.

'And then a man naturally loves his own wife too, even if it is not bearable to love her.'

'Or one leaves her, like Aaron,' said Lilly.

'And seeks another woman, so,' said the Marchese.

'Does he seek another woman?' said Lilly. 'Do you, Aaron?'

'I don't *want* to,' said Aaron. 'But – I can't stand by myself in the middle of the world and in the middle of people, and know I am quite by myself, and nowhere to go, and nothing to hold on to. I can for a day or two – But then, it becomes unbearable as well. You get frightened. You feel you might go funny – as you would if you stood on this balcony wall with all the space beneath you.'

'Can't one be alone – quite alone?' said Lilly.

'But no – it is absurd. Like Saint Simeon Stylites on a pillar. But it is absurd!' cried the Italian.

'I don't mean like Simeon Stylites. I mean can't one live with one's wife, and be fond of her: and with one's friends, and enjoy their company: and with the world and everything, pleasantly: and yet *know* that one is alone? Essentially, at the very core of me, alone. Eternally alone. And choosing to be alone. Not sentimental or *lonely*. Alone, choosing to be alone, because by one's own nature one is alone. The being with another person is secondary,' said Lilly.

'One is alone,' said Argyle, 'in all but love. In all but love, my dear fellow. And then I agree with you.'

'No,' said Lilly, 'in love most intensely of all, alone.'

'Completely incomprehensible,' said Argyle. 'Amounts to nothing.'

'One man is but a part. How can he be so alone?' said the Marchese.

'In so far as he is a single individual soul, he *is* alone – *ipso facto.* In so far as I am I, and only I am I, and I am only I, in so far, I am inevitably and eternally alone, and it is my last blessedness to know it, and to accept it, and to live with this as the core of my self-knowledge.'

'My dear boy, you are becoming metaphysical, and that is as bad as softening of the brain,' said Argyle.

'All right,' said Lilly.

'And,' said the Marchese, 'it may be so by *reason.* But in the heart – ? Can the heart ever beat quite alone? Plop! Plop! Can the heart beat quite alone, alone in all the atmosphere, all the space of the universe? Plop! Plop! Plop! Quite alone in all the space?' A slow smile came over the Italian's face. 'It is impossible. It may beat *against* the heart of other men, in anger, all in pressure against the others. It may beat hard, like iron, saying it is independent. But this is only beating against the heart of mankind, not alone. But either with or against the heart of mankind, or the heart of someone, mother, wife, friend, children – so must the heart of every man beat. It is so.'

'It beats alone in its own silence,' said Lilly.

The Italian shook his head.

'We'd better be going inside, anyhow,' said Argyle. 'Some of you will be taking cold.'

'Aaron,' said Lilly. 'Is it true for you?'

'Nearly,' said Aaron, looking into the quiet, half-amused, yet frightening eyes of the other man. 'Or it has been.'

'A miss is as good as a mile,' laughed Lilly, rising and picking up his chair to take indoors. And the laughter of his voice was so like a simple, deliberate amiability, that Aaron's heart really stood still for a second. He knew that Lilly *was* alone – as far as he, Aaron, was concerned. Lilly was alone – and out of his isolation came his words, indifferent as to whether they came or not. And he left his friends utterly to their own choice. Utterly to their own choice. Aaron felt that Lilly was *there*, existing in life, yet neither asking for connection nor preventing any connection. He was present, he was the real centre of the group. And yet he asked nothing of them, and he imposed nothing. He left each to himself, and he himself remained just himself: neither more nor less. And there was a finality about it, which was at once maddening and fascinating. Aaron felt angry, as if he were half insulted by the other man's placing the gift of friendship or connection so quietly back in the giver's hands. Lilly would receive no gift of friendship in equality. Neither would he violently refuse it. He let it lie unmarked. And yet at the same time Aaron knew that he could depend on the other man for help, nay, almost for life itself – so long as it entailed no breaking of the intrinsic isolation of Lilly's soul. But this condition was also hateful. And there was also a great fascination in it.

18

THE MARCHESA

So Aaron dined with the Marchesa and Manfredi. He was quite startled when his hostess came in: she seemed like somebody else. She seemed like a demon, her hair on her brows, her terrible modern elegance. She wore a wonderful gown of thin blue velvet, of a lovely colour, with some kind of gauzy gold-threaded filament down the sides. It was terribly modern, short, and showed her legs and her shoulders and breast and all her beautiful white arms. Round her throat was a collar of dark-blue sapphires. Her hair was done low, almost to the brows, and heavy, like an Aubrey Beardsley drawing. She was most carefully made up – yet with that touch of exaggeration, lips slightly too red, which was quite intentional, and which frightened Aaron. He thought her wonderful, and sinister. She affected him with a touch of horror. She sat down opposite him, and her beautifully shapen legs, in frail, goldish stockings, seemed to glisten metallic naked, thrust from out of the wonderful, wonderful skin, like periwinkle-blue velvet. She had tapestry shoes, blue and gold: and almost one could see her toes: metallic naked. The gold-threaded gauze slipped at her side. Aaron could not help watching the naked-seeming arch of her foot. It was as if she were dusted with dark gold-dust upon her marvellous nudity.

She must have seen his face, seen that he was *ébloui*.

'You brought the flute?' she said, in that toneless, melancholy, unstriving voice of hers. Her voice alone was the same: direct and bare and quiet.

'Yes.'

'Perhaps I shall sing later on, if you'll accompany me. Will you?'

'I thought you hated accompaniments.'

'Oh no – not just unison. I don't mean accompaniment. I mean unison. I don't know how it will be. But will you try?'

'Yes, I'll try.'

'Manfredi is just bringing the cocktails. Do you think you'd prefer orange in yours?'

'I'll have mine as you have yours.'

'I don't take orange in mine. Won't you smoke?'

The strange, naked, remote-seeming voice! And then the beautiful firm limbs thrust out in that dress, and nakedly dusky as with gold-dust. Her beautiful woman's legs, slightly glistening, duskily. His one abiding instinct was to touch them, to kiss them. He had never know a woman exercise such power over him. It was a bare, occult force, something he could not cope with.

Manfredi came in with the little tray. He was still in uniform.

'Hello!' cried the little Italian. 'Glad to see you – Well, everything all right? Glad to hear it. How is the cocktail, Nan?'

'Yes,' she said. 'All right.'

'One drop too much peach, eh?'

'No, all right.'

'Ah,' and the little officer seated himself, stretching his gaitered legs as if gaily. He had a curious smiling look on his face, that Aaron thought also diabolical – and almost handsome. Suddenly the odd, laughing, satanic beauty of the little man was visible.

'Well, and what have you been doing with yourself?' said he. 'What did you do yesterday?'

'Yesterday?' said Aaron. 'I went to the Uffizi.'

'To the Uffizi? Well! And what did you think of it?'

'Very fine.'

'I think it is. I think it is. What pictures did you look at?'

'I was with Dekker. We looked at most, I believe.'

'And what do you remember best?'

'I remember Botticelli's Venus on the shell.'

'Yes! Yes! –' said Manfredi. 'I like her. But I like others better. You thought her a pretty woman, yes?'

'No – not particularly pretty. But I like her body. And I like the fresh air. I like the fresh air, the summer sea air all through it – through her as well.'

'And her face?' asked the Marchesa, with a slow, ironic smile.

'Yes – she's a bit baby-faced,' said Aaron.

'Trying to be more innocent than her own common-sense will let her,' said the Marchesa.

'I don't agree with you, Nan,' said her husband. 'I think it is just that wistfulness and innocence which makes her the true Venus: the true modern Venus. She chooses *not* to know too much. And that is her attraction. Don't you agree, Aaron? Excuse me, but everybody speaks of you as Aaron. It seems to come naturally. Most people speak of me as Manfredi too, because it is easier, perhaps, than Del Torre. So if you find it easier, use it. Do you mind that I call you Aaron?'

'Not at all. I hate Misters, always.'

'Yes, so do I. I like one name only.'

The little officer seemed very winning and delightful to Aaron this evening – and Aaron began to like him extremely. But the dominating consciousness in the room was the woman's.

'*Do* you agree, Mr Sisson?' said the Marchesa. 'Do you agree that the mock-innocence and the sham wistfulness of Botticelli's Venus are her great charm?'

'I don't think she is at all charming, as a person,' said Aaron. 'As a particular woman, she makes no impression on me at all. But as a picture – and the fresh air, particularly the fresh air. She doesn't seem so much a woman, you know, as the kind of out-of-doors morning-feeling at the sea-side.'

'Quite! A sort of sea-scape of a woman. With a perfectly sham innocence. Are you as keen on innocence as Manfredi is?'

'Innocence?' said Aaron. 'It's the sort of thing I don't have much feeling about.'

'Ah, I know you,' laughed the soldier wickedly. 'You are the sort of man who wants to be Antony to Cleopatra. Ha-ha!'

Aaron winced as if struck. Then he too smiled, flattered. Yet he felt he had been struck. Did he want to be Antony to Cleopatra? Without knowing, he was watching the Marchesa. And she was looking away, but knew he was watching her. And at last she turned her eyes to his, with a slow, dark smile, full of pain and fuller still of knowledge. A strange, dark, silent look of knowledge she gave him: from so far away, it seemed. And he felt all the bonds that held him melting away. His eyes remained fixed and gloomy, but with his mouth he smiled back at her. And he was terrified. He knew he was sinking towards her – sinking towards her. And he was terrified. But at the back of his mind, also, he knew there was Lilly, whom he might depend on. And also, he wanted to sink towards her. The flesh and blood of him simply melted out, in desire towards her. Cost what may, he must come to her. And yet he knew at the same time that, cost what may, he must keep the power to recover himself from her. He must have his cake and eat it.

And she became Cleopatra to him. 'Age cannot wither her, nor custom stale –' To his instinctive, unwilled fancy, she was Cleopatra.

They went in to dinner, and he sat on her right hand. It was a smallish table. with a very few daisy-flowers: everything rather frail and sparse. The food the same – nothing very heavy, all rather exquisite. They drank hock. And he was aware of her beautiful arms, and her bosom; her low-crowded, thick hair, parted in the centre: the sapphires on her throat, the heavy rings on her fingers: and the paint on her lips, the fard. Something deep, deep at the bottom of him hovered upon her, cleaved to her. Yet he was as if sightless, in a stupor. Who was she, what was she? He had lost all his grasp. Only he sat there, with his face turned to hers, or to her; all the time. And she talked to him. But she never looked at him.

Indeed she said little. It was the husband who talked. His manner towards Aaron was almost caressive. And Aaron liked it. The woman was silent mostly, and seemed remote. And Aaron felt his life ebb towards her. He felt the marvellousness, the rich beauty of her arms and breast. And the thought of her gold-dusted smooth limbs beneath the table made him feel almost an idiot.

The second wine was a gold-coloured Moselle, very soft and rich and beautiful. She drank this with pleasure, as one who understands. And for dessert there was a dish of cacchi – that orange-coloured, pulpy Japanese fruit – persimmons. Aaron had never eaten these before. Soft, almost slimy, of a wonderful colour, and of a flavour that had sunk from harsh astringency down to that first decay-sweetness which is all autumn-rich. The Marchese loved them, and scooped them out with his spoon. But she ate none.

Aaron did not know what they talked about, what was said. If someone had taken his mind away altogether, and left him with nothing but a body and a spinal consciousness, it would have been the same.

But at coffee the talk turned to Manfredi's duties. He would not be free from the army for some time yet. On the morrow, for example, he had to be out and away before it was day. He said he hated it, and wanted to be a free man once more. But it seemed to Aaron he would be a very bored man, once he was free. And then they drifted on to talk of the palazzo in which was their apartment.

'We've got such a fine terrace – you can see it from your house where you are,' said Manfredi. 'Have you noticed it?'

'No,' said Aaron.

'Near that tuft of palm trees. Don't you know?'

'No,' said Aaron.

'Let us go out and show it him,' said the Marchesa.

Manfredi fetched her a cloak, and they went through various doors, then up some steps. The terrace was broad and open. It looked straight across the river at the opposite Lungarno: and there was the thin-necked tower of the Palazzo Vecchio, and the great dome of the cathedral in the distance, in shadow-bulk in the cold-aired night of stars. Little trams were running brilliant over the flat new bridge on the right. And from a garden just below rose a tuft of palm trees.

'You see,' said the Marchesa, coming and standing close to Aaron, so that she just touched him, 'you can know the terrace, just by these palm trees. And you are in the Nardini just across there, are you? On the top floor, you said?'

'Yes the top floor – one of the middle windows, I think.'

'One that is always open now – and the others are shut. I have noticed it, not connecting it with you.'

'Yes, my window is always open.'

She was leaning very slightly against him, as he stood. And he knew, with the same kind of inevitability with which he knew he would one day die, that he would be the lover of this woman. Nay, that he *was* her lover already.

'Don't take cold,' said Manfredi.

She turned at once indoors. Aaron caught a faint whiff of perfume from the little orange trees in tubs round the wall.

'Will you get the flute?' she said as they entered.

'And will you sing?' he answered.

'Play first,' she said.

He did as she wished. As the other night, he went into the big music-room to play. And the stream of sound came out with the quick wild imperiousness of the pipe. It had an immediate effect on her. She seemed to relax the peculiar, drug-like tension which was upon her at all ordinary times. She seemed to go still, and yielding. Her red mouth looked as if it might moan with relief. She sat with her chin dropped on her breast, listening. And she did not move. But she sat softly, breathing rather quick, like one who has been hurt, and is soothed. A certain womanly naturalness seemed to soften her.

And the music of the flute came quick, rather brilliant like a call-note, or like a long quick message, half command. To her it was like a pure male voice – as a blackbird's when he calls: a pure male voice, not only calling, but telling her something, telling her something, and soothing her soul to sleep. It was like the fire-music putting Brünnhilde to sleep. But the pipe did not flicker and sink. It seemed to cause a natural relaxation in her soul, a peace. Perhaps it was more like waking to a sweet, morning-awakening, after a night of tormented, painful tense sleep. Perhaps more like that.

When Aaron came in, she looked at him with a gentle, fresh smile that seemed to make the fard on her face look like a curious tiredness, which now she might recover from. And as the last time, it was difficult for her to identify this man with the voice of the flute. It was rather difficult. Except that, perhaps, between his brows was something of a doubt, and in his bearing an aloofness that made her dread he might go away and not come back. She could see it in him, that he might go away and not come back.

She said nothing to him, only just smiled. And the look of knowledge in her eyes seemed, for the moment, to be contained in another look: a look of faith, and at last happiness. Aaron's heart stood still. Now, in her moment's mood of faith and at last peace, life-trust, he was perhaps more terrified of her than in her previous sinister elegance. His spirit started and shrank. What was she going to ask of him?

'I am so anxious that you should come to play one Saturday morning,' said

Manfredi. 'With an accompaniment, you know. I should like so much to hear you with the piano accompaniment.'

'Very well,' said Aaron.

'Will you really come? And will you practise with me, so that I can accompany you?' said Manfredi eagerly.

'Yes. I will,' said Aaron.

'Oh, good! Oh, good! Look here, come in on Friday morning and let us both look through the music.'

'If Mr Sisson plays for the public,' said the Marchesa, 'he must not do it for charity. He must have the proper fee.'

'No, I don't want it,' said Aaron.

'But you must earn money, mustn't you?' said she.

'I must,' said Aaron. 'But I can do it somewhere else.'

'No. If you play for the public, you must have your earnings. When you play for me, it is different.'

'Of course,' said Manfredi. 'Every man must have his wage. I have mine from the Italian Government –'

After a while, Aaron asked the Marchesa if she would sing.

'Shall I?' she said.

'Yes, do.'

'Then I will sing alone first, to let you see what you think of it – I shall be like Trilby – I won't say like Yvette Gilbert, because I daren't. So I will be like Trilby, and sing a little French song. Though not Malbrouk, and without a Svengali to keep me in tune.'

She went near the door, and stood with her hands by her side. There was something wistful, almost pathetic now, in her elegance.

'Derrière chez mon père
Vole vole mon coeur, vole!
Derrière chez mon père
Il y a un pommier doux.
Tout doux, et iou
Et iou, tout doux.
Il y a un pommier doux.

Trois belles princesses
Vole vole mon coeur, vole!
Trois belles princesses
Sont assis dessous.
Tout doux, et iou
Et iou, tout doux.
Sont assis dessous.

She had a beautiful, strong, sweet voice. But it was faltering, stumbling, and sometimes it seemed to drop almost to speech. After three verses she faltered to an end, bitterly chagrined.

'No,' she said. 'It's no good. I can't sing.' And she dropped in her chair.

'A lovely little tune,' said Aaron. 'Haven't you got the music?'

She rose, not answering, and found him a little book.

'What do the words mean?' he asked her.

She told him. And then he took his flute.

'You don't mind if I play it, do you?' he said.

So he played the tune. It was so simple. And he seemed to catch the lilt and the timbre of her voice.

'Come and sing it while I play,' he said.

'I can't sing,' she said, shaking her head rather bitterly.

'But let us try,' said he, disappointed.

'I know I can't,' she said. But she rose.

He remained sitting at the little table, the book propped up under the reading-lamp. She stood at a little distance, unhappy.

'I've always been like that,' she said. 'I could never sing music, unless I had a thing drilled into me, and then it wasn't singing any more.'

But Aaron wasn't heeding. His flute was at his mouth, he was watching her. He sounded the note, but she did not begin. She was twisting her handkerchief. So he played the melody alone. At the end of the verse, he looked up at her again, and a half-mocking smile played in his eyes. Again he sounded the note, a challenge. And this time, as at his bidding, she began to sing. The flute instantly swung with a lovely soft firmness into the soul, and she wavered only for a minute or two. Then her soul and her voice got free, and she sang – she sang as she wanted to sing, as she had always wanted to sing, without that awful scotch, that impediment inside her own soul, which prevented her.

She sang free, with the flute gliding along with her. And oh, how beautiful it was for her! How beautiful it was to sing the little song in the sweetness of her own spirit. How sweet it was to move pure and unhampered at last in the music! The lovely ease and lilt of her own soul in its motion through the music! She wasn't aware of the flute. She didn't know there was anything except her own pure lovely song-drift. Her soul seemed to breathe as a butterfly breathes, as it rests on a leaf and slowly breathes its wings. For the first time! For the first time her soul drew its own deep breath. All her life, the breath had caught half-way. And now she breathed full, deep, to the deepest extent of her being.

And oh, it was so wonderful, she was dazed. The song ended, she stood with a dazed, happy face, like one just coming awake. And on the fard on her face seemed like old night-crust, the bad sleep. New and luminous she looked out. And she looked at Aaron with a proud smile.

'Bravo, Nan! That was what you wanted,' said her husband.

'It was, wasn't it?' she said, turning a wondering, glowing face to him.

His face looked strange and withered and gnome-like at the moment.

She went and sat in her chair, quite silent, as if in a trance. The two men also sat quite still. And in the silence, a little drama played itself between the three, of which they knew definitely nothing. But Manfredi knew that Aaron had done what he himself never could do, for this woman. And yet the woman was his own woman, not Aaron's. And so, he was displaced. Aaron, sitting there, glowed with a sort of triumph. He had performed a little miracle, and felt himself a little wonder-worker, to whom reverence was due. And as in a dream the woman sat, feeling what a joy it was to float and move like a swan in the high air, flying upon the wings of her own spirit. She was as a swan which never before could get its wings quite open, and so which never could get up into the open, where alone it can sing. For swans, and storks make their music only when they are high, high up in the air. Then they can give sound to their strange spirits. And so she.

Aaron and Manfredi kept their faces averted from one another and hardly spoke to one another. It was as if two invisible hands pushed their faces apart, away, averted. And Aaron's face glimmered with a little triumph, and a little grimace of obstinacy. And the Italian's face looked old, rather monkey-like, and of a deep, almost stone-bare bitterness. The woman looked wondering from one man to the other – wondering. The glimmer of the open flower, the wonder-look, still lasted. And Aaron said in his heart, what a goodly woman, what a woman to taste and enjoy. Ah, what a woman to enjoy! And was it not his privilege? Had he not gained it?

His manhood, or rather his maleness, rose powerfully in him, in a sort of mastery. He felt his own power, he felt suddenly his own virile title to strength and reward. Suddenly, and newly flushed with his own male super-power, he was going to have his reward. The woman was his reward. So it was, in him. And he cast it over in his mind. He wanted her – ha, didn't he! But the husband sat there, like a soap-stone Chinese monkey, greyish-green. So, it would have to be another time.

He rose, therefore, and took his leave.

'But you'll let us do that again, won't you?' said she.

'When you tell me, I'll come,' said he.

'Then I'll tell you soon,' said she.

So he left, and went home to his own place, and there to his own remote room. As he laid his flute on the table he looked at it and smiled. He remembered that Lilly had called it Aaron's Rod.

'So you blossom, do you? – and thorn as well,' said he.

For such a long time he had been gripped inside himself, and withheld. For such a long time it had been hard and unyielding, so hard and unyielding. He had wanted nothing, his desire had kept itself back, fast back. For such a long time his desire for women had withheld itself, hard and resistant. All his deep, desirous blood had been locked, he had wanted nobody, and nothing. And it had been hard to live, so. Without desire, without any movement of passionate love, only gripped back in recoil! That was an experience to endure.

And now came his desire back. But strong, fierce as iron. Like the strength of an eagle with the lightning in its talons. Something to glory in, something overweening, the powerful male passion, arrogant, royal, Jove's thunderbolt. Aaron's black rod of power, blossoming again with red Florentine lilies and fierce thorns. He moved about in the splendour of his own male lightning, invested in the thunder of the male passion-power. He had got it back, the male godliness, the male godhead.

So he slept, and dreamed violent dreams of strange, black strife, something like the street-riot in Milan, but more terrible. In the morning, however, he cared nothing about his dreams. As soon as it was really light, he rose, and opened his window wide. It was a grey, slow morning. But he saw neither the morning nor the river nor the woman walking on the gravel river-bed with her goose nor the green hill up to San Miniato. He watched the tuft of palm trees, and the terrace beside it. He could just distinguish the terrace clearly, among the green of foliage. So he stood at his window for a full hour, and did not move. Motionless, planted, he stood and watched that terrace across the Arno. But like a statue.

After an hour or so, he looked at his watch. It was nine o'clock. So he rang for his coffee, and meanwhile still stood watching the terrace across. He felt his turn had come. The phoenix had risen in fire again, out of the ashes.

Therefore at ten o'clock he went over the bridge. He wrote on the back of his card a request, would she please let him have the little book of songs, that he might practise them over. The manservant went, and came back with the request that Aaron should wait. So Aaron entered, while the man took his hat.

The manservant spoke only French and Spanish, no English. He was a

Spaniard, with greyish hair and stooping shoulders and dark, mute-seeming eyes. He spoke as little as possible. The Marchesa had inherited him from her father.

Aaron sat in the little sitting-room and waited. After a rather long time the Marchesa came in – wearing a white, thin blouse and a blue skirt. She was hardly made-up at all. She had an odd, pleased, yet brooding look on her face as she gave Aaron her hand. Something brooded between her brows. And her voice was strange, with a strange, secret undertone, that he could not understand. He looked up at her. And his face was bright, and his knees, as he sat, were like the knees of the gods.

'You wanted the book of *chansons*?' she said.

'I wanted to learn your tunes,' he replied.

'Yes. Look – here it is!' And she brought him the little yellow book. It was just a hand-book, with melody and words only, no accompaniment. So she stood offering him the book, but waiting, as if for something else, and standing as if with another meaning.

He opened the leaves at random.

'But I ought to know which ones you sing,' said he, rising and standing by her side with the open book.

'Yes,' she said, looking over his arm. He turned the pages one by one. '*Trois jeunes tambours*,' said she. 'Yes, that ... Yes, *En passant par la Lorraine* ... *Auprès de ma blonde* ... Oh, I like that one so much –' He stood and went over the tune in his mind.

'Would you like me to play it?' he said.

'Very much,' said she.

So he got his flute, propped up the book against a vase, and played the tune, whilst she hummed it fragmentarily. But as he played, he felt that he did not cast the spell over her. There was no connection. She was in some mysterious way withstanding him. She was withstanding him, and his male super-power, and his thunderbolt desire. She was, in some indescribable way, throwing cold water over his phoenix newly risen from the ashes of its nest in flames.

He realized that she did not want him to play. She did not want him to look at the songs. So he put the book away, and turned round, rather baffled, not quite sure what was happening, yet feeling she was withstanding him. He glanced at her face: it was inscrutable: it was her Cleopatra face once more, yet with something new and warm in it. He could not understand it. What was it in her face that puzzled him? Almost angered him? But she could not rob him of his male power, she could not divest him of his concentrated force.

'Won't you take off your coat?' she said, looking at him with strange, large dark eyes. A strange woman, he could not understand her. Yet, as he sat down again, having removed his overcoat, he felt her looking at his limbs, his physical body. And this went against him, he did not want it. Yet quite fixed in him too was the desire for her, her beautiful white arms, her whole soft white body. And such desire he would not contradict or allow to be contradicted. It was his will also. Her whole soft white body – to possess it in its entirety, its fullness.

'What have you got to do this morning?' she asked him.

'Nothing,' he said. 'Have you?' He lifted his head and looked at her.

'Nothing at all,' said she.

And then they sat in silence, he with his head dropped. Then again he looked at her.

'Shall we be lovers?' he said.

She sat with her face averted, and did not answer. His heart struck heavily, but he did not relax.

'Shall we be lovers?' came his voice once more, with the faintest touch of irony.

Her face gradually grew dusky. And he wondered very much to see it.

'Yes,' said she, still not looking at him. 'If you wish.'

'I do wish,' he said. And all the time he sat with his eyes fixed on her face, and she sat with her face averted.

'Now?' he said. 'And where?'

Again she was silent for some moments, as if struggling with herself. Then she looked at him, a long, strange, dark look, incomprehensible, and which he did not like.

'You don't want emotions? You don't want me to say things, do you?' he said.

A faint ironic smile came on her face.

'I know what all that is worth,' she said, with curious calm equanimity. 'No, I want none of that.'

'Then –?'

But now she sat gazing on him with wide, heavy, incomprehensible eyes. It annoyed him.

'What do you want to see in me?' he asked, with a smile, looking steadily back again.

And now she turned aside her face once more, and once more the dusky colour came in her cheek. He waited.

'Shall I go away?' he said at length.

'Would you rather?' she said, keeping her face averted.

'No,' he said.

Then again she was silent.

'Where shall I come to you?' he said.

She paused a moment still, then answered:

'I'll go to my room.'

'I don't know which it is,' he said.

'I'll show it you,' she said.

'And then I shall come to you in ten minutes. In ten minutes,' he reiterated.

So she rose, and led the way out of the little salon. He walked with her to the door of her room, bowed his head as she looked at him, holding the door handle; and then he turned and went back to the drawing-room, glancing at his watch.

In the drawing-room he stood quite still, with his feet apart, and waited. He stood with his hands behind him, and his feet apart, quite motionless, planted and firm. So the minutes went by unheeded, He looked at his watch. The ten minutes were just up. He had heard footsteps and doors. So he decided to give her another five minutes. He wished to be quite sure that she had had her own time for her own movements.

Then at the end of the five minutes he went straight to her room, entered, and locked the door behind him. She was lying in bed, with her back to him.

He found her strange, not as he had imagined her. Not powerful, as he had imagined her. Strange, in his arms she seemed almost small and childish, whilst in daily life she looked a full, womanly woman. Strange, the naked way she clung to him! Almost like a sister, a younger sister! Or like a child! It filled him with a curious wonder, almost a bewilderment. In the dark sightlessness of passion, she seemed almost like a clinging child in his arms. And yet, like a child who in some deep and essential way mocked him. In some strange incomprehensible way, as a girl-child blindly obstinate in her deepest nature, she was against him. He felt she was not his woman. Through him went the feeling, 'This is not my woman.'

When, after a long sleep, he awoke and came fully to himself, with that click of awakedness which is the end, the first shades were closing on the afternoon. He got up, and reached for his watch.

'Quarter-past four,' he said.

Her eyes stretched wide with surprise as she looked at him. But she said nothing. The same strange and wide, perhaps insatiable child-like curiosity was in her eyes as she watched him. He dressed very quickly. And her eyes were wide, and she said no single word.

But when he was dressed, and bent over her to say good-bye, she put her arms round him, that seemed such frail and childish arms now, yet withal so deadly in power. Her soft arms round his neck, her tangle of hair over his face. And yet, even as he kissed her, he felt her deadly. He wanted to be gone. He wanted to get out of her arms and her clinging and her tangle of hair and her curiosity and her strange and hateful power.

'You'll come again. We'll be like this again?' she whispered.

And it was hard for him to realize that this was that other woman, who had sat so silently on the sofa, so darkly and reservedly, at the tea at Algy's.

'Yes! I will! Good-bye now!' And he kissed her, and walked straight out of the room. Quickly he took his coat and his hat, quickly, and left the house. In his nostrils was still the scent with which the bed linen was faintly scented – he did not know what it was. But now he wiped his face and his mouth, to wipe it away.

He had eaten nothing since coffee that morning, and was hungry, faint feeling. And his face, and his mind, felt withered. Curiously he felt blasted – as if blighted by some electricity. And he knew, he knew quite well he was only in possession of a tithe of his natural faculties. And in his male spirit he felt himself hating her: hating her deeply, damnably. But he said to himself: 'No, I won't hate her. I won't hate her.'

So he went on, over the Ponte Vecchio, where the jewellers' windows on the bridge were already blazing with light, on into the town. He wanted to eat something, so he decided to go to a shop he knew, where one could stand and eat good tiny rolls split into truffle or salami sandwiches, and drink marsala. So one after the other he ate little truffle rolls, and drank a few glasses of marsala. And then he did not know what to do. He did not want to eat any more. He had had what he wanted. His hunger had been more nervous than sensual.

So he went into the street. It was just growing dark and the town was lighting up. He felt curiously blazed, as if some flame or electric power had gone through him and withered his vital tissue. Blazed, as if some kind of electric flame had run over him and withered him. His brain felt withered, his mind had only one of its many-sighted eyes left open and unscorched. So many of the eyes of his mind were scorched now and sightless.

Yet a restlessness was in his nerves. What should he do? He remembered he had a letter in his pocket from Sir William Franks. Sir William had still teased him about his fate and his providence, in which he, Aaron, was supposed to trust. 'I shall be very glad to hear from you, and to know how your benevolent Providence – or was yours a Fate – has treated you since we saw you –'

So, Aaron turned away, and walked to the post office. There he took paper, and sat down at one of the tables in the writing-room, and wrote his answer. It was very strange, writing thus when most of his mind's eyes were scorched, and it seemed he could hardly see to hold the pen, to drive it straight across the paper. Yet write he must. And most of his faculties being quenched or blasted for the moment, he wrote perhaps his greatest, or his innermost truth. 'I don't want my Fate or my Providence to treat me well. I don't want kindness or love. I don't believe in harmony and people loving one another. I believe in the fight and nothing else. I believe in the fight which is in everything. And if it is a question of women, I believe in the fight of love, even if it blinds me. And if it is a question of the world, I believe in fighting it and in having it hate me, even if it breaks my legs. I want the world to hate me, because I can't bear the thought that it might love me. For of all things love is the most deadly to me, and especially from such a repulsive world as I think this is....'

Well, here was a letter for a poor old man to receive. But, in the dryness of his withered mind, Aaron got it out of himself. When a man writes a letter to himself, it is a pity to post it to somebody else. Perhaps the same is true of a book.

His letter written, however, he stamped it and sealed it and put it in the box. That made it final. Then he turned towards home. One fact remained unbroken in the debris of his consciousness: that in the town was Lilly: and that when he needed, he could go to Lilly: also, that in the world was Lottie, his wife: and that against Lottie, his heart burned with a deep, deep, almost unreachable bitterness. Like a deep burn on his deepest soul, Lottie. And like a fate which he resented, yet which steadied him, Lilly.

He went home and lay on his bed. He had enough self-command to hear the gong and go down to dinner. White and abstract-looking, he sat and ate his dinner. And then, thank God, he could go to bed, alone, in his own cold bed, alone, thank God. To be alone in the night! For this he was unspeakably thankful.

19

CLEOPATRA, BUT NOT ANTONY

Aaron awoke in the morning feeling better, but still only a part himself. The night alone had restored him. And the need to be alone still was his greatest need. He felt an intense resentment against the Marchesa. He felt that somehow, she had given him a scorpion. And his instinct was to hate her. And yet he avoided hating her. He remembered Lilly – and the saying that one must possess oneself, and be alone in possession of oneself. And somehow, under the influence of Lilly, he refused to follow the reflex of his own passion. He refused to hate the Marchesa. He *did* like her. He *did* esteem her. And after all, she too was struggling with her fate. He had a genuine sympathy with her. Nay, he was not going to hate her.

But he could not see her. He could not bear the thought that she might call and see him. So he took the tram to Settignano, and walked away all day into the country, having bread and sausage in his pocket. He sat for long hours among the cypress trees of Tuscany. And never had any trees seemed so like ghosts, like soft, strange, pregnant presences. He lay and watched tall cypresses breathing and communicating, faintly moving and as it were walking in the small wind. And his soul seemed to leave him and to go far away, far back, perhaps, to where life was all different and time passed otherwise than time passes now. As in clairvoyance he perceived it: that our life is only a fragment of the shell of life. That there has been and will be life, human life such as we do not begin to conceive. Much that is life has passed away from men, leaving us all mere bits. In the dark, mindful silence and inflection of the cypress trees, lost races, lost languages, lost human ways of feeling and of knowing. Men have known as we can no more known, have felt as we can no more feel. Great life-realities gone into the darkness. But the cypresses commemorate. In the afternoon, Aaron felt the cypresses rising dark about him, like so many high visitants from an old, lost, lost subtle world, where men had the wonder of demons about them, the aura of demons, such as still clings to the cypresses, in Tuscany.

All day, he did not make up his mind what he was going to do. His first impulse was never to see her again. And this was his intention all day. But as he went home in the tram he softened, and thought, nay, that would not be fair. For how had he treated him, otherwise than generously.

She had been generous, and the other thing, that he felt blasted afterwards, which was his experience, that was fate, and not her fault. So he must see her again. He must not act like a churl. But he would tell her – he would tell her that he was a married man, and that though he had left his wife, and though he had no dogma of fidelity, still, the years of marriage had made a married man of him, and any other woman than his wife was a strange woman to him, a violation. 'I will tell her,' he said to himself, 'that at the bottom of my heart I love Lottie still, and that I can't help it. I believe that is true. It isn't love, perhaps. But it is marriage. I am married to Lottie. And that means I can't be married to another woman. It isn't my nature. And perhaps I can't bear to live with Lottie now, because I am married and not in love. When a man is married, he is not in love. A husband is not a lover. Lilly told me that: and I know it's true now. Lilly told me that a husband cannot be a lover, and a lover cannot be a husband. And that women will only have lovers now, and never a husband. Well, I am a husband, if I am anything. And I shall never be a lover again, not while I live. No, not to anybody. I haven't it in me. I am a husband, and so it is finished with me as a lover. I can't be a lover any more, just as I can't be aged twenty any more. I am a man now, not an adolescent. And to my sorrow I am a husband to a woman who wants a lover: always a lover. But all women want lovers. And I can't be it any more. I don't want to. I have finished that. Finished for ever: unless I become senile –'

Therefore next day he gathered up his courage. He would not have had courage unless he had known that he was not alone. The other man was in the town, and from this fact he derived his strength: the fact that Lilly was there. So at tea-time he went over the river, and rang at her door. Yes, she was at home, and she had other visitors. She was wearing a beautiful soft afternoon dress, again of a blue, like chicory-flowers, a pale, *warm* blue. And she had cornflowers in her belt: heaven knows where she had got them.

She greeted Aaron with some of a childish shyness. He could tell that she was glad he had come, and that she had wondered at his not coming sooner. She introduced him to her visitors: two young ladies and one old lady and one elderly Italian count. The conversation was mostly in French or Italian, so Aaron was rather out of it.

However, the visitors left fairly early, so Aaron stayed them out. When they had gone, he asked:

'Where is Manfredi?'

'He will come in soon. At about seven o'clock.'

Then there was a silence again.

'You are dressed fine today,' he said to her.

'Am I?' she smiled.

He was never able to make out quite what she felt, what she was feeling. But she had a quiet little air of proprietorship in him, which he did not like.

'You will stay to dinner tonight, won't you?' she said.

'No – not tonight,' he said. And then, awkwardly, he added: 'You know. I think it is better if we are friends – not lovers. You know – I don't feel free. I feel my wife, I suppose, somewhere inside me. And I can't help it –'

She bent her head and was silent for some moments. Then she lifted her face and looked at him oddly.

'Yes,' she said. 'I am sure you love your wife.'

The reply rather staggered him – and to tell the truth, annoyed him.

'Well,' he said. 'I don't know about love. But when one has been married for ten years – and I did love her – then – some sort of bond or something grows. I think some sort of connection grows between us, you know. And it isn't natural, quite, to break it. Do you know what I mean?'

She paused for a moment. Then, very softly, almost gently, she said:

'Yes, I do. I know so well what you mean.'

He was really surprised at her soft acquiescence. What *did* she mean?

'But we can be friends, can't we?' he said.

'Yes, I hope so. Why, yes! I should be sorry if we couldn't be friends.'

After which speech he felt that everything was all right – everything was A1. And when Manfredi came home, the first sound he heard was the flute and his wife's singing.

'I'm so glad you've come,' his wife said to him. 'Shall we go into the sala and have real music? Will you play?'

'I should love to,' replied the husband.

Behold them then in the big drawing-room, and Aaron and the Marchese practising together, and the Marchesa singing an Italian folk-song while her husband accompanied her on the pianoforte. But her singing was rather strained and forced. Still, they were quite a little family, and it seemed quite nice. As soon as she could, the Marchesa left the two men together, whilst she sat apart. Aaron and Manfredi went through old Italian and old German music, tried one thing and then another, and seemed quite like brothers. They arranged a piece which they should play together on a Saturday morning, eight days hence.

The next day, Saturday, Aaron went to one of the Del Torre music mornings. There was a string quartette – and a violin soloist – and the Marchese at the piano. The audience, some dozen or fourteen friends, sat at the near end of the room, or in the smaller salotto, whilst the musicians performed at the farther end of the room. The Lillys were there, both Tanny and her husband. But apart from these, Aaron knew nobody, and felt uncomfortable.

The Marchesa gave her guests little sandwiches and glasses of wine or marsala or vermouth, as they chose. And she was quite the hostess: the well-bred and very simple, but still the conventional hostess. Aaron did not like it. And he could see that Lilly too was unhappy. In fact, the little man bolted the moment he could, dragging after him the indignant Tanny, who was so looking forward to the excellent little sandwiches. But no – Lilly just rudely bolted. Aaron followed as soon as he could.

'Will you come to dinner tomorrow evening?' said his hostess to him as he was leaving. And he agreed. He had really resented seeing her as a conventional hostess, attending so charmingly to all the other people, and treating him so merely as one of the guests, among many others. So that when at the last moment she quietly invited him to dinner next day, he was flattered and accepted at once.

The next day was Sunday – the seventh day after his coming together with the Marchesa – which had taken place on the Monday. And already he was feeling much less dramatic in his decision to keep himself apart from her, to be merely friends. Already the memory of the last time was fanning up in him, not as a warning but as a terrible incitement. Again the naked desire was getting hold of him, with that peculiar brutal powerfulness which startled him and also pleased him.

So that, by the time Sunday morning came, his recoil had exhausted itself, and he was ready again, eager again, but more wary this time. He sat in his room alone in the morning, playing his flute, playing over from memory the tunes she loved, and imagining how he and she would get into unison in the evening. His flute, his Aaron's rod, would blossom once again with splendid scarlet flowers, the red Florentine lilies. It was curious, the passion he had for her: just unalloyed desire, and nothing else. Something he had not known in his life before. Previously there had been always *some* personal quality, some sort of personal tenderness. But here, none. She did not seem to want it. She seemed to hate it, indeed. No, all he felt was stark, naked desire, without a single pretention. True enough, his last experience had been a warning to him. His desire and himself likewise had broken rather disastrously under the proving. But not finally broken. He was ready again. And with all the sheer powerful insolence of desire he looked forward to the evening. For he almost expected Manfredi would not be there. The officer had said something about having to go to Padua on the Saturday afternoon.

So Aaron went skipping off to his appointment, at seven o'clock. Judge of his chagrin, then, when he found already seated in the salotto an elderly, quite well-known, very cultured and very well-connected English authoress. She was charming, in her white hair and dress of soft white wool and white lace, with a long chain of filigree gold beads, like bubbles. She was charming in her old-fashioned manners too, as if the world were still safe and stable, like a garden in which delightful culture and choice ideas bloomed safe from wind and weather. Alas, never was Aaron more conscious of the crude collapse in the world than when he listened to this animated young-seeming lady from the safe days of the seventies. All the old culture and choice ideas seemed like blowing bubbles. And dear old Corinna Wade, she seemed to be blowing bubbles still, as she sat there so charming in her soft white dress, and talked with her bright animation about the influence of woman in Parliament and the influence of woman in the Periclean day. Aaron listened spell-bound, watching the bubbles float round his head, and almost hearing them go pop.

To complete the party arrived an elderly littérateur who was more proud of his social not-very-important standing than of his literature. In fact he was one of those English snobs of the old order, living abroad. Perfectly well dressed for the evening, his grey hair and his prim face was the most well-dressed thing to be met in North Italy.

'Oh, so glad to see you, Mr ffrench. I didn't know you were in Florence again. You make that journey from Venice so often. I wonder you don't get tired of it,' cried Corinna Wade.

'No,' he said. 'So long as duty to England calls me to Florence, I shall come to Florence. But I can *live* in no town but Venice.'

'No, I suppose you can't. Well, there *is* something special about Venice: having no streets and no carriages, and moving about in a gondola. I suppose it is all much more soothing.'

'Much less nerve-racking, yes. And then there is a quality in the whole life. Of course I see few English people in Venice – only the old Venetian families, as a rule.'

'Ah yes. That must be very interesting. They are very exclusive still, the Venetian *noblesse*?' said Miss Wade.

'Oh very exclusive,' said Mr ffrench. 'That is one of the charms. Venice is really altogether exclusive. It excludes the world, really, and defies time and modern movement. Yes, in spite of the steamers on the canal, and the tourists.'

'That is so. That is so. Venice is a strange backwater. And the old families are very proud still, in these democratic days. They have a great opinion of themselves, I am told.'

'Well,' said Mr ffrench. 'Perhaps you know the rhyme:

> "Veneziano gran' Signore
> Padovano buon' dottore.
> Vicenzese mangia il gatto
> Veronese tutto matto –"'

'How very amusing!' said Miss Wade. '*Veneziano* gran' signore. The Venetian is a great gentleman! Yes I know they are all convinced of it. Really, how very amusing, in these advanced days. To be born a Venetian, is to be born a great gentleman! But this outdoes divine right of kings.'

'To be born a Venetian *gentleman* is to be born a great gentleman,' said Mr ffrench, rather fussily.

'You seriously think so?' said Miss Wade. 'Well now, what do you base your opinion on?'

Mr ffrench gave various bases for his opinion.

'Yes – interesting. Very interesting. Rather like the Byzantines – lingering on into far other ages. Anna Comnena always charmed me very much. *How* she despised the flower of the north – even Tancred! And so the lingering Venetian families! And you, in your palazzo on the Grand Canal: you are a northern barbarian civilized into the old Venetian Signoria. But how very romantic a situation!'

It was really amusing to see the old maid, how she skirmished and hit out so gaily, like an old jaunty free-lance: and to see the old bachelor, how prim he was, and nervy and fussy and precious, like an old maid.

But need we say that Mr Aaron felt very much out of it. He sat and listened, with a sardonic small smile on his face and a sardonic gleam in his blue eyes, that looked so very blue on such an occasion. He made the two elderly people uncomfortable with his silence: his democratic silence, Miss Wade might have said.

However, Miss Wade lived out towards Galuzzo, so she rose early, to catch her tram. And Mr ffrench gallantly and properly rose to accompany her, to see her safe on board. Which left Aaron and the Marchesa alone.

'What time is Manfredi coming back?' said he.

'Tomorrow,' replied she.

There was a pause.

'Why do you have those people?' he asked.

'Who?'

'Those two who were here this evening.'

'Miss Wade and Mr ffrench? Oh, I like Miss Wade so very much. She is so refreshing.'

'Those old people,' said Aaron. 'They licked the sugar off the pill, and go on as if everything was toffee. And we've got to swallow the pill. It's easy to be refreshing –'

'No, don't say anything against her. I like her so much.'

'And him?'

'Mr ffrench! Well, he's perhaps a little like the princess who felt the pea through three feather-beds. But he can be quite witty, and an excellent conversationalist too. Oh yes, I like him quite well.'

'Matter of taste,' said Aaron.

They had not much to say to one another. The time passed, in the pauses. He looked at his watch.

'I shall have to go,' he said.

'Won't you stay?' she said in a small, muted voice.

'Stay all night?' he said.

'Won't you?'

'Yes,' he said quietly. Did he not feel the strength of his desire on him?

After which she said no more. Only she offered him whisky and soda, which he accepted.

'Go then,' he said to her. 'And I'll come to you. Shall I come in fifteen minutes?'

She looked at him with strange, slow dark eyes. And he could not understand.

'Yes,' she said. And she went.

And again, this night as before, she seemed strangely small and clinging in his arms. And this night he felt his passion drawn from him as if a long, live nerve were drawn out from his body, a long, live thread of electric fire.

This night he slept with a deeper obliviousness than before. But ah, as it grew towards morning, how he wished he could be alone.

They must stay together till the day was light. And she seemed to love clinging to him and curling strangely on his breast. He could never reconcile it with her who was a hostess entertaining her guests. How could she now in a sort of little ecstasy curl herself and nestle herself on his, Aaron's breast, tangling his face all over with her hair? He verily believed that this was what she really wanted of him: to curl herself on his naked breast, to make herself small, small, to feel his arms round her, and his slow, still, breathing, lifting her, while he himself was remote, silent, in some way inaccessible. This seemed almost to make her beside herself with gratification. But why, why? Was it because he was one of her own race, and she, as it were, crept right home to him?

He did not know. He only knew it had nothing to do with him: and that, save out of *complaisance*, he did not want it. But did he not want it? – the magic feeling of phallic immortality. But at the same time it simply blasted his own central life. It simply blighted him.

And she clung to him closer. Strange, she was afraid of him! Of his actual male physique she was afraid as of a fetish. Fetish afraid, and fetish-fascinated. Or was her fear only a delightful game of cat and mouse? Or was the fear genuine, and the delight the greater: a sort of sacrilege? The fear, and the dangerous, sacrilegious power over that which she feared.

In some way she was not afraid of him at all. In some other way she used him as a mere magic implement, used him with the most amazing priestess-craft. Himself, the individual man which he was, this she ignored with an indifference that was startling to him.

He forgot, perhaps, that this was how he had treated her. His famous desire for her, what it had been but this same attempt to strike a magic fire out of her, for his own ecstasy. They were playing the same game of fire. In him, however, there was always something, all the time something hard and reckless and defiant, which stood apart. She was absolutely gone in her own incantations. She was absolutely gone, like a priestess utterly involved in her own terrible rites. And he was part of the ritual only, God and victim in one. God and victim. All the time, God and victim. When his aloof soul realized, amid the incantation, how he was being used – not as himself, but as something quite different: God and victim; then he dilated with intense surprise, and his remote soul stood up tall and knew itself alone. He did not want it – not at all. He knew he was apart. And he looked back over the whole mystery of their love contact. Only his soul was apart.

He was aware of the strength and beauty and god-likeness that his breast was then to her – the magic. But himself, he stood far off, like Moses' sister Miriam. She would drink the one drop of his innermost heart's blood, and he would be carrion. As Cleopatra killed her lovers in the morning. Surely they knew that death was their just climax. They had approached the climax. Accept then.

But his soul stood apart, and could have nothing to do with it. If he had *really* been tempted, he would have gone on, and she might have had his central heart's blood. Yes, and thrown away the carrion. He would have been willing.

But fatally, he was not tempted. His soul stood apart and decided. At the bottom of his soul he disliked her. Or if not her, then her whole motive. Her whole life-mode. He was neither God nor victim: neither more nor less than himself. His soul, in its isolation as she lay there on his breast, chose it so with the soul's inevitability. So, there was no temptation.

When it was sufficiently light, he kissed her and left her. Quietly he left the silent flat. He had some difficulty in unfastening the various locks and bars and catches of the massive doors downstairs, and began, in irritation and anger, to feel he was a prisoner, that he was locked in. But suddenly the ponderous door came loose, and he was out in the street. The door shut heavily behind him, with a shudder. He was out in the morning streets of Florence.

20

THE BROKEN ROD

The day was rainy. Aaron stayed indoors alone, and copied music and slept. He felt the same stunned, withered feeling as before, but less intensely, less disastrously, this time. He knew now, without argument or thought, that he would never go again to the Marchesa: not as a lover. He would go away from it all. He did not dislike her. But he would never see her again. A great gulf had opened, leaving him alone on the far side.

He did not go out till after dinner. When he got downstairs he found the heavy night-door closed. He wondered: then remembered the Signorina's fear of riots and disturbances. As again he fumbled with the catches, he felt that the doors of Florence were trying to prevent his egress. However, he got out.

It was a very dark night, about nine o'clock, and deserted seeming. He was struck by the strange, deserted feeling of the city's atmosphere: Yet he noticed before him, at the foot of the statue, three men, one with a torch: a long torch with naked flames. The men were stooping over something dark, the man with the torch bending forward too. It was a dark, weird little group, like Medieval Florence. Aaron lingered on his doorstep, watching. He could not see what they were doing. But now, the two were crouching down; over a long dark object on the ground, and the one with the torch bending also to look. What was it? They were just at the foot of the statue, a dark little group under the big pediment, the torch-flames weirdly flickering as the torch-bearer moved and stopped lower to the two crouching men, who seemed to be kneeling.

Aaron felt his blood stir. There was something dark and mysterious, stealthy, in the little scene. It was obvious the men did not want to draw attention, they were so quiet and furtive-seeming. And an eerie instinct prevented Aaron's going nearer to look. Instead, he swerved on to the Lungarno, and went along the top of the square, avoiding the little group in the centre. He walked the deserted dark-seeming street by the river, then turned inwards, into the city. He was going to the Piazza Vittoria Emmanuele, to sit in the café which is the centre of Florence at night. There he could sit for an hour, and drink his vermouth and watch the Florentines.

As he went along one of the dark, rather narrow streets, he heard a hurrying of feet behind him. Glancing round, he saw the torch-bearer coming along at a trot, holding his flaming torch up in front of him as he trotted down the middle of the narrow dark street. Aaron shrank under the wall. The trotting torch-bearer drew near, and now Aaron perceived the other two men slowly trotting behind, stealthily, bearing a stretcher on which a body was wrapped up, completely and darkly covered. The torch-bearer passed, the men with the stretcher passed too, hastily and stealthily, the flickering flames revealing them. They took no notice of Aaron, no notice of anything, but trotted softly on towards the centre of the city. Their queer, quick footsteps echoed down the distance. Then Aaron too resumed his way.

He came to the large, brilliantly-lighted café. It was Sunday evening, and the place was full. Men, Florentines, many, many men sat in groups and in twos and threes at the little marble tables. They were mostly in dark clothes or black overcoats. They had mostly been drinking just a cup of coffee – others, however, had glasses of wine or liquor. But mostly it was just a little coffee-tray with a tiny coffee-pot and a cup and saucer. There was a faint film of tobacco smoke. And the men were all talking: talking, talking with that peculiar intensity of the Florentines. Aaron felt the intense, compressed sound of many half-secret voices. For the little groups and couples abated their voices, none wished that others should hear what they said.

Aaron was looking for a seat – there was no table to himself – when suddenly someone took him by the arm. It was Argyle.

'Come along, now! Come and join us. Here, this way! Come along!'

Aaron let himself be led away towards a corner. There sat Lilly and a strange man: called Levison. The room was warm. Aaron could never bear to be too hot. After sitting a minute, he rose and took off his coat, and hung it on a stand near the window. As he did so he felt the weight of his flute – it was still in his pocket. And he wondered if it was safe to leave it.

'I suppose no one will steal from the overcoat pockets,' he said, as he sat down.

'My dear chap, they'd steal the gold filling out of your teeth, if you happened to yawn,' said Argyle. 'Why, have you left valuables in your overcoat?'

'My flute,' said Aaron.

'Oh, they won't steal that,' said Argyle.

'Besides,' said Lilly, 'we should see anyone who touched it.'

And so they settled down to the vermouth.

'Well,' said Argyle, 'what have you been doing with yourself, eh? I haven't seen a glimpse of you for a week. Been going to the dogs, eh? I can see I shall have to take you in hand, and commence my work of reform. Oh, I'm a great reformer, a Zwingli and Savonarola in one. I couldn't count the number of people I've led into the right way. It takes some finding, you know. Strait is the gate – damned strait sometimes. A damned tight squeeze ...' Argyle was somewhat intoxicated. He spoke with a slight slur, and laughed, really tickled at his own jokes. The man Levison smiled acquiescent. But Lilly was not listening. His brow was heavy and he seemed abstracted. He hardly noticed Aaron's arrival.

'Did you see the row yesterday?' asked Levison.

'No,' said Aaron. 'What was it?'

'It was the Socialists. They were making a demonstration against the imprisonment of one of the railway-strikers. I was there. They went on all right with a good bit of howling and gibing: a lot of young louts, you know. And the shop-keepers shut up shop, and nobody showed the Italian flag, of course. Well, when they came to the Via Benedetto Croce, there were a few mounted carabinieri. So they stopped the procession, and the sergeant said that the crowd could continue, could go on where they like, but would they not go down the Via Verrocchio, because it was being repaired, the roadway was all up, and there were piles of cobble-stones. These might prove a temptation and lead to trouble. So would the demonstrators not take that road – they might take any other they liked. Well, the very moment he had finished, there was a revolver shot, he made a noise, and fell forward over his horse's nose. One of the anarchists had shot him. Then there was hell let loose, the carabinieri fired back, and people were bolting and fighting like devils. I cleared out, myself. But my God – what do you think of it?'

'Seems pretty mean,' said Aaron.

'Mean! He had just spoken them fair – they could go where they liked, only would they not go down the one road, because of the heap of stones. And they let him finish. And then shot him dead.'

'Was he dead?' said Aaron.

'Yes – killed outright, the *Nazione* says.'

There was a silence. The drinkers in the café all continued to talk vehemently, casting uneasy glances.

'Well,' said Argyle, 'if you let loose the dogs of war you mustn't expect them to come to heel again in five minutes.'

'But there's no fair play about it, not a bit,' said Levison.

'Ah, my dear fellow, are you still so young and callow that you cherish the illusion of fair play?' said Argyle.

'Yes, I am,' said Levison.

'Live longer and grow wiser,' said Argyle, rather contemptuously.

'Are you a Socialist?' asked Levison.

'Am I my aunt Tabitha's dachshund bitch called Bella,' said Argyle, in his musical, indifferent voice. 'Yes, Bella's her name. And if you can tell me a demneder name for a dog, I shall listen, I assure you, attentively.'

'But you haven't got an aunt called Tabitha,' said Aaron.

'Haven't I? Oh, haven't I? I've got *two* aunts called Tabitha: if not more.'

'They aren't of any vital importance to you, are they?' said Levison.

'Not the very least in the world – if it hadn't been that my elder Aunt Tabitha had christened her dachshund bitch Bella. I cut myself off from the family after that. Oh, I turned over a new leaf, with not a family name on it. Couldn't stand Bella amongst the rest.'

'You must have strained most of the gnats out of your drink, Argyle,' said Lilly, laughing.

'Assiduously! Assiduously! I can't stand these little vermin. Oh, I am quite indifferent about swallowing a camel or two – or even a whole string of dromedaries. How charmingly Eastern that sounds! But gnats! Not for anything in the world would I swallow one.'

'*You're* a bit of a Socialist though, aren't you?' persisted Levison, now turning to Lilly.

'No,' said Lilly. 'I was.'

'And am no more,' said Argyle sarcastically. 'My dear fellow, the only hope of salvation for the world lies in the reinstitution of slavery.'

'What kind of slavery?' asked Levison.

'Slavery! *Slavery!* When I say *slavery* I don't mean any of your damned modern reform cant. I mean solid sound slavery on which the Greek and the Roman world rested. *Far* finer worlds than ours, my dear chap! Oh *far* finer! And can't be done without slavery. Simply can't be done. Oh, they'll all come to realize it, when they've had a bit more of this democratic washer-women business.'

Levison was laughing, with a slight sneer down his nose.

'Anyhow, there's no immediate danger – or hope, if you prefer it – of the re-instituting of classic slavery,' he said.

'Unfortunately no. We are all such fools,' said Argyle.

'Besides,' said Levison, 'who would you make slaves of?'

'Everybody, my dear chap: beginning with the idealists and the theorizing Jews, and after them your nicely-bred gentlemen, and then perhaps your profiteers, and Rothschilds, and *all* politicians, and ending up with the proletariat,' said Argyle.

'Then who would be the masters? – the professional classes, doctors and lawyers and so on?'

'What? Masters? They would be the sewerage slaves, as being those who had made most stinks.'

There was a moment's silence.

'The only fault I have to find with your system,' said Levison, rather acidly, 'is that there would be only one master, and everybody else slaves.'

'Do you call that a fault? What do you want with more than one master? Are you asking for several? Well, perhaps there's cunning in *that*. Cunning devils, cunning devils, these theorizing slaves –' and Argyle pushed his face with a devilish leer into Aaron's face. 'Cunning devils!' he reiterated, with a slight tipsy slur. 'Epictetus wasn't the last of 'em – nor the first. Oh, not by any means, not by any means.'

Here Lilly could not avoid a slight spasm of amusement.

'But returning to serious conversation,' said Levison, turning his rather sallow face to Lilly. 'I think you'll agree with me that Socialism is the inevitable next step –'

Lilly waited for some time without answering. Then he said, with unwilling attention to the question:

'I suppose it's the logically inevitable next step.'

'Yes – logically inevitable – and humanly inevitable at the same time. Some form of Socialism is bound to come, no matter how you postpone it or try variations,' said Levison.

'All right, let it come,' said Lilly. 'It's not my affair, neither to help it nor to keep it back, or even to try varying it.'

'There I don't follow you,' said Levison. 'Suppose you were in Russia now –'

'I watch it I'm not.'

'But you're in Italy, which isn't far off. Supposing a Socialist revolution takes place all round you. Won't that force the problem on you? It is every man's problem,' persisted Levison.

'Not mine,' said Lilly.

'How shall you escape it?' said Levison.

'Because to me it is no problem. To Bolsh or not to Bolsh, as far as my mind goes, presents no problem. Not any more than to be or not to be. To be or not to be is simply no problem –'

'No, I quite agree, that since you are already existing, and since death is ultimately inevitable, to be or not to be is no sound problem,' said Levison. 'But the parallel isn't true of Socialism. That is not a problem of existence, but of a certain mode of existence which centuries of thought and action on the part of Europe have now made logically inevitable for Europe. And therefore there is a problem. There is more than a problem, there is a dilemma. Either we must go to the logical conclusion – or –'

'Somewhere else,' said Lilly.

'Yes – yes. Precisely! But *where* else? That's the one half of the problem: supposing you do not agree to a logical progression in human social activity. Because after all, human society through the course of ages only enacts, spasmodically but still inevitably, the logical development of a given idea.'

'Well, then, I tell you. The idea and the ideal has for me gone dead – dead as carrion –'

'Which idea, which ideal precisely?'

'The ideal of love, the ideal that it is better to give than to receive, the ideal of liberty, the ideal of the brotherhood of man, the ideal of the sanctity of human life, the ideal of what we call goodness, charity, benevolence, public spiritedness, the ideal of sacrifice for a cause, the ideal of unity and unanimity – all the lot – all the whole beehive of ideals – has all got the modern bee-disease, and gone putrid, stinking. And when the ideal is dead and putrid, the logical sequence is only stink. Which, for me, is the truth concerning the ideal of good, peaceful, loving humanity and its logical sequence in Socialism and equality, equal opportunity or whatever you like. By this time he stinketh – and I'm sorry for any Christus who brings him to life again, to stink livingly for another thirty years: the beastly Lazarus of our idealism.'

'That may be true for you –'

'But it's true for nobody else,' said Lilly. 'All the worse for them. Let them die of the bee-disease.'

'Not only that,' persisted Levison, 'but what is your alternative? Is it merely nihilism?'

'My alternative,' said Lilly, 'is an alternative for no one but myself, so I'll keep my mouth shut about it.'

'That isn't fair.'

'I tell you, the ideal of fairness stinks with the rest. I have no obligation to say what I think.'

'Yes, if you enter into conversation, you have –'

'Bah, then I didn't enter into conversation. The only thing is, I agree in the rough with Argyle. You've got to have a sort of slavery again. People are not *men*: they are insects and instruments, and their destiny is slavery. They are too many for me, and so what I think is ineffectual. But ultimately they will be brought to agree – after sufficient extermination – and then they will elect for themselves a proper and healthy and energetic slavery.'

'I should like to know what you mean by slavery. Because to me it is impossible that slavery should be healthy and energetic. You seem to have some other idea in your mind, and you merely use the word slavery out of exasperation –'

'I mean it none the less. I mean a real committal of the life-issue of inferior beings to the responsibility of a superior being.'

'It'll take a bit of knowing, who are the inferior and which is the superior,' said Levison sarcastically.

'Not a bit. It is written between a man's brows, which he is.'

'I'm afraid we shall all read differently.'

'So long as we're liars.'

'And putting that question aside: I presume that you mean that this committal of the life-issue of inferior beings to someone higher shall be made voluntarily – a sort of voluntary self-gift of the inferiors –'

'Yes – more or less – and a voluntary acceptance. For it's no pretty gift, after all. But once made it must be held fast by genuine power. Oh yes – no playing and fooling about with it. Permanent and very efficacious power.'

'You mean military power?'

'I do, of course.'

Here Levison smiled a long, slow, subtle smile of ridicule. It all seemed to him the preposterous pretentiousness of a megalomaniac – one whom, after a while, humanity would probably have the satisfaction of putting into prison, or into a lunatic asylum. And Levison felt strong, overwhelmingly strong, in the huge social power with which he, insignificant as he was, was armed against such criminal-imbecile pretensions as those above set forth. Prison or the lunatic asylum. The face of the fellow gloated in these two inevitable engines of his disapproval.

'It will take you some time before you'll get your doctrines accepted,' he said.

'Accepted! I'd be sorry. I don't want a lot of swine snouting and sniffing at me with their acceptance. Bah, Levison – one can easily make a fool of you. Do you take this as my gospel?'

'I take it you are speaking seriously.'

Here Lilly broke into that peculiar, gay, whimsical smile.

'But I should say the blank opposite with just as much fervour,' he declared.

'Do you mean to say you don't *mean* what you've been saying?' said Levison, now really looking angry.

'Why, I'll tell you the real truth,' said Lilly. 'I think every man is a sacred and holy individual, *never* to be violated. I think there is only one thing I hate to the verge of madness, and that is *bullying*. To see any living creature *bullied*, in *any* way, almost makes a murderer of me. That is true. Do you believe it –?'

'Yes,' said Levison unwillingly. 'That may be true as well. You have no doubt, like most of us, got a complex nature which –'

CRASH!

There intervened one awful minute of pure shock, when the soul was in darkness.

Out of this shock Aaron felt himself issuing amid a mass of terrible sensations: the fearful blow of the explosion, the noise of glass, the hoarse howl of people, the rushing of men, the sudden gulf, the awful gulfing whirpool of horror in the social life.

He stood in agony and semi-blindness amid a chaos. Then as he began to recover his consciousness, he found himself standing by a pillar some distance from where he had been sitting: he saw a place where tables and chairs were all upside down, legs in the air, amid débris of glass and breakage: he saw the café almost empty, nearly everybody gone: he saw the owner, or the manager, advancing aghast to the place of débris: he saw Lilly standing not far off, white as a sheet, and as if unconscious. And still he had no idea of what had happened. He thought perhaps something had broken down. He could not understand.

Lilly began to look round. He caught Aaron's eye. And then Aaron began to approach his friend.

'What is it?' he asked.

'A bomb,' said Lilly.

The manager, and one old waiter, and three or four youths had now advanced to the place of débris. And now Aaron saw that a man was lying there – and horror, blood was running across the floor of the café. Men began now hastily to return to the place. Some seized their hats and departed again at once. But many began to crowd in – a black eager crowd of men pressing to where the bomb had burst – where the man was lying. It was rather dark, some of the lamps were broken – but enough still shone. Men surged in with that eager, excited zest of people, when there has been an accident. Grey carabinieri, and carabinieri in the cocked hat and fine Sunday uniform pressed forward officiously.

'Let us go,' said Lilly.

And he went to the far corner, where his hat hung. But Aaron looked in vain for his own hat. The bomb had fallen near the stand where he had hung it and his overcoat.

'My hat and coat?' he said to Lilly.

Lilly, not very tall, stood on tiptoe. Then he climbed on a chair and looked round. Then he squeezed past the crowd.

Aaron followed. On the other side of the crowd excited angry men were wrestling over overcoats that were mixed up with a broken marble table-top. Aaron spied his own black hat under the sofa near the wall. He waited his turn and then in the confusion pressed forward to where the coats were. Someone had dragged out his, and it lay on the floor under many feet. He managed, with a struggle, to get it from under the feet of the crowd. He felt at once for his flute. But his trampled, torn coat had no flute in its pocket. He pushed and struggled, caught sight of a section and picked it up. But it was split right down, two silver stops were torn out, and a long thin spelk of wood was curiously torn off. He looked at it, and his heart stood still. No need to look for the rest.

He felt utterly, utterly overcome – as if he didn't care what became of him any further. He didn't care whether he were hit by a bomb, or whether he himself threw the next bomb, and hit somebody. He just didn't care any more about anything in life or death. It was as if the reins of his life slipped from his hands, and he would let everything run where it would, so long as it did run.

Then he became aware of Lilly's eyes on him – and automatically he joined the little man.

'Let us go,' said Lilly.

And they pushed their way through the door. The police were just marching across the square. Aaron and Lilly walked in the opposite direction. Groups of people were watching. Suddenly Lilly swerved – in the middle of the road was a large black glisten of blood, trickling horribly. A wounded man had run from the blow and fallen here.

Aaron did not know where he was going. But in the Via Tornabuoni Lilly turned towards the Arno, and soon they were on the Ponte Santa Trinità.

'Who threw the bomb?' said Aaron.

'I suppose an anarchist.'

'It's all the same,' said Aaron.

The two men, as if unable to walk any farther, leaned on the broad parapet of the bridge and looked at the water in the darkness of the still, deserted night. Aaron still had his flute section in his hand, his overcoat over his arm.

'Is that your flute?' asked Lilly.

'Bit of it. Smashed.'

'Let me look.'

He looked, and gave it back.

'No good,' he said.

'Oh no,' said Aaron.

'Throw it in the river, Aaron,' said Lilly.

Aaron turned and looked at him.

'Throw it in the river,' repeated Lilly. 'It's an end.'

Aaron nervelessly dropped the flute into the stream. The two men stood leaning on the bridge-parapet, as if unable to move.

'We shall have to go home,' said Lilly. 'Tanny may hear of it and be anxious.'

Aaron was quite dumbfounded by the night's event: the loss of his flute. Here was a blow he had not expected. And the loss was for him symbolistic. It chimed with something in his soul: the bomb, the smashed flute, the end.

'There goes Aaron's Rod, then,' he said to Lilly.

'It'll grow again. It's a reed, a water-plant. You can't kill it,' said Lilly, unheeding.

'And me?'

'You'll have to live without a rod, meanwhile.'

To which pleasant remark Aaron made no reply.

21

WORDS

He went home to bed: and dreamed a strange dream. He dreamed that he was in a country with which he was not acquainted. Night was coming on, and he had nowhere to sleep. So he passed the mouth of a sort of cave or house, in which a woman, an old woman, sat. Therefore he entered, and though he could not understand the language, still his second self understood. The cave was a house: and men came home from work. His second self assumed that they were tinminers.

He wandered uneasily to and fro, no one taking any particular notice of him. And he realized that there was a whole vast country spreading, a sort of underworld country, spreading away beyond him. He wandered from vast apartment to apartment, down narrow corridors like the roads in a mine. In one of the great square rooms, the men were going to eat. And it seemed to him that what they were going to eat was a man, a naked man. But his second self knew that what appeared to his eyes as a man was really a man's skin stuffed tight with prepared meat, as the skin of a Bologna sausage. This did not prevent his seeing the naked man who was to be eaten walk slowly and stiffly across the gangway and down the corridor. He saw him from behind. It was a big and handsome man in the prime of life, quite naked and perhaps stupid. But, of course, he was only a skin stuffed with meat, whom the grey tinminers were going to eat.

Aaron, the dream-Aaron, turned another way, and strayed among the vast square rooms, cavern apartments. He came into one room where there were many children, all in white gowns. And they were all busily putting themselves to bed, in the many beds scattered about the room at haphazard. And each child went to bed with a wreath of flowers on its head, white flowers and pink, so it seemed. So there they all lay, in their flower-crowns in the vast space of the rooms. And Aaron went away.

He could not remember the following part. Only he seemed to have passed through many grey domestic apartments, where were all women, all greyish in their clothes and appearance, being wives of the underground tinminers. The men were away and the dream-Aaron remembered with fear the food they were to eat.

The next thing he could recall was that he was in a boat. And now he was most definitely two people. His invisible, *conscious* self, what we have called his second self, hovered as it were before the prow of the boat, seeing and knowing, but unseen. His other self, the palpable Aaron, sat as a passenger in the boat, which was being rowed by the unknown people of this underworld. They stood up as they thrust the boat along. Other passengers were in the boat too, women as well, but all of the unknown people, and not noticeable.

The boat was upon a great lake in the underworld country, a lake of dark-blue water, but crystal clear and very beautiful in colour. The second or invisible Aaron sat in the prow and watched the fishes swimming suspended in the clear, beautiful dark-blue water. Some were pale fish, some frightening-looking, like centipedes swimming, and some were dark fish, of definite form, and delightful to watch.

The palpable or visible Aaron sat at the side of the boat, on the end of the middle seat, with his naked right elbow leaning out over the side. And now the boat entered upon shallows. The impalpable Aaron in the bows saw the whitish clay of the bottom swirl up in clouds at each thrust of the oars, whitish clayey clouds which would envelope the strange fishes in a sudden mist. And on the right hand of the course stakes stood up in the water, at intervals, to mark the course.

The boat must pass very near these stakes, almost touching. And Aaron's naked elbow was leaning right over the side. As they approached the first stake, the boatmen all uttered a strange cry of warning, in a foreign language. The flesh-and-blood Aaron seemed not even to hear. The invisible Aaron heard, but did not comprehend the words of the cry. So the naked elbow struck smartly against the stake as the boat passed.

The rowers rowed on. And still the flesh-and-blood Aaron sat with his arm over the side. Another stake was nearing. 'Will he heed, will he heed?' thought the anxious second self. The rowers gave the strange warning cry. He did not heed, and again the elbow struck against the stake as the boat passed.

And yet the flesh-and-blood Aaron sat on and made no sign. There were stakes all along this shallow part of the lake. Beyond was deep water again. The invisible Aaron was becoming anxious. 'Will he never hear? Will he never heed? Will he never understand?' he thought. And he watched in pain for the next stake. But still the flesh-and-blood Aaron sat on, and though the rowers cried so acutely that the invisible Aaron almost understood their very language, still the Aaron seated at the side heard nothing, and his elbow struck against the third stake.

This was almost too much. But after a few moments, as the boat rowed on, the palpable Aaron changed his position as he sat, and drew in his arm: though even now he was not aware of any need to do so. The invisible Aaron breathed with relief in the bows, the boat swung steadily on, into the deep, unfathomable water again.

They were drawing near a city. A lake city, like Mexico. They must have reached a city, because when Aaron woke up and tried to piece together the dream of which these are mere fragments, he could remember having just seen an idol. An Astarte he knew it as, seated by the road, and in her open lap were some eggs: smallish hen's eggs, and one or two bigger eggs, like swan's, and one single little roll of bread. These lay in the lap of the roadside Astarte ... And then he could remember no more.

He woke, and for a minute tried to remember what he had been dreaming, and what it all meant. But he quickly relinquished the effort. So he looked at his watch: it was only half-past three. He had one of those American watches with luminous, phosphorescent figures and fingers. And tonight he felt afraid of its eerily shining face.

He was awake a long time in the dark – for two hours, thinking and not thinking, in that barren state which is not sleep, nor yet full wakefulness, and which is a painful strain. At length he went to sleep again, and did not wake till past eight o'clock. He did not ring for his coffee till nine.

Outside was a bright day – but he hardly heeded it. He lay profitlessly thinking. With the breaking of the flute, that which was slowly breaking had finally shattered at last. And there was nothing ahead: no plan, no prospect. He knew quite well that people would help him: Francis Dekker or Angus Guest or the Marchese or Lilly. They would get him a new flute, and find him engagements. But what was the good? His flute was broken, and broken finally. The bomb had settled it. The bomb had settled it and everything. It was an end, no matter how he tried to patch things up. The only thing he felt was a thread of destiny attaching him to Lilly. The rest had all gone as bare and bald as the dead orb of the moon. So he made up his mind, if he could, to make some plan that would bring his life together with that of his evanescent friend.

Lilly was a peculiar bird. Clever and attractive as he undoubtedly was, he was perhaps the most objectionable person to know. It was stamped on his peculiar face. Aaron thought of Lilly's dark, ugly face, which had something that lurked in it as a creature under leaves. Then the thought of the wide-apart eyes, with their curious candour and surety. The peculiar, half-veiled surety, as if nothing, nothing could overcome him. It made people angry, this look of silent, indifferent assurance. 'Nothing can touch him on the quick, nothing can really *get* at him,' they felt at last. And they felt it with resentment, almost with hate. They wanted to be able to get at him. For he was so open-seeming, so very outspoken. He gave himself away so much. And he had no money to fall back on. Yet he gave himself away so easily, paid such attention, almost deference to any chance friend. So they all thought: Here is a wise person who finds me the wonder which I really am. And lo and behold, after he had given them the trial, and found their inevitable limitations, he departed and ceased to heed their wonderful existence. Which, to say the least of it, was fraudulent and damnable. It was then, after his departure, that they realized his basic indifference to them, and his silent arrogance. A silent arrogance that knew all their wisdom, and left them to it.

Aaron had been through it all. He had started by thinking Lilly a peculiar little freak: gone on to think him a wonderful chap, and a bit pathetic: progressed, and found him generous, but overbearing: then cruel and intolerant, allowing no man to have a soul of his own: then terribly arrogant, throwing a fellow aside like an old glove which is in holes at the finger-ends. And all the time, which was most beastly, seeing through one. All the time, freak and outsider as he was, Lilly *knew*. He knew, and his soul was against the whole world.

Driven to bay, and forced to choose. Forced to choose, not between life and death, but between the world and the uncertain, assertive Lilly. Forced to choose, and yet, in the world, having nothing left to choose. For in the world there was nothing left to choose, unless he would give in and try for success. Aaron knew well enough that if he liked to do a bit of buttering, people would gladly make a success of him, and give him money and success. He could become quite a favourite.

But no! If he had to give in to something: if he really had to give in, and it seemed he had: then he would rather give in to the devilish little Lilly than to the beastly people of the world. If he had to give in, then it should be to no woman, and to no social ideal, and to no special institution. No! – if he had to yield his wilful independence, and give himself, then he would rather give himself to the little, individual *man* than to any of the rest. For to tell the truth, in the man was something incomprehensible, which had dominion over him, if he chose to allow it.

As he lay pondering this over, escaping from the *cul de sac* in which he had been running for so long, by yielding to one of his pursuers: yielding to the peculiar mastery of one man's nature rather than to the quicksands of woman or the stinking bog of society: yielding, since yield he must, in some direction or other: yielding in a new direction now, to one strange and incalculable little individual: as Aaron lay so relaxing, finding a peculiar delight in giving his soul to his mind's hero, the self-same hero tapped and entered.

'I wondered,' he said, 'if you'd like to walk into the country with me: it is such a nice day. I thought you might have gone out already. But here you are in bed like a woman who's had a baby. You're all right, are you?'

'Yes,' said Aaron. 'I'm all right.'

'Miserable about your flute? Ah well, there are more flutes. Get up then.' And Lilly went to the window, and stood looking out at the river.

'We're going away on Thursday,' he said.

'Where to?' said Aaron.

'Naples. We've got a little house there for the winter – in the country, not far from Sorrento – I must get a bit of work done, now the winter is coming. And forget all about everything and just live with life. What's the good of running after life, when we've got it in us, if nobody prevents us and obstructs us?'

Aaron felt very queer.

'But for how long will you settle down –?' he asked.

'Oh, only for the winter. I am a vagrant really: or a migrant. I must migrate. Do you think a cuckoo in Africa and a cuckoo in Essex is one *and* the same bird? Anyhow, I know I must oscillate between north and south, so oscillate I do. It's just my nature. All people don't have the same needs.'

'Perhaps not,' said Aaron, who had risen and was sitting on the side of the bed.

'I would very much like to try life in another continent, among another race. I feel Europe becoming like a cage to me. Europe may be all right in herself. But I find myself chafing. Another year I shall get out. I shall leave Europe. I begin to feel caged.'

'I guess there are others that feel caged, as well as you,' said Aaron.

'I guess there are.'

'And maybe they haven't a chance to get out.'

Lilly was silent a moment. Then he said:

'Well, I didn't make life and society. I can only go my own way.'

Aaron too was silent. A deep disappointment was settling over his spirit.

'Will you be alone all winter?'

'Just myself and Tanny,' he answered. 'But people always turn up.'

'And then next year, what will you do?'

'Who knows? I may sail far off. I should like to. I should like to try quite a new life-mode. This is finished in me – and yet perhaps it is absurd to go further. I'm rather sick of seekers. I hate a seeker.'

'What,' said Aaron rather sarcastically – 'those who are looking for a new religion?'

'Religion – and love – and all that. It's a disease now.'

'Oh, I don't know,' said Aaron. 'Perhaps the lack of love and religion is the disease.'

'Ah – bah! The grinding of the old millstones of love and God is what ails us, when there's no more grist between the stones. We've ground love very small. Time to forget it. Forget the very words religion, and God, and love – then have a shot at a new mode. But the very words rivet us down and don't let us move. Rivets, and we can't get them out.'

'And where should we be if we could?' said Aaron.

'We might begin to be ourselves, anyhow.'

'And what does that mean?' said Aaron. 'Being yourself – what does it mean?'

'To me, everything.'

'And to most folks, nothing. They've got to have a goal.'

'There is no goal. I loathe goals more than any other impertinence. Gaols, they are. Bah – jails and jailers! gaols and gaolers –'

'Wherever you go, you'll find people with their noses tied to some goal,' said Aaron.

'Their wagon hitched to a star – which goes round and round like an ass in a gin,' laughed Lilly. 'Be damned to it.'

Aaron got himself dressed, and the two men went out, took a tram and went into the country. Aaron could not help it – Lilly put his back up. They came to a little inn near a bridge, where a broad stream rustled bright and shallow. It was a sunny, warm day, and Aaron and Lilly had a table outside under the thin leaves at the top of the bank above the river. The yellow leaves were falling – the Tuscan sky was turquoise blue. In the stream below three naked boys still adventurously bathed, and lay flat on the shingle in the sun. A wagon with two pale, loving, velvety oxen drew slowly down the hill, looking at each step as if they were going to come to rest, to move no more. But still they stepped forward. Till they came to the inn, and there they stood at rest. Two old women were picking the last acorns under three scrubby oak trees, whilst a girl with bare feet drove her two goats and a sheep up from the water-side towards the women. The girl wore a dress that had been blue, perhaps indigo, but which had faded to the beautiful lavender-purple colour which is so common, and which always reminded Lilly of purple anemones in the south.

The two friends sat in the sun and drank red wine. It was midday. From the thin, square belfry on the opposite hill the bells had rung. The old women and the girl squatted under the trees eating their bread and figs. The boys were dressing, fluttering into their shirts on the stream's shingle. A big girl went past, with somebody's dinner tied in a red kerchief and perched on her head. It was one of the most precious hours: the hour of pause, noon, and the sun, and the quiet acceptance of the world. At such a time everything seems to fall into a true relationship, after the strain of work and of urge.

Aaron looked at Lilly, and saw the same odd, distant look on his face as on the face of some animal when it lies awake and alert, yet perfectly at one with its surroundings. It was something quite different from happiness: an alert enjoyment of rest, an intense and satisfying sense of centrality. As a dog when it basks in the sun with one eye open and winking: or a rabbit quite still and wide-eyed, with a faintly-twitching nose. Not passivity, but alert enjoyment of being central, life-central in one's own little circumambient world.

They sat thus still – or lay under the trees – for an hour and a half. Then Lilly paid the bill, and went on.

'What am I going to do this winter, do you think?' Aaron asked.

'What do you want to do?'

'Nay, that's what I want to know.'

'Do you want anything? I mean, does something drive you from inside?'

'I can't just rest,' said Aaron.

'Can't you settle down to something? – to a job, for instance?'

'I've not found the job I could settle down to, yet,' said Aaron.

'Why not?'

'It's just my nature.'

'Are you a seeker? Have you got a divine urge, or need?'

'How do I know?' laughed Aaron. 'Perhaps I've got a *damned* urge, at the bottom of me. I'm sure it's nothing divine.'

'Very well then. Now, in life, there are only two great dynamic urges – do you believe me?'

'How do I know?' laughed Aaron. 'Do you want to be believed?'

'No, I don't care a straw. Only for your own sake, you'd better believe me.'

'All right then – what about it?'

'Well then, there are only two great dynamic urges in *life*: love and power.'

'Love and power?' said Aaron. 'I don't see power as so very important.'

'You don't see because you don't look. But that's not the point. What sort of urge is your urge? Is it the love urge?'

'I don't know,' said Aaron.

'Yes, you do. You know that you have got an urge, don't you?'

'Yes –' rather unwillingly Aaron admitted it.

'Well then, what is it? Is it that you want to love, or to be obeyed?'

'A bit of both.'

'All right – a bit of both. And what are you looking for in love? A woman whom you can love, and who will love you, out and out and all in all and happy ever after sort of thing.'

'That's what I started out for, perhaps,' laughed Aaron.

'And now you know it's all my eye!' Aaron looked at Lilly, unwilling to admit it. Lilly began to laugh.

'You know it well enough,' he said. 'It's one of your lost illusions, my boy. Well then, what next? Is it a God you're after? Do you want a God you can strive to and attain, through love, and live happy ever after, countless millions of eternities, immortality and all that? Is this your little dodge?'

Again Aaron looked at Lilly with that odd double look of mockery and unwillingness to give himself away.

'All right then. You've got a love-urge that urges you to God, have you? Then go and join the Buddhists in Burma, or the newest fangled Christians in Europe. Go and stick your head in a bush of Nirvana or spiritual perfection. Trot off.'

'I won't,' said Aaron.

'You must. If you've got a love-urge, then give it its fulfilment.'

'I haven't got a love-urge.'

'You have. You want to get excited in love. You want to be carried away in love. You want to whoosh off in a nice little love-whoosh and lose yourself. Don't deny it. I know you do. You want passion to sweep you off on wings of fire till you surpass yourself, and like the swooping eagle swoop right into the sun. I know you, my love-boy.'

'Not any more – not any more. I've been had too often,' laughed Aaron.

'Bah, it's a lesson men never learn. No matter how sick they make themselves with love, they always rush for more, like a dog to his vomit.'

'Well, what am I to do then, if I'm not to love?' cried Aaron.

'You want to go on, from passion to passion, from ecstasy to ecstasy, from triumph to triumph, till you can whoosh away into glory, beyond yourself, all bonds loosened and happy ever after. Either that or Nirvana, opposite side of the medal.'

'There's probably more hate than love in me,' said Aaron.

'That's the recoil of the same urge. The anarchist, the criminal, the murderer, he is only the extreme lover acting on the recoil. But it is love: only in recoil. It flies back, the love-urge, and becomes a horror.'

'All right then. I'm a criminal and a murderer,' said Aaron.

'No, you're not. But you're a love-urger. And perhaps on the recoil just now. But listen to me. It's no good thinking the love-urge is the one and only. *Niente!* you can whoosh if you like, and get excited and carried away loving a woman, or humanity, or God. Swoop away in the love direction till you lose yourself. But that's where you're had. You can't lose yourself. You can try. But you might just as well try to swallow yourself. You'll only bite your fingers off in the attempt. You can't lose yourself, neither in woman nor humanity nor in God! You've always got yourself on your hands in the end: and a very raw and jaded and humiliated and nervous-neurasthenic self it is, too, in the end. A very nasty thing to wake up to is one's own raw self after an excessive love-whoosh. Look even at President Wilson: he love-whooshed for humanity, and found in the end he'd only got a very sorry self on his hands.

'So leave off. Leave off, my boy. Leave off love-whooshing. You can't lose yourself, so stop trying. The responsibility is on your own shoulders all the time, and no God which man has ever struck can take it off. You *are* yourself and so *be* yourself. Stick to it and abide by it. Passion or no passion, ecstasy or no ecstasy, urge or no urge, there's no goal outside you, where you can consumate like an eagle flying into the sun, or a moth into a candle. There's no goal outside you – and there's no God outside you. No God, whom you can get to and rest in. None. It's a case of

> Trot, trot to market, to buy a penny bun,
> And trot trot back again, as fast as you can run.

But there's no God outside you, whom you can rise to or sink to or swoop away to. You can't even gum yourself to a divine Nirvana moon. There is no goal outside you. None.

'There is only one thing, your own very self. So you'd better stick to it. You can't be any bigger than just yourself, so you needn't drag God in. You've got one job, and no more. There inside you lies your own very self, like a germinating egg, your precious Easter egg of your own soul. There it is, developing bit by bit, from one single egg-cell which you were at your conception in your mother's womb, on and on to the strange and peculiar complication in unity which never stops till you die – if then. You've got an innermost, integral unique self, and since it's the only thing you have got or ever will have, don't go trying to lose it. You've got to develop it, from the egg into the chicken, and from the chicken into the one-and-only phoenix, of which there can only be one at a time in the universe. There can only be one of you at a time in the universe – and one of me. So don't forget it. Your own single oneness is your destiny. Your destiny comes from within, from your own self-form. And you can't know it beforehand, neither your destiny nor your self-form. You can only develop it. You can only stick to your own very self, and *never* betray it. And by so sticking, you develop the one and only phoenix of your own self, and you unfold your own destiny, as a dandelion unfolds itself into a dandelion, and not into a stick of celery.

'Remember this, my boy: you've never got to deny the Holy Ghost which is inside you, your own soul's self. Never. Or you'll catch it. And you've never got to think you'll dodge the responsibility of your own soul's self, by loving or sacrificing or Nirvaning – or even anarchizing and throwing bombs. You never will . . .'

Aaron was silenced for a moment by this flood of words. Then he said, smiling:

'So I'd better sit tight on my soul, till it hatches, had I?'

'Oh yes. If your soul's urge urges you to love, then love. But always know that what you are doing is the fulfilling of your own soul's impulse. It's no good trying to act by prescription: not a bit. And it's no use getting into frenzies. If you've got to go in for love and passion, go in for them. But they aren't the goal. They're a mere means: a life-means, if you will. The only goal is the fulfilling of your own soul's active desire and suggestion. Be passionate as much as ever it is your nature to be passionate, and deeply sensual as far as you can be. Small souls have a small sensuality, deep souls a deep one. But remember, all the time, the responsibility is upon your own head, it all rests with your own lonely soul, the responsibility for your own action.'

'I never said it didn't,' said Aaron.

'You never said it did. You never accepted. You thought there was something outside, to justify you: God, or a creed, or a prescription. But remember, your soul inside you is your only Godhead. It develops your actions within you as a tree develops its own new cells. And the cells push on into buds and boughs and flowers. And these are your passion and your acts and your thoughts and expressions, your developing consciousness. You don't know beforehand, and you can't. You can only stick to your own soul through thick and thin.

'You are your own Tree of Life, roots and limbs and trunk. Somewhere within the wholeness of the tree lies the very self, the quick: its own innate Holy Ghost. And this Holy Ghost puts forth new buds, and pushes past old limits, and shakes off a whole body of dying leaves. And the old limits hate being empassed, and the old leaves hate to fall. But they must, if the tree-soul says so. . . .'

They had sat down again during this harangue, under a white wall. Aaron listened more to the voice than the words. It was more the sound value which entered his soul, the tone, the strange speech-music which sank into him. The sense he hardly heeded. And yet he understood, he knew. He understood, oh, so much more deeply than if he had listened with his head. And he answered an objection from the bottom of his soul.

'But you talk,' he said, 'as if we were like trees, alone by ourselves in the world. We aren't. If we love, it needs another person than ourselves. And if we hate, and even if we talk.'

'Quite,' said Lilly. 'And that's just the point. We've got to love and hate moreover – and even talk. But we haven't got to fix on any one of the modes, and say that's the only mode. It is such imbecility to say that love and love alone must rule. It is so obviously not the case. Yet we try and make it so.'

'I feel that,' said Aaron. 'It's all a lie.'

'It's worse. It's a half lie. But listen. I told you there were two urges – two great life-urges, didn't I? There may be more. But it comes on me so strongly, now, that there are two: love, and power. And we've been trying to work ourselves, at least as individuals, from the love-urge exclusively, hating the power-urge, and repressing it. And now I find we've got to accept the very thing we've hated.

'We've exhausted our love-urge, for the moment. And yet we try to force it to continue working. So we get inevitably anarchy and murder. It's no good. We've got to accept the power motive, accept it in deep responsibility, do you understand me? It is a great life motive. It was the great dark power-urge which kept Egypt so intensely living for so many centuries. It is a vast dark source of life and strength in us now, waiting either to issue into true action, or to burst into cataclysm. Power – the power-urge. The will-to-power – but not in Nietzsche's sense. Not intellectual power. Not mental power. Not conscious will-power. Not even wisdom. But dark, living, fructifying power. Do you know what I mean?'

'I don't know,' said Aaron.

'Take what you call love, for example. In the real way of love, the positive aim is to make the other person – or persons – happy. It devotes itself to the other or to others. But change the mode. Let the urge be the urge of power. Then the great desire is not happiness, neither of the beloved nor of oneself. Happiness is only one of many states, and it is horrible to think of fixing us down to one state. The urge of power does not seek for happiness any more than for any other state. It urges from within, darkly, for the displacing of the old leaves, the inception of the new. It is powerful and self-central, not seeking its centre outside, in some God or some beloved, but acting indomitably from within itself.

'And, of course, there must be one who urges, and one who is impelled. Just as in love there is beloved and a lover: the man is supposed to be the lover, the woman the beloved. Now, in the urge of power, it is the reverse. The woman must submit, but deeply, deeply submit. Not to any foolish fixed authority, not to any foolish and arbitrary will. But to something deep, deeper. To the soul in its dark motion of power and pride. We must reverse the poles. The woman must now submit – but deeply, deeply, and richly! No subservience. None of that. No slavery. A deep, unfathomable free submission.'

'You'll never get it,' said Aaron.

'You will, if you abandon the love idea and the love motive, and if you stand apart, and never bully, never force the conscious will. That's where Nietzsche was wrong. His was the conscious and benevolent will, in fact, the love-will. But the deep power-urge is not conscious of its aims: and it is certainly not consciously benevolent or love-directed. Whatever else happens, somewhere, sometime, the deep power-urge in a man will have to issue forth again, and woman will submit, livingly, not subjectively.'

'She never will,' persisted Aaron. 'Anything else will happen, but not that.'

'She will,' said Lilly, 'once man disengages himself from the love-mode, and stands clear. Once he stands clear, and the other great urge begins to flow in him, then the woman won't be able to resist. Her own soul will wish to yield itself.'

'Woman yield –?' Aaron re-echoed.

'Woman – and man too. Yield to the deep power-soul in the individual man, and obey implicitly. I don't go back on what I said before. I do believe that every man must fulfil his own soul, every woman must be herself, herself only, not some man's instrument, or some embodied theory. But the mode of our being is such that we can only live and have our being whilst we are implicit in one of the great dynamic modes. We *must* either love, or rule. And once the love-mode changes, as change it must, for we are worn out and becoming evil in its persistence, then the other mode will take place in us. And there will be profound, profound obedience in place of this love-crying, obedience to the incalculable power-urge. And men must submit to the greater soul in a man, for their guidance: and women must submit to the positive power-soul in man, for their being.'

'You'll never get it,' said Aaron.

'You will, when all men want it. All men say, they want a leader. Then let them in their souls *submit* to some greater soul than theirs. At present, when they say they want a leader, they mean they want an instrument, like Lloyd George. A mere instrument for their use. But it's more than that. It's the reverse. It's the deep, fathomless submission to the heroic soul in a greater man. You, Aaron, you too have the need to submit. You, too, have the need livingly to yield to a more heroic soul, to give yourself. You know you have. And you know it isn't love. It is life-submission. And you know it. But you kick against the pricks. And perhaps you'd rather die than yield. And so, die you must. It is your affair.'

There was a long pause. Then Aaron looked up into Lilly's face. It was dark and remote-seeming. It was like a Byzantine eikon at the moment.

'And whom shall I submit to?' he said.

'Your soul will tell you,' replied the other.

D.H. LAWRENCE

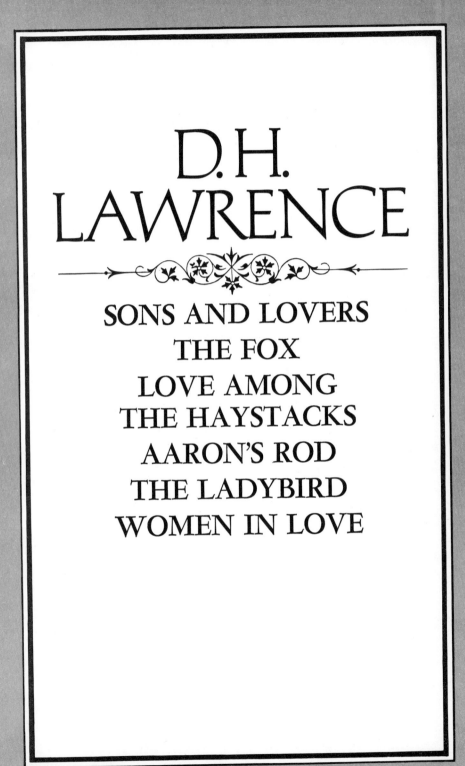

SONS AND LOVERS

THE FOX

LOVE AMONG
THE HAYSTACKS

AARON'S ROD

THE LADYBIRD

WOMEN IN LOVE

How many swords had Lady Beveridge in her pierced heart! Yet there always seemed room for another. Since she had determined that her heart of pity and kindness should never die. If it had not been for this determination she herself might have died of sheer agony, in the years 1916 and 1917, when her boys were killed, and her brother, and death seemed to be mowing with wide swaths through her family. But let us forget.

Lady Beveridge loved humanity, and come what might, she would continue to love it. Nay, in the human sense, she would love her enemies. Not the criminals among the enemy, the men who committed atrocities. But the men who were enemies through no choice of their own. She would be swept into no general hate.

Somebody had called her the soul of England. It was not ill said, though she was half Irish. But of an old, aristocratic, loyal family famous for its brilliant men. And she, Lady Beveridge, had for years as much influence on the tone of English politics as any individual alive. The close friend of the real leaders in the House of Lords and in the Cabinet, she was content that the men should act, so long as they breathed from her as from the rose of life the pure fragrance of truth and genuine love. She had no misgiving regarding her own spirit.

She, she would never lower her delicate silken flag. For instance, throughout all the agony of the war she never forgot the enemy prisoners; she was determined to do her best for them. During the first years she still had influence. But during the last years of the war power slipped out of the hands of her and her sort, and she found she could do nothing any more: almost nothing. Then it seemed as if the many swords had gone home into the heart of this little, unyielding Mater Dolorosa. The new generation jeered at her. She was a shabby, old-fashioned little aristocrat, and her drawing-room was out of date.

But we anticipate. The years 1916 and 1917 were the years when the old spirit died for ever in England. But Lady Beveridge struggled on. She was being beaten.

It was in the winter of 1917 – or in the late autumn. She had been for a fortnight sick, stricken, paralysed by the fearful death of her youngest boy. She felt she *must* give in, and just die. And then she remembered how many others were lying in agony.

So she rose, trembling, frail, to pay a visit to the hospital where lay the enemy sick and wounded, near London. Countess Beveridge was still a privileged woman. Society was beginning to jeer at this little, worn bird of an out-of-date righteousness and aesthetic. But they dared not think ill of her.

She ordered the car and went alone. The Earl, her husband, had taken his gloom to Scotland. So, on a sunny, wan November morning Lady Beveridge descended at the hospital, Hurst Place. The guard knew her, and saluted as she passed. Ah, she was used to such deep respect! It was strange that she felt it so bitterly, when the respect became shallower. But she did. It was the beginning of the end to her.

The matron went with her into the ward. Alas, the beds were all full, and men were even lying on pallets on the floor. There was a desperate, crowded dreariness and helplessness in the place: as if nobody wanted to make a sound or utter a word. Many of the men were haggard and unshaven, one was delirious, and talking fitfully in the Saxon dialect. It went to Lady Beveridge's heart. She had been educated in Dresden, and had had many dear friendships in the city. Her children also had been educated there. She heard the Saxon dialect with pain.

She was a little, frail, bird-like woman, elegant, but with that touch of the blue-stocking of the 'Nineties which was unmistakable. She fluttered delicately from bed to bed, speaking in perfect German, but with a thin, English intonation: and always asking if there was anything she could do. The men were mostly officers and gentlemen. They made little requests which she wrote down in a book. Her long, pale, rather worn face, and her nervous little gestures somehow inspired confidence.

One man lay quite still, with his eyes shut. He had a black beard. His face was rather small and sallow. He might be dead. Lady Beveridge looked at him earnestly, and fear came into her face.

'Why, Count Dionys!' she said, fluttered. 'Are you asleep?'

It was Count Johann Dionys Psanek, a Bohemian. She had known him when he was a boy, and only in the spring of 1914 he and his wife had stayed with Lady Beveridge in her country house in Leicestershire.

His black eyes opened: large, black, unseeing eyes, with curved black lashes. He was a small man, small as a boy, and his face too was rather small. But all the lines were fine, as if they had been fired with a keen male energy. Now the yellowish swarthy paste of his flesh seemed dead, and the fine black brows seemed drawn on the face of one dead. The eyes, however, were alive: but only just alive, unseeing and unknowing.

'You know me, Count Dionys? You know me, don't you?' said Lady Beveridge, bending forward over the bed.

There was no reply for some time. Then the black eyes gathered a look of recognition, and there came the ghost of a polite smile.

'Lady Beveridge.' The lips formed the words. There was practically no sound.

'I am so glad you can recognize me. And I am so sorry you are hurt. I am so sorry.'

The black eyes watched her from that terrible remoteness of death, without changing.

'There is nothing I can do for you? Nothing at all?' she said, always speaking German.

And after a time, and from a distance, came the answer from his eyes, a look of weariness, of refusal, and a wish to be left alone; he was unable to strain himself into consciousness. His eyelids dropped.

'I am so sorry,' she said. 'If ever there is anything I can do –'

The eyes opened again, looking at her. He seemed at last to hear, and it was as if his eyes made the last weary gesture of a polite bow. Then slowly his eyelids closed again.

Poor Lady Beveridge felt another sword-thrust of sorrow in her heart, as she stood looking down at the motionless face, and at the black fine beard. The black hairs came out of his skin thin and fine, not very close together. A queer, dark, aboriginal little face he had, with a fine little nose: not an Aryan, surely. And he was going to die.

He had a bullet through the upper part of his chest, and another bullet had broken one of his ribs. He had been in hospital five days.

Lady Beveridge asked the matron to ring her up if anything happened. Then she drove away, saddened. Instead of going to Beveridge House, she went to her daughter's flat near the park – near Hyde Park. Lady Daphne was poor. She had married a commoner, son of one of the most famous politicians in England, but a man with no money. And Earl Beveridge had wasted most of the large fortune that had come to him, so that the daughter had very little, comparatively.

Lady Beveridge suffered, going in the narrow doorway into the rather ugly flat. Lady Daphne was sitting by the electric fire in the small yellow drawing-room, talking to a visitor. She rose at once, seeing her little mother.

'Why, mother, ought you to be out? I'm sure not.'

'Yes, Daphne darling. Of course I ought to be out.'

'How are you?' The daugher's voice was slow and sonorous, protective, sad. Lady Daphne was tall, only twenty-five years old. She had been one of the beauties, when the war broke out, and her father had hoped she would make a splendid match. Truly, she had married fame: but without money. Now, sorrow, pain, thwarted passion had done her great damage. Her husband was missing in the East. Her baby had been born dead. Her two darling brothers were dead. And she was ill, always ill.

A tall, beautifully-built girl, she had the fine stature of her father. Her shoulders were still straight. But how thin her white throat! She wore a simple black frock stitched with coloured wool round the top, and held in a loose coloured girdle: otherwise no ornaments. And her face was lovely, fair, with a soft exotic white complexion and delicate pink cheeks. Her hair was soft and heavy, of a lovely pallid gold colour, ash-blonde. Her hair, her complexion were so perfectly cared for as to be almost artificial, like a hot-house flower.

But alas, her beauty was a failure. She was threatened with phthisis, and was far too thin. Her eyes were the saddest part of her. They had slightly reddened rims, nerve-worn, with heavy, veined lids that seemed as if they did not want to keep up. The eyes themselves were large and of a beautiful green-blue colour. But they were full, languid, almost glaucous.

Standing as she was, a tall, finely-built girl, looking down with affectionate care on her mother, she filled the heart with ashes. The little pathetic mother, so wonderful in her way, was not really to be pitied for all her sorrow. Her life was in her sorrows, and her efforts on behalf of the sorrows of others. But Daphne was not born for grief and philanthropy. With her splendid frame, and her lovely, long, strong legs, she was Artemis or Atlanta rather than Daphne. There was a certain width of brow and even of chin that spoke a strong, reckless nature, and the curious, distraught slant of her eyes told of a wild energy dammed up inside her.

That was what ailed her: her own wild energy. She had it from her father, and from her father's desperate race. The earldom had begun with a riotous, dare-devil border soldier, and this was the blood that flowed on. And alas, what was to be done with it?

Daphne had married an adorable husband: truly an adorable husband. Whereas she needed a dare-devil. But in her *mind* she hated all dare-devils: she had been brought up by her mother to admire only the good.

So, her reckless, anti-philanthropic passion could find no outlet – and *should* find no outlet, she thought. So her own blood turned against her, beat on her own nerves, and destroyed her. It was nothing but frustration and anger which made her ill, and made the doctors fear consumption. There it was, drawn on her rather wide mouth: frustration, anger, bitterness. There it was the same in the roll of her green-blue eyes, a slanting, averted look: the same anger furtively turning back on itself. This anger reddened her eyes and shattered her nerves. And yet her whole will was fixed in her adoption of her mother's creed, and in condemnation of her handsome, proud, brutal father, who had made so much misery in the family. Yes, her will was fixed in the determination that life should be gentle and good and benevolent. Whereas her blood was reckless, the blood of dare-devils. Her will was the stronger of the two. But her blood had its revenge on her. So it is with strong natures today: shattered from the inside.

'You have no news, darling?' asked the mother.

'No. My father-in-law had information that British prisoners had been brought into Hasrun, and that details would be forwarded by the Turks. And there was a rumour from some Arab prisoners that Basil was one of the British brought in wounded.'

'When did you hear this?'

'Primrose came in this morning.'

'Then we can hope, dear.'

'Yes.'

Never was anything more dull and bitter than Daphne's affirmative of hope. Hope had become almost a curse to her. She wished there need be no such thing. Ha, the torment of hoping, and the *insult* to one's soul. Like the importunate widow dunning her for deserts. Why could it not all be just clean disaster, and have done with it? This dilly-dallying with despair was worse than despair. She had hoped so much: ah, for her darling brothers she had hoped with such anguish. And the two she loved best were dead. So were most others she had hoped for, dead. Only this uncertainty about her husband still rankling.

'You feel better, dear?' said the little, unquenched mother.

'Rather better,' came the resentful answer.

'And your night?'

'No better.'

There was a pause.

'You are coming to lunch with me, Daphne darling?'

'No, mother dear. I promised to lunch at the Howards with Primrose. But I needn't go for a quarter of an hour. Do sit down.'

Both women seated themselves near the electric fire. There was that bitter pause, neither knowing what to say. Then Daphne roused herself to look at her mother.

'Are you sure you were fit to go out?' she said. 'What took you out so suddenly?'

'I went to Hurst Place, dear. I had the men on my mind, after the way the newspapers have been talking.'

'Why ever do you read the newspapers!' blurted Daphne, with a certain burning, acid anger. 'Well,' she said, more composed. 'And do you feel better now you've been?'

'So many people suffer besides ourselves, darling.'

'I know they do. Makes it all the worse. It wouldn't matter if it were only just us. At least, it would matter, but one could bear it more easily. To be just one of a crowd all in the same state.'

'And some even worse, dear.'

'Oh, quite! And the worse it is for all, the worse it is for one.'

'Is that so, darling? Try not to see too darkly. I feel if I can give just a little bit of myself to help the others – you know – it alleviates me. I feel that what I can give to the men lying there, Daphne, I give to my own boys. I can only help them now through helping others. But I can still do that, Daphne, my girl.'

And the mother put her little white hand into the long, white, cold hand of her daughter. Tears came to Daphne's eyes, and a fearful stony grimace to her mouth.

'It's so wonderful of you that you can feel like that,' she said.

'But you feel the same, my love. I know you do.'

'No, I don't. Everyone I see suffering these same awful things, it makes me wish more for the end of the world. And I quite see that the world won't end –'

'But it will get better, dear. This time it's like a great sickness – like a terrible pneumonia tearing the breast of the world.'

'Do you believe it will get better? I don't.'

'It will get better. Of course it will get better. It is perverse to think otherwise, Daphne. Remember what *has* been before, even in Europe. Ah, Daphne, we must take a bigger view.'

'Yes, I suppose we must.'

The daughter spoke rapidly, from the lips, in a resonant, monotonous tone. The mother spoke from the heart.

'And Daphne, I found an old friend among the men at Hurst Place.'

'Who?'

'Little Count Dionys. You remember him?'

'Quite. What's wrong?'

'Wounded rather badly – through the chest. So ill.'

'Did you speak to him?'

'Yes. I recognized him in spite of his beard.'

'Beard!'

'Yes – a black beard. I suppose he could not be shaven. It seems strange that he is still alive, poor man.'

'Why strange? He isn't old. How old is he?'

'Between thirty and forty. But so ill, so wounded, Daphne. And so small. So small, so sallow – *smorto*, you know the Italian word. The way dark people look. There is something so distressing in it.'

'Does he look *very* small now – uncanny?' asked the daughter.

'No, not uncanny. Something of the terrible far-awayness of a child that is very ill and can't tell you what hurts it. Poor Count Dionys. Daphne. I didn't know, dear, that his eyes were so black, and his lashes so curved and long. I had never thought of him as beautiful.'

'Nor I. Only a little comical. Such a dapper little man.'

'Yes. And yet now, Daphne, there is something remote and in a sad way heroic in his dark face. Something primitive.'

'What did he say to you?'

'He couldn't speak to me. Only with his lips, just my name.'

'So bad as that?'

'Oh yes. They are afraid he will die.'

'Poor Count Dionys. I liked him. He was a bit like a monkey, but he had his points. He gave me a thimble on my seventeenth birthday. Such an amusing thimble.'

'I remember, dear.'

'Unpleasant wife, though. Wonder if he minds dying far away from her. Wonder if she knows.'

'I think not. They didn't even know his name properly. Only that he was a colonel of such and such a regiment.'

'Fourth Cavalry,' said Daphne. 'Poor Count Dionys. Such a lovely name, I always thought: Count Johann Dionys Psanek. Extraordinary dandy he was. And an amazingly good dancer, small, yet electric. Wonder if he minds dying.'

'He was so full of life, in his own little animal way. They say small people are always conceited. But he doesn't look conceited now, dear. Something ages old in his face – and, yes, a certain beauty, Daphne.'

'You mean long lashes.'

'No. So still, so solitary – and ages old, in his race. I suppose he must belong to one of those curious little aboriginal races of Central Europe. I felt quite new beside him.'

'Now nice of you,' said Daphne.

Nevertheless, next day Daphne telephoned to Hurst Place to ask for news of him. He was about the same. She telephoned every day. Then she was told he was a little stronger. The day she received the message that her husband was wounded and a prisoner in Turkey, and that his wounds were healing, she forgot to telephone for news of the little enemy Count. And the following day she telephoned that she was coming to the hospital to see him.

He was awake, more restless, more in physical excitement. They could see the nausea of pain round his nose. His face seemed to Daphne curiously hidden behind the black beard, which nevertheless was thin, each hair coming thin and fine, singly, from the sallow, slightly translucent skin. In the same way his moustache made a thin black line round his mouth. His eyes were wide open, very black, and of no legible expression. He watched the two women coming down the crowded, dreary room, as if he did not see them. His eyes seemed too wide.

It was a cold day, and Daphne was huddled in a black sealskin coat with a skunk collar pulled up to her ears, and a dull gold cap with wings pulled down on her brow. Lady Beveridge wore her sable coat, and had that odd, untidy elegance which was natural to her, rather like a ruffled chicken.

Daphne was upset by the hospital. She looked from right to left in spite of herself, and everything gave her a dull feeling of horror: the terror of these sick, wounded enemy men. She loomed tall and obtrusive in her furs by the bed, her little mother at her side.

'I hope you don't mind my coming!' she said in German to the sick man. Her tongue felt rusty, speaking the language.

'Who is it then?' he asked.

'It is my daughter, Lady Daphne. You remembered *me*, Lady Beveridge! This is my daughter, whom you knew in Saxony. She was so sorry to hear you were wounded.'

The black eyes rested on the little lady. Then they returned to the looming figure of Daphne. And a certain fear grew on the low, sick brow. It was evident the presence loomed and frightened him. He turned his face aside. Daphne noticed how his fine black hair grew uncut over his small, animal ears.

'You don't remember me, Count Dionys?' she said dully.

'Yes,' he said. But he kept his face averted.

She stood there feeling confused and miserable, as if she had made a *faux pas* in coming.

'Would you rather be left alone?' she said. 'I'm sorry.'

Her voice was monotonous. She felt suddenly stifled in her closed furs, and threw her coat open, showing her thin white throat and plain black slip dress on her flat breast. He turned again unwillingly to look at her. He looked at her as if she were some strange creature standing near him.

'Good-bye,' she said. 'Do get better.'

She was looking at him with a queer, slanting, downward look of her heavy eyes as she turned away. She was still a little red round the eyes, with nervous exhaustion.

'You are so tall,' he said, still frightened.

'I was always tall,' she replied, turning half to him again.

'And I, small,' he said.

'I am so glad you are getting better,' she said.

'I am not glad,' he said.

'Why? I'm sure you are. Just as we are glad because we want you to get better.'

'Thank you,' he said. 'I have wished to die.'

'Don't do that, Count Dionys. Do get better,' she said, in the rather deep, laconic manner of her girlhood. He looked at her with a further look of recognition. But his short, rather pointed nose was lifted with the disgust and weariness of pain, his brows were tense. He watched her with that curious flame of suffering which is forced to give a little outside attention, but which speaks only to itself.

'Why did they not let me die?' he said. 'I wanted death now.'

'No,' she said. 'You mustn't. You must live. If we *can* live we must.'

'I wanted death,' he said.

'Ah, well,' she said, 'even death we can't have when we want it, or when we think we want it.'

'That is true,' he said, watching her with the same wide black eyes. 'Please to sit down. You are too tall as you stand.'

It was evident he was a little frightened still by her looming, overhanging figure.

'I am sorry I am too tall,' she said, taking a chair which a man-nurse had brought her. Lady Beveridge had gone away to speak with the men. Daphne sat down, not knowing what to say further. The pitch-black look in the Count's wide eyes puzzled her.

'Why do you come here? Why does your lady mother come?' he said.

'To see if we can do anything,' she answered.

'When I am well, I will thank your ladyship.'

'All right,' she replied. 'When you are well I will let my lord the Count thank me. Please do get well.'

'We are enemies,' he said.

'Who? You and I and my mother?'

'Are we not? The most difficult thing is to be sure of anything. If they had let me die!'

'This is at least ungrateful, Count Dionys.'

'*Lady Daphne!* Yes. *Lady Daphne!* Beautiful, the name is. You are always called Lady Daphne? I remember you were so bright a maiden.'

'More or less,' she said, answering his question.

'Ach! We should all have new names now. I thought of a name for myself, but I have forgotten it. No longer Johann Dionys. That is shot away. I am Karl or Wilhelm or Ernst or Georg. Those are names I hate. Do you hate them?'

'I don't like them – but I don't hate them. And you mustn't leave off being Count Johann Dionys. If you do I shall have to leave off being Daphne. I like your name so much.'

'Lady Daphne! Lady Daphne!' he repeated. 'Yes, it rings well, it sounds beautiful to me. I think I talk foolishly. I hear myself talking foolishly to you.' He looked at her anxiously.

'Not at all,' she said.

'Ach! I have a head on my shoulders that is like a child's windmill, and I can't prevent its making foolish words. Please to go away, not to hear me. I can hear myself.'

'Can't I do anything for you?' she asked.

'No, no! No, no! If I could be buried deep, very deep down, where everything is forgotten! But they draw me up, back to the surface. I would not mind if they buried me alive, if it were very deep, and dark, and the earth heavy above.'

'Don't say that,' she replied, rising.

'No, I am saying it when I don't wish to say it. Why am I here? Why am I here? Why have I survived into this? Why can I not stop talking?'

He turned his face aside. The black, fine, elfish hair was so long, and pushed up in tufts from the smooth brown nape of his neck. Daphne looked at him in sorrow. He could not turn his body. He could only move his head. And he lay with his face averted, the fine hair of his beard coming up strange from under his chin and from his throat, up to the socket of his ear. He lay quite still in this position. And she turned away, looking for her mother. She had suddenly realized that the bonds, the connections between him and his life in the world had broken, and he lay there a bit of loose, palpitating humanity, shot away from the body of humanity.

It was ten days before she went to the hospital again. She had wanted never to go again, to forget him, as one tries to forget incurable things. But she could not forget him. He came again and again into her mind. She had to go back. She had heard that he was recovering very slowly.

He really looked better. His eyes were not so wide open, they had lost that black, inky exposure which had given him such an unnatural look, unpleasant. He watched her guardedly. She had taken off her furs, and wore only her dress and a dark, soft feather toque.

'How are you?' she said, keeping her face averted, unwilling to meet his eyes.

'Thank you, I am better. The nights are not so long.'

She shuddered, knowing what long nights meant. He saw the worn look in her face too, the reddened rims of her eyes.

'Are you not well? Have you some trouble?' he asked her.

'No, no,' she answered.

She had brought a handful of pinky, daisy-shaped flowers.

'Do you care for flowers?' she asked.

He looked at them. Then he slowly shook his head.

'No,' he said. 'If I am on horseback, riding through the marshes or through the hills, I like to see them below me. But not here. Not now. Please do not bring flowers into this grave. Even in gardens, I do not like them. When they are upholstery to human life.'

'I will take them away again,' she said.

'Please do. Please give them to the nurse.'

Daphne paused.

'Perhaps,' she said, 'you wish I would not come to disturb you.'

He looked into her face.

'No,' he said. 'You are like a flower behind a rock, near an icy water. No, you do not live too much. I am afraid I cannot talk sensibly. I wish to hold my mouth shut. If I open it, I talk this absurdity. It escapes from my mouth.'

'It is not so very absurd,' she said.

But he was silent – looking away from her.

'I want you to tell me if there is really nothing I can do for you,' she said.

'Nothing,' he answered.

'If I can write any letter for you.'

'None,' he answered.

'But your wife and your two children. Do they know where you are?'

'I should think not.'

'And where are they?'

'I do not know. Probably they are in Hungary.'

'Not at your home?'

'My castle was burnt down in a riot. My wife went to Hungary with the children. She has her relatives there. She went away from me. I wished it too. Alas for her, I wished to be dead. Pardon me the personal tone.'

Daphne looked down at him – the queer, obstinate little fellow.

'But you have somebody you wish to tell – somebody you want to hear from?'

'Nobody. Nobody. I wish the bullet had gone through my heart. I wish to be dead. It is only I have a devil in my body that will not die.'

She looked at him as he lay with closed, averted face.

'Surely it is not a devil which keeps you alive,' she said. 'It is something good.'

'No, a devil,' he said.

She sat looking at him with a long, slow, wondering look.

'Must one hate a devil that makes one live?' she asked.

He turned his eyes to her with a touch of a satiric smile.

'If one lives, no,' he said.

She looked away from him the moment he looked at her. For her life she could not have met his dark eyes direct.

She left him, and he lay still. He neither read nor talked throughout the long winter nights and the short winter days. He only lay for hours with black, open eyes, seeing everything around with a touch of disgust, and heeding nothing.

Daphne went to see him now and then. She never forgot him for long. He seemed to come into her mind suddenly, as if by sorcery.

One day he said to her:

'I see you are married. May I ask you who is your husband?'

She told him. She had had a letter also from Basil. The Count smiled slowly.

'You can look forward,' he said, 'to a happy reunion and new, lovely children, Lady Daphne. Is it not so?'

'Yes, of course,' she said.

'But you are ill,' he said to her.

'Yes – rather ill.'

'Of what?'

'Oh!' she answered fretfully, turning her face aside. 'They talk about lungs.' She hated speaking of it. 'Why, how do you know I am ill?' she added quickly.

Again he smiled slowly.

'I see it in your face, and hear it in your voice. One would say the Evil One had cast a spell on you.'

'Oh no,' she said hastily. 'But do I look ill?'

'Yes. You look as if something had struck you across the face, and you could not forget it.'

'Nothing has,' she said. 'Unless it's the war.'

'The war!' he repeated.

'Oh, well, don't let us talk of it,' she said.

Another time he said to her:

'The year has turned – the sun must shine at last, even in England. I am afraid of getting well too soon. I am a prisoner, am I not? But I wish the sun would shine. I wish the sun would shine on my face.'

'You won't always be a prisoner. The war will end. And the sun *does* shine even in the winter in England,' she said.

'I wish it would shine on my face,' he said.

So that when in February there came a blue, bright morning, the morning that suggests yellow crocuses and the smell of a mezereon tree and the smell of damp, warm earth, Daphne hastily got a taxi and drove out to the hospital.

'You have come to put me in the sun,' he said the moment he saw her.

'Yes, that's what I came for,' she said.

She spoke to the matron, and had his bed carried out where there was a big window that came low. There he was put full in the sun. Turning, he could see the blue sky and the twinkling tops of purplish, bare trees.

'The world! The world!' he murmured.

He lay with his eyes shut, and the sun on his swarthy, transparent, immobile face. The breath came and went through his nostrils invisibly. Daphne wondered how he could lie so still, how he could look so immobile. It was true as her mother had said: he looked as if he had been cast in the mould when the metal was white hot, all his lines were so clean. So small, he was, and in his way perfect.

Suddenly his dark eyes opened and caught her looking.

'The sun makes even anger open like a flower,' he said.

'Whose anger?' she said.

'I don't know. But I can make flowers, looking through my eyelashes. Do you know how?'

'You mean rainbows?'

'Yes, flowers.'

And she saw him, with a curious smile on his lips, looking through his almost closed eyelids at the sun.

'The sun is neither English nor German nor Bohemian,' he said. 'I am a subject of the sun. I belong to the fire-worshippers.'

'Do you?' she replied.

'Yes, truly, by tradition.' He looked at her smiling. 'You stand there like a flower that will melt,' he added.

She smiled slowly at him with a slow, cautious look of her eyes, as if she feared something.

'I am much more solid than you imagine,' she said.

Still he watched her.

'One day,' he said, 'before I go, let me wrap your hair round my hands, will you?' He lifted his thin, short, dark hands. 'Let me wrap your hair round my hands, like a bandage. They hurt me. I don't know what it is. I think it is all the gun explosions. But if you let me wrap your hair round my hands. You know, it is the hermetic gold – but so much of water in it, of the moon. That will soothe my hands. One day, will you?'

'Let us wait till the day comes,' she said.

'Yes,' he answered, and was still again.

'It troubles me,' he said after a while, 'that I complain like a child, and ask for things. I feel I have lost my manhood for the time being. The continual explosions of guns and shells! It seems to have driven my soul out of me like a bird frightened away at last. But it will come back, you know. And I am so grateful to you; you are good to me when I am soulless, and you don't take advantage of me. Your soul is quiet and heroic.'

'Don't,' she said. 'Don't talk!'

The expression of shame and anguish and disgust crossed his face.

'It is because I can't help it,' he said. 'I have lost my soul, and I can't stop talking to you. I can't stop. But I don't talk to anyone else. I try not to talk, but I can't prevent it. Do you draw the words out of me?'

Her wide, green-blue eyes seemed like the heart of some curious, full-open flower, some Christmas rose with its petals of snow and flush. Her hair glinted heavy, like water-gold. She stood there passive and indomitable with the wide-eyed persistence of her wintry, blonde nature.

Another day when she came to see him, he watched her for a time, then he said:

'Do they all tell you you are lovely, you are beautiful?'

'Not quite all,' she replied.

'But your husband?'

'He has said so.'

'Is he gentle? Is he tender? Is he a dear lover?'

She turned her face aside, displeased.

'Yes,' she replied curtly.

He did not answer. And when she looked again he was lying with his eyes shut, a faint smile seeming to curl round his short, transparent nose. She could faintly see the flesh through his beard, as water through reeds. His black hair was brushed smooth as glass, his black eyebrows glinted like a curve of black glass on the swarthy opalescence of his brow.

Suddenly he spoke, without opening his eyes.

'You have been very kind to me,' he said.

'Have I? Nothing to speak of.'

He opened his eyes and looked at her.

'Everything finds its mate,' he said. 'The ermine and the pole-cat and the buzzard. One thinks so often that only the dove and the nightingale and the stag with his antlers have gentle mates. But the pole-cat and the ice-bears of the north have their mates. And a white she-bear lies with her cubs under a rock as a snake lies hidden, and the male bear slowly swims back from the sea, like a clot of snow or a shadow of a white cloud passing on the speckled sea. I have seen her too, and I did not shoot her, nor him when he landed with fish in his mouth, wading wet and slow and yellow-white over the black stones.'

'You have been in the North Sea?'

'Yes. And with the Eskimo in Siberia, and across the Tundras. And a white sea-hawk makes a nest on a high stone, and sometimes looks out with her white head over the edge of the rocks. It is not only a world of men, Lady Daphne.'

'Not by any means,' said she.

'Else it were a sorry place.'

'It is bad enough,' said she.

'Foxes have their holes. They have even their mates, Lady Daphne, that they bark to and are answered. And an adder finds his female. Psanek means an outlaw; did you know?'

'I did not.'

'Outlaws and brigands, have often the finest woman-mates.'

'They do,' she said.

'I will be Psanek, Lady Daphne. I will not be Johann Dionys any more. I will be Psanek. The law has shot me through.'

'You might be Psanek and Johann and Dionys as well,' she said.

'With the sun on my face? Maybe,' he said, looking to the sun.

There were some lovely days in the spring of 1918. In March the Count was able to get up. They dressed him in a simple, dark-blue uniform. He was not very thin, only swarthy-transparent, now his beard was shaven and his hair was cut. His smallness made him noticeable, but he was masculine, perfect in his small stature. All the smiling dapperness that had made him seem like a monkey to Daphne when she was a girl had gone now. His eyes were dark and haughty; he seemed to keep inside his own reserves, speaking to nobody if he could help it, neither to the nurses nor the visitors nor to his fellow-prisoners, fellow-officers. He seemed to put a shadow between himself and them, and from across this shadow he looked with his dark, beautifully-fringed eyes, as a proud little beast from the shadow of its lair. Only to Daphne he laughed and chatted.

She sat with him one day in March on the terrace of the hospital, on a morning when white clouds went endlessly and magnificently about a blue sky, and the sunshine felt warm after the blots of shadow.

'When you had a birthday, and you were seventeen, didn't I give you a thimble?' he asked her.

'Yes. I have it still.'

'With a gold snake at the bottom, and a Mary-beetle of green stone at the top, to push the needle with.'

'Yes.'

'Do you ever use it?'

'No. I sew so rarely.'

'Would it displease you to sew something for me?'

'You won't admire my stitches. What would you wish me to sew?'

'Sew me a shirt that I can wear. I have never before worn shirts from a shop, with a maker's name inside. It is very distasteful to me.'

She looked at him – his haughty little brows.

'Shall I ask my maid to do it?' she said.

'Oh, please, no! Oh, please, no, do not trouble. No, please, I would not want it unless you sewed it yourself, with the Psanek thimble.'

She paused before she answered. Then came her slow:

'Why?'

He turned and looked at her with dark, searching eyes.

'I have no reason,' he said, rather haughtily.

She left the matter there. For two weeks she did not go to see him. Then suddenly one day she took the bus down Oxford Street and brought some fine white flannel. She decided he must wear flannel.

That afternoon she drove out to Hurst Place. She found him sitting on the terrace, looking across the garden at the red suburb of London smoking fumily in the near distance, interrupted by patches of uncovered ground and a flat, tin-roofed laundry.

'Will you give me the measurements for your shirt?' she said.

'The number of the neck-band of this English shirt is fifteen. If you ask the matron she will give you the measurement. It is a little too large, too long in the sleeves, you see,' and he shook his shirt cuff over his wrist. 'Also too long altogether.'

'Mine will probably be unwearable when I've made them,' said she.

'Oh no. Let your maid direct you. But please do not let her sew them.'

'Will you tell my why you want me to do it?'

'Because I am a prisoner, in other people's clothes, and I have nothing of my own. All the things I touch are distasteful to me. If your maid sews for me, it will still be the same. Only you might give me what I want, something that buttons round my throat and on my wrists.'

'And in Germany – or in Austria?'

'My mother sewed for me. And after her, my mother's sister, who was the head of my house.'

'Not your wife?'

'Naturally not. She would have been insulted. She was never more than a guest in my house. In my family there are old traditions – but with me they have come to an end. I had best try to revive them.'

'Beginning with traditions of shirts?'

'Yes. In our family the shirt should be made and washed by a woman of our own blood: but when we marry, by the wife. So when I married I had sixty shirts, and many other things – sewn by my mother and my aunt, all with my initial, and the ladybird, which is our crest.'

'And where did they put the initial?'

'Here!' He put his finger on the back of his neck, on the swarthy, transparent skin. 'I fancy I can feel the embroidered ladybird still. On our linen we had no crown: only the ladybird.'

She was silent, thinking.

'You will forgive what I ask you?' he said, 'since I am a prisoner and can do no other, and since fate has made you so that you understand the world as I understand it. It is not really indelicate, what I ask you. There will be a ladybird on your finger when you sew, and those who wear the ladybird understand.'

'I suppose,' she mused, 'it is as bad to have your bee in your shirt as in your bonnet.'

He looked at her with round eyes.

'Don't you know what it is to have a bee in your bonnet?' she said.

'No.'

'To have a bee buzzing among your hair! To be out of your wits,' she smiled at him.

'So!' he said. 'Ah, the Psaneks have had a ladybird in their bonnets for many hundred years.'

'Quite, quite mad,' she said.

'It may be,' he answered. 'But with my wife I was quite sane for ten years. Now give me the madness of the ladybird. The world I was sane about has gone raving. The ladybird I was mad with is wise still.'

'At least, when I sew the shirts, if I sew them,' she said, 'I shall have the ladybird at my finger's end.'

'You want to laugh at me.'

'But surely you know you are funny, with your family insect.'

'My family insect? Now you want to be rude to me.'

'How many spots must it have?'

'Seven.'

'Three on each wing. And what do I do with the odd one?'

'You put that one between its teeth, like the cake for Cerberus.'

'I'll remember that.'

When she brought the first shirt, she gave it to the matron. Then she found Count Dionys sitting on the terrace. It was a beautiful spring day. Near at hand were tall elm trees and some rooks cawing.

'What a lovely day!' she said. 'Are you liking the world any better?'

'The world?' he said, looking up at her with the same old discontent and disgust on his fine, transparent nose.

'Yes,' she replied, a shadow coming over her face.

'Is this the world – all those little red-brick boxes in rows, where the couples of little people live, who decree my destiny?'

'You don't like England?'

'Ah, England! Little houses like little boxes, each with its domestic Englishman and his domestic wife, each ruling the world because all are alike, so alike.'

'But England isn't all houses.'

'Fields then! Little fields with innumerable hedges. Like a net with an irregular mesh, pinned down over this island and everything under the net. Ah, Lady Daphne, forgive me. I am ungrateful. I am so full of bile, of spleen, you say. My only wisdom is to keep my mouth shut.'

'Why do you hate everything?' she said, her own face going bitter.

'Not everything. If I were free! If I were outside the law. Ah, Lady Daphne, how does one get outside the law?'

'By going inside oneself,' she said. 'Not outside.'

His face took on a greater expression of disgust.

'No, no. I am a man, I am a man, even if I am little. I am not a spirit, that coils itself inside a shell. In my soul is anger, anger, anger. Give me room for my anger. Give me room for that.'

His black eyes tooked keenly into hers. She rolled her eyes as if in a half-trance. And in a monotonous, tranced voice she said:

'Much better get over your anger. And *why* are you angry?'

'There is no why. If it were love, you would not ask me, *why do you love*? But it is anger, anger, anger. What else can I call it? And there is no why.'

Again he looked at her with his dark, sharp questioning, tormented eyes.

'Can't you get rid of it?' she said, looking aside.

'If a shell exploded and blew me into a thousand fragments,' he said, 'it would not destroy the anger that is in me. I know that. No, it will never dissipate. And to die is no release. The anger goes on gnashing and whimpering in death. Lady Daphne, Lady Daphne, we have used up all the love, and this is what is left.'

'Perhaps *you* have used up all your love,' she replied. 'You are not everybody.'

'I know it. I speak for me and you.'

'Not for me,' she said rapidly.

He did not answer, and they remained silent.

At length she turned her eyes slowly to him.

'Why do you say you speak for me?' she said, in an accusing tone.

'Pardon me. I was hasty.'

But a faint touch of superciliousness in his tone showed he meant what he had said. She mused, her brow cold and stony.

'And why do you tell *me* about your anger?' she said. 'Will that make it better?'

'Even the adder finds his mate. And she has as much poison in her mouth as he.'

She gave a little sudden squirt of laughter.

'Awfully poetic thing to say about me,' she said.

He smiled, but with the same corrosive quality.

'Ah,' he said, 'you are not a dove. You are a wild-cat with open eyes, half dreaming on a bough, in a lonely place, as I have seen her. And I ask myself – What are her memories, then?'

'I wish I were a wild-cat,' she said suddenly.

He eyed her shrewdly, and did not answer.

'You want more war?' she said to him bitterly.

'More trenches? More Big Berthas, more shells and poison-gas, more machine-drilled science-manoeuvred so-called armies? Never. Never. I would rather work in a factory that makes boots and shoes. And I would rather deliberately starve to death than work in a factory that makes boots and shoes.'

'Then what do you want?'

'I want my anger to have room to grow.'

'How?'

'I do not know. That is why I sit here, day after day. I wait.'

'For your anger to have room to grow?'

'For that.'

'Good-bye, Count Dionys.'

'Good-bye, Lady Daphne.'

She had determined never to go and see him again. She had no sign from him. Since she had begun the second shirt, she went on with it. And then she hurried to finish it, because she was starting a round of visits that would end in the summer sojourn in Scotland. She intended to post the shirt. But after all, she took it herself.

She found Count Dionys had been removed from Hurst Place to Voynich Hall, where other enemy officers were interned. The being thwarted made her more determined. She took the train next day to go to Voynich Hall.

When he came into the ante-room where he was to receive her, she felt at once the old influence of his silence and his subtle power. His face had still that swarthy-transparent look of one who is unhappy, but his bearing was proud and reserved. He kissed her hand politely, leaving her to speak.

'How are you?' she said. 'I didn't know you were here. I am going away for the summer.'

'I wish you a pleasant time,' he said. They were speaking English.

'I brought the other shirt,' she said. 'It is finished at last.'

'That is a greater honour than I dared expect,' he said.

'I'm afraid it may be more honourable than useful. The other didn't fit, did it?'

'Almost,' he said. 'It fitted the spirit, if not the flesh,' he smiled.

'I'd rather it had been the reverse, for once,' she said. 'Sorry.'

'I would not have it one stitch different.'

'Can we sit in the garden?'

'I think we may.'

They sat on a bench. Other prisoners were playing croquet not far off. But these two were left comparatively alone.

'Do you like it better here?' she said.

'I have nothing to complain of,' he said.

'And the anger?'

'It is doing well, I thank you,' he smiled.

'You mean getting better?'

'Making strong roots,' he said, laughing.

'Ah, so long as it only makes roots!' she said.

'And your ladyship, how is she?'

'My ladyship is rather better,' she replied.

'Much better, indeed,' he said, looking into her face.

'Do you mean I *look* much better?' she asked quickly.

'Very much. It is your beauty you think of. Well, your beauty is almost itself again.'

'Thanks.'

'You brood on your beauty as I on my anger. Ah, your ladyship, be wise, and make friends with your anger. That is the way to let your beauty blossom.'

'I was not unfriendly with you, was I?' she said.

'With me?' His face flickered with a laugh. 'Am I your anger? Your vicar in wrath? So then, be friends with the angry me, your ladyship. I ask nothing better.'

'What is the use,' she said, 'being friends with the *angry* you? I would much rather be friends with the happy you.'

'That little animal is extinct,' he laughed. 'And I am glad of it.'

'But what remains? Only the angry you? Then it is no use my trying to be friends.'

'You remember, dear Lady Daphne, that the adder does not suck his poison all alone, and the pole-cat knows where to find his she pole-cat. You remember that each one has his own dear mate,' he laughed. 'Dear, deadly mate.'

'And what if I do remember those bits of natural history, Count Dionys?'

'The she-adder is dainty, delicate, and carries her poison lightly. The wild-cat has wonderful green eyes that she closes with memory like a screen. The ice-bear hides like a snake with her cubs, and her snarl is the strangest thing in the world.'

'Have you ever heard me snarl?' she asked suddenly.

He only laughed, and looked away.

They were silent. And immediately the strange thrill of secrecy was between them. Something had gone beyond sadness into another, secret, thrilling communion which she would never admit.

'What do you do all day here?' she asked.

'Play chess, play this foolish croquet, play billiards, and read, and wait, and remember.'

'What do you wait for?'

'I don't know.'

'And what do you remember?'

'Ah, that. Shall I tell you what amuses me? Shall I tell you a secret?'

'Please don't, if it's anything that matters.'

'It matters to nobody but me. Will you hear it?'

'If it does not implicate me in any way.'

'It does not. Well, I am a member of a certain old secret society – no, don't look at me, nothing frightening – only a society like the free-masons.'

'And?'

'And – well, as you know, one is initiated into certain so-called secrets and rites. My family has always been initiated. So I am an initiate too. Does it interest you?'

'Why, of course.'

'Well. I was always rather thrilled by these secrets. Or some of them. Some seemed to me far-fetched. The ones that thrilled me even never had any relation to actual life. When you knew me in Dresden and Prague, you would not have thought me a man invested with awful secret knowledge, now would you?'

'Never.'

'No. It was just a little exciting side-show. And I was a grimacing little society man. But now they become true. It becomes true.'

'The secret knowledge?'

'Yes.'

'What, for instance?'

'Take actual fire. It will bore you. Do you want to hear?'

'Go on.'

'This is what I was taught. The true fire is invisible. Flame, and the red fire we see burning, has its back to us. It is running away from us. Does that mean anything to you?'

'Yes.'

'Well then, the yellowness of sunshine – light itself – that is only the glancing aside of the real original fire. You know that is true. There would be no light if there was no refraction, no bits of dust and stuff to turn the dark fire into visibility. You know that's a fact. And that being so, even the sun is dark. It is only his jacket of dust that makes him visible. You know that too. And the true sunbeams coming towards us flow darkly, a moving darkness of the genuine fire. The sun is dark, the sunshine flowing to us is dark. And light is only the inside-turning away of the sun's directness that was coming to us. Does that interest you at all?'

'Yes,' she said dubiously.

'Well, we've got the world inside out. The true living world of fire is dark, throbbing, darker than blood. Our luminous world that we go by is only the reverse of this.'

'Yes, I like that,' she said.

'Well! Now listen. The same with love. This white love that we have is the same. It is only the reverse, the whited sepulchre of the true love. True love is dark, a throbbing together in darkness, like the wild-cat in the night, when the green screen opens and her eyes are on the darkness.'

'No, I don't see that,' she said in a slow, clanging voice.

'You, and your beauty – that is only the inside-out of you. The real you is the wild-cat invisible in the night, with red fire perhaps coming out of its wide, dark eyes. Your beauty is your whited sepulchre.'

'You mean cosmetics,' she said. 'I've got none on today – not even powder.'
He laughed.

'Very good,' he said. 'Consider me. I used to think myself small but handsome, and the ladies used to admire me moderately, never very much. A trim little fellow, you know. Well, that was just the inside-out of me. I am a black tom-cat howling in the night, and it is then that fire comes out of me. This me you look at is my whited sepulchre. What do you say?'

She was looking into his eyes. She could see the darkness swaying in the depths. She perceived the invisible, cat-like fire stirring deep inside them, felt it coming towards her. She turned her face aside. Then he laughed, showing his strong white teeth, that seemed a little too large, rather dreadful.

She rose to go.

'Well,' she said. 'I shall have the summer in which to think about the world inside-out. Do write if there is anything to say. Write to Thoresway. Good-bye!'

'Ah, your eyes!' he said. 'They are like jewels of stone.'

Being away from the Count, she put him out of her mind. Only she was sorry for him a prisoner in that sickening Voynich Hall. But she did not write. Nor did he.

As a matter of fact, her mind was now much more occupied with her husband. All arrangements were being made to effect his exchange. From month to month she looked for his return. And so she thought of him.

Whatever happened to her, she thought about it, thought and thought a great deal. The consciousness of her mind was like tablets of stone weighing her down. And whoever would make a new entry into her must break these tablets of stone piece by piece. So it was that in her own way she thought often enough of the Count's world inside-out. A curious latency stirred in her consciousness that was not yet an idea.

He said her eyes were like jewels of stone. What a horrid thing to say! What did he want her eyes to be like? He wanted them to dilate and become all black pupil, like a cat's at night. She shrank convulsively from the thought, and tightened her breast.

He said her beauty was her whited sepulchre. Even that, she knew what he meant. The invisibility of her he wanted to love. But ah, her pearl-like beauty was so dear to her, and it was so famous in the world.

He said her white love was like moonshine, harmful, the reverse of love. He meant Basil, of course. Basil always said she was the moon. But then Basil loved her for that. The ecstasy of it! She shivered, thinking of her husband. But it had also made her nerve-worn, her husband's love. Ah, nerve-worn.

What then would the Count's love be like? Something so secret and different. She would not be lovely and a queen to him. He hated her loveliness. The wild-cat has its mate. The little wild-cat that he was. Ah!

She caught her breath, determined not to think. When she thought of Count Dionys she felt the world slipping away from her. She would sit in front of a mirror, looking at her wonderful cared-for face that had appeared in so many society magazines. She loved it so, it made her feel so vain. And she looked at her blue-green eyes – the eyes of the wild-cat on a bough. Yes, the lovely blue-green iris drawn tight like a screen. Supposing it should relax. Supposing it should unfold, and open out the dark depths, the dark, dilated pupil! Supposing it should?

Never! She always caught herself back. She felt she might be killed before she could give way to that relaxation that the Count wanted of her. She could not. She just could not. At the very thought of it some hypersensitive nerve started with a great twinge in her breast; she drew back, forced to keep her guard. Ah no, Monsieur le Comte, you shall never take her ladyship off her guard.

She disliked the thought of the Count. An impudent little fellow. An impertinent little fellow! A little madman, really. A little outsider. No, no. She would think of her husband: an adorable, tall, well-bred Englishman, so easy and simple, and with the amused look in his blue eyes. She thought of the cultured, casual trail of his voice. It set her nerves on fire. She thought of his strong, easy body – beautiful, white-fleshed, with the fine springing of warm-brown hair like tiny flames. He was the Dionysos, full of sap, milk and honey, and northern golden wine: he, her husband. Not that little unreal Count. Ah, she dreamed of her husband, of the love-days, and the honeymoon, the lovely, simple intimacy. Ah, the marvellous revelation of that intimacy, when he left himself to her so generously. Ah, she was his wife for this reason, that he had given himself to her so greatly, so generously. Like an ear of corn he was there for her gathering – her husband, her own, lovely, English husband. Ah, when would he come again, when would he come again!

She had letters from him – and how he loved her. Far away, his life was all hers. All hers, flowing to her as the beam flows from a white star right down to us, to our heart. Her lover, her husband.

He was now expecting to come home soon. It had all been arranged. 'I hope you won't be disappointed in me when I do get back,' he wrote. 'I am afraid I am no longer the plump and well-looking young man I was. I've got a big scar at the side of my mouth, and I'm as thin as a starved rabbit, and my hair's going grey. Doesn't sound attractive, does it? And it isn't attractive. But once I can get out of this infernal place, and once I can be with you again, I shall come in for my second blooming. The very thought of being quietly in the same house with you, quiet and in peace, makes me realize that if I've been through hell, I have known heaven on earth and can hope to know it again. I am a miserable brute to look at now. But I have faith in you. You will forgive my appearance, and that alone will make me feel handsome.'

She read this letter many times. She was not afraid of his scar or his looks. She would love him all the more.

Since she had started making shirts – those two for the Count had been an enormous labour, even though her maid had come to her assistance forty times: but since she had started making shirts, she thought she might continue. She had some good suitable silk: her husband liked silk underwear.

But still she used the Count's thimble. It was gold outside and silver inside, and was too heavy. A snake was coiled round the base, and at the top, for pressing the needle, was inlet a semi-translucent apple-green stone, perhaps jade, carved like a scarab, with little dots. It was too heavy. But then she sewed so slowly. And she liked to feel her hand heavy, weighted. And as she sewed she thought about her husband, and she felt herself in love with him. She thought of him, how beautiful he was, and how she would love him now he was thin: she would love him all the more. She would love to trace his bones, as if to trace his living skeleton. The thought made her rest her hands in her lap, and drift into a muse. Then she felt the weight of the thimble on her finger, and took it off, and sat looking at the green stone. The ladybird. The ladybird. And if only her husband would come soon, soon. It was wanting him that made her so ill. Nothing but that. She had wanted him so badly. She wanted now. Ah, if she could go to him now, and find him, wherever he was, and see him and touch him and take all his love.

As she mused, she put the thimble down in front of her, took up a little silver pencil from her work-basket, and on a bit of blue paper that had been the band of a small skein of silk she wrote the lines of the silly little song:

> *'Wenn ich ein Vöglein wär'*
> *Und auch zwei Flüglein hätt'*
> *Flög' ich zu dir –'*

That was all she could get on her bit of pale-blue paper.

> 'If I were a little bird
> And had two little wings
> I'd fly to thee –'

Silly enough, in all conscience. But she did not translate it, so it did not seem quite so silly.

At that moment her maid announced Lady Bingham – her husband's sister. Daphne crumpled up the bit of paper in a flurry, and in another minute Primrose, his sister, came in. The newcomer was not a bit like a primrose, being long-faced and clever, smart, but not a bit elegant, in her new clothes.

'Daphne dear, what a domestic scene! I suppose it's rehearsal. Well, you may as well rehearse, he's with Admiral Burns on the *Ariadne*. Father just heard from the Admiralty: quite fit. He'll be here in a day or two. Splendid, isn't it? And the war is going to end. At least it seems like it. You'll be safe of your man now, dear. Thank heaven when it's all over. What are you sewing?'

'A shirt,' said Daphne.

'A shirt! Why, how clever of you. I should never know which end to begin. Who showed you?'

'Millicent.'

'And how did *she* know? She's no business to know how to sew shirts: nor cushions nor sheets either. Do let me look. Why, how perfectly marvellous you are! – every bit by hand too. Basil isn't worth it, dear, really he isn't. Let him order his shirts in Oxford Street. Your business is to be beautiful, not to sew shirts. What a dear little pin-poppet, or rather needle-woman! I say, a satire on us, that is. But what a darling, with mother-of-pearl wings to her skirts! And darling little gold-eyed needles inside her. You screw her head off, and you find she's full of pins and needles. Woman for you! Mother says won't you come to lunch tomorrow. And won't you come to Brassey's to tea with me at this minute. Do, there's a dear. I've got a taxi.'

Daphne bundled her sewing loosely together.

When she tried to do a bit more, two days later, she could not find her thimble. She asked her maid, whom she could absolutely trust. The girl had not seen it. She searched everywhere. She asked her nurse – who was now her housekeeper – and footman. No, nobody had seen it. Daphne even asked her sister-in-law.

'Thimble, darling? No, I don't remember a thimble. I remember a dear little needle-lady, whom I thought such a precious satire on us women. I didn't notice a thimble.'

Poor Daphne wandered about in a muse. She did not want to believe it lost. It had been like a talisman to her. She tried to forget it. Her husband was coming, quite soon, quite soon. But she could not raise herself to joy. She had lost her thimble. It was as if Count Dionys accused her in her sleep of something, she did not quite know what.

And though she did not really want to go to Voynich Hall, yet like a fatality she went, like one doomed. It was already late autumn, and some lovely days. This was the last of the lovely days. She was told that Count Dionys was in the small park, finding chestnuts. She went to look for him. Yes, there he was in his blue uniform stooping over the brilliant yellow leaves of the sweet chestnut tree, that lay around him like a fallen nimbus of glowing yellow, under his feet, as he kicked and rustled, looking for the chestnut burrs. And with his short, brown hands he was pulling out the small chestnuts and putting them in his pockets. But as she approached he peeled a nut to eat it. His teeth were white and powerful.

'You remind me of a squirrel laying in a winter store,' said she.

'Ah, Lady Daphne – I was thinking, and did not hear you.'

'I thought you were gathering chestnuts – even eating them.'

'Also!' he laughed. He had a dark, sudden charm when he laughed, showing his rather large white teeth. She was not quite sure whether she found him a little repulsive.

'Were you *really* thinking?' she said, in her slow, resonant way.

'Very truly.'

'And weren't you enjoying the chestnut a bit?'

'Very much. Like sweet milk. Excellent, excellent.' He had the fragments of the nut between his teeth, and bit them finely. 'Will you take one too.' He held out the little, pointed brown nuts on the palm of his hand.

She looked at them doubtfully.

'Are they as tough as they always were?' she said.

'No, they are fresh and good. Wait, I will peel one for you.'

They strayed about through the thin clump of trees.

'You have had a pleasant summer; you are strong?'

'Almost *quite* strong,' said she. 'Lovely summer, thanks. I suppose it's no good asking you if you have been happy?'

'Happy?' He looked at her direct. His eyes were black, and seemed to examine her. She always felt he had a little contempt of her. 'Oh yes,' he said, smiling. 'I have been very happy.'

'So glad.'

They drifted a little farther, and he picked up an apple-green chestnut burr out of the yellow-brown leaves, handling it with sensitive fingers that still suggested paws to her.

'How did you succeed in being happy?' she said.

'How shall I tell you? I felt that the same power which put up the mountains could pull them down again – no matter how long it took.'

'And was that all?'

'Was it not enough?'

'I should say decidedly too little.'

He laughed broadly, showing the strong, negroid teeth.

'You do not know all it means,' he said.

'The thought that the mountains were going to be pulled down?' she said. 'It will be so long after my day.'

'Ah, you are bored,' he said. 'But I – I found the God who pulls things down: especially the things that men have put up. Do they not say that life is a search after God, Lady Daphne? I have found my God.'

'The god of destruction,' she said, blanching.

'Yes – not the devil of destruction, but the god of destruction. The blessed god of destruction. It is strange' – he stood before her, looking up at her – 'but I have found my God. The god of anger, who throws down the steeples and the factory chimneys. Ah, Lady Daphne, he is a man's God, he is a man's God. I have found my God, Lady Daphne.'

'Apparently. And how are you going to serve him?'

A naïve glow transfigured his face.

'Oh, I will help. With my heart I will help while I can do nothing with my hands. I say to my heart: Beat, hammer, beat with little strokes. Beat, hammer of God, beat them down. Beat it all down.'

Her brows knitted, her face took on a look of discontent.

'Beat what down?' she asked harshly.

'The world, the world of man. Not the trees – these chestnuts, for example' – he looked up at them, at the tufts and loose pinions of yellow – 'not these – nor the chattering sorcerers, the squirrels – nor the hawk that comes. Not those.'

'You mean beat England?' she said.

'Ah, no. Ah, no. Not England any more than Germany – perhaps not as much. Not Europe any more than Asia.'

'Just the end of the world?'

'No, no. No, no. What grudge have I against a world where little chestnuts are so sweet as these! Do you like yours? Will you take another?'

'No, thanks.'

'What grudge have I against a world where even the hedges are full of berries, bunches of black berries that hang down, and red berries that thrust up. Never would I hate the world. But the world of man. Lady Daphne' – his voice sank to a whisper – '*I hate it.* Zzz!' he hissed. 'Strike, little heart! Strike, strike, hit, smite! Oh, Lady Daphne!' – his eyes dilated with a ring of fire.

'What?' she said, scared.

'I believe in the power of my red, dark heart. God has put the hammer in my breast – the little eternal hammer. Hit – hit – hit! It hits on the world of man. It hits, it hits! And it hears the thin sound of cracking. The thin sound of cracking. Hark!'

He stood still and made her listen. It was late afternoon. The strange laugh of his face made the air seem dark to her. And she could easily have believed that she heard a faint, fine shivering, cracking, through the air, a delicate crackling noise.

'You hear it? Yes? Oh, may I live long! May I live long, so that my hammer may strike and strike, and the cracks go deeper, deeper! Ah, the world of man! Ah, the joy, the passion in every heart-beat! Strike home, strike true, strike sure. Strike to destroy it. Strike! Strike! To destroy the world of man. Ah, God. Ah, God, prisoner of peace. Do I not know you, Lady Daphne? Do I not? Do I not?'

She was silent for some moments, looking away at the twinkling lights of a station beyond.

'Not the white plucked lily of your body. I have gathered no flower for my ostentatious life. But in the cold dark, your lily root, Lady Daphne. Ah, yes, you will know it all your life, that I know where your root lies buried, with its sad, sad quick of life. What does it matter!'

They had walked slowly towards the house. She was silent. Then at last she said, in a peculiar voice:

'And you would never want to kiss me?'

'Ah, no!' he answered sharply.

She held out her hand.

'Good-bye, Count Dionys,' she drawled, fashionably. He bowed over her hand, but did not kiss it.

'Good-bye, Lady Daphne.'

She went away, with her brow set hard. And henceforth she thought only of her husband, of Basil. She made the Count die out of her. Basil was coming, he was near. He was coming back from the East, from war and death. Ah, he had been through awful fire of experience. He would be something new, something she did not know. He was something new, a stronger lover who had been through terrible fire, and had come out strange and new, like a god. Ah, new and terrible his love would be, pure and intensified by the awful fire of suffering. A new lover – a new bridegroom – a new, supernatural wedding-night. She shivered in anticipation, waiting for her husband. She hardly noticed the wild excitement of the Armistice. She was waiting for something more wonderful to her.

And yet the moment she heard his voice on the telephone, her heart contracted with fear. It was his well-known voice, deliberate, diffident, almost drawling, with the same subtle suggestion of deference, and the rather exaggerated Cambridge intonation, up and down. But there was a difference, a new icy note that went through her veins like death.

'Is that you, Daphne? I shall be with you in half an hour. Is that all right for you? Yes, I've just landed, and shall come straight to you. Yes, a taxi. Shall I be too sudden for you, darling? No? Good, oh, good! Half an hour, then! I say, Daphne? There won't be anyone else there, will there? Quite alone! Good! I can ring up Dad afterwards. Yes, splendid, splendid. Sure you're all right, my darling? I'm at death's door till I see you. Yes. Good-bye – half an hour. Good-bye.'

When Daphne had hung up the receiver she sat down almost in a faint. What was it that so frightened her? His terrible, terrible altered voice, like cold, blue steel. She had no time to think. She rang for her maid.

'Oh, my lady, it isn't bad news?' cried Millicent, when she caught sight of her mistress white as death.

'No, good news. Major Apsley will be here in half an hour. Help me to dress.

Ring to Murry's first to send in some roses, red ones, and some lilac-coloured iris – two dozen of each, at once.'

Daphne went to her room. She didn't know what to wear, she didn't know how she wanted her hair dressed. She spoke hastily to her maid. She chose a violet-coloured dress. She did not know what she was doing. In the middle of dressing the flowers came, and she left off to put them in the bowls. So that when she heard his voice in the hall, she was still standing in front of the mirror reddening her lips and wiping it away again.

'Major Apsley, my lady!' murmured the maid, in excitement.

'Yes, I can hear. Go and tell him I shall be *one* minute.'

Daphne's voice had become slow and sonorous, like bronze, as it always did when she was upset. Her face looked almost haggard, and in vain she dabbed with the rouge.

'How does he look?' she asked curtly, when her maid came back.

'A long scar here,' said the maid, and she drew her finger from the left-hand corner of her mouth into her cheek, slanting downwards.

'Make him look very different?' asked Daphne.

'Not so *very* different, my lady,' said Millicent gently. 'His eyes are the same, I think.' The girl also was distressed.

'All right,' said Daphne. She looked at herself a long, last look as she turned away from the mirror. The sight of her own face made her feel almost sick. She had seen so much of herself. And yet even now she was fascinated by the heavy droop of her lilac-veined lids over her slow, strange, large, green-blue eyes. They *were* mysterious-looking. And she gave herself a long, sideways glance, curious and Chinese. How was it possible there was a touch of the Chinese in her face? – she so purely an English blonde, an Aphrodite of the foam, as Basil had called her in poetry. Ah well! She left off her thoughts and went through the hall to the drawing-room.

He was standing nervously in the middle of the room in his uniform. She hardly glanced at his face – and saw only the scar.

'Hullo, Daphne,' he said, in a voice full of the expected emotion. He stepped forward and took her in his arms, and kissed her forehead.

'So glad! So glad it's happened at last,' she said, hiding her tears.

'So glad what has happened, darling?' he asked, in his deliberate manner.

'That you're back.' Her voice had the bronze resonance, she spoke rather fast.

'Yes, I'm back, Daphne darling – as much of me as there is to bring back.'

'Why?' she said. 'You've come back whole, surely?' She was frightened.

'Yes, apparently I have. Apparently. But don't let's talk of that. Let's talk of you, darling. How are you? Let me look at you. You are thinner, you are older. But you are more wonderful than ever. Far more wonderful.'

'How?' said she.

'I can't exactly say how. You were only a girl. Now you are a woman. I suppose it's all that's happened. But you are wonderful as a woman, Daphne darling – more wonderful than all that's happened. I couldn't have believed you'd be so wonderful. I'd forgotten – or else I'd never known. I say, I'm a lucky chap really. Here I am, alive and well, and I've got you for a wife. It's brought you out like a flower. I say, darling, there is more now that Venus of the foam – grander. How beautiful you are! But you look like the beauty of all life – as if you were moon-mother of the world – Aphrodite. God is good to me after all, darling. I ought never to utter a single complaint. How lovely you are –

how lovely you are, my darling! I'd forgotten you – and I thought I knew you
so well. Is it true that you belong to me? Are you really mine?'

They were seated on the yellow sofa. He was holding her hand, and his eyes
were going up and down, from her face to her throat and her breast. The sound
of his words, and the strong, cold desire in his voice excited her, pleased her,
and made her heart freeze. She turned and looked into his light blue eyes. They
had no longer the amused light, nor the young look. They burned with a hard,
focused light, whitish.

'It's all right. You are mine, aren't you, Daphne darling?' came his cultured,
musical voice, that had always the well-bred twang of diffidence.

She looked back into his eyes.

'Yes, I am yours,' she said, from the lips.

'Darling! Darling!' he murmured, kissing her hand.

Her heart beat suddenly so terribly, as if her breast would be ruptured, and
she rose in one movement and went across the room. She leaned her hand on
the mantelpiece and looked down at the electric fire. She could hear the faint,
faint noise of it. There was silence for a few moments.

Then she turned and looked at him. He was watching her intently. His face
was gaunt, and there was a curious deathly sub-pallor, though his cheeks were
not white. The scar ran livid from the side of his mouth. It was not so very big.
But it seemed like a scar in him himself, in his brain, as it were. In his eyes was
that hard, white, focused light that fascinated her and was terrible to her. He
was different. He was like death; like risen death. She felt she dared not touch
him. White death was still upon him. She could tell that he shrank with a kind
of agony from contact. 'Touch me not, I am not yet ascended unto the Father.'
Yet for contact he had come. Something, someone seemed to be looking over
his shoulder. His own young ghost looking over his shoulder. Oh, God! She
closed her eyes, seeming to swoon. He remained leaning forward on the sofa,
watching her.

'Aren't you well, darling?' he asked. There was a strange, incomprehensible
coldness in his very fire. He did not move to come near her.

'Yes, I'm well. It is only that after all it is so sudden. Let me get used to you,'
she said, turning aside her face from him. She felt utterly like a victim of his
white, awful face.

'I suppose I must be a bit of a shock to you,' he said. 'I hope you won't leave
off loving me. It won't be that, will it?'

The strange coldness in his voice! And yet the white, uncanny fire.

'No, I shan't leave off loving you,' she admitted, in a low tone, as if almost
ashamed. She *dared* not have said otherwise. And the saying it made it true.

'Ah, if you're sure of that,' he said. 'I'm a pretty unlovely sight to behold, I
know, with this wound-scar. But if you can forgive it me, darling. Do you think
you can?' There was something like compulsion in his tone.

She looked at him, and shivered slightly.

'I love you – more than before,' she said hurriedly.

'Even the scar?' came his terrible voice, inquiring.

She glanced again, with that slow, Chinese side-look, and felt she would die.

'Yes,' she said, looking away at nothingness. It was an awful moment to her.
A little, slightly imbecile smile widened on his face.

He suddenly knelt at her feet, and kissed the toe of her slipper, and kissed the
instep, and kissed the ankle in the thin, black stocking.

'I knew,' he said in a muffled voice. 'I knew you would make good. I knew if I

had to kneel, it was before you. I knew you were divine, you were the one –
Cybele – Isis. I knew I was your slave. I knew. It has all been just a long
initiation. I had to learn how to worship you.'

He kissed her feet again and again, without the slightest self-consciousness,
or the slightest misgiving. Then he went back to the sofa, and sat there looking
at her, saying:

'It isn't love, it is worship. Love between me and you will be a sacrament,
Daphne. That's what I had to learn. You are beyond me. A mystery to me. My
God, how great it all is. How marvellous!'

She stood with her hand on the mantelpiece, looking down and not
answering. She was frightened – almost horrified: but she was thrilled deep
down to her soul. She really felt she could glow white and fill the universe like
the moon, like Astarte, like Isis, like Venus. The grandeur of her own pale
power. The man religiously worshipped her, not merely amorously. She was
ready for him – for the sacrament of his supreme worship.

He sat on the sofa with his hands spread on the yellow brocade and pushing
downwards behind him, down between the deep upholstery of the back and
the seat. He had long, white hands with pale freckles. And his fingers touched
something. With his long white fingers he groped and brought it out. It was the
lost thimble. And inside it was the bit of screwed-up blue paper.

'I say, is that *your* thimble?' he asked.

She started, and went hurriedly forward for it.

'Where was it?' she said, agitated.

But he did not give it to her. He turned it round and pulled out the bit of blue
paper. He saw the faint pencil marks on the screwed-up ball, and unrolled the
band of paper, and slowly deciphered the verse.

> *'Wenn ich ein Vöglein wär'*
> *Und auch zwei Flüglein hätt'*
> *Flög' ich zu dir –'*

'How awfully touching that is,' he said. A *Vöglein* with two little *Flüglein*!
But what a precious darling child you are! Whom did you want to fly to, if you
were a *Vöglein*?' He looked up at her with a curious smile.

'I can't remember,' she said, turning aside her head.

'I hope it was to me,' he said. 'Anyhow, I shall consider it was, and shall love
you all the more for it. What a darling child! A *Vöglein* if you please, with two
little wings! Why, how beautifully absurd of you, darling!'

He folded the scrap of paper carefully, and put it in his pocket-book, keeping
the thimble all the time between his knees.

'Tell me when you lost it, Daphne,' he said, examining the bauble.

'About a month ago – or two months.'

'About a month ago – or two months. And what were you sewing? Do you
mind if I ask? I like to think of you then. I was still in that beastly El Hasrun.
What were you sewing, darling, two months ago, when you lost your thimble?'

'A shirt.'

'I say, a shirt! Whose shirt?'

'Yours.'

'There. Now we've run it to earth. Were you really sewing a shirt for me! Is it
finished? Can I put it on at this minute?'

'That one isn't finished, but the first one is.'

'I say, darling, let me go and put it on. To think I should have it next my

skin! I shall feel you all round me, all over me. I say how marvellous that will
be! Won't you come?'

'Won't you give me the thimble?' she said.

'Yes, of course. What a noble thimble too! Who gave it you?'

'Count Dionys Psanek.'

'Who was he?'

'A Bohemian Count, in Dresden. He once stayed with us in Thoresway –
with a tall wife. Didn't you meet them?'

'I don't think I did. I don't think I did. I don't remember. What was he like?'

'A little man with black hair and a rather low, dark forehead – rather dressy.'

'No, I don't remember him at all. So he gave it you. Well, I wonder where he
is now? Probably rotted, poor devil.'

'No, he's interned in Voynich Hall. Mother and I have been to see him
several times. He was awfully badly wounded.'

'Poor little beggar! In Voynich Hall! I'll look at him before he goes. Odd
thing, to give you a thimble. Odd gift! You were a girl then, though. Do you
think he had it made, or do you think he found it in a shop?'

'I think it belonged to the family. The ladybird at the top is part of their crest
– and the snake as well, I think.'

'A ladybird! Funny thing for a crest. Americans would call it a bug. I must
look at him before he goes. And you were sewing a shirt for me! And then you
posted me this little letter into the sofa. Well, I'm awfully glad I received it, and
that it didn't go astray in the post, like so many things. *'Wenn ich ein Vöglein
wär''* – you perfect child! But that is the beauty of a woman like you: you are so
superb and beyond worship, and then such an exquisite naïve child. Who
could help worshipping you and loving you: immortal and mortal together.
What, you want the thimble? Here! Wonderful, wonderful white fingers. Ah,
darling, you are more goddess than child, you long, limber Isis with sacred
hands. White, white, and immortal! Don't tell me your hands could die,
darling: your wonderful Proserpine fingers. They are immortal as February
and snowdrops. If you lift your hands the spring comes. I *can't* help kneeling
before you, darling. I am no more than a sacrifice to you, an offering. I *wish*
I could die in giving myself to you, give you all my blood on your altar, for
ever.'

She looked at him with a long, slow look, as he turned his face to her. His
face was white with ecstasy. And she was not afraid. Somewhere, saturnine, she
knew it was absurd. But she chose not to know. A certain swoon-sleep was on
her. With her slow, green-blue eyes she looked down on his ecstasized face,
almost benign. But in her right hand unconsciously she held the thimble fast,
she only gave him her left hand. He took her hand and rose to his feet in that
curious priestly ecstasy which made him more than a man or a soldier, far, far
more than a lover to her.

Nevertheless, his home-coming made her begin to be ill again. Afterwards,
after his love, she had to bear herself in torment. To her shame and her
heaviness, she knew she was not strong enough, or pure enough, to bear this
awful outpouring adoration-lust. It was not her fault she felt weak and fretful
afterwards, as if she wanted to cry and be fretful and petulant, wanted someone
to save her. She could not turn to Basil, her husband. After his ecstasy of
adoration-lust for her, she recoiled from him. Alas, she was not the goddess,
the superb person he named her. She was flawed with the fatal humility of her
age. She could not harden her heart and burn her soul pure of this humility,

this misgiving. She could not finally believe in her own woman-godhead – only in her own female mortality.

That fierce power of being alone, even with your lover, the fierce power of the woman *in excelsis* – alas, she could not keep it. She could rise to the height for the time, the incandescent, transcendent, moon-fierce womanhood. But alas, she could not stay intensified and resplendent in her white, womanly powers, her female mystery. She relaxed, she lost her glory, and became fretful. Fretful and ill and never to be soothed. And then naturally her man became ashy and somewhat acrid, while she ached with nerves, and could not eat.

Of course she began to dream about Count Dionys: to yearn wistfully for him. And it was absolutely a fatal thought to her that he was going away. When she thought that – that he was leaving England soon – going away into the dark for ever – then the last spark seemed to die in her. She felt her soul perish, whilst she herself was worn and soulless like a prostitute. A prostitute goddess. And her husband, the gaunt, white, intensified priest of her, who never ceased from being before her like a lust.

'Tomorrow,' she said to him, gathering her last courage and looking at him with a side look, 'I want to go to Voynich Hall.'

'What, to see Count Psanek? Oh, good! Yes, very good! I'll come along as well. I should like very much to see him. I suppose he'll be getting sent back before long.'

It was a fortnight before Christmas, very dark weather. Her husband was in khaki. She wore her black furs and a black lace veil over her face, so that she seemed mysterious. But she lifted the veil and looped it behind, so that it made a frame for her face. She looked very lovely like that – her face pure like the most white hellebore flower, touched with winter pink, amid the blackness of her drapery and furs. Only she was rather too much like the picture of modern beauty: too much the actual thing. She had half an idea that Dionys would hate her for her effective loveliness. He would see it and hate it. The thought was like a bitter balm to her. For herself, she loved her loveliness almost with obsession.

The Count came cautiously forward, glancing from the lovely figure of Lady Daphne to the gaunt well-bred Major at her side. Daphne was so beautiful in her dark furs, the black lace of her veil thrown back over her close-fitting, dull-gold-threaded hat, and her face fair like a winter flower in a cranny of darkness. But on her face, that was smiling with a slow self-satisfaction of beauty and of knowledge that she was dangling the two men, and setting all the imprisoned officers wildly on the alert, the Count could read that acridity of dissatisfaction and of inefficiency. And he looked away to the livid scar on the Major's cheek.

'Count Dionys, I wanted to bring my husband to see you. May I introduce him to you? Major Apsley – Count Dionys Psanek.'

The two men shook hands rather stiffly.

'I can sympathize with you being fastened up in this place,' said Basil in his slow, easy fashion. 'I hated it, I assure you, out there in the East.'

'But your conditions were much worse than mine,' smiled the Count.

'Well, perhaps they were. But prison is prison, even if it were heaven itself.'

'Lady Apsley has been the one angel of my heaven,' smiled the Count.

'I'm afraid I was as inefficient as most angels,' said she.

The small smile never left the Count's dark face. It was true as she said, he was low-browed, the black hair growing low on his brow, and his eyebrows making a thick bow above his dark eyes, which had again long black lashes. So that the upper part of his face seemed very dusky-black. His nose was small and somewhat translucent. There was a touch of mockery about him, which was intensified even by his small, energetic stature. He was still carefully dressed in the dark-blue uniform, whose shabbiness could not hinder the dark flame of life which seemed to glow through the cloth from his body. He was not thin – but still had a curious swarthy translucency of skin in his low-browed face.

'What would you have been more?' he laughed, making equivocal dark eyes at her.

'Oh, of course, a delivering angel – a cinema heroine,' she replied, closing her eyes and turning her face aside.

All the while the white-faced, tall Major watched the little man with a fixed, half-smiling scrutiny. The Count seemed to notice. He turned to the Englishman.

'I am glad that I can congratulate you, Major Apsley, on your safe and happy return to your home.'

'Thanks. I hope I may be able to congratulate you in the same way before long.'

'Oh yes,' said the Count. 'Before long I shall be shipped back.'

'Have you any news of your family?' interrupted Daphne.

'No news,' he replied briefly, with sudden gravity.

'It seems you'll find a fairish mess out in Austria,' said Basil.

'Yes, probably. It is what we had to expect,' replied the Count.

'Well, I don't know. Sometimes things do turn out for the best. I feel that's as good as true in my case,' said the Major.

'Things have turned out for the best?' said the Count, with an intonation of polite enquiry.

'Yes. Just for me personally, I mean – to put it quite selfishly. After all, what we've learned is that a man can only speak for himself. And I feel it's been dreadful, but it's not been lost. It was like an ordeal one had to go through,' said Basil.

'You mean the war?'

'The war and everything that went with it.'

'And when you've been through the ordeal?' politely enquired the Count.

'Why, you arrive at a higher state of consciousness, and therefore of life. And so, of course, at a higher plane of love. A surprisingly higher plane of love, that you had never suspected the existence of before.'

The Count looked from Basil to Daphne, who was posing her head a little self-consciously.

'Then indeed the war has been a valuable thing,' he said.

'Exactly!' cried Basil. 'I am another man.'

'And Lady Apsley?' queried the Count.

'Oh' – her husband faced round to her – 'she is *absolutely* another woman – and *much* more wonderful, more marvellous.'

The Count smiled and bowed slightly.

'When we knew her ten years ago, we should have said then that it was impossible,' said he, 'for her to be more wonderful.'

'Oh, quite!' returned the husband. 'It always seems impossible. And the impossible is always happening. As a matter of fact, I think the war has opened another circle of life to us – a wider ring.'

'It may be so,' said the Count.

'You don't feel it so yourself?' The Major looked with his keen, white attention into the dark, low-browed face of the other man. The Count looked smiling at Daphne.

'I am only a prisoner still, Major, therefore I feel my ring quite small.'

'Yes, of course you do. Of course. Well, I do hope you won't be a prisoner much longer. You must be dying to get back into your own country.'

'Yes, I shall be glad to be free. Also,' he smiled. 'I shall miss my prison and my visits from the angels.'

Even Daphne could not be sure he was mocking her. It was evident the visit was unpleasant to him. She could see he did not like Basil. Nay, more, she could feel that the presence of her tall, gaunt, idealistic husband was hateful to the little swarthy man. But he passed it all off in smiles and polite speeches.

On the other hand, Basil was as if fascinated by the Count. He watched him absorbedly all the time, quite forgetting Daphne. She knew this. She knew that she was quite gone out of her husband's consciousness, like a lamp that has been carried away into another room. There he stood completely in the dark, as far as she was concerned, and all his attention focused on the other man. On his pale, gaunt face was a fixed smile of amused attention.

'But don't you get awfully bored,' he said, 'between the visits?'

The Count looked up with an affectation of frankness.

'No, I do not,' he said. 'I can brood, you see, on the things that come to pass.'

'I think that's where the harm comes in,' replied the Major. 'One sits and broods, and is cut off from everything, and one loses one's contact with reality. That's the effect it had on me, being a prisoner.'

'Contact with reality – what is that?'

'Well – contact with anybody, really – or anything.'

'Why must one have contact?'

'Well, because one must,' said Basil.

The Count smiled slowly.

'But I can sit and watch fate flowing, like black water, deep down in my own soul,' he said. 'I feel that there, in the dark of my own soul, things are happening.'

'That may be. But whatever happens, it is only one thing, really. It is a contact between your own soul and the soul of one other being, or of many other beings. Nothing else can happen to man. That's how I figured it out for myself. I may be wrong. But that's how I figured it out when I was wounded and a prisoner.'

The Count's face had gone dark and serious.

'But is this contact an aim in itself?' he asked.

'Well' – said the Major – he had taken his degree in philosophy – 'it seems to me it is. It results inevitably in some form of activity. But the cause and the origin and the life-impetus of all action, activity, whether constructive or destructive, seems to me to be in the dynamic contact between human beings. You bring to pass a certain dynamic contact between men, and you get war. Another sort of dynamic contact, and you get them all building a cathedral, as they did in the Middle Ages.'

'But was not the war, or the cathedral, the real aim, and the emotional contact just the means?' said the Count.

'I don't think so,' said the Major, his curious white passion beginning to glow through his face. The three were seated in a little card-room, left alone by courtesy by the other men. Daphne was still draped in her dark, too-becoming drapery. But alas, she sat now ignored by both men. She might just as well have been an ugly little nobody, for all the notice that was taken of her. She sat in the window-seat of the dreary small room with a look of discontent on her exotic, rare face, that was like a delicate white and pink hot-house flower. From time to time she glanced with long, slow looks from man to man: from her husband, whose pallid, intense, white glowing face was pressed forward across the table to the Count, who sat back in his chair, as if in opposition, and whose dark face seemed clubbed together in a dark, unwilling stare. Her husband was *quite* unaware of anything but his own white identity. But the Count still had a grain of secondary consciousness which hovered round and remained aware of the woman in the window-seat. The whole of his face, and his forward-looking attention was concentrated on Basil. But somewhere at the back of him he kept track of Daphne. She sat uneasy, in discontent, as women always do sit when men are locked together in a combustion of words. At the same time, she followed the argument. It was curious that, while her sympathy at this moment was with the Count, it was her husband whose words she believed to be true. The contact, the emotional contact was the real thing, the so-called 'aim' was only a by-product. Even wars and cathedrals, in her mind, were only by-products. The real thing was what the warriors and cathedral-builders had had in common, as a great uniting feeling: the thing they felt for one another, and for their women in particular, of course.

'There are a great many kinds of contact, nevertheless,' said Dionys.

'Well, do you know,' said the Major, 'it seems to me there is really only one supreme contact, the contact of love. Mind you, the love may take on an infinite variety of forms. And in my opinion, no form of love is wrong, so long as it *is* love, and you yourself *honour* what you are doing. Love has an extraordinary variety of forms! And that is all that there is in life, it seems to me. But I grant you, if you deny the *variety* of love you deny love altogether. If you try to specialize love into one set of accepted feelings, you wound the very soul of love. Love *must* be multiform, else it is just tyranny, just death.'

'But why call it all *love*?' said the Count.

'Because it seems to me it *is* love: the great power that draws human beings together, no matter what the result of the contact may be. Of course there is hate, but hate is only the recoil of love.'

'Do you think the old Egypt was established on love?' asked Dionys.

'Why, of course! And perhaps the most multiform, the most comprehensive love that the world has seen. All that we suffer from now is that our way of love is narrow, exclusive, and therefore not love at all; more like death and tyranny.'

The Count slowly shook his head, smiling slowly and as if sadly.

'No,' he said. 'No. It is no good. You must use another word than love.'

'I don't agree at all,' said Basil.

'What word then?' blurted Daphne.

The Count looked at her.

'Obedience, submission, faith, belief, responsibility, power,' he said slowly, picking out the words slowly, as if searching for what he wanted, and never quite finding it. He looked with his quiet dark eyes into her eyes. It was curious, she disliked his words intensely, but she liked him. On the other hand, she believed absolutely what her husband said, yet her physical sympathy was against him.

'Do you agree, Daphne?' asked Basil.

'Not a bit,' she replied, with a heavy look at her husband.

'Nor I,' said Basil. 'It seems to me, if you love, there is no obedience nor submission, except to the soul of love. If you mean obedience, submission, and all the rest, to the soul of love itself, I quite agree. But if you mean obedience, submission of one person to another, and one man having power over others – I don't agree, and never shall. It seems to me just there where we have gone wrong. Kaiser Wilhelm II wanted power –'

'No, no,' said the Count. 'He was a mountebank. He had no conception of the sacredness of power.'

'He proved himself very dangerous.'

'Oh yes. But peace can be even more dangerous still.'

'Tell me, then. Do you believe that you, as an aristocrat, should have feudal power over a few hundreds of other men, who happen to be born serfs, or not aristocrats?'

'Not as a hereditary aristocrat, but as a *man* who is by nature an aristocrat,' said the Count, 'it is my sacred duty to hold the lives of other men in my hands, and to shape the issue. But I can never fulfil my destiny till men will willingly put their lives in my hands.'

'You don't expect them to, do you?' smiled Basil.

'At this moment, no.'

'Or at any moment!' The Major was sarcastic.

'At a certain moment the men who are really living will come beseeching to put their lives into the hands of the greater men among them, beseeching the greater men to take the sacred responsibility of power.'

'Do you think so? Perhaps you mean men will at last begin to choose leaders whom they will *love*,' said Basil. 'I wish they would.'

'No, I mean that they will at last yield themselves before men who are greater than they: become vassals by choice.'

'Vassals!' exclaimed Basil, smiling. 'You are still in the feudal ages, Count.'

'Vassals. Not to any hereditary aristocrat – Hohenzollern or Hapsburg or Psanek,' smiled the Count. 'But to the man whose soul is born single, able to be alone, to choose and to command. At last the masses will come to such men and say: "You are greater than we. Be our lords. Take our life and our death in your hands, and dispose of us according to your will. Because we see a light in your face, and a burning on your mouth."'

The Major smiled for many moments, really piqued and amused, watching the Count, who did not turn a hair.

'I say, you must be awfully naïve, Count, if you believe the modern masses are ever going to behave like that. I assure you, they never will.'

'If they did,' said the Count, 'would you call it a new reign of love, or something else?'

'Well, of course, it would contain an element of love. There would have to be an element of love in their feeling for their leaders.'

'Do you think so? I thought that love assumed an equality in difference. I thought that love gave to every man the right to judge the acts of other men – "This was not an act of love, therefore it was wrong." Does not democracy, and love, give to every man this right?'

'Certainly,' said Basil.

'Ah, but my chosen aristocrat would say to those who chose him: "If you choose me, you give up forever your right to judge me. If you have truly chosen to follow me, you have thereby rejected all your right to criticise me. You can no longer either approve or disapprove of me. You have performed the sacred act of choice. Henceforth you can only obey."'

'They wouldn't be able to help criticising, for all that,' said Daphne, blurting in her say.

He looked at her slowly, and for the first time in her life she was doubtful of what she was saying.

'The day of Judas,' he said, 'ends with the day of love.'

Basil woke up from a sort of trance.

'I think, of course, Count,' he said, 'that it's an awfully amusing idea. A retrogression slap back to the Dark Ages.'

'Not so,' said the Count. 'Men – the mass of men – were never before free to perform the sacred act of choice. Today – soon – they may be free.'

'Oh, I don't know. Many tribes chose their kings and chiefs.'

'Men have never before been quite free to choose: and to know what they are doing.'

'You mean they've only made themselves free in order voluntarily to saddle themselves with new lords and masters?'

'I do mean that.'

'In short, life is just a vicious circle?'

'Not at all. An ever-widening circle, as you say. Always more wonderful.'

'Well, it's all frightfully interesting and amusing – don't you think so, Daphne? By the way, Count, where would women be? Would they be allowed to criticise their husbands?'

'Only before marriage,' smiled the Count. 'Not after.'

'Splendid!' said Basil. 'I'm all for that bit of your scheme, Count. I hope you're listening, Daphne.'

'Oh yes. But then I've only married *you*. I've got my right to criticise all the other men,' she said in a dull, angry voice.

'Exactly. Clever of you! So the Count won't get off! Well now, what do you think of the Count's aristocratic scheme for the future, Daphne? Do you approve?'

'Not at all. But then little men have always wanted power,' she said cruelly.

'Oh, big men as well, for that matter,' said Basil, conciliatory.

'I have been told before,' smiled the Count, 'little men are always bossy. I am afraid I have offended Lady Daphne?'

'No,' she said. 'Not really. I'm amused, really. But I always dislike any suggestion of bullying.'

'Indeed, so do I,' said he.

'The Count didn't mean bullying, Daphne,' said Basil. 'Come, there is really an allowable distinction between responsible power and bullying.'

'When men put their heads together about it,' said she.

She was haughty and angry, as if she were afraid of losing something. The Count smiled mischievously at her.

'You are offended, Lady Daphne? But why? You are safe from any spark of my dangerous and extensive authority.'

Basil burst into a roar of laughter.

'It *is* rather funny, you to be talking of power and of not being criticised,' he said. 'But I should like to hear more: I would like to hear more.'

As they drove home, he said to his wife:

'You know I like that little man. He's a quaint little bantam. And he sets one thinking.'

Lady Daphne froze to four degrees below zero, under the north wind of this statement, and not another word was to be thawed out of her.

Curiously enough, it was now Basil who was attracted by the Count, and Daphne who was repelled. Not that she was so bound up in her husband. Not at all. She was feeling rather sore against men altogether. But as so often happens, in this life based on the wicked triangle, Basil could only follow his enthusiasm for the Count in his wife's presence. When the two men were alone together, they were awkward, resistant, they could hardly get out a dozen words to one another. When Daphne was there, however, to complete the circuit of the opposing currents, things went like a house on fire.

This, however, was not much consolation to Lady Daphne. Merely to sit as a passive medium between two men who are squibbing philosophical nonsense to one another: no, it was not good enough! She almost hated the Count: low-browed little fellow, belonging to the race of prehistoric slaves. But her grudge against her white-faced, spiritually intense husband was sharp as vinegar. Let down: she was let down between the pair of them.

What next? Well, what followed was entirely Basil's fault. The winter was passing: it was obvious the war was really over, that Germany was finished. The Hohenzollern had fizzled out like a very poor squib, the Hapsburg was popping feebly in obscurity, the Romanov was smudged out without a sputter. So much for imperial royalty. Henceforth democratic peace.

The Count, of course, would be shipped back now like returned goods that had no market any more. There was a world peace ahead. A week or two, and Voynich Hall would be empty.

Basil, however, could not let matters follow their simple course. He was awfully intrigued by the Count. He wanted to entertain him as a guest before he went. And Major Apsley could get anything in reason, at this moment. So he obtained permission for the poor little Count to stay a fortnight at Thoresway, before being shipped back to Austria. Earl Beveridge, whose soul was black as ink since the war, would never have allowed the little alien enemy to enter his house, had it not been for the hatred which had been aroused in him, during the last two years, by the degrading spectacle of the so-called patriots who had been howling their mongrel indecency in the public face. These mongrels had held the Press and the British public in abeyance for almost two years. Their one aim was to degrade and humiliate anything that was proud or dignified remaining in England. It was almost the worst nightmare of all, this coming to the top of a lot of public filth which was determined to suffocate the souls of all dignified men.

Hence, the Earl, who never intended to be swamped by unclean scum, whatever else happened to him, stamped his heels in the ground and stood on his own feet. When Basil said to him, would he allow the Count to have a fortnight's decent peace in Thoresway before all was finished, Lord Beveridge gave a slow consent, scandal or no scandal. Indeed, it was really to defy scandal that he took such a step. For the thought of his dead boys was bitter to him: and the thought of England fallen under the paws of smelly mongrels was bitterer still.

Lord Beveridge was at Thoresway to receive the Count, who arrived escorted by Basil. The English Earl was a big, handsome man, rather heavy, with a dark, sombre face that would have been haughty if haughtiness had not been made so ridiculous. He was a passionate man, with a passionate man's sensitiveness, generosity, and instinctive overbearing. But *his* dark, passionate nature, and his violent sensitiveness had been subjected now to fifty-five years subtle repression, condemnation, repudiation, till he had almost come to believe in his own wrongness. His little, frail wife, all love for humanity, she was the genuine article. Himself, he was labelled selfish, sensual, cruel, etc. etc. So by now he always seemed to be standing aside, in the shadow, letting himself be obliterated by the pallid rabble of the democratic hurry. That was the impression he gave, of a man standing back, half-ashamed, half-haughty, semi-hidden in the dark background.

He was a little on the defensive as Basil came in with the Count.

'Ah – how do you do, Count Psanek?' he said, striding largely forward and holding out his hand. Because he was the father of Daphne, the Count felt a certain tenderness for the taciturn Englishman.

'You do me too much honour, my lord, receiving me in your house,' said the small Count proudly.

The Earl looked at him slowly, without speaking: seemed to look down on him, in every sense of the words.

'We are still men, Count. We are not beasts altogether.'

'You wish to say that my countrymen are so very nearly beasts, Lord Beveridge?' smiled the Count, curling his fine nose.

Again the Earl was slow in replying.

'You have a low opinion of my manners, Count Psanek.'

'But perhaps a just appreciation of your meaning, Lord Beveridge,' smiled the Count, with the same reckless little look of contempt on his nose.

Lord Beveridge flushed dark, with all his native anger offended.

'I am glad Count Psanek makes my own meaning clear to me,' he said.

'I beg your pardon a thousand times, my lord, if I give offence in doing so,' replied the Count.

The Earl went black, and felt a fool. He turned his back on the Count. And then he turned round again, offering his cigar-case.

'Will you smoke?' he said. There was kindness in his tone.

'Thank you,' said the Count, taking a cigar.

'I dare say,' said Lord Beveridge, 'that all men are beasts in some way. I am afraid I have fallen into the common habit of speaking by rote, and not what I really mean. Won't you take a seat?'

'It is only as a prisoner that I have learned that I am *not* truly a beast. No, I am myself. I am not a beast,' said the Count, seating himself.

The Earl eyed him curiously.

'Well,' he said, smiling, 'I suppose it is best to come to a decision about it.'

'It is necessary, if one is to be safe from vulgarity.'

The Earl felt a twinge of accusation. With his agate-brown, hard-looking eyes he watched the black-browed little Count.

'You are probably right,' he said.

But he turned his face aside.

They were five people at dinner – Lady Beveridge was there as hostess.

'Ah, Count Dionys,' she said with a sigh, 'do you really feel that the war is over?'

'Oh yes,' he replied quickly. 'This war is over. The armies will go home. *Their* cannon will not sound any more. Never again like this.'

'Ah, I hope so,' she sighed.

'I am sure,' he said.

'You think there'll be no more war?' said Daphne.

For some reason she had made herself very fine, in her newest dress of silver and black and pink-chenille, with bare shoulders, and her hair fashionably done. The Count in his shabby uniform turned to her. She was nervous, hurried. Her slim white arm was near him, with the bit of silver at the shoulder. Her skin was white like a hot-house flower. Her lips moved hurriedly.

'Such a war as this there will never be again,' he said.

'What makes you so sure?' she replied, glancing into his eyes.

'The machine of war has got out of control. We shall never start it again, till it has fallen to pieces. We shall be afraid.'

'Will everybody be afraid?' said she, looking down and pressing back her chin.

'I think so.'

'We will hope so,' said Lady Beveridge.

'Do you mind if I ask you, Count,' said Basil, 'what you feel about the way the war has ended? The way it has ended for *you*, I mean.'

'You mean that Germany and Austria have lost the war? It was bound to be. We have all lost the war. All Europe.'

'I agree there,' said Lord Beveridge.

'We've all lost the war?' said Daphne, turning to look at him.

There was pain on his dark, low-browed face. He suffered having the sensitive woman beside him. Her skin had a hot-house delicacy that made his head go round. Her shoulders were broad, rather thin, but the skin was white and so sensitive, so hot-house delicate. It affected him like the perfume of some white, exotic flower. And she seemed to be sending her heart towards him. It was as if she wanted to press her breast to his. From the breast she loved him, and sent out love to him. And it made him unhappy; he wanted to be quiet, and to keep his honour before these hosts.

He looked into her eyes, his own eyes dark with knowledge and pain. She, in her silence and her brief words seemed to be holding them all under her spell. She seemed to have cast a certain muteness on the table, in the midst of which she remained silently master, leaning forward to her plate, and silently mastering them all.

'Don't I think we've all lost the war?' he replied, in answer to her question. 'It was a war of suicide. Nobody could win it. It was suicide for all of us.'

'Oh, I don't know,' she replied. 'What about America and Japan?'

'They don't count. They only helped *us* to commit suicide. They did not enter vitally.'

There was such a look of pain on his face, and such a sound of pain in his voice, that the other three closed their ears, shut off from attending. Only Daphne was making him speak. It was she who was drawing the soul out of him, trying to read the future in him as the augurs read the future in the quivering entrails of the sacrificed beast. She looked direct into his face, searching his soul.

'You think Europe has committed suicide?' she said.

'Morally.'

'Only morally?' came her slow, bronze-like words, so fatal.

'That is enough,' he smiled.

'Quite,' she said, with a slow droop of her eyelids. Then she turned away her face. But he felt the heart strangling inside his breast. What was she doing now? What was she thinking? She filled him with uncertainty and with uncanny fear.

'At least,' said Basil, 'those infernal guns are quiet.'

'For ever,' said Dionys.

'I wish I could believe you, Count,' said the Major.

The talk became more general – or more personal. Lady Beveridge asked Dionys about his wife and family. He knew nothing save that they had gone to Hungary in 1916, when his own house was burnt down. His wife might even have gone to Bulgaria with Prince Bogorik. He did not know.

'But your children, Count!' cried Lady Beveridge.

'I do not know. Probably in Hungary, with their grandmother. I will go when I get back.'

'But have you never *written*? – never inquired?'

'I could not write. I shall know soon enough – everything.'

'You have no son?'

'No. Two girls.'

'Poor things!'

'Yes.'

'I say, isn't it an odd thing to have a ladybird on your crest?' asked Basil, to cheer up the conversation.

'Why queer? Charlemagne had bees. And it is a Marienkäfer – a Mary-beetle. The beetle of Our Lady. I think it is quite a heraldic insect, Major,' smiled the Count.

'You're proud of it?' said Daphne, suddenly turning to look at him again, with her slow, pregnant look.

'I am, you know. It has such a long genealogy – our spotted beetle. Much longer than the Psaneks. I think, you know, it is a descendant of the Egyptian scarabeus, which is a very mysterious emblem. So I connect myself with the Pharaohs: just through my ladybird.'

'You feel your ladybird has crept through so many ages,' she said.

'Imagine it!' he laughed.

'The scarab *is* a piquant insect,' said Basil.

'Do you know Fabre?' put in Lord Beveridge. 'He suggests that the beetle rolling a little ball of dung before him, in a dry old field, must have suggested to the Egyptians the First Principle that set the globe rolling. And so the scarab became the symbol of the creative principle – or something like that.'

'That the earth is a tiny ball of dry dung is good,' said Basil.

'Between the claws of a ladybird,' added Daphne.

'That is what it is, to go back to one's origin,' said Lady Beveridge.

'Perhaps they meant that it was the principle of decomposition which first set the ball rolling,' said the Count.

'The ball would have to be *there* first,' said Basil.

'Certainly. But it hadn't started to roll. Then the principle of decomposition started it.' The Count smiled as if it were a joke.

'I am no Egyptologist,' said Lady Beveridge, 'so I can't judge.'

The Earl and Countess Beveridge left next day. Count Dionys was left with the two young people in the house. It was a beautiful Elizabethan mansion, not very large, but with those magical rooms that are all a twinkle of small-paned windows, looking out from the dark panelled interior. The interior was cosy, panelled to the ceiling, and the ceiling moulded and touched with gold. And then the great square bow of the window with its little panes intervening like magic between oneself and the world outside, the crest in stained glass crowning its colour, the broad window-seat cushioned in faded green. Dionys wandered round the house like a little ghost, through the succession of small and large twinkling sitting-rooms and lounge rooms in front, down the long, wide corridor with the wide stair-head at each end, and up the narrow stairs to the bedrooms above, and on to the roof.

It was early spring, and he loved to sit on the leaded pale-grey roof that had its queer seats and slopes, a little pale world in itself. Then to look down over the garden and the sloping lawn to the ponds massed round with trees, and away to the elms and furrows and hedges of the shires. On the left of the house was the farmstead, with ricks and great-roofed barns and dark-red cattle. Away to the right, beyond the park, was a village among trees, and the spark of a grey church spire.

He liked to be alone, feeling his soul heavy with its own fate. He would sit for hours watching the elm trees standing in rows like giants, like warriors across the country. The Earl had told him that the Romans had brought these elms to Britain. And he seemed to see the spirit of the Romans in them still. Sitting there alone in the spring sunshine, in the solitude of the roof, he saw the glamour of this England of hedgerows and elm trees, and the labourers with slow horses slowly drilling the sod, crossing the brown furrow: and the roofs of the village, with the church steeple rising beside a big black yew tree: and the chequer of fields away to the distance.

And the charm of the old manor around him, the garden with its grey stone walls and yew hedges – broad, broad yew hedges – and a peacock pausing to glitter and scream in the busy silence of an English spring, when celandines open their yellow under the hedges, and violets are in the secret, and by the broad paths of the garden polyanthus and crocuses vary the velvet and flame, and bits of yellow wallflower shake raggedly, with a wonderful triumphance, out of the cracks of the wall. There was a fold somewhere near, and he could hear the treble bleat of the growing lambs, and the deeper, contented baa-ing of the ewes.

This was Daphne's home, where she had been born. She loved it with an ache of affection. But now it was hard to forget her dead brothers. She wandered about in the sun, with two old dogs paddling after her. She talked with everybody – gardener, groom, stableman, with the farm-hands. That filled a large part of her life – straying round talking with the work-people. They were, of course, respectful to her – but not at all afraid of her. They knew she was poor, that she could not afford a car, nor anything. So they talked to her very freely: perhaps a little too freely. Yet she let it be. It was her one passion at Thoresway to hear the dependants talk and talk – about everything. The curious feeling of intimacy across a breach fascinated her. Their lives fascinated her: what they thought, what they *felt*. These, what they felt. That fascinated her. There was a gamekeeper she could have loved – an impudent, ruddy-faced, laughing, ingratiating fellow; she could have loved him, if he had not been isolated beyond the breach of his birth, her culture, her consciousness. Her *consciousness* seemed to make a great gulf between her and the lower classes, the unconscious classes. She accepted it as her doom. She could never meet in real contact anyone but a super-conscious, finished being like herself: or like her husband. Her father had some of the unconscious blood-warmth of the lower classes. But he was like a man who is damned. And the Count, of course. The Count had something that was hot and invisible, a dark flame of life that might warm the cold white fire of her own blood, But –

They avoided each other. All three, they avoided one another. Basil, too, went off alone. Or he immersed himself in poetry. Sometimes he and the Count played billiards. Sometimes all three walked in the park. Often Basil and Daphne walked to the village, to post. But truly, they avoided one another, all three. The days slipped by.

At evening they sat together in the small west room that had books and a piano and comfortable shabby furniture of faded rose-coloured tapestry: a shabby room. Sometimes Basil read aloud: sometimes the Count played the piano. And they talked. And Daphne stitch by stitch went on with a big embroidered bedspread, which she might finish if she lived long enough. But they always went to bed early. They were nearly always avoiding one another.

Dionys had a bedroom in the east bay – a long way from the rooms of the others. He had a habit, when he was quite alone, of singing, or rather crooning to himself the old songs of his childhood. It was only when he felt he was quite alone: when other people seemed to fade out of him, and all the world seemed to dissolve into darkness, and there was nothing but himself, his own soul, alive in the middle of his own small night, isolate for ever. Then, half unconscious, he would croon in a small, high-pitched, squeezed voice, a sort of high dream-voice, the songs of his childhood dialect. It was a curious noise: the sound of a man who is alone in his own blood: almost the sound of a man who is going to be executed.

Daphne heard the sound one night when she was going downstairs again with the corridor lantern to find a book. She was a bad sleeper, and her nights were a torture to her. She, too, like a neurotic, was nailed inside her own fretful self-consciousness. But she had a very keen ear. So she started as she heard the small, bat-like sound of the Count's singing to himself. She stood in the midst of the wide corridor, that was wide as a room, carpeted with a faded lavender-coloured carpet, with a piece of massive dark furniture at intervals by the wall, and an oak arm-chair and sometimes a faded, reddish Oriental rug. The big horn lantern which stood at nights at the end of the corridor she held in her hand. The intense 'peeping' sound of the Count, like a witchcraft, made her forget everything. She could not understand a word, of course. She could not understand the noise even. After listening for a long time, she went on downstairs. When she came back again he was still, and the light was gone from under his door.

After this, it became almost an obsession to her to listen for him. She waited with fretful impatience for ten o'clock, when she could retire. She waited more fretfully still for the maid to leave her, and for her husband to come and say good night. Basil had the room across the corridor. And then in resentful impatience she waited for the sounds of the house to become still. Then she opened her door to listen.

And far away, as if from far, far away in the unseen, like a ventriloquist sound or a bat's uncanny peeping, came the frail, almost inaudible sound of the Count's singing to himself before he went to bed. It *was* inaudible to anyone but herself. But she, by concentration, seemed to hear supernaturally. She had a low arm-chair by the door, and there, wrapped in a huge old black silk shawl, she sat and listened. At first she could not hear. That is, she could hear the sound. But it was only a sound. And then, gradually, gradually she began to follow the thread of it. It was like a thread which she followed out of the world: out of the world. And as she went, slowly, by degrees, far, far away, down the thin thread of his singing, she knew peace – she knew forgetfulness. She could pass beyond the world, away beyond where her soul balanced like a bird on wings, and was perfected.

So it was, in her upper spirit. But underneath was a wild, wild yearning, actually to go, actually to be given. Actually to go, actually to die the death, actually to cross the border and be gone, to be gone. To be gone from this herself, from this Daphne, to be gone from father and mother, brothers and husband, and home and land and world: to be gone. To be gone to the call from the beyond: the call. It was the Count calling. He was calling her. She was sure he was calling her. Out of herself, out of her world, he was calling her.

Two nights she sat just inside her room, by the open door, and listened. Then when he finished she went to sleep, a queer, light, bewitched sleep. In the day she was bewitched. She felt strange and light, as if pressure had been removed from around her. Some pressure had been clamped round her all her life. She had never realized it till now; now it was removed, and her feet felt so light, and her breathing delicate and exquisite. There had always been a pressure against her breathing. Now she breathed delicate and exquisite, so that it was a delight to breathe. Life came in exquisite breaths, quickly, as if it delighted to come to her.

The third night he was silent – though she waited and waited till the small hours of the morning. He was silent, he did not sing. And then she knew the terror and blackness of the feeling that he might never sing any more. She waited like one doomed, throughout the day. And when the night came she trembled. It was her greatest nervous terror, lest her spell should be broken, and she should be thrown back to what she was before.

Night came, and the kind of swoon upon her. Yes, and the call from the night. The call! She rose helplessly and hurried down the corridor. The light was under his door. She sat down in the big oak arm-chair that stood near his door, and huddled herself tight in her black shawl. The corridor was dim with the big, star-studded yellow lantern-light. Away down she could see the lamp-light in her doorway; she had left her door ajar.

But she saw nothing. Only she wrapped herself close in the black shawl, and listened to the sound from the room. It called. Oh, it called her! Why could she not go? Why could she not cross through the closed door.

Then the noise ceased. And then the light went out, under the door of his room. Must she go back? Must she go back? Oh, impossible. As impossible as that the moon should go back on her tracks, once she has risen. Daphne sat on, wrapped in her black shawl. If it must be so, she would sit on through eternity. Return she never could.

And then began the most terrible song of all. It began with a rather dreary, slow, horrible sound, like death. And then suddenly came a real call – fluty, and a kind of whistling and a strange whirr at the changes, most imperative, and utterly inhuman. Daphne rose to her feet. And at the same moment up rose the whistling throb of a summons out of the death moan.

Daphne tapped low and rapidly at the door. 'Count! Count!' she whispered. The sound inside ceased. The door suddenly opened. The pale, obscure figure of Dionys.

'Lady Daphne!' he said in astonishment, automatically standing aside.

'You called,' she murmured rapidly, and she passed intent into his room.

'No, I did not call,' he said gently, his hand on the door still.

'Shut the door,' she said abruptly.

He did as he was bid. The room was in complete darkness. There was no moon outside. She could not see him.

'Where can I sit down?' she said abruptly.

'I will take you to the couch,' he said, putting out his hand and touching her in the dark. She shuddered.

She found the couch and sat down. It was quite dark.

'What are you singing?' she said rapidly.

'I am so sorry. I did not think anyone could hear.'

'What was it you were singing?'

'A song of my country.'

'Had it any words?'

'Yes, it is a woman who was a swan, and who loved a hunter by the marsh. So she became a woman and married him and had three children. Then in the night one night the king of the swans called to her to come back, or else he would die. So slowly she turned into a swan again, and slowly she opened her wide, wide wings, and left her husband and her children.'

There was silence in the dark room. The Count had been really startled, startled out of his mood of the song into the day-mood of human convention. He was distressed and embarrassed by Daphne's presence in his dark room. She, however, sat on and did not make a sound. He, too, sat down in a chair by the window. It was everywhere dark. A wind was blowing in gusts outside. He could see nothing inside his room: only the faint, faint strip of light under the door. But he could feel her presence in the darkness. It was uncanny, to feel her near in the dark, and not to see any sign of her, nor to hear any sound.

She had been wounded in her bewitched state by the contact with the everyday human being in him. But now she began to relapse into her spell, as she sat there in the dark. And he, too, in the silence, felt the world sinking away from him once more, leaving him once more alone on a darkened earth, with nothing between him and the infinite dark space. Except now her presence. Darkness answering to darkness, and deep answering to deep. An answer, near to him, and invisible.

But he did not know what to do. He sat still and silent as she was still and silent. The darkness inside the room seemed alive like blood. He had no power to move. The distance between them seemed absolute.

Then suddenly, without knowing, he went across in the dark, feeling for the end of the couch. And he sat beside her on the couch. But he did not touch her. Neither did she move. The darkness flowed about them thick like blood, and time seemed dissolved in it. They sat with the small, invisible distance between them, motionless, speechless, thoughtless.

Then suddenly he felt her finger-tips touch his arm, and a flame went over him that left him no more a man. He was something seated in flame, in flame unconscious, seated erect, like an Egyptian King-god in the statues. Her finger-tips slid down him, and she herself slid down in a strange, silent rush, and he felt her face against his closed feet and ankles, her hands pressing his ankles. He felt her brow and hair against his ankles, her face against his feet, and there she clung in the dark, as if in space below him. He still sat erect and motionless. Then he bent forward and put his hand on her hair.

'Do you come to me?' he murmured. 'Do you come to me?'

The flame that enveloped him seemed to sway him silently.

'Do you really come to me?' he repeated. 'But we have nowhere to go.'

He felt his bare feet wet with her tears. Two things were struggling in him, the sense of eternal solitude, like space, and the rush of dark flame that would throw him out of his solitude towards her.

He was thinking too. He was thinking of the future. He had no future in the world: of that he was conscious. He had no future in his life. Even if he lived on, it would only be a kind of enduring. But he felt that in the after-life the inheritance was his. He felt the after-life belonged to him.

Future in the world he could not give her. Life in the world he had not to offer her. Better go on alone. Surely better go on alone.

But then the tears on his feet: and her face that would face him as he left her! No, no. The next life was his. He was master of the after-life. Why fear for this life? Why not take the soul she offered him? Now and for ever, for the life that would come when they both were dead. Take her into the underworld. Take her into the dark Hades with him, like Francesca and Paolo. And in hell hold her fast, queen of the underworld, himself master of the underworld. Master of the life to come. Father of the soul that would come after.

'Listen,' he said to her softly. 'Now you are mine. In the dark you are mine. And when you die you are mine. But in the day you are not mine, because I have no power in the day. In the night, in the dark, and in death, you are mine. And that is for ever. No matter if I must leave you. I shall come again from time to time. In the dark you are mine. But in the day I cannot claim you. I have no power in the day, and no place. So remember. When the darkness comes, I shall always be in the darkness of you. And as long as I live, from time to time I shall come to find you, when I am able to, when I am not a prisoner. But I shall have to go away soon. So don't forget – you are the night wife of the ladybird, while you live and even when you die.'

Later, when he took her back to her room, he saw her door still ajar.

'You shouldn't leave a light in your room.' he murmured.

In the morning there was a curious remote look about him. He was quieter than ever, and seemed very far away. Daphne slept late. She had a strange feeling as if she had slipped off all her cares. She did not care, she did not grieve, she did not fret any more. All that had left her. She felt she could sleep, sleep, sleep – for ever. Her face, too, was very still, with a delicate look of virginity that she had never had before. She had always been Aphrodite, the self-conscious one. And her eyes, the green-blue, had been like slow, living jewels, resistant. Now they had unfolded from the hard flower-bud, and had the wonder, and the stillness of a quiet night.

Basil noticed it at once.

'You're different, Daphne,' he said. 'What are you thinking about?'

'I wasn't thinking,' she said, looking at him with candour.

'What were you doing then?'

'What does one do when one doesn't think? Don't make me puzzle it out, Basil.'

'Not a bit of it, if you don't want to.'

But he was puzzled by her. The sting of his ecstatic love for her seemed to have left him. Yet he did not know what else to do but to make love to her. She went very pale. She submitted to him, bowing her head because she was his wife. But she looked at him with fear, with sorrow, with real suffering. He could feel the heaving of her breast, and knew she was weeping. But there were no tears on her face, she was only death-pale. Her eyes were shut.

'Are you in pain?' he asked her.

'No, no!' She opened her eyes, afraid lest she had disturbed him. She did not want to disturb him.

He was puzzled. His own ecstatic, deadly love for her had received a check. He was out of the reckoning.

He watched her when she was with the Count. Then she seemed so meek – so maidenly – so different from what he had known of her. She was so still, like a virgin girl. And it was this quiet, intact quality of Virginity in her which puzzled him most, puzzled his emotions and his ideas. He became suddenly ashamed to make love to her. And because he was ashamed, he said to her as he stood in her room that night:

'Daphne, are you in love with the Count?'

He was standing by the dressing-table, uneasy. She was seated in a low chair by the tiny dying wood fire. She looked up at him with wide, slow eyes. Without a word, with wide, soft, dilated eyes she watched him. What was it that made him feel all confused. He turned his face aside, away from her wide, soft eyes.

'Pardon me, dear. I didn't intend to ask such a question. Don't take any notice of it,' he said. And he strode away and picked up a book. She lowered her head and gazed abstractedly into the fire, without a sound. Then he looked at her again, at her bright hair that the maid had plaited for the night. Her plait hung down over her soft pinkish wrap. His heart softened to her as he saw her sitting there. She seemed like his sister. The excitement of desire had left him, and now he seemed to see clear and feel true for the first time in his life. She was like a dear, dear sister to him. He felt that she was his blood-sister, nearer to him than he had imagined any woman could be. So near – so dear – and all the sex and the desire gone. He didn't want it – he hadn't wanted it. This new pure feeling was so much more wonderful.

He went to her side.

'Forgive me, darling,' he said, 'for having questioned you.'

She looked up at him with the wide eyes, without a word. His face was good and beautiful. Tears came to her eyes.

'You have the right to question me,' she said sadly.

'No,' he said. 'No, darling. I have no right to question you. Daphne! Daphne, darling! It shall be as *you* wish, between us. Shall it? Shall it be as you wish?'

'You are the husband, Basil,' she said sadly.

'Yes, darling. But' – he went on his knees beside her – 'perhaps, darling, something has changed in us. I feel as if I ought never to touch you again – as if I never *wanted* to touch you – in that way. I feel it was wrong, darling. Tell me what you think.'

'Basil, don't be angry with me.'

'It isn't anger; it's pure love, darling – it is.'

'Let us not come any nearer to one another than this, Basil – physically – shall we?' she said. 'And don't be angry with me, will you?'

'Why,' he said. 'I think myself the sexual part has been a mistake. I had rather love you – as I love now. I *know* that this is true love. The other was always a bit whipped up. I *know* I love you now, darling: now I'm free from that other. But what if it comes upon me, that other, Daphne?'

'I am always your wife,' she said quietly. 'I am always your wife. I want always to obey you, Basil: what you wish.'

'Give me your hand, dear.'

She gave him her hand. But the look in her eyes at the same time warned him and frightened him. He kissed her hand and left her.

It was to the Count she belonged. This had decided itself in her down to the depths of her soul. If she could not marry him and be his wife in the world, it had nevertheless happened to her for ever. She could no more question it. Question had gone out of her.

Strange how different she had become – a strange new quiescence. The last days were slipping past. He would be going away – Dionys: he with the still remote face, the man she belonged to in the dark and in the light, for ever. He would be going away. He said it must be so. And she acquiesced. The grief was deep, deep inside her. He must go away. Their lives could not be one life, in this world's day. Even in her anguish she knew it was so. She knew he was right. He was for her infallible. He spoke the deepest soul in her.

She never *saw* him as a lover. When she saw him, he was the little officer, a prisoner, quiet, claiming nothing in all the world. And when she went to him as his lover, his wife, it was always dark. She only knew his voice and his contact in darkness. 'My wife in darkness,' he said to her. And in this too she believed him. She would not have contradicted him, no, not for anything on earth: lest, contradicting him she should lose the dark treasure of stillness and bliss which she kept in her breast even when her heart was wrung with the agony of knowing he must go.

No, she had found this wonderful thing after she had heard him singing: she had suddenly collapsed away from her old self into this darkness, this peace, this quiescence that was like a full dark river flowing eternally in her soul. She had gone to sleep from the *nuit blanche* of her days. And Basil, wonderful, had changed almost at once. She feared him, lest he might change back again. She would always have him to fear. But deep inside her she only feared for this love of hers for the Count: this dark, everlasting love that was like a full river flowing for ever inside her. Ah, let that not be broken.

She was so still inside her. She could sit so still, and feel the day slowly, richly changing to night. And she wanted nothing, she was short of nothing. If only Dionys need not go away! If only he need not go away!

But he said to her, the last morning:

'Don't forget me. Always remember me. I leave my soul in your hands and your womb. Nothing can ever separate us, unless we betray one another. If you have to give yourself to your husband, do so, and obey him. If you are true to me, innerly, innerly true, he will not hurt us. He is generous, be generous to him. And never fail to believe in me. Because even on the other side of death I shall be watching for you. I shall be king in Hades when I am dead. And you will be at my side. You will never leave me any more, in the after-death. So don't be afraid in life. Don't be afraid. If you have to cry tears, cry them. But in your heart of hearts know that I shall come again, and that I have taken you for ever. And so, in your heart of hearts be still, be still, since you are the wife of the ladybird.' He laughed as he left her, with his own beautiful, fearless laugh. But they were strange eyes that looked after him.

He went in the car with Basil back to Voynich Hall.

'I believe Daphne will miss you,' said Basil.

The Count did not reply for some moments.

'Well, if she does,' he said, 'there will be no bitterness in it.'

'Are you sure?' smiled Basil.

'Why – if we are sure of anything,' smiled the Count.

'She's changed, isn't she?'

'Is she?'

'Yes, she's quite changed since you came, Count.'

'She does not seem to me so very different from the girl of seventeen whom I knew.'

'No – perhaps not. I didn't know her then. But she's very different from the wife I have known.'

'A regrettable difference?'

'Well – no, not as far as she goes. She is much quieter inside herself. You know, Count, something of me died in the war. I feel it will take me an eternity to sit and think about it all.'

'I hope you may think it out to your satisfaction, Major.'

'Yes, I hope so too. But that is how it has left me – feeling as if I needed eternity now to brood about it all, you know. Without the need to act – or even to love, really. I suppose love is action.'

'Intense action,' said the Count.

'Quite so. I know really how I feel. I only ask of life to spare me from further effort of action of any sort – even love. And then to fulfil myself, brooding through eternity. Of course, I don't mind *work*, mechanical action. That in itself is a form of inaction.'

'A man can only be happy following his own inmost need,' said the Count.

'Exactly!' said Basil. 'I will lay down the law for nobody, not even for myself. And live my day –'

'Then you will be happy in your own way. I find it so difficult to keep from laying the law down for myself,' said the Count. 'Only the thought of death and the after life saves me from doing it any more.'

'As the thought of eternity helps me,' said Basil. 'I suppose it amounts to the same thing.'

D.H. LAWRENCE

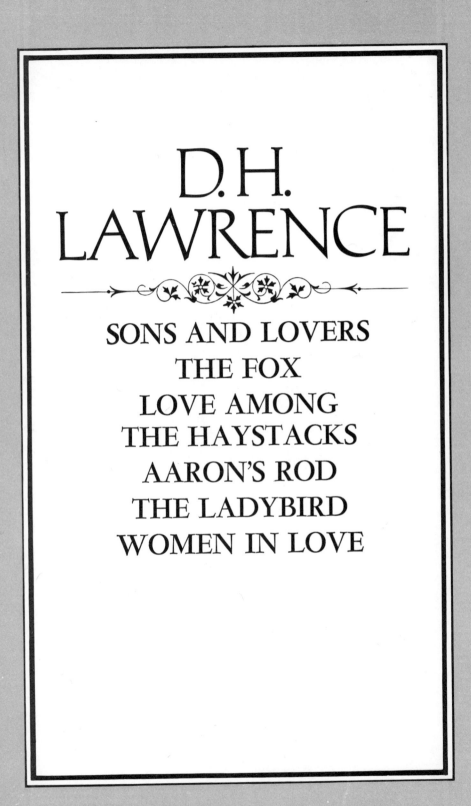

SONS AND LOVERS

THE FOX

LOVE AMONG
THE HAYSTACKS

AARON'S ROD

THE LADYBIRD

WOMEN IN LOVE

1

SISTERS

Ursula and Gudrun Brangwen sat one morning in the window-bay of their father's house in Beldover, working and talking. Ursula was stitching a piece of brightly-coloured embroidery, and Gudrun was drawing upon a board which she held on her knee. They were mostly silent, talking as their thoughts strayed through their minds.

'Ursula,' said Gudrun, 'don't you *really want* to get married?' Ursula laid her embroidery in her lap and looked up. Her face was calm and considerate.

'I don't know,' she replied. 'It depends how you mean.'

Gudrun was slightly taken aback. She watched her sister for some moments.

'Well,' she said, ironically, 'it usually means one thing! But don't you think, anyhow, you'd be –' she darkened slightly – 'in a better position than you are in now.'

A shadow came over Ursula's face.

'I might,' she said. 'But I'm not sure.'

Again Gudrun paused, slightly irritated. She wanted to be quite definite.

'You don't think one needs the *experience* of having been married?' she asked.

'Do you think it need *be* an experience?' replied Ursula.

'Bound to be, in some way or other,' said Gudrun, coolly. 'Possibly undesirable, but bound to be an experience of some sort.'

'Not really,' said Ursula. 'More likely to be the end of experience.'

Gudrun sat very still, to attend to this.

'Of course,' she said, 'there's *that* to consider.' This brought the conversation to a close. Gudrun, almost angrily, took up her rubber and began to rub out part of her drawing. Ursula stitched absorbedly.

'You wouldn't consider a good offer?' asked Gudrun.

'I think I've rejected several,' said Ursula.

'*Really!*' Gudrun flushed dark – 'But anything really worth while? Have you *really*?'

'A thousand a year, and an awfully nice man. I liked him awfully,' said Ursula.

'Really! But weren't you fearfully tempted?'

'In the abstract but not in the concrete,' said Ursula. 'When it comes to the point, one isn't even tempted – oh, if I were tempted, I'd marry like a shot. I'm only tempted *not* to.' The faces of both sisters suddenly lit up with amusement.

'Isn't it an amazing thing,' cried Gudrun, 'how strong the temptation is, not to!' They both laughed, looking at each other. In their hearts they were frightened.

There was a long pause, whilst Ursula stitched and Gudrun went on with her sketch. The sisters were women, Ursula twenty-six, and Gudrun twenty-five. But both had the remote, virgin look of modern girls, sisters of Artemis rather than of Hebe. Gudrun was very beautiful, passive, soft-skinned, soft-limbed. She wore a dress of dark-blue silky stuff, with ruches of blue and green linen lace in the neck and sleeves; and she had emerald-green stockings. Her look of confidence and diffidence contrasted with Ursula's sensitive expectancy. The provincial people, intimidated by Gudrun's perfect sang-froid and exclusive bareness of manner, said of her: 'She is a smart woman.' She had just come back from London, where she had spent several years, working at an art-school, as a student, and living a studio life.

'I was hoping now for a man to come along,' Gudrun said, suddenly catching her underlip between her teeth, and making a strange grimace, half sly smiling, half anguish. Ursula was afraid.

'So you have come home, expecting him here?' she laughed.

'Oh my dear,' cried Gudrun, strident, 'I wouldn't go out of my way to look for him. But if there did happen to come along a highly attractive individual of sufficient means – well –' she tailed off ironically. Then she looked searchingly at Ursula, as if to probe her. 'Don't you find yourself getting bored?' she asked of her sister. 'Don't you find, that things fail to materialize? *Nothing materializes!* Everything withers in the bud.'

'What withers in the bud?' asked Ursula.

'Oh, everything – oneself – things in general.' There was a pause, whilst each sister vaguely considered her fate.

'It does frighten one,' said Ursula, and again there was a pause. 'But do you hope to get anywhere by just marrying?'

'It seems to be the inevitable next step,' said Gudrun. Ursula pondered this, with a little bitterness. She was a class mistress herself, in Willey Green Grammar School, as she had been for some years.

'I know,' she said, 'it seems like that when one thinks in the abstract. But really imagine it: imagine any man one knows, imagine him coming home to one every evening, and saying "Hello", and giving one a kiss –'

There was a blank pause.

'Yes,' said Gudrun, in a narrowed voice. 'It's just impossible. The man makes it impossible.'

'Of course there's children –' said Ursula doubtfully.

Gudrun's face hardened.

'Do you *really* want children, Ursula?' she asked coldly. A dazzled, baffled look came on Ursula's face.

'One feels it is still beyond one,' she said.

'*Do* you feel like that?' asked Gudrun. 'I get no feeling whatever from the thought of bearing children.'

Gudrun looked at Ursula with a mask-like, expressionless face. Ursula knitted her brows.

'Perhaps it isn't genuine,' she faltered. 'Perhaps one doesn't really want them, in one's soul – only superficially.' A hardness came over Gudrun's face. She did not want to be too definite.

'When one thinks of other people's children –' said Ursula.

Again Gudrun looked at her sister, almost hostile.

'Exactly,' she said, to close the conversation.

The two sisters worked on in silence. Ursula having always that strange brightness of an essential flame that is caught, meshed, contravened. She lived a good deal by herself, to herself, working, passing on from day to day, and always thinking, trying to lay hold on life, to grasp it in her own understanding. Her active living was suspended, but underneath, in the darkness, something was coming to pass. If only she could break through the last integuments! She seemed to try and put her hands out, like an infant in the womb, and she could not, not yet. Still she had a strange prescience, an intimation of something yet to come.

She laid down her work and looked at her sister. She thought Gudrun so *charming*, so infinitely charming, in her softness and her fine, exquisite richness of texture and delicacy of line. There was a certain playfulness about her too, such a piquancy or ironic suggestion, such an untouched reserve. Ursula admired her with all her soul.

'Why did you come home, Prune?' she asked.

Gudrun knew she was being admired. She sat back from her drawing and looked at Ursula, from under her finely-curved lashes.

'Why did I come back, Ursula?' she repeated. 'I have asked myself a thousand times.'

'And don't you know?'

'Yes, I think I do. I think my coming back home was just *reculer pour mieux sauter*.'

And she looked with a long, slow look of knowledge at Ursula.

'I know!' cried Ursula, looking slightly dazzled and falsified, and as if she did *not* know. 'But where can one jump to?'

'Oh, it doesn't matter,' said Gudrun, somewhat superbly. 'If one jumps over the edge, one is bound to land somewhere.'

'But isn't it very risky?' asked Ursula.

A slow mocking smile dawned on Gudrun's face.

'Ah!' she said, laughing. 'What is it all but words!' And so again she closed the conversation. But Ursula was still brooding.

'And how do you find home, now you have come back to it?' she asked.

Gudrun paused for some moments, coldly, before answering. Then, in a cold truthful voice, she said:

'I find myself completely out of it.'

'And father?'

Gudrun looked at Ursula, almost with resentment, as if brought to bay.

'I haven't thought about him: I've refrained,' she said coldly.

'Yes,' wavered Ursula; and the conversation was really at an end. The sisters found themselves confronted by a void, a terrifying chasm, as if they had looked over the edge.

They worked on in silence for some time, Gudrun's cheek was flushed with repressed emotion. She resented its having been called into being.

'Shall we go and look at that wedding?' she asked at length, in a voice that was too casual.

'Yes!' cried Ursula, too eagerly, throwing aside her sewing and leaping up, as if to escape something, thus betraying the tension of the situation and causing a friction of dislike to go over Gudrun's nerves.

As she went upstairs, Ursula was aware of the house, of her home round about her. And she loathed it, the sordid, too-familiar place! She was afraid at the depth of her feeling against the home, the milieu, the whole atmosphere and condition of this obsolete life. Her feeling frightened her.

The two girls were soon walking swiftly down the main road of Beldover, a wide street, part shops, part dwelling-houses, utterly formless and sordid, without poverty. Gudrun, new from her life in Chelsea and Sussex, shrank cruelly from this amorphous ugliness of a small colliery town in the Midlands. Yet forward she went, through the whole sordid gamut of pettiness, the long amorphous, gritty street. She was exposed to every stare, she passed on through a stretch of torment. It was strange that she should have chosen to come back and test the full effect of this shapeless, barren ugliness upon herself. Why had she wanted to submit herself to it, did she still want to submit herself to it, the insufferable torture of these ugly, meaningless people, this defaced countryside? She felt like a beetle toiling in the dust. She was filled with repulsion.

They turned off the main road, past a black patch of common-garden, where sooty cabbage stumps stood shameless. No one thought to be ashamed. No one was ashamed of it all.

'It is like a country in an underworld,' said Gudrun. 'The colliers bring it above-ground with them, shovel it up. Ursula it's marvellous, it's really marvellous – it's really wonderful, another world. The people are all ghouls, and everything is ghostly. Everything is a ghoulish replica of the real world, a replica, a ghoul, all soiled, everything sordid. It's like being mad, Ursula.'

The sisters were crossing a black path through a dark, soiled field. On the left was a large landscape, a valley with collieries, and opposite hills with cornfields and woods, all blackened with distance, as if seen through a veil of crape. White and black smoke rose up in steady columns, magic within the dark air. Near at hand came the long rows of dwellings, approaching curved up the hill-slope, in straight lines along the brow of the hill. They were of darkened red brick, brittle, with dark slate roofs. The path on which the sisters walked was black, trodden-in by the feet of the recurrent colliers, and bounded from the field by iron fences; the stile that led again into the road was rubbed shiny by the moleskins of the passing miners. Now the two girls were going between some rows of dwellings, of the poorer sort. Women, their arms folded over their coarse aprons, standing gossiping at the end of their block, stared after the Brangwen sisters with that long, unwearying stare of aborigines; children called out names.

Gudrun went on her way half dazed. If this were human life, if these were human beings, living in a complete world, then what was her own world, outside? She was aware of her grass-green stockings, her large grass-green velour hat, her full soft coat, of a strong blue colour. And she felt as if she were treading in the air, quite unstable, her heart was contracted, as if at any minute she might be precipitated to the ground. She was afraid.

She clung to Ursula, who, through long usage, was inured to this violation of a dark, uncreated, hostile world. But all the time her heart was crying, as if in the midst of some ordeal: 'I want to go back, I want to go away, I want not to know it, not to know that this exists.' Yet she must go forward.

Ursula could feel her suffering.

'You hate this, don't you?' she asked.

'It bewilders me,' stammered Gudrun.

'You won't stay long,' replied Ursula.

And Gudrun went along, grasping at release.

They drew away from the colliery region, over the curve of the hill, into the purer country of the other side, towards Willey Green. Still the faint glamour of blackness persisted over the fields and the wooded hills, and seemed darkly to gleam in the air. It was a spring day, chilly, with snatches of sunshine. Yellow celandines showed out from the hedge-bottoms, and in the cottage gardens of Willey Green, currant-bushes were breaking into leaf, and little flowers were coming white on the grey alyssum that hung over the stone walls.

Turning, they passed down the high-road, that went between high banks towards the church. There, in the lowest bend of the road, low under the trees, stood a little group of expectant people, waiting to see the wedding. The daughter of the chief mine-owner of the district, Thomas Crich, was getting married to a naval officer.

'Let us go back,' said Gudrun, swerving away. 'There are all those people.' And she hung wavering in the road.

'Never mind them,' said Ursula, 'they're all right. They all know me, they don't matter.'

'But must we go through them?' asked Gudrun.

'They're quite all right, really,' said Ursula, going forward. And together the two sisters approached the group of uneasy, watchful common people. They were chiefly women, colliers' wives of the more shiftless sort. They had watchful, underworld faces.

The two sisters held themselves tense, and went straight towards the gate. The women made way for them, but barely sufficient, as if grudging to yield ground. The sisters passed in silence through the stone gateway and up the steps, on the red carpet, a policeman estimating their progress.

'What price the stockings!' said a voice at the back of Gudrun. A sudden fierce anger swept over the girl, violent and murderous. She would have liked them all annihilated, cleared away, so that the world was left clear for her. How she hated walking up the churchyard path, along the red carpet, continuing in motion, in their sight.

'I won't go into the church,' she said suddenly, with such final decision that Ursula immediately halted, turned round, and branched off up a small side path which led to the little private gate of the Grammar School, whose grounds adjoined those of the church.

Just inside the gate of the school shrubbery, outside the churchyard, Ursula sat down for a moment on the low stone wall under the laurel bushes, to rest. Behind her, the large red building of the school rose up peacefully, the windows all open for the holiday. Over the shrubs, before her, were the pale roofs and tower of the old church. The sisters were hidden by the foliage.

Gudrun sat down in silence. Her mouth was shut close, her face averted. She was regretting bitterly that she had ever come back. Ursula looked at her, and thought how amazingly beautiful she was, flushed with discomfiture. But she caused a constraint over Ursula's nature, a certain weariness. Ursula wished to be alone, freed from the tightness, the enclosure of Gudrun's presence.

'Are we going to stay here?' asked Gudrun.

'I was only resting a minute,' said Ursula, getting up as if rebuked. 'We will stand in the corner by the fives-court, we shall see everything from there.'

For the moment, the sunshine fell brightly into the churchyard, there was a vague scent of sap and of spring, perhaps of violets from off the graves. Some white daisies were out, bright as angels. In the air, the unfolding leaves of a copper-beech were blood-red.

Punctually at eleven o'clock, the carriages began to arrive. There was a stir in the crowd at the gate, a concentration as a carriage drove up, wedding guests were mounting up the steps and passing along the red carpet to the church. They were all gay and excited because the sun was shining.

Gudrun watched them closely, with objective curiosity. She saw each one as a complete figure, like a character in a book, or a subject in a picture, or a marionette in a theatre, a finished creation. She loved to recognize their various characteristics, to place them in their true light, give them their own surroundings, settle them for ever as they passed before her along the path to the church. She knew them, they were finished, sealed and stamped and finished with, for her. There was none that had anything unknown, unresolved, until the Criches themselves began to appear. Then her interest was piqued. Here was something not quite so preconcluded.

There came the mother, Mrs Crich, with her eldest son Gerald. She was a queer unkempt figure, in spite of the attempts that had obviously been made to bring her into line for the day. Her face was pale, yellowish, with a clear, transparent skin, she leaned forward rather, her features were strongly marked, handsome, with a tense, unseeing, predative look. Her colourless hair was untidy, wisps floating down on to her sac coat of dark blue silk, from under her blue silk hat. She looked like a woman with a monomania, furtive almost, but heavily proud.

Her son was of a fair, sun-tanned type, rather above middle height, well-made, and almost exaggeratedly well-dressed. But about him also was the strange, guarded look, the unconscious glisten, as if he did not belong to the same creation as the people about him. Gudrun lighted on him at once. There was something northern about him that magnetized her. In his clear northern flesh and his fair hair was a glisten like sunshine refracted through crystals of ice. And he looked so new, unbroached, pure as an arctic thing. Perhaps he was thirty years old, perhaps more. His gleaming beauty, maleness, like a young, good-humoured, smiling wolf, did not blind her to the significant, sinister stillness in his bearing, the lurking danger of his unsubdued temper. 'His totem is the wolf,' she repeated to herself. 'His mother is an old, unbroken wolf.' And then she experienced a keen paroxysm, a transport, as if she had made some incredible discovery, known to nobody else on earth. A strange transport took possession of her, all her veins were in a paroxysm of violent sensation. 'Good God!' she exclaimed to herself, 'what is this?' And then, a moment after, she was saying assuredly, 'I shall know more of that man.' She was tortured with desire to see him again, a nostalgia, a necessity to see him again, to make sure it was not all a mistake, that she was not deluding herself, that she really felt this strange and overwhelming sensation on his account, this knowledge of him in her essence, this powerful apprehension of him. 'Am I *really* singled out for him in some way, is there really some pale gold, arctic light that envelops only us two?' she asked herself. And she could not believe it, she remained in a muse, scarcely conscious of what was going on around.

The bridesmaids were here, and yet the bridegroom had not come. Ursula wondered if something was amiss, and if the wedding would yet all go wrong. She felt troubled, as if it rested upon her. The chief bridesmaids had arrived. Ursula watched them come up the steps. One of them she knew, a tall, slow, reluctant woman with a weight of fair hair and a pale, long face. This was Hermione Roddice, a friend of the Criches. Now she came along, with her head held up, balancing an enormous flat hat of pale yellow velvet, on which were streaks of ostrich feathers, natural and grey. She drifted forward as if scarcely conscious, her long blanched face lifted up, not to see the world. She was rich. She wore a dress of silky, frail velvet, of pale yellow colour, and she carried a lot of small rose-coloured cyclamens. Her shoes and stockings were of brownish grey, like the feathers on her hat, her hair was heavy, she drifted along with a peculiar fixity of the hips, a strange unwilling motion. She was impressive, in her lovely pale-yellow and brownish-rose, yet macabre, something repulsive. People were silent when she passed, impressed, roused, wanting to jeer, yet for some reason silenced. Her long, pale face, that she carried lifted up, somewhat in the Rossetti fashion, seemed almost drugged, as if a strange mass of thoughts coiled in the darkness within her, and she was never allowed to escape.

Ursula watched her with fascination. She knew her a little. She was the most remarkable woman in the Midlands. Her father was a Derbyshire Baronet of the old school, she was a woman of the new school, full of intellectuality, and heavy, nerve-worn with consciousness. She was passionately interested in reform, her soul was given up to the public cause. But she was a man's woman, it was the manly world that held her.

She had various intimacies of mind and soul with various men of capacity. Ursula knew, among these men, only Rupert Birkin, who was one of the school-inspectors of the county. But Gudrun had met others, in London. Moving with her artist friends in different kinds of society, Gudrun had already come to know a good many people of repute and standing. She had met Hermione twice, but they did not take to each other. It would be queer to meet again down here in the Midlands, where their social standing was so diverse, after they had known each other on terms of equality in the houses of sundry acquaintances in town. For Gudrun had been a social success, and had her friends among the slack aristocracy that keeps touch with the arts.

Hermione knew herself to be well-dressed; she knew herself to be the social equal, if not far the superior, of anyone she was likely to meet in Willey Green. She knew she was accepted in the world of culture and of intellect. She was a *Kulturträger*, a medium for the culture of ideas. With all that was highest, whether in society or in thought or in public action, or even in art, she was at one, she moved among the foremost, at home with them. No one could put her down, no one could make mock of her, because she stood among the first, and those that were against her were below her, either in rank, or in wealth, or in high association of thought and progress and understanding. So, she was invulnerable. All her life, she had sought to make herself invulnerable, unassailable, beyond reach of the world's judgment.

And yet her soul was tortured, exposed. Even walking up the path to the church, confident as she was that in every respect she stood beyond all vulgar judgment, knowing perfectly that her appearance was complete and perfect, according to the first standards, yet she suffered a torture, under her confidence and her pride, feeling herself exposed to wounds and to mockery and to despite. She always felt vulnerable, vulnerable, there was always a secret chink in her armour. She did not know herself what it was. It was a lack of robust self, she had no natural sufficiency, there was a terrible void, a lack, a deficiency of being within her.

And she wanted someone to close up this deficiency, to close it up for ever. She craved for Rupert Birkin. When he was there, she felt complete, she was sufficient, whole. For the rest of time she was established on the sand, built over a chasm, and, in spite of all her vanity and securities, any common maid-servant of positive, robust temper could fling her down this bottomless pit of insufficiency, by the slightest movement of jeering or contempt. And all the while the pensive, tortured women piled up her own defences of aesthetic knowledge, and culture, and world-visions, and disinterestedness. Yet she could never stop up the terrible gap of insufficiency.

If only Birkin would form a close and abiding connection with her, she would be safe during this fretful voyage of life. He could make her sound and triumphant over the very angels of heaven. If only he would do it! But she was tortured with fear, with misgiving. She made herself beautiful, she strove so hard to come to that degree of beauty and advantage, when he should be convinced. But always there was a deficiency.

He was perverse too. He fought her off, he always fought her off. The more she strove to bring him to her, the more he battled her back. And they had been lovers now, for years. Oh, it was so wearying, so aching; she was so tired. But still she believed in herself. She knew he was trying to leave her. She knew he was trying to break away from her finally, to be free. But still she believed in her strength to keep him, she believed in her own higher knowledge. His own knowledge was high, she was the central touchstone of truth. She only needed his conjunction with her.

And this, this conjunction with her, which was his highest fulfilment also, with the perverseness of a wilful child, he wanted to deny. With the wilfulness of an obstinate child, he wanted to break the holy connection that was between them.

He would be at this wedding; he was to be groom's man. He would be in the church, waiting. He would know when she came. She shuddered with nervous apprehension and desire as she went through the church-door. He would be there, surely he would see how beautiful her dress was, surely he would see how she had made herself beautiful for him. He would understand, he would be able to see how she was made for him, the first, how she was, for him, the highest. Surely at last he would be able to accept his highest fate, he would not deny her.

In a little convulsion of too-tired yearning, she entered the church and looked slowly along her cheeks for him, her slender body convulsed with agitation. As best man, he would be standing beside the altar. She looked slowly, deferring in her certainty.

And then, he was not there. A terrible storm came over her, as if she were drowning. She was possessed by a devastating hopelessness. And she approached mechanically to the altar. Never had she known such a pang of utter and final hopelessness. It was beyond death, so utterly null, desert.

The bridegroom and the groom's man had not yet come. There was a growing consternation outside. Ursula felt almost responsible. She could not bear it that the bride should arrive and no groom. The wedding must not be a fiasco, it must not.

But here was the bride's carriage, adorned with ribbons and cockades. Gaily the grey horses curvetted to their destination at the church-gate, a laughter in the whole movement. Here was the quick of all laughter and pleasure. The door of the carriage was thrown open, to let out the very blossom of the day. The people on the roadway murmured faintly with the discontented murmuring of a crowd.

The father stepped out first into the air of the morning, like a shadow. He was a tall, thin, careworn man, with a thin black beard that was touched with grey. He waited at the door of the carriage patiently, self-obliterated.

In the opening of the doorway was a shower of fine foliage and flowers, a whiteness of satin and lace, and a sound of a gay voice saying:

'How do I get out?'

A ripple of satisfaction ran through the expectant people. They pressed near to receive her, looking with zest at the stooping blonde head with its flower buds, and at the delicate, white, tentative foot that was reaching down to the step of the carriage. There was a sudden foaming rush, and the bride like a sudden self-rush, floating all white beside her father in the morning shadow of trees, her veil flowing with laughter.

'That's done it!' she said.

She put her hand on the arm of her careworn, sallow father, and frothing her light draperies, proceeded over the eternal red carpet. Her father, mute and yellowish, his black beard making him look more careworn, mounted the steps stiffly, as if his spirit were absent; but the laughing mist of the bride went along with him undiminished.

And no bridegroom had arrived! It was intolerable for her. Ursula, her heart strained with anxiety, was watching the hill beyond; the white, descending road, that should give sight of him. There was a carriage. It was running. It had just come into sight. Yes, it was he. Ursula turned towards the bride and the people, and from her place of vantage, gave an inarticulate cry. She wanted to warn them that he was coming. But her cry was inarticulate and inaudible, and she flushed deeply, between her desire and her wincing confusion.

The carriage rattled down the hill, and drew near. There was a shout from the people. The bride, who had just reached the top of the steps, turned round gaily to see what was the commotion. She saw a confusion among the people, a cab pulling up, and her lover dropping out of the carriage, and dodging among the horses and into the crowd.

'Tibs! Tibs!' she cried in her sudden, mocking excitement, standing high on the path in the sunlight and waving her bouquet. He, dodging with his hat in his hand, had not heard.

'Tibs!' she cried again, looking down to him.

He glanced up, unaware, and saw the bride and her father standing on the path above him. A queer, startled look went over his face. He hesitated for a moment. Then he gathered himself together for a leap, to overtake her.

'Ah-h-h!' came her strange, intaken cry, as, on the reflex, she started, turned and fled, scudding with an unthinkable swift beating of her white feet and fraying of her white garments, towards the church. Like a hound the young man was after her, leaping the steps and swinging past her father, his supple haunches working like those of a hound that bears down on the quarry.

'Ay, after her!' cried the vulgar women below, carried suddenly into the sport.

She, her flowers shaken from her like froth, was steadying herself to turn the angle of the church. She glanced behind, and with a wild cry of laughter and challenge, veered, poised, and was gone beyond the grey stone buttress. In another instant the bridegroom, bent forward as he ran, had caught the angle of the silent stone with his hand, and had swung himself out of sight, his supple, strong loins vanishing in pursuit.

Instantly cries and exclamations of excitement burst from the crowd at the gate. And then Ursula noticed again the dark, rather stooping figure of Mr Crich, waiting suspended on the path, watching with expressionless face the flight to the church. It was over, and he turned round to look behind him, at the figure of Rupert Birkin, who at once came forward and joined him.

'We'll bring up the rear,' said Birkin, a faint smile on his face.

'Ay!' replied the father laconically. And the two men turned together up the path.

Birkin was as thin as Mr Crich, pale and ill-looking. His figure was narrow but nicely made. He went with a slight trail of one foot, which came only from self-consciousness. Although he was dressed correctly for his part, yet there was an innate incongruity which caused a slight ridiculousness in his appearance. His nature was clever and separate, he did not fit at all in the conventional occasion. Yet he subordinated himself to the common idea, travestied himself.

He affected to be quite ordinary, perfectly and marvellously commonplace. And he did it so well, taking the tone of his surroundings, adjusting himself quickly to his interlocutor and his circumstance, that he achieved a verisimilitude of ordinary commonplaceness that usually propitiated his onlookers for the moment, disarmed them from attacking his singleness.

Now he spoke quite easily and pleasantly to Mr Crich, as they walked along the path; he played with situations like a man on a tight-rope: but always on a tight-rope, pretending nothing but ease.

'I'm sorry we are so late,' he was saying. 'We couldn't find a button-hook, so it took us a long time to button our boots. But you were to the moment.'

'We are usually to time,' said Mr Crich.

'And I'm always late,' said Birkin. 'But today I was *really* punctual, only accidentally not so. I'm sorry.'

The two men were gone, there was nothing more to see, for the time. Ursula was left thinking about Birkin. He piqued her, attracted her, and annoyed her.

She wanted to know him more. She had spoken with him once or twice, but only in his official capacity as inspector. She thought he seemed to acknowledge some kinship between her and him, a natural, tacit understanding, a using of the same language. But there had been no time for the understanding to develop. And something kept her from him, as well as attracted her to him. There was a certain hostility, a hidden ultimate reserve in him, cold and inaccessible.

Yet she wanted to know him.

'What do you think of Rupert Birkin?' she asked, a little reluctantly, of Gudrun. She did not want to discuss him.

'What do I think of Rupert Birkin?' repeated Gudrun. 'I think he's attractive – decidedly attractive. What I can't stand about him is his way with other people – his way of treating any little fool as if she were his greatest consideration. One feels so awfully sold, oneself.'

'Why does he do it?' said Ursula.

'Because he has no real critical faculty – of people, at all events,' said Gudrun. 'I tell you, he treats any little fool as he treats me or you – and it's such an insult.'

'Oh, it is,' said Ursula. 'One must discriminate.'

'One *must* discriminate,' repeated Gudrun. 'But he's a wonderful chap, in other respects – a marvellous personality. But you can't trust him.'

'Yes,' said Ursula vaguely. She was always forced to assent to Gudrun's pronouncements, even when she was not in accord altogether.

The sisters sat silent, waiting for the wedding party to come out. Gudrun was impatient of talk. She wanted to think about Gerald Crich. She wanted to see if the strong feeling she had got from him was real. She wanted to have herself ready.

Inside the church, the wedding was going on. Hermione Roddice was thinking only of Birkin. He stood near her. She seemed to gravitate physically towards him. She wanted to stand touching him. She could hardly be sure he was near her, if she did not touch him. Yet she stood subjected through the wedding service.

She had suffered so bitterly when he did not come, that still she was dazed. Still she was gnawed as by a neuralgia, tormented by his potential absence from her. She had awaited him in a faint delirium of nervous torture. As she stood bearing herself pensively, the rapt look on her face, that seemed spiritual, like the angels, but which came from torture, gave her a certain poignancy that tore his heart with pity. He saw her bowed head, her rapt face, the face of an almost demoniacal ecstatic. Feeling him looking, she lifted her face and sought his eyes, her own beautiful grey eyes flaring him a great signal. But he avoided her look, she sank her head in torment and shame, the gnawing at her heart going on. And he too was tortured with shame, and ultimate dislike, and with acute pity for her, because he did not want to meet her eyes, he did not want to receive her flare of recognition.

The bride and bridegroom were married, the party went into the vestry. Hermione crowded involuntarily up against Birkin, to touch him. And he endured it.

Outside, Gudrun and Ursula listened for their father's playing on the organ. He would enjoy playing a wedding march. Now the married pair were coming! The bells were ringing, making the air shake. Ursula wondered if the trees and the flowers could feel the vibration, and what they thought of it, this strange motion in the air. The bride was quite demure on the arm of the bridegroom, who stared up into the sky before him, shutting and opening his eyes unconsciously, as if he were neither here nor there. He looked rather comical, blinking and trying to be in the scene, when emotionally he was violated by his exposure to a crowd. He looked a typical naval officer, manly, and up to his duty.

Birkin came with Hermione. She had a rapt, triumphant look, like the fallen angels restored, yet still subtly demoniacal, now she held Birkin by the arm. And he was expressionless, neutralized, possessed by her as if it were his fate, without question.

Gerald Crich came, fair, good-looking, healthy, with a great reserve of energy. He was erect and complete, there was a strange stealth glistening through his amiable, almost happy appearance. Gudrun rose sharply and went away. She could not bear it. She wanted to be alone, to know this strange, sharp inoculation that had changed the whole temper of her blood.

2

SHORTLANDS

The Brangwens went home to Beldover, the wedding party gathered at Shortlands, the Criches' home. It was a long, low old house, a sort of manor farm, that spread along the top of a slope just beyond the narrow little lake of Willey Water. Shortlands looked across a sloping meadow that might be a park, because of the large, solitary trees that stood here and there, across the water of the narrow lake, at the wooded hill that successfully hid the colliery valley beyond, but did not quite hide the rising smoke. Nevertheless, the scene was rural and picturesque, very peaceful, and the house had a charm of its own.

It was crowded now with the family and the wedding guests. The father, who was not well, withdrew to rest. Gerald was host. He stood in the homely entrance hall, friendly and easy, attending to the men. He seemed to take pleasure in his social functions, he smiled, and was abundant in hospitality.

The women wandered about in a little confusion, chased hither and thither by the three married daughters of the house. All the while there could be heard the characteristic, imperious voice of one Crich woman or another calling 'Helen, come here a minute,' 'Marjory, I want you – here.' 'Oh, I say, Mrs Witham –' There was a great rustling of skirts, swift glimpses of smartly-dressed women, a child danced through the hall and back again, a maidservant came and went hurriedly.

Meanwhile the men stood in calm little groups, chatting, smoking, pretending to pay no heed to the rustling animation of the women's world. But they could not really talk, because of the glassy ravel of women's excited, cold laughter and running voices. They waited, uneasy, suspended, rather bored. But Gerald remained as if genial and happy, unaware that he was waiting or unoccupied, knowing himself the very pivot of the occasion.

Suddenly Mrs Crich came noiselessly into the room, peering about with her strong, clear face. She was still wearing her hat, and her sac coat of blue silk.

'What is it, mother?' said Gerald.

'Nothing, nothing!' she answered vaguely. And she went straight towards Birkin, who was talking to a Crich brother-in-law.

'How do you do, Mr Birkin,' she said, in her low voice, that seemed to take no count of her guests. She held out her hand to him.

'Oh Mrs Crich,' replied Birkin, in his readily-changing voice, 'I couldn't come to you before.'

'I don't know half the people here,' she said, in her low voice. Her son-in-law moved uneasily away.

'And you don't like strangers?' laughed Birkin. 'I myself can never see why one should take account of people, just because they happen to be in the room with one: why *should* I know they are there?'

'Why indeed, why indeed!' said Mrs Crich, in her low, tense voice. 'Except that they *are* there. *I* don't know people whom I find in the house. The children introduce them to me – "Mother, this is Mr So-and-so." I am no further. What has Mr So-and-so to do with his own name? – and what have I to do with either him or his name!'

She looked up at Birkin. She startled him. He was flattered too that she came to talk to him, for she took hardly any notice of anybody. He looked down at her tense clear face, with its heavy features, but he was afraid to look into her heavy-seeing blue eyes. He noticed instead how her hair looped in slack, slovenly strands over her rather beautiful ears, which were not quite clean. Neither was her neck perfectly clean. Even in that he seemed to belong to her, rather than to the rest of the company; though, he thought to himself, he was always well washed, at any rate at the neck and ears.

He smiled faintly, thinking these things. Yet he was tense, feeling that he and the elderly, estranged woman were conferring together like traitors, like enemies within the camp of the other people. He resembled a deer, that throws one ear back upon the trail behind, and one ear forward, to know what is ahead.

'People don't really matter,' he said, rather unwilling to continue.

The mother looked up at him with sudden, dark interrogation, as if doubting his sincerity.

'How do you mean, *matter*?' she asked sharply.

'Not many people are anything at all,' he answered, forced to go deeper than he wanted to. 'They jingle and giggle. It would be much better if they were just wiped out. Essentially, they don't exist, they aren't there.'

She watched him steadily while he spoke.

'But we don't imagine them,' she said sharply.

'There's nothing to imagine, that's why they don't exist.'

'Well,' she said, 'I would hardly go as far as that. There they are, whether they exist or no. It doesn't rest with me to decide on their existence. I only know that I can't be expected to take count of them all. You can't expect me to know them, just because they happen to be there. As far as *I* go they might as well not be there.'

'Exactly,' he replied.

'Mightn't they?' she asked again.

'Just as well,' he repeated. And there was a little pause.

'Except that they *are* there, and that's a nuisance,' she said. 'There are my sons-in-law,' she went on, in a sort of monologue. 'Now Laura's got married, there's another. And I really don't know John from James yet. They come up to me and call me mother. I know what they will say – "How are you, mother?" I ought to say, "I am not your mother, in any sense." But what is the use? There they are. I have had children of my own. I suppose I know them from another woman's children.'

'One would suppose so,' he said.

She looked at him, somewhat surprised, forgetting perhaps that she was talking to him. And she lost her thread.

She looked round the room, vaguely. Birkin could not guess what she was looking for, nor what she was thinking. Evidently she noticed her sons.

'Are my children all there?' she asked him abruptly.

He laughed, startled, afraid perhaps.

'I scarcely know them, except Gerald,' he replied.

'Gerald!' she exclaimed. 'He's the most wanting of them all. You'd never think it, to look at him now, would you?'

'No,' said Birkin.

The mother looked across at her eldest son, stared at him heavily for some time.

'Ay,' she said, in an incomprehensible monosyllable, that sounded profoundly cynical. Birkin felt afraid, as if he dared not realize. And Mrs Crich moved away, forgetting him. But she returned on her traces.

'I should like him to have a friend,' she said. 'He has never had a friend.'

Birkin looked down into her eyes, which were blue, and watching heavily. He could not understand them. 'Am I my brother's keeper?' he said to himself, almost flippantly.

Then he remembered, with a slight shock, that that was Cain's cry. And Gerald was Cain, if anybody. Not that he was Cain, either, although he had slain his brother. There was such a thing as pure accident, and the consequences did not attach to one, even though one had killed one's brother in such wise. Gerald as a boy had accidentally killed his brother. What then? Why seek to draw a brand and a curse across the life that had caused the accident? A man can live by accident, and die by accident. Or can he not? Is every man's life subject to pure accident, is it only the race, the genus, the species, that has a universal reference? Or is this not true, is there no such thing as pure accident? Has *everything* that happens a universal significance? Has it? Birkin, pondering as he stood there, had forgotten Mrs Crich, as she had forgotten him.

He did not believe that there was any such thing as accident. It all hung together, in the deepest sense.

Just as he had decided this, one of the Crich daughters came up, saying:

'Won't you come and take your hat off, mother dear? We shall be sitting down to eat in a minute, and it's a formal occasion, darling, isn't it?' She drew her arm through her mother's, and they went away. Birkin immediately went to talk to the nearest man.

The gong sounded for the luncheon. The men looked up, but no move was made to the dining-room. The women of the house seemed not to feel that the sound had meaning for them. Five minutes passed by. The elderly manservant, Crowther, appeared in the doorway exasperatedly. He looked with appeal at Gerald. The latter took up a large, curved conch shell, that lay on a shelf, and without reference to anybody, blew a shattering blast. It was a strange rousing noise, that made the heart beat. The summons was almost magical. Everybody came running, as if at a signal. And then the crowd in one impulse moved to the dining-room.

Gerald waited for a moment, for his sister to play hostess. He knew his mother would pay no attention to her duties. But his sister merely crowded to her seat. Therefore the young man, slightly too dictatorial, directed the guests to their places.

There was a moment's lull, as everybody looked at the *hors d'oeuvres* that were being handed round. And out of this lull, a girl of thirteen or fourteen, with her long hair down her back, said in a calm, self-possessed voice:

'Gerald, you forget father, when you make that unearthly noise.'

'Do I?' he answered. And then, to the company, 'Father is lying down, he is not quite well.'

'How is he, really?' called one of the married daughters, peeping round the immense wedding cake that towered up in the middle of the table shedding its artificial flowers.

'He has no pain, but he feels tired,' replied Winifred, the girl with the hair down her back.

The wine was filled, and everybody was talking boisterously. At the far end of the table sat the mother, with her loosely-looped hair. She had Birkin for a neighbour. Sometimes she glanced fiercely down the rows of faces, bending forwards and staring unceremoniously. And she would say in a low voice to Birkin:

'Who is that young man?'

'I don't know,' Birkin answered discreetly.

'Have I seen him before?' she asked.

'I don't think so. *I* haven't,' he replied. And she was satisfied. Her eyes closed wearily, a peace came over her face, she looked like a queen in repose. Then she started, a little social smile came on her face, for a moment she looked the pleasant hostess. For a moment she bent graciously, as if everyone were welcome and delightful. And then immediately the shadow came back, a sullen, eagle look was on her face, she glanced from under her brows like a sinister creature at bay, hating them all.

'Mother,' called Diana, a handsome girl a little older than Winifred, 'I may have wine, mayn't I!'

'Yes, you may have wine,' replied the mother automatically, for she was perfectly indifferent to the question.

And Diana beckoned to the footman to fill her glass.

'Gerald shouldn't forbid me,' she said calmly, to the company at large.

'All right, Di,' said her brother amiably. And she glanced challenge at him as she drank from her glass.

There was a strange freedom, that almost amounted to anarchy, in the house. It was rather a resistance to authority, than liberty. Gerald had some command, by mere force of personality, not because of any granted position. There was a quality in his voice, amiable but dominant, that cowed the others, who were all younger than he.

Hermione was having a discussion with the bridegroom about nationality.

'No,' she said, 'I think that the appeal to patriotism is a mistake. It is like one house of business rivalling another house of business.'

'Well, you can hardly say that, can you!' exclaimed Gerald, who had a real *passion* for discussion. 'You couldn't call a race a business concern, could you? – and nationality roughly corresponds to race, I think. I think it is *meant* to.'

There was a moment's pause. Gerald and Hermione were always strangely but politely and evenly inimical.

'*Do* you think race corresponds with nationality?' she asked musingly, with expressionless indecision.

Birkin knew she was waiting for him to participate. And dutifully he spoke up.

'I think Gerald is right – race is the essential element in nationality, in Europe at least,' he said.

Again Hermione paused, as if to allow this statement to cool. Then she said with strange assumption of authority:

'Yes, but even so, is the patriotic appeal an appeal to the racial instinct? Is it not rather an appeal to the proprietary instinct, the *commercial* instinct? And isn't this what we mean by nationality?'

'Probably,' said Birkin, who felt that such a discussion was out of place and out of time.

But Gerald was now on the scent of argument.

'A race may have its commercial aspect,' he said. 'In fact it must. It is like a family. You *must* make provision. And to make provision you have got to strive against other families, other nations. I don't see why you shouldn't.'

Again Hermione made a pause, domineering and cold, before she replied: 'Yes, I think it is always wrong to provoke a spirit of rivalry. It makes bad blood. And bad blood accumulates.'

'But you can't do away with the spirit of emulation altogether?' said Gerald. 'It is one of the necessary incentives to production and improvement.'

'Yes,' came Hermione's sauntering response. 'I think you can do away with it.'

'I must say,' said Birkin, 'I detest the spirit of emulation.' Hermione was biting a piece of bread, pulling it from between her teeth with her fingers, in a slow, slightly derisive movement. She turned to Birkin.

'You do hate it, yes,' she said, intimate and gratified.

'Detest it,' he repeated.

'Yes,' she murmured, assured and satisfied.

'But,' Gerald insisted, 'you don't allow one man to take away his neighbour's living, so why should you allow one nation to take away the living from another nation?'

There was a long slow murmur from Hermione before she broke into speech, saying with a laconic indifference:

'It is not always a question of possessions, is it? It is not all a question of goods?'

Gerald was nettled by this implication of vulgar materialism.

'Yes, more or less,' he retorted. 'If I go and take a man's hat from off his head, that hat becomes a symbol of that man's liberty. When he fights me for his hat, he is fighting me for his liberty.'

Hermione was nonplussed.

'Yes,' she said, irritated. 'But that way of arguing by imaginary instances is not supposed to be genuine, is it? A man does *not* come and take my hat from off my head, does he?'

'Only because the law prevents him,' said Gerald.

'Not only,' said Birkin. 'Ninety-nine men out of a hundred don't want my hat.'

'That's a matter of opinion,' said Gerald.

'Or the hat,' laughed the bridegroom.

'And if he does want my hat, such as it is,' said Birkin, 'why, surely it is open to me to decide, which is a greater loss to me, my hat, or my liberty as a free and indifferent man. If I am compelled to offer fight, I lose the latter. It is a question which is worth more to me, my pleasant liberty of conduct, or my hat.'

'Yes,' said Hermione, watching Birkin strangely. 'Yes.'

'But would you let somebody come and snatch your hat off your head?' the bride asked of Hermione.

The face of the tall straight woman turned slowly and as if drugged to this new speaker.

'No,' she replied, in a low inhuman tone, that seemed to contain a chuckle. 'No, I shouldn't let anybody take my hat off my head.'

'How would you prevent it?' asked Gerald.

'I don't know,' replied Hermione slowly. 'Probably I should kill him.'

There was a strange chuckle in her tone, a dangerous and convincing humour in her bearing.

'Of course,' said Gerald, 'I can see Rupert's point. It is a question to him whether his hat or his peace of mind is more important.'

'Peace of body,' said Birkin.

'Well, as you like there,' replied Gerald. 'But how are you going to decide this for a nation?'

'Heaven preserve me,' laughed Birkin.

'Yes, but suppose you have to?' Gerald persisted.

'Then it is the same. If the national crown-piece is an old hat, then the thieving gent may have it.'

'But *can* the national or racial hat be an old hat?' insisted Gerald.

'Pretty well bound to be, I believe,' said Birkin.

'I'm not so sure,' said Gerald.

'I don't agree, Rupert,' said Hermione.

'All right,' said Birkin.

'I'm all for the old national hat,' laughed Gerald.

'And a fool you look in it,' cried Diana, his pert sister who was just in her teens.

'Oh, we're quite out of our depths with these old hats,' cried Laura Crich. 'Dry up now, Gerald. We're going to drink toasts. Let us drink toasts. Toasts – glasses, glasses – now then, toasts! Speech! Speech!'

Birkin, thinking about race or national death, watched his glass being filled with champagne. The bubbles broke at the rim, the man withdrew, and feeling a sudden thirst at the sight of the fresh wine, Birkin drank up his glass. A queer little tension in the room roused him. He felt a sharp constraint.

'Did I do it by accident, or on purpose?' he asked himself. And he decided that, according to the vulgar phrase, he had done it 'accidentally on purpose'. He looked round at the hired footman. And the hired footman came, with a silent step of cold servant-like disapprobation. Birkin decided that he detested toasts, and footmen, and assemblies, and mankind altogether, in most of its aspects. Then he rose to make a speech. But he was somehow disgusted.

At length it was over, the meal. Several men strolled out into the garden. There was a lawn, and flower-beds, and at the boundary an iron fence shutting off the little field or park. The view was pleasant; a highroad curving round the edge of a low lake, under the trees. In the spring air, the water gleamed and the opposite woods were purplish with new life. Charming Jersey cattle came to the fence, breathing hoarsely from their velvet muzzles at the human beings, expecting perhaps a crust.

Birkin leaned on the fence. A cow was breathing wet hotness on his hand.

'Pretty cattle, very pretty,' said Marshall, one of the brothers-in-law. 'They give the best milk you can have.'

'Yes,' said Birkin.

'Eh, my little beauty, eh, my beauty!' said Marshall, in a queer high falsetto voice, that caused the other man to have convulsions of laughter in his stomach.

'Who won the race, Lupton?' he called to the bridegroom, to hide the fact that he was laughing.

The bridegroom took his cigar from his mouth.

'The race?' he exclaimed. Then a rather thin smile came over his face. He did not want to say anything about the flight to the church door. 'We got there together. At least she touched first, but I had my hand on her shoulder.'

'What's this?' asked Gerald.

Birkin told him about the race of the bride and the bridegroom.

'H'm!' said Gerald, in disapproval. 'What made you late then?'

'Lupton would talk about the immortality of the soul,' said Birkin, 'and then he hadn't got a button-hook.'

'Oh, God!' cried Marshall. 'The immortality of the soul on your wedding day! Hadn't you got anything better to occupy your mind?'

'What's wrong with it?' asked the bridegroom, a clean-shaven naval man, flushing sensitively.

'Sounds as if you were going to be executed instead of married. *The immortality of the soul!*' repeated the brother-in-law, with most killing emphasis.

But he fell quite flat.

'And what did you decide?' asked Gerald, at once pricking up his ears at the thought of a metaphysical discussion.

'You don't want a soul today, my boy,' said Marshall. 'It'd be in your road.'

'Christ! Marshall, go and talk to somebody else,' cried Gerald, with sudden impatience.

'By God, I'm willing,' said Marshall, in a temper. 'Too much bloody soul and talk altogether –'

He withdrew in a dudgeon, Gerald staring after him with angry eyes, that grew gradually calm and amiable as the stoutly-built form of the other man passed into the distance.

'There's one thing, Lupton,' said Gerald, turning suddenly to the bridegroom. 'Laura won't have brought such a fool into the family as Lottie did.'

'Comfort yourself with that,' laughed Birkin.

'I take no notice of them,' laughed the bridegroom.

'What about this race then – who began it?' Gerald asked.

'We were late. Laura was at the top of the churchyard steps when our cab came up. She saw Lupton bolting towards her. And she fled. But why do you look so cross? Does it hurt your sense of the family dignity?'

'It does, rather,' said Gerald. 'If you're doing a thing, do it properly, and if you're not going to do it properly, leave it alone.'

'Very nice aphorism,' said Birkin.

'Don't you agree?' asked Gerald.

'Quite,' said Birkin. 'Only it bores me rather, when you become aphoristic.'

'Damn you, Rupert, you want all the aphorisms your own way,' said Gerald.

'No. I want them out of the way, and you're always shoving them in it.'

Gerald smiled grimly at this humorism. Then he made a little gesture of dismissal with his eyebrows.

'You don't believe in having any standard of behaviour at all, do you?' he challenged Birkin, censoriously.

'Standard – no. I hate standards. But they're necessary for the common ruck. Anybody who is anything can just be himself and do as he likes.'

'But what do you mean by being himself?' said Gerald. 'Is that an aphorism or a cliché?'

'I mean just doing what you want to do. I think it was perfect good form in Laura to bolt from Lupton to the church door. It was almost a masterpiece in good form. It's the hardest thing in the world to act spontaneously on one's impulses – and it's the only really gentlemanly thing to do – provided you're fit to do it.'

'You don't expect me to take you seriously, do you?' asked Gerald.

'Yes, Gerald, you're one of the very few people I do expect that of.'

'Then I'm afraid I can't come up to your expectations here, at any rate. You think people should just do as they like.'

'I think they always do. But I should like them to like the purely individual thing in themselves, which makes them act in singleness. And they only like to do the collective thing.'

'And I,' said Gerald grimly, 'shouldn't like to be in a world of people who acted individually and spontaneously, as you call it. We should have everybody cutting everybody else's throat in five minutes.'

'That means *you* would like to be cutting everybody's throat,' said Birkin.

'How does that follow?' asked Gerald crossly.

'No man,' said Birkin, 'cuts another man's throat unless he wants to cut it, and unless the other man wants it cutting. This is a complete truth. It takes two people to make a murder: a murderer and a murderee. And a murderee is a man who is murderable. And a man who is murderable is a man who in a profound if hidden lust desires to be murdered.'

'Sometimes you talk pure nonsense,' said Gerald to Birkin. 'As a matter of fact, none of us wants our throat cut, and most other people would like to cut it for us – some time or other –'

'It's a nasty view of things, Gerald,' said Birkin, 'and no wonder you are afraid of yourself and your own unhappiness.'

'How am I afraid of myself?' said Gerald; 'and I don't think I am unhappy.'

'You seem to have a lurking desire to have your gizzard slit, and imagine every man has his knife up his sleeve for you,' Birkin said.

'How do you make that out?' said Gerald.

'From you,' said Birkin.

There was a pause of strange enmity between the two men, that was very near to love. It was always the same between them; always their talk brought them into a deadly nearness of contact, a strange, perilous intimacy which was either hate or love, or both. They parted with apparent unconcern, as if their going apart were a trivial occurrence. And they really kept it to the level of trivial occurrence. Yet the heart of each burned from the other. They burned with each other, inwardly. This they would never admit. They intended to keep their relationship a casual free-and-easy friendship, they were not going to be so unmanly and unnatural as to allow any heart-burning between them. They had not the faintest belief in deep relationship between men and men, and their disbelief prevented any development of their powerful but suppressed friendliness.

3

CLASS-ROOM

A school-day was drawing to a close. In the class-room the last lesson was in progress, peaceful and still. It was elementary botany. The desks were littered with catkins, hazel and willow, which the children had been sketching. But the sky had come over dark, as the end of the afternoon approached: there was scarcely light to draw any more. Ursula stood in front of the class, leading the children by questions to understand the structure and the meaning of the catkins.

A heavy, copper-coloured beam of light came in at the west window, gilding the outlines of the children's heads with red gold, and falling on the wall opposite in a rich, ruddy illumination. Ursula, however, was scarcely conscious of it. She was busy, the end of the day was here, the work went on as a peaceful tide that is at flood, hushed to retire.

This day had gone by like so many more, in an activity that was like a trance. At the end there was a little haste, to finish what was in hand. She was pressing the children with questions, so that they should know all they were to know, by the time the gong went. She stood in shadow in front of the class, with catkins in her hand, and she leaned towards the children, absorbed in the passion of instruction.

She heard, but did not notice the click of the door. Suddenly she started. She saw, in the shaft of ruddy, copper-coloured light near her, the face of a man. It was gleaming like fire, watching her, waiting for her to be aware. It startled her terribly. She thought she was going to faint. All her suppressed, subconscious fear sprang into being, with anguish.

'Did I startle you?' said Birkin, shaking hands with her. 'I thought you had heard me come in.'

'No,' she faltered, scarcely able to speak. He laughed, saying he was sorry. She wondered why it amused him.

'It is so dark,' he said. 'Shall we have the light?'

And moving aside, he switched on the strong electric lights. The class-room was distinct and hard, a strange place after the soft dim magic that filled it before he came. Birkin turned curiously to look at Ursula. Her eyes were round and wondering, bewildered, her mouth quivered slightly. She looked like one who is suddenly wakened. There was a living, tender beauty, like a tender light of dawn shining from her face. He looked at her with a new pleasure, feeling gay in his heart, irresponsible.

'You are doing catkins?' he asked, picking up a piece of hazel from a scholar's desk in front of him. 'Are they as far out as this? I hadn't noticed them this year.'

He looked absorbedly at the tassel of hazel in his hand.

'The red ones too!' he said, looking at the flickers of crimson that came from the female bud.

Then he went in among the desks, to see the scholars' books. Ursula watched his intent progress. There was a stillness in his motion that hushed the activities of her heart. She seemed to be standing aside in arrested silence, watching him move in another concentrated world. His presence was so quiet, almost like a vacancy in the corporate air.

Suddenly he lifted his face to her, and her heart quickened at the flicker of his voice.

'Give them some crayons, won't you?' he said, 'so that they can make the gynaecious flowers red, and the androgynous yellow. I'd chalk them in plain, chalk in nothing else, merely the red and the yellow. Outline scarcely matters in this case. There is just the one fact to emphasize.'

'I haven't any crayons,' said Ursula.

'There will be some somewhere – red and yellow, that's all you want.'

Ursula sent out a boy on a quest.

'It will make the books untidy,' she said to Birkin, flushing deeply.

'Not very,' he said. 'You must mark in these things obviously. It's the fact you want to emphasize, not the subjective impression to record. What's the fact? – red little spiky stigmas of the female flower, dangling yellow male catkin, yellow pollen flying from one to the other. Make a pictorial record of the fact, as a child does when drawing a face – two eyes, one nose, mouth with teeth – so –' And he drew a figure on the blackboard.

At that moment another vision was seen through the glass panels of the door. It was Hermione Roddice. Birkin went and opened to her.

'I saw your car,' she said to him. 'Do you mind my coming to find you? I wanted to see you when you were on duty.'

She looked at him for a long time, intimate and playful, then she gave a short little laugh. And then only she turned to Ursula, who, with all the class, had been watching the little scene between the lovers.

'How do you do, Miss Brangwen,' sang Hermione, in her low, odd, singing fashion, that sounded almost as if she were poking fun. 'Do you mind my coming in?'

Her grey, almost sardonic eyes rested all the while on Ursula, as if summing her up.

'Oh no,' said Ursula.

'Are you *sure*?' repeated Hermione, with complete sang froid, and an odd, half-bullying effrontery.

'Oh no, I like it awfully,' laughed Ursula, a little bit excited and bewildered, because Hermione seemed to be compelling her, coming very close to her, as if intimate with her; and yet, how could she be intimate?

This was the answer Hermione wanted. She turned satisfied to Birkin.

'What are you doing?' she sang, in her casual, inquisitive fashion.

'Catkins,' he replied.

'Really!' she said. 'And what do you learn about them?' She spoke all the while in a mocking, half teasing fashion, as if making game of the whole business. She picked up a twig of the catkin, piqued by Birkin's attention to it.

She was a strange figure in the class-room, wearing a large, old cloak of greenish cloth, on which was a raised pattern of dull gold. The high collar, and the inside of the cloak, was lined with dark fur. Beneath she had a dress of fine lavender-coloured cloth, trimmed with fur, and her hat was close-fitting, made of fur and of the dull, green-and-gold figured stuff. She was tall and strange, she looked as if she had come out of some new, bizarre picture.

'Do you know the little red ovary flowers, that produce the nuts? Have you ever noticed them?' he asked her. And he came close and pointed them out to her, on the sprig she held.

'No,' she replied. 'What are they?'

'Those are the little seed-producing flowers, and the long catkins, they only produce pollen, to fertilize them.'

'Do they, do they!' repeated Hermione, looking closely.

'From those little red bits, the nuts come; if they receive pollen from the long danglers.'

'Little red flames, little red flames,' murmured Hermione to herself. And she remained for some moments looking only at the small buds out of which the red flickers of the stigma issued.

'Aren't they beautiful? I think they're so beautiful,' she said, moving close to Birkin, and pointing to the red filaments with her long, white finger.

'Had you never noticed them before?' he asked.

'No, never before,' she replied.

'And now you will always see them,' he said.

'Now I shall always see them,' she repeated. 'Thank you so much for showing me. I think they're so beautiful – little red flames –'

Her absorption was strange, almost rhapsodic. Both Birkin and Ursula were suspended. The little red pistillate flowers had some strange, almost mystic-passionate attraction for her.

The lesson was finished, the books were put away, at last the class was dismissed. And still Hermione sat at the table, with her chin in her hand, her elbow on the table, her long white face pushed up, not attending to anything.

Birkin had gone to the window, and was looking from the brilliantly-lighted room on to the grey, colourless outside, where rain was noiselessly falling. Ursula put away her things in the cupboard.

At length Hermione rose and came near to her.

'Your sister has come home?' she said.

'Yes,' said Ursula.

'And does she like being back in Beldover?'

'No,' said Ursula.

'No, I wonder she can bear it. It takes all my strength, to bear the ugliness of this district, when I stay here. Won't you come and see me? Won't you come with your sister to stay at Breadalby for a few days? – do –'

'Thank you very much,' said Ursula.

'Then I will write to you,' said Hermione. 'You think your sister will come? I should be so glad. I think she is wonderful. I think some of her work is really wonderful. I have two water-wagtails, carved in wood, and painted – perhaps you have seen it?'

'No,' said Ursula.

'I think it is perfectly wonderful – like a flash of instinct –'

'Her little carvings *are* strange,' said Ursula.

'Perfectly beautiful – full of primitive passion –'

'Isn't it queer that she always likes little things? – she must always work small things, that one can put between one's hands, birds and tiny animals. She likes to look through the wrong end of the opera-glasses, and see the world that way – why is it, do you think?'

Hermione looked down at Ursula with that long, detached scrutinizing gaze that excited the younger woman.

'Yes,' said Hermione at length. 'It is curious. The little things seem to be more subtle to her –'

'But they aren't, are they? A mouse isn't any more subtle than a lion, is it?'

Again Hermione looked down at Ursula with that long scrutiny, as if she were following some train of thought of her own, and barely attending to the other's speech.

'I don't know,' she replied.

'Rupert, Rupert,' she sang mildly, calling him to her. He approached in silence.

'Are little things more subtle than big things?' she asked, with the odd grunt of laughter in her voice, as if she were making game of him in the question.

'Dunno,' he said.

'I hate subtleties,' said Ursula.

Hermione looked at her slowly.

'Do you?' she said.

'I always think they are a sign of weakness,' said Ursula, up in arms, as if her prestige were threatened.

Hermione took no notice. Suddenly her face puckered, her brow was knit with thought, she seemed twisted in troublesome effort for utterance.

'Do you really think, Rupert,' she asked, as if Ursula were not present, 'do you really think it is worth while? Do you really think the children are better for being roused to consciousness?'

A dark flash went over his face, a silent fury. He was hollow-cheeked and pale, almost unearthly. And the woman, with her serious, conscience-harrowing question tortured him on the quick.

'They are not roused to consciousness,' he said. 'Consciousness comes to them, willy-nilly.'

'But do you think they are better for having it quickened, stimulated? Isn't it better that they should remain unconscious of the hazel, isn't it better that they should see as a whole, without all this pulling to pieces, all this knowledge?'

'Would you rather, for yourself, know or not know, that the little red flowers are there, putting out for the pollen?' he asked harshly. His voice was brutal, scornful, cruel.

Hermione remained with her face lifted up, abstracted. He hung silent in irritation.

'I don't know,' she replied, balancing mildly. 'I don't know.'

'But knowing is everything to you, it is all your life,' he broke out. She slowly looked at him.

'Is it?' she said.

'To know, that is your all, that is your life – you have only this, this knowledge,' he cried. 'There is only one tree, there is only one fruit, in your mouth.'

Again she was some time silent.

'Is there?' she said at last, with the same untouched calm. And then in a tone of whimsical inquisitiveness: 'What fruit, Rupert?'

'The eternal apple,' he replied in exasperation, hating his own metaphors.

'Yes,' she said. There was a look of exhaustion about her. For some moments there was silence. Then, pulling herself together with a convulsed movement, Hermione resumed, in a sing-song, casual voice.

'But leaving me apart, Rupert; do you think the children are better, richer, happier, for all this knowledge; do you really think they are? Or is it better to leave them untouched, spontaneous. Hadn't they better be animals, simple animals, crude, violent, *anything*, rather than this self-consciousness, this incapacity to be spontaneous.'

They thought she had finished. But with a queer rumbling in her throat she resumed, 'Hadn't they better be anything than grow up crippled, crippled in their souls, crippled in their feelings – so thrown back – so turned back on themselves – incapable –' Hermione clenched her fist like one in a trance – 'of any spontaneous action, always deliberate, always burdened with choice, never carried away.'

Again they thought she had finished. But just as he was going to reply, she resumed her queer rhapsody – 'never carried away, out of themselves, always conscious, always self-conscious, always aware of themselves. Isn't *anything* better than this? Better be animals, mere animals with no mind at all, than this, this *nothingness* –'

'But do you think it is knowledge that makes us unliving and self-conscious?' he asked irritably.

She opened her eyes and looked at him slowly.

'Yes,' she said. She paused, watching him all the while, her eyes vague. Then she wiped her fingers across her brow, with a vague weariness. It irritated him bitterly. 'It is the mind,' she said, 'and that is death.' She raised her eyes slowly to him: 'Isn't the mind –' she said, with the convulsed movement of her body, 'isn't it our death? Doesn't it destroy all our spontaneity, all our instincts? Are not the young people growing up today, really dead before they have a chance to live?'

'Not because they have too much mind, but too little,' he said brutally.

'Are you *sure*?' she cried. 'It seems to me the reverse. They are over-conscious, burdened to death with consciousness.'

'Imprisoned within a limited, false set of concepts,' he cried.

But she took no notice of this, only went on with her own rhapsodic interrogation.

'When we have knowledge, don't we lose everything but knowledge?' she asked pathetically. 'If I know about the flower, don't I lose the flower and have only the knowledge? Aren't we exchanging the substance for the shadow, aren't we forfeiting life for this dead quality of knowledge? And what does it mean to me after all? What does all this knowing mean to me? It means nothing.'

'You are merely making words,' he said; 'knowledge means everything to you. Even you animalism, you want it in your head. You don't want to *be* an animal, you want to observe your own animal functions, to get a mental thrill out of them. It is all purely secondary – and more decadent than the most hidebound intellectualism. What is it but the worst and last form of intellectualism, this love of yours for passion and the animal instincts? Passion and the instincts – you want them hard enough, but through your head, in your consciousness. It all takes place in your head, under that skull of yours. Only you won't be conscious of what *actually* is: you want the lie that will match the rest of your furniture.'

Hermione set hard and poisonous against this attack. Ursula stood covered with wonder and shame. It frightened her, to see how they hated each other.

'It's all that Lady of Shalott business,' he said, in his strong abstract voice. He seemed to be charging her before the unseeing air. 'You've got that mirror, your own fixed will, your immortal understanding, your own tight conscious world, and there is nothing beyond it. There, in the mirror, you must have everything. But now you have come to all your conclusions, you want to go back and be like a savage, without knowledge. You want a life of pure sensation and "passion".'

He quoted the last word satirically against her. She sat convulsed with fury and violation, speechless, like a striken pythoness of the Greek oracle.

'But your passion is a lie,' he went on violently. 'It isn't passion at all, it is your *will*. It's your bullying will. You want to clutch things and have them in your power. You want to have things in your power. And why? Because you haven't got any real body, any dark sensual body of life. You have no sensuality. You have only your will and your conceit of consciousness, and your lust for power, to *know*.'

He looked at her in mingled hate and contempt, also in pain because she suffered, and in shame because he knew he tortured her. He had an impulse to kneel and plead for forgiveness. But a bitterer red anger burned up to fury in him. He became unconscious of her, he was only a passionate voice speaking.

'Spontaneous!' he cried. 'You and spontaneity! You, the most deliberate thing that ever walked or crawled! You'd be verily deliberately spontaneous – that's you. Because you want to have everything in your own volition, your deliberate voluntary consciousness. You want it all in that loathsome little skull of yours, that ought to be cracked like a nut. For you'll be the same till it *is* cracked, like an insect in its skin. If one cracked your skull perhaps one might get a spontaneous, passionate woman out of you, with real sensuality. As it is, what you want is pornography – looking at yourself in mirrors, watching your naked animal actions in mirrors, so that you can have it all in your consciousness, make it all mental.'

There was a sense of violation in the air, as if too much was said, the unforgivable. Yet Ursula was concerned now only with solving her own problems, in the light of his words. She was pale and abstracted.

'But do you really *want* sensuality?' she asked puzzled.

Birkin looked at her, and became intent in his explanation.

'Yes,' he said, 'that and nothing else, at this point. It is a fulfilment – the great dark knowledge you can't have in your head – the dark involuntary being. It is death to one's self – but it is the coming into being of another.'

'But how? How can you have knowledge not in your head?' she asked, quite unable to interpret his phrases.

'In the blood,' he answered; 'when the mind and the known world is drowned in darkness – everything must go – there must be the deluge. Then you find yourself in a palpable body of darkness, a demon –'

'But why should I be a demon –?' she asked.

' *"Woman wailing for her demon lover"* –' he quoted – 'why, I don't know.'

Hermione roused herself as from a death – annihilation.

'He is such a *dreadful* satanist, isn't he?' she drawled to Ursula, in a queer resonant voice, that ended in a shrill little laugh of pure ridicule. The two women were jeering at him, jeering him into nothingness. The laugh of the shrill, triumphant female sounded from Hermione, jeering him as if he were a neuter.

'No,' he said. 'You are the real devil who won't let life exist.'

She looked at him with a long, slow look, malevolent, supercilious.

'You know all about it, don't you?' she said, with slow, cold, cunning mockery.

'Enough,' he replied, his face fixing fine and clear like steel. A horrible despair, and at the same time a sense of release, liberation, came over Hermione. She turned with a pleasant intimacy to Ursula.

'You are sure you will come to Breadalby?' she said, urging.

'Yes, I should like to very much,' replied Ursula.

Hermione looked down at her, gratified, reflecting, and strangely absent, as if possessed, as if not quite there.

'I'm so glad,' she said, pulling herself together. 'Some time in about a fortnight. Yes? I will write to you here, at the school, shall I? Yes. And you'll be sure to come? Yes. I shall be so glad. Good-bye! Good-bye!'

Hermione held out her hand and looked into the eyes of the other woman. She knew Ursula as an immediate rival, and the knowledge strangely exhilarated her. Also she was taking leave. It always gave her a sense of strength, advantage, to be departing and leaving the other behind. Moreover she was taking the man with her, if only in hate.

Birkin stood aside, fixed and unreal. But now, when it was his turn to bid good-bye, he began to speak again.

'There's the whole difference in the world,' he said, 'between the actual sensual being and the vicious mental-deliberate profligacy our lot goes in for. In our night-time, there's always the electricity switched on, we watch ourselves, we get it all in the head, really. You've got to lapse out before you can know what sensual reality is, lapse into unknowingness, and give up your volition. You've got to do it. You've got to learn not-to-be, before you can come into being.

'But we have got such a conceit of ourselves – that's where it is. We are so conceited, and so unproud. We've got no pride, we're all conceit, so conceited in our own papier-mâché realized selves. We'd rather die than give up our little self-righteous self-opinionated self-will.'

There was silence in the room. Both women were hostile and resentful. He sounded as if he were addressing a meeting. Hermione merely paid no attention, stood with her shoulders tight in a shrug of dislike.

Ursula was watching him as if furtively, not really aware of what she was seeing. There was a great physical attractiveness in him – a curious hidden richness, that came through his thinness and his pallor like another voice, conveying another knowledge of him. It was in the curves of his brows and his chin, rich, fine, exquisite curves, the powerful beauty of life itself. She could not say what it was. But there was a sense of richness and of liberty.

'But we are sensual enough, without making ourselves so, aren't we?' she asked, turning to him with a certain golden laughter flickering under her greenish eyes, like a challenge. And immediately the queer, careless, terribly attractive smile came over his eyes and brows, though his mouth did not relax.

'No,' he said, 'we aren't. We're too full of ourselves.'

'Surely it isn't a matter of conceit,' she cried.

'That and nothing else.'

She was frankly puzzled.

'Don't you think that people are most conceited of all about their sensual powers?' she asked.

'That's why they aren't sensual – only sensuous – which is another matter. They're *always* aware of themselves – and they're so conceited, that rather than release themselves, and live in another world, from another centre, they'd –'

'You want your tea, don't you,' said Hermione, turning to Ursula with a gracious kindliness. 'You've worked all day –'

Birkin stopped short. A spasm of anger and chagrin went over Ursula. His face set. And he bade good-bye, as if he had ceased to notice her.

They were gone. Ursula stood looking at the door for some moments. Then she put out the lights. And having done so, she sat down again in her chair, absorbed and lost. And then she began to cry, bitterly, bitterly weeping: but whether for misery or joy, she never knew.

4

DIVER

The week passed away. On the Saturday it rained, a soft drizzling rain that held off at times. In one of the intervals Gudrun and Ursula set out for a walk, going towards Willey Water. The atmosphere was grey and translucent, the birds sang sharply on the young twigs, the earth would be quickening and hastening in growth. The two girls walked swiftly, gladly, because of the soft, subtle rush of morning that filled the wet haze. By the road the blackthorn was in blossom, white and wet, its tiny amber grains burning faintly in the white smoke of blossom. Purple twigs were darkly luminous in the grey air, high hedges glowed like living shadows, hovering nearer, coming into creation. The morning was full of a new creation.

When the sisters came to Willey Water, the lake lay all grey and visionary, stretching into the moist, translucent vista of trees and meadow. Fine electric activity in sound came from the dumbles below the road, the birds piping one against the other, and water mysteriously plashing, issuing from the lake.

The two girls drifted swiftly along. In front of them, at the corner of the lake, near the road, was a mossy boat-house under a walnut tree, and a little landing-stage where a boat was moored, wavering like a shadow on the still grey water, below the green, decayed poles. All was shadowy with coming summer.

Suddenly, from the boat-house, a white figure ran out, frightening in its swift sharp transit, across the old landing-stage. It launched in a white arc through the air, there was a bursting of the water, and among the smooth ripples a swimmer was making out to space, in a centre of faintly heaving motion. The whole otherworld, wet and remote, he had to himself. He could move into the pure translucency of the grey, uncreated water.

Gudrun stood by the stone wall, watching.

'How I envy him,' she said, in low, desirous tones.

'Ugh!' shivered Ursula. 'So cold!'

'Yes, but how good, how really fine, to swim out there!' The sisters stood watching the swimmer move farther into the grey, moist, full space of the water, pulsing with his own small, invading motion, and arched over with mist and dim woods.

'Don't you wish it were you?' asked Gudrun, looking at Ursula.

'I do,' said Ursula. 'But I'm not sure – it's so wet.'

'No,' said Gudrun, reluctantly. She stood watching the motion on the bosom of the water, as if fascinated. He, having swum a certain distance, turned round and was swimming on his back, looking along the water at the two girls by the wall. In the faint wash of motion, they could see his ruddy face, and could feel him watching them.

'It is Gerald Crich,' said Ursula.

'I know,' replied Gudrun.

And she stood motionless gazing over the water at the face which washed up and down on the flood, as he swam steadily. From his separate element he saw them and he exulted to himself because of his own advantage, his possession of a world to himself. He was immune and perfect. He loved his own vigorous, thrusting motion, and the violent impulse of the very cold water against his limbs, buoying him up. He could see the girls watching him a way off, outside, and that pleased him. He lifted his arm from the water, in a sign to them.

'He is waving,' said Ursula.

'Yes,' replied Gudrun. They watched him. He waved again, with a strange movement of recognition across the difference.

'Like a Nibelung,' laughed Ursula. Gudrun said nothing, only stood still looking over the water.

Gerald suddenly turned, and was swimming away swiftly, with a side stroke. He was alone now, alone and immune in the middle of the waters, which he had all to himself. He exulted in his isolation in the new element, unquestioned and unconditioned. He was happy, thrusting with his legs and all his body, without bond or connection anywhere, just himself in the watery world.

Gudrun envied him almost painfully. Even this momentary possession of pure isolation and fluidity seemed to her so terribly desirable that she felt herself as if damned, out there on the high-road.

'God, what it is to be a man!' she cried.

'What?' exclaimed Ursula in surprise.

'The freedom, the liberty, the mobility!' cried Gudrun, strangely flushed and brilliant. 'You're a man, you want to do a thing, you do it. You haven't the *thousand* obstacles a woman has in front of her.'

Ursula wondered what was in Gudrun's mind, to occasion this outburst. She could not understand.

'What do you want to do?' she asked.

'Nothing,' cried Gudrun, in swift refutation. 'But supposing I did. Supposing I want to swim up that water. It is impossible, it is one of the impossibilities of life, for me to take my clothes off now and jump in. But isn't it *ridiculous*, doesn't it simply prevent our living!'

She was so hot, so flushed, so furious, that Ursula was puzzled.

The two sisters went on, up the road. They were passing between the trees just below Shortlands. They looked up at the long, low house, dim and glamorous in the wet morning, its cedar trees slanting before the windows. Gudrun seemed to be studying it closely.

'Don't you think it's attractive, Ursula?' asked Gudrun.

'Very,' said Ursula. 'Very peaceful and charming.'

'It has form, too – it has a period.'

'What period?'

'Oh, eighteenth century, for certain; Dorothy Wordsworth and Jane Austen, don't you think?'

Ursula laughed.

'Don't you think so?' repeated Gudrun.

'Perhaps. But I don't think the Criches fit the period. I know Gerald is putting in a private electric plant, for lighting the house, and is making all kinds of latest improvements.'

Gudrun shrugged her shoulders swiftly.

'Of course,' she said, 'that's quite inevitable.'

'Quite,' laughed Ursula. 'He is several generations of youngness at one go. They hate him for it. He takes them all by the scruff of the neck, and fairly flings them along. He'll have to die soon, when he's made every possible improvement, and there will be nothing more to improve. He's got *go*, anyhow.'

'Certainly, he's got go,' said Gudrun. 'In fact I've never seen a man that showed signs of so much. The unfortunate thing is, where does his *go* go to, what becomes of it?'

'Oh I know,' said Ursula. 'It goes in applying the latest appliances!'

'Exactly,' said Gudrun.

'You know he shot his brother?' said Ursula.

'Shot his brother?' cried Gudrun, frowning as if in disapprobation.

'Didn't you know? Oh yes! – I thought you knew. He and his brother were playing together with a gun. He told his brother to look down the gun, and it was loaded, and blew the top of his head off. Isn't it a horrible story?'

'How fearful!' cried Gudrun. 'But it is long ago?'

'Oh yes, they were quite boys,' said Ursula. 'I think it is one of the most horrible stories I know.'

'And he of course did not know that the gun was loaded?'

'Yes. You see it was an old thing that had been lying in the stable for years. Nobody dreamed it would ever go off, and of course, no one imagined it was loaded. But isn't it dreadful, that it should happen?'

'Frightful!' cried Gudrun. 'And isn't it horrible too to think of such a thing happening to one when one was a child, and having to carry the responsibility of it all through one's life. Imagine it, two boys playing together – then this comes upon them, for no reason whatever – out of the air. Ursula, it's very frightening! Oh, it's one of the things I can't bear. Murder, that is thinkable, because there's a will behind it. But a thing like that to *happen* to one –'

'Perhaps there *was* an unconscious will behind it,' said Ursula. 'This playing at killing has some primitive *desire* for killing in it, don't you think?'

'Desire!' said Gudrun, coldly, stiffening a little. 'I can't see that they were even playing at killing. I suppose one boy said to the other, "You look down the barrel while I pull the trigger, and see what happens." It seems to me the purest form of accident.'

'No,' said Ursula. 'I couldn't pull the trigger of the emptiest gun in the world, not if someone were looking down the barrel. One instinctively doesn't do it – one can't.'

Gudrun was silent for some moments, in sharp disagreement.

'Of course,' she said coldly. 'If one is a woman, and grown up, one's instinct prevents one. But I cannot see how that applies to a couple of boys playing together.'

Her voice was cold and angry.

'Yes,' persisted Ursula. At that moment they heard a woman's voice a few yards off say loudly:

'Oh damn the thing!' They went forward and saw Laura Crich and Hermione Roddice in the field on the other side of the hedge, and Laura Crich struggling with the gate, to get out. Ursula at once hurried up and helped to lift the gate.

'Thanks so much,' said Laura, looking up flushed and amazon-like, yet rather confused. 'It isn't right on the hinges.'

'No,' said Ursula. 'And they're so heavy.'

'Surprising!' cried Laura.

'How do you do,' sang Hermione, from out of the field, the moment she could make her voice heard. 'It's nice now. Are you going for a walk? Yes. Isn't the young green beautiful? So beautiful – quite burning. Good morning – good morning – you'll come and see me? thank you so much – next week – yes – good-bye, g-o-o-d-b-y-e.'

Gudrun and Ursula stood and watched her slowly waving her head up and down, and waving her hand slowly in dismissal, smiling a strange affected smile, making a tall queer, frightening figure, with her heavy fair hair slipping to her eyes. Then they moved off, as if they had been dismissed like inferiors. The four women parted.

As soon as they had gone far enough, Ursula said, her cheeks burning:

'I do think she's impudent.'

'Who, Hermione Roddice?' asked Gudrun. 'Why?'

'The way she treats one – impudence!'

'Why, Ursula, what did you notice that was so impudent?' asked Gudrun rather coldly.

'Her whole manner. Oh, it's impossible, the way she tries to bully one. Pure bullying. She's an impudent woman. "You'll come and see me," as if we should be falling over ourselves for the privilege.'

'I can't understand, Ursula, what you are so much put out about,' said Gudrun, in some exasperation. 'One knows those women are impudent – these free women who have emancipated themselves from the aristocracy.'

'But it is so *unnecessary* – so vulgar,' cried Ursula.

'No, I don't see it. And if I did – *pour moi elle n'existe pas*. I don't grant her the power to be impudent to me.'

'Do you think she likes you?' asked Ursula.

'Well, no, I shouldn't think she did.'

'Then why does she ask you to go to Breadalby and stay with her?'

Gudrun lifted her shoulders in a low shrug.

'After all, she's got the sense to know we're not just the ordinary run,' said Gudrun. 'Whatever she is, she's not a fool. And I'd rather have somebody I detested than the ordinary woman who keeps to her own set. Hermione Roddice does risk herself in some respects.'

Ursula pondered this for a time.

'I doubt it,' she replied. 'Really she risks nothing. I suppose we ought to admire her for knowing she *can* invite us – school teachers – and risk nothing.'

'Precisely!' said Gudrun. 'Think of the myriads of women that daren't do it. She makes the most of her privileges – that's something. I suppose, really, we should do the same, in her place.'

'No,' said Ursula. 'No. It would bore me. I couldn't spend my time playing her games. It's infra dig.'

The two sisters were like a pair of scissors, snipping off everything that came athwart them; or like a knife and a whetstone, the one sharpened against the other.

'Of course,' cried Ursula suddenly, 'she ought to thank her stars if we will go and see her. You are perfectly beautiful, a thousand times more beautiful than ever she is or was, and to my thinking, a thousand times more beautifully dressed, for she never looks fresh and natural, like a flower, always old, thought-out; and we are more intelligent than most people.'

'Undoubtedly!' said Gudrun.

'And it ought to be admitted, simply,' said Ursula.

'Certainly it ought,' said Gudrun. 'But you'll find that the really chic thing is to be so absolutely ordinary, so perfectly commonplace and like the person in the street, that you really are a masterpiece of humanity, not the person in the street actually, but the artistic creation of her –'

'How awful!' cried Ursula.

'Yes, Ursula, it *is* awful, in most respects. You daren't be anything that isn't amazingly *à terre*, so much *à terre* that it is the artistic creation of ordinariness.'

'It's very dull to create oneself into nothing better,' laughed Ursula.

'Very dull!' retorted Gudrun. 'Really, Ursula, it *is* dull, that's just the word. One longs to be high-flown, and make speeches like Corneille, after it.'

Gudrun was becoming flushed and excited over her own cleverness.

'Strut,' said Ursula. 'One wants to strut, to be a swan among geese.'

'Exactly,' cried Gudrun, 'a swan among geese.'

'They are all so busy playing the ugly duckling,' cried Ursula, with mocking laughter. 'And I don't feel a bit like a humble and pathetic ugly duckling. I do feel like a swan among geese – I can't help it. They make one feel so. And I don't care what *they* think of me. *Je m'en fiche.*'

Gudrun looked up at Ursula with a queer, uncertain envy and dislike.

'Of course, the only thing to do is to despise them all – just all,' she said.

The sisters went home again, to read and talk and work, and wait for Monday, for school. Ursula often wondered what else she waited for, besides the beginning and end of the school week, and the beginning and end of the holidays. This was a whole life! Sometimes she had periods of tight horror, when it seemed to her that her life would pass away and be gone, without having been more than this. But she never really accepted it. Her spirit was active, her life like a shoot that is growing steadily, but which has not get come above ground.

5

IN THE TRAIN

One day at this time Birkin was called to London. He was not very fixed in his abode. He had rooms in Nottingham, because his work lay chiefly in that town. But often he was in London, or in Oxford. He moved about a great deal, his life seemed uncertain, without any definite rhythm, any organic meaning.

On the platform of the railway station he saw Gerald Crich, reading a newspaper, and evidently waiting for the train. Birkin stood some distance off, among the people. It was against his instinct to approach anybody.

From time to time, in a manner characteristic of him, Gerald lifted his head and looked round. Even though he was reading the newspaper closely, he must keep a watchful eye on his external surroundings. There seemed to be a dual consciousness running in him. He was thinking vigorously of something he read in the newspaper, and at the same time his eye ran over the surfaces of the life round him, and he missed nothing. Birkin, who was watching him, was irritated by his duality. He noticed too, that Gerald seemed always to be at bay against everybody, in spite of his queer, genial, social manner when roused.

Now Birkin started violently at seeing this genial look flash on to Gerald's face, at seeing Gerald approaching with hand outstretched.

'Hallo, Rupert, where are you going?'

'London. So are you, I suppose.'

'Yes –'

Gerald's eyes went over Birkin's face in curiosity.

'We'll travel together if you like,' he said.

'Don't you usually go first?' asked Birkin.

'I can't stand the crowd,' replied Gerald. 'But third'll be all right. There's a restaurant car, we can have some tea.'

The two men looked at the station clock, having nothing further to say.

'What were you reading in the paper?' Birkin asked.

Gerald looked at him quickly.

'Isn't it funny, what they *do* put in the newspapers,' he said. 'Here are two leaders –' he held out his *Daily Telegraph*, 'full of the ordinary newspaper cant –' he scanned the columns down – 'and then there's this little – I dunno what you'd call it, essay, almost – appearing with the leaders, and saying there must arise a man who will give new values to things, give us new truths, a new attitude to life, or else we shall be a crumbling nothingness in a few years, a country in ruin –'

'I suppose that's a bit of newspaper cant, as well,' said Birkin.

'It sounds as if the man meant it, and quite genuinely,' said Gerald.

'Give it to me,' said Birkin, holding out his hand for the paper.

The train came, and they went on board, sitting on either side of a little table, by the window, in the restaurant car. Birkin glanced over his paper, then looked up at Gerald, who was waiting for him.

'I believe the man means it,' he said, 'as far as he means anything.'

'And do you think it's true? Do you think we really want a new gospel?' asked Gerald.

Birkin shrugged his shoulders.

'I think the people who say they want a new religion are the last to accept anything new. They want novelty right enough. But to stare straight at this life that we've brought upon ourselves and rejected, absolutely smash up the old idols of ourselves, that we sh'll never do. You've got very badly to want to get rid of the old before anything new will appear – even in the self.'

Gerald watched him closely.

'You think we ought to break up this life, just start and let fly?' he asked.

'This life. Yes I do. We've got to bust it completely, or shrivel inside it, as in a tight skin. For it won't expand any more.'

There was a queer little smile in Gerald's eyes, a look of amusement, calm and curious.

'And how do you propose to begin? I suppose you mean, reform the whole order of society?' he asked.

Birkin had a slight, tense frown between the brows. He too was impatient of the conversation.

'I don't propose at all,' he replied. 'When we really want to go for something better, we shall smash the old. Until then, any sort of proposal, or making proposals, is no more than a tiresome game for self-important people.'

The little smile began to die out of Gerald's eyes, and he said, looking with a cool stare at Birkin:

'So you really think things are very bad?'

'Completely bad.'

The smile appeared again.

'In what way?'

'Every way,' said Birkin. 'We are such dreary liars. Our one idea is to lie to ourselves. We have an ideal of a perfect world, clean and straight and sufficient. So we cover the earth with foulness; life is a blotch of labour, like insects scurrying in filth, so that your collier can have a pianoforte in his parlour, and you can have a butler and a motor-car in your up-to-date house, and as a nation we can sport the Ritz, or the Empire, Gaby Deslys and the Sunday newspapers. It is very dreary.'

Gerald took a little time to re-adjust himself after this tirade.

'Would you have us live without houses – return to nature?' he asked.

'I would have nothing at all. People only do what they want to do – and what they are capable of doing. If they were capable of anything else, there would be something else.'

Again Gerald pondered. He was not going to take offence at Birkin.

'Don't you think the collier's *pianoforte*, as you call it, is a symbol for something very real, a real desire for something higher, in the collier's life?'

'Higher!' cried Birkin. 'Yes. Amazing heights of upright grandeur. It makes him so much higher in his neighbouring collier's eyes. He sees himself reflected in the neighbouring opinion, like in a Brocken mist, several feet taller on the strength of the pianoforte, and he is satisfied. He lives for the sake of that Brocken spectre, the reflection of himself in the human opinion. You do the same. If you are of high importance to humanity you are of high importance to yourself. That is why you work so hard at the mines. If you can produce coal to cook five thousand dinners a day, you are five thousand times more important than if you cooked only your own dinner.'

'I suppose I am,' laughed Gerald.

'Can't you see,' said Birkin, 'that to help my neighbour to eat is no more than eating myself. "I eat, thou eatest, he eats, we eat, you eat, they eat" – and what then? Why should every man decline the whole verb. First person singular is enough for me.'

'You've got to start with material things,' said Gerald. Which statement Birkin ignored.

'And we've got to live for *something*, we're not just cattle that can graze and have done with it,' said Gerald.

'Tell me,' said Birkin. 'What do you live for?'

Gerald's face went baffled.

'What do I live for?' he repeated. 'I suppose I live to work, to produce something, in so far as I am a purposive being. Apart from that, I live because I am living.'

'And what's your work? Getting so many more thousands of tons of coal out of the earth every day. And when we've got all the coal we want, and all the plush furniture, and pianofortes, and the rabbits are all stewed and eaten, and we're all warm and our bellies are filled and we're listening to the young lady performing on the pianoforte – what then? What then, when you've made a real fair start with your material things?'

Gerald sat laughing at the words and the mocking humour of the other man. But he was cogitating too.

'We haven't got there yet,' he replied. 'A good many people are still waiting for the rabbit and the fire to cook it.'

'So while you get the coal I must chase the rabbit?' said Birkin, mocking at Gerald.

'Something like that,' said Gerald.

Birkin watched him narrowly. He saw the perfect good-humoured callousness, even strange, glistening malice, in Gerald, glistening through the plausible ethics of productivity.

'Gerald,' he said, 'I rather hate you.'

'I know you do,' said Gerald. 'Why do you?'

Birkin mused inscrutably for some minutes.

'I should like to know if you are conscious of hating me,' he said at last. 'Do you ever consciously detest me – hate me with mystic hate? There are odd moments when I hate you starrily.'

Gerald was rather taken aback, even a little disconcerted. He did not quite know what to say.

'I may, of course, hate you sometimes,' he said. 'But I'm not aware of it – never acutely aware of it, that is.'

'So much the worse,' said Birkin.

Gerald watched him with curious eyes. He could not quite make him out.

'So much the worse, is it?' he repeated.

There was a silence between the two men for some time, as the train ran on. In Birkin's face was a little irritable tension, a sharp knitting of the brows, keen and difficult. Gerald watched him warily, carefully, rather calculatingly, for he could not decide what he was after.

Suddenly Birkin's eyes looked straight and overpowering into those of the other man.

'What do you think is the aim and object of your life, Gerald?' he asked.

Again Gerald was taken aback. He could not think what his friend was getting at. Was he poking fun, or not?

'At this moment, I couldn't say off-hand,' he replied, with faintly ironic humour.

'Do you think to live is the be-all and the end-all of life?' Birkin asked, with direct, attentive seriousness.

'Of my own life?' said Gerald.

'Yes.'

There was a really puzzled pause.

'I can't say,' said Gerald. 'It hasn't been, so far.'

'What has your life been, so far?'

'Oh – finding out things for myself – and getting experiences – and making things *go.*'

Birkin knitted his brows like sharply moulded steel.

'I find,' he said, 'that one needs someone *really* pure single activity – I should call love a single pure activity. But I *don't* really love anybody – not now.'

'Have you ever really loved anybody?' asked Gerald.

'Yes and no,' replied Birkin.

'Not finally?' said Gerald.

'Finally – finally – no,' said Birkin.

'Nor I,' said Gerald.

'And do you want to?' said Birkin.

Gerald looked with a long, twinkling, almost sardonic look into the eyes of the other man.

'I don't know,' he said.

'I do – I want to love,' said Birkin.

'You do?'

'Yes. I want the finality of love.'

'The finality of love,' repeated Gerald. And he waited for a moment.

'Just one woman?' he added. The evening light, flooding yellow along the fields, lit up Birkin's face with a tense, abstract steadfastness. Gerald still could not make it out.

'Yes, one woman,' said Birkin.

But to Gerald it sounded as if he were insistent rather than confident.

'I don't believe a woman, and nothing but a woman, will ever make my life,' said Gerald.

'Not the centre and core of it – the love between you and a woman?' asked Birkin.

Gerald's eyes narrowed with a queer dangerous smile as he watched the other man.

'I never quite feel it that way,' he said.

'You don't? Then wherein does life centre, for you?'

'I don't know – that's what I want somebody to tell me. As far as I can make out, it doesn't centre at all. It is artificially held *together* by the social mechanism.'

Birkin pondered as if he would crack something.

'I know,' he said, 'it just doesn't centre. The old ideals are dead as nails – nothing there. It seems to me there remains only this perfect union with a woman – sort of ultimate marriage – and there isn't anything else.'

'And you mean if there isn't the woman, there's nothing?' said Gerald.

'Pretty well that – seeing there's no God.'

'Then we're hard put to it,' said Gerald. And he turned to look out of the window at the flying, golden landscape.

Birkin could not help seeing how beautiful and soldierly his face was, with a certain courage to be indifferent.

'You think it's heavy odds against us?' said Birkin.

'If we've got to make our life up out of a woman, one woman, woman only, yes I do,' said Gerald. 'I don't believe I shall ever make up *my* life, at that rate.'

Birkin watched him almost angrily.

'You are a born unbeliever,' he said.

'I only feel what I feel,' said Gerald. And he looked again at Birkin almost sardonically, with his blue, manly, sharp-lighted eyes. Birkin's eyes were at the moment full of anger. But swiftly they became troubled, doubtful, then full of a warm, rich affectionateness and laughter.

'It troubles me very much, Gerald,' he said, wrinkling his brows.

'I can see it does,' said Gerald, uncovering his mouth in a manly, quick, soldierly laugh.

Gerald was held unconsciously by the other man. He wanted to be near him, he wanted to be within his sphere of influence. There was something very congenial to him in Birkin. But yet, beyond this, he did not take much notice. He felt that he, himself, Gerald, had harder and more durable truths than any the other man knew. He felt himself older, more knowing. It was the quick-changing warmth and vitality and brilliant warm utterance he loved in his friend. It was the rich play of words and quick interchange of feelings he enjoyed. The real content of the words he never really considered: he himself knew better.

Birkin knew this. He knew that Gerald wanted to be *fond* of him without taking him seriously. And this made him go hard and cold. As the train ran on, he sat looking at the land, and Gerald fell away, became as nothing to him.

Birkin looked at the land, at the evening, and was thinking: 'Well, if mankind is destroyed, if our race is destroyed like Sodom, and there is this beautiful evening with the luminous land and trees, I am satisfied. That which informs it all is there, and can never be lost. After all, what is mankind but just one expression of the incomprehensible? And if mankind passes away, it will only mean that this particular expression is completed and done. That which is expressed, and that which is to be expressed, cannot be diminished. There it is, in the shining evening. Let mankind pass away – time it did. The creative utterances will not cease, they will only be there. Humanity doesn't embody the utterance of the incomprehensible any more. Humanity is a dead letter. There will be a new embodiment, in a new way. Let humanity disappear as quick as possible.'

Gerald interrupted him by asking:

'Where are you staying in London?'

Birkin looked up.

'With a man in Soho. I pay part of the rent of a house, and stop there when I like.'

'Good idea – have a place more or less your own,' said Gerald.

'Yes. But I don't care for it much. I'm tired of the people I am bound to find there.'

'What kind of people?'

'Art – music – London Bohemia – the most pettifogging calculating Bohemia that ever reckoned its pennies. But there are a few decent people, decent in some respects. They are really very thorough rejecters of the world – perhaps they live only in the gesture of rejection and negation – but negatively something, at any rate.'

'What are they? – painters, musicians?'

'Painters, musicians, writers – hangers-on, models, advanced young people, anybody who is openly at outs with the conventions, and belongs to nowhere particularly. They are often young fellows down from the University, and girls who are living their own lives, as they say.'

'All loose?' said Gerald.

Birkin could see his curiosity roused.

'In one way. Most bound, in another. For all their shockingness, all on one note.'

He looked at Gerald, and saw how his blue eyes were lit up with a little flame of curious desire. He saw too how good-looking he was. Gerald was attractive, his blood seemed fluid and electric. His blue eyes burned with a keen, yet cold light, there was a certain beauty, a beautiful passivity in all his body, his moulding.

'We might see something of each other – I am in London for two or three days,' said Gerald.

'Yes,' said Birkin, 'I don't want to go to the theatre, or the music-hall – you'd better come round and see what you can make of Halliday and his crowd.'

'Thanks – I should like to,' laughed Gerald. 'What are you doing tonight?'

'I promised to meet Halliday at the Pompadour. It's a bad place, but there is nowhere else.'

'Where is it?' asked Gerald.

'Piccadilly Circus.'

'Oh yes – well, shall I come round there?'

'By all means, it might amuse you.'

The evening was falling. They had passed Bedford. Birkin watched the country, and was filled with a sort of hopelessness. He always felt this, on approaching London. His dislike of mankind, of the mass of mankind, amounted almost to an illness.

> "'Where the quiet coloured end of evening smiles
> Miles and miles –'"

he was murmuring to himself, like a man condemned to death. Gerald, who was very subtly alert, wary in all his senses, leaned forward and asked smilingly:

'What were you saying?' Birkin glanced at him, laughed, and repeated:

"'Where the quiet coloured end of evening smiles.
  Miles and miles,
Over pastures where the something something sheep
  Half asleep –'"

Gerald also looked now at the country. And Birkin, who, for some reason was now tired and dispirited, said to him:

'I always feel doomed when the train is running into London. I feel such a despair, so hopeless, as if it were the end of the world.'

'Really!' said Gerald. 'And does the end of the world frighten you?'

Birkin lifted his shoulders in a slow shrug.

'I don't know,' he said. 'It does while it hangs imminent and doesn't fall. But people give me a bad feeling – very bad.'

There was a roused glad smile in Gerald's eyes.

'Do they?' he said. And he watched the other man critically.

In a few minutes the train was running through the disgrace of outspread London. Everybody in the carriage was on the alert, waiting to escape. At last they were under the huge arch of the station, in the tremendous shadow of the town. Birkin shut himself together – he was in now.

The two men went together in a taxi-cab.

'Don't you feel like one of the damned?' asked Birkin, as they sat in a little, swiftly-running enclosure, and watched the hideous great street.

'No,' laughed Gerald.

'It is real death,' said Birkin.

6

CREME DE MENTHE

They met again in the café several hours later. Gerald went through the push doors into the large, lofty room where the faces and heads of the drinkers showed dimly through the haze of smoke, reflected more dimly, and repeated ad infinitum in the great mirrors on the walls, so that one seemed to enter a vague, dim world of shadowy drinkers humming within an atmosphere of blue tobacco smoke. There was, however, the red plush of the seats to give substance within the bubble of pleasure.

Gerald moved in his slow, observant, glistening-attentive motion down between the tables and the people whose shadowy faces looked up as he passed. He seemed to be entering in some strange element, passing into an illuminated new region, among a host of licentious souls. He was pleased, and entertained. He looked over all the dim, evanescent, strangely illuminated faces that bent across the tables. Then he saw Birkin rise and signal to him.

At Birkin's table was a girl with bobbed, blonde hair cut short in the artist fashion, hanging straight and curving slightly inwards to her ears. She was small and delicately made, with fair colouring and large, innocent, blue eyes. There was a delicacy, almost a floweriness in all her form, and at the same time a certain attractive grossness of spirit, that made a little spark leap instantly alight in Gerald's eyes.

Birkin, who looked muted, unreal, his presence left out, introduced her as

Miss Darrington. She gave her hand with a sudden, unwilling movement, looking all the while at Gerald with a dark, exposed stare. A glow came over him as he sat down.

The waiter appeared. Gerald glanced at the glasses of the other two. Birkin was drinking something green, Miss Darrington had a small liqueur glass that was empty save for a tiny drop.

'Won't you have some more –?'

'Brandy,' she said, sipping her last drop and putting down the glass. The waiter disappeared.

'No,' she said to Birkin. 'He doesn't know I'm back. He'll be terwified when he see me here.'

She spoke her r's like w's, lisping with a slightly babyish pronunciation which was at once affected and true to her character. Her voice was dull and toneless.

'Where is he then?' asked Birkin.

'He's doing a private show at Lady Snellgrove's,' said the girl. 'Warens is there too.'

There was a pause.

'Well, then,' said Birkin, in a dispassionate protective manner, 'what do you intend to do?'

The girl paused sullenly. She hated the question.

'I don't intend to do anything,' she replied. 'I shall look for some sittings tomorrow.'

'Who shall you go to?' asked Birkin.

'I shall go to Bentley's first. But I believe he's angwy with me for running away.'

'That is from the Madonna?'

'Yes. And then if he doesn't want me. I know I can get work with Carmarthen.'

'Carmarthen?'

'Frederick Carmarthen – he does photographs.'

'Chiffon and shoulders –'

'Yes. But he's awfully decent.' There was a pause.

'And what are you going to do about Julius?' he asked.

'Nothing,' she said. 'I shall just ignore him.'

'You've done with him altogether?' But she turned aside her face sullenly, and did not answer the question.

Another young man came hurrying up to the table.

'Hallo, Birkin! Hallo, Minette, when did you come back?' he said eagerly.

'Today.'

'Does Halliday know?'

'I don't know. I don't care either.'

'Ha-ha! The wind still sits in that quarter, does it? Do you mind if I come over to this table?'

'I'm talking to Wupert, do you mind?' she replied, coolly and yet appealingly, like a child.

'Open confession – good for the soul, eh?' said the young man. 'Well, so long.'

And giving a sharp look at Birkin and at Gerald, the young man moved off, with a swing of his coat skirts.

All this time Gerald had been completely ignored. And yet he felt that the girl was physically aware of his proximity. He waited, listened, and tried to piece together the conversation.

'Are you staying at the house?' the girl asked, of Birkin.

'For three days,' replied Birkin. 'And you?'

'I don't know yet. I can always go to Bertha's.' There was a silence.

Suddenly the girl turned to Gerald, and said, in a rather formal, polite voice, with the distant manner of a woman who accepts her position as a social inferior, yet assumes intimate *camaraderie* with the male she addresses:

'Do you know London well?'

'I can hardly say,' he laughed. 'I've been up a good many times, but I was never in this place before.'

'You're not an artist, then?' she said, in a tone that placed him an outsider.

'No,' he replied.

'He's a soldier, and an explorer, and a Napoleon of industry,' said Birkin, giving Gerald his credentials for Bohemia.

'Are you a soldier?' asked the girl, with a cold yet lively curiosity.

'No, I resigned my commission,' said Gerald, 'some years ago.'

'He was in the last war,' said Birkin.

'Were you really?' said the girl.

'And then he explored the Amazon,' said Birkin, 'and now he is ruling over coal-mines.'

The girl looked at Gerald with steady, calm curiosity. He laughed, hearing himself described. He felt proud too, full of male strength. His blue, keen eyes were lit up with laughter, his ruddy face, with its sharp fair hair, was full of satisfaction, and glowing with life. He piqued her.

'How long are you staying?' she asked him.

'A day or two,' he replied. 'But there is no particular hurry.'

Still she stared into his face with that slow, full gaze which was so curious and so exciting to him. He was acutely and delightfully conscious of himself, of his own attractiveness. He felt full of strength, able to give off a sort of electric power. And he was aware of her blue, exposed-looking eyes upon him. She had beautiful eyes, flower-like, fully opened, naked in their looking at him. And on them there seemed to float a curious iridescence, a sort of film of disintegration, and sullenness, like oil on water. She wore no hat in the heated café, her loose, simple jumper was strung on a string round her neck. But it was made of rich yellow crêpe-de-chine, that hung heavily and softly from her young throat and her slender wrists. Her appearance was simple and complete, really beautiful, because of her regularity and form, her shiny yellow hair falling curved and level on either side of her head, her straight, small, softened features, provoking in the slight fullness of their curves, her slender neck and the simple, rich-coloured smock hanging on her slender shoulders. She was very still, almost null, in her manner, apart and watchful.

She appealed to Gerald strongly. He felt an awful, enjoyable power over her, an instinctive cherishing very near to cruelty. For she was a victim. He felt that she was in his power, and he was generous. The electricity was turgid and voluptuously rich, in his limbs. He would be able to destroy her utterly in the strength of his discharge. But she was waiting in her separation, given.

They talked banalities for some time. Suddenly Birkin said:

'There's Julius!' and he half rose to his feet, motioning to the newcomer. The girl, with a curious, almost evil motion, looked round over her shoulder without moving her body. Gerald watched her fair, close hair swing over her ears. He felt her watching intensely the man who was approaching, so he looked too. He saw a swarthy, slender young man with rather long, solid black hair hanging from under his black hat, moving cumbrously down the room, his face lit up with a smile at once naïve and warm, and vapid. He approached towards Birkin with a haste of welcome.

It was not till he was quite close that he perceived the girl. He recoiled, went green, and said, in a high squealing voice:

'Minette, what are *you* doing here?'

The café looked up like animals when they hear a cry. Halliday hung motionless, an almost imbecile smile flickering palely on his face. The girl only stared at him with an ice-cold look in which flared an unfathomable hell of knowledge, and a certain impotence. She was limited by him.

'Why have you come back?' repeated Halliday, in the same high, hysterical voice. 'I told you not to come back.'

The girl did not answer, only stared in the same ice-blank, heavy fashion, straight at him, as he stood recoiled, as if for safety, against the next table.

'You know you wanted her to come back – come and sit down,' said Birkin to him.

'No, I didn't want her to come back, and I told her not to come back. What have you come for, Minette?'

'For nothing from *you*,' she said in a heavy voice of resentment.

'Then why have you come back at *all*?' cried Halliday, his voice rising to a kind of squeal.

'She comes as she likes,' said Birkin. 'Are you going to sit down, or are you not?'

'No, I won't sit down with Minette,' cried Halliday.

'I won't hurt you, you needn't be afraid,' she said to him, very curtly, and yet with a sort of protectiveness towards him, in her voice.

Halliday came and sat at the table, putting his hand on his heart, and crying:

'Oh, it's given me such a turn! Minette, I wish you wouldn't do these things. Why did you come back?'

'Not for anything from you,' she repeated.

'You've said that before,' he cried in a high voice.

She turned completely away from him, to Gerald Crich, whose eyes were shining with a subtle amusement.

'Were you ever vewy much afwaid of the savages?' she asked in her calm, dull, childish voice.

'No – never very much afraid. On the whole they're harmless – they're not born yet, you can't feel really afraid of them. You know you can manage them.'

'Do you weally? Aren't they very fierce?'

'Not very. There aren't many fierce things, as a matter of fact. There aren't many things, neither people nor animals, that have it in them to be really dangerous.'

'Except in herds,' interrupted Birkin.

'Aren't there really?' she said. 'Oh, I thought savages were all so dangerous, they'd have your life before you could look round.'

'Did you?' he laughed. 'They are over-rated, savages. They're too much like other people, not exciting, after the first acquaintance.'

'Oh, it's not so very wonderfully brave then, to be an explorer?'

'No. It's more a question of hardships than of terrors.'

'Oh! And weren't you ever afraid?'

'In my life? I don't know. Yes, I'm afraid of some things – of being shut up, locked up anywhere – or being fastened. I'm afraid of being bound hand and foot.'

She looked at him steadily with her naïve eyes, that rested on him and roused him so deeply, that it left his upper self quite calm. It was rather delicious, to feel her drawing his self-revelations from him, as from the very innermost dark marrow of his body. She wanted to know. And her eyes seemed to be looking through into his naked organism. He felt, she was compelled to him, she was fated to come into contact with him, must have the seeing him and knowing him. And this roused a curious exultance. Also he felt, she must relinquish herself into his hands, and be subject to him. She was so profane, slave-like, watching him, absorbed by him. It was not that she was interested in what he said; she was absorbed by his self-revelation, by *him*, she wanted the secret of him, the experience of his male being.

Gerald's face was lit up with an uncanny smile, full of light and rousedness, yet unconscious. He sat with his arms on the table, his sun-browned, rather sinister hands, that were animal and yet very shapely and attractive, pushed forward towards her. And they fascinated her. And she knew, she watched her own fascination.

Other men had come to the table, to talk with Birkin and Halliday. Gerald said in a low voice, apart, to Minette:

'Where have you come back from?'

'From the country,' replied Minette, in a very low, yet fully resonant voice. Her face closed hard. Continually she glanced at Halliday, and then a flare came over her eyes. The heavy, fair young man ignored her completely; he was really afraid of her. For some moments she would be unaware of Gerald. He had not conquered her yet.

'And what has Halliday to do with it?' he asked, his voice still muted.

She would not answer for some seconds. Then she said, unwillingly:

'He made me go and live with him, and now he wants to throw me over. And yet he won't let me go to anybody else. He wants me to live hidden in the country. And then he says I persecute him, that he can't get rid of me.'

'Doesn't know his own mind,' said Gerald.

'He hasn't any mind, so he can't know it,' she said. 'He waits for what somebody tells him to do. He never does anything he wants to do himself – because he doesn't know what he wants. He's a perfect baby.'

Gerald looked at Halliday for some moments, watching the soft, rather degenerate face of the young man. Its very softness was an attraction; it was a soft, warm nature, into which one might plunge with gratification.

'But he has no hold over you, has he?' Gerald asked.

'You see he *made* me go and live with him, when I didn't want to,' she replied. 'He came and cried to me, tears, you never saw so many, saying *he couldn't* bear it unless I went back to him. And he wouldn't go away, he would have stayed for ever. He made me go back. Then every time he behaves in this fashion. And now I'm going to have a baby, he wants to give me a hundred pounds and send me into the country, so that he would never see me nor hear of me again. But I'm not going to do it, after –'

A queer look came over Gerald's face.

'Are you going to have a child?' he asked incredulous. It seemed, to look at her, impossible, she was so young and so far in spirit from any childbearing.

She looked full into his face, and her blue, inchoate eyes had now a furtive look, and a look of a knowledge of evil, dark and indomitable. A flame ran secretly to his heart.

'Yes,' she said. 'Isn't it beastly?'

'Don't you want it?' he asked.

'I don't,' she replied emphatically.

'But –' he said, 'how long have you known?'

'Ten weeks,' she said.

All the time she kept her eyes full upon him. He remained silent, thinking. Then, switching off and becoming cold, he asked, in a voice full of considerate kindness:

'Is there anything we can eat here? Is there anything you would like?'

'Yes,' she said, 'I should adore some oysters.'

'All right,' he said. 'We'll have oysters.' And he beckoned to the waiter.

Halliday took no notice, until the little plate was set before her. Then suddenly he cried:

'Minette, you can't eat oysters when you're drinking brandy.'

'What has it got to do with you?' she asked.

'Nothing, nothing,' he cried. 'But you can't eat oysters when you're drinking brandy.'

'I'm not drinking brandy,' she replied, and she sprinkled the last drops of her liqueur over his face. He gave an odd squeal. She sat looking at him, as if indifferent.

'Minette, why do you do that?' he cried in panic. He gave Gerald the impression that he was terrified of her, and that he loved his terror. He seemed to relish his own horror and hatred of her, turn it over and extract every flavour from it, in real panic. Gerald thought him a strange fool, and yet piquant.

'But Minette,' said another man, in a very small, quick Eton voice, 'you promised not to hurt him.'

'I haven't hurt him,' she answered.

'What will you drink?' the young man asked. He was dark, and smooth-skinned, and full of a stealthy vigour.

'I don't like porter, Maxim,' she replied.

'You must ask for champagne,' came the whispering gentlemanly voice of the other.

Gerald suddenly realized that this was a hint to him.

'Shall we have champagne?' he asked, laughing.

'Yes, please, dwy,' she lisped childishly.

Gerald watched her eating the oysters. She was delicate and finicking in her eating, her fingers were fine and seemed very sensitive in the tips, so she put her food apart with fine, small motions, she ate carefully, delicately. It pleased him very much to see her, and it irritated Birkin. They were all drinking champagne. Maxim, the prim young Russian with the smooth, warm-coloured face and black, oiled hair was the only one who seemed to be perfectly calm and sober. Birkin was white and abstract, unnatural, Gerald was smiling with a constant bright, amused, cold light in his eyes, leaning a little protectively towards Minette, who was very handsome, and soft, unfolded like some fair ice-flower in dreadful flowering nakedness, vainglorious now, flushed with wine and with the excitement of men. Halliday looked foolish. One glass of wine was enough to make him drunk and giggling. Yet there was always a pleasant, warm naïveté about him, that made him attractive.

'I'm not afwaid of anything except black-beetles,' said Minette, looking up suddenly and staring with her round eyes, on which there seemed an unseeing film of flame, fully upon Gerald. He laughed dangerously, from the blood. Her childish speech caressed his nerves, and her burning, filmed eyes, turned now full upon him, oblivious of all her antecedents, gave him a sort of licence.

'I'm not,' she protested. 'I'm not afraid of other things. But black-beetles – ugh!' she shuddered convulsively, as if the very thought were too much to bear.

'Do you mean,' said Gerald, with the punctiliousness of a man who has been drinking, 'that you are afraid of the sight of a black-beetle, or you are afraid of a black-beetle biting you, or doing you some harm?'

'Do they bite?' cried the girl.

'How perfectly loathsome!' exclaimed Halliday.

'I don't know,' replied Gerald, looking round the table. 'Do black-beetles bite? But that isn't the point. Are you afraid of their biting, or is it a metaphysical antipathy?'

The girl was looking full upon him all the time with inchoate eyes.

'Oh, I think they're beastly, they're horrid,' she cried. 'If I see one, it gives me the creeps all over. If one were to crawl on me. I'm *sure* I should die – I'm sure I should.'

'I hope not,' whispered the young Russian.

'I'm sure I should, Maxim,' she asseverated.

'Then one won't crawl on you,' said Gerald, smiling and knowing. In some strange way he understood her.

'It's metaphysical, as Gerald says,' Birkin stated.

There was a little pause of uneasiness.

'And are you afraid of nothing else, Minette?' asked the young Russian, in his quick, hushed, elegant manner.

'Not weally,' she said. 'I am afwaid of some things, but not weally the same. I'm not afwaid of *blood.*'

'Not afwaid of blood!' exclaimed a young man with a thick, pale, jeering face, who had just come to the table and was drinking whisky.

Minette turned on him a sulky look of dislike, low and ugly.

'Aren't you really afraid of blood?' the other persisted, a sneer all over his face.

'No, I'm not,' she retorted.

'Why, have you ever seen blood, except in a dentist's spittoon?' jeered the young man.

'I wasn't speaking to you,' she replied rather superbly.

'You can answer me, can't you?' he said.

For reply, she suddenly jabbed a knife across his thick, pale hand. He started up with a vulgar curse.

'Show's what you are,' said Minette in contempt.

'Curse you,' said the young man, standing by the table and looking down at her with acrid malevolence.

'Stop that,' said Gerald, in quick, instinctive command.

The young man stood looking down at her with sardonic contempt, a cowed, self-conscious look on his thick, pale face. The blood began to flow from his hand.

'Oh, how horrible, take it away!' squealed Halliday, turning green and averting his face.

'D'you feel ill?' asked the sardonic young man, in some concern. 'Do you feel ill, Julius? Garn, it's nothing, man, don't give her the pleasure of letting her think she's performed a feat – don't give her the satisfaction, man – it's just what she wants.'

'Oh!' squealed Halliday.

'He's going to cat, Maxim,' said Minette warningly. The suave young Russian rose and took Halliday by the arm, leading him away. Birkin, white and diminished, looked on as if he were displeased. The wounded, sardonic young man moved away, ignoring his bleeding hand in the most conspicuous fashion.

'He's an awful coward, really,' said Minette to Gerald. 'He's got such an influence over Julius.'

'Who is he?' asked Gerald.

'He's a Jew, really. I can't bear him.'

'Well, he's quite unimportant. But what's wrong with Halliday?'

'Julius's the most awful coward you've ever seen,' she cried. 'He always faints if I lift a knife – he's tewwified of me.'

'H'm!' said Gerald.

'They're all afwaid of me,' she said. 'Only the Jew thinks he's going to show his courage. But he's the biggest coward of them all, really, because he's afwaid what people will think about him – and Julius doesn't care about that.'

'They've a lot of valour between them,' said Gerald good-humouredly.

Minette looked at him with a slow, slow smile. She was very handsome, flushed, and confident in dreadful knowledge. Two little points of light glinted on Gerald's eyes.

'Why do they call you Minette? Because you're like a cat?' he asked her.

'I expect so,' she said.

The smile grew more intense on his face.

'You are, rather; – or a young, female panther.'

'Oh God, Gerald!' said Birkin, in some disgust.

They both looked uneasily at Birkin.

'You're silent tonight, Wupert,' she said to him, with a slight insolence, being safe with the other man.

Halliday was coming back, looking forlorn and sick.

'Minette,' he said, 'I wish you wouldn't do these things – Oh!' He sank in his chair with a groan.

'You'd better go home,' she said to him.

'I *will* go home,' he said. 'But won't you all come along. Won't you come round to the flat?' he said to Gerald. 'I should be so glad if you would. Do – that'll be splendid. I say?' He looked round for a waiter. 'Get me a taxi.' Then he groaned again. 'Oh, I do feel – perfectly ghastly! Minette, you see what you do to me.'

'Then why are you such an idiot?' she said with sullen calm.

'But I'm not an idiot! Oh, how awful! Do come, everybody, it will be so splendid. Minette, you are coming. What? Oh, but you *must* come, yes, you must. What? Oh, my dear girl, don't make a fuss now, I feel perfectly – Oh, it's so ghastly – Ho! – er! Oh!'

'You know you can't drink,' she said to him, coldly.

'I tell you it isn't drink – it's your disgusting behaviour, Minette, it's nothing else. Oh, how awful! Libidnikov, do let us go.'

'He's only drunk one glass – only one glass,' came the rapid, hushed voice of the young Russian.

They all moved off to the door. The girl kept near to Gerald, and seemed to be at one in her motion with him. He was aware of this, and filled with demon-satisfaction that his motion held good for two. He held her in the hollow of his will, and she was soft, secret, invisible in her stirring there.

They crowded five of them into the taxi-cab. Halliday lurched in first, and dropped into his seat against the other window. Then Minette took her place, and Gerald sat next to her. They heard the young Russian giving orders to the driver, then they were all seated in the dark, crowded close together, Halliday groaning and leaning out of the window. They felt the swift, muffled motion of the car.

Minette sat near to Gerald, and she seemed to become soft, subtly to infuse herself into his bones, as if she were passing into him in a black, electric flow. Her being suffused into his veins like a magnetic darkness, and concentrated at the base of his spine like a fearful source of power. Meanwhile her voice sounded out reedy and nonchalant, as she talked indifferently with Birkin and with Maxim. Between her and Gerald was this silence and this black, electric comprehension in the darkness. Then she found his hand, and grasped it in her own firm, small clasp. It was so utterly dark, and yet such a naked statement, that rapid vibrations ran through his blood and over his brain, he was no longer responsible. Still her voice rang on like a bell, tinged with a tone of mockery. And as she swung her head, her fine mane of hair just swept his face, and all his nerves were on fire, as with a subtle friction of electricity. But the great centre of his force held steady, a magnificent pride to him, at the base of his spine.

They arrived at a street of quiet houses, went up a garden path, and presently a door was being opened for them by a dark-skinned servant. Gerald looked in surprise, wondering if he were a gentleman, one of the Orientals down from Oxford, perhaps. But no, he was the man-servant.

'Make tea, Hasan,' said Halliday.

'There is a room for me?' said Birkin.

To both of which questions the man grinned, and murmured.

He made Gerald uncertain, because, being tall and slender and reticent, he looked like a gentleman.

'Who is your servant?' he asked of Halliday. 'He looks a swell.'

'Oh yes – that's because he's dressed in another man's clothes. He's anything but a swell really. We found him in the road, starving. So I took him here, and another man gave him clothes. He's anything but what he seems to be – his only advantage is that he can't speak English and can't understand it, so he's perfectly safe.'

'He's very dirty,' said the young Russian swiftly and silently.

Directly, the man appeared in the doorway.

'What is it?' said Halliday.

The man grinned and murmured shyly:

'Want to speak to master.'

Gerald watched curiously. The fellow in the doorway was good-looking and clean-limbed, his bearing was calm, he looked elegant, aristocratic. Yet he was half a savage, grinning foolishly. Halliday went out into the corridor to speak with him.

'What?' they heard his voice. 'What? What do you say? Tell me again. What? Want money? Want *more* money? But what do you want money for?' There was the confused sound of the Arab's talking, then Halliday appeared in the room, smiling also foolishly, and saying:

'He says he wants money to buy underclothing. Can anybody lend me a shilling? Oh thanks, a shilling will do to buy all the underclothes he wants.' He took the money from Gerald and went out into the passage again, where they heard him saying. 'You can't want more money, you had three and six yesterday. You mustn't ask for any more. Bring the tea in quickly.'

Gerald looked round the room. It was an ordinary London sitting-room in a house evidently taken furnished, rather haphazard but pleasant. But there were several statues, wood-carvings from the West Pacific, strange and disturbing, the carved natives looked almost like the foetus of a human being. One was a woman sitting naked in a strange posture, and looking tortured, her abdomen stuck out. The young Russian explained that she was sitting in child-birth, clutching the ends of the band that hung from her neck, one in each hand, so that she could bear down, and help labour. The strange, transfixed, rudimentary face of the woman again reminded Gerald of a foetus, it was also rather wonderful, conveying the suggestion of the extreme of physical sensation, beyond the limits of mental consciousness.

'Aren't they rather obscene?' he asked, disapproving.

'I don't know,' murmured the other rapidly. 'I have never defined the obscene. I think they are very good.'

Gerald turned away. There were one or two new pictures in the room, in the Futurist manner; there was a large piano. And these, with some ordinary London lodging-house furniture of the better sort, completed the whole.

Minette had taken off her hat and coat, and was seated on the sofa. She was evidently quite at home in the house, but uncertain, suspended. She did not quite know her position. Her alliance for the time being was with Gerald, and she did not know how far this was admitted by any of the men. She was considering how she could carry off the situation. She was determined to have her experience. Now, at this eleventh hour, she was not to be baulked. Her face was flushed as with battle, her eye was brooding but inevitable.

The man came in with tea and a bottle of Kümmel. He set the tray on a little table before the couch.

'Minette,' said Halliday, 'pour out the tea.'

She did not move.

'Won't you do it?' Halliday repeated, in a state of nervous apprehension.

'I've not come back here as it was before,' she said. 'I only came because the others wanted me to, not for your sake.'

'My dear Minette, you know you are your own mistress. I don't want you to do anything but use the flat for your own convenience – you know it, I've told you so many times.'

She did not reply, but silently, reservedly reached for the tea-pot. They all sat round and drank tea. Gerald could feel the electric connection between him and her so strongly, as she sat there quiet and withheld, that another set of conditions altogether had come to pass. Her silence and her immutability perplexed him. *How* was he going to come to her? And yet he felt it quite inevitable. He trusted completely to the current that held them. His perplexity was only superficial, new conditions reigned, the old were surpassed; here one did as one was possessed to do, no matter what it was.

Birkin rose. It was nearly one o'clock.

'I'm going to bed,' he said. 'Gerald, I'll ring you up in the morning at your place – or you ring me up here.'

'Right,' said Gerald, and Birkin went out.

When he was well gone, Halliday said in a stimulated voice, to Gerald:

'I say, won't you stay here – oh do!'

'You can't put everybody up,' said Gerald.

'Oh but I can, perfectly – there are three more beds besides mine – do stay, won't you. Everything is quite ready – there is always somebody here – I always put people up – I love having the house crowded.'

'But there are only two rooms,' said Minette, in a cold, hostile voice, 'now Rupert's here.'

'I know there are only two rooms,' said Halliday, in his odd, high way of speaking. 'But what does that matter? There is the studio –'

He was smiling rather foolishly, and he spoke eagerly, with an insinuating determination.

'Julius and I will share one room,' said the Russian in his discreet, precise voice. Halliday and he were friends since Eton.

'It's very simple,' said Gerald, rising and pressing back his arms, stretching himself. Then he went again to look at one of the pictures. Every one of his limbs was turgid with electric force, and his back was tense like a tiger's with slumbering fire. He was very proud.

Minette rose. She gave a black look at Halliday, fierce and deadly, which brought the rather foolish, pleased smile to that young man's face. Then she went out of the room, with a cold Good night to them all generally.

There was a brief interval, they heard a door close, then Maxim said, in his refined voice:

'That's all right.'

He looked significantly at Gerald, and said again, with a silent nod:

'That's all right – you're all right.'

Gerald looked at the smooth, ruddy, comely face, and at the strange, significant eyes, and it seemed as if the voice of the young Russian, so small and perfect, sounded in the blood rather than in the air.

'*I'm* all right then,' said Gerald.

'Yes! Yes! You're all right,' said the Russian.

Halliday continued to smile, and to say nothing.

Suddenly Minette appeared again in the door, her small, childish face looking sullen and vindictive.

'I know you want to catch me out,' came her cold, rather resonant voice. 'But I don't care, I don't care how much you catch me out.'

She turned and was gone again. She had been wearing a loose dressing-gown of purple silk, tied round her waist. She looked so small and childish and vulnerable, almost pitiful. And yet the looks of her eyes made Gerald feel drowned in some potent darkness that almost frightened him.

The men lit another cigarette and talked casually.

7

TOTEM

In the morning Gerald woke late. He had slept heavily. Minette was still asleep, sleeping childishly and pathetically. There was something small and curled up and defenceless about her, that roused an unsatisfied flame of passion in the young man's blood, a devouring avid pity. He looked at her again. But it would be too cruel to wake her. He subdued himself, and went away.

Hearing voices coming from the sitting-room, Halliday talking to Libidnikov, he went to the door and glanced in. He had on a silk wrap of a beautiful bluish colour, with an amethyst hem.

To his surprise he saw the two young men by the fire, stark naked. Halliday looked up, rather pleased.

'Good morning,' he said. 'Oh – did you want towels?' And stark naked he went out into the hall, striding a strange, white figure between the unliving furniture. He came back with the towels, and took his former position, crouching seated before the fire on the fender.

'Don't you love to feel the fire on your skin?' he said.

'It *is* rather pleasant,' said Gerald.

'How perfectly splendid it must be to be in a climate where one could do without clothing altogether,' said Halliday.

'Yes,' said Gerald, 'if there weren't so many things that sting and bite.'

'That's a disadvantage,' murmured Maxim.

Gerald looked at him, and with a slight revulsion saw the human animal, golden skinned and bare, somehow humiliating. Halliday was different. He had a rather heavy, slack, broken beauty, dark and firm. He was like a Christ in a Pietà. The animal was not there at all, only the heavy, broken beauty. And Gerald realized how Halliday's eyes were beautiful too, so hazel-yellow and warm and confused, broken also in their expression. The fireglow fell on his heavy, rather bowed shoulders, he sat slackly crouched on the fender, his face was uplifted, weak, perhaps slightly disintegrate, and yet with a moving beauty of its own.

'Of course,' said Maxim, 'you've been in hot countries where the people go about naked.'

'Oh really!' exclaimed Halliday. 'Where?'

'South America – Amazon,' said Gerald.

'Oh but how perfectly splendid! It's one of the things I want most to do – to live from day to day without *ever* putting on any sort of clothing whatever. If I could do that, I should feel I had lived.'

'But why?' said Gerald. 'I can't see that it makes so much difference.'

'Oh, I think it would be perfectly splendid. I'm sure life would be entirely another thing – entirely different, and perfectly wonderful.'

'But why?' asked Gerald. 'Why should it?'

'Oh – one would *feel* things instead of merely looking at them. I should feel the air move against me, and feel the things I touched, instead of having only to look at them. I'm sure life is all wrong because it has become much too visual – we can neither hear nor feel nor understand, we can only see. I'm sure that is entirely wrong.'

'Yes, that is true, that is true,' said the Russian.

Gerald glanced at him, and saw him, his suave, golden coloured body with the black hair growing fine and freely, like tendrils, and his limbs like smooth plant-stems. He was so healthy and well-made, why did he make one ashamed, why did one feel repelled? Why should Gerald even dislike it, why did it seem to him to detract from his own dignity. Was that all a human being amounted to? So uninspired! thought Gerald.

Birkin suddenly appeared in the doorway, in white pyjamas and wet hair, and a towel over his arm. He was aloof and white, and somehow evanescent.

'There's the bath-room now, if you want it,' he said generally, and was going away again, when Gerald called:

'I say, Rupert!'

'What?' The single white figure appeared again, a presence in the room.

'What do you think of that figure there? I want to know,' Gerald asked.

Birkin, white and strangely ghostly, went over to the carved figure of the savage woman in labour. Her nude, protuberant body crouched in a strange, clutching posture, her hands gripping the ends of the band, above her breast.

'It is art,' said Birkin.

'Very beautiful, it's very beautiful,' said the Russian.

They all drew near to look. Gerald looked at the group of men, the Russian golden and like a water-plant, Halliday tall and heavily, brokenly beautiful, Birkin very white and indefinite, not to be assigned, as he looked closely at the carven woman. Strangely elated, Gerald also lifted his eyes to the face of the wooden figure. And his heart contracted.

He saw vividly with his spirit the grey, forward-stretching face of the savage woman, dark and tense, abstracted in utter physical stress. It was a terrible face, void, peaked, abstracted almost into meaningless by the weight of sensation beneath. He saw Minette in it. As in a dream, he knew her.

'Why is it art?' Gerald asked, shocked, resentful.

'It conveys a complete truth,' said Birkin. 'It contains the whole truth of that state, whatever you feel about it.'

'But you can't call it *high* art,' said Gerald.

'High! There are centuries and hundreds of centuries of development in a straight line, behind that carving; it is an awful pitch of culture, of a definite sort.'

'What culture?' Gerald asked, in opposition. He hated the sheer barbaric thing.

'Pure culture in sensation, culture in the physical consciousness, really ultimate *physical* consciousness, mindless, utterly sensual. It is so sensual as to be final, supreme.'

But Gerald resented it. He wanted to keep certain illusions, certain ideas like clothing.

'You like the wrong things, Rupert,' he said, 'things against yourself.'

'Oh, I know, this isn't everything,' Birkin replied, moving away.

When Gerald went back to his room from the bath, he also carried his clothes. He was so conventional at home, that when he was really away, and on the loose, as now, he enjoyed nothing so much as full outrageousness. So he strode with his blue silk wrap over his arm and felt defiant.

Minette lay in her bed, motionless, her round, blue eyes like stagnant, unhappy pools. He could only see the dead, bottomless pools of her eyes. Perhaps she suffered. The sensation of her inchoate suffering roused the old sharp flame in him, a mordant pity, a passion almost of cruelty.

'You are awake now,' he said to her.

'What time is it?' came her muted voice.

She seemed to flow back, almost like liquid, from his approach, to sink helplessly away from him. Her inchoate look of a violated slave, whose fulfilment lies in her further and further violation, made his nerves quiver with acutely desirable sensation. After all, his was the only will, she was the passive substance of his will. He tingled with the subtle, biting sensation. And then he knew, he must go away from her, there must be pure separation between them.

It was a quiet and ordinary breakfast, the four men all looking very clean and bathed. Gerald and the Russian were both correct and *comme il faut* in appearance and manner, Birkin was gaunt and sick, and looked a failure in his attempt to be a properly dressed man, like Gerald and Maxim. Halliday wore tweeds and a green flannel shirt, and a rag of a tie, which was just right for him. The Arab brought in a great deal of soft toast, and looked exactly the same as he had looked the night before, statically the same.

At the end of the breakfast Minette appeared, in a purple silk wrap with a shimmering sash. She had recovered herself somewhat, but was mute and lifeless still. It was a torment to her when anybody spoke to her. Her face was like a small, fine mask, sinister too, masked with unwilling suffering. It was almost midday. Gerald rose and went away to his business, glad to get out. But he had not finished. He was coming back again at evening, they were all dining together, and he had booked seats for the party, excepting Birkin, at a music-hall.

At night they came back to the house very late again, again flushed with drink. Again the Arab – who invariably disappeared between the hours of ten and twelve at night – came in silently and inscrutably with tea, bending in a slow, strange, leopard-like fashion to put the tray softly on the table. His face was immutable, aristocratic-looking, tinged slightly with grey under the skin; he was young and good-looking. But Birkin felt a slight sickness, looking at him, and feeling the slight greyness as an ash or a corruption, in the aristocratic inscrutability of expression a nauseating, bestial stupidity.

Again they talked cordially and rousedly together. But already a certain friability was coming over the party, Birkin was mad with irritation, Halliday was turning in an insane hatred against Gerald, Minette was becoming hard and cold, like a flint knife, and Halliday was laying himself out to her. And her intention, ultimately, was to capture Halliday, to have complete power over him.

In the morning they all stalked and lounged about again. But Gerald could feel a strange hostility to himself in the air. It roused his obstinacy, and he stood up against it. He hung on for two more days. The result was a nasty and insane scene with Halliday on the fourth evening. Halliday turned with absurd animosity upon Gerald, in the café. There was a row. Gerald was on the point of knocking-in Halliday's face; when he was filled with sudden disgust and indifference, and he went away, leaving Halliday in a foolish state of gloating triumph, Minette hard and established, and Maxim standing clear. Birkin was absent, he had gone out of town again.

Gerald was piqued because he had left without giving Minette money. It was true, he did not know whether she wanted money or not. But she might have been glad of ten pounds, and he would have been *very* glad to give them to her. Now he felt in a false position. He went away chewing his lips to get at the ends of his short clipped moustache. He knew Minette was merely glad to be rid of him. She had got her Halliday whom she wanted. She wanted him completely in her power. Then she would marry him. She wanted to marry him. She had set her will on marrying Halliday. She never wanted to hear of Gerald again; unless, perhaps, she were in difficulty; because after all, Gerald was what she called a man, and these others, Halliday, Libidnikov, Birkin, the whole Bohemian set, they were only half men. But it was half men she could deal with. She felt sure of herself with them. The real men, like Gerald, put her in her place too much.

Still, she respected Gerald, she really respected him. She had managed to get his address, so that she could appeal to him in time of distress. She knew he wanted to give her money. She would perhaps write to him on that inevitable rainy day.

8

BREADALBY

Breadalby was a Georgian house with Corinthian pillars, standing among the softer, greener hills of Derbyshire, not far from Cromford. In front, it looked over a lawn, over a few trees, down to a string of fish-ponds in the hollow of the silent park. At the back were trees, among which were to be found the stables, and the big kitchen garden, behind which was a wood.

It was a very quiet place, some miles from the high-road, back from the Derwent Valley, outside the show scenery. Silent and forsaken, the golden stucco showed between the trees, the house-front looked down the park, unchanged and unchanging.

Of late, however, Hermione had lived a good deal at the house. She had turned away from London, away from Oxford, towards the silence of the country. Her father was mostly absent, abroad, she was either alone in the house, with her visitors, of whom there were always several, or she had with her her brother, a bachelor, and a Liberal member of Parliament. He always came down when the House was not sitting, seemed always to be present in Breadalby, although he was most conscientious in his attendance to duty.

The summer was just coming in when Ursula and Gudrun went to stay the second time with Hermione. Coming along in the car, after they had entered the park, they looked across the dip, where the fish-ponds lay in silence, at the pillared front of the house, sunny and small like an English drawing of the old school, on the brow of the green hill, against the trees. There were small figures on the green lawn, women in lavender and yellow moving to the shade of the enormous, beautifully balanced cedar tree.

'Isn't it complete!' said Gudrun. 'It is as final as an old aquatint.' She spoke with some resentment in her voice, as if she were captivated unwillingly, as if she must admire against her will.

'Do you love it?' asked Ursula.

'I don't *love* it, but in its way, I think it is quite complete.'

The motor-car ran down the hill and up again in one breath, and they were curving to the side door. A parlour-maid appeared, and then Hermione, coming forward with her pale face lifted, and her hands outstretched, advancing straight to the newcomers, her voice singing:

'Here you are – I'm so glad to see you –' she kissed Gudrun – 'so glad to see you –' she kissed Ursula and remained with her arm round her. 'Are you very tired?'

'Not at all tired,' said Ursula.

'Are you tired, Gudrun?'

'Not at all, thanks,' said Gudrun.

'No –' drawled Hermione. And she stood and looked at them. The two girls were embarrassed because she would not move into the house, but must have her little scene of welcome there on the path. The servants waited.

'Come in,' said Hermione at last, having fully taken in the pair of them. Gudrun was the more beautiful and attractive, she had decided again, Ursula was more physical, more womanly. She admired Gudrun's dress more. It was of green poplin, with a loose coat above it, of broad, dark-green and dark-brown stripes. The hat was of a pale, greenish-straw, the colour of new hay, and it had a plaited ribbon of black and orange, the stockings were dark green, the shoes black. It was a good get-up, at once fashionable and individual. Ursula, in dark blue, was more ordinary, though she also looked well.

Hermione herself wore a dress of prune-coloured silk, with coral beads and coral-coloured stockings. But her dress was both shabby and soiled, even rather dirty.

'You would like to see your rooms now, wouldn't you! Yes. We will go up now, shall we?'

Ursula was glad when she could be left alone in her room. Hermione lingered so long, made such a stress on one. She stood so near to one, pressing herself near upon one, in a way that was most embarrassing and oppressive. She seemed to hinder one's workings.

Lunch was served on the lawn, under the great tree, whose thick, blackish boughs came down close to the grass. There were present a young Italian woman, slight and fashionable, a young, athletic-looking Miss Bradley, a learned, dry Baronet of fifty, who was always making witticisms and laughing at them heartily in a harsh, horse-laugh, there was Rupert Birkin, and then a woman secretary, a Fräulein März, young and slim and pretty.

The food was very good, that was one thing. Gudrun, critical of everything, gave it her full approval. Ursula loved the situation, the white table by the cedar tree, the scent of new sunshine, the little vision of the leafy park, with far-off deer feeding peacefully. There seemed a magic circle drawn about the place, shutting out the present, enclosing the delightful, precious past, trees and deer and silence, like a dream.   .

But in spirit she was unhappy. The talk went on like a rattle of small artillery, always slightly sententious, with a sententiousness that was only emphasized by the continual crackling of a witticism, the continual spatter of verbal jest, designed to give a tone of flippancy to a stream of conversation that was all critical and general, a canal of conversation rather than a stream.

The attitude was mental and very wearying. Only the elderly sociologist, whose mental fibre was so tough as to be insentient, seemed to be thoroughly happy. Birkin was down in the mouth. Hermione appeared, with amazing persistence, to wish to ridicule him and make him look ignominious in the eyes of everybody. And it was surprising how she seemed to succeed, how helpless he seemed against her. He looked completely insignificant. Ursula and Gudrun, both very unused, were mostly silent, listening to the slow, rhapsodic sing-song of Hermione, or the verbal sallies of Sir Joshua, or the prattle of Fräulein, or the responses of the other two women.

Luncheon was over, coffee was brought out on the grass, the party left the table and sat about in lounge chairs, in the shade or in the sunshine as they wished. Fräulein departed into the house, Hermione took up her embroidery, the little Contessa took a book, Miss Bradley was weaving a basket out of fine grass, and there they all were on the lawn in the early summer afternoon, working leisurely and spattering with half-intellectual, deliberate talk.

Suddenly there was the sound of the brakes and the shutting off of a motor-car.

'There's Salsie!' sang Hermione, in her slow, amusing sing-song. And laying down her work, she rose slowly, and slowly passed over the lawn, round the bushes, out of sight.

'Who is it?' asked Gudrun.

'Mr Roddice – Miss Roddice's brother – at least, I suppose it's he,' said Sir Joshua.

'Salsie, yes, it is her brother,' said the little Contessa, lifting her head for a moment from her book, and speaking as if to give information, in her slightly deepened, guttural English.

They all waited. And then round the bushes came the tall form of Alexander Roddice, striding romantically like a Meredith hero who remembers Disraeli. He was cordial with everybody, he was at once a host, with an easy, off-hand hospitality that he had learned for Hermione's friends. He had just come down from London, from the House. At once the atmosphere of the House of Commons made itself felt over the lawn: the Home Secretary had said such and such a thing, and he, Roddice, on the other hand, thought such and such a thing, and had said so-and-so to the P.M.

Now Hermione came round the bushes with Gerald Crich. He had come along with Alexander. Gerald was presented to everybody, was kept by Hermione for a few moments in full view, then he was led away, still by Hermione. He was evidently her guest of the moment.

There had been a split in the Cabinet; the Minister for Education had resigned owing to adverse criticism. This started a conversation on education.

'Of course,' said Hermione, lifting her face like a rhapsodist, 'there *can* be no reason, no *excuse* for education, except the joy and beauty of knowledge in itself.' She seemed to rumble and ruminate with subterranean thoughts for a minute, then she proceeded: 'Vocational education *isn't* education, it is the close of education.'

Gerald, on the brink of discussion, sniffed the air with delight and prepared for action.

'Not necessarily,' he said. 'But isn't education really like gymnastics, isn't the end of education the production of a well-trained, vigorous, energetic mind?'

'Just as athletics produce a healthy body, ready for anything,' cried Miss Bradley, in hearty accord.

Gudrun looked at her in silent loathing.

'Well –' rumbled Hermione, 'I don't know. To me the pleasure of knowing is *so* great, so *wonderful* – nothing has meant so much to me in all life, as certain knowledge – no, I am sure – nothing.'

'What knowledge, for example, Hermione?' asked Alexander.

Hermione lifted her face and rumbled –

'M – m – m – I don't know... But one thing was the stars, when I really understood something about the stars. One feels so *uplifted*, so *unbounded*...'

Birkin looked at her in a white fury.

'What do you want to feel unbounded for?' he said sarcastically. 'You don't want to *be* unbounded.'

Hermione recoiled in offence.

'Yes, but one does have that limitless feeling,' said Gerald. 'It's like getting on top of the mountain and seeing the Pacific.'

'Silent upon a peak in Dariayn,' murmured the Italian, lifting her face for a moment from her book.

'Not necessarily in Darien,' said Gerald, while Ursula began to laugh.

Hermione waited for the dust to settle, and then she said, untouched:

'Yes, it is the greatest thing in life – *to know*. It is really to be happy, to be *free*.'

'Knowledge is, of course, liberty,' said Mattheson.

'In compressed tabloids,' said Birkin, looking at the dry, stiff little body of the Baronet. Immediately Gudrun saw the famous sociologist as a flat bottle, containing tabloids of compressed liberty. That pleased her. Sir Joshua was labelled and placed for ever in her mind.

'What does that mean, Rupert?' sang Hermione, in a calm snub.

'You can only have knowledge, strictly,' he replied, 'of things concluded, in the past. It's like bottling the liberty of last summer in the bottled gooseberries.'

'*Can* one have knowledge only of the past?' asked the Baronet, pointedly. 'Could we call our knowledge of the laws of gravitation for instance, knowledge of the past?'

'Yes,' said Birkin.

'There is a most beautiful thing in my book,' suddenly piped the little Italian woman. 'It says the man came to the door and threw his eyes down the street.'

There was a general laugh in the company. Miss Bradley went and looked over the shoulder of the Contessa.

'See!' said the Contessa.

'Bazarov came to the door and threw his eyes hurriedly down the street,' she read.

Again there was a loud laugh, the most startling of which was the Baronet's, which rattled out like a clatter of falling stones.

'What is the book?' asked Alexander, promptly.

'Fathers and Sons, by Turgenev,' said the little foreigner, pronouncing every syllable distinctly. She looked at the cover, to verify herself.

'An old American edition,' said Birkin.

'Ha! – of course – translated from the French,' said Alexander, with a fine declamatory voice. '*Bazarov ouvra la porte et jeta les yeux dans la rue.*'

He looked brightly round the company.

'I wonder what the "hurriedly" was,' said Ursula.

They all began to guess.

And then, to the amazement of everybody, the maid came hurrying with a large tea-tray. The afternoon had passed so swiftly.

After tea, they were all gathered for a walk.

'Would you like to come for a walk?' said Hermione to each of them, one by one. And they all said yes, feeling somehow like prisoners marshalled for exercise. Birkin only refused.

'Will you come for a walk, Rupert?'

'No, Hermione.'

'But are you *sure*?'

'Quite sure.' There was a second's hesitation.

'And why not?' sang Hermione's question. It made her blood run sharp, to be thwarted in even so trifling a matter. She intended them all to walk with her in the park.

'Because I don't like trooping off in a gang,' he said.

Her voice rumbled in her throat for a moment. Then she said, with a curious stray calm:

'Then we'll leave a little boy behind, if he's sulky.'

And she looked really gay, while she insulted him. But it merely made him stiff.

She trailed off to the rest of the company, only turning to wave her handkerchief to him, and to chuckle with laughter, singing out:

'Good-bye, good-bye, little boy.'

'Good-bye, impudent hag,' he said to himself.

They all went through the park. Hermione wanted to show them the wild daffodils on a little slope. 'This way, this way,' sang her leisurely voice at intervals. And they had all to come this way. The daffodils were pretty, but who could see them? Ursula was stiff all over with resentment by this time, resentment of the whole atmosphere. Gudrun, mocking and objective, watched and registered everything.

They looked at the shy deer, and Hermione talked to the stag, as if he too were a boy she wanted to wheedle and fondle. He was male, so she must exert some kind of power over him. They trailed home by the fish-ponds, and Hermione told them about the quarrel of two male swans, who had striven for the love of the one lady. She chuckled and laughed as she told how the ousted lover had sat with his head buried under his wing, on the gravel.

When they arrived back at the house, Hermione stood on the lawn and sang out, in a strange, small, high voice that carried very far:

'Rupert! Rupert!' the first syllable was high and slow, the second dropped down. 'Roo-o-opert.'

But there was no answer. A maid appeared.

'Where is Mr Birkin, Alice?' asked the mild straying voice of Hermione. But under the straying voice, what a persistent, almost insane *will*!

'I think he's in his room, madame.'

'Is he?'

Hermione went slowly up the stairs, along the corridor, singing out in her high, small call:

'Ru-oo-pert! Ru-oo-pert!'

She came to his door, and tapped, still crying: 'Roo-pert.'

'Yes,' sounded his voice at last.

'What are you doing?'

The question was mild and curious.

There was no answer. Then he opened the door.

'We've come back,' said Hermione. 'The daffodils are *so* beautiful.'

'Yes,' he said, 'I've seen them.'

She looked at him with her long, slow, impassive look, along her cheeks.

'Have you?' she echoed. And she remained looking at him. She was stimulated above all things by this conflict with him, when he was like a sulky boy, helpless, and she had him safe at Breadalby. But underneath she knew the split was coming, and her hatred of him was subconscious and intense.

'What were you doing?' she reiterated, in her mild, indifferent tone. He did not answer, and she made her way, almost unconsciously into his room. He had taken a Chinese drawing of geese from the boudoir, and was copying it, with much skill and vividness.

'You are copying the drawing,' she said, standing near the table, and looking down at his work. 'Yes. How beautifully you do it! You like it very much, don't you?'

'It's a marvellous drawing,' he said.

'Is it? I'm so glad you like it, because I've always been fond of it. The Chinese Ambassador gave it me.'

'I know,' he said.

'But why do you copy it?' she asked, casual and sing-song. 'Why not do something original?'

'I want to know it,' he replied. 'One gets more of China, copying this picture, than reading all the books.'

'And what do you get?'

She was at once roused, she laid as it were violent hands on him, to extract his secrets from him. She *must* know. It was a dreadful tyranny, an obsession in her, to know all he knew. For some time he was silent, hating to answer her. Then, compelled, he began:

'I know what centres they live from – what they perceive and feel – the hot, stinging centrality of a goose in the flux of cold water and mud – the curious bitter stinging heat of a goose's blood, entering their own blood like an inoculation of corruptive fire – fire of the cold-burning mud – the lotus mystery.'

Hermione looked at him along her narrow, pallid cheeks. Her eyes were strange and drugged, heavy under their heavy, drooping lids. Her thin bosom shrugged convulsively. He stared back at her, devilish and unchanging. With another strange, sick convulsion, she turned away, as if she were sick, could feel dissolution setting-in in her body. For with her mind she was unable to attend to his words; he caught her, as it were, beneath all her defences, and destroyed her with some insidious occult potency.

'Yes,' she said, as if she did not know what she were saying. 'Yes,' and she swallowed, and tried to regain her mind. But she could not, she was witless, decentralized. Use all her will as she might, she could not recover. She suffered the ghastliness of dissolution, broken and gone in a horrible corruption. And he stood and looked at her unmoved. She strayed out, pallid and preyed upon like a ghost, like one attacked by the tomb-influences which dog us. And she was gone like a corpse, that has no presence, no connection. He remained hard and vindictive.

Hermione came down to dinner strange and sepulchral, her eyes heavy and full of sepulchral darkness, strength. She had put on a dress of stiff old greenish brocade, that fitted tight and made her look tall and rather terrible, ghastly. In the gay light of the drawing-room she was uncanny and oppressive. But seated in the half-light of the dining-room, sitting stiffly before the shaded candles on the table, she seemed a power, a presence. She listened and attended with a drugged attention.

The party was gay and extravagant in appearance, everybody had put on evening dress except Birkin and Joshua Mattheson. The little Italian Contessa wore a dress of tissue, of orange and gold and black velvet in soft wide stripes, Gudrun was emerald green with strange net-work, Ursula was in yellow with dull silver veiling, Miss Bradley was of grey, crimson and jet, Fräulein März wore pale blue. It gave Hermione a sudden convulsive sensation of pleasure, to see these rich colours under the candle-light. She was aware of the talk going on, ceaselessly, Joshua's voice dominating; of the ceaseless pitter-patter of women's light laughter and responses; of the brilliant colours and the white table and the shadow above and below; and she seemed in a swoon of gratification, convulsed with pleasure, and yet sick, like a *revenant*. She took very little part in the conversation, yet she heard it all, it was all hers.

They all went together into the drawing-room, as if they were one family, easily, without any attention to ceremony. Fräulein handed the coffee, everybody smoked cigarettes, or else long warden pipes of white clay, of which a sheaf was provided.

'Will you smoke? – cigarettes or pipe?' asked Fräulein prettily. There was a circle of people, Sir Joshua with his eighteenth-century appearance, Gerald the amused, handsome young Englishman, Alexander tall and the handsome politician, democratic and lucid, Hermione strange like a long Cassandra, and the women lurid with colour, all dutifully smoking their long white pipes, and sitting in a half-moon in the comfortable, soft-lighted drawing-room, round the logs that flickered on the marble hearth.

The talk was very often political or sociological, and interesting, curiously anarchistic. There was an accumulation of powerful force in the room, powerful and destructive. Everything seemed to be thrown into the melting-pot, and it seemed to Ursula they were all witches, helping the pot to bubble. There was an elation and a satisfaction in it all, but it was cruelly exhausting for the newcomers, this ruthless mental pressure, this powerful, consuming, destructive mentality that emanated from Joshua and Hermione and Birkin and dominated the rest.

But a sickness, a fearful nausea gathered possession of Hermione. There was a lull in the talk, as it was arrested by her unconscious but all-powerful will.

'Salsie, won't you play something?' said Hermione, breaking off completely. 'Won't somebody dance? Gudrun, you will dance, won't you? I wish you would. *Anche tu, Palestra, ballerai? – si, per piacere*. You too, Ursula.'

Hermione rose and slowly pulled the gold-embroidered band that hung by the mantel, clinging to it for a moment, then releasing it suddenly. Like a priestess she looked, unconscious, sunk in a heavy half-trance.

A servant came, and soon reappeared with armfuls of silk robes and shawls and scarves, mostly Oriental, things that Hermione, with her love for beautiful extravagant dress, had collected gradually.

'The three women will dance together,' she said.

'What shall it be?' asked Alexander, rising briskly.

'Vergini Delle Rocchette,' said the Contessa at once.

'They are so languid,' said Ursula.

'The three witches from Macbeth,' suggested Fräulein usefully. It was finally decided to do Naomi and Ruth and Orpah. Ursula was Naomi, Gudrun was Ruth, the Contessa was Orpah. The idea was to make a little ballet, in the style of the Russian Ballet of Pavlova and Nijinsky.

The Contessa was ready first, Alexander went to the piano, a space was cleared. Orpah, in beautiful Oriental clothes, began slowly to dance the death of her husband. Then Ruth came, and they wept together, and lamented, then Naomi came to comfort them. It was all done in dumb show, the women danced their emotion in gesture and motion. The little drama went on for a quarter of an hour.

Ursula was beautiful as Naomi. All her men were dead, it remained to her only to stand alone in indomitable assertion, demanding nothing. Ruth, woman-loving, loved her. Orpah, a vivid, sensational, subtle widow, would go back to the former life, a repetition. The inter-play between the women was real and rather frightening. It was strange to see how Gudrun clung with heavy, desperate passion to Ursula, yet smiled with subtle malevolence against her, how Ursula accepted silently, unable to provide any more either for herself or for the other, but dangerous and indomitable, refuting her grief.

Hermione loved to watch. She could see the Contessa's rapid, stoat-like sensationalism, Gudrun's ultimate but treacherous cleaving to the woman in her sister, Ursula's dangerous helplessness, as if she were helplessly weighted, and unreleased.

'That was very beautiful,' everybody cried with one accord. But Hermione writhed in her soul, knowing what she could not know. She cried out for more dancing, and it was her will that set the Contessa and Birkin moving mockingly in Malbrouk.

Gerald was excited by the desperate cleaving of Gudrun to Naomi. The essence of that female, subterranean recklessness and mockery penetrated his blood. He could not forget Gudrun's lifted, offered, cleaving, reckless, yet withal mocking weight. And Birkin, watching like a hermit crab from its hole, had seen the brilliant frustration and helplessness of Ursula. She was rich, full of dangerous power. She was like a strange unconscious bud of powerful womanhood. He was unconsciously drawn to her. She was his future.

Alexander played some Hungarian music, and they all danced, seized by the spirit. Gerald was marvellously exhilarated at finding himself in motion, moving towards Gudrun, dancing with feet that could not yet escape from the waltz and the two-step, but feeling his force stir along his limbs and his body, out of captivity. He did not know yet how to dance their convulsive, rag-time sort of dancing, but he knew how to begin. Birkin, when he could get free from the weight of the people present, whom he disliked, danced rapidly and with a real gaiety. And how Hermione hated him for this irresponsible gaiety.

'Now I see,' cried the Contessa excitedly, watching his purely gay motion, which he had all to himself. 'Mr Birkin, he is a changer.'

Hermione looked at her slowly, and shuddered, knowing that only a foreigner could have seen and have said this.

'*Cosa vuol'dire*, Palestra?' she asked, sing-song.

'Look,' said the Contessa, in Italian. 'He is not a man, he is a chameleon, a creature of change.'

'He is not a man, he is treacherous, not one of us,' said itself over in Hermione's consciousness. And her soul writhed in the black subjugation to him, because of his power to escape, to exist, other than she did, because he was not consistent, not a man, less than a man. She hated him in a despair that shattered her and broke her down, so that she suffered sheer dissolution like a corpse, and was unconscious of everything save the horrible sickness of dissolution that was taking place within her, body and soul.

The house being full, Gerald was given the smaller room, really the dressing-room, communicating with Birkin's bedroom. When they all took their candles and mounted the stairs, where the lamps were burning subduedly, Hermione captured Ursula and brought her into her own bedroom, to talk to her. A sort of constraint came over Ursula in the big, strange bedroom. Hermione seemed to be bearing down on her, awful and inchoate, making some appeal. They were looking at some Indian silk shirts, gorgeous and sensual in themselves, their shape, their almost corrupt gorgeousness. And Hermione came near, and her bosom writhed, and Ursula was for a moment blank with panic. And for a moment Hermione's haggard eyes saw the fear on the face of the other, there was again a sort of crash, a crashing down. And Ursula picked up a shirt of rich red and blue silk, made for a young princess of fourteen, and was crying mechanically:

'Isn't it wonderful – who would dare to put those two strong colours together –'

Then Hermione's maid entered silently and Ursula, overcome with dread, escaped, carried away by powerful impulse.

Birkin went straight to bed. He was feeling happy, and sleepy. Since he had danced he was happy. But Gerald would talk to him. Gerald, in evening dress, sat on Birkin's bed when the other lay down, and must talk.

'Who are those two Brangwens?' Gerald asked.

'They live in Beldover.'

'In Beldover! Who are they then?'

'Teachers in the Grammar School.'

There was a pause.

'They are!' exclaimed Gerald at length. 'I thought I had seen them before.'

'It disappoints you?' said Birkin.

'Disappoints me! No – but how is it Hermione has them here?'

'She knew Gudrun in London – that's the younger one, the one with the darker hair – she's an artist – does sculpture and modelling.'

'She's not a teacher in the Grammar School, then – only the other?'

'Both – Gudrun art mistress, Ursula a class mistress.'

'And what's the father?'

'Handicraft instructor in the schools.'

'Really!'

'Class-barriers are breaking down!'

Gerald was always uneasy under the slightly jeering tone of the other.

'That their father is handicraft instructor in a school! What does it matter to me?'

Birkin laughed. Gerald looked at his face, as it lay there laughing and bitter and indifferent on the pillow, and he could not go away.

'I don't suppose you will see very much more of Gudrun at least. She is a restless bird, she'll be gone in a week or two,' said Birkin.

'Where will she go?'

'London, Paris, Rome – heaven knows. I always expect her to sheer off to Damascus or San Francisco; she's a bird of paradise. God knows what she's got to do with Beldover. It goes by contraries, like dreams.'

Gerald pondered for a few moments.

'How do you know her so well?' he asked.

'I knew her in London,' he replied, 'in the Algernon Strange set. She'll know about Minette and Libidnikov and the rest – even if she doesn't know them personally. She was never quite that set – more conventional, in a way. I've known her for two years, I suppose.'

'And she makes money, apart from her teaching?' asked Gerald.

'Some – irregularly. She can sell her models. She has a certain réclame.'

'How much for?'

'A guinea, ten guineas.'

'And are they good? What are they?'

'I think sometimes they are marvellously good. That is hers, those two wagtails in Hermione's boudoir – you've seen them – they are carved in wood and painted.'

'I thought it was savage carving again.'

'No, hers. That's what they are – animals and birds, sometimes odd small people in everyday dress, really rather wonderful when they come off. They have a sort of funniness that is quite unconscious and subtle.'

'She might be a well-known artist one day?' mused Gerald.

'She might. But I think she won't. She drops her art if anything else catches her. Her contrariness prevents her taking it seriously – she must never be too serious, she feels she might give herself away. And she won't give herself away – she's always on the defensive. That's what I can't stand about her type. By the way, how did things go off with Minette after I left you? I haven't heard anything.'

'Oh, rather disgusting. Halliday turned objectionable, and I only just saved myself from jumping on his stomach, in a real old-fashioned row.'

Birkin was silent.

'Of course,' he said, 'Julius is somewhat insane. On the one hand he's had religious mania, and on the other, he is fascinated by obscenity. Either he is a pure servant, washing the feet of Christ, or else he is making obscene drawings of Jesus – action and reaction – and between the two, nothing. He is really insane. He wants a pure lily, another girl, with a Botticelli face, on the one hand, and on the other, he *must* have Minette, just to defile himself with her.'

'That's what I can't make out,' said Gerald. 'Does he love her, Minette, or doesn't he?'

'He neither does nor doesn't. She is the harlot, the actual harlot of adultery to him. And he's got a craving to throw himself into the filth of her. Then he gets up and calls on the name of the lily of purity, the baby-faced girl, and so enjoys himself all round. It's the old story – action and reaction, and nothing between.'

'I don't know,' said Gerald, after a pause, 'that he does insult Minette so very much. She strikes me as being rather foul.'

'But I thought you liked her,' exclaimed Birkin. 'I always felt fond of her. I never had anything to do with her, personally, that's true.'

'I liked her all right, for a couple of days,' said Gerald. 'But a week of her would have turned me over. There's a certain smell about the skin of those women, that in the end is sickening beyond words – even if you like it at first.'

'I know,' said Birkin. Then he added, rather fretfully, 'But go to bed, Gerald. God knows what time it is.'

Gerald looked at his watch, and at length rose off the bed, and went to his room. But he returned in a few minutes, in his shirt.

'One thing,' he said, seating himself on the bed again. 'We finished up rather stormily, and I never had time to give her anything.'

'Money?' said Birkin. 'She'll get what she wants from Halliday or from one of her acquaintances.'

'But then,' said Gerald, 'I'd rather give her her dues and settle the account.'

'She doesn't care.'

'No, perhaps not. But one feels the account is left open, and would rather it were closed.'

'Would you?' said Birkin. He was looking at the white legs of Gerald, as the latter sat on the side of the bed in his shirt. They were white-skinned, full, muscular legs, handsome and decided. Yet they moved Birkin with a sort of pathos, tenderness, as if they were childish.

'I think I'd rather close the account,' said Gerald, repeating himself vaguely.

'It doesn't matter one way or another,' said Birkin.

'You always say it doesn't matter,' said Gerald, a little puzzled, looking down at the face of the other man affectionately.

'Neither does it,' said Birkin.

'But she was a decent sort, really –'

'Render unto Caesarina the things that are Caesarina's,' said Birkin, turning aside. It seemed to him Gerald was talking for the sake of talking. 'Go away, it wearies me – it's too late at night,' he said.

'I wish you'd tell me something that *did* matter,' said Gerald, looking down all the time at the face of the other man, waiting for something. But Birkin turned his face aside.

'All right then, go to sleep,' said Gerald, and he laid his hand affectionately on the other man's shoulder, and went away.

In the morning when Gerald awoke and heard Birkin move, he called out: 'I still think I ought to give Minette some money.'

'Oh, God!' said Birkin, 'don't be so matter-of-fact. Close the account in your own soul, if you like. It is there you can't close it.'

'How do you know I can't?'

'Knowing you.'

Gerald meditated for some moments.

'It seems to me the right thing to do, you know, with the Minettes, is to pay them.'

'And the right thing for mistresses: keep them. And the right thing for wives: live under the same roof with them. *Integer vitae scelerisque purus –*' said Birkin.

'There's no need to be nasty about it,' said Gerald.

'It bores me. I'm not interested in your peccadilloes.'

'And I don't care whether you are or not – I am.'

The morning was again sunny. The maid had been in and brought the water, and had drawn the curtains. Birkin, sitting up in bed, looked lazily and pleasantly out on the park, that was so green and deserted, romantic, belonging to the past. He was thinking how lovely, how sure, how formed, how final all the things of the past were – the lovely accomplished past – this house, so still and golden, the park slumbering its centuries of peace. And then, what a snare and a delusion, this beauty of static things – what a horrible, dead prison Breadalby really was, what an intolerable confinement, the peace! Yet it was better than the sordid scrambling conflict of the present. If only one might create the future after one's own heart – for a little pure truth, a little unflinching application of simple truth to life, the heart cried out ceaselessly.

'I can't see what you will leave me at all, to be interested in,' came Gerald's voice from the lower room. 'Neither the Minettes, nor the mines, nor anything else.'

'You be interested in what you can, Gerald. Only I'm not interested myself,' said Birkin.

'What am I to do at all, then?' came Gerald's voice.

'What you like. What am I to do myself?'

In the silence Birkin could feel Gerald musing this fact.

'I'm blest if I know,' came the good-humoured answer.

'You see,' said Birkin, 'part of you wants Minette, and nothing but Minette, part of you wants the mines, the business, and nothing but the business – and there you are – all in bits –'

'And part of me wants something else,' said Gerald, in a queer, quiet, real voice.

'What?' said Birkin, rather surprised.

'That's what I hoped you could tell me,' said Gerald.

There was a silence for some time.

'I can't tell you – I can't find my own way, let alone yours. You might marry,' Birkin replied.

'Who – Minette?' asked Gerald.

'Perhaps,' said Birkin. And he rose and went to the window.

'That is your panacea,' said Gerald. 'But you haven't even tried it on yourself yet, and you are sick enough.'

'I am,' said Birkin. 'Still, I shall come right.'

'Through marriage?'

'Yes,' Birkin answered obstinately.

'And no,' added Gerald. 'No, no, no, my boy.'

There was a silence between them, and a strange tension of hostility. They always kept a gap, a distance between them, they wanted always to be free each of the other. Yet there was a curious heart-straining towards each other.

'*Salvator femininus,*' said Gerald, satirically.

'Why not?' said Birkin.

'No reason at all,' said Gerald, 'if it really works. But whom will you marry?'

'A woman,' said Birkin.

'Good,' said Gerald.

Birkin and Gerald were the last to come down to breakfast. Hermione liked everybody to be early. She suffered when she felt her day was diminished, she felt she had missed her life. She seemed to grip the hours by the throat, to force her life from them. She was rather pale and ghastly, as if left behind, in the morning. Yet she had her power, her will was strangely pervasive. With the entrance of the two young men a sudden tension was felt.

She lifted her face, and said, in her amused sing-song:

'Good morning! Did you sleep well? I'm so glad.'

And she turned away, ignoring them. Birkin, who knew her well, saw that she intended to discount his existence.

'Will you take what you want from the sideboard?' said Alexander, in a voice slightly suggesting disapprobation. 'I hope the things aren't cold. Oh no! Do you mind putting out the flame under the chafing-dish, Rupert? Thank you.'

Even Alexander was rather authoritative where Hermione was cool. He took his tone from her, inevitably. Birkin sat down and looked at the table. He was so used to this house, to this room, to this atmosphere, through years of intimacy, and now he felt in complete opposition to it all, it had nothing to do with him. How well he knew Hermione, as she sat there, erect and silent and somewhat bemused, and yet so potent, so powerful! He knew her statically, so finally, that it was almost like a madness. It was difficult to believe one was not mad, that one was not a figure in the hall of kings in some

Egyptian tomb, where the dead all sat immemorial and tremendous. How utterly he knew Joshua Mattheson, who was talking in his harsh, yet rather mincing voice, endlessly, endlessly, always with a strong mentality working, always interesting, and yet always known, everything he said known beforehand, however novel it was, and clever. Alexander the up-to-date host, so bloodlessly free-and-easy, Fräulein so prettily chiming in just as she should, the little Italian Countess taking notice of everybody, only playing her little game, objective and cold, like a weasel watching everything, and extracting her own amusement, never giving herself in the slightest; then Miss Bradley, heavy and rather subservient, treated with cool, almost amused contempt by Hermione, and therefore slighted by everybody – how known it all was, like a game with the figures set out, the same figures, the Queen of chess, the knights, the pawns, the same now as they were hundreds of years ago, the same figures moving round in one of the innumerable permutations that make up the game. But the game is known, its going on is like a madness, it is so exhausted.

There was Gerald, an amused look on his face; the game pleased him. There was Gudrun, watching with steady, large, hostile eyes; the game fascinated her, and she loathed it. There was Ursula, with a slightly startled look on her face, as if she were hurt, and the pain were just outside her consciousness.

Suddenly Birkin got up and went out.

'That's enough,' he said to himself involuntarily.

Hermione knew his motion, though not in her consciousness. She lifted her heavy eyes and saw him lapse suddenly away, on a sudden, unknown tide, and the waves broke over her. Only her indomitable will remained static and mechanical, she sat at the table making her musing, stray remarks. But the darkness had covered her, she was like a ship that has gone down. It was finished for her too, she was wrecked in the darkness. Yet the unfailing mechanism of her will worked on, she had that activity.

'Shall we bathe this morning?' she said, suddenly looking at them all.

'Splendid,' said Joshua. 'It is a perfect morning.'

'Oh, it is beautiful,' said Fräulein.

'Yes, let us bathe,' said the Italian woman.

'We have no bathing-suits,' said Gerald.

'Have mine,' said Alexander. 'I must go to church and read the lessons. They expect me.'

'Are you a Christian?' asked the Italian Countess, with sudden interest.

'No,' said Alexander. 'I'm not. But I believe in keeping up the old institutions.'

'They are so beautiful,' said Fräulein daintily.

'Oh, they are,' cried Miss Bradley.

They all trailed out on to the lawn. It was a sunny, soft morning in early summer, when life ran in the world subtly, like a reminiscence. The church bells were ringing a little way off, not a cloud was in the sky, the swans were like lilies on the water below, the peacocks walked with long, prancing steps across the shadow and into the sunshine of the grass. One wanted to swoon into the by-gone perfection of it all.

'Good-bye,' called Alexander, waving his gloves cheerily, and he disappeared behind the bushes, on his way to church.

'Now,' said Hermione, 'shall we all bathe?'

'I won't,' said Ursula.

'You don't want to?' said Hermione, looking at her slowly.

'No. I don't want to,' said Ursula.

'Nor I,' said Gudrun.

'What about my suit?' asked Gerald.

'I don't know,' laughed Hermione, with an odd, amused intonation. 'Will a handkerchief do – a large handkerchief?'

'That will do,' said Gerald.

'Come along then,' sang Hermione.

The first to run across the lawn was the little Italian, small and like a cat, her white legs twinkling as she went, ducking slightly her head, that was tied in a gold silk kerchief. She tripped through the gate and down the grass, and stood, like a tiny figure of ivory and bronze, at the water's edge, having dropped off her towelling, watching the swans, which came up in surprise. Then out ran Miss Bradley, like a large, soft plum in her dark-blue suit. Then Gerald came, a scarlet silk kerchief round his loins, his towels over his arms. He seemed to flaunt himself a little in the sun, lingering and laughing, strolling easily, looking white but natural in his nakedness. Then came Sir Joshua, in an overcoat, and lastly Hermione, striding with stiff grace from out of a great mantle of purple silk, her head tied up in purple and gold. Handsome was her stiff, long body, her straight-stepping white legs, there was a static magnificence about her as she let the cloak float loosely away from her striding. She crossed the lawn like some strange memory, and passed slowly and statelily towards the water.

There were three ponds, in terraces descending the valley, large and smooth and beautiful, lying in the sun. The water ran over a little stone wall, over small rocks, splashing down from one pond to the level below. The swans had gone out on to the opposite bank, the reeds smelled sweet, a faint breeze touched the skin.

Gerald had dived in, after Sir Joshua, and had swum to the end of the pond. There he climbed out and sat on the wall. There was a dive, and the little Countess was swimming like a rat, to join him. They both sat in the sun, laughing and crossing their arms on their breasts. Sir Joshua swam up to them, and stood near them, up to his arm-pits in the water. Then Hermione and Miss Bradley swam over, and they sat in a row on the embankment.

'Aren't they terrifying? Aren't they really terrifying?' said Gudrun. 'Don't they look saurian? They are just like great lizards. Did you ever see anything like Sir Joshua? But really, Ursula, he belongs to the primeval world, when great lizards crawled about.'

Gudrun looked in dismay on Sir Joshua, who stood up to the breast in the water, his long, greyish hair washed down into his eyes, his neck set into thick, crude shoulders. He was talking to Miss Bradley, who, seated on the bank above, plump and big and wet, looked as if she might roll and slither in the water almost like one of the slithering sea-lions in the Zoo.

Ursula watched in silence. Gerald was laughing happily, between Hermione and the Italian. He reminded her of Dionysus, because his hair was really yellow, his figure so full and laughing. Hermione, in her large, stiff, sinister grace, leaned near him, frightening, as if she were not responsible for what she might do. He knew a certain danger in her, a convulsive madness. But he only laughed the more, turning often to the little Countess, who was flashing up her face at him.

They all dropped into the water, and were swimming together like a shoal of seals. Hermione was powerful and unconscious in the water, large and slow and powerful, Palestra was quick and silent as a water-rat, Gerald wavered and flickered, a white natural shadow. Then, one after the other, they waded out, and went up to the house.

But Gerald lingered a moment to speak to Gudrun.

'You don't like the water?' he said.

She looked at him with a long, slow inscrutable look, as he stood before her negligently, the water standing in beads all over his skin.

'I like it very much,' she replied.

He paused, expecting some sort of explanation.

'And you swim?'

'Yes, I swim.'

Still he would not ask her why she would not go in then. He could feel something ironic in her. He walked away, piqued for the first time.

'Why wouldn't you bathe?' he asked her again, later, when he was once more the properly-dressed young Englishman.

She hesitated a moment before answering, opposing his persistence.

'Because I didn't like the crowd,' she replied.

He laughed, her phrase seemed to re-echo in his consciousness. The flavour of her slang was piquant to him. Whether he would or not, she signified the real world to him. He wanted to come up to her standards, fulfil her expectations. He knew that her criterion was the only one that mattered. The others were all outsiders, instinctively, whatever they might be socially. And Gerald could not help it, he was bound to strive to come up to her criterion, fulfil her idea of a man and a human being.

After lunch, when all the others had withdrawn, Hermione and Gerald and Birkin lingered, finishing their talk. There had been some discussion, on the whole quite intellectual and artificial, about a new state, a new world of man. Supposing this old social state *were* broken and destroyed, then, out of the chaos, what then?

The great social idea, said Sir Joshua, was the *social* equality of man. No, said Gerald, the idea was, that every man was fit for his own little bit of a task – let him do that, and then please himself. The unifying principle was the work in hand. Only work, the business of production, held men together. It was mechanical, but then society *was* a mechanism. Apart from work they were isolated, free to do as they liked.

'Oh!' cried Gudrun. 'Then we shan't have names any more – we shall be like the Germans, nothing but Herr Obermeister and Herr Untermeister. I can imagine it – "I am Mrs Colliery-Manager Crich – I am Mrs Member-of-Parliament Roddice. I am Miss Art-Teacher Brangwen." Very pretty that.'

'Things would work very much better, Miss Art-Teacher Brangwen,' said Gerald.

'What things, Mr Colliery-Manager Crich? The relation between you and me, *par exemple*?'

'Yes, for example,' cried the Italian. 'That which is between men and women – !'

'That is non-social,' said Birkin, sarcastically.

'Exactly,' said Gerald. 'Between me and a woman, the social question does not enter. It is my own affair.'

'A ten-pound note on it,' said Birkin.

'You don't admit that a woman is a social being?' asked Ursula of Gerald.

'She is both,' said Gerald. 'She is a social being, as far as society is concerned. But for her own private self, she is a free agent, it is her own affair, what she does.'

'But won't it be rather difficult to arrange the two halves?' asked Ursula.

'Oh no,' replied Gerald. 'They arrange themselves naturally – we see it now, everywhere.'

'Don't you laugh so pleasantly till you're out of the wood,' said Birkin. Gerald knitted his brows in momentary irritation.

'Was I laughing?' he said.

'*If,*' said Hermione at last, 'we could only realize that in the *spirit* we are all one, all equal in the spirit, all brothers there – the rest wouldn't matter, there would be no more of this carping and envy and this struggle for power, which destroys, only destroys.'

This speech was received in silence, and almost immediately the party rose from the table. But when the others had gone, Birkin turned round in bitter declamation, saying:

'It is just the opposite, just the contrary, Hermione. We are all different and unequal in spirit – it is only the *social* differences that are based on accidental material conditions. We are all abstractly or mathematically equal, if you like. Every man has hunger and thirst, two eyes, one nose and two legs. We're all the same in point of number. But spiritually there is pure difference and neither equality nor inequality counts. It is upon these two bits of knowledge that you must found a state. Your democracy is an absolute lie – your brotherhood of man is a pure falsity, if you apply it further than the mathematical abstraction. We all drank milk first, we all eat bread and meat, we all want to ride in motor-cars – therein lies the beginning and the end of the brotherhood of man. But no equality.

'But I, myself who am myself, what have I to do with equality with any other man or woman? In the spirit, I am as separate as one star is from another, as different in quality and quantity. Establish a state on *that*. One man isn't any better than another, not because they are equal, but because they are intrinsically *other,* that there is no term of comparison. The minute you begin to compare, one man is seen to be far better than another, all the inequality you can imagine is there by nature. I want every man to have his share in the world's goods, so that I am rid of his importunity, so that I can tell him: "Now you've got what you want – you've got your fair share of the world's gear. Now, you one-mouthed fool, mind yourself and don't obstruct me."'

Hermione was looking at him with leering eyes, along her cheeks. He could feel violent waves of hatred and loathing of all he said, coming out of her. It was dynamic hatred and loathing, coming strong and black out of the unconsciousness. She heard his words in her unconscious self, *consciously* she was as if deafened, she paid no heed to them.

'It *sounds* like megalomania, Rupert,' said Gerald, genially.

Hermione gave a queer, grunting sound. Birkin stood back.

'Yes, let it,' he said suddenly, the whole tone gone out of his voice, that had been so insistent, bearing everybody down. And he went away.

But he felt, later, a little compunction. He had been violent, cruel with poor Hermione. He wanted to recompense her, to make it up. He had hurt her, he had been vindictive. He wanted to be on good terms with her again.

He went into her boudoir, a remote and very cushiony place. She was sitting at her table writing letters. She lifted her face abstractedly when he entered, watched him go to the sofa, and sit down. Then she looked down at her paper again.

He took up a large volume which he had been reading before, and became minutely attentive to his author. His back was towards Hermione. She could not go on with her writing. Her whole mind was a chaos, darkness breaking in upon it, and herself struggling to gain control with her will, as a swimmer struggles with the swirling water. But in spite of her efforts she was borne down, darkness seemed to break over her, she felt as if her heart was bursting. The terrible tension grew stronger and stronger, it was most fearful agony, like being walled up.

And then she realized that his presence was the wall, his presence was destroying her. Unless she could break out, she must die most fearfully, walled up in horror. And he was the wall. She must break down the wall – she must break him down before her, the awful obstruction of him who obstructed her life to the last. It must be done, or she must perish most horribly.

Terrible shocks ran over her body, like shocks of electricity, as if many volts of electricity suddenly struck her down. She was aware of him sitting silently there, an unthinkable evil obstruction. Only this blotted out her mind, pressed out her very breathing, his silent, stooping back, the back of his head.

A terrible voluptuous thrill ran down her arms – she was going to know her voluptuous consummation. Her arms quivered and were strong, immeasurably and irresistibly strong. What delight, what delight in strength, what delirium of pleasure! She was going to have her consummation of voluptuous ecstasy at last. It was coming! In utmost terror and agony, she knew it was upon her now, in extremity of bliss. Her hand closed on a blue, beautiful ball of lapis lazuli that stood on her desk for a paper-weight. She rolled it round in her hand as she rose silently. Her heart was a pure flame in her breast, she was purely unconscious in ecstasy. She moved towards him and stood behind him for a moment in ecstasy. He, closed within the spell, remained motionless and unconscious.

Then swiftly, in a flame that drenched down her body like fluid lightning and gave her a perfect, unutterable consummation, unutterable satisfaction, she brought down the ball of jewel stone with all her force, crash on his head. But her fingers were in the way and deadened the blow. Nevertheless, down went his head on the table on which his book lay, the stone slid aside and over his ear, it was one convulsion of pure bliss for her, lit up by the crushed pain of her fingers. But it was not somehow complete. She lifted her arm high to aim once more, straight down on the head that lay dazed on the table. She must smash it, it must be smashed before her ecstasy was consummated, fulfilled for ever. A thousand lives, a thousand deaths mattered nothing now, only the fulfilment of this perfect ecstasy.

She was not swift, she could only move slowly. A strong spirit in him woke him and made him lift his face and twist to look at her. Her arm was raised, the hand clasping the ball of lapis lazuli. It was her left hand, he realized again with horror that she was left-handed. Hurriedly, with a burrowing motion, he covered his head under the thick volume of Thucydides, and the blow came down, almost breaking his neck, and shattering his heart.

He was shattered, but he was not afraid. Twisting round to face her he pushed the table over and got away from her. He was like a flask that is smashed to atoms, he seemed to himself that he was all fragments, smashed to bits. Yet his movements were perfectly coherent and clear, his soul was entire and unsurprised.

'No you don't, Hermione,' he said in a low voice. 'I don't let you.'

He saw her standing tall and livid and attentive, the stone clenched tense in her hand.

'Stand away and let me go,' he said, drawing near to her.

As if pressed back by some hand, she stood away, watching him all the time without changing, like a neutralized angel confronting him.

'It is no good,' he said, when he had gone past her. 'It isn't I who will die. You hear?'

He kept his face to her as he went out, lest she should strike again. While he was on his guard, she dared not move. And he was on his guard, she was powerless. So he had gone, and left her standing.

She remained perfectly rigid, standing as she was for a long time. Then she staggered to the couch and lay down, and went heavily to sleep. When she awoke, she remembered what she had done, but it seemed to her, she had only hit him, as any woman might do, because he tortured her. She was perfectly right. She knew that, spiritually, she was right. In her own infallible purity, she had done what must be done. She was right, she was pure. A drugged, almost sinister religious expression became permanent on her face.

Birkin, barely conscious, and yet perfectly direct in his motion, went out of the house and straight across the park, to the open country, to the hills. The brilliant day had become overcast, spots of rain were falling. He wandered on to a wild valley-side, where were thickets of hazel, many flowers, tufts of heather, and little clumps of young fir-trees, budding with soft paws. It was rather wet everywhere, there was a stream running down at the bottom of the valley, which was gloomy, or seemed gloomy. He was aware that he could not regain his consciousness, that he was moving in a sort of darkness.

Yet he wanted something. He was happy in the wet hill-side, that was overgrown and obscure with bushes and flowers. He wanted to touch them all, to saturate himself with the touch of them all. He took off his clothes, and sat down naked among the primroses, moving his feet softly among the primroses, his legs, his knees, his arms right up to the arm-pits, lying down and letting them touch his belly, his breasts. It was such a fine, cool, subtle touch all over him, he seemed to saturate himself with their contact.

But they were too soft. He went through the long grass to a clump of young fir-trees, that were no higher than a man. The soft sharp boughs beat upon him, as he moved in keen pangs against them, threw little cold showers of drops on his belly, and beat his loins with their clusters of soft-sharp needles. There was a thistle which pricked him vividly, but not too much, because all his movements were too discriminate and soft. To lie down and roll in the sticky, cool young hyacinths, to lie on one's belly and cover one's back with handfuls of fine wet grass, soft as a breath, soft and more delicate and more beautiful than the touch of any woman; and then to sting one's thigh against the living dark bristles of the fir-boughs; and then to feel the light whip of the hazel on one's shoulders, stinging, and then to clasp the silvery birch-trunk against one's breast, its smoothness, its hardness, its vital knots and ridges – this was good, this was all very good, very satisfying. Nothing else would do, nothing else would satisfy, except this coolness and subtlety of vegetation travelling into one's blood. How fortunate he was, that there was this lovely, subtle, responsive vegetation, waiting for him, as he waited for it; how fulfilled he was, how happy!

As he dried himself a little with his handkerchief, he thought about Hermione and the blow. He could feel a pain on the side of his head. But after all, what did it matter? What did Hermione matter, what did people matter altogether? There was this perfect cool loneliness, so lovely and fresh and unexplored. Really, what a mistake he had made, thinking he wanted people, thinking he wanted a woman. He did not want a woman – not in the least. The leaves and the primroses and the trees, they were really lovely and cool and desirable, they really came into the blood and were added on to him. He was enriched now immeasurably, and so glad.

It was quite right of Hermione to want to kill him. What had he to do with her? Why should he pretend to have anything to do with human beings at all? Here was his world, he wanted nobody and nothing but the lovely, subtle, responsive vegetation, and himself, his own living self.

It was necessary to go back into the world. That was true. But that did not matter, so one knew where one belonged. He knew now where he belonged. This was his place, his marriage place. The world was extraneous.

He climbed out of the valley, wondering if he were mad. But if so, he preferred his own madness, to the regular sanity. He rejoiced in his own madness, he was free. He did not want that old sanity of the world, which was become so repulsive. He rejoiced in the new-found world of his madness. It was so fresh and delicate and so satisfying.

As for the certain grief he felt at the same time, in his soul, that was only the remains of an old ethic, that bade a human being adhere to humanity. But he was weary of the old ethic, of the human being, and of humanity. He loved now the soft, delicate vegetation, that was so cool and perfect. He would overlook the old grief, he would put away the old ethic, he would be free in his new state.

He was aware of the pain in his head becoming more and more difficult every minute. He was walking now along the road to the nearest station. It was raining and he had no hat. But then plenty of cranks went out nowadays without hats, in the rain.

He wondered again how much of his heaviness of heart, a certain depression, was due to fear, fear lest anybody should have seen him naked lying against the vegetation. What a dread he had of mankind, of other people! It amounted almost to horror, to a sort of dream terror – his horror of being observed by some other people. If he were on an island, like Alexander Selkirk, with only the creatures and the trees, he would be free and glad, there would be none of this heaviness, this misgiving. He could love the vegetation and be quite happy and unquestioned, by himself.

He had better send a note to Hermione: she might trouble about him, and he did not want the onus of this. So at the station, he wrote saying:

'I will go on to town – I don't want to come back to Breadalby for the present. But it is quite all right – I don't want you to mind having biffed me, in the least. Tell the others it is just one of my moods. You were quite right, to biff me – because I know you wanted to. So there's the end of it.'

In the train, however, he felt ill. Every motion was insufferable pain, and he was sick. He dragged himself from the station into a cab, feeling his way step by step, like a blind man, and held up only by a dim will.

For a week or two he was ill, but he did not let Hermione know, and she thought he was sulking; there was a complete estrangement between them. She became rapt, abstracted in her conviction of exclusive righteousness. She lived in and by her own self-esteem, conviction of her own rightness of spirit.

9

COAL-DUST

Going home from school in the afternoon, the Brangwen girls descended the hill between the picturesque cottages of Willey Green till they came to the railway crossing. There they found the gate shut, because the colliery train was rumbling nearer. They could hear the small locomotive panting hoarsely as it advanced with caution between the embankments. The one-legged man in the little signal-hut by the road stared out from his security, like a crab from a snail-shell.

Whilst the two girls waited, Gerald Crich trotted up on a red Arab mare. He rode well and softly, pleased with the delicate quivering of the creature between his knees. And he was very picturesque, at least in Gudrun's eyes, sitting soft and close on the slender red mare, whose long tail flowed on the air. He saluted the two girls, and drew up at the crossing to wait for the gate, looking down the railway for the approaching train. In spite of her ironic smile at his picturesqueness, Gudrun liked to look at him. He was well set and easy, his face with its warm tan showed up his whitish, coarse moustache, and his blue eyes were full of sharp light as he watched the distance.

The locomotive chuffed slowly between the banks, hidden. The mare did not like it. She began to wince away, as if hurt by the unknown noise. But Gerald pulled her back and held her head to the gate. The sharp blasts of the chuffing engine broke with more and more force on her. The repeated sharp blows of unknown, terrifying noise struck through her till she was rocking with terror. She recoiled like a spring let go. But a glistening, half-smiling look came into Gerald's face. He brought her back again, inevitably.

The noise was released, the little locomotive with her clanking steel connecting-rod emerged on the highroad, clanking sharply. The mare rebounded like a drop of water from hot iron. Ursula and Gudrun pressed back into the hedge, in fear. But Gerald was heavy on the mare, and forced her back. It seemed as if he sank into her magnetically, and could thrust her back against herself.

'The fool!' cried Ursula loudly. 'Why doesn't he ride away till it's gone by?'

Gudrun was looking at him with black-dilated, spellbound eyes. But he sat glistening and obstinate, forcing the wheeling mare, which spun and swerved like a wind, and yet could not get out of the grasp of his will, nor escape from the mad clamour of terror that resounded through her, as the trucks thumped slowly, heavily, horrifying, one after the other, one pursuing the other, over the rails of the crossing.

The locomotive, as if wanting to see what could be done, put on the brakes, and back came the trucks rebounding on the iron buffers, striking like horrible cymbals, clashing nearer and nearer in frightful strident concussions. The mare opened her mouth and rose slowly, as if lifted up on a wind of terror. Then suddenly her fore-feet struck out, as she convulsed herself utterly away from the horror. Back she went, and the two girls clung to each other, feeling she must fall backwards on top of him. But he leaned forward, his face shining with fixed amusement, and at last he brought her down, sank her down, and was bearing her back to the mark. But as strong as the pressure of his compulsion was the repulsion of her utter terror, throwing her back away from the railway, so that she spun round and round on two legs, as if she were in the centre of some whirlwind. It made Gudrun faint with poignant dizziness, which seemed to penetrate to her heart.

'No – ! No – ! Let her go! Let her go, you fool, you *fool* – !' cried Ursula at the top of her voice, completely outside herself. And Gudrun hated her bitterly for being outside herself. It was unendurable that Ursula's voice was so powerful and naked.

A sharpened look came on Gerald's face. He bit himself down on the mare like a keen edge biting home, and *forced* her round. She roared as she breathed, her nostrils were two wide, hot holes, her mouth was apart, her eyes frenzied. It was a repulsive sight. But he held on her unrelaxed, with an almost mechanical relentlessness, keen as a sword pressing into her. Both man and horse were sweating with violence. Yet he seemed calm as a ray of cold sunshine.

Meanwhile the eternal trucks were rumbling on, very slowly, treading one after the other, one after the other, like a disgusting dream that has no end. The connecting chains were grinding and squeaking as the tension varied, the mare pawed and struck away mechanically now, her terror fulfilled in her, for now the man encompassed her; her paws were blind and pathetic as she beat the air, the man closed round her, and brought her down, almost as if she were part of his own physique.

'And she's bleeding! She's bleeding!' cried Ursula, frantic with opposition and hatred of Gerald. She alone understood him perfectly, in pure opposition.

Gudrun looked and saw the trickles of blood on the sides of the mare, and she turned white. And then on the very wound the bright spurs came down, pressing relentlessly. The world reeled and passed into nothingness for Gudrun, she could not know any more.

When she recovered, her soul was calm and cold, without feeling. The trucks were still rumbling by, and the man and the mare were still fighting. But she herself was cold and separate, she had no more feeling for them. She was quite hard and cold and indifferent.

They could see the top of the hooded guard's-van approaching, the sound of the trucks was diminishing, there was hope of relief from the intolerable noise. The heavy panting of the half-stunned mare sounded automatically, the man seemed to be relaxing confidently, his will bright and unstained. The guard's-van came up, and passed slowly, the guard staring out in his transition on the spectacle in the road. And through the man in the closed wagon Gudrun could see the whole scene spectacularly, isolated and momentary, like a vision isolated in eternity.

Lovely, grateful silence seemed to trail behind the receding train. How sweet the silence is! Ursula looked with hatred on the buffers of the diminishing wagon. The gate-keeper stood ready at the door of his hut, to proceed to open the gate. But Gudrun sprang suddenly forward, in front of the struggling horse, threw off the latch and flung the gates asunder, throwing one-half to the keeper, and running with the other half forwards. Gerald suddenly let go the horse and leaped forwards, almost on to Gudrun. She was not afraid. As he jerked aside the mare's head, Gudrun cried, in a strange, high voice, like a gull, or like a witch screaming out from the side of the road:

'I should think you're proud.'

The words were distinct and formed. The man, twisting aside on his dancing horse, looked at her in some surprise, some wondering interest. Then the mare's hoofs had danced three times on the drum-like sleepers of the crossing, and man and horse were bounding springily, unequally up the road.

The two girls watched them go. The gate-keeper hobbled thudding over the logs of the crossing, with his wooden leg. He had fastened the gate. Then he also turned, and called to the girls:

'A masterful young jockey, that'll have his own road, if ever anybody would.'

'Yes,' cried Ursula, in her hot, overbearing voice. 'Why couldn't he take the horse away, till the trucks had gone by? He's a fool, and a bully. Does he think it's manly, to torture a horse? It's a living thing, why should he bully it and torture it?'

There was a pause, then the gate-keeper shook his head, and replied:

'Yes, it's as nice a little mare as you could set eyes on – beautiful little thing, beautiful. Now you couldn't see his father treat any animal like that – not you. They're as different as they welly can be, Gerald Crich and his father – two different men, different made.'

Then there was a pause.

'But why does he do it?' cried Ursula, 'why does he? Does he think he's grand, when he's bullied a sensitive creature, ten times as sensitive as himself?'

Again there was a cautious pause. Then again the man shook his head, as if he would say nothing, but would think the more.

'I expect he's got to train the mare to stand to anything,' he replied. 'A pure-bred Harab – not the sort of breed as is used to round here – different sort from our sort altogether. They say as he got her from Constantinople.'

'He would!' said Ursula. 'He'd better have left her to the Turks, I'm sure they would have had more decency towards her.'

The man went in to drink his can of tea, the girls went on down the lane, that was deep in soft black dust. Gudrun was as if numbed in her mind by the sense of indomitable soft weight of the man, bearing down into the living body of the horse: the strong, indomitable thighs of the blond man clenching the palpitating body of the mare into pure control; a sort of soft white magnetic domination from the loins and thighs and calves, enclosing and encompassing the mare heavily into unutterable subordination, soft-blood-subordination, terrible.

On the left, as the girls walked silently, the coal-mine lifted its great mounds and its patterned head-stocks, the black railway with the trucks at rest looked like a harbour just below, a large bay of railroad with anchored wagons.

Near the second level-crossing, that went over many bright rails, was a farm belonging to the collieries, and a great round globe of iron, a disused boiler, huge and rusty and perfectly round, stood silently in a paddock by the road. The hens were pecking round it, some chickens were balanced on the drinking trough, wagtails flew away in among trucks, from the water.

On the other side of the wide crossing, by the road-side, was a heap of pale-grey stones for mending the roads, and a cart standing, and a middle-aged

man with whiskers round his face was leaning on his shovel, talking to a
young man in gaiters, who stood by the horse's head. Both men were facing
the crossing.

They saw the two girls appear, small, brilliant figures in the near distance,
in the strong light of the late afternoon. Both wore light, gay summer dresses.
Ursula had an orange-coloured knitted coat, Gudrun a pale yellow. Ursula
wore canary yellow stockings, Gudrun bright rose. The figures of the two
women seemed to glitter in progress over the wide bay of the railway crossing,
white and orange and yellow and rose glittering in motion across a hot world
silted with coal-dust.

The two men stood quite still in the heat, watching. The elder was a short,
hard-faced energetic man of middle age, the younger a labourer of twenty-
three or so. They stood in silence watching the advance of the sisters. They
watched whilst the girls drew near, and whilst they passed, and whilst they
receded down the dusty road, that had dwellings on one side, and dusty young
corn on the other.

Then the elder man, with the whiskers round his face, said in a prurient
manner to the young man:

'What price that, eh? She'll do, won't she?'

'Which?' asked the young man, eagerly, with a laugh.

'Her with the red stockings. What d' you say? I'd give my week's wages for
five minutes; what! – just for five minutes.'

Again the young man laughed.

'Your missis 'ud have summat to say to you,' he replied.

Gudrun had turned round and looked at the two men. They were to her
sinister creatures, standing watching after her, by the heap of pale grey slag.
She loathed the man with whiskers round his face.

'You're first class, you are,' the man said to her, and to the distance.

'Do you think it would be worth a week's wages?' said the younger man,
musing.

'Do I? I'd put 'em bloody-well down this second –'

The younger man looked after Gudrun and Ursula objectively, as if he
wished to calculate what there might be, that was worth his week's wages. He
shook his head with fatal misgiving.

'No,' he said. 'It's not worth that to me.'

'Isn't?' said the man. 'By God, if it isn't to me!'

And he went on shovelling his stones.

The girls descended between the houses with slate roofs and blackish brick
walls. The heavy gold glamour of approaching sunset lay over all the colliery
district, and the ugliness overlaid with beauty was like a narcotic to the
senses. On the roads silted with black dust, the rich light fell more warmly,
more heavily, over all the amorphous squalor a kind of magic was cast, from
the glowing close of day.

'It has a foul kind of beauty, this place,' said Gudrun, evidently suffering
from fascination. 'Can't you feel in some way, a thick, hot attraction in it? I
can. And it quite stupefies me.'

They were passing between blocks of miners' dwellings. In the back yards
of several dwellings a miner could be seen washing himself in the open on this
hot evening, naked down to the loins, his great trousers of moleskin slipping
almost away. Miners already cleaned were sitting on their heels, with their
backs near the walls, talking and silent in pure physical well-being, tired, and

taking physical rest. Their voices sounded out with strong intonation, and the broad dialect was curiously caressing to the blood. It seemed to envelop Gudrun in a labourer's caress, there was in the whole atmosphere, a resonance of physical men, a glamorous thickness of labour and maleness, surcharged in the air. But it was universal in the district, and therefore unnoticed by the inhabitants.

To Gudrun, however, it was potent and half-repulsive. She could never tell why Beldover was so utterly different from London and the south, why one's whole feelings were different, why one seemed to live in another sphere. Now she realized that this was the world of powerful, underworld men who spent most of their time in the darkness. In their voices she could hear the voluptuous resonance of darkness, the strong, dangerous underworld, mindless, inhuman. They sounded also like strange machines, heavy, oiled. The voluptuousness was like that of machinery, cold and iron.

It was the same every evening when she came home, she seemed to move through a wave of disruptive force, that was given off from the presence of thousands of vigorous, underworld, half-automatized colliers, and which went to the brain and the heart, awaking a fatal desire, and a fatal callousness.

There came over her a nostalgia for the place. She hated it, she knew how utterly cut off it was, how hideous and how sickeningly mindless. Sometimes she beat her wings like a new Daphne, turning not into a tree but a machine. And yet she was overcome by the nostalgia. She struggled to get more and more into accord with the atmosphere of the place, she craved to get her satisfaction of it.

She felt herself drawn out at evening into the main street of the town, that was uncreated and ugly, and yet surcharged with this same potent atmosphere of intense, dark callousness. There were always miners about. They moved with their strange, distorted dignity, a certain beauty, and unnatural stillness in their bearing, a look of abstraction and half resignation in their pale, often gaunt faces. They belonged to another world, they had a strange glamour, their voices were full of an intolerable deep resonance, like a machine's burring, a music more maddening than the sirens' long ago.

She found herself, with the rest of the common women, drawn out on Friday evenings to the little market. Friday was pay-day for the colliers, and Friday night was market night. Every woman was abroad, every man was out, shopping with his wife, or gathering with his pals. The pavements were dark for miles around with people coming in; the little market-place on the crown of the hill, and the main street of Beldover were black with thickly-crowded men and women.

It was dark, the market-place was hot with kerosene flares, which threw a ruddy light on the grave faces of the purchasing wives, and on the pale abstract faces of the men. The air was full of the sound of criers and of people talking, thick streams of people moved on the pavements towards the solid crowd of the market. The shops were blazing and packed with women, in the streets were men, mostly men, miners of all ages. Money was spent with almost lavish freedom.

The carts that came could not pass through. They had to wait, the driver calling and shouting, till the dense crowd would make way. Everywhere, young fellows from the outlying districts were making conversation with the girls, standing in the road and at the corners. The doors of the public-houses were open and full of light, men passed in and out in a continual stream, everywhere men were calling out to one another, or crossing to meet one another, or standing in little gangs and circles, discussing, endlessly discussing. The sense of talk, buzzing, jarring, half-secret, the endless mining, and political wrangling, vibrated in the air like discordant machinery. And it was their voices which affected Gudrun almost to swooning. They aroused a strange, nostalgic ache of desire, something almost demoniacal, never to be fulfilled.

Like any other common girl of the district, Gudrun strolled up and down, up and down the length of the brilliant two-hundred paces of the pavement nearest the market-place. She knew it was a vulgar thing to do; her father and mother could not bear it; but the nostalgia came over her, she must be among the people. Sometimes she sat among the louts in the cinema: rakish-looking, unattractive louts they were. Yet she must be among them.

And, like any other common lass, she found her 'boy'. It was an electrician, one of the electricians introduced according to Gerald's new scheme. He was an earnest, clever man, a scientist with a passion for sociology. He lived alone in a cottage, in lodgings, in Willey Green. He was a gentleman, and sufficiently well-to-do. His landlady spread the reports about him; he *would* have a large wooden tub in his bedroom, and every time he came in from work, he *would* have pails and pails of water brought up, to bathe in, then he put on clean shirt and under-clothing *every* day, and clean silk socks; fastidious and exacting he was in these respects, but in every other way, most ordinary and unassuming.

Gudrun knew all these things. The Brangwens' house was one to which the gossip came naturally and inevitably. Palmer was in the first place a friend of Ursula's. But in his pale, elegant, serious face there showed the same nostalgia that Gudrun felt. He too must walk up and down the street on Friday evening. So he walked with Gudrun, and a friendship was struck up between them. But he was not in love with Gudrun; he *really* wanted Ursula, but for some strange reason, nothing could happen between her and him. He liked to have Gudrun about, as a fellow-mind – but that was all. And she had no real feeling for him. He was a scientist, he had to have a woman to back him. But he was really impersonal, he had the fineness of an elegant piece of machinery. He was too cold, too destructive to care really for women, too great an egoist. He was polarized by the men. Individually he detested and despised them. In the mass they fascinated him, as machinery fascinated him. They were a new sort of machinery to him – but incalculable, incalculable.

So Gudrun strolled the streets with Palmer, or went to the cinema with him. And his long, pale, rather elegant face flickered as he made his sarcastic remarks. There they were, the two of them: two elegants in one sense: in the other sense, two units, absolutely adhering to the people, teeming with the distorted colliers. The same secret seemed to be working in the souls of all alike, Gudrun, Palmer, the rakish young bloods, the gaunt, middle-aged men. All had a secret sense of power, and of inexpressible destructiveness, and of fatal half-heartedness, a sort of rottenness in the will.

Sometimes Gudrun would start aside, see it all, see how she was sinking in. And then she was filled with a fury of contempt and anger. She felt she was sinking into one mass with the rest – all so close and intermingled and breathless. It was horrible. She stifled. She prepared for flight, feverishly she flew to her work. But soon she let go. She started off into the country – the darkish, glamorous country. The spell was beginning to work again.

10

SKETCH-BOOK

One morning the sisters were sketching by the side of Willey Water, at the remote end of the lake. Gudrun had waded out to a gravelly shoal, and was seated like a Buddhist, staring fixedly at the water-plants that rose succulent from the mud of the low shores. What she could see was mud, soft, oozy, watery mud, and from its festering chill, water-plants rose up, thick and cool and fleshy, very straight and turgid, thrusting out their leaves at right angles, and having dark lurid colours, dark green and blotches of black-purple and bronze. But she could feel their turgid fleshy structure as in a sensuous vision, she *knew* how they rose out of the mud, she *knew* how they thrust out from themselves, how they stood stiff and succulent against the air.

Ursula was watching the butterflies, of which there were dozens near the water, little blue ones suddenly snapping out of nothingness into a jewel-life, a large black-and-red one standing upon a flower and breathing with his soft wings, intoxicatingly, breathing pure, ethereal sunshine; two white ones wrestling in the low air; there was a halo round them; ah, when they came tumbling nearer they were orange-tips, and it was the orange that had made the halo. Ursula rose and drifted away, unconscious like the butterflies.

Gudrun, absorbed in a stupor of apprehension of surging water-plants, sat crouched on the shoal, drawing, not looking up for a long time, and then staring unconsciously, absorbedly at the rigid, naked, succulent stems. Her feet were bare, her hat lay on the bank opposite.

She started out of her trance, hearing the knocking of oars. She looked round. There was a boat with a gaudy Japanese parasol, and a man in white, rowing. The woman was Hermione, and the man was Gerald. She knew it instantly. And instantly she perished in the keen *frisson* of anticipation, an electric vibration in her veins, intense, much more intense than that which was always humming low in the atmosphere of Beldover.

Gerald was her escape from the heavy slough of the pale, underworld, automatic colliers. He started out of the mud. He was master. She saw his back, the movement of his white loins. But not that – it was the whiteness he seemed to enclose as he bent forwards, rowing. He seemed to stoop to something. His glistening, whitish hair seemed like the electricity of the sky.

'There's Gudrun,' came Hermione's voice floating distinct over the water. 'We will go and speak to her. Do you mind?'

Gerald looked round and saw the girl standing by the water's edge, looking at him. He pulled the boat towards her, magnetically, without thinking of her. In his world, his conscious world, she was still nobody. He knew that Hermione had a curious pleasure in treading down all the social differences, at least apparently, and he left it to her.

'How do you do, Gudrun?' sang Hermione, using the Christian name in the fashionable manner. 'What are you doing?'

'How do you do, Hermione? I *was* sketching.'

'Were you?' The boat drifted nearer, till the keel ground on the bank. 'May we see? I should like to *so* much.'

It was no use resisting Hermione's deliberate intention.

'Well –' said Gudrun reluctantly, for she always hated to have her unfinished work exposed – 'there's nothing in the least interesting.'

'Isn't there? But let me see, will you?'

Gudrun reached out the sketch-book, Gerald stretched from the boat to take it. And as he did so, he remembered Gudrun's last words to him, and her face lifted up to him as he sat on the swerving horse. An intensification of pride went over his nerves, because he felt, in some way she was compelled by him. The exchange of feeling between them was strong and apart from their consciousness.

And as if in a spell, Gudrun was aware of his body, stretching and surging like the marsh-fire, stretching towards her, his hand coming straight forward like a stem. Her voluptuous, acute apprehension of him made the blood faint in her veins, her mind went dim and unconscious. And he rocked on the water perfectly, like the rocking of phosphorescence. He looked round at the boat. It was drifting off a little. He lifted the oar to bring it back. And the exquisite pleasure of slowly arresting the boat, in the heavy-soft water, was complete as a swoon.

'*That's* what you have done,' said Hermione, looking searchingly at the plants on the shore, and comparing with Gudrun's drawing. Gudrun looked round in the direction of Hermione's long, pointing finger. 'That is it, isn't it?' repeated Hermione needing confirmation.

'Yes,' said Gudrun automatically, taking no real heed.

'Let me look,' said Gerald, reaching forward for the book. But Hermione ignored him, he must not presume, before she had finished. But he, his will as unthwarted and as unflinching as hers, stretched forward till he touched the book. A little shock, a storm of revulsion against him, shook Hermione unconsciously. She released the book when he had not properly got it, and it tumbled against the side of the boat and bounced into the water.

'There!' sang Hermione, with a strange ring of malevolent victory. 'I'm so sorry, so awfully sorry. Can't you get it, Gerald?'

This last was said in a note of anxious sneering that made Gerald's veins tingle with fine hate for her. He leaned far out of the boat, reaching down into the water. He could feel his position was ridiculous, his loins exposed behind him.

'It is of no importance,' came the strong, clanging voice of Gudrun. She seemed to touch him. But he reached further, the boat swayed violently. Hermione, however, remained unperturbed. He grasped the book, under the water, and brought it up, dripping.

'I'm so dreadfully sorry – dreadfully sorry,' repeated Hermione. 'I'm afraid it was all my fault.'

'It's of no importance – really, I assure you – it doesn't matter in the least,' said Gudrun loudly, with emphasis, her face flushed scarlet. And she held out her hand impatiently for the wet book, to have done with the scene. Gerald gave it to her. He was not quite himself.

'I'm so dreadfully sorry,' repeated Hermione, till both Gerald and Gudrun were exasperated. 'Is there nothing that can be done?'

'In what way?' asked Gudrun, with cool irony.

'Can't we save the drawings?'

There was a moment's pause, wherein Gudrun made evident all her refutation of Hermione's persistence.

'I assure you,' said Gudrun, with cutting distinctness, 'the drawings are quite as good as ever they were, for my purpose. I want them only for reference.'

'But can't I give you a new book? I wish you'd let me do that. I feel so truly sorry. I feel it was all my fault.'

'As far as I saw,' said Gudrun, 'it wasn't your fault at all. If there was any *fault*, it was Mr Crich's. But the whole thing is *entirely* trivial, and it really is ridiculous to take any notice of it.'

Gerald watched Gudrun closely, whilst she repulsed Hermione. There was a body of cold power in her. He watched her with an insight that amounted to clairvoyance. He saw her a dangerous, hostile spirit, that could stand undiminished and unabated. It was so finished, and of such perfect gesture, moreover.

'I'm awfully glad if it doesn't matter,' he said; 'if there's no real harm done.'

She looked back at him, with her fine blue eyes, and signalled full into his spirit, as she said, her voice ringing with intimacy almost caressive now it was addressed to him:

'Of course, it doesn't matter in the *least*.'

The bond was established between them, in that look, in her tone. In her tone, she made the understanding clear – they were of the same kind, he and she, a sort of diabolic freemasonry subsisted between them. Henceforward, she knew, she had her power over him. Wherever they met, they would be secretly associated. And he would be helpless in the association with her. Her soul exulted.

'Good-bye! I'm so glad you forgive me. Gooood-bye!'

Hermione sang her farewell, and waved her hand. Gerald automatically took the oar and pushed off. But he was looking all the time, with a glimmering, subtly-smiling admiration in his eyes, at Gudrun, who stood on the shoal shaking the wet book in her hand. She turned away and ignored the receding boat. But Gerald looked back as he rowed, beholding her, forgetting what he was doing.

'Aren't we going too much to the left?' sang Hermione, as she sat ignored under her coloured parasol.

Gerald looked round without replying, the oars balanced and glancing in the sun.

'I think it's all right,' he said good-humouredly, beginning to row again without thinking of what he was doing. And Hermione disliked him extremely for his good-humoured obliviousness, she was nullified, she could not regain ascendancy.

11

AN ISLAND

Meanwhile Ursula had wandered on from Willey Water along the course of the bright little stream. The afternoon was full of larks' singing. On the bright hill-sides was a subdued smoulder of gorse. A few forget-me-nots flowered by the water. There was a rousedness and a glancing everywhere.

She strayed absorbedly on, over the brooks. She wanted to go to the mill-pond above. The big mill-house was deserted, save for a labourer and his wife who lived in the kitchen. So she passed through the empty farm-yard and through the wilderness of a garden, and mounted the bank by the sluice. When she got to the top, to see the old, velvety surface of the pond before her, she noticed a man on the bank, tinkering with a punt. It was Birkin sawing and hammering away.

She stood at the head of the sluice, looking at him. He was unaware of anybody's presence. He looked very busy, like a wild animal, active and intent. She felt she ought to go away, he would not want her. He seemed to be so much occupied. But she did not want to go away. Therefore she moved along the bank till he would look up.

Which he soon did. The moment he saw her, he dropped his tools and came forward, saying:

'How do you do? I'm making the punt water-tight. Tell me if you think it is right.'

She went along with him.

'You are your father's daughter, so you can tell me if it will do,' he said.

She bent to look at the patched punt.

'I am sure I am my father's daughter,' she said, fearful of having to judge. 'But I don't know anything about carpentry. It *looks* right, don't you think?'

'Yes, I think. I hope it won't let me to the bottom, that's all. Though even so, it isn't a great matter, I should come up again. Help me to get it into the water, will you?'

With combined efforts they turned over the heavy punt and set it afloat.

'Now,' he said, 'I'll try it and you can watch what happens. Then if it carries, I'll take you over to the island.'

'Do,' she cried, watching anxiously.

The pond was large, and had that perfect stillness and the dark lustre of very deep water. There were two small islands overgrown with bushes and a few trees, towards the middle. Birkin pushed himself off, and veered clumsily in the pond. Luckily the punt drifted so that he could catch hold of a willow bough, and pull it to the island.

'Rather overgrown,' he said, looking into the interior, 'but very nice. I'll come and fetch you. The boat leaks a little.'

In a moment he was with her again, and she stepped into the wet punt.

'It'll float us all right,' he said, and manoeuvred again to the island.

They landed under a willow tree. She shrank from the little jungle of rank plants before her, evil-smelling figwort and hemlock. But he explored into it.

'I shall mow this down,' he said, 'and then it will be romantic – like Paul et Virginie.'

'Yes, one could have lovely Watteau picnics here,' cried Ursula with enthusiasm.

His face darkened.

'I don't want Watteau picnics here,' he said.

'Only your Virginie,' she laughed.

'Virginie enough,' he smiled wryly. 'No, I don't want her either.'

Ursula looked at him closely. She had not seen him since Breadalby. He was very thin and hollow, with a ghastly look in his face.

'You have been ill, haven't you?' she asked, rather repulsed.

'Yes,' he replied coldly.

They had sat down under the willow tree, and were looking at the pond, from their retreat on the island.

'Has it made you frightened?' she asked.

'What of?' he asked, turning his eyes to look at her. Something in him, inhuman and unmitigated, disturbed her, and shook her out of her ordinary self.

'It *is* frightening to be very ill, isn't it?' she said.

'It isn't pleasant,' he said. 'Whether one is really afraid of death or not, I have never decided. In one mood, not a bit, in another, very much.'

'But doesn't it make you feel ashamed? I think it makes one so ashamed, to be ill – illness is so terribly humiliating, don't you think?'

He considered for some minutes.

'May-be,' he said. 'Though one knows all the time one's life isn't really right, at the source. That's the humiliation. I don't see that the illness counts so much, after that. One is ill because one doesn't live properly – can't. It's the failure to live that makes one ill, and humiliates one.'

'But do you fail to live?' she asked, almost jeering.

'Why, yes – I don't make much of a success of my days. One seems always to be bumping one's nose against the blank wall ahead.'

Ursula laughed. She was frightened, and when she was frightened she always laughed and pretended to be jaunty.

'Your poor nose!' she said, looking at that feature of his face.

'No wonder it's ugly,' he replied.

She was silent for some minutes, struggling with her own self-deception. It was an instinct in her, to deceive herself.

'But *I'm* happy – I think life is *awfully* jolly,' she said.

'Good,' he answered, with a certain cold indifference.

She reached for a bit of paper which had wrapped a small piece of chocolate she had found in her pocket, and began making a boat. He watched her without heeding her. There was something strangely pathetic and tender in her moving, unconscious finger-tips, that were agitated and hurt, really.

'I *do* enjoy things – don't you?' she asked.

'Oh yes! But it infuriates me that I can't get right, at the really growing part of me. I feel all tangled and messed up, and I *can't* get straight anyhow. I don't know what really to *do*. One must do something somewhere.'

'Why should you always be *doing*?' she retorted. 'It is so plebeian. I think it is much better to be really patrician, and to do nothing but just be oneself, like a walking flower.'

'I quite agree,' he said, 'if one has burst into blossom. But I can't get my flower to blossom anyhow. Either it is blighted in the bud, or has got the smother-fly, or it isn't nourished. Curse it, it isn't even a bud. It is a contravened knot.'

Again she laughed. He was so very fretful and exasperated. But she was anxious and puzzled. How was one to get out, anyhow. There must be a way out somewhere.

There was a silence, wherein she wanted to cry. She reached for another bit of chocolate paper, and began to fold another boat.

'And why is it,' she asked at length, 'that there is no flowering, no dignity of human life now?'

'The whole idea is dead. Humanity itself is dry-rotten, really. There are myriads of human beings hanging on the bush – and they look very nice and rosy, your healthy young men and women. But they are apples of Sodom, as a matter of fact, Dead Sea Fruit, gall-apples. It isn't true that they have any significance – their insides are full of bitter, corrupt ash.'

'But there *are* good people,' protested Ursula.

'Good enough for the life of today. But mankind is a dead tree, covered with fine brilliant galls of people.'

Ursula could not help stiffening herself against this, it was too picturesque and final. But neither could she help making him go on.

'And if it is so, *why* is it?' she asked, hostile. They were rousing each other to a fine passion of opposition.

'Why, why are people all balls of bitter dust? Because they won't fall off the tree when they're ripe. They hang on to their old positions when the position is overpast, till they become infested with little worms and dry-rot.'

There was a long pause. His voice had become hot and very sarcastic. Ursula was troubled and bewildered, they were both oblivious of everything but their own immersion.

'But even if everybody is wrong – where are *you* right?' she cried, 'where are you any better?'

'I? – I'm not right,' he cried back. 'At least my only rightness lies in the fact that I know it. I detest what I am, outwardly. I loathe myself as a human being. Humanity is a huge aggregate lie, and a huge lie is less than a small truth. Humanity is less, far less than the individual, because the individual may sometimes be capable of truth, and humanity is a tree of lies. And they say that love is the greatest thing; they persist in *saying* this, the foul liars, and just look at what they do! Look at all the millions of people who repeat every minute that love is the greatest, and charity is the greatest – and see what they are doing all the time. By their works ye shall know them, for dirty liars and cowards, who daren't stand by their own actions, much less by their own words.'

'But,' said Ursula sadly, 'that doesn't alter the fact that love is the greatest, does it? What they *do* doesn't alter the truth of what they say, does it?'

'Completely, because if what they say *were* true, then they couldn't help fulfilling it. But they maintain a lie, and so they run amok at last. It's a lie to say that love is the greatest. You might as well say that hate is the greatest, since the opposite of everything balances. What people want is hate – hate and nothing but hate. And in the name of righteousness and love, they get it. They distil themselves with nitro-glycerine, all the lot of them, out of very love. It's the lie that kills. If we want hate, let us have it – death, murder, torture, violent destruction – let us have it: but not in the name of love. But I abhor humanity, I wish it was swept away. It could go, and there would be no *absolute* loss, if every human being perished tomorrow. The reality would be untouched. Nay, it would be better. The real tree of life would then be rid of the most ghastly, heavy crop of Dead Sea Fruit, the intolerable burden of myriad simulacra of people, an infinite weight of mortal lies.'

'So you'd like everybody in the world destroyed?' said Ursula.

'I should indeed.'

'And the world empty of people?'

'Yes truly. You yourself, don't you find it a beautiful clean thought, a world empty of people, just uninterrupted grass, and a hare sitting up?'

The pleasant sincerity of his voice made Ursula pause to consider her own proposition. And really it *was* attractive: a clean, lovely, humanless world. It was the *really* desirable. Her heart hesitated, and exulted. But still, she was dissatisfied with *him*.

'But,' she objected, 'you'd be dead yourself, so what good would it do you?'

'I would die like a shot, to know that the earth would really be cleaned of all the people. It is the most beautiful and freeing thought. Then there would *never* be another foul humanity created, for a universal defilement.'

'No,' said Ursula, 'there would be nothing.'

'What! Nothing? Just because humanity was wiped out? You flatter yourself. There'd be everything.'

'But how, if there were no people?'

'Do you think that creation depends on *man*! It merely doesn't. There are the trees and the grass and birds. I much prefer to think of the lark rising up in the morning upon a humanless world. Man is a mistake, he must go. There is the grass, and hares and adders, and the unseen hosts, actual angels that go about freely when a dirty humanity doesn't interrupt them – and good pure-tissued demons: very nice.'

It pleased Ursula, what he said, pleased her very much, as a phantasy. Of course it was only a pleasant fancy. She herself knew too well the actuality of humanity, its hideous actuality. She knew it could not disappear so cleanly and conveniently. It had a long way to go yet, a long and hideous way. Her subtle, feminine, demoniacal soul knew it well.

'If only man was swept off the face of the earth, creation would go on so marvellously, with a new start, non-human. Man is one of the mistakes of creation – like the ichthyosauri. If only he were gone again, think what lovely things would come out of the liberated days; – things straight out of the fire.'

'But man will never be gone,' she said, with insidious, diabolical knowledge of the horrors of persistence. 'The world will go with him.'

'Ah no,' he answered, 'not so. I believe in the proud angels and the demons that are our fore-runners. They will destroy us, because we are not proud enough. The ichthyosauri were not proud: they crawled and floundered as we do. And besides, look at elder-flowers and bluebells – they are a sign that pure creation takes place – even the butterfly. But humanity never gets beyond the caterpillar stage – it rots in the chrysalis, it never will have wings. It is anti-creation, like monkeys and baboons.'

Ursula watched him as he talked. There seemed a certain impatient fury in him, all the while, and at the same time a great amusement in everything, and a final tolerance. And it was this tolerance she mistrusted, not the fury. She saw that, all the while, in spite of himself, he would have to be trying to save the world. And this knowledge, whilst it comforted her heart somewhere with a little self-satisfaction, stability, yet filled her with a certain sharp contempt and hate of him. She wanted him to herself, she hated the Salvator Mundi touch. It was something diffuse and generalized about him, which she could not stand. He would behave in the same way, say the same things, give himself as completely to anybody who came along, anybody and everybody who liked to appeal to him. It was despicable, a very insidious form of prostitution.

'But,' she said, 'you believe in individual love, even if you don't believe in loving humanity – ?'

'I don't believe in love at all – that is, any more than I believe in hate, or in grief. Love is one of the emotions like all the others – and so it is all right whilst you feel it. But I can't see how it becomes an absolute. It is just part of human relationships, no more. And it is only part of *any* human relationship. And why one should be required *always* to feel it, any more than one always feels sorrow or distant joy, I cannot conceive. Love isn't a desideratum – it is an emotion you feel or you don't feel, according to circumstance.'

'Then why do you care about people at all,' she asked, 'if you don't believe in love? Why do you bother about humanity?'

'Why do I? Because I can't get away from it.'

'Because you love it,' she persisted.

It irritated him.

'If I do love it,' he said, 'it is my disease.'

'But it is a disease you don't want to be cured of,' she said, with some cold sneering.

He was silent now, feeling she wanted to insult him.

'And if you don't believe in love, what *do* you believe in?' she asked, mocking. 'Simply in the end of the world, and grass?'

He was beginning to feel a fool.

'I believe in the unseen hosts,' he said.

'And nothing else? You believe in nothing visible, except grass and birds? Your world is a poor show.'

'Perhaps it is,' he said, cool and superior now he was offended, assuming a certain insufferable aloof superiority, and withdrawing into his distance.

Ursula disliked him. But also she felt she had lost something. She looked at him as he sat crouched on the bank. There was a certain priggish Sunday-school stiffness over him, priggish and detestable. And yet, at the same time, the moulding of him was so quick and attractive, it gave such a great sense of freedom: the moulding of his brows, his chin, his whole physique, something so alive, somewhere, in spite of the look of sickness.

And it was this duality in feeling which he created in her, that made a fine hate of him quicken in her bowels. There was his wonderful, desirable life-rapidity, the rare quality of an utterly desirable man: and there was at the same time this ridiculous, mean effacement into a Salvator Mundi and a Sunday-school teacher, a prig of the stiffest type.

He looked up at her. He saw her face strangely enkindled, as if suffused from within by a powerful sweet fire. His soul was arrested in wonder. She was enkindled in her own living fire. Arrested in wonder and in pure, perfect attraction, he moved towards her. She sat like a strange queen, almost supernatural in her glowing smiling richness.

'The point about love,' he said, his consciousness quickly adjusting itself, 'is that we hate the word because we have vulgarized it. It ought to be prescribed, tabooed from utterance, for many years, till we get a new, better idea.'

There was a beam of understanding between them.

'But it always means the same thing,' she said.

'Ah, God, no, let it not mean that any more,' he cried. 'Let the old meanings go.'

'But still it is love,' she persisted. A strange, wicked yellow light shone at him in her eyes.

He hesitated, baffled, withdrawing.

'No,' he said, 'it isn't. Spoken like that, never in the world. You've no business to utter the word.'

'I must leave it to you, to take it out of the Ark of the Covenant at the right moment,' she mocked.

Again they looked at each other. She suddenly sprang up, turned her back to him, and walked away. He too rose slowly and went to the water's edge, where, crouching, he began to amuse himself unconsciously. Picking a daisy he dropped it on the pond, so that the stem was a keel, the flower floated like a little water-lily, staring with its open face up to the sky. It turned slowly round, in a slow, slow Dervish dance, as it veered away.

He watched it, then dropped another daisy into the water, and after that another, and sat watching them with bright, absolved eyes, crouching near on the bank. Ursula turned to look. A strange feeling possessed her, as if something were taking place. But it was all intangible. And some sort of control was being put on her. She could not know. She could only watch the brilliant little discs of the daisies veering slowly in travel on the dark, lustrous water. The little flotilla was drifting into the light, a company of white specks in the distance.

'Do let us go to the shore, to follow them,' she said, afraid of being any longer imprisoned on the island. And they pushed off in the punt.

She was glad to be on the free land again. She went along the bank towards the sluice. The daisies were scattered broadcast on the pond, tiny radiant things, like an exaltation, points of exaltation here and there. Why did they move her so strongly and mystically?

'Look,' he said, 'your boat of purple paper is escorting them, and they are a convoy of rafts.'

Some of the daisies came slowly towards her, hesitating, making a shy bright little cotillon on the dark clear water. Their gay bright candour moved her so much as they came near, that she was almost in tears.

'Why are they so lovely,' she cried. 'Why do I think them so lovely?'

'They are nice flowers,' he said, her emotional tones putting a constraint on him.

'You know that a daisy is a company of florets, a concourse, become individual. Don't the botanists put it highest in the line of development? I believe they do.'

'The compositae, yes, I think so,' said Ursula, who was never very sure of anything. Things she knew perfectly well, at one moment, seemed to become doubtful the next.

'Explain it so, then,' he said. 'The daisy is a perfect little democracy, so it's the highest of flowers, hence its charm.'

'No,' she cried, 'no – never. It isn't democratic.'

'No,' he admitted. 'It's the golden mob of the proletariat, surrounded by a showy white fence of the idle rich.'

'How hateful – your hateful social orders!' she cried.

'Quite! It's a daisy – we'll leave it alone.'

'Do. Let it be a dark horse for once,' she said: 'if anything can be a dark horse to you,' she added satirically.

They stood aside, forgetful. As if a little stunned, they both were motionless, barely conscious. The little conflict into which they had fallen had torn their consciousness and left them like two impersonal forces, there in contact.

He became aware of the lapse. He wanted to say something, to get on to a new more ordinary footing.

'You know,' he said, 'that I am having rooms here at the mill? Don't you think we can have some good times?'

'Oh, are you?' she said, ignoring all his implication of admitted intimacy.
He adjusted himself at once, became normally distant.

'If I find I can live sufficiently by myself,' he continued, 'I shall give up my work altogether. It has become dead to me. I don't believe in the humanity I pretend to be part of, I don't care a straw for the social ideals I live by, I hate the dying organic form of social mankind – so it can't be anything but trumpery, to work at education. I shall drop it as soon as I am clear enough – tomorrow perhaps – and be by myself.'

'Have you enough to live on?' asked Ursula.

'Yes – I've about four hundred a year. That makes it easy for me.'

There was a pause.

'And what about Hermione?' asked Ursula.

'That's over, finally – a pure failure, and never could have been anything else.'

'But you still know each other?'

'We could hardly pretend to be strangers, could we?'

There was a stubborn pause.

'But isn't that a half-measure?' asked Ursula at length.

'I don't think so,' he said. 'You'll be able to tell me if it is.'

Again there was a pause of some minutes' duration. He was thinking.

'One must throw everything away, everything – let everything go, to get the one last thing one wants,' he said.

'What thing?' she asked in challenge.

'I don't know – freedom together,' he said.

She had wanted him to say 'love'.

There was heard a loud barking of the dogs below. He seemed disturbed by it. She did not notice. Only she thought he seemed uneasy.

'As a matter of fact,' he said, in rather a small voice, 'I believe that is Hermione come now, with Gerald Crich. She wanted to see the rooms before they are furnished.'

'I know,' said Ursula. 'She will superintend the furnishing for you.'

'Probably. Does it matter?'

'Oh no, I should think not,' said Ursula. 'Though personally, I can't bear her. I think she is a lie, if you like, you who are always talking about lies.' Then she ruminated for a moment, when she broke out: 'Yes, and I do mind if she furnishes your rooms – I do mind. I mind that you keep her hanging on at all.'

He was silent now, frowning.

'Perhaps,' he said. 'I don't *want* her to furnish the rooms here – and I don't keep her hanging on. Only, I needn't be churlish to her, need I? At any rate, I shall have to go down and see them now. You'll come, won't you?'

'I don't think so,' she said coldly and irresolutely.

'Won't you? Yes, do. Come and see the rooms as well. Do come.'

12

CARPETING

He set off down the bank, and she went unwillingly with him. Yet she would not have stayed away, either.

'We know each other well, you and I, already,' he said. She did not answer.

In the large darkish kitchen of the mill, the labourer's wife was talking shrilly to Hermione and Gerald, who stood, he in white and she in a glistening bluish foulard, strangely luminous in the dusk of the room; whilst from the cages on the walls, a dozen or more canaries sang at the top of their voices. The cages were all placed round a small square window at the back, where the sunshine came in, a beautiful beam, filtering through green leaves of a tree. The voice of Mrs Salmon shrilled against the noise of the birds, which rose ever more wild and triumphant, and the woman's voice went up and up against them, and the birds replied with wild animation.

'Here's Rupert!' shouted Gerald in the midst of the din. He was suffering badly, being very sensitive in the ear.

'O-o-h them birds, they won't let you speak –!' shrilled the labourer's wife in disgust. 'I'll cover them up.'

And she darted here and there, throwing a duster, an apron, a towel, a table-cloth over the cages of the birds.

'Now will you stop it, and let a body speak for your row,' she said, still in a voice that was too high.

The party watched her. Soon the cages were covered, they had a strange funereal look. But from under the towels odd defiant trills and bubblings still shook out.

'Oh, they won't go on,' said Mrs Salmon reassuringly. 'They'll go to sleep now.'

'Really,' said Hermione politely.

'They will,' said Gerald. 'They will go to sleep automatically, now the impression of evening is produced.'

'Are they so easily deceived?' cried Ursula.

'Oh yes,' replied Gerald. 'Don't you know the story of Fabre, who, when he was a boy, put a hen's head under her wing, and she straight away went to sleep? It's quite true.'

'And did that make him a naturalist?' asked Birkin.

'Probably,' said Gerald.

Meanwhile Ursula was peeping under one of the cloths. There sat the canary in a corner, bunched and fluffed up for sleep.

'How ridiculous!' she cried. 'It really thinks the night has come! How absurd! Really, how can one have any respect for a creature that is so easily taken in!'

'Yes,' sang Hermione, coming also to look. She put her hand on Ursula's arm and chuckled a low laugh. 'Yes, doesn't he look comical?' she chuckled. 'Like a stupid husband.'

Then, with her hand still on Ursula's arm, she drew her away, saying, in her mild sing-song:

'How did you come here? We saw Gudrun too.'

'I came to look at the pond,' said Ursula, 'and I found Mr Birkin there.'

'Did you? This is quite a Brangwen land, isn't it?'

'I'm afraid I hoped so,' said Ursula. 'I ran here for refuge, when I saw you down the lake, just putting off.'

'Did you! And now we've run you to earth.'

Hermione's eyelids lifted with an uncanny movement, amused but overwrought. She had always her strange, rapt look, unnatural and irresponsible.

'I was going on,' said Ursula. 'Mr Birkin wanted me to see the rooms. Isn't it delightful to live here? It is perfect.'

'Yes,' said Hermione, abstractedly. Then she turned right away from Ursula, ceased to know her existence.

'How do you feel, Rupert?' she sang in a new, affectionate tone to Birkin.

'Very well,' he replied.

'Were you quite comfortable?' The curious, sinister, rapt look was on Hermione's face, she shrugged her bosom in a convulsed movement, and seemed like one half in a trance.

'Quite comfortable,' he replied.

There was a long pause, whilst Hermione looked at him for a long time, from under her heavy, drugged eyelids.

'And you think you'll be happy here?' she said at last.

'I'm sure I shall.'

'I'm sure I shall do anything for him as I can,' said the labourer's wife. 'And I'm sure our mester will; so I *hope* as he'll find himself comfortable.'

Hermione turned and looked at her slowly.

'Thank you so much,' she said, and then she turned completely away again. She recovered her position, and lifting her face towards him, and addressing him exclusively, she said:

'Have you measured the rooms?'

'No,' he said, 'I've been mending the punt.'

'Shall we do it now?' she said slowly, balanced and dispassionate.

'Have you got a tape measure, Mrs Salmon?' he said, turning to the woman.

'Yes, sir, I think I can find one,' replied the woman, bustling immediately to a basket. 'This is the only one I've got, if it will do.'

Hermione took it, though it was offered to him.

'Thank you so much,' she said. 'It will do very nicely. Thank you so much.' Then she turned to Birkin, saying with a little gay movement: 'Shall we do it now, Rupert?'

'What about the others, they'll be bored,' he said reluctantly.

'Do you mind?' said Hermione, turning to Ursula and Gerald vaguely.

'Not in the least,' they replied.

'Which room shall we do first?' she said, turning again to Birkin, with the same gaiety, now she was going to *do* something with him.

'We'll take them as they come,' he said.

'Should I be getting your teas ready, while you do that?' said the labourer's wife, also gay because *she* had something to do.

'Would you?' said Hermione, turning to her with the curious motion of intimacy that seemed to envelop the woman, draw her almost to Hermione's breast, and which left the others standing apart. 'I should be so glad. Where shall we have it?'

'Where would you like it? Shall it be in here, or out on the grass?'

'Where shall we have tea?' sang Hermione to the company at large.

'On the bank by the pond. And *we'll* carry the things up, if you'll just get them ready, Mrs Salmon,' said Birkin.

'All right,' said the pleased woman.

The party moved down the passage into the front room. It was empty, but clean and sunny. There was a window looking on to the tangled front garden.

'This is the dining-room,' said Hermione. 'We'll measure it this way, Rupert – you go down there –'

'Can't I do it for you,' said Gerald, coming to take the end of the tape.

'No, thank you,' cried Hermione, stooping to the ground in her bluish, brilliant foulard. It was a great joy to her to *do* things, and to have the ordering of the job, with Birkin. He obeyed her subduedly. Ursula and Gerald looked on. It was a peculiarity of Hermione's, that at every moment, she had one intimate, and turned all the rest of those present into onlookers. This raised her into a state of triumph.

They measured and discussed in the dining-room, and Hermione decided what the floor coverings must be. It sent her into a strange, convulsed anger, to be thwarted. Birkin always let her have her way, for the moment.

Then they moved across, through the hall, to the other front room, that was a little smaller than the first.

'This is the study,' said Hermione. 'Rupert, I have a rug that I want you to have for here. Will you let me give it to you? Do – I want to give it you.'

'What is it like?' he asked ungraciously.

'You haven't seen it. It is chiefly rose red, then blue, a metallic, mid-blue, and a very soft dark blue. I think you would like it. Do you think you would?'

'It sounds very nice,' he replied. 'What is it? Oriental? With a pile?'

'Yes. Persian! It is made of camel's hair, silky. I think it is called Bergamos – twelve feet by seven – Do you think it will do?'

'It would *do*,' he said. 'But why should you give me an expensive rug? I can manage perfectly well with my old Oxford Turkish.'

'But may I give it to you? Do let me.'

'How much did it cost?'

She looked at him, and said:

'I don't remember. It was quite cheap.'

He looked at her, his face set.

'I don't want to take it, Hermione,' he said.

'Do let me give it to the rooms,' she said, going up to him and putting her hand on his arm lightly, pleadingly. 'I shall be so disappointed.'

'You know I don't want you to give me things,' he repeated helplessly.

'I don't want to give you *things*,' she said teasingly. 'But will you have this?'

'All right,' he said, defeated, and she triumphed.

They went upstairs. There were two bedrooms to correspond with the rooms downstairs. One of them was half furnished, and Birkin had evidently slept there. Hermione went round the room carefully, taking in every detail, as if absorbing the evidence of his presence, in all the inanimate things. She felt the bed and examined the coverings.

'Are you *sure* you were quite comfortable?' she said, pressing the pillow.

'Perfectly,' he replied coldly.

'And were you warm? There is no down quilt. I am sure you need one. You mustn't have a great pressure of clothes.'

'I've got one,' he said. 'It is coming down.'

They measured the rooms, and lingered over every consideration. Ursula stood at the window and watched the woman carrying the tea up the bank to the pond. She hated the palaver Hermione made, she wanted to drink tea, she wanted anything but this fuss and business.

At last they all mounted the grassy bank, to the picnic. Hermione poured out tea. She ignored now Ursula's presence. And Ursula, recovering from her ill-humour, turned to Gerald saying:

'Oh, I hated you so much the other day, Mr Crich.'

'What for?' said Gerald, wincing slightly away.

'For treating your horse so badly. Oh, I hated you so much!'

'What did he do?' sang Hermione.

'He made his lovely sensitive Arab horse stand with him at the railway-crossing whilst a horrible lot of trucks went by; and the poor thing, she was in a perfect frenzy, a perfect agony. It was the most horrible sight you can imagine.'

'Why did you do it, Gerald?' asked Hermione, calm and interrogative.

'She must learn to stand – what use is she to me in this country if she shies and goes off every time an engine whistles.'

'But why inflict unnecessary torture?' said Ursula. 'Why make her stand all that time at the crossing? You might just as well have ridden back up the road, and saved all that horror. Her sides were bleeding where you had spurred her. It was too horrible – !'

Gerald stiffened.

'I have to use her,' he replied. 'And if I'm going to be sure of her at *all*, she'll have to learn to stand noises.'

'Why should she?' cried Ursula in a passion. 'She is a living creature, why should she stand anything, just because you choose to make her? She has as much right to her own being, as you have to yours.'

'There I disagree,' said Gerald. 'I consider that mare is there for my use. Not because I bought her, but because that is the natural order. It is more natural for a man to take a horse and use it as he likes, than for him to go down on his knees to it, begging it to do as it wishes, and to fulfil its own marvellous nature.'

Ursula was just breaking out, when Hermione lifted her face and began, in her musing sing-song:

'I do think – I do really think we must have the *courage* to use the lower animal life for our needs. I do think there is something wrong, when we look on every living creature as if it were ourselves. I do feel, that it is false to project our own feelings on every animate creature. It is a lack of discrimination, a lack of criticism.'

'Quite,' said Birkin sharply. 'Nothing is so detestable as the maudlin attributing of human feelings and consciousness to animals.'

'Yes,' said Hermione wearily, 'we must really take a position. Either we are going to use the animals, or they will use us.'

'That's a fact,' said Gerald. 'A horse has got a will like a man, though it has no *mind*, strictly. And if your will isn't master, then the horse is master of you. And this is a thing I can't help. I can't help being master of the horse.'

'If only we could learn how to use our will,' said Hermione, 'we could do anything. The will can cure anything, and put anything right. That I am convinced of – if only we use the will properly, intelligibly.'

'What do you mean by using the will properly?' said Birkin.

'A very great doctor taught me,' she said, addressing Ursula and Gerald vaguely. 'He told me, for instance, that to cure oneself of a bad habit, one should *force* oneself to do it, when one would not do it; – make oneself do it – and then the habit would disappear.'

'How do you mean?' said Gerald.

'If you bite your nails, for example. Then, when you don't want to bite your nails, bite them, make yourself bite them. And you would find the habit was broken.'

'Is that so?' said Gerald.

'Yes. And in so many things, I have *made* myself well. I was a very queer and nervous girl. And by learning to use my will, simply by using my will, I *made* myself right.'

Ursula looked all the while at Hermione, as she spoke in her slow, dispassionate, and yet strangely tense voice. A curious thrill went over the younger woman. Some strange, dark, convulsive power was in Hermione, fascinating and repelling.

'It is fatal to use the will like that,' cried Birkin harshly, 'disgusting. Such a will is an obscenity.'

Hermione looked at him for a long time, with her shadowed, heavy eyes. Her face was soft and pale and thin, almost phosphorescent, her jaw was lean.

'I'm sure it isn't,' she said at length. There always seemed an interval, a strange split between what she seemed to feel and experience, and what she actually said and thought. She seemed to catch her thoughts at length from off the surface of a maelstrom of chaotic black emotions and reactions, and Birkin was always filled with repulsion, she caught so infallibly, her will never failed her. Her voice was always dispassionate and tense, and perfectly confident. Yet she shuddered with a sense of nausea, a sort of sea-sickness that always threatened to overwhelm her mind. But her mind remained unbroken, her will was still perfect. It almost sent Birkin mad. But he would never, never dare to break her will, and let loose the maelstrom of her subconsciousness, and see her in her ultimate madness. Yet he was always striking at her.

'And of course,' he said to Gerald, 'horses *haven't* got a complete will, like human beings. A horse has no *one* will. Every horse, strictly, has two wills. With one will, it wants to put itself in the human power completely – and with the other, it wants to be free, wild. The two wills sometimes lock – you know that, if ever you've felt a horse bolt, while you've been driving it.'

'I have felt a horse bolt while I was driving it,' said Gerald, 'but it didn't make me know it had two wills. I only knew it was frightened.'

Hermione had ceased to listen. She simply became oblivious when these subjects were started.

'Why should a horse want to put itself in the human power?' asked Ursula. 'That is quite incomprehensible to me. I don't believe it ever wanted it.'

'Yes it did. It's the last, perhaps highest, love-impulse: resign your will to the higher being,' said Birkin.

'What curious notions you have of love,' jeered Ursula.

'And woman is the same as horses: two wills act in opposition inside her. With one will, she wants to subject herself utterly. With the other she wants to bolt, and pitch her rider to perdition.'

'Then I'm a bolter,' said Ursula, with a burst of laughter.

'It's a dangerous thing to domesticate even horses, let alone women,' said Birkin. 'The dominant principle has some rare antagonists.'

'Good thing too,' said Ursula.

'Quite,' said Gerald, with a faint smile. 'There's more fun.'

Hermione could bear no more. She rose, saying in her easy sing-song:

'Isn't the evening beautiful! I get filled sometimes with such a great sense of beauty, that I feel I can hardly bear it.'

Ursula, to whom she had appealed, rose with her, moved to the last impersonal depths. And Birkin seemed to her almost a monster of hateful arrogance. She went with Hermione along the bank of the pond, talking of beautiful, soothing things, picking the gentle cowslips.

'Wouldn't you like a dress,' said Ursula to Hermione, 'of this yellow spotted with orange – a cotton dress?'

'Yes,' said Hermione, stopping and looking at the flower, letting the thought come home to her and soothe her. 'Wouldn't it be pretty? I should *love* it.'

And she turned smiling to Ursula, in a feeling of real affection.

But Gerald remained with Birkin, wanting to probe him to the bottom, to know what he meant by the dual will in horses. A flicker of excitement danced on Gerald's face.

Hermione and Ursula strayed on together, united in a sudden bond of deep affection and closeness.

'I really do not want to be forced into all this criticism and analysis of life. I really *do* want to see things in their entirety, with their beauty left to them, and their wholeness, their natural holiness. Don't you feel it, don't you feel you *can't* be tortured into any more knowledge?' said Hermione, stopping in front of Ursula, and turning to her with clenched fists thrust downwards.

'Yes,' said Ursula. 'I do. I am sick of all this poking and prying.'

'I'm so glad you are. Sometimes,' said Hermione, again stopping arrested in her progress and turning to Ursula, 'sometimes I wonder if I *ought* to submit to all this realization, if I am not being weak in rejecting it. But I feel I *can't* – I *can't*. It seems to destroy *everything*. All the beauty and the – and the true holiness is destroyed – and I feel I can't live without them.'

'And it would be simply wrong to live without them,' cried Ursula. 'No, it is so *irreverent* to think that everything must be realized in the head. Really, something must be left to the Lord, there always is and always will be.'

'Yes,' said Hermione, reassured like a child, 'it should, shouldn't it? And Rupert –' she lifted her face to the sky, in a muse – 'he *can* only tear things to pieces. He really *is* like a boy who must pull everything to pieces to see how it is made. And I can't think it is right – it does seem so irreverent, as you say.'

'Like tearing open a bud to see what the flower will be like,' said Ursula.

'Yes. And that kills everything, doesn't it? It doesn't allow any possibility of flowering.'

'Of course not,' said Ursula. 'It is purely destructive.'

'It is, isn't it!'

Hermione looked long and slow at Ursula, seeming to accept confirmation from her. Then the two women were silent. As soon as they were in accord, they began mutually to mistrust each other. In spite of herself, Ursula felt herself recoiling from Hermione. It was all she could do to restrain her revulsion.

They returned to the men, like two conspirators who have withdrawn to come to an agreement. Birkin looked up at them. Ursula hated him for his cold watchfulness. But he said nothing.

'Shall we be going?' said Hermione. 'Rupert, you are coming to Shortlands to dinner? Will you come at once, will you come now, with us?'

'I'm not dressed,' replied Birkin. 'And you know Gerald stickles for convention.'

'I don't stickle for it,' said Gerald. 'But if you'd got as sick as I have of rowdy go-as-you-please in the house, you'd prefer it if people were peaceful and conventional, at least at meals.'

'All right,' said Birkin.

'But can't we wait for you while you dress?' persisted Hermione.

'If you like.'

He rose to go indoors. Ursula said she would take her leave.

'Only,' she said, turning to Gerald, 'I must say that, however man is lord of the beast and the fowl, I still don't think he has any right to violate the feelings of the inferior creation. I still think it would have been much more sensible and nice of you if you'd trotted back up the road while the train went by, and been considerate.'

'I see,' said Gerald, smiling, but somewhat annoyed. 'I must remember another time.'

'They all think I'm an interfering female,' thought Ursula to herself, as she went away. But she was in arms against them.

She ran home plunged in thought. She had been very much moved by Hermione, she had really come into contact with her, so that there was a sort of league between the two women. And yet she could not bear her. But she put the thought away. 'She's really good,' she said to herself. 'She really wants what is right.' And she tried to feel at one with Hermione, and to shut off from Birkin. She was strictly hostile to him. But she was held to him by some bond, some deep principle. This at once irritated her and saved her.

Only now and again, violent little shudders would come over her, out of her subconsciousness, and she knew it was the fact that she had stated her challenge to Birkin, and he had, consciously or unconsciously, accepted. It was a fight to the death between them – or to new life: though in what the conflict lay, no one could say.

13

MINO

The days went by, and she received no sign. Was he going to ignore her, was he going to take no further notice of her secret? A dreary weight of anxiety and acrid bitterness settled on her. And yet Ursula knew she was only deceiving herself, and that he *would* proceed. She said no word to anybody.

Then, sure enough, there came a note from him, asking if she would come to tea, with Gudrun, to his rooms in town.

'Why does he ask Gudrun as well?' she asked herself at once. 'Does he want to protect himself, or does he think I would not go alone?'

She was tormented by the thought that he wanted to protect himself. But at the end of all, she only said to herself:

'I don't want Gudrun to be there, because I want him to say something more to me. So I shan't tell Gudrun anything about it, and I shall go alone. Then I shall know.'

She found herself sitting on the tram-car, mounting up the hill going out of the town, to the place where he had his lodging. She seemed to have passed into a kind of dream world, absolved from the conditions of actuality. She watched the sordid streets of the town go by beneath her, as if she were a spirit disconnected from the material universe. What had it all to do with her? She was palpitating and formless within the flux of the ghost life. She could not consider any more, what anybody would say of her or think about her. People had passed out of her range, she was absolved. She had fallen strange and dim, out of the sheath of the material life, as a berry falls from the only world it has ever known, down out of the sheath on to the real unknown.

Birkin was standing in the middle of the room, when she was shown in by the landlady. He too was moved outside himself. She saw him agitated and shaken, a frail, unsubstantial body silent like the node of some violent force, that came out from him and shook her almost into a swoon.

'You are alone?' he said.

'Yes – Gudrun could not come.'

He instantly guessed why.

And they were both seated in silence, in the terrible tension of the room. She was aware that it was a pleasant room, full of light and very restful in its form – aware also of a fuchsia tree, with dangling scarlet and purple flowers.

'How nice the fuchsias are!' she said, to break the silence.

'Aren't they! Did you think I had forgotten what I said?'

A swoon went over Ursula's mind.

'I don't want you to remember it – if you don't want to,' she struggled to say, through the dark mist that covered her.

There was silence for some moments.

'No,' he said. 'It isn't that. Only – if we are going to know each other, we must pledge ourselves for ever. If we are going to make a relationship, even of friendship, there must be something final and irrevocable about it.'

There was a clang of mistrust and almost anger in his voice. She did not answer. Her heart was too much contracted. She could not have spoken.

Seeing she was not going to reply, he continued, almost bitterly, giving himself away:

'I can't say it is love I have to offer – and it isn't love I want. It is something much more impersonal and harder – and rarer.'

There was a silence, out of which she said:

'You mean you don't love me?'

She suffered furiously, saying that.

'Yes, if you like to put it like that. Though perhaps that isn't true. I don't know. At any rate, I don't feel the emotion of love for you – no, and I don't want to. Because it gives out in the last issues.'

'Love gives out in the last issues?' she asked, feeling numb to the lips.

'Yes, it does. At the very last, one is alone, beyond the influence of love. There is a real impersonal me, that is beyond love, beyond any emotional relationship. So it is with you. But we want to delude ourselves that love is the root. It isn't. It is only the branches. The root is beyond love, a naked kind of isolation, an isolated me, that does *not* meet and mingle, and never can.'

She watched him with wide, troubled eyes. His face was incandescent in its abstract earnestness.

'And you mean you can't love?' she asked, in trepidation.

'Yes, if you like. I have loved. But there is a beyond, where there is not love.'

She could not submit to this. She felt it swooning over her. But she could not submit.

'But how do you know – if you have never *really* loved?' she asked.

'It is true what I say; there is a beyond, in you, in me, which is further than love, beyond the scope, as stars are beyond the scope of vision, some of them.'

'Then there is no love,' cried Ursula.

'Ultimately, no, there is something else. But, ultimately, there *is* no love.'

Ursula was given over to this statement for some moments. Then she half rose from her chair, saying, in a final, repellent voice:

'Then let me go home – what am I doing here?'

'There is the door,' he said. 'You are a free agent.'

He was suspended finely and perfectly in this extremity. She hung motionless for some seconds, then she sat down again.

'If there is no love, what is there?' she cried, almost jeering.

'Something,' he said, looking at her, battling with his soul, with all his might.

'What?'

He was silent for a long time, unable to be in communication with her while she was in this state of opposition.

'There is,' he said, in a voice of pure abstraction, 'a final me which is stark and impersonal and beyond responsibility. So there is a final you. And it is there I would want to meet you – not in the emotional, loving plane – but there beyond, where there is no speech and no terms of agreement. There we are two stark, unknown beings, two utterly strange creatures, I would want to approach you, and you me. And there could be no obligation, because there is no standard for action there, because no understanding has been reaped from that plane. It is quite inhuman – so there can be no calling to book, in any form whatsoever – because one is outside the pale of all that is accepted, and nothing known applies. One can only follow the impulse, taking that which lies in front, and responsible for nothing, asking for nothing, giving nothing, only each taking according to the primal desire.'

Ursula listened to this speech, her mind dumb and almost senseless, what he said was so unexpected and so untoward.

'It is just purely selfish,' she said.

'If it is pure, yes. But it isn't selfish at all. Because I don't *know* what I want of you. I deliver *myself* over to the unknown, in coming to you, I am without reserves or defences, stripped entirely, into the unknown. Only there needs the pledge between us, that we will both cast off everything, cast off ourselves even, and cease to be, so that that which is perfectly ourselves can take place in us.'

She pondered along her own line of thought.

'But it is because you love me, that you want me?' she persisted.

'No it isn't. It is because I believe in you – if I *do* believe in you.'

'Aren't you sure?' she laughed, suddenly hurt.

He was looking at her steadfastly, scarcely heeding what she said.

'Yes, I must believe in you, or else I shouldn't be here saying this,' he replied. 'But that is all the proof I have. I don't feel any very strong belief at this particular moment.'

She disliked him for this sudden relapse into weariness and faithlessness.

'But don't you think me good-looking?' she persisted in a mocking voice.

He looked at her, to see if he felt that she was good-looking.

'I don't *feel* that you're good-looking,' he said.

'Not even attractive?' she mocked, bitingly.

He knitted his brows in sudden exasperation.

'Don't you see that it's not a question of visual appreciation in the least,' he cried. 'I don't *want* to see you. I've seen plenty of women, I'm sick and weary of seeing them. I want a woman I don't see.'

'I'm sorry I can't oblige you by being invisible,' she laughed.

'Yes,' he said, 'you are invisible to me, if you don't force me to be visually aware of you. But I don't want to see you or hear you.'

'What did you ask me to tea for, then?' she mocked.

But he would take no notice of her. He was talking to himself.

'I want to find you, where you don't know your own existence, the you that your common self denies utterly. But I don't want your good looks, and I don't want your womanly feelings, and I don't want your thoughts nor opinions nor your ideas – they are all bagatelles to me.'

'You are very conceited, Monsieur,' she mocked. 'How do you know what my womanly feelings are, or my thoughts or my ideas? You don't even know what I think of you now.'

'Nor do I care in the slightest.'

'I think you are very silly. I think you want to tell me you love me, and you go all this way round to do it.'

'All right,' he said, looking up with sudden exasperation. 'Now go away then, and leave me alone. I don't want any more of your meretricious persiflage.'

'Is it really persiflage?' she mocked, her face really relaxing into laughter. She interpreted it, that he had made a deep confession of love to her. But he was so absurd in his words, also.

They were silent for many minutes, she was pleased and elated like a child. His concentration broke, he began to look at her simply and naturally.

'What I want is a strange conjunction with you –' he said quietly; '– not meeting and mingling; – you are quite right: – but an equilibrium, a pure balance of two single beings: – as the stars balance each other.'

She looked at him. He was very earnest, and earnestness was always rather ridiculous, commonplace, to her. It made her feel unfree and uncomfortable. Yet she liked him so much. But why drag in the stars.

'Isn't this rather sudden?' she mocked.

He began to laugh.

'Best to read the terms of the contract, before we sign,' he said.

A young grey cat that had been sleeping on the sofa jumped down and stretched, rising on its long legs, and arching its slim back. Then it sat considering for a moment, erect and kingly. And then, like a dart, it had shot out of the room, through the open window-doors, and into the garden.

'What's he after?' said Birkin rising.

The young cat trotted lordly down the path, waving his tail. He was an ordinary tabby with white paws, a slender young gentleman. A crouching, fluffy, brownish-grey cat was stealing up the side of the fence. The Mino walked statelily up to her, with manly nonchalance. She crouched before him and pressed herself on the ground in humility, a fluffy soft outcast, looking up at him with wild eyes that were green and lovely as great jewels. He looked casually down on her. So she crept a few inches further, proceeding on her way to the back door, crouching in a wonderful, soft, self-obliterating manner, and moving like a shadow.

He, going statelily on his slim legs, walked after her, then suddenly, for pure excess, he gave her a light cuff with his paw on the side of her face. She ran off a few steps, like a blown leaf along the ground, then crouched unobtrusively, in submissive, wild patience. The Mino pretended to take no notice of her. He blinked his eyes superbly at the landscape. In a minute she drew herself together and moved softly, a fleecy brown-grey shadow, a few paces forward. She began to quicken her pace, in a moment she would be gone like a dream, when the young grey lord sprang before her, and gave her a light handsome cuff. She subsided at once, submissively.

'She is a wild cat,' said Birkin. 'She has come in from the woods.'

The eyes of the stray cat flared round for a moment, like great green fires staring at Birkin. Then she had rushed in a soft swift rush, halfway down the garden. There she paused to look round. The Mino turned his face in pure superiority to his master, and slowly closed his eyes, standing in statuesque young perfection. The wild cat's round, green, wondering eyes were staring all the while like uncanny fires. Then again, like a shadow, she slid towards the kitchen.

In a lovely springing leap, like a wind, the Mino was upon her, and had boxed her twice, very definitely, with a white, delicate fist. She sank and slid back, unquestioning. He walked after her, and cuffed her once or twice, leisurely, with sudden little blows of his magic white paws.

'Now why does he do that?' cried Ursula in indignation.

'They are on intimate terms,' said Birkin.

'And is that why he hits her?'

'Yes,' laughed Birkin, 'I think he wants to make it quite obvious to her.'

'Isn't it horrid of him!' she cried; and going out into the garden she called to the Mino:

'Stop it, don't bully. Stop hitting her.'

The stray cat vanished like a swift, invisible shadow. The Mino glanced at Ursula, then looked from her disdainfully to his master.

'Are you a bully, Mino?' Birkin asked.

The young slim cat looked at him, and slowly narrowed its eyes. Then it glanced away at the landscape, looking into the distance as if completely oblivious of the two human beings.

'Mino,' said Ursula, 'I don't like you. You are a bully like all males.'

'No,' said Birkin, 'he is justified. He is not a bully. He is only insisting to the poor stray that she shall acknowledge him as a sort of fate, her own fate: because you can see she is fluffy and promiscuous as the wind. I am with him entirely. He wants superfine stability.'

'Yes, I know!' cried Ursula. 'He wants his own way – I know what your fine words work down to – bossiness, I call it, bossiness.'

The young cat again glanced at Birkin in disdain of the noisy woman.

'I quite agree with you, Miciotto,' said Birkin to the cat. 'Keep your male dignity, and your higher understanding.'

Again the Mino narrowed his eyes as if he were looking at the sun. Then, suddenly affecting to have no connection at all with the two people, he went trotting off, with assumed spontaneity and gaiety, his tail erect, his white feet blithe.

'Now he will find the belle sauvage once more, and entertain her with his superior wisdom,' laughed Birkin.

Ursula looked at the man who stood in the garden with his hair blowing and his eyes smiling ironically, and she cried:

'Oh, it makes me so cross, the assumption of male superiority! And it is such a lie! One wouldn't mind if there were any justification for it.'

'The wild cat,' said Birkin, 'doesn't mind. She perceives that it is justified.'

'Does she!' cried Ursula. 'And tell it to the Horse Marines.'

'To them also.'

'It is just like Gerald Crich with his horse – a lust for bullying – a real *Wille zur Macht* – so base, so petty.'

'I agree that the *Wille zur Macht* is a base and petty thing. But with the Mino, it is the desire to bring this female cat into a pure stable equilibrium, a transcendent and abiding *rapport* with the single male. Whereas without him, as you see, she is a mere stray, a fluffy sporadic bit of chaos. It is a *volonté de pouvoir*, if you like, a win to ability, taking *pouvoir* as a verb.'

'Ah – ! Sophistries! It's the old Adam.'

'Oh yes. Adam kept Eve in the indestructible paradise, when he kept her single with himself, like a star in its orbit.'

'Yes – yes –' cried Ursula, pointing her finger at him. 'There you are – a star in its orbit! A satellite – a satellite of Mars – that's what she is to be! There – there – you've given yourself away! You want a satellite, Mars and his satellite! You've said it – you've said it – you've dished yourself!'

He stood smiling in frustration and amusement and irritation and admiration and love. She was so quick, and so lambent, like discernible fire, and so vindictive, and so rich in her dangerous flamy sensitiveness.

'I've not said it at all,' he replied, 'if you will give me a chance to speak.'

'No, no!' she cried. 'I won't let you speak. You've said it, a satellite, you're not going to wriggle out of it. You've said it.'

'You'll never believe now that I *haven't* said it,' he answered. 'I neither implied nor indicated nor mentioned a satellite, nor intended a satellite, never.'

'*You prevaricator!*' she cried, in real indignation.

'Tea is ready, sir,' said the landlady from the doorway.

They both looked at her, very much as the cats had looked at them, a little while before.

'Thank you, Mrs Daykin.'

An interrupted silence fell over the two of them, a moment of breach.

'Come and have tea,' he said.

'Yes, I should love it,' she replied, gathering herself together.

They sat facing each other across the tea table.

'I did not say, nor imply, a satellite. I meant two single equal stars balanced in conjunction –'

'You gave yourself away, you gave away your little game completely,' she cried, beginning at once to eat. He saw that she would take no further heed of his expostulation, so he began to pour the tea.

'What *good* things to eat!' she cried.

'Take your own sugar,' he said.

He handed her her cup. He had everything so nice, such pretty cups and plates, painted with mauve-lustre and green, also shapely bowls and glass plates, and old spoons, on a woven cloth of pale grey and black and purple. It was very rich and fine. But Ursula could see Hermione's influence.

'Your things are so lovely!' she said, almost angrily.

'*I* like them. It gives me real pleasure to use things that are attractive in themselves – pleasant things. And Mrs Daykin is good. She thinks everything is wonderful, for my sake.'

'Really,' said Ursula, 'landladies are better than wives, nowadays. They certainly *care* a great deal more. It is much more beautiful and complete here now, than if you were married.'

'But think of the emptiness within,' he laughed.

'No,' she said. 'I am jealous that men have such perfect landladies and such beautiful lodgings. There is nothing left them to desire.'

'In the house-keeping way, we'll hope not. It is disgusting, people marrying for a home.'

'Still,' said Ursula, 'a man has very little need for a woman now, has he?'

'In outer things, maybe – except to share his bed and bear his children. But essentially, there is just the same need as there ever was. Only nobody takes the trouble to be essential.'

'How essential?' she said.

'I do think,' he said, 'that the world is only held together by the mystic conjunction, the ultimate unison between people – a bond. And the immediate bond is between man and woman.'

'But it's such old hat,' said Ursula. 'Why should love be a bond? No, I'm not having any.'

'If you are walking westward,' he said, 'you forfeit the northern and eastward and southern direction. If you admit a unison, you forfeit all the possibilities of chaos.'

'But love is freedom,' she declared.

'Don't cant to me,' he replied. 'Love is a direction which excludes all other directions. It's a freedom *together*, if you like.'

'No,' she said, 'love includes everything.'

'Sentimental cant,' he replied. 'You want the state of chaos, that's all. It is ultimate nihilism, this freedom-in-love business, this freedom which is love and love which is freedom. As a matter of fact, if you enter into a pure unison, it is irrevocable, and it is never pure till it is irrevocable. And it is one way, like the path of a star.'

'Ha!' she cried bitterly. 'It is the old dead morality.'

'No,' he said, 'it is the law of creation. One is committed. One must commit oneself to a conjunction with the other – for ever. But it is not selfless – it is a maintaining of the self in mystic balance and integrity – like a star balanced with another star.'

'I don't trust you when you drag in the stars,' she said. 'If you were quite true, it wouldn't be necessary to be so far-fetched.'

'Don't trust me then,' he said, angry. 'It is enough that I trust myself.'

'And that is where you make another mistake,' she replied. 'You *don't* trust yourself. You don't fully believe yourself what you are saying. You don't really want this conjunction, otherwise you wouldn't talk so much about it, you'd get it.'

He was suspended for a moment, arrested.

'How?' he said.

'By just loving,' she retorted in defiance.

He was still a moment, in anger. Then he said:

'I tell you, I don't believe in love like that. I tell you, you want love to administer to your egoism, to subserve you. Love is a process of subservience with you – and with everybody. I hate it.'

'No,' she cried, pressing back her head like a cobra, her eyes flashing. 'It is a process of pride – I want to be proud –'

'Proud and subservient, proud and subservient, I know you,' he retorted dryly. 'Proud and subservient, then subservient to the proud – I know you and your love. It is a tick-tack, tick-tack, a dance of opposites.'

'Are you sure?' she mocked wickedly, 'what my love is?'

'Yes, I am,' he retorted.

'So cocksure!' she said. 'How can anybody ever be right, who is so cocksure? It shows you are wrong.'

He was silent in chagrin.

They had talked and struggled till they were both wearied out.

'Tell me about yourself and your people,' he said.

And she told him about the Brangwens, and about her mother, and about Skrebensky, her first love, and about her later experiences. He sat very still, watching her as she talked. And he seemed to listen with reverence. Her face was beautiful and full of baffled light as she told him all the things that had hurt her or perplexed her so deeply. He seemed to warm and comfort his soul at the beautiful light of her nature.

'If she *really* could pledge herself,' he thought to himself, with passionate insistence but hardly any hope. Yet a curious little irresponsible laughter appeared in his heart.

'We have all suffered so much,' he mocked, ironically.

She looked up at him, and a flash of wild gaiety went over her face, a strange flash of yellow light coming from her eyes.

'Haven't we!' she cried, in a high, reckless cry. 'It is almost absurd, isn't it?'

'Quite absurd,' he said. 'Suffering bores me, any more.'

'So it does me.'

He was almost afraid of the mocking recklessness of her splendid face. Here was one who would go to the whole lengths of heaven or hell, whichever she had to go. And he mistrusted her, he was afraid of a woman capable of such abandon, such dangerous thoroughness of destructivity. Yet he chuckled within himself also.

She came over to him and put her hand on his shoulder, looking down at him with strange golden-lighted eyes, very tender, but with a curious devilish look lurking underneath.

'Say you love me, say "my love" to me,' she pleaded.

He looked back into her eyes, and saw. His face flickered with sardonic comprehension.

'I love you right enough,' he said grimly. 'But I want it to be something else.'

'But why? But why?' she insisted, bending her wonderful luminous face to him. 'Why isn't it enough?'

'Because we can go one better,' he said, putting his arms round her.

'No, we can't,' she said, in a strong, voluptuous voice of yielding. 'We can only love each other. Say "my love" to me, say it, say it.'

She put her arms round his neck. He enfolded her, and kissed her subtly, murmuring in a subtle voice of love, and irony, and submission:

'Yes – my love, yes – my love. Let love be enough then. I love you then – I love you. I'm bored by the rest.'

'Yes,' she murmured, nestling very sweet and close to him.

14

WATER-PARTY

Every year Mr Crich gave a more or less public water-party on the lake. There was a little pleasure-launch on Willey Water and several rowing-boats, and guests could take tea either in the marquee that was set up in the grounds of the house, or they could picnic in the shade of the great walnut tree at the boat-house by the lake. This year the staff of the Grammar School was invited, along with the chief officials of the firm. Gerald and the younger Criches did not care for this party, but it become customary now, and it pleased the father, as being the only occasion when he could gather some people of the district together in festivity with him. For he loved to give pleasure to his dependants and to those poorer than himself. But his children preferred the company of their equals in wealth. They hated their inferiors' humility or gratitude or awkwardness.

Nevertheless they were willing to attend at this festival, as they had done almost since they were children, the more so, as they all felt a little guilty now, and unwilling to thwart their father any more, since he was so ill in health. Therefore, quite cheerfully Laura prepared to take her mother's place as hostess, and Gerald assumed responsibility for the amusements on the water.

Birkin had written to Ursula saying he expected to see her at the party, and Gudrun, although she scorned the patronage of the Criches, would nevertheless accompany her mother and father if the weather were fine.

The day came blue and full of sunshine, with little wafts of wind. The sisters both wore dresses of white crêpe, and hats of soft grass. But Gudrun had a sash of brilliant black and pink and yellow colour wound broadly round her waist, and she had pink silk stockings, and black and pink and yellow decoration on the brim of her hat, weighing it down a little. She carried also a yellow silk coat over her arm, so that she looked remarkable, like a painting from the Salon. Her appearance was a sore trial to her father, who said angrily:

'Don't you think you might as well get yourself up for a Christmas cracker, an' ha' done with it?'

But Gudrun looked handsome and brilliant, and she wore her clothes in pure defiance. When people stared at her, and giggled after her, she made a point of saying loudly, to Ursula:

'*Regarde, regarde ces gens-là! Ne sont-ils pas des hiboux incroyables?*' And with the words of French in her mouth, she would look over her shoulder at the giggling party.

'No, really, it's impossible!' Ursula would reply distinctly. And so the two girls took it out of their universal enemy. But their father became more and more enraged.

Ursula was all snowy white, save that her hat was pink, and entirely without trimming, and her shoes were dark red, and she carried an orange-coloured coat. And in this guise they were walking all the way to Shortlands, their father and mother going in front.

They were laughing at their mother, who, dressed in a summer material of black and purple stripes, and wearing a hat of purple straw, was setting forth with much more of the shyness and trepidation of a young girl than her daughters ever felt, walking demurely beside her husband, who, as usual, looked rather crumpled in his best suit, as if he were the father of a young family and had been holding the baby whilst his wife got dressed.

'Look at the young couple in front,' said Gudrun calmly. Ursula looked at her mother and father, and was suddenly seized with uncontrollable laughter. The two girls stood in the road and laughed till the tears ran down their faces, as they caught sight again of the shy, unworldly couple of their parents going on ahead.

'We are roaring at you, mother,' called Ursula, helplessly following after her parents.

Mrs Brangwen turned round with a slightly puzzled exasperated look. 'Oh indeed!' she said. 'What is there so very funny about *me*, I should like to know?'

She could not understand that there could be anything amiss with her appearance. She had a perfect calm sufficiency, an easy indifference to any criticism whatsoever, as if she were beyond it. Her clothes were always rather odd, and as a rule slip-shod, yet she wore them with a perfect ease and satisfaction. Whatever she had on, so long as she was barely tidy, she was right, beyond remark; such an aristocrat she was by instinct.

'You look so stately, like a country Baroness,' said Ursula, laughing with a little tenderness at her mother's naïve puzzled air.

'*Just* like a country Baroness!' chimed in Gudrun. Now the mother's natural hauteur became self-conscious, and the girls shrieked again.

'Go home, you pair of idiots, great giggling idiots!' cried the father inflamed with irritation.

'Mm-m-er!' booed Ursula, pulling a face at his crossness.

The yellow lights danced in his eyes, he leaned forward in real rage.

'Don't be so silly as to take any notice of the great gabies,' said Mrs Brangwen, turning on her way.

'I'll see if I'm going to be followed by a pair of giggling, yelling jackanapes –' he cried vengefully.

The girls stood still, laughing helplessly at his fury, upon the path beside the hedge.

'Why you're as silly as they are, to take any notice,' said Mrs Brangwen also becoming angry now he was really enraged.

'There are some people coming, father,' cried Ursula, with mocking warning. He glanced round quickly, and went on to join his wife, walking stiff with rage. And the girls followed, weak with laughter.

When the people had passed by, Brangwen cried in a loud, stupid voice:

'I'm going back home if there's any more of this. I'm damned if I'm going to be made a fool of in this fashion, in the public road.'

He was really out of temper. At the sound of his blind, vindictive voice, the laughter suddenly left the girls, and their hearts contracted with contempt. They hated his words 'in the public road'. What did they care for the public road? But Gudrun was conciliatory.

'But we weren't laughing to *hurt* you,' she cried, with an uncouth gentleness which made her parents uncomfortable. 'We were laughing because we're fond of you.'

'We'll walk on in front, if they are *so* touchy,' said Ursula, angry. And in this wise they arrived at Willey Water. The lake was blue and fair, the meadows sloped down in sunshine on one side, the thick dark woods dropped steeply on the other. The little pleasure-launch was fussing out from the shore, twanging its music, crowded with people, flapping its paddles. Near the boat-house was a throng of gaily-dressed persons, small in the distance. And on the high-road, some of the common people were standing along the hedge, looking at the festivity beyond, enviously, like souls not admitted to paradise.

'My eye!' said Gudrun, sotto voce, looking at the motley of guests, 'there's a pretty crowd if you like! Imagine yourself in the midst of that, my dear.'

Gudrun's apprehensive horror of people in the mass unnerved Ursula. 'It looks rather awful,' she said anxiously.

'And imagine what they'll be like – *imagine*!' said Gudrun, still in that unnerving, subdued voice. Yet she advanced determinedly.

'I suppose we can get away from them,' said Ursula anxiously.

'We're in a pretty fix if we can't,' said Gudrun. Her extreme ironic loathing and apprehension was very trying to Ursula.

'We needn't stay,' she said.

'I certainly shan't stay five minutes among that little lot,' said Gudrun. They advanced nearer, till they saw policemen at the gates.

'Policemen to keep you in, too!' said Gudrun. 'My word, this is a beautiful affair.'

'We'd better look after father and mother,' said Ursula anxiously.

'Mother's *perfectly* capable of getting through this little celebration,' said Gudrun with some contempt.

But Ursula knew that her father felt uncouth and angry and unhappy, so she was far from her ease. They waited outside the gate till their parents came up. The tall, thin man in his crumpled clothes was unnerved and irritable as a boy, finding himself on the brink of this social function. He did not feel a gentleman, he did not feel anything except pure exasperation.

Ursula took her place at his side, they gave their tickets to the policeman, and passed in on to the grass, four abreast; the tall, hot, ruddy-dark man with his narrow boyish brow drawn with irritation, the fresh-faced, easy woman, perfectly collected though her hair was slipping on one side, then Gudrun, her eyes round and dark and staring, her full soft face impassive, almost sulky, so that she seemed to be backing away in antagonism even whilst she was advancing; and then Ursula, with the odd, brilliant, dazzled look on her face, that always came when she was in some false situation.

Birkin was the good angel. He came smiling to them with his affected social grace, that somehow was never *quite* right. But he took off his hat and smiled at them with a real smile in his eyes, so that Brangwen cried out heartily in relief:

'How do you do? You're better, are you?'

'Yes, I'm better. How do you do, Mrs Brangwen? I know Gudrun and Ursula very well.'

His eyes smiled full of natural warmth. he had a soft, flattering manner with women, particularly with women who were not young.

'Yes,' said Mrs Brangwen, cool but yet gratified. 'I have heard them speak of you often enough.'

He laughed. Gudrun looked aside, feeling she was being belittled. People were standing about in groups, some women were sitting in the shade of the walnut tree, with cups of tea in their hands, a waiter in evening dress was hurrying round, some girls were simpering with parasols, some young men, who had just come in from rowing, were sitting cross-legged on the grass, coatless, their shirt-sleeves rolled up in manly fashion, their hands resting on their white flannel trousers, their gaudy ties floating about, as they laughed and tried to be witty with the young damsels.

'Why,' thought Gudrun churlishly, 'don't they have the manners to put their coats on, and not to assume such intimacy in their appearance.'

She abhorred the ordinary young man, with his hair plastered back, and his easy-going chumminess.

Hermione Roddice came up, in a handsome gown of white lace, trailing an enormous silk shawl blotched with great embroidered flowers, and balancing an enormous plain hat on her head. She looked striking, astonishing, almost macabre, so tall, with the fringe of her great cream-coloured vividly-blotched shawl trailing on the ground after her, her thick hair coming low over her eyes, her face strange and long and pale, and the blotches of brilliant colour drawn round her.

'Doesn't she look *weird*!' Gudrun heard some girls titter behind her. And she could have killed them.

'How do you do!' sang Hermione, coming up very kindly, and glancing slowly over Gudrun's father and mother. It was a trying moment, exasperating for Gudrun. Hermione was really so strongly entrenched in her class superiority, she could come up and know people out of simple curiosity, as if they were creatures on exhibition. Gudrun would do the same herself. But she resented being in the position when somebody might do it to her.

Hermione, very remarkable, and distinguishing the Brangwens very much, led them along to where Laura Crich stood receiving the guests.

'This is Mrs Brangwen,' sang Hermione, and Laura, who wore a stiff embroidered linen dress, shook hands and said she was glad to see her. Then Gerald came up, dressed in white, with a black and brown blazer, and looking handsome. He too was introduced to the Brangwen parents, and immediately he spoke to Mrs Brangwen as if she were a lady, and to Brangwen as if he were *not* a gentleman. Gerald was so obvious in his demeanour. He had to shake hands with his left hand, because he had hurt his right, and carried it, bandaged up, in the pocket of his jacket. Gudrun was *very* thankful that none of her party asked him what was the matter with the hand.

The steam launch was fussing in, all its music jingling, people calling excitedly from on board. Gerald went to see to the debarkation, Birkin was getting tea for Mrs Brangwen, Brangwen had joined a Grammar-School group, Hermione was sitting down by their mother, the girls went to the landing-stage to watch the launch come in.

She hooted and tooted gaily, then her paddles were silent, the ropes were thrown ashore, she drifted in with a little bump. Immediately the passengers crowded excitedly to come ashore.

'Wait a minute, wait a minute,' shouted Gerald in sharp command.

They must wait till the boat was tight on the ropes, till the small gangway was put out. Then they streamed ashore, clamouring as if they had come from America.

'Oh, it's *so* nice!' the young girls were crying. 'It's quite lovely.'

The waiters from on board ran out to the boat-house with baskets, the captain lounged on the little bridge. Seeing all safe, Gerald came to Gudrun and Ursula.

'You wouldn't care to go on board for the next trip, and have tea there?' he asked.

'No, thanks,' said Gudrun coldly.

'You don't care for the water?'

'For the water? Yes, I like it very much.'

He looked at her, his eyes searching.

'You don't care for going on a launch, then?'

She was slow in answering, and then she spoke slowly.

'No,' she said. 'I can't say that I do.' Her colour was high, she seemed angry about something.

'*Un peu trop de monde,*' said Ursula, explaining.

'Eh? *Trop de monde!*' He laughed shortly. 'Yes, there's a fair number of 'em.'

Gudrun turned on him brilliantly.

'Have you ever been from Westminster Bridge to Richmond on one of the Thames steamers?' she cried.

'No,' he said, 'I can't say I have.'

'Well, it's one of the most *vile* experiences I've ever had.' She spoke rapidly and excitedly, the colour high in her cheeks. 'There was absolutely nowhere to sit down, nowhere, a man just above sang 'Rocked in the Cradle of the Deep' the *whole* way; he was blind and he had a small organ, one of those portable organs, and he expected money; so you can imagine what *that* was like; there came a constant smell of luncheon from below, and puffs of hot oily machinery; the journey took hours and hours and hours; and for miles, literally for miles, dreadful boys ran with us on the shore, in that *awful* Thames mud, going in *up to the waist* – they had their trousers turned back, and they went up to their hips in that indescribable Thames mud, their faces always turned to us, and screaming, exactly like carrion creatures, screaming "'Ere y'are sir, 'ere y'are sir, 'ere y'are sir", exactly like some foul carrion objects, perfectly obscene; and paterfamilias on board, laughing when the boys went right down in that awful mud, occasionally throwing them a ha-penny. And if you'd seen the intent look on the faces of these boys, and the way they darted in the filth when a coin was flung – really, no vulture or jackal could dream of approaching them, for foulness. I *never* would go on a pleasure boat again – never.'

Gerald watched her all the time she spoke, his eyes glittering with faint rousedness. It was not so much what she said; it was she herself who roused him, roused him with a small, vivid pricking.

'Of course,' he said, 'every civilized body is bound to have its vermin.'

'Why?' cried Ursula. '*I* don't have vermin.'

'And it's not that – it's the *quality* of the whole thing – paterfamilias laughing and thinking it sport, and throwing the ha'pennies, and mater-familias spreading her fat little knees and eating, continually eating –' replied Gudrun.

'Yes,' said Ursula. 'It isn't the boys so much who are vermin; it's the people themselves, the whole body politic, as you call it.'

Gerald laughed.

'Never mind,' he said. 'You shan't go on the launch.'

Gudrun flushed quickly at his rebuke.

There were a few moments of silence. Gerald, like a sentinel, was watching the people who were going on to the boat. He was very good-looking and self-contained, but his air of soldierly alertness was rather irritating.

'Will you have tea here then, or go across to the house, where there's a tent on the lawn?' he asked.

'Can't we have a rowing-boat, and get out?' asked Ursula, who was always rushing in too fast.

'To get out?' smiled Gerald.

'You see,' said Gudrun, flushing at Ursula's outspoken rudeness, 'we don't know the people, we are almost *complete* strangers here.'

'Oh, I can soon set you up with a few acquaintances,' he said easily.

Gudrun looked at him, to see if it were ill-meant. Then she smiled at him.

'Ah,' she said, 'you know what we mean. Can't we go up there, and explore that coast?' She pointed to a grove on the hillock of the meadow-side, near the shore, halfway down the lake. 'That looks perfectly lovely. We might even bathe. Isn't it beautiful in this light! Really, it's like one of the reaches of the Nile – as one imagines the Nile.'

Gerald smiled at her factitious enthusiasm for the distant spot.

'You're sure it's far enough off?' he asked ironically, adding at once: 'Yes, you might go there, if we could get a boat. They seem to be all out.'

He looked round the lake and counted the rowing-boats on its surface.

'How lovely it would be!' cried Ursula wistfully.

'And don't you want tea?' he said.

'Oh,' said Gudrun, 'we could just drink a cup, and be off.'

He looked from one to the other, smiling. He was somewhat offended – yet sporting.

'Can you manage a boat pretty well?' he asked.

'Yes,' replied Gudrun coldly, 'pretty well.'

'Oh yes,' cried Ursula. 'We can both of us row like water-spiders.'

'You can? There's a light little canoe of mine, that I didn't take out for fear somebody should drown themselves. Do you think you'd be safe in that?'

'Oh, perfectly,' said Gudrun.

'What an angel!' cried Ursula.

'Don't, for *my* sake, have an accident – because I'm responsible for the water.'

'Sure,' pledged Gudrun.

'Besides, we can both swim quite well,' said Ursula.

'Well – then I'll get them to put you up a tea-basket, and you can picnic all to yourselves – that's the idea, isn't it?'

'How fearfully good! How frightfully nice if you could!' cried Gudrun warmly, her colour flushing up again. It made the blood stir in his veins, the subtle way she turned to him and infused her gratitude into his body.

'Where's Birkin?' he said, his eyes twinkling. 'He might help me to get it down.'

'But what about your hand? Isn't it hurt?' asked Gudrun, rather muted, as if avoiding the intimacy. This was the first time the hurt had been mentioned. The curious way she skirted round the subject sent a new, subtle caress through his veins. He took his hand out of his pocket. It was bandaged. He looked at it, then put it in his pocket again. Gudrun quivered at the sight of the wrapped-up paw.

'Oh, I can manage with one hand. The canoe is as light as a feather,' he said. 'There's Rupert! – Rupert!'

Birkin turned from his social duties and came towards them.

'What have you done to it?' asked Ursula, who had been aching to put the question for the last half-hour.

'To my hand?' said Gerald. 'I trapped it in some machinery.'

'Ugh!' said Ursula. 'And did it hurt much?'

'Yes,' he said. 'It did at the time. It's getting better now. It crushed the fingers.'

'Oh,' cried Ursula, as if in pain, 'I hate people who hurt themselves. I can *feel* it.' And she shook her hand.

'What do you want?' said Birkin.

The two men carried down the slim brown boat, and set it on the water.

'You're quite sure you'll be safe in it?' Gerald asked.

'Quite sure,' said Gudrun. 'I wouldn't be so mean as to take it, if there was the slightest doubt. But I've had a canoe at Arundel, and I assure you I'm perfectly safe.'

So saying, having given her word like a man, she and Ursula entered the frail craft, and pushed gently off. The two men stood watching them. Gudrun was paddling. She knew the men were watching her, and it made her slow and rather clumsy. The colour flew in her face like a flag.

'Thanks awfully,' she called back to him, from the water, as the boat slid away. 'It's lovely – like sitting in a leaf.'

He laughed at the fancy. Her voice was shrill and strange, calling from the distance. He watched her as she paddled away. There was something childlike about her, trustful and deferential, like a child. He watched her all the while, as she rowed. And to Gudrun it was a real delight, in make-belief, to be the childlike, clinging woman to the man who stood there on the quay, so good-looking and efficient in his white clothes, and moreover the most important man she knew at the moment. She did not take any notice of the wavering, indistinct, lambent Birkin, who stood at his side. One figure at a time occupied the field of her attention.

The boat rustled lightly along the water. They passed the bathers whose striped tents stood between the willows of the meadow's edge, and drew along the open shore, past the meadows that sloped golden in the light of the already late afternoon. Other boats were stealing under the wooden shore opposite, they could hear people's laughter and voices. But Gudrun rowed on towards the clump of trees that balanced perfect in the distance, in the golden light.

The sisters found a little place where a tiny stream flowed into the lake, with reeds and flowery marsh of pink willow herb, and a gravelly bank to the side. Here they ran delicately ashore, with their frail boat, the two girls took off their shoes and stockings and went through the water's edge to the grass. The tiny ripples of the lake were warm and clear, they lifted their boat on to the bank, and looked round with joy. They were quite alone in a forsaken little stream-mouth, and on the knoll just behind was the clump of trees.

'We will bathe just for a moment,' said Ursula, 'and then we'll have tea.'

They looked round. Nobody could notice them, or could come up in time to see them. In less than a minute Ursula had thrown off her clothes and had slipped naked into the water, and was swimming out. Quickly, Gudrun joined her. They swam silently and blissfully for a few minutes, circling round their little stream-mouth. Then they slipped ashore and ran into the grove again, like nymphs.

'How lovely it is to be free,' said Ursula, running swiftly here and there between the tree-trunks, quite naked, her hair blowing loose. The grove was of beech-trees, big and splendid, a steel-grey scaffolding of trunks and boughs, with level sprays of strong green here and there, whilst through the northern side the distance glimmered open as through a window.

When they had run and danced themselves dry, the girls quickly dressed and sat down to the fragrant tea. They sat on the northern side of the grove, in the yellow sunshine facing the slope of the grassy hill, alone in a little wild world of their own. The tea was hot and aromatic, there were delicious little sandwiches of cucumber and of caviare, and winy cakes.

'Are you happy, Prune?' cried Ursula in delight, looking at her sister.

'Ursula, I'm perfectly happy,' replied Gudrun gravely, looking at the westering sun.

'So am I.'

When they were together, doing the things they enjoyed, the two sisters were quite complete in a perfect world of their own. And this was one of the perfect moments of freedom and delight, such as children alone know, when all seems a perfect and blissful adventure.

When they had finished tea, the two girls sat on, silent and serene. Then Ursula, who had a beautiful strong voice, began to sing to herself, softly: *'Annchen von Tharau.'* Gudrun listened, as she sat beneath the trees, and the yearning came into her heart. Ursula seemed so peaceful and sufficient unto herself, sitting there unconsciously crooning her song, strong and un-questioned at the centre of her own universe. And Gudrun felt herself outside. Always this desolating, agonized feeling, that she was outside of life, an onlooker, whilst Ursula was a partaker, caused Gudrun to suffer from a sense of her own negation, and made her, that she must always demand the other to be aware of her, to be in connection with her.

'Do you mind if I do Dalcroze to that tune, Hurtler?' she asked in a curious muted tone, scarce moving her lips.

'What did you say?' asked Ursula, looking up in peaceful surprise.

'Will you sing while I do Dalcroze?' said Gudrun, suffering at having to repeat herself.

Ursula thought a moment, gathering her straying wits together.

'While you do –?' she asked vaguely.

'Dalcroze movements,' said Gudrun, suffering tortures of self-consciousness, even because of her sister.

'Oh, Dalcroze! I couldn't catch the name. *Do* – I should love to see you,' cried Ursula, with childish surprised brightness. 'What shall I sing?'

'Sing anything you like, and I'll take the rhythm from it.'

But Ursula could not for her life think of anything to sing. However, she suddenly began, in a laughing, teasing voice:

'My love – is a high-born lady –'

Gudrun, looking as if some invisible chain weighed on her hands and feet, began slowly to dance in the eurhythmic manner, pulsing and fluttering rhythmically with her feet making slower, regular gestures with her hands and arms, now spreading her arms wide, now raising them above her head, now flinging them softly apart, and lifting her face, her feet all the time beating and running to the measure of the song, as if it were some strange incantation, her white, rapt form drifting here and there in a strange impulsive rhapsody, seeming to be lifted on a breeze of incantation, shuddering with strange little runs. Ursula sat on the grass, her mouth open in her singing, her eyes laughing as if she thought it was a great joke, but a yellow light flashing up in them, as she caught some of the unconscious ritualistic suggestion of the complex shuddering and waving and drifting of her sister's white form, that was clutched in pure, mindless, tossing rhythm, and a will set powerful in a kind of hypnotic influence.

'My love is a high-born lady – She is-s-s – rather dark than shady –' rang out Ursula's laughing, satiric song, and quicker, fiercer went Gudrun in the dance, stamping as if she were trying to throw off some bond, flinging her hands suddenly and stamping again, then rushing with face uplifted and throat full and beautiful, and eyes half closed, sightless. The sun was low and yellow, sinking down, and in the sky floated a thin, ineffectual moon.

Ursula was quite absorbed in her song, when suddenly Gudrun stopped and said mildly, ironically:

'Ursula!'

'Yes?' said Ursula, opening her eyes out of the trance.

Gudrun was standing still and pointing, a mocking smile on her face, towards the side.

'Ugh!' cried Ursula in sudden panic, starting to her feet.

'They're quite all right,' rang out Gudrun's sardonic voice.

On the left stood a little cluster of Highland cattle, vividly coloured and fleecy in the evening light, their horns branching into the sky, pushing forward their muzzles inquisitively, to know what it was all about. Their eyes glittered through their tangle of hair, their naked nostrils were full of shadow.

'Won't they do anything?' cried Ursula in fear.

Gudrun, who was usually frightened of cattle, now shook her head in a queer, half-doubtful, half-sardonic motion, a faint smile round her mouth.

'Don't they look charming, Ursula?' cried Gudrun, in a high, strident voice, something like the scream of a seagull.

'Charming,' cried Ursula in trepidation. 'But won't they do anything to us?'

Again Gudrun looked back at her sister with an enigmatic smile, and shook her head.

'I'm sure they won't,' she said, as if she had to convince herself also, and yet, as if she were confident of some secret power in herself, and had to put it to the test. 'Sit down and sing again,' she called in her high, strident voice.

'I'm frightened,' cried Ursula, in a pathetic voice, watching the group of sturdy short cattle, that stood with their knees planted, and watched with their dark, wicked eyes, through the matted fringe of their hair. Nevertheless, she sank down again, in her former posture.

'They are quite safe,' came Gudrun's high call. 'Sing something, you've only to sing something.'

It was evident she had a strange passion to dance before the sturdy, handsome cattle.

Ursula began to sing, in a false quavering voice:

'Way down in Tennessee –'

She sounded purely anxious. Nevertheless, Gudrun, with her arms outspread and her face uplifted, went in a strange palpitating dance towards the cattle, lifting her body towards them as if in a spell, her feet pulsing as if in some little frenzy of unconscious sensation, her arms, her wrists, her hands stretching and heaving and falling and reaching and reaching and falling, her breasts lifted and shaken towards the cattle, her throat exposed as in some voluptuous ecstasy towards them, whilst she drifted imperceptibly nearer, an uncanny white figure, towards them, carried away in its own rapt trance, ebbing in strange fluctuations upon the cattle, that waited, and ducked their heads a little in sudden contraction from her, watching all the time as if hypnotized, their bare horns branching in the clear light, as the white figure of the woman ebbed upon them, in the slow hypnotizing convulsion of the dance. She could feel them just in front of her, it was as if she had the electric pulse from their breasts running into her hands. Soon she would touch them, actually touch them. A terrible shiver of fear and pleasure went through her. And all the while Ursula, spell-bound, kept up her high-pitched thin, irrelevant song, which pierced the fading evening like an incantation.

Gudrun could hear the cattle breathing heavily with helpless fear and fascination. Oh, they were brave little beasts, these wild Scotch bullocks, wild and fleecy. Suddenly one of them snorted, ducked its head, and backed.

'Hue! Hi-eee!' came a sudden loud shout from the edge of the grove. The cattle broke and fell back quite spontaneously, went running up the hill, their fleece waving like fire to their motion. Gudrun stood suspended out on the grass, Ursula rose to her feet.

It was Gerald and Birkin come to find them, and Gerald had cried out to frighten off the cattle.

'What do you think you're doing?' he now called, in a high, wondering vexed tone.

'Why have you come?' came back Gudrun's strident cry of anger.

'What do you think you were doing?' Gerald repeated, automatically.

'We were doing eurhythmics,' laughed Ursula, in a shaken voice.

Gudrun stood aloof looking at them with large dark eyes of resentment, suspended for a few moments. Then she walked away up the hills, after the cattle, which had gathered in a little, spell-bound cluster higher up.

'Where are you going?' Gerald called after her. And he followed her up the hill-side. The sun had gone behind the hill, and shadows were clinging to the earth, the sky above was full of travelling light.

'A poor song for a dance,' said Birkin to Ursula, standing before her with a sardonic, flickering laugh on his face. And in another second, he was singing softly to himself, and dancing a grotesque step-dance in front of her, his limbs and body shaking loose, his face flickering palely, a constant thing, whilst his feet beat a rapid mocking tattoo, and his body seemed to hang all loose and quaking in between, like a shadow.

'I think we've all gone mad,' she said, laughing rather frightened.

'Pity we aren't madder,' he answered, as he kept up the incessant shaking dance. Then suddenly he leaned up to her and kissed her fingers lightly, putting his face to hers and looking into her eyes with a pale grin. She stepped back, affronted.

'Offended –?' he asked ironically, suddenly going quite still and reserved again. 'I thought you liked the light fantastic.'

'Not like that,' she said, confused and bewildered, almost affronted. Yet somewhere inside her she was fascinated by the sight of his loose, vibrating body, perfectly abandoned to its own dropping and swinging, and by the pallid, sardonic-smiling face above. Yet automatically she stiffened herself away, and disapproved. It seemed almost an obscenity, in a man who talked as a rule so very seriously.

'Why not like that?' he mocked. And immediately he dropped again into the incredibly rapid, slack-waggling dance, watching her malevolently. And moving in the rapid, stationary dance he came a little nearer, and reached forward with an incredibly mocking, satiric gleam on his face, and would have kissed her again, had she not started back.

'No, don't!' she cried, really afraid.

'Cordelia after all,' he said satirically. She was stung, as if this were an insult. She knew he intended it as such, and it bewildered her.

'And you,' she cried in retort, 'why do you always take your soul in your mouth, so frightfully full?'

'So that I can spit it out the more readily,' he said, pleased by his own retort.

Gerald Crich, his face narrowing to an intent gleam, followed up the hill with quick strides, straight after Gudrun. The cattle stood with their noses together on the brow of a slope, watching the scene below, the men in white hovering about the white forms of the women, watching above all Gudrun, who was advancing slowly towards them. She stood a moment, glancing back at Gerald, and then at the cattle.

Then in a sudden motion, she lifted her arms and rushed sheer upon the long-horned bullocks, in shuddering irregular runs, pausing for a second and looking at them, then lifting her hands and running forward with a flash, till they ceased pawing the ground, and gave way, snorting with terror, lifting their heads from the ground and flinging themselves away, galloping off into the evening, becoming tiny in the distance, and still not stopping.

Gudrun remained staring after them, with a mask-like defiant face.

'Why do you want to drive them mad?' asked Gerald, coming up with her.

She took no notice of him, only averted her face from him.

'It's not safe, you know,' he persisted. 'They're nasty, when they do turn.'

'Turn where? Turn away?' she mocked loudly.

'No,' he said, 'turn against you.'

'Turn against *me*?' she mocked.

He could make nothing of this.

'Anyway, they gored one of the farmer's cows to death the other day,' he said.

'What do I care?' she said.

'*I* cared though,' he replied, 'seeing that they're my cattle.'

'How are they yours! You haven't swallowed them. Give me one of them now,' she said, holding out her hand.

'You know where they are,' he said, pointing over the hill. 'You can have one if you'd like it sent to you later on.'

She looked at him inscrutably.

'You think I'm afraid of you and your cattle, don't you?' she asked.

His eyes narrowed dangerously. There was a faint domineering smile on his face.

'Why should I think that?' he said.

She was watching him all the time with her dark, dilated, inchoate eyes. She leaned forward and swung round her arm, catching him a light blow on the face with the back of her hand.

'That's why,' she said, mocking.

And she felt in her soul an unconquerable desire for deep violence against him. She shut off the fear and dismay that filled her conscious mind. She wanted to do as she did, she was not going to be afraid.

He recoiled from the slight blow on his face. He became deadly pale, and a dangerous flame darkened his eyes. For some seconds he could not speak, his lungs were so suffused with blood, his heart stretched almost to bursting with a great gush of ungovernable emotion. It was as if some reservoir of black emotion had burst within him, and swamped him.

'You have struck the first blow,' he said at last, forcing the words from his lungs, in a voice so soft and low, it sounded like a dream within her, not spoken in the outer air.

'And I shall strike the last,' she retorted involuntarily, with confident assurance. He was silent, he did not contradict her.

She stood negligently, staring away from him, into the distance. On the edge of her consciousness the question was asking itself, automatically:

'Why *are* you behaving in this *impossible* and ridiculous fashion.' But she was sullen, she half shoved the question out of herself. She could not get it clean away, so she felt self-conscious.

Gerald, very pale, was watching her closely. His eyes were lit up with intent lights, absorbed and gleaming. She turned suddenly on him.

'It's you who make me behave like this, you know,' she said, almost suggestive.

'I? How?' he said.

But she turned away, and set off towards the lake. Below, on the water, lanterns were coming alight, faint ghosts of warm flame floating in the pallor of the first twilight. The earth was spread with darkness, like lacquer, overhead was a pale sky, all primrose, and the lake was pale as milk in one part. Away at the landing-stage, tiniest points of coloured rays were stringing themselves in the dusk. The launch was being illuminated. All round, shadow was gathering from the trees.

Gerald, white like a presence in his summer clothes, was following down the open grassy slope. Gudrun waited for him to come up. Then she softly put out her hand and touched him, saying softly:

'Don't be angry with me.'

A flame flew over him, and he was unconscious. Yet he stammered:

'I'm not angry with you. I'm in love with you.'

His mind was gone, he grasped for sufficient mechanical control, to save himself. She laughed a silvery little mockery, yet intolerably caressive.

'That's one way of putting it,' she said.

The terrible swooning burden on his mind, the awful swooning, the loss of all his control, was too much for him. He grasped her arm in his one hand, as if his hand were iron.

'It's all right, then, is it?' he said, holding her arrested.

She looked at the face with the fixed eyes, set before her, and her blood ran cold.

'Yes, it's all right,' she said softly, as if drugged, her voice crooning and witch-like.

He walked on beside her, a striding, mindless body. But he recovered a little as he went. He suffered badly. He had killed his brother when a boy, and was set apart, like Cain.

They found Birkin and Ursula sitting together by the boats, talking and laughing. Birkin had been teasing Ursula.

'Do you smell this little marsh?' he said, sniffing the air. He was very sensitive to scents, and quick in understanding them.

'It's rather nice,' she said.

'No,' he replied, 'alarming.'

'Why alarming?' she laughed.

'It seethes and seethes, a river of darkness,' he said, 'putting forth lilies and snakes, and the *ignis fatuus*, and rolling all the time onward. That's what we never take into count – that it rolls onwards.'

'What does?'

'The other river, the black river. We always consider the silver river of life, rolling on and quickening all the world to a brightness, on and on to heaven, flowing into a bright eternal sea, a heaven of angels thronging. But the other is our real reality –'

'But what other? I don't see any other,' said Ursula.

'It is your reality, nevertheless,' he said; 'that dark river of dissolution. You see it rolls in us just as the other rolls – the black river of corruption. And our flowers are of this – our sea-born Aphrodite, all our white phosphorescent flowers of sensuous perfection, all our reality, nowadays.'

'You mean that Aphrodite is really deathly?' asked Ursula.

'I mean she is the flowering mystery of the death-process, yes,' he replied. 'When the stream of synthetic creation lapses, we find ourselves part of the inverse process, the blood of destructive creation. Aphrodite is born in the first spasm of universal dissolution – then the snakes and swans and lotus – marsh-flowers – and Gudrun and Gerald – born in the process of destructive creation.'

'And you and me –?' she asked.

'Probably,' he replied. 'In part, certainly. Whether we are that, *in toto*, I don't yet know.'

'You mean we are flowers of dissolution – *fleurs du mal*? I don't feel as if I were,' she protested.

He was silent for a time.

'I don't feel as if we were, *altogether*,' he replied. 'Some people are pure flowers of dark corruption – lilies. But there ought to be some roses, warm and flamy. You know Herakleitos says "a dry soul is best". I know so well what that means. Do you?'

'I'm not sure,' Ursula replied. 'But what if people *are* all flowers of dissolution – when they're flowers at all – what difference does it make?'

'No difference – and all the difference. Dissolution rolls on, just as production does,' he said. 'It is a progressive process – and it ends in universal nothing – the end of the world, if you like. But why isn't the end of the world as good as the beginning?'

'I suppose it isn't,' said Ursula, rather angry.

'Oh yes, ultimately,' he said. 'It means a new cycle of creation after – but not for us. If it is the end, then we are of the end – *fleurs du mal*, if you like. If we are *fleurs du mal*, we are not roses of happiness, and there you are.'

'But I think I am,' said Ursula. 'I think I am a rose of happiness.'

'Ready-made?' he asked ironically.

'No – real,' she said, hurt.

'If we are the end, we are not the beginning,' he said.

'Yes, we are,' she said. 'The beginning comes out of the end.'

'After it, not out of it. After us, not out of us.'

'You are a devil, you know, really,' she said. 'You want to destroy our hope. You *want* us to be deathly.'

'No,' he said, 'I only want us to *know* what we are.'

'Ha!' she cried in anger. 'You only want us to know death.'

'You're quite right,' said the soft voice of Gerald, out of the dusk behind.

Birkin rose. Gerald and Gudrun came up. They all began to smoke, in the moments of silence. One after another, Birkin lighted their cigarettes. The match flickered in the twilight, and they were all smoking peacefully by the water-side. The lake was dim, the light dying from off it, in the midst of the dark land. The air all round was intangible, neither here nor there, and there was an unreal noise of banjoes, or suchlike music.

As the golden swim of light overhead died out, the moon gained brightness, and seemed to begin to smile forth her ascendancy. The dark woods on the opposite shore melted into universal shadow. And amid this universal under-shadow, there was a scattered intrusion of lights. Far down the lake were fantastic pale strings of colour, like beads of wan fire, green and red and yellow. The music came out in a little puff, as the launch, all illuminated, veered into the great shadow, stirring her outlines of half-living lights, puffing out her music in little drifts.

All were lighting up. Here and there, close against the faint water, and at the far end of the lake, where the water lay milky in the last whiteness of the sky, and there was no shadow, solitary, frail flames of lanterns floated from the unseen boats. There was a sound of oars, and a boat passed from the pallor into the darkness under the wood, where her lanterns seemed to kindle into fire, hanging in ruddy lovely globes. And again, in the lake, shadowy red gleams hovered in reflection about the boat. Everywhere were these noiseless ruddy creatures of fire drifting near the surface of the water, caught at by the rarest scarce visible reflections.

Birkin brought the lanterns from the bigger boat, and the four shadowy white figures gathered round, to light them. Ursula held up the first, Birkin lowered the light from the rosy, glowing cup of his hands, into the depths of the lantern. It was kindled, and they all stood back to look at the great blue moon of light that hung from Ursula's hand, casting a strange gleam on her face. It flickered, and Birkin went bending over the well of light. His face shone out like an apparition, so unconscious, and again, something demoni-acal. Ursula was dim and veiled, looming over him.

'That is all right,' said his voice softly.

She held up the lantern. It had a flight of storks streaming through a turquoise sky of light, over a dark earth.

'This is beautiful,' she said.

'Lovely,' echoed Gudrun, who wanted to hold one also and lift it up full of beauty.

'Light one for me,' she said. Gerald stood by her, incapacitated. Birkin lit the lantern she held up. Her heart beat with anxiety, to see how beautiful it would be. It was primrose yellow, with tall straight flowers growing darkly from their dark leaves, lifting their heads into the primrose day, while butterflies hovered about them, in the pure clear light.

Gudrun gave a little cry of excitement, as if pierced with delight.

'Isn't it beautiful, oh, isn't it beautiful!'

Her soul was really pierced with beauty, she was translated beyond herself. Gerald leaned near to her, into her zone of light, as if to see. He came close to her, and stood touching her, looking with her at the primrose-shining globe. And she turned her face to his, that was faintly bright in the light of the lantern, and they stood together in one luminous union, close together and ringed round with light, all the rest excluded.

Birkin looked away, and went to light Ursula's second lantern. It had a pale ruddy sea-bottom, with black crabs and sea-weed moving sinuously under a transparent sea, that passed into flamy ruddiness above.

'You've got the heavens above, and the waters under the earth,' said Birkin to her.

'Anything but the earth itself,' she laughed, watching his live hands that hovered to attend to the light.

'I'm dying to see what my second one is,' cried Gudrun, in a vibrating rather strident voice, that seemed to repel the others from her.

Birkin went and kindled it. It was of a lovely deep blue colour, with a red floor, and a great white cuttle-fish flowing in white soft streams all over it. The cuttle-fish had a face that stared straight from the heart of the light, very fixed and coldly intent.

'How truly terrifying!' exclaimed Gudrun, in a voice of horror. Gerald, at her side, gave a low laugh.

'But isn't it really fearful!' she cried in dismay.

Again he laughed, and said:

'Change it with Ursula, for the crabs.'

Gudrun was silent for a moment.

'Ursula,' she said, 'could you bear to have this fearful thing?'

'I think the colouring is *lovely*,' said Ursula.

'So do I,' said Gudrun. 'But could you *bear* to have it swinging to your boat? Don't you want to destroy it *at once*?'

'Oh no,' said Ursula. 'I don't want to destroy it.'

'Well, do you mind having it instead of the crabs? Are you sure you don't mind?'

Gudrun came forward to exchange lanterns.

'No,' said Ursula, yielding up the crabs and receiving the cuttle-fish.

Yet she could not help feeling rather resentful at the way in which Gudrun and Gerald should assume a right over her, a precedence.

'Come then,' said Birkin. 'I'll put them on the boat.'

He and Ursula were moving away to the big boat.

'I suppose you'll row me back, Rupert,' said Gerald, out of the pale shadow of the evening.

'Won't you go with Gudrun in the canoe?' said Birkin. 'It'll be more interesting.'

There was a moment's pause. Birkin and Ursula stood dimly, with their swinging lanterns, by the water's edge. The world was all illusive.

'Is that all right?' said Gudrun to him.

'It'll suit *me* very well,' he said. 'But what about you, and the rowing? I don't see why you should pull me.'

'Why not?' she said. 'I can pull you as well as I could pull Ursula.'

By her tone he could tell she wanted to have him in the boat to herself, and that she was subtly gratified that she should have power over them both. He gave himself, in a strange, electric submission.

She handed him the lanterns, whilst she went to fix the cane at the end of the canoe. He followed after her, and stood with the lanterns dangling against his white-flannelled thighs, emphasizing the shadow around.

'Kiss me before we go,' came his voice softly from out of the shadow above.

She stopped her work in real, momentary astonishment.

'But why?' she exclaimed, in pure surprise.

'Why?' he echoed ironically.

And she looked at him fixedly for some moments. Then she leaned forward and kissed him, with a slow, luxurious kiss, lingering on the mouth. And then she took the lanterns from him, while he stood swooning with the perfect fire that burned in all his joints.

They lifted the canoe into the water, Gudrun took her place, and Gerald pushed off.

'Are you sure you don't hurt your hand, doing that?' she asked, solicitous. 'Because I could have done it *perfectly*.'

'I don't hurt myself,' he said in a low, soft voice, that caressed her with inexpressible beauty.

And she watched him as he sat near her, very near to her, in the stern of the canoe, his legs coming towards hers, his feet touching hers. And she paddled softly, lingeringly, longing for him to say something meaningful to her. But he remained silent.

'You like this, do you?' she said, in a gentle, solicitous voice.

He laughed shortly.

'There is a space between us,' he said, in the same low, unconscious voice, as if something were speaking out of him. And she was as if magically aware of their being balanced in separation, in the boat. She swooned with acute comprehension and pleasure.

'But I'm very near,' she said caressively, gaily.

'Yet distant, distant,' he said.

Again she was silent with pleasure, before she answered, speaking with a reedy, thrilled voice:

'Yet we cannot very well change, whilst we are on the water.' She caressed him subtly and strangely, having him completely at her mercy.

A dozen or more boats on the lake swung their rosy and moon-like lanterns low on the water, that reflected as from a fire. In the distance, the steamer twanged and thrummed and washed with her faintly-splashing paddles, trailing her strings of coloured lights, and occasionally lighting up the whole scene luridly with an effusion of fireworks, Roman candles and sheafs of stars and other simple effects, illuminating the surface of the water, and showing the boats creeping round, low down. Then the lovely darkness fell again, the lanterns and the little threaded lights glimmered softly, there was a muffled knocking of oars and a waving of music.

Gudrun paddled almost imperceptibly. Gerald could see, not far ahead, the rich blue and the rose globes of Ursula's lanterns swaying softly cheek to cheek as Birkin rowed, and iridescent, evanescent gleams chasing in the wake. He was aware, too, of his own delicately coloured lights casting their softness behind him.

Gudrun rested her paddle and looked round. The canoe lifted with the lightest ebbing of the water. Gerald's white knees were very near to her.

'Isn't it beautiful!' she said softly, as if reverently.

She looked at him, as he leaned back against the faint crystal of the lantern-light. She could see his face, although it was a pure shadow. But it was a piece of twilight. And her breast was keen with passion for him, he was so beautiful in his male stillness and mystery. It was a certain pure effluence of maleness, like an aroma from his softly, firmly moulded contours, a certain rich perfection of his presence, that touched her with an ecstasy, a thrill of pure intoxication. She loved to look at him. For the present she did not want to touch him, to know the further, satisfying substance of his living body. He was purely intangible, yet so near. Her hands lay on the paddle like slumber, she only wanted to see him, like a crystal shadow, to feel his essential presence.

'Yes,' he said vaguely. 'It is very beautiful.'

He was listening to the faint near sounds, the dropping of water-drops from the oar-blades, the slight drumming of the lanterns behind him, as they rubbed against one another, the occasional rustling of Gudrun's full skirt, an alien land noise. His mind was almost submerged, he was almost transfused, lapsed out for the first time in his life, into the things about him. For he always kept such a keen attentiveness, concentrated and unyielding in himself. Now he had let go, imperceptibly he was melting into oneness with the whole. It was like pure, perfect sleep, his first great sleep of life. He had been so insistent, so guarded, all his life. But here was sleep, and peace, and perfect lapsing out.

'Shall I row to the landing-stage?' asked Gudrun wistfully.

'Anywhere,' he answered. 'Let it drift.'

'Tell me then, if we are running into anything,' she replied, in that very quiet, toneless voice of sheer intimacy.

'The lights will show,' he said.

So they drifted almost motionless, in silence. He wanted silence, pure and whole. But she was uneasy yet for some word, for some assurance.

'Nobody will miss you?' she asked, anxious for some communication.

'Miss me?' he echoed. 'No! Why?'

'I wondered if anybody would be looking for you.'

'Why should they look for me?' And then he remembered his manners. 'But perhaps you want to get back,' he said, in a changed voice.

'No, I don't want to get back,' she replied. 'No, I assure you.'

'You're quite sure it's all right for you?'

'Perfectly all right.'

And again they were still. The launch twanged and hooted, somebody was singing. Then as if the night smashed, suddenly there was a great shout, a confusion of shouting, warring on the water, then the horrid noise of paddles reversed and churned violently.

Gerald sat up, and Gudrun looked at him in fear.

'Somebody in the water,' he said, angrily, and desperately, looking keenly across the dusk. 'Can you row up?'

'Where, to the launch?' asked Gudrun, in nervous panic.

'Yes.'

'You'll tell me if I don't steer straight,' she said, in nervous apprehension.

'You keep pretty level,' he said, and the canoe hastened forward.

The shouting and the noise continued, sounding horrid through the dusk, over the surface of the water.

'Wasn't this *bound* to happen?' said Gudrun, with heavy hateful irony. But he hardly heard, and she glanced over her shoulder to see her way. The half-dark waters were sprinkled with lovely bubbles of swaying lights, the launch did not look far off. She was rocking her lights in the early night. Gudrun rowed as hard as she could. But now that it was a serious matter, she seemed uncertain and clumsy in her stroke, it was difficult to paddle swiftly. She glanced at his face. He was looking fixedly into the darkness, very keen and alert and single in himself, instrumental. Her heart sank, she seemed to die a death. 'Of course,' she said to herself, 'nobody will be drowned. Of course they won't. It would be too extravagant and sensational.' But her heart was cold, because of his sharp impersonal face. It was as if he belonged naturally to dread and catastrophe, as if he were himself again.

Then there came a child's voice, a girl's high, piercing shriek:

'Di – Di – Di – Di – Oh Di – Oh Di – Oh Di!'

The blood ran cold in Gudrun's veins.

'It's Diana, is it,' muttered Gerald. 'The young monkey, she'd have to be up to some of her tricks.'

And he glanced again at the paddle, the boat was not going quickly enough for him. It made Gudrun almost helpless at the rowing, this nervous stress. She kept up with all her might. Still the voices were calling and answering.

'Where, where? There you are – that's it. Which? No – No-o-o. Damn it all, here, *here* –' Boats were hurrying from all directions to the scene, coloured lanterns could be seen waving close to the surface of the lake, reflections swaying after them in uneven haste. The steamer hooted again, for some unknown reason. Gudrun's boat was travelling quickly, the lanterns were swinging behind Gerald.

And then again came the child's high, screaming voice, with a note of weeping and impatience in it now:

'Di – Oh Di – Oh Di – Di – !'

It was a terrible sound, coming through the obscure air of the evening.

'You'd be better if you were in bed, Winnie,' Gerald muttered to himself.

He was stooping unlacing his shoes, pushing them off with the foot. Then he threw his soft hat into the bottom of the boat.

'You can't go into the water with your hurt hand,' said Gudrun, panting, in a low voice of horror.

'What? It won't hurt.'

He had struggled out of his jacket, and had dropped it between his feet. He sat bare-headed, in all white now. He felt the belt at his waist. They were nearing the launch, which stood still big above them, her myriad lamps making lovely darts, and sinuous running tongues of ugly red and green and yellow light on the lustrous dark water, under the shadow.

'Oh get her out! Oh Di, *darling*! Oh get her out! Oh Daddy, Oh Daddy!' moaned the child's voice, in distraction. Somebody was in the water, with a lifebelt. Two boats paddled near, their lanterns swinging ineffectually, the boats nosing round.

'Hi there – Rockley! – hi there!'

'Mr Gerald!' came the captain's terrified voice. 'Miss Diana's in the water.'

'Anybody gone in for her?' came Gerald's sharp voice.

'Young Doctor Brindell, sir.'

'Where?'

'Can't see no signs of them, sir. Everybody's looking, but there's nothing so far.'

There was a moment's ominous pause.

'Where did she go in?'

'I think – about where that boat is,' came the uncertain answer, 'that one with red and green lights.'

'Row there,' said Gerald quietly to Gudrun.

'Get her out, Gerald, oh get her out,' the child's voice was crying anxiously. He took no heed.

'Lean back that way,' said Gerald to Gudrun, as he stood up in the frail boat. 'She won't upset.'

In another moment, he had dropped clean down, soft and plumb, into the water. Gudrun was swaying violently in her boat, the agitated water shook with transient lights, she realized that it was faintly moonlight, and that he was gone. So it was possible to be gone. A terrible sense of fatality robbed her of all feeling and thought. She knew he was gone out of the world, there was merely the same world, and absence, his absence. The night seemed large and vacuous. Lanterns swayed here and there, people were talking in an undertone on the launch and in the boats. She could hear Winifred moaning: *'Oh do find her Gerald, do find her,'* and someone trying to comfort the child. Gudrun paddled aimlessly here and there. The terrible, massive, cold, boundless surface of the water terrified her beyond words. Would he never come back? She felt she must jump into the water too, to know the horror also.

She started, hearing someone say: 'There he is.' She saw the movement of his swimming, like a water-rat. And she rowed involuntarily to him. But he was near another boat, a bigger one. Still she rowed towards him. She must be very near. She saw him – he looked like a seal. He looked like a seal as he took hold of the side of the boat. His fair hair was washed down on his round head, his face seemed to glisten suavely. She could hear him panting.

Then he clambered into the boat. Oh, and the beauty of the subjection of his loins, white and dimly luminous as he climbed over the side of the boat, made her want to die, to die. The beauty of his dim and luminous loins as he climbed into the boat, his back rounded and soft – ah, this was too much for her, too final a vision. She knew it, and it was fatal. The terrible hopelessness of fate, and of beauty, such beauty!

He was not like a man to her, he was an incarnation, a great phase of life. She saw him press the water out of his face, and look at the bandage on his hand. And she knew it was all no good, and that she would never go beyond him, he was the final approximation of life to her.

'Put the lights out, we shall see better,' came his voice, sudden and mechanical and belonging to the world of man. She could scarcely believe there was a world of man. She leaned round and blew out her lanterns. They were difficult to blow out. Everywhere the lights were gone save the coloured points on the sides of the launch. The bluey-grey, early night spread level around, the moon was overhead, there were shadows of boats here and there.

Again there was a splash, and he was gone under. Gudrun sat, sick at heart, frightened of the great, level surface of the water, so heavy and deadly. She was so alone, with the level, unliving field of the water stretching beneath her. It was not a good isolation, it was a terrible, cold separation of suspense. She was suspended upon the surface of the insidious reality until such time as she also should disappear beneath it.

Then she knew, by a stirring of voices, that he had climbed out again, into a boat. She sat wanting connection with him. Strenuously she claimed her connection with him, across the invisible space of the water. But round her heart was an isolation unbearable, through which nothing would penetrate.

'Take the launch in. It's no use keeping her there. Get lines for the dragging,' came the decisive, instrumental voice, that was full of the sound of the world.

The launch began gradually to beat the waters.

'Gerald! Gerald!' came the wild crying voice of Winifred. He did not answer. Slowly the launch drifted round in a pathetic, clumsy circle, and slunk away to the land, retreating into the dimness. The wash of her paddles grew duller. Gudrun rocked in her light boat, and dipped the paddle automatically to steady herself.

'Gudrun?' called Ursula's voice.

'Ursula!'

The boats of the two sisters pulled together.

'Where is Gerald?' said Gudrun.

'He's dived again,' said Ursula plaintively. 'And I know he ought not, with his hurt hand and everything.'

'I'll take him in home this time,' said Birkin.

The boats swayed again from the wash of the steamer. Gudrun and Ursula kept a look-out for Gerald.

'There he is!' cried Ursula, who had the sharpest eyes. He had not been long under. Birkin pulled towards him, Gudrun followed. He swam slowly, and caught hold of the boat with his wounded hand. It slipped, and he sank back.

'Why don't you help him?' cried Ursula sharply.

He came again, and Birkin leaned to help him into the boat. Gudrun again watched Gerald climb out of the water, but this time slowly, heavily, with the blind clambering motions of an amphibious beast, clumsy. Again the moon shone with faint luminosity on his white wet figure, on the stooping back and the rounded loins. But it looked defeated now, his body, it clambered and fell with slow clumsiness. He was breathing hoarsely too, like an animal that is suffering. He sat slack and motionless in the boat, his head blunt and blind like a seal's, his whole appearance inhuman, unknowing. Gudrun shuddered as she mechanically followed his boat. Birkin rowed without speaking to the landing-stage.

'Where are you going?' Gerald asked suddenly, as if just waking up.

'Home,' said Birkin.

'Oh no!' said Gerald imperiously. 'We can't go home while they're in the water. Turn back again, I'm going to find them.' The women were frightened, his voice was so imperative and dangerous, almost mad, not to be opposed.

'No,' said Birkin. 'You can't.' There was a strange fluid compulsion in his voice. Gerald was silent in a battle of wills. It was as if he would kill the other man. But Birkin rowed evenly and/ unswerving, with an inhuman inevitability.

'Why should you interfere?' said Gerald, in hate.

Birkin did not answer. He rowed towards the land. And Gerald sat mute, like a dumb beast, panting, his teeth chattering, his arms inert, his head like a seal's head.

They came to the landing-stage. Wet and naked looking, Gerald climbed up the few steps. There stood his father, in the night.

'Father!' he said.

'Yes, my boy? Go home and get those things off.'

'We shan't save them, father,' said Gerald.

'There's hope yet, my boy.'

'I'm afraid not. There's no knowing where they are. You can't find them. And there's a current, as cold as hell.'

'We'll let the water out,' said the father. 'Go home you and look to yourself. See that he's looked after, Rupert,' he added in a neutral voice.

'Well, father, I'm sorry. I'm sorry. I'm afraid it's my fault. But it can't be helped; I've done what I could for the moment. I could go on diving, of course – not much, though – and not much use –'

He moved away barefoot, on the planks of the platform. Then he trod on something sharp.

'Of course, you've got no shoes on,' said Birkin.

'His shoes are here!' cried Gudrun from below. She was making fast her boat.

Gerald waited for them to be brought to him. Gudrun came with them. He pulled them on his feet.

'If you once die,' he said, 'then when it's over, it's finished. Why come to life again? There's room under that water there for thousands.'

'Two is enough,' she said, murmuring.

He dragged on his second shoe. He was shivering violently, and his jaw shook as he spoke.

'That's true,' he said, 'maybe. But it's curious how much room there seems, a whole universe under there; and as cold as hell, you're as helpless as if your head was cut off.' He could scarcely speak, he shook so violently. 'There's one thing about our family, you know,' he continued. 'Once anything goes wrong, it can never be put right again – not with us. I've noticed it all my life – you can't put a thing right, once it has gone wrong.'

They were walking across the high-road to the house.

'And do you know, when you are down there, it is so cold, actually, and so endless, so different really from what it is on top, so endless – you wonder how it is so many are alive, why we're up here. Are you going? I shall see you again, shan't I? Good night, and thank you. Thank you very much.'

The two girls waited a while, to see if there were any hope. The moon shone clearly overhead, with almost impertinent brightness, the small dark boats clustered on the water, there were voices and subdued shouts. But it was all to no purpose. Gudrun went home when Birkin returned.

He was commissioned to open the sluice that let out the water from the lake, which was pierced at one end, near the high-road, thus serving as a reservoir to supply with water the distant mines, in case of necessity. 'Come with me,' he said to Ursula, 'and then I will walk home with you, when I've done this.'

He called at the water-keeper's cottage and took the key of the sluice. They went through a little gate from the high-road, to the head of the water, where there was a great stone basin which received the overflow, and a flight of stone steps descended into the depths of the water itself. At the head of the steps was the lock of the sluice-gate.

The night was silver-grey and perfect, save for the scattered restless sound of voices. The grey sheen of the moonlight caught the stretch of water, dark boats plashed and moved. But Ursula's mind ceased to be receptive, everything was unimportant and unreal.

Birkin fixed the iron handle of the sluice, and turned it with a wrench. The cogs began slowly to rise. He turned and turned, like a slave, his white figure became distinct. Ursula looked away. She could not bear to see him winding heavily and laboriously, bending and rising mechanically like a slave, turning the handle.

Then, a real shock to her, there came a loud splashing of water from out of the dark, tree-filled hollow beyond the road, a splashing that deepened rapidly to a harsh roar, and then became a heavy, booming noise of a great body of water falling solidly all the time. It occupied the whole of the night, this great steady booming of water, everything was drowned within it, drowned and lost. Ursula seemed to have to struggle for her life. She put her hands over her ears, and looked at the high bland moon.

'Can't we go now?' she cried to Birkin, who was watching the water on the steps, to see if it would get any lower. It seemed to fascinate him. He looked at her and nodded.

The little dark boats had moved nearer, people were crowding curiously along the hedge by the high-road, to see what was to be seen. Birkin and Ursula went to the cottage with the key, then turned their backs on the lake. She was in great haste. She could not bear the terrible crushing boom of the escaping water.

'Do you think they are dead?' she cried in a high voice, to make herself heard.

'Yes,' he replied.

'Isn't it horrible!'

He paid no heed. They walked up the hill, farther and farther away from the noise.

'Do you mind very much?' she asked him.

'I don't mind about the dead,' he said, 'once they are dead. The worst of it is, they cling on to the living, and won't let go!'

She pondered for a time.

'Yes,' she said. 'The *fact* of death doesn't really seem to matter much, does it?'

'No,' he said. 'What does it matter if Diana Crich is alive or dead?'

'Doesn't it?' she said, shocked.

'No, why should it? Better she were dead – she'll be much more real. She'll be positive in death. In life she was a fretting, negated thing.'

'You are rather horrible,' murmured Ursula.

'No! I'd rather Diana Crich were dead. Her living somehow was all wrong. As for the young man, poor devil – he'll find his way out quickly instead of slowly. Death is all right – nothing better.'

'Yet you don't want to die,' she challenged him.

He was silent for a time. Then he said, in a voice that was frightening to her in its change:

'I should like to be through with it – I should like to be through with the death process.'

'And aren't you?' asked Ursula nervously.

They walked on for some way in silence, under the trees. Then he said slowly, as if afraid:

'There is life which belongs to death, and there is life which isn't death. One is tired of the life that belongs to death – our kind of life. But whether it is finished, God knows. I want love that is like sleep, like being born again, vulnerable as a baby that just comes into the world.'

Ursula listened, half attentive, half avoiding what he said. She seemed to catch the drift of his statement, and then she drew away. She wanted to hear, but she did not want to be implicated. She was reluctant to yield there, where he wanted her, to yield as it were her very identity.

'Why should love be like sleep?' she asked sadly.

'I don't know. So that it is like death – I *do* want to die from this life – and yet it is more than life itself. One is delivered over like a naked infant from the womb, all the old defences, and the old body gone, and new air around one, that has never been breathed before.'

She listened, making out what he said. She knew, as well as he knew, that words themselves do not convey meaning, that they are but a gesture we make, a dumb show like any other. And she seemed to feel his gesture through her blood, and she drew back, even though her desire sent her forward.

'But,' she said gravely, 'didn't you say you wanted something that was *not* love – something beyond love?'

He turned in confusion. There was always confusion in speech. Yet it must be spoken. Whichever way one moved, if one were to move forwards, one must break a way through. And to know, to give utterance, was to break a way through the walls of the prison as the infant in labour strives through the walls of the womb. There is no new movement now, without the breaking through of the old body, deliberately, in knowledge, in the struggle to get out.

'I don't want love,' he said. 'I don't want to know you. I want to be gone out of myself, and you to be lost to yourself, so we are found different. One shouldn't talk when one is tired and wretched. One Hamletizes, and it seems a lie. Only believe me when I show you a bit of healthy pride and insouciance. I hate myself serious.'

'Why shouldn't you be serious?' she said.

He thought for a minute, then he said sulkily:

'I don't know.' Then they walked on in silence, at outs. He was vague and lost.

'Isn't it strange,' she said, suddenly putting her hand on his arm, with a loving impulse, 'how we always talk like this! I suppose we do love each other, in some way.'

'Oh yes,' he said; 'too much.'

She laughed almost gaily.

'You'd have to have it your own way, wouldn't you?' she teased. 'You could never take it on trust.'

He changed, laughed softly, and turned and took her in his arms, in the middle of the road.

'Yes,' he said softly.

And he kissed her face and brow, slowly, gently, with a sort of delicate happiness which surprised her extremely, and to which she could not respond. They were soft, blind kisses, perfect in their stillness. Yes she held back from them. It was like strange moths, very soft and silent, settling on her from the darkness of her soul. She was uneasy. She drew away.

'Isn't somebody coming?' she said.

So they looked down the dark road, then set off again walking towards Beldover. Then suddenly, to show him she was no shallow prude, she stopped and held him tight, hard against her, and covered his face with hard, fierce kisses of passion. In spite of his otherness, the old blood beat up in him.

'Not this, not this,' he whimpered to himself, as the first perfect mood of softness and sleep-loveliness ebbed back away from the rushing of passion that came up to his limbs and over his face as she drew him. And soon he was a perfect hard flame of passionate desire for her. Yet in the small core of the flame was an unyielding anguish of another thing. But this also was lost; he only wanted her, with an extreme desire that seemed inevitable as death, beyond question.

Then, satisfied and shattered, fulfilled and destroyed, he went home away from her, drifting vaguely through the darkness, lapsed into the old fire of burning passion. Far away, far away, there seemed to be a small lament in the darkness. But what did it matter? What did it matter, what did anything matter save this ultimate and triumphant experience of physical passion, that had blazed up anew like a new spell of life. 'I was becoming quite dead-alive, nothing but a word-bag,' he said in triumph, scorning his other self. Yet somewhere far off and small, the other hovered.

The men were still dragging the lake when he got back. He stood on the bank and heard Gerald's voice. The voice was still booming in the night, the moon was fair, the hills beyond were elusive. The lake was sinking. There came the raw smell of the banks, in the night air.

Up at Shortlands there were lights in the windows, as if nobody had gone to bed. On the landing-stage was the old doctor, the father of the young man who was lost. He stood quite silent, waiting. Birkin also stood and watched, Gerald came up in a boat.

'You still here, Rupert?' he said. 'We can't get them. The bottom slopes, you know, very steep. The water lies between two very sharp slopes, with little branch valleys, and God knows where the drift will take you. It isn't as if it was a level bottom. You never know where you are, with the dragging.'

'Is there any need for you to be working?' said Birkin. 'Wouldn't it be much better if you went to bed?'

'To bed! Good God, do you think I should sleep? We'll find 'em, before I go away from here.'

'But the men would find them just the same without you – why should you insist?'

Gerald looked up at him. Then he put his hands affectionately on Birkin's shoulder, saying:

'Don't you bother about me, Rupert. If there's anybody's health to think about, it's yours, not mine. How do you feel yourself?'

'Very well. But you, you spoil your own chance of life – you waste your best self.'

Gerald was silent for a moment. Then he said:

'Waste it? What else is there to do with it?'

'But leave this, won't you? You force yourself into horrors, and put a mill-stone of beastly memories round your neck. Come away now.'

'A mill-stone of beastly memories!' Gerald repeated. Then he put his hand again affectionately on Birkin's shoulder. 'God, you've got such a telling way of putting things, Rupert, you have.'

Birkin's heart sank. He was irritated and weary of having a telling way of putting things.

'Won't you leave it? Come over to my place' – he urged as one urges a drunken man.

'No,' said Gerald coaxingly, his arm across the other man's shoulder. 'Thanks very much, Rupert – I shall be glad to come tomorrow, if that'll do. You understand, don't you? I want to see this job through. But I'll come tomorrow, right enough. Oh, I'd rather come and have a chat with you than – than do anything else, I verily believe. Yes, I would. You mean a lot to me, Rupert, more than you know.'

'What do I mean, more than I know?' asked Birkin irritably. He was acutely aware of Gerald's hand on his shoulder. And he did not want this altercation. He wanted the other man to come out of the ugly misery.

'I'll tell you another time,' said Gerald coaxingly.

'Come along with me now – I want you to come,' said Birkin.

There was a pause, intense and real. Birkin wondered why his own heart beat so heavily. Then Gerald's fingers gripped hard and communicative into Birkin's shoulder, as he said:

'No, I'll see this job through, Rupert. Thank you – I know what you mean. We're all right, you know, you and me.'

'I may be all right, but I'm not sure you're not, mucking about here,' said Birkin. And he went away.

The bodies of the dead were not recovered till towards dawn. Diana had her arms tight round the neck of the young man, choking him.

'She killed him,' said Gerald.

The moon sloped down the sky and sank at last. The lake was sunk to quarter size, it had horrible raw banks of clay, that smelled of raw rottenish water. Dawn roused faintly behind the eastern hill. The water still boomed through the sluice.

As the birds were whistling for the first morning, and the hills at the back of the desolate lake stood radiant with the new mists, there was a straggling procession up to Shortlands, men bearing the bodies on a stretcher, Gerald going beside them, the two grey-bearded fathers following in silence. Indoors the family was all sitting up, waiting. Somebody must go to tell the mother, in her room. The doctor in secret struggled to bring back his son, till he himself was exhausted.

Over all the outlying district was a hush of dreadful excitement on that Sunday morning. The colliery people felt as if this catastrophe had happened directly to themselves, indeed they were more shocked and frightened than if their own men had been killed. Such a tragedy in Shortlands, the high home of the district! One of the young mistresses, persisting in dancing on the cabin roof of the launch, wilful young madam, drowned in the midst of the festival, with the young doctor! Everywhere on the Sunday morning, the colliers wandered about, discussing the calamity. At all the Sunday dinners of the people, there seemed a strange presence. It was as if the angel of death were very near, there was a sense of the supernatural in the air. The men had excited, startled faces, the women looked solemn, some of them had been crying. The children enjoyed the excitement at first. There was an intensity in the air, almost magical. Did all enjoy it? Did all enjoy the thrill?

Gudrun had wild ideas of rushing to comfort Gerald. She was thinking all the time of the perfect comforting, reassuring thing to say to him. She was shocked and frightened, but she put that away, thinking of how she should deport herself with Gerald: act her part. That was the real thrill: how she should act her part.

Ursula was deeply and passionately in love with Birkin, and she was capable of nothing. She was perfectly callous about all the talk of the accident, but her estranged air looked like trouble. She merely sat by herself, whenever she could, and longed to see him again. She wanted him to come to the house – she would not have it otherwise, he must come at once. She was waiting for him. She stayed indoors all day, waiting for him to knock at the door. Every minute, she glanced automatically at the window. He would be there.

15

SUNDAY EVENING

As the day wore on, the life-blood seemed to ebb away from Ursula, and within the emptiness a heavy despair gathered. Her passion seemed to bleed to death, and there was nothing. She sat suspended in a state of complete nullity, harder to bear than death.

'Unless something happens,' she said to herself, in the perfect lucidity of final suffering, 'I shall die. I am at the end of my line of life.'

She sat crushed and obliterated in a darkness that was the border of death. She realized how all her life she had been drawing nearer and nearer to this brink, where there was no beyond, from which one had to leap like Sappho into the unknown. The knowledge of the imminence of death was like a drug. Darkly, without thinking at all, she knew that she was near to death. She had travelled all her life along the line of fulfilment, and it was nearly concluded. She knew all she had to know, she had experienced all she had to experience, she was fulfilled in a kind of bitter ripeness, there remained only to fall from the tree into death. And one must fulfil one's development to the end, must carry the adventure to its conclusion. And the next step was over the border into death. So it was then! There was a certain peace in the knowledge.

After all, when one was fulfilled, one was happiest in falling into death, as a bitter fruit plunges in its ripeness downwards. Death is a great consummation, a consummating experience. It is a development from life. That we know, while we are yet living. What then need we think for further? One can never see beyond the consummation. It is enough that death is a great and conclusive experience. Why should we ask what comes after the experience, when the experience is still unknown to us? Let us die, since the great experience is the one that follows now upon all the rest, death, which is the next great crisis in front of which we have arrived. If we wait, if we baulk the issue, we do but hang about the gates in undignified uneasiness. There it is, in front of us, as in front of Sappho, the illimitable space. Thereinto goes the journey. Have we not the courage to go on with our journey, must we cry 'I daren't'? On ahead we will go, into death, and whatever death may mean. If a man can see the next step to be taken, why should he fear the next but one? Why ask about the next but one? Of the next step we are certain. It is the step into death.

'I shall die – I shall quickly die,' said Ursula to herself, clear as if in a trance, clear, calm, and certain beyond human certainty. But somewhere behind, in the twilight, there was a bitter weeping and a hopelessness. That must not be attended to. One must go where the unfaltering spirit goes, there must be no baulking the issue, because of fear. No baulking the issue, no listening to the lesser voices. If the deepest desire be now, to go on into the unknown of death, shall one forfeit the deepest truth for one more shallow?

'Then let it end,' she said to herself. It was a decision. It was not a question of taking one's life – she would *never* kill herself, that was repulsive and violent. It was a question of *knowing* the next step. And the next step led into the space of death. Did it? – or was there –'

Her thoughts drifted into unconsciousness, she sat as if asleep beside the fire. And then the thought came back. The space of death! Could she give herself to it? Ah, yes – it was a sleep. She had had enough. So long she had held out and resisted. Now was the time to relinquish, not to resist any more.

In a kind of spiritual trance, she yielded, she gave way, and all was dark. She could feel, within the darkness, the terrible assertion of her body, the unutterable anguish of dissolution, the only anguish that is too much, the far-off awful nausea of dissolution set in within the body.

'Does the body correspond so immediately with the spirit?' she asked herself. And she knew, with the clarity of ultimate knowledge, that the body is only one of the manifestations of the spirit, the transmutation of the integral spirit is the transmutation of the physical body as well. 'Unless I set my will, unless I absolve myself from the rhythm of life, fix myself and remain static, cut off from living, absolved within my own will. But better die than live mechanically a life that is a repetition of repetitions. To die is to move on with the invisible. To die is also a joy, a joy of submitting to that which is greater than the known; namely, the pure unknown. That is a joy. But to live mechanized and cut off within the motion of the will, to live as an entity absolved from the unknown, that is shameful and ignominious. There is no ignominy in death. There is complete ignominy in an unreplenished, mechanized life. Life indeed may be ignominious, shameful to the soul. But death is never a shame. Death itself, like the illimitable space, is beyond our sullying.'

Tomorrow was Monday. Monday, the beginning of another school-week! Another shameful, barren school-week, mere routine and mechanical activity. Was not the adventure of death infinitely preferable? Was not death infinitely more lovely and noble than such a life? A life of barren routine, without inner meaning, without any real significance. How sordid life was, how it was a terrible shame to the soul, to live now! How much cleaner and more dignified to be dead! One could not bear any more of this shame of sordid routine and mechanical nullity. One might come to fruit in death. She had had enough. For where was life to be found? No flowers grow upon busy machinery, there is no sky to a routine, there is no space to a rotary motion.

And all life was a rotary motion, mechanized, cut off from reality. There was nothing to look for from life – it was the same in all countries and all peoples. The only window was death. One could look out on to the great dark sky of death with emotion, as one had looked out of the class-room window as a child, and seen perfect freedom in the outside. Now one was not a child, and one knew that the soul was a prisoner within this sordid vast edifice of life, and there was no escape, save in death.

But what a joy! What a gladness to think that whatever humanity did, it could not seize hold of the kingdom of death, to nullify that. The sea they turned into a murderous alley and a soiled road of commerce, disputed like the dirty land of a city every inch of it. The air they claimed too, shared it up, parcelled it out to certain owners, they trespassed in the air to fight for it. Everything was gone, walled in, with spikes on top of the walls, and one must ignominiously creep between the spiky walls through a labyrinth of life.

But the great dark, illimitable kingdom of death, there humanity was put to scorn. So much they could do upon earth, the multifarious little gods that they were. But the kingdom of death put them all to scorn, they dwindled into their true vulgar silliness in face of it.

How beautiful, how grand and perfect death was, how good to look forward to. There one would wash off all the lies and ignominy and dirt that had been put upon one here, a perfect bath of cleanness and glad refreshment, and go unknown, unquestioned, unabased. After all, one was rich, if only in the promise of perfect death. It was a gladness above all, that this remained to look forward to, the pure inhuman otherness of death.

Whatever life might be, it could not take away death, the inhuman transcendent death. Oh, let us ask no question of it, what it is or is not. To know is human, and in death we do not know, we are not human. And the joy of this compensates for all the bitterness of knowledge and the sordidness of our humanity. In death we shall not be human, and we shall not know. The promise of this is our heritage, we look forward like heirs to their majority.

Ursula sat quite still and quite forgotten, alone by the fire in the drawing-room. The children were playing in the kitchen, all the others were gone to church. And she was gone into the ultimate darkness of her own soul.

She was startled by hearing the bell ring, away in the kitchen, the children came scudding along the passage in delicious alarm.

'Ursula, there's somebody.'

'I know. Don't be silly,' she replied. She too was startled, almost frightened. She dared hardly go to the door.

Birkin stood on the threshold, his rain-coat turned up to his ears. He had come now, now she was gone far away. She was aware of the rainy night behind him.

'Oh, is it you?' she said.

'I am glad you are at home,' he said in a low voice, entering the house.

'They are all gone to church.'

He took off his coat and hung it up. The children were peeping at him round the corner.

'Go and get undressed now, Billy and Dora,' said Ursula. 'Mother will be back soon, and she'll be disappointed if you're not in bed.'

The children, in a sudden angelic mood, retired without a word. Birkin and Ursula went into the drawing-room. The fire burned low. He looked at her and wondered at the luminous delicacy of her beauty, and the wide shining of her eyes. He watched from a distance, with wonder in his heart, she seemed transfigured with light.

'What have you been doing all day?' he asked her.

'Only sitting about,' she said.

He looked at her. There was a change in her. But she was separate from him. She remained apart, in a kind of brightness. They both sat silent in the soft light of the lamp. He felt he ought to go away again, he ought not to have come. Still he did not gather enough resolution to move. But he was *de trop*, her mood was absent and separate.

Then there came the voices of the two children calling shyly outside the door, softly, with self-excited timidity:

'Ursula! Ursula!'

She rose and opened the door. On the threshold stood the two children in their long nightgowns, with wide-eyed, angelic faces. They were being very good for the moment, playing the rôle perfectly of two obedient children.

'Shall you take us to bed!' said Billy, in a loud whisper.

'Why, you *are* angels tonight,' she said softly. 'Won't you come and say good night to Mr Birkin?'

The children merged shyly into the room, on bare feet. Billy's face was wide and grinning, but there was a great solemnity of being good in his round blue eyes. Dora, peeping from the floss of her fair hair, hung back like some tiny Dryad, that has no soul.

'Will you say good night to me?' asked Birkin, in a voice that was strangely soft and smooth. Dora drifted away at once, like a leaf lifted on a breath of wind. But Billy went softly forward, slow and willing, lifting his pinched-up mouth implicitly to be kissed. Ursula watched the full, gathered lips of the man gently touch those of the boy, so gently. Then Birkin lifted his fingers and touched the boy's round, confiding cheek, with a faint touch of love. Neither spoke. Billy seemed angelic like a cherub boy, or like an acolyte, Birkin was a tall, grave angel looking down to him.

'Are you going to be kissed?' Ursula broke in, speaking to the little girl. But Dora edged away like a tiny Dryad that will not be touched.

'Won't you say good night to Mr Birkin? Go, he's waiting for you,' said Ursula. But the girl-child only made a little motion away from him.

'Silly Dora, silly Dora!' said Ursula.

Birkin felt some mistrust and antagonism in the small child. He could not understand it.

'Come then,' said Ursula. 'Let us go before mother comes.'

'Who'll hear us say our prayers?' asked Billy anxiously.

'Whom you like.'

'Won't you?'

'Yes, I will.'

'Ursula?'

'Well, Billy?'

'Is it *whom* you like?'

'That's it.'

'Well, what is *whom*?'

'It's the accusative of who.'

There was a moment's contemplative silence, then the confiding:

'Is it?'

Birkin smiled to himself as he sat by the fire. When Ursula came down he sat motionless, with his arms on his knees. She saw him, how he was motionless and ageless, like some crouching idol, some image of a deathly religion. He looked round at her, and his face, very pale and unreal, seemed to gleam with a whiteness almost phosphorescent.

'Don't you feel well?' she asked, in indefinable repulsion.

'I hadn't thought about it.'

'But don't you know without thinking about it?'

He looked at her, his eyes dark and swift, and he saw her revulsion. He did not answer her question.

'Don't you know whether you are unwell or not, without thinking about it?' she persisted.

'Not always,' he said coldly.

'But don't you think that's very wicked?'

'Wicked?'

'Yes. I think it's *criminal* to have so little connection with your own body that you don't even know when you are ill.'

He looked at her darkly.

'Yes,' he said.

'Why don't you stay in bed when you are seedy? You look perfectly ghastly.'

'Offensively so?' he asked ironically.

'Yes, quite offensive. Quite repelling.'

'Ah! Well, that's unfortunate.'

'And it's raining, and it's a horrible night. Really, you shouldn't be forgiven for treating your body like it – you *ought* to suffer, a man who takes as little notice of his body as that.'

'– takes as little notice of his body as that,' he echoed mechanically.

This cut her short, and there was silence.

The others came in from church, and the two had the girls to face, then the mother and Gudrun, and then the father and the boy.

'Good evening,' said Brangwen, faintly surprised. 'Came to see me, did you?'

'No,' said Birkin, 'not about anything in particular, that is. The day was dismal, and I thought you wouldn't mind if I called in.'

'It *has* been a depressing day,' said Mrs Brangwen sympathetically. At that moment the voices of the children were heard calling from upstairs: 'Mother! Mother!' She lifted her face and answered mildly into the distance: 'I shall come up to you in a minute, Doysie.' Then to Birkin: 'There is nothing fresh at Shortlands, I suppose? Ah,' she sighed, 'no, poor things, I should think not.'

'You've been over there today, I suppose?' asked the father.

'Gerald came round to tea with me, and I walked back with him. The house is over-excited and unwholesome, I thought.'

'I should think they were people who hadn't much restraint,' said Gudrun.

'Or too much,' Birkin answered.

'Oh yes, I'm sure,' said Gudrun, almost vindictively, 'one or the other.'

'They all feel they ought to behave in some unnatural fashion,' said Birkin. 'When people are in grief, they would do better to cover their faces and keep in retirement, as in the old days.'

'Certainly!' cried Gudrun, flushed and inflammable. 'What can be worse

than this public grief – what is more horrible, more false! If *grief* is not private,
and hidden, what is?'

'Exactly,' he said. 'I felt ashamed when I was there and they were all going
about in a lugubrious false way, feeling they must not be natural or ordinary.'

'Well –' said Mrs Brangwen, offended at this criticism, 'it isn't so easy to
bear a trouble like that.'

And she went upstairs to the children

He remained only a few minutes longer, then took his leave. When he was
gone Ursula felt such a poignant hatred of him, that all her brain seemed
turned into a sharp crystal of fine hatred. Her whole nature seemed sharpened
and intensified into a pure dart of hate. She could not imagine what it was. It
merely took hold of her, the most poignant and ultimate hatred, pure and
clear and beyond thought. She could not think of it at all, she was translated
beyond herself. It was like a possession. She felt she was possessed. And for
several days she went about possessed by this exquisite force of hatred against
him. It surpassed anything she had ever known before, it seemed to throw her
out of the world into some terrible region where nothing of her old life held
good. She was quite lost and dazed, really dead to her own life.

It was so completely incomprehensible and irrational. She did not know
why she hated him, her hate was quite abstract. She had only realized with a
shock that stunned her, that she was overcome by this pure transportation.
He was the enemy, fine as a diamond, and as hard and jewel-like, the
quintessence of all that was inimical.

She thought of his face, white and purely wrought, and of his eyes that had
such a dark, constant will of assertion, and she touched her own forehead, to
feel if she were mad, she was so transfigured in white flame of essential hate.

It was not temporal, her hatred, she did not hate him for this or for that; she
did not want to do anything to him, to have any connection with him. Her
relation was ultimate and utterly beyond words, the hate was so pure and
gem-like. It was as if he were a beam of essential enmity, a beam of light that
did not only destroy her, but denied her altogether, revoked her whole world.
She saw him as a clear stroke of uttermost contradiction, a strange gem-like
being whose existence defined her own non-existence. When she heard he was
ill again, her hatred only intensified itself a few degrees, if that were possible.
It stunned her and annihilated her, but she could not escape it. She could not
escape this transfiguration of hatred that had come upon her.

16

MAN TO MAN

He lay sick and unmoved, in pure opposition to everything. He knew how
near to breaking was the vessel that held his life. He knew also how strong and
durable it was. And he did not care. Better a thousand times take one's chance
with death, than accept a life one did not want. But best of all to persist and
persist and persist for ever, till one were satisfied in life.

He knew that Ursula was referred back to him. He knew his life rested with
her. But he would rather not live than accept the love she proffered. The old

way of love seemed a dreadful bondage, a sort of conscription. What it was in him he did not know, but the thought of love, marriage, and children, and a life lived together, in the horrible privacy of domestic and connubial satisfaction, was repulsive. He wanted something clearer, more open, cooler, as it were. The hot narrow intimacy between man and wife was abhorrent. The way they shut their doors, these married people, and shut themselves into their own exclusive alliance with each other, even in love, disgusted him. It was a whole community of mistrustful couples insulated in private houses or private rooms, always in couples, and no further life, no further immediate, no disinterested relationship admitted: a kaleidoscope of couples, disjoined, separatist, meaningless entities of married couples. True, he hated promiscuity even worse than marriage, and a liaison was only another kind of coupling, reactionary from the legal marriage. Reaction was a greater bore than action.

On the whole, he hated sex, it was such a limitation. It was sex that turned a man into a broken half of a couple, the woman into the other broken half. And he wanted to be single in himself, the woman single in herself. He wanted sex to revert to the level of the other appetites, to be regarded as a functional process, not as a fulfilment. He believed in sex marriage. But beyond this, he wanted a further conjunction, where man had being and woman had being, two pure beings, each constituting the freedom of the other, balancing each other like two poles of one force, like two angels, or two demons.

He wanted so much to be free, not under the compulsion of any need for unification, or tortured by unsatisfied desire. Desire and aspiration should find their object without all this torture, as now, in a world of plenty of water, simple thirst is inconsiderable, satisfied almost unconsciously. And he wanted to be with Ursula as free as with himself, single and clear and cool, yet balanced, polarized with her. The merging, the clutching, the mingling of love was become madly abhorrent to him.

But it seemed to him, woman was always so horrible and clutching, she had such a lust for possession, a greed of self-importance in love. She wanted to have, to own, to control, to be dominant. Everything must be referred back to her, to Woman, the Great Mother of everything, out of whom proceeded everything and to whom everything must finally be rendered up.

It filled him with almost insane fury, this calm assumption of the Magna Mater, that all was hers, because she had borne it. Man was hers because she had borne him. A Mater Dolorosa, she had borne him, a Magna Mater, she now claimed him again, soul and body, sex, meaning, and all. He had a horror of the Magna Mater, she was detestable.

She was on a very high horse again was woman, the Great Mother. Did he not know it in Hermione. Hermione, the humble, the subservient, what was she all the while but the Mater Dolorosa, in her subservience, claiming with horrible, insidious arrogance and female tyranny, her own again, claiming back the man she had borne in suffering. By her very suffering and humility she bound her son with chains, she held him her everlasting prisoner.

And Ursula, Ursula was the same – or the inverse. She too was the awful, arrogant queen of life, as if she were a queen bee on whom all the rest depended. He saw the yellow flare in her eyes, he knew the unthinkable overweening assumption of primacy in her. She was unconscious of it herself. She was only too ready to knock her head on the ground before a man. But this was only when she was so certain of her man, that she could worship him as a woman worships her own infant, with a worship of perfect possession.

It was intolerable, this possession at the hands of woman. Always a man must be considered as the broken-off fragment of a woman, and the sex was the still aching scar of the laceration. Man must be added on to a woman, before he had any real place or wholeness.

And why? Why should we consider ourselves, men and women, as broken fragments of one whole? It is not true. We are not broken fragments of one whole. Rather we are the singling away into purity and clear being, of things that were mixed. Rather the sex is that which remains in us of the mixed, the unresolved. And passion is the further separating of this mixture, that which is manly being taken into the being of the man, that which is womanly passing to the woman, till the two are clear and whole as angels, the admixture of sex in the highest sense surpassed, leaving two single beings constellated together like two stars.

In the old age, before sex was, we were mixed, each one a mixture. The process of singling into individuality resulted into the great polarization of sex. The womanly drew to one side, the manly to the other. But the separation was imperfect even then. And so our world-cycle passes. There is now to come the new day, when we are beings each of us, fulfilled in difference. The man is pure man, the woman pure woman, they are perfectly polarized. But there is no longer any of the horrible merging, mingling self-abnegation of love. There is only the pure duality of polarization, each one free from any contamination of the other. In each, the individual is primal, sex is subordinate, but perfectly polarized. Each has a single, separate being, with its own laws. The man has his pure freedom, the woman hers. Each acknowledges the perfection of the polarized sex-circuit. Each admits the different nature in the other.

So Birkin meditated whilst he was ill. He liked sometimes to be ill enough to take to his bed. For then he got better very quickly, and things came to him clear and sure.

Whilst he was laid up, Gerald came to see him. The two men had a deep, uneasy feeling for each other. Gerald's eyes were quick and restless, his whole manner tense and impatient, he seemed strung up to some activity. According to conventionality, he wore black clothes, he looked formal, handsome and *comme il faut*. His hair was fair almost to whiteness, sharp like splinters of light, his face was keen and ruddy, his body seemed full of northern energy.

Gerald really loved Birkin, though he never quite believed in him. Birkin was too unreal; – clever, whimsical, wonderful, but not practical enough. Gerald felt that his own understanding was much sounder and safer. Birkin was delightful, a wonderful spirit, but after all, not to be taken seriously, not quite to be counted as a man among men.

'Why are you laid up again?' he asked kindly, taking the sick man's hand. It was always Gerald who was protective, offering the warm shelter of his physical strength.

'For my sins, I suppose,' Birkin said, smiling a little ironically.

'For your sins? Yes, probably that is so. You should sin less, and keep better in health?'

'You'd better teach me.'

He looked at Gerald with ironic eyes.

'How are things with you?' asked Birkin.

'With me?' Gerald looked at Birkin, saw he was serious, and a warm light came into his eyes.

'I don't know that they're any different. I don't see how they could be. There's nothing to change.'

'I suppose you are conducting the business as successfully as ever, and ignoring the demand of the soul.'

'That's it,' said Gerald. 'At least as far as the business is concerned. I couldn't say about the soul, I'm sure.'

'No.'

'Surely you don't expect me to?' laughed Gerald.

'No. How are the rest of your affairs progressing, apart from the business?'

'The rest of my affairs? What are those? I couldn't say; I don't know what you refer to.'

'Yes, you do,' said Birkin. 'Are you gloomy or cheerful? And what about Gudrun Brangwen?'

'What about her?' A confused look came over Gerald. 'Well,' he added, 'I don't know. I can only tell you she gave me a hit over the face last time I saw her.'

'A hit over the face! What for?'

'That I couldn't tell you, either.'

'Really! But when?'

'The night of the party – when Diana was drowned. She was driving the cattle up the hill, and I went after her – you remember.'

'Yes, I remember. But what made her do that? You didn't definitely ask her for it, I suppose?'

'I? No, not that I know of. I merely said to her that it was dangerous to drive those Highland bullocks – as it *is*. She turned in such a way, and said – "I suppose you think I'm afraid of you and your cattle, don't you?" So I asked her "why"? and for answer she flung me a back-hander across the face.'

Birkin laughed quickly, as if it pleased him. Gerald looked at him, wondering, and began to laugh as well, saying:

'I didn't laugh at the time, I assure you. I was never so taken aback in my life.'

'And weren't you furious?'

'Furious? I should think I was. I'd have murdered her for two pins.'

'H'm!' ejaculated Birkin. 'Poor Gudrun, wouldn't she suffer afterwards for having given herself away!' He was hugely delighted.

'Would she suffer?' asked Gerald, also amused now.

Both men smiled in malice and amusement.

'Badly, I should think; seeing how self-conscious she is.'

'She is self-conscious, is she? Then what made her do it? For I certainly think it was quite uncalled-for, and quite unjustified.'

'I suppose it was a sudden impulse.'

'Yes, but how do you account for her having such an impulse? I'd done her no harm.'

Birkin shook his head.

'The Amazon suddenly came up in her, I suppose,' he said.

'Well,' replied Gerald, 'I'd rather it had been the Orinoco.'

They both laughed at the poor joke. Gerald was thinking how Gudrun had said she would strike the last blow too. But some reserve made him keep this back from Birkin.

'And you resent it?' Birkin asked.

'I don't resent it. I don't care a tinker's curse about it.' He was silent a moment, then he added, laughing, 'No, I'll see it through, that's all. She seemed sorry afterwards.'

'Did she? You've not met since that night?'

Gerald's face clouded.

'No,' he said. 'We've been – you can imagine how it's been, since the accident.'

'Yes. Is it calming down?'

'I don't know. It's a shock, of course. But I don't believe mother minds. I really don't believe she takes any notice. And what's so funny, she used to be all for the children – nothing mattered, nothing whatever mattered but the children. And now, she doesn't take any more notice than if it was one of the servants.'

'No? Did it upset *you* very much?'

'It's a shock. But I don't feel it very much, really. I don't feel any different. We've all got to die, and it doesn't seem to make any great difference, anyhow, whether you die or not. I can't feel any *grief*, you know. It leaves me cold. I can't quite account for it.'

'You don't care if you die or not?' asked Birkin.

Gerald looked at him with eyes blue as the blue-fibred steel of a weapon. He felt awkward, but indifferent. As a matter of fact, he did care terribly, with a great fear.

'Oh,' he said, 'I don't want to die, why should I? But I never trouble. The question doesn't seem to be on the carpet for me at all. It doesn't interest me, you know.'

'*Timor mortis conturbat me,*' quoted Birkin, adding – 'No, death doesn't really seem the point any more. It curiously doesn't concern one. It's like an ordinary tomorrow.'

Gerald looked closely at his friend. The eyes of the two men met, and an unspoken understanding was exchanged.

Gerald narrowed his eyes, his face was cool and unscrupulous as he looked at Birkin, impersonally, with a vision that ended in a point in space, strangely keen-eyed and yet blind.

'If death isn't the point,' he said, in a strangely abstract, cold, fine voice – 'what is?' He sounded as if he had been found out.

'What is?' re-echoed Birkin. And there was a mocking silence.

'There's a long way to go, after the point of intrinsic death, before we disappear,' said Birkin.

'There is,' said Gerald. 'But what sort of way?' He seemed to press the other man for knowledge which he himself knew far better than Birkin did.

'Right down the slopes of degeneration – mystic, universal degeneration. There are many stages of pure degradation to go through: age-long. We live on long after our death, and progressively, in progressive devolution.'

Gerald listened with a faint, fine smile on his face, all the time, as if, somewhere, he knew so much better than Birkin, all about this: as if his own knowledge were direct and personal, whereas Birkin's was a matter of observation and inference, not quite hitting the nail on the head: – though aiming near enough at it. But he was not going to give himself away. If Birkin could get at the secrets, let him. Gerald would never help him. Gerald would be a dark horse to the end.

'Of course,' he said, with a startling change of conversation, 'it is father who really feels it. It will finish him. For him the world collapses. All his care now is for Winnie – he must save Winnie. He says she ought to be sent away to school, but she won't hear of it, and he'll never do it. Of course she *is* in rather a queer way. We're all of us curiously bad at living. We can do things – but we can't get on with life at all. It's curious – a family failing.'

'She oughtn't to be sent away to school,' said Birkin, who was considering a new proposition.

'She oughtn't? Why?'

'She's a queer child – a special child, more special even than you. And in my opinion special children should never be sent away to school. Only moderately ordinary children should be sent to school – so it seems to me.'

'I'm inclined to think just the opposite. I think it would probably make her more normal if she went away and mixed with other children.'

'She wouldn't mix, you see. *You* never really mixed, did you? And she wouldn't be willing even to pretend to. She's proud and solitary, and naturally apart. If she has a single nature, why do you want to make her gregarious?'

'No, I don't want to make her anything. But I think school would be good for her.'

'Was it good for you?'

Gerald's eyes narrowed uglily. School had been torture to him. Yet he had not questioned whether one should go through this torture. He seemed to believe in education through subjection and torment.

'I hated it at the time, but I can see it was necessary,' he said. 'It brought me into line a bit – and you can't live unless you do come into line somewhere.'

'Well,' said Birkin, 'I begin to think that you can't live unless you keep entirely out of the line. It's no good trying to toe the line, when your one impulse is to smash up the line. Winnie is a special nature, and for special natures you must give a special world.'

'Yes, but where's your special world?' said Gerald.

'Make it. Instead of chopping yourself down to fit the world, chop the world down to fit yourself. As a matter of fact, two exceptional people make another world. You and I, we make another, separate world. You don't *want* a world same as your brothers-in-law. It's just the special quality you value. Do you *want* to be normal or ordinary? It's a lie. You want to be free and extraordinary, in an extraordinary world of liberty.'

Gerald looked at Birkin with subtle eyes of knowledge. But he would never openly admit what he felt. He knew more than Birkin, in one direction – much more. And this gave him his gentle love for the other man, as if Birkin were in some way young, innocent, child-like; so amazingly clever, but incurably innocent.

'Yet you are so banal as to consider me chiefly a freak,' said Birkin pointedly.

'A freak!' exclaimed Gerald, startled. And his face opened suddenly, as if lighted with simplicity, as when a flower opens out of the cunning bud. 'No – I never consider you a freak.' And he watched the other man with strange eyes, that Birkin could not understand. 'I feel,' Gerald continued, 'that there is always an element of uncertainty about you – perhaps you are uncertain about yourself. But I'm never sure of you. You can go away and change as easily as if you had no soul.'

He looked at Birkin with penetrating eyes. Birkin was amazed. He thought he had all the soul in the world. He stared in amazement. And Gerald, watching, saw the amazing attractive goodliness of his eyes, a young, spontaneous goodness that attracted the other man infinitely, yet filled him with bitter chagrin, because he mistrusted it so much. He knew Birkin could do without him – could forget, and not suffer. This was always present in Gerald's consciousness, filling him with bitter unbelief: this consciousness of the young, animal-like spontaneity of detachment. It seemed almost like hypocrisy and lying, sometimes, oh, often, on Birkin's part, to talk so deeply and importantly.

Quite other things were going through Birkin's mind. Suddenly he saw himself confronted with another problem – the problem of love and eternal conjunction between two men. Of course this was necessary – it had been a necessity inside himself all his life – to love a man purely and fully. Of course he had been loving Gerald all along, and all along denying it.

He lay in the bed and wondered, whilst his friend sat beside him, lost in brooding. Each man was gone in his own thoughts.

'You know how the old German knights used to swear a *Blutbruderschaft*,' he said to Gerald, with quite a new happy activity in his eyes.

'Make a little wound in their arms, and rub each other's blood into the cut?' said Gerald.

'Yes – and swear to be true to each other, of one blood, all their lives. That is what we ought to do. No wounds, that is obsolete. But we ought to swear to love each other, you and I, implicitly, and perfectly, finally, without any possibility of going back on it.'

He looked at Gerald with clear, happy eyes of discovery. Gerald looked down at him, attracted, so deeply bondaged in fascinated attraction, that he was mistrustful, resenting the bondage, hating the attraction.

'We will swear to each other, one day, shall we?' pleaded Birkin. 'We will swear to stand by each other – be true to each other – ultimately – infallibly – give to each other, organically – without possibility of taking back.'

Birkin sought hard to express himself. But Gerald hardly listened. His face shone with a certain luminous pleasure. He was pleased. But he kept his reserve. He held himself back.

'Shall we swear to each other, one day?' said Birkin, putting out his hand towards Gerald.

Gerald just touched the extended fine, living hand, as if withheld and afraid.

'We'll leave it till I understand it better,' he said, in a voice of excuse.

Birkin watched him. A little sharp disappointment, perhaps a touch of contempt came into his heart.

'Yes,' he said. 'You must tell me what you think, later. You know what I mean? Not sloppy emotionalism. An impersonal union that leaves one free.'

They lapsed both into silence. Birkin was looking at Gerald all the time. He seemed now to see, not the physical, animal man, which he usually saw in Gerald, and which usually he liked so much, but the man himself, complete, and as if fated, doomed, limited. This strange sense of fatality in Gerald, as if he were limited to one form of existence, one knowledge, one activity, a sort of fatal halfness, which to himself seemed wholeness, always overcame Birkin after their moments of passionate approach, and filled him with a sort of contempt, or boredom. It was the insistence on the limitation which so bored

Birkin in Gerald. Gerald could never fly away from himself, in real indifferent gaiety. He had a clog, a sort of monomania.

There was silence for a time. Then Birkin said, in a lighter tone, letting the stress of the contact pass:

'Can't you get a good governess for Winifred? – somebody exceptional?'

'Hermione Roddice suggested we should ask Gudrun to teach her to draw and to model in clay. You know Winnie is astonishingly clever with that plasticine stuff. Hermione declares she is an artist.' Gerald spoke in the usual animated, chatty manner, as if nothing unusual had passed. But Birkin's manner was full of reminder.

'Really! I didn't know that. Oh well then, if Gudrun *would* teach her, it would be perfect – couldn't be anything better – if Winifred is an artist. Because Gudrun somewhere is one. And every true artist is the salvation of every other.'

'I thought they got on so badly, as a rule.'

'Perhaps. But only artists produce for each other the world that is fit to live in. If you can arrange *that* for Winifred, it is perfect.'

'But you think she wouldn't come?'

'I don't know. Gudrun is rather self-opinionated. She won't go cheap anywhere. Or if she does, she'll pretty soon take herself back. So whether she would condescend to do private teaching, particularly here, in Beldover, I don't know. But it would be just the thing. Winifred has got a special nature. And if you can put into her way the means of being self-sufficient, that is the best thing possible. She'll never get on with the ordinary life. You find it difficult enough yourself, and she is several skins thinner than you are. It is awful to think what her life will be like unless she does find a means of expression, some way of fulfilment. You can see what mere leaving it to fate brings. You can see how much marriage is to be trusted to – look at your own mother.'

'Do you think mother is abnormal?'

'No! I think she only wanted something more, or other than the common run of life. And not getting it, she has gone wrong perhaps.'

'After producing a brood of wrong children,' said Gerald gloomily.

'No more wrong than any of the rest of us,' Birkin replied. 'The most normal people have the worst subterranean selves, take them one by one.'

'Sometimes I think it is a curse to be alive,' said Gerald, with sudden impotent anger.

'Well,' said Birkin, 'why not! Let it be a curse sometimes to be alive – at other times it is anything but a curse. You've got plenty of zest in it really.'

'Less than you'd think,' said Gerald, revealing a strange poverty in his look at the other man.

There was silence, each thinking his own thoughts.

'I don't see what she has to distinguish between teaching at the Grammar School and coming to teach Win,' said Gerald.

'The difference between a public servant and a private one. The only nobleman today, king and only aristocrat, is the public, the public. You are quite willing to serve the public – but to be a private tutor –'

'I don't want to serve either –'

'No! And Gudrun will probably feel the same.'

Gerald thought for a few minutes. Then he said:

'At all events, father won't make her feel like a private servant. He will be fussy and grateful enough.'

'So he ought. And so ought all of you. Do you think you can hire a woman like Gudrun Brangwen with money? She is your equal like anything – probably your superior.'

'Is she?' said Gerald.

'Yes, and if you haven't the guts to know it, I hope she'll leave you to your own devices.'

'Nevertheless,' said Gerald, 'if she is my equal, I wish she weren't a teacher, because I don't think teachers as a rule are my equal.'

'Nor do I, damn them. But am I a teacher because I teach, or a parson because I preach?'

Gerald laughed. He was always uneasy on this score. He did not *want* to claim social superiority, yet he *would* not claim intrinsic personal superiority, because he would never base his standard of values on pure being. So he wobbled upon a tacit assumption of social standing. Now Birkin wanted him to accept the fact of intrinsic difference between human beings, which he did not intend to accept. It was against his social honour, his principle. He rose to go.

'I've been neglecting my business all this while,' he said, smiling.

'I ought to have reminded you before,' Birkin replied, laughing and mocking.

'I knew you'd say something like that,' laughed Gerald, rather uneasily. 'Did you?'

'Yes, Rupert. It wouldn't do for us all to be like you are – we should soon be in the cart. When I am above the world, I shall ignore all businesses.'

'Of course, we're not in the cart now,' said Birkin, satirically.

'Not as much as you make out. At any rate, we have enough to eat and drink –'

'And be satisfied,' added Birkin.

Gerald came near the bed and stood looking down at Birkin whose throat was exposed, whose tossed hair fell attractively on the warm brow, above the eyes that were so unchallenged and still in the satirical face. Gerald, full-limbed and turgid with energy, stood unwilling to go, he was held by the presence of the other man. He had not the power to go away.

'So,' said Birkin. 'Good-bye.' And he reached out his hand from under the bed-clothes, smiling with a glimmering look.

'Good-bye,' said Gerald, taking the warm hand of his friend in a firm grasp. 'I shall come again. I miss you down at the mill.'

'I'll be there in a few days,' said Birkin.

The eyes of the two men met again. Gerald's, that were keen as a hawk's, were suffused now with warm light and with unadmitted love, Birkin looked back as out of a darkness, unsounded and unknown, yet with a kind of warmth, that seemed to flow over Gerald's brain like a fertile sleep.

'Good-bye then. There's nothing I can do for you?'

'Nothing, thanks.'

Birkin watched the black-clothed form of the other man move out of the door, the bright head was gone, he turned over to sleep.

THE INDUSTRIAL MAGNATE

In Beldover, there was both for Ursula and for Gudrun an interval. It seemed to Ursula as if Birkin had gone out of her for the time, he had lost his significance, he scarcely mattered in her world. She had her own friends, her own activities, her own life. She turned back to the old ways with zest, away from him.

And Gudrun, after feeling every moment in all her veins conscious of Gerald Crich, connected even physically with him, was now almost indifferent to the thought of him. She was nursing new schemes for going away and trying a new form of life. All the time, there was something in her urging her to avoid the final establishing of a relationship with Gerald. She felt it would be wiser and better to have no more than a casual acquaintance with him.

She had a scheme for going to St Petersburg, where she had a friend who was a sculptor like herself, and who lived with a wealthy Russian whose hobby was jewel-making. The emotional, rather rootless life of the Russians appealed to her. She did not want to go to Paris. Paris was dry, and essentially boring. She would like to go to Rome, Munich, Vienna, or to St Petersburg or Moscow. She had a friend in St Petersburg and a friend in Munich. To each of these she wrote, asking about rooms.

She had a certain amount of money. She had come home partly to save, and now she had sold several pieces of work, she had been praised in various shows. She knew she could become quite the 'go' if she went to London. But she knew London, she wanted something else. She had seventy pounds, of which nobody knew anything. She would move soon, as soon as she heard from her friends. Her nature, in spite of her apparent placidity and calm, was profoundly restless.

The sisters happened to call in a cottage in Willey Green to buy honey. Mrs Kirk, a stout, pale, sharp-nosed woman, sly, honied, with something shrewish and cat-like beneath, asked the girls into her too cosy, too tidy kitchen. There was a cat-like comfort and cleanliness everywhere.

'Yes, Miss Brangwen,' she said, in her slightly whining, insinuating voice, 'and how do you like being back in the old place, then?'

Gudrun, whom she addressed, hated her at once.

'I don't care for it,' she replied abruptly.

'You don't? Ay, well, I suppose you found a difference from London. You like life, and big, grand places. Some of us has to be content with Willey Green and Beldover. And what do you think of our Grammar School, as there's so much talk about?'

'What do I think of it?' Gudrun looked round at her slowly. 'Do you mean, do I think it's a good school?'

'Yes. What is your opinion of it?'

'I *do* think it's a good school.'

Gudrun was very cold and repelling. She knew the common people hated the school.

'Ay, you do, then! I've heard so much, one way and the other. It's nice to know what those that's in it feel. But opinions vary, don't they? Mr Crich up at Highclose is all for it. Ay, poor man, I'm afraid he's not long for this world. He's very poorly.'

'Is he worse?' asked Ursula.

'Eh, yes – since they lost Miss Diana. He's gone off to a shadow. Poor man, he's had a world of trouble.'

'Has he?' asked Gudrun, faintly ironic.

'He has, a world of trouble. And as nice and kind a gentleman as ever you could wish to meet. His children don't take after him.'

'I suppose they take after their mother?' said Ursula.

'In many ways.' Mrs Kirk lowered her voice a little. 'She was a proud haughty lady when she came into these parts – my word, she was that! She mustn't be looked at, and it was worth your life to speak to her.' The woman made a dry, sly face.

'Did you know her when she was first married?'

'Yes, I knew her. I nursed three of her children. And proper little terrors they were, little fiends – that Gerald was a demon if ever there was one, a proper demon, ay, at six months old.' A curious malicious, sly tone came into the woman's voice.

'Really,' said Gudrun.

'That wilful, masterful – he'd mastered one nurse at six months. Kick, and scream, and struggle like a demon. Many's the time I've pinched his little bottom for him, when he was a child in arms. Ay, and he'd have been better if he'd had it pinched oftener. But she wouldn't have them corrected – no-o, wouldn't hear of it. I can remember the rows she had with Mr Crich, my word. When he'd got worked up, properly worked up till he could stand no more, he'd lock the study door and whip them. But she paced up and down all the while like a tiger outside, like a tiger, with very murder in her face. She had a face that could *look* death. And when the door was opened, she'd go in with her hands lifted – "What have you been doing to *my* children, you coward." She was like one out of her mind. I believe he was frightened of her; he had to be driven mad before he'd lift a finger. Didn't the servants have a life of it! And didn't we used to be thankful when one of them caught it. They were the torment of your life.'

'Really!' said Gudrun.

'In every possible way. If you wouldn't let them smash their pots on the table, if you wouldn't let them drag the kitten about with a string round its neck, if you wouldn't give them whatever they asked for, every mortal thing – then there was a shine on, and their mother coming in asking – "What's the matter with him? What have you done to him? What is it, darling?" And then she'd turn on you as if she'd trample you under her feet. But she didn't trample on me. I was the only one that could do anything with her demons – for she wasn't going to be bothered with them herself. No, *she* took no trouble for them. But they must just have their way, they mustn't be spoken to. And Master Gerald was the beauty. I left when he was a year and a half, I could stand no more. But I pinched his little bottom for him when he was in arms, I did, when there was no holding him, and I'm not sorry I did –'

Gudrun went away in fury and loathing. The phrase, "I pinched his little bottom for him," sent her into a white, stony fury. She could not bear it, she wanted to have the woman taken out at once and strangled. And yet there the phrase was lodged in her mind for ever, beyond escape. She felt, one day, she would *have* to tell him, to see how he took it. And she loathed herself for the thought.

But at Shortlands the life-long struggle was coming to a close. The father was ill and was going to die. He had bad internal pains, which took away all his attentive life, and left him with only a vestige of his consciousness. More and more a silence came over him, he was less and less acutely aware of his surroundings. The pain seemed to absorb his activity. He knew it was there, he knew it would come again. It was like something lurking in the darkness within him. And he had not the power, or the will, to seek it out and to know it. There it remained in the darkness, the great pain, tearing him at times, and then being silent. And when it tore him he crouched in silent subjection under it, and when it left him alone again, he refused to know of it. It was within the darkness, let it remain unknown. So he never admitted it, except in a secret corner of himself, where all his never-revealed fears and secrets were accumulated. For the rest, he had a pain, it went away, it made no difference. It even stimulated him, excited him.

But it gradually absorbed his life. Gradually it drew away all his potentiality, it bled him into the dark, it weaned him of life and drew him away into the darkness. And in this twilight of his life little remained visible to him. The business, his work, that was gone entirely. His public interests had disappeared as if they had never been. Even his family had become extraneous to him, he could only remember, in some slight non-essential part of himself, that such and such were his children. But it was historical fact, not vital to him. He had to make an effort to know their relation to him. Even his wife barely existed. She indeed was like the darkness, like the pain within him. By some strange association, the darkness that contained the pain and the darkness that contained his wife were identical. All his thoughts and understandings became blurred and fused, and now his wife and the consuming pain were the same dark secret power against him, that he never faced. He never drove the dread out of its lair within him. He only knew that there was a dark place, and something inhabiting this darkness which issued from time to time and rent him. But he dared not penetrate and drive the beast into the open. He had rather ignore its existence. Only, in his vague way, the dread was his wife, the destroyer, and it was the pain, the destruction, a darkness which was one and both.

He very rarely saw his wife. She kept to her room. Only occasionally she came forth, with her head stretched forward, and in her low, possessed voice, she asked him how he was. And he answered her, in the habit of more than thirty years: 'Well, I don't think I'm any the worse, dear.' But he was frightened of her, underneath this safeguard of habit, frightened almost to the verge of death.

But all his life, he had been so constant to his lights, he had never broken down. He would die even now without breaking down, without knowing what his feelings were, towards her. All his life, he had said: 'Poor Christiana, she has such a strong temper.' With unbroken will, he had stood by this position with regard to her, he had substituted pity for all his hostility, pity had been his shield and his safeguard, and his infallible weapon. And still, in his consciousness, he was sorry for her, her nature was so violent and so impatient.

But now his pity, with his life, was wearing thin, and the dread almost amounting to horror, was rising into being. But before the armour of his pity really broke, he would die, as an insect when its shell is cracked. This was his final resource. Others would live on, and know the living death, the ensuing process of hopeless chaos. He would not. He denied death its victory.

He had been so constant to his lights, so constant to charity, and to his love for his neighbour. Perhaps he had loved his neighbour even better than himself – which is going one further than the commandment. Always, this flame had burned in his heart, sustaining him through everything, the welfare of the people. He was a large employer of labour, he was a great mine-owner. And he had never lost this from his heart, that in Christ he was one with his workmen. Nay, he had felt inferior to them, as if they through poverty and labour were nearer to God than he. He had always the unacknowledged belief that it was his workmen, the miners, who held in their hands the means of salvation. To move nearer to God, he must move towards his miners, his life must gravitate towards theirs. They were, unconsciously, his idol, his God made manifest. In them he worshipped the highest, the great, sympathetic, mindless Godhead of humanity.

And all the while, his wife had opposed him like one of the great demons of hell. Strange, like a bird of prey, with the fascinating beauty and abstraction of a hawk, she had beat against the bars of his philanthropy, and like a hawk in a cage, she had sunk into silence. By force of circumstance, because all the world combined to make the cage unbreakable, he had been too strong for her, he had kept her prisoner. And because she was his prisoner, his passion for her had always remained keen as death. He had always loved her, loved her with intensity. Within the cage, she was denied nothing, she was given all licence.

But she had gone almost mad. Of wild and overweening temper, she could not bear the humiliation of her husband's soft, half-appealing kindness to everybody. He was not deceived by the poor. He knew they came and sponged on him, and whined to him, the worst sort; the majority, luckily for him, were much too proud to ask for anything, much too independent to come knocking at his door. But in Beldover, as everywhere else, there were the whining, parasitic, foul human beings who come crawling after charity, and feeding on the living body of the public like lice. A kind of fire would go over Christiana Crich's brain, as she saw two more pale-faced, creeping women in objectionable black clothes, cringing lugubriously up the drive to the door. She wanted to set the dogs on them, 'Hi Rip! Hi Ring! Ranger! At 'em, boys, set 'em off.' But Crowther, the butler, with all the rest of the servants, was Mr Crich's man. Nevertheless, when her husband was away, she would come down like a wolf on the crawling supplicants: 'What do you people want? There is nothing for you here. You have no business on the drive at all. Simpson, drive them away and let no more of them through the gate.'

The servants had to obey her. And she would stand watching with an eye like the eagle's, whilst the groom in clumsy confusion drove the lugubrious persons down the drive, as if they were rusty fowls, scuttling before him.

But they learned to know, from the lodge-keeper, when Mr Crich was away, and they timed their visits. How many times, in the first years, would Crowther knock softly at the door: 'Person to see you, sir.'

'What name?'

'Grocock, sir.'

'What do they want?' The question was half impatient, half gratified. He liked hearing appeals to his charity.

'About a child, sir.'

'Show them into the library, and tell them they shouldn't come after eleven o'clock in the morning.'

'Why do you get up from dinner? – send them off,' his wife would say abruptly.

'Oh, I can't do that. It's no trouble just to hear what they have to say.'

'How many more have been here today? why don't you establish open house for them? They would soon oust me and the children.'

'You know, dear, it doesn't hurt me to hear what they have to say. And if they really are in trouble – well, it is my duty to help them out of it.'

'It's your duty to invite all the rats in the world to gnaw at your bones.'

'Come, Christiana, it isn't that. Don't be uncharitable.'

But she suddenly swept out of the room, and out to the study. There sat the meagre charity-seekers, looking as if they were at the doctor's.

'Mr Crich can't see you. He can't see you at this hour. Do you think he is your property, that you can come whenever you like? You must go away, there is nothing for you here.'

The poor people rose in confusion. But Mr Crich, pale and black-bearded and deprecating, came behind her, saying:

'Yes, I don't like you coming as late as this. I'll hear any of you in the morning part of the day, but I can't really do with you after. What's amiss then, Gittens. How is your Missis?'

'Why, she's sunk very low, Mester Crich, she's a'most gone, she is –'

Sometimes, it seemed to Mrs Crich as if her husband were some subtle funeral bird, feeding on the miseries of the people. It seemed to her he was never satisfied unless there was some sordid tale being poured out to him which he drank in with a sort of mournful, sympathetic satisfaction. He would have no *raison d'être* if there were no lugubrious miseries in the world, as an undertaker would have no meaning if there were no funerals.

Mrs Crich recoiled back upon herself, she recoiled away from this world of creeping democracy. A band of tight, baleful exclusion fastened round her heart, her isolation was fierce and hard, her antagonism was passive but terribly pure, like that of a hawk in a cage. As the years went on, she lost more and more count of the world, she seemed rapt in some glittering abstraction, almost purely unconscious. She would wander about the house and about the surrounding country, staring keenly and seeing nothing. She rarely spoke, she had no connection with the world. And she did not even think. She was consumed in a fierce tension of opposition, like the negative pole of a magnet.

And she bore many children. For, as time went on, she never opposed her husband in word or deed. She took no notice of him, externally. She submitted to him, let him take what he wanted and do as he wanted with her. She was like a hawk that sullenly submits to everything. The relation between her and her husband was wordless and unknown, but it was deep, awful, a relation of utter interdestruction. And he, who triumphed in the world, he became more and more hollow in his vitality, the vitality was bled from within him, as by some haemorrhage. She was hulked like a hawk in a cage, but her heart was fierce and undiminished within her, though her mind was destroyed.

So to the last he would go to her and hold her in his arms sometimes, before his strength was all gone. The terrible white, destructive light that burned in her eyes only excited and roused him. Till he was bled to death, and then he dreaded her more than anything. But he always said to himself, how happy he had been, how he had loved her with a pure and consuming love ever since he had known her. And he thought of her as pure, chaste; the white flame which was known to him alone, the flame of her sex, was a white flower of snow to his mind. She was a wonderful white snow-flower, which he had desired infinitely. And now he was dying with all his ideas and interpretations intact. They would only collapse when the breath left his body. Till then they would be pure truths for him. Only death would show the perfect completeness of the lie. Till death, she was his white snow-flower. He had subdued her, and her subjugation was to him an infinite chastity in her, a virginity which he could never break, and which dominated him as by a spell.

She had let go the outer world, but within herself she was unbroken and unimpaired. She only sat in her room like a moped, dishevelled hawk, motionless, mindless. Her children, for whom she had been so fierce in her youth, now meant scarcely anything to her. She had lost all that, she was quite by herself. Only Gerald, the gleaming, had some existence for her. But of late years, since he had become head of the business, he too was forgotten. Whereas the father, now he was dying, turned for compassion to Gerald. There had always been opposition between the two of them. Gerald had feared and despised his father, and to a great extent had avoided him all through boyhood and young manhood. And the father had felt very often a real dislike of his eldest son, which, never wanting to give way to, he had refused to acknowledge. He had ignored Gerald as much as possible, leaving him alone.

Since, however, Gerald had come home and assumed responsibility in the firm, and had proved such a wonderful director, the father, tired and weary of all outside concerns, had put all his trust of these things in his son, implicitly, leaving everything to him, and assuming a rather touching dependence on the young enemy. This immediately roused a poignant pity and allegiance in Gerald's heart, always shadowed by contempt and by unadmitted enmity. For Gerald was in reaction against Charity; and yet he was dominated by it, it assumed supremacy in the inner life, and he could not confute it. So he was partly subject to that which his father stood for, but he was in reaction against it. Now he could not save himself. A certain pity and grief and tenderness for his father overcame him, in spite of the deeper, more sullen hostility.

The father won shelter from Gerald through compassion. But for love he had Winifred. She was his youngest child, she was the only one of his children whom he had ever closely loved. And her he loved with all the great, overweening, sheltering love of a dying man. He wanted to shelter her infinitely, infinitely, to wrap her in warmth and love and shelter, perfectly. If he could save her she should never know one pain, one grief, one hurt. He had been so right all his life, so constant in his kindness and his goodness. And this was his last passionate righteousness, his love for the child Winifred. Some things troubled him yet. The world had passed away from him, as his strength ebbed. There were no more poor and injured and humble to protect and succour. These were all lost to him. There were no more sons and daughters to trouble him, and to weigh on him as an unnatural responsibility. These too had faded out of reality. All these things had fallen out of his hands, and left him free.

There remained the covert fear and horror of his wife, as she sat mindless and strange in her room, or as she came forth with slow, prowling step, her head bent forward. But this he put away. Even his life-long righteousness, however, would not quite deliver him from the inner horror. Still, he could keep it sufficiently at bay. It would never break forth openly. Death would come first.

Then there was Winifred! If only he could be sure about her, if only he could be sure. Since the death of Diana, and the development of his illness, his craving for surety with regard to Winifred amounted almost to obsession. It was as if, even dying, he must have some anxiety, some responsibility of love, of Charity, upon his heart.

She was an odd, sensitive, inflammable child, having her father's dark hair and quiet bearing, but being quite detached, momentaneous. She was like a changeling indeed, as if her feelings did not matter to her, really. She often seemed to be talking and playing like the gayest and most childish of children, she was full of the warmest, most delightful affection for a few things – for her father, and for her animals in particular. But if she heard that her beloved kitten Leo had been run over by the motor-car she put her head on one side, and replied, with a faint contraction like resentment on her face: 'Has he?' Then she took no more notice. She only disliked the servant who would force bad news on her, and wanted her to be sorry. She wished not to know, and that seemed her chief motive. She avoided her mother, and most of the members of her family. She *loved* her Daddy, because he wanted her always to be happy, and because he seemed to become young again, and irresponsible in her presence. She liked Gerald, because he was so self-contained. She loved people who would make life a game for her. She had an amazing instinctive critical faculty, and was a pure anarchist, a pure aristocrat at once. For she accepted her equals wherever she found them, and she ignored with blithe indifference her inferiors, whether they were her brothers and sisters, or whether they were wealthy guests of the house, or whether they were the common people or the servants. She was quite single and by herself, deriving from nobody. It was as if she were cut off from all purpose or continuity, and existed simply moment by moment.

The father, as by some strange final illusion, felt as if all his fate depended on his ensuring to Winifred her happiness. She who could never suffer, because she never formed vital connections, she who could lose the dearest things of her life and be just the same the next day, the whole memory dropped out, as if deliberately, she whose will was so strangely and easily free, anarchistic, almost nihilistic, who like a soulless bird flits on its own will, without attachment or responsibility beyond the moment, who in her every motion snapped the threads of serious relationship with blithe, free hands, really nihilistic, because never troubled, she must be the object of her father's final passionate solicitude.

When Mr Crich heard that Gudrun Brangwen might come to help Winifred with her drawing and modelling he saw a road to salvation for his child. He believed that Winifred had talent, he had seen Gudrun, he knew that she was an exceptional person. He could give Winifred into her hands as into the hands of a right being. Here was a direction and a positive force to be lent to his child, he need not leave her directionless and defenceless. If he could but graft the girl on to some tree of utterance before he died, he would have fulfilled his responsibility. And here it could be done. He did not hesitate to appeal to Gudrun.

Meanwhile, as the father drifted more and more out of life, Gerald experienced more and more a sense of exposure. His father after all had stood for the living world to him. Whilst his father lived Gerald was not responsible for the world. But now his father was passing away, Gerald found himself left exposed and unready before the storm of living, like the mutinous first mate of a ship that has lost his captain, and who sees only a terrible chaos in front of him. He did not inherit an established order and a living idea. The whole unifying idea of mankind seemed to be dying with his father, the centralizing force that had held the whole together seemed to collapse with his father, the parts were ready to go asunder in terrible disintegration. Gerald was as if left on board of a ship that was going asunder beneath his feet, he was in charge of a vessel whose timbers were all coming apart.

He knew that all his life he had been wrenching at the frame of life to break it apart. And now, with something of the terror of a destructive child, he saw himself on the point of inheriting his own destruction. And during the last months, under the influence of death, and of Birkin's talk, and of Gudrun's penetrating being, he had lost entirely that mechanical certainty that had been his triumph. Sometimes spasms of hatred came over him, against Birkin and Gudrun and that whole set. He wanted to go back to the dullest conservatism, to the most stupid of conventional people. He wanted to revert to the strictest Toryism. But the desire did not last long enough to carry him into action.

During his childhood and his boyhood he had wanted a sort of savagedom. The days of Homer were his ideal, when a man was chief of an army of heroes, or spent his years in wonderful Odyssey. He hated remorselessly the circumstances of his own life, so much that he never really saw Beldover and the colliery valley. He turned his face entirely away from the blackened mining region that stretched away on the right hand of Shortlands, he turned entirely to the country and the woods beyond Willey Water. It was true that the panting and rattling of the coal-mines could always be heard at Shortlands. But from his earliest childhood, Gerald had paid no heed to this. He had ignored the whole of the industrial sea which surged in coal-blackened tides against the grounds of the house. The world was really a wilderness where one hunted and swam and rode. He rebelled against all authority. Life was a condition of savage freedom.

Then he had been sent away to school, which was so much death to him. He refused to go to Oxford, choosing a German university. He had spent a certain time at Bonn, at Berlin, and at Frankfurt. There, a curiosity had been aroused in his mind. He wanted to see and to know, in a curious objective fashion, as if it were an amusement to him. Then he must try war. Then he must travel into the savage regions that had so attracted him.

The result was, he found humanity very much alike everywhere, and to a mind like his, curious and cold, the savage was duller, less exciting than the European. So he took hold of all kinds of sociological ideas, and ideas of reform. But they never went more than skin-deep, they were never more than a mental amusement. Their interest lay chiefly in the reaction against the positive order, the destructive reaction.

He discovered at last a real adventure in the coal-mines. His father asked him to help in the firm. Gerald had been educated in the science of mining, and it had never interested him. Now, suddenly, with a sort of exultation, he laid hold of the world.

There was impressed photographically on his consciousness the great industry. Suddenly, it was real, he was part of it. Down the valley ran the colliery railway, linking mine with mine. Down the railway ran the trains, short trains of heavily laden trucks, long trains of empty wagons, each one bearing in big white letters the initials:

'C. B. & Co.'

These white letters on all the wagons he had seen since his first childhood, and it was as if he had never seen them, they were so familiar, and so ignored. Now at last he saw his own name written on the wall. Now he had a vision of power.

So many wagons, bearing his initial, running all over the country. He saw them as he entered London in the train, he saw them at Dover. So far his power ramified. He looked at Beldover, at Selby, at Whatmore, at Lethley Bank, the great colliery villages which depended entirely on his mines. They were hideous and sordid, during his childhood they had been sores in his consciousness. And now he saw them with pride. Four raw new towns, and many ugly industrial hamlets were crowded under his dependence. He saw the stream of miners flowing along the causeways from the mines at the end of the afternoon, thousands of blackened, slightly distorted human beings with red mouths, all moving subjugate to his will. He pushed slowly in his motor-car through the little market-top on Friday nights in Beldover, through a solid mass of human beings that were making their purchases and doing their weekly spending. They were all subordinate to him. They were ugly and uncouth, but they were his instruments. He was the God of the machine. They made way for his motor-car automatically, slowly.

He did not care whether they made way with alacrity, or grudgingly. He did not care what they thought of him. His vision had suddenly crystallized. Suddenly he had conceived the pure instrumentality of mankind. There had been so much humanitarianism, so much talk of sufferings and feelings. It was ridiculous. The sufferings and feelings of individuals did not matter in the least. They were mere conditions, like the weather. What mattered was the pure instumentality of the individual. As a man as of a knife: does it cut well? Nothing else mattered.

Everything in the world has its function, and is good or not good in so far as it fulfils this function more or less perfectly. Was a miner a good miner? Then he was complete. Was a manager a good manager? That was enough. Gerald himself, who was responsible for all this industry, was he a good director? If he were, he had fulfilled his life. The rest was by-play.

The mines were there, they were old. They were giving out, it did not pay to work the seams. There was talk of closing down two of them. It was at this point that Gerald arrived on the scene.

He looked around. There lay the mines. They were old, obsolete. They were like old lions, no more good. He looked again. Pah! the mines were nothing but the clumsy efforts of impure minds. There they lay, abortions of a half-trained mind. Let the idea of them be swept away. He cleared his brain of them, and thought only of the coal in the under earth. How much was there?

There was plenty of coal. The old workings could not get at it, that was all. Then break the neck of the old workings. The coal lay there in its seams, even though the seams were thin. There it lay, inert matter, as it had always lain, since the beginning of time, subject to the will of man. The will of man was the determining factor. Man was the arch-god of earth. His mind was obedient to serve his will. Man's will was the absolute, the only absolute.

And it was his will to subjugate Matter to his own ends. The subjugation itself was the point, the fight was the be-all, the fruits of victory were mere results. It was not for the sake of money that Gerald took over the mines. He did not care about money, fundamentally. He was neither ostentatious nor luxurious, neither did he care about social position, not finally. What he wanted was the pure fulfilment of his own will in the struggle with the natural conditions. His will was now, to take the coal out of the earth, profitably. The profit was merely the condition of victory, but the victory itself lay in the feat achieved. He vibrated with zest before the challenge. Every day he was in the mines, examining, testing, he consulted experts, he gradually gathered the whole situation into his mind, as a general grasps the plan of his campaign.

Then there was need for a complete break. The mines were run on an old system, an obsolete idea. The initial idea had been, to obtain as much money from the earth as would make the owners comfortably rich, would allow the workmen sufficient wages and good conditions, and would increase the wealth of the country altogether. Gerald's father, following in the second generation, having a sufficient fortune, had thought only of the men. The mines, for him, were primarily great fields to produce bread and plenty for all the hundreds of human beings gathered about them. He had lived and striven with his fellow owners to benefit the men every time. And the men had been benefited in their fashion. There were few poor, and few needy. All was plenty, because the mines were good and easy to work. And the miners, in those days, finding themselves richer than they might have expected, felt glad and triumphant. They thought themselves well off, they congratulated themselves on their good fortune, they remembered how their fathers had starved and suffered, and they felt that better times had come. They were grateful to those others, the pioneers, the new owners, who had opened out the pits, and let forth this stream of plenty.

But man is never satisfied, and so the miners, from gratitude to their owners, passed on to murmuring. Their sufficiency decreased with knowledge, they wanted more. Why should the master be so out-of-all-proportion rich?

There was a crisis when Gerald was a boy, when the Masters' Federation closed down the mines because the men would not accept a reduction. This lock-out had forced home the new conditions to Thomas Crich. Belonging to the Federation, he had been compelled by his honour to close the pits against his men. He, the father, the Patriarch, was forced to deny the means of life to his sons, his people. He, the rich man who would hardly enter heaven because of his possessions, must now turn upon the poor, upon those who were nearer Christ than himself, those who were humble and despised and closer to perfection, those who were manly and noble in their labours, and must say to them: 'Ye shall neither labour nor eat bread.'

It was this recognition of the state of war which really broke his heart. He wanted his industry to be run on love. Oh, he wanted love to be the directing power even of the mines. And now, from under the cloak of love, the sword was cynically drawn, the sword of mechanical necessity.

This really broke his heart. He must have the illusion and now the illusion was destroyed. The men were not against *him*, but they were against the masters. It was war, and willy-nilly he found himself on the wrong side, in his own conscience. Seething masses of miners met daily, carried away by a new religious impulse. The idea flew through them: 'All men are equal on earth,' and they would carry the idea to its material fulfilment. After all, is it not the teaching of Christ? And what is an idea, if not the germ of action in the material world. 'All men are equal in spirit, they are all sons of God. Whence then this obvious *disquality*?' It was a religious creed pushed to its material conclusion. Thomas Crich at least had no answer. He could but admit, according to his sincere tenets, that the disquality was wrong. But he could not give up his goods, which were the stuff of disquality. So the men would fight for their rights. The last impulses of the last religious passion left on earth, the passion for equality, inspired them.

Seething mobs of men marched about, their faces lighted up as for holy war, with a smoke of cupidity. How disentangle the passion for equality from the passion of cupidity, when begins the fight for equality of possessions? But the God was the machine. Each man claimed equality in the Godhead of the great productive machine. Every man equally was part of this Godhead. But somehow, somewhere, Thomas Crich knew this was false. When the machine is the Godhead, and production or work is worship, then the most mechanical mind is purest and highest, the representative of God on earth. And the rest are subordinate, each according to his degree.

Riots broke out, Whatmore pit-head was in flames. This was the pit farthest in the country, near the woods. Soldiers came. From the windows of Shortlands, on that fatal day, could be seen the flare of fire in the sky not far off, and now the little colliery train, with the workmen's carriages which were used to convey the miners to the distant Whatmore, was crossing the valley full of soldiers, full of red-coats. Then there was the far-off sound of firing, then the later news that the mob was dispersed, one man was shot dead, the fire was put out.

Gerald, who was a boy, was filled with the wildest excitement and delight. He longed to go with the soldiers to shoot the men. But he was not allowed to go out of the lodge gates. At the gates were stationed sentries with guns. Gerald stood near them in delight, whilst gangs of derisive miners strolled up and down the lanes, calling and jeering:

'Now then, three ha'porth o' coppers, let's see thee shoot thy gun.' Insults were chalked on the walls and the fences, the servants left.

And all this while Thomas Crich was breaking his heart, and giving away hundreds of pounds in charity. Everywhere there was free food, a surfeit of free food. Anybody could have bread for asking, and a loaf cost only three-ha'pence. Every day there was a free tea somewhere, the children had never had so many treats in their lives. On Friday afternoon great basketfuls of buns and cakes were taken into the schools, and great pitchers of milk, the schoolchildren had what they wanted. They were sick with eating too much cake and milk.

And then it came to an end, and the men went back to work. But it was never the same as before. There was a new situation created, a new idea reigned. Even in the machine, there should be equality. No part should be subordinate to any other part: all should be equal. The instinct for chaos had entered. Mystic equality lies in abstraction, not in having or in doing, which are processes. In function and process, one man, one part, must of necessity be subordinate to another. It is a condition of being. But the desire for chaos had risen, and the idea of mechanical equality was the weapon of disruption which should execute the will of men, the will for chaos.

Gerald was a boy at the time of the strike, but he longed to be a man, to fight the colliers. The father, however, was trapped between two half-truths, and broken. He wanted to be a pure Christian, one and equal with all men. He even wanted to give away all he had, to the poor. Yet he was a great promoter of industry, and he knew perfectly that he must keep his goods and keep his authority. This was as divine a necessity in him, as the need to give away all he possessed – more divine, even, since this was the necessity he acted upon. Yet because he did *not* act on the other ideal, it dominated him, he was dying of chagrin because he must forfeit it. He wanted to be a father of loving kindness and sacrificial benevolence. The colliers shouted to him about his thousands a year. They would not be deceived.

When Gerald grew up in the ways of the world, he shifted the position. He did not care about the equality. The whole Christian attitude of love and self-sacrifice was old hat. He knew that position and authority were the right thing in the world, and it was useless to cant about it. They were the right thing, for the simple reason that they were functionally necessary. They were not the be-all and the end-all. It was like being part of a machine. He himself happened to be a controlling, central part, the masses of men were the parts variously controlled. This was merely as it happened. As well get excited because a central hub drives a hundred outer wheels – or because the whole universe wheels round the sun. After all, it would be mere silliness to say that the moon and the earth and Saturn and Jupiter and Venus have just as much right to be the centre of the universe, each of them separately, as the sun. Such an assertion is made merely in the desire of chaos.

Without bothering to *think* to a conclusion, Gerald jumped to a conclusion. He abandoned the whole democratic-equality problem as a problem of silliness. What mattered was the great social productive machine. Let that work perfectly, let it produce a sufficiency of everything, let every man be given a rational portion, greater or less according to his functional degree or magnitude, and then, provision made, let the devil supervene, let every man look after his own amusements and appetites, so long as he interfered with nobody.

So Gerald set himself to work, to put the great industry in order. In his travels, and in his accompanying readings, he had come to the conclusion that the essential secret of life was harmony. He did not define to himself at all clearly what harmony was. The word pleased him, he felt he had come to his own conclusions. And he proceeded to put his philosophy into practice by forcing order into the established world, translating the mystic word harmony into the practical word organization.

Immediately he *saw* the firm, he realized what he could do. He had a fight to fight with Matter, with the earth and the coal it enclosed. This was the sole idea, to turn upon the inanimate matter of the underground, and reduce it to his will. And for this fight with matter, one must have perfect instruments in perfect organization, a mechanism so subtle and harmonious in its workings that it represents the single mind of man, and by its relentless repetition of given movement, will accomplish a purpose irresistibly, inhumanly. It was this inhuman principle in the mechanism he wanted to construct that inspired Gerald with an almost religious exaltation. He, the man, could interpose a perfect, changeless, godlike medium between himself and the Matter he had to subjugate. There were two opposites, his will and the resistant Matter of the earth. And between these he could establish the very expression of his will, the incarnation of his power, a great and perfect machine, a system, an activity of pure order, pure mechanical repetition, repetition *ad infinitum*, hence eternal and infinite. He found his eternal and his infinite in the pure machine-principle of perfect co-ordination into one pure, complex, infinitely repeated motion, like the spinning of a wheel; but a productive spinning, as the revolving of the universe may be called a productive spinning, a productive repetition through eternity, to infinity. And this is the God-motion, this productive repetition *ad infinitum*. And Gerald was the God of the machine, *Deus ex Machina*. And the whole productive will of man was the Godhead.

He had his life-work now, to extend over the earth a great and perfect system in which the will of man ran smooth and unthwarted, timeless, a Godhead in process. He had to begin with the mines. The terms were given: first the resistant Matter of the underground; then the instruments of its subjugation, instruments human and metallic; and finally his own pure will, his own mind. It would need a marvellous adjustment of myriad instruments, human, animal, metallic, kinetic, dynamic, a marvellous casting of myriad tiny wholes into one great perfect entirety. And then, in this case there was perfection attained, the will of the highest was perfectly fulfilled, the will of mankind was perfectly enacted; for was not mankind mystically con-tradistinguished against inanimate Matter, was not the history of mankind just the history of the conquest of the one by the other?

The miners were overreached. While they were still in the toils of divine equality of man, Gerald had passed on, granted essentially their case, and proceeded in his quality of human being to fulfil the will of mankind as a whole. He merely represented the miners in a higher sense when he perceived that the only way to fulfil perfectly the will of man was to establish the perfect, inhuman machine. But he represented them very essentially, they were far behind, out of date, squabbling for their material equality. The desire had already transmuted into this new and greater desire, for a perfect intervening mechanism between man and Matter, the desire to translate the Godhead into pure mechanism.

As soon as Gerald entered the firm, the convulsion of death ran through the old system. He had all his life been tortured by a furious and destructive demon, which possessed him sometimes like an insanity. This temper now entered like a virus into the firm, and there were cruel eruptions. Terrible and inhuman were his examinations into every detail; there was no privacy he would spare, no old sentiment but he would turn it over. The old grey managers, the old grey clerks, the doddering old pensioners, he looked at them, and removed them as so much lumber. The whole concern seemed like a hospital of invalid employees. He had no emotional qualms. He arranged what pensions were necessary, he looked for efficient substitutes, and when these were found, he substituted them for the old hands.

'I've a pitiful letter here from Letherington,' his father would say, in a tone of deprecation and appeal. 'Don't you think the poor fellow might keep on a little longer. I always fancied he did very well.'

'I've got a man in his place now, father. He'll be happier out of it, believe me. You think his allowance is plenty, don't you?'

'It is not the allowance that he wants, poor man. He feels it very much, that he is superannuated. Says he thought he had twenty more years of work in him yet.'

'Not of this kind of work I want. He doesn't understand.'

The father sighed. He wanted not to know any more. He believed the pits would have to be overhauled if they were to go on working. And after all, it would be worst in the long run for everybody, if they must close down. So he could make no answer to the appeals of his old and trusty servants, he could only repeat 'Gerald says'.

So the father drew more and more out of the light. The whole frame of the real life was broken for him. He had been right according to his lights. And his lights had been those of the great religion. Yet they seemed to have become obsolete, to be superseded in the world. He could not understand. He only withdrew with his lights into an inner room, into the silence. The beautiful candles of belief, that would not do to light the world any more, they would still burn sweetly and sufficiently in the inner room of his soul, and in the silence of his retirement.

Gerald rushed into the reform of the firm, beginning with the office. It was needful to economize severely, to make possible the great alterations he must introduce.

'What are these widows' coals?' he asked.

'We have always allowed all widows of men who worked for the firm a load of coals every three months.'

'They must pay cost price henceforth. The firm is not a charity institution, as everybody seems to think.'

Widows, these stock figures of sentimental humanitarianism, he felt a dislike at the thought of them. They were almost repulsive. Why were they not immolated on the pyre of the husband, like the sati in India? At any rate, let them pay the cost of their coals.

In a thousand ways he cut down the expenditure, in ways so fine as to be hardly noticeable to the men. The miners must pay for the cartage of their coals, heavy cartage too; they must pay for their tools, for the sharpening, for the care of lamps, for the many trifling things that made the bill of charges against every man mount up to a shilling or so in the week. It was not grasped very definitely by the miners, though they were sore enough. But it saved hundreds of pounds every week for the firm.

Gradually Gerald got hold of everything. And then began the great reform. Expert engineers were introduced in every department. An enormous electric plant was installed, both for lighting and for haulage underground, and for power. The electricity was carried into every mine. New machinery was brought from America, such as the miners had never seen before, great iron men, as the cutting machines were called, and unusual appliances. The working of the pits was thoroughly changed, all the control was taken out of the hands of the miners, the butty system was abolished. Everything was run on the most accurate and delicate scientific method, educated and expert men were in control everywhere, the miners were reduced to mere mechanical instruments. They had to work hard, much harder than before, the work was terrible and heart-breaking in its mechanicalness.

But they submitted to it all. The joy went out of their lives, the hope seemed to perish as they became more and more mechanized. And yet they accepted the new conditions. They even got a further satisfaction out of them. At first they hated Gerald Crich, they swore to do something to him, to murder him. But as time went on, they accepted everything with some fatal satisfaction. Gerald was their high priest, he represented the religion they really felt. His father was forgotten already. There was a new world, a new order, strict, terrible, inhuman, but satisfying in its very destructiveness. The men were satisfied to belong to the great and wonderful machine, even whilst it destroyed them. It was what they wanted. It was the highest that man had produced, the most wonderful and superhuman. They were exalted by belonging to this great and superhuman system which was beyond feeling or reason, something really godlike. Their hearts died within them, but their souls were satisfied. It was what they wanted. Otherwise Gerald could never have done what he did. He was just ahead of them in giving them what they wanted, this participation in a great and perfect system that subjected life to pure mathematical principles. This was a sort of freedom, the sort they really wanted. It was the first great step in undoing, the first great phase of chaos, the substitution of the mechanical principle for the organic, the destruction of the organic purpose, the organic unity, and the subordination of every organic unit to the great mechanical purpose. It was pure organic disintegration and pure mechanical organization. This is the first and finest state of chaos.

Gerald was satisfied. He knew the colliers said they hated him. But he had long ceased to hate them. When they streamed past him at evening, their heavy boots slurring on the pavement wearily, their shoulders slightly distorted, they took no notice of him, they gave him no greeting whatever, they passed in a grey-black stream of unemotional acceptance. They were not important to him, save as instruments, nor he to them, save as a supreme instrument of control. As miners they had their being, he had his being as director. He admired their qualities. But as men, personalities, they were just accidents, sporadic little unimportant phenomena. And tacitly, the men agreed to this. For Gerald agreed to it in himself.

He had succeeded. He had converted the industry into a new and terrible purity. There was a greater output of coal than ever, the wonderful and delicate system ran almost perfectly. He had a set of really clever engineers, both mining and electrical, and they did not cost much. A highly educated man cost very little more than a workman. His managers, who were all rare men, were no more expensive than the old bungling fools of his father's days, who were merely colliers promoted. His chief manager, who had twelve hundred a year, saved the firm at least five thousand. The whole system was now so perfect that Gerald was hardly necessary any more.

It was so perfect that sometimes a strange fear came over him, and he did not know what to do. He went on for some years in a sort of trance of activity. What he was doing seemed supreme, he was almost like a divinity. He was a pure and exalted activity.

But now he had succeeded – he had finally succeeded. And once or twice lately, when he was alone in the evening and had nothing to do, he had suddenly stood up in terror, not knowing what he was. And he went to the mirror and looked long and closely at his own face, at his own eyes, seeking for something. He was afraid, in mortal dry fear, but he knew not what of. He looked at his own face. There it was, shapely and healthy and the same as ever, yet somehow, it was not real, it was a mask. He dared not touch it, for fear it should prove to be only a composition mask. His eyes were blue and keen as ever, and as firm in their sockets. Yet he was not sure that they were not blue false bubbles that would burst in a moment and leave clear annihilation. He could see the darkness in them, as if they were only bubbles of darkness. He was afraid that one day he would break down and be a purely meaningless babble lapping round a darkness.

But his will yet held good, he was able to go away and read, and think about things. He liked to read books about the primitive man, books of anthropology, and also works of speculative philosophy. His mind was very active. But it was like a bubble floating in the darkness. At any moment it might burst and leave him in chaos. He would not die. He knew that. He would go on living, but the meaning would have collapsed out of him, his divine reason would be gone. In a strangely indifferent, sterile way, he was frightened. But he could not react even to the fear. It was as if his centres of feelings were drying up. He remained calm, calculative and healthy, and quite freely deliberate, even whilst he felt, with faint, small but final sterile horror, that his mystic reason was breaking, giving way now, at this crisis.

And it was a strain. He knew there was no equilibrium. He would have to go in some direction, shortly, to find relief. Only Birkin kept the fear definitely off him, saved him his quick sufficiency in life, by the odd mobility and changeableness which seemed to contain the quintessence of faith. But then Gerald must always come away from Birkin, as from a Church service, back to the outside real world of work and life. There it was, it did not alter, and words were futilities. He had to keep himself in reckoning with the world of work and material life. And it became more and more difficult, such a strange pressure was upon him, as if the very middle of him were a vacuum, and outside were an awful tension.

He had found his most satisfactory relief in women. After a debauch with some desperate woman, he went on quite easy and forgetful. The devil of it was, it was so hard to keep up his interest in women nowadays. He didn't care about them any more. A Pussum was all right in her way, but she was an exceptional case, and even she mattered extremely little. No, women, in that sense, were useless to him any more. He felt that his *mind* needed acute stimulation, before he could be physically roused.

18

RABBIT

Gudrun knew that it was a critical thing for her to go to Shortlands. She knew it was equivalent to accepting Gerald Crich as a lover. And though she hung back, disliking the condition, yet she knew she would go on. She equivocated. She said to herself, in torment recalling the blow and the kiss, 'After all, what is it? What is a kiss? What even is a blow? It is an instant, vanished at once. I can go to Shortlands just for a time, before I go away, if only to see what it is like.' For she had an insatiable curiosity to see and to know everything.

She also wanted to know what Winifred was really like. Having heard the child calling from the steamer in the night, she felt some mysterious connection with her.

Gudrun talked with the father in the library. Then he sent for his daughter. She came accompanied by Mademoiselle.

'Winnie, this is Miss Brangwen, who will be so kind as to help you with your drawing and making models of your animals,' said the father.

The child looked at Gudrun for a moment with interest, before she came forward, and with face averted offered her hand. There was a complete *sang*

froid and indifference under Winifred's childish reserve, a certain irresponsible callousness.

'How do you do?' said the child, not lifting her face.

'How do you do?' said Gudrun.

Then Winifred stood aside, and Gudrun was introduced to Mademoiselle.

'You have a fine day for your walk,' said Mademoiselle, in a bright manner.

'*Quite* fine,' said Gudrun.

Winifred was watching from her distance. She was as if amused, but rather
unsure as yet what this new person was like. She saw so many new persons,
and so few who became real to her. Mademoiselle was of no count whatever,
the child merely put up with her, calmly and easily, accepting her little
authority with faint scorn, compliant out of childish arrogance of
indifference.

'Well, Winifred,' said the father, 'aren't you glad Miss Brangwen has come?
She makes animals and birds in wood and in clay, that the people in London
write about in the papers, praising them to the skies.'

Winifred smiled slightly.

'Who told you, Daddy?' she asked.

'Who told me? Hermione told me, and Rupert Birkin.'

'Do you know them?' Winifred asked of Gudrun, turning to her with faint
challenge.

'Yes,' said Gudrun.

Winifred readjusted herself a little. She had been ready to accept Gudrun as
a sort of servant. Now she saw it was on terms of friendship they were
intended to meet. She was rather glad. She had so many half inferiors, whom
she tolerated with perfect good-humour.

Gudrun was very calm. She also did not take these things very seriously. A
new occasion was mostly spectacular to her. However, Winifred was a
detached, ironic child, she would never attach herself. Gudrun liked her and
was intrigued by her. The first meetings went off with a certain humiliating
clumsiness. Neither Winifred nor her instructress had any social grace.

Soon, however, they met in a kind of make-believe world. Winifred did not
notice human beings unless they were like herself, playful and slightly
mocking. She would accept nothing but the world of amusement, and the
serious people of her life were the animals she had for pets. On those she
lavished, almost ironically, her affection and her companionship. To the rest
of the human scheme she submitted with a faint bored indifference.

She had a Pekinese dog called Looloo, which she loved.

'Let us draw Looloo,' said Gudrun, 'and see if we can get his Looliness,
shall we?'

'Darling!' cried Winifred, rushing to the dog, that sat with comtemplative
sadness on the hearth, and kissing its bulging brow. 'Darling one, will you be
drawn? Shall its mummy draw its portrait?' Then she chuckled gleefully, and
turning to Gudrun, said: 'Oh, let's!'

They proceeded to get pencils and paper, and were ready.

'Beautifullest,' cried Winifred, hugging the dog, 'sit still while its mummy
draws its beautiful portrait.' The dog looked up at her with grievous
resignation in its large, prominent eyes. She kissed it fervently, and said: 'I
wonder what mine will be like. It's sure to be awful.'

As she sketched she chuckled to herself, and cried out at times:

'Oh, darling, you're so beautiful!'

And again chuckling, she rushed to embrace the dog, in penitence, as if she were doing him some subtle injury. He sat all the time with the resignation and fretfulness of ages on his dark velvety face. She drew slowly, with a wicked concentration in her eyes, her head on one side, an intense stillness over her. She was as if working the spell of some enchantment. Suddenly she had finished. She looked at the dog, and then at her drawing, and then cried, with real grief for the dog, and at the same time with a wicked exultation:

'My beautiful, why did they?'

She took her paper to the dog, and held it under his nose. He turned his head aside as in chagrin and mortification, and she impulsively kissed his velvety bulging forehead.

''s a Loolie, 's a little Loozie! Look at his portrait, darling, look at his portrait, that his mother has done of him.' She looked at her paper and chuckled. Then, kissing the dog once more, she rose and came gravely to Gudrun, offering her the paper.

It was a grotesque little diagram of a grotesque little animal, so wicked and so comical, a slow smile came over Gudrun's face, unconsciously. And at her side Winifred chuckled with glee, and said.

'It isn't like him, is it? He's much lovelier than that. He's *so* beautiful – mmm, Looloo, my sweet darling.' And she flew off to embrace the chagrined little dog. He looked up at her with reproachful, saturnine eyes, vanquished in his extreme agedness of being. Then she flew back to her drawing, and chuckled with satisfaction.

'It isn't like him, is it?' she said to Gudrun.

'Yes, it's very like him,' Gudrun replied.

The child treasured her drawing, carried it about with her, and showed it, with a silent embarrassment, to everybody.

'Look,' she said, thrusting the paper into her father's hand.

'Why, that's Looloo!' he exclaimed. And he looked down in surprise, hearing the almost inhuman chuckle of the child at his side.

Gerald was away from home when Gudrun first came to Shortlands. But the first morning he came back he watched for her. It was a sunny, soft morning, and he lingered in the garden paths, looking at the flowers that had come out during his absence. He was clean and fit as ever, shaven, his fair hair scrupulously parted at the side, bright in the sunshine, his short, fair moustache closely clipped, his eyes with their humorous kind twinkle, which was so deceptive. He was dressed in black, his clothes sat well on his well-nourished body. Yet as he lingered before the flower-beds in the morning sunshine, there was a certain isolation, a fear about him, as of something wanting.

Gudrun came up quickly, unseen. She was dressed in blue, with woollen yellow stockings, like the Bluecoat boys. He glanced up in surprise. Her stockings always disconcerted him, the pale-yellow stockings and the heavy, heavy black shoes. Winifred, who had been playing about the garden with Mademoiselle and the dogs, came flitting towards Gudrun. The child wore a dress of black-and-white stripes. Her hair was rather short, cut round and hanging level in her neck.

'We're going to do Bismarck, aren't we?' she said, linking her hand through Gudrun's arm.

'Yes, we're going to do Bismarck. Do you want to?'

'Oh yes – oh, I do! I want most awfully to do Bismarck. He looks *so* splendid this morning, so *fierce*. He's almost as big as a lion.' And the child chuckled sardonically at her own hyperbole. 'He's a real king, he really is.'

'*Bon jour, Mademoiselle,*' said the little French governess, wavering up with a slight bow, a bow of the sort that Gudrun loathed, insolent.

'*Winifred veut tant faire le portrait de Bismarck –!* Oh, *mais toute la matinée – "We will do Bismarck this morning!"* – *Bismarck, Bismarck, toujours Bismarck! C'est un lapin, n'est-ce pas, mademoiselle?*'

'*Oui, c'est un grand lapin blanc et noir. Vous ne l'avez pas vu?*' said Gudrun in her good, but rather heavy French.

'*Non, mademoiselle, Winifred n'a jamais voulu me le faire voir. Tant de fois je le lui ai demandé, Qu'est ce donc que ce Bismarck, Winifred?* Mais elle n'a pas voulu me le dire. Son Bismarck, c'était un mystère.*'

'*Oui, c'est un mysterè, vraiment un mysterè!* Miss Brangwen, say that Bismarck is a mystery,' cried Winifred.

'Bismarck, is a mystery, Bismarck, *c'est un mysterè, der Bismarck, er ist ein Wunder,*' said Gudrun, in mocking incantation.

'*Ja, er ist ein Wunder,*' repeated Winifred, with odd seriousness, under which lay a wicked chuckle.

'*Ist er auch ein Wunder?*' came the slightly insolent sneering of Mademoiselle.

'*Doch!*' said Winifred briefly, indifferent.

'*Doch ist er nicht ein König,* Beesmarck, he was not a king, Winifred, as you have said. He was only – *il n'était que chancelier.*'

'*Qu'est ce qu'un chancelier?*' said Winifred, with slightly contemptuous indifference.

'A chancelier is a chancellor, and a chancellor is, I believe, a sort of judge,' said Gerald, coming up and shaking hands with Gudrun. 'You'll have made a song of Bismarck soon,' said he.

Mademoiselle waited, and discreetly made her inclination, and her greeting.

'So they wouldn't let you see Bismarck, Mademoiselle?' he said.

'*Non, Monsieur.*'

'Ay, very mean of them. What are you going to do to him, Miss Brangwen? I want him sent to the kitchen and cooked.'

'Oh no,' cried Winifred.

'We're going to draw him,' said Gudrun.

'Draw him and quarter him and dish him up,' he said, being purposely fatuous.

'Oh no,' cried Winifred with emphasis, chuckling.

Gudrun detected the tang of mockery in him, and she looked up and smiled into his face. He felt his nerves caressed. Their eyes met in knowledge.

'How do you like Shortlands?' he asked.

'Oh, very much,' she said, with nonchalance.

'Glad you do. Have you noticed these flowers?'

He led her along the path. She followed intently. Winifred came, and the governess lingered in the rear. They stopped before some veined salpiglossis flowers.

'Aren't they wonderful?' she cried, looking at them absorbedly. Strange how her reverential, almost ecstatic admiration of the flowers caressed his nerves. She stooped down, and touched the trumpets, with infinitely fine and delicate-touching finger-tips. It filled him with ease to see her. When she rose, her eyes, hot with the beauty of the flowers, looked into his.

'What are they?' she asked.

'Sort of petunia, I suppose,' he answered. 'I don't really know them.'

'They are quite strangers to me,' she said.

They stood together in a false intimacy, a nervous contact. And he was in love with her.

She was aware of Mademoiselle standing near, like a little French beetle, observant and calculating. She moved away with Winifred, saying they would go to find Bismarck.

Gerald watched them go, looking all the while at the soft, full, still body of Gudrun, in its silky cashmere. How silky and rich and soft her body must be. An excess of appreciation came over his mind, she was the all-desirable, the all-beautiful. He wanted only to come to her, nothing more. He was only this, this being that should come to her, and be given to her.

At the same time he was finely and acutely aware of Mademoiselle's neat, brittle finality of form. She was like some elegant beetle with thin ankles, perched on her high heels, her glossy black dress perfectly correct, her dark hair done high and admirably. How repulsive her completeness and her finality was! He loathed her.

Yet he did admire her. She was perfectly correct. And it did rather annoy him, that Gudrun came dressed in startling colours, like a macaw, when the family was in mourning. Like a macaw she was! He watched the lingering way she took her feet from the ground. And her ankles were pale yellow, and her dress a deep blue. Yet it pleased him. It pleased him very much. He felt the challenge in her very attire – she challenged the whole world. And he smiled as to the note of a trumpet.

Gudrun and Winifred went through the house to the back, where were the stables and the out-buildings. Everywhere was still and deserted. Mr Crich had gone out for a short drive, the stable-man had just led round Gerald's horse. The two girls went to the hutch that stood in a corner, and looked at the great black-and-white rabbit.

'Isn't he beautiful! Oh, do look at him listening! Doesn't he look silly!' she laughed quickly, then added: 'Oh, do let's do him listening, do let us, he listens with so much of himself; – don't you, darling Bismarck?'

'Can we take him out?' said Gudrun.

'He's very strong. He really is extremely strong.' She looked at Gudrun, her head on one side, in odd calculating mistrust.

'But we'll try, shall we?'

'Yes, if you like. But he's a fearful kicker!'

They took the key to unlock the door. The rabbit exploded in a wild rush round the hutch.

'He scratches most awfully sometimes,' cried Winifred in excitement. 'Oh, do look at him, isn't he wonderful!' The rabbit tore round the hutch in a flurry. 'Bismarck!' cried the child, in rousing excitement. 'How *dreadful* you are! You are beastly.' Winifred looked up at Gudrun with some misgiving in her wild excitement. Gudrun smiled sardonically with her mouth. Winifred made a strange crooning noise of unaccountable excitement. 'Now he's still!' she cried, seeing the rabbit settle down in a far corner of the hutch. 'Shall we take him now?' she whispered excitedly, mysteriously, looking up at Gudrun and edging very close. 'Shall we get him now? –' she chuckled wickedly to herself.

They unlocked the door of the hutch. Gudrun thrust in her arm and seized the great, lusty rabbit as it crouched still, she grasped its long ears. It set its four feet flat, and thrust back. There was a long scraping sound as it was hauled forward, and in another instant it was in mid-air, lunging wildly, its body flying like a spring coiled and released, as it lashed out, suspended from the ears. Gudrun held the black-and-white tempest at arms' length, averting her face. But the rabbit was magically strong, it was all she could do to keep her grasp. She almost lost her presence of mind.

'Bismarck, Bismarck, you are behaving terribly,' said Winifred in a rather frightened voice. 'Oh, do put him down, he's beastly.'

Gudrun stood for a moment astounded by the thunderstorm that had sprung into being in her grip. Then her colour came up, a heavy rage came over her like a cloud. She stood shaken as a house in a storm, and utterly overcome. Her heart was arrested with fury at the mindlessness and the bestial stupidity of this struggle, her wrists were badly scored by the claws of the beast, a heavy cruelty welled up in her.

Gerald came round as she was trying to capture the flying rabbit under her arm. He saw, with subtle recognition, her sullen passion of cruelty.

'You should let one of the men do that for you,' he said, hurrying up.

'Oh, he's *so* horrid!' cried Winifred, almost frantic.

He held out his nervous, sinewy hand and took the rabbit by the ears from Gudrun.

'It's most *fearfully* strong,' she cried in a high voice, like the crying of a seagull, strange and vindictive.

The rabbit made itself into a ball in the air and lashed out, flinging itself into a bow. It really seemed demoniacal. Gudrun saw Gerald's body tighten, saw a sharp blindness come into his eyes.

'I know these beggars of old,' he said.

The long, demon-like beast lashed out again, spread on the air as if it were flying, looking something like a dragon, then closing up again, inconceivably powerful and explosive. The man's body, strung to its efforts, vibrated strongly. Then a sudden sharp, white-edged wrath came up in him. Swift as lightning he drew back and brought his free hand down like a hawk on the neck of the rabbit. Simultaneously, there came the unearthly abhorrent scream of a rabbit in the fear of death. It made one immense writhe, tore his wrists and his sleeves in a final convulsion, all its belly flashed white in a whirlwind of paws, and then he had slung it round and had it under his arm, fast. It cowered and skulked. His face was gleaming with a smile.

'You wouldn't think there was all that force in a rabbit,' he said, looking at Gudrun. And he saw her eyes black as night in her pallid face, she looked almost unearthly. The scream of the rabbit, after the violent tussle, seemed to have torn the veil of her consciousness. He looked at her, and the whitish, electric gleam in his face intensified.

'I don't really like him,' Winifred was crooning. 'I don't care for him as I do for Loozie. He's hateful really.'

A smile twisted Gudrun's face as she recovered. She knew she was revealed.

'Don't they make the most fearful noise when they scream?' she cried, the high note in her voice like a seagull's cry.

'Abominable,' he said.

'He shouldn't be so silly when he has to be taken out,' Winifred was saying, putting out her hand and touching the rabbit tentatively, as it skulked under his arm, motionless as if it were dead.

'He's not dead, is he, Gerald?' she asked.

'No, he ought to be,' he said.

'Yes, he ought!' cried the child, with a sudden flush of amusement. And she touched the rabbit with more confidence. 'His heart is beating *so* fast. Isn't he funny? He really is.'

'Where do you want him?' asked Gerald.

'In the little green court,' she said.

Gudrun looked at Gerald with strange, darkened eyes, strained with underworld knowledge, almost supplicating, like those of a creature which is at his mercy, yet which is his ultimate victor. He did not know what to say to her. He felt the mutual hellish recognition. And he felt he ought to say something to cover it. He had the power of lightning in his nerves, she seemed like a soft recipient of his magical, hideous white fire. He was unconfident, he had qualms of fear.

'Did he hurt you?' he asked.

'No,' she said.

'He's an insensible beast,' he said, turning his face away.

They came to the little court, which was shut in by old red walls in whose crevices wallflowers were growing. The grass was soft and fine and old, a level floor carpeting the court, the sky was blue overhead. Gerald tossed the rabbit down. It crouched still and would not move. Gudrun watched it with faint horror.

'Why doesn't it move?' she cried.

'It's skulking,' he said.

She looked up at him, and a slight sinister smile contracted her white face.

'Isn't it a *fool*!' she cried. 'Isn't it a sickening *fool*?' The vindictive mockery in her voice made his brain quiver. Glancing up at him, into his eyes, she revealed again the mocking, white-cruel recognition. There was a league between them, abhorrent to them both. They were implicated with each other in abhorrent mysteries.

'How many scratches have you?' he asked, showing his hard forearm, white and hard and torn in red gashes.

'How really vile!' she cried, flushing with a sinister vision. 'Mine is nothing.'

She lifted her arm and showed a deep red score down the silken white flesh.

'What a devil!' he exclaimed. But it was as if he had had knowledge of her in the long red rent of her forearm, so silken and soft. He did not want to touch her. He would have to make himself touch her, deliberately. The long, shallow red rip seemed torn across his own brain, tearing the surface of his ultimate consciousness, letting through the for ever unconscious, unthinkable red ether of the beyond, the obscene beyond.

'It doesn't hurt you very much, does it?' he asked, solicitous.

'Not at all,' she cried.

And suddenly the rabbit, which had been crouching as if it were a flower, so still and soft, suddenly burst into life. Round and round the court it went, as if shot from a gun, round and round like a furry meteorite, in a tense hard circle that seemed to bind their brains. They all stood in amazement, smiling uncannily, as if the rabbit were obeying some unknown incantation. Round and round it flew, on the grass under the old red walls like a storm.

And then quite suddenly it settled down, hobbled among the grass, and sat considering, its nose twitching like a bit of fluff in the wind. After having considered for a few minutes, a soft bunch with a black, open eye, which perhaps was looking at them, perhaps was not, it hobbled calmly forward and began to nibble the grass with that mean motion of a rabbit's quick eating.

'It's mad,' said Gudrun. 'It is most decidedly mad.'

He laughed.

'The question is,' he said, 'what is madness? I don't suppose it is rabbit-mad.'

'Don't you think it is?' she asked.

'No. That's what it is to be a rabbit.'

There was a queer, faint, obscene smile over his face. She looked at him and saw him, and knew that he was initiate as she was initiate. This thwarted her, and contravened her, for the moment.

'God be praised we aren't rabbits,' she said in a high, shrill voice.

The smile intensified a little on his face.

'Not rabbits?' he said, looking at her fixedly.

Slowly her face relaxed into a smile of obscene recognition.

'Ah, Gerald,' she said in a strong, slow, almost man-like way. '– All that, and more.' Her eyes looked up at him with shocking nonchalance.

He felt again as if she had hit him across the face – or rather as if she had torn him across the breast, dully, finally. He turned aside.

'Eat, eat, my darling!' Winifred was softly conjuring the rabbit, and creeping forward to touch it. It hobbled away from her. 'Let its mother stroke its fur then, darling, because it is so mysterious –'

19

MOONY

After his illness Birkin went to the south of France for a time. He did not write, nobody heard anything of him. Ursula, left alone, felt as if everything were lapsing out. There seemed to be no hope in the world. One was a tiny little rock with the tide of nothingness rising higher and higher. She herself was real, and only herself – just like a rock in a wash of flood-water. The rest was all nothingness. She was hard and indifferent, isolated in herself.

There was nothing for it now, but contemptuous, resistant indifference. All the world was lapsing into a grey wish-wash of nothingness, she had no contact and no connection anywhere. She despised and detested the whole show. From the bottom of her heart, from the bottom of her soul, she despised and detested people, adult people. She loved only children and animals: children she loved passionately, but coldly. They made her want to hug them, to protect them, to give them life. But this very love, based on pity and despair, was only a bondage and a pain to her. She loved best of all the animals, that were single and unsocial as she herself was. She loved the horses and cows in the field. Each was single and to itself, magical. It was not referred away to some detestable social principle. It was incapable of soulfulness and tragedy, which she detested so profoundly.

She could be very pleasant and flattering, almost subservient, to people she met. But no one was taken in. Instinctively each felt her contemptuous mockery of the human being in himself, or herself. She had a profound grudge against the human being. That which the word 'human' stood for was despicable and repugnant to her.

Mostly her heart was closed in this hidden, unconscious strain of contemptuous ridicule. She thought she loved, she thought she was full of love. This was her idea of herself. But the strange brightness of her presence, a marvellous radiance of intrinsic vitality, was a luminousness of supreme repudiation, nothing but repudiation.

Yet, at moments, she yielded and softened, she wanted pure love, only pure love. This other, this state of constant unfailing repudiation, was a strain, a suffering also. A terrible desire for pure love overcame her again.

She went out one evening, numbed by this constant essential suffering. Those who are timed for destruction must die now. The knowledge of this reached a finality, a finishing in her. And the finality released her. If fate would carry off in death or downfall all those who are timed to go, why need she trouble, why repudiate any further. She was free of it all, she could seek a new union elsewhere.

Ursula set off to Willey Green, towards the mill. She came to Willey Water. It was almost full again, after its period of emptiness. Then she turned off through the woods. The night had fallen, it was dark. But she forgot to be afraid, she who had such great sources of fear. Among the trees, far from any human beings, there was a sort of magic peace. The more one could find a pure loneliness, with no taint of people, the better one felt. She was in reality terrified, horrified in her apprehension of people.

She started, noticing something on her right hand, between the tree-trunks. It was like a great presence, watching her, dodging her. She started violently. It was only the moon, risen through the thin trees. But it seemed so mysterious, with its white and deathly smile. And there was no avoiding it. Night or day, one could not escape the sinister face, triumphant and radiant like this moon, with a high smile. She hurried on, cowering from the white planet. She would just see the pond at the mill before she went home.

Not wanting to go through the yard, because of the dogs, she turned off along the hill-side to descend on the pond from above. The moon was transcendent over the bare, open space, she suffered from being exposed to it. There was a glimmer of nightly rabbits across the ground. The night was as clear as crystal, and very still. She could hear a distant coughing of a sheep.

So she swerved doen to the steep, tree-hidden bank above the pond, where the alders twisted their roots. She was glad to pass into the shade out of the moon. There she stood, at the top of the fallen-away bank, her hand on the rough trunk of a tree, looking at the water, that was perfect in its stillness, floating the moon upon it. But for some reason she disliked it. It did not give her anything. She listened for the hoarse rustle of the sluice. And she wished for something else out of the night, she wanted another night, not this moon-brilliant hardness. She could feel her soul crying out in her, lamenting desolately.

She saw a shadow moving by the water. It would be Birkin. He had come back then, unawares. She accepted it without remark, nothing mattered to her. She sat down among the roots of the alder tree, dim and veiled, hearing the sound of the sluice like dew distilling audibly into the night. The islands were dark and half revealed, the reeds were dark also, only some of them had a little frail fire of reflection. A fish leaped secretly, revealing the light in the pond. This fire of the chill night breaking constantly on to the pure darkness, repelled her. She wished it were perfectly dark, perfectly, and noiseless and without motion. Birkin, small and dark also, his hair tinged with moonlight, wandered nearer. He was quite near, and yet he did not exist in her. He did not know she was there. Supposing he did something he would not wish to be seen doing, thinking he was quite private? But there, what did it matter? What did the small privacies matter? How could it matter, what he did? How can there be any secrets, we are all the same organisms? How can there be any secrecy, when everything is known to all of us?

He was touching unconsciously the dead husks of flowers as he passed by, and talking disconnectedly to himself.

'You can't go away,' he was saying. 'There *is* no away. You only withdraw upon yourself.'

He threw a dead flower-husk on to the water.

'An antiphony – they lie, and you sing back to them. There wouldn't have to be any truth, if there weren't any lies. Then one needn't assert anything –'

He stood still, looking at the water, and throwing upon it the husks of the flowers.

'Cybele – curse her! The accused Syria Dea! Does one begrudge it her? What else is there – ?'

Ursula wanted to laugh loudly and hysterically, hearing his isolated voice speaking out. It was so ridiculous.

He stood staring at the water. Then he stooped and picked up a stone, which he threw sharply at the pond. Ursula was aware of the bright moon leaping and swaying, all distorted, in her eyes. It seemed to shoot out arms of fire like a cuttle-fish, like a luminous polyp, palpitating strongly before her.

And his shadow on the border of the pond was watching for a few moments, then he stooped and groped on the ground. Then again there was a burst of sound, and a burst of brilliant light, the moon had exploded on the water, and was flying asunder in flakes of white and dangerous fire. Rapidly, like white birds, the fires all broken rose across the pond, fleeing in clamorous confusion, battling with the flock of dark waves that were forcing their way in. The furthest waves of light, fleeing out, seemed to be clamouring against the shore for escape, the waves of darkness came in heavily, running under towards the centre. But at the centre, the heart of all, was still a vivid, incandescent quivering of a white moon not quite destroyed, a white body of fire writhing and striving and not even now broken open, not yet violated. It seemed to be drawing itself together with strange, violent pangs, in blind effort. It was getting stronger, it was re-asserting itself, the inviolable moon. And the rays were hastening in in thin lines of light, to return to the strengthened moon, that shook upon the water in triumphant reassumption.

Birkin stood and watched, motionless, till the pond was almost calm, the moon was almost serene. Then, satisfied of so much, he looked for more stones. She felt his invisible tenacity. And in a moment again, the broken lights scattered in explosion over her face, dazzling her; and then, almost immediately, came the second shot. The moon leapt up white and burst through the air. Darts of bright light shot asunder, darkness swept over the centre. There was no moon, only a battlefield of broken lights and shadows, running close together. Shadows, dark and heavy, struck again and again across the place where the heart of the moon had been, obliterating it altogether. The white fragments pulsed up and down, and could not find where to go, apart and brilliant on the water like the petals of a rose that a wind has blown far and wide.

Yet again, they were flickering their way to the centre, finding the path blindly, enviously. And again, all was still, as Birkin and Ursula watched. The waters were loud on the shore. He saw the moon regathering itself insidiously, saw the heart of the rose intertwining vigorously and blindly, calling back the scattered fragments, winning home the fragments, in a pulse and in effort of return.

And he was not satisfied. Like a madness, he must go on. He got large stones, and threw them, one after the other, at the white-burning centre of the moon, till there was nothing but a rocking of hollow noise, and a pond surged up, no moon any more, only a few broken flakes tangled and glittering broadcast in the darkness, without aim or meaning, a darkened confusion, like a black and white kaleidoscope tossed at random. The hollow night was rocking and crashing with noise, and from the sluice came sharp, regular flashes of sound. Flakes of light appeared here and there, glittering tormented among the shadows, far off, in strange places; among the dripping shadow of the willow on the island. Birkin stood and listened and was satisfied.

Ursula was dazed, her mind was all gone. She felt she had fallen to the ground and was spilled out, like water on the earth. Motionless and spent, she remained in the gloom. Though even now she was aware, unseeing, that in the darkness was a little tumult of ebbing flakes of light, a cluster dancing secretly in a round, twining and coming steadily together. They were gathering a heart again, they were coming once more into being. Gradually the fragments caught together re-united, heaving, rocking, dancing, falling back as in panic, but working their way home again persistently, making semblance of fleeing away when they had advanced, but always flickering nearer, a little closer to the mark, the cluster growing mysteriously larger and brighter, as gleam after gleam fell in with the whole, until a ragged rose, a distorted, frayed moon was shaking upon the waters again, re-asserted, renewed, trying to recover from its convulsion, to get over the disfigurement and the agitation, to be whole and composed, at peace.

Birkin lingered vaguely by the water. Ursula was afraid that he would stone the moon again. She slipped from her seat and went down to him, saying:

'You won't throw stones at it any more, will you?'

'How long have you been there?'

'All the time. You won't throw any more stones, will you?'

'I wanted to see if I could make it be quite gone off the pond,' he said.

'Yes, it was horrible, really. Why should you hate the moon? It hasn't done you any harm, has it?'

'Was it hate?' he said.

And they were silent for a few minutes.

'When did you come back?' she said.

'Today.'

'Why did you never write?'

'I could find nothing to say.'

'Why was there nothing to say?'

'I don't know. Why are there no daffodils now?'

'No.'

Again there was a space of silence. Ursula looked at the moon. It had gathered itself together, and was quivering slightly.

'Was it good for you to be alone?' she asked.

'Perhaps. Not that I know much. But I got over a good deal. Did you do anything important?'

'No. I looked at England, and thought I'd done with it.'

'Why England?' he asked in surprise.

'I don't know, it came like that.'

'It isn't a question of nations,' he said. 'France is far worse.'

'Yes, I know. I felt I'd done with it all.'

They went and sat down on the roots of the trees, in the shadow. And being silent, he remembered the beauty of her eyes, which were sometimes filled with light, like spring, suffused with wonderful promise. So he said to her, slowly, with difficulty:

'There is a golden light in you, which I wish you would give me.' It was as if he had been thinking of this for some time.

She was startled, she seemed to leap clear of him. Yet also she was pleased.

'What kind of a light?' she asked.

But he was shy, and did not say any more. So the moment passed for this time. And gradually a feeling of sorrow came over her.

'My life is unfulfilled,' she said.

'Yes,' he answered briefly, not wanting to hear this.

And I feel as if nobody could ever really love me,' she said.

But he did not answer.

'You think, don't you,' she said slowly, 'that I only want physical things? It isn't true. I want you to serve my spirit.'

'I know you do. I know you don't want physical things by themselves. But, I want you to give me – to give your spirit to me – that golden light which is you – which you don't know – give it me –'

After a moment's silence she replied:

'But how can I, you don't love me! You only want your own ends. You don't want to serve *me*, and yet you want me to serve you. It is so one-sided!'

It was a great effort to him to maintain this conversation, and to press for the thing he wanted from her, the surrender of her spirit.

'It is different,' he said. 'The two kinds of service are so different. I serve you in another way – not through *yourself* – somewhere else. But I want us to be together without bothering about ourselves – to be really together because we *are* together, as if it were a phenomenon, not a thing we have to maintain by our own effort.'

'No,' she said, pondering. 'You are just egocentric. You never have any enthusiasm, you never come out with any spark towards me. You want yourself, really, and your own affairs. And you want me just to be there, to serve you.'

But this only made him shut off from her.

'Ah well,' he said, 'words make no matter, anyway. The thing *is* between us, or it isn't.'

'You don't even love me,' she cried.

'I do,' he said angrily. 'But I want –' His mind saw again the lovely golden light of spring transfused through her eyes, as through some wonderful window. And he wanted her to be with him there, in this world of proud indifference. But what was the good of telling her he wanted this company in proud indifference. What was the good of talking, anyway? It must happen beyond the sound of words. It was merely ruinous to try to work her by conviction. This was a paradisal bird that could never be netted, it must fly by itself to the heart.

'I always think I am going to be loved – and then I am let down. You *don't* love me, you know. You don't want to serve me. You only want yourself.'

A shiver of rage went over his veins, at this repeated: 'You don't want to serve me.' All the paradisal disappeared from him.

'No,' he said, irritated, 'I don't want to serve you, because there is nothing there to serve. What you want me to serve is nothing, mere nothing. It isn't even you, it is your female quality. And I wouldn't give a straw for your female ego – it's a rag doll.'

'Ha!' she laughed in mockery. 'That's all you think of me, is it? And then you have the impudence to say you love me!'

She rose in anger, to go home.

'You want the paradisal unknowing,' she said, turning round on him as he still sat half visible in the shadow. 'I know what that means, thank you. You want me to be your thing, never to criticize you or to have anything to say for myself. You want me to be a mere *thing* for you! No, thank you! *If* you want that, there are plenty of women who will give it to you. There are plenty of women who will lie down for you to walk over them – *go* to them then, if that's what you want – go to them.'

'No,' he said, outspoken with anger. 'I want you to drop your assertive *will*, your frightened apprehensive self-insistence, that is what I want. I want you to trust yourself so implicitly that you can let yourself go.'

'Let myself go!' she re-echoed in mockery. '*I* can let myself go easily enough. It is you who can't let yourself go, it is you who hang on to yourself as if it were your only treasure. *You – you* are the Sunday school teacher – *You –* you preacher.'

The amount of truth that was in this made him stiff and unheeding of her.

'I don't mean let yourself go in the Dionysic ecstatic way,' he said. 'I know you can do that. But I hate ecstasy, Dionysic or any other. It's like going round in a squirrel cage. I want you not to care about yourself, just to be there and not to care about yourself, not to insist – be glad and sure and indifferent.'

'Who insists?' she mocked. 'Who is it that keeps on insisting? It isn't *me*!'

There was a weary, mocking bitterness in her voice. He was silent for some time.

'I know,' he said. 'While ever either of us insists to the other, we are all wrong. But there we are, the accord doesn't come.'

They sat in stillness under the shadow of the trees by the bank. The night was white around them, they were in the darkness, barely conscious.

Gradually, the stillness and peace came over them. She put her hand tentatively on his. Their hands clasped softly and silently in peace.

'Do you really love me?' she said.

He laughed.

'I call that your war-cry,' he replied, amused.

'Why!' she cried, amused and really wondering.

'Your insistence – Your war-cry – "A Brangwen, A Brangwen" – an old battle-cry. Yours is "Do you love me? Yield knave, or die."'

'No,' she said, pleading, 'not like that. Not like that. But I must know that you love me, mustn't I?'

'Well then, know it and have done with it.'

'But do you?'

'Yes, I do. I love you, and I know it's final. It is final, so why say any more about it.'

She was silent for some moments, in delight and doubt.

'Are you sure?' she said, nestling happily near to him.

'Quite sure – so now have done – accept it and have done.'

She was nestled quite close to him.

'Have done with what?' she murmured happily.

'With bothering,' he said.

She clung nearer to him. He held her close, and kissed her softly, gently. It was such peace and heavenly freedom, just to fold her and kiss her gently, and not to have any thoughts or any desires or any will, just to be still with her, to be perfectly still and together, in a peace that was not sleep, but content in bliss. To be content in bliss, without desire or insistence anywhere, this was heaven: to be together in happy stillness.

For a long time she nestled to him, and he kissed her softly, her hair, her face, her ears, gently, softly, like dew falling. But this warm breath on her ears disturbed her again, kindled the old destructive fires. She cleaved to him, and he could feel his blood changing like quicksilver.

'But we'll be still, shall we?' he said.

'Yes,' she said, as if submissively.

And she continued to nestle against him.

But in a little while she drew away and looked at him.

'I must be going home,' she said.

'Must you – how sad,' he replied.

She leaned forward and put up her mouth to be kissed.

'Are you really sad?' she murmured, smiling.

'Yes,' he said, 'I wish we could stay as we were, always.'

'Always! Do you?' she murmured, as he kissed her. And then, out of a full throat, she crooned: 'Kiss me! Kiss me!' And she cleaved close to him. He kissed her many times. But he too had his idea and his will. He wanted only gentle communion, no other, no passion now. So that soon she drew away, put on her hat and went home.

The next day, however, he felt wistful and yearning. He thought he had been wrong, perhaps. Perhaps he had been wrong to go to her with an idea of what he wanted. Was it really only an idea, or was it the interpretation of a profound yearning? If the latter, how was it he was always talking about sensual fulfilment? The two did not agree very well.

Suddenly he found himself face to face with a situation. It was as simple as this: fatally simple. On the one hand, he knew he did not want a further sensual experience – something deeper, darker, than ordinary life could give. He remembered the African fetishes he had seen at Halliday's so often. There came back to him one, a statuette about two feet high, a tall, slim, elegant figure from West Africa, in dark wood, glossy and suave. It was a woman, with hair dressed high, like a melon-shaped dome. He remembered her vividly: she was one of his soul's intimates. Her body was long and elegant, her face was crushed tiny like a beetle's, she had rows of round heavy collars, like a column of quoits, on her neck. He remembered her: her astonishing cultured elegance, her diminished, beetle face, the astounding long elegant body, on short, ugly legs, with such protuberant buttocks, so weighty and unexpected below her slim long loins. She knew what he himself did not know. She had thousands of years of purely sensual, purely unspiritual knowledge behind her. It must have been thousands of years since her race had died, mystically: that is, since the relation between the senses and the outspoken mind had broken, leaving the experience all in one sort, mystically sensual. Thousands of years ago, that which was imminent in himself must have taken place in these Africans: the goodness, the holiness, the desire for creation and productive happiness must have lapsed, leaving the single impulse for knowledge in one sort, mindless progressive knowledge through the senses, knowledge arrested and ending in the senses, mystic knowledge in disintegration and dissolution, knowledge such as the beetles have, which live purely within the world of corruption and cold dissolution. This was why her face looked like a beetle's: this was why the Egyptians worshipped the ball-rolling scarab: because of the principle of knowledge in dissolution and corruption.

There is a long way we can travel, after the death-break: after that point when the soul in intense suffering breaks, breaks away from its organic hold like a leaf that falls. We fall from the connection with life and hope, we lapse from pure integral being, from creation and liberty, and we fall into the long, long African process of purely sensual understanding, knowledge in the mystery of dissolution.

He realized now that this is a long process – thousands of years it takes, after the death of the creative spirit. He realized that there were great mysteries to be unsealed, sensual, mindless, dreadful mysteries, far beyond the phallic cult. How far, in their inverted culture, had these West Africans gone beyond phallic knowledge? Very, very far. Birkin recalled again the female figure: the elongated, long, long body, the curious unexpected heavy buttocks, the long, imprisoned neck, the face with tiny features like a beetle's. This was far beyond any phallic knowledge, sensual subtle realities far beyond the scope of phallic investigation.

There remained this way, this awful African process, to be fulfilled. It would be done differently by the white races. The white races, having the Arctic north behind them, the vast abstraction of ice and snow, would fulfil a mystery of ice-destructive knowledge, snow-abstract annihilation. Whereas the West Africans, controlled by the burning death-abstraction of the Sahara, had been fulfilled in sun-destruction, the putrescent mystery of sun-rays.

Was this then all that remained? Was there left now nothing but to break off from the happy creative being, was the time up? Is our day of creative life finished? Does there remain to us only the strange, awful afterwards of the knowledge in dissolution, the African knowledge, but different in us, who are blond and blue-eyed from the north?

Birkin thought of Gerald. He was one of these strange white wonderful demons from the north, fulfilled in the destructive frost mystery. And was he fated to pass away in this knowledge, this one process of frost-knowledge, death by perfect cold? Was he a messenger, an omen of the universal dissolution into whiteness and snow?

Birkin was frightened. He was tired too, when he had reached this length of speculation. Suddenly his strange, strained attention gave way, he could not attend to these mysteries any more. There was another way, the way of freedom. There was the paradisal entry into pure, single being, the individual soul taking precedence over love and desire for union, stronger than any pangs of emotion, a lovely stage of free proud singleness, which accepted the obligation of the permanent connection with others, and with the other, submits to the yoke and leash of love, but never forfeits its own proud individual singleness, even while it loves and yields.

There was the other way, the remaining way. And he must run to follow it. He thought of Ursula, how sensitive and delicate she really was, her skin so over-fine, as if one skin were wanting. She was really so marvellously gentle and sensitive. Why did he ever forget it? He must go to her at once. He must ask her to marry him. They must marry at once, and so make a definite pledge, enter into a definite communion. He must set out at once and ask her, this moment. There was no moment to spare.

He drifted on swiftly to Beldover, half unconscious of his own movement. He saw the town on the slope of the hill, not straggling, but as if walled-in with the straight, final streets of miner's dwellings, making a great square, and it looked like Jerusalem to his fancy. The world was all strange and transcendent.

Rosalind opened the door to him. She started slightly, as a young girl will, and said:

'Oh, I'll tell father.'

With which she disappeared, leaving Birkin in the hall, looking at some reproductions from Picasso, lately introduced by Gudrun. He was admiring the almost wizard, sensuous apprehension of the earth, when Will Brangwen appeared, rolling down his shirt-sleeves.

'Well,' said Brangwen, 'I'll get a coat.' And he too disappeared for a moment. Then he returned and opened the door of the drawing-room, saying:

'You must excuse me, I was just doing a bit of work in the shed. Come inside, will you?'

Birkin entered and sat down. He looked at the bright, reddish face of the other man, at the narrow brow and the very bright eyes, and at the rather sensual lips that unrolled wide and expansive under the black cropped moustache. How curious it was that this was a human being! What Brangwen thought himself to be, how meaningless it was, confronted with the reality of him. Birkin could see only a strange, inexplicable, almost patternless collection of passions and desires and suppressions and traditions and mechanical ideas, all cast unfused and disunited into this slender, bright-faced man of nearly fifty, who was as unresolved now as he was at twenty, and as uncreated. How could he be the parent of Ursula, when he was not created himself. He was not a parent. A slip of living flesh had been transmitted through him, but the spirit had not come from him. The spirit had not come from any ancestor, it had come out of the unknown. A child is the child of the mystery, or it is uncreated.

'The weather's not so bad as it has been,' said Brangwen, after waiting a moment. There was no connection between the two men.

'No,' said Birkin. 'It was full moon two days ago.'

'Oh! You believe in the moon then, affecting the weather?'

'No, I don't think I do. I don't really know enough about it.'

'You know what they say? The moon and the weather may change together, but the change of the moon won't change the weather.'

'Is that it?' said Birkin. 'I hadn't heard it.'

There was a pause. Then Birkin said:

'Am I hindering you? I called to see Ursula, really. Is she at home?'

'I don't believe she is. I believe she's gone to the library. I'll just see.'

Birkin could hear him inquiring in the dining-room.

'No,' he said, coming back. 'But she won't be long. You wanted to speak to her?'

Birkin looked across at the other man with curious calm, clear eyes.

'As a matter of fact,' he said, 'I wanted to ask her to marry me.'

A point of light came on the golden-brown eyes of the elder man.

'O-oh?' he said, looking at Birkin, then dropping his eyes before the calm, steadily watching look of the other. 'Was she expecting you then?'

'No,' said Birkin.

'No? I didn't know anything of this sort was on foot –' Brangwen smiled awkwardly.

Birkin looked back at him, and said to himself: 'I wonder why it should be "on foot"!' Aloud he said:

'No, it's perhaps rather sudden.' At which, thinking of his relationship with Ursula, he added – 'but I don't know –'

'Quite sudden, is it? Oh!' said Brangwen, rather baffled and annoyed.

'In one way,' replied Birkin, '– not in another.'

There was a moment's pause, after which Brangwen said:

'Well, she pleases herself –'

'Oh yes!' said Birkin calmly.

A vibration came into Brangwen's strong voice as he replied:

'Though I shouldn't want her to be in too big a hurry, either. It's no good looking around afterwards, when it's too late.'

'Oh, it need never be too late,' said Birkin, 'as far as that goes.'

'How do you mean?' asked the father.

'If one repents being married, the marriage is at an end,' said Birkin.

'You think so?'

'Yes.'

'Ay, well, that may be your way of looking at it.'

Birkin, in silence, thought to himself: 'So it may. As for *your* way of looking at it, William Brangwen, it needs a little explaining.'

'I suppose,' said Brangwen, 'you know what sort of people we are? What sort of a bringing-up she's had?'

'"She",' thought Birkin to himself, remembering his childhood's corrections, 'is the cat's mother.'

'Do I know what sort of a bringing-up she's had?' he said aloud.

He seemed to annoy Brangwen intentionally.

'Well,' he said, 'she's had everything that's right for a girl to have – as far as possible, as far as we could give it her.'

'I'm sure she has,' said Birkin, which caused a perilous full-stop. The father was becoming exasperated. There was something naturally irritant to him in Birkin's mere presence.

'And I don't want to see her going back on it all,' he said, in a clanging voice.

'Why?' said Birkin.

This monosyllable exploded in Brangwen's brain like a shot.

'Why! *I* don't believe in your new-fangled ways and new-fangled ideas – in and out like a frog in a gallipot. It would never do for me.'

Birkin watched him with steady emotionless eyes. The radical antagonism in the two men was rousing.

'Yes, but are my ways and ideas new-fangled?' asked Birkin.

'Are they?' Brangwen caught himself up. 'I'm not speaking of you in particular,' he said. 'What I mean is that my children have been brought up to think and do according to the religion I was brought up in myself, and I don't want to see them going away from *that*.'

There was a dangerous pause.

'And beyond that – ?' asked Birkin.

The father hesitated, he was in a nasty position.

'Eh? What do you mean? All I want to say is that my daughter' – he tailed off into silence, overcome by futility. He knew that in some way he was off the track.

'Of course,' said Birkin, 'I don't want to hurt anybody or influence anybody. Ursula does exactly as she pleases.'

There was a complete silence, because of the utter failure in mutual understanding. Birkin felt bored. Her father was not a coherent human being, he was a roomful of old echoes. The eyes of the younger man rested on the face of the elder. Brangwen looked up, and saw Birkin looking at him. His face was covered with inarticulate anger and humiliation and sense of inferiority in strength.

'And as for beliefs, that's one thing,' he said. 'But I'd rather see my daughters dead tomorrow than that they should be at the beck and call of the first man that likes to come and whistle for them.'

A queer painful light came into Birkin's eyes.

'As to that,' he said, 'I only know that it's much more likely that it's I who am at the beck and call of the woman, than she at mine.'

Again there was a pause. The father was somewhat bewildered.

'I know,' he said, 'she'll please herself – she always has done. I've done my best for them, but that doesn't matter. They've got themselves to please, and if they can help it they'll please nobody *but* themselves. But she's a right to consider her mother, and me as well –'

Brangwen was thinking his own thoughts.

'And I tell you this much, I would rather bury them than see them getting into a lot of loose ways such as you see everywhere nowadays. I'd rather bury them –'

'Yes, but, you see,' said Birkin slowly, rather wearily, bored again by this new turn, 'they won't give either you or me the chance to bury them, because they're not to be buried.'

Brangwen looked at him in a sudden flare of impotent anger.

'Now, Mr Birkin,' he said, 'I don't know what you've come here for, and I don't know what you're asking for. But my daughters are my daughters – and it's *my* business to look after them while I can.'

Birkin's brows knitted suddenly, his eyes concentrated in mockery. But he remained perfectly stiff and still. There was a pause.

'I've nothing against your marrying Ursula,' Brangwen began at length. 'It's got nothing to do with me, she'll do as she likes, me or no me.'

Birkin turned away, looking out of the window and letting go his consciousness. After all, what good was this? It was hopeless to keep it up. He would sit on till Ursula came home, then speak to her, then go away. He would not accept trouble at the hands of her father. It was all unnecessary, and he himself need not have provoked it.

The two men sat in complete silence, Birkin almost unconscious of his own whereabouts. He had come to ask her to marry him – well then, he would wait on, and ask her. As for what she said, whether she accepted or not, he did not think about it. He would say what he had come to say, and that was all he was conscious of. He accepted the complete insignificance of this household for him. But everything now was as if fated. He could see one thing ahead, and no more. From the rest, he was absolved entirely for the time being. It had to be left to fate and chance to resolve the issues.

At length they heard the gate. They saw her coming up the steps with a bundle of books under her arm. Her face was bright and abstracted as usual, with the abstraction, that look of being not quite *there*, not quite present to the facts of reality, that galled her father so much. She had a maddening faculty of assuming a light of her own, which excluded the reality, and within which she looked radiant as if in sunshine.

They heard her go into the dining-room and drop her armful of books on the table.

'Did you bring me that Girl's Own?' cried Rosalind.

'Yes, I brought it. But I forgot which one it was you wanted.'

'You would,' cried Rosalind angrily. 'It's right for a wonder.'

Then they heard her say something in a lowered tone.

'Where?' cried Ursula.

Again her sister's voice was muffled.

Brangwen opened the door and called in his strong, brazen voice:
'Ursula.'

She appeared in a moment, wearing her hat.

'Oh, how do you do!' she cried, seeing Birkin, and all dazzled as if taken by surprise. He wondered at her, knowing she was aware of his presence. She had her queer, radiant, breathless manner, as if confused by the actual world, unreal to it, having a complete bright world of her self alone.

'Have I interrupted a conversation?' she asked.

'No, only a complete silence,' said Birkin.

'Oh,' said Ursula vaguely, absent. Their presence was not vital to her, she was withheld, she did not take them in. It was a subtle insult that never failed to exasperate her father.

'Mr Birkin came to speak to *you*, not to me,' said her father.

'Oh, did he!' she exclaimed vaguely, as if it did not concern her. Then, recollecting herself, she turned to him rather radiantly, but still quite superficially, and said: 'Was it anything special?'

'I hope so,' he said ironically.

'– To propose to you, according to all accounts,' said her father.

'Oh,' said Ursula.

'Oh,' mocked her father, imitating her. 'Have you nothing more to say?'

She winced as if violated.

'Did you really come to propose to me?' she asked of Birkin, as if it were a joke.

'Yes,' he said. 'I suppose I came to propose.' He seemed to fight shy of the last word.

'Did you?' she cried, with her vague radiance. He might have been saying anything whatsoever. She seemed pleased.

'Yes,' he answered. 'I wanted to – I wanted you to agree to marry me.'

She looked at him. His eyes were flickering with mixed lights, wanting something of her, yet not wanting it. She shrank a little, as if she were exposed to his eyes, and as if it were a pain to her. She darkened, her soul clouded over, she turned aside. She had been driven out of her own radiant, single world. And she dreaded contact, it was almost unnatural to her at these times.

'Yes,' she said vaguely, in a doubting, absent voice.

Birkin's heart contracted swiftly, in a sudden fire of bitterness. It all meant nothing to her. He had been mistaken again. She was in some self-satisfied world of her own. He and his hopes were accidentals, violations to her. It drove her father to a pitch of mad exasperation. He had had to put up with this all his life from her.

'Well, what do you say?' he cried.

She winced. Then she glanced down at her father, half frightened, and she said:

'I didn't speak, did I?' as if she were afraid she might have committed herself.

'No,' said her father, exasperated. 'But you needn't look like an idiot. You've got your wits, haven't you?'

She ebbed away in silent hostility.

'I've got my wits, what does that mean?' she repeated in a sullen voice of antagonism.

'You heard what was asked you, didn't you?' cried her father in anger.

'Of course I heard.'

'Well then, can't you answer?' thundered her father.

'Why should I?'

At the impertinence of this retort, he went stiff. But he said nothing.

'No,' said Birkin, to help out the occasion, 'there's no need to answer at once. You can say when you like.'

Her eyes flashed with a powerful light.

'Why should I say anything?' she cried. 'You do this off your *own* bat, it has nothing to do with me. Why do you both want to bully me?'

'Bully you! Bully you!' cried her father in bitter, rancorous anger. 'Bully you! Why, it's a pity you can't be bullied into some sense and decency. Bully you! *You'll* see to that, you self-willed creature.'

She stood suspended in the middle of the room, her face glimmering and dangerous. She was set in satisfied defiance. Birkin looked up at her. He too was angry.

'But no one is bullying you,' he said in a very soft dangerous voice also.

'Oh yes,' she cried. 'You both want to force me into something.'

'That is an illusion of yours,' he said ironically.

'Illusion!' cried her father. 'A self-opinionated fool, that's what she is.'

Birkin rose, saying:

'However, we'll leave it for the time being.'

And without another word, he walked out of the house.

'You fool! You fool!' her father cried to her, with extreme bitterness. She left the room, and went upstairs, singing to herself. But she was terribly fluttered, as after some dreadful fight. From her window, she could see Birkin going up the road. He went in such a blithe drift of rage that her mind wondered over him. He was ridiculous, but she was afraid of him. She was as if escaped from some danger.

Her father sat below, powerless in humiliation and chagrin. It was as if he were possessed with all the devils, after one of these unaccountable conflicts with Ursula. He hated her as if his only reality were in hating her to the last degree. He had all hell in his heart. But he went away to escape himself. He knew he must despair, yield, give in to despair, and have done.

Ursula's face closed, she completed herself against them all. Recoiling upon herself, she became hard and self-completed, like a jewel. She was bright and invulnerable, quite free and happy, perfectly liberated in her self-possession. Her father had to learn not to see her blithe obliviousness, or it would have sent him mad. She was so radiant with all things in her possession of perfect hostility.

She would go on now for days like this, in this bright frank state of seemingly pure spontaneity, so essentially oblivious of the existence of anything but herself, but so ready and facile in her interest. Ah, it was a bitter thing for a man to be near her, and her father cursed his fatherhood. But he must learn not to see her, not to know.

She was perfectly stable in resistance when she was in this state: so bright and radiant and attractive in her pure opposition, so very pure, and yet mistrusted by everybody, disliked on every hand. It was her voice, curiously clear and repellent, that gave her away. Only Gudrun was in accord with her. It was at these times that the intimacy between the two sisters was most complete, as if their intelligence were one. They felt a strong, bright bond of understanding between them surpassing everything else. And during all these days of blind bright abstraction and intimacy of his two daughters, the father seemed to breathe an air of death, as if he were destroyed in his very being. He was irritable to madness, he could not rest, his daughters seemed to be destroying him. But he was inarticulate and helpless against them. He was forced to breathe the air of his own death. He cursed them in his soul, and only wanted that they should be removed from him.

They continued radiant in their easy female transcendency, beautiful to look at. They exchanged confidences, they were intimate in their revelations to the last degree, giving each other at last every secret. They withheld nothing, they told everything, till they were over the border of evil. And they armed each other with knowledge, they extracted the subtlest flavours from the apple of knowledge. It was curious how their knowledge was complementary, that of each to that of the other.

Ursula saw her men as sons, pitied their yearning and admired their courage, and wondered over them as a mother wonders over her child, with a certain delight in their novelty. But to Gudrun, they were the opposite camp. She feared them and despised them, and respected their activities even over-much.

'Of course,' she said easily, 'there is a quality of life in Birkin which is quite remarkable. There is an extraordinary rich spring of life in him, really amazing, the way he can give himself to things. But there are so many things in life that he simply doesn't know. Either he is not aware of their existence at all, or he dismisses them as merely negligible – things which are vital to the other person. In a way, he is not clever enough, he is too intense in spots.'

'Yes,' cried Ursula, 'too much of a preacher. He is really a priest.'

'Exactly! He can't hear what anybody else has to say – he simply cannot hear. His voice is so loud.'

'Yes. He cries you down.'

'He cries you down,' repeated Gudrun. 'And by mere force of violence. And of course it is hopeless. Nobody is convinced by violence. It makes talking to him impossible – and living with him I should think would be more than impossible.'

'You don't think one could live with him?' asked Ursula.

'I think it would be too wearing, too exhausting. One would be shouted down every time, and rushed into his way without any choice. He would want to control you entirely. He cannot allow that there is any other mind than his own. And then the real clumsiness of his mind is its lack of self-criticism. No, I think it would be perfectly intolerable.'

'Yes,' assented Ursula vaguely. She only half agreed with Gudrun. 'The nuisance is,' she said, 'that one would find almost any man intolerable after a fortnight.'

'It's perfectly dreadful,' said Gudrun. 'But Birkin – he is too positive. He couldn't bear it if you called your soul your own. Of him that is strictly true.'

'Yes,' said Ursula. 'You must have *his* soul.'

'Exactly! And what can you conceive more deadly?' This was all so true, that Ursula felt jarred to the bottom of her soul with ugly distaste.

She went on, with the discord jarring and jolting through her, in the most barren of misery.

Then there started a revulsion from Gudrun. She finished life off so thoroughly, she made things so ugly and so final. As a matter of fact, even if it were as Gudrun said, about Birkin, other things were true as well. But Gudrun would draw two lines under him and cross him out like an account that is settled. There he was, summed up, paid for, settled, done with. And it was such a lie. This finality of Gudrun's, this dispatching of people and things in a sentence, it was all such a lie. Ursula began to revolt from her sister.

One day as they were walking along the lane, they saw a robin sitting on the top twig of a bush, singing shrilly. The sisters stood to look at him. An ironical smile flickered on Gudrun's face.

'Doesn't he feel important?' smiled Gudrun.

'Doesn't he!' exclaimed Ursula, with a little ironical grimace. 'Isn't he a little Lloyd George of the air!'

'Isn't he! Little Lloyd George of the air! That's just what they are,' cried Gudrun in delight. Then for days, Ursula saw the persistent, obtrusive birds, as stout, short politicians lifting up their voices from the platform, little men who must make themselves heard at any cost.

But even from this there came the revulsion. Some yellow-hammers suddenly shot along the road in front of her. And they looked to her so uncanny and inhuman, like flaring yellow barbs shooting through the air on some weird, living errand, that she said to herself: 'After all, it is impudence to call them little Lloyd Georges. They are really unknown to us, they are the unknown forces. It is impudence to look at them as if they were the same as human beings. They are of another world. How stupid anthropomorphism is! Gudrun is really impudent, insolent, making herself the measure of everything, making everything come down to human standards. Rupert is quite right, human beings are boring, painting the universe with their own image. The universe is non-human, thank God.' It seemed to her irreverence, destructive of all true life, to make little Lloyd Georges of the birds. It was such a lie towards the robins and such a defamation. Yet she had done it herself. But under Gudrun's influence: so she exonerated herself.

So she withdrew away from Gudrun and from that which she stood for, she turned in spirit towards Birkin again. She had not seen him since the fiasco of his proposal. She did not want to, because she did not want the question of her acceptance thrust upon her. She knew what Birkin meant when he asked her to marry him; vaguely, without putting it into speech, she knew. She knew what kind of love, what kind of surrender he wanted. And she was not at all sure that this was the kind of love that she herself wanted. She was not at all sure that it was this mutual unison in separateness that she wanted. She wanted unspeakable intimacies. She wanted to have him, utterly, finally to have him as her own, oh, so unspeakably, in intimacy. To drink him down – ah, like a life-draught. She made great professions, to herself, of her willingness to warm his foot-soles between her breasts, after the fashion of that nauseous Meredith poem. But only on condition that he, her lover, loved her absolutely, with complete self-abandon. And subtly enough, she knew he would never abandon himself *finally* to her. He did not believe in final self-abandonment. He said it openly. It was his challenge. She was prepared to fight him for it. For she believed in an absolute surrender to love. She believed that love far surpassed the individual. He said the individual was *more* than love, or than any relationship. For him, the bright, single soul accepted love as one of its conditions, a condition of its own equilibrium. She believed that love was *everything*. Man must render himself up to her. He must be quaffed to the dregs by her. Let him be *her man* utterly, and she in return would be his humble slave – whether she wanted it or not.

20

GLADIATORIAL

After the fiasco of the proposal, Birkin had hurried blindly away from Beldover, in a whirl of fury. He felt he had been a complete fool, that the whole scene had been a farce of the first water. But that did not trouble him at all. He was deeply, mockingly angry that Ursula persisted always in this old cry: 'Why do you want to bully me?' and in her bright, insolent abstraction.

He went straight to Shortlands. There he found Gerald standing with his back to the fire, in the library, as motionless as a man is who is completely and emptily restless, utterly hollow. He had done all the work he wanted to do – and now there was nothing. He could go out in the car, he could run to town. But he did not want to go out in the car, he did not want to run to town, he did not want to call on the Thirlbys. He was suspended motionless, in an agony of inertia, like a machine that is without power.

This was very bitter to Gerald, who had never known what boredom was, who had gone from activity to activity, never at a loss. Now, gradually, everything seemed to be stopping in him. He did not want any more to do the things that offered. Something dead within him just refused to respond to any suggestion. He cast over in his mind what it would be possible to do to save himself from this misery of nothingness, relieve the stress of this hollowness. And there were only three things left that would rouse him, make him live. One was to drink or smoke hashish, the other was to be soothed by Birkin, and the third was women. And there was no one for the moment to drink with. Nor was there a woman. And he knew Birkin was out. So there was nothing to do but to bear the stress of his own emptiness.

When he saw Birkin his face lit up in a sudden, wonderful smile.

'By God, Rupert,' he said, 'I'd just come to the conclusion that nothing in the world mattered except somebody to take the edge off one's being alone: the right somebody.'

The smile in his eyes was very astonishing as he looked at the other man. It was the pure gleam of relief. His face was pallid and even haggard.

'The right woman, I suppose you mean,' said Birkin spitefully.

'Of course, for choice. Failing that, an amusing man.'

He laughed as he said it. Birkin sat down near the fire.

'What were you doing?' he asked.

'I? Nothing. I'm in a bad way just now, everything's on edge, and I can neither work nor play. I don't know whether it's a sign of old age, I'm sure.'

'You mean you are bored?'

'Bored, I don't know. I can't apply myself. And I feel the devil is either very present inside me or dead.'

Birkin glanced up and looked in his eyes.

'You should try hitting something,' he said.

Gerald smiled.

'Perhaps,' he said. 'So long as it was something worth hitting.'

'Quite!' said Birkin in his soft voice. There was a long pause during which each could feel the presence of the other.

'One has to wait,' said Birkin.

'Ah, God! Waiting! What are we waiting for?'

'Some old Johnny says there are three cures for *ennui*, sleep, drink, and travel,' said Birkin.

'All cold eggs,' said Gerald. 'In sleep, you dream, in drink you curse, and in travel you yell at a porter. No, work and love are the two. When you're not at work you should be in love.'

'Be it then,' said Birkin.

'Give me the object,' said Gerald. 'The possibilities of love exhaust themselves.'

'Do they? And then what?'

'Then you die,' said Gerald.

'So you ought,' said Birkin.

'I don't see it,' replied Gerald. He took his hands out of his trousers pockets and reached for a cigarette. He was tense and nervous. He lit the cigarette over a lamp, reaching forward and drawing steadily. He was dressed for dinner, as usual in the evening, although he was alone.

'There's a third one even to your two,' said Birkin. 'Work, love, and fighting. You forget the fight.'

'I suppose I do,' said Gerald. 'Did you ever do any boxing – ?'

'No, I don't think I did,' said Birkin.

'Ay –' Gerald lifted his head and blew the smoke slowly into the air.

'Why?' said Birkin.

'Nothing. I thought we might have a round. It is perhaps true that I want something to hit. It's a suggestion.'

'So you think you might as well hit me?' said Birkin.

'You? Well – ! Perhaps – ! In a friendly kind of way, of course.'

'Quite!' said Birkin bitingly.

Gerald stood leaning back against the mantelpiece. He looked down at Birkin, and his eyes flashed with a sort of terror like the eyes of a stallion, that are bloodshot and overwrought, turned glancing backwards in a stiff terror.

'I feel that if I don't watch myself, I shall find myself doing something silly,' he said.

'Why not do it?' said Birkin coldly.

Gerald listened with quick impatience. He kept glancing down at Birkin, as if looking for something from the other man.

'I used to do some Japanese wrestling,' said Birkin. 'A Jap lived in the same house with me in Heidelberg, and he taught me a little. But I was never much good at it.'

'You did!' exclaimed Gerald. 'That's one of the things I've never ever seen done. You mean jiu-jitsu, I suppose?'

'Yes. But I am no good at those things – they don't interest me.'

'They don't? They do me. What's the start?'

'I'll show you what I can, if you like,' said Birkin.

'You will?' A queer, smiling look tightened Gerald's face for a moment as he said, 'Well, I'd like it very much.'

'Then we'll try jiu-jitsu. Only you can't do much in a starched shirt.'

'Then let us strip, and do it properly. Hold a minute –' He rang the bell and waited for the butler.

'Bring a couple of sandwiches and a syphon,' he said to the man, 'and then don't trouble me any more tonight – or let anybody else.'

The man went. Gerald turned to Birkin with his eyes lighted.

'And you used to wrestle with a Jap?' he said. 'Did you strip?'

'Sometimes.'

'You did! What was he like then, as a wrestler?'

'Good, I believe. I am no judge. He was very quick and slippery and full of electric fire. It is a remarkable thing what a curious sort of fluid force they seem to have in them, those people – not like a human grip – like a polyp –'

Gerald nodded.

'I should imagine so,' he said, 'to look at them. They repel me, rather.'

'Repel and attract, both. They are very repulsive when they are cold, and they look grey. But when they are hot and roused, there is a definite attraction – a curious kind of full electric fluid – like eels.'

'Well –, yes –, probably.'

The man brought in the tray and set it down.

'Don't come in any more,' said Gerald.

The door closed.

'Well then,' said Gerald; 'shall we strip and begin? Will you have a drink first?'

'No, I don't want one.'

'Neither do I.'

Gerald fastened the door and pushed the furniture aside. The room was large, there was plenty of space, it was thickly carpeted. Then he quickly threw off his clothes and waited for Birkin. The latter, white and thin, came over to him. Birkin was more a presence than a visible object; Gerald was aware of him completely, but not really visually. Whereas Gerald himself was concrete and noticeable, a piece of pure final substance.

'Now,' said Birkin, 'I will show you what I learned, and what I remember. You let me take you so –' And his hands closed on the naked body of the other man. In another moment he had Gerald swung over lightly and balanced against his knee, head downwards. Relaxed, Gerald sprang to his feet with eyes glittering.

'That's smart,' he said. 'Now try again.'

So the two men began to struggle together. They were very dissimilar. Birkin was tall and narrow, his bones were very thin and fine. Gerald was much heavier and more plastic. His bones were strong and round, his limbs were rounded, all his contours were beautifully and fully moulded. He seemed to stand with a proper, rich weight on the face of the earth, whilst Birkin seemed to have the centre of gravitation in his own middle. And Gerald had a rich, frictional kind of strength, rather mechanical, but sudden and invincible, whereas Birkin was abstract as to be almost intangible. He impinged invisibly upon the other man, scarcely seeming to touch him, like a garment, and then suddenly piercing in a tense fine grip that seemed to penetrate into the very quick of Gerald's being.

They stopped, they discussed methods, they practiced grips and throws, they became accustomed to each other, to each other's rhythm, they got a kind of mutual physical understanding. And then again they had a real struggle. They seemed to drive their white flesh deeper and deeper against each other, as if they would break into a oneness. Birkin had a great subtle energy, that would press upon the other man with an uncanny force, weigh him like a spell put upon him. Then it would pass, and Gerald would heave free, with white, heaving, dazzling movements.

So the two men entwined and wrestled with each other, working nearer and nearer. Both were white and clear, but Gerald flushed smart red where he was touched, and Birkin remained white and tense. He seemed to penetrate into Gerald's more solid, more diffuse bulk, to interfuse his body through the body of the other, as if to bring it subtly into subjection, always seizing with some rapid necromantic foreknowledge every motion of the other flesh, converting and counteracting it, playing upon the limbs and trunk of Gerald like some hard wind. It was as if Birkin's whole physical intelligence interpenetrated into Gerald's body, as if his fine, sublimated energy entered into the flesh of the fuller man, like some potency, casting a fine net, a prison, through the muscles into the very depths of Gerald's physical being.

So they wrestled swiftly, rapturously, intent and mindless at last, two essential white figures working into a tighter, closer oneness of struggle, with a strange, octopus-like knotting and flashing of limbs in the subdued light of the room; a tense white knot of flesh gripped in silence between the walls of old brown books. Now and again came a sharp gasp of breath, or a sound like a sigh, then the rapid thudding of movement on the thickly-carpeted floor, then the strange sound of flesh escaping under flesh. Often, in the white interlaced knot of violent living being that swayed silently, there was no head to be seen, only the swift, tight limbs, the solid white backs, the physical junction of two bodies clinched into oneness. Then would appear the gleaming, ruffled head of Gerald, as the struggle changed, then for a moment the dun-coloured, shadow-like head of the other man would lift up from the conflict, the eyes wide and dreadful and sightless.

At length Gerald lay back inert on the carpet, his breast rising in great slow panting, whilst Birkin kneeled over him, almost unconscious. Birkin was much more exhausted. He caught little, short breaths, he could scarcely breathe any more. The earth seemed to tilt and sway, and a complete darkness was coming over his mind. He did not know what happened. He slid forward quite unconscious over Gerald, and Gerald did not notice. Then he was half conscious again, aware only of the strange tilting and sliding of the world.

The world was sliding, everything was sliding off into the darkness. And he was sliding, endlessly, endlessly away.

He came to consciousness again, hearing an immense knocking outside. What could be happening, what was it, the great hammer-stroke resounding through the house? He did not know. And then it came to him that it was his own heart beating. But that seemed impossible, the noise was outside. No, it was inside himself, it was his own heart. And the beating was painful, so strained, surcharged. He wondered if Gerald heard it. He did not know whether he were standing or lying or falling.

When he realized that he had fallen prostrate upon Gerald's body he wondered, he was surprised. But he sat up, steadying himself with his hand and waiting for his heart to become stiller and less painful. It hurt very much, and took away his consciousness.

Gerald, however, was still less conscious than Birkin. They waited dimly, in a sort of not-being, for many uncounted, unknown minutes.

'Of course –' panted Gerald, 'I didn't have to be rough – with you – I had to keep back – my force –'

Birkin heard the sound as if his own spirit stood behind him, outside him, and listened to it. His body was in a trance of exhaustion, his spirit heard thinly. His body could not answer. Only he knew his heart was getting quieter. He was divided entirely between his spirit, which stood outside, and knew, and his body, that was a plunging, unconscious stroke of blood.

'I could have thrown you – using violence –' panted Gerald. 'But you beat me right enough.'

'Yes,' said Birkin, hardening his throat and producing the words in the tension there, 'you're much stronger than I – you could beat me – easily.'

Then he relaxed again to the terrible plunging of his heart and his blood.

'It surprised me,' panted Gerald, 'what strength you've got. Almost supernatural.'

'For a moment,' said Birkin.

He still heard as if it were his own disembodied spirit hearing, standing at some distance behind him. It drew nearer, however, his spirit. And the violent striking of blood in his chest was sinking quieter, allowing his mind to come back. He realized that he was leaning with all his weight on the soft body of the other man. It startled him, because he thought he had withdrawn. He recovered himself and sat up. But he was still vague and unestablished. He put out his hand to steady himself. It touched the hand of Gerald, that was lying out on the floor. And Gerald's hand closed warm and sudden over Birkin's, they remained exhausted and breathless, the one hand clasped closely over the other. It was Birkin whose hand, in swift response, had closed in a strong, warm clasp over the hand of the other. Gerald's clasp had been sudden and momentaneous.

The normal consciousness, however, was returning, ebbing back. Birkin could breathe almost naturally again. Gerald's hand slowly withdrew, Birkin slowly, dazedly rose to his feet and went towards the table. He poured out a whisky and soda. Gerald also came for a drink.

'It was a real set-to, wasn't it?' said Birkin, looking at Gerald with darkened eyes.

'God, yes,' said Gerald. He looked at the delicate body of the other man, and added: 'It wasn't too much for you, was it?'

'No. One ought to wrestle and strive and be physically close. It makes one sane.'

'You do think so?'

'I do. Don't you?'

'Yes,' said Gerald.

There were long spaces of silence between their words. The wrestling had some deep meaning to them – an unfinished meaning.

'We are mentally, spiritually intimate, therefore we should be more or less physically intimate too – it is more whole.'

'Certainly it is,' said Gerald. Then he laughed pleasantly, adding: 'It's rather wonderful to me.' He stretched out his arms handsomely.

'Yes,' said Birkin. 'I don't know why one should have to justify oneself.'

'No.'

The two men began to dress.

'I think also that you are beautiful,' said Birkin to Gerald, 'and that is enjoyable too. One should enjoy what is given.'

'You think I am beautiful – how do you mean, physically?' asked Gerald, his eyes glistening.

'Yes. You have a northern kind of beauty, like light refracted from snow – and a beautiful, plastic form. Yes, that is there to enjoy as well. We should enjoy everything.'

Gerald laughed in his throat, and said:

'That's certainly one way of looking at it. I can say this much, I feel better. It has certainly helped me. Is this the *Bruderschaft* you wanted?'

'Perhaps. Do you think this pledges anything?'

'I don't know,' laughed Gerald.

'At any rate, one feels freer and more open now – and that is what we want.'

'Certainly,' said Gerald.

They drew to the fire, with the decanters and the glasses and the food.

'I always eat a little before I go to bed,' said Gerald. 'I sleep better.'

'I should not sleep so well,' said Birkin.

'No? There you are, we are not alike. I'll put a dressing-gown on.' Birkin remained alone, looking at the fire. His mind had reverted to Ursula. She seemed to return again into his consciousness. Gerald came down wearing a gown of broad-barred, thick black-and-green silk, brilliant and striking.

'You are very fine,' said Birkin, looking at the full robe.

'It was a caftan in Bokhara,' said Gerald. 'I like it.'

'I like it too.'

Birkin was silent, thinking how scrupulous Gerald was in his attire, how expensive too. He wore silk socks, and studs of fine workmanship, and silk underclothing, and silk braces. Curious! This was another of the differences between them. Birkin was careless and unimaginative about his own appearance.

'Of course you,' said Gerald, as if he had been thinking; 'there's something curious about you. You're curiously strong. One doesn't expect it, it is rather surprising.'

Birkin laughed. He was looking at the handsome figure of the other man, blond and comely in the rich robe, and he was half thinking of the difference between it and himself – so different; as far, perhaps, apart as man from woman, yet in another direction. But really it was Ursula, it was the woman who was gaining ascendance over Birkin's being at this moment. Gerald was becoming dim again, lapsing out of him.

'Do you know,' he said suddenly, 'I went and proposed to Ursula Brangwen tonight, that she should marry me.'

He saw the blank shining wonder come over Gerald's face.

'You did?'

'Yes. Almost formally – speaking first to her father, as it should be, in the world – though that was accident – or mischief.'

Gerald only stared in wonder, as if he did not grasp.

'You don't mean to say that you seriously went and asked her father to let you marry her?'

'Yes,' said Birkin, 'I did.'

'What, had you spoken to her before about it, then?'

'No, not a word. I suddenly thought I would go there and ask her – and her father happened to come instead of her – so I asked him first.'

'If you could have her?' concluded Gerald.

'Ye-es, that.'

'And you didn't speak to her?'

'Yes. She came in afterwards. So it was put to her as well.'

'It was! And what did she say then? You're an engaged man?'

'No – she only said she didn't want to be bullied into answering.'

'She what?'

'Said she didn't want to be bullied into answering.'

'"Said she didn't want to be bullied into answering!" Why, what did she mean by that?'

Birkin raised his shoulders. 'Can't say,' he answered. 'Didn't want to be bothered just then, I suppose.'

'But is this really so? And what did you do then?'

'I walked out of the house and came here.'

'You came straight here?'

'Yes.'

Gerald stared in amazement and amusement. He could not take it in.

'But is this really true, as you say it now?'

'Word for word.'

'It is?'

He leaned back in his chair, filled with delight and amusement.

'Well, that's good,' he said. 'And so you came here to wrestle with your good angel, did you?'

'Did I?' said Birkin.

'Well, it looks like it. Isn't that what you did?'

Now Birkin could not follow Gerald's meaning.

'And what's going to happen?' said Gerald. 'You're going to keep open the proposition, so to speak.'

'I suppose so. I vowed to myself I would see them all to the devil. But I suppose I shall ask her again, in a little while.'

Gerald watched him steadily.

'So you're fond of her then?' he asked.

'I think – I love her,' said Birkin, his face going very still and fixed.

Gerald glistened for a moment with pleasure, as if it were something done specially to please him. Then his face assumed a fitting gravity, and he nodded his head slowly.

'You know,' he said, 'I always believed in love – true love. But where does one find it nowadays?'

'I don't know,' said Birkin.

'Very rarely,' said Gerald. Then, after a pause, 'I've never felt it myself – not what I should call love. I've gone after women – and been keen enough over some of them. But I've never felt *love*. I don't believe I've ever felt as much *love* for a woman as I have for you – not *love*. You understand what I mean?'

'Yes. I'm sure you've never loved a woman.'

'You feel that, do you? And do you think I ever shall? You understand what I mean?' He put his hand to his breast, closing his fist there, as if he would draw something out. 'I mean that – that – I can't express what it is, but I know it.'

'What is it, then?' asked Birkin.

'You see, I can't put it into words. I mean, at any rate, something abiding, something that can't change –'

His eyes were bright and puzzled.

'Now do you think I shall ever feel that for a woman?' he said anxiously.

Birkin looked at him and shook his head.

'I don't know,' he said. 'I could not say.'

Gerald had been on the *qui vive*, as awaiting his fate. Now he drew back in his chair.

'No,' he said, 'and neither do I, and neither do I.'

'We are different, you and I,' said Birkin. 'I can't tell your life.'

'No,' said Gerald, 'no more can I. But I tell you – I begin to doubt it.'

'That you will ever love a woman?'

'Well – yes – what you would truly call love –'

'You doubt it?'

'Well – I begin to.'

There was a long pause.

'Life has all kinds of things,' said Birkin. 'There isn't only one road.'

'Yes, I believe that too. I believe it. And mind you, I don't care how it is with me – I don't care how it is – so long as I don't feel –' he paused, and a blank, barren look passed over his face, to express his feeling – 'so long as I feel I've *lived*, somehow – and I don't care how it is – but I want to feel that –'

'Fulfilled,' said Birkin.

'We-ell, perhaps it is fulfilled; I don't use the same words as you.'

'It is the same.'

21

THRESHOLD

Gudrun was away in London, having a little show of her work with a friend, and looking round, preparing for flight from Beldover. Come what might, she would be on the wing in a very short time. She received a letter from Winifred Crich, ornamented with drawings.

'Father also has been to London, to be examined by the doctors. It made him very tired. They say he must rest a very great deal, so he is mostly in bed. He brought me a lovely tropical parrot in faïence, of Dresden ware, also a man ploughing, and two mice climbing up a stalk, also in faïence. The mice were Copenhagen ware. They are the best, but mice don't shine so much, otherwise they are very good, their tails are slim and long. They all shine nearly like glass. Of course it is the glaze, but I don't like it. Gerald likes the man ploughing the best, his trousers are torn, he is ploughing with an ox, being, I suppose, a German peasant. It is all grey and white, white shirt and grey trousers, but very shiny and clean. Mr Birkin likes the girl best, under the hawthorn blossom, with a lamb, and with daffodils painted on her skirts, in the drawing-room. But that is silly, because the lamb is not a real lamb, and she is silly too.

'Dear Miss Brangwen, are you coming back soon, you are very much missed here. I enclose a drawing of father sitting up in bed. He says he hopes you are not going to forsake us. Oh dear, Miss Brangwen, I am sure you won't. Do come back and draw the ferrets, they are the most lovely noble darlings in the world. We might carve them in holly-wood, playing against a background of green leaves. Oh, do let us, for they are most beautiful.

'Father says we might have a studio. Gerald says we could easily have a beautiful one over the stables, it would only need windows to be put in the slant of the roof, which is a simple matter. Then you could stay here all day and work, and we could live in the studio, like two real artists, like the man in the picture in the hall, with the frying-pan and the walls all covered with drawings. I long to be free, to live the free life of an artist. Even Gerald told father that only an artist is free, because he lives in a creative world of his own –'

Gudrun caught the drift of the family intentions, in this letter. Gerald wanted her to be attached to the household at Shortlands, he was using Winifred as his stalking-horse. The father thought only of his child, he saw a rock of salvation in Gudrun. And Gudrun admired him for his perspicacity. The child, moreover, was really exceptional. Gudrun was quite content. She was quite willing, given a studio, to spend her days at Shortlands. She disliked the Grammar School already thoroughly, she wanted to be free. If a studio were provided, she would be free to go on with her work, she would await the turn of events with complete serenity. And she was really interested in Winifred, she would be quite glad to understand the girl.

So there was quite a little festivity on Winifred's account, the day Gudrun returned to Shortlands.

'You should make a bunch of flowers to give to Miss Brangwen when she arrives,' Gerald said, smiling to his sister.

'Oh no,' cried Winifred, 'it's silly.'

'Not at all. It is a very charming and ordinary attention.'

'Oh, it *is* silly,' protested Winifred, with all the extreme *mauvaise honte* of her years. Nevertheless, the idea appealed to her. She wanted very much to carry it out. She flitted round the green-houses and the conservatory looking wistfully at the flowers on their stems. And the more she looked, the more she *longed* to have a bunch of the blossoms she saw, the more fascinated she became with her little vision of ceremony, and the more consumedly shy and self-conscious she grew, till she was almost beside herself. She could not get the idea out of her mind. It was as if some haunting challenge prompted her, and she had not enough courage to take it up. So again she drifted into the green-houses, looking at the lovely roses in their pots, and at the virginal cyclamens, and at the mystic white clusters of a creeper. The beauty, oh, the beauty of them, and oh, the paradisal bliss, if she should have a perfect bouquet and could give it to Gudrun the next day. Her passion and her complete indecision almost made her ill.

At last she slid to her father's side.

'Daddie –' she said.

'What, my precious?'

But she hung back, the tears almost coming to her eyes, in her sensitive confusion. Her father looked at her, and his heart ran hot with tenderness, an anguish of poignant love.

'What do you want to say to me, my love?'

'Daddie – !' her eyes smiled laconically – 'isn't it silly if I give Miss Brangwen some flowers when she comes?'

The sick man looked at the bright, knowing eyes of his child, and his heart burned with love.

'No, darling, that's not silly. It's what they do to queens.'

This was not very reassuring to Winifred. She half suspected that queens in themselves were a silliness. Yet she so wanted her little romantic occasion.

'Shall I then?' she asked.

'Give Miss Brangwen some flowers? Do, Birdie. Tell Wilson I say you are to have what you want.'

The child smiled a small, subtle, unconscious smile to herself, in anticipation of her way.

'But I won't get them till tomorrow,' she said.

'Not till tomorrow, Birdie. Give me a kiss then –'

Winifred silently kissed the sick man, and drifted out of the room. She again went the round of the green-houses and the conservatory, informing the gardener, in her high, peremptory, simple fashion, of what she wanted, telling him all the blooms she had selected.

'What do you want these for?' Wilson asked.

'I want them,' she said. She wished servants did not ask questions.

'Ay, you've said as much. But what do you want them for, for decoration, or to send away, or what?'

'I want them for a presentation bouquet.'

'A presentation bouquet! Who's coming then? – the Duchess of Portland?'

'No.'

'Oh, not her? Well, you'll have a rare poppy-show if you put all the things you've mentioned into your bouquet.'

'Yes, I want a rare poppy-show.'

'You do! Then there's no more to be said.'

The next day Winifred, in a dress of silvery velvet and holding a gaudy bunch of flowers in her hand, waited with keen impatience in the schoolroom, looking down the drive for Gudrun's arrival. It was a wet morning. Under her nose was the strange fragrance of hot-house flowers, the bunch was like a little fire to her, she seemed to have a strange new fire in her heart. This slight sense of romance stirred her like an intoxicant.

At last she saw Gudrun coming, and she ran downstairs to warn her father and Gerald. They, laughing at her anxiety and gravity, came with her into the hall. The man-servant came hastening to the door, and there he was, relieving Gudrun of her umbrella, and then of her raincoat. The welcoming party hung back till their visitor entered the hall.

Gudrun was flushed with the rain, her hair was blown in loose little curls, she was like a flower just opened in the rain, the heart of the blossom just newly visible, seeming to emit a warmth of retained sunshine. Gerald winced in spirit, seeing her so beautiful and unknown. She was wearing a soft blue dress, and her stockings were of dark red.

Winifred advanced with odd, stately formality.

'We are so glad you've come back,' she said. 'These are your flowers.' She presented the bouquet.

'Mine!' cried Gudrun. She was suspended for a moment, then a vivid flush went over her, she was as if blinded for a moment with a flame of pleasure. Then her eyes, strange and flaming, lifted and looked at the father, and at Gerald. And again Gerald shrank in spirit, as if it would be more than he could bear, as her hot, exposed eyes rested on him. There was something so revealed, she was revealed beyond bearing, to his eyes. He turned his face aside. And he felt he would not be able to avert her. And he writhed under the imprisonment.

Gudrun put her face into the flowers.

'But how beautiful they are!' she said, in a muffled voice. Then, with a strange, suddenly revealed passion, she stooped and kissed Winifred.

Mr Crich went forward with his hand held out to her.

'I was afraid you were going to run away from us,' he said playfully.

Gudrun looked up at him with a luminous, roguish, unknown face.

'Really!' she replied. 'No, I didn't want to stay in London.'

Her voice seemed to imply that she was glad to get back to Shortlands, her tone was warm and subtly caressing.

'That is a good thing,' smiled the father. 'You see, you are very welcome here among us.'

Gudrun only looked into his face with dark-blue, warm, shy eyes. She was unconsciously carried away by her own power.

'And you look as if you came home in every possible triumph,' Mr Crich continued, holding her hand.

'No,' she said, glowing strangely. 'I haven't had any triumph till I came here.'

'Ah, come, come! We're not going to hear any of those tales. Haven't we read notices in the newspaper, Gerald?'

'You came off pretty well,' said Gerald to her, shaking hands. 'Did you sell anything?'

'No,' she said, 'not much.'

'Just as well,' he said.

She wondered what he meant. But she was all aglow with her reception, carried away by this little flattering ceremonial on her behalf.

'Winifred,' said the father, 'have you a pair of shoes for Miss Brangwen? You had better change at once –'

Gudrun went out with her bouquet in her hand.

'Quite a remarkable young woman,' said the father to Gerald, when she had gone.

'Yes,' replied Gerald briefly, as if he did not like the observation.

Mr Crich liked Gudrun to sit with him for half an hour. Usually he was ashy and wretched, with all the life gnawed out of him. But as soon as he rallied, he liked to make believe that he was just as before, quite well and in the midst of life – not of the outer world, but in the midst of a strong essential life. And to this belief, Gudrun contributed perfectly. With her, he could get by stimulation those precious half-hours of strength and exaltation and pure freedom, when he seemed to live more than he had ever lived.

She came to him as he lay propped up in the library. His face was like yellow wax, his eyes darkened, as it were sightless. His black beard, now streaked with grey, seemed to spring out of the waxy flesh of a corpse. Yet the atmosphere about him was energetic and playful. Gudrun subscribed to this perfectly. To her fancy, he was just an ordinary man. Only his rather terrible appearance was photographed upon her soul, away beneath her consciousness. She knew that, in spite of his playfulness, his eyes could not change from their darkened vacancy, they were the eyes of a man who is dead.

'Ah, this is Miss Brangwen,' he said, suddenly rousing as she entered, announced by the man-servant. 'Thomas, put Miss Brangwen a chair here – that's right.' He looked at her soft, fresh face with pleasure. It gave him the illusion of life. 'Now, you will have a glass of sherry and a little piece of cake. Thomas –'

'No, thank you,' said Gudrun. And as soon as she had said it, her heart sank horribly. The sick man seemed to fall into a gap of death, at her contradiction. She ought to play up to him, not to contravene him. In an instant she was smiling her rather roguish smile.

'I don't like sherry very much,' she said. 'But I like almost anything else.'

The sick man caught at this straw instantly.

'Not sherry! No! Something else! What then? What is there, Thomas?'

'Port wine – curaçao –'

'I would love some curaçao –' said Gudrun, looking at the sick man confidingly.

'You would. Well then, Thomas, curaçao – and a little cake or a biscuit?'

'A biscuit,' said Gudrun. She did not want anything, but she was wise.

'Yes.'

He waited till she was settled with her little glass and her biscuit. Then he was satisfied.

'You have heard the plan,' he said with some excitement, 'for a studio for Winifred over the stables?'

'No!' exclaimed Gudrun, in mock wonder.

'Oh! – I thought Winnie wrote it to you in her letter!'

'Oh – yes – of course. But I thought perhaps it was only her own little idea –' Gudrun smiled subtly, indulgently. The sick man smiled also, elated.

'Oh no. It is a real project. There is a good room under the roof of the stables – with sloping rafters. We had thought of converting it into a studio.'

'How *very* nice that would be!' cried Gudrun, with excited warmth. The thought of the rafters stirred her.

'You think it would? Well, it can be done.'

'But how perfectly splendid for Winifred! Of course, it is just what is needed, if she is to work at all seriously. One must have one's workshop, otherwise one never ceases to be an amateur.'

'Is that so? Yes. Of course, I should like you to share it with Winifred.'

'Thank you *so* much.'

Gudrun knew all these things already, but she must look shy and very grateful, as if overcome.

'Of course, what I should like best would be if you could give up your work at the Grammar School and just avail yourself of the studio, and work there – well, as much or as little as you liked –'

He looked at Gudrun with dark, vacant eyes. She looked back at him as if full of gratitude. These phrases of a dying man were so complete and natural, coming like echoes through his dead mouth.

'And as to your earnings – you don't mind taking from me what you have taken from the Education Committee, do you? I don't want you to be a loser.'

'Oh,' said Gudrun, 'if I can have the studio and work there, I can earn money enough, really I can.'

'Well,' he said, pleased to be the benefactor, 'we can see about all that. You wouldn't mind spending your days here?'

'If there were a studio to work in,' said Gudrun, 'I could ask for nothing better.'

'Is that so?'

He was really very pleased. But already he was getting tired. She could see the grey, awful semi-consciousness of mere pain and dissolution coming over him again, the torture coming into the vacancy of his darkened eyes. It was not over yet, this process of death. She rose softly, saying:

'Perhaps you will sleep. I must look for Winifred.'

She went out, telling the nurse that she had left him. Day by day the tissue of the sick man was further and further reduced, nearer and nearer the process came, towards the last knot which held the human being in its unity. But this knot was hard and unrelaxed, the will of the dying man never gave way. He might be dead in nine-tenths, yet the remaining tenth remained unchanged, till it too was torn apart. With his will he held the unit of himself firm, but the circle of his power was ever and ever reduced, it would be reduced to a point at last, then swept away.

To adhere to life, he must adhere to human relationships, and he caught at every straw. Winifred, the butler, the nurse, Gudrun, these were the people who meant all to him, in these last resources. Gerald, in his father's presence, stiffened with repulsion. It was so, to a less degree, with all the other children except Winifred. They could not see anything but the death, when they looked at their father. It was as if some subterranean dislike overcame them. They could not see the familiar face, hear the familiar voice. They were overwhelmed by the antipathy of visible and audible death. Gerald could not breathe in his father's presence. He must get out at once. And so, in the same way, the father could not bear the presence of his son. It sent a final irritation through the soul of the dying man.

The studio was made ready, Gudrun and Winifred moved in. They enjoyed so much the ordering and the appointing of it. And now they need hardly be in the house at all. They had their meals in the studio, they lived there safely. For the house was becoming dreadful. There were two nurses in white, flitting silently about, like heralds of death. The father was confined to his bed, there was a come and go of *sotto-voce* sisters and brothers and children.

Winifred was her father's constant visitor. Every morning, after breakfast, she went into his room when he was washed and propped up in bed, to spend half an hour with him.

'Are you better, Daddie?' she asked him invariably.

And invariably he answered:

'Yes, I think I'm a little better, pet.'

She held his hand in both her own, lovingly and protectively. And this was very dear to him.

She ran in again as a rule at lunch-time, to tell him the course of events, and every evening, when the curtains were drawn, and his room was cosy, she spent a long time with him. Gudrun was gone home, Winifred was alone in the house; she liked best to be with her father. They talked and prattled at random, he always as if he were well, just the same as when he was going about. So that Winifred, with a child's subtle instinct for avoiding the painful things, behaved as if nothing serious was the matter. Instinctively, she withheld her attention, and was happy. Yet in her remoter soul, she knew as well as the adults knew: perhaps better.

Her father was quite well in his make-believe with her. But when she went away, he relapsed under the misery of his dissolution. But still there were these bright moments, though as his strength waned, his faculty for attention grew weaker, and the nurse had to send Winifred away, to save him from exhaustion.

He never admitted that he was going to die. He knew it was so, he knew it was the end. Yet even to himself he did not admit it. He hated the fact, mortally. His will was rigid. He could not bear being overcome by death. For him there was no death. And yet, at times, he felt a great need to cry out and to wail and complain. He would have liked to cry aloud to Gerald, so that his son should be horrified out of his composure. Gerald was instinctively aware of this, and he recoiled, to avoid any such thing. This uncleanness of death repelled him too much. One should die quickly, like the Romans, one should be master of one's fate in dying as in living. He was convulsed in the clasp of this death of his father's, as in the coils of the great serpent of Laocoön. The great serpent had got the father, and the son was dragged into the embrace of horrifying death along with him. He resisted always. And in some strange way he was a tower of strength to his father.

The last time the dying man asked to see Gudrun he was grey with near death. Yet he must see someone, he must, in the intervals of consciousness, catch into connection with the living world, lest he should have to accept his own situation. Fortunately he was most of his time dazed and half gone. And he spent many hours dimly thinking of the past, as it were, dimly re-living his old experiences. But there were times even to the end when he was capable of realizing what was happening to him in the present, the death that was on him. And these were the times when he called in outside help, no matter whose. For to realize this death that he was dying was a death beyond death, never to be borne. It was an admission never to be made.

Gudrun was shocked by his appearance, and by the darkened, almost disintegrated eyes, that still were unconquered and firm.

'Well,' he said in his weakened voice, 'and how are you and Winifred getting on?'

'Oh, very well indeed,' replied Gudrun.

There were slight dead gaps in the conversation, as if the ideas called up were only elusive straws floating on the dark chaos of the sick man's dying.

'The studio answers all right?' he said.

'Splendid. It couldn't be more beautiful and perfect,' said Gudrun.

She waited for what he would say next.

'And you think Winifred has the makings of a sculptor?'

It was strange how hollow the words were, meaningless.

'I'm sure she has. She will do good things one day.'

'Ah! Then her life won't be altogether wasted, you think?'

Gudrun was rather surprised.

'Sure it won't!' she exclaimed softly.

'That's right.'

Again Gudrun waited for what he would say.

'You find life pleasant, it is good to live, isn't it?' he asked, with a pitiful faint smile that was almost too much for Gudrun.

'Yes,' she smiled – she would lie at random – 'I get a pretty good time, I believe.'

'That's right. A happy nature is a great asset.'

Again Gudrun smiled, though her soul was dry with repulsion. Did one have to die like this – having the life extracted forcibly from one, whilst one smiled and made conversation to the end? Was there no other way? Must one go through all the horror of this victory over death, the triumph of the integral will, that would not be broken till it disappeared utterly? One must, it was the only way. She admired the self-possession and the control of the dying man exceedingly. But she loathed the death itself. She was glad the everyday world held good, and she need not recognize anything beyond.

'You are quite all right here? – nothing we can do for you? – nothing you find wrong in your position?'

'Except that you are too good to me,' said Gudrun.

'Ah, well, the fault of that lies with yourself,' he said, and he felt a little exultation, that he had made this speech. He was still so strong and living! But the nausea of death began to creep back on him, in reaction.

Gudrun went away, back to Winifred. Mademoiselle had left, Gudrun stayed a good deal at Shortlands, and a tutor came in to carry on Winifred's education. But he did not live in the house, he was connected with the Grammar School.

One day, Gudrun was to drive with Winifred and Gerald and Birkin to town in the car. It was a dark, showery day. Winifred and Gudrun were ready and waiting at the door. Winifred was very quiet, but Gudrun had not noticed. Suddenly the child asked, in a voice of unconcern:

'Do you think my father's going to die, Miss Brangwen?'

Gudrun started.

'I don't know,' she replied.

'Don't you truly?'

'Nobody knows for certain. He *may* die, of course.'

The child pondered for a few moments, then she asked:

'But do you *think* he will die?'

It was put almost like a question in geography or science, insistent, as if she would force an admission from the adult. The watchful, slightly triumphant child was almost diabolical.

'Do I think he will die?' repeated Gudrun. 'Yes, I do.'

But Winifred's large eyes were fixed on her, and the girl did not move.

'He is very ill,' said Gudrun.

A small smile came over Winifred's face, subtle and sceptical.

'*I* don't believe he will,' the child asserted mockingly, and she moved away into the drive. Gudrun watched the isolated figure, and her heart stood still. Winifred was playing with a little rivulet of water, absorbedly as if nothing had been said.

'I've made a proper dam,' she said, out of the moist distance.

Gerald came to the door from out of the hall behind.

'It is just as well she doesn't choose to believe it,' he said.

Gudrun looked at him. Their eyes met; and they exchanged a sardonic understanding.

'Just as well,' said Gudrun.

He looked at her again, and a fire flickered up in his eyes.

'Best to dance while Rome burns, since it must burn, don't you think?' he said.

She was rather taken aback. But, gathering herself together, she replied:

'Oh – better dance than wail, certainly.'

'So I think.'

And they both felt the subterranean desire to let go, to fling away everything, and lapse into a sheer unrestraint, brutal and licentious. A strange black passion surged up pure in Gudrun. She felt strong. She felt her hands so strong, as if she could tear the world asunder with them. She remembered the abandonments of Roman licence, and her heart grew hot. She knew she wanted this herself also – or something, something equivalent. Ah, if that which was unknown and suppressed in her were once let loose, what an orgiastic and satisfying event it would be. And she wanted it, she trembled slightly from the proximity of the man, who stood just behind her, suggestive of the same black licentiousness that rose in herself. She wanted it with him, this unacknowledged frenzy. For a moment the clear perception of this preoccupied her, distinct and perfect in its final reality. Then she shut it off completely, saying:

'We might as well go down to the lodge after Winifred – we can get in the car there.'

'So we can,' he answered, going with her.

They found Winifred at the lodge admiring the litter of pure-bred white puppies. The girl looked up, and there was a rather ugly, unseeing cast in her eyes as she turned to Gerald and Gudrun. She did not want to see them.

'Look!' she cried. 'Three new puppies! Marshall says this one seems perfect. Isn't it a sweetling? But it isn't so nice as its mother.' She turned to caress the fine white bull-terrier bitch that stood uneasily near her.

'My dearest Lady Crich,' she said, 'you are beautiful as an angel on earth. Angel – angel – don't you think she's good enough and beautiful enough to go to heaven, Gudrun? They will be in heaven, won't they – and *especially* my darling Lady Crich! Mrs Marshall, I say!'

'Yes, Miss Winifred?' said the woman, appearing at the door.

'Oh, do call this one Lady Winifred, if she turns out perfect, will you? Do tell Marshall to call it Lady Winifred.'

'I'll tell him – but I'm afraid that's a gentleman puppy, Miss Winifred.'

'Oh *no!*' There was the sound of a car. 'There's Rupert!' cried the child, and she ran to the gate.

Birkin, driving his car, pulled up outside the lodge gate.

'We're ready!' cried Winifred. 'I want to sit in front with you, Rupert. May I?'

'I'm afraid you'll fidget about and fall out,' he said.

'No, I won't. I do want to sit in front next to you. It makes my feet so lovely and warm, from the engines.'

Birkin helped her up, amused at sending Gerald to sit by Gudrun in the body of the car.

'Have you any news, Rupert?' Gerald called, as they rushed along the lanes.

'News?' exclaimed Birkin.

'Yes.' Gerald looked at Gudrun, who sat by his side, and he said, his eyes narrowly laughing, 'I want to know whether I ought to congratulate him, but I can't get anything definite out of him.'

Gudrun flushed deeply.

'Congratulate him on what?' she asked.

'There was some mention of an engagement – at least, he said something to me about it.'

Gudrun flushed darkly.

'You mean with Ursula?' she said, in challenge.

'Yes. That is so, isn't it?'

'I don't think there's any engagement,' said Gudrun coldly.

'That so? Still no developments, Rupert?' he called.

'Where? Matrimonial? No.'

'How's that?' called Gudrun.

Birkin glanced quickly round. There was irritation in his eyes also.

'Why?' he replied. 'What do you think of it, Gudrun?'

'Oh,' she cried, determined to fling her stone also into the pool, since they had begun, 'I don't think she wants an engagement. Naturally, she's a bird that prefers the bush.' Gudrun's voice was clear and gong-like. It reminded Rupert of her father's, so strong and vibrant.

'And I,' said Birkin, his face playful but yet determined, 'I want a binding contract, and am not keen on love, particularly free love.'

They were both amused. *Why* this public avowal? Gerald seemed suspended a moment, in amusement.

'Love isn't good enough for you?' he called.

'No!' shouted Birkin.

'Ha, well, that's being over-refined,' said Gerald, and the car ran through the mud.

'What's the matter, really?' said Gerald, turning to Gudrun.

This was an assumption of a sort of intimacy that irritated Gudrun almost like an affront. It seemed to her that Gerald was deliberately insulting her, and infringing on the decent privacy of them all.

'What is it?' she said, in her high, repellent voice. 'Don't ask me! – I know nothing about *ultimate* marriage, I assure you: or even penultimate.'

'Only the ordinary unwarrantable brand!' replied Gerald. 'Just so – same here. I am no expert on marriage and degrees of ultimateness. It seems to be a bee that buzzes loudly in Rupert's bonnet.'

'Exactly! But that is his trouble, exactly! Instead of wanting a woman for herself, he wants his *ideas* fulfilled. Which, when it comes to actual practice, is not good enough.'

'Oh no. Best go slap for what's womanly in woman, like a bull at a gate.' Then he seemed to glimmer in himself. 'You think love is the ticket, do you?' he asked.

'Certainly, while it lasts – you only can't insist on permanency,' came Gudrun's voice, strident above the noise.

'Marriage or no marriage, ultimate or penultimate or just so-so? – take the love as you find it.'

'As you please, or as you don't please,' she echoed. 'Marriage is a social arrangement, I take it, and has nothing to do with the question of love.'

His eyes were flickering on her all the time. She felt as if he were kissing her freely and malevolently. It made the colour burn in her cheeks, but her heart was quite firm and unfailing.

'You think Rupert is off his head a bit?' Gerald asked.

Her eyes flashed with acknowledgement.

'As regards a woman, yes,' she said, 'I do. There *is* such a thing as two people being in love for the whole of their lives – perhaps. But marriage is neither here nor there, even then. If they are in love, well and good. If not – why break eggs about it!'

'Yes,' said Gerald. 'That's how it strikes me. But what about Rupert?'

'I can't make out – neither can he nor anybody. He seems to think that if you marry you can get through marriage into a third heaven, or something – all very vague.'

'Very! And who wants a third heaven? As a matter of fact, Rupert has a great yearning to be *safe* – to tie himself to the mast.'

'Yes. It seems to me he's mistaken there too,' said Gudrun. 'I'm sure a mistress is more likely to be faithful than a wife – just because she is her *own* mistress. No – he says he believes that a man and wife can go further than any other two beings – but *where*, is not explained. They can know each other, heavenly and hellish, but particularly hellish, so perfectly that they go beyond heaven and hell – into – there it all breaks down – into nowhere.'

'Into Paradise, he says,' laughed Gerald.

Gudrun shrugged her shoulders. '*Je m'en fiche* of your Paradise!' she said.

'Not being a Mohammedan,' said Gerald. Birkin sat motionless, driving the car, quite unconscious of what they said. And Gudrun, sitting immediately behind him, felt a sort of ironic pleasure in thus exposing him.

'He says,' she added, with a grimace of irony, 'that you can find an eternal equilibrium in marriage, if you accept the unison, and still leave yourself separate, don't try to fuse.'

'Doesn't inspire me,' said Gerald.

'That's just it,' said Gudrun.

'I believe in love, in a real *abandon*, if you're capable of it,' said Gerald.

'So do I,' said she.

'And so does Rupert, too – though he is always shouting.'

'No,' said Gudrun. 'He won't abandon himself to the other person. You can't be sure of him. That's the trouble, I think.'

'Yet he wants marriage! Marriage – *et puis?*'

'*Le Paradis!*' mocked Gudrun.

Birkin, as he drove, felt a creeping of the spine, as if somebody were threatening his neck. But he shrugged with indifference. It began to rain. Here was a change. He stopped the car and got down to put up the hood.

22

WOMAN TO WOMAN

They came to the town, and left Gerald at the railway station. Gudrun and Winifred were to come to tea with Birkin, who expected Ursula also. In the afternoon, however, the first person to turn up was Hermione. Birkin was out, so she went in the drawing-room, looking at his books and papers, and playing on the piano. Then Ursula arrived. She was surprised, unpleasantly so, to see Hermione, of whom she had heard nothing for some time.

'It is a surprise to see you,' she said.

'Yes,' said Hermione – 'I've been away at Aix –'

'Oh, for your health?'

'Yes.'

The two women looked at each other. Ursula resented Hermione's long, grave, downward-looking face. There was something of the stupidity and the unlightened self-esteem of a horse in it. 'She's got a horse-face,' Ursula said to herself, 'she runs between blinkers.' It did seem as if Hermione, like the moon, had only one side to her penny. There was no obverse. She stared out all the time on the narrow, but to her, complete world of the extant consciousness. In the darkness, she did not exist. Like the moon, one half of her was lost to life. Her self was all in her head, she did not know what it was spontaneously to run or move, like a fish in the water, or a weasel on the grass. She must always *know*.

But Ursula only suffered from Hermione's one-sidedness. She only felt Hermione's cool evidence, which seemed to put her down as nothing. Hermione, who brooded and brooded till she was exhausted with the ache of her effort at consciousness, spent and ashen in her body, who gained so slowly and with such effort her final and barren conclusions of knowledge, was apt, in the presence of other women, whom she thought simply female, to wear the conclusions of her bitter assurance like jewels which conferred on her an unquestionable distinction, established her in a higher order of life. She was apt, mentally, to condescend to women such as Ursula, whom she regarded as purely emotional. Poor Hermione, it was her one possession, this aching certainty of hers, it was her only justification. She must be confident here, for God knows, she felt rejected and deficient enough elsewhere. In the life of thought, of the spirit, she was one of the elect. And she wanted to be universal. But there was a devastating cynicism at the bottom of her. She did not believe in her own universals – they were sham. She did not believe in the inner life – it was a trick, not a reality. She did not believe in the spiritual world – it was an affectation. In the last resort, she believed in Mammon, the flesh, and the devil – these at least were not sham. She was a priestess without belief, without conviction, suckled in a creed outworn, and condemned to the reiteration of mysteries that were not divine to her. Yet there was no escape. She was a leaf upon a dying tree. What help was there then, but to fight still for the old, withered truths, to die for the old, outworn belief, to be a sacred and inviolate priestess of desecrated mysteries? The old great truths *had* been true. And she was a leaf of the old great tree of knowledge that was withering now. To the old and last truth then she must be faithful even though cynicism and mockery took place at the bottom of her soul.

'I am so glad to see you,' she said to Ursula, in her slow voice, that was like an incantation. 'You and Rupert have become quite friends?'

'Oh yes,' said Ursula. 'He is always somewhere in the background.'

Hermione paused before she answered. She saw perfectly well the other woman's vaunt: it seemed truly vulgar.

'Is he?' she said slowly, and with perfect equanimity. 'And do you think you will marry?'

The question was so calm and mild, so simple and bare and dispassionate that Ursula was somewhat taken aback, rather attracted. It pleased her almost like a wickedness. There was some delightful naked irony in Hermione.

'Well,' replied Ursula, '*He* wants to, awfully, but I'm not so sure.'

Hermione watched her with slow, calm eyes. She noted this new expression of vaunting. How she envied Ursula a certain unconscious positivity! even her vulgarity!

'Why aren't you sure?' she asked, in her easy sing-song. She was perfectly at her ease, perhaps even rather happy in this conversation. 'You don't really love him?'

Ursula flushed a little at the mild impertinence of this question. And yet she could not definitely take offence. Hermione seemed so calmly and sanely candid. After all, it was rather great to be able to be so sane.

'He says it isn't love he wants,' she replied.

'What is it then?' Hermione was slow and level.

'He wants me really to accept him in marriage.'

Hermione was silent for some time, watching Ursula with slow, pensive eyes.

'Does he?' she said at length, without expression. Then, rousing, 'And what is it you don't want? You don't want marriage?'

'No – I don't – not really. I don't want to give the sort of *submission* he insists on. He wants me to give myself up – and I simply don't feel that I *can* do it.'

Again there was a long pause before Hermione replied:

'Not if you don't want to.' Then again there was silence. Hermione shuddered with a strange desire. Ah, if only he had asked *her* to subserve him, to be his slave! She shuddered with desire.

'You see, I can't –'

'But exactly in what does –'

They had both begun at once, they both stopped. Then Hermione, assuming priority of speech, resumed as if wearily:

'To what does he want you to submit?'

'He says he wants me to accept him non-emotionally, and finally – I really don't know *what* he means. He says he wants the demon part of himself to be mated – physically – not the human being. You see, he says one thing one day, and another the next – and he always contradicts himself –'

'And always thinks about himself, and his own dissatisfaction,' said Hermione slowly.

'Yes,' cried Ursula. 'As if there were no one but himself concerned. That makes it so impossible.'

But immediately she began to retract.

'He insists on my accepting God knows what in *him*,' she resumed. 'He wants me to accept *him* as – as an absolute – But it seems to me he doesn't want to *give* anything. He doesn't want real warm intimacy – he won't have it – he rejects it. He won't let me think, really, and he won't let me *feel* – he hates feelings.'

There was a long pause, bitter for Hermione. Ah, if only he would have made this demand of her? Her he *drove* into thought, drove inexorably into knowledge – and then execrated her for it.

'He wants me to sink myself,' Ursula resumed, 'not to have any being of my own –'

'Then why doesn't he marry an odalisk?' said Hermione in her mild sing-song, 'if it is that he wants.' Her long face looked sardonic and amused.

'Yes,' said Ursula vaguely. After all, the tiresome thing was, he did not want an odalisk, he did not want a slave. Hermione would have been his slave – there was in her a horrible desire to prostrate herself before a man – a man who worshipped her, however, and admitted her as the supreme thing. He did not want an odalisk. He wanted a woman to *take* something from him, to give herself up so much that she could take the last realities of him, the last facts, the last physical facts, physical and unbearable.

And if she did, would he acknowledge her? Would he be able to acknowledge her through everything, or would he use her just as his instrument, use her for his own private satisfaction, not admitting her? That was what the other men had done. They had wanted their own show, and they would not admit her, they turned all she was into nothingness. Just as Hermione now betrayed herself as a woman. Hermione was like a man, she believed only in men's things. She betrayed the woman in herself. And Birkin, would he acknowledge, or would he deny her?

'Yes,' said Hermione, as each woman came out of her own separate reverie. 'It would be a mistake – I think it would be a mistake –'

'To marry him?' asked Ursula.

'Yes,' said Hermione slowly – 'I think you need a man – soldierly, strong-willed –' Hermione held out her hand and clenched it with rhapsodic intensity. 'You should have a man like the old heroes – you need to stand behind him as he goes into battle, you need to *see* his strength, and to *hear* his shout – You need a man physically strong, and virile in his will, *not* a sensitive man –' There was a break, as if the pythoness had uttered the oracle, and now the woman went on, in a rhapsody-wearied voice: 'And you see, Rupert isn't this, he isn't. He is frail in health and body, he needs great, great care. Then he is so changeable and unsure of himself – it requires the greatest patience and understanding to help him. And I don't think you are patient. You would have to be prepared to suffer – dreadfully. I can't *tell* you how much suffering it would take to make him happy. He lives an *intensely* spiritual life, at times – too, too wonderful. And then come the reactions. I can't speak of what I have been through with him. We have been together so long, I really do know him, I *do* know what he is. And I feel I must say it; I feel it would be perfectly *disastrous* for you to marry him – for you even more than for him.' Hermione lapsed into bitter reverie. 'He is so uncertain, so unstable – he wearies, and then reacts. I couldn't *tell* you what his reactions are. I couldn't *tell* you the agony of them. That which he affirms and loves one day – a little later he turns on it in a fury of destruction. He is never constant, always this awful, dreadful reaction. Always the quick change from good to bad, bad to good. And nothing is so devastating, nothing – '

'Yes,' said Ursula humbly, 'you must have suffered.'

An unearthly light came on Hermione's face. She clenched her hand like one inspired.

'And one must be willing to suffer – willing to suffer for him hourly, daily – if you are going to help him, if he is to keep true to anything at all –'

'And I don't *want* to suffer hourly and daily,' said Ursula. 'I don't, I should be ashamed. I think it is degrading not to be happy.'

Hermione stopped and looked at her a long time.

'Do you?' she said at last. And this utterance seemed to her a mark of

Ursula's far distance from herself. For to Hermione suffering was the greatest reality, come what might. Yet she too had a creed of happiness.

'Yes,' she said. 'One *should* be happy –' But it was a matter of will.

'Yes,' said Hermione, listlessly now, 'I can only feel that it would be disastrous, disastrous – at least, to marry in a hurry. Can't you be together without marriage? Can't you go away and live somewhere without marriage? I do feel that marriage would be fatal for both of you. I think for you even more than for him – and I think of his health –'

'Of course,' said Ursula, '*I* don't care about marriage – it isn't really important to me – it's he who wants it.'

'It is his idea for the moment,' said Hermione, with that weary finality and a sort of *si jeunesse savait* infallibility.

There was a pause. Then Ursula broke into faltering challenge.

'You think I'm merely a physical woman, don't you?'

'No, indeed,' said Hermione. 'No, indeed! But I think you are vital and young – it isn't a question of years, or even of experience – it is almost a question of race. Rupert is race-old, he comes of an old race – and you seem to me so young, you come of a young, inexperienced race.'

'Do I!' said Ursula. 'But I think he is awfully young, on one side.'

'Yes, perhaps – childish in many respects. Nevertheless –'

They both lapsed into silence. Ursula was filled with deep resentment and a touch of hopelessness. 'It isn't true,' she said to herself, silently addressing her adversary. 'It isn't true. And it is *you* who want a physically strong, bullying man, not I. It is you who want an unsensitive man, not I. You *don't* know anything about Rupert, not really, in spite of the years you have had with him. You don't give him a woman's love, you give him an ideal love, and that is why he reacts away from you. You don't know. You only know the dead things. Any kitchen-maid would know something about him, you don't know. What do you think your knowledge is but dead understanding, that doesn't mean a thing. You are so false, and untrue, how could you know anything? What is the good of your talking about love – you untrue spectre of a woman! How can you know anything, when you don't believe? You don't believe in yourself and your own womanhood, so what good is your conceited, shallow cleverness – !'

The two women sat on in antagonistic silence. Hermione felt injured, that all her good intention, all her offering, only left the other woman in vulgar antagonism. But then, Ursula could not understand, never would understand, could never be more than the usual jealous and unreasonable female, with a good deal of powerful female emotion, female attraction, and a fair amount of female understanding, but no mind. Hermione had decided long ago that where there was no mind, it was useless to appeal for reason – one had merely to ignore the ignorant. And Rupert – he had now reacted towards the strongly female, healthy, selfish woman – it was his reaction for the time being – there was no helping it at all. It was all a foolish backward and forward, a violent oscillation that would at length be too violent for his coherency, and he would smash and be dead. There was no saving him. This violent and directionless reaction between animalism and spiritual truth would go on in him till he tore himself in two between the opposite directions, and disappeared meaninglessly out of life. It was no good – he too was without unity, without *mind*, in the ultimate stages of living; not quite man enough to make a destiny for a woman.

They sat on till Birkin came in and found them together. He felt at once the antagonism in the atmosphere, something radical and insuperable, and he bit his lip. But he affected a bluff manner.

'Hello, Hermione, are you back again? How do you feel?'

'Oh, better. And how are you – you don't look well –'

'Oh! – I believe Gudrun and Winnie Crich are coming in to tea. At least they said they were. We shall be a tea-party. What train did you come by, Ursula?'

It was rather annoying to see him trying to placate both women at once. Both women watched him, Hermione with deep resentment and pity for him, Ursula very impatient. He was nervous and apparently in quite good spirits, chattering the conventional commonplaces. Ursula was amazed and indignant at the way he made small-talk; he was adept as any *fat* in Christendom. She became quite stiff, she would not answer. It all seemed to her so false and so belittling. And still Gudrun did not appear.

'I think I shall go to Florence for the winter,' said Hermione at length.

'Will you?' he answered. 'But it is so cold there.'

'Yes, but I shall stay with Palestra. It is quite comfortable.'

'What takes you to Florence?'

'I don't know,' said Hermione slowly. Then she looked at him with her slow, heavy gaze. 'Barnes is starting his school of aesthetics, and Olandese is going to give a set of discourses on the Italian national policy –'

'Both rubbish,' he said.

'No, I don't think so,' said Hermione.

'Which do you admire, then?'

'I admire both. Barnes is a pioneer. And then I am interested in Italy, in her coming to national consciousness.'

'I wish she'd come to something different from national consciousness, then,' said Birkin; 'especially as it only means a sort of commercial-industrial consciousness. I hate Italy and her national rant. And I think Barnes is an amateur.'

Hermione was silent for some moments, in a state of hostility. But yet, she had got Birkin back again into her world! How subtle her influence was, she seemed to start his irritable attention into her direction exclusively, in one minute. He was her creature.

'No,' she said, 'you are wrong.' Then a sort of tension came over her, she raised her face like the pythoness inspired with oracles, and went on in rhapsodic manner: *'Il Sandro mi scrive che ha accolto il piu grande entusiasmo, tutti i giovani e fanciulle e ragazzi, sono tutti –'* She went on in Italian, as if, in thinking of the Italians she thought in their language.

He listened with a shade of distaste to her rhapsody, then he said:

'For all that, I don't like it. Their nationalism is just industrialism – that and a shallow jealousy I detest so much.'

'I think you are wrong – I think you are wrong –' said Hermione. 'It seems to me purely spontaneous and beautiful, the modern Italian's *passion*, for it is a passion, for Italy, L'Italia –'

'Do you know Italy well?' Ursula asked of Hermione. Hermione hated to be broken in upon in this manner. Yet she answered mildly:

'Yes, pretty well. I spent several years of my girlhood there with my mother. My mother died in Florence.'

'Oh.'

There was a pause, painful to Ursula and to Birkin. Hermione, however, seemed abstracted and calm. Birkin was white, his eyes glowed as if he were in a fever, he was far too overwrought. How Ursula suffered in this tense atmosphere of strained wills! Her head seemed bound round by iron bands.

Birkin rang the bell for tea. They could not wait for Gudrun any longer. When the door was opened, the cat walked in.

'Micio! Micio!' called Hermione in her slow, deliberate sing-song. The young cat turned to look at her, then, with his slow and stately walk he advanced to her side.

'*Vieni – vieni quá,*' Hermione was saying in her strange caressive, protective voice, as if she were always the elder, the mother superior. '*Vieni dire Buon' Giorno alla zia. Mi ricordi, mi ricordi bene – non è vero, piccolo? E vero che mi ricordi? E vero?*' And slowly she rubbed his head, slowly and with ironic indifference.

'Does he understand Italian?' said Ursula, who knew nothing of the language.

'Yes,' said Hermione at length. 'His mother was Italian. She was born in my waste-paper basket in Florence on the morning of Rupert's birthday. She was his birthday present.'

Tea was brought in. Birkin poured out for them. It was strange how inviolable was the intimacy which existed between him and Hermione. Ursula felt that she was an outsider. The very tea-cups and the old silver was a bond between Hermione and Birkin. It seemed to belong to an old, past world which they had inhabited together, and in which Ursula was a foreigner. She was almost a parvenue in their old cultured milieu. Her convention was not their convention, their standards were not her standards. But theirs were established, they had the sanction and the grace of age. He and she together, Hermione and Birkin, were people of the same old tradition, the same withered deadening culture. And she, Ursula, was an intruder. So they always made her feel.

Hermione poured a little cream into a saucer. The simple way she assumed her rights in Birkin's room maddened and discouraged Ursula. There was a fatality about it, as if it were bound to be. Hermione lifted the cat and put the cream before him. He planted his two paws on the edge of the table and bent his gracious young head to drink.

'*Sicuro che capisce italiano,*' sang Hermione, '*non l'avrà dimenticato, la lingua della Mamma.*'

She lifted the cat's head with her long, slow, white fingers, not letting him drink, holding him in her power. It was always the same, this joy in power she manifested, peculiarly in power over any male being. He blinked forbearingly, with a male, bored expression, licking his whiskers. Hermione laughed in her short, grunting fashion.

'*Ecco, il bravo ragazzo, com' è superbo, questo!*'

She made a vivid picture, so calm and strange with the cat. She had a true static impressiveness, she was a social artist in some ways.

The cat refused to look at her, indifferently avoided her fingers, and began to drink again, his nose down to the cream, perfectly balanced, as he lapped with his odd little click.

'It's bad for him, teaching him to eat at table,' said Birkin.

'Yes,' said Hermione, easily assenting.

Then, looking down at the cat, she resumed her old, mocking, humorous sing-song.

'Ti imparano fare brutte cose, brutte cose –'

She lifted the Mino's white chin on her forefinger slowly. The young cat looked round with a supremely forbearing air, avoided seeing anything, withdrew his chin, and began to wash his face with his paw. Hermione grunted her laughter, pleased.

'Bel giovanetto –' she said.

The cat reached forward again and put his fine white paw on the edge of the saucer. Hermione lifted it down with delicate slowness. This deliberate, delicate carefulness of movement reminded Ursula of Gudrun.

'No! *Non è permesso di mettere il zampino nel tondinetto. Non piace al babbo. Un signor gatto così selvatico – !'*

And she kept her finger on the softly planted paw of the cat, and her voice had the same whimsical, humorous note of bullying.

Ursula had her nose out of joint. She wanted to go away now. It all seemed no good. Hermione was established for ever, she herself was ephemeral and had not yet even arrived.

'I will go now,' she said suddenly.

Birkin looked at her almost in fear – he so dreaded her anger. 'But there is no need for such hurry,' he said.

'Yes,' she answered. 'I will go.' And turning to Hermione, before there was time to say any more, she held out her hand and said 'Good-bye'.

'Good-bye –' sang Hermione, detaining the hand. 'Must you really go now?'

'Yes, I think I'll go,' said Ursula, her face set and averted from Hermione's eyes.

'You think you will –'

But Ursula had got her hand free. She turned to Birkin with a quick, almost jeering 'Good-bye', and she was opening the door before he had time to do it for her.

When she got outside the house she ran down the road in fury and agitation. It was strange, the unreasoning rage and violence Hermione roused in her, by her very presence. Ursula knew she gave herself away to the other woman, she knew she looked ill-bred, uncouth, exaggerated. But she did not care. She only ran up the road, lest she should go back and jeer in the faces of the two she had left behind. For they outraged her.

23

EXCURSE

Next day Birkin sought Ursula out. It happened to be the half-day at the Grammar School. He appeared towards the end of the morning, and asked her, would she drive with him in the afternoon. She consented. But her face was closed and unresponding, and his heart sank.

The afternoon was fine and dim. He was driving the motor-car, and she sat beside him. But still her face was closed against him, unresponding. When she became like this, like a wall against him, his heart contracted.

His life now seemed so reduced that he hardly cared any more. At moments it seemed to him he did not care a straw whether Ursula or Hermione or anybody else existed or did not exist. Why bother! Why strive for a coherent, satisfied life? Why not drift on in a series of accidents – like a picaresque novel? Why not? Why bother about human relationships? Why take them seriously – male or female? Why form any serious connections at all? Why not be casual, drifting along, taking all for what it was worth?

And yet, still, he was damned and doomed to the old effort at serious living.

'Look,' he said, 'what I bought.' The car was running along a broad white road between autumn trees.

He gave her a little bit of screwed-up paper. She took it and opened it.

'How lovely,' she cried.

She examined the gift.

'How perfectly lovely!' she cried again. 'But why do you give them me?' She put the question offensively.

His face flickered with bored irritation. He shrugged his shoulders slightly.

'I wanted to,' he said coolly.

'But why? Why should you?'

'Am I called on to find reasons?' he asked.

There was a silence, whilst she examined the rings that had been screwed up in the paper.

'I think they are *beautiful*,' she said, 'especially this. This is wonderful –'

It was a round opal, red and fiery, set in a circle of tiny rubies.

'You like that best?' he said.

'I think I do.'

'I like the sapphire,' he said.

'This?'

It was a rose-shaped, beautiful sapphire, with small brilliants.

'Yes,' she said, 'it is lovely.' She held it in the light. 'Yes, perhaps it *is* the best –'

'The blue –' he said.

'Yes, wonderful –'

He suddenly swung the car out of the way of a farm-cart. It tilted on the bank. He was a careless driver, yet very quick. But Ursula was frightened. There was always that something regardless in him which terrified her. She suddenly felt he might kill her, by making some dreadful accident with the motor-car. For a moment she was stony with fear.

'Isn't it rather dangerous, the way you drive?' she asked him.

'No, it isn't dangerous,' he said. And then, after a pause: 'Don't you like the yellow ring at all?'

It was a squarish topaz set in a frame of steel, or some other similar mineral, finely wrought.

'Yes,' she said, 'I do like it. But why did you buy these rings?'

'I wanted them. They are second-hand.'

'You bought them for yourself?'

'No. Rings look wrong on my hands.'

'Why did you buy them then?'

'I bought them to give to you.'

'But why? Surely you ought to give them to Hermione! You belong to her.'

He did not answer. She remained with the jewels shut in her hand. She wanted to try them on her fingers, but something in her would not let her.

And, moreover, she was afraid her hands were too large, she shrank from the mortification of a failure to put them on any but her little finger. They travelled in silence through the empty lanes.

Driving in a motor-car excited her, she forgot his presence even.

'Where are we?' she asked suddenly.

'Not far from Worksop.'

'And where are we going?'

'Anywhere.'

It was the answer she liked.

She opened her hand to look at the rings. They gave her *such* pleasure, as they lay, the three circles, with their knotted jewels, entangled in her palm. She would have to try them on. She did so secretly, unwilling to let him see, so that he should not know her finger was too large for them. But he saw, nevertheless. He always saw, if she wanted him not to. It was another of his hateful, watchful characteristics.

Only the opal, with its thin wire loop, would go on her ring finger. And she was superstitious. No, there was ill-portent enough, she would not accept this ring from him in pledge.

'Look,' she said, putting forward her hand, that was half closed and shrinking. 'The others don't fit me.'

He looked at the red-glinting, soft stone on her over-sensitive skin.

'Yes,' he said.

'But opals are unlucky, aren't they?' she said wistfully.

'No. I prefer unlucky things. Luck is vulgar. Who wants what *luck* would bring? I don't.'

'But why?' she laughed.

And, consumed with a desire to see how the other rings would look on her hand, she put them on her little finger.

'They can be made a little bigger,' he said.

'Yes,' she replied doubtfully. And she sighed. She knew that, in accepting the rings, she was accepting a pledge. Yet fate seemed more than herself. She looked again at the jewels. They were very beautiful to her eyes – not as ornament, or wealth, but as tiny fragments of loveliness.

'I'm glad you bought them,' she said, putting her hand, half unwillingly, gently on his arm.

He smiled slightly. He wanted her to come to him. But he was angry at the bottom of his soul, and indifferent. He knew she had a passion for him, really. But it was not finally interesting. There were depths of passion when one became impersonal and indifferent, unemotional. Whereas Ursula was still at the emotional personal level – always so abominably personal. He had taken her as he had never been taken himself. He had taken her at the roots of her darkness and shame – like a demon, laughing over the fountain of mystic corruption which was one of the sources of her being, laughing, shrugging, accepting, accepting finally. As for her, when would she so much go beyond herself as to accept him at the quick of death?

She now became quite happy. The motor-car ran on, the afternoon was soft and dim. She talked with lively interest, analysing people and their motives – Gudrun, Gerald. He answered vaguely. He was not very much interested any more in personalities and in people – people were all different, but they were all enclosed nowadays in a definite limitation, he said; there were only about two great ideas, two great streams of activity remaining, with various forms of reaction therefrom. The reactions were all varied in various people, but they followed a few great laws, and intrinsically there was no difference. They acted and reacted involuntarily according to a few great laws, and once the laws, the great principles, were known, people were no longer mystically interesting. They were all essentially alike, the differences were only variations on a theme. None of them transcended the given terms.

Ursula did not agree – people were still an adventure to her – but – perhaps not as much as she tried to persuade herself. Perhaps there was something mechanical, now, in her interest. Perhaps also her interest was destructive, her analysing was a real tearing to pieces. There was an under-space in her where she did not care for people and their idiosyncrasies, even to destroy them. She seemed to touch for a moment this under-silence in herself, she became still, and she turned for a moment purely to Birkin.

'Won't it be lovely to go home in the dark?' she said. 'We might have tea rather late – shall we? – and have high tea? Wouldn't that be rather nice?'

'I promised to be at Shortlands for dinner,' he said.

'But – it doesn't matter – you can go tomorrow –'

'Hermione is there,' he said, in rather an uneasy voice. 'She is going away in two days. I suppose I ought to say good-bye to her. I shall never see her again.'

Ursula drew away, closed in a violent silence. He knitted his brows, and his eyes began to sparkle again in anger.

'You don't mind, do you?' he asked irritably.

'No, I don't care. Why should I? Why should I mind?' Her tone was jeering and offensive.

'That's what I ask myself,' he said; 'why *should* you mind! But you seem to.' His brows were tense with violent irritation.

'I *assure* you I don't, I don't mind in the least. Go where you belong – it's what I want you to do.'

'Ah, you fool!' he cried, 'with your "go where you belong". It's finished between Hermione and me. She means much more to *you*, if it comes to that, than she does to me. For you can only revolt in pure reaction from her – and to be her opposite is to be her counterpart.'

'Ah, opposite!' cried Ursula. 'I know your dodges. I am not taken in by your word-twisting. You belong to Hermione and her dead show. Well, if you do, you do. I don't blame you. But then you've nothing to do with me.'

In his inflamed, overwrought exasperation he stopped the car, and they sat there, in the middle of the country lane, to have it out. It was a crisis of war between them, so they did not see the ridiculousness of their situation.

'If you weren't a fool, if only you weren't a fool,' he cried in bitter despair, 'you'd see that one could be decent, even when one has been wrong. I *was* wrong to go on all those years with Hermione – it was a deathly process. But after all, one can have a little human decency. But no, you would tear my soul out with your jealousy at the very mention of Hermione's name.'

'I jealous! *I* – jealous! You *are* mistaken if you think that. I'm not jealous in the least of Hermione, she is nothing to me, not *that*!' And Ursula snapped her fingers. 'No, it's you who are a liar. It's you who must return, like a dog to his vomit. It is what Hermione *stands for* that I *hate*. I *hate* it. It is lies, it is false, it is death. But you want it, you can't help it, you can't help yourself. You belong to that old, deathly way of living – then go back to it. But don't come to me, for I've nothing to do with it.'

And in the stress of her violent emotion, she got down from the car and went to the hedgerow, picking unconsciously some flesh-pink spindleberries, some of which were burst, showing their orange seeds.

'Ah, you are a fool,' he cried bitterly, with some contempt.

'Yes, I am. I *am* a fool. And thank God for it. I'm too big a fool to swallow your cleverness. God be praised. You go to your women – go to them – they are your sort – you've always had a string of them trailing after you – and you always will. Go to your spiritual brides – but don't come to me as well, because I'm not having any, thank you. You're not satisfied, are you? Your spiritual brides can't give you what you want, they aren't common and fleshy enough for you, aren't they? So you come to me, and keep them in the background! You will marry me for daily use. But you'll keep yourself well provided with spiritual brides in the background. I know your dirty little game.' Suddenly a flame ran over her, and she stamped her foot madly on the road, and he winced, afraid that she would strike him. 'And *I, I'm* not spiritual enough, *I'm* not as spiritual as that Hermione – !' Her brows knitted, her eyes blazed like a tiger's. 'Then *go* to her, that's all I say, *go* to her, *go*. Ha, she spiritual – *spiritual*, she! A dirty materialist as she is. *She* spiritual? What does she care for, what is her spirituality? What *is* it?' Her fury seemed to blaze out and burn his face. He shrank a little. 'I tell you it's *dirt, dirt,* and nothing *but* dirt. And it's dirt you want, you crave for it. Spiritual! Is *that* spiritual, her bullying, her conceit, her sordid materialism? She's a fishwife, a fishwife, she is such a materialist. And all so sordid. What does she work out to, in the end, with all her social passion, as you call it. Social passion – what social passion has she? – show it me! – where is it? She wants petty, immediate *power*, she wants the illusion that she is a great woman, that is all. In her soul she's a devilish unbeliever, common as dirt. That's what she is at the bottom. And all the rest is pretence – but you love it. You love the sham spirituality, it's your food. And why? Because of the dirt underneath. Do you think I don't know the foulness of your sex life – and hers? – I do. And it's that foulness you want, you liar. Then have it, have it. You're such a liar.'

She turned away, spasmodically tearing the twigs of spindleberry from the hedge, and fastening them, with vibrating fingers, in the bosom of her coat.

He stood watching in silence. A wonderful tenderness burned in him at the sight of her quivering, so sensitive fingers: and at the same time he was full of rage and callousness.

'This is a degrading exhibition,' he said coolly.

'Yes, degrading indeed,' she said. 'But more to me than to you.'

'Since you choose to degrade yourself,' he said. Again the flash came over her face, the yellow lights concentrated in her eyes.

'*You!*' she cried. 'You! You truth-lover! You purity-monger! It *stinks*, your truth and your purity. It stinks of the offal you feed on, you scavenger dog, you eater of corpses. You are foul, *foul* – and you must know it. Your purity, your candour, your goodness – yes, thank you, we've had some. What you are is a foul, deathly thing, obscene, that's what you are, obscene and perverse. You, and love! You may well say, you don't want love. No, you want *yourself*, and dirt and death – that's what you want. You are so *perverse*, so death-eating. And then –'

'There's a bicycle coming,' he said, writhing under her loud denunciation.

She glanced down the road.

'I don't care,' she cried.

Nevertheless she was silent. The cyclist, having heard the voices raised in altercation, glanced curiously at the man and the woman, and at the standing motor-car as he passed.

'– Afternoon,' he said cheerfully.

'Good afternoon,' replied Birkin coldly.

They were silent as the man passed into the distance.

A clearer look had come over Birkin's face. He knew she was in the main right. He knew he was perverse, so spiritual on the one hand, and in some strange way, degraded on the other. But was she herself any better? Was anybody any better?

'It may all be true, lies and stink and all,' he said. 'But Hermione's spiritual intimacy is no rottener than your emotional-jealous intimacy. One can preserve the decencies, even to one's enemies: for one's own sake. Hermione is my enemy – to her last breath! That's why I must bow her off the field.'

'You! You and your enemies and your bows! A pretty picture you make of yourself. But it takes nobody in but yourself. I *jealous! I!* What I say,' her voice sprang into flame, 'I say because it is *true*, do you see, because you are *you*, a foul and false liar, a whited sepulchre. That's why I say it. And *you* hear it.'

'And be grateful,' he added, with a satirical grimace.

'Yes,' she cried, 'and if you have a spark of decency in you, be grateful.'

'Not having a spark of decency, however –' he retorted.

'No,' she cried, 'you haven't a *spark*. And so you can go your way, and I'll go mine. It's no good, not the slightest. So you can leave me now, I don't want to go any farther with you – leave me –'

'You don't even know where you are,' he said.

'Oh, don't bother, I assure you I shall be all right. I've got ten shillings in my purse, and that will take me back from anywhere *you* have brought me to.' She hesitated. The rings were still on her fingers, two on her little finger, one on her ring finger. Still she hesitated.

'Very good,' he said. 'The only hopeless thing is a fool.'

'You are quite right,' she said.

Still she hesitated. Then an ugly, malevolent look came over her face, she pulled the rings from her fingers and tossed them at him. One touched his face, the others hit his coat, and they scattered into the mud.

'And take your rings,' she said, 'and go and buy yourself a female elsewhere – there are plenty to be had, who will be quite glad to share your spiritual mess – or to have your physical mess, and leave your spiritual mess to Hermione.'

With which she walked away, desultorily, up the road. He stood motionless, watching her sullen, rather ugly walk. She was sullenly picking and pulling at the twigs of the hedge as she passed. She grew smaller, she seemed to pass out of his sight. A darkness came over his mind. Only a small, mechanical speck of consciousness hovered near him.

He felt tired and weak. Yet also he was relieved. He gave up his old position. He went and sat on the bank. No doubt Ursula was right. It was true, really, what she said. He knew that his spirituality was concomitant of a process of depravity, a sort of pleasure in self-destruction. There really *was* a certain stimulant in self-destruction, for him – especially when it was translated spiritually. But then he knew it – he knew it, and had done. And was not Ursula's way of emotional intimacy, emotional and physical, was it not just as dangerous as Hermione's abstract spiritual intimacy?

Fusion, fusion, this horrible fusion of two beings, which every woman and most men insisted on, was it not nauseous and horrible anyhow, whether it was a fusion of the spirit or of the emotional body? Hermione saw herself as the perfect Idea, to which all men must come: and Ursula was the perfect Womb, the bath of birth, to which all men must come! And both were horrible. Why could they not remain individuals, limited by their own limits? Why this dreadful all-comprehensiveness, this hateful tyranny? Why not leave the other being free, why try to absorb, or melt, or merge? One might abandon oneself utterly to the *moments*, but not to any other being.

He could not bear to see the rings lying in the pale mud of the road. He picked them up and wiped them unconsciously on his hands. They were the little tokens of the reality of beauty, the reality of happiness in warm creation. But he had made his hands all dirty and gritty.

There was a darkness over his mind. The terrible knot of consciousness that had persisted there like an obsession was broken, gone, his life was dissolved in darkness over his limbs and his body. But there was a point of anxiety in his heart now. He wanted her to come back. He breathed lightly and regularly like an infant, that breathes innocently, beyond the touch of responsibility.

She was coming back. He saw her drifting desultorily under the high hedge, advancing towards him slowly. He did not move, he did not look again. He was as if asleep, at peace, slumbering and utterly relaxed.

She came up and stood before him, hanging her head.

'See what a flower I found you,' she said, wistfully holding a piece of purple-red bell-heather under his face. He saw the clump of coloured bells, and the tree-like, tiny branch: also her hands, with their over-fine, over-sensitive skin.

'Pretty!' he said, looking up at her with a smile, taking the flower. Everything had become simple again, quite simple, the complexity gone into nowhere. But he badly wanted to cry: except that he was weary and bored by emotion.

Then a hot passion of tenderness for her filled his heart. He stood up and looked into her face. It was new, and oh, so delicate in its luminous wonder and fear. He put his arms round her, and she hid her face on his shoulder.

It was peace, just simple peace, as he stood holding her quietly there on the open lane. It was peace at last. The old, detestable world of tension had passed away at last, his soul was strong and at ease.

She looked up at him. The wonderful yellow light in her eyes now was soft and yielded, they were at peace with each other. He kissed her softly, many, many times. A laugh came into her eyes.

'Did I abuse you?' she asked.

He smiled too, and took her hand, that was so soft and given.

'Never mind,' she said, 'it is all for the good.' He kissed her again, softly, many times.

'Isn't it?' she said.

'Certainly,' he replied. 'Wait! I shall have my own back.'

She laughed suddenly, with a wild catch in her voice, and flung her arms around him.

'You are mine, my love, aren't you?' she cried, straining him close.

'Yes,' he said softly.

His voice was so soft and final, she went very still, as if under a fate which had taken her. Yes, she acquiesced – but it was accomplished without her acquiescence. He was kissing her quietly, repeatedly, with a soft, still happiness that almost made her heart stop beating.

'My love!' she cried, lifting her face and looking with frightened, gentle wonder of bliss. Was it all real? But his eyes were beautiful and soft and immune from stress or excitement, beautiful and smiling lightly to her, smiling with her. She hid her face on his shoulder, hiding before him, because he could see her so completely. She knew he loved her, and she was afraid, she was in a strange element, a new heaven round about her. She wished he were passionate, because in passion she was at home. But this was so still and frail, as space is more frightening than force.

Again, quickly, she lifted her head.

'Do you love me?' she said quickly, impulsively.

'Yes,' he replied, not heeding her motion, only her stillness.

She knew it was true. She broke away.

'So you ought,' she said, turning round to look at the road. 'Did you find the rings?'

'Yes.'

'Where are they?'

'In my pocket.'

She put her hand into his pocket and took them out.

She was restless.

'Shall we go?' she said.

'Yes,' he answered. And they mounted to the car once more, and left behind them this memorable battle-field.

They drifted through the wild, late afternoon in a beautiful motion that was smiling and transcendent. His mind was sweetly at ease, the life flowed through him as from some new fountain, he was as if born out of the cramp of a womb.

'Are you happy?' she asked him, in her strange, delighted way.

'Yes,' he said.

'So am I,' she cried in sudden ecstasy, putting her arm round him and clutching him violently against her, as he steered the motor-car.

'Don't drive much more,' she said. 'I don't want you to be always doing something.'

'No,' he said. 'We'll finish this little trip, and then we'll be free.'

'We will, my love, we will,' she cried in delight, kissing him as he turned to her.

He drove on in a strange new wakefulness, the tension of his consciousness broken. He seemed to be conscious all over, all his body awake with a simple, glimmering awareness, as if he had just come awake, like a thing that is born, like a bird when it comes out of an egg, into a new universe.

They dropped down a long hill in the dusk, and suddenly Ursula recognized on her right hand, below in the hollow, the form of Southwell Minster.

'Are we here!' she cried with pleasure.

The rigid, sombre, ugly cathedral was settling under the gloom of the coming night, as they entered the narrow town, the golden lights showed like slabs of revelation in the shop-windows.

'Father came here with mother,' she said, 'when they first knew each other. He loves it – he loves the Minster. Do you?'

'Yes. It looks like quartz crystals sticking up out of the dark hollow. We'll have our high tea at the Saracen's Head.'

As they descended, they heard the Minster bells playing a hymn, when the hour had struck six.

> 'Glory to thee my God this night
> For all the blessings of the light –'

So, to Ursula's ear, the tune fell out, drop by drop, from the unseen sky on to the dusky town. It was like dim, bygone centuries sounding. It was all so far off. She stood in the old yard of the inn, smelling of straw and stables and petrol. Above, she could see the first stars. What was it all? This was no actual world, it was the dream-world of one's childhood – a great circumscribed reminiscence. The world had become unreal. She herself was a strange, transcendent reality.

They sat together in a little parlour by the fire.

'Is it?' she replied, laughing, but unassured.

'What?'

'Everything – is everything true?'

'The best is true,' he said, grimacing at her.

'Is it?' she replied, laughing, but unassured.

She looked at him. He seemed still so separate. New eyes were opened in her soul. She saw a strange creature from another world in him. It was as if she were enchanted, and everything were metamorphosed. She recalled again the old magic of the Book of Genesis, where the sons of God saw the daughters of men, that they were fair. And he was one of these, one of these strange creatures from the beyond, looking down at her, and seeing she was fair.

He stood on the hearth-rug looking at her, at her face that was upturned exactly like a flower, a fresh, luminous flower, glinting faintly golden with the dew of the first light. And he was smiling faintly as if there were no speech in the world, save the silent delight of flowers in each other. Smilingly they delighted in each other's presence, not to be thought of, even known. But his eyes had a faintly ironical contraction.

And she was drawn to him strangely, as in a spell. Kneeling on the hearth-rug before him, she put her arms round his loins, and put her face against his thighs. Riches! Riches! She was overwhelmed with a sense of a heavenful of riches.

'We love each other,' she said in delight.

'More than that,' he answered, looking down at her with his glimmering, easy face.

Unconsciously, with her sensitive finger-tips, she was tracing the back of his thighs, following some mysterious life-flow there. She had discovered something, something more than wonderful, more wonderful than life itself. It was the strange mystery of his life-motion, there, at the back of the thighs, down the flanks. It was a strange reality of his being, the very stuff of being, there in the straight downflow of the thighs. It was here she discovered him one of the sons of God such as were in the beginning of the world, not a man, something other, something more.

This was release at last. She had had lovers, she had known passion. But this was neither love nor passion. It was the daughters of men coming back to the sons of God, the strange inhuman sons of God who are in the beginning.

Her face was now one dazzle of released, golden light, as she looked up at him and laid her hands full on his thighs, behind, as he stood before her. He looked down at her with a rich bright brow like a diadem above his eyes. She was beautiful as a new marvellous flower opened at his knees, a paradisal flower she was, beyond womanhood, such a flower of luminousness. Yet something was tight and unfree in him. He did not like this crouching, this radiance – not altogether.

It was all achieved for her. She had found one of the sons of God from the Beginning, and he had found one of the first most luminous daughters of men.

She traced with her hands the line of his loins and thighs, at the back, and a living fire ran through her, from him, darkly. It was a dark flood of electric passion she released from him, drew into herself. She had established a rich new circuit, a new current of passional electric energy, between the two of them, released from the darkest poles of the body and established in perfect circuit. It was a dark fire of electricity that rushed from him to her, and flooded them both with rich peace, satisfaction.

'My love,' she cried, lifting her face to him, her eyes, her mouth open in transport.

'My love,' he answered, bending and kissing her, always kissing her.

She closed her hands over the full, rounded body of his loins, as he stooped over her, she seemed to touch the quick of the mystery of darkness that was bodily him. She seemed to faint beneath, and he seemed to faint, stooping over her. It was a perfect passing away for both of them, and at the same time the most intolerable accession into being, the marvellous fullness of immediate gratification, overwhelming, outflooding from the source of the deepest life-force, the darkest, deepest, strangest life-source of the human body, at the back and base of the loins.

After a lapse of stillness, after the rivers of strange dark fluid richness had passed over her, flooding, carrying away her mind and flooding down her spine and down her knees, past her feet, a strange flood, sweeping away everything and leaving her an essential new being, she was left quite free, she was free in complete ease, her complete self. So she rose, stilly and blithe, smiling at him. He stood before her, glimmering, so awfully real, that her heart almost stopped beating. He stood there in his strange, whole body, that had its marvellous fountains, like the bodies of the sons of God who were in the beginning. There were strange fountains of his body, more mysterious and potent than any she had imagined or known, more satisfying, ah, finally, mystically-physically satisfying. She had thought there was no source deeper than the phallic source. And now, behold, from the smitten rock of the man's body, from the strange marvellous flanks and thighs, deeper, further in mystery than the phallic source, came the floods of ineffable darkness and ineffable riches.

They were glad, and they could forget perfectly. They laughed and went to the meal provided. There was a venison pasty, of all things, a large broad-faced cut ham, eggs and cresses and red beetroot, and medlars and apple-tart, and tea.

'What *good* things!' she cried with pleasure. 'How noble it looks! – shall I pour out the tea? –'

She was usually nervous and uncertain at performing these public duties, such as giving tea. But today she forgot, she was at her ease, entirely forgetting to have misgivings. The tea-pot poured beautifully from a proud slender spout. Her eyes were warm with smiles as she gave him his tea. She had learned at last to be still and perfect.

'Everything is ours,' she said to him.

'Everything,' he answered.

She gave a queer little crowing sound of triumph.

'I'm so glad!' she cried, with unspeakable relief.

'So am I,' he said. 'But I'm thinking we'd better get out of our responsibilities as quick as we can.'

'What responsibilities?' she asked, wondering.

'We must drop our jobs, like a shot.'

A new understanding dawned into her face.

'Of course,' she said, 'there's that.'

'We must get out,' he said. 'There's nothing for it but to get out, quick.'

She looked at him doubtfully across the table.

'But where?' she said.

'I don't know,' he said. 'We'll just wander about for a bit.'

Again she looked at him quizzically.

'I should be perfectly happy at the Mill,' she said.

'It's very near the old thing,' he said. 'Let us wander a bit.'

His voice could be so soft and happy-go-lucky, it went through her veins like an exhilaration. Nevertheless, she dreamed of a valley, and wild gardens, and peace. She had a desire too for splendour – an aristocratic extravagant splendour. Wandering seemed to her like restlessness, dissatisfaction.

'Where will you wander to?' she asked.

'I don't know. I feel as if I would just meet you and we'd set off – just towards the distance.'

'But where can one go?' she asked anxiously. 'After all, there *is* only the world, and none of it is very distant.'

'Still,' he said, 'I should like to go with you – nowhere. It would be rather wandering just to nowhere. That's the place to get to – nowhere. One wants to wander away from the world's somewheres, into our own nowhere.'

Still she meditated.

'You see, my love,' she said, 'I'm so afraid that while we are only people, we've got to take the world that's given – because there isn't any other.'

'Yes, there is,' he said. 'There's somewhere where we can be free – somewhere where one needn't wear much clothes – none even – where one meets a few people who have gone through enough, and can take things for granted – where you can be yourself, without bothering. There is somewhere – there are one or two people –'

'But where – ?' she sighed.

'Somewhere – anywhere. Let's wander off. That's the thing to do – let's wander off.'

'Yes –' she said, thrilled at the thought of travel. But to her it was only travel.

'To be free,' he said. 'To be free, in a free place, with a few other people!'

'Yes,' she said wistfully. Those 'few other people' depressed her.

'It isn't really a locality, though,' he said. 'It's a perfected relation between you and me, and others – the perfect relation – so that we are free together.'

'It is, my love, isn't it,' she said. 'It's you and me. It's you and me, isn't it?' She stretched out her arms to him. He went across and stooped to kiss her face. Her arms closed round him again, her hands spread upon his shoulders, moving slowly there, moving slowly on his back, down his back slowly, with a strange recurrent, rhythmic motion, yet moving slowly down, pressing mysteriously over his loins, over his flanks. The sense of the awfulness of riches that could never be impaired flooded her mind like a swoon, a death in most marvellous possession, mystic-sure. She possessed him so utterly and intolerably that she herself lapsed out. And yet she was only sitting still in the chair, with her hands pressed upon him, and lost.

Again he softly kissed her.

'We shall never go apart again,' he murmured quietly. And she did not speak, but only pressed her hands firmer down upon the source of darkness in him.

They decided, when they woke again from the pure swoon, to write their resignations from the world of work there and then. She wanted this.

He rang the bell and ordered note-paper without a printed address. The waiter cleared the table.

'Now then,' he said, 'yours first. Put your home address, and the date – then "Director of Education, Town Hall – Sir –" Now then! – I don't know how one really stands – I suppose one could get out of it in less than a month – Anyhow, "Sir – I beg to resign my post as classmistress in the Willey Green Grammar School. I should be very grateful if you would liberate me as soon as possible, without waiting for the expiration of the month's notice." That'll do. Have you got it? Let me look. "Ursula Brangwen." Good! Now I'll write mine. I ought to give them three months, but I can plead health. I can arrange it all right.'

He sat and wrote out his formal resignation.

'Now,' he said, when the envelopes were sealed and addressed, 'shall we post them here, both together? I know Jackie will say, "Here's a coincidence!" when he receives them in all their identity. Shall we let him say it, or not?'

'I don't care,' she said.

'No –?' he said, pondering.

'It doesn't matter, does it?' she said.

'Yes,' he replied. 'Their imaginations shall not work on us. I'll post yours here, mine after, I cannot be implicated in their imaginings.'

He looked at her with his strange, non-human singleness.

'Yes, you are right,' she said.

She lifted her face to him, all shining and open. It was as if he might enter straight into the source of her radiance. His face became a little distracted.

'Shall we go?' he said.

'As you like,' she replied.

They were soon out of the little town and running through the uneven lanes of the country. Ursula nestled near him, into his constant warmth, and watched the pale-lit revelation racing ahead, the visible night. Sometimes it was a wide old road, with grass-spaces on either side, flying magic and elfin in the greenish illumination, sometimes it was trees looming overhead, sometimes it was bramble bushes, sometimes the walls of a crew-yard and the butt of a barn.

'Are you going to Shortlands to dinner?' Ursula asked him suddenly. He started.

'Good God!' he said. 'Shortlands! Never again. Not that. Besides, we should be too late.'

'Where are we going then – to the Mill?'

'If you like. Pity to go anywhere on this good dark night. Pity to come out of it, really. Pity we can't stop in the good darkness. It is better than anything ever would be – this good immediate darkness.'

She sat wondering. The car lurched and swayed. She knew there was no leaving him, the darkness held them both and contained them, it was not to be surpassed. Besides, she had a full mystic knowledge of his suave loins of darkness, dark-clad and suave, and in this knowledge there was some of the inevitability and the beauty of fate, fate which one asks for, which one accepts in full.

He sat still like an Egyptian Pharaoh, driving the car. He felt as if he were seated in immemorial potency, like the great carven statues of real Egypt, as real and as fulfilled with subtle strength, as these are, with a vague inscrutable smile on the lips. He knew what it was to have the strange and magical current of force in his back and loins, and down his legs, force so perfect that it stayed him immobile, and left his face subtly, mindlessly smiling. He knew what it was to be awake and potent in that other basic mind, the deepest physical mind. And from this source he had a pure and magic control, magical, mystical, a force in darkness, like electricity.

It was very difficult to speak, it was so perfect to sit in this pure living silence, subtle, full of unthinkable knowledge and unthinkable force, upheld immemorially in timeless force, like the immobile, supremely potent Egyptians, seated for ever in their living, subtle silence.

'We need not go home,' he said. 'This car has seats that let down and make a bed, and we can lift the hood.'

She was glad and frightened. She cowered near to him.

'But what about them at home?' she said.

'Send a telegram.'

Nothing more was said. They ran on in silence. But with a sort of second consciousness he steered the car towards a destination. For he had the free intelligence to direct his own ends. His arms and his breast and his head were rounded and living like those of the Greek, he had not the unawakened straight arms of the Egyptian, nor the sealed, slumbering head. A lambent intelligence played secondarily above his pure Egyptian concentration in darkness.

They came to a village that lined along the road. The car crept slowly along, until he saw the post office. Then he pulled up.

'I will send a telegram to your father,' he said. 'I will merely say "Spending the night in town", shall I?'

'Yes,' she answered. She did not want to be disturbed into taking thought.

She watched him move into the post office. It was also a shop, she saw. Strange, he was. Even as he went into the lighted, public place he remained dark and magic, the living silence seemed the body of reality in him, subtle, potent, indiscoverable. There he was! In a strange uplift of elation she saw him, the being never to be revealed, awful in its potency, mystic and real. This dark, subtle reality of him, never to be translated, liberated her into perfection, her own perfect being. She too was dark and fulfilled in silence.

He came out, throwing some packages into the car.

'There is some bread, and cheese, and raisins, and apples, and hard chocolate,' he said, in his voice that was as if laughing, because of the unblemished stillness and force which was the reality in him. She would have to touch him. To speak, to see, was nothing. It was a travesty to look and to comprehend the man there. Darkness and silence must fall perfectly on her, then she could know mystically, in unrevealed touch. She must lightly, mindlessly connect with him, have the knowledge which is death of knowledge, the reality of surety in not knowing.

Soon they had run on again into the darkness. She did not ask where they were going, she did not care. She sat in a fullness and a pure potency that was like apathy, mindless and immobile. She was next to him, and hung in a pure rest, as a star is hung, balanced unthinkably. Still there remained a dark lambency of anticipation. She would touch him. With perfect fine finger-tips of reality she would touch the reality in him, the suave, pure, untranslatable reality of his loins of darkness. To touch, mindlessly in darkness to come in pure touching upon the living reality of him, his suave perfect loins and thighs of darkness, this was her sustaining anticipation.

And he too waited in the magical steadfastness of suspense, for her to take this knowledge of him as he had taken it of her. He knew her darkly, with the fullness of dark knowledge. Now she would know him, and he too would be liberated. He would be night-free, like an Egyptian, steadfast in perfectly suspended equilibrium, pure mystic nodality of physical being. They would give each other this star-equilibrium which alone is freedom.

She saw that they were running among trees – great old trees with dying bracken undergrowth. The palish, gnarled trunks showed ghostly, and like old priests in the hovering distance, the fern rose magical and mysterious. It was a night all darkness, with low cloud. The motor-car advanced slowly.

'Where are we?' she whispered.

'In Sherwood Forest.'

It was evident he knew the place. He drove softly, watching. Then they came to a green road between the trees. They turned cautiously round, and were advancing between the oaks of the forest, down a green lane. The green lane widened into a little circle of grass, where there was a small trickle of water at the bottom of a sloping bank. The car stopped.

'We will stay here,' he said, 'and put out the lights.'

He extinguished the lamps at once, and it was pure night, with shadows of trees like realities of other nightly being. He threw a rug on to the bracken, and they sat in stillness and mindless silence. There were faint sounds from the wood, but no disturbance, no possible disturbance, the world was under a strange ban, a new mystery had supervened. They threw off their clothes, and he gathered her to him, and found her, found the pure lambent reality of her for ever invisible flesh. Quenched, inhuman, his fingers upon her unrevealed nudity were the fingers of silence upon silence, the body of mysterious night upon the body of mysterious night, the night masculine and feminine, never to be seen with the eye, or known with the mind, only known as a palpable revelation of living otherness.

She had her desire of him, she touched, she received the maximum of unspeakable communication in touch, dark, subtle, positively silent, a magnificent gift and give again, a perfect acceptance and yielding, a mystery, the reality of that which can never be known, vital, sensual reality that can never be transmuted into mind content, but remains outside, living body of darkness and silence and subtlety, the mystic body of reality. She had her desire fulfilled. He had his desire fulfilled. For she was to him what he was to her, the immemorial magnificence of mystic, palpable, real otherness.

They slept the chilly night through under the hood of the car, a night of unbroken sleep. It was already high day when he awoke. They looked at each other and laughed, then looked away, filled with darkness and secrecy. Then they kissed and remembered the magnificence of the night. It was so magnificent, such an inheritance of a universe of dark reality, that they were afraid to seem to remember. They hid away the remembrance and the knowledge.

24

DEATH AND LOVE

Thomas Crich died slowly, terribly slowly. It seemed impossible to everybody that the thread of life could be drawn out so thin, and yet not break. The sick man lay unutterably weak and spent, kept alive by morphia and by drinks, which he sipped slowly. He was only half conscious – a thin strand of consciousness linking the darkness of death with the light of day. Yet his will was unbroken, he was integral, complete. Only he must have perfect stillness about him.

Any presence but that of the nurses was a strain and an effort to him now. Every morning Gerald went into the room, hoping to find his father passed away at last. Yet always he saw the same transparent face, the same dread dark hair on the waxen forehead, and the awful, inchoate dark eyes, which seemed to be decomposing into formless darkness, having only a tiny grain of vision within them.

And always, as the dark, inchoate eyes turned to him, there passed through Gerald's bowels a burning stroke of revolt, that seemed to resound through his whole being, threatening to break his mind with its clangour, and making him mad.

Every morning, the son stood there, erect and taut with life, gleaming in his blondness. The gleaming blondness of his strange, imminent being put the father into a fever of fretful irritation. He could not bear to meet the uncanny, downward look of Gerald's blue eyes. But it was only for a moment. Each on the brink of departure, the father and son looked at each other, then parted.

For a long time Gerald preserved a perfect *sang froid*, he remained quite collected. But at last, fear undermined him. He was afraid of some horrible collapse in himself. He had to stay and see this thing through. Some perverse will made him watch his father drawn over the borders of life. And yet, now, every day, the great red-hot stroke of horrified fear through the bowels of the son struck a further inflammation. Gerald went about all day with a tendency to cringe, as if there were the point of a sword of Damocles pricking the nape of his neck.

There was no escape – he was bound up with his father, he had to see him through. And the father's will never relaxed or yielded to death. It would have to snap when death at last snapped it – if it did not persist after a physical death. In the same way, the will of the son never yielded. He stood firm and immune, he was outside this death and this dying.

It was a trial by ordeal. Could he stand and see his father slowly dissolve and disappear in death, without once yielding his will, without once relenting before the omnipotence of death. Like a Red Indian undergoing torture, Gerald would experience the whole process of slow death without wincing or flinching. He even triumphed in it. He somehow *wanted* this death, even forced it. It was as if he himself were dealing the death, even when he most recoiled in horror. Still, he would deal it, he would triumph through death.

But in the stress of this ordeal, Gerald too lost his hold on the outer, daily life. That which was much to him, came to mean nothing. Work, pleasure – it was all left behind. He went on more or less mechanically with his business, but this activity was all extraneous. The real activity was this ghastly wrestling for death in his own soul. And his own will should triumph. Come what might, he would not bow down or submit or acknowledge a master. He had no master in death.

But as the fight went on, and all that he had been and was continued to be destroyed, so that life was a hollow shell all round him, roaring and clattering like the sound of the sea, a noise in which he participated externally, and inside this hollow shell was all the darkness and fearful space of death, he knew he would have to find reinforcements, otherwise he would collapse inwards upon the great dark void which circled at the centre of his soul. His will held his outer life, his outer mind, his outer being unbroken and unchanged. But the pressure was too great. He would have to find something to make good the equilibrium. Something must come with him into the hollow void of death in his soul, fill it up, and so equalise the pressure within to the pressure without. For day by day he felt more and more like a bubble filled with darkness, round which whirled the iridescence of his consciousness, and upon which the pressure of the outer world, the outer life, roared vastly.

In this extremity his instinct led him to Gudrun. He threw away everything now – he only wanted the relation established with her. He would follow her to the studio, to be near her, to talk to her. He would stand about the room, aimlessly picking up the implements, the lumps of clay, the little figures she had cast – they were whimsical and grotesque – looking at them without perceiving them. And she felt him following her, dogging her heels like a doom. She held away from him, and yet she knew he drew always a little nearer, a little nearer.

'I say,' he said to her one evening, in an odd, unthinking, uncertain way, 'won't you stay to dinner tonight? I wish you would.'

She started slightly. He spoke to her like a man making a request of another man.

'They'll be expecting me at home,' she said.

'Oh, they won't mind, will they?' he said. 'I should be awfully glad if you'd stay.'

Her long silence gave consent at last.

'I'll tell Thomas, shall I?' he said.

'I must go almost immediately after dinner,' she said.

It was a dark, cold evening. There was no fire in the drawing-room, they sat in the library. He was mostly silent, absent, and Winifred talked little. But when Gerald did rouse himself, he smiled and was pleasant and ordinary with her. Then there came over him again the long blanks, of which he was not aware.

She was very much attracted by him. He looked so preoccupied, and his strange, blank silences, which she could not read, moved her and made her wonder over him, made her feel reverential towards him.

But he was very kind. He gave her the best things at the table, he had a bottle of slightly sweet, delicious golden wine brought out for dinner, knowing she would prefer it to the burgundy. She felt herself esteemed, needed almost.

As they took coffee in the library, there was a soft, very soft knocking at the door. He started, and called, 'Come in.' The timbre of his voice, like something vibrating at high pitch, unnerved Gudrun. A nurse in white entered, half hovering, in the doorway like a shadow. She was very good-looking, but strangely enough, shy and self-mistrusting.

'The doctor would like to speak to you, Mr Crich,' she said in her low, discreet voice.

'The doctor!' he said, starting up. 'Where is he?'

'He is in the dining-room.'

'Tell him I'm coming.'

He drank up his coffee and followed the nurse, who had dissolved like a shadow.

'Which nurse was that?' asked Gudrun.

'Miss Inglis – I like her best,' replied Winifred.

After a while Gerald came back, looking absorbed by his own thoughts, and having some of that tension and abstraction which is seen in a slightly drunken man. He did not say what the doctor had wanted him for, but stood before the fire, with his hands behind his back, and his face open and as if rapt. Not that he was really thinking – he was only arrested in pure suspense inside himself, and thoughts wafted through his mind without order.

'I must go now and see Mama,' said Winifred, 'and see Dadda before he goes to sleep.'

She bade them both good night.

Gudrun also rose to take her leave.

'You needn't go yet, need you?' said Gerald, glancing quickly at the clock. 'It is early yet. I'll walk down with you when you go. Sit down, don't hurry away.'

Gudrun sat down, as if, absent as he was, his will had power over her. She felt almost mesmerized. He was strange to her, something unknown. What was he thinking, what was he feeling, as he stood there so rapt, saying nothing? He kept her – she could feel that. He would not let her go. She watched him in humble submissiveness.

'Had the doctor anything new to tell you?' she asked softly, at length, with that gentle, timid sympathy which touched a keen fibre in his heart. He lifted his eyebrows with a negligent indifferent expression.

'No – nothing new,' he replied, as if the question were quite casual, trivial. 'He says the pulse is very weak indeed, very intermittent – but that doesn't necessarily mean much, you know.'

He looked down at her. Her eyes were dark and soft and unfolded, with a stricken look that roused him.

'No,' she murmured at length. 'I don't understand anything about these things.'

'Just as well not,' he said. 'I say, won't you have a cigarette? – do!' He quickly fetched the box and held her a light. Then he stood before her on the hearth again.

'No,' he said, 'we've never had much illness in the house, either – not till father.' He seemed to meditate a while. Then looking down at her, with strangely communicative blue eyes that filled her with dread, he continued: 'It's something you don't reckon with, you know, till it is there. And then you realize that it was there all the time – it was always there – you understand what I mean? – the possibility of this incurable illness, this slow death.'

He moved his feet uneasily on the marble hearth and put his cigarette to his mouth, looking up at the ceiling.

'I know,' murmured Gudrun: 'it is dreadful.'

He smoked without knowing. Then he took the cigarette from his lips, bared his teeth, and putting the tip of his tongue between his teeth, spat off a grain of tobacco, turning slightly aside, like a man who is alone, or who is lost in thought.

'I don't know what the effect actually *is* on one,' he said, and again he looked down at her. Her eyes were dark and stricken with knowledge, looking into his. He saw her submerged, and he turned aside his face. 'But I absolutely am not the same. There's nothing left, if you understand what I mean. You seem to be clutching at the void – and at the same time you are void yourself. And so you don't know what to *do*.'

'No,' she murmured. A heavy thrill ran down her nerves, heavy, almost pleasure, almost pain. 'What can be done?' she added.

He turned and flipped the ash from his cigarette on to the great marble hearth-stones, that lay bare in the room, without fender or bar.

'I don't know, I'm sure,' he replied. 'But I do think you've got to find some way of resolving the situation – not because you want to, but because you've *got* to, otherwise you're done. The whole of everything, and yourself included, is just on the point of caving in, and you are just holding it up with your hands. Well, it's a situation that obviously can't continue. You can't stand holding the roof up with your hands for ever. You know that sooner or later you'll *have* to let go. Do you understand what I mean? And so something's got to be done, or there's a universal collapse – as far as you yourself are concerned.'

He shifted slightly on the hearth, crunching a cinder under his heel. He looked down at it. Gudrun was aware of the beautiful old marble panels of the fireplace, swelling softly carved, round him and above him. She felt as if she were caught at last by fate, imprisoned in some horrible and fatal trap.

'But what *can* be done?' she murmured humbly. 'You must use me if I can be of any help at all – but how can I? I don't see how I *can* help you.'

He looked down at her critically.

'I don't want you to *help*,' he said, slightly irritated, 'because there's nothing to be *done*. I only want sympathy, do you see: I want somebody I can talk to sympathetically. That eases the strain. And there *is* nobody to talk to sympathetically. That's the curious thing. There *is* nobody. There's Rupert Birkin. But then he *isn't* sympathetic, he wants to *dictate*. And that is no use whatsoever.'

She was caught in a strange snare. She looked down at her hands.

Then there was the sound of the door softly opening. Gerald started. He was chagrined. It was his starting that really startled Gudrun. Then he went forward, with quick, graceful, intentional courtesy.

'Oh, mother!' he said. 'How nice of you to come down. How are you?'

The elderly woman, loosely and bulkily wrapped in a purple gown, came forward silently, slightly hulked, as usual. Her son was at her side. He pushed her up a chair, saying: 'You know Miss Brangwen, don't you?'

The mother glanced at Gudrun indifferently.

'Yes,' she said. Then she turned her wonderful, forget-me-not blue eyes up to her son, as she slowly sat down in the chair he had brought her.

'I came to ask you about your father,' she said, in her rapid, scarcely audible voice. 'I didn't know you had company.'

'No? Didn't Winifred tell you? Miss Brangwen stayed to dinner to make us a little more lively –'

Mrs Crich turned slowly round to Gudrun and looked at her, but with unseeing eyes.

'I'm afraid it would be no treat to her.' Then she turned again to her son. 'Winifred tells me the doctor had something to say about your father. What is it?'

'Only that the pulse is very weak – misses altogether a good many times – so that he might not last the night out,' Gerald replied.

Mrs Crich sat perfectly impassive, as if she had not heard. Her bulk seemed hunched in the chair, her fair hair hung slack over her ears. But her skin was clear and fine, her hands, as she sat with them forgotten and folded, were quite beautiful, full of potential energy. A great mass of energy seemed decaying up in that silent, hulking form.

She looked up at her son as he stood, keen and soldierly, near to her. Her eyes were most wonderfully blue, bluer than forget-me-nots. She seemed to have a certain confidence in Gerald, and to feel a certain motherly mistrust of him.

'How are *you*?' she muttered in her strangely quiet voice, as if nobody should hear but him. 'You're not getting into a state, are you? You're not letting it make you hysterical?'

The curious challenge in the last words startled Gudrun.

'I don't think so, mother,' he answered, rather coldly cheery. 'Somebody's got to see it through, you know.'

'Have they? Have they?' answered his mother rapidly. 'Why should *you* take it on yourself? What have you got to do, seeing it through. It will see itself through. You are not needed.'

'No, I don't suppose I can do any good,' he answered. 'It's just how it affects us, you see.'

'You like to be affected – don't you? It's quite nuts for you? You would have to be important. You have no need to stop at home. Why don't you go away!'

These sentences, evidently the ripened grain of many dark hours, took Gerald by surprise.

'I don't think it's any good going away now, mother, at the last minute,' he said coldly.

'You take care,' replied his mother. 'You mind *yourself* – that's your business. You take too much on yourself. You mind yourself, or you'll find yourself in Queer Street, that's what will happen to you. You're hysterical, always were.'

'I'm all right, mother,' he said. 'There's no need to worry about *me*, I assure you.'

'Let the dead bury their dead – don't go and bury yourself along with them – that's what I tell you. I know you well enough.'

He did not answer this, not knowing what to say. The mother sat bunched up in silence, her beautiful white hands, that had no rings whatsoever, clasping the pommels of her arm-chair.

'You can't do it,' she said, almost bitterly. 'You haven't the nerve. You're as weak as a cat, really – always were. Is this young woman staying here?'

'No,' said Gerald. 'She is going home tonight.'

'Then she'd better have the dog-cart. Does she go far?'

'Only to Beldover.'

'Ah!' The elderly woman never looked at Gudrun, yet she seemed to take knowledge of her presence.

'You are inclined to take too much on yourself, Gerald,' said the mother, pulling herself to her feet, with a little difficulty.

'Will you go, mother?' he asked politely.

'Yes, I'll go up again,' she replied. Turning to Gudrun, she bade her 'Good night'. Then she went slowly to the door, as if she were unaccustomed to walking. At the door she lifted her face to him implicitly. He kissed her.

'Don't come any further with me,' she said in her barely audible voice. 'I don't want you any further.'

He bade her good night, watched her across to the stairs and mount slowly. Then he closed the door and came back to Gudrun. Gudrun rose also, to go.

'A queer being, my mother,' he said.

'Yes,' replied Gudrun.

'She has her own thoughts.'

'Yes,' said Gudrun.

Then they were silent.

'You want to go?' he asked. 'Half a minute, I'll just have a horse put in –'

'No,' said Gudrun. 'I want to walk.'

He had promised to walk with her down the long, lonely mile of drive, and she wanted this.

'You might *just* as well drive,' he said.

'I'd *much rather* walk,' she asserted, with emphasis.

'You would! Then I will come along with you. You know where your things are? I'll put boots on.'

He put on a cap and an overcoat over his evening dress. They went out into the night.

'Let us light a cigarette,' he said, stopping in a sheltered angle of the porch. 'You have one too.'

So, with the scent of tobacco on the night air, they set off down the dark drive that ran between close-cut hedges through sloping meadows.

He wanted to put his arm round her. If he could put his arm round her, and draw her against him as they walked, he would equilibrate himself. For now he felt like a pair of scales, the half of which tips down and down into an indefinite void. He must recover some sort of balance. And here was the hope and the perfect recovery.

Blind to her, thinking only of himself, he slipped his arm softly round her waist, and drew her to him. Her heart fainted, feeling herself taken. But then, his arm was so strong, she quailed under its powerful close grasp. She died a little death, and was drawn against him as they walked down the stormy darkness. He seemed to balance her perfectly in opposition to himself, in their dual motion of walking. So, suddenly, he was liberated and perfect, strong, heroic.

He put his hand to his mouth and threw his cigarette away, a gleaming point, into the unseen hedge. Then he was quite free to balance her.

'That's better,' he said, with exultancy.

The exultation in his voice was like a sweetish, poisonous drug to her. Did she then mean so much to him! She sipped the poison.

'Are you happier?' she asked wistfully.

'Much better,' he said in the same exultant voice, 'and I was rather far gone.'

She nestled against him. He felt her all soft and warm, she was the rich, lovely substance of his being. The warmth and motion of her walk suffused through him wonderfully.

'I'm *so* glad if I help you,' she said.

'Yes,' he answered. 'There's nobody else could do it, if you wouldn't.'

'That is true,' she said to herself, with a thrill of strange, fatal elation.

As they walked, he seemed to lift her nearer and nearer to himself, till she moved upon the firm vehicle of his body. He was so strong, so sustaining, and he could not be opposed. She drifted along in a wonderful interfusion of physical motion, down the dark, blowy hill-side. Far across shone the little yellow lights of Beldover, many of them, spread in a thick patch on another dark hill. But he and she were walking in perfect, isolated darkness, outside the world.

'But how much do you care for me!' came her voice, almost querulous. 'You see, I don't know, I don't understand!'

'How much!' His voice rang with a painful elation. 'I don't know either – but everything.' He was startled by his own declaration. It was true. So he stripped himself of every safeguard, in making this admission to her. He cared everything for her – she was everything.

'But I can't believe it,' said her low voice, amazed, trembling. She was trembling with doubt and exultance. This was the thing she wanted to hear, only this. Yet now she heard it, heard the strange clapping vibration of truth in his voice as he said it, she could not believe. She could not believe – she did not believe. Yet she believed, triumphantly, with fatal exultance.

'Why not?' he said. 'Why don't you believe it? It's true. It is true, as we stand at this moment –' he stood still with her in the wind; 'I care for nothing on earth, or in heaven, outside this spot where we are. And it isn't my own presence I care about, it is all yours. I'd sell my soul a hundred times – but I couldn't bear not to have you here. I couldn't bear to be alone. My brain would burst. It is true.' He drew her closer to him, with definite movement.

'No,' she murmured, afraid. Yet this was what she wanted. Why did she lose courage?

They resumed their strange walk. They were such strangers – and yet they were so frightfully, unthinkably near. It was like a madness. Yet it was what she wanted, it was what she wanted. They had descended the hill, and now they were coming to the square arch where the road passed under the colliery railway. The arch, Gudrun knew, had walls of squared stone, mossy on one side with water that trickled down, dry on the other side. She had stood under it to hear the train rumble thundering over the logs overhead. And she knew that under this dark and lonely bridge the young colliers stood in the darkness with their sweethearts, in rainy weather. And so she wanted to stand under the bridge with *her* sweetheart, and be kissed under the bridge in the invisible darkness. Her steps dragged as she drew near.

So, under the bridge, they came to a standstill, and he lifted her upon his breast. His body vibrated taut and powerful as he closed upon her and crushed her, breathless and dazed and destroyed, crushed her upon his breast. Ah, it was terrible, and perfect. Under this bridge, the colliers pressed their lovers to their breast. And now, under the bridge, the master of them all pressed her to himself! And how much more powerful and terrible was his embrace than theirs, how much more concentrated and supreme his love was, than theirs in the same sort! She felt she would swoon, die, under the vibrating, inhuman tension of his arms and his body – she would pass away. Then the unthinkable high vibration slackened and became more undulating. He slackened and drew her with him to stand with his back to the wall.

She was almost unconscious. So the colliers' lovers would stand with their backs to the walls, holding their sweethearts and kissing them as she was being kissed. Ah, but would their kisses be fine and powerful as the kisses of the firm-mouthed master? Even the keen, short-cut moustache – the colliers would not have that.

And the colliers' sweethearts would, like herself, hang their heads back limp over their shoulder, and look out from the dark archway at the close patch of yellow lights on the unseen hill in the distance, or at the vague form of trees, and at the buildings of the colliery wood-yard, in the other direction.

His arms were fast around her, he seemed to be gathering her into himself, her warmth, her softness, her adorable weight, drinking in the suffusion of her physical being, avidly. He lifted her, and seemed to pour her into himself, like wine into a cup.

'This is worth everything,' he said in a strange, penetrating voice.

So she relaxed, and seemed to melt, to flow into him, as if she were some infinitely warm and precious suffusion filling into his veins, like an intoxicant. Her arms were round his neck, he kissed her and held her perfectly suspended, she was all slack and flowing into him, and he was the firm, strong cup that receives the wine of her life. So she lay cast upon him, stranded, lifted up against him, melting and melting under his kisses, melting into his limbs and bones, as if he were soft iron becoming surcharged with her electric life.

Till she seemed to swoon, gradually her mind went, and she passed away, everything in her was melted down and fluid, and she lay still, become contained by him, sleeping in him as lightning sleeps in a pure, soft stone. So she was passed away and gone in him, and he was perfected.

When she opened her eyes again and saw the patch of lights in the distance, it seemed to her strange that the world still existed, that she was standing under the bridge resting her head on Gerald's breast. Gerald – who was he? He was the exquisite adventure, the desirable unknown to her.

She looked up, and in the darkness saw his face above her, his shapely, male face. There seemed a faint, white light emitted from him, a white aura, as if he were a visitor from the unseen. She reached up, like Eve reaching to the apples on the tree of knowledge, and she kissed him, though her passion was a transcendent fear of the thing he was, touching his face with her infinitely delicate, encroaching, wondering fingers. Her fingers went over the mould of his face, over his features. How perfect and foreign he was – ah, how dangerous! Her soul thrilled with complete knowledge. This was the glistening, forbidden apple, this face of a man. She kissed him, putting her fingers over his face, his eyes, his nostrils, over his brows and his ears, to his neck, to know him, to gather him in by touch. He was so firm and shapely, with such satisfying, inconceivable shapeliness, strange yet unutterably clear. He was such an unutterable enemy, yet glistening with uncanny white fire. She wanted to touch him and touch him and touch him, till she had him all in her hands, till she had strained him into her knowledge. Ah, if she could have the precious *knowledge* of him, she would be filled, and nothing could deprive her of this. For he was so unsure, so risky in the common world of day.

'You are so *beautiful*,' she murmured in her throat.

He wondered, and was suspended. But she felt him quiver, and she came down involuntarily nearer upon him. He could not help himself. Her fingers had him under their power. The fathomless, fathomless desire they could evoke in him was deeper than death, where he had no choice.

But she knew now, and it was enough. For the time, her soul was destroyed with the exquisite shock of his invisible fluid lightning. She knew. And this knowledge was a death from which she must recover. How much more of him was there to know? Ah, much, much, many days harvesting for her large, yet perfectly subtle and intelligent hands upon the field of his living, radio-active body. Ah, her hands were eager, greedy for knowledge. But for the present it was enough, enough, as much as her soul could bear. Too much, and she would shatter herself, she would fill the fine vial of her soul too quickly, and it would break. Enough now – enough for the time being. There were all the after days when her hands, like birds, could feed upon the fields of his mystical plastic form – till then enough.

And even he was glad to be checked, rebuked, held back. For to desire is better than to possess, the finality of the end was dreaded as deeply as it was desired.

They walked on towards the town, towards where the lamps threaded singly, at long intervals, down the dark high-road of the valley. They came at length to the gate of the drive.

'Don't come any further,' she said.

'You'd rather I didn't?' he asked, relieved. He did not want to go up the public streets with her, his soul all naked and alight as it was.

'Much rather – good night.' She held out her hand. He grasped it, then touched the perilous, potent fingers with his lips.

'Good night,' he said. 'Tomorrow.'

And they parted. He went home full of the strength and the power of living desire.

But the next day, she did not come, she sent a note that she was kept indoors by a cold. Here was a torment! But he possessed his soul in some sort of patience, writing a brief answer, telling her how sorry he was not to see her.

The day after this, he stayed at home – it seemed so futile to go down to the office. His father could not live the week out. And he wanted to be at home, suspended.

Gerald sat on a chair by the window in his father's room. The landscape outside was black and winter-sodden. His father lay grey and ashen on the bed, a nurse moved silently in her white dress, neat and elegant, even beautiful. There was a scent of eau-de-Cologne in the room. The nurse went out of the room, Gerald was alone with death, facing the winter-black landscape.

'Is there much more water in Denley?' came the faint voice, determined and querulous, from the bed. The dying man was asking about a leakage from Willey Water into one of the pits.

'Some more – we shall have to run off the lake,' said Gerald.

'Will you?' The faint voice filtered to extinction. There was dead stillness. The grey-faced, sick man lay with eyes closed, more dead than death. Gerald looked away. He felt his heart was seared, it would perish if this went on much longer.

Suddenly he heard a strange noise. Turning round, he saw his father's eyes wide open, strained and rolling in a frenzy of inhuman struggling. Gerald started to his feet, and stood transfixed in horror.

'Wha-a-ah-h-h!' came a horrible choking rattle from his father's throat, the fearful, frenzied eye, rolling awfully in its wild, fruitless search for help, passed blindly over Gerald, then up came the dark blood and mess pumping over the face of the agonized being. The tense body relaxed, the head fell aside, down the pillow.

Gerald stood transfixed, his soul echoing in horror. He would move, but he could not. He could not move his limbs. His brain seemed to re-echo, like a pulse.

The nurse in white softly entered. She glanced at Gerald, then at the bed.

'Ah!' came her soft whimpering cry, and she hurried forward to the dead man. 'Ah-h!' came the slight sound of her agitated distress, as she stood bending over the bedside. Then she recovered, turned, and came for towel and sponge. She was wiping the dead face carefully, and murmuring, almost whimpering, very softly: 'Poor Mr Crich! – Poor Mr Crich! – Oh, poor Mr Crich!'

'Is he dead?' clanged Gerald's sharp voice.

'Oh yes, he's gone,' replied the soft, moaning voice of the nurse, as she looked up at Gerald's face. She was young and beautiful and quivering. A strange sort of grin went over Gerald's face, over the horror. And he walked out of the room.

He was going to tell his mother. On the landing he met his brother Basil.

'He's gone, Basil,' he said, scarcely able to subdue his voice, not to let an unconscious, frightening exultation sound through.

'What?' cried Basil, going pale.

Gerald nodded. Then he went on to his mother's room.

She was sitting in her purple gown, sewing, very slowly sewing, putting in a stitch, then another stitch. She looked up at Gerald with her blue, undaunted eyes.

'Father's gone,' he said.

'He's dead? Who says so?'

'Oh, you know, mother, if you see him.'

She put her sewing down and slowly rose.

'Are you going to see him?' he asked.

'Yes,' she said.

By the bedside the children already stood in a weeping group.

'Oh, mother!' cried the daughters, almost in hysterics, weeping loudly.

But the mother went forward. The dead man lay in repose, as if gently asleep, so gently, so peacefully, like a young man sleeping in purity. He was still warm. She stood looking at him in gloomy, heavy silence for some time.

'Ay,' she said bitterly, at length, speaking as if to the unseen witnesses of the air. 'You're dead.' She stood for some minutes in silence, looking down. 'Beautiful,' she asserted, 'beautiful as if life had never touched you – never touched you. God send I look different. I hope I shall look my years when I am dead. Beautiful, beautiful,' she crooned over him. 'You can see him in his teens, with his first beard on his face. A beautiful soul, beautiful –' Then there was a tearing in her voice as she cried: 'None of you look like this when you are dead! Don't let it happen again.' It was a strange, wild command from out of the unknown. Her children moved unconsciously together, in a nearer group, at the dreadful command in her voice. The colour was flushed bright in her cheek, she looked awful and wonderful. 'Blame me, blame me if you like, that he lies there like a lad in his teens, with his first beard on his face. Blame me if you like. But you none of you know.' She was silent in intense silence. Then there came in a low, tense voice: 'If I thought that the children I bore would lie looking like that in death, I'd strangle them when they were infants, yes –'

'No, mother,' came the strange, clarion voice of Gerald from the background, 'we are different, we don't blame you.'

She turned and looked full in his eyes. Then she lifted her hands in a strange half-gesture of mad despair.

'Pray!' she said strongly. 'Pray for yourselves to God, for there's no help for you from your parents.'

'Oh, mother!' cried her daughters wildly.

But she had turned and gone, and they all went quickly away from each other.

When Gudrun heard that Mr Crich was dead, she felt rebuked. She had stayed away lest Gerald should think her too easy of winning. And now, he was in the midst of trouble, whilst she was cold.

The following day she went up as usual to Winifred, who was glad to see her, glad to get away into the studio. The girl had wept, and then, too frightened, had turned aside to avoid any more tragic eventuality. She and Gudrun resumed work as usual in the isolation of the studio, and this seemed an immeasurable happiness, a pure world of freedom, after the aimlessness and misery of the house. Gudrun stayed on till evening. She and Winifred had dinner brought up to the studio, where they ate in freedom, away from all the people in the house.

After dinner Gerald came up. The great high studio was full of shadow and a fragrance of coffee. Gudrun and Winifred had a little table near the fire at the far end, with a white lamp whose light did not travel far. They were a tiny world to themselves, the two girls surrounded by lovely shadows, the beams and rafters shadowy overhead, the benches and implements shadowy down the studio.

'You are cosy enough here,' said Gerald, going up to them.

There was a low brick fireplace, full of fire, an old blue Turkish rug, the little oak table with the lamp and the white-and-blue cloth and the dessert, and Gudrun making coffee in an odd brass coffee-maker, and Winifred scalding a little milk in a tiny saucepan.

'Have you had coffee?' said Gudrun.

'I have, but I'll have some more with you,' he replied.

'Then you must have it in a glass – there are only two cups,' said Winifred.

'It is the same to me,' he said, taking a chair and coming into the charmed circle of the girls. How happy they were, how cosy and glamorous it was with them, in a world of lofty shadows! The outside world, in which he had been transacting funeral business all the day, was completely wiped out. In an instant he snuffed glamour and magic.

They had all their things very dainty, two odd and lovely little cups, scarlet and solid gilt, and a little black jug with scarlet discs, and the curious coffee machine, whose spirit-flame flowed steadily, almost invisibly. There was the effect of rather sinister richness, in which Gerald at once escaped himself.

They all sat down, and Gudrun carefully poured out the coffee.

'Will you have milk?' she asked calmly, yet nervously poising the little black jug with its big red dots. She was always so completely controlled, yet so bitterly nervous.

'No, I won't,' he replied.

So, with a curious humility, she placed him the little cup of coffee, and herself took the awkward tumbler. She seemed to want to serve him.

'Why don't you give me the glass – it is so clumsy for you,' he said. He would much rather have had it, and seen her daintily served. But she was silent, pleased with the disparity, with her self-abasement.

'You are quite *en ménage*,' he said.

'Yes. We aren't really at home to visitors,' said Winifred.

'You're not? Then I'm an intruder?'

For once he felt his conventional dress was out of place, he was an outsider.

Gudrun was very quiet. She did not feel drawn to talk to him. At this stage silence was best – or mere light words. It was best to leave serious things aside. So they talked gaily and lightly till they heard the man below lead out the horse, and call it to 'Back-back!' into the dog-cart that was to take Gudrun home. So she put on her things and shook hands with Gerald, without once meeting his eyes. And she was gone.

The funeral was detestable. Afterwards, at the tea-table, the daughters kept saying – 'He was a good father to us – the best father in the world' – or else – 'We shan't easily find another man as good as father was.'

Gerald acquiesced in all this. It was the right conventional attitude, and, as far as the world went, he believed in the conventions. He took it as a matter of course. But Winifred hated everything, and hid in the studio, and cried her heart out, and wished Gudrun would come.

Luckily everybody was going away. The Criches never stayed long at home. By dinner-time, Gerald was left quite alone. Even Winifred was carried off to London for a few days with her sister Laura.

But when Gerald was really left alone, he could not bear it. One day passed by, and another. And all the time he was like a man hung in chains over the edge of an abyss. Struggle as he might, he could not turn himself to the solid earth, he could not get footing. He was suspended on the edge of a void, writhing. Whatever he thought of, was the abyss – whether it were friends or strangers, or work or play, it all showed him only the same bottomless void, in which his heart swung perishing. There was no escape, there was nothing to grasp hold of. He must writhe on the edge of the chasm, suspended in chains of invisible physical life.

At first he was quiet, he kept still, expecting the extremity to pass away, expecting to find himself released into the world of the living, after this extremity of penance. But it did not pass, and a crisis gained upon him.

As the evening of the third day came on, his heart rang with fear. He could not bear another night. Another night was coming on, for another night he was to be suspended in chain of physical life, over the bottomless pit of nothingness. And he could not bear it. He could not bear it. He was frightened deeply, and coldly, frightened in his soul. He did not believe in his own strength any more. He could not fall into this infinite void and rise again. If he fell, he would be gone for ever. He must withdraw, he must seek reinforcements. He did not believe in his own single self any further than this.

After dinner, faced with the ultimate experience of his own nothingness, he turned aside. He pulled on his boots, put on his coat, and set out to walk in the night.

It was dark and misty. He went through the wood, stumbling and feeling his way to the Mill. Birkin was away. Good – he was half glad. He turned up the hill, and stumbled blindly over the wild slopes, having lost the path in the complete darkness. It was boring. Where was he going? No matter. He stumbled on till he came to a path again. Then he went on through another wood. His mind became dark, he went on automatically. Without thought or sensation, he stumbled unevenly on, out into the open again, fumbling for stiles, losing the path, and going along the hedges of the fields till he came to the outlet.

And at last he came to high road. It had distracted him to struggle blindly through the maze of darkness. But now, he must take a direction. And he did not even know where he was. But he must take a direction now. Nothing would be resolved by merely walking, walking away. He had to take a direction.

He stood still on the road that was high in the utterly dark night, and he did not know where he was. It was a strange sensation, his heart beating, and ringed round with the utterly unknown darkness. So he stood for some time.

Then he heard footsteps, and saw a small, swinging light. He immediately went towards this. It was a miner.

'Can you tell me,' he said, 'where this road goes?'

'Road? Ay, it goes ter Whatmore.'

'Whatmore? Oh, thank you, that's right. I thought I was wrong. Good night.'

'Good night,' replied the broad voice of the miner.

Gerald guessed where he was. At least, when he came to Whatmore, he would know. He was glad to be on a high road. He walked forward as in a sleep of decision.

That was Whatmore Village –? Yes, the King's Head – and there the hall gates. He descended the steep hill almost running. Winding through the hollow, he passed the Grammar School, and came to Willey Green Church. The churchyard! He halted.

Then in another moment he had clambered up the wall and was going among the graves. Even in this darkness he could see the heaped pallor of old white flowers at his feet. This then was the grave. He stooped down. The flowers were cold and clammy. There was a raw scent of chrysanthemums and tuberoses, deadened. He felt the clay beneath, and shrank, it was so horribly cold and sticky. He stood away in revulsion.

Here was one centre then, here in the complete darkness beside the unseen, raw grave. But there was nothing for him here. No, he had nothing to stay here for. He felt as if some of the clay were sticking cold and unclean on his heart. No, enough of this.

Where then? – home? Never! It was no use going there. That was less than no use. It could not be done. There was somewhere else to go. Where?

A dangerous resolve formed in his heart, like a fixed idea. There was Gudrun – she would be safe in her home. But he could get at her – he would get at her. He would not go back tonight till he had come to her, if it cost him his life. He staked his all on this throw.

He set off walking straight across the fields towards Beldover. It was so dark, nobody could ever see him. His feet were wet and cold, heavy with clay. But he went on persistently, like a wind, straight forward, as if to his fate. There were great gaps in his consciousness. He was conscious that he was at Winthorpe hamlet, but quite unconscious how he had got there. And then, as in a dream, he was in the long street of Beldover, with its street-lamps.

There was a noise of voices, and of a door shutting loudly, and being barred, and of men talking in the night. The 'Lord Nelson' had just closed, and the drinkers were going home. He had better ask one of these where she lived – for he did not know the side streets at all.

'Can you tell me where Somerset Drive is?' he asked of one of the uneven men.

'Where what?' replied the tipsy miner's voice.

'Somerset Drive.'

'Somerset Drive! – I've heard o' such a place, but I couldn't for my life say where it is. Who might you be wanting?'

'Mr Brangwen – William Brangwen.'

'William Brangwen –?'

'Who teaches at the Grammar School at Willey Green – his daughter teaches there too.'

'O-o-o-oh, Brangwen! *Now* I've got you. Of *course*, William Brangwen! Yes, yes, he's got two lasses as teachers, aside hisself. Ay, that's him – that's him! Why, certainly I know where he lives, back your life I do! Yi – *what* place do they ca' it?'

'Somerset Drive,' repeated Gerald patiently. He knew his own colliers fairly well.

'Somerset Drive, for certain!' said the collier, swinging his arm as if catching something up. 'Somerset Drive – yi! I couldn't for my life lay hold o' the lercality o' the place. Yis, I know the place, to be sure I do –'

He turned unsteadily on his feet and pointed up the dark, nigh-deserted road.

'You go up theer – an' you ta'e th' first – yi, th' first turnin' on your left – o' that side – past Withamses tuffy shop –'

'*I* know,' said Gerald.

'Ay! You go down a bit, past wheer th' water-man lives – and then Somerset Drive, as they ca' it, branches off on 't right hand side – an' there's nowt but three houses in it, no more than three, I believe – an' I'm a'most certain as theirs is th' last – th' last o' th' three – you see –'

'Thank you very much,' said Gerald. 'Good night.'

And he started off, leaving the tipsy man there standing rooted.

Gerald went past the dark shops and houses, most of them sleeping now, and twisted round to the little blind road that ended on a field of darkness. He slowed down as he neared his goal, not knowing how he should proceed. What if the house were closed in darkness?

But it was not. He saw a big lighted window, and heard voices, then a gate banged. His quick ears caught the sound of Birkin's voice, his keen eyes made out Birkin, with Ursula standing in a pale dress on the step of the garden path. Then Ursula stepped down and came along the road, holding Birkin's arm.

Gerald went across into the darkness and they dawdled past him, talking happily, Birkin's voice low, Ursula's high and distinct. Gerald went quickly to the house.

The blinds were drawn before the big lighted window of the dining-room. Looking up the path at the side he could see the door left open, shedding a soft, coloured light from the hall lamp. He went quickly and silently up the path, and looked up into the hall. There were pictures on the walls, and the antlers of a stag – and the stairs going up on one side – and just near the foot of the stairs the half opened door of the dining-room.

With heart drawn fine, Gerald stepped into the hall, whose floor was of coloured tiles, went quickly and looked into the large, pleasant room. In a chair by the fire, the father sat asleep, his head tilted back against the side of the big oak chimney-piece, his ruddy face seen foreshortened, the nostrils open, the mouth fallen a little. It would take the merest sound to wake him.

Gerald stood a second suspended. He glanced down the passage behind him. It was all dark. Again he was suspended. Then he went swiftly upstairs. His senses were so finely, almost supernaturally keen, that he seemed to cast his own will over the half-unconscious house.

He came to the first landing. There he stood, scarcely breathing. Again, corresponding to the door below, there was a door again. That would be the mother's room. He could hear her moving about in the candle-light. She would be expecting her husband to come up. He looked along the dark landing.

Then, silently, on infinitely careful feet, he went along the passage, feeling the wall with the extreme tips of his fingers. There was a door. He stood and listened. He could hear two people's breathing. It was not that. He went stealthily forward. There was another door, slightly open. The room was in darkness. Empty. There there was the bathroom, he could smell the soap and the heat. Then at the end another bedroom – one soft breathing. This was she.

With an almost occult carefulness he turned the doorhandle and opened the door an inch. It creaked slightly. Then he opened it another inch – then another. His heart did not beat, he seemed to create a silence about himself, an obliviousness.

He was in the room. Still the sleeper breathed softly. It was very dark. He felt his way forward inch by inch, with his feet and hands. He touched the bed, he could hear the sleeper. He drew nearer, bending close as if his eyes would disclose whatever there was. And then, very near to his face, to his fear, he saw the round, dark head of a boy.

He recovered, turned round, saw the door afar, a faint light revealed. And he retreated swiftly, drew the door to without fastening it, and passed rapidly down the passage. At the head of the stairs he hesitated. There was still time to flee.

But it was unthinkable. He would maintain his will. He turned past the door of the parental bedroom like a shadow, and was climbing the second flight of stairs. They creaked under his weight – it was exasperating. Ah, what disaster, if the mother's door opened just beneath him, and she saw him! It would have to be, if it were so. He held the control still.

He was not quite up these stairs when he heard a quick running of feet below, the outer door was closed and locked, he heard Ursula's voice, then the father's sleepy exclamation. He pressed on swiftly to the upper landing.

Again a door was ajar, a room was empty. Feeling his way forward, with the tips of his fingers, travelling rapidly, like a blind man, anxious lest Ursula should come upstairs, he found another door. There, with his preternaturally fine senses alert, he listened. He heard someone moving in bed. This would be she.

Softly now, like one who has only one sense, the tactile sense, he turned the latch. It clicked. He held still. The bedclothes rustled. His heart did not beat. Then again he drew the latch back, and very gently pushed the door. It made a sticking noise as it gave.

'Ursula?' said Gudrun's voice, frightened. He quickly opened the door and pushed it behind him.

'Is it you, Ursula?' came Gudrun's frightened voice. He heard her sitting up in bed. In another moment she would scream.

'No, it's me,' he said, feeling his way towards her. 'It is I, Gerald.'

She sat motionless in her bed in sheer astonishment. She was too astonished, too much taken by surprise, even to be afraid.

'Gerald!' she echoed, in blank amazement. He had found his way to the bed, and his outstretched hand touched her warm breast blindly. She shrank away.

'Let me make a light,' she said, springing out.

He stood perfectly motionless. He heard her touch the match box, he heard her fingers in their movement. Then he saw her in the light of a match, which she held to the candle. The light rose in the room, then sank to a small dimness, as the flame sank down on the candle, before it mounted again.

She looked at him as he stood near the other side of the bed. His cap was pulled low over his brow, his black overcoat was buttoned close up to his chin. His face was strange and luminous. He was inevitable as a supernatural being. When she had seen him, she knew. She knew there was something fatal in the situation, and she must accept it. Yet she must challenge him.

'How did you come up?' she asked.

'I walked up the stairs – the door was open.'

She looked at him.

'I haven't closed this door, either,' he said. She walked swiftly across the room and closed her door softly, and locked it. Then she came back.

She was wonderful, with startled eyes and flushed cheeks, and her plait of hair rather short and thick down her back, and her long, fine white night-dress falling to her feet.

She saw that his boots were all clayey, even his trousers were plastered with clay. And she wondered if he had made footprints all the way up. He was a very strange figure, standing in her bedroom, near the tossed bed.

'Why have you come?' she asked, almost querulous.

'I wanted to,' he replied.

And this she could see from his face. It was fate.

'You are so muddy,' she said in distaste, but gently.

He looked down at his feet.

'I was walking in the dark,' he replied. But he felt vividly elated. There was a pause. He stood on one side of the tumbled bed, she on the other. He did not even take his cap from his brows.

'And what do you want of me?' she challenged.

He looked aside and did not answer. Save for the extreme beauty and mystic attractiveness of this distinct, strange face, she would have sent him away. But his face was too wonderful and undiscovered to her. It fascinated her with the fascination of pure beauty, cast a spell on her, like nostalgia, an ache.

'What do you want of me?' she repeated in an estranged voice.

He pulled off his cap in a movement of dream-liberation and went across to her. But he could not touch her because she stood barefoot in her night-dress, and he was muddy and damp. Her eyes, wide and large and wondering, watched him, and asked him the ultimate question.

'I came – because I must,' he said. 'Why do you ask?'

She looked at him in doubt and wonder.

'I must ask,' she said.

He shook his head slightly.

'There is no answer,' he replied, with strange vacancy.

There was about him a curious and almost godlike air of simplicity and naïve directness. He reminded her of an apparition, the young Hermes.

'But why did you come to me?' she persisted.

'Because – it has to be so. If there weren't you in the world, then *I* shouldn't be in the world, either.'

She stood looking at him with large, wide, wondering, stricken eyes. His eyes were looking steadily into hers all the time, and he seemed fixed in an odd supernatural steadfastness. She sighed. She was lost now. She had no choice.

'Won't you take off your boots?' she said. 'They must be wet.'

He dropped his cap on a chair, unbuttoned his overcoat, lifting up his chin to unfasten the throat buttons. His short, keen hair was ruffled. He was so beautifully blond, like wheat. He pulled off his overcoat.

Quickly he pulled off his jacket, pulled loose his black tie, and was unfastening his studs, which were headed each with a pearl. She listened, watching, hoping no one would hear the starched linen crackle. It seemed to snap like pistol-shots.

He had come for vindication. She let him hold her in his arms, clasp her close against him. He found in her an infinite relief. Into her he poured all his pent-up darkness and corrosive death, and he was whole again. It was wonderful, marvellous, it was a miracle. This was the ever-recurrent miracle of his life, at the knowledge of which he was lost in an ecstasy of relief and wonder. And she, subject, received him as a vessel filled with his bitter potion of death. She had no power at this crisis to resist. The terrible frictional violence of death filled her, and she received it in an ecstasy of subjection, in throes of acute, violent sensation.

As he drew nearer to her, he plunged deeper into her enveloping soft warmth, a wonderful creative heat that penetrated his veins and gave him life again. He felt himself dissolving and sinking to rest in the bath of her living strength. It seemed as if her heart in her breast were a second unconquerable sun, into the glow and creative strength of which he plunged further and further. All his veins, that were murdered and lacerated, healed softly as life came pulsing in, stealing invisibly into him as if it were the all-powerful effluence of the sun. His blood, which seemed to have been drawn back into death, came ebbing on the return, surely, beautifully, powerfully.

He felt his limbs growing fuller and flexible with life, his body gained an unknown strength. He was a man again, strong and rounded. And he was a child, so soothed and restored and full of gratitude.

And she, she was the great bath of life, he worshipped her. Mother and substance of all life she was. And he, child and man, received of her and was made whole. His pure body was almost killed. But the miraculous, soft effluence of her breast suffused over him, over his seared, damaged brain, like a healing lymph, like a soft, soothing flow of life itself, perfect as if he were bathed in the womb again.

His brain was hurt, seared, the tissue was as if destroyed. He had not known how hurt he was, how his tissue, the very tissue of his brain was damaged by the corrosive flood of death. Now, as the healing lymph of her effluence flowed through him, he knew how destroyed he was, like a plant whose tissue is burst from inwards by a frost.

He buried his small, hard head between her breasts and pressed her breasts against him with his hands. And she with quivering hands pressed his head against her, as he lay suffused out, and she lay fully conscious. The lovely creative warmth flooded through him like a sleep of fecundity within the womb. Ah, if only she would grant him the flow of this living effluence, he would be restored, he would be complete again. He was afraid she would deny him before it was finished. Like a child at the breast, he cleaved intensely to her, and she could not put him away. And his seared, ruined membrane relaxed, softened, that which was seared and stiff and blasted yielded again, became soft and flexible, palpitating with new life. He was infinitely grateful, as to God, or as an infant is at its mother's breast. He was glad and grateful like a delirium, as he felt his own wholeness come over him again, as he felt the full, unutterable sleep coming over him, the sleep of complete exhaustion and restoration.

But Gudrun lay wide awake, destroyed into perfect consciousness. She lay motionless, with wide eyes staring motionless into the darkness, whilst he was sunk away in sleep, his arms round her.

She seemed to be hearing waves break on a hidden shore, long, slow, gloomy waves, breaking with the rhythm of fate, so monotonously that it seemed eternal. This endless breaking of slow, sullen waves of fate held her life a possession, whilst she lay with dark, wide eyes looking into the darkness. She could see so far, as far as eternity – yet she saw nothing. She was suspended in perfect consciousness – and of what was she conscious?

This mood of extremity, when she lay staring into eternity, utterly suspended, and conscious of everything, to the last limits, passed and left her uneasy. She had lain so long motionless. She moved, she became self-conscious. She wanted to look at him, to see him.

But she dared not make a light, because she knew he would wake, and she did not want to break his perfect sleep, that she knew he had got of her.

She disengaged herself softly and rose up a little to look at him. There was a faint light, it seemed to her, in the room. She could just distinguish his features, as he slept the perfect sleep. In this darkness, she seemed to see him so distinctly. But he was far off, in another world. Ah, she could shriek with torment, he was so far off, and perfected, in another world. She seemed to look at him as at a pebble far away under clear dark water. And here was she, left with all the anguish of consciousness, whilst he was sunk deep into the other element of mindless, remote, living shadow-gleam. He was beautiful, far off, and perfected. They would never be together. Ah, this awful, inhuman distance which would always be interposed between her and the other being!

There was nothing to do but to lie still and endure. She felt an overwhelming tenderness for him, and a dark, under-stirring of jealous hatred, that he should lie so perfect and immune, in another world, whilst she was tormented with violent wakefulness, cast out in the outer darkness.

She lay in intense and vivid consciousness, an exhausting superconsciousness. The church clock struck the hours, it seemed to her, in quick succession. She heard them distinctly in the tension of her vivid consciousness. And he slept as if time were one moment, unchanging and unmoving.

She was exhausted, wearied. Yet she must continue in this state of violent active superconsciousness. She was conscious of everything – her childhood, her girlhood, all the forgotten incidents, all the unrealized influences and all the happenings she had not understood, pertaining to herself, to her family, to her friends, her lovers, her acquaintances, everybody. It was as if she drew a glittering rope of knowledge out of the sea of darkness, drew and drew and drew it out of the fathomless depths of the past, and still it did not come to an end, there was no end to it, she must haul and haul at the rope of glittering consciousness, pull it out phosphorescent from the endless depths of the unconsciousness, till she was weary, aching, exhausted, and fit to break, and yet she had not done.

Ah, if only she might wake him! She turned uneasily. When could she rouse him and send him away? When could she disturb him? And she relapsed into her activity of automatic consciousness, that would never end.

But the time was drawing near when she could wake him. It was like a release. The clock had struck four, outside in the night. Thank God the night had passed almost away. At five he must go, and she would be released. Then she could relax and fill her own place. Now she was driven up against his perfect sleeping motion like a knife white-hot on a grindstone. There was something monstrous about him, about his juxtaposition against her.

The last hour was the longest. And yet, at last it passed. Her heart leapt with relief – yes, there was the slow, strong stroke of the church clock – at last, after this night of eternity. She waited to catch each slow, fatal reverberation. 'Three – four – five!' There, it was finished. A weight rolled off her.

She raised herself, leaned over him tenderly, and kissed him. She was sad to wake him. After a few moments, she kissed him again. But he did not stir. The darling, he was so deep in sleep! What a shame to take him out of it. She let him lie a little longer. But he must go – he must really go.

With full over-tenderness she took his face between her hands and kissed his eyes. The eyes opened, he remained motionless, looking at her. Her heart stood still. To hide her face from his dreadful opened eyes, in the darkness, she bent down and kissed him, whispering:

'You must go, my love.'

But she was sick with terror, sick.

He put his arms round her. Her heart sank.

'But you must go, my love. It's late.'

'What time is it?' he said.

Strange, his man's voice. She quivered. It was an intolerable oppression to her.

'Past five o'clock,' she said.

But he only closed his arms round her again. Her heart cried within her in torture. She disengaged herself firmly.

'You really must go,' she said.

'Not for a minute,' he said.

She lay still, nestling against him, but unyielding.

'Not for a minute,' he repeated, clasping her closer.

'Yes,' she said, unyielding. 'I'm afraid if you stay any longer.'

There was a certain coldness in her voice that made him release her, and she broke away, rose and lit the candle. That then was the end.

He got up. He was warm and full of life and desire. Yet he felt a little bit ashamed, humiliated, putting on his clothes before her, in the candle-light. For he felt revealed, exposed to her, at a time when she was in some way against him. It was all very difficult to understand. He dressed himself quickly, without collar or tie. Still he felt full and complete, perfected. She thought it humiliating to see a man dressing: the ridiculous shirt, the ridiculous trousers and braces. But again an idea saved her.

'It is like a workman getting up to go to work,' thought Gudrun. 'And I am like a workman's wife.' But an ache like nausea was upon her: a nausea of him.

He pushed his collar and tie into his overcoat pocket. Then he sat down and pulled on his boots. They were sodden, as were his socks and trouser-bottoms. But he himself was quick and warm.

'Perhaps you ought to have put your boots on downstairs,' she said.

At once, without answering, he pulled them off again and stood holding them in his hand. She had thrust her feet into slippers, and flung a loose robe round her. She was ready. She looked at him as he stood waiting, his black coat buttoned to the chin, his cap pulled down, his boots in his hand. And the passionate almost hateful fascination revived in her for a moment. It was not exhausted. His face was so warm-looking, wide-eyed and full of newness, so perfect. She felt old, old. She went to him heavily to be kissed. He kissed her quickly. She wished his warm, expressionless beauty did not so fatally put a spell on her, compel her and subjugate her. It was a burden upon her, that she resented, but could not escape. Yet when she looked at his straight man's brows, and at his rather small, well-shaped nose, and at his blue, indifferent eyes, she knew her passion for him was not yet satisfied, perhaps never could be satisfied. Only now she was weary, with an ache like nausea. She wanted him gone.

They went downstairs quickly. It seemed they made a prodigious noise. He followed her as, wrapped in her vivid green wrap, she preceded him with the light. She suffered badly with fear, lest her people should be roused. He hardly cared. He did not care now who knew. And she hated this in him. One *must* be cautious. One must preserve oneself.

She led the way to the kitchen. It was neat and tidy, as the woman had left it. He looked up at the clock – twenty minutes past five! Then he sat down on a chair to put on his boots. She waited, watching his every movement. She wanted it to be over, it was a great nervous strain on her.

He stood up – she unbolted the back door and looked out. A cold, raw night, not yet dawn, with a piece of a moon in the vague sky. She was glad she need not go out.

'Good-bye then,' he murmured.

'I'll come to the gate,' she said.

And again she hurried on in front, to warn him of the steps. And at the gate, once more she stood on the step whilst he stood below her.

'Good-bye,' she whispered.

He kissed her dutifully and turned away.

She suffered torments hearing his firm tread going so distinctly down the road. Ah, the insensitiveness of that firm tread!

She closed the gate and crept quickly and noiselessly back to bed. When she was in her room, and the door closed, and all safe, she breathed freely, and a great weight fell off her. She nestled down in bed, in the groove his body had made, in the warmth he had left. And excited, worn out, yet still satisfied, she fell soon into a deep, heavy sleep.

Gerald walked quickly through the raw darkness of the coming dawn. He met nobody. His mind was beautifully still and thoughtless, like a still pool, and his body full and warm and rich. He went quickly along towards Shortlands in a grateful self-sufficiency.

25

MARRIAGE OR NOT

The Brangwen family was not going to move from Beldover. It was necessary now for the father to be in town.

Birkin had taken out a marriage licence, yet Ursula deferred from day to day. She would not fix any definite time – she still wavered. Her month's notice to leave the Grammar School was in its third week. Christmas was not far off.

Gerald waited for the Ursula–Birkin marriage. It was something crucial to him.

'Shall we make it a double-barrelled affair?' he said to Birkin one day.

'Who for the second shot?' asked Birkin.

'Gudrun and me,' said Gerald, the venturesome twinkle in his eyes.

Birkin looked at him steadily, as if somewhat taken aback.

'Serious – or joking?' he asked.

'Oh, serious. Shall I? Shall Gudrun and I rush in along with you?'

'Do by all means,' said Birkin. 'I didn't know you'd got that length.'

'What length?' said Gerald, looking at the other man, and laughing. 'Oh yes, we've gone all the lengths.'

'There remains to put it on a broad social basis, and to achieve a high moral purpose,' said Birkin.

'Something like that: the length and breadth and height of it,' replied Gerald, smiling.

'Oh well,' said Birkin, 'it's a very admirable step to take, I should say.'

Gerald looked at him closely.

'Why aren't you enthusiastic?' he asked. 'I thought you were such dead nuts on marriage.'

Birkin lifted his shoulders.

'One might as well be dead nuts on noses. There are all sorts of noses, snub and otherwise –'

Gerald laughed.

'And all sorts of marriage, also snub and otherwise?' he said.

'And you think if I marry, it will be snub?' asked Gerald quizzically, his head a little on one side.

Birkin laughed quickly.

'How do I know what it will be!' he said. 'Don't lambaste me with my own parallels –'

Gerald pondered a while.

'But I should like to know your opinion, exactly,' he said.

'On your marriage? – or marrying? Why should you want my opinion? I've got no opinions. I'm not interested in legal marriage, one way or another. It's a mere question of convenience.'

Still Gerald watched him closely.

'More than that, I think,' he said seriously. 'However, you may be bored by the ethics of marriage, yet really to marry, in one's own personal case, is something critical, final –'

'You mean there is something final in going to the registrar with a woman?'

'If you're coming back with her, I do,' said Gerald. 'It is in some way irrevocable.'

'Yes, I agree,' said Birkin.

'No matter how one regards legal marriage, yet to enter into the married state, in one's own personal instance, is final –'

'I believe it is,' said Birkin, 'somewhere.'

'The question remains, then, should one do it,' said Gerald.

Birkin watched him narrowly, with amused eyes.

'You are like Lord Bacon, Gerald,' he said. 'You argue it like a lawyer – or like Hamlet's to-be-or-not-to-be. If I were you I would *not* marry: but ask Gudrun, not me. You're not marrying me, are you?'

Gerald did not heed the latter part of this speech.

'Yes,' he said, 'one must consider it coldly. It is something critical. One comes to the point where one must take a step in one direction or another. And marriage is one direction –'

'And what is the other?' asked Birkin quickly.

Gerald looked up at him with hot, strangely-conscious eyes, that the other man could not understand.

'I can't say,' he replied. 'If I knew *that* –' He moved uneasily on his feet and did not finish.

'You mean if you knew the alternative?' asked Birkin. 'And since you don't know it, marriage is a *pis aller*.'

Gerald looked up at Birkin with the same hot, constrained eyes.

'One does have the feeling that marriage is a *pis aller*,' he admitted.

'Then don't do it,' said Birkin. 'I tell you,' he went on, 'the same as I've said before, marriage in the old sense seems to me repulsive. *Egoïsme à deux* is nothing to it. It's a sort of tacit hunting in couples: the world all in couples, each couple in its own little house, watching its own little interests, and stewing in its own little privacy – it's the most repulsive thing on earth.'

'I quite agree,' said Gerald. 'There's something inferior about it. But as I say, what's the alternative.'

'One should avoid this *home* instinct. It's not an instinct, it's a habit of cowardliness. One should never have a *home*.'

'I agree really,' said Gerald. 'But there's no alternative.'

'We've got to find one. I do believe in a permanent union between a man and a woman. Chopping about is merely an exhaustive process. But a permanent relation between a man and a woman isn't the last word – it certainly isn't.'

'Quite,' said Gerald.

'In fact,' said Birkin, 'because the relation between men and women is made the supreme and exclusive relationship, that's where all the tightness and meanness and insufficiency comes in.'

'Yes, I believe you,' said Gerald.

'You've got to take down the love-and-marriage ideal from its pedestal. We want something broader. I believe in the *additional* perfect relationship between man and man – additional to marriage.'

'I can never see how they can be the same,' said Gerald.

'Not the same – but equally important, equally creative, equally sacred, if you like.'

'I know,' said Gerald, 'you believe something like that. Only I can't *feel* it, you see.' He put his hand on Birkin's arm, with a sort of deprecating affection. And he smiled as if triumphantly.

He was ready to be doomed. Marriage was like a doom to him. He was willing to condemn himself in marriage, to become like a convict condemned to the mines of the underworld, living no life in the sun, but having a dreadful subterranean activity. He was willing to accept this. And marriage was the seal of his condemnation. He was willing to be sealed thus in the underworld, like a soul damned but living for ever in damnation. But he would not make any pure relationship with any other soul. He could not. Marriage was not the committing of himself into a relationship with Gudrun. It was a committing of himself in acceptance of the established world, he would accept the established order, in which he did not livingly believe, and then he would retreat to the underworld for his life. This he would do.

The other way was to accept Rupert's offer of alliance, to enter into the bond of pure trust and love with the other man, and then subsequently with the woman. If he pledged himself with the man he would later be able to pledge himself with the woman: not merely in legal marriage, but in absolute, mystic marriage.

Yet he could not accept the offer. There was a numbness upon him, a numbness either of unborn, absent volition or of atrophy. Perhaps it was the absence of volition. For he was strangely elated at Rupert's offer. Yet he was still more glad to reject it, not to be committed.

26

A CHAIR

There was a jumble market every Monday afternoon in the old market-place in town. Ursula and Birkin strayed down there one afternoon. They had been talking of furniture, and they wanted to see if there was any fragment they would like to buy, amid the heaps of rubbish collected on the cobble-stones.

The old market-square was not very large, a mere bare patch of granite setts, usually with a few fruit-stalls under a wall. It was in a poor quarter of the town. Meagre houses stood down one side, there was a hosiery factory, a great blank with myriad oblong windows at the end, a street of little shops with flagstone pavement down the other side, and, for a crowning monument, the public baths, of new red brick, with a clock-tower. The people who moved about seemed stumpy and sordid, the air seemed to smell rather dirty, there was a sense of many mean streets ramifying off into warrens of meanness. Now and again a great chocolate-and-yellow tramcar ground round a difficult bend under the hosiery factory.

Ursula was superficially thrilled when she found herself out among the common people, in the jumbled place piled with old bedding, heaps of old iron, shabby crockery in pale lots, muffled lots of unthinkable clothing. She and Birkin went unwillingly down the narrow aisle between the rusty wares. He was looking at the goods, she at the people.

She excitedly watched a young woman who was going to have a baby, and who was turning over a mattress and making a young man, down-at-heel and dejected, feel it also. So secretive and active and anxious the young woman seemed, so reluctant, slinking, the young man. He was going to marry her because she was having a child.

When they had felt the mattress, the young woman asked the old man seated on a stool among his wares how much it was. He told her, and she turned to the young man. The latter was ashamed and self-conscious. He turned his face away, though he left his body standing there, and muttered aside. And again the woman anxiously and actively fingered the mattress and added up in her mind and bargained with the old, unclean man. All the while the young man stood by, shamefaced and down-at-heel, submitting.

'Look,' said Birkin, 'there is a pretty chair.'

'Charming!' cried Ursula. 'Oh, charming.'

It was an arm-chair of simple wood, probably birch, but of such fine delicacy of grace, standing there on the sordid stones, it almost brought tears to the eyes. It was square in shape, of the purest, slender lines, and four short lines of wood in the back, that reminded Ursula of harp-strings.

'It was once,' said Birkin, 'gilded – and it had a cane seat. Somebody has nailed this wooden seat in. Look, here is a trifle of the red that underlay the gilt. The rest is all black, except where the wood is worn pure and glossy. It is the fine unity of the lines that is so attractive. Look, how they run and meet and counteract. But of course the wooden seat is wrong – it destroys the perfect lightness and unity in tension the cane gave. I like it though –'

'Ah yes,' said Ursula, 'so do I.'

'How much is it?' Birkin asked the man.

'Ten shillings.'

'And you will send it –?'

It was bought.

'So beautiful, so pure!' Birkin said. 'It almost breaks my heart.' They walked along between the heaps of rubbish. 'My beloved country – it had something to express even when it made that chair.'

'And hasn't it now?' asked Ursula. She was always angry when he took this tone.

'No, it hasn't. When I see that clear, beautiful chair, and I think of England, even Jane Austen's England – it had living thoughts to unfold even then, and pure happiness in unfolding them. And now, we can only fish among the rubbish-heaps for the remnants of their old expression. There is no production in us now, only sordid and foul mechanicalness.'

'It isn't true,' cried Ursula. 'Why must you always praise the past at the expense of the present? *Really*, I don't think so much of Jane Austen's England. It was materialistic enough, if you like –'

'It could afford to be materialistic,' said Birkin, 'because it had the power to be something other – which we haven't. We are materialistic because we haven't the power to be anything else – try as we may, we can't bring off anything but materialism: mechanism, the very soul of materialism.'

Ursula was subdued into angry silence. She did not heed what he said. She was rebelling against something else.

'And I hate your past. I'm sick of it,' she cried. 'I believe I even hate that old chair, though it *is* beautiful. It isn't *my* sort of beauty. I wish it had been smashed up when its day was over, not left to preach the beloved past to us. I'm sick of the beloved past.'

'Not so sick as I am of the accursed present,' he said.

'Yes, just the same. I hate the present – but I don't want the past to take its place – I don't want that old chair.'

He was rather angry for a moment. Then he looked at the sky shining beyond the tower of the public baths, and he seemed to get over it all. He laughed.

'All right,' he said, 'then let us not have it. I'm sick of it all, too. At any rate, one can't go on living on the old bones of beauty.'

'One can't,' she cried. 'I *don't* want old things.'

'The truth is, we don't want things at all,' he replied. 'The thought of a house and furniture of my own is hateful to me.'

This startled her for a moment. Then she replied:

'So it is to me. But one must live somewhere.'

'Not somewhere – anywhere,' he said. 'One should just live anywhere – not have a definite place. I don't want a definite place. As soon as you get a room, and it is *complete*, you want to run from it. Now my rooms at the Mill are quite complete, I want them at the bottom of the sea. It is a horrible tyranny of a fixed milieu, where each piece of furniture is a commandment-stone.'

She clung to his arm as they walked away from the market.

'But what are you going to do?' she said. 'We must live somehow. And I do want some beauty in my surroundings. I want a sort of natural *grandeur* even, *splendour*.'

'You'll never get it in houses and furniture – or even clothes. Houses and furniture and clothes, they are all terms of an old base world, a detestable society of man. And if you have a Tudor house and old, beautiful furniture, it is only the past perpetuated on top of you, horrible. And if you have a perfect modern house done for you by Poiret, it is something else perpetuated on top of you. It is all horrible. It is all possessions, possessions, bullying you and turning you into a generalization. You have to be like Rodin, Michael Angelo, and leave a piece of raw rock unfinished to your figure. You must leave your surroundings sketchy, unfinished, so that you are never contained, never confined, never dominated from the outside.'

She stood in the street contemplating.

'And we are never to have a complete place of our own – never a home?' she said.

'Pray God, in this world, no,' he answered.

'But there's only this world,' she objected.

He spread out his hands with a gesture of indifference.

'Meanwhile, then, we'll avoid having things of our own,' he said.

'But you've just bought a chair,' she said.

'I can tell the man I don't want it,' he replied.

She pondered again. Then a queer little movement twitched her face.

'No,' she said, 'we don't want it. I'm sick of old things.'

'New ones as well,' he said.

They retraced their steps.

There – in front of some furniture, stood the young couple, the woman who was going to have a baby and the narrow-faced youth. She was fair, rather short, stout. He was of medium height, attractively built. His dark hair fell sideways over his brow from under his cap, he stood strangely aloof, like one of the damned.

'Let us give it to *them*,' whispered Ursula. 'Look, they are getting a home together.'

'*I* won't aid and abet them in it,' he said petulantly, instantly sympathizing with the aloof, furtive youth, against the active, procreant female.

'Oh yes,' cried Ursula. 'It's right for them – there's nothing else for them.'

'Very well,' said Birkin, 'you offer it to them. I'll watch.'

Ursula went rather nervously to the young couple who were discussing an iron washstand – or rather, the man was glancing furtively and wonderingly, like a prisoner, at the abominable article, whilst the woman was arguing.

'We bought a chair,' said Ursula, 'and we don't want it. Would you have it? We should be glad if you would.'

The young couple looked round at her, not believing that she could be addressing them.

'Would you care for it?' repeated Ursula. 'It's really *very* pretty – but – but –' she smiled rather dazzlingly.

The young couple only stared at her, and looked significantly at each other to know what to do. And the man curiously obliterated himself, as if he could make himself invisible as a rat can.

'We wanted to *give* it to you,' explained Ursula, now overcome with confusion and dread of them. She was attracted by the young man. He was a still, mindless creature, hardly a man at all, a creature that the towns have produced, strangely pure-bred and fine in one sense, furtive, quick, subtle. His lashes were dark and long and fine over his eyes, that had no mind in them, only a dreadful kind of subject, inward consciousness, glazed and dark. His dark brows and all his lines were finely drawn. He would be a dreadful, but wonderful lover to a woman, so marvellously contributed. His legs would be marvellously subtle and alive, under the shapeless trousers, he had some of the fineness and stillness and silkiness of a dark-eyed, silent rat.

Ursula had apprehended him with a fine *frisson* of attraction. The full-built woman was staring offensively. Again Ursula forgot him.

'Won't you have the chair?' she said.

The man looked at her with a sideways look of appreciation, yet far off, almost insolent. The woman drew herself up. There was a certain coster-monger richness about her. She did not know what Ursula was after, she was on her guard, hostile. Birkin approached, smiling wickedly at seeing Ursula so nonplussed and frightened.

'What's the matter?' he said, smiling. His eyelids had dropped slightly, there was about him the same suggestive, mocking secrecy that was in the bearing of the two city creatures. The man jerked his head a little on one side, indicating Ursula, and said, with curious amiable, jeering warmth:

'What she warnt? – eh?' An odd smile writhed his lips.

Birkin looked at him from under his slack, ironical eyelids.

'To give you a chair – that – with the label on it,' he said, pointing.

The man looked at the object indicated. There was a curious hostility in male, outlawed understanding between the two men.

'What's she warnt to give it *us* for, guv'nor,' he replied in a tone of free intimacy that insulted Ursula.

'Thought you'd like it – it's a pretty chair. We bought it and don't want it. No need for you to have it, don't be frightened,' said Birkin, with a wry smile.

The man glanced up at him, half inimical, half recognizing.

'Why don't you want it for yourselves, if you've just bought it?' asked the woman coolly. ''Taint good enough for you, now you've had a look at it. Frightened it's got something in it, eh?'

She was looking at Ursula admiringly, but with some resentment.

'I'd never thought of that,' said Birkin. 'But no, the wood's too thin everywhere.'

'You see,' said Ursula, her face luminous and pleased. '*We* are just going to get married, and we thought we'd buy things. Then we decided just now, that we wouldn't have furniture, we'd go abroad.'

The full-built, slightly blowsy city girl looked at the fine face of the other woman with appreciation. They appreciated each other. The youth stood aside, his face expressionless and timeless, the thin line of the black moustache drawn strangely suggestive over his rather wide, closed mouth. He was impassive, abstract, like some dark suggestive presence, a gutter presence.

'It's all right to be some folks,' said the city girl, turning to her own young man. He did not look at her, but he smiled with the lower part of his face, putting his head aside in an odd gesture of assent. His eyes were unchanging, glazed with darkness.

'Cawsts something to chynge your mind,' he said in an incredibly low accent.

'Only ten shillings this time,' said Birkin.

The man looked up at him with a grimace of a smile, furtive, unsure.

'Cheap at 'arf a quid, guv'nor,' he said. 'Not like getting divawced.'

'We're not married yet,' said Birkin.

'No, no more aren't we,' said the young woman loudly. 'But we shall be a Saturday.'

Again she looked at the young man with a determined, protective look, at once overbearing and very gentle. He grinned sicklily, turning away his head. She had got his manhood, but Lord, what did he care! He had a strange furtive pride and slinking singleness.

'Good luck to you,' said Birkin.

'Same to you,' said the young woman. Then, rather tentatively: 'When's yours coming off, then?'

Birkin looked round at Ursula.

'It's for the lady to say,' he replied. 'We go to the registrar the moment she's ready.'

Ursula laughed, covered with confusion and bewilderment.

'No 'urry,' said the young man, grinning suggestive.

'Oh, don't break your neck to get there,' said the young woman. ''Slike when you're dead – you're a long time married.'

The young man turned aside as if this hit him.

'The longer the better, let us hope,' said Birkin.

'That's it, guv'nor,' said the young man admiringly. 'Enjoy it while it larsts – niver whip a dead donkey.'

'Only when he's shamming dead,' said the young woman, looking at her young man with caressive tenderness of authority.

'Aw, there's a difference,' he said satirically.

'What about the chair?' said Birkin.

'Yes, all right,' said the woman.

They trailed off to the dealer, the handsome but abject young fellow hanging a little aside.

'That's it,' said Birkin. 'Will you take it with you or have the address altered?'

'Oh, Fred can carry it. Make him do what he can for the dear old 'ome.'

'Mike use of 'im,' said Fred, grimly humorous, as he took the chair from the dealer. His movements were graceful, yet curiously abject, slinking.

' 'Ere's mother's cosy chair,' he said. 'Warnts a cushion.' And he stood it down on the market stones.

'Don't you think it's pretty?' laughed Ursula.

'Oh, I do,' said the young woman.

' 'Ave a sit in it, you'll wish you'd kept it,' said the young man.

Ursula promptly sat down in the middle of the market-place.

'Awfully comfortable,' she said. 'But rather hard. You try it.' She invited the young man to a seat. But he turned uncouthly, awkwardly aside, glancing up at her with quick bright eyes, oddly suggestive, like a quick, live rat.

'Don't spoil him,' said the young woman. 'He's not used to arm-chairs, 'e isn't.'

The young man turned away and said, with averted grin:

'Only warnts legs on 'is.'

The four parted. The young woman thanked them.

'Thank you for the chair – it'll last till it gives way.'

'Keep it for an ornyment,' said the young man.

'Good afternoon – good afternoon,' said Ursula and Birkin.

'Goo'-luck to you,' said the young man, glancing and avoiding Birkin's eyes as he turned aside his head.

The two couples went asunder, Ursula clinging to Birkin's arm. When they had gone some distance, she glanced back and saw the young man going beside the full, easy young woman. His trousers sank over his heels, he moved with a sort of slinking evasion, more crushed with odd self-consciousness now he had the slim old arm-chair to carry, his arm over the back, the four fine, square tapering legs swaying perilously near the granite setts of the pavement. And yet he was somewhere indomitable and separate, like a quick, vital rat. He had a queer, subterranean beauty, repulsive too.

'How strange they are!' said Ursula.

'Children of men,' he said. 'They remind me of Jesus: "The meek shall inherit the earth".'

'But they aren't the meek,' said Ursula.

'Yes, I don't know why, but they are,' he replied.

They waited for the tram-car. Ursula sat on top and looked out on the town. The dusk was just dimming the hollows of crowded houses.

'And are they going to inherit the earth?' she said.

'Yes – they.'

'Then what are we going to do?' she asked. 'We're not like them – are we? We're not the meek?'

'No. We've got to live in the chinks they leave us.'

'How horrible!' cried Ursula. 'I don't want to live in chinks.'

'Don't worry,' he said. 'They are the children of man, they like market-places and street corners best. That leaves plenty of chinks.'

'All the world,' she said.

'Ah, no – but some room.'

The tram-car mounted slowly up the hill, where the ugly winter-grey masses of houses looked like a vision of hell that is cold and angular. They sat and looked. Away in the distance was an angry redness of sunset. It was all cold, somehow small, crowded, and like the end of the world.

'I don't mind it even then,' said Ursula, looking at the repulsiveness of it all. 'It doesn't concern me.'

'No more it does,' he replied, holding her hand. 'One needn't see. One goes one's way. In my world it is sunny and spacious –'

'It is, my love, isn't it?' she cried, hugging near to him on the top of the tram-car, so that the other passengers stared at them.

'And we will wander about on the face of the earth,' he said, 'and we'll look at the world beyond just this bit.'

There was a long silence. Her face was radiant like gold as she sat thinking.

'I don't want to inherit the earth,' she said. 'I don't want to inherit anything.'

He closed his hand over hers.

'Neither do I. I want to be disinherited.'

She clasped his fingers closely.

'We won't care about *anything*,' she said.

He sat still and laughed.

'And we'll be married, and have done with them,' she added.

Again he laughed.

'It's one way of getting rid of everything,' she said, 'to get married.'

'And one way of accepting the whole world,' he added.

'A whole other world, yes,' she said happily.

'Perhaps there's Gerald – and Gudrun –' he said.

'If there is there is, you see,' she said. 'It's no good our worrying. We can't really alter them, can we?'

'No,' he said. 'One has no right to try – not with the best intentions in the world.'

'Do you try to force them?' she asked.

'Perhaps,' he said. 'Why should I want him to be free, if it isn't his business?'

She paused for a time.

'We can't *make* him happy, anyhow,' she said. 'He'd have to be it of himself.'

'I know,' he said. 'But we want other people with us, don't we?'

'Why should we?' she asked.

'I don't know,' he said uneasily. 'One has a hankering after a sort of further fellowship.'

'But why?' she insisted. 'Why should you hanker after other people? Why should you need them?'

This hit him right on the quick. His brows knitted.

'Does it end with just our two selves?' he asked, tense.

'Yes – what more do you want? If anybody likes to come along, let them. But why must you run after them?'

His face was tense and unsatisfied.

'You see,' he said, 'I always imagine our being really happy with some few other people – a little freedom with people.'

She pondered for a moment.

'Yes, one does want that. But it must *happen*. You can't do anything for it with your will. You always seem to think you can force the flowers to come out. People must love us because they love us – you can't *make* them.'

'I know,' he said. 'But must one take no steps at all? Must one just go as if one were alone in the world – the only creature in the world?'

'You've got me,' she said. 'Why should you *need* others? Why must you force people to agree with you? Why can't you be single by yourself, as you are always saying? You try to bully Gerald – as you tried to bully Hermione. You must learn to be alone. And it's so horrid of you. You've got me. And yet you want to force other people to love you as well. You do try to bully them to love you. And even then you don't want their love.'

His face was full of real perplexity.

'Don't I?' he said. 'It's the problem I can't solve. I *know* I want a perfect and complete relationship with you: and we've nearly got it – we really have. But beyond that. *Do* I want a real, ultimate relationship with Gerald? Do I want a final, almost extra-human relationship with him – a relationship in the ultimate of me and him – or don't I?'

She looked at him for a long time with strange bright eyes, but she did not answer.

27

FLITTING

That evening Ursula returned home very bright-eyed and wondrous – which irritated her people. Her father came home at supper-time, tired after the evening class, and the long journey home. Gudrun was reading, the mother sat in silence.

Suddenly Ursula said to the company at large in a bright voice: 'Rupert and I are going to be married tomorrow.'

Her father turned round stiffly.

'You what?' he said.

'Tomorrow!' echoed Gudrun.

'Indeed!' said the mother.

But Ursula only smiled wonderfully and did not reply.

'Married tomorrow!' cried her father harshly. 'What are you talking about?'

'Yes,' said Ursula. 'Why not?' Those two words from her always drove him mad. 'Everything is all right – we shall go to the registrar's office –'

There was a second's hush in the room after Ursula's blithe vagueness.

'*Really*, Ursula!' said Gudrun.

'Might we ask why there has been all this secrecy?' demanded the mother, rather superbly.

'But there hasn't,' said Ursula. 'You knew.'

'Who knew?' now cried the father. 'Who knew? What do you mean by your "you knew"?'

He was in one of his stupid rages, she instantly closed against him.

'Of course you knew,' she said coolly. 'You knew we were going to get married.'

There was a dangerous pause.

'We knew you were going to get married, did we? Knew! Why, does anybody know anything about *you*, you shifty bitch!'

'Father!' cried Gudrun, flushing deep in violent remonstrance. Then in a cold but gentle voice, as if to remind her sister to be tractable: 'But isn't it a *fearfully* sudden decision, Ursula?' she asked.

'No, not really,' replied Ursula, with the same maddening cheerfulness. 'He's been *wanting* me to agree for weeks – he's had the licence ready. Only I – I wasn't ready in myself. Now I am ready – is there anything to be disagreeable about?'

'Certainly not,' said Gudrun, but in a tone of cold reproof. 'You are perfectly free to do as you like.'

'"Ready in yourself" – *yourself*, that's all that matters, isn't it! "I wasn't ready in myself,"' he mimicked her phrase offensively. 'You and *yourself*, you're of some importance, aren't you?'

She drew herself up and set back her throat, her eyes shining yellow and dangerous.

'I am to myself,' she said, wounded and mortified. 'I know I am not to anybody else. You only wanted to *bully* me – you never cared for my happiness.'

He was leaning forward watching her, his face intense like a spark.

'Ursula, what are you saying? Keep your tongue still,' cried her mother.

Ursula swung round and the lights in her eyes flashed.

'No, I won't,' she cried. 'I won't hold my tongue and be bullied. What does it matter which day I get married – what does it *matter*! It doesn't affect anybody but myself.'

Her father was tense and gathered together like a cat about to spring.

'Doesn't it?' he cried, coming nearer to her. She shrank away.

'No, how can it?' she replied, shrinking but stubborn.

'It doesn't matter to *me*, then, what you do – what becomes of you?' he cried, in a strange voice like a cry.

The mother and Gudrun stood back as if hypnotized.

'No,' stammered Ursula. Her father was very near to her. 'You only want to –'

She knew it was dangerous, and she stopped. He was gathered together, every muscle ready.

'What?' he challenged.

'Bully me,' she muttered, and even as her lips were moving, his hand had caught her smack at the side of the face and she was sent up against the door.

'Father!' cried Gudrun in a high voice, 'it is impossible!'

He stood unmoving. Ursula recovered, her hand was on the door-handle. She slowly drew herself up. He seemed doubtful now.

'It's true,' she declared, with brilliant tears in her eyes, her head lifted up in defiance. 'What has your love meant, what did it ever mean? – bullying and denial – it did –'

He was advancing again with strange, tense movements, and clenched fist, and the face of a murderer. But swift as lightning she had flashed out of the door, and they heard her running upstairs.

He stood for a moment looking at the door. Then, like a defeated animal, he turned and went back to his seat by the fire.

Gudrun was very white. Out of the intense silence the mother's voice was heard saying, cold and angry:

'Well, you shouldn't take so much notice of her.'

Again the silence fell, each followed a separate set of emotions and thoughts.

Suddenly the door opened again: Ursula, dressed in hat and furs, with a small valise in her hand:

'Good-bye!' she said in her maddening, bright, almost mocking tone. 'I'm going.'

And in the next instant the door was closed, they heard the outer door, then her quick steps down the garden path, then the gate banged, and her light footfall was gone. There was a silence like death in the house.

Ursula went straight to the station, hastening heedlessly on winged feet. There was no train, she must walk on to the junction. As she went through the darkness, she began to cry, and she wept bitterly, with a dumb, heart-broken, child's anguish, all the way on the road, and in the train. Time passed unheeded and unknown, she did not know where she was, nor what was taking place. Only she wept from fathomless depths of hopeless, hopeless grief, the terrible grief of a child, that knows no extenuation.

Yet her voice had the same defensive brightness as she spoke to Birkin's landlady at the door.

'Good evening! Is Mr Birkin in? Can I see him?'

'Yes, he's in. He's in his study.'

Ursula slipped past the woman. His door opened. He had heard her voice.

'Hello!' he exclaimed in surprise, seeing her standing there with the valise in her hand, and marks of tears on her face. She was the one who wept without showing many traces, like a child.

'Do I look a sight?' she said, shrinking.

'No – why? Come in.' He took the bag from her hand and they went into the study.

There – immediately, her lips began to tremble like those of a child that remembers again, and the tears came rushing up.

'What's the matter?' he asked, taking her in his arms. She sobbed violently on his shoulder whilst he held her still, waiting.

'What's the matter?' he said again, when she was quieter. But she only pressed her face farther into his shoulder, in pain, like a child that cannot tell.

'What is it, then?' he asked.

Suddenly she broke away, wiped her eyes, regained her composure, and went and sat in a chair.

'Father hit me,' she announced, sitting bunched up, rather like a ruffled bird, her eyes very bright.

'What for?' he said.

She looked away and would not answer. There was a pitiful redness about her sensitive nostrils and her quivering lips.

'Why?' he repeated in his strange, soft, penetrating voice.

She looked round at him rather defiantly.

'Because I said I was going to be married tomorrow, and he bullied me.'

'Why did he bully you?'

Her mouth dropped again, she remembered the scene once more, the tears came up.

'Because I said he didn't care – and he doesn't; it's only his domineeringness that's hurt –' she said, her mouth pulled awry by her weeping all the time she spoke, so that he almost smiled, it seemed so childish. Yet it was not childish, it was a mortal conflict, a deep wound.

'It isn't quite true,' he said. 'And even so, you shouldn't *say* it.'

'It *is* true – it *is* true,' she wept, 'and I won't be bullied by his pretending it's love – when it *isn't* – he doesn't care, how can he – no, he can't –'

He sat in silence. She moved him beyond himself.

'Then you shouldn't rouse him, if he can't,' replied Birkin quietly.

'And I *have* loved him, I have,' she wept. 'I've loved him always, and he's always done this to me, he has –'

'It's been a love opposition, then,' he said. 'Never mind – it will be all right. It's nothing desperate.'

'Yes,' she wept, 'it is, it is.'

'Why?'

'I shall never see him again –'

'Not immediately. Don't cry, you had to break with him, it had to be – don't cry.'

He went over to her and kissed her fine, fragile hair, touching her wet cheeks gently.

'Don't cry,' he repeated, 'don't cry any more.'

He held her head close against him, very close and quiet.

At last she was still. Then she looked up, her eyes wide and frightened.

'Don't you want me?' she asked.

'Want you?' His darkened, steady eyes puzzled her and did not give her play.

'Do you wish I hadn't come?' she asked, anxious now again for fear she might be out of place.

'No,' he said. 'I wish there hadn't been the violence – so much ugliness – but perhaps it was inevitable.'

She watched him in silence. He seemed deadened.

'But where shall I stay?' she asked, feeling humiliated.

He thought for a moment.

'Here, with me,' he said. 'We're married as much today as we shall be tomorrow.'

'But –'

'I'll tell Mrs Varley,' he said. 'Never mind now.'

He sat looking at her. She could feel his darkened steady eyes looking at her all the time. It made her a little bit frightened. She pushed her hair off her forehead nervously.

'Do I look ugly?' she said.

And she blew her nose again.

A small smile came round his eyes.

'No,' he said, 'fortunately.'

And he went across to her and gathered her like a belonging in his arms. She was so tenderly beautiful, he could not bear to see her, he could only bear to hide her against himself. Now, washed all clean by her tears, she was new and frail like a flower just unfolded, a flower so new, so tender, so made perfect by inner light, that he could not bear to look at her, he must hide her against himself, cover his eyes against her. She had the perfect candour of creation, something translucent and simple, like a radiant, shining flower that moment unfolded in primal blessedness. She was so new, so wonder-clear, so undimmed. And he was so old, so steeped in heavy memories. Her soul was new, undefined and glimmering with the unseen. And his soul was dark and gloomy, it had only one grain of living hope, like a grain of mustard seed. But this one living grain in him matched the perfect youth in her.

'I love you,' he whispered as he kissed her, and trembled with pure hope, like a man who is born again to a wonderful, lively hope far exceeding the bounds of death.

She could not know how much it meant to him, how much he meant by the few words. Almost childish, she wanted proof, and statement, even over-statement, for everything seemed still uncertain, unfixed to her.

But the passion of gratitude with which he received her into his soul, the extreme, unthinkable gladness of knowing himself living and fit to unite with her, he, who was so nearly dead, who was so near to being gone with the rest of his race down the slope of mechanical death, could never be understood by her. He worshipped her as age worships youth, he gloried in her because, in his one grain of faith, he was young as she, he was her proper mate. This marriage with her was his resurrection and his life.

All this she could not know. She wanted to be made much of, to be adored. There were infinite distances of silence between them. How could he tell her of the immanence of her beauty, that was not form, or weight, or colour, but something like a strange, golden light! How could he know himself what her beauty lay in, for him. He said: 'Your nose is beautiful, your chin is adorable.' But it sounded like lies, and she was disappointed, hurt. Even when he said, whispering with truth, 'I love you, I love you,' it was not the real truth. It was something beyond love, such a gladness of having surpassed oneself, of having transcended the old existence. How could he say 'I' when he was something new and unknown, not himself at all? This I, this old formula of the age, was a dead letter.

In the new, superfine bliss, a peace superseding knowledge, there was no I and you, there was only the third, unrealized wonder, the wonder of existing not as oneself, but in a consummation of my being and of her being in a new one, a new, paradisal unit regained from the duality. How can I say 'I love you' when I have ceased to be, and you have ceased to be: we are both caught up and transcended into a new oneness where everything is silent, because there is nothing to answer, all is perfect and at one. Speech travels between the separate parts. But in the perfect One there is perfect silence of bliss.

They were married by law on the next day, and she did as he bade her, she wrote to her father and mother. Her mother replied, not her father.

She did not go back to school. She stayed with Birkin in his rooms, or at the Mill, moving with him as he moved. But she did not see anybody, save Gudrun and Gerald. She was all strange and wondering as yet, but relieved as by dawn.

Gerald sat talking to her one afternoon in the warm study down at the Mill. Rupert had not yet come home.

'You are happy?' Gerald asked her, with a smile.

'Very happy!' she cried, shrinking a little in her brightness.

'Yes, one can see it.'

'Can one?' cried Ursula in surprise.

He looked up at her with a communicative smile.

'Oh yes, plainly.'

She was pleased. She meditated a moment.

'And can you see that Rupert is happy as well?'

He lowered his eyelids and looked aside.

'Oh yes,' he said.

'Really!'

'Oh yes.'

He was very quiet, as if it were something not to be talked about by him. He seemed sad.

She was very sensitive to suggestion. She asked the question he wanted her to ask.

'Why don't you be happy as well?' she said. 'You could be just the same.'

He paused a moment.

'With Gudrun?' he asked.

'Yes!' she cried, her eyes glowing. But there was a strange tension, an emphasis, as if they were asserting their wishes, against the truth.

'You think Gudrun would have me, and we should be happy?' he said.

'Yes, I'm *sure*!' she cried.

Her eyes were round with delight. Yet underneath she was constrained, she knew her own insistence.

'Oh, I'm *so* glad,' she added.

He smiled.

'What makes you glad?' he said.

'For *her* sake,' she replied. 'I'm sure you'd – you're the right man for her.'

'You are?' he said. 'And do you think she would agree with you?'

'Oh yes!' she exclaimed hastily. Then, upon reconsideration, very uneasy: 'Though Gudrun isn't so very simple, is she? One doesn't know her in five minutes, does one? She's not like me in that.' She laughed at him with her strange, open, dazzled face.

'You think she's not much like you?' Gerald asked.

She knitted her brows.

'Oh, in many ways she is. But I never know what she will do when anything new comes.'

'You don't?' said Gerald. He was silent for some moments. Then he moved tentatively. 'I was going to ask her, in any case, to go away with me at Christmas,' he said in a very small, cautious voice.

'Go away with you? For a time, you mean?'

'As long as she likes,' he said, with a deprecating movement.

They were both silent for some minutes.

'Of course,' said Ursula at last, 'she *might* just be willing to rush into marriage. You can see.'

'Yes,' smiled Gerald. 'I can see. But in case she won't – do you think she would go abroad with me for a few days – or for a fortnight?'

'Oh yes,' said Ursula. 'I'd ask her.'

'Do you think we might all go together?'

'All of us?' Again Ursula's face lighted up. 'It would be rather fun, don't you think?'

'Great fun,' he said.

'And then you could see,' said Ursula.

'What?'

'How things went. I think it is best to take the honeymoon before the wedding – don't you?'

She was pleased with this *mot*. He laughed.

'In certain cases,' he said. 'I'd rather it were so in my own case.'

'Would you!' exclaimed Ursula. Then doubtingly, 'Yes, perhaps you're right. One should please oneself.'

Birkin came in a little later, and Ursula told him what had been said.

'Gudrun!' exclaimed Birkin. 'She's a born mistress, just as Gerald is a born lover – *amant en titre*. If as somebody says all women are either wives or mistresses, then Gudrun is a mistress.'

'And all men either lovers or husbands,' cried Ursula. 'But why not both?'

'The one excludes the other,' he laughed.

'Then I want a lover,' cried Ursula.

'No, you don't,' he said.

'But I do,' she wailed.

He kissed her and laughed.

It was two days after this that Ursula was to go to fetch her things from the house in Beldover. The removal had taken place, the family had gone. Gudrun had rooms in Willey Green.

Ursula had not seen her parents since her marriage. She wept over the rupture, yet what was the good of making it up! Good or not good, she could not go to them. So her things had been left behind and she and Gudrun were to walk over for them in the afternoon.

It was a wintry afternoon, with red in the sky, when they arrived at the house. The windows were dark and blank, already the place was frightening. A stark, void entrance-hall struck a chill to the hearts of the girls.

'I don't believe I dare have come in alone,' said Ursula. 'It frightens me.'

'Ursula!' cried Gudrun. 'Isn't it amazing! Can you believe you lived in this place and never felt it? How I lived here a day without dying of terror, I cannot conceive!'

They looked in the big dining-room. It was a good-sized room, but now a cell would have been lovelier. The large bay windows were naked, the floor was stripped, and a border of dark polish went round the tract of pale boarding. In the faded wall-paper were dark patches where furniture had stood, where pictures had hung. The sense of walls, dry, thin, flimsy-seeming walls, and a flimsy flooring, pale with its artificial black edges, was neutralizing to the mind. Everything was null to the senses, there was enclosure without substance, for the walls were dry and papery. Where were they standing, on earth, or suspended in some cardboard box? In the hearth was burnt paper and scraps of half-burnt paper.

'Imagine that we passed our days here!' said Ursula.

'I know,' cried Gudrun. 'It is too appalling. What must we be like, if we are the contents of *this*!'

'Vile!' said Ursula. 'It really is.'

And she recognized half-burnt covers of *Vogue* – half-burnt representations of women in gowns – lying under the grate.

They went to the drawing-room. Another piece of shut-in air; without weight or substance, only a sense of intolerable papery imprisonment in nothingness. The kitchen did look more substantial, because of the red-tiled floor and the stove, but it was cold and horrid.

The two girls tramped hollowly up the bare stairs. Every sound re-echoed under their hearts. They tramped down the bare corridor. Against the wall of Ursula's bedroom were her things – a trunk, a work-basket, some books, loose coats, a hat-box, standing desolate in the universal emptiness of the dusk.

'A cheerful sight, aren't they?' said Ursula, looking down at her forsaken possessions.

'Very cheerful,' said Gudrun.

The two girls set to, carrying everything down to the front door. Again and again they made the hollow, re-echoing transit. The whole place seemed to resound about them with a noise of hollow, empty futility. In the distance the empty, invisible rooms sent forth a vibration almost of obscenity. They almost fled with the last articles into the out-of-door.

But it was cold. They were waiting for Birkin, who was coming with the car. They went indoors again, and upstairs to their parents' front bedroom, whose windows looked down on the road, and across the country at the black-barred sunset, black and red barred, without light.

They sat down in the window-seat to wait. Both girls were looking over the room. It was void, with a meaninglessness that was almost dreadful.

'Really,' said Ursula, 'this room *couldn't* be sacred, could it?'

Gudrun looked over it with slow eyes.

'Impossible,' she replied.

'When I think of their lives – father's and mother's, their love, and their marriage, and all of us children, and our bringing-up – would you have such a life, Prune?'

'I wouldn't, Ursula.'

'It all seems so *nothing* – their two lives – there's no meaning in it. Really, if they had *not* met, and *not* married, and not lived together – it wouldn't have mattered, would it?'

'Of course – you can't tell,' said Gudrun.

'No. But if I thought my life was going to be like it – Prune,' she caught Gudrun's arm, 'I should run.'

Gudrun was silent for a few moments.

'As a matter of fact, one cannot contemplate the ordinary life – one cannot contemplate it,' replied Gudrun. 'With you, Ursula, it is quite different. You will be out of it all, with Birkin. He's a special case. But with the ordinary man, who has his life fixed in one place, marriage is just impossible. There may be, and there *are*, thousands of women who want it, and could conceive of nothing else. But the very thought of it sends me *mad*. One must be free, above all, one must be free. One may forfeit everything else, but one must be free – one must not become 7, Pinchbeck Street – or Somerset Drive – or Shortlands. No man will be sufficient to make that good – no man! To marry, one must have a free lance or nothing, a comrade-in-arms, a Glücksritter. A man with a position in the social world – well, it is just impossible, impossible!'

'What a lovely word – a Glücksritter!' said Ursula. 'So much nicer than a soldier of fortune.'

'Yes, isn't it?' said Gudrun. 'I'd tilt the world with a Glücksritter. But a home, and establishment! Ursula, what would it mean? – think!'

'I know,' said Ursula. 'We've had one home – that's enough for me.'

'Quite enough,' said Gudrun.

'The little grey home in the west,' quoted Ursula ironically.

'Doesn't it sound grey, too,' said Gudrun grimly.

They were interrupted by the sound of the car. There was Birkin. Ursula was surprised that she felt so lit up, that she became suddenly so free from the problems of grey homes in the west.

They heard his heels click on the hall pavement below.

'Hello!' he called, his voice echoing alive through the house. Ursula smiled to herself. *He* was frightened of the place too.

'Hello! Here we are,' she called downstairs. And they heard him quickly running up.

'This is a ghostly situation,' he said.

'These houses don't have ghosts – they've never had any personality, and only a place with personality can have a ghost,' said Gudrun.

'I suppose so. Are you both weeping over the past?'

'We are,' said Gudrun, grimly.

Ursula laughed.

'Not weeping that it's gone, but weeping that it ever *was*,' she said.

'Oh,' he replied, relieved.

He sat down for a moment. There was something in his presence, Ursula thought, lambent and alive. It made even the impertinent structure of this null house disappear.

'Gudrun says she could not bear to be married and put into a house,' said Ursula meaningful – they knew this referred to Gerald.

He was silent for some moments.

'Well,' he said, 'if you know beforehand you couldn't stand it, you're safe.'

'Quite!' said Gudrun.

'Why *does* every woman think her aim in life is to have a hubby and a little grey home in the west? Why is this the goal of life? Why should it be?' said Ursula.

'*Il faut avoir le respect de ses bêtises,*' said Birkin.

'But you needn't have the respect for the *bêtise* before you've committed it,' laughed Ursula.

'Ah then, *des bêtises du papa?*'

'*Et de la maman,*' added Gudrun satirically.

'*Et des voisins,*' said Ursula.

They all laughed, and rose. It was getting dark. They carried the things to the car. Gudrun locked the door of the empty house. Birkin had lighted the lamps of the automobile. It all seemed very happy, as if they were setting out.

'Do you mind stopping at Coulsons. I have to leave the key there,' said Gudrun.

'Right,' said Birkin, and they moved off.

They stopped in the main street. The shops were just lighted, the last miners were passing home along the causeways, half-visible shadows in their grey pit-dirt, moving through the blue air. But their feet rang harshly in manifold sound, along the pavement.

How pleased Gudrun was to come out of the shop, and enter the car, and be borne swiftly away into the down-hill of palpable dusk, with Ursula and Birkin! What an adventure life seemed at this moment! How deeply, how suddenly she envied Ursula! Life for her was so quick, and an open door – so reckless as if not only this world, but the world that was gone and the world to come were nothing to her. Ah, if she could be *just like that*, it would be perfect.

For always, except in her moments of excitement, she felt a want within herself. She was unsure. She had felt that now, at last, in Gerald's strong and violent love, she was living fully and finally. But when she compared herself with Ursula, already her soul was jealous, unsatisfied. She was not satisfied – she was never to be satisfied.

What was she short of now? It was marriage – it was the wonderful stability of marriage. She did not want it, let her say what she might. She had been lying. The old idea of marriage was right even now – marriage and the home. Yet her mouth gave a little grimace at the words. She thought of Gerald and Shortlands – marriage and the home! Ah well, let it rest! He meant a great deal to her – but –! Perhaps it was not in her to marry. She was one of life's outcasts, one of the drifting lives that have no root. No, no – it could not be so. She suddenly conjured up a rosy room, with herself in a beautiful gown, and a handsome man in evening dress who held her in his arms in the firelight, and kissed her. This picture she entitled 'Home'. It would have done for the Royal Academy.

'Come with us to tea – *do*,' said Ursula, as they ran nearer to the cottage of Willey Green.

'Thanks awfully – but I *must* go in –' said Gudrun. She wanted very much to go on with Ursula and Birkin. That seemed like life indeed to her. Yet a certain perversity would not let her.

'Do come – yes, it would be so nice,' pleaded Ursula.

'I'm awfully sorry – I should love to – but I can't – really –'

She descended from the car in trembling haste.

'Can't you really!' came Ursula's regretful voice.

'No, really I can't,' responded Gudrun's pathetic, chagrined words out of the dusk.

'All right, are you?' called Birkin.

'Quite!' said Gudrun. 'Good night!'

'Good night,' they called.

'Come whenever you like, we shall be glad,' called Birkin.

'Thank you very much,' called Gudrun, in the strange, twanging voice of lonely chagrin that was very puzzling to him. She turned away to her cottage gate, and they drove on. But immediately she stood to watch them, as the car ran vague into the distance. And as she went up the path to her strange house, her heart was full of incomprehensible bitterness.

In her parlour was a long-case clock, and inserted into its dial was a ruddy, round, slant-eyed, joyous-painted face, that wagged over with the most ridiculous ogle when the clock ticked, and back again with the same absurd glad-eye at the next tick. All the time the absurd smooth, brown-ruddy face gave her an obtrusive 'glad-eye'. She stood for minutes, watching it, till a sort of maddened disgust overcame her, and she laughed at herself hollowly. And still it rocked, and gave her the glad-eye from one side, then from the other, from one side, then from the other. Ah, how unhappy she was! In the midst of her most active happiness, ah, how unhappy she was. She glanced at the table.

Gooseberry jam, and the same home-made cake with too much soda in it! Still, gooseberry jam was good, and one so rarely got it.

All the evening she wanted to go to the Mill. But she coldly refused to allow herself. She went the next afternoon instead. She was happy to find Ursula alone. It was a lovely, intimate secluded atmosphere. They talked endlessly and delightedly. 'Aren't you *fearfully* happy here?' said Gudrun to her sister glancing at her own bright eyes in the mirror. She always envied, almost with resentment, the strange positive fullness that subsisted in the atmosphere around Ursula and Birkin.

'How really beautifully this room is done,' she said aloud. 'This hard plaited matting – what a lovely colour it is, the colour of cool light!'

And it seemed to her perfect.

'Ursula,' she said at length, in a voice of question and detachment, 'did you know that Gerald Crich had suggested our going away all together at Christmas?'

'Yes, he's spoken to Rupert.'

A deep flush dyed Gudrun's cheek. She was silent a moment, as if taken aback, and not knowing what to say.

'But don't you think,' she said at last, 'it is *amazingly cool*!'

Ursula laughed.

'I like him for it,' she said.

Gudrun was silent. It was evident that, whilst she was almost mortified by Gerald's taking the liberty of making such a suggestion to Birkin, yet the idea itself attracted her strongly.

'There's a rather lovely simplicity about Gerald, I think,' said Ursula, 'so defiant, somehow! Oh, I think he's *very* lovable.'

Gudrun did not reply for some moments. She had still to get over the feeling of insult at the liberty taken with her freedom.

'What did Rupert say – do you know?' she asked.

'He said it would be most awfully jolly,' said Ursula.

Again Gudrun looked down, and was silent.

'Don't you think it would?' said Ursula, tentatively. She was never quite sure how many defences Gudrun was having round herself.

Gudrun raised her face with difficulty and held it averted.

'I think it *might* be awfully jolly, as you say,' she replied. 'But don't you think it was an unpardonable liberty to take – to talk of such things to Rupert – who after all – you see what I mean, Ursula – they might have been two men arranging an outing with some little *type* they'd picked up. Oh, I think it's unforgivable, quite!' She used the French word *'type'*.

Her eyes flashed, her soft face was flushed and sullen. Ursula looked on, rather frightened, frightened most of all because she thought Gudrun seemed rather common, really like a little *type*. But she had not the courage quite to think this – not right out.

'Oh no,' she cried, stammering. 'Oh no – not at all like that – oh no! No, I think it's rather beautiful, the friendship between Rupert and Gerald. They just are simple – they say anything to each other, like brothers.'

Gudrun flushed deeper. She could not *bear* it that Gerald gave her away – even to Birkin.

'But do you think even brothers have any right to exchange confidences of that sort?' she asked, with deep anger.

'Oh yes,' said Ursula. 'There's never anything said that isn't perfectly straightforward. No, the thing that's amazed me most in Gerald – how perfectly simple and direct he can be! And you know, it takes rather a big man. Most of them *must* be indirect, they are such cowards.'

But Gudrun was still silent with anger. She wanted the absolute secrecy kept, with regard to her movements.

'Won't you go?' said Ursula. 'Do, we might all be so happy! There is something I *love* about Gerald – he's *much* more lovable than I thought him. He's free, Gudrun, he really is.'

Gudrun's mouth was still closed, sullen and ugly. She opened it at length.

'Do you know where he proposes to go?' she asked.

'Yes – to the Tyrol, where he used to go when he was in Germany – a lovely place where students go, small and rough and lovely, for winter sport!'

Through Gudrun's mind went the angry thought – 'they know everything.'

'Yes,' she said aloud, 'about forty kilometres from Innsbruck, isn't it?'

'I don't know exactly where – but it would be lovely, don't you think, high in the perfect snow –?'

'Very lovely!' said Gudrun, sarcastically.

Ursula was put out.

'Of course,' she said, 'I think Gerald spoke to Rupert so that it shouldn't seem like an outing with a *type* –'

'I know, of course,' said Gudrun, 'that he quite commonly does take up with that sort.'

'Does he!' said Ursula. 'Why how do you know?'

'I know of a model in Chelsea,' said Gudrun coldly.

Now Ursula was silent.

'Well,' she said at last, with a doubtful laugh, 'I hope he has a good time with her.' At which Gudrun looked more glum.

28

GUDRUN IN THE POMPADOUR

Christmas drew near, all four prepared for flight. Birkin and Ursula were busy packing their few personal things, making them ready to be sent off, to whatever country and whatever place they might choose at last. Gudrun was very much excited. She loved to be on the wing.

She and Gerald, being ready first, set off via London and Paris to Innsbruck, where they would meet Ursula and Birkin. In London they stayed one night. They went to the music-hall, and afterwards to the Pompadour Café.

Gudrun hated the Café, yet she always went back to it, as did most of the artists of her acquaintance. She loathed its atmosphere of petty vice and petty jealousy and petty art. Yet she always called in again, when she was in town. It was, as if she *had* to return to this small, slow central whirlpool of disintegration and dissolution: just give it a look.

She sat with Gerald drinking some sweetish liqueur, and staring with black, sullen looks at the various groups of people at the tables. She would greet nobody, but young men nodded to her frequently, with a kind of sneering familiarity. She cut them all. And it gave her pleasure to sit there, cheeks flushed, eyes black and sullen, seeing them all objectively, as put away from her, like creatures in some menagerie of apish degraded souls. God, what a foul crew they were! Her blood beat black and thick in her veins with rage and loathing. Yet she must sit and watch, watch. One or two people came to speak to her. From every side of the Café, eyes turned half furtively, half jeeringly at her, men looking over their shoulders, women under their hats.

The old crowd was there, Carlyon in his corner with his pupils and his girl, Halliday and Libidnikov and the Pussum – they were all there. Gudrun watched Gerald. She watched his eyes linger a moment on Halliday, on Halliday's party. These last were on the look-out – they nodded to him, he nodded again. They giggled and whispered among themselves. Gerald watched them with the steady twinkle in his eyes. They were urging Minette to something.

She at last rose. She was wearing a curious dress of dark silk with long pale rays, a curious rayed effect. She was thinner, her eyes were perhaps wider, more disintegrated. Otherwise she was just the same. Gerald watched her with the same steady twinkle in his eyes as she came across. She held out her thin fair hand to him.

'How are you?' she said.

He shook hands with her, but remained seated, and let her stand near him, against the table. She nodded coldly to Gudrun, whom she did not know to speak to, but well enough by sight and reputation.

'I am very well,' said Gerald. 'And you?'

'Oh I'm all wight. What about Wupert?'

'Rupert? He's very well, too.'

'Yes, I don't mean that. What about him being married?'

'Oh – yes, he is married.'

Minette's eyes had a hot flash.

'Oh, he's weally bwought it off then, has he? When was he married?'

'A week or two ago.'

'Weally! He's never written.'

'No.'

'No. Don't you think it's too bad?'

This last was in a tone of challenge. Minette let it be known by her tone, that she was aware of Gudrun's listening.

'I suppose he didn't feel like it,' replied Gerald.

'But why didn't he?' pursued Minette.

This was received in silence. There was an ugly, mocking persistence in the small, beautiful figure of the short-haired girl, as she stood near Gerald.

'Are you staying in town long?' she asked.

'Tonight only.'

'Oh, only tonight. Are you coming over to speak to Julius?'

'Not tonight.'

'Oh very well. I'll tell him then.' Then came her touch of diablerie. 'You're looking awf'lly fit.'

'Yes – I feel it.' Gerald was quite calm and easy, a spark of satiric amusement in his eye.

'Are you having a good time?'

This was a direct blow for Gudrun, spoken in a level, toneless voice of callous ease.

'Yes,' he replied, quite colourlessly.

'I'm awf'lly sorry you aren't coming round. You aren't very faithful to your fwiends.'

'Not very,' he said.

She nodded them both 'Good night', and went back slowly to her own set. Gudrun watched her curious walk, stiff and jerking at the loins. They heard her level, toneless voice distinctly.

'He won't come over; – he is otherwise engaged,' it said. There was more laughter and lowered voices and mockery at the table.

'Is she a friend of yours?' said Gudrun, looking calmly at Gerald.

'I've stayed at Halliday's with Birkin,' he said, meeting her slow, calm eyes. And she knew that Minette was one of his mistresses – and he knew she knew.

She looked round, and called for the waiter. She wanted an iced cocktail, of all things. This amused Gerald – he wondered what was up.

The Halliday party was tipsy, and malicious. They were talking out loudly about Birkin, ridiculing him on every point, particularly on his marriage.

'Oh, *don't* make me think of Birkin,' Halliday was squealing. 'He makes me perfectly sick. He is as bad as Jesus. "Lord, *what* must I do to be saved!"'

He giggled to himself tipsily.

'Do you remember,' came the quick voice of the Russian, 'the letters he used to send. "Desire is holy –"'

'Oh yes!' cried Halliday. 'Oh, how perfectly splendid. Why, I've got one in my pocket. I'm sure I have.'

He took out various papers from his pocket book.

'I'm sure I've – *hic! Oh dear!* – got one.'

Gerald and Gudrun were watching absorbedly.

'Oh yes, how perfectly – *hic!* – splendid! Don't make me laugh, Minette, it gives me the hiccup. Hic! –' They all giggled.

'What did he say in that one?' Minette asked, leaning forward, her close fair hair falling and swinging against her face. There was something curiously indecent about her small, longish, fair skull, particularly when the ears showed.

'Wait – oh, do wait! *No-o*, I won't give it to you, I'll read it aloud. I'll read you the choice bits – hic! Oh dear! Do you think if I drink water it would take off this hiccup? *Hic!* Oh, I feel perfectly helpless.'

'Isn't that the letter about uniting the dark and the light – and the Flux of Corruption?' asked Maxim, in his precise, quick voice.

'I believe so,' said Minette.

'Oh, is it? I'd forgotten – *hic!* – it was that one,' Halliday said, opening the letter. '*Hic!* Oh yes. How perfectly splendid! This is one of the best. "There is a phrase in every race –"' he read in the sing-song, slow, distinct voice of a clergyman reading the Scriptures, '"when the desire for destruction overcomes every other desire. In the individual, this desire is ultimately a desire for destruction in the self" – *hic!* –' he paused and looked up.

'I hope he's going ahead with the destruction of himself,' said the quick voice of the Russian. Halliday giggled, and lolled his head back, vaguely.

'There's not much to destroy in him,' said Minette. 'He's so thin already, there's only a fag-end to start on.'

'Oh, isn't it beautiful! I love reading it! I believe it has cured my hiccup!' squealed Halliday. 'Do let me go on. "It is a desire for the reduction-process in oneself, a reducing back to the origin, a return along the Flux of Corruption, to the original rudimentary conditions of being – !" Oh, but I *do* think it is wonderful. It almost supersedes the Bible –'

'Yes – Flux of Corruption,' said the Russian, 'I remember that phrase.'

'Oh, he was always talking about Corruption,' said Minette. 'He must be corrupt himself, to have it so much on his mind.'

'Exactly!' said the Russian.

'Do let me go on! Oh, this is a perfectly wonderful piece! But do listen to this. "And in the great retrogression, the reducing back of the created body of life, we get knowledge, and beyond knowledge, the phosphorescent ecstasy of acute sensation.' Oh, I do think these phrases are too absurdly wonderful. Oh, but don't you think they *are* – they're nearly as good as Jesus. "And if, Julius, you want this ecstasy of reduction with Minette, you must go on till it is fulfilled. But surely there is in you also, somewhere, the living desire for positive creation, relationships in ultimate faith, when all this process of active corruption, with all its flowers of mud, is transcended, and more or less finished –" I do wonder what the flowers of mud are. Minette, you are a flower of mud.'

'Thank you – and what are you?'

'Oh, I'm another, surely, according to this letter! We're all flowers of mud – *Fleurs – hic! du mal!* It's perfectly wonderful, Birkin harrowing Hell – harrowing the Pompadour – *Hic!*'

'Go on – go on,' said Maxim. 'What comes next? It's really very interesting.'

'I think it's awful cheek to write like that,' said Minette.

'Yes – yes, so do I,' said the Russian. 'He is a megalomaniac, of course, it is a form of religious mania. He thinks he is the Saviour of man – go on reading.'

'Surely,' Halliday intoned, ' "surely goodness and mercy hath followed me all the days of my life –" ' he broke off and giggled. Then he began again, intoning like a clergyman. ' "Surely there will come an end in us to this desire – for the constant going apart – this passion for putting asunder – everything – ourselves, reducing ourselves part from part – reacting in intimacy only for destruction – using sex as a great reducing agent, reducing the two great elements of male and female from their highly complex unity – reducing the old ideas, going back to the savages for our sensations – always seeking to *lose* ourselves in some ultimate black sensation, mindless and infinite – burning only with destructive fires, ranging on with the hope of being burnt out utterly –" '

'I want to go,' said Gudrun to Gerald, as she signalled the waiter. Her eyes were flashing, her cheeks were flushed. The strange effect of Birkin's letter read aloud in a perfect clerical sing-song, clear and resonant, phrase by phrase, made the blood mount into her head as if she were mad.

She rose, whilst Gerald was paying the bill, and walked over to Halliday's table. They all glanced up at her.

'Excuse me,' she said. 'Is that a genuine letter you are reading?'

'Oh yes,' said Halliday. 'Quite genuine.'

'May I see?'

Smiling foolishly he handed it to her, as if hypnotized.

'Thank you,' she said.

And she turned and walked out of the Café with the letter, all down the brilliant room, between the tables, in her measured fashion. It was some moments before anybody realized what was happening.

From Halliday's table came half articulate cries, then somebody booed, then all the far end of the place began booing after Gudrun's retreating form. She was fashionably dressed in blackish-green and silver, her hat was brilliant green, like the sheen on an insect, but the brim was soft dark green, a falling edge with fine silver, her coat was dark green, lustrous, with a high collar of grey fur, and great fur cuffs, the edge of her dress showed silver and black velvet, her stockings and shoes were silver grey. She moved with slow, fashionable indifference to the door. The porter opened obsequiously for her, and at her nod, hurried to the edge of the pavement and whistled for a taxi. The two lights of a vehicle almost immediately curved round towards her, like two eyes.

Gerald had followed in wonder, amid all the booing, not having caught her misdeed. He heard Minette's voice saying:

'Go and get it back from her. I never heard of such a thing! Go and get it back from her. Tell Gerald Crich – there he goes – go and make him give it up.'

Gudrun stood at the door of the taxi, which the man held open for her.

'To the hotel?' she asked, as Gerald came out, hurriedly.

'Where you like,' he answered.

'Right!' she said. Then to the driver, 'Wagstaff's – Barton Street.'

The driver bowed his head, and put down the flag.

Gudrun entered the taxi, with the deliberate cold movement of a woman who is well-dressed and contemptuous in her soul. Yet she was frozen with overwrought feelings. Gerald followed her.

'You've forgotten the man,' she said coolly, with a slight nod of her hat. Gerald gave the porter a shilling. The man saluted. They were in motion.

'What was all the row about?' asked Gerald, in wondering excitement.

'I walked away with Birkin's letter,' she said, and he saw the crushed paper in her hand.

His eyes glittered with satisfaction.

'Ah!' he said. 'Splendid! A set of jackasses!'

'I could have *killed* them!' she cried in passion. '*Dogs!* – they are dogs! Why is Rupert such a *fool* as to write such letters to them? Why does he give himself away to such canaille? It's a thing that *cannot be borne.*'

Gerald wondered over her strange passion.

And she could not rest any longer in London. They must go by the morning train from Charing Cross. As they drew over the bridge, in the train, having glimpses of the river between the great iron girders, she cried:

'I feel I could *never* see this foul town again – I couldn't *bear* to come back to it.'

29

CONTINENTAL

Ursula went on in an unreal suspense, the last weeks before going away. She was not herself – she was not anything. She was something that is going to be – soon – soon – very soon. But as yet, she was only imminent.

She went to see her parents. It was a rather stiff, sad meeting, more like a verification of separateness than a reunion. But they were all vague and indefinite with one another, stiffened in the fate that moved them apart.

She did not really come to until she was on the ship crossing from Dover to Ostend. Dimly she had come down to London with Birkin, London had been a vagueness, so had the train journey to Dover. It was all like a sleep.

And now, at last, as she stood in the stern of the ship, in a pitch-dark, rather blowy night, feeling the motion of the sea, and watching the small, rather desolate little lights that twinkled on the shores of England, as on the shores of nowhere, watched them sinking smaller and smaller on the profound and living darkness, she felt her soul stirring to awake from its anaesthetic sleep.

'Let us go forward, shall we?' said Birkin. He wanted to be at the tip of their projection. So they left off looking at the faint sparks that glimmered out of nowhere, in the far distance, called England, and turned their faces to the unfathomed night in front.

They went right to the bows of the softly plunging vessel. In the complete obscurity, Birkin found a comparatively sheltered nook, where a great rope was coiled up. It was quite near the very point of the ship, near the black, unpierced space ahead. Here they sat down, folded together, folded round with the same rug, creeping in nearer and ever nearer to one another, till it seemed they had crept right into each other, and become one substance. It was very cold, and the darkness was palpable.

One of the ship's crew came along the deck, dark as the darkness, not really visible. They then made out the faintest pallor of his face. He felt their presence, and stopped, unsure – then bent forward. When his face was near them, he saw the faint pallor of their faces. Then he withdrew like a phantom. And they watched him without making any sound.

They seemed to fall away into the profound darkness. There was no sky, no earth, only one unbroken darkness, into which, with a soft, sleeping motion, they seemed to fall like one closed seed of life falling through dark, fathomless space.

They had forgotten where they were, forgotten all that was and all that had been, conscious only in their hearts, and there conscious only of this pure trajectory through the surpassing darkness. The ship's prow cleaved on, with a faint noise of cleavage, into the complete night, without knowing, without seeing, only surging on.

In Ursula the sense of the unrealized world ahead triumphed over everything. In the midst of this profound darkness, there seemed to glow on her heart the effulgence of a paradise unknown and unrealized. Her heart was full of the most wonderful light, golden like honey of darkness, sweet like the warmth of day, a light which was not shed on the world, only on the unknown paradise towards which she was going, a sweetness of habitation, a delight of living quite unknown, but hers infallibly. In her transport she lifted her face suddenly to him, and he touched it with his lips. So cold, so fresh, so sea-clear her face was, it was like kissing a flower that grows near the surf.

But he did not know the ecstasy of bliss in fore-knowledge that she knew. To him, the wonder of this transit was overwhelming. He was falling through a gulf of infinite darkness, like a meteorite plunging across the chasm between the worlds. The world was torn in two, and he was plunging like an unlit star through the ineffable rift. What was beyond was not yet for him. He was overcome by the trajectory.

In a trance he lay enfolding Ursula round about. His face was against her fine, fragile hair, he breathed its fragrance with the sea and the profound night. And his soul was at peace; yielded, as he fell into the unknown. This was the first time that an utter and absolute peace had entered his heart, now, in this final transit out of life.

When there came some stir on the deck, they roused. They stood up. How stiff and cramped they were in the night-time! And yet the paradisal glow on her heart, and the unutterable peace of darkness in his, this was the all-in-all.

They stood up and looked ahead. Low lights were seen down the darkness. This was the world again. It was not the bliss of her heart, nor the peace of his. It was the superficial unreal world of fact. Yet not quite the old world. For the peace and the bliss in their hearts was enduring.

Strange and desolate above all things, like disembarking from the Styx into the desolated underworld, was this landing at night. There was the raw, half-lighted, covered-in vastness of the dark place, boarded and hollow underfoot, with only desolation everywhere. Ursula had caught sight of the big, pallid, mystic letters 'OSTEND' standing in the darkness. Everybody was hurrying with a blind, insect-like intentness through the dark grey air, porters were calling in un-English English, then trotting with heavy bags, their colourless blouses looking ghostly as they disappeared; Ursula stood at a long, low, zinc-covered barrier along with hundreds of other spectral people, and all the way down the vast, raw darkness was this low stretch of open bags and spectral people, whilst, on the other side of the barrier, pallid officials in peaked caps and moustaches were turning the underclothing in the bags, then scrawling a chalk-mark.

It was done. Birkin snapped the hand-bags, off they went, the porter coming behind. They were through a great doorway, and in the open night again – ah, a railway platform! Voices were still calling in inhuman agitation through the dark-grey air, spectres were running along the darkness between the train.

'Köln – Berlin –' Ursula made out on the boards hung on the high train on one side.

'Here we are,' said Birkin. And on her side she saw: 'Elsass – Lothringen – Luxembourg, Metz – Basle.'

'That was it, Basle!'

The porter came up.

'*A Bâle – deuxième classe? – Voilà!*' And he clambered into the high train. They followed. The compartments were already some of them taken. But many were dim and empty. The luggage was stowed, the porter was tipped.

'*Nous avons encore – ?*' said Birkin, looking at his watch and at the porter.

'Encore une demi-heure.' With which, in his blue blouse, he disappeared. He was ugly and insolent.

'Come,' said Birkin. 'It is cold. Let us eat.'

There was a coffee-wagon on the platform. They drank hot, watery coffee and ate the long rolls, split, with ham between, which were such a wide bite that it almost dislocated Ursula's jaw; and they walked beside the high trains. It was all so strange, so extremely desolate, like the underworld, grey, grey, dirt grey, desolate, forlorn, nowhere – grey, dreary nowhere.

At last they were moving through the night. In the darkness Ursula made out the flat fields, the wet, flat, dreary darkness of the Continent. They pulled up surprisingly soon – Bruges! Then on through the level darkness, with glimpses of sleeping farms and thin poplar trees and deserted high-roads. She sat dismayed, hand in hand with Birkin. He pale, immobile like a *revenant* himself, looked sometimes out of the window, sometimes closed his eyes. Then his eyes opened again, dark as the darkness outside.

A flash of a few lights on the darkness – Ghent station! A few more spectres moving outside on the platform – then the bell – then motion again through the level darkness. Ursula saw a man with a lantern come out of a farm by the railway and cross to the dark farm-buildings. She thought of the Marsh, the old, intimate farm life at Cossethay. My God, how far was she projected from her childhood, how far was she still to go! In one lifetime one travelled through aeons. The great chasm of memory from her childhood in the intimate country surroundings of Cossethay and the Marsh Farm – she remembered the servant Tilly, who used to give her bread and butter sprinkled with brown sugar in the old living-room where the grandfather clock had two pink roses in a basket painted above the figures on the face – and now when she was travelling into the unknown with Birkin, an utter stranger – was so great, that it seemed she had no identity, that the child she had been, playing in Cossethay churchyard, was a little creature of history, not really herself.

They were at Brussels – half an hour for breakfast. They got down. On the great station clock it said six o'clock. They had coffee and rolls and honey in the vast desert refreshment-room, so dreary, always so dreary, dirty, so spacious, such desolation of space. But she washed her face and hands in hot water and combed her hair – that was a blessing.

Soon they were in the train again and moving on. The greyness of dawn began. There were several people in the compartment, large florid Belgian business-men with long brown beards, talking incessantly in an ugly French she was too tired to follow.

It seemed the train ran by degrees out of the darkness into a faint light, then beat after beat into the day. Ah, how weary it was! Faintly, the trees showed, like shadows. Then a house, white, had a curious distinctness. How was it? Then she saw a village – there were always houses passing.

This was an old world she was still journeying through, winter-heavy and dreary. There was plough-land and pasture, and copses of bare trees, copses of bushes, and homesteads naked and work-bare. No new earth had come to pass.

She looked at Birkin's face. It was white and still and eternal, too eternal. She linked her fingers imploringly in his under the cover of her rug. His fingers responded, his eyes looked back at her. How dark, like a night, his eyes were, like another world beyond! Oh, if he were the world as well, if only the world were he! If only he could call a world into being, that should be their own world!

The Belgians left, the train ran on, through Luxembourg, through Alsace-Lorraine, through Metz. But she was blind, she could see no more. Her soul did not look out.

They came at last to Basle, to the hotel. It was all a drifting trance, from which she never came to. They went out in the morning before the train departed. She saw the street, the river, she stood on the bridge. But it all meant nothing. She remembered some shops – one full of pictures, one with orange velvet and ermine. But what did these signify? – nothing.

She was not at ease till they were in the train again. Then she was relieved. So long as they were moving onwards, she was satisfied. They came to Zürich, then, before very long, ran under the mountains that were deep in snow. At last she was drawing near. This was the other world now.

Innsbruck was wonderful, deep in snow, and evening. They drove in an open sledge over the snow: the train had been so hot and stifling. And the hotel, with the golden light glowing under the porch, seemed like a home.

They laughed with pleasure when they were in the hall. The place seemed full and busy.

'Do you know if Mr and Mrs Crich – English – from Paris, have arrived?' Birkin asked in German.

The porter reflected a moment, and was just going to answer when Ursula caught sight of Gudrun sauntering down the stairs, wearing her dark glossy coat with grey fur.

'Gudrun! Gudrun!' she called, waving up the well of the staircase. 'Shu-hu!'

Gudrun looked over the rail, and immediately lost her sauntering, diffident air. Her eyes flashed.

'Really – Ursula!' she cried. And she began to move downstairs as Ursula ran up. They met at a turn and kissed with laughter and exclamations inarticulate and stirring.

'But!' cried Gudrun, mortified. 'We thought it was *tomorrow* you were coming! I wanted to come to the station.'

'No, we've come today!' cried Ursula. 'Isn't it lovely here!'

'Adorable!' said Gudrun. 'Gerald's just gone out to get something. Ursula, aren't you *fearfully* tired?'

'No, not so very. But I look a filthy sight, don't I?'

'No, you don't. You look almost perfectly fresh. I like that fur cap *immensely!*' She glanced over Ursula, who wore a big soft coat with a collar of deep, soft, blond fur and a soft blond cap of fur.

'And you!' cried Ursula. 'What do you think *you* look like!'

Gudrun assumed an unconcerned, expressionless face.

'Do you like it?' she said.

'It's *very* fine!' cried Ursula, perhaps with a touch of satire.

'Go up – or come down,' said Birkin. For there the sisters stood, Gudrun with her hand on Ursula's arm, on the turn of the stairs halfway to the first landing, blocking the way, and affording full entertainment to the whole of the hall below, from the door porter to the plump Jew in black clothes.

The two young women slowly mounted, followed by Birkin and the waiter.

'First floor?' asked Gudrun, looking back over her shoulder.

'Second, Madam – the lift!' the waiter replied. And he darted to the elevator to forestall the two women. But they ignored him, as, chattering without

heed, they set to mount the second flight. Rather chagrined, the waiter
followed.

It was curious, the delight of the sisters in each other, at this meeting. It was
as if they met in exile and united their solitary forces against all the world.
Birkin looked on with some mistrust and wonder.

When they had bathed and changed, Gerald came in. He looked shining
like the sun on frost.

'Go with Gerald and smoke,' said Ursula to Birkin. 'Gudrun and I want to
talk.'

Then the sisters sat in Gudrun's bedroom and talked clothes and experiences. Gudrun told Ursula the experience of the Birkin letter in the café.
Ursula was shocked and frightened.

'Where is the letter?' she asked.

'I kept it,' said Gudrun.

'You'll give it me, won't you?' she said.

But Gudrun was silent for some moments before she replied:

'Do you really want it, Ursula?'

'I want to read it,' said Ursula.

'Certainly,' said Gudrun.

Even now she could not admit, to Ursula, that she wanted to keep it as a
memento or a symbol. But Ursula knew, and was not pleased. So the subject
was switched off.

'What did you do in Paris?' asked Ursula.

'Oh,' said Gudrun laconically – 'the usual things. We had a *fine* party one
night in Fanny Bath's studio.'

'Did you? And you and Gerald were there! Who else? Tell me about it.'

'Well,' said Gudrun. 'There's nothing particular to tell. You know Fanny is
frightfully in love with that painter, Billy Macfarlane. He was there – so
Fanny spared nothing, she spent *very* freely. It was really remarkable! Of
course, everybody got fearfully drunk – but in an interesting way, not like that
filthy London crowd. The fact is these were all people that matter, which
makes all the difference. There was a Roumanian, a fine chap. He got
completely drunk, and climbed to the top of a high studio ladder, and gave
the most marvellous address – really, Ursula, it was wonderful! He began in
French – *La vie, c'est une affaire d'âmes impériales* – in a most beautiful voice
– he was a fine-looking chap – but he had got into Roumanian before he had
finished, and not a soul understood. But Donald Gilchrist was worked to a
frenzy. He dashed his glass to the ground and declared, by God, he was glad
he had been born, by God, it was a miracle to be alive. And do you know,
Ursula, so it was –' Gudrun laughed rather hollowly.

'But how was Gerald among them all?' asked Ursula.

'Gerald! Oh, my word, he came out like a dandelion in the sun! *He's* a
whole saturnalia in himself, once he is roused. I shouldn't like to say whose
waist his arm did not go round. Really, Ursula, he seems to reap the women
like a harvest. There wasn't one that would have resisted him. It was too
amazing! Can you understand it?'

Ursula reflected, and a dancing light came into her eyes.

'Yes,' she said. 'I can. He is such a whole-hogger.'

'Whole-hogger! I should think so!' exclaimed Gudrun. 'But it is true,
Ursula, every woman in the room was ready to surrender to him. Chanticleer
isn't in it – even Fanny Bath, who is *genuinely* in love with Billy Macfarlane! I

never was more amazed in my life! And you know, afterwards – I felt I was a whole *roomful* of women. I was no more myself to him than I was Queen Victoria. I was a whole roomful of women at once. It was most astounding! But my eye, I'd caught a Sultan that time –'

Gudrun's eyes were flashing, her cheek was hot, she looked strange, exotic, satiric. Ursula was fascinated at once – and yet uneasy.

They had to get ready for dinner. Gudrun came down in a daring gown of vivid green silk and tissue of gold, with green velvet bodice and a strange black-and-white band round her hair. She was really brilliantly beautiful and everybody noticed her. Gerald was in that full-blooded, gleaming state when he was most handsome. Birkin watched them with quick, laughing, half-sinister eyes, Ursula quite lost her head. There seemed a spell, almost a blinding spell, cast round their table, as if they were lighted up more strongly than the rest of the dining-room.

'Don't you love to be in this place?' cried Gudrun. 'Isn't the snow wonderful! Do you notice how it exalts everything? It is simply marvellous. One really does feel *übermenschlich* – more than human.'

'One does,' cried Ursula. 'But isn't that partly the being out of England?'

'Oh, of course,' cried Gudrun. 'One could never feel like this in England, for the simple reason that the damper is *never* lifted off one, there. It is quite impossible really to let go, in England, of that I am assured.'

And she turned again to the food she was eating. She was fluttering with vivid intensity.

'It's quite true,' said Gerald, 'it never is *quite* the same in England. But perhaps we don't want it to be – perhaps it's like bringing the light a little too near the powder-magazine, to let go altogether, in England. One is afraid what might happen, if *everybody else* let go.'

'My God!' cried Gudrun. 'But wouldn't it be wonderful if all England *did* suddenly go off like a display of fireworks.'

'It couldn't,' said Ursula. 'They are all too damp, the powder is damp in them.'

'I'm not so sure of that,' said Gerald.

'Nor I,' said Birkin. 'When the English really begin to go off, *en masse*, it'll be time to shut your ears and run.'

'They never will,' said Ursula.

'We'll see,' he replied.

'Isn't it marvellous,' said Gudrun, 'how thankful one can be, to be out of one's country. I cannot believe myself, I am so transported, the moment I set foot on a foreign shore. I say to myself: 'Here steps a new creature into life.'

'Don't be too hard on poor old England,' said Gerald. 'Though we curse it, we love it really.'

To Ursula there seemed a fund of cynicism in these words.

'We may,' said Birkin. 'But it's a damnably uncomfortable love: like a love for an aged parent who suffers horribly from a complication of diseases, for which there is no hope.'

Gudrun looked at him with dilated dark eyes.

'You think there is no hope?' she asked in her pertinent fashion.

But Birkin backed away. He would not answer such a question.

'Any hope of England's becoming real? God knows. It's a great actual unreality now, an aggregation into unreality. It might be real, if there were no Englishmen.'

'You think the English will have to disappear?' persisted Gudrun. It was strange, her pointed interest in his answer. It might have been her own fate she was inquiring after. Her dark, dilated eyes rested on Birkin, as if she could conjure the truth of the future out of him, as out of some instrument of divination.

He was pale. Then, reluctantly, he answered:

'Well – what else is in front of them but disappearance? They've got to disappear from their own special brand of Englishness, anyhow.'

Gudrun watched him as if in a hypnotic state, her eyes wide and fixed on him.

'But in what way do you mean, disappear? – ' she persisted.

'Yes, do you mean a change of heart?' put in Gerald.

'I don't mean anything, why should I?' said Birkin. 'I'm an Englishman, and I've paid the price of it. I can't talk about England – I can only speak for myself.'

'Yes,' said Gudrun slowly, 'you love England immensely, *immensely*, Rupert.'

'And leave her,' he replied.

'No, not for good. You'll come back,' said Gerald, nodding sagely.

'They say the lice crawl off a dying body,' said Birkin, with a glare of bitterness. 'So I leave England.'

'Ah, but you'll come back,' said Gudrun, with a sardonic smile.

'*Tant pis pour moi,*' he replied.

'Isn't he angry with his mother country!' laughed Gerald, amused.

'Ah, a patriot!' said Gudrun, with something like a sneer.

Birkin refused to answer any more.

Gudrun watched him still for a few seconds. Then she turned away. It was finished, her spell of divination in him. She felt already purely cynical. She looked at Gerald. He was wonderful like a piece of radium to her. She felt she could consume herself and know *all*, by means of this fatal, living metal. She smiled to herself at her fancy. And what would she do with herself when she had destroyed herself? For if spirit, if integral being is destructible, Matter is indestructible.

He was looking bright and abstracted, puzzled, for the moment. She stretched out her beautiful arm, with its fluff of green tulle, and touched his chin with her subtle, artist's fingers.

'What are they then?' she asked, with a strange, knowing smile.

'What?' he replied, his eyes suddenly dilating with wonder.

'Your thoughts.'

Gerald looked like a man coming awake.

'I think I had none,' he said.

'Really!' she said, with grave laughter in her voice.

And to Birkin it was as if she killed Gerald, with that touch.

'Ah, but,' cried Gudrun, 'let us drink to Britannia – let us drink to Britannia.'

It seemed there was wild despair in her voice. Gerald laughed and filled the glasses.

'I think Rupert means,' he said, 'that *nationally* all Englishmen must die, so that they can exist individually and –'

'Super-nationally –' put in Gudrun, with a slight ironic grimace, raising her glass.

The next day they descended at the tiny railway station of Hohenhausen at the end of the tiny valley railway. It was snow everywhere, a white, perfect cradle of snow, new and frozen, sweeping up on either side, black crags, and white sweeps of silver towards the blue pale heavens.

As they stepped out on the naked platform, with only snow around and above, Gudrun shrank as if it chilled her heart.

'My God, Jerry,' she said, turning to Gerald with sudden intimacy, 'you've done it now.'

'What?'

She made a faint gesture, indicating the world on either hand.

'Look at it!'

She seemed afraid to go on. He laughed.

They were in the heart of the mountains. From high above, on either side, swept down the white fold of snow, so that one seemed small and tiny in a valley of pure concrete heaven, all strangely radiant and changeless and silent.

'It makes one feel so small and alone,' said Ursula, turning to Birkin and laying her hand on his arm.

'You're not sorry you've come, are you?' said Gerald to Gudrun.

She looked doubtful. They went out of the station between banks of snow.

'Ah,' said Gerald, sniffing the air in elation, 'this is perfect. There's our sledge. We'll walk a bit – we'll run up the road.'

Gudrun, always doubtful, dropped her heavy coat on the sledge, as he did his, and they set off. Suddenly she threw up her head and set off scudding along the road of snow, pulling her cap down over her ears. Her blue, bright dress fluttered in the wind, her thick scarlet stockings were brilliant above the whiteness. Gerald watched her: she seemed to be rushing towards her fate, and leaving him behind. He let her get some distance, then, loosening his limbs, he went after her.

Everywhere was deep and silent snow. Great snow-eaves weighed down the broad-roofed Tyrolese houses that were sunk to the window-sashes in snow. Peasant women, full-skirted, wearing each a cross-over shawl and thick snow-boots, turned in the way to look at the soft, determined girl running with such heavy fleetness from the man who was overtaking her, but not gaining any power over her.

They passed the inn with its painted shutters and balcony, a few cottages, half buried in the snow; then the snow-buried silent saw-mill by the roofed bridge, which crossed the hidden stream, over which they ran into the very depth of the untouched sheets of snow. It was a silence and a sheer whiteness exhilarating to madness. But the perfect silence was most terrifying, isolating the soul, surrounding the heart with frozen air.

'It's a marvellous place, for all that,' said Gudrun, looking into his eyes with a strange, meaning look. His soul leapt.

'Good,' he said.

A fierce electric energy seemed to flow over all his limbs, his muscles were surcharged, his hands felt hard with strength. They walked along rapidly up the snow-road, that was marked by withered branches of trees stuck in at intervals. He and she were separate, like opposite poles of one fierce energy. But they felt powerful enough to leap over the confines of life into the forbidden places and back again.

Birkin and Ursula were running along also over the snow. He had disposed of the luggage, and they had a little start of the sledges. Ursula was excited and happy, but she kept turning suddenly to catch hold of Birkin's arm, to make sure of him.

'This is something I never expected,' she said. 'It is a different world, here.'

They went on into a snow meadow. There they were overtaken by the sledge that came tinkling through the silence. It was another mile before they came upon Gudrun and Gerald on the steep up-climb, beside the pink, half-buried shrine.

Then they passed into a gulley, where were walls of black rock and a river filled with snow, and a still blue sky above. Through a covered bridge they went, drumming roughly over the boards, crossing the snow-bed once more, then slowly up and up, the horses walking swiftly, the driver cracking his long whip as he walked beside, and calling his strange wild *hue-hue!*, the walls of rock passing slowly by till they emerged again between slopes and masses of snow. Up and up, gradually they went, through the cold shadow-radiance of the afternoon, silenced by the imminence of the mountains, the luminous, dazing sides of snow that rose above them and fell away beneath.

They came forth at last in a little high table-land of snow, where stood the last peaks of snow like the heart petals of an open rose. In the midst of the last deserted valleys of heaven stood a lonely building with brown wooden walls and white heavy roof, deep and deserted in the waste of snow, like a dream. It stood like a rock that had rolled down from the last steep slopes, a rock that had taken the form of a house, and was now half buried. It was unbelievable that one could live there uncrushed by all this terrible waste of whiteness and silence and clear, upper, ringing cold.

Yet the sledges ran up in fine style, people came to the door laughing and excited, the floor of the hostel rang hollow, the passage was wet with snow, it was a real, warm interior.

The newcomers tramped up the bare wooden stairs, following the serving woman. Gudrun and Gerald took the first bedroom. In a moment they found themselves alone in a bare, smallish, close-shut room that was all of golden-coloured wood, floor, walls, ceiling, door, all of the same warm gold panelling of oiled pine. There was a window opposite the door, but low down, because the roof sloped. Under the slope of the ceiling were the table with wash-hand-bowl and jug, and across, another table with mirror. On either side the door were two beds piled high with an enormous blue-checked overbolster, enormous.

This was all – no cupboard, none of the amenities of life. Here they were shut up together in this cell of golden-coloured wood, with two blue checked beds. They looked at each other and laughed, frightened by this naked nearness of isolation.

A man knocked and came in with the luggage. He was a sturdy fellow with flattish cheek-bones, rather pale, and with coarse fair moustache. Gudrun watched him put down the bags in silence, then tramp heavily out.

'It isn't too rough, is it?' Gerald asked.

The bedroom was not very warm, and she shivered slightly.

'It is wonderful,' she equivocated. 'Look at the colour of this panelling – it's wonderful, like being inside a nut.'

He was standing watching her, feeling his short-cut moustache, leaning back slightly and watching her with his keen, undaunted eyes, dominated by the constant passion, that was like a doom upon him.

She went and crouched down in front of the window, curious.

'Oh, but this – !' she cried involuntarily, almost in pain.

In front was a valley shut in under the sky, the last huge slopes of snow and black rock, and at the end, like the navel of the earth, a white-folded wall, and two peaks glimmering in the late light. Straight in front ran the cradle of silent snow, between the great slopes that were fringed with a little roughness of pine trees, like hair, round the base. But the cradle of snow ran on to the eternal closing-in, where the walls of snow and rock rose impenetrable, and the mountain peaks above were in heaven immediate. This was the centre, the knot, the navel of the world, where the earth belonged to the skies, pure, unapproachable, impassable.

It filled Gudrun with a strange rapture. She crouched in front of the window, clenching her face in her hands, in a sort of trance. At last she had arrived, she had reached her place. Here at last she folded her venture and settled down like a crystal in the navel of snow and was gone.

Gerald bent above her and was looking out over her shoulder. Already he felt he was alone. She was gone. She was completely gone, and there was icy vapour round his heart. He saw the blind valley, the great cul-de-sac of snow and mountain peaks under the heaven. And there was no way out. The terrible silence and cold and the glamorous whiteness of the dusk wrapped him round, and she remained crouching before the window, as at a shrine, a shadow.

'Do you like it?' he asked in a voice that sounded detached and foreign. At least she might acknowledge he was with her. But she only averted her soft, mute face a little from his gaze. And he knew that there were tears in her eyes, her own tear, tears of her strange religion, that put him to nought.

Quite suddenly, he put his hand under her chin and lifted up her face to him. Her dark blue eyes, in their wetness of tears, dilated as if she was startled in her very soul. They looked at him through their tears in terror and a little horror. His light blue eyes were keen, small-pupilled and unnatural in their vision. Her lips parted as she breathed with difficulty.

The passion came up in him, stroke after stroke, like the ringing of a bronze bell, so strong and unflawed and indomitable. His knees tightened to bronze as he hung above her soft face, whose lips parted and whose eyes dilated in a strange violation. In the grasp of his hand her chin was unutterably soft and silken. He felt strong as winter, his hands were living metal, invincible and not to be turned aside. His heart rang like a bell clanging inside him.

He took her up in his arms. She was soft and inert, motionless. All the while her eyes, in which the tears had not yet dried, were dilated as if in a kind of swoon of fascination and helplessness. He was super-humanly strong and unflawed, as if invested with supernatural force.

He lifted her close and folded her against him. Her softness, her inert, relaxed weight lay against his own surcharged, bronze-like limbs in a heaviness of desirability that would destroy him, if he were not fulfilled. She moved convulsively, recoiling away from him. His heart went up like a flame of ice, he closed over her like steel. He would destroy her rather than be denied.

But the overweening power of his body was too much for her. She relaxed again, and lay loose and soft, panting in a little delirium. And to him, she was so sweet, she was such bliss of release, that he would have suffered a whole eternity of torture rather than forgo one second of this pang of unsurpassable bliss.

'My God,' he said to her, his face drawn and strange, transfigured, 'what next?'

She lay perfectly still, with a still, child-like face and dark eyes, looking at him. She was lost, fallen right away.

'I shall always love you,' he said, looking at her.

But she did not hear. She lay, looking at him as at something she could never understand, never: as a child looks at a grown-up person, without hope of understanding, only submitting.

He kissed her, kissed her eyes shut, so that she could not look any more. He wanted something now, some recognition, some sign, some admission. But she only lay silent and child-like and remote, like a child that is overcome and cannot understand, only feels lost. He kissed her again, giving up.

'Shall we go down and have coffee and *Kuchen*?' he asked.

The twilight was falling slate-blue at the window. She closed her eyes, closed away the monotonous level of dead wonder, and opened them again to the everyday world.

'Yes,' she said briefly, regaining her will with a click. She went again to the window. Blue evening had fallen over the cradle of snow and over the great pallid slopes. But in the heaven the peaks of snow were rosy, glistening like transcendent, radiant spikes of blossom in the heavenly upper world, so lovely and beyond.

Gudrun saw all their loveliness, she *knew* how immortally beautiful they were, great pistils of rose-coloured, snow-fed fire in the blue twilight of the heaven. She could *see* it, she knew it, but she was not of it. She was divorced, debarred, a soul shut out.

With a last look of remorse, she turned away, and was doing her hair. He had unstrapped the luggage and was waiting, watching her. She knew he was watching her. It made her a little hasty and feverish in her precipitation.

They went downstairs, both with a strange other-world look on their faces, and with a glow in their eyes. They saw Birkin and Ursula sitting at the long table in a corner, waiting for them.

'How good and simple they look together,' Gudrun thought jealously. She envied them some spontaneity, a childish sufficiency to which she herself could never approach. They seemed such children to her.

'Such good *Kranzkuchen*!' cried Ursula greedily. 'So good!'

'Right,' said Gudrun. 'Can we have *Kaffee mit Kranzkuchen*?' she added to the waiter.

And she seated herself on the bench beside Gerald. Birkin, looking at them, felt a pain of tenderness for them.

'I think the place is really wonderful, Gerald,' he said; '*prachtvoll* and *wunderbar* and *wunderschön* and *unbeschreiblich* and all the other German adjectives.'

Gerald broke into a slight smile.

'*I* like it.' he said.

The tables, of white scrubbed wood, were placed round three sides of the room, as in a *Gasthaus*. Birkin and Ursula sat with their backs to the wall, which was of oiled wood, and Gerald and Gudrun sat in the corner next them, near to the stove. It was a fairly large place, with a tiny bar, just like a country inn, but quite simple and bare, and all of oiled wood, ceilings and walls and floor, the only furniture being the tables and benches going round three sides, the great green stove, and the bar and the doors on the fourth side. The windows were double, and quite uncurtained. It was early evening.

The coffee came – hot and good – and a whole ring of cake.

'A whole *Kuchen*!' cried Ursula. 'They give you more than us! I want some of yours.'

There were other people in the place, ten altogether, so Birkin had found out: two artists, three students, a man and wife, and a Professor and two daughters – all Germans. The four English people, being newcomers, sat in their coign of vantage to watch. The Germans peeped in at the door, called a word to the waiter, and went away again. It was not meal-time, so they did not come into this dining-room, but betook themselves, when their boots were changed, to the *Reunionsaal*.

The English visitors could hear the occasional twanging of a zither, the strumming of a piano, snatches of laughter and shouting and singing, a faint vibration of voices. The whole building being of wood, it seemed to carry every sound, like a drum, but instead of increasing each particular noise, it decreased it, so that the sound of the zither seemed tiny, as if a diminutive zither were playing somewhere, and it seemed the piano must be a small one, like a little spinet.

The host came when the coffee was finished. He was a Tyrolese, broad, rather flat-cheeked, with a pale, pock-marked skin and flourishing moustaches.

'Would you like to go to the *Reunionsaal* to be introduced to the other ladies and gentlemen?' he asked, bending forward and smiling, showing his large, strong teeth. His blue eyes went quickly from one to the other – he was not quite sure of his ground with these English people. He was unhappy too because he spoke no English and he was not sure whether to try his French.

'Shall we go to the *Reunionsaal*, and be introduced to the other people?' repeated Gerald, laughing.

There was a moment's hesitation.

'I suppose we'd better – better break the ice,' said Birkin.

The women rose, rather flushed. And the *Wirt's* black, beetle-like, broad-shouldered figure went on ignominiously in front, towards the noise. He opened the door and ushered the four strangers into the play-room.

Instantly a silence fell, a slight embarrassment came over the company. The newcomers had a sense of many blond faces looking their way. Then the host was bowing to a short, energetic-looking man with large moustaches, and saying in a low voice:

'*Herr Professor, darf ich vorstellen –*'

The Herr Professor was prompt and energetic. He bowed low to the English people, smiling, and began to be a comrade at once.

'*Nehmen die Herrschaften teil an unserer Unterhaltung?*' he said, with a vigorous suavity, his voice curling up in the question.

The four English people smiled, lounging with an attentive uneasiness in the middle of the room. Gerald, who was spokesman, said that they would willingly take part in the entertainment. Gudrun and Ursula, laughing, excited, felt the eyes of all the men upon them, and they lifted their heads and looked nowhere, and felt royal.

The Professor announced the names of those present, *sans cérémonie*. There was a bowing to the wrong people and to the right people. Everybody was there except the man and wife. The two tall, clear-skinned, athletic daughters of the professor, with their plain-cut, dark blue blouses and loden skirts, their rather long, strong necks, their clear blue eyes and carefully banded hair, and their blushes, bowed and stood back; the three students bowed very low, in the humble hope of making an impression of extreme good breeding; then there was a thin, dark-skinned man with full eyes, an odd creature, like a child, and like a troll, quick, detached; he bowed slightly; his companion, a large fair young man, stylishly dressed, blushed to the eyes and bowed very low.

It was over.

'Herr Loerke was giving us a recitation in the Cologne dialect,' said the Professor.

'He must forgive us for interrupting him,' said Gerald, 'we should like very much to hear it.'

There was instantly a bowing and an offering of seats. Gudrun and Ursula, Gerald and Birkin sat in the deep sofas against the wall. The room was of naked oiled panelling, like the rest of the house. It had a piano, sofas and chairs, and a couple of tables with books and magazines. In its complete absence of decoration, save for the big, blue stove, it was cosy and pleasant.

Herr Loerke was the little man with the boyish figure and the round, full, sensitive-looking head, and the quick, full eyes, like a mouse's. He glanced swiftly from one to the other of the strangers, and held himself aloof.

'Please go on with the recitation,' said the Professor suavely, with his slight authority. Loerke, who was sitting hunched on the piano-stool, blinked and did not answer.

'It would be a great pleasure,' said Ursula, who had been getting the sentence ready, in German, for some minutes.

Then, suddenly, the small, unresponding man swung aside, towards his previous audience and broke forth, exactly as he had broken off; in a controlled, mocking voice, giving an imitation of a quarrel between an old Cologne woman and a railway guard.

His body was slight and unformed, like a boy's, but his voice was mature, sardonic, its movement had the flexibility of essential energy, and of a mocking penetrating understanding. Gudrun could not understand a word of his monologue, but she was spell-bound watching him. He must be an artist, nobody else could have such fine adjustment and singleness. The Germans were doubled up with laughter, hearing his strange droll words, his droll phrases of dialect. And in the midst of their paroxysms, they glanced with deference at the four English strangers, the elect. Gudrun and Ursula were forced to laugh. The room rang with shouts of laughter. The blue eyes of the Professor's daughters were swimming over with laughter-tears, their clear cheeks were flushed crimson with mirth, their father broke out in the most astonishing peals of hilarity, the students bowed their heads on their knees in excess of joy. Ursula looked round amazed, the laughter was bubbling out of her involuntarily. She looked at Gudrun. Gudrun looked at her, and the two sisters burst out laughing, carried away. Loerke glanced at them swiftly, with his full eyes. Birkin was sniggering involuntarily. Gerald Crich sat erect, with a glistening look of amusement on his face. And the laughter crashed out again, in wild paroxysms, the Professor's daughters were reduced to shaking helplessness, the veins of the Professor's neck were swollen, his face was purple, he was strangled in ultimate, silent spasms of laughter. The students were shouting half-articulated words that tailed off in helpless explosions. Then suddenly the rapid patter of the artist ceased, there were little whoops of subsiding mirth, Ursula and Gudrun were wiping their eyes, and the Professor was crying loudly.

'*Das war ausgezeichnet, das war famos –*'

'*Wirklich famos,*' echoed his exhausted daughters, faintly.

'And we couldn't understand it,' cried Ursula.

'*Oh leider, leider!*' cried the Professor.

'You couldn't understand it?' cried the Students, let loose at last in speech with the newcomers. '*Ja, das ist wirklich schade, das ist schade, gnädige Frau. Wissen Sie –*'

The mixture was made, the newcomers were stirred into the party, like new ingredients, the whole room was alive. Gerald was in his element, he talked freely and excitedly, his face glistened with a strange amusement. Perhaps even Birkin, in the end, would break forth. He was shy and withheld, though full of attention.

Ursula was prevailed upon to sing 'Annie Lowrie', as the Professor called it. There was a hush of *extreme* deference. She had never been so flattered in her life. Gudrun accompanied her on the piano, playing from memory.

Ursula had a beautiful ringing voice, but usually no confidence, she spoiled everything. This evening she felt conceited and untrammelled. Birkin was well in the background, she shone almost in reaction, the Germans made her feel fine and infallible, she was liberated into overweening self-confidence. She felt like a bird flying in the air, as her voice soared out, enjoying herself extremely in the balance and flight of the song, like the motion of a bird's wings that is up in the wind, sliding and playing on the air, she played with sentimentality, supported by rapturous attention. She was very happy, singing that song by herself, full of a conceit of emotion and power, working upon all those people and upon herself, exerting herself with gratification, giving immeasurable gratification to the Germans.

At the end, the Germans were all touched with admiring, delicious melancholy, they praised her in soft, reverent voices, they could not say too much.

'*Wie schön, wie rührend! Ach, die Schottischen Lieder, sie haben so viel Stimmung! Aber die gnädige Frau hat eine* wunderbare *Stimme; die gnädige Frau ist wirklich eine Künstlerin, aber wirklich!*'

She was dilated and brilliant, like a flower in the morning sun. She felt Birkin looking at her, as if he were jealous of her, and her breasts thrilled, her veins were all golden. She was as happy as the sun that has just opened above clouds. And everybody seemed so admiring and radiant, it was perfect.

After dinner she wanted to go out for a minute, to look at the world. The company tried to dissuade her – it was so terribly cold. But just to look, she said.

They all four wrapped up warmly, and found themselves in a vague, unsubstantial outdoors of dim snow and ghosts of an upper-world, that made strange shadows before the stars. It was indeed cold, bruisingly, frighteningly, unnaturally cold Ursula could not believe the air in her nostrils. It seemed conscious, malevolent, purposive in its intense murderous coldness.

Yet it was wonderful, an intoxication, a silence of dim, unrealized snow, of the invisible intervening between her and the visible, between her and the flashing stars. She could see Orion sloping up. How wonderful he was, wonderful enough to make one cry aloud.

And all around was this cradle of snow, and there was firm snow underfoot, that struck with heavy cold through her bootsoles. It was night, and silence. She imagined she could hear the stars. She imagined distinctly she could hear the celestial, musical motion of the stars, quite near at hand. She seemed like a bird flying amongst their harmonious motion.

And she clung close to Birkin. Suddenly she realized she did not know what he was thinking. She did not know where he was ranging.

'My love!' she said, stopping to look at him.

His face was pale, his eyes dark, there was a faint spark of starlight on them. And he saw her face soft and upturned to him, very near. He kissed her softly.

'What then?' he asked.

'Do you love me?' she asked.

'Too much,' he answered quietly.

She clung a little closer.

'Not too much,' she pleaded.

'Far too much,' he said, almost sadly.

'And does it make you sad, that I am everything to you?' she asked, wistful. He held her close to him, kissing her, and saying, scarcely audible:

'No, but I feel like a beggar – I feel poor.'

She was silent, looking at the stars now. Then she kissed him.

'Don't be a beggar,' she pleaded, wistfully. 'It isn't ignominious that you love me.'

'It is ignominious to feel poor, isn't it?' he replied.

'Why? Why should it be?' she asked. He only stood still, in the terribly cold air that moved invisibly over the mountain-tops, folding her round with his arms.

'I couldn't bear this cold, eternal place without you,' he said. 'I couldn't bear it, it would kill the quick of my life.'

She kissed him again, suddenly.

'Do you hate it?' she asked, puzzled, wondering.

'If I couldn't come near to you, if you weren't here, I should hate it. I couldn't bear it,' he answered.

'But the people are nice,' she said.

'I mean the stillness, the cold, the frozen eternality,' he said.

She wondered. Then her spirit came home to him, nestling unconscious in him.

'Yes, it is good we are warm and together,' she said.

And they turned home again. They saw the golden lights of the hotel glowing out in the night of snow-silence, small in the hollow, like a cluster of yellow berries. It seemed like a bunch of sun-sparks, tiny and orange in the midst of the snow-darkness. Behind, was a high shadow of a peak, blotting out the stars, like a ghost.

They drew near to their home. They saw a man come from the dark building, with a lighted lantern which swung golden, and made that his dark feet walked in a halo of snow. He was a small, dark figure in the darkened snow. He unlatched the door of an outhouse. A smell of cows, hot, animal, almost like beef, came out on the heavily cold air. There was a glimpse of two cattle in their dark stalls, then the door was shut again, and not a chink of light showed. It had reminded Ursula again of home, of the Marsh, of her childhood, and of the journey to Brussels, and, strangely, of Anton Skrebensky.

Oh, God, could one bear it, this past which was gone down the abyss? Could she bear, that it ever had been! She looked round this silent, upper world of snow and stars and powerful cold. There was another world, like views on a magic lantern; The Marsh, Cossethay, Ilkeston, lit up with a common, unreal light. There was a shadowy unreal Ursula, a whole shadow-play of an unreal life. It was as unreal, and circumscribed, as a magic-lantern show. She wished the slides could all be broken. She wished it could be gone for ever, like a lantern-slide which was broken. She wanted to have no past. She wanted to have come down from the slopes of heaven to this place, with Birkin, not to have toiled out of the murk of her childhood and her upbringing, slowly, all soiled. She felt that memory was a dirty trick played upon her. What was this decree, that she should 'remember'! Why not a bath of pure oblivion, a new birth, without any recollections or blemish of a past life. She was with Birkin, she had just come into life, here in the high snow, against the stars. What had she to do with parents and antecedents? She knew herself new and unbegotten, she had no father, no mother, no anterior connections, she was herself, pure and silvery, she belonged only to the oneness with Birkin, a oneness that struck deeper notes, sounding into the heart of the universe, the heart of reality, where she had never existed before.

Even Gudrun was a separate unit, separate, separate, having nothing to do with this self, this Ursula, in her new world of reality. That old shadow-world, the actuality of the past – ah, let it go! She rose free on the wings of her new condition.

Gudrun and Gerald had not come in. They had walked up the valley straight in front of the house, not like Ursula and Birkin, on to the little hill at the right. Gudrun was driven by a strange desire. She wanted to plunge on and on, till she came to the end of the valley of snow. Then she wanted to climb the wall of white finality, climb over, into the peaks that sprang up like sharp petals in the heart of the frozen, mysterious navel of the world. She felt that there, over the strange blind, terrible wall of rocky snow, there in the navel of the mystic world, among the final cluster of peaks, there, in the infolded navel of it all, was her consummation. If she could but come there, alone, and pass into the infolded navel of eternal snow and of uprising, immortal peaks of snow and rock, she would be a oneness with all, she would be herself the eternal, infinite silence, the sleeping, timeless, frozen centre of the All.

They went back to the house, to the *Reunionsaal*. She was curious to see what was going on. The men there made her alert, roused her curiosity. It was a new taste of life for her, they were so prostrate before her, yet so full of life.

The party was boisterous; they were dancing all together, dancing the *Schuhplatteln*, the Tyrolese dance of the clapping hands and tossing the partner in the air at the crisis. The Germans were all proficient – they were from Munich chiefly. Gerald also was quite passable. There were three zithers twanging away in a corner. It was a scene of great animation and confusion. The Professor was initiating Ursula into the dance, stamping, clapping, and swinging her high, with amazing force and zest. When the crisis came even Birkin was behaving manfully with one of the Professor's fresh, strong daughters, who was exceedingly happy. Everybody was dancing, there was the most boisterous turmoil.

Gudrun looked on with delight. The solid wooden floor resounded to the knocking heels of the men, the air quivered with the clapping hands and the zither music, there was a golden dust about the hanging lamps.

Suddenly the dance finished, Loerke and the students rushed out to bring in drinks. There was an excited clamour of voices, a clinking of mug-lids, a great crying of *'Prosit – Prosit!'* Loerke was everywhere at once, like a gnome, suggesting drinks for the women, making an obscure, slightly risky joke with the men, confusing and mystifying the waiter.

He wanted very much to dance with Gudrun. From the first moment he had seen her, he wanted to make a connection with her. Instinctively she felt this, and she waited for him to come up. But a kind of sulkiness kept him away from her, so she thought he disliked her.

'Will you *schuhpletteln, gnädige Frau?*' said the large, fair youth, Loerke's companion. He was too soft, too humble for Gudrun's taste. But she wanted to dance, and the fair youth, who was called Leitner, was handsome enough in his uneasy, slightly abject fashion, a humility that covered a certain fear. She accepted him as a partner.

The zithers sounded out again, the dance began. Gerald led them, laughing, with one of the Professor's daughters. Ursula danced with one of the students, Birkin with the other daughter of the Professor, the Professor with Frau Kramer, and the rest of the men danced together, with quite as much zest as if they had had women partners.

Because Gudrun had danced with the well-built, soft youth, his companion, Loerke, was more pettish and exasperated than ever, and would not even notice her existence in the room. This piqued her, but she made up to herself by dancing with the Professor, who was strong as a mature well-seasoned bull, and as full of coarse energy. She could not bear him, critically, and yet she enjoyed being rushed through the dance, and tossed up into the air, on his coarse, powerful impetus. The Professor enjoyed it too, he eyed her with strange, large blue eyes, full of galvanic fire. She hated him for the seasoned, semi-paternal animalism with which he regarded her, but she admired his weight of strength.

The room was charged with excitement and strong, animal emotion. Loerke was kept away from Gudrun, to whom he wanted to speak, as by a hedge of thorns, and he felt a sardonic ruthless hatred for this young love-companion, Leitner, who was his penniless dependant. He mocked the youth, with an acid ridicule, that made Leitner red in the face and impotent with resentment.

Gerald, who had now got the dance perfectly, was dancing again with the younger of the Professor's daughters, who was almost dying of virgin excitement, because she thought Gerald so handsome, so superb. He had her in his power, as if she were a palpitating bird, a fluttering, flushing, bewildered creature. And it made him smile, as she shrank convulsively between his hands, violently, when he must throw her into the air. At the end, she was so overcome with prostrate love for him, that she could scarcely speak sensibly at all.

Birkin was dancing with Ursula. There were odd little fires playing in his eyes, he seemed to have turned into something wicked and flickering, mocking, suggestive, quite impossible. Ursula was frightened of him, and fascinated. Clear, before her eyes, as in a vision, she could see the sardonic licentious mockery of his eyes, he moved towards her with subtle, animal, indifferent approach. The strangeness of his hands, which came quick and cunning, inevitably to the vital place beneath her breasts, and, lifting with mocking, suggestive impulse, carried her through the air as if without strength, through black magic, made her swoon with fear. For a moment she revolted, it was horrible. She would break the spell. But before the resolution had formed she had submitted again, yielded to her fear. He knew all the time what he was doing, she could see it in his smiling, concentrated eyes. It was his responsibility, she would leave it to him.

When they were alone in the darkness, she felt the strange licentiousness of him hovering upon her. She was troubled and repelled. Why should he turn like this.

'What is it?' she asked in dread.

But his face only glistened on her, unknown, horrible. And yet she was fascinated. Her impulse was to repel him violently, break from this spell of mocking brutishness. But she was too fascinated, she wanted to submit, she wanted to know. What would he do to her?

He was so attractive, and so repulsive at once. The sardonic suggestivity that flickered over his face and looked from his narrowed eyes, made her want to hide, to hide herself away from him and watch him from somewhere unseen.

'Why are you like this?' she demanded again, rousing against him with sudden force and animosity.

The flickering fires in his eyes concentrated as he looked into her eyes. Then the lids drooped with a faint motion of satiric contempt. Then they rose again to the same remorseless suggestivity. And she gave way, he might do as he would. His licentiousness was repulsively attractive. But he was self-responsible, she would see what it was.

They might do as they liked – this she realized as she went to sleep. How could anything that gave one satisfaction be excluded? What was degrading? Who cared? Degrading things were real, with a different reality. And he was so unabashed and unrestrained. Wasn't it rather horrible, a man who could be so soulful and spiritual, now to be so – she baulked at her own thoughts and memories: then she added – so bestial? So bestial, they two! – so degraded! She winced. But after all, why not? She exulted as well. Why not be bestial, and go the whole round of experience? She exulted in it. She was bestial. How good it was to be really shameful! There would be no shameful thing she had not experienced. Yet she was unabashed, she was herself. Why not? She was free, when she knew everything, and no dark shameful things were denied her.

Gudrun, who had been watching Gerald in the *Reunionsaal*, suddenly thought:

'He should have all the women he can – it is his nature. It is absurd to call him monogamous – he is naturally promiscuous. That is his nature.'

The thought came to her involuntarily. It shocked her somewhat. It was as if she had seen some new *Mene! Mene!* upon the wall. Yet it was merely true. A voice seemed to have spoken it to her so clearly, that for the moment she believed in inspiration.

'It is really true,' she said to herself again.

She knew quite well she had believed it all along. She knew it implicitly. But she must keep it dark – almost from herself. She must keep it completely secret. It was knowledge for her alone, and scarcely even to be admitted to herself.

The deep resolve formed in her, to combat him. One of them must triumph over the other. Which should it be? Her soul steeled itself with strength.

Almost she laughed within herself, at her confidence. It woke a certain keen, half contemptuous pity, tenderness for him: she was so ruthless.

Everybody retired early. The Professor and Loerke went into a small lounge to drink. They both watched Gudrun go along the landing by the railing upstairs.

'*Ein schönes Frauenzimmer*,' said the Professor.

'*Ja!*' asserted Loerke, shortly.

Gerald walked with his queer, long wolf-steps across the bedroom to the window, stooped and looked out, then rose again, and turned to Gudrun, his eyes sharp with an abstract smile. He seemed very tall to her, she saw the glisten of his whitish eyebrows, that met between his brows.

'How do you like it?' he said.

He seemed to be laughing inside himself, quite unconsciously. She looked at him. He was a phenomenon to her, not a human being: a sort of creature, greedy.

'I like it very much,' she replied.

'Who do you like best downstairs?' he asked, standing tall and glistening above her, with his glistening stiff hair erect.

'Who do I like best?' she repeated, wanting to answer his question, and finding it difficult to collect herself. 'Why I don't know, I don't know enough about them yet, to be able to say. Who do *you* like best?'

'Oh, I don't care – I don't like or dislike any of them. It doesn't matter about me. I wanted to know about you.'

'But why?' she asked, going rather pale. The abstract, unconscious smile in his eyes was intensified.

'I wanted to know,' he said.

She turned aside, breaking the spell. In some strange way, she felt he was getting power over her.

'Well, I can't tell you already,' she said.

She went to the mirror to take out the hairpins from her hair. She stood before the mirror every night for some minutes, brushing her fine dark hair. It was part of the inevitable ritual of her life.

He followed her, and stood behind her. She was busy with bent head, taking out the pins and shaking her warm hair loose. When she looked up, she saw him in the glass, standing behind her, watching unconsciously, not consciously seeing her, and yet watching, with fine-pupilled eyes that *seemed* to smile, and which were not really smiling.

She started. It took all her courage for her to continue brushing her hair, as usual, for her to pretend she was at her ease. She was far, far from being at her ease with him. She beat her brains wildly for something to say to him.

'What are your plans for tomorrow?' she asked nonchalantly, whilst her heart was beating so furiously, her eyes were so bright with strange nervousness, she felt he could not but observe. But she knew also that he was completely blind, blind as a wolf looking at her. It was a strange battle between her ordinary consciousness and his uncanny, black-art consciousness.

'I don't know,' he replied, 'what would you like to do?'

He spoke emptily, his mind was sunk away.

'Oh,' she said, with easy protestation, 'I'm ready for anything – anything will be fine for *me*, I'm sure.'

And to herself she was saying: 'God, why am I so nervous – why are you so nervous, you fool. If he sees it I'm done for for ever – you *know* you're done for for ever, if he sees the absurd state you're in.'

And she smiled to herself as if it were all child's play. Meanwhile her heart was plunging, she was almost fainting. She could see him, in the mirror, as he stood there behind her, tall and over-arching – blond and terribly frightening. She glanced at his reflection with furtive eyes, willing to give anything to save him from knowing she could see him. He did not know she could see his reflection. He was looking unconsciously, glisteningly down at her head, from which the hair fell loose, as she brushed it with wild, nervous hand. She held her head aside and brushed and brushed her hair madly. For her life, she could not turn round and face him. For her life, *she could not*. And the knowledge made her almost sink to the ground in a faint, helpless, spent. She was aware of his frightening, impending figure standing close behind her, she was aware of his hard, strong, unyielding chest, close upon her back. And she felt she could not bear it any more, in a few minutes she would fall down at his feet, grovelling at his feet, and letting him destroy her.

The thought pricked up all her sharp intelligence and presence of mind. She dared not turn round to him – and there he stood motionless, unbroken. Summoning all her strength, she said, in a full, resonant, nonchalant voice that was forced out with all her remaining self-control:

'Oh, would you mind looking in that bag behind there and giving me my –'

Here her power fell inert. 'My what – my what – ?' she screamed in silence to herself.

But he had started round, surprised and startled that she should ask him to look in her bag, which she always kept so *very* private to herself. She turned now, her face white, her dark eyes blazing with uncanny, overwrought excitement. She saw him stooping to the bag, undoing the loosely buckled strap, unattentive.

'Your what?' he asked.

'Oh, a little enamel box – yellow – with a design of a cormorant plucking her breast –'

She went towards him, stooping her beautiful, bare arm, and deftly turned some of her things, disclosing the box, which was exquisitely painted.

'That is it, see,' she said, taking it from under his eyes.

And he was baffled now. He was left to fasten up the bag, whilst she swiftly did up her hair for the night, and sat down to unfasten her shoes. She would not turn her back to him any more.

He was baffled, frustrated, but unconscious. She had the whip hand over him now. She knew he had not realized her terrible panic. Her heart was beating heavily still. Fool, fool that she was, to get into such a state! How she thanked God for Gerald's obtuse blindness. Thank God he could see nothing.

She sat slowly unlacing her shoes, and he too commenced to undress. Thank God that crisis was over. She felt almost fond of him now, almost in love with him.

'Ah, Gerald,' she laughed, caressively, teasingly. 'Ah, what a fine game you played with the Professor's daughter – didn't you now?'

'What game?' he asked, looking round.

'*Isn't* she in love with you – oh *dear*, isn't she in love with you!' said Gudrun, in her gayest, most attractive mood.

'I shouldn't think so,' he said.

'Shouldn't think so!' she teased. 'Why the poor girl is lying at this moment overwhelmed, dying with love for you. She thinks you're *wonderful* – oh marvellous, beyond what man has ever been. *Really,* isn't it funny?'

'Why funny, what is funny?' he asked.

'Why to see you working it on her,' she said, with a half reproach that confused the male conceit in him. 'Really, Gerald, the poor girl – !'

'I did nothing to her,' he said.

'Oh, it was too shameful, the way you simply swept her off her feet.'

'That was *Schuhplatteln,*' he replied, with a bright grin.

'Ha – ha – ha!' laughed Gudrun.

Her mockery quivered through his muscles with curious re-echoes. When he slept he seemed to crouch down in the bed, lapped up in his own strength, that yet was hollow.

And Gudrun slept strongly, a victorious sleep. Suddenly, she was almost fiercely awake. The small timber room glowed with the dawn, that came upwards from the low window. She could see down the valley when she lifted her head: the snow with a pinkish, half-revealed magic, the fringe of pine trees at the bottom of the slope. And one tiny figure moved over the vaguely-illuminated space.

She glanced at his watch; it was seven o'clock. He was still completely asleep. And she was so hard awake, it was almost frightening – a hard, metallic wakefulness. She lay looking at him.

He slept in the subjection of his own health and defeat. She was overcome by a sincere regard for him. Till now, she was afraid before him. She lay and thought about him, what he was, what he represented in the world. A fine, independent will, he had. She thought of the revolution he had worked in the mines, in so short a time. She knew that if he were confronted with any problem, any hard actual difficulty, he would overcome it. If he laid hold of any idea, he would carry it through. He had the faculty of making order out of confusion. Only let him grip hold of a situation, and he would bring to pass an inevitable conclusion.

For a few moments she was borne away on the wild wings of ambition. Gerald, with his force of will and his power for comprehending the actual world, should be set to solve the problems of the day, the problem of industrialism in the modern world. She knew he would, in the course of time, effect the changes he desired, he could reorganize the industrial system. She knew he could do it. As an instrument, in these things, he was marvellous, she had never seen any man with his potentiality. He was unaware of it, but she knew.

He only needed to be hitched on, he needed that his hand should be set to the task, because he was so unconscious. And this she could do. She would marry him, he would go into Parliament in the Conservative interest, he would clear up the great muddle of labour and industry. He was so superbly fearless, masterful, he knew that every problem could be worked out, in life as in geometry. And he would care neither about himself nor about anything but the pure working out of the problem. He was very pure, really.

Her heart beat fast, she flew away on wings of elation, imagining a future. He would be a Napoleon of peace, or a Bismarck – and she the woman behind him. She had read Bismarck's letters, and had been deeply moved by them. And Gerald would be freer, more dauntless than Bismarck.

But even as she lay in fictitious transport, bathed in the strange, false sunshine of hope in life, something seemed to snap in her, and a terrible cynicism began to gain upon her, blowing in like a wind. Everything turned to irony with her: the last flavour of everything was ironical. When she felt her pang of undeniable reality, this was when she knew the hard irony of hopes and ideas.

She lay and looked at him, as he slept. He was sheerly beautiful, he was a perfect instrument. To her mind, he was a pure, inhuman, almost super-human instrument. His instrumentality appealed so strongly to her, she wished she were God, to use him as a tool.

And at the same instant, came the ironical question: 'What for?' She thought of the colliers' wives, with their linoleum and their lace curtains and their little girls in high-laced boots. She thought of the wives and daughters of the pit-managers, their tennis-parties, and their terrible struggles to be superior each to the other, in the social scale. There was Shortlands with its meaningless distinction, the meaningless crowd of the Criches. There was London, the House of Commons, the extant social world. My God!

Young as she was, Gudrun had touched the whole pulse of social England. She had no ideas of rising in the world. She knew, with the perfect cynicism of cruel youth, that to rise in the world meant to have one outside show instead of another, the advance was like having a spurious half-crown instead of a spurious penny. The whole coinage of valuation was spurious. Yet, of course, her cynicism knew well enough that, in a world where spurious coin was current, a bad sovereign was better than a bad farthing. But rich and poor, she despised both alike.

Already she mocked at herself for her dreams. They could be fulfilled easily enough. But she recognized too well, in her spirit, the mockery of her own impulses. What did she care, that Gerald had created a richly-paying industry out of an old worn-out concern? What did she care? The worn-out concern and the rapid, splendidly organized industry, they were bad money. Yet, of course, she cared a great deal, outwardly – and outwardly was all that mattered, for inwardly was a bad joke.

Everything was intrinsically a piece of irony to her. She leaned over Gerald and said in her heart, with compassion:

'Oh, my dear, my dear, the game isn't worth even you. You are a fine thing really – why should you be used on such a poor show!'

Her heart was breaking with pity and grief for him. And at the same moment, a grimace came over her mouth of mocking irony at her own unspoken tirade. Ah, what a farce it was! She thought of Parnell and Katherine O'Shea. Parnell! After all, who can take the nationalization of Ireland seriously? Who can take political Ireland really seriously, whatever it does? And who can take political England seriously? Who can? Who can care a straw, really, how the old patched-up Constitution is tinkered at any more? Who cares a button for our national ideas, any more than for our national bowler hat? Aha, it is all old hat, it is all old bowler hat!

That's all it is, Gerald, my young hero. At any rate, we'll spare ourselves the nausea of stirring the old broth any more. You be beautiful, my Gerald, and reckless. There *are* perfect moments. Wake up, Gerald, wake up, convince me of the perfect moments. Oh, convince me, I need it.

He opened his eyes, and looked at her. She greeted him with a mocking, enigmatic smile in which was a poignant gaiety. Over his face went the reflection of the smile, he smiled, too, purely unconsciously.

That filled her with extraordinary delight, to see the smile cross his face, reflected from her face. She remembered that was how a baby smiled. It filled her with extraordinary radiant delight.

'You've done it,' she said.

'What?' he asked, dazed.

'Convinced me.'

And she bent down, kissing him passionately, passionately, so that he was bewildered. He did not ask her of what he had convinced her, thought he meant to. He was glad she was kissing him. She seemed to be feeling for his very heart to touch the quick of him. And he wanted her to touch the quick of his being, he wanted that most of all.

Outside, somebody was singing in a manly, reckless, handsome voice:

> 'Mach mir auf, mach mir auf, du Stolze,
> Mach mir ein Feuer von Holze.
> Vom Regen bin ich nass
> Vom Regen bin ich nass –'

Gudrun knew that that song would sound through her eternity, sung in a manly, reckless, mocking voice. It marked one of her supreme moments, the supreme pangs of her nervous gratification. There it was, fixed in eternity for her.

The day came fine and bluish. There was a light wind blowing among the mountain-tops, keen as a rapier where it touched, carrying with it a fine dust of snow powder. Gerald went out with the fine, blind face of a man who is in his state of fulfilment. Gudrun and he were in perfect static unity this morning, but unseeing and unwitting. They went out with a toboggan, leaving Ursula and Birkin to follow.

Gudrun was all scarlet and royal blue – a scarlet jersey and cap, and a royal blue skirt and stockings. She went gaily over the white snow, with Gerald beside her, in white and grey, pulling the little toboggan. They grew small in the distance of snow, climbing the steep slope.

For Gudrun herself, she seemed to pass altogether into the whiteness of the snow, she became a pure, thoughtless crystal. When she reached the top of the slope, in the wind, she looked round, and saw peak beyond peak of rock and snow, bluish, transcendent in heaven. And it seemed to her like a garden, with the peaks for pure flowers, and her heart gathering them. She had no separate consciousness for Gerald.

She held on to him as they went sheering down over the keen slope. She felt as if her senses were being whetted on some fine grindstone that was keen as flame. The snow sprinted on either side, like sparks from a blade that is being sharpened, the whiteness round about ran swifter, swifter, in pure flame the white slope flew against her, and she fused like one molten, dancing globule, rushed through a white intensity. Then there was a great swerve at the bottom when they swung, as it were, in a fall to earth in the diminishing motion.

They came to rest. But when she rose to her feet, she could not stand. She gave a strange cry, turned and clung to him, sinking her face on his breast, fainting in him. Utter oblivion came over her as she lay for a few moments abandoned against him.

'What is it?' he was saying. 'Was it too much for you?'

But she heard nothing.

When she came to, she stood up and looked round, astonished. Her face was white, her eyes brilliant and large.

'What is it?' he repeated. 'Did it upset you?'

She looked at him with her brilliant eyes that seemed to have undergone some transfiguration, and she laughed, with a terrible merriment.

'No,' she cried, with triumphant joy. 'It was the complete moment of my life.'

And she looked at him with her dazzling, overweening laughter, like one possessed. A fine blade seemed to enter his heart, but he did not care, or take any notice.

But they climbed up the slope again, and they flew down through the white flame again splendidly, splendidly. Gudrun was laughing and flashing, powdered with snow-crystals, Gerald worked perfectly. He felt he could guide the toboggan to a hairbreadth, almost he could make it pierce into the air and right into the very heart of the sky. It seemed to him the flying sledge was but his strength spread out, he had but to move his arms, the motion was his own. They explored the great slopes, to find another slide. He felt there must be something better than they had known. And he found what he desired, a perfect long, fierce sweep, sheering past the foot of a rock and into the trees at the base. It was dangerous, he knew. But then he knew also he would direct the sledge between his fingers.

The first days passed in an ecstasy of physical motion, sleighing, ski-ing, skating, moving in an intensity of speed and white light that surpassed life itself, and carried the souls of the human beings beyond into an inhuman abstraction of velocity and weight and eternal, frozen snow.

Gerald's eyes became hard and strange, and as he went by on his skis he was more like some powerful, fateful sigh than a man, his muscles elastic in a perfect, soaring trajectory, his body projected in pure flight, mindless, soulless, whirling along one perfect line of force.

Luckily there came a day of snow, when they must all stay indoors: otherwise Birkin said they would all lose their faculties, and begin to utter themselves in cries and shrieks, like some strange, unknown species of snow-creatures.

It happened in the afternoon that Ursula sat in the *Reunionsaal* talking to Loerke. The latter had seemed unhappy lately. He was lively and full of mischievous humour, as usual.

But Ursula had thought he was sulky about something. His partner, too, the big, fair, good-looking youth, was ill at ease, going about as if he belonged to nowhere, and was kept in some sort of subjection, against which he was rebelling.

Loerke had hardly talked to Gudrun. His associate, on the other hand, had paid her constantly a soft, over-deferential attention. Gudrun wanted to talk to Loerke. He was a sculptor, and she wanted to hear his view of his art. And his figure attracted her. There was the look of a little wastrel about him that intrigued her, and an old man's look that interested her, and then, beside this, an uncanny singleness, a quality of being by himself, not in contact with anybody else, that marked out an artist to her. He was a chatterer, a magpie, a maker of mischievous word-jokes, that were sometimes very clever, but which often were not. And she could see in his brown, gnome's eyes the black look of inorganic misery which lay behind all his small buffoonery.

His figure interested her – the figure of a boy, almost a street arab. He made no attempt to conceal it. He always wore a simple loden suit, with knee breeches. His legs were thin, and he made no attempt to disguise the fact:

which was of itself remarkable in a German. And he never ingratiated himself anywhere, not in the slightest, but kept to himself, for all his apparent playfulness.

Leitner, his companion, was a great sportsman, very handsome with his big limbs and his blue eyes. Loerke would go tobogganing or skating in little snatches, but he was indifferent. And his fine, thin nostrils, the nostrils of a pure-bred street arab, would quiver with contempt at Leitner's splothering gymnastic displays. It was evident that the two men who had travelled and lived together, sharing the same bedroom, had now reached the stage of loathing. Leitner hated Loerke with an injured, writhing, impotent hatred, and Loerke treated Leitner with a fine-quivering contempt and sarcasm. Soon the two would have to go apart.

Already they were rarely together. Leitner ran attaching himself to somebody or other, always deferring, Loerke was a good deal alone. Out of doors he wore a Westphalian cap, a close brown velvet head with big brown velvet flaps down over his ears, so that he looked like a lop-eared rabbit or a troll. His face was brown-red, with a dry, bright skin, that seemed to crinkle with his mobile expressions. His eyes were arresting – brown, full, like a rabbit's, or like a troll's, or like the eyes of a lost being, having a strange, dumb, depraved look of knowledge and a quick spark of uncanny fire. Whenever Gudrun had tried to talk to him he had shied away unresponsive, looking at her with his watchful dark eyes, but entering into no relation with her. He had made her feel that her slow French and her slower German were hateful to him. As for his own inadequate English, he was much too awkward to try it at all. But he understood a good deal of what was said, nevertheless. And Gudrun, piqued, left him alone.

This afternoon, however, she came into the lounge as he was talking to Ursula. His fine, black hair somehow reminded her of a bat, thin as it was on his full, sensitive-looking head, and worn away at the temples. He sat hunched up, as if his spirit were bat-like. And Gudrun could see he was making some slow confidence to Ursula, unwilling, a slow, grudging, scanty self-revelation. She went and sat by her sister.

He looked at her, then looked away again, as if he took no notice of her. But as a matter of fact, she interested him deeply.

'Isn't it interesting, Prune,' said Ursula, turning to her sister, 'Herr Loerke is doing a great frieze for a factory in Cologne, for the outside, the street.'

She looked at him, at his thin, brown, nervous hands, that were prehensile, and somehow like talons, like 'griffes', inhuman.

'*What in?*' she asked.

'*Aus was?*' repeated Ursula.

'*Granit,*' he replied.

It had become immediately a laconic series of question and answer between fellow craftsmen.

'What is the relief?' asked Gudrun.

'Alto relievo.'

'And at what height?'

It was very interesting to Gudrun to think of his making the great granite frieze for a great granite factory in Cologne. She got from him some notion of the design. It was a representation of a fair, with peasants and artisans in an orgy of enjoyment, drunk and absurd in their modern dress, whirling ridiculously in roundabouts, gaping at shows, kissing and staggering and rolling in knots, swinging in swing-boats, and firing down shooting-galleries, a frenzy of chaotic motion.

There was a swift discussion of technicalities. Gudrun was very much impressed.

'But how wonderful, to have such a factory!' cried Ursula. 'Is the whole building fine?'

'Oh yes,' he replied. 'The frieze is part of the whole architecture. Yes, it is a colossal thing.'

Then he seemed to stiffen, shrugged his shoulders, and went on:

'Sculpture and architecture must go together. The day for irrelevant statues, as for wall pictures, is over. As a matter of fact, sculpture is always part of an architectural conception. And since churches are all museum stuff, since industry is our business, now, then let us make our places of industry our art – our factory area our Parthenon, *ecco!*'

Ursula pondered.

'I suppose,' she said, 'there is no *need* for our great works to be so hideous.'

Instantly he broke into motion.

'There you are!' he cried, 'there you are! There is not only *no need* for our places of work to be ugly, but their ugliness ruins the work, in the end. Men will not go on submitting to such intolerable ugliness. In the end it will hurt too much, and they will wither because of it. And this will wither the *work* as well. They will think the work itself is ugly: the machines, the very act of labour. Whereas the machinery and the acts of labour are extremely, maddeningly beautiful. But this will be the end of our civilization, when people will not work because work has become so intolerable to their senses, it nauseates them too much, they would rather starve. *Then* we shall see the hammer used only for smashing, then we shall see it. Yet here we are – we have the opportunity to make beautiful factories, beautiful machine-houses – we have the opportunity – '

Gudrun could only partly understand. She could have cried with vexation.

'What does he say?' she asked Ursula. And Ursula translated, stammering and brief. Loerke watched Gudrun's face to see her judgment.

'And do you think then,' said Gudrun, 'that art should serve industry?'

'Art should *interpret* industry as art once interpreted religion,' he said.

'But does your fair interpret industry?' she asked him.

'Certainly. What is man doing when he is at a fair like this? He is fulfilling the counterpart of labour – the machine works him instead of he the machine. He enjoys the mechanical motion in his own body.'

'But is there nothing but work – mechanical work?' said Gudrun.

'Nothing but work!' he repeated, leaning forward, his eyes two darknesses, with needle-points of light. 'No, it is nothing but this, serving a machine, or enjoying the motion of a machine – motion, that is all. You have never worked for hunger, or you would know what god governs us.'

Gudrun quivered and flushed. For some reason she was almost in tears.

'No, I have not worked for hunger,' she replied, 'but I have worked!'

'*Travaillé – lavorato?*' he asked. '*E che lavoro – che lavoro? Quel travail est-ce que vous avez fait?*'

He broke into a mixture of Italian and French, instinctively using a foreign language when he spoke to her.

'You have never worked as the world works,' he said to her, with sarcasm.

'Yes,' she said. 'I have. And I do – I work now for my daily bread.'

He paused, looked at her steadily, then dropped the subject entirely. She seemed to him to be trifling.

'But have *you* ever worked as the world works?' Ursula asked him.

He looked at her untrustful.

'Yes,' he replied, with a surly bark. 'I have known what it was to lie in bed for three days, because I had nothing to eat.'

Gudrun was looking at him with large, grave eyes that seemed to draw the confession from him as the marrow from his bones. All his nature held him back from confessing. And yet her large, grave eyes upon him seemed to open some valve in his veins, and involuntarily he was telling.

'My father was a man who did not like work, and we had no mother. We lived in Austria, Polish Austria. How did we live? Ha! – somehow! Mostly in a room with three other families – one set in each corner – and the w.c. in the middle of the room – a pan with a plank on it – ha! I had two brothers and a sister – and there might be a woman with my father. He was a free being, in his way – would fight with any man in the town – a garrison town – and was a little man too. But he wouldn't work for anybody – set his heart against it, and wouldn't.'

'And how did you live then?' asked Ursula.

He looked at her – then, suddenly, at Gudrun.

'Do you understand?' he asked.

'Enough,' she replied.

Their eyes met for a moment. Then he looked away. He would say no more.

'And how did you become a sculptor?' asked Ursula.

'How did I become a sculptor –' He paused. *'Dunque –'* he resumed in a changed manner, and beginning to speak French – 'I became old enough – I used to steal from the market-place. Later I went to work – imprinted the stamp on clay bottles before they were baked. It was an earthenware bottle factory. There I began making models. One day I had had enough. I lay in the sun and did not go to work. Then I walked to Munich – then I walked to Italy – begging, begging everything.

'The Italians were very good to me – they were good and honourable to me. From Bozen to Rome, almost every night I had a meal and a bed, perhaps of straw, with some peasant. I love the Italian people with all my heart.

'Dunque, adesso – maintenant – I earn a thousand pounds in a year, or I earn two thousand –'

He looked down at the ground, his voice tailing off into silence.

Gudrun looked at his fine, thin, shiny skin, reddish-brown from the sun, drawn tight over his full temples; and at his thin hair –, and at the thick, coarse, brush-like moustache, cut short about his mobile, rather shapeless mouth.

'How old are you?' she asked.

He looked up at her with his full, elfin eyes startled.

'Wie alt?' he repeated. And he hesitated. It was evidently one of his reticences.

'How old are *you*?' he replied, without answering.

'I am twenty-six,' she answered.

'Twenty-six,' he repeated, looking into her eyes. He paused. Then he said: *'Und Ihr Herr Gemahl, wie alt is er?'*

'Who?' asked Gudrun.

'Your husband,' said Ursula, with a certain irony.

'I haven't got a husband,' said Gudrun in English. In German she answered:

'He is thirty-one.'

But Loerke was watching closely, with his uncanny, full, suspicious eyes. Something in Gudrun seemed to accord with him. He was really like one of the 'little people' who have no soul, who has found his mate in a human being. But he suffered in his discovery. She too was fascinated by him, fascinated, as if some strange creature, a rabbit or a bat, or a brown seal, had begun to talk to her. But also, she knew what he was unconscious of, his tremendous power of understanding, of apprehending her living motion. He did not know his own power. He did not know how, with his full, submerged, watchful eyes, he could look into her and see her, what she was, see her secrets. He would only want her to be herself – he knew her verily, with a subconscious, sinister knowledge, devoid of illusions and hopes.

To Gudrun, there was in Loerke the rock bottom of all life. Everybody else had their illusion, must have their illusion, their before and after. But he, with a perfect stoicism, did without any before and after, dispensed with all illusion. He did not deceive himself in the last issue. In the last issue he cared about nothing, he was troubled about nothing, he made not the slightest attempt to be at one with anything. He existed a pure, unconnected will, stoical and momentaneous. There was only his work.

It was curious, too, how his poverty, the degradation of his earlier life, attracted her. There was something insipid and tasteless to her in the idea of a gentleman, a man who had gone the usual course through school and university. A certain violent sympathy, however, came up in her for this mud-child. He seemed to be the very stuff of the underworld of life. There was no going beyond him.

Ursula too was attracted by Loerke. In both sisters he commanded a certain homage. But there were moments when to Ursula he seemed indescribably inferior, false, a vulgarism.

Both Birkin and Gerald disliked him, Gerald ignoring him with some contempt, Birkin exasperated.

'What do the women find so impressive in that little brat?' Gerald asked.

'God alone knows,' replied Birkin, 'unless it's some sort of appeal he makes to them, which flatters them and has such a power over them.'

Gerald looked up in surprise.

'*Does* he make an appeal to them?' he asked.

'Oh yes,' replied Birkin. 'He is the perfectly subjected being, existing almost like a criminal. And the women rush towards that, like a current of air towards a vacuum.'

'Funny they should rush to that,' said Gerald.

'Makes one mad, too,' said Birkin. 'But he has the fascination of pity and repulsion for them, a little obscene monster of the darkness that he is.'

Gerald stood still, suspended in thought.

'What *do* women want at the bottom?' he asked.

Birkin shrugged his shoulders.

'God knows,' he said. 'Some satisfaction in basic repulsion, it seems to me. They seem to creep down some ghastly tunnel of darkness, and will never be satisfied till they've come to the end.'

Gerald looked out into the mist of fine snow that was blowing by. Everywhere was blind today, horribly blind.

'And what *is* the end?' he asked.

Birkin shook his head.

'I've not got there yet, so I don't know. Ask Loerke, he's pretty near. He is a good many stages farther than either you or I can go.'

'Yes, but stages farther in what?' cried Gerald, irritated.

Birkin sighed, and gathered his brows into a knot of anger.

'Stages farther in social hatred,' he said. 'He lives like a rat in the river of corruption, just where it falls over into the bottomless pit. He's farther on than we are. He hates the ideal more acutely. He *hates* the ideal utterly, yet it still dominates him. I expect he is a Jew – or part Jewish.'

'Probably,' said Gerald.

'He is a gnawing little negation, gnawing at the roots of life.'

'But why does anybody care about him?' cried Gerald.

'Because they hate the ideal also in their souls. They want to explore the sewers, and he's the wizard rat that swims ahead.'

Still Gerald stood and stared at the blind haze of snow outside.

'I don't understand your terms, really,' he said in a flat, doomed voice. 'But it sounds a rum sort of desire.'

'I suppose we want the same,' said Birkin. 'Only we want to take a quick jump downwards, in a sort of ecstasy – and he ebbs with the stream, the sewer stream.'

Meanwhile Gudrun and Ursula waited for the next opportunity to talk to Loerke. It was no use beginning when the men were there. Then they could get into no touch with the isolated little sculptor. He had to be alone with them. And he preferred Ursula to be there, as a sort of transmitter to Gudrun.

'Do you do nothing but architectural sculpture?' Gudrun asked him one evening.

'Not now,' he replied. 'I have done all sorts – except portraits – I never did portraits. But other things –'

'What kind of things?' asked Gudrun.

He paused a moment, then rose and went out of the room. He returned almost immediately with a little roll of paper, which he handed to her. She unrolled it. It was a photogravure reproduction of a statuette, signed F. Loerke.

'That is quite an early thing – *not* mechanical,' he said, 'more popular.'

The statuette was of a naked girl, small, finely made, sitting on a great naked horse. The girl was young and tender, a mere bud. She was sitting sideways on the horse, her face in her hands, as if in shame and grief, in a little abandon. Her hair, which was short and must be flaxen, fell forward, divided, half covering her hands.

Her limbs were young and tender. Her legs, scarcely formed yet, the legs of a maiden just passing towards cruel womanhood, dangled childishly over the side of the powerful horse, pathetically, the small feet folded one over the other, as if to hide. But there was no hiding. There she was exposed naked on the naked flank of the horse.

The horse stood stock still, stretched in a kind of start. It was a massive, magnificent stallion, rigid with pent-up power. Its neck was arched and terrible, like a sickle, its flanks were pressed back, rigid with power.

Gudrun went pale, and a darkness came over her eyes, like shame, she looked up with a certain supplication, almost slave-like. He glanced at her and jerked his head a little.

'How big is it?' she asked in a toneless voice, persisting in appearing casual and unaffected.

'How big?' he replied, glancing again at her. 'Without pedestal – so high' – he measured with his hand – 'with pedestal, so –'

He looked at her steadily. There was a little brusque, turgid contempt for her in his swift gesture, and she seemed to cringe a little.

'And what is it done in?' she asked, throwing back her head and looking at him with affected coldness.

He still gazed at her steadily, and his dominance was not shaken.

'Bronze – green bronze.'

'Green bronze!' repeated Gudrun, coldly accepting his challenge. She was thinking of the slender, immature, tender limbs of the girl, smooth and cold in green bronze.

'Yes, beautiful,' she murmured, looking up at him with a certain dark homage.

He closed his eyes and looked aside, triumphant.

'Why,' said Ursula, 'did you make the horse so stiff? It is as stiff as a block.'

'Stiff?' he repeated, in arms at once.

'Yes. *Look* how stock and stupid and brutal it is. Horses are sensitive, quite delicate and sensitive, really.'

He raised his shoulders, spread his hands in a shrug of slow indifference, as much as to inform her she was an amateur and an impertinent nobody.

'*Wissen Sie,*' he said, with an insulting patience and condescension in his voice, 'that horse is a certain *form*, part of a whole form. It is part of a work of art, a piece of form. It is not a picture of a friendly horse to which you give a lump of sugar, do you see – it is part of a work of art, it has no relation to anything outside that work of art.'

Ursula, angry at being treated quite so insultingly *de haut en bas*, from the height of esoteric art to the depth of general exoteric amateurism, replied, hotly, flushing and lifting her face.

'But it *is* a picture of a horse, nevertheless.'

He lifted his shoulders in another shrug.

'As you like – it is not a picture of a cow, certainly.'

Here Gudrun broke in, flushed and brilliant, anxious to avoid any more of this, any more of Ursula's foolish persistence in giving herself away.

'What do you mean by "it is a picture of a horse"?' she cried at her sister. 'What do you mean by a horse? You mean an idea you have in *your* head, and which you want to see represented. There is another idea altogether, quite another idea. Call it a horse if you like, or say it is not a horse. I have just as much right to say that *your* horse isn't a horse, that it is a falsity of your own make-up.'

Ursula wavered, baffled. Then her words came.

'But why does he have this idea of a horse?' she said. 'I know it is his idea. I know it is a picture of himself, really –'

Loerke snorted with rage.

'A picture of myself!' he repeated in derision. '*Wissen sie, gnädige Frau,* that is a *Kunstwerk*, a work of art. It is a work of art, it is a picture of nothing, of absolutely nothing. It has nothing to do with anything but itself, it has no relation with the everyday world of this and other, there is no connection between them, absolutely none, they are two different and distinct planes of existence, and to translate one into the other is worse than foolish, it is a darkening of all counsel, a making confusion everywhere. Do you see, you *must not* confuse the relative work of action with the absolute world of art. That you *must not do.*'

'That is quite true,' cried Gudrun, let loose in a sort of rhapsody. 'The two things are quite and permanently apart, they have nothing to do with one another. *I* and my art, they have *nothing* to do with each other. My art stands in another world, I am in this world.'

Her face was flushed and transfigured. Loerke, who was sitting with his head ducked, like some creature at bay, looked up at her swiftly, almost furtively, and murmured:

'*Ja – so ist es, so ist es.*'

Ursula was silent after this outburst. She was furious. She wanted to poke a hole into them both.

'It isn't a word of it true. of all this harangue you have made me,' she replied flatly. 'The horse is a picture of your own stock, stupid brutality, and the girl was a girl you loved and tortured and then ignored.'

He looked up at her with a small smile of contempt in his eyes. He would not trouble to answer this last charge.

Gudrun too was silent in exasperated contempt. Ursula *was* such an insufferable outsider, rushing in where angels would fear to tread. But then – fools must be suffered, if not gladly.

But Ursula was persistent too.

'As for your world of art and your world of reality,' she replied, 'you have to separate the two, because you can't bear to know what you are. You can't bear to realize what a stock, stiff, hide-bound brutality you *are* really, so you say "it's the world of art". The world of art is only the truth about the real world, that's all – but you are too far gone to see it.'

She was white and trembling, intent. Gudrun and Loerke sat in stiff dislike of her. Gerald too, who had come up in the beginning of the speech, stood looking at her in complete disapproval and opposition. He felt she was undignified, she put a sort of vulgarity over the esotericism which gave man his last distinction. He joined his forces with the other two. They all three wanted her to go away. But she sat on in silence, her soul weeping, throbbing violently, her fingers twisting her handkerchief.

The others maintained a dead silence, letting the display of Ursula's obtrusiveness pass by. Then Gudrun asked, in a voice that was quite cool and casual, as if resuming a casual conversation:

'Was the girl a model?'

'*Nein, sie war kein Modell. Sie war eine kleine Malschülerin.*'

'An art student!' replied Gudrun.

And how the situation revealed itself to her! She saw the girl art student, unformed and of pernicious recklessness, too young, her straight flaxen hair cut short, hanging just into her neck, curving inwards slightly, because it was rather thick; and Loerke, the well-known master-sculptor, and the girl, probably well brought up and of good family, thinking herself so great to be his mistress. Oh, how well she knew the common callousness of it all. Dresden, Paris, or London, what did it matter? She knew it.

'Where is she now?' Ursula asked.

Loerke raised his shoulders to convey his complete ignorance and indifference.

'That is already six years ago,' he said; 'she will be twenty-three years old, no more good.'

Gerald had picked up the picture and was looking at it. It attracted him also. He saw on the pedestal that the piece was called 'Lady Godiva'.

'But this isn't Lady Godiva,' he said, smiling good-humouredly. 'She was the middle-aged wife of some Earl or other, who covered herself with her long hair.'

'*A la* Maud Allan,' said Gudrun, with a mocking grimace.

'Why Maud Allan?' he replied. 'Isn't it so? I always thought the legend was that.'

'Yes, Gerald dear, I'm quite *sure* you've got the legend perfectly.'

She was laughing at him, with a little, mock-caressive contempt.

'To be sure, I'd rather see the woman than the hair,' he laughed in return.

'Wouldn't you just!' mocked Gudrun.

Ursula rose and went away, leaving the three together.

Gudrun took the picture again from Gerald, and sat looking at it closely.

'Of course,' she said, turning to tease Loerke now, 'you *understood* your little *Malschülerin*.'

He raised his eyebrows and his shoulders in a complacent shrug.

'The little girl?' asked Gerald, pointing to the figure.

Gudrun was sitting with the picture in her lap. She looked up at Gerald, full into his eyes, so that he seemed to be blinded.

'*Didn't* he understand her!' she said to Gerald in a slightly mocking, humorous playfulness. 'You've only to look at the feet – *aren't* they darling, so pretty and tender – oh, they're really wonderful, they are really –'

She lifted her eyes slowly, with a hot, flaming look into Loerke's eyes. His soul was filled with her burning recognition, he seemed to grow more uppish and lordly.

Gerald looked at the small, sculptured feet. They were turned together, half covering each other in pathetic shyness and fear. He looked at them a long time, fascinated. Then, in some pain, he put the picture away from him. He felt full of barrenness.

'What was her name?' Gudrun asked Loerke.

'Annette von Weck,' Loerke replied, reminiscent. '*Ja, sie war hübsch*. She was pretty – but she was tiresome. She was a nuisance – not for a minute would she keep still – not until I'd slapped her hard and made her cry – then she'd sit for five minutes.'

He was thinking over the work, his work, the all important to him.

'Did you really slap her?' asked Gudrun coolly.

He glanced back at her, reading her challenge.

'Yes, I did,' he said, nonchalant, 'harder than I have ever beat anything in my life. I had to, I had to. It was the only way I got the work done.'

Gudrun watched him with large, dark-filled eyes for some moments. She seemed to be considering his very soul. Then she looked down in silence.

'Why did you have such a young Godiva then?' asked Gerald. 'She is so small, besides, on the horse – not big enough for it – such a child.'

A queer spasm went over Loerke's face.

'Yes,' he said. 'I don't like them any bigger, any older. Then they are beautiful at sixteen, seventeen, eighteen – after that, they are no use to me.'

There was a moment's pause.

'Why not?' asked Gerald.

Loerke shrugged his shoulders.

'I don't find them interesting – or beautiful – they are no good to me, for my work.'

'Do you mean to say a woman isn't beautiful after she is twenty?' asked Gerald.

'For me, no. Before twenty, she is small and fresh and tender and slight. After that – let her be what she likes, she has nothing for me. The Venus of Milo is a bourgeoise – so are they all.'

'And you don't care for women at all after twenty?' asked Gerald.

'They are no good to me, they are of no use in my art,' Loerke repeated impatiently. 'I don't find them beautiful.'

'You are an epicure,' said Gerald, with a slight sarcastic laugh.

'And what about men?' asked Gudrun suddenly.

'Yes, they are good at all ages,' replied Loerke. 'A man should be big and powerful – whether he is old or young is of no account, so he has the size, something of massiveness and – and stupid form.'

Ursula went out alone into the world of pure, new snow. But the dazzling whiteness seemed to beat upon her till it hurt her, she felt the cold was slowly strangling her soul. Her head felt dazed and numb.

Suddenly she wanted to go away. It occurred to her like a miracle, that she might go away into another world. She had felt so doomed up here in the eternal snow, as if there were no beyond.

Now suddenly, as by a miracle she remembered that away beyond, below her, lay the dark fruitful earth, that towards the south there were stretches of land dark with orange trees and cypress, grey with olives, that ilex trees lifted wonderful plumy tufts in shadow against a blue sky. Miracle of miracles! – this utterly silent, frozen world of the mountain-tops was not universal! One might leave it and have done with it. One might go away.

She wanted to realize the miracle at once. She wanted at this instant to have done with the snow world, the terrible, static ice-built mountain-tops. She wanted to see the dark earth, to smell its earthy fecundity, to see the patient wintry vegetation, to feel the sunshine touch a response in the buds.

She went back gladly to the house, full of hope. Birkin was reading, lying in bed.

'Rupert,' she said, bursting in on him. 'I want to go away.'

He looked up at her slowly.

'Do you?' he replied mildly.

She sat by him and put her arms round his neck. It surprised her that he was so little surprised.

'Don't *you*?' she asked troubled.

'I hadn't thought about it,' he said. 'But I'm sure I do.'

She sat up, suddenly erect.

'I hate it,' she said. 'I hate the snow, and the unnaturalness of it, the unnatural light it throws on everybody, the ghastly glamour, the unnatural feelings it makes everybody have.'

He lay still and laughed, meditating.

'Well,' he said, 'we can go away – we can go tomorrow. We'll go tomorrow to Verona, and find Romeo and Juliet, and sit in the amphitheatre – shall we?'

Suddenly she hid her face against his shoulder with perplexity and shyness. He lay so untrammelled.

'Yes,' she said softly, filled with relief. She felt her soul had new wings, now he was so uncaring. 'I shall love to be Romeo and Juliet,' she said. 'My love!'

'Though a fearfully cold wind blows in Verona,' he said, 'from out of the Alps. We shall have the smell of the snow in our noses.'

She sat up and looked at him.

'Are you glad to go?' she asked, troubled.

His eyes were inscrutable and laughing. She hid her face against his neck, clinging close to him, pleading:

'Don't laugh at me – don't laugh at me.'

'Why how's that?' he laughed, putting his arms round her.

'Because I don't want to be laughed at,' she whispered.

He laughed more, as he kissed her delicate, finely perfumed hair.

'Do you love me?' she whispered, in wild seriousness.

'Yes,' he answered, laughing.

Suddenly she lifted her mouth to be kissed. Her lips were taut and quivering and strenuous, his were soft, deep and delicate. He waited a few moments in the kiss. Then a shade of sadness went over his soul.

'Your mouth is so hard,' he said, in faint reproach.

'And yours is so soft and nice,' she said gladly.

'But why do you always grip your lips?' he asked, regretful.

'Never mind,' she said swiftly. 'It is my way.'

She knew he loved her; she was sure of him. Yet she could not let go a certain hold over herself, she could not bear him to question her. She gave herself up in delight to being loved by him. She knew that, in spite of his joy when she abandoned herself, he was a little bit saddened too. She could give herself up to his activity. But she could not be herself, she *dared* not come forth quite nakedly to his nakedness, abandoning all adjustment, lapsing in pure faith with him. She abandoned herself to *him*, or she took hold of him and gathered her joy of him. And she enjoyed him fully. But they were never *quite* together, at the same moment, one was always a little left out. Nevertheless she was glad in hope, glorious and free, full of life and liberty. And he was still and soft and patient, for the time.

They made their preparations to leave the next day. First they went to Gudrun's room, where she and Gerald were just dressed ready for the evening indoors.

'Prune,' said Ursula, 'I think we shall go away tomorrow. I can't stand the snow any more. It hurts my skin and my soul.'

'Does it really hurt your soul, Ursula?' asked Gudrun, in some surprise. 'I can't believe quite it hurts your skin – it is *terrible*. But I thought it was *admirable* for the soul.'

'No, not for mine. It just injures it,' said Ursula.

'Really!' cried Gudrun.

There was a silence in the room. And Ursula and Birkin could feel that Gudrun and Gerald were relieved by their going.

'You will go south?' said Gerald, a little ring of uneasiness in his voice.

'Yes,' said Birkin, turning away. There was a queer, indefinable hostility between the two men, lately. Birkin was on the whole dim and indifferent, drifting along in a dim, easy flow, unnoticing and patient, since he came abroad, whilst Gerald on the other hand, was intense and gripped into white light, *agonistes*. The two men revoked one another.

Gerald and Gudrun were very kind to the two who were departing, solicitous for their welfare as if they were two children. Gudrun came to

Ursula's bedroom with three pairs of the coloured stockings for which she was notorious, and she threw them on the bed. But these were thick silk stockings, vermilion, cornflower blue, and grey, bought in Paris. The grey ones were knitted, seamless and heavy. Ursula was in raptures. She knew Gudrun must be feeling *very* loving, to give away such treasures.

'I can't take them from you, Prune,' she cried. 'I can't possibly deprive you of them – the jewels.'

'*Aren't* they jewels!' cried Gudrun, eyeing her gifts with an envious eye. '*Aren't* they real lambs!'

'Yes, you *must* keep them,' said Ursula.

'I don't *want* them, I've got three more pairs. I *want* you to keep them – I want you to have them. They're yours, there –'

And with trembling, excited hands she put the coveted stockings under Ursula's pillow.

'One gets the greatest joy of all out of really lovely stockings,' said Ursula.

'One does,' replied Gudrun; 'the greatest joy of all.'

And she sat down in the chair. It was evident she had come for a last talk. Ursula, not knowing what she wanted, waited in silence.

'Do you *feel*, Ursula,' Gudrun began, rather sceptically, 'that you are going-away-for-ever, never-to-return, sort of thing?'

'Oh, we shall come back,' said Ursula. 'It isn't a question of train journeys.'

'Yes, I know. But spiritually, so to speak, you are going away from us all?'

Ursula quivered.

'I don't know a bit what is going to happen,' she said. 'I only know we are going somewhere.'

Gudrun waited.

'And you are glad?' she asked.

Ursula meditated for a moment.

'I believe I am *very* glad,' she replied.

But Gudrun read the unconscious brightness on her sister's face, rather than the uncertain tones of her speech.

'But don't you think you'll *want* the old connection with the world – father and the rest of us, and all that it means, England and the world of thought – don't you think you'll *need* that, really to make a world?'

Ursula was silent, trying to imagine.

'I think,' she said at length, involuntarily, 'that Rupert is right – one wants a new space to be in, and one falls away from the old.'

Gudrun watched her sister with impassive face and steady eyes.

'One wants a new space to be in, I quite agree,' she said. 'But *I* think that a new world is a development from this world, and that to isolate oneself with one other person, isn't to find a new world at all, but only to secure oneself in one's illusions.'

Ursula looked out of the window. In her soul she began to wrestle, and she was frightened. She was always frightened of words, because she knew that mere word-force could always make her believe what she did not believe.

'Perhaps,' she said, full of mistrust, of herself and everybody. 'But,' she added, 'I do think that one can't have anything new whilst one cares for the old – do you know what I mean? – even fighting the old is belonging to it. I know, one is tempted to stop with the world, just to fight it. But then it isn't worth it.'

Gudrun considered herself.

'Yes,' she said. 'In a way, one is of the world if one lives in it. But isn't it really an illusion to think you can get out of it? After all, a cottage in the Abruzzi, or wherever it may be, isn't a new world. No, the only thing to do with the world, is to see it through.'

Ursula looked away. She was so frightened of argument.

'But there *can* be something else, can't there?' she said. 'One can see it through in one's soul, long enough before it sees itself through in actuality. And then, when one has seen one's soul, one is something else.'

'*Can* one see it through in one's soul?' asked Gudrun. 'If you mean that you can see to the end of what will happen, I don't agree. I really can't agree. And anyhow, you can't suddenly fly off on to a new planet, because you think you can see to the end of this.'

Ursula suddenly straightened herself.

'Yes,' she said. 'Yes – one knows. One has no more connections here. One has a sort of other self, that belongs to a new planet, not to this. You've got to hop off.'

Gudrun reflected for a few moments. Then a smile of ridicule, almost of contempt, came over her face.

'And what will happen when you find yourself in space?' she cried in derision. 'After all, the great ideas of the world are the same there. You above everybody can't get away from the fact that love, for instance, is the supreme thing, in space as well as on earth.'

'No,' said Ursula, 'it isn't. Love is too human and little. I believe in something inhuman, of which love is only a little part. I believe what we must fulfil comes out of the unknown to us, and it is something infinitely more than love. It isn't so merely *human*.'

Gudrun looked at Ursula with steady, balancing eyes. She admired and despised her sister so much, both! Then, suddenly she averted her face, saying coldly, uglily:

'Well, I've got no further than love, yet.'

Over Ursula's mind flashed the thought: 'Because you never *have* loved, you can't get beyond it.'

Gudrun rose, came over to Ursula and put her arm round her neck.

'Go and find your new world, dear,' she said, her voice clanging with false benignity. 'After all, the happiest voyage is the quest of Rupert's Blessed Isles.'

Her arm rested round Ursula's neck, her fingers on Ursula's cheek for a few moments. Ursula was supremely uncomfortable meanwhile. There was an insult in Gudrun's protective patronage that was really too hurting. Feeling her sister's resistance, Gudrun drew awkwardly away, turned over the pillow, and disclosed the stockings again.

'Ha – ha!' she laughed, rather hollowly. 'How we do talk indeed – new worlds and old – !'

And they passed to the familiar worldly subjects.

Gerald and Birkin had walked on ahead, waiting for the sledge to overtake them, conveying the departing guests.

'How much longer will you stay here?' asked Birkin, glancing up at Gerald's very red, almost blank face.

'Oh, I can't say,' Gerald replied. 'Till we get tired of it.'

'You're not afraid of the snow melting first?' asked Birkin.

Gerald laughed.

'Does it melt?' he said.

'Things are all right with you then?' said Birkin.

Gerald screwed up his eyes a little.

'All right?' he said. 'I never know what those common words mean. All right and all wrong, don't they become synonymous, somewhere?'

'Yes, I suppose. How about going back?' asked Birkin.

'Oh, I don't know. We may never get back. I don't look before and after,' said Gerald.

'*Nor* pine for what is not,' said Birkin.

Gerald looked into the distance, with the small-pupilled, abstract eyes of a hawk.

'No. There's something final about this. And Gudrun seems like the end to me. I don't know – but she seems so soft, her skin like silk, her arms heavy and soft. And it withers my consciousness, somehow, it burns the pith of my mind.' He went on a few paces, staring ahead, his eyes fixed, looking like a mask used in ghastly religions of the barbarians. 'It blasts your soul's eye,' he said, 'and leaves you sightless. Yet you *want* to be sightless, you *want* to be blasted, you don't want it any different.'

He was speaking as if in a trance, verbal and blank. Then suddenly he braced himself up with a kind of rhapsody, and looked at Birkin with vindictive, cowed eyes saying:

'Do you know what it is to suffer when you are with a woman? She's so beautiful, so perfect, you find her *so good*, it tears you like a silk, and every stroke and bit cuts hot – ha, that perfection, when you blast yourself, you blast yourself! And then –' he stopped on the snow and suddenly opened his clenched hands – 'it's nothing – your brain might have gone charred as rags – and –' he looked round into the air with a queer histrionic movement – 'it's blasting – you understand what I mean – it is a great experience, something final – and then – you're shrivelled as if struck by electricity.' He walked on in silence. It seemed like bragging, but like a man in extremity bragging truthfully.

'Of course,' he resumed, 'I wouldn't *not* have had it! It's a complete experience. And she's a wonderful woman. But – how I hate her somewhere! It's curious –'

Birkin looked at him, at his strange, scarcely conscious face. Gerald seemed blank before his own words.

'But you've had enough now?' said Birkin. 'You have had your experience. Why work on an old wound?'

'Oh,' said Gerald, 'I don't know. It's not finished –'

And the two walked on.

'I've loved you, as well as Gudrun, don't forget,' said Birkin bitterly. Gerald looked at him strangely, abstractedly.

'Have you?' he said, with icy scepticism. 'Or do you think you have?' He was hardly responsible for what he said.

The sledge came. Gudrun dismounted and they all made their farewell. They wanted to go apart, all of them. Birkin took his place, and the sledge drove away leaving Gudrun and Gerald standing on the snow, waving. Something froze Birkin's heart, seeing them standing there in the isolation of the snow, growing smaller and more isolated.

30

SNOWED UP

When Ursula and Birkin were gone, Gudrun felt herself free in her contest with Gerald. As they grew more used to each other, he seemed to press upon her more and more. At first she could manage him, so that her own will was always left free. But very soon, he began to ignore her female tactics, he dropped his respect for her whims and her privacies, he began to exert his own will blindly, without submitting to hers.

Already a vital conflict had set in, which frightened them both. But he was alone, whilst already she had begun to cast round for external resource.

When Ursula had gone, Gudrun felt her own existence had become stark and elemental. She went and crouched alone in her bedroom, looking out of the window at the big, flashing stars. In front was the faint shadow of the mountain-knot. That was the pivot. She felt strange and inevitable, as if she were centred upon the pivot of all existence, there was no further reality.

Presently Gerald opened the door. She knew he would not be long before he came. She was rarely alone, he pressed upon her like a frost, deadening her.

'Are you alone in the dark?' he said. And she could tell by his tone he resented it, he resented this isolation she had drawn round herself. Yet, feeling static and inevitable, she was kind towards him.

'Would you like to light the candle?' she asked.

He did not answer, but came and stood behind her, in the darkness.

'Look,' she said, 'at that lovely star up there. Do you know its name?'

He crouched beside her, to look through the low window.

'No,' he said. 'It is very fine.'

'*Isn't* it beautiful! Do you notice how it darts different coloured fires – it flashes really superbly –'

They remained in silence. With a mute, heavy gesture she put her hand on his knee, and took his hand.

'Are you regretting Ursula?' he asked.

'No, not at all,' she said. Then, in a slow mood, she asked:

'How much do you love me?'

He stiffened himself further against her.

'How much do you think I do?' he asked.

'I don't know,' she replied.

'But what is your opinion?' he asked.

There was a pause. At length, in the darkness, came her voice, hard and indifferent:

'Very little indeed,' she said coldly, almost flippant.

His heart went icy at the sound of her voice.

'Why don't I love you?' he asked, as if admitting the truth of her accusation, yet hating her for it.

'I don't know why you don't – I've been good to you. You were in a *fearful* state when you came to me.'

Her heart was beating to suffocate her, yet she was strong and unrelenting.

'When was I in a fearful state?' he asked.

'When you first came to me. I *had* to take pity on you. But it was never love.'

It was that statement 'It was never love', which sounded in his ears with madness.

'Why must you repeat it so often, that there is no love?' he said in a voice strangled with rage.

'Well you don't *think* you love, do you?' she asked.

He was silent with cold passion of anger.

'You don't think you *can* love me, do you?' she repeated almost with a sneer.

'No,' he said.

'You know you never *have* loved me, don't you?'

'I don't know what you mean by the word "love",' he replied.

'Yes, you do. You know all right that you have never loved me. Have you, do you think?'

'No,' he said, prompted by some barren spirit of truthfulness and obstinacy.

'And you never *will* love me,' she said finally, 'will you?'

There was a diabolic coldness in her, too much to bear.

'No,' he said.

'Then,' she replied, 'what have you against me?'

He was silent in cold, frightened rage and despair. 'If only I could kill her,' his heart was whispering repeatedly. 'If only I could kill her – I should be free.'

It seemed to him that death was the only severing of this Gordian knot.

'Why do you torture me?' he said.

She flung her arms round his neck.

'Ah, I don't want to torture you,' she said pityingly, as if she were comforting a child. The impertinence made his veins go cold, he was insensible. She held her arms round his neck, in a triumph of pity. And her pity for him was as cold as stone, its deepest motive was hate of him, and fear of his power over her, which she must always counterfoil.

'Say you love me,' she pleaded. 'Say you will love me for ever – won't you – won't you?'

But it was her voice only that coaxed him. Her senses were entirely apart from him, cold and destructive of him. It was her overbearing *will* that insisted.

'Won't you say you'll love me always?' she coaxed. 'Say it, even if it isn't true – say it Gerald, do.'

'I will love you always,' he repeated, in real agony, forcing the words out.

She gave him a quick kiss.

'Fancy your actually having said it,' she said with a touch of raillery.

He stood as if he had been beaten.

'Try to love me a little more, and to want me a little less,' she said, in a half contemptuous, half coaxing tone.

The darkness seemed to be swaying in waves across his mind, great waves of darkness plunging across his mind. It seemed to him he was degraded at the very quick, made of no account.

'You mean you don't want me?' he said.

'You are so insistent, and there is so little grace in you, so little fineness. You are so crude. You break me – you only waste me – it is horrible to me.'

'Horrible to you?' he repeated.

'Yes. Don't you think I might have a room to myself, now Ursula has gone? You can say you want a dressing-room.'

'You do as you like – you can leave altogether if you like,' he managed to articulate.

'Yes, I know that,' she replied. 'So can you. You can leave me whenever you like – without notice even.'

The great tides of darkness were swinging across his mind, he could hardly stand upright. A terrible weariness overcame him, he felt he must lie on the floor. Dropping off his clothes, he got into bed, and lay like a man suddenly overcome by drunkenness, the darkness lifting and plunging as if he were lying upon a black, giddy sea. He lay still in this strange, horrific reeling for some time, purely unconscious.

At length she slipped from her own bed and came over to him. He remained rigid, his back to her. He was all but unconscious.

She put her arms round his terrifying, insentient body, and laid her cheek against his hard shoulder.

'Gerald,' she whispered. 'Gerald.'

There was no change in him. She caught him against her. She pressed her breasts against his shoulders, she kissed his shoulder, through the sleeping jacket. Her mind wondered, over his rigid, unliving body. She was bewildered, and insistent, only her will was set for him to speak to her.

'Gerald, my dear!' she whispered, bending over him, kissing his ear.

Her warm breath playing, flying rhythmically over his ear, seemed to relax the tension. She could feel his body gradually relaxing a little, losing its terrifying, unnatural rigidity. Her hands clutched his limbs, his muscles, going over him spasmodically.

The hot blood began to flow again through his veins, his limbs relaxed.

'Turn round to me,' she whispered, forlorn with insistence and triumph.

So at last he was given again, warm and flexible. He turned and gathered her in his arms. And feeling her soft against him, so perfectly and wondrously soft and recipient, his arms tightened on her. She was as if crushed, powerless in him. His brain seemed hard and invincible now like a jewel, there was no resisting him.

His passion was awful to her, tense and ghastly, and impersonal, like a destruction, ultimate. She felt it would kill her. She was being killed.

'My God, my God,' she cried, in anguish, in his embrace, feeling her life being killed within her. And when he was kissing her, soothing her, her breath came slowly, as if she were really spent, dying.

'Shall I die, shall I die?' she repeated to herself.

And in the night, and in him, there was no answer to the question.

And yet, next day, the fragment of her which was not destroyed remained intact and hostile, she did not go away, she remained to finish the holiday, admitting nothing. He scarcely ever left her alone, but followed her like a shadow, he was like a doom upon her, a continual 'thou shalt', 'thou shalt not'. Sometimes it was he who seemed strongest, whilst she was almost gone, creeping near the earth like a spent wind; sometimes it was the reverse. But always it was this eternal see-saw, one destroyed that the other might exist, one ratified because the other was nulled.

'In the end,' she said to herself, 'I shall go away from him.'

'I can be free of her,' he said to himself in his paroxysms of suffering.

And he set himself to be free. He even prepared to go away, to leave her in the lurch. But for the first time there was a flaw in his will.

'Where shall I go?' he asked himself.

'Can't you be self-sufficient?' he replied to himself, putting himself upon his pride.

'Self-sufficient!' he repeated.

It seemed to him that Gudrun was sufficient unto herself, closed round and completed, like a thing in a case. In the calm, static reason of his soul, he recognized this, and admitted it was her right, to be closed round upon herself, self-complete, without desire. He realized it, he admitted it, it only needed one last effort on his own part, to win for himself the same completeness. He knew that it only needed one convulsion of his will for him to be able to turn upon himself also, to close upon himself as a stone fixes upon itself, and is impervious, self-completed, a thing isolated.

This knowledge threw him into a terrible chaos. Because, however much he might mentally *will* to be immune and self-complete, the desire for this state was lacking, and he could not create it. He could see that, to exist at all, he must be perfectly free of Gudrun, leave her if she wanted to be left, demand nothing of her, have no claim upon her.

But then, to have no claim upon her, he must stand by himself, in sheer nothingness. And his brain turned to nought at the idea. It was a state of nothingness. On the other hand, he might give in, and fawn to her. Or, finally, he might kill her. Or he might become just indifferent, purposeless, dissipated, momentaneous. But his nature was too serious, not gay enough or subtle enough for mocking licentiousness.

A strange rent had been torn in him; like a victim that is torn open and given to the heavens, so he had been torn apart and given to Gudrun. How should he close again? This wound, this strange, infinitely-sensitive opening of his soul, where he was exposed, like an open flower, to all the universe, and in which he was given to his complement, the other, the unknown, this wound, this disclosure, this unfolding of his own covering, leaving him incomplete, limited, unfinished, like an open flower under the sky, this was his cruellest joy. Why then should he forgo it? Why should he close up and become impervious, immune, like a partial thing in a sheath, when he had broken forth, like a seed that has germinated, to issue forth in being, embracing the unrealized heavens.

He would keep the unfinished bliss of his own yearning even through the torture she inflicted upon him. A strange obstinacy possessed him. He would not go away from her whatever she said or did. A strange, deathly yearning carried him along with her. She was the determinating influence of his very being, though she treated him with contempt, repeated rebuffs and denials, still he would never be gone, since in being near her, even, he felt the quickening, the going forth in him, the release, the knowledge of his own limitation and the magic of the promise, as well as the mystery of his own destruction and annihilation.

She tortured the open heart of him even as he turned to her. And she was tortured herself. It may have been her will was stronger. She felt, with horror, as if he tore at the bud of her heart, tore it open, like an irreverent persistent being. Like a boy who pulls off a fly's wings, or tears open a bud to see what is in the flower, he tore at her privacy, at her very life, he would destroy her as an immature bud, torn open, is destroyed.

She might open towards him, a long while hence, in her dreams, when she was a pure spirit. But now she was not to be violated and ruined. She closed against him fiercely.

They climbed together, at evening, up the high slope, to see the sun set. In the finely breathing, keen wind they stood and watched the yellow sun sink in crimson and disappear. Then in the east the peaks and ridges glowed with living rose, incandescent like immortal flowers against a brown-purple sky, a miracle, whilst down below the world was a bluish shadow, and above, like an annunciation, hovered a rosy transport in mid-air.

To her it was so beautiful, it was a delirium, she wanted to gather the glowing, eternal peaks to her breast, and die. He saw them, saw they were beautiful. But there arose no clamour in his breast, only a bitterness that was visionary in itself. He wished the peaks were grey and unbeautiful, so that she should not get her support from them. Why did she betray the two of them so terribly, in embracing the glow of the evening? Why did she leave him standing there, with the ice-wind blowing through his heart, like death, to gratify herself among the rosy snow-tips?

'What does the twilight matter?' he said. 'Why do you grovel before it? Is it so important to you?'

She winced in violation and in fury.

'Go away,' she cried, 'and leave me to it. It is beautiful, beautiful,' she sang in strange, rhapsodic tones. 'It is the most beautiful thing I have ever seen in my life. Don't try to come between it and me. Take yourself away, you are out of place –'

He stood back a little, and left her standing there, statue-like, transported into the mystic glowing east. Already the rose was fading, large white stars were flashing out. He waited. He would forgo everything but the yearning.

'That was the most perfect thing I have ever seen,' she said in cold, brutal tones, when at last she turned round to him. 'It amazes me that you should want to destroy it. If you can't see it yourself, why try to debar me?' But in reality, he had destroyed it for her, she was straining after a dead effect.

'One day,' he said, softly, looking up at her, 'I shall destroy *you*, as you stand looking at the sunset; because you are such a liar.'

There was a soft, voluptuous promise to himself in the words. She was chilled but arrogant.

'Ha!' she said. 'I am not afraid of your threats!'

She denied herself to him, she kept her room rigidly private to herself. But he waited on, in a curious patience, belonging to his yearning for her.

'In the end,' he said to himself with real voluptuous promise, 'when it reaches that point, I shall do away with her.' And he trembled delicately in every limb, in anticipation, as he trembled in his most violent accesses of passionate approach to her, trembling with too much desire.

She had a curious sort of allegiance with Loerke, all the while now, something insidious and traitorous. Gerald knew of it. But in the unnatural state of patience, and the unwillingness to harden himself against her, in which he found himself, he took no notice, although her soft kindliness to the other man, whom he hated as a noxious insect, made him shiver again with an access of the strange shuddering that came over him repeatedly.

He left her alone only when he went ski-ing, a sport he loved, and which she did not practise. Then he seemed to sweep out of life, to be a projectile into the beyond. And often, when he went away, she talked to the little German sculptor. They had an invariable topic, in their art.

They were almost of the same ideas. He hated Mestrovic, was not satisfied with the Futurists, he liked the West African wooden figures, the Aztec art, Mexican and Central American. He saw the grotesque, and a curious sort of mechanical motion intoxicated him, a confusion in nature. They had a curious game with each other, Gudrun and Loerke, of infinite suggestivity, strange and leering, as if they had some esoteric understanding of life, that they alone were initiated into the fearful central secrets, that the world dared not know. Their whole correspondence was in a strange, barely comprehensible suggestivity, they kindled themselves at the subtle lust of the Egyptians or the Mexicans. The whole game was one of subtle inter-suggestivity, and they wanted to keep it on the plane of suggestion. From their verbal and physical nuances they got the highest satisfaction in the nerves, from a queer interchange of half-suggested ideas, looks, expressions and gestures, which were quite intolerable, though incomprehensible, to Gerald. He had no terms in which to think of their commerce, his terms were much too gross.

The suggestion of primitive art was their refuge, and the inner mysteries of sensation their object of worship. Art and Life were to them the Reality and the Unreality.

'Of course,' said Gudrun, 'life doesn't *really* matter – it is one's art which is central. What one does in one's life has *peu de rapport*, it doesn't signify much.'

'Yes, that is so, exactly,' replied the sculptor. 'What one does in one's art, that is the breath of one's being. What one does in one's life, that is a bagatelle for the outsiders to fuss about.'

It was curious what a sense of elation and freedom Gudrun found in this communication. She felt established for ever. Of course Gerald was *bagatelle*. Love was one of the temporal things in her life, except in so far as she was an artist. She thought of Cleopatra – Cleopatra must have been an artist; she reaped the essential from a man, she harvested the ultimate sensation, and threw away the husk; and Mary Stuart, and the great Rachel, panting with her lovers after the theatre, these were the exoteric exponents of love. After all, what was the lover but fuel for the transport of this subtle knowledge, for a female art, the art of pure, perfect knowledge in sensuous understanding.

One evening Gerald was arguing with Loerke about Italy and Tripoli. The Englishman was in a strange, inflammable state, the German was excited. It was a contest of words, but it meant a conflict of spirit between the two men. And all the while Gudrun could see in Gerald an arrogant English contempt for a foreigner. Although Gerald was quivering, his eyes flashing, his face flushed, in his argument there was a brusqueness, a savage contempt in his manner, that made Gudrun's blood flare up, and made Loerke keen and mortified. For Gerald came down like a sledge-hammer with his assertions, anything the little German said was merely contemptible rubbish.

At last Loerke turned to Gudrun, raising his hands in helpless irony, a shrug of ironical dismissal, something appealing and child-like.

'*Sehen sie, gnädige Frau –*' he began.

'*Bitte sagen Sie nicht immer, gnädige Frau,*' cried Gudrun, her eyes flashing, her cheeks burning. She looked like a vivid Medusa. Her voice was loud and clamorous, the other people in the room were startled.

'Please don't call me Mrs Crich,' she cried aloud.

The name, in Loerke's mouth particularly, had been an intolerable humiliation and constraint upon her these many days.

The two men looked at her in amazement. Gerald went white at the cheek-bones.

'What shall I say, then?' asked Loerke, with soft, mocking insinuation.

'*Sagen Sie nur nicht das,*' she muttered, her cheeks flushed crimson. 'Not that, at least.'

She saw, by the dawning look on Loerke's face, that he had understood. She was *not* Mrs Crich! So-o-, that explained a great deal.

'*Soll ich Fräulein sagen?*' he asked malevolently.

'I am not married,' she said, with some hauteur.

Her heart was fluttering now, beating like a bewildered bird. She knew she had dealt a cruel wound, and she could not bear it.

Gerald sat erect, perfectly still, his face pale and calm, like the face of a statue. He was unaware of her, or of Loerke or anybody. He sat perfectly still in an unalterable calm. Loerke, meanwhile, was crouching and glancing up from under his ducked head.

Gudrun was tortured for something to say, to relieve the suspense. She twisted her face in a smile and glanced knowingly, almost sneering, at Gerald.

'Truth is best,' she said to him, with a grimace.

But now again she was under his domination; now, because she had dealt him this blow; because she had destroyed him, and she did not know how he had taken it. She watched him. He was interesting to her. She had lost her interest in Loerke.

Gerald rose at length and went over in a leisurely still movement to the professor. The two began a conversation on Goethe.

She was rather piqued by the simplicity of Gerald's demeanour this evening. He did not seem angry or disgusted, only he looked curiously innocent and pure, really beautiful. Sometimes it came upon him, this look of clear distance, and it always fascinated her.

She waited, troubled, throughout the evening. She thought he would avoid her, or give some sign. But he spoke to her simply and unemotionally, as he would to anyone else in the room. A certain peace, an abstraction possessed his soul.

She went to his room, hotly, violently in love with him. He was so beautiful and inaccessible. He kissed her, he was a lover to her. And she had extreme pleasure of him. But he did not come to, he remained remote and candid, unconscious. She wanted to speak to him. But this innocent, beautiful state of unconsciousness that had come upon him prevented her. She felt tormented and dark.

In the morning, however, he looked at her with a little aversion, some horror and some hatred darkening into his eyes. She withdrew on to her old ground. But still he would not gather himself together against her.

Loerke was waiting for her now. The little artist, isolated in his own complete envelope, felt that here at last was a woman from whom he could get something. He was uneasy all the while, waiting to talk with her subtly contriving to be near her. Her presence filled him with keenness and excitement, he gravitated cunningly towards her, as if she had some unseen force of attraction.

He was not in the least doubtful of himself, as regards Gerald. Gerald was one of the outsiders. Loerke only hated him for being rich and proud and of fine appearance. All these things, however, riches, pride of social standing, handsome physique, were externals. When it came to the relation with a woman such as Gudrun, he Loerke, had an approach and a power that Gerald never dreamed of.

How should Gerald hope to satisfy a woman of Gudrun's calibre? Did he think that pride or masterful will or physical strength would help him? Loerke knew a secret beyond these things. The greatest power is the one that is subtle and adjusts itself, not one which blindly attacks. And he, Loerke, had understanding where Gerald was a calf. He, Loerke could penetrate into depths far out of Gerald's knowledge. Gerald was left behind like a postulant in the ante-room of this temple of mysteries, this woman. But he, Loerke, could he not penetrate into the inner darkness, find the spirit of the woman in its inner recess, and wrestle with it there, the central serpent that is coiled at the core of life.

What was it, after all, that a woman wanted? Was it mere social effect, fulfilment of ambition in the social world, in the community of mankind? Was it even a union in love and goodness? Did she want 'goodness'? Who but a fool would accept this of Gudrun? This was but the street view of her wants. Cross the threshold, and you found her completely, completely cynical about the social world and its advantages. Once inside the house of her soul, and there was a pungent atmosphere of corrosion, an inflamed darkness of sensation, and a vivid, subtle, critical consciousness, that saw the world distorted, horrific.

What then, what next? Was it sheer blind force of passion that would satisfy her now? Not this, but the subtle thrills of extreme sensation in reduction. It was an unbroken will reacting against her unbroken will in a myriad subtle thrills of reduction, the last subtle activities of analysis and breaking down, carried out in the darkness of her, whilst the outside form, the individual, was utterly unchanged, even sentimental in its poses.

But between two particular people, any two people on earth, the range of pure sensational experience is limited. The climax of sensual reaction, once reached in any direction, is reached finally, there is no going on. There is only repetition possible, or the going apart of the two protagonists, or the subjugating of the one will to the other, or death.

Gerald had penetrated all the outer places of Gudrun's soul. He was to her the most crucial instance of the existing world, the *ne plus ultra* of the world of man as it existed for her. In him she knew the world, and had done with it. Knowing him finally she was the Alexander seeking new worlds. But there *were* no new worlds, there were no more *men*, there were only creatures, little, ultimate *creatures* like Loerke. The world was finished now, for her. There was only the inner, individual darkness, sensation within the ego, the obscene religious mystery of ultimate reduction, the mystic frictional activities of diabolic reducing down, disintegrating the vital organic body of life.

All this Gudrun knew in her subconsciousness, not in her mind. She knew her next step – she knew what she should move on to when she left Gerald. She was afraid of Gerald, that he might kill her. But she did not intend to be killed. A fine thread still united her to him. It should not be *her* death which broke it. She had farther to go, a farther, slow, exquisite experience to reap, unthinkable subtleties of sensation to know, before she was finished.

Of the last series of subtleties, Gerald was not capable. He could not touch the quick of her. But where his ruder blows could not penetrate, the fine, insinuating blade of Loerke's insect-like comprehension could. At least, it was time for her now to pass over to the other, the creature, the final craftsman. She knew that Loerke, in his innermost soul, was detached from everything, for him there was neither heaven nor earth nor hell. He admitted no allegiance, he gave no adherence anywhere. He was single and, by abstraction from the rest, absolute in himself.

Whereas in Gerald's soul there still lingered some attachment to the rest, to the whole. And this was his limitation. He was limited, *borné*, subject to his necessity, in the last issue, for goodness, for righteousness, for oneness with the ultimate purpose. That the ultimate purpose might be the perfect and subtle experience of the process of death, the will being kept unimpaired, that was not allowed in him. And this was his limitation.

There was a hovering triumph in Loerke, since Gudrun had denied her marriage with Gerald. The artist seemed to hover like a creature on the wing, waiting to settle. He did not approach Gudrun violently, he was never ill-timed. But carried on by a sure instinct in the complete darkness of his soul, he corresponded mystically with her, imperceptibly, but palpably.

For two days, he talked to her, continued the discussions of art, of life, in which they both found such pleasure. They praised the bygone things, they took a sentimental, childish delight in the achieved perfections of the past. Particularly they liked the late eighteenth century, the period of Goethe and of Shelley, and Mozart.

They played with the past, and with the great figures of the past, a sort of little game of chess, or marionettes, all to please themselves. They had all the great men for their marionettes, and they two were the God of the show, working it all. As for the future, that they never mentioned except one laughed out some mocking dream of the destruction of the world by a ridiculous catastrophe of man's invention: a man invented such a perfect explosive that it blew the earth in two, and the two halves set off in different directions through space, to the dismay of the inhabitants: or else the people of the world divided into two halves, and each half decided *it* was perfect and right, the other half was wrong and must be destroyed; so another end of the world. Or else, Loerke's dream of fear, the world went cold, and snow fell everywhere, and only white creatures, Polar bears, white foxes, and men like awful white snow-birds, persisted in ice cruelty.

Apart from these stories, they never talked of the future. They delighted most either in mocking imaginations of destruction or in sentimental, fine marionette shows of the past. It was a sentimental delight to reconstruct the world of Goethe at Weimar, or of Schiller and poverty and faithful love, or to see again Jean Jacques in his quakings, or Voltaire at Ferney, or Frederick the Great reading his own poetry.

They talked together for hours, of literature and sculpture and painting, amusing themselves with Flaxman and Blake and Fuseli, with tenderness, and with Feuerbach and Böcklin. It would take them a lifetime, they felt, to live again, *in petto*, the lives of the great artists. But they preferred to stay in the eighteenth and the nineteenth centuries.

They talked in a mixture of languages. The ground-work was French, in either case. But he ended most of his sentences in a stumble of English and a conclusion of German, she skilfully wove herself to her end in whatever phrase came to her. She took a peculiar delight in this conversation. It was full of odd, fantastic expression, of double meanings, of evasions, of suggestive vagueness. It was a real physical pleasure to her to make this thread of conversation out of the different-coloured strands of three languages.

And all the while they two were hovering, hesitating round the flame of some invisible declaration. He wanted it, but was held back by some inevitable reluctance. She wanted it also, but she wanted to put it off, to put it off indefinitely, she still had some pity for Gerald, some connection with him. And the most fatal of all, she had the reminiscent sentimental compassion for herself in connection with him. Because of what *had* been, she felt herself held to him by immortal, invisible threads – because of what *had* been, because of his coming to her that first night, into her own house, in his extremity, because –

Gerald was gradually overcome with a revulsion of loathing for Loerke. He did not take the man seriously, he despised him merely, except as he felt in Gudrun's veins the influence of the little creature. It was this that drove Gerald wild, the feeling in Gudrun's veins of Loerke's presence, Loerke's being, flowing dominant through her.

'What makes you so smitten with that little vermin?' he asked, really puzzled. For he, man-like, could not see anything attractive or important *at all* in Loerke. Gerald expected to find some handsomeness or nobleness to account for a woman's subjection. But he saw none here, only an insect-like repulsiveness.

Gudrun flushed deeply. It was these attacks she would never forgive.

'What do you mean?' she replied. 'My God, what a mercy I am *not* married to you!'

Her voice of flouting and contempt scotched him. He was brought up short. But he recovered himself.

'Tell me, only tell me,' he reiterated in a dangerous, narrowed voice – 'tell me what it is that fascinates you in him.'

'I am not fascinated,' she said, with cold, repelling innocence.

'Yes, you are. You are fascinated by that little dry snake, like a bird gaping ready to fall down its throat.'

She looked at him with black fury.

'I don't choose to be discussed by you,' she said.

'It doesn't matter whether you choose or not,' he replied, 'that doesn't alter the fact that you are ready to fall down and kiss the feet of that little insect. And I don't want to prevent you – do it, fall down and kiss his feet. But I want to know what it is that fascinates you – what is it?'

She was silent, suffused with black rage.

'How *dare* you come brow-beating me,' she cried, 'how dare you, you little squire, you bully. What right have you over me, do you think?'

His face was white and gleaming, she knew by the light in his eyes that she was in his power – the wolf. And because she was in his power, she hated him with a power that she wondered did not kill him. In her will she killed him as he stood, effaced him.

'It is not a question of right,' said Gerald, sitting down on a chair. She watched the change in his body. She saw his clenched, mechanical body moving there like an obsession. Her hatred of him was tingled with fatal contempt.

'It's not a question of my right over you – though I *have* some right, remember. I want to know, I only want to know what it is that subjugates you to that little scum of a sculptor downstairs, what it is that brings you down like a humble maggot, in worship of him. I want to know what you creep after.'

She stood over against the window, listening. Then she turned round.

'Do you?' she said, in her most easy, most cutting voice. 'Do you want to know what it is in him? It's because he has some understanding of a woman, because he is not stupid. That's why it is.'

A queer, sinister, animal-like smile came over Gerald's face.

'But what understanding is it?' he said. 'The understanding of a flea, a hopping flea with a proboscis. Why should you crawl abject before the understanding of a flea?'

There passed through Gudrun's mind Blake's representation of the soul of a flea. She wanted to fit it to Loerke. Blake was a clown too. But it was necessary to answer Gerald.

'Don't you think the understanding of a flea is more interesting than the understanding of a fool?' she asked.

'A fool!' he repeated.

'A fool, a conceited fool – a *Dummkopf*,' she replied, adding the German word.

'Do you call me a fool?' he replied. 'Well, wouldn't I rather be the fool I am than that flea downstairs?'

She looked at him. A certain blunt, blind stupidity in him palled on her soul, limiting her.

'You give yourself away by that last,' she said.

He sat and wondered.

'I shall go away soon,' he said.

She turned on him.

'Remember,' she said, 'I am completely independent of you – completely. You make your arrangements, I make mine.'

He pondered this.

'You mean we are strangers from this minute?' he asked.

She halted and flushed. He was putting her in a trap, forcing her hand. She turned round on him.

'Strangers,' she said, 'we can never be. But if you *want* to make any movement apart from me, then I wish you to know you are perfectly free to do so. Do not consider me in the slightest.'

Even so slight an implication that she needed him and was depending on him still was sufficient to rouse his passion. As he sat a change came over his body, the hot, molten stream mounted involuntarily through his veins. He groaned inwardly, under its bondage, but he loved it. He looked at her with clear eyes, waiting for her.

She knew at once, and was shaken with cold revulsion. *How* could he look at her with those clear, warm, waiting eyes, waiting for her, even now? What had been said between them, was it not enough to put them worlds asunder, to freeze them for ever apart! And yet he was all transfused and roused, waiting for her.

It confused her. Turning her head aside, she said:

'I shall always *tell* you, whenever I am going to make any change –'

And with this she moved out of the room.

He sat suspended in a fine recoil of disappointment, that seemed gradually to be destroying his understanding. But the unconscious state of patience persisted in him. He remained motionless, without thought or knowledge, for a long time. Then he rose and went downstairs to play at chess with one of the students. His face was open and clear, with a certain innocent *laisser-aller* that troubled Gudrun most, made her almost afraid of him, whilst she disliked him deeply for it.

It was after this that Loerke, who had never yet spoken to her personally, began to ask her of her state.

'You are not married at all, are you?' he asked.

She looked full at him.

'Not in the least,' she replied, in her measured way. Loerke laughed, wrinkling up his face oddly. There was a thin wisp of his hair straying on his forehead, she noticed that his skin was of a clear brown colour, his hands, his wrists. And his hands seemed closely prehensile. He seemed like topaz, so strangely brownish and pellucid.

'Good,' he said.

Still it needed some courage for him to go on.

'Was Mrs Birkin your sister?' he asked.

'Yes.'

'And was *she* married?'

'She was married.'

'Have you parents, then?'

'Yes,' said Gudrun, 'we have parents.'

And she told him, briefly, laconically, her position. He watched her closely, curiously, all the while.

'So!' he exclaimed, with some surprise. 'And the Herr Crich, is he rich?'

'Yes, he is rich, a coal owner.'

'How long has your friendship with him lasted?'

'Some months.'

There was a pause.

'Yes, I am surprised,' he said at length. 'The English, I thought they were so – cold. And what do you think to do when you leave here?'

'What do I think to do?' she repeated.

'Yes. You cannot go back to the teaching. No' – he shrugged his shoulders – 'that is impossible. Leave that to the *canaille* who can do nothing else. You, for your part – you know, you are a wonderful woman, *eine seltsame Frau*. Why deny it – why make any question of it? You are an extraordinary woman, why should you follow the ordinary course, the ordinary life?'

Gudrun sat looking at her hands, flushed. She was pleased that he said, so simply, that she was a remarkable woman. He would not say that to flatter her – he was far too self-opinionated and objective by nature. He said it as he would say a piece of sculpture was remarkable, because he knew it was so.

And it gratified her to hear it from him. Other people had such a passion to make everything of one degree, of one pattern. In England it was chic to be perfectly ordinary. And it was a relief to her to be acknowledged extraordinary. Then she need not fret about the common standards.

'You see,' she said, 'I have no money whatsoever.'

'Ach, money!' he cried, lifting his shoulders. 'When one is grown up, money is lying about at one's service. It is only when one is young that it is rare. Take no thought for money – that always lies to hand.'

'Does it?' she said, laughing.

'Always. The Gerald will give you a sum if you ask him for it –'

She flushed deeply.

'I will ask anybody else,' she said, with some difficulty – 'but not him.'
Loerke looked closely at her.

'Good,' he said. 'Then let it be somebody else. Only don't go back to that
England, that school. No, that is stupid.'

Again there was a pause. He was afraid to ask her outright to go with him,
he was not even quite sure he wanted her; and she was afraid to be asked. He
begrudged his own isolation, was *very* chary of sharing his life, even for a day.

'The only other place I know is Paris,' she said, 'and I can't stand that.'

She looked with her wide, steady eyes full at Loerke. He lowered his head
and averted his face.

'Paris, no!' he said. 'Between the *religion d'amour*, and the latest 'ism, and
the new turning to Jesus, one had better ride on a carrousel all day. But come
to Dresden. I have a studio there – I can give you work – oh, that would be
easy enough. I haven't seen any of your things, but I believe in you. Come to
Dresden – that is a fine town to be in, and as good a life as you can expect of a
town. You have everything there, without the foolishness of Paris or the beer
of Munich.'

He sat and looked at her coldly. What she liked about him was that he
spoke to her simple and flat, as to himself. He was a fellow craftsman, a fellow
being to her, first.

'No – Paris,' he resumed, 'it makes me sick. Pah – *l'amour*. I detest it.
L'amour, l'amore, die Liebe – I detest it in every language. Women and love,
there is no greater tedium,' he cried.

She was slightly offended. And yet this was her own basic feeling. Men and
love – there was no greater tedium.

'I think the same,' she said.

'A bore,' he repeated. 'What does it matter whether I wear this hat or
another. So love. I needn't wear a hat at all, only for convenience. Neither
need I love except for convenience. I tell you what, *gnädige Frau –*' and he
leaned towards her – then he made a quick odd gesture, as of striking
something aside – '*gnädige Fräulein*, never mind – I tell you what, I would give
everything, everything, all your love, for a little companionship in intelligence –' his eyes flickered darkly, evilly at her. 'You understand?' he asked,
with a faint smile. 'It wouldn't matter if she were a hundred years old, a
thousand – it would be all the same to me, so that she can *understand*.' He
shut his eyes with a little snap.

Again Gudrun was rather offended. Did he not think her good-looking,
then? Suddenly she laughed.

'I shall have to wait about eighty years to suit you at that,' she said. 'I am
ugly enough, aren't I?'

He looked at her with an artist's sudden, critical, estimating eye.

'You are beautiful,' he said, 'and I am glad of it. But it isn't that – it isn't
that,' he cried, with emphasis that flattered her. 'It is that you have a certain
wit, it is the kind of understanding. For me, I am little, *chétif*, insignificant.
Good! Do not ask me to be strong and handsome, then. But it is the *me*' – he
put his fingers to his mouth oddly – 'it is the *me* that is looking for a mistress,
and my *me* is waiting for the *thee* of the mistress, for the match to my
particular intelligence. You understand?'

'Yes,' she said, 'I understand.'

'As for the other, this *amour*' – he made a gesture, dashing his hand aside,
as if to dash away something troublesome – 'it is unimportant, unimportant.

Does it matter whether I drink white wine this evening or whether I drink nothing? It *does not matter*, it does not matter. So this love, this *amour*, this *baiser*. Yes or no, *soit ou soit pas*, today, tomorrow, or never, it is all the same, it does not matter – no more than the white wine.'

He ended with an odd dropping of the head in a desperate negation. Gudrun watched him steadily. She had gone pale.

Suddenly she stretched over and seized his hand in her own.

'That is true,' she said, in rather a high, vehement voice, 'that is true for me too. It is the understanding that matters.'

He looked up at her almost frightened, furtive. Then he nodded a little sullenly. She let go his hand: he had made not the lightest response. And they sat in silence.

'Do you know,' he said, suddenly looking at her with dark, self-important, prophetic eyes, 'your fate and mine, they will run together till –' and he broke off in a little grimace.

'Till when?' she asked, blanched, her lips going white. She was terribly susceptible to these evil prognostications, but he only shook his head.

'I don't know,' he said, 'I don't know.'

Gerald did not come in from his ski-ing until nightfall, he missed the coffee and cake that she took at four o'clock. The snow was in perfect condition, he had travelled a long way, by himself, among the snow ridges, on his skis, he had climbed high, so high that he could see over the top of the pass five miles distant, could see the Marienhütte, the hostel on the crest of the pass, half buried in snow, and over into the deep valley beyond, to the dusk of the pine trees. One could go that way home; but he shuddered with nausea at the thought of home; – one could travel on skis down there, and come to the old imperial road, below the pass. But why come to any road? he revolted at the thought of finding himself in the world again. He must stay up there in the snow for ever. He had been happy by himself, high up there alone, travelling swiftly on skis, taking far flights and skimming past the dark rocks veined with brilliant snow.

But he felt something icy gathering at his heart. This strange mood of patience and innocence which had persisted in him for some days was passing away, he would be left again a prey to the horrible passions and tortures.

So he came down reluctantly, snow-burned, snow-estranged, to the house in the hollow, between the knuckles of the mountain-tops. He saw its lights shining yellow, and he held back, wishing he need not go in to confront those people, to hear the turmoil of voices and to feel the confusion of other presences. He was isolated as if there were a vacuum round his heart, or a sheath of pure ice.

The moment he saw Gudrun something jolted in his soul. She was looking rather lofty and superb, smiling slowly and graciously to the Germans. A sudden desire leapt in his heart to kill her. He thought, what a perfect voluptuous fulfilment it would be to kill her. His mind was absent all the evening, estranged by the snow and his passion. But he kept the idea constant within him, what a perfect voluptuous consummation it would be to strangle her, to strangle every spark of life out of her, till she lay completely inert, soft, relaxed for ever, a soft heap lying dead between his hands, utterly dead. Then he would have had her finally and for ever; there would be such a perfect voluptuous finality.

Gudrun was unaware of what he was feeling, he seemed so quiet and amiable, as usual. His amiability even made her feel brutal towards him.

She went into his room when he was partially undressed. She did not notice the curious, glad gleam of pure hatred, with which he looked at her. She stood near the door, with her hand behind her.

'I have been thinking, Gerald,' she said, with an insulting nonchalance, 'that I shall not go back to England.'

'Oh,' he said, 'where will you go then?'

But she ignored his question. She had her own logical statement to make, and it must be made as she had thought it.

'I can't see the use of going back,' she continued. 'It is over between me and you –'

She paused for him to speak. But he said nothing. He was only talking to himself, saying: 'Over, is it? I believe it is over. But it isn't finished. Remember, it isn't finished. We must put some sort of a finish on it. There must be a conclusion, there must be finality.'

So he talked to himself, but aloud he said nothing whatever.

'What has been, has been,' she continued. 'There is nothing that I regret. I hope you regret nothing –'

She waited for him to speak.

'Oh, I regret nothing,' he said, accommodatingly.

'Good then,' she answered, 'good then. Then neither of us cherishes any regrets, which is as it should be.'

'Quite as it should be,' he said aimlessly.

She paused to gather up her thread again.

'Our attempt has been a failure,' she said. 'But we can try again elsewhere.'

A little flicker of rage ran through his blood. It was as if she were rousing him, goading him. Why must she do it?

'Attempt at what?' he asked.

'At being lovers, I suppose,' she said, a little baffled, yet so trivial she made it all seem.

'Our attempt at being lovers has been a failure?' he repeated aloud.

To himself he was saying, 'I ought to kill her here. There is only this left, for me to kill her.' A heavy, overcharged desire to bring about her death possessed him. She was unaware.

'Hasn't it?' she asked. 'Do you think it has been a success?'

Again the insult of the flippant question ran through his blood like a current of fire.

'It had some of the elements of success, our relationship,' he replied. 'It – might have come off.'

But he paused before concluding the last phrase. Even as he began the sentence, he did not believe in what he was going to say. He knew it never could have been a success.

'No,' she replied. 'You cannot love.'

'And you?' he asked.

Her wide, dark-filled eyes were fixed on him like two moons of darkness.

'I couldn't love *you*,' she said, with stark, cold truth.

A blinding flash went over his brain, his body jolted. His heart had burst into flame. His consciousness was gone into his wrists, into his hands. He was one blind, incontinent desire to kill her. His wrists were bursting, there would be no satisfaction till his hands had closed on her.

But even before his body swerved forward on her, a sudden, cunning comprehension was expressed on her face, and in a flash she was out of the door. She ran in one flash to her room and locked herself in. She was afraid, but confident. She knew her life trembled on the edge of an abyss. But she was curiously sure of her footing. She knew her cunning could outwit him.

She trembled, as she stood in her room, with excitement and awful exhilaration. She knew she could outwit him. She could depend on her presence of mind, and on her wits. But it was a fight to the death, she knew it now. One slip, and she was lost. She had a strange, tense, exhilarated sickness in her body, as one who is in peril of falling from a great height, but who does not look down, does not admit the fear.

'I will go away the day after tomorrow,' she said.

She only did not want Gerald to think that she was afraid of him, that she was running away because she was afraid of him. She was not afraid of him, fundamentally. She knew it was her safeguard to avoid his physical violence. But even physically she was not afraid of him. She wanted to prove it to him. When she had proved it, that, whatever he was, she was not afraid of him; when she had proved *that*, she could leave him for ever. But meanwhile the fight between them, terrible as she knew it to be, was inconclusive. And she wanted to be confident in herself. However many terrors she might have, she would be unafraid, uncowed by him. He could never cow her, nor dominate her, nor have any right over her; this she would maintain until she had proved it. Once it was proved, she was free of him for ever.

But she had not proved it yet, neither to him nor to herself. And this was what still bound her to him. She was bound to him, she could not live beyond him. She sat up in bed, closely wrapped up, for many hours, thinking endlessly to herself. It was as if she would never have done weaving the great provision of her thoughts.

'It isn't as if he really loved me,' she said to herself. 'He doesn't. Every woman he comes across he wants to make her in love with him. He doesn't even know that he is doing it. But there he is, before every woman he unfurls his male attractiveness, displays his great desirability, he tries to make every woman think how wonderful it would be to have him for a lover. His very ignoring of the women is part of the game. He is never *unconscious* of them. He should have been a cockerel, so he could strut before fifty females, all his subjects. But really, his Don Juan does *not* interest me. I could play Dona Juanita a million times better than he plays Juan. He bores me, you know. His maleness bores me. Nothing is so boring, so inherently stupid and stupidly conceited. Really, the fathomless conceit of these men, it is ridiculous – the little strutters.

'They are all alike. Look at Birkin. Built out of the limitation of conceit they are, and nothing else. Really, nothing but their ridiculous limitation and intrinsic insignificance could make them so conceited.

'As for Loerke, there is a thousand times more in him than in Gerald. Gerald is so limited, there is a dead end to him. He would grind on at the old mills for ever. And really, there is no corn between the millstones any more. They grind on and on, when there is nothing to grind – saying the same things, believing the same things, acting the same things. Oh, my God, it would wear out the patience of a stone.

'I don't worship Loerke, but at any rate, he is a free individual. He is not stiff with conceit of his own maleness. He is not grinding dutifully at the old mills. Oh God, when I think of Gerald, and his work – those offices at

Beldover, and the mines – it makes my heart sick. What *have* I to do with it – and him thinking he can be a lover to a woman! One might as well ask it of a self-satisfied lamp-post. These men, with their eternal jobs – and their eternal mills of God that keep on grinding at nothing! It is too boring, just boring. However did I come to take him seriously at all!

'At least in Dresden, one will have one's back to it all. And there will be amusing things to do. It will be amusing to go to these eurhythmic displays, and the German opera, the German theatre. It *will* be amusing to take part in German Bohemian life. And Loerke *is* an artist, he is a free individual. One will escape from so much, that is the chief thing, escape so much hideous boring repetition of vulgar actions, vulgar phrases, vulgar postures. I don't delude myself that I shall find an elixir of life in Dresden. I know I shan't. But I shall get away from people who have their own homes and their own children and their own acquaintances and their own this and their own that. I shall be among people who *don't* own things and who haven't got a home and a domestic servant in the background, who *haven't* got a standing and a status and a degree and a close circle of friends of the same. Oh God, the wheels within wheels of people, it makes one's head tick like a clock, with a very madness of dead mechanical monotony and meaninglessness. How I *hate* life, how I hate it. How I hate the Geralds, that they can offer one nothing else.

'Shortlands! – Heavens! Think of living there, one week, then the next, and *then the third* –

'No, I won't think of it – it is too much –'

And she broke off, really terrified, really unable to bear any more.

The thought of the mechanical succession of day following day, day following day, *ad infinitum*, was one of the things that made her heart palpitate with a real approach of madness. The terrible bondage of this tick-tack of time, this twitching of the hands of the clock, this eternal repetition of hours and days – oh God, it was too awful to contemplate. And there was no escape from it, no escape.

She almost wished Gerald were with her to save her from the terror of her own thoughts. Oh, how she suffered, lying there alone, confronted by the terrible clock, with its eternal tick-tack. All life, all life resolved itself into this: tick-tack, tick-tack, tick-tack; then the striking of the hour; then the tick-tack, tick-tack, and the twitching of the clock-fingers.

Gerald could not save her from it. He, his body, his motion, his life – it was the same ticking, the same twitching across the dial, a horrible mechanical twitching forward over the face of the hours. What were his kisses, his embraces. She could hear their tick-tack, tick-tack.

Ha – ha – she laughed to herself, so frightened that she was trying to laugh it off – ha – ha, how maddening it was, to be sure, to be sure!

Then, with a fleeting self-conscious motion, she wondered if she would be very much surprised, on rising in the morning, to realize that her hair had turned white. She had *felt* it turning white so often, under the intolerable burden of her thoughts, and her sensations. Yet there it remained, brown as ever, and there she was herself, looking a picture of health.

Perhaps she was healthy. Perhaps it was only her unabateable health that left her so exposed to the truth. If she were sickly she would have her illusions, imaginations. As it was, there was no escape. She must always see and know and never escape. She could never escape. There she was, placed before the clock-face of life. And if she turned round as in a railway station, to look at the bookstall, still she could see, with her very spine, she could see the clock, always the great white clock-face. In vain she fluttered the leaves of books, or made statuettes in clay. She knew she was not *really* reading. She was not *really* working. She was watching the fingers twitch across the eternal, mechanical, monotonous clock-face of time. She never really lived, she only watched. Indeed, she was like a little, twelve-hour clock, *vis-à-vis* with the enormous clock of eternity – there she was, like Dignity and Impudence, or Impudence and Dignity.

The picture pleased her. Didn't her face really look like a clock dial – rather roundish and often pale, and impassive. She would have got up to look in the mirror, but the thought of the sight of her own face, that was like a twelve-hour clock dial, filled her with such deep terror, that she hastened to think of something else.

Oh, why wasn't somebody kind to her? Why wasn't there somebody who would take her in their arms, and hold her to their breast, and give her rest, pure, deep, healing rest. Oh, why wasn't there somebody to take her in their arms and fold her safe and perfect, for sleep. She wanted so much this perfect enfolded sleep. She lay always so unsheathed in sleep. She would lie always unsheathed in sleep, unrelieved, unsaved. Oh, how could she bear it, this endless unrelief, this eternal unrelief.

Gerald! Could he fold her in his arms and sheathe her in sleep? Ha! He needed putting to sleep himself – poor Gerald. That was all he needed. What did he do, he made the burden for her greater, the burden of her sleep was the more intolerable, when he was there. He was an added weariness upon her unripening nights, her unfruitful slumbers. Perhaps he got some repose from her. Perhaps he did. Perhaps this was what he was always dogging her for, like a child that is famished, crying for the breast. Perhaps this was the secret of his passion, his for ever unquenched desire for her – that he needed her to put him to sleep, to give him repose.

What then! Was she his mother? Had she asked for a child, whom she must nurse through the nights, for her lover. She despised him, she despised him, she hardened her heart. An infant crying in the night, this Don Juan.

Ooh, but how she hated the infant crying in the night. She would murder it gladly. She would stifle it and bury it, as Hetty Sorrell did. No doubt Hetty Sorrell's infant cried in the night – no doubt Arthur Donnithorne's infant would. Ha – the Arthur Donnithornes, the Geralds of this world. So manly by day, yet all the while, such a crying of infants in the night. Let them turn into mechanisms, let them. Let them become instruments, pure machines, pure wills, that work like clockwork, in perpetual repetition. Let them be this, let them be taken up entirely in their work, let them be perfect parts of a great machine, having a slumber of constant repetition. Let Gerald manage his firm. There he would be satisfied, as satisfied as a wheel-barrow that goes backwards and forwards along a plank all day – she had seen it.

The wheel-barrow – the one humble wheel – the unit of the firm. Then the cart, with two wheels; then the truck, with four; then the donkey-engine, with eight, then the winding-engine, with sixteen, and so on, till it came to the miner, with a thousand wheels, and then the electrician, with three thousand, and the underground manager, with twenty thousand, and the general manager with a hundred thousand little wheels working away to complete his make-up, and then Gerald, with a million wheels and cogs and axles.

Poor Gerald, such a lot of little Wheels to his make-up! He was more intricate than a chronometer-watch. But oh heavens, what weariness! What weariness, God above! A chronometer-watch – a beetle – her soul fainted with utter ennui, from the thought. So many wheels to count and consider and calculate! Enough, enough – there was an end to man's capacity for complications, even. Or perhaps there was no end.

Meanwhile Gerald sat in his room, reading. When Gudrun was gone, he was left stupefied with arrested desire. He sat on the side of the bed for an hour, stupefied, little strands of consciousness appearing and reappearing. But he did not move, for a long time he remained inert, his head dropped on his breast.

Then he looked up and realized that he was going to bed. He was cold. Soon he was lying down in the dark.

But what he could not bear was the darkness. The solid darkness confronting him drove him mad. So he rose, and made a light. He remained seated for a while, staring in front. He did not think of Gudrun, he did not think of anything.

Then suddenly he went downstairs for a book. He had all his life been in terror of the nights that should come, when he could not sleep. He knew that this would be too much for him, to have to face nights of sleeplessness and of horrified watching the hours.

So he sat for hours in bed, like a statue, reading. His mind, hard and acute, read on rapidly, his body, understood nothing. In a state of rigid unconsciousness, he read on through the night, till morning, when, weary and disgusted in spirit, disgusted most of all with himself, he slept for two hours.

Then he got up, hard and full of energy. Gudrun scarcely spoke to him, except at coffee when she said:

'I shall be leaving tomorrow.'

'We will go together as far as Innsbruck, for appearance's sake?' he asked.

'Perhaps,' she said.

She said 'Perhaps' between the sips of her coffee. And the sound of her taking her breath in the word was nauseous to him. He rose quickly to be away from her.

He went and made arrangements for the departure on the morrow. Then, taking some food, he set out for the day on the skis. Perhaps, he said to the *Wirt*, he would go up to the Marienhütte, perhaps to the village below.

To Gudrun this day was full of a promise like spring. She felt an approaching release, a new fountain of life rising up in her. It gave her pleasure to dawdle through her packing, it gave her pleasure to dip into books, to try on her different garments, to look at herself in the glass. She felt a new lease of life was come upon her, and she was happy like a child, very attractive and beautiful to everybody, with her soft, luxuriant figure, and her happiness. Yet underneath was death itself.

In the afternoon she had to go out with Loerke. Her tomorrow was perfectly vague before her. This was what gave her pleasure. She might be going to England with Gerald, she might be going to Dresden with Loerke, she might be going to Munich, to a girl-friend she had there. Anything might come to pass on the morrow. And today was the white, snowy iridescent threshold of all possibility. All possibility – that was the charm to her, the lovely, iridescent, indefinite charm – pure illusion. All possibility – because death was inevitable, and *nothing* was possible but death.

She did not want things to materialize, to take any definite shape. She wanted, suddenly, at one moment of the journey tomorrow, to be wafted into an utterly new course, by some utterly unforeseen event, or motion. So that, although she wanted to go out with Loerke for the last time into the snow, she did not want to be serious or business-like.

And Loerke was not a serious figure. In his brown velvet cap, that made his head as round as a chestnut, with the brown velvet flaps loose and wild over his ears, and a wisp of elf-like, thin black hair blowing above his full, elf-like dark eyes, the shiny, transparent brown skin crinkling up into odd grimaces on his small-featured face, he looked an odd little boy-man, a bat. But in his figure, in the greeny loden suit, he looked *chétif* and puny, still strangely different from the rest.

He had taken a little toboggan, for the two of them, and they trudged between the blinding slopes of snow, that burned their now hardening faces, laughing in an endless sequence of quips and jests and polyglot fancies. The fancies were the reality to both of them, they were both so happy, tossing about the little coloured balls of verbal humour and whimsicality. Their natures seemed to sparkle in full interplay, they were enjoying a pure game. And they wanted to keep it on the level of a game, their relationship: *such* a fine game.

Loerke did not take the tobogganing very seriously. He put no fire and intensity into it, as Gerald did. Which pleased Gudrun. She was weary, oh so weary of Gerald's gripped intensity of physical motion. Loerke let the sledge go wildly, and gaily, like a flying leaf, and when, at a bend, he pitched both her and him out into the snow, he only waited for them both to pick themselves up unhurt off the keen white ground, to be laughing and pert as a pixie. She knew he would be making ironical, playful remarks as he wandered in hell – if he were in the humour. And that pleased her immensely. It seemed like a rising above the dreariness of actuality, the monotony of contingencies.

They played till the sun went down, in pure amusement, careless and timeless. Then, as the little sledge twirled riskily to rest at the bottom of the slope:

'Wait!' he said suddenly, and he produced from somewhere a large thermos flask, a packet of Keks, and a bottle of Schnapps.

'Oh, Loerke,' she cried. 'What an inspiration! What a *comble de joie indeed*! What is the Schnapps?'

He looked at it, and laughed.

'*Heidelbeer!*' he said.

'No! From the bilberries under the snow. Doesn't it look as if it were distilled from snow. Can you –' she sniffed, and sniffed at the bottle – 'can you smell bilberries? Isn't it wonderful? It is exactly as if one could smell them through the snow.'

She stamped her foot lightly on the ground. He kneeled down and whistled, and put his ear to the snow. As he did so his black eyes twinkled up.

'Ha! Ha!' she laughed, warmed by the whimsical way in which he mocked at her verbal extravagances. He was always teasing her, mocking her ways. But as he in his mockery was even more absurd than she in her extravagances, what could one do but laugh and feel liberated.

She could feel their voices, hers and his, ringing silvery like bells in the frozen, motionless air of the first twilight. How perfect it was, how *very* perfect it was, this silvery isolation and interplay.

She sipped the hot coffee, whose fragrance flew around them like bees

murmuring around flowers, in the snowy air, she drank tiny sips of the
Heidelbeerwasser, she ate the cold, sweet, creamy wafers. How good everything was! How perfect everything tasted and smelled and sounded, here in
this utter stillness of snow and falling twilight.

'You are going away tomorrow?' his voice came at last.

'Yes.'

There was a pause, when the evening seemed to rise in its silent, ringing
pallor infinitely high, to the infinite which was near at hand.

'*Wohin?*'

That was the question – *wohin?* Whither? *Wohin?* What a lovely word! She
never wanted it answered. Let it chime for ever.

'I don't know,' she said, smiling at him.

He caught the smile from her.

'One never does,' he said.

'One never does,' she repeated.

There was a silence, wherein he ate biscuits rapidly, as a rabbit eats
leaves.

'But,' he laughed, 'where will you take a ticket to?'

'Oh heaven!' she cried. 'One must take a ticket.'

Here was a blow. She saw herself at the wicket, at the railway station. Then
a relieving thought came to her. She breathed freely.

'But one needn't go,' she cried.

'Certainly not,' he said.

'I mean one needn't go where one's ticket says.'

That struck him. One might take a ticket, so as not to travel to the
destination it indicated. One might break off, and avoid the destination. A
point located. That was an idea!

'Then take a ticket to London,' he said. 'One should never go there.'

'Right,' she answered.

He poured a little coffee into a tin can.

'You won't tell me where you will go?' he asked.

'Really and truly,' she said, 'I don't know. It depends which way the wind
blows.'

He looked at her quizzically, then he pursed up his lips, like Zephyrus,
blowing across the snow.

'It goes towards Germany,' he said.

'I believe so,' she laughed.

Suddenly, they were aware of a vague white figure near them. It was
Gerald. Gudrun's heart leapt in sudden terror, profound terror. She rose to
her feet.

'They told me where you were,' came Gerald's voice, like a judgment in the
whitish air of twilight.

'*Maria!* You look like a ghost,' exclaimed Loerke.

Gerald did not answer. His presence was unnatural and ghostly to them.

Loerke shook the flask – then he held it inverted over the snow. Only a few
brown drops trickled out.

'All gone!' he said.

To Gerald, the smallish, odd figure of the German was distinct and
objective, as if seen through field glasses. And he disliked the small figure
exceedingly, he wanted it removed.

Then Loerke rattled the box which held the biscuits.

'Biscuits there are still,' he said.

And reaching from his seated posture in the sledge, he handed them to Gudrun. She fumbled, and took one. He would have held them to Gerald, but Gerald so definitely did not want to be offered a biscuit, that Loerke, rather vaguely, put the box aside. Then he took up the small bottle and held it to the light.

'Also there is some Schnapps,' he said to himself.

Then suddenly, he elevated the bottle gallantly in the air, a strange, grotesque figure leaning towards Gudrun, and said:

'*Gnädiges Fräulein,*' he said, '*wohl –*'

There was a crack, the bottle was flying, Loerke had started back, the three stood quivering in violent emotion.

Loerke turned to Gerald, a devilish leer on his bright-skinned face.

'Well done!' he said, in a satirical demoniac frenzy. '*C'est le sport, sans doute.*'

The next instant he was sitting ludicrously in the snow, Gerald's fist having rung against the side of his head. But Loerke pulled himself together, rose, quivering, looking full at Gerald, his body weak and furtive, but his eyes demoniacal with satire.

'*Vive le héros, vive –*'

But he flinched as, in a black flash, Gerald's fist came upon him, banged into the other side of his head, and sent him aside like a broken straw.

But Gudrun moved forward. She raised her clenched hand high, and brought it down, with a great downward stroke on to the face and on to the breast of Gerald.

A great astonishment burst upon him, as if the air had broken. Wide, wide his soul opened, in wonder, feeling the pain. Then it laughed, turning, with strong hands outstretched, at last to take the apple of his desire. At last he could finish his desire.

He took the throat of Gudrun between his hands, that were hard and indomitably powerful. And her throat was beautifully, so beautifully soft, save that, within, he could feel the slippery chords of her life. And this he crushed, this he could crush. What bliss! Oh what bliss, at last, what satisfaction, at last! The pure zest of satisfaction filled his soul. He was watching the unconsciousness come into her swollen face, watching the eyes roll back. How ugly she was! What a fulfilment, what a satisfaction! How good this was, oh how good it was, what a God-given gratification, at last! He was unconscious of her fighting and struggling. The struggling was her reciprocal lustful passion in this embrace, the more violent it became, the greater the frenzy of delight, till the zenith was reached, the crisis, the struggle was overborne, her movement became softer, appeased.

Loerke roused himself on the snow, too dazed and hurt to get up. Only his eyes were conscious.

'*Monsieur!*' he said in his thin, roused voice: '*Quand vous aurez fini –*'

A revulsion of contempt and disgust came over Gerald's soul. The disgust went to the very bottom of him, a nausea. Ah, what was he doing, to what depths was he letting himself go! As if he cared about her enough to kill her, to have her life on his hands!

A weakness ran over his body, a terrible relaxing, a thaw, a decay of strength. Without knowing, he had let go his grip, and Gudrun had fallen to her knees. Must he see, must he know?

A fearful weakness possessed him, his joints were turned to water. He drifted, as on a wind, veered, and went drifting away.

'I didn't want it, really,' was the last confession of disgust in his soul, as he drifted up the slope, weak, finished, only sheering off unconsciously from any further contact. 'I've had enough – I want to go to sleep. I've had enough.' He was sunk under a sense of nausea.

He was weak, but he did not want to rest, he wanted to go on and on, to the end. Never again to stay, till he came to the end, that was all the desire that remained to him. So he drifted on and on, unconscious and weak, not thinking of anything, so long as he could keep in action.

The twilight spread a weird, unearthly light overhead, bluish-rose in colour, the cold blue night sank on the snow. In the valley below, behind, in the great bed of snow, were two small figures; Gudrun dropped on her knees, like one executed, and Loerke sitting propped up near her. That was all.

Gerald stumbled on up the slope of snow, in the bluish darkness, always climbing, always unconsciously climbing, weary though he was. On his left was a steep slope with black rocks and fallen masses of rock and veins of snow slashing in and about the blackness of rock, veins of snow slashing vaguely in and about the blackness of rock. Yet there was no sound, all this made no noise.

To add to his difficulty, a small bright moon shone brilliantly just ahead, on the right, a painful brilliant thing that was always there, unremitting, from which there was no escape. He wanted so to come to the end – he had had enough. Yet he did not sleep.

He surged painfully up, sometimes having to cross a slope of black rock, that was blown bare of snow. Here he was afraid of falling, very much afraid of falling. And high up here on the crest, moved a wind that almost overpowered him with a sleep-heavy iciness. Only it was not here, the end, and he must go on. His indefinite nausea would not let him stay.

Having gained one ridge, he saw the vague shadow of something higher in front. Always higher, always higher. He knew he was following the track towards the summit of the slopes, where was the Marienhütte, and the descent on the other side. But he was not really conscious. He only wanted to go on, to go on whilst he could, to move, to keep going, that was all, to keep going, until it was finished. He had lost all his sense of place. And yet in the remaining instinct of life, his feet sought the track where the skis had gone.

He slithered down a sheer snow slope. That frightened him. He had no alpenstock, nothing. But having come safely to rest, he began to walk on in the illuminated darkness. It was as cold as sleep. He was between two ridges in a hollow. So he swerved. Should he climb the other ridge or wander along the hollow? How frail the thread of his being was stretched! He would perhaps climb the ridge. The snow was firm and simple. He went along. There was something standing out of the snow. He approached with dimmest curiosity.

It was a half-buried crucifix, a little Christ under a little sloping hood at the top of a pole. He sheered away. Somebody was going to murder him. He had a great dread of being murdered. But it was a dread which stood outside him like his own ghost.

Yet why be afraid? It was bound to happen. To be murdered! He looked round in terror at the snow, the rocking, pale, shadowy slopes of the upper world. He was bound to be murdered, he could see it. This was the moment when the death was uplifted, and there was no escape.

Lord Jesus, was it then bound to be – Lord Jesus! He could feel the blow descending, he knew he was murdered. Vaguely wandering forward, his hands lifted as if to feel what would happen, he was waiting for the moment when he would stop, when it would cease. It was not over yet.

He had come to the hollow basin of snow, surrounded by sheer slopes and precipices, out of which rose a track that brought one to the top of the mountain. But he wandered unconsciously, till he slipped and fell down, and as he fell something broke in his soul, and immediately he went to sleep.

31

EXEUNT

When they brought the body home the next morning, Gudrun was shut up in her room. From her window she saw men coming along with a burden over the snow. She sat still and let the minutes go by.

There came a tap at her door. She opened. There stood a woman, saying softly, oh, far too reverently:

'They have found him, madam!'

'Il est mort?'

'Yes – hours ago.'

Gudrun did not know what to say. What should she say? What should she feel? What should she do? What did they expect of her? She was coldly at a loss.

'Thank you,' she said, and she shut the door of her room. The woman went away mortified. Not a word, not a tear – ha! Gudrun was cold, a cold woman.

Gudrun sat on in her room, her face pale and impassive. What was she to do? She could not weep and make a scene. She could not alter herself. She sat motionless, hiding from people. Her one motive was to avoid actual contact with events. She only wrote out a long telegram to Ursula and Birkin.

In the afternoon, however, she rose suddenly to look for Loerke. She glanced with apprehension at the door of the room that had been Gerald's. Not for worlds would she enter there.

She found Loerke sitting alone in the lounge. She went straight up to him.

'It isn't true, is it?' she said.

He looked up at her. A small smile of misery twisted his face. He shrugged his shoulders.

'True?' he echoed.

'We haven't killed him?' she asked.

He disliked her coming to him in such a manner. He raised his shoulders wearily.

'It has happened,' he said.

She looked at him. He sat crushed and frustrated for the time being, quite as emotionless and barren as herself. My God! this was a barren tragedy, barren, barren.

She returned to her room to wait for Ursula and Birkin. She wanted to get away, only to get away. She could not think or feel until she had got away, till she was loosed from this position.

The day passed, the next day came. She heard the sledge, saw Ursula and Birkin alight, and she shrank from these also.

Ursula came straight up to her.

'Gudrun!' she cried, the tears running down her cheeks. And she took her sister in her arms. Gudrun hid her face on Ursula's shoulder, but still she could not escape the cold devil of irony that froze her soul.

'Ha, ha!' she thought, 'this is the right behaviour.'

But she could not weep, and the sight of her cold, pale, impassive face soon stopped the fountain of Ursula's tears. In a few moments, the sisters had nothing to say to each other.

'Was it very vile to be dragged back here again?' Gudrun asked at length.

Ursula looked up in some bewilderment.

'I never thought of it,' she said.

'I felt a beast, fetching you,' said Gudrun. 'But I simply couldn't see people. That is too much for me.'

'Yes,' said Ursula, chilled.

Birkin tapped and entered. His face was white and expressionless. She knew he knew. He gave her his hand, saying:

'The end of *this* trip, at any rate.'

Gudrun glanced at him, afraid.

There was silence between the three of them, nothing to be said. At length Ursula asked in a small voice:

'Have you seen him?'

He looked back at Ursula with a hard, cold look, and did not trouble to answer.

'Have you seen him?' she repeated.

'I have,' he said coldly.

Then he looked at Gudrun.

'Have you done anything?' he said.

'Nothing,' she replied, 'nothing.'

She shrank in cold disgust from making any statement.

'Loerke says that Gerald came to you when you were sitting on the sledge at the bottom of the Rudelbahn, that you had words, and Gerald walked away. What were the words about? I had better know, so that I can satisfy the authorities, if necessary.'

Gudrun looked up at him, white, childlike, mute with trouble.

'There weren't even any words,' she said. 'He knocked Loerke down and stunned him, he half strangled me, then he went away.'

To herself she was saying:

'A pretty little sample of the eternal triangle!' And she turned ironically away, because she knew that the fight had been between Gerald and herself and that the presence of the third party was a mere contingency – an inevitable contingency perhaps, but a contingency none the less. But let them have it as an example of the eternal triangle, the trinity of hate. It would be simpler for them.

Birkin went away, his manner cold and abstracted. But she knew he would do things for her, nevertheless, he would see her through. She smiled slightly to herself, with contempt. Let him do the work, since he was so extremely *good* at looking after other people.

Birkin went again to Gerald. He had loved him. And yet he felt chiefly disgust at the inert body lying there. It was so inert, so coldly dead, a carcase,

Birkin's bowels seemed to turn to ice. He had to stand and look at the frozen dead body that had been Gerald.

It was the frozen carcase of a dead male. Birkin remembered a rabbit which he had once found frozen like a board on the snow. It had been rigid like a dried board when he picked it up. And now this was Gerald, stiff as a board, curled up as if for sleep, yet with the horrible hardness somehow evident. It filled him with horror. The room must be made warm, the body must be thawed. The limbs would break like glass or like wood if they had to be straightened.

He reached and touched the dead face. And the sharp, heavy bruise of ice bruised his living bowels. He wondered if he himself were freezing too, freezing from the inside. In the short blond moustache the life breath was frozen into a block of ice beneath the silent nostrils. And this was Gerald!

Again he touched the sharp, almost glittering fair hair of the frozen body. It was icy-cold, almost venomous. Birkin's heart began to freeze. He had loved Gerald. Now he looked at the shapely, strange-coloured face, with the small, fine, pinched nose and the manly cheeks, saw it frozen like an ice pebble – yet he had loved it. What was one to think or feel? His brain was beginning to freeze, his blood was turning to ice-water. So cold, so cold, a heavy, bruising cold pressing on his arms from outside, and a heavier cold congealing within him, in his heart and in his bowels.

He went over the snow slopes to see where the death had been. At last he came to the great shallow among the precipices and slopes, near the summit of the pass. It was a grey day, the third day of greyness and stillness. All was white, icy, pallid, save for the scoring of black rocks that jutted like roots sometimes, and sometimes were in naked faces. In the distance a slope sheered down from a peak, with many black rockslides.

It was like a shallow pot lying among the stone and snow of the upper world. In this pot Gerald had gone to sleep. At the far end, the guides had driven iron stakes deep into the snow-wall, so that, by means of the great rope attached, they could haul themselves up the massive snow-front, out on to the jagged summit of the pass, naked to heaven, where the Marienhütte hid among the naked rocks. Round about, spiked, slashed snow-peaks pricked the heaven.

Gerald might have found this rope. He might have hauled himself up to the crest. He might have heard the dogs in the Marienhütte, and found shelter. He might have gone on down the steep, steep fall of the south side, down into the dark valley with its pines, on to the great Imperial road leading south to Italy.

He might! And what then? The Imperial road! The south? Italy? What then? Was it a way out? It was only a way in again. Birkin stood high in the painful air, looking at the peaks and the way south. Was it any good going south, to Italy? Down the old, old Imperial road?

He turned away. Either the heart would break or cease to care. Best cease to care. Whatever the mystery which has brought forth man and the universe, it is a non-human mystery, it has its own great ends, man is not the criterion. Best leave it all to the vast, creative, non-human mystery. Best strive with oneself only, not with the universe.

'God cannot do without man.' It was a saying of some great French religious teacher. But surely this is false. God can do without man. God could do without the ichthyosauri and the mastodon. These monsters failed creatively to develop, so God, the creative mystery, dispensed with them. In the same way the mystery could dispense with man, should he too fail creatively to change and develop. The eternal creative mystery could dispose of man, and replace him with a finer created being. Just as the horse has taken the place of the mastodon.

It was very consoling to Birkin to think this. If humanity ran into a cul-de-sac, and expended itself, the timeless creative mystery would bring forth some other being, finer, more wonderful, some new, more lovely race, to carry on the embodiment of creation. The game was never up. The mystery of creation was fathomless, infallible, inexhaustible, for ever. Races came and went, species passed away, but ever new species arose, more lovely, or equally lovely, always surpassing wonder. The fountain-head was incorruptible and unsearchable. It had no limits. It could bring forth miracles, create utter new races and new species in its own hour, new forms of consciousness, new forms of body, new units of being. To be man was as nothing compared to the possibilities of the creative mystery. To have one's pulse beating direct from the mystery, this was perfection, unutterable satisfaction. Human or inhuman mattered nothing. The perfect pulse throbbed with indescribable being, miraculous unborn species.

Birkin went home again to Gerald. He went into the room and sat down on the bed. Dead, dead and cold!

> 'Imperial Cæsar dead and turned to clay
> Would stop a hole to keep the wind away.'

There was no response from that which had been Gerald. Strange, congealed, icy substance – no more. No more!

Terribly weary, Birkin went away, about the day's business. He did it all quietly, without bother. To rant, to rave, to be tragic, to make situations – it was all too late. Best be quiet, and bear one's soul in patience and in fullness.

But when he went in again, at evening, to look at Gerald between the candles, because of his heart's hunger, suddenly his heart contracted, his own candle all but fell from his hand, as, with a strange whimpering cry, the tears broke out. He sat down in a chair, shaken by a sudden access. Ursula, who had followed him, recoiled aghast from him as he sat with sunken head and body convulsively shaken, making a strange, horrible sound of tears.

'I didn't want it to be like this – I didn't want it to be like this,' he cried to himself. Ursula could but think of the Kaiser's: *'Ich habe es nicht gewollt.'* She looked almost with horror on Birkin.

Suddenly he was silent. But he sat with his head dropped to hide his face. Then furtively he wiped his face with his fingers. Then suddenly he lifted his head and looked straight at Ursula with dark, almost vengeful eyes.

'He should have loved me,' he said. 'I offered him.'

She, afraid, white, with mute lips, answered:

'What difference would it have made!'

'It would!' he said. 'It would.'

He forgot her and turned to look at Gerald. With head oddly lifted, like a man who draws his head back from an insult, half haughtily, he watched the cold, mute, material face. It had a bluish cast. It sent a shaft like ice through the heart of the living man. Cold, mute, material! Birkin remembered how once Gerald had clutched his hand with a warm, momentaneous grip of final love. For one second – then let go again, let go for ever. If he had kept true to that clasp, death would not have mattered. Those who die, and dying still can love, still believe, do not die. They live still in the beloved. Gerald might still have been living in the spirit with Birkin, even after death. He might have lived with his friend, a further life.

But now he was dead, like clay, like bluish, corruptible ice. Birkin looked at the pale fingers, the inert mass. He remembered a dead stallion he had seen: a dead mass of maleness, repugnant. He remembered also the beautiful face of one whom he had loved, and who had died still having the faith to yield to the mystery. That dead face was beautiful, no one could call it cold, mute, material. No one could remember it without gaining faith in the mystery, without the soul's warming with new, deep life trust.

And Gerald! The denier! He left the heart cold, frozen, hardly able to beat. Gerald's father had looked wistful, to break the heart: but not this last terrible look of cold, mute Matter. Birkin watched and watched.

Ursula stood aside watching the living man stare at the frozen face of the dead man. Both faces were unmoved and unmoving. The candle-flames flickered in the frozen air in the intense silence.

'Haven't you seen enough?' she said.

He got up.

'It's a bitter thing to me,' he said.

'What – that he's dead?' she said.

His eyes just met hers. He did not answer.

'You've got me,' she said.

He smiled and kissed her.

'If I die,' he said, 'you'll know I haven't left you.'

'And me?' she cried.

'And you won't have left me,' he said. 'We shan't have any need to despair, in death.'

She took hold of his hand.

'But need you despair over Gerald?' she said.

'Yes,' he answered.

They went away. Gerald was taken to England to be buried. Birkin and Ursula accompanied the body, along with one of Gerald's brothers. It was the Crich brothers and sisters who insisted on the burial in England. Birkin wanted to leave the dead man in the Alps, near the snow. But the family was strident, loudly insistent.

Gudrun went to Dresden. She wrote no particulars of herself. Ursula stayed at the Mill with Birkin for a week or two. They were both very quiet.

'Did you need Gerald?' she asked one evening.

'Yes,' he said.

'Aren't I enough for you?' she asked.

'No,' he said. 'You are enough for me, as far as a woman is concerned. You are all women to me. But I wanted a man friend, as eternal as you and I are eternal.'

'Why aren't I enough?' she said. 'You are enough for me. I don't want anybody else but you. Why isn't it the same with you?'

'Having you, I can live all my life without anybody else, any other sheer intimacy. But to make it complete, really happy, I wanted eternal union with a man too: another kind of love,' he said.

'I don't believe it,' she said. 'It's an obstinacy, a theory, a perversity.'

'Well –' he said.

'You can't have two kinds of love. Why should you!'

'It seems as if I can't,' he said. 'Yet I wanted it.'

'You can't have it, because it's false, impossible,' she said.

'I don't believe that,' he answered.